PERCY JACKSON & THE OLYMPIANS

BOOK I

THE LIGHTNING THIEF

RICK RIORDAN

MW00756922

SCHOLASTIC INC.

New York Toronto London Auckland Sydney
Mexico City New Delhi Hong Kong Buenos Aires

ISBN 0-439-86130-6

Copyright © 2005 by Rick Riordan. All rights reserved. Published by Scholastic Inc., 557 Broadway, New York, NY 10012, by arrangement with Hyperion Books for Children, an imprint of Disney Children's Book Group, LLC. SCHOLASTIC and associated logos are trademarks and/or registered trademarks of Scholastic Inc.

12 11 10 9   13 14 15 16/0

Printed in the U.S.A.   40

First Scholastic printing, March 2006

To Haley,
who heard the story first

CONTENTS

I ⚡ I ACCIDENTALLY VAPORIZE MY PRE-ALGEBRA TEACHER

Look, I didn't want to be a half-blood.

If you're reading this because you think you might be one, my advice is: close this book right now. Believe whatever lie your mom or dad told you about your birth, and try to lead a normal life.

Being a half-blood is dangerous. It's scary. Most of the time, it gets you killed in painful, nasty ways.

If you're a normal kid, reading this because you think it's fiction, great. Read on. I envy you for being able to believe that none of this ever happened.

But if you recognize yourself in these pages—if you feel something stirring inside—stop reading immediately. You might be one of us. And once you know that, it's only a matter of time before *they* sense it too, and they'll come for you.

Don't say I didn't warn you.

My name is Percy Jackson.

I'm twelve years old. Until a few months ago, I was a boarding student at Yancy Academy, a private school for troubled kids in upstate New York.

Am I a troubled kid?

Yeah. You could say that.

I could start at any point in my short miserable life to prove it, but things really started going bad last May, when our sixth-grade class took a field trip to Manhattan— twenty-eight mental-case kids and two teachers on a yellow school bus, heading to the Metropolitan Museum of Art to look at ancient Greek and Roman stuff.

I know—it sounds like torture. Most Yancy field trips were.

But Mr. Brunner, our Latin teacher, was leading this trip, so I had hopes.

Mr. Brunner was this middle-aged guy in a motorized wheelchair. He had thinning hair and a scruffy beard and a frayed tweed jacket, which always smelled like coffee. You wouldn't think he'd be cool, but he told stories and jokes and let us play games in class. He also had this awesome collection of Roman armor and weapons, so he was the only teacher whose class didn't put me to sleep.

I hoped the trip would be okay. At least, I hoped that for once I wouldn't get in trouble.

Boy, was I wrong.

See, bad things happen to me on field trips. Like at my fifth-grade school, when we went to the Saratoga battlefield, I had this accident with a Revolutionary War cannon. I wasn't aiming for the school bus, but of course I got expelled anyway. And before that, at my fourth-grade school, when we took a behind-the-scenes tour of the Marine World shark pool, I sort of hit the wrong lever on the catwalk and our class took an unplanned swim. And the time before that . . . Well, you get the idea.

This trip, I was determined to be good.

All the way into the city, I put up with Nancy Bobofit, the freckly, redheaded kleptomaniac girl, hitting my best friend Grover in the back of the head with chunks of peanut butter-and-ketchup sandwich.

Grover was an easy target. He was scrawny. He cried when he got frustrated. He must've been held back several grades, because he was the only sixth grader with acne and the start of a wispy beard on his chin. On top of all that, he was crippled. He had a note excusing him from PE for the rest of his life because he had some kind of muscular disease in his legs. He walked funny, like every step hurt him, but don't let that fool you. You should've seen him run when it was enchilada day in the cafeteria.

Anyway, Nancy Bobofit was throwing wads of sandwich that stuck in his curly brown hair, and she knew I couldn't do anything back to her because I was already on probation. The headmaster had threatened me with death by in-school suspension if anything bad, embarrassing, or even mildly entertaining happened on this trip.

"I'm going to kill her," I mumbled.

Grover tried to calm me down. "It's okay. I like peanut butter."

He dodged another piece of Nancy's lunch.

"That's it." I started to get up, but Grover pulled me back to my seat.

"You're already on probation," he reminded me. "You know who'll get blamed if anything happens."

Looking back on it, I wish I'd decked Nancy Bobofit

right then and there. In-school suspension would've been nothing compared to the mess I was about to get myself into.

Mr. Brunner led the museum tour.

He rode up front in his wheelchair, guiding us through the big echoey galleries, past marble statues and glass cases full of really old black-and-orange pottery.

It blew my mind that this stuff had survived for two thousand, three thousand years.

He gathered us around a thirteen-foot-tall stone column with a big sphinx on the top, and started telling us how it was a grave marker, a *stele*, for a girl about our age. He told us about the carvings on the sides. I was trying to listen to what he had to say, because it was kind of interesting, but everybody around me was talking, and every time I told them to shut up, the other teacher chaperone, Mrs. Dodds, would give me the evil eye.

Mrs. Dodds was this little math teacher from Georgia who always wore a black leather jacket, even though she was fifty years old. She looked mean enough to ride a Harley right into your locker. She had come to Yancy halfway through the year, when our last math teacher had a nervous breakdown.

From her first day, Mrs. Dodds loved Nancy Bobofit and figured I was devil spawn. She would point her crooked finger at me and say, "Now, honey," real sweet, and I knew I was going to get after-school detention for a month.

One time, after she'd made me erase answers out of old math workbooks until midnight, I told Grover I didn't think Mrs. Dodds was human. He looked at me, real serious, and said, "You're absolutely right."

Mr. Brunner kept talking about Greek funeral art.

Finally, Nancy Bobofit snickered something about the naked guy on the stele, and I turned around and said, "Will you *shut up?*"

It came out louder than I meant it to.

The whole group laughed. Mr. Brunner stopped his story.

"Mr. Jackson," he said, "did you have a comment?"

My face was totally red. I said, "No, sir."

Mr. Brunner pointed to one of the pictures on the stele. "Perhaps you'll tell us what this picture represents?"

I looked at the carving, and felt a flush of relief, because I actually recognized it. "That's Kronos eating his kids, right?"

"Yes," Mr. Brunner said, obviously not satisfied. "And he did this because . . ."

"Well . . ." I racked my brain to remember. "Kronos was the king god, and—"

"God?" Mr. Brunner asked.

"Titan," I corrected myself. "And . . . he didn't trust his kids, who were the gods. So, um, Kronos ate them, right? But his wife hid baby Zeus, and gave Kronos a rock to eat instead. And later, when Zeus grew up, he tricked his dad, Kronos, into barfing up his brothers and sisters—"

"Eeew!" said one of the girls behind me.

"—and so there was this big fight between the gods and the Titans," I continued, "and the gods won."

Some snickers from the group.

Behind me, Nancy Bobofit mumbled to a friend, "Like we're going to use this in real life. Like it's going to say on our job applications, 'Please explain why Kronos ate his kids.'"

"And why, Mr. Jackson," Brunner said, "to paraphrase Miss Bobofit's excellent question, does this matter in real life?"

"Busted," Grover muttered.

"Shut up," Nancy hissed, her face even brighter red than her hair.

At least Nancy got packed, too. Mr. Brunner was the only one who ever caught her saying anything wrong. He had radar ears.

I thought about his question, and shrugged. "I don't know, sir."

"I see." Mr. Brunner looked disappointed. "Well, half credit, Mr. Jackson. Zeus did indeed feed Kronos a mixture of mustard and wine, which made him disgorge his other five children, who, of course, being immortal gods, had been living and growing up completely undigested in the Titan's stomach. The gods defeated their father, sliced him to pieces with his own scythe, and scattered his remains in Tartarus, the darkest part of the Underworld. On that happy note, it's time for lunch. Mrs. Dodds, would you lead us back outside?"

The class drifted off, the girls holding their stomachs, the guys pushing each other around and acting like doofuses.

Grover and I were about to follow when Mr. Brunner said, "Mr. Jackson."

I knew that was coming.

I told Grover to keep going. Then I turned toward Mr. Brunner. "Sir?"

Mr. Brunner had this look that wouldn't let you go—intense brown eyes that could've been a thousand years old and had seen everything.

"You must learn the answer to my question," Mr. Brunner told me.

"About the Titans?"

"About real life. And how your studies apply to it."

"Oh."

"What you learn from me," he said, "is vitally important. I expect you to treat it as such. I will accept only the best from you, Percy Jackson."

I wanted to get angry, this guy pushed me so hard.

I mean, sure, it was kind of cool on tournament days, when he dressed up in a suit of Roman armor and shouted: "What ho!" and challenged us, sword-point against chalk, to run to the board and name every Greek and Roman person who had ever lived, and their mother, and what god they worshipped. But Mr. Brunner expected me to be as good as everybody else, despite the fact that I have dyslexia and attention deficit disorder and I had never made above a C− in my life. No—he didn't expect me to be *as good*; he expected me to be *better*. And I just couldn't learn all those names and facts, much less spell them correctly.

I mumbled something about trying harder, while Mr.

Brunner took one long sad look at the stele, like he'd been at this girl's funeral.

He told me to go outside and eat my lunch.

The class gathered on the front steps of the museum, where we could watch the foot traffic along Fifth Avenue.

Overhead, a huge storm was brewing, with clouds blacker than I'd ever seen over the city. I figured maybe it was global warming or something, because the weather all across New York state had been weird since Christmas. We'd had massive snow storms, flooding, wildfires from lightning strikes. I wouldn't have been surprised if this was a hurricane blowing in.

Nobody else seemed to notice. Some of the guys were pelting pigeons with Lunchables crackers. Nancy Bobofit was trying to pickpocket something from a lady's purse, and, of course, Mrs. Dodds wasn't seeing a thing.

Grover and I sat on the edge of the fountain, away from the others. We thought that maybe if we did that, everybody wouldn't know we were from *that* school—the school for loser freaks who couldn't make it elsewhere.

"Detention?" Grover asked.

"Nah," I said. "Not from Brunner. I just wish he'd lay off me sometimes. I mean—I'm not a genius."

Grover didn't say anything for a while. Then, when I thought he was going to give me some deep philosophical comment to make me feel better, he said, "Can I have your apple?"

I didn't have much of an appetite, so I let him take it.

I watched the stream of cabs going down Fifth Avenue, and thought about my mom's apartment, only a little ways uptown from where we sat. I hadn't seen her since Christmas. I wanted so bad to jump in a taxi and head home. She'd hug me and be glad to see me, but she'd be disappointed, too. She'd send me right back to Yancy, remind me that I had to try harder, even if this was my sixth school in six years and I was probably going to be kicked out again. I wouldn't be able to stand that sad look she'd give me.

Mr. Brunner parked his wheelchair at the base of the handicapped ramp. He ate celery while he read a paperback novel. A red umbrella stuck up from the back of his chair, making it look like a motorized café table.

I was about to unwrap my sandwich when Nancy Bobofit appeared in front of me with her ugly friends—I guess she'd gotten tired of stealing from the tourists—and dumped her half-eaten lunch in Grover's lap.

"Oops." She grinned at me with her crooked teeth. Her freckles were orange, as if somebody had spray-painted her face with liquid Cheetos.

I tried to stay cool. The school counselor had told me a million times, "Count to ten, get control of your temper." But I was so mad my mind went blank. A wave roared in my ears.

I don't remember touching her, but the next thing I knew, Nancy was sitting on her butt in the fountain, screaming, "Percy pushed me!"

Mrs. Dodds materialized next to us.

Some of the kids were whispering: "Did you see—"

"—the water—"

"—like it grabbed her—"

I didn't know what they were talking about. All I knew was that I was in trouble again.

As soon as Mrs. Dodds was sure poor little Nancy was okay, promising to get her a new shirt at the museum gift shop, etc., etc., Mrs. Dodds turned on me. There was a triumphant fire in her eyes, as if I'd done something she'd been waiting for all semester. "Now, honey—"

"I know," I grumbled. "A month erasing workbooks."

That wasn't the right thing to say.

"Come with me," Mrs. Dodds said.

"Wait!" Grover yelped. "It was me. *I* pushed her."

I stared at him, stunned. I couldn't believe he was trying to cover for me. Mrs. Dodds scared Grover to death.

She glared at him so hard his whiskery chin trembled.

"I don't think so, Mr. Underwood," she said.

"But—"

"You—*will*—stay—here."

Grover looked at me desperately.

"It's okay, man," I told him. "Thanks for trying."

"Honey," Mrs. Dodds barked at me. *"Now."*

Nancy Bobofit smirked.

I gave her my deluxe I'll-kill-you-later stare. Then I turned to face Mrs. Dodds, but she wasn't there. She was standing at the museum entrance, way at the top of the steps, gesturing impatiently at me to come on.

How'd she get there so fast?

I have moments like that a lot, when my brain falls asleep or something, and the next thing I know I've missed something, as if a puzzle piece fell out of the universe and left me staring at the blank place behind it. The school counselor told me this was part of the ADHD, my brain misinterpreting things.

I wasn't so sure.

I went after Mrs. Dodds.

Halfway up the steps, I glanced back at Grover. He was looking pale, cutting his eyes between me and Mr. Brunner, like he wanted Mr. Brunner to notice what was going on, but Mr. Brunner was absorbed in his novel.

I looked back up. Mrs. Dodds had disappeared again. She was now inside the building, at the end of the entrance hall.

Okay, I thought. She's going to make me buy a new shirt for Nancy at the gift shop.

But apparently that wasn't the plan.

I followed her deeper into the museum. When I finally caught up to her, we were back in the Greek and Roman section.

Except for us, the gallery was empty.

Mrs. Dodds stood with her arms crossed in front of a big marble frieze of the Greek gods. She was making this weird noise in her throat, like growling.

Even without the noise, I would've been nervous. It's weird being alone with a teacher, especially Mrs. Dodds. Something about the way she looked at the frieze, as if she wanted to pulverize it . . .

"You've been giving us problems, honey," she said.

I did the safe thing. I said, "Yes, ma'am."

She tugged on the cuffs of her leather jacket. "Did you really think you would get away with it?"

The look in her eyes was beyond mad. It was evil.

She's a teacher, I thought nervously. It's not like she's going to hurt me.

I said, "I'll—I'll try harder, ma'am."

Thunder shook the building.

"We are not fools, Percy Jackson," Mrs. Dodds said. "It was only a matter of time before we found you out. Confess, and you will suffer less pain."

I didn't know what she was talking about.

All I could think of was that the teachers must've found the illegal stash of candy I'd been selling out of my dorm room. Or maybe they'd realized I got my essay on *Tom Sawyer* from the Internet without ever reading the book and now they were going to take away my grade. Or worse, they were going to make me read the book.

"Well?" she demanded.

"Ma'am, I don't . . ."

"Your time is up," she hissed.

Then the weirdest thing happened. Her eyes began to glow like barbecue coals. Her fingers stretched, turning into talons. Her jacket melted into large, leathery wings. She wasn't human. She was a shriveled hag with bat wings and claws and a mouth full of yellow fangs, and she was about to slice me to ribbons.

Then things got even stranger.

Mr. Brunner, who'd been out in front of the museum a minute before, wheeled his chair into the doorway of the gallery, holding a pen in his hand.

"What ho, Percy!" he shouted, and tossed the pen through the air.

Mrs. Dodds lunged at me.

With a yelp, I dodged and felt talons slash the air next to my ear. I snatched the ballpoint pen out of the air, but when it hit my hand, it wasn't a pen anymore. It was a sword—Mr. Brunner's bronze sword, which he always used on tournament day.

Mrs. Dodds spun toward me with a murderous look in her eyes.

My knees were jelly. My hands were shaking so bad I almost dropped the sword.

She snarled, "Die, honey!"

And she flew straight at me.

Absolute terror ran through my body. I did the only thing that came naturally: I swung the sword.

The metal blade hit her shoulder and passed clean through her body as if she were made of water. *Hisss!*

Mrs. Dodds was a sand castle in a power fan. She exploded into yellow powder, vaporized on the spot, leaving nothing but the smell of sulfur and a dying screech and a chill of evil in the air, as if those two glowing red eyes were still watching me.

I was alone.

There was a ballpoint pen in my hand.

Mr. Brunner wasn't there. Nobody was there but me.

My hands were still trembling. My lunch must've been contaminated with magic mushrooms or something.

Had I imagined the whole thing?

I went back outside.

It had started to rain.

Grover was sitting by the fountain, a museum map tented over his head. Nancy Bobofit was still standing there, soaked from her swim in the fountain, grumbling to her ugly friends. When she saw me, she said, "I hope Mrs. Kerr whipped your butt."

I said, "Who?"

"Our *teacher*. Duh!"

I blinked. We had no teacher named Mrs. Kerr. I asked Nancy what she was talking about.

She just rolled her eyes and turned away.

I asked Grover where Mrs. Dodds was.

He said, "Who?"

But he paused first, and he wouldn't look at me, so I thought he was messing with me.

"Not funny, man," I told him. "This is serious."

Thunder boomed overhead.

I saw Mr. Brunner sitting under his red umbrella, reading his book, as if he'd never moved.

I went over to him.

He looked up, a little distracted. "Ah, that would be my pen. Please bring your own writing utensil in the future, Mr. Jackson."

I handed Mr. Brunner his pen. I hadn't even realized I

was still holding it.

"Sir," I said, "where's Mrs. Dodds?"

He stared at me blankly. "Who?"

"The other chaperone. Mrs. Dodds. The pre-algebra teacher."

He frowned and sat forward, looking mildly concerned. "Percy, there is no Mrs. Dodds on this trip. As far as I know, there has never been a Mrs. Dodds at Yancy Academy. Are you feeling all right?"

2 ⚡ THREE OLD LADIES KNIT THE SOCKS OF DEATH

I was used to the occasional weird experience, but usually they were over quickly. This twenty-four/seven hallucination was more than I could handle. For the rest of the school year, the entire campus seemed to be playing some kind of trick on me. The students acted as if they were completely and totally convinced that Mrs. Kerr—a perky blond woman whom I'd never seen in my life until she got on our bus at the end of the field trip—had been our pre-algebra teacher since Christmas.

Every so often I would spring a Mrs. Dodds reference on somebody, just to see if I could trip them up, but they would stare at me like I was psycho.

It got so I almost believed them—Mrs. Dodds had never existed.

Almost.

But Grover couldn't fool me. When I mentioned the name Dodds to him, he would hesitate, then claim she didn't exist. But I knew he was lying.

Something was going on. Something *had* happened at the museum.

I didn't have much time to think about it during the days, but at night, visions of Mrs. Dodds with talons and leathery wings would wake me up in a cold sweat.

The freak weather continued, which didn't help my mood. One night, a thunderstorm blew out the windows in my dorm room. A few days later, the biggest tornado ever spotted in the Hudson Valley touched down only fifty miles from Yancy Academy. One of the current events we studied in social studies class was the unusual number of small planes that had gone down in sudden squalls in the Atlantic that year.

I started feeling cranky and irritable most of the time. My grades slipped from Ds to Fs. I got into more fights with Nancy Bobofit and her friends. I was sent out into the hallway in almost every class.

Finally, when our English teacher, Mr. Nicoll, asked me for the millionth time why I was too lazy to study for spelling tests, I snapped. I called him an old sot. I wasn't even sure what it meant, but it sounded good.

The headmaster sent my mom a letter the following week, making it official: I would not be invited back next year to Yancy Academy.

Fine, I told myself. Just fine.

I was homesick.

I wanted to be with my mom in our little apartment on the Upper East Side, even if I had to go to public school and put up with my obnoxious stepfather and his stupid poker parties.

And yet . . . there were things I'd miss at Yancy. The view of the woods out my dorm window, the Hudson River in the distance, the smell of pine trees. I'd miss Grover, who'd been a good friend, even if he was a little strange. I worried how he'd survive next year without me.

I'd miss Latin class, too—Mr. Brunner's crazy tournament days and his faith that I could do well.

As exam week got closer, Latin was the only test I studied for. I hadn't forgotten what Mr. Brunner had told me about this subject being life-and-death for me. I wasn't sure why, but I'd started to believe him.

The evening before my final, I got so frustrated I threw the *Cambridge Guide to Greek Mythology* across my dorm room. Words had started swimming off the page, circling my head, the letters doing one-eighties as if they were riding skateboards. There was no way I was going to remember the difference between Chiron and Charon, or Polydictes and Polydeuces. And conjugating those Latin verbs? Forget it.

I paced the room, feeling like ants were crawling around inside my shirt.

I remembered Mr. Brunner's serious expression, his thousand-year-old eyes. *I will accept only the best from you, Percy Jackson.*

I took a deep breath. I picked up the mythology book.

I'd never asked a teacher for help before. Maybe if I talked to Mr. Brunner, he could give me some pointers. At least I could apologize for the big fat F I was about to score on his exam. I didn't want to leave Yancy Academy with him thinking I hadn't tried.

I walked downstairs to the faculty offices. Most of them were dark and empty, but Mr. Brunner's door was ajar, light from his window stretching across the hallway floor.

I was three steps from the door handle when I heard voices inside the office. Mr. Brunner asked a question. A voice that was definitely Grover's said ". . . worried about Percy, sir."

I froze.

I'm not usually an eavesdropper, but I dare you to try not listening if you hear your best friend talking about you to an adult.

I inched closer.

". . . alone this summer," Grover was saying. "I mean, a Kindly One in the *school*! Now that we know for sure, and *they* know too—"

"We would only make matters worse by rushing him," Mr. Brunner said. "We need the boy to mature more."

"But he may not have time. The summer solstice deadline—"

"Will have to be resolved without him, Grover. Let him enjoy his ignorance while he still can."

"Sir, he *saw* her. . . ."

"His imagination," Mr. Brunner insisted. "The Mist over the students and staff will be enough to convince him of that."

"Sir, I . . . I can't fail in my duties again." Grover's voice was choked with emotion. "You know what that would mean."

"You haven't failed, Grover," Mr. Brunner said kindly. "I should have seen her for what she was. Now let's just worry about keeping Percy alive until next fall—"

The mythology book dropped out of my hand and hit the floor with a thud.

Mr. Brunner went silent.

My heart hammering, I picked up the book and backed down the hall.

A shadow slid across the lighted glass of Brunner's office door, the shadow of something much taller than my wheelchair-bound teacher, holding something that looked suspiciously like an archer's bow.

I opened the nearest door and slipped inside.

A few seconds later I heard a slow *clop-clop-clop*, like muffled wood blocks, then a sound like an animal snuffling right outside my door. A large, dark shape paused in front of the glass, then moved on.

A bead of sweat trickled down my neck.

Somewhere in the hallway, Mr. Brunner spoke. "Nothing," he murmured. "My nerves haven't been right since the winter solstice."

"Mine neither," Grover said. "But I could have sworn . . ."

"Go back to the dorm," Mr. Brunner told him. "You've got a long day of exams tomorrow."

"Don't remind me."

The lights went out in Mr. Brunner's office.

I waited in the dark for what seemed like forever.

Finally, I slipped out into the hallway and made my way back up to the dorm.

Grover was lying on his bed, studying his Latin exam notes like he'd been there all night.

"Hey," he said, bleary-eyed. "You going to be ready for this test?"

I didn't answer.

"You look awful." He frowned. "Is everything okay?"

"Just . . . tired."

I turned so he couldn't read my expression, and started getting ready for bed.

I didn't understand what I'd heard downstairs. I wanted to believe I'd imagined the whole thing.

But one thing was clear: Grover and Mr. Brunner were talking about me behind my back. They thought I was in some kind of danger.

The next afternoon, as I was leaving the three-hour Latin exam, my eyes swimming with all the Greek and Roman names I'd misspelled, Mr. Brunner called me back inside.

For a moment, I was worried he'd found out about my eavesdropping the night before, but that didn't seem to be the problem.

"Percy," he said. "Don't be discouraged about leaving Yancy. It's . . . it's for the best."

His tone was kind, but the words still embarrassed me. Even though he was speaking quietly, the other kids finishing the test could hear. Nancy Bobofit smirked at me and made sarcastic little kissing motions with her lips.

I mumbled, "Okay, sir."

"I mean . . ." Mr. Brunner wheeled his chair back and forth, like he wasn't sure what to say. "This isn't the right place for you. It was only a matter of time."

My eyes stung.

Here was my favorite teacher, in front of the class, telling me I couldn't handle it. After saying he believed in me all year, now he was telling me I was destined to get kicked out.

"Right," I said, trembling.

"No, no," Mr. Brunner said. "Oh, confound it all. What I'm trying to say . . . you're not normal, Percy. That's nothing to be—"

"Thanks," I blurted. "Thanks a lot, sir, for reminding me."

"Percy—"

But I was already gone.

On the last day of the term, I shoved my clothes into my suitcase.

The other guys were joking around, talking about their vacation plans. One of them was going on a hiking trip to Switzerland. Another was cruising the Caribbean for a month. They were juvenile delinquents, like me, but they were *rich* juvenile delinquents. Their daddies were executives, or ambassadors, or celebrities. I was a nobody, from a family of nobodies.

They asked me what I'd be doing this summer and I told them I was going back to the city.

What I didn't tell them was that I'd have to get a summer job walking dogs or selling magazine subscriptions, and spend my free time worrying about where I'd go to school in the fall.

"Oh," one of the guys said. "That's cool."

They went back to their conversation as if I'd never existed.

The only person I dreaded saying good-bye to was Grover, but as it turned out, I didn't have to. He'd booked a ticket to Manhattan on the same Greyhound as I had, so there we were, together again, heading into the city.

During the whole bus ride, Grover kept glancing nervously down the aisle, watching the other passengers. It occurred to me that he'd always acted nervous and fidgety when we left Yancy, as if he expected something bad to happen. Before, I'd always assumed he was worried about getting teased. But there was nobody to tease him on the Greyhound.

Finally I couldn't stand it anymore.

I said, "Looking for Kindly Ones?"

Grover nearly jumped out of his seat. "Wha—what do you mean?"

I confessed about eavesdropping on him and Mr. Brunner the night before the exam.

Grover's eye twitched. "How much did you hear?"

"Oh . . . not much. What's the summer solstice deadline?"

He winced. "Look, Percy . . . I was just worried for you, see? I mean, hallucinating about demon math teachers . . ."

"Grover—"

"And I was telling Mr. Brunner that maybe you were overstressed or something, because there was no such person as Mrs. Dodds, and . . ."

"Grover, you're a really, really bad liar."

His ears turned pink.

From his shirt pocket, he fished out a grubby business card. "Just take this, okay? In case you need me this summer."

The card was in fancy script, which was murder on my dyslexic eyes, but I finally made out something like:

Grover Underwood
Keeper

Half-Blood Hill
Long Island, New York
(800) 009-0009

"What's Half—"

"Don't say it aloud!" he yelped. "That's my, um . . . summer address."

My heart sank. Grover had a summer home. I'd never considered that his family might be as rich as the others at Yancy.

"Okay," I said glumly. "So, like, if I want to come visit your mansion."

He nodded. "Or . . . or if you need me."

"Why would I need you?"

It came out harsher than I meant it to.

Grover blushed right down to his Adam's apple. "Look, Percy, the truth is, I—I kind of have to protect you."

I stared at him.

All year long, I'd gotten in fights, keeping bullies away

from him. I'd lost sleep worrying that he'd get beaten up next year without me. And here he was acting like he was the one who defended *me*.

"Grover," I said, "what exactly are you protecting me from?"

There was a huge grinding noise under our feet. Black smoke poured from the dashboard and the whole bus filled with a smell like rotten eggs. The driver cursed and limped the Greyhound over to the side of the highway.

After a few minutes clanking around in the engine compartment, the driver announced that we'd all have to get off. Grover and I filed outside with everybody else.

We were on a stretch of country road—no place you'd notice if you didn't break down there. On our side of the highway was nothing but maple trees and litter from passing cars. On the other side, across four lanes of asphalt shimmering with afternoon heat, was an old-fashioned fruit stand.

The stuff on sale looked really good: heaping boxes of bloodred cherries and apples, walnuts and apricots, jugs of cider in a claw-foot tub full of ice. There were no customers, just three old ladies sitting in rocking chairs in the shade of a maple tree, knitting the biggest pair of socks I'd ever seen.

I mean these socks were the size of sweaters, but they were clearly socks. The lady on the right knitted one of them. The lady on the left knitted the other. The lady in the middle held an enormous basket of electric-blue yarn.

All three women looked ancient, with pale faces

wrinkled like fruit leather, silver hair tied back in white bandannas, bony arms sticking out of bleached cotton dresses.

The weirdest thing was, they seemed to be looking right at me.

I looked over at Grover to say something about this and saw that the blood had drained from his face. His nose was twitching.

"Grover?" I said. "Hey, man—"

"Tell me they're not looking at you. They are, aren't they?"

"Yeah. Weird, huh? You think those socks would fit me?"

"Not funny, Percy. Not funny at all."

The old lady in the middle took out a huge pair of scissors—gold and silver, long-bladed, like shears. I heard Grover catch his breath.

"We're getting on the bus," he told me. "Come on."

"What?" I said. "It's a thousand degrees in there."

"Come on!" He pried open the door and climbed inside, but I stayed back.

Across the road, the old ladies were still watching me. The middle one cut the yarn, and I swear I could hear that *snip* across four lanes of traffic. Her two friends balled up the electric-blue socks, leaving me wondering who they could possibly be for—Sasquatch or Godzilla.

At the rear of the bus, the driver wrenched a big chunk of smoking metal out of the engine compartment. The bus shuddered, and the engine roared back to life.

The passengers cheered.

"Darn right!" yelled the driver. He slapped the bus with his hat. "Everybody back on board!"

Once we got going, I started feeling feverish, as if I'd caught the flu.

Grover didn't look much better. He was shivering and his teeth were chattering.

"Grover?"

"Yeah?"

"What are you not telling me?"

He dabbed his forehead with his shirt sleeve. "Percy, what did you see back at the fruit stand?"

"You mean the old ladies? What is it about them, man? They're not like . . . Mrs. Dodds, are they?"

His expression was hard to read, but I got the feeling that the fruit-stand ladies were something much, much worse than Mrs. Dodds. He said, "Just tell me what you saw."

"The middle one took out her scissors, and she cut the yarn."

He closed his eyes and made a gesture with his fingers that might've been crossing himself, but it wasn't. It was something else, something almost—older.

He said, "You saw her snip the cord."

"Yeah. So?" But even as I said it, I knew it was a big deal.

"This is not happening," Grover mumbled. He started chewing at his thumb. "I don't want this to be like the last time."

"What last time?"

"Always sixth grade. They never get past sixth."

"Grover," I said, because he was really starting to scare me. "What are you talking about?"

"Let me walk you home from the bus station. Promise me."

This seemed like a strange request to me, but I promised he could.

"Is this like a superstition or something?" I asked.

No answer.

"Grover—that snipping of the yarn. Does that mean somebody is going to die?"

He looked at me mournfully, like he was already picking the kind of flowers I'd like best on my coffin.

3 GROVER UNEXPECTEDLY LOSES HIS PANTS

Confession time: I ditched Grover as soon as we got to the bus terminal.

I know, I know. It was rude. But Grover was freaking me out, looking at me like I was a dead man, muttering "Why does this always happen?" and "Why does it always have to be sixth grade?"

Whenever he got upset, Grover's bladder acted up, so I wasn't surprised when, as soon as we got off the bus, he made me promise to wait for him, then made a beeline for the restroom. Instead of waiting, I got my suitcase, slipped outside, and caught the first taxi uptown.

"East One-hundred-and-fourth and First," I told the driver.

A word about my mother, before you meet her.

Her name is Sally Jackson and she's the best person in the world, which just proves my theory that the best people have the rottenest luck. Her own parents died in a plane crash when she was five, and she was raised by an uncle who didn't care much about her. She wanted to be a novelist, so she spent high school working to save enough money for a college with a good creative-writing program. Then her uncle got cancer, and she had to quit school her senior year to take care of him. After he died, she was left with no money, no family, and no diploma.

The only good break she ever got was meeting my dad.

I don't have any memories of him, just this sort of warm glow, maybe the barest trace of his smile. My mom doesn't like to talk about him because it makes her sad. She has no pictures.

See, they weren't married. She told me he was rich and important, and their relationship was a secret. Then one day, he set sail across the Atlantic on some important journey, and he never came back.

Lost at sea, my mom told me. Not dead. Lost at sea.

She worked odd jobs, took night classes to get her high school diploma, and raised me on her own. She never complained or got mad. Not even once. But I knew I wasn't an easy kid.

Finally, she married Gabe Ugliano, who was nice the first thirty seconds we knew him, then showed his true colors as a world-class jerk. When I was young, I nicknamed him Smelly Gabe. I'm sorry, but it's the truth. The guy reeked like moldy garlic pizza wrapped in gym shorts.

Between the two of us, we made my mom's life pretty hard. The way Smelly Gabe treated her, the way he and I got along . . . well, when I came home is a good example.

I walked into our little apartment, hoping my mom would be home from work. Instead, Smelly Gabe was in the living room, playing poker with his buddies. The television blared ESPN. Chips and beer cans were strewn all over the carpet.

Hardly looking up, he said around his cigar, "So, you're home."

"Where's my mom?"

"Working," he said. "You got any cash?"

That was it. No *Welcome back. Good to see you. How has your life been the last six months?*

Gabe had put on weight. He looked like a tuskless walrus in thrift-store clothes. He had about three hairs on his head, all combed over his bald scalp, as if that made him handsome or something.

He managed the Electronics Mega-Mart in Queens, but he stayed home most of the time. I don't know why he hadn't been fired long before. He just kept on collecting paychecks, spending the money on cigars that made me nauseous, and on beer, of course. Always beer. Whenever I was home, he expected me to provide his gambling funds. He called that our "guy secret." Meaning, if I told my mom, he would punch my lights out.

"I don't have any cash," I told him.

He raised a greasy eyebrow.

Gabe could sniff out money like a bloodhound, which was surprising, since his own smell should've covered up everything else.

"You took a taxi from the bus station," he said. "Probably paid with a twenty. Got six, seven bucks in change. Somebody expects to live under this roof, he ought to carry his own weight. Am I right, Eddie?"

Eddie, the super of the apartment building, looked at me with a twinge of sympathy. "Come on, Gabe," he said. "The kid just got here."

"Am I *right*?" Gabe repeated.

Eddie scowled into his bowl of pretzels. The other two guys passed gas in harmony.

"Fine," I said. I dug a wad of dollars out of my pocket and threw the money on the table. "I hope you lose."

"Your report card came, brain boy!" he shouted after me. "I wouldn't act so snooty!"

I slammed the door to my room, which really wasn't my room. During school months, it was Gabe's "study." He didn't study anything in there except old car magazines, but he loved shoving my stuff in the closet, leaving his muddy boots on my windowsill, and doing his best to make the place smell like his nasty cologne and cigars and stale beer.

I dropped my suitcase on the bed. Home sweet home.

Gabe's smell was almost worse than the nightmares about Mrs. Dodds, or the sound of that old fruit lady's shears snipping the yarn.

But as soon as I thought that, my legs felt weak. I remembered Grover's look of panic—how he'd made me promise I wouldn't go home without him. A sudden chill rolled through me. I felt like someone—something—was looking for me right now, maybe pounding its way up the stairs, growing long, horrible talons.

Then I heard my mom's voice. "Percy?"

She opened the bedroom door, and my fears melted.

My mother can make me feel good just by walking into

the room. Her eyes sparkle and change color in the light. Her smile is as warm as a quilt. She's got a few gray streaks mixed in with her long brown hair, but I never think of her as old. When she looks at me, it's like she's seeing all the good things about me, none of the bad. I've never heard her raise her voice or say an unkind word to anyone, not even me or Gabe.

"Oh, Percy." She hugged me tight. "I can't believe it. You've grown since Christmas!"

Her red-white-and-blue Sweet on America uniform smelled like the best things in the world: chocolate, licorice, and all the other stuff she sold at the candy shop in Grand Central. She'd brought me a huge bag of "free samples," the way she always did when I came home.

We sat together on the edge of the bed. While I attacked the blueberry sour strings, she ran her hand through my hair and demanded to know everything I hadn't put in my letters. She didn't mention anything about my getting expelled. She didn't seem to care about that. But was I okay? Was her little boy doing all right?

I told her she was smothering me, and to lay off and all that, but secretly, I was really, really glad to see her.

From the other room, Gabe yelled, "Hey, Sally—how about some bean dip, huh?"

I gritted my teeth.

My mom is the nicest lady in the world. She should've been married to a millionaire, not to some jerk like Gabe.

For her sake, I tried to sound upbeat about my last days at Yancy Academy. I told her I wasn't too down about the expulsion. I'd lasted almost the whole year this time. I'd made some new friends. I'd done pretty well in Latin. And honestly, the fights hadn't been as bad as the headmaster said. I liked Yancy Academy. I really did. I put such a good spin on the year, I almost convinced myself. I started choking up, thinking about Grover and Mr. Brunner. Even Nancy Bobofit suddenly didn't seem so bad.

Until that trip to the museum . . .

"What?" my mom asked. Her eyes tugged at my conscience, trying to pull out the secrets. "Did something scare you?"

"No, Mom."

I felt bad lying. I wanted to tell her about Mrs. Dodds and the three old ladies with the yarn, but I thought it would sound stupid.

She pursed her lips. She knew I was holding back, but she didn't push me.

"I have a surprise for you," she said. "We're going to the beach."

My eyes widened. "Montauk?"

"Three nights—same cabin."

"When?"

She smiled. "As soon as I get changed."

I couldn't believe it. My mom and I hadn't been to Montauk the last two summers, because Gabe said there wasn't enough money.

Gabe appeared in the doorway and growled, "Bean dip, Sally? Didn't you hear me?"

I wanted to punch him, but I met my mom's eyes and I understood she was offering me a deal: be nice to Gabe for a little while. Just until she was ready to leave for Montauk. Then we would get out of here.

"I was on my way, honey," she told Gabe. "We were just talking about the trip."

Gabe's eyes got small. "The trip? You mean you were serious about that?"

"I knew it," I muttered. "He won't let us go."

"Of course he will," my mom said evenly. "Your step-father is just worried about money. That's all. Besides," she added, "Gabriel won't have to settle for bean dip. I'll make him enough seven-layer dip for the whole weekend. Guacamole. Sour cream. The works."

Gabe softened a bit. "So this money for your trip . . . it comes out of your clothes budget, right?"

"Yes, honey," my mother said.

"And you won't take my car anywhere but there and back."

"We'll be very careful."

Gabe scratched his double chin. "Maybe if you hurry with that seven-layer dip . . . And maybe if the kid apologizes for interrupting my poker game."

Maybe if I kick you in your soft spot, I thought. And make you sing soprano for a week.

But my mom's eyes warned me not to make him mad.

Why did she put up with this guy? I wanted to scream. Why did she care what he thought?

"I'm sorry," I muttered. "I'm really sorry I interrupted your incredibly important poker game. Please go back to it right now."

Gabe's eyes narrowed. His tiny brain was probably trying to detect sarcasm in my statement.

"Yeah, whatever," he decided.

He went back to his game.

"Thank you, Percy," my mom said. "Once we get to Montauk, we'll talk more about . . . whatever you've forgotten to tell me, okay?"

For a moment, I thought I saw anxiety in her eyes—the same fear I'd seen in Grover during the bus ride—as if my mom too felt an odd chill in the air.

But then her smile returned, and I figured I must have been mistaken. She ruffled my hair and went to make Gabe his seven-layer dip.

An hour later we were ready to leave.

Gabe took a break from his poker game long enough to watch me lug my mom's bags to the car. He kept griping and groaning about losing her cooking—and more important, his '78 Camaro—for the whole weekend.

"Not a scratch on this car, brain boy," he warned me as I loaded the last bag. "Not one little scratch."

Like I'd be the one driving. I was twelve. But that didn't matter to Gabe. If a seagull so much as pooped on his paint job, he'd find a way to blame me.

Watching him lumber back toward the apartment building, I got so mad I did something I can't explain. As Gabe reached the doorway, I made the hand gesture I'd seen Grover make on the bus, a sort of warding-off-evil gesture, a clawed hand over my heart, then a shoving movement toward Gabe. The screen door slammed shut so hard it whacked him in the butt and sent him flying up the staircase as if he'd been shot from a cannon. Maybe it was just the wind, or some freak accident with the hinges, but I didn't stay long enough to find out.

I got in the Camaro and told my mom to step on it.

Our rental cabin was on the south shore, way out at the tip of Long Island. It was a little pastel box with faded curtains, half sunken into the dunes. There was always sand in the sheets and spiders in the cabinets, and most of the time the sea was too cold to swim in.

I loved the place.

We'd been going there since I was a baby. My mom had been going even longer. She never exactly said, but I knew why the beach was special to her. It was the place where she'd met my dad.

As we got closer to Montauk, she seemed to grow younger, years of worry and work disappearing from her face. Her eyes turned the color of the sea.

We got there at sunset, opened all the cabin's windows, and went through our usual cleaning routine. We walked on the beach, fed blue corn chips to the seagulls, and munched on blue jelly beans, blue saltwater taffy, and all the other free samples my mom had brought from work.

I guess I should explain the blue food.

See, Gabe had once told my mom there was no such thing. They had this fight, which seemed like a really small thing at the time. But ever since, my mom went out of her way to eat blue. She baked blue birthday cakes. She mixed blueberry smoothies. She bought blue-corn tortilla chips and brought home blue candy from the shop. This—along with keeping her maiden name, Jackson, rather than calling herself Mrs. Ugliano—was proof that she wasn't totally suckered by Gabe. She did have a rebellious streak, like me.

When it got dark, we made a fire. We roasted hot dogs and marshmallows. Mom told me stories about when she was a kid, back before her parents died in the plane crash. She told me about the books she wanted to write someday, when she had enough money to quit the candy shop.

Eventually, I got up the nerve to ask about what was always on my mind whenever we came to Montauk—my father. Mom's eyes went all misty. I figured she would tell me the same things she always did, but I never got tired of hearing them.

"He was kind, Percy," she said. "Tall, handsome, and powerful. But gentle, too. You have his black hair, you know, and his green eyes."

Mom fished a blue jelly bean out of her candy bag. "I wish he could see you, Percy. He would be so proud."

I wondered how she could say that. What was so great about me? A dyslexic, hyperactive boy with a D+ report card, kicked out of school for the sixth time in six years.

"How old was I?" I asked. "I mean . . . when he left?"

She watched the flames. "He was only with me for one summer, Percy. Right here at this beach. This cabin."

"But . . . he knew me as a baby."

"No, honey. He knew I was expecting a baby, but he never saw you. He had to leave before you were born."

I tried to square that with the fact that I seemed to remember . . . something about my father. A warm glow. A smile.

I had always assumed he knew me as a baby. My mom had never said it outright, but still, I'd felt it must be true. Now, to be told that he'd never even seen me . . .

I felt angry at my father. Maybe it was stupid, but I resented him for going on that ocean voyage, for not having the guts to marry my mom. He'd left us, and now we were stuck with Smelly Gabe.

"Are you going to send me away again?" I asked her. "To another boarding school?"

She pulled a marshmallow from the fire.

"I don't know, honey." Her voice was heavy. "I think . . . I think we'll have to do something."

"Because you don't want me around?" I regretted the words as soon as they were out.

My mom's eyes welled with tears. She took my hand, squeezed it tight. "Oh, Percy, no. I—I *have* to, honey. For your own good. I have to send you away."

Her words reminded me of what Mr. Brunner had said—that it was best for me to leave Yancy.

"Because I'm not normal," I said.

"You say that as if it's a bad thing, Percy. But you don't realize how important you are. I thought Yancy Academy would be far enough away. I thought you'd finally be safe."

"Safe from what?"

She met my eyes, and a flood of memories came back to me—all the weird, scary things that had ever happened to me, some of which I'd tried to forget.

During third grade, a man in a black trench coat had stalked me on the playground. When the teachers threatened to call the police, he went away growling, but no one believed me when I told them that under his broad-brimmed hat, the man only had one eye, right in the middle of his head.

Before that—a really early memory. I was in preschool, and a teacher accidentally put me down for a nap in a cot that a snake had slithered into. My mom screamed when she came to pick me up and found me playing with a limp, scaly rope I'd somehow managed to strangle to death with my meaty toddler hands.

In every single school, something creepy had happened, something unsafe, and I was forced to move.

I knew I should tell my mom about the old ladies at the fruit stand, and Mrs. Dodds at the art museum, about my weird hallucination that I had sliced my math teacher into dust with a sword. But I couldn't make myself tell her. I had a strange feeling the news would end our trip to Montauk, and I didn't want that.

"I've tried to keep you as close to me as I could," my mom said. "They told me that was a mistake. But there's only one other option, Percy—the place your father wanted to send you. And I just . . . I just can't stand to do it."

"My father wanted me to go to a special school?"

"Not a school," she said softly. "A summer camp."

My head was spinning. Why would my dad—who

hadn't even stayed around long enough to see me born—talk to my mom about a summer camp? And if it was so important, why hadn't she ever mentioned it before?

"I'm sorry, Percy," she said, seeing the look in my eyes. "But I can't talk about it. I—I couldn't send you to that place. It might mean saying good-bye to you for good."

"For good? But if it's only a summer camp . . ."

She turned toward the fire, and I knew from her expression that if I asked her any more questions she would start to cry.

That night I had a vivid dream.

It was storming on the beach, and two beautiful animals, a white horse and a golden eagle, were trying to kill each other at the edge of the surf. The eagle swooped down and slashed the horse's muzzle with its huge talons. The horse reared up and kicked at the eagle's wings. As they fought, the ground rumbled, and a monstrous voice chuckled somewhere beneath the earth, goading the animals to fight harder.

I ran toward them, knowing I had to stop them from killing each other, but I was running in slow motion. I knew I would be too late. I saw the eagle dive down, its beak aimed at the horse's wide eyes, and I screamed, *No!*

I woke with a start.

Outside, it really was storming, the kind of storm that cracks trees and blows down houses. There was no horse or eagle on the beach, just lightning making false daylight, and twenty-foot waves pounding the dunes like artillery.

With the next thunderclap, my mom woke. She sat up, eyes wide, and said, "Hurricane."

I knew that was crazy. Long Island never sees hurricanes this early in the summer. But the ocean seemed to have forgotten. Over the roar of the wind, I heard a distant bellow, an angry, tortured sound that made my hair stand on end.

Then a much closer noise, like mallets in the sand. A desperate voice—someone yelling, pounding on our cabin door.

My mother sprang out of bed in her nightgown and threw open the lock.

Grover stood framed in the doorway against a backdrop of pouring rain. But he wasn't . . . he wasn't exactly Grover.

"Searching all night," he gasped. "What were you thinking?"

My mother looked at me in terror—not scared of Grover, but of why he'd come.

"Percy," she said, shouting to be heard over the rain. "What happened at school? What didn't you tell me?"

I was frozen, looking at Grover. I couldn't understand what I was seeing.

"O Zeu kai alloi theoi!" he yelled. "It's right behind me! Didn't you *tell* her?"

I was too shocked to register that he'd just cursed in Ancient Greek, and I'd understood him perfectly. I was too shocked to wonder how Grover had gotten here by himself in the middle of the night. Because Grover didn't have his pants on—and where his legs should be . . . where his legs should be . . .

My mom looked at me sternly and talked in a tone she'd never used before: "*Percy.* Tell me *now!*"

I stammered something about the old ladies at the fruit stand, and Mrs. Dodds, and my mom stared at me, her face deathly pale in the flashes of lightning.

She grabbed her purse, tossed me my rain jacket, and said, "Get to the car. Both of you. *Go!*"

Grover ran for the Camaro—but he wasn't running, exactly. He was trotting, shaking his shaggy hindquarters, and suddenly his story about a muscular disorder in his legs made sense to me. I understood how he could run so fast and still limp when he walked.

Because where his feet should be, there were no feet. There were cloven hooves.

4 ⚡ MY MOTHER TEACHES ME BULLFIGHTING

We tore through the night along dark country roads. Wind slammed against the Camaro. Rain lashed the windshield. I didn't know how my mom could see anything, but she kept her foot on the gas.

Every time there was a flash of lightning, I looked at Grover sitting next to me in the backseat and I wondered if I'd gone insane, or if he was wearing some kind of shag-carpet pants. But, no, the smell was one I remembered from kindergarten field trips to the petting zoo—lanolin, like from wool. The smell of a wet barnyard animal.

All I could think to say was, "So, you and my mom . . . know each other?"

Grover's eyes flitted to the rearview mirror, though there were no cars behind us. "Not exactly," he said. "I mean, we've never met in person. But she knew I was watching you."

"Watching me?"

"Keeping tabs on you. Making sure you were okay. But I wasn't faking being your friend," he added hastily. "I *am* your friend."

"Um . . . what *are* you, exactly?"

"That doesn't matter right now."

"It doesn't matter? From the waist down, my best friend is a donkey—"

Grover let out a sharp, throaty *"Blaa-ha-ha!"*

I'd heard him make that sound before, but I'd always assumed it was a nervous laugh. Now I realized it was more of an irritated bleat.

"Goat!" he cried.

"What?"

"I'm a *goat* from the waist down."

"You just said it didn't matter."

"Blaa-ha-ha! There are satyrs who would trample you underhoof for such an insult!"

"Whoa. Wait. Satyrs. You mean like . . . Mr. Brunner's myths?"

"Were those old ladies at the fruit stand a *myth*, Percy? Was Mrs. Dodds a myth?"

"So you *admit* there was a Mrs. Dodds!"

"Of course."

"Then why—"

"The less you knew, the fewer monsters you'd attract," Grover said, like that should be perfectly obvious. "We put Mist over the humans' eyes. We hoped you'd think the Kindly One was a hallucination. But it was no good. You started to realize who you are."

"Who I—wait a minute, what do you mean?"

The weird bellowing noise rose up again somewhere behind us, closer than before. Whatever was chasing us was still on our trail.

"Percy," my mom said, "there's too much to explain and not enough time. We have to get you to safety."

"Safety from what? Who's after me?"

"Oh, nobody much," Grover said, obviously still miffed about the donkey comment. "Just the Lord of the Dead and a few of his blood-thirstiest minions."

"Grover!"

"Sorry, Mrs. Jackson. Could you drive faster, please?"

I tried to wrap my mind around what was happening, but I couldn't do it. I knew this wasn't a dream. I had no imagination. I could never dream up something this weird.

My mom made a hard left. We swerved onto a narrower road, racing past darkened farmhouses and wooded hills and PICK YOUR OWN STRAWBERRIES signs on white picket fences.

"Where are we going?" I asked.

"The summer camp I told you about." My mother's voice was tight; she was trying for my sake not to be scared. "The place your father wanted to send you."

"The place you didn't want me to go."

"Please, dear," my mother begged. "This is hard enough. Try to understand. You're in danger."

"Because some old ladies cut yarn."

"Those weren't old ladies," Grover said. "Those were the Fates. Do you know what it means—the fact they appeared in front of you? They only do that when you're about to . . . when someone's about to die."

"Whoa. You said 'you.'"

"No I didn't. I said 'someone.'"

"You meant 'you.' As in *me*."

"I meant *you*, like 'someone.' Not you, *you*."

"Boys!" my mom said.

She pulled the wheel hard to the right, and I got a glimpse of a figure she'd swerved to avoid—a dark fluttering shape now lost behind us in the storm.

"What was that?" I asked.

"We're almost there," my mother said, ignoring my question. "Another mile. Please. Please. Please."

I didn't know where *there* was, but I found myself leaning forward in the car, anticipating, wanting us to arrive.

Outside, nothing but rain and darkness—the kind of empty countryside you get way out on the tip of Long Island. I thought about Mrs. Dodds and the moment when she'd changed into the thing with pointed teeth and leathery wings. My limbs went numb from delayed shock. She really *hadn't* been human. She'd meant to kill me.

Then I thought about Mr. Brunner . . . and the sword he had thrown me. Before I could ask Grover about that, the hair rose on the back of my neck. There was a blinding flash, a jaw-rattling *boom!*, and our car exploded.

I remember feeling weightless, like I was being crushed, fried, and hosed down all at the same time.

I peeled my forehead off the back of the driver's seat and said, "Ow."

"Percy!" my mom shouted.

"I'm okay. . . ."

I tried to shake off the daze. I wasn't dead. The car hadn't really exploded. We'd swerved into a ditch. Our driver's-side doors were wedged in the mud. The roof had cracked open like an eggshell and rain was pouring in.

Lightning. That was the only explanation. We'd been blasted right off the road. Next to me in the backseat was a big motionless lump. "Grover!"

He was slumped over, blood trickling from the side of his mouth. I shook his furry hip, thinking, No! Even if you are half barnyard animal, you're my best friend and I don't want you to die!

Then he groaned "Food," and I knew there was hope.

"Percy," my mother said, "we have to . . ." Her voice faltered.

I looked back. In a flash of lightning, through the mud-spattered rear windshield, I saw a figure lumbering toward us on the shoulder of the road. The sight of it made my skin crawl. It was a dark silhouette of a huge guy, like a football player. He seemed to be holding a blanket over his head. His top half was bulky and fuzzy. His upraised hands made it look like he had horns.

I swallowed hard. "Who is—"

"Percy," my mother said, deadly serious. "Get out of the car."

My mother threw herself against the driver's-side door. It was jammed shut in the mud. I tried mine. Stuck too. I looked up desperately at the hole in the roof. It might've been an exit, but the edges were sizzling and smoking.

"Climb out the passenger's side!" my mother told me. "Percy—you have to run. Do you see that big tree?"

"What?"

Another flash of lightning, and through the smoking hole in the roof I saw the tree she meant: a huge, White House Christmas tree–sized pine at the crest of the nearest hill.

"That's the property line," my mom said. "Get over that hill and you'll see a big farmhouse down in the valley. Run and don't look back. Yell for help. Don't stop until you reach the door."

"Mom, you're coming too."

Her face was pale, her eyes as sad as when she looked at the ocean.

"No!" I shouted. "You *are* coming with me. Help me carry Grover."

"Food!" Grover moaned, a little louder.

The man with the blanket on his head kept coming toward us, making his grunting, snorting noises. As he got closer, I realized he *couldn't* be holding a blanket over his head, because his hands—huge meaty hands—were swinging at his sides. There was no blanket. Meaning the bulky, fuzzy mass that was too big to be his head . . . was his head. And the points that looked like horns . . .

"He doesn't want *us*," my mother told me. "He wants you. Besides, I can't cross the property line."

"But . . ."

"We don't have time, Percy. Go. Please."

I got mad, then—mad at my mother, at Grover the goat, at the thing with horns that was lumbering toward us slowly and deliberately like, like a bull.

I climbed across Grover and pushed the door open into the rain. "We're going together. Come on, Mom."

"I told you—"

"Mom! I am not leaving you. Help me with Grover."

I didn't wait for her answer. I scrambled outside, dragging Grover from the car. He was surprisingly light, but I couldn't have carried him very far if my mom hadn't come to my aid.

Together, we draped Grover's arms over our shoulders and started stumbling uphill through wet waist-high grass.

Glancing back, I got my first clear look at the monster. He was seven feet tall, easy, his arms and legs like something from the cover of *Muscle Man* magazine—bulging biceps and triceps and a bunch of other 'ceps, all stuffed like baseballs under vein-webbed skin. He wore no clothes except underwear—I mean, bright white Fruit of the Looms—which would've looked funny, except that the top half of his body was so scary. Coarse brown hair started at about his belly button and got thicker as it reached his shoulders.

His neck was a mass of muscle and fur leading up to his enormous head, which had a snout as long as my arm, snotty nostrils with a gleaming brass ring, cruel black eyes, and horns—enormous black-and-white horns with points you just couldn't get from an electric sharpener.

I recognized the monster, all right. He had been in one of the first stories Mr. Brunner told us. But he couldn't be real.

I blinked the rain out of my eyes. "That's—"

"Pasiphae's son," my mother said. "I wish I'd known how badly they want to kill you."

"But he's the Min—"

"Don't say his name," she warned. "Names have power."

The pine tree was still way too far—a hundred yards uphill at least.

I glanced behind me again.

The bull-man hunched over our car, looking in the windows—or not looking, exactly. More like snuffling, nuzzling. I wasn't sure why he bothered, since we were only about fifty feet away.

"Food?" Grover moaned.

"Shhh," I told him. "Mom, what's he doing? Doesn't he see us?"

"His sight and hearing are terrible," she said. "He goes by smell. But he'll figure out where we are soon enough."

As if on cue, the bull-man bellowed in rage. He picked up Gabe's Camaro by the torn roof, the chassis creaking and groaning. He raised the car over his head and threw it down the road. It slammed into the wet asphalt and skidded in a shower of sparks for about half a mile before coming to a stop. The gas tank exploded.

Not a scratch, I remembered Gabe saying.

Oops.

"Percy," my mom said. "When he sees us, he'll charge. Wait until the last second, then jump out of the way—directly sideways. He can't change directions very well once he's charging. Do you understand?"

"How do you know all this?"

"I've been worried about an attack for a long time. I should have expected this. I was selfish, keeping you near me."

"Keeping me near you? But—"

Another bellow of rage, and the bull-man started tromping uphill.

He'd smelled us.

The pine tree was only a few more yards, but the hill was getting steeper and slicker, and Grover wasn't getting any lighter.

The bull-man closed in. Another few seconds and he'd be on top of us.

My mother must've been exhausted, but she shouldered Grover. "Go, Percy! Separate! Remember what I said."

I didn't want to split up, but I had the feeling she was right—it was our only chance. I sprinted to the left, turned, and saw the creature bearing down on me. His black eyes glowed with hate. He reeked like rotten meat.

He lowered his head and charged, those razor-sharp horns aimed straight at my chest.

The fear in my stomach made me want to bolt, but that wouldn't work. I could never outrun this thing. So I held my ground, and at the last moment, I jumped to the side.

The bull-man stormed past like a freight train, then bellowed with frustration and turned, but not toward me this time, toward my mother, who was setting Grover down in the grass.

We'd reached the crest of the hill. Down the other side I could see a valley, just as my mother had said, and the lights of a farmhouse glowing yellow through the rain. But that was half a mile away. We'd never make it.

The bull-man grunted, pawing the ground. He kept

eyeing my mother, who was now retreating slowly downhill, back toward the road, trying to lead the monster away from Grover.

"Run, Percy!" she told me. "I can't go any farther. Run!"

But I just stood there, frozen in fear, as the monster charged her. She tried to sidestep, as she'd told me to do, but the monster had learned his lesson. His hand shot out and grabbed her by the neck as she tried to get away. He lifted her as she struggled, kicking and pummeling the air.

"Mom!"

She caught my eyes, managed to choke out one last word: "Go!"

Then, with an angry roar, the monster closed his fists around my mother's neck, and she dissolved before my eyes, melting into light, a shimmering golden form, as if she were a holographic projection. A blinding flash, and she was simply . . . gone.

"No!"

Anger replaced my fear. Newfound strength burned in my limbs—the same rush of energy I'd gotten when Mrs. Dodds grew talons.

The bull-man bore down on Grover, who lay helpless in the grass. The monster hunched over, snuffling my best friend, as if he were about to lift Grover up and make him dissolve too.

I couldn't allow that.

I stripped off my red rain jacket.

"Hey!" I screamed, waving the jacket, running to one side of the monster. "Hey, stupid! Ground beef!"

"Raaaarrrrr!" The monster turned toward me, shaking his meaty fists.

I had an idea—a stupid idea, but better than no idea at all. I put my back to the big pine tree and waved my red jacket in front of the bull-man, thinking I'd jump out of the way at the last moment.

But it didn't happen like that.

The bull-man charged too fast, his arms out to grab me whichever way I tried to dodge.

Time slowed down.

My legs tensed. I couldn't jump sideways, so I leaped straight up, kicking off from the creature's head, using it as a springboard, turning in midair, and landing on his neck.

How did I do that? I didn't have time to figure it out. A millisecond later, the monster's head slammed into the tree and the impact nearly knocked my teeth out.

The bull-man staggered around, trying to shake me. I locked my arms around his horns to keep from being thrown. Thunder and lightning were still going strong. The rain was in my eyes. The smell of rotten meat burned my nostrils.

The monster shook himself around and bucked like a rodeo bull. He should have just backed up into the tree and smashed me flat, but I was starting to realize that this thing had only one gear: forward.

Meanwhile, Grover started groaning in the grass. I wanted to yell at him to shut up, but the way I was getting tossed around, if I opened my mouth I'd bite my own tongue off.

"Food!" Grover moaned.

The bull-man wheeled toward him, pawed the ground again, and got ready to charge. I thought about how he had squeezed the life out of my mother, made her disappear in a flash of light, and rage filled me like high-octane fuel. I got both hands around one horn and I pulled backward with all my might. The monster tensed, gave a surprised grunt, then—*snap!*

The bull-man screamed and flung me through the air. I landed flat on my back in the grass. My head smacked against a rock. When I sat up, my vision was blurry, but I had a horn in my hands, a ragged bone weapon the size of a knife.

The monster charged.

Without thinking, I rolled to one side and came up kneeling. As the monster barreled past, I drove the broken horn straight into his side, right up under his furry rib cage.

The bull-man roared in agony. He flailed, clawing at his chest, then began to disintegrate—not like my mother, in a flash of golden light, but like crumbling sand, blown away in chunks by the wind, the same way Mrs. Dodds had burst apart.

The monster was gone.

The rain had stopped. The storm still rumbled, but only in the distance. I smelled like livestock and my knees were shaking. My head felt like it was splitting open. I was weak and scared and trembling with grief. I'd just seen my mother vanish. I wanted to lie down and cry, but there was Grover, needing my help, so I managed to haul him up and stagger down into the valley, toward the lights of the farmhouse. I was crying, calling for my mother, but I held on to Grover—I wasn't going to let him go.

The last thing I remember is collapsing on a wooden porch, looking up at a ceiling fan circling above me, moths flying around a yellow light, and the stern faces of a familiar-looking bearded man and a pretty girl, her blond hair curled like a princess's. They both looked down at me, and the girl said, "He's the one. He must be."

"Silence, Annabeth," the man said. "He's still conscious. Bring him inside."

5 ⚡ I PLAY PINOCHLE WITH A HORSE

I had weird dreams full of barnyard animals. Most of them wanted to kill me. The rest wanted food.

I must've woken up several times, but what I heard and saw made no sense, so I just passed out again. I remember lying in a soft bed, being spoon-fed something that tasted like buttered popcorn, only it was pudding. The girl with curly blond hair hovered over me, smirking as she scraped drips off my chin with the spoon.

When she saw my eyes open, she asked, "What will happen at the summer solstice?"

I managed to croak, "What?"

She looked around, as if afraid someone would over-hear. "What's going on? What was stolen? We've only got a few weeks!"

"I'm sorry," I mumbled, "I don't . . ."

Somebody knocked on the door, and the girl quickly filled my mouth with pudding.

The next time I woke up, the girl was gone.

A husky blond dude, like a surfer, stood in the corner of the bedroom keeping watch over me. He had blue eyes—at least a dozen of them—on his cheeks, his forehead, the backs of his hands.

* * *

When I finally came around for good, there was nothing weird about my surroundings, except that they were nicer than I was used to. I was sitting in a deck chair on a huge porch, gazing across a meadow at green hills in the distance. The breeze smelled like strawberries. There was a blanket over my legs, a pillow behind my neck. All that was great, but my mouth felt like a scorpion had been using it for a nest. My tongue was dry and nasty and every one of my teeth hurt.

On the table next to me was a tall drink. It looked like iced apple juice, with a green straw and a paper parasol stuck through a maraschino cherry.

My hand was so weak I almost dropped the glass once I got my fingers around it.

"Careful," a familiar voice said.

Grover was leaning against the porch railing, looking like he hadn't slept in a week. Under one arm, he cradled a shoe box. He was wearing blue jeans, Converse hi-tops and a bright orange T-shirt that said CAMP HALF-BLOOD. Just plain old Grover. Not the goat boy.

So maybe I'd had a nightmare. Maybe my mom was okay. We were still on vacation, and we'd stopped here at this big house for some reason. And . . .

"You saved my life," Grover said. "I . . . well, the least I could do . . . I went back to the hill. I thought you might want this."

Reverently, he placed the shoe box in my lap.

Inside was a black-and-white bull's horn, the base jagged

from being broken off, the tip splattered with dried blood. It hadn't been a nightmare.

"The Minotaur," I said.

"Um, Percy, it isn't a good idea—"

"That's what they call him in the Greek myths, isn't it?" I demanded. "The Minotaur. Half man, half bull."

Grover shifted uncomfortably. "You've been out for two days. How much do you remember?"

"My mom. Is she really . . ."

He looked down.

I stared across the meadow. There were groves of trees, a winding stream, acres of strawberries spread out under the blue sky. The valley was surrounded by rolling hills, and the tallest one, directly in front of us, was the one with the huge pine tree on top. Even that looked beautiful in the sunlight.

My mother was gone. The whole world should be black and cold. Nothing should look beautiful.

"I'm sorry," Grover sniffled. "I'm a failure. I'm—I'm the worst satyr in the world."

He moaned, stomping his foot so hard it came off. I mean, the Converse hi-top came off. The inside was filled with Styrofoam, except for a hoof-shaped hole.

"Oh, Styx!" he mumbled.

Thunder rolled across the clear sky.

As he struggled to get his hoof back in the fake foot, I thought, Well, that settles it.

Grover was a satyr. I was ready to bet that if I shaved his curly brown hair, I'd find tiny horns on his head. But I was too miserable to care that satyrs existed, or even minotaurs.

All that meant was my mom really had been squeezed into nothingness, dissolved into yellow light.

I was alone. An orphan. I would have to live with . . . Smelly Gabe? No. That would never happen. I would live on the streets first. I would pretend I was seventeen and join the army. I'd do something.

Grover was still sniffling. The poor kid—poor goat, satyr, whatever—looked as if he expected to be hit.

I said, "It wasn't your fault."

"Yes, it was. I was supposed to *protect* you."

"Did my mother ask you to protect me?"

"No. But that's my job. I'm a keeper. At least . . . I was."

"But why . . ." I suddenly felt dizzy, my vision swimming.

"Don't strain yourself," Grover said. "Here."

He helped me hold my glass and put the straw to my lips.

I recoiled at the taste, because I was expecting apple juice. It wasn't that at all. It was chocolate-chip cookies. Liquid cookies. And not just any cookies—my mom's homemade blue chocolate-chip cookies, buttery and hot, with the chips still melting. Drinking it, my whole body felt warm and good, full of energy. My grief didn't go away, but I felt as if my mom had just brushed her hand against my cheek, given me a cookie the way she used to when I was small, and told me everything was going to be okay.

Before I knew it, I'd drained the glass. I stared into it, sure I'd just had a warm drink, but the ice cubes hadn't even melted.

"Was it good?" Grover asked.

I nodded.

"What did it taste like?" He sounded so wistful, I felt guilty.

"Sorry," I said. "I should've let you taste."

His eyes got wide. "No! That's not what I meant. I just . . . wondered."

"Chocolate-chip cookies," I said. "My mom's. Home-made."

He sighed. "And how do you feel?"

"Like I could throw Nancy Bobofit a hundred yards."

"That's good," he said. "That's good. I don't think you could risk drinking any more of that stuff."

"What do you mean?"

He took the empty glass from me gingerly, as if it were dynamite, and set it back on the table. "Come on. Chiron and Mr. D are waiting."

The porch wrapped all the way around the farmhouse.

My legs felt wobbly, trying to walk that far. Grover offered to carry the Minotaur horn, but I held on to it. I'd paid for that souvenir the hard way. I wasn't going to let it go.

As we came around the opposite end of the house, I caught my breath.

We must've been on the north shore of Long Island, because on this side of the house, the valley marched all the way up to the water, which glittered about a mile in the distance. Between here and there, I simply couldn't process everything I was seeing. The landscape was dotted with buildings that looked like ancient Greek architecture—an open-air pavilion, an amphitheater, a circular arena—except that they all looked brand new, their white marble columns sparkling in the sun. In a nearby sandpit, a dozen high school—age kids and satyrs played volleyball. Canoes glided across a small lake. Kids in bright orange T-shirts like Grover's were chasing each other around a cluster of cabins nestled in the woods. Some shot targets at an archery range. Others rode horses down a wooded trail, and, unless I was hallucinating, some of their horses had wings.

Down at the end of the porch, two men sat across from each other at a card table. The blond-haired girl who'd spoon-fed me popcorn-flavored pudding was leaning on the porch rail next to them.

The man facing me was small, but porky. He had a red nose, big watery eyes, and curly hair so black it was almost purple. He looked like those paintings of baby angels—what do you call them, hubbubs? No, cherubs. That's it. He looked like a cherub who'd turned middle-aged in a trailer park. He wore a tiger-pattern Hawaiian shirt, and he would've fit right in at one of Gabe's poker parties, except I got the feeling this guy could've out-gambled even my step-father.

"That's Mr. D," Grover murmured to me. "He's the camp director. Be polite. The girl, that's Annabeth Chase. She's just a camper, but she's been here longer than just about anybody. And you already know Chiron. . . ."

He pointed at the guy whose back was to me.

First, I realized he was sitting in the wheelchair. Then I

recognized the tweed jacket, the thinning brown hair, the scraggly beard.

"Mr. Brunner!" I cried.

The Latin teacher turned and smiled at me. His eyes had that mischievous glint they sometimes got in class when he pulled a pop quiz and made all the multiple choice answers *B*.

"Ah, good, Percy," he said. "Now we have four for pinochle."

He offered me a chair to the right of Mr. D, who looked at me with bloodshot eyes and heaved a great sigh. "Oh, I suppose I must say it. Welcome to Camp Half-Blood. There. Now, don't expect me to be glad to see you."

"Uh, thanks." I scooted a little farther away from him because, if there was one thing I had learned from living with Gabe, it was how to tell when an adult has been hitting the happy juice. If Mr. D was a stranger to alcohol, I was a satyr.

"Annabeth?" Mr. Brunner called to the blond girl.

She came forward and Mr. Brunner introduced us. "This young lady nursed you back to health, Percy. Annabeth, my dear, why don't you go check on Percy's bunk? We'll be putting him in cabin eleven for now."

Annabeth said, "Sure, Chiron."

She was probably my age, maybe a couple of inches taller, and a whole lot more athletic looking. With her deep tan and her curly blond hair, she was almost exactly what I thought a stereotypical California girl would look like, except her eyes ruined the image. They were startling gray, like storm clouds; pretty, but intimidating, too, as if she were analyzing the best way to take me down in a fight.

She glanced at the minotaur horn in my hands, then back at me. I imagined she was going to say, *You killed a minotaur!* or *Wow, you're so awesome!* or something like that.

Instead she said, "You drool when you sleep."

Then she sprinted off down the lawn, her blond hair flying behind her.

"So," I said, anxious to change the subject. "You, uh, work here, Mr. Brunner?"

"Not Mr. Brunner," the ex–Mr. Brunner said. "I'm afraid that was a pseudonym. You may call me Chiron."

"Okay." Totally confused, I looked at the director. "And Mr. D . . . does that stand for something?"

Mr. D stopped shuffling the cards. He looked at me like I'd just belched loudly. "Young man, names are powerful things. You don't just go around using them for no reason."

"Oh. Right. Sorry."

"I must say, Percy," Chiron-Brunner broke in, "I'm glad to see you alive. It's been a long time since I've made a house call to a potential camper. I'd hate to think I've wasted my time."

"House call?"

"My year at Yancy Academy, to instruct you. We have satyrs at most schools, of course, keeping a lookout. But Grover alerted me as soon as he met you. He sensed you were something special, so I decided to come upstate. I convinced the other Latin teacher to . . . ah, take a leave of absence."

I tried to remember the beginning of the school year. It seemed like so long ago, but I did have a fuzzy memory of there being another Latin teacher my first week at Yancy. Then, without explanation, he had disappeared and Mr. Brunner had taken the class.

"You came to Yancy just to teach me?" I asked.

Chiron nodded. "Honestly, I wasn't sure about you at first. We contacted your mother, let her know we were keeping an eye on you in case you were ready for Camp Half-Blood. But you still had so much to learn. Nevertheless, you made it here alive, and that's always the first test."

"Grover," Mr. D said impatiently, "are you playing or not?"

"Yes, sir!" Grover trembled as he took the fourth chair, though I didn't know why he should be so afraid of a pudgy little man in a tiger-print Hawaiian shirt.

"You *do* know how to play pinochle?" Mr. D eyed me suspiciously.

"I'm afraid not," I said.

"I'm afraid not, *sir*," he said.

"Sir," I repeated. I was liking the camp director less and less.

"Well," he told me, "it is, along with gladiator fighting and Pac-Man, one of the greatest games ever invented by humans. I would expect all *civilized* young men to know the rules."

"I'm sure the boy can learn," Chiron said.

"Please," I said, "what is this place? What am I doing here? Mr. Brun—Chiron—why would you go to Yancy Academy just to teach me?"

Mr. D snorted. "I asked the same question."

The camp director dealt the cards. Grover flinched every time one landed in his pile.

Chiron smiled at me sympathetically, the way he used to in Latin class, as if to let me know that no matter what my average was, *I* was his star student. He expected *me* to have the right answer.

"Percy," he said. "Did your mother tell you nothing?"

"She said . . ." I remembered her sad eyes, looking out over the sea. "She told me she was afraid to send me here, even though my father had wanted her to. She said that once I was here, I probably couldn't leave. She wanted to keep me close to her."

"Typical," Mr. D said. "That's how they usually get killed. Young man, are you bidding or not?"

"What?" I asked.

He explained, impatiently, how you bid in pinochle, and so I did.

"I'm afraid there's too much to tell," Chiron said. "I'm afraid our usual orientation film won't be sufficient."

"Orientation film?" I asked.

"No," Chiron decided. "Well, Percy. You know your friend Grover is a satyr. You know"—he pointed to the horn in the shoe box—"that you have killed the Minotaur. No small feat, either, lad. What you may not know is that great powers are at work in your life. Gods—the forces you call the Greek gods—are very much alive."

I stared at the others around the table.

I waited for somebody to yell, *Not!* But all I got was Mr. D yelling, "Oh, a royal marriage. Trick! Trick!" He cackled as he tallied up his points.

"Mr. D," Grover asked timidly, "if you're not going to eat it, could I have your Diet Coke can?"

"Eh? Oh, all right."

Grover bit a huge shard out of the empty aluminum can and chewed it mournfully.

"Wait," I told Chiron. "You're telling me there's such a thing as God."

"Well, now," Chiron said. "God—capital *G*, God. That's a different matter altogether. We shan't deal with the metaphysical."

"Metaphysical? But you were just talking about—"

"Ah, gods, plural, as in, great beings that control the forces of nature and human endeavors: the immortal gods of Olympus. That's a smaller matter."

"Smaller?"

"Yes, quite. The gods we discussed in Latin class."

"Zeus," I said. "Hera. Apollo. You mean them."

And there it was again—distant thunder on a cloudless day.

"Young man," said Mr. D, "I would really be less casual about throwing those names around, if I were you."

"But they're stories," I said. "They're—myths, to explain

lightning and the seasons and stuff. They're what people believed before there was science."

"Science!" Mr. D scoffed. "And tell me, Perseus Jackson"—I flinched when he said my real name, which I never told anybody—"what will people think of your 'science' two thousand years from now?" Mr. D continued. "Hmm? They will call it primitive mumbo jumbo. That's what. Oh, I love mortals—they have absolutely no sense of perspective. They think they've come so-o-o far. And have they, Chiron? Look at this boy and tell me."

I wasn't liking Mr. D much, but there was something about the way he called me mortal, as if . . . he wasn't. It was enough to put a lump in my throat, to suggest why Grover was dutifully minding his cards, chewing his soda can, and keeping his mouth shut.

"Percy," Chiron said, "you may choose to believe or not, but the fact is that *immortal* means immortal. Can you imagine that for a moment, never dying? Never fading? Existing, just as you are, for all time?"

I was about to answer, off the top of my head, that it sounded like a pretty good deal, but the tone of Chiron's voice made me hesitate.

"You mean, whether people believed in you or not," I said.

"Exactly," Chiron agreed. "If you were a god, how would you like being called a myth, an old story to explain lightning? What if I told you, Perseus Jackson, that someday people would call *you* a myth, just created to explain how little boys can get over losing their mothers?"

My heart pounded. He was trying to make me angry for some reason, but I wasn't going to let him. I said, "I wouldn't like it. But I don't believe in gods."

"Oh, you'd better," Mr. D murmured. "Before one of them incinerates you."

Grover said, "P-please, sir. He's just lost his mother. He's in shock."

"A lucky thing, too," Mr. D grumbled, playing a card. "Bad enough I'm confined to this miserable job, working with boys who don't even believe!"

He waved his hand and a goblet appeared on the table, as if the sunlight had bent, momentarily, and woven the air into glass. The goblet filled itself with red wine.

My jaw dropped, but Chiron hardly looked up.

"Mr. D," he warned, "your restrictions."

Mr. D looked at the wine and feigned surprise.

"Dear me." He looked at the sky and yelled, "Old habits! Sorry!"

More thunder.

Mr. D waved his hand again, and the wineglass changed into a fresh can of Diet Coke. He sighed unhappily, popped the top of the soda, and went back to his card game.

Chiron winked at me. "Mr. D offended his father a while back, took a fancy to a wood nymph who had been declared off-limits."

"A wood nymph," I repeated, still staring at the Diet Coke can like it was from outer space.

"Yes," Mr. D confessed. "Father loves to punish me. The first time, Prohibition. Ghastly! Absolutely horrid ten years! The second time—well, she really was pretty, and I couldn't stay away—the second time, he sent me here. Half-Blood Hill. Summer camp for brats like you. 'Be a better influence,' he told me. 'Work with youths rather than tearing them down.' Ha! Absolutely unfair."

Mr. D sounded about six years old, like a pouting little kid.

"And . . ." I stammered, "your father is . . ."

"*Di immortales*, Chiron," Mr. D said. "I thought you taught this boy the basics. My father is Zeus, of course."

I ran through D names from Greek mythology. Wine. The skin of a tiger. The satyrs that all seemed to work here. The way Grover cringed, as if Mr. D were his master.

"You're Dionysus," I said. "The god of wine."

Mr. D rolled his eyes. "What do they say, these days, Grover? Do the children say, 'Well, duh!'?"

"Y-yes, Mr. D."

"Then, well, duh! Percy Jackson. Did you think I was Aphrodite, perhaps?"

"You're a god."

"Yes, child."

"A god. You."

He turned to look at me straight on, and I saw a kind of purplish fire in his eyes, a hint that this whiny, plump little man was only showing me the tiniest bit of his true nature. I saw visions of grape vines choking unbelievers to death, drunken warriors insane with battle lust, sailors screaming as their hands turned to flippers, their faces elongating into dolphin snouts. I knew that if I pushed him,

Mr. D would show me worse things. He would plant a disease in my brain that would leave me wearing a strait-jacket in a rubber room for the rest of my life.

"Would you like to test me, child?" he said quietly.

"No. No, sir."

The fire died a little. He turned back to his card game. "I believe I win."

"Not quite, Mr. D," Chiron said. He set down a straight, tallied the points, and said, "The game goes to me."

I thought Mr. D was going to vaporize Chiron right out of his wheelchair, but he just sighed through his nose, as if he were used to being beaten by the Latin teacher. He got up, and Grover rose, too.

"I'm tired," Mr. D said. "I believe I'll take a nap before the sing-along tonight. But first, Grover, we need to talk, *again*, about your less-than-perfect performance on this assignment."

Grover's face beaded with sweat. "Y-yes, sir."

Mr. D turned to me. "Cabin eleven, Percy Jackson. And mind your manners."

He swept into the farmhouse, Grover following miserably.

"Will Grover be okay?" I asked Chiron.

Chiron nodded, though he looked a bit troubled. "Old Dionysus isn't really mad. He just hates his job. He's been . . . ah, grounded, I guess you would say, and he can't stand waiting another century before he's allowed to go back to Olympus."

"Mount Olympus," I said. "You're telling me there really is a palace there?"

"Well now, there's Mount Olympus in Greece. And then there's the home of the gods, the convergence point of their powers, which did indeed used to be on Mount Olympus. It's still called Mount Olympus, out of respect to the old ways, but the palace moves, Percy, just as the gods do."

"You mean the Greek gods are here? Like . . . in *America*?"

"Well, certainly. The gods move with the heart of the West."

"The what?"

"Come now, Percy. What you call 'Western civilization.' Do you think it's just an abstract concept? No, it's a living force. A collective consciousness that has burned bright for thousands of years. The gods are part of it. You might even say they are the source of it, or at least, they are tied so tightly to it that they couldn't possibly fade, not unless all of Western civilization were obliterated. The fire started in Greece. Then, as you well know—or as I hope you know, since you passed my course—the heart of the fire moved to Rome, and so did the gods. Oh, different names, perhaps— Jupiter for Zeus, Venus for Aphrodite, and so on—but the same forces, the same gods."

"And then they died."

"Died? No. Did the West die? The gods simply moved, to Germany, to France, to Spain, for a while. Wherever the flame was brightest, the gods were there. They spent several centuries in England. All you need to do is look at the architecture. People do not forget the gods. Every place they've ruled, for the last three thousand years, you can see them in paintings, in statues, on the most important buildings. And yes, Percy, of course they are now in your United States. Look at your symbol, the eagle of Zeus. Look at the statue of Prometheus in Rockefeller Center, the Greek facades of your government buildings in Washington. I defy you to find any American city where the Olympians are not prominently displayed in multiple places. Like it or not—and believe me, plenty of people weren't very fond of Rome, either—America is now the heart of the flame. It is the great power of the West. And so Olympus is here. And we are here."

It was all too much, especially the fact that *I* seemed to be included in Chiron's *we*, as if I were part of some club.

"Who are you, Chiron? Who . . . who am I?"

Chiron smiled. He shifted his weight as if he were going to get up out of his wheelchair, but I knew that was impossible. He was paralyzed from the waist down.

"Who are you?" he mused. "Well, that's the question we all want answered, isn't it? But for now, we should get you a bunk in cabin eleven. There will be new friends to meet. And plenty of time for lessons tomorrow. Besides, there will be s'mores at the campfire tonight, and I simply adore chocolate."

And then he did rise from his wheelchair. But there was something odd about the way he did it. His blanket fell away from his legs, but the legs didn't move. His waist kept getting longer, rising above his belt. At first, I thought he was wearing very long, white velvet underwear, but as he kept rising out of the chair, taller than any man, I realized that the velvet underwear wasn't underwear; it was the front of an animal, muscle and sinew under coarse white fur. And the wheelchair wasn't a chair. It was some kind of container, an enormous box on wheels, and it must've been magic, because there's no way it could've held all of him. A leg came out, long and knobby-kneed, with a huge polished hoof. Then another front leg, then hindquarters, and then the box was empty, nothing but a metal shell with a couple of fake human legs attached.

I stared at the horse who had just sprung from the wheelchair: a huge white stallion. But where its neck should be was the upper body of my Latin teacher, smoothly grafted to the horse's trunk.

"What a relief," the centaur said. "I'd been cooped up in there so long, my fetlocks had fallen asleep. Now, come, Percy Jackson. Let's meet the other campers."

6 I BECOME SUPREME LORD OF THE BATHROOM

Once I got over the fact that my Latin teacher was a horse, we had a nice tour, though I was careful not to walk behind him. I'd done pooper-scooper patrol in the Macy's Thanksgiving Day Parade a few times, and, I'm sorry, I did not trust Chiron's back end the way I trusted his front.

We passed the volleyball pit. Several of the campers nudged each other. One pointed to the minotaur horn I was carrying. Another said, "That's *him.*"

Most of the campers were older than me. Their satyr friends were bigger than Grover, all of them trotting around in orange CAMP HALF-BLOOD T-shirts, with nothing else to cover their bare shaggy hindquarters. I wasn't normally shy, but the way they stared at me made me uncomfortable. I felt like they were expecting me to do a flip or something.

I looked back at the farmhouse. It was a lot bigger than I'd realized—four stories tall, sky blue with white trim, like an upscale seaside resort. I was checking out the brass eagle weather vane on top when something caught my eye, a shadow in the uppermost window of the attic gable. Something had moved the curtain, just for a second, and I got the distinct impression I was being watched.

"What's up there?" I asked Chiron.

He looked where I was pointing, and his smile faded. "Just the attic."

"Somebody lives there?"

"No," he said with finality. "Not a single living thing."

I got the feeling he was being truthful. But I was also sure something had moved that curtain.

"Come along, Percy," Chiron said, his lighthearted tone now a little forced. "Lots to see."

We walked through the strawberry fields, where campers were picking bushels of berries while a satyr played a tune on a reed pipe.

Chiron told me the camp grew a nice crop for export to New York restaurants and Mount Olympus. "It pays our expenses," he explained. "And the strawberries take almost no effort."

He said Mr. D had this effect on fruit-bearing plants: they just went crazy when he was around. It worked best with wine grapes, but Mr. D was restricted from growing those, so they grew strawberries instead.

I watched the satyr playing his pipe. His music was causing lines of bugs to leave the strawberry patch in every direction, like refugees fleeing a fire. I wondered if Grover could work that kind of magic with music. I wondered if he was still inside the farmhouse, getting chewed out by Mr. D.

"Grover won't get in too much trouble, will he?" I asked Chiron. "I mean . . . he was a good protector. Really."

Chiron sighed. He shed his tweed jacket and draped it over his horse's back like a saddle. "Grover has big dreams,

Percy. Perhaps bigger than are reasonable. To reach his goal, he must first demonstrate great courage by succeeding as a keeper, finding a new camper and bringing him safely to Half-Blood Hill."

"But he did that!"

"I might agree with you," Chiron said. "But it is not my place to judge. Dionysus and the Council of Cloven Elders must decide. I'm afraid they might not see this assignment as a success. After all, Grover lost you in New York. Then there's the unfortunate . . . ah . . . fate of your mother. And the fact that Grover was unconscious when you dragged him over the property line. The council might question whether this shows any courage on Grover's part."

I wanted to protest. None of what happened was Grover's fault. I also felt really, really guilty. If I hadn't given Grover the slip at the bus station, he might not have gotten in trouble.

"He'll get a second chance, won't he?"

Chiron winced. "I'm afraid that *was* Grover's second chance, Percy. The council was not anxious to give him another, either, after what happened the first time, five years ago. Olympus knows, I advised him to wait longer before trying again. He's still so small for his age. . . ."

"How old is he?"

"Oh, twenty-eight."

"What! And he's in sixth grade?"

"Satyrs mature half as fast as humans, Percy. Grover has been the equivalent of a middle school student for the past six years."

"That's horrible."

"Quite," Chiron agreed. "At any rate, Grover is a late bloomer, even by satyr standards, and not yet very accomplished at woodland magic. Alas, he was anxious to pursue his dream. Perhaps now he will find some other career. . . ."

"That's not fair," I said. "What happened the first time? Was it really so bad?"

Chiron looked away quickly. "Let's move along, shall we?"

But I wasn't quite ready to let the subject drop. Something had occurred to me when Chiron talked about my mother's fate, as if he were intentionally avoiding the word *death*. The beginnings of an idea—a tiny, hopeful fire—started forming in my mind.

"Chiron," I said. "If the gods and Olympus and all that are real . . ."

"Yes, child?"

"Does that mean the Underworld is real, too?"

Chiron's expression darkened.

"Yes, child." He paused, as if choosing his words carefully. "There is a place where spirits go after death. But for now . . . until we know more . . . I would urge you to put that out of your mind."

"What do you mean, 'until we know more'?"

"Come, Percy. Let's see the woods."

As we got closer, I realized how huge the forest was. It took up at least a quarter of the valley, with trees so tall and thick, you could imagine nobody had been in there since the Native Americans.

Chiron said, "The woods are stocked, if you care to try your luck, but go armed."

"Stocked with what?" I asked. "Armed with what?"

"You'll see. Capture the flag is Friday night. Do you have your own sword and shield?"

"My own—?"

"No," Chiron said. "I don't suppose you do. I think a size five will do. I'll visit the armory later."

I wanted to ask what kind of summer camp had an armory, but there was too much else to think about, so the tour continued. We saw the archery range, the canoeing lake, the stables (which Chiron didn't seem to like very much), the javelin range, the sing-along amphitheater, and the arena where Chiron said they held sword and spear fights.

"Sword and spear fights?" I asked.

"Cabin challenges and all that," he explained. "Not lethal. Usually. Oh, yes, and there's the mess hall."

Chiron pointed to an outdoor pavilion framed in white Grecian columns on a hill overlooking the sea. There were a dozen stone picnic tables. No roof. No walls.

"What do you do when it rains?" I asked.

Chiron looked at me as if I'd gone a little weird. "We still have to eat, don't we?" I decided to drop the subject.

Finally, he showed me the cabins. There were twelve of them, nestled in the woods by the lake. They were arranged in a U, with two at the base and five in a row on either side. And they were without doubt the most bizarre collection of buildings I'd ever seen.

Except for the fact that each had a large brass number above the door (odds on the left side, evens on the right), they looked absolutely nothing alike. Number nine had smokestacks, like a tiny factory. Number four had tomato vines on the walls and a roof made out of real grass. Seven seemed to be made of solid gold, which gleamed so much in the sunlight it was almost impossible to look at. They all faced a commons area about the size of a soccer field, dotted with Greek statues, fountains, flower beds, and a couple of basketball hoops (which were more my speed).

In the center of the field was a huge stone-lined firepit. Even though it was a warm afternoon, the hearth smoldered. A girl about nine years old was tending the flames, poking the coals with a stick.

The pair of cabins at the head of the field, numbers one and two, looked like his-and-hers mausoleums, big white marble boxes with heavy columns in front. Cabin one was the biggest and bulkiest of the twelve. Its polished bronze doors shimmered like a hologram, so that from different angles lightning bolts seemed to streak across them. Cabin two was more graceful somehow, with slimmer columns garlanded with pomegranates and flowers. The walls were carved with images of peacocks.

"Zeus and Hera?" I guessed.

"Correct," Chiron said.

"Their cabins look empty."

"Several of the cabins are. That's true. No one ever stays in one or two."

Okay. So each cabin had a different god, like a mascot.

Twelve cabins for the twelve Olympians. But why would some be empty?

I stopped in front of the first cabin on the left, cabin three.

It wasn't high and mighty like cabin one, but long and low and solid. The outer walls were of rough gray stone studded with pieces of seashell and coral, as if the slabs had been hewn straight from the bottom of the ocean floor. I peeked inside the open doorway and Chiron said, "Oh, I wouldn't do that!"

Before he could pull me back, I caught the salty scent of the interior, like the wind on the shore at Montauk. The interior walls glowed like abalone. There were six empty bunk beds with silk sheets turned down. But there was no sign anyone had ever slept there. The place felt so sad and lonely, I was glad when Chiron put his hand on my shoulder and said, "Come along, Percy."

Most of the other cabins were crowded with campers.

Number five was bright red—a real nasty paint job, as if the color had been splashed on with buckets and fists. The roof was lined with barbed wire. A stuffed wild boar's head hung over the doorway, and its eyes seemed to follow me. Inside I could see a bunch of mean-looking kids, both girls and boys, arm wrestling and arguing with each other while rock music blared. The loudest was a girl maybe thirteen or fourteen. She wore a size XXXL CAMP HALF-BLOOD T-shirt under a camouflage jacket. She zeroed in on me and gave me an evil sneer. She reminded me of Nancy Bobofit, though the camper girl was much bigger and tougher looking, and her hair was long and stringy, and brown instead of red.

I kept walking, trying to stay clear of Chiron's hooves. "We haven't seen any other centaurs," I observed.

"No," said Chiron sadly. "My kinsmen are a wild and barbaric folk, I'm afraid. You might encounter them in the wilderness, or at major sporting events. But you won't see any here."

"You said your name was Chiron. Are you really . . ."

He smiled down at me. "*The* Chiron from the stories? Trainer of Hercules and all that? Yes, Percy, I am."

"But, shouldn't you be dead?"

Chiron paused, as if the question intrigued him. "I honestly don't know about *should* be. The truth is, I *can't* be dead. You see, eons ago the gods granted my wish. I could continue the work I loved. I could be a teacher of heroes as long as humanity needed me. I gained much from that wish . . . and I gave up much. But I'm still here, so I can only assume I'm still needed."

I thought about being a teacher for three thousand years. It wouldn't have made my Top Ten Things to Wish For list.

"Doesn't it ever get boring?"

"No, no," he said. "Horribly depressing, at times, but never boring."

"Why depressing?"

Chiron seemed to turn hard of hearing again.

"Oh, look," he said. "Annabeth is waiting for us."

* * *

The blond girl I'd met at the Big House was reading a book in front of the last cabin on the left, number eleven.

When we reached her, she looked me over critically, like she was still thinking about how much I drooled.

I tried to see what she was reading, but I couldn't make out the title. I thought my dyslexia was acting up. Then I realized the title wasn't even English. The letters looked Greek to me. I mean, literally Greek. There were pictures of temples and statues and different kinds of columns, like those in an architecture book.

"Annabeth," Chiron said, "I have masters' archery class at noon. Would you take Percy from here?"

"Yes, sir."

"Cabin eleven," Chiron told me, gesturing toward the doorway. "Make yourself at home."

Out of all the cabins, eleven looked the most like a regular old summer camp cabin, with the emphasis on *old*. The threshold was worn down, the brown paint peeling. Over the doorway was one of those doctor's symbols, a winged pole with two snakes wrapped around it. What did they call it . . . ? A caduceus.

Inside, it was packed with people, both boys and girls, way more than the number of bunk beds. Sleeping bags were spread all over on the floor. It looked like a gym where the Red Cross had set up an evacuation center.

Chiron didn't go in. The door was too low for him. But when the campers saw him they all stood and bowed respectfully.

"Well, then," Chiron said. "Good luck, Percy. I'll see you at dinner."

He galloped away toward the archery range.

I stood in the doorway, looking at the kids. They weren't bowing anymore. They were staring at me, sizing me up. I knew this routine. I'd gone through it at enough schools.

"Well?" Annabeth prompted. "Go on."

So naturally I tripped coming in the door and made a total fool of myself. There were some snickers from the campers, but none of them said anything.

Annabeth announced, "Percy Jackson, meet cabin eleven."

"Regular or undetermined?" somebody asked.

I didn't know what to say, but Annabeth said, "Undetermined."

Everybody groaned.

A guy who was a little older than the rest came forward. "Now, now, campers. That's what we're here for. Welcome, Percy. You can have that spot on the floor, right over there."

The guy was about nineteen, and he looked pretty cool. He was tall and muscular, with short-cropped sandy hair and a friendly smile. He wore an orange tank top, cutoffs, sandals, and a leather necklace with five different-colored clay beads. The only thing unsettling about his appearance was a thick white scar that ran from just beneath his right eye to his jaw, like an old knife slash.

"This is Luke," Annabeth said, and her voice sounded different somehow. I glanced over and could've sworn she was blushing. She saw me looking, and her expression hardened again. "He's your counselor for now."

"For now?" I asked.

"You're undetermined," Luke explained patiently. "They don't know what cabin to put you in, so you're here. Cabin eleven takes all newcomers, all visitors. Naturally, we would. Hermes, our patron, is the god of travelers."

I looked at the tiny section of floor they'd given me. I had nothing to put there to mark it as my own, no luggage, no clothes, no sleeping bag. Just the Minotaur's horn. I thought about setting that down, but then I remembered that Hermes was also the god of thieves.

I looked around at the campers' faces, some sullen and suspicious, some grinning stupidly, some eyeing me as if they were waiting for a chance to pick my pockets.

"How long will I be here?" I asked.

"Good question," Luke said. "Until you're determined."

"How long will that take?"

The campers all laughed.

"Come on," Annabeth told me. "I'll show you the volleyball court."

"I've already seen it."

"Come on."

She grabbed my wrist and dragged me outside. I could hear the kids of cabin eleven laughing behind me.

When we were a few feet away, Annabeth said, "Jackson, you have to do better than that."

"What?"

She rolled her eyes and mumbled under her breath, "I can't believe I thought you were the one."

"What's your problem?" I was getting angry now. "All I know is, I kill some bull guy—"

"Don't talk like that!" Annabeth told me. "You know how many kids at this camp wish they'd had your chance?"

"To get killed?"

"To fight the Minotaur! What do you think we train for?"

I shook my head. "Look, if the thing I fought really was *the* Minotaur, the same one in the stories . . ."

"Yes."

"Then there's only one."

"Yes."

"And he died, like, a gajillion years ago, right? Theseus killed him in the labyrinth. So . . ."

"Monsters don't die, Percy. They can be killed. But they don't die."

"Oh, thanks. That clears it up."

"They don't have souls, like you and me. You can dispel them for a while, maybe even for a whole lifetime if you're lucky. But they are primal forces. Chiron calls them archetypes. Eventually, they re-form."

I thought about Mrs. Dodds. "You mean if I killed one, accidentally, with a sword—"

"The Fur . . . I mean, your math teacher. That's right. She's still out there. You just made her very, very mad."

"How did you know about Mrs. Dodds?"

"You talk in your sleep."

"You almost called her something. A Fury? They're Hades' torturers, right?"

Annabeth glanced nervously at the ground, as if she expected it to open up and swallow her. "You shouldn't call them by name, even here. We call them the Kindly Ones, if we have to speak of them at all."

"Look, is there anything we *can* say without it thundering?" I sounded whiny, even to myself, but right then I didn't care. "Why do I have to stay in cabin eleven, anyway? Why is everybody so crowded together? There are plenty of empty bunks right over there."

I pointed to the first few cabins, and Annabeth turned pale. "You don't just choose a cabin, Percy. It depends on who your parents are. Or . . . your parent."

She stared at me, waiting for me to get it.

"My mom is Sally Jackson," I said. "She works at the candy store in Grand Central Station. At least, she used to."

"I'm sorry about your mom, Percy. But that's not what I mean. I'm talking about your other parent. Your dad."

"He's dead. I never knew him."

Annabeth sighed. Clearly, she'd had this conversation before with other kids. "Your father's not dead, Percy."

"How can you say that? You know him?"

"No, of course not."

"Then how can you say—"

"Because I know *you*. You wouldn't be here if you weren't one of us."

"You don't know anything about me."

"No?" She raised an eyebrow. "I bet you moved around

from school to school. I bet you were kicked out of a lot of them."

"How—"

"Diagnosed with dyslexia. Probably ADHD, too."

I tried to swallow my embarrassment. "What does that have to do with anything?"

"Taken together, it's almost a sure sign. The letters float off the page when you read, right? That's because your mind is hardwired for ancient Greek. And the ADHD—you're impulsive, can't sit still in the classroom. That's your battle-field reflexes. In a real fight, they'd keep you alive. As for the attention problems, that's because you see too much, Percy, not too little. Your senses are better than a regular mortal's. Of course the teachers want you medicated. Most of them are monsters. They don't want you seeing them for what they are."

"You sound like . . . you went through the same thing?"

"Most of the kids here did. If you weren't like us, you couldn't have survived the Minotaur, much less the ambrosia and nectar."

"Ambrosia and nectar."

"The food and drink we were giving you to make you better. That stuff would've killed a normal kid. It would've turned your blood to fire and your bones to sand and you'd be dead. Face it. You're a half-blood."

A half-blood.

I was reeling with so many questions I didn't know where to start.

Then a husky voice yelled, "Well! A newbie!"

I looked over. The big girl from the ugly red cabin was sauntering toward us. She had three other girls behind her, all big and ugly and mean looking like her, all wearing camo jackets.

"Clarisse," Annabeth sighed. "Why don't you go polish your spear or something?"

"Sure, Miss Princess," the big girl said. "So I can run you through with it Friday night."

"*Erre es korakas!*" Annabeth said, which I somehow understood was Greek for 'Go to the crows!' though I had a feeling it was a worse curse than it sounded. "You don't stand a chance."

"We'll pulverize you," Clarisse said, but her eye twitched. Perhaps she wasn't sure she could follow through on the threat. She turned toward me. "Who's this little runt?"

"Percy Jackson," Annabeth said, "meet Clarisse, Daughter of Ares."

I blinked. "Like . . . the war god?"

Clarisse sneered. "You got a problem with that?"

"No," I said, recovering my wits. "It explains the bad smell."

Clarisse growled. "We got an initiation ceremony for newbies, Prissy."

"Percy."

"Whatever. Come on, I'll show you."

"Clarisse—" Annabeth tried to say.

"Stay out of it, wise girl."

Annabeth looked pained, but she did stay out of it, and

I didn't really want her help. I was the new kid. I had to earn my own rep.

I handed Annabeth my minotaur horn and got ready to fight, but before I knew it, Clarisse had me by the neck and was dragging me toward a cinder-block building that I knew immediately was the bathroom.

I was kicking and punching. I'd been in plenty of fights before, but this big girl Clarisse had hands like iron. She dragged me into the girls' bathroom. There was a line of toilets on one side and a line of shower stalls down the other. It smelled just like any public bathroom, and I was thinking—as much as I *could* think with Clarisse ripping my hair out—that if this place belonged to the gods, they should've been able to afford classier johns.

Clarisse's friends were all laughing, and I was trying to find the strength I'd used to fight the Minotaur, but it just wasn't there.

"Like he's 'Big Three' material," Clarisse said as she pushed me toward one of the toilets. "Yeah, right. Minotaur probably fell over laughing, he was so stupid looking."

Her friends snickered.

Annabeth stood in the corner, watching through her fingers.

Clarisse bent me over on my knees and started pushing my head toward the toilet bowl. It reeked like rusted pipes and, well, like what goes into toilets. I strained to keep my head up. I was looking at the scummy water, thinking, I will not go into that. I won't.

Then something happened. I felt a tug in the pit of my stomach. I heard the plumbing rumble, the pipes shudder. Clarisse's grip on my hair loosened. Water shot out of the toilet, making an arc straight over my head, and the next thing I knew, I was sprawled on the bathroom tiles with Clarisse screaming behind me.

I turned just as water blasted out of the toilet again, hitting Clarisse straight in the face so hard it pushed her down onto her butt. The water stayed on her like the spray from a fire hose, pushing her backward into a shower stall.

She struggled, gasping, and her friends started coming toward her. But then the other toilets exploded, too, and six more streams of toilet water blasted them back. The showers acted up, too, and together all the fixtures sprayed the camouflage girls right out of the bathroom, spinning them around like pieces of garbage being washed away.

As soon as they were out the door, I felt the tug in my gut lessen, and the water shut off as quickly as it had started.

The entire bathroom was flooded. Annabeth hadn't been spared. She was dripping wet, but she hadn't been pushed out the door. She was standing in exactly the same place, staring at me in shock.

I looked down and realized I was sitting in the only dry spot in the whole room. There was a circle of dry floor around me. I didn't have one drop of water on my clothes. Nothing.

I stood up, my legs shaky.

Annabeth said, "How did you . . ."

"I don't know."

We walked to the door. Outside, Clarisse and her friends were sprawled in the mud, and a bunch of other campers had gathered around to gawk. Clarisse's hair was flattened across her face. Her camouflage jacket was sopping and she smelled like sewage. She gave me a look of absolute hatred. "You are dead, new boy. You are totally dead."

I probably should have let it go, but I said, "You want to gargle with toilet water again, Clarisse? Close your mouth."

Her friends had to hold her back. They dragged her toward cabin five, while the other campers made way to avoid her flailing feet.

Annabeth stared at me. I couldn't tell whether she was just grossed out or angry at me for dousing her.

"What?" I demanded. "What are you thinking?"

"I'm thinking," she said, "that I want you on my team for capture the flag."

7 ⚡ MY DINNER GOES UP IN SMOKE

Word of the bathroom incident spread immediately. Wherever I went, campers pointed at me and murmured something about toilet water. Or maybe they were just staring at Annabeth, who was still pretty much dripping wet.

She showed me a few more places: the metal shop (where kids were forging their own swords), the arts-and-crafts room (where satyrs were sandblasting a giant marble statue of a goat-man), and the climbing wall, which actually consisted of two facing walls that shook violently, dropped boulders, sprayed lava, and clashed together if you didn't get to the top fast enough.

Finally we returned to the canoeing lake, where the trail led back to the cabins.

"I've got training to do," Annabeth said flatly. "Dinner's at seven-thirty. Just follow your cabin to the mess hall."

"Annabeth, I'm sorry about the toilets."

"Whatever."

"It wasn't my fault."

She looked at me skeptically, and I realized it *was* my fault. I'd made water shoot out of the bathroom fixtures. I didn't understand how. But the toilets had responded to me. I had become one with the plumbing.

"You need to talk to the Oracle," Annabeth said.

"Who?"

"Not who. What. The Oracle. I'll ask Chiron."

I stared into the lake, wishing somebody would give me a straight answer for once.

I wasn't expecting anybody to be looking back at me from the bottom, so my heart skipped a beat when I noticed two teenage girls sitting cross-legged at the base of the pier, about twenty feet below. They wore blue jeans and shimmering green T-shirts, and their brown hair floated loose around their shoulders as minnows darted in and out. They smiled and waved as if I were a long-lost friend.

I didn't know what else to do. I waved back.

"Don't encourage them," Annabeth warned. "Naiads are terrible flirts."

"Naiads," I repeated, feeling completely overwhelmed. "That's it. I want to go home now."

Annabeth frowned. "Don't you get it, Percy? You *are* home. This is the only safe place on earth for kids like us."

"You mean, mentally disturbed kids?"

"I mean *not human*. Not totally human, anyway. Half-human."

"Half-human and half-what?"

"I think you know."

I didn't want to admit it, but I was afraid I did. I felt a tingling in my limbs, a sensation I sometimes felt when my mom talked about my dad.

"God," I said. "Half-god."

Annabeth nodded. "Your father isn't dead, Percy. He's one of the Olympians."

"That's . . . crazy."

"Is it? What's the most common thing gods did in the old stories? They ran around falling in love with humans and having kids with them. Do you think they've changed their habits in the last few millennia?"

"But those are just—" I almost said *myths* again. Then I remembered Chiron's warning that in two thousand years, *I* might be considered a myth. "But if all the kids here are half-gods—"

"Demigods," Annabeth said. "That's the official term. Or half-bloods."

"Then who's your dad?"

Her hands tightened around the pier railing. I got the feeling I'd just trespassed on a sensitive subject.

"My dad is a professor at West Point," she said. "I haven't seen him since I was very small. He teaches American history."

"He's human."

"What? You assume it has to be a male god who finds a human female attractive? How sexist is that?"

"Who's your mom, then?"

"Cabin six."

"Meaning?"

Annabeth straightened. "Athena. Goddess of wisdom and battle."

Okay, I thought. Why not?

"And my dad?"

"Undetermined," Annabeth said, "like I told you before. Nobody knows."

"Except my mother. She knew."

"Maybe not, Percy. Gods don't always reveal their identities."

"My dad would have. He loved her."

Annabeth gave me a cautious look. She didn't want to burst my bubble. "Maybe you're right. Maybe he'll send a sign. That's the only way to know for sure: your father has to send you a sign claiming you as his son. Sometimes it happens."

"You mean sometimes it doesn't?"

Annabeth ran her palm along the rail. "The gods are busy. They have a lot of kids and they don't always . . . Well, sometimes they don't care about us, Percy. They ignore us."

I thought about some of the kids I'd seen in the Hermes cabin, teenagers who looked sullen and depressed, as if they were waiting for a call that would never come. I'd known kids like that at Yancy Academy, shuffled off to boarding school by rich parents who didn't have the time to deal with them. But gods should behave better.

"So I'm stuck here," I said. "That's it? For the rest of my life?"

"It depends," Annabeth said. "Some campers only stay the summer. If you're a child of Aphrodite or Demeter, you're probably not a real powerful force. The monsters might ignore you, so you can get by with a few months of summer training and live in the mortal world the rest of the year. But for some of us, it's too dangerous to leave. We're year-rounders. In the mortal world, we attract monsters. They sense us. They come to challenge us. Most of the time, they'll ignore us until we're old enough to cause trouble—about ten or eleven years old, but after that, most demigods either make their way here, or they get killed off. A few manage to survive in the outside world and become famous. Believe me, if I told you the names, you'd know them. Some don't even realize they're demigods. But very, very few are like that."

"So monsters can't get in here?"

Annabeth shook her head. "Not unless they're intentionally stocked in the woods or specially summoned by somebody on the inside."

"Why would anybody want to summon a monster?"

"Practice fights. Practical jokes."

"Practical jokes?"

"The point is, the borders are sealed to keep mortals and monsters out. From the outside, mortals look into the valley and see nothing unusual, just a strawberry farm."

"So . . . you're a year-rounder?"

Annabeth nodded. From under the collar of her T-shirt she pulled a leather necklace with five clay beads of different colors. It was just like Luke's, except Annabeth's also had a big gold ring strung on it, like a college ring.

"I've been here since I was seven," she said. "Every August, on the last day of summer session, you get a bead for surviving another year. I've been here longer than most of the counselors, and they're all in college."

"Why did you come so young?"

She twisted the ring on her necklace. "None of your business."

"Oh." I stood there for a minute in uncomfortable silence. "So . . . I could just walk out of here right now if I wanted to?"

"It would be suicide, but you could, with Mr. D's or Chiron's permission. But they wouldn't give permission until the end of the summer session unless . . ."

"Unless?"

"You were granted a quest. But that hardly ever happens. The last time . . ."

Her voice trailed off. I could tell from her tone that the last time hadn't gone well.

"Back in the sick room," I said, "when you were feeding me that stuff—"

"Ambrosia."

"Yeah. You asked me something about the summer solstice."

Annabeth's shoulders tensed. "So you *do* know something?"

"Well . . . no. Back at my old school, I overheard Grover and Chiron talking about it. Grover mentioned the summer solstice. He said something like we didn't have much time, because of the deadline. What did that mean?"

She clenched her fists. "I wish I knew. Chiron and the satyrs, they know, but they won't tell me. Something is wrong in Olympus, something pretty major. Last time I was there, everything seemed so *normal.*"

"You've been to Olympus?"

"Some of us year-rounders—Luke and Clarisse and I and a few others—we took a field trip during winter solstice. That's when the gods have their big annual council."

"But . . . how did you get there?"

"The Long Island Railroad, of course. You get off at Penn Station. Empire State Building, special elevator to the six hundredth floor." She looked at me like she was sure I must know this already. "You *are* a New Yorker, right?"

"Oh, sure." As far as I knew, there were only a hundred and two floors in the Empire State Building, but I decided not to point that out.

"Right after we visited," Annabeth continued, "the weather got weird, as if the gods had started fighting. A couple of times since, I've overheard satyrs talking. The best I can figure out is that something important was stolen. And if it isn't returned by summer solstice, there's going to be trouble. When you came, I was hoping . . . I mean— Athena can get along with just about anybody, except for Ares. And of course she's got the rivalry with Poseidon. But, I mean, aside from that, I thought we could work together. I thought you might know something."

I shook my head. I wished I could help her, but I felt too hungry and tired and mentally overloaded to ask any more questions.

"I've got to get a quest," Annabeth muttered to herself. "I'm *not* too young. If they would just tell me the problem . . ."

I could smell barbecue smoke coming from somewhere

nearby. Annabeth must've heard my stomach growl. She told me to go on, she'd catch me later. I left her on the pier, tracing her finger across the rail as if drawing a battle plan.

Back at cabin eleven, everybody was talking and horsing around, waiting for dinner. For the first time, I noticed that a lot of the campers had similar features: sharp noses, upturned eyebrows, mischievous smiles. They were the kind of kids that teachers would peg as troublemakers. Thankfully, nobody paid much attention to me as I walked over to my spot on the floor and plopped down with my minotaur horn.

The counselor, Luke, came over. He had the Hermes family resemblance, too. It was marred by that scar on his right cheek, but his smile was intact.

"Found you a sleeping bag," he said. "And here, I stole you some toiletries from the camp store."

I couldn't tell if he was kidding about the stealing part. I said, "Thanks."

"No prob." Luke sat next to me, pushed his back against the wall. "Tough first day?"

"I don't belong here," I said. "I don't even believe in gods."

"Yeah," he said. "That's how we all started. Once you start believing in them? It doesn't get any easier."

The bitterness in his voice surprised me, because Luke seemed like a pretty easygoing guy. He looked like he could handle just about anything.

"So your dad is Hermes?" I asked.

He pulled a switchblade out of his back pocket, and for a second I thought he was going to gut me, but he just scraped the mud off the sole of his sandal. "Yeah. Hermes."

"The wing-footed messenger guy."

"That's him. Messengers. Medicine. Travelers, merchants, thieves. Anybody who uses the roads. That's why you're here, enjoying cabin eleven's hospitality. Hermes isn't picky about who he sponsors."

I figured Luke didn't mean to call me a nobody. He just had a lot on his mind.

"You ever meet your dad?" I asked.

"Once."

I waited, thinking that if he wanted to tell me, he'd tell me. Apparently, he didn't. I wondered if the story had anything to do with how he got his scar.

Luke looked up and managed a smile. "Don't worry about it, Percy. The campers here, they're mostly good people. After all, we're extended family, right? We take care of each other."

He seemed to understand how lost I felt, and I was grateful for that, because an older guy like him—even if he was a counselor—should've steered clear of an uncool middle-schooler like me. But Luke had welcomed me into the cabin. He'd even stolen me some toiletries, which was the nicest thing anybody had done for me all day.

I decided to ask him my last big question, the one that had been bothering me all afternoon. "Clarisse, from Ares, was joking about me being 'Big Three' material. Then

Annabeth . . . twice, she said I might be 'the one.' She said I should talk to the Oracle. What was that all about?"

Luke folded his knife. "I hate prophecies."

"What do you mean?"

His face twitched around the scar. "Let's just say I messed things up for everybody else. The last two years, ever since my trip to the Garden of the Hesperides went sour, Chiron hasn't allowed any more quests. Annabeth's been dying to get out into the world. She pestered Chiron so much he finally told her he already knew her fate. He'd had a prophecy from the Oracle. He wouldn't tell her the whole thing, but he said Annabeth wasn't destined to go on a quest yet. She had to wait until . . . somebody special came to the camp."

"Somebody special?"

"Don't worry about it, kid," Luke said. "Annabeth wants to think every new camper who comes through here is the omen she's been waiting for. Now, come on, it's dinnertime."

The moment he said it, a horn blew in the distance. Somehow, I knew it was a conch shell, even though I'd never heard one before.

Luke yelled, "Eleven, fall in!"

The whole cabin, about twenty of us, filed into the commons yard. We lined up in order of seniority, so of course I was dead last. Campers came from the other cabins, too, except for the three empty cabins at the end, and cabin eight, which had looked normal in the daytime, but was now starting to glow silver as the sun went down.

We marched up the hill to the mess hall pavilion. Satyrs joined us from the meadow. Naiads emerged from the canoeing lake. A few other girls came out of the woods— and when I say out of the woods, I mean *straight* out of the woods. I saw one girl, about nine or ten years old, melt from the side of a maple tree and come skipping up the hill.

In all, there were maybe a hundred campers, a few dozen satyrs, and a dozen assorted wood nymphs and naiads.

At the pavilion, torches blazed around the marble columns. A central fire burned in a bronze brazier the size of a bathtub. Each cabin had its own table, covered in white cloth trimmed in purple. Four of the tables were empty, but cabin eleven's was way overcrowded. I had to squeeze on to the edge of a bench with half my butt hanging off.

I saw Grover sitting at table twelve with Mr. D, a few satyrs, and a couple of plump blond boys who looked just like Mr. D. Chiron stood to one side, the picnic table being way too small for a centaur.

Annabeth sat at table six with a bunch of serious-looking athletic kids, all with her gray eyes and honey-blond hair.

Clarisse sat behind me at Ares's table. She'd apparently gotten over being hosed down, because she was laughing and belching right alongside her friends.

Finally, Chiron pounded his hoof against the marble floor of the pavilion, and everybody fell silent. He raised a glass. "To the gods!"

Everybody else raised their glasses. "To the gods!"

Wood nymphs came forward with platters of food:

grapes, apples, strawberries, cheese, fresh bread, and yes, barbecue! My glass was empty, but Luke said, "Speak to it. Whatever you want—nonalcoholic, of course."

I said, "Cherry Coke."

The glass filled with sparkling caramel liquid.

Then I had an idea. "*Blue* Cherry Coke."

The soda turned a violent shade of cobalt.

I took a cautious sip. Perfect.

I drank a toast to my mother.

She's not gone, I told myself. Not permanently, anyway. She's in the Underworld. And if that's a real place, then someday . . .

"Here you go, Percy," Luke said, handing me a platter of smoked brisket.

I loaded my plate and was about to take a big bite when I noticed everybody getting up, carrying their plates toward the fire in the center of the pavilion. I wondered if they were going for dessert or something.

"Come on," Luke told me.

As I got closer, I saw that everyone was taking a portion of their meal and dropping it into the fire, the ripest strawberry, the juiciest slice of beef, the warmest, most buttery roll.

Luke murmured in my ear, "Burnt offerings for the gods. They like the smell."

"You're kidding."

His look warned me not to take this lightly, but I couldn't help wondering why an immortal, all-powerful being would like the smell of burning food.

Luke approached the fire, bowed his head, and tossed in a cluster of fat red grapes. "Hermes."

I was next.

I wished I knew what god's name to say.

Finally, I made a silent plea. *Whoever you are, tell me. Please.*

I scraped a big slice of brisket into the flames.

When I caught a whiff of the smoke, I didn't gag.

It smelled nothing like burning food. It smelled of hot chocolate and fresh-baked brownies, hamburgers on the grill and wildflowers, and a hundred other good things that shouldn't have gone well together, but did. I could almost believe the gods could live off that smoke.

When everybody had returned to their seats and finished eating their meals, Chiron pounded his hoof again for our attention.

Mr. D got up with a huge sigh. "Yes, I suppose I'd better say hello to all you brats. Well, hello. Our activities director, Chiron, says the next capture the flag is Friday. Cabin five presently holds the laurels."

A bunch of ugly cheering rose from the Ares table.

"Personally," Mr. D continued, "I couldn't care less, but congratulations. Also, I should tell you that we have a new camper today. Peter Johnson."

Chiron murmured something.

"Er, Percy Jackson," Mr. D corrected. "That's right. Hurrah, and all that. Now run along to your silly campfire. Go on."

Everybody cheered. We all headed down toward the amphitheater, where Apollo's cabin led a sing-along. We sang camp songs about the gods and ate s'mores and joked around, and the funny thing was, I didn't feel that anyone was staring at me anymore. I felt that I was home.

Later in the evening, when the sparks from the campfire were curling into a starry sky, the conch horn blew again, and we all filed back to our cabins. I didn't realize how exhausted I was until I collapsed on my borrowed sleeping bag.

My fingers curled around the Minotaur's horn. I thought about my mom, but I had good thoughts: her smile, the bedtime stories she would read me when I was a kid, the way she would tell me not to let the bedbugs bite.

When I closed my eyes, I fell asleep instantly.

That was my first day at Camp Half-Blood.

I wish I'd known how briefly I would get to enjoy my new home.

8 WE CAPTURE A FLAG

The next few days I settled into a routine that felt almost normal, if you don't count the fact that I was getting lessons from satyrs, nymphs, and a centaur.

Each morning I took Ancient Greek from Annabeth, and we talked about the gods and goddesses in the present tense, which was kind of weird. I discovered Annabeth was right about my dyslexia: Ancient Greek wasn't that hard for me to read. At least, no harder than English. After a couple of mornings, I could stumble through a few lines of Homer without too much headache.

The rest of the day, I'd rotate through outdoor activities, looking for something I was good at. Chiron tried to teach me archery, but we found out pretty quick I wasn't any good with a bow and arrow. He didn't complain, even when he had to desnag a stray arrow out of his tail.

Foot racing? No good either. The wood-nymph instructors left me in the dust. They told me not to worry about it. They'd had centuries of practice running away from lovesick gods. But still, it was a little humiliating to be slower than a tree.

And wrestling? Forget it. Every time I got on the mat, Clarisse would pulverize me.

"There's more where that came from, punk," she'd mumble in my ear.

The only thing I really excelled at was canoeing, and that wasn't the kind of heroic skill people expected to see from the kid who had beaten the Minotaur.

I knew the senior campers and counselors were watching me, trying to decide who my dad was, but they weren't having an easy time of it. I wasn't as strong as the Ares kids, or as good at archery as the Apollo kids. I didn't have Hephaestus's skill with metalwork or—gods forbid—Dionysus's way with vine plants. Luke told me I might be a child of Hermes, a kind of jack-of-all-trades, master of none. But I got the feeling he was just trying to make me feel better. He really didn't know what to make of me either.

Despite all that, I liked camp. I got used to the morning fog over the beach, the smell of hot strawberry fields in the afternoon, even the weird noises of monsters in the woods at night. I would eat dinner with cabin eleven, scrape part of my meal into the fire, and try to feel some connection to my real dad. Nothing came. Just that warm feeling I'd always had, like the memory of his smile. I tried not to think too much about my mom, but I kept wondering: if gods and monsters were real, if all this magical stuff was possible, surely there was some way to save her, to bring her back. . . .

I started to understand Luke's bitterness and how he seemed to resent his father, Hermes. So okay, maybe gods had important things to do. But couldn't they call once in a while, or thunder, or something? Dionysus could make Diet Coke appear out of thin air. Why couldn't my dad, whoever he was, make a phone appear?

Thursday afternoon, three days after I'd arrived at Camp Half-Blood, I had my first sword-fighting lesson. Everybody from cabin eleven gathered in the big circular arena, where Luke would be our instructor.

We started with basic stabbing and slashing, using some straw-stuffed dummies in Greek armor. I guess I did okay. At least, I understood what I was supposed to do and my reflexes were good.

The problem was, I couldn't find a blade that felt right in my hands. Either they were too heavy, or too light, or too long. Luke tried his best to fix me up, but he agreed that none of the practice blades seemed to work for me.

We moved on to dueling in pairs. Luke announced he would be my partner, since this was my first time.

"Good luck," one of the campers told me. "Luke's the best swordsman in the last three hundred years."

"Maybe he'll go easy on me," I said.

The camper snorted.

Luke showed me thrusts and parries and shield blocks the hard way. With every swipe, I got a little more battered and bruised. "Keep your guard up, Percy," he'd say, then whap me in the ribs with the flat of his blade. "No, not that far up!" *Whap!* "Lunge!" *Whap!* "Now, back!" *Whap!*

By the time he called a break, I was soaked in sweat. Everybody swarmed the drinks cooler. Luke poured ice water on his head, which looked like such a good idea, I did the same.

Instantly, I felt better. Strength surged back into my arms. The sword didn't feel so awkward.

"Okay, everybody circle up!" Luke ordered. "If Percy doesn't mind, I want to give you a little demo."

Great, I thought. Let's all watch Percy get pounded.

The Hermes guys gathered around. They were suppressing smiles. I figured they'd been in my shoes before and couldn't wait to see how Luke used me for a punching bag. He told everybody he was going to demonstrate a disarming technique: how to twist the enemy's blade with the flat of your own sword so that he had no choice but to drop his weapon.

"This is difficult," he stressed. "I've had it used against me. No laughing at Percy, now. Most swordsmen have to work years to master this technique."

He demonstrated the move on me in slow motion. Sure enough, the sword clattered out of my hand.

"Now in real time," he said, after I'd retrieved my weapon. "We keep sparring until one of us pulls it off. Ready, Percy?"

I nodded, and Luke came after me. Somehow, I kept him from getting a shot at the hilt of my sword. My senses opened up. I saw his attacks coming. I countered. I stepped forward and tried a thrust of my own. Luke deflected it easily, but I saw a change in his face. His eyes narrowed, and he started to press me with more force.

The sword grew heavy in my hand. The balance wasn't

right. I knew it was only a matter of seconds before Luke took me down, so I figured, What the heck?

I tried the disarming maneuver.

My blade hit the base of Luke's and I twisted, putting my whole weight into a downward thrust.

Clang.

Luke's sword rattled against the stones. The tip of my blade was an inch from his undefended chest.

The other campers were silent.

I lowered my sword. "Um, sorry."

For a moment, Luke was too stunned to speak.

"Sorry?" His scarred face broke into a grin. "By the gods, Percy, why are you sorry? Show me that again!"

I didn't want to. The short burst of manic energy had completely abandoned me. But Luke insisted.

This time, there was no contest. The moment our swords connected, Luke hit my hilt and sent my weapon skidding across the floor.

After a long pause, somebody in the audience said, "Beginner's luck?"

Luke wiped the sweat off his brow. He appraised at me with an entirely new interest. "Maybe," he said. "But I wonder what Percy could do with a balanced sword. . . ."

Friday afternoon, I was sitting with Grover at the lake, resting from a near-death experience on the climbing wall. Grover had scampered to the top like a mountain goat, but the lava had almost gotten me. My shirt had smoking holes in it. The hairs had been singed off my forearms.

We sat on the pier, watching the naiads do underwater basket-weaving, until I got up the nerve to ask Grover how his conversation had gone with Mr. D.

His face turned a sickly shade of yellow.

"Fine," he said. "Just great."

"So your career's still on track?"

He glanced at me nervously. "Chiron t-told you I want a searcher's license?"

"Well . . . no." I had no idea what a searcher's license was, but it didn't seem like the right time to ask. "He just said you had big plans, you know . . . and that you needed credit for completing a keeper's assignment. So did you get it?"

Grover looked down at the naiads. "Mr. D suspended judgment. He said I hadn't failed or succeeded with you yet, so our fates were still tied together. If you got a quest and I went along to protect you, and we both came back alive, then maybe he'd consider the job complete."

My spirits lifted. "Well, that's not so bad, right?"

"*Blaa-ha-ha!* He might as well have transferred me to stable-cleaning duty. The chances of you getting a quest . . . and even if you did, why would you want *me* along?"

"Of course I'd want you along!"

Grover stared glumly into the water. "Basket-weaving . . . Must be nice to have a useful skill."

I tried to reassure him that he had lots of talents, but that just made him look more miserable. We talked about canoeing and swordplay for a while, then debated the pros and cons of the different gods. Finally, I asked him about the four empty cabins.

"Number eight, the silver one, belongs to Artemis," he said. "She vowed to be a maiden forever. So of course, no kids. The cabin is, you know, honorary. If she didn't have one, she'd be mad."

"Yeah, okay. But the other three, the ones at the end. Are those the Big Three?"

Grover tensed. We were getting close to a touchy subject. "No. One of them, number two, is Hera's," he said. "That's another honorary thing. She's the goddess of marriage, so of course she wouldn't go around having affairs with mortals. That's her husband's job. When we say the Big Three, we mean the three powerful brothers, the sons of Kronos."

"Zeus, Poseidon, Hades."

"Right. You know. After the great battle with the Titans, they took over the world from their dad and drew lots to decide who got what."

"Zeus got the sky," I remembered. "Poseidon the sea, Hades the Underworld."

"Uh-huh."

"But Hades doesn't have a cabin here."

"No. He doesn't have a throne on Olympus, either. He sort of does his own thing down in the Underworld. If he did have a cabin here . . ." Grover shuddered. "Well, it wouldn't be pleasant. Let's leave it at that."

"But Zeus and Poseidon—they both had, like, a bazillion kids in the myths. Why are their cabins empty?"

Grover shifted his hooves uncomfortably. "About sixty years ago, after World War II, the Big Three agreed they wouldn't sire any more heroes. Their children were just too powerful. They were affecting the course of human events too much, causing too much carnage. World War II, you know, that was basically a fight between the sons of Zeus and Poseidon on one side, and the sons of Hades on the other. The winning side, Zeus and Poseidon, made Hades swear an oath with them: no more affairs with mortal women. They all swore on the River Styx."

Thunder boomed.

I said, "That's the most serious oath you can make."

Grover nodded.

"And the brothers kept their word—no kids?"

Grover's face darkened. "Seventeen years ago, Zeus fell off the wagon. There was this TV starlet with a big fluffy eighties hairdo—he just couldn't help himself. When their child was born, a little girl named Thalia . . . well, the River Styx is serious about promises. Zeus himself got off easy because he's immortal, but he brought a terrible fate on his daughter."

"But that isn't fair! It wasn't the little girl's fault."

Grover hesitated. "Percy, children of the Big Three have powers greater than other half-bloods. They have a strong aura, a scent that attracts monsters. When Hades found out about the girl, he wasn't too happy about Zeus breaking his oath. Hades let the worst monsters out of Tartarus to torment Thalia. A satyr was assigned to be her keeper when she was twelve, but there was nothing he could do. He tried to escort her here with a couple of other half-bloods she'd befriended. They almost made it. They got all the way to the top of that hill."

He pointed across the valley, to the pine tree where I'd fought the minotaur. "All three Kindly Ones were after them, along with a hoard of hellhounds. They were about to be overrun when Thalia told her satyr to take the other two half-bloods to safety while she held off the monsters. She was wounded and tired, and she didn't want to live like a hunted animal. The satyr didn't want to leave her, but he couldn't change her mind, and he had to protect the others. So Thalia made her final stand alone, at the top of that hill. As she died, Zeus took pity on her. He turned her into that pine tree. Her spirit still helps protect the borders of the valley. That's why the hill is called Half-Blood Hill."

I stared at the pine in the distance.

The story made me feel hollow, and guilty too. A girl my age had sacrificed herself to save her friends. She had faced a whole army of monsters. Next to that, my victory over the Minotaur didn't seem like much. I wondered, if I'd acted differently, could I have saved my mother?

"Grover," I said, "have heroes really gone on quests to the Underworld?"

"Sometimes," he said. "Orpheus. Hercules. Houdini."

"And have they ever returned somebody from the dead?"

"No. Never. Orpheus came close. . . . Percy, you're not seriously thinking—"

"No," I lied. "I was just wondering. So . . . a satyr is always assigned to guard a demigod?"

Grover studied me warily. I hadn't persuaded him that I'd really dropped the Underworld idea. "Not always. We go undercover to a lot of schools. We try to sniff out the half-bloods who have the makings of great heroes. If we find one with a very strong aura, like a child of the Big Three, we alert Chiron. He tries to keep an eye on them, since they could cause really huge problems."

"And you found me. Chiron said you thought I might be something special."

Grover looked as if I'd just led him into a trap. "I didn't . . . Oh, listen, don't think like that. If you *were*—you know—you'd never *ever* be allowed a quest, and I'd never get my license. You're probably a child of Hermes. Or maybe even one of the minor gods, like Nemesis, the god of revenge. Don't worry, okay?"

I got the idea he was reassuring himself more than me.

That night after dinner, there was a lot more excitement than usual.

At last, it was time for capture the flag.

When the plates were cleared away, the conch horn sounded and we all stood at our tables.

Campers yelled and cheered as Annabeth and two of her siblings ran into the pavilion carrying a silk banner. It was about ten feet long, glistening gray, with a painting of a barn owl above an olive tree. From the opposite side of the pavilion, Clarisse and her buddies ran in with another banner, of identical size, but gaudy red, painted with a bloody spear and a boar's head.

I turned to Luke and yelled over the noise, "Those are the flags?"

"Yeah."

"Ares and Athena always lead the teams?"

"Not always," he said. "But often."

"So, if another cabin captures one, what do you do— repaint the flag?"

He grinned. "You'll see. First we have to get one."

"Whose side are we on?"

He gave me a sly look, as if he knew something I didn't. The scar on his face made him look almost evil in the torchlight. "We've made a temporary alliance with Athena. Tonight, we get the flag from Ares. And *you* are going to help."

The teams were announced. Athena had made an alliance with Apollo and Hermes, the two biggest cabins. Apparently, privileges had been traded—shower times, chore schedules, the best slots for activities—in order to win support.

Ares had allied themselves with everybody else: Dionysus, Demeter, Aphrodite, and Hephaestus. From what I'd seen, Dionysus's kids were actually good athletes, but there were only two of them. Demeter's kids had the edge with nature skills and outdoor stuff, but they weren't very aggressive. Aphrodite's sons and daughters I wasn't too worried about. They mostly sat out every activity and checked their reflections in the lake and did their hair and gossiped. Hephaestus's kids weren't pretty, and there were only four of them, but they were big and burly from working in the metal shop all day. They might be a problem. That, of course, left Ares's cabin: a dozen of the biggest, ugliest, meanest kids on Long Island, or anywhere else on the planet.

Chiron hammered his hoof on the marble.

"Heroes!" he announced. "You know the rules. The creek is the boundary line. The entire forest is fair game. All magic items are allowed. The banner must be prominently displayed, and have no more than two guards. Prisoners may be disarmed, but may not be bound or gagged. No killing or maiming is allowed. I will serve as referee and battlefield medic. Arm yourselves!"

He spread his hands, and the tables were suddenly covered with equipment: helmets, bronze swords, spears, oxhide shields coated in metal.

"Whoa," I said. "We're really supposed to use these?"

Luke looked at me as if I were crazy. "Unless you want to get skewered by your friends in cabin five. Here—Chiron thought these would fit. You'll be on border patrol."

My shield was the size of an NBA backboard, with a big caduceus in the middle. It weighed about a million pounds. I could have snowboarded on it fine, but I hoped nobody seriously expected me to run fast. My helmet, like all the helmets on Athena's side, had a blue horsehair plume on top. Ares and their allies had red plumes.

Annabeth yelled, "Blue team, forward!"

We cheered and shook our swords and followed her down the path to the south woods. The red team yelled taunts at us as they headed off toward the north.

I managed to catch up with Annabeth without tripping over my equipment. "Hey."

She kept marching.

"So what's the plan?" I asked. "Got any magic items you can loan me?"

Her hand drifted toward her pocket, as if she were afraid I'd stolen something.

"Just watch Clarisse's spear," she said. "You don't want that thing touching you. Otherwise, don't worry. We'll take the banner from Ares. Has Luke given you your job?"

"Border patrol, whatever that means."

"It's easy. Stand by the creek, keep the reds away. Leave the rest to me. Athena always has a plan."

She pushed ahead, leaving me in the dust.

"Okay," I mumbled. "Glad you wanted me on your team."

It was a warm, sticky night. The woods were dark, with fireflies popping in and out of view. Annabeth stationed me next to a little creek that gurgled over some rocks, then she and the rest of the team scattered into the trees.

Standing there alone, with my big blue-feathered helmet and my huge shield, I felt like an idiot. The bronze sword, like all the swords I'd tried so far, seemed balanced wrong. The leather grip pulled on my hand like a bowling ball.

There was no way anybody would actually attack me, would they? I mean, Olympus had to have liability issues, right?

Far away, the conch horn blew. I heard whoops and yells in the woods, the clanking of metal, kids fighting. A blue-plumed ally from Apollo raced past me like a deer, leaped through the creek, and disappeared into enemy territory.

Great, I thought. I'll miss all the fun, as usual.

Then I heard a sound that sent a chill up my spine, a low canine growl, somewhere close by.

I raised my shield instinctively; I had the feeling something was stalking me.

Then the growling stopped. I felt the presence retreating.

On the other side of the creek, the underbrush exploded. Five Ares warriors came yelling and screaming out of the dark.

"Cream the punk!" Clarisse screamed.

Her ugly pig eyes glared through the slits of her helmet. She brandished a five-foot-long spear, its barbed metal tip flickering with red light. Her siblings had only the standard-issue bronze swords—not that that made me feel any better.

They charged across the stream. There was no help in sight. I could run. Or I could defend myself against half the Ares cabin.

I managed to sidestep the first kid's swing, but these guys were not as stupid the Minotaur. They surrounded me, and Clarisse thrust at me with her spear. My shield deflected the point, but I felt a painful tingling all over my body. My hair stood on end. My shield arm went numb, and the air burned.

Electricity. Her stupid spear was electric. I fell back.

Another Ares guy slammed me in the chest with the butt of his sword and I hit the dirt.

They could've kicked me into jelly, but they were too busy laughing.

"Give him a haircut," Clarisse said. "Grab his hair."

I managed to get to my feet. I raised my sword, but Clarisse slammed it aside with her spear as sparks flew. Now both my arms felt numb.

"Oh, wow," Clarisse said. "I'm scared of this guy. Really scared."

"The flag is that way," I told her. I wanted to sound angry, but I was afraid it didn't come out that way.

"Yeah," one of her siblings said. "But see, we don't care about the flag. We care about a guy who made our cabin look stupid."

"You do that without my help," I told them. It probably wasn't the smartest thing to say.

Two of them came at me. I backed up toward the creek, tried to raise my shield, but Clarisse was too fast. Her spear stuck me straight in the ribs. If I hadn't been wearing an armored breastplate, I would've been shish-ke-babbed. As it was, the electric point just about shocked my teeth out of my mouth. One of her cabinmates slashed his sword across my arm, leaving a good-size cut.

Seeing my own blood made me dizzy—warm and cold at the same time.

"No maiming," I managed to say.

"Oops," the guy said. "Guess I lost my dessert privilege."

He pushed me into the creek and I landed with a splash. They all laughed. I figured as soon as they were through being amused, I would die. But then something happened. The water seemed to wake up my senses, as if I'd just had a bag of my mom's double-espresso jelly beans.

Clarisse and her cabinmates came into the creek to get me, but I stood to meet them. I knew what to do. I swung the flat of my sword against the first guy's head and knocked his helmet clean off. I hit him so hard I could see his eyes vibrating as he crumpled into the water.

Ugly Number Two and Ugly Number Three came at me. I slammed one in the face with my shield and used my sword to shear off the other guy's horsehair plume. Both of them backed up quick. Ugly Number Four didn't look really anxious to attack, but Clarisse kept coming, the point of her spear crackling with energy. As soon as she thrust, I caught the shaft between the edge of my shield and my sword, and I snapped it like a twig.

"Ah!" she screamed. "You idiot! You corpse-breath worm!"

She probably would've said worse, but I smacked her between the eyes with my sword-butt and sent her stumbling backward out of the creek.

Then I heard yelling, elated screams, and I saw Luke racing toward the boundary line with the red team's banner lifted high. He was flanked by a couple of Hermes guys covering his retreat, and a few Apollos behind them, fighting off the Hephaestus kids. The Ares folks got up, and Clarisse muttered a dazed curse.

"A trick!" she shouted. "It was a trick."

They staggered after Luke, but it was too late. Everybody converged on the creek as Luke ran across into friendly territory. Our side exploded into cheers. The red banner shimmered and turned to silver. The boar and spear were replaced with a huge caduceus, the symbol of cabin eleven. Everybody on the blue team picked up Luke and started carrying him around on their shoulders. Chiron cantered out from the woods and blew the conch horn.

The game was over. We'd won.

I was about to join the celebration when Annabeth's voice, right next to me in the creek, said, "Not bad, hero."

I looked, but she wasn't there.

"Where the heck did you learn to fight like that?" she asked. The air shimmered, and she materialized, holding a Yankees baseball cap as if she'd just taken it off her head.

I felt myself getting angry. I wasn't even fazed by the fact that she'd just been invisible. "You set me up," I said. "You put me here because you knew Clarisse would come after me, while you sent Luke around the flank. You had it all figured out."

Annabeth shrugged. "I told you. Athena always, always has a plan."

"A plan to get me pulverized."

"I came as fast as I could. I was about to jump in, but . . ." She shrugged. "You didn't need help."

Then she noticed my wounded arm. "How did you do that?"

"Sword cut," I said. "What do you think?"

"No. It *was* a sword cut. Look at it."

The blood was gone. Where the huge cut had been, there was a long white scratch, and even that was fading. As I watched, it turned into a small scar, and disappeared.

"I—I don't get it," I said.

Annabeth was thinking hard. I could almost see the gears turning. She looked down at my feet, then at Clarisse's broken spear, and said, "Step out of the water, Percy."

"What—"

"Just do it."

I came out of the creek and immediately felt bone tired. My arms started to go numb again. My adrenaline rush left me. I almost fell over, but Annabeth steadied me.

"Oh, Styx," she cursed. "This is *not* good. I didn't want . . . I assumed it would be Zeus. . . ."

Before I could ask what she meant, I heard that canine growl again, but much closer than before. A howl ripped through the forest.

The campers' cheering died instantly. Chiron shouted something in Ancient Greek, which I would realize, only later, I had understood perfectly: *"Stand ready! My bow!"*

Annabeth drew her sword.

There on the rocks just above us was a black hound the size of a rhino, with lava-red eyes and fangs like daggers.

It was looking straight at me.

Nobody moved except Annabeth, who yelled, "Percy, run!"

She tried to step in front of me, but the hound was too fast. It leaped over her—an enormous shadow with teeth—and just as it hit me, as I stumbled backward and felt its razor-sharp claws ripping through my armor, there was a cascade of thwacking sounds, like forty pieces of paper being ripped one after the other. From the hound's neck sprouted a cluster of arrows. The monster fell dead at my feet.

By some miracle, I was still alive. I didn't want to look underneath the ruins of my shredded armor. My chest felt warm and wet, and I knew I was badly cut. Another second, and the monster would've turned me into a hundred pounds of delicatessen meat.

Chiron trotted up next to us, a bow in his hand, his face grim.

"*Di immortales!*" Annabeth said. "That's a hellhound from the Fields of Punishment. They don't . . . they're not supposed to . . ."

"Someone summoned it," Chiron said. "Someone inside the camp."

Luke came over, the banner in his hand forgotten, his moment of glory gone.

Clarisse yelled, "It's all Percy's fault! Percy summoned it!"

"Be quiet, child," Chiron told her.

We watched the body of the hellhound melt into shadow, soaking into the ground until it disappeared.

"You're wounded," Annabeth told me. "Quick, Percy, get in the water."

"I'm okay."

"No, you're not," she said. "Chiron, watch this."

I was too tired to argue. I stepped back into the creek, the whole camp gathering around me.

Instantly, I felt better. I could feel the cuts on my chest closing up. Some of the campers gasped.

"Look, I—I don't know why," I said, trying to apologize. "I'm sorry. . . ."

But they weren't watching my wounds heal. They were staring at something above my head.

"Percy," Annabeth said, pointing. "Um . . ."

By the time I looked up, the sign was already fading, but I could still make out the hologram of green light, spinning and gleaming. A three-tipped spear: a trident.

"Your father," Annabeth murmured. "This is *really* not good."

"It is determined," Chiron announced.

All around me, campers started kneeling, even the Ares cabin, though they didn't look happy about it.

"My father?" I asked, completely bewildered.

"Poseidon," said Chiron. "Earthshaker, Stormbringer, Father of Horses. Hail, Perseus Jackson, Son of the Sea God."

9 I AM OFFERED
     A QUEST

The next morning, Chiron moved me to cabin three.

I didn't have to share with anybody. I had plenty of room for all my stuff: the Minotaur's horn, one set of spare clothes, and a toiletry bag. I got to sit at my own dinner table, pick all my own activities, call "lights out" whenever I felt like it, and not listen to anybody else.

And I was absolutely miserable.

Just when I'd started to feel accepted, to feel I had a home in cabin eleven and I might be a normal kid—or as normal as you can be when you're a half-blood—I'd been separated out as if I had some rare disease.

Nobody mentioned the hellhound, but I got the feeling they were all talking about it behind my back. The attack had scared everybody. It sent two messages: one, that I was the son of the Sea God; and two, monsters would stop at nothing to kill me. They could even invade a camp that had always been considered safe.

The other campers steered clear of me as much as possible. Cabin eleven was too nervous to have sword class with me after what I'd done to the Ares folks in the woods, so my lessons with Luke became one-on-one. He pushed me harder than ever, and wasn't afraid to bruise me up in the process.

"You're going to need all the training you can get," he promised, as we were working with swords and flaming torches. "Now let's try that viper-beheading strike again. Fifty more repetitions."

Annabeth still taught me Greek in the mornings, but she seemed distracted. Every time I said something, she scowled at me, as if I'd just poked her between the eyes.

After lessons, she would walk away muttering to herself: "Quest . . . Poseidon? . . . Dirty rotten . . . Got to make a plan . . ."

Even Clarisse kept her distance, though her venomous looks made it clear she wanted to kill me for breaking her magic spear. I wished she would just yell or punch me or something. I'd rather get into fights every day than be ignored.

I knew somebody at camp resented me, because one night I came into my cabin and found a mortal newspaper dropped inside the doorway, a copy of the *New York Daily News*, opened to the Metro page. The article took me almost an hour to read, because the angrier I got, the more the words floated around on the page.

BOY AND MOTHER STILL MISSING AFTER FREAK CAR ACCIDENT

BY EILEEN SMYTHE

Sally Jackson and son Percy are still missing one week after their mysterious disappearance. The family's badly burned '78 Camaro was discovered last Saturday on a north Long Island road with the roof ripped off and the front axle broken. The car had flipped and skidded for several hundred feet before exploding.

Mother and son had gone for a weekend vacation to Montauk, but left hastily, under mysterious circumstances. Small traces of blood were found in the car and near the scene of the wreck, but there were no other signs of the missing Jacksons. Residents in the rural area reported seeing nothing unusual around the time of the accident.

Ms. Jackson's husband, Gabe Ugliano, claims that his stepson, Percy Jackson, is a troubled child who has been kicked out of numerous boarding schools and has expressed violent tendencies in the past.

Police would not say whether son Percy is a suspect in his mother's disappearance, but they have not ruled out foul play. Below are recent pictures of Sally Jackson and Percy. Police urge anyone with information to call the following toll-free crime-stoppers hotline.

The phone number was circled in black marker.

I wadded up the paper and threw it away, then flopped down in my bunk bed in the middle of my empty cabin.

"Lights out," I told myself miserably.

That night, I had my worst dream yet.

I was running along the beach in a storm. This time,

there was a city behind me. Not New York. The sprawl was different: buildings spread farther apart, palm trees and low hills in the distance.

About a hundred yards down the surf, two men were fighting. They looked like TV wrestlers, muscular, with beards and long hair. Both wore flowing Greek tunics, one trimmed in blue, the other in green. They grappled with each other, wrestled, kicked and head-butted, and every time they connected, lightning flashed, the sky grew darker, and the wind rose.

I had to stop them. I didn't know why. But the harder I ran, the more the wind blew me back, until I was running in place, my heels digging uselessly in the sand.

Over the roar of the storm, I could hear the blue-robed one yelling at the green-robed one, *Give it back! Give it back!* Like a kindergartner fighting over a toy.

The waves got bigger, crashing into the beach, spraying me with salt.

I yelled, *Stop it! Stop fighting!*

The ground shook. Laughter came from somewhere under the earth, and a voice so deep and evil it turned my blood to ice.

Come down, little hero, the voice crooned. *Come down!*

The sand split beneath me, opening up a crevice straight down to the center of the earth. My feet slipped, and darkness swallowed me.

I woke up, sure I was falling.

I was still in bed in cabin three. My body told me it was morning, but it was dark outside, and thunder rolled across the hills. A storm was brewing. I hadn't dreamed that.

I heard a clopping sound at the door, a hoof knocking on the threshold.

"Come in?"

Grover trotted inside, looking worried. "Mr. D wants to see you."

"Why?"

"He wants to kill . . . I mean, I'd better let him tell you."

Nervously, I got dressed and followed, sure that I was in huge trouble.

For days, I'd been half expecting a summons to the Big House. Now that I was declared a son of Poseidon, one of the Big Three gods who weren't supposed to have kids, I figured it was a crime for me just to be alive. The other gods had probably been debating the best way to punish me for existing, and now Mr. D was ready to deliver their verdict.

Over Long Island Sound, the sky looked like ink soup coming to a boil. A hazy curtain of rain was coming in our direction. I asked Grover if we needed an umbrella.

"No," he said. "It never rains here unless we want it to."

I pointed at the storm. "What the heck is that, then?"

He glanced uneasily at the sky. "It'll pass around us. Bad weather always does."

I realized he was right. In the week I'd been here, it had never even been overcast. The few rain clouds I'd seen had skirted right around the edges of the valley.

But this storm . . . this one was huge.

At the volleyball pit, the kids from Apollo's cabin were playing a morning game against the satyrs. Dionysus's twins were walking around in the strawberry fields, making the plants grow. Everybody was going about their normal business, but they looked tense. They kept their eyes on the storm.

Grover and I walked up to the front porch of the Big House. Dionysus sat at the pinochle table in his tiger-striped Hawaiian shirt with his Diet Coke, just as he had on my first day. Chiron sat across the table in his fake wheelchair. They were playing against invisible opponents—two sets of cards hovering in the air.

"Well, well," Mr. D said without looking up. "Our little celebrity."

I waited.

"Come closer," Mr. D said. "And don't expect me to kowtow to you, mortal, just because old Barnacle-Beard is your father."

A net of lightning flashed across the clouds. Thunder shook the windows of the house.

"Blah, blah, blah," Dionysus said.

Chiron feigned interest in his pinochle cards. Grover cowered by the railing, his hooves clopping back and forth.

"If I had my way," Dionysus said, "I would cause your molecules to erupt in flames. We'd sweep up the ashes and be done with a lot of trouble. But Chiron seems to feel this would be against my mission at this cursed camp: to keep you little brats safe from harm."

"Spontaneous combustion *is* a form of harm, Mr. D," Chiron put in.

"Nonsense," Dionysus said. "Boy wouldn't feel a thing.

Nevertheless, I've agreed to restrain myself. I'm thinking of turning you into a dolphin instead, sending you back to your father."

"Mr. D—" Chiron warned.

"Oh, all right," Dionysus relented. "There's one more option. But it's deadly foolishness." Dionysus rose, and the invisible players' cards dropped to the table. "I'm off to Olympus for the emergency meeting. If the boy is still here when I get back, I'll turn him into an Atlantic bottlenose. Do you understand? And Perseus Jackson, if you're at all smart, you'll see that's a much more sensible choice than what Chiron feels you must do."

Dionysus picked up a playing card, twisted it, and it became a plastic rectangle. A credit card? No. A security pass.

He snapped his fingers.

The air seemed to fold and bend around him. He became a hologram, then a wind, then he was gone, leaving only the smell of fresh-pressed grapes lingering behind.

Chiron smiled at me, but he looked tired and strained. "Sit, Percy, please. And Grover."

We did.

Chiron laid his cards on the table, a winning hand he hadn't gotten to use.

"Tell me, Percy," he said. "What did you make of the hellhound?"

Just hearing the name made me shudder.

Chiron probably wanted me to say, *Heck, it was nothing. I eat hellhounds for breakfast.* But I didn't feel like lying.

"It scared me," I said. "If you hadn't shot it, I'd be dead."

"You'll meet worse, Percy. Far worse, before you're done."

"Done . . . with what?"

"Your quest, of course. Will you accept it?"

I glanced at Grover, who was crossing his fingers.

"Um, sir," I said, "you haven't told me what it is yet."

Chiron grimaced. "Well, that's the hard part, the details."

Thunder rumbled across the valley. The storm clouds had now reached the edge of the beach. As far as I could see, the sky and the sea were boiling together.

"Poseidon and Zeus," I said. "They're fighting over something valuable . . . something that was stolen, aren't they?"

Chiron and Grover exchanged looks.

Chiron sat forward in his wheelchair. "How did you know that?"

My face felt hot. I wished I hadn't opened my big mouth. "The weather since Christmas has been weird, like the sea and the sky are fighting. Then I talked to Annabeth, and she'd overheard something about a theft. And . . . I've also been having these dreams."

"I knew it," Grover said.

"Hush, satyr," Chiron ordered.

"But it is his quest!" Grover's eyes were bright with excitement. "It must be!"

"Only the Oracle can determine." Chiron stroked his bristly beard. "Nevertheless, Percy, you are correct. Your father and Zeus are having their worst quarrel in centuries.

They are fighting over something valuable that was stolen. To be precise: a lightning bolt."

I laughed nervously. "A *what?*"

"Do not take this lightly," Chiron warned. "I'm not talking about some tinfoil-covered zigzag you'd see in a second-grade play. I'm talking about a two-foot-long cylinder of high-grade celestial bronze, capped on both ends with god-level explosives."

"Oh."

"Zeus's master bolt," Chiron said, getting worked up now. "The symbol of his power, from which all other lightning bolts are patterned. The first weapon made by the Cyclopes for the war against the Titans, the bolt that sheered the top off Mount Etna and hurled Kronos from his throne; the master bolt, which packs enough power to make mortal hydrogen bombs look like firecrackers."

"And it's missing?"

"Stolen," Chiron said.

"By who?"

"By *whom,*" Chiron corrected. Once a teacher, always a teacher. "By you."

My mouth fell open.

"At least"—Chiron held up a hand—"that's what Zeus thinks. During the winter solstice, at the last council of the gods, Zeus and Poseidon had an argument. The usual nonsense: 'Mother Rhea always liked you best,' 'Air disasters are more spectacular than sea disasters,' et cetera. Afterward, Zeus realized his master bolt was missing, taken from the throne room under his very nose. He immediately blamed Poseidon. Now, a god cannot usurp another god's symbol of power directly—that is forbidden by the most ancient of divine laws. But Zeus believes your father convinced a human hero to take it."

"But I didn't—"

"Patience and listen, child," Chiron said. "Zeus has good reason to be suspicious. The forges of the Cyclopes are under the ocean, which gives Poseidon some influence over the makers of his brother's lightning. Zeus believes Poseidon has taken the master bolt, and is now secretly having the Cyclopes build an arsenal of illegal copies, which might be used to topple Zeus from his throne. The only thing Zeus wasn't sure about was which hero Poseidon used to steal the bolt. Now Poseidon has openly claimed you as his son. You were in New York over the winter holidays. You could easily have snuck into Olympus. Zeus believes he has found his thief."

"But I've never even been to Olympus! Zeus is crazy!"

Chiron and Grover glanced nervously at the sky. The clouds didn't seem to be parting around us, as Grover had promised. They were rolling straight over our valley, sealing us in like a coffin lid.

"Er, Percy . . . ?" Grover said. "We don't use the *c*-word to describe the Lord of the Sky."

"Perhaps *paranoid*," Chiron suggested. "Then again, Poseidon has tried to unseat Zeus before. I believe that was question thirty-eight on your final exam. . . ." He looked at me as if he actually expected me to remember question thirty-eight.

How could anyone accuse me of stealing a god's weapon? I couldn't even steal a slice of pizza from Gabe's poker party without getting busted. Chiron was waiting for an answer.

"Something about a golden net?" I guessed. "Poseidon and Hera and a few other gods . . . they, like, trapped Zeus and wouldn't let him out until he promised to be a better ruler, right?"

"Correct," Chiron said. "And Zeus has never trusted Poseidon since. Of course, Poseidon denies stealing the master bolt. He took great offense at the accusation. The two have been arguing back and forth for months, threatening war. And now, you've come along—the proverbial last straw."

"But I'm just a kid!"

"Percy," Grover cut in, "if you were Zeus, and you already thought your brother was plotting to overthrow you, then your brother suddenly admitted he had broken the sacred oath he took after World War II, that he's fathered a new mortal hero who might be used as a weapon against you. . . . Wouldn't that put a twist in your toga?"

"But I didn't do anything. Poseidon—my dad—he didn't really have this master bolt stolen, did he?"

Chiron sighed. "Most thinking observers would agree that thievery is not Poseidon's style. But the Sea God is too proud to try convincing Zeus of that. Zeus has demanded that Poseidon return the bolt by the summer solstice. That's June twenty-first, ten days from now. Poseidon wants an apology for being called a thief by the same date. I hoped that diplomacy might prevail, that Hera or Demeter or Hestia would make the two brothers see sense. But your arrival has inflamed Zeus's temper. Now neither god will back down. Unless someone intervenes, unless the master bolt is found and returned to Zeus before the solstice, there will be war. And do you know what a full-fledged war would look like, Percy?"

"Bad?" I guessed.

"Imagine the world in chaos. Nature at war with itself. Olympians forced to choose sides between Zeus and Poseidon. Destruction. Carnage. Millions dead. Western civilization turned into a battleground so big it will make the Trojan War look like a water-balloon fight."

"Bad," I repeated.

"And you, Percy Jackson, would be the first to feel Zeus's wrath."

It started to rain. Volleyball players stopped their game and stared in stunned silence at the sky.

I had brought this storm to Half-Blood Hill. Zeus was punishing the whole camp because of me. I was furious.

"So I have to find the stupid bolt," I said. "And return it to Zeus."

"What better peace offering," Chiron said, "than to have the son of Poseidon return Zeus's property?"

"If Poseidon doesn't have it, where is the thing?"

"I believe I know." Chiron's expression was grim. "Part of a prophecy I had years ago . . . well, some of the lines make sense to me, now. But before I can say more, you must officially take up the quest. You must seek the counsel of the Oracle."

"Why can't you tell me where the bolt is beforehand?"

"Because if I did, you would be too afraid to accept the challenge."

I swallowed. "Good reason."

"You agree then?"

I looked at Grover, who nodded encouragingly.

Easy for him. I was the one Zeus wanted to kill.

"All right," I said. "It's better than being turned into a dolphin."

"Then it's time you consulted the Oracle," Chiron said. "Go upstairs, Percy Jackson, to the attic. When you come back down, assuming you're still sane, we will talk more."

Four flights up, the stairs ended under a green trap-door.

I pulled the cord. The door swung down, and a wooden ladder clattered into place.

The warm air from above smelled like mildew and rotten wood and something else . . . a smell I remembered from biology class. Reptiles. The smell of snakes.

I held my breath and climbed.

The attic was filled with Greek hero junk: armor stands covered in cobwebs; once-bright shields pitted with rust; old leather steamer trunks plastered with stickers saying ITHAKA, CIRCE'S ISLE, and LAND OF THE AMAZONS. One long table was stacked with glass jars filled with pickled *things*—severed hairy claws, huge yellow eyes, various other parts of monsters. A dusty mounted trophy on the wall looked like a giant snake's head, but with horns and a full set of shark's teeth. The plaque read, HYDRA HEAD #1, WOODSTOCK, N.Y., 1969.

By the window, sitting on a wooden tripod stool, was the most gruesome memento of all: a mummy. Not the wrapped-in-cloth kind, but a human female body shriveled to a husk. She wore a tie-dyed sundress, lots of beaded necklaces, and a headband over long black hair. The skin of her face was thin and leathery over her skull, and her eyes were glassy white slits, as if the real eyes had been replaced by marbles; she'd been dead a long, long time.

Looking at her sent chills up my back. And that was before she sat up on her stool and opened her mouth. A green mist poured from the mummy's mouth, coiling over the floor in thick tendrils, hissing like twenty thousand snakes. I stumbled over myself trying to get to the trap-door, but it slammed shut. Inside my head, I heard a voice, slithering into one ear and coiling around my brain: *I am the spirit of Delphi, speaker of the prophecies of Phoebus Apollo, slayer of the mighty Python. Approach, seeker, and ask.*

I wanted to say, *No thanks, wrong door, just looking for the bathroom.* But I forced myself to take a deep breath.

The mummy wasn't alive. She was some kind of gruesome receptacle for something else, the power that was now swirling around me in the green mist. But its presence didn't feel evil, like my demonic math teacher Mrs. Dodds or the Minotaur. It felt more like the Three Fates I'd seen knitting the yarn outside the highway fruit stand: ancient, powerful, and definitely *not* human. But not particularly interested in killing me, either.

I got up the courage to ask, "What is my destiny?"

The mist swirled more thickly, collecting right in front of me and around the table with the pickled monster-part jars. Suddenly there were four men sitting around the table, playing cards. Their faces became clearer. It was Smelly Gabe and his buddies.

My fists clenched, though I knew this poker party couldn't be real. It was an illusion, made out of mist.

Gabe turned toward me and spoke in the rasping voice of the Oracle: *You shall go west, and face the god who has turned.*

His buddy on the right looked up and said in the same voice: *You shall find what was stolen, and see it safely returned.*

The guy on the left threw in two poker chips, then said: *You shall be betrayed by one who calls you a friend.*

Finally, Eddie, our building super, delivered the worst line of all: *And you shall fail to save what matters most, in the end.*

The figures began to dissolve. At first I was too stunned to say anything, but as the mist retreated, coiling into a huge green serpent and slithering back into the mouth of the mummy, I cried, "Wait! What do you mean? What friend? What will I fail to save?"

The tail of the mist snake disappeared into the mummy's mouth. She reclined back against the wall. Her mouth closed tight, as if it hadn't been open in a hundred years. The attic was silent again, abandoned, nothing but a room full of mementos.

I got the feeling that I could stand here until I had cobwebs, too, and I wouldn't learn anything else.

My audience with the Oracle was over.

"Well?" Chiron asked me.

I slumped into a chair at the pinochle table. "She said I would retrieve what was stolen."

Grover sat forward, chewing excitedly on the remains of a Diet Coke can. "That's great!"

"What did the Oracle say *exactly*?" Chiron pressed. "This is important."

My ears were still tingling from the reptilian voice. "She . . . she said I would go west and face a god who had turned. I would retrieve what was stolen and see it safely returned."

"I knew it," Grover said.

Chiron didn't look satisfied. "Anything else?"

I didn't want to tell him.

What friend would betray me? I didn't have that many.

And the last line—I would fail to save what mattered most. What kind of Oracle would send me on a quest and tell me, *Oh, by the way, you'll fail.*

How could I confess that?

"No," I said. "That's about it."

He studied my face. "Very well, Percy. But know this: the Oracle's words often have double meanings. Don't dwell on them too much. The truth is not always clear until events come to pass."

I got the feeling he knew I was holding back something bad, and he was trying to make me feel better.

"Okay," I said, anxious to change topics. "So where do I go? Who's this god in the west?"

"Ah, think, Percy," Chiron said. "If Zeus and Poseidon weaken each other in a war, who stands to gain?"

"Somebody else who wants to take over?" I guessed.

"Yes, quite. Someone who harbors a grudge, who has been unhappy with his lot since the world was divided eons ago, whose kingdom would grow powerful with the deaths of millions. Someone who hates his brothers for forcing him into an oath to have no more children, an oath that both of them have now broken."

I thought about my dreams, the evil voice that had spoken from under the ground. "Hades."

Chiron nodded. "The Lord of the Dead is the only possibility."

A scrap of aluminum dribbled out of Grover's mouth. "Whoa, wait. Wh-what?"

"A Fury came after Percy," Chiron reminded him. "She watched the young man until she was sure of his identity, then tried to kill him. Furies obey only one lord: Hades."

"Yes, but—but Hades hates *all* heroes," Grover protested. "Especially if he has found out Percy is a son of Poseidon. . . ."

"A hellhound got into the forest," Chiron continued. "Those can only be summoned from the Fields of Punishment, and it had to be summoned by someone within the camp. Hades must have a spy here. He must suspect Poseidon will try to use Percy to clear his name. Hades would very much like to kill this young half-blood before he can take on the quest."

"Great," I muttered. "That's two major gods who want to kill me."

"But a quest to . . ." Grover swallowed. "I mean, couldn't the master bolt be in some place like Maine? Maine's very nice this time of year."

"Hades sent a minion to steal the master bolt," Chiron insisted. "He hid it in the Underworld, knowing full well that Zeus would blame Poseidon. I don't pretend to understand the Lord of the Dead's motives perfectly, or why he chose this time to start a war, but one thing is certain. Percy must go to the Underworld, find the master bolt, and reveal the truth."

A strange fire burned in my stomach. The weirdest thing was: it wasn't fear. It was anticipation. The desire for revenge. Hades had tried to kill me three times so far, with the Fury, the Minotaur, and the hellhound. It was his fault my mother had disappeared in a flash of light. Now he was trying to frame me and my dad for a theft we hadn't committed.

I was ready to take him on.

Besides, if my mother was in the Underworld . . .

Whoa, boy, said the small part of my brain that was still sane. You're a kid. Hades is a god.

Grover was trembling. He'd started eating pinochle cards like potato chips.

The poor guy needed to complete a quest with me so he could get his searcher's license, whatever that was, but how could I ask him to do this quest, especially when the Oracle said I was destined to fail? This was suicide.

"Look, if we know it's Hades," I told Chiron, "why can't we just tell the other gods? Zeus or Poseidon could go down to the Underworld and bust some heads."

"Suspecting and knowing are not the same," Chiron said. "Besides, even if the other gods suspect Hades—and I imagine Poseidon does—they couldn't retrieve the bolt themselves. Gods cannot cross each other's territories except by invitation. That is another ancient rule. Heroes, on the other hand, have certain privileges. They can go anywhere, challenge anyone, as long as they're bold enough and strong enough to do it. No god can be held responsible for a hero's actions. Why do you think the gods always operate through humans?"

"You're saying I'm being used."

"I'm saying it's no accident Poseidon has claimed you now. It's a very risky gamble, but he's in a desperate situation. He needs you."

My dad needs me.

Emotions rolled around inside me like bits of glass in a kaleidoscope. I didn't know whether to feel resentful or grateful or happy or angry. Poseidon had ignored me for twelve years. Now suddenly he needed me.

I looked at Chiron. "You've known I was Poseidon's son all along, haven't you?"

"I had my suspicions. As I said . . . I've spoken to the Oracle, too."

I got the feeling there was a lot he wasn't telling me about his prophecy, but I decided I couldn't worry about that right now. After all, I was holding back information too.

"So let me get this straight," I said. "I'm supposed to go to the Underworld and confront the Lord of the Dead."

"Check," Chiron said.

"Find the most powerful weapon in the universe."

"Check."

"And get it back to Olympus before the summer solstice, in ten days."

"That's about right."

I looked at Grover, who gulped down the ace of hearts.

"Did I mention that Maine is very nice this time of year?" he asked weakly.

"You don't have to go," I told him. "I can't ask that of you."

"Oh . . ." He shifted his hooves. "No . . . it's just that satyrs and underground places . . . well . . ."

He took a deep breath, then stood, brushing the shredded cards and aluminum bits off his T-shirt. "You saved my life, Percy. If . . . if you're serious about wanting me along, I won't let you down."

I felt so relieved I wanted to cry, though I didn't think that would be very heroic. Grover was the only friend I'd ever had for longer than a few months. I wasn't sure what good a satyr could do against the forces of the dead, but I felt better knowing he'd be with me.

"All the way, G-man." I turned to Chiron. "So where do we go? The Oracle just said to go west."

"The entrance to the Underworld is always in the west. It moves from age to age, just like Olympus. Right now, of course, it's in America."

"Where?"

Chiron looked surprised. "I thought that would be obvious enough. The entrance to the Underworld is in Los Angeles."

"Oh," I said. "Naturally. So we just get on a plane—"

"No!" Grover shrieked. "Percy, what are you thinking? Have you ever been on a plane in your life?"

I shook my head, feeling embarrassed. My mom had never taken me anywhere by plane. She'd always said we didn't have the money. Besides, her parents had died in a plane crash.

"Percy, think," Chiron said. "You are the son of the Sea God. Your father's bitterest rival is Zeus, Lord of the Sky. Your mother knew better than to trust you in an airplane. You would be in Zeus's domain. You would never come down again alive."

Overhead, lightning crackled. Thunder boomed.

"Okay," I said, determined not to look at the storm. "So, I'll travel overland."

"That's right," Chiron said. "Two companions may accompany you. Grover is one. The other has already volunteered, if you will accept her help."

"Gee," I said, feigning surprise. "Who else would be stupid enough to volunteer for a quest like this?"

The air shimmered behind Chiron.

Annabeth became visible, stuffing her Yankees cap into her back pocket.

"I've been waiting a long time for a quest, seaweed brain," she said. "Athena is no fan of Poseidon, but if you're going to save the world, I'm the best person to keep you from messing up."

"If you do say so yourself," I said. "I suppose you have a plan, wise girl?"

Her cheeks colored. "Do you want my help or not?"

The truth was, I did. I needed all the help I could get.

"A trio," I said. "That'll work."

"Excellent," Chiron said. "This afternoon, we can take you as far as the bus terminal in Manhattan. After that, you are on your own."

Lightning flashed. Rain poured down on the meadows that were never supposed to have violent weather.

"No time to waste," Chiron said. "I think you should all get packing."

10 ⚡ I RUIN A PERFECTLY GOOD BUS

It didn't take me long to pack. I decided to leave the Minotaur horn in my cabin, which left me only an extra change of clothes and a toothbrush to stuff in a backpack Grover had found for me.

The camp store loaned me one hundred dollars in mortal money and twenty golden drachmas. These coins were as big as Girl Scout cookies and had images of various Greek gods stamped on one side and the Empire State Building on the other. The ancient mortal drachmas had been silver, Chiron told us, but Olympians never used less than pure gold. Chiron said the coins might come in handy for nonmortal transactions—whatever that meant. He gave Annabeth and me each a canteen of nectar and a Ziploc bag full of ambrosia squares, to be used only in emergencies, if we were seriously hurt. It was god food, Chiron reminded us. It would cure us of almost any injury, but it was lethal to mortals. Too much of it would make a half-blood very, very feverish. An overdose would burn us up, literally.

Annabeth was bringing her magic Yankees cap, which she told me had been a twelfth-birthday present from her mom. She carried a book on famous classical architecture, written in Ancient Greek, to read when she got bored, and a long bronze knife, hidden in her shirt sleeve. I was sure the knife would get us busted the first time we went through a metal detector.

Grover wore his fake feet and his pants to pass as human. He wore a green rasta-style cap, because when it rained his curly hair flattened and you could just see the tips of his horns. His bright orange backpack was full of scrap metal and apples to snack on. In his pocket was a set of reed pipes his daddy-goat had carved for him, even though he only knew two songs: Mozart's Piano Concerto no. 12 and Hilary Duff's "So Yesterday," both of which sounded pretty bad on reed pipes.

We waved good-bye to the other campers, took one last look at the strawberry fields, the ocean, and the Big House, then hiked up Half-Blood Hill to the tall pine tree that used to be Thalia, daughter of Zeus.

Chiron was waiting for us in his wheelchair. Next to him stood the surfer dude I'd seen when I was recovering in the sick room. According to Grover, the guy was the camp's head of security. He supposedly had eyes all over his body so he could never be surprised. Today, though, he was wearing a chauffeur's uniform, so I could only see extra peepers on his hands, face and neck.

"This is Argus," Chiron told me. "He will drive you into the city, and, er, well, keep an eye on things."

I heard footsteps behind us.

Luke came running up the hill, carrying a pair of basketball shoes.

"Hey!" he panted. "Glad I caught you."

Annabeth blushed, the way she always did when Luke was around.

"Just wanted to say good luck," Luke told me. "And I thought . . . um, maybe you could use these."

He handed me the sneakers, which looked pretty normal. They even smelled kind of normal.

Luke said, *"Maia!"*

White bird's wings sprouted out of the heels, startling me so much, I dropped them. The shoes flapped around on the ground until the wings folded up and disappeared.

"Awesome!" Grover said.

Luke smiled. "Those served me well when I was on my quest. Gift from Dad. Of course, I don't use them much these days. . . ." His expression turned sad.

I didn't know what to say. It was cool enough that Luke had come to say good-bye. I'd been afraid he might resent me for getting so much attention the last few days. But here he was giving me a magic gift. . . . It made me blush almost as much as Annabeth.

"Hey, man," I said. "Thanks."

"Listen, Percy . . ." Luke looked uncomfortable. "A lot of hopes are riding on you. So just . . . kill some monsters for me, okay?"

We shook hands. Luke patted Grover's head between his horns, then gave a good-bye hug to Annabeth, who looked like she might pass out.

After Luke was gone, I told her, "You're hyperventilating."

"Am not."

"You let him capture the flag instead of you, didn't you?"

"Oh . . . why do I want to go anywhere with you, Percy?"

She stomped down the other side of the hill, where a white SUV waited on the shoulder of the road. Argus followed, jingling his car keys.

I picked up the flying shoes and had a sudden bad feeling. I looked at Chiron. "I won't be able to use these, will I?"

He shook his head. "Luke meant well, Percy. But taking to the air . . . that would not be wise for you."

I nodded, disappointed, but then I got an idea. "Hey, Grover. You want a magic item?"

His eyes lit up. "Me?"

Pretty soon we'd laced the sneakers over his fake feet, and the world's first flying goat boy was ready for launch.

"Maia!" he shouted.

He got off the ground okay, but then fell over sideways so his backpack dragged through the grass. The winged shoes kept bucking up and down like tiny broncos.

"Practice," Chiron called after him. "You just need practice!"

"Aaaaa!" Grover went flying sideways down the hill like a possessed lawn mower, heading toward the van.

Before I could follow, Chiron caught my arm. "I should have trained you better, Percy," he said. "If only I had more time. Hercules, Jason—they all got more training."

"That's okay. I just wish—"

I stopped myself because I was about to sound like a

brat. I was wishing my dad had given me a cool magic item to help on the quest, something as good as Luke's flying shoes, or Annabeth's invisible cap.

"What am I thinking?" Chiron cried. "I can't let you get away without this."

He pulled a pen from his coat pocket and handed it to me. It was an ordinary disposable ballpoint, black ink, removable cap. Probably cost thirty cents.

"Gee," I said. "Thanks."

"Percy, that's a gift from your father. I've kept it for years, not knowing you were who I was waiting for. But the prophecy is clear to me now. You are the one."

I remembered the field trip to the Metropolitan Museum of Art, when I'd vaporized Mrs. Dodds. Chiron had thrown me a pen that turned into a sword. Could this be . . . ?

I took off the cap, and the pen grew longer and heavier in my hand. In half a second, I held a shimmering bronze sword with a double-edged blade, a leather-wrapped grip, and a flat hilt riveted with gold studs. It was the first weapon that actually felt balanced in my hand.

"The sword has a long and tragic history that we need not go into," Chiron told me. "Its name is Anaklusmos."

"'Riptide,'" I translated, surprised the Ancient Greek came so easily.

"Use it only for emergencies," Chiron said, "and only against monsters. No hero should harm mortals unless absolutely necessary, of course, but this sword wouldn't harm them in any case."

I looked at the wickedly sharp blade. "What do you mean it wouldn't harm mortals? How could it not?"

"The sword is celestial bronze. Forged by the Cyclopes, tempered in the heart of Mount Etna, cooled in the River Lethe. It's deadly to monsters, to any creature from the Underworld, provided they don't kill you first. But the blade will pass through mortals like an illusion. They simply are not important enough for the blade to kill. And I should warn you: as a demigod, you can be killed by either celestial or normal weapons. You are twice as vulnerable."

"Good to know."

"Now recap the pen."

I touched the pen cap to the sword tip and instantly Riptide shrank to a ballpoint pen again. I tucked it in my pocket, a little nervous, because I was famous for losing pens at school.

"You can't," Chiron said.

"Can't what?"

"Lose the pen," he said. "It is enchanted. It will always reappear in your pocket. Try it."

I was wary, but I threw the pen as far as I could down the hill and watched it disappear in the grass.

"It may take a few moments," Chiron told me. "Now check your pocket."

Sure enough, the pen was there.

"Okay, that's *extremely* cool," I admitted. "But what if a mortal sees me pulling out a sword?"

Chiron smiled. "Mist is a powerful thing, Percy."

"Mist?"

"Yes. Read *The Iliad*. It's full of references to the stuff. Whenever divine or monstrous elements mix with the mortal world, they generate Mist, which obscures the vision of humans. You will see things just as they are, being a half-blood, but humans will interpret things quite differently. Remarkable, really, the lengths to which humans will go to fit things into their version of reality."

I put Riptide back in my pocket.

For the first time, the quest felt real. I was actually leaving Half-Blood Hill. I was heading west with no adult supervision, no backup plan, not even a cell phone. (Chiron said cell phones were traceable by monsters; if we used one, it would be worse than sending up a flare.) I had no weapon stronger than a sword to fight off monsters and reach the Land of the Dead.

"Chiron . . ." I said. "When you say the gods are immortal . . . I mean, there was a time *before* them, right?"

"Four ages before them, actually. The Time of the Titans was the Fourth Age, sometimes called the Golden Age, which is definitely a misnomer. This, the time of Western civilization and the rule of Zeus, is the Fifth Age."

"So what was it like . . . before the gods?"

Chiron pursed his lips. "Even I am not old enough to remember that, child, but I know it was a time of darkness and savagery for mortals. Kronos, the lord of the Titans, called his reign the Golden Age because men lived innocent and free of all knowledge. But that was mere propaganda. The Titan king cared nothing for your kind except as appetizers or a source of cheap entertainment. It was only in the early reign of Lord Zeus, when Prometheus the good Titan brought fire to mankind, that your species began to progress, and even then Prometheus was branded a radical thinker. Zeus punished him severely, as you may recall. Of course, eventually the gods warmed to humans, and Western civilization was born."

"But the gods can't die now, right? I mean, as long as Western civilization is alive, they're alive. So . . . even if I failed, nothing could happen so bad it would mess up *everything*, right?"

Chiron gave me a melancholy smile. "No one knows how long the Age of the West will last, Percy. The gods are immortal, yes. But then, so were the Titans. *They* still exist, locked away in their various prisons, forced to endure endless pain and punishment, reduced in power, but still very much alive. May the Fates forbid that the gods should ever suffer such a doom, or that we should ever return to the darkness and chaos of the past. All we can do, child, is follow our destiny."

"Our destiny . . . assuming we know what that is."

"Relax," Chiron told me. "Keep a clear head. And remember, you may be about to prevent the biggest war in human history."

"Relax," I said. "I'm very relaxed."

When I got to the bottom of the hill, I looked back. Under the pine tree that used to be Thalia, daughter of Zeus, Chiron was now standing in full horse-man form, holding his bow high in salute. Just your typical summer-camp send-off by your typical centaur.

* * *

Argus drove us out of the countryside and into western Long Island. It felt weird to be on a highway again, Annabeth and Grover sitting next to me as if we were normal carpoolers. After two weeks at Half-Blood Hill, the real world seemed like a fantasy. I found myself staring at every McDonald's, every kid in the back of his parents' car, every billboard and shopping mall.

"So far so good," I told Annabeth. "Ten miles and not a single monster."

She gave me an irritated look. "It's bad luck to talk that way, seaweed brain."

"Remind me again—why do you hate me so much?"

"I don't hate you."

"Could've fooled me."

She folded her cap of invisibility. "Look . . . we're just not supposed to get along, okay? Our parents are rivals."

"Why?"

She sighed. "How many reasons do you want? One time my mom caught Poseidon with his girlfriend in Athena's temple, which is *hugely* disrespectful. Another time, Athena and Poseidon competed to be the patron god for the city of Athens. Your dad created some stupid saltwater spring for his gift. My mom created the olive tree. The people saw that her gift was better, so they named the city after her."

"They must really like olives."

"Oh, forget it."

"Now, if she'd invented pizza—*that* I could understand."

"I said, forget it!"

In the front seat, Argus smiled. He didn't say anything, but one blue eye on the back of his neck winked at me.

Traffic slowed us down in Queens. By the time we got into Manhattan it was sunset and starting to rain.

Argus dropped us at the Greyhound Station on the Upper East Side, not far from my mom and Gabe's apartment. Taped to a mailbox was a soggy flyer with my picture on it: HAVE YOU SEEN THIS BOY?

I ripped it down before Annabeth and Grover could notice.

Argus unloaded our bags, made sure we got our bus tickets, then drove away, the eye on the back of his hand opening to watch us as he pulled out of the parking lot.

I thought about how close I was to my old apartment. On a normal day, my mom would be home from the candy store by now. Smelly Gabe was probably up there right now, playing poker, not even missing her.

Grover shouldered his backpack. He gazed down the street in the direction I was looking. "You want to know why she married him, Percy?"

I stared at him. "Were you reading my mind or something?"

"Just your emotions." He shrugged. "Guess I forgot to tell you satyrs can do that. You were thinking about your mom and your stepdad, right?"

I nodded, wondering what else Grover might've forgotten to tell me.

"Your mom married Gabe for *you*," Grover told me. "You call him 'Smelly,' but you've got no idea. The guy has this aura. . . . Yuck. I can smell him from here. I can smell traces of him on you, and you haven't been near him for a week."

"Thanks," I said. "Where's the nearest shower?"

"You should be grateful, Percy. Your stepfather smells so repulsively human he could mask the presence of any demigod. As soon as I took a whiff inside his Camaro, I knew: Gabe has been covering your scent for years. If you hadn't lived with him every summer, you probably would've been found by monsters a long time ago. Your mom stayed with him to protect you. She was a smart lady. She must've loved you a lot to put up with that guy—if that makes you feel any better."

It didn't, but I forced myself not to show it. I'll see her again, I thought. She isn't gone.

I wondered if Grover could still read my emotions, mixed up as they were. I was glad he and Annabeth were with me, but I felt guilty that I hadn't been straight with them. I hadn't told them the real reason I'd said yes to this crazy quest.

The truth was, I didn't care about retrieving Zeus's lightning bolt, or saving the world, or even helping my father out of trouble. The more I thought about it, I resented Poseidon for never visiting me, never helping my mom, never even sending a lousy child-support check. He'd only claimed me because he needed a job done.

All I cared about was my mom. Hades had taken her unfairly, and Hades was going to give her back.

You will be betrayed by one who calls you a friend, the Oracle whispered in my mind. *You will fail to save what matters most in the end.*

Shut up, I told it.

The rain kept coming down.

We got restless waiting for the bus and decided to play some Hacky Sack with one of Grover's apples. Annabeth was unbelievable. She could bounce the apple off her knee, her elbow, her shoulder, whatever. I wasn't too bad myself.

The game ended when I tossed the apple toward Grover and it got too close to his mouth. In one mega goat bite, our Hacky Sack disappeared—core, stem, and all.

Grover blushed. He tried to apologize, but Annabeth and I were too busy cracking up.

Finally the bus came. As we stood in line to board, Grover started looking around, sniffing the air like he smelled his favorite school cafeteria delicacy—enchiladas.

"What is it?" I asked.

"I don't know," he said tensely. "Maybe it's nothing."

But I could tell it wasn't nothing. I started looking over my shoulder, too.

I was relieved when we finally got on board and found seats together in the back of the bus. We stowed our backpacks. Annabeth kept slapping her Yankees cap nervously against her thigh.

As the last passengers got on, Annabeth clamped her hand onto my knee. "Percy."

An old lady had just boarded the bus. She wore a crumpled velvet dress, lace gloves, and a shapeless orange-knit hat that shadowed her face, and she carried a big paisley purse. When she tilted her head up, her black eyes glittered, and my heart skipped a beat.

It was Mrs. Dodds. Older, more withered, but definitely the same evil face.

I scrunched down in my seat.

Behind her came two more old ladies: one in a green hat, one in a purple hat. Otherwise they looked exactly like Mrs. Dodds—same gnarled hands, paisley handbags, wrinkled velvet dresses. Triplet demon grandmothers.

They sat in the front row, right behind the driver. The two on the aisle crossed their legs over the walkway, making an X. It was casual enough, but it sent a clear message: nobody leaves.

The bus pulled out of the station, and we headed through the slick streets of Manhattan. "She didn't stay dead long," I said, trying to keep my voice from quivering. "I thought you said they could be dispelled for a lifetime."

"I said if you're *lucky*," Annabeth said. "You're obviously not."

"All three of them," Grover whimpered. *"Di immortales!"*

"It's okay," Annabeth said, obviously thinking hard. "The Furies. The three worst monsters from the Underworld. No problem. No problem. We'll just slip out the windows."

"They don't open," Grover moaned.

"A back exit?" she suggested.

There wasn't one. Even if there had been, it wouldn't

have helped. By that time, we were on Ninth Avenue, heading for the Lincoln Tunnel.

"They won't attack us with witnesses around," I said. "Will they?"

"Mortals don't have good eyes," Annabeth reminded me. "Their brains can only process what they see through the Mist."

"They'll see three old ladies killing us, won't they?"

She thought about it. "Hard to say. But we can't count on mortals for help. Maybe an emergency exit in the roof . . . ?"

We hit the Lincoln Tunnel, and the bus went dark except for the running lights down the aisle. It was eerily quiet without the sound of the rain.

Mrs. Dodds got up. In a flat voice, as if she'd rehearsed it, she announced to the whole bus: "I need to use the restroom."

"So do I," said the second sister.

"So do I," said the third sister.

They all started coming down the aisle.

"I've got it," Annabeth said. "Percy, take my hat."

"What?"

"You're the one they want. Turn invisible and go up the aisle. Let them pass you. Maybe you can get to the front and get away."

"But you guys—"

"There's an outside chance they might not notice us," Annabeth said. "You're a son of one of the Big Three. Your smell might be overpowering."

"I can't just leave you."

"Don't worry about us," Grover said. "Go!"

My hands trembled. I felt like a coward, but I took the Yankees cap and put it on.

When I looked down, my body wasn't there anymore.

I started creeping up the aisle. I managed to get up ten rows, then duck into an empty seat just as the Furies walked past.

Mrs. Dodds stopped, sniffing, and looked straight at me. My heart was pounding.

Apparently she didn't see anything. She and her sisters kept going.

I was free. I made it to the front of the bus. We were almost through the Lincoln Tunnel now. I was about to press the emergency stop button when I heard hideous wailing from the back row.

The old ladies were not old ladies anymore. Their faces were still the same—I guess those couldn't get any uglier—but their bodies had shriveled into leathery brown hag bodies with bat's wings and hands and feet like gargoyle claws. Their handbags had turned into fiery whips.

The Furies surrounded Grover and Annabeth, lashing their whips, hissing: "Where is it? Where?"

The other people on the bus were screaming, cowering in their seats. They saw *something*, all right.

"He's not here!" Annabeth yelled. "He's gone!"

The Furies raised their whips.

Annabeth drew her bronze knife. Grover grabbed a tin can from his snack bag and prepared to throw it.

What I did next was so impulsive and dangerous I should've been named ADHD poster child of the year.

The bus driver was distracted, trying to see what was going on in his rearview mirror.

Still invisible, I grabbed the wheel from him and jerked it to the left. Everybody howled as they were thrown to the right, and I heard what I hoped was the sound of three Furies smashing against the windows.

"Hey!" the driver yelled. "Hey—whoa!"

We wrestled for the wheel. The bus slammed against the side of the tunnel, grinding metal, throwing sparks a mile behind us.

We careened out of the Lincoln Tunnel and back into the rainstorm, people and monsters tossed around the bus, cars plowed aside like bowling pins.

Somehow the driver found an exit. We shot off the highway, through half a dozen traffic lights, and ended up barreling down one of those New Jersey rural roads where you can't believe there's so much nothing right across the river from New York. There were woods to our left, the Hudson River to our right, and the driver seemed to be veering toward the river.

Another great idea: I hit the emergency brake.

The bus wailed, spun a full circle on the wet asphalt, and crashed into the trees. The emergency lights came on. The door flew open. The bus driver was the first one out, the passengers yelling as they stampeded after him. I stepped into the driver's seat and let them pass.

The Furies regained their balance. They lashed their

whips at Annabeth while she waved her knife and yelled in Ancient Greek, telling them to back off. Grover threw tin cans.

I looked at the open doorway. I was free to go, but I couldn't leave my friends. I took off the invisible cap. "Hey!"

The Furies turned, baring their yellow fangs at me, and the exit suddenly seemed like an excellent idea. Mrs. Dodds stalked up the aisle, just as she used to do in class, about to deliver my F— math test. Every time she flicked her whip, red flames danced along the barbed leather.

Her two ugly sisters hopped on top of the seats on either side of her and crawled toward me like huge nasty lizards.

"Perseus Jackson," Mrs. Dodds said, in an accent that was definitely from somewhere farther south than Georgia. "You have offended the gods. You shall die."

"I liked you better as a math teacher," I told her.

She growled.

Annabeth and Grover moved up behind the Furies cautiously, looking for an opening.

I took the ballpoint pen out of my pocket and uncapped it. Riptide elongated into a shimmering double-edged sword.

The Furies hesitated.

Mrs. Dodds had felt Riptide's blade before. She obviously didn't like seeing it again.

"Submit now," she hissed. "And you will not suffer eternal torment."

"Nice try," I told her.

"Percy, look out!" Annabeth cried.

Mrs. Dodds lashed her whip around my sword hand while the Furies on the either side lunged at me.

My hand felt like it was wrapped in molten lead, but I managed not to drop Riptide. I stuck the Fury on the left with its hilt, sending her toppling backward into a seat. I turned and sliced the Fury on the right. As soon as the blade connected with her neck, she screamed and exploded into dust. Annabeth got Mrs. Dodds in a wrestler's hold and yanked her backward while Grover ripped the whip out of her hands.

"Ow!" he yelled. "Ow! Hot! Hot!"

The Fury I'd hilt-slammed came at me again, talons ready, but I swung Riptide and she broke open like a piñata.

Mrs. Dodds was trying to get Annabeth off her back. She kicked, clawed, hissed and bit, but Annabeth held on while Grover got Mrs. Dodds's legs tied up in her own whip. Finally they both shoved her backward into the aisle. Mrs. Dodds tried to get up, but she didn't have room to flap her bat wings, so she kept falling down.

"Zeus will destroy you!" she promised. "Hades will have your soul!"

"*Braccas meas vescimini!*" I yelled.

I wasn't sure where the Latin came from. I think it meant "Eat my pants!"

Thunder shook the bus. The hair rose on the back of my neck.

"Get out!" Annabeth yelled at me. "Now!" I didn't need any encouragement.

We rushed outside and found the other passengers wandering around in a daze, arguing with the driver, or running around in circles yelling, "We're going to die!" A Hawaiian-shirted tourist with a camera snapped my photograph before I could recap my sword.

"Our bags!" Grover realized. "We left our—"

BOOOOOM!

The windows of the bus exploded as the passengers ran for cover. Lightning shredded a huge crater in the roof, but an angry wail from inside told me Mrs. Dodds was not yet dead.

"Run!" Annabeth said. "She's calling for reinforcements! We have to get out of here!"

We plunged into the woods as the rain poured down, the bus in flames behind us, and nothing but darkness ahead.

II   WE VISIT THE GARDEN GNOME EMPORIUM

In a way, it's nice to know there are Greek gods out there, because you have somebody to blame when things go wrong. For instance, when you're walking away from a bus that's just been attacked by monster hags and blown up by lightning, and it's raining on top of everything else, most people might think that's just really bad luck; when you're a half-blood, you understand that some divine force really is trying to mess up your day.

So there we were, Annabeth and Grover and I, walking through the woods along the New Jersey riverbank, the glow of New York City making the night sky yellow behind us, and the smell of the Hudson reeking in our noses.

Grover was shivering and braying, his big goat eyes turned slit-pupiled and full of terror. "Three Kindly Ones. All three at once."

I was pretty much in shock myself. The explosion of bus windows still rang in my ears. But Annabeth kept pulling us along, saying: "Come on! The farther away we get, the better."

"All our money was back there," I reminded her. "Our food and clothes. Everything."

"Well, maybe if you hadn't decided to jump into the fight—"

"What did you want me to do? Let you get killed?"

"You didn't need to protect me, Percy. I would've been fine."

"Sliced like sandwich bread," Grover put in, "but fine."

"Shut up, goat boy," said Annabeth.

Grover brayed mournfully. "Tin cans . . . a perfectly good bag of tin cans."

We sloshed across mushy ground, through nasty twisted trees that smelled like sour laundry.

After a few minutes, Annabeth fell into line next to me. "Look, I . . ." Her voice faltered. "I appreciate your coming back for us, okay? That was really brave."

"We're a team, right?"

She was silent for a few more steps. "It's just that if you died . . . aside from the fact that it would really suck for you, it would mean the quest was over. This may be my only chance to see the real world."

The thunderstorm had finally let up. The city glow faded behind us, leaving us in almost total darkness. I couldn't see anything of Annabeth except a glint of her blond hair.

"You haven't left Camp Half-Blood since you were seven?" I asked her.

"No . . . only short field trips. My dad—"

"The history professor."

"Yeah. It didn't work out for me living at home. I mean, Camp Half-Blood *is* my home." She was rushing her words out now, as if she were afraid somebody might try to stop her. "At camp you train and train. And that's all cool and everything, but the real world is where the monsters are. That's where you learn whether you're any good or not."

If I didn't know better, I could've sworn I heard doubt in her voice.

"You're pretty good with that knife," I said.

"You think so?"

"Anybody who can piggyback-ride a Fury is okay by me."

I couldn't really see, but I thought she might've smiled.

"You know," she said, "maybe I should tell you . . . Something funny back on the bus . . ."

Whatever she wanted to say was interrupted by a shrill *toot-toot-toot*, like the sound of an owl being tortured.

"Hey, my reed pipes still work!" Grover cried. "If I could just remember a 'find path' song, we could get out of these woods!"

He puffed out a few notes, but the tune still sounded suspiciously like Hilary Duff.

Instead of finding a path, I immediately slammed into a tree and got a nice-size knot on my head.

Add to the list of superpowers I did *not* have: infrared vision.

After tripping and cursing and generally feeling miserable for another mile or so, I started to see light up ahead: the colors of a neon sign. I could smell food. Fried, greasy, excellent food. I realized I hadn't eaten anything unhealthy since I'd arrived at Half-Blood Hill, where we lived on grapes, bread, cheese, and extra-lean-cut nymph-prepared barbecue. This boy needed a double cheeseburger.

We kept walking until I saw a deserted two-lane road through the trees. On the other side was a closed-down gas station, a tattered billboard for a 1990s movie, and one open business, which was the source of the neon light and the good smell.

It wasn't a fast-food restaurant like I'd hoped. It was one of those weird roadside curio shops that sell lawn flamingos and wooden Indians and cement grizzly bears and stuff like that. The main building was a long, low warehouse, surrounded by acres of statuary. The neon sign above the gate was impossible for me to read, because if there's anything worse for my dyslexia than regular English, it's red cursive neon English.

To me, it looked like: *ATNYU MES GDERAN GOMEN MEPROUIM.*

"What the heck does that say?" I asked.

"I don't know," Annabeth said.

She loved reading so much, I'd forgotten she was dyslexic, too.

Grover translated: "Aunty Em's Garden Gnome Emporium."

Flanking the entrance, as advertised, were two cement garden gnomes, ugly bearded little runts, smiling and waving, as if they were about to get their picture taken.

I crossed the street, following the smell of the hamburgers.

"Hey . . ." Grover warned.

"The lights are on inside," Annabeth said. "Maybe it's open."

"Snack bar," I said wistfully.

"Snack bar," she agreed.

"Are you two crazy?" Grover said. "This place is weird."

We ignored him.

The front lot was a forest of statues: cement animals, cement children, even a cement satyr playing the pipes, which gave Grover the creeps.

"*Bla-ha-ha!*" he bleated. "Looks like my Uncle Ferdinand!"

We stopped at the warehouse door.

"Don't knock," Grover pleaded. "I smell monsters."

"Your nose is clogged up from the Furies," Annabeth told him. "All I smell is burgers. Aren't you hungry?"

"Meat!" he said scornfully. "I'm a vegetarian."

"You eat cheese enchiladas and aluminum cans," I reminded him.

"Those are vegetables. Come on. Let's leave. These statues are . . . looking at me."

Then the door creaked open, and standing in front of us was a tall Middle Eastern woman—at least, I assumed she was Middle Eastern, because she wore a long black gown that covered everything but her hands, and her head was completely veiled. Her eyes glinted behind a curtain of black gauze, but that was about all I could make out. Her coffee-colored hands looked old, but well-manicured and elegant, so I imagined she was a grandmother who had once been a beautiful lady.

Her accent sounded vaguely Middle Eastern, too. She

said, "Children, it is too late to be out all alone. Where are your parents?"

"They're . . . um . . ." Annabeth started to say.

"We're orphans," I said.

"Orphans?" the woman said. The word sounded alien in her mouth. "But, my dears! Surely not!"

"We got separated from our caravan," I said. "Our circus caravan. The ringmaster told us to meet him at the gas station if we got lost, but he may have forgotten, or maybe he meant a different gas station. Anyway, we're lost. Is that food I smell?"

"Oh, my dears," the woman said. "You must come in, poor children. I am Aunty Em. Go straight through to the back of the warehouse, please. There is a dining area."

We thanked her and went inside.

Annabeth muttered to me, "Circus caravan?"

"Always have a strategy, right?"

"Your head is full of kelp."

The warehouse was filled with more statues—people in all different poses, wearing all different outfits and with different expressions on their faces. I was thinking you'd have to have a pretty huge garden to fit even one of these statues, because they were all life-size. But mostly, I was thinking about food.

Go ahead, call me an idiot for walking into a strange lady's shop like that just because I was hungry, but I do impulsive stuff sometimes. Plus, you've never smelled Aunty Em's burgers. The aroma was like laughing gas in the dentist's chair—it made everything else go away. I barely noticed Grover's nervous whimpers, or the way the statues' eyes seemed to follow me, or the fact that Aunty Em had locked the door behind us.

All I cared about was finding the dining area. And sure enough, there it was at the back of the warehouse, a fast-food counter with a grill, a soda fountain, a pretzel heater, and a nacho cheese dispenser. Everything you could want, plus a few steel picnic tables out front.

"Please, sit down," Aunty Em said.

"Awesome," I said.

"Um," Grover said reluctantly, "we don't have any money, ma'am."

Before I could jab him in the ribs, Aunty Em said, "No, no, children. No money. This is a special case, yes? It is my treat, for such nice orphans."

"Thank you, ma'am," Annabeth said.

Aunty Em stiffened, as if Annabeth had done something wrong, but then the old woman relaxed just as quickly, so I figured it must've been my imagination.

"Quite all right, Annabeth," she said. "You have such beautiful gray eyes, child." Only later did I wonder how she knew Annabeth's name, even though we had never introduced ourselves.

Our hostess disappeared behind the snack counter and started cooking. Before we knew it, she'd brought us plastic trays heaped with double cheeseburgers, vanilla shakes, and XXL servings of French fries.

I was halfway through my burger before I remembered to breathe.

Annabeth slurped her shake.

Grover picked at the fries, and eyed the tray's waxed paper liner as if he might go for that, but he still looked too nervous to eat.

"What's that hissing noise?" he asked.

I listened, but didn't hear anything. Annabeth shook her head.

"Hissing?" Aunty Em asked. "Perhaps you hear the deep-fryer oil. You have keen ears, Grover."

"I take vitamins. For my ears."

"That's admirable," she said. "But please, relax."

Aunty Em ate nothing. She hadn't taken off her head-dress, even to cook, and now she sat forward and interlaced her fingers and watched us eat. It was a little unsettling, having someone stare at me when I couldn't see her face, but I was feeling satisfied after the burger, and a little sleepy, and I figured the least I could do was try to make small talk with our hostess.

"So, you sell gnomes," I said, trying to sound interested.

"Oh, yes," Aunty Em said. "And animals. And people. Anything for the garden. Custom orders. Statuary is very popular, you know."

"A lot of business on this road?"

"Not so much, no. Since the highway was built . . . most cars, they do not go this way now. I must cherish every customer I get."

My neck tingled, as if somebody else was looking at me. I turned, but it was just a statue of a young girl holding an Easter basket. The detail was incredible, much better than you see in most garden statues. But something was wrong with her face. It looked as if she were startled, or even terrified.

"Ah," Aunty Em said sadly. "You notice some of my creations do not turn out well. They are marred. They do not sell. The face is the hardest to get right. Always the face."

"You make these statues yourself?" I asked.

"Oh, yes. Once upon a time, I had two sisters to help me in the business, but they have passed on, and Aunty Em is alone. I have only my statues. This is why I make them, you see. They are my company." The sadness in her voice sounded so deep and so real that I couldn't help feeling sorry for her.

Annabeth had stopped eating. She sat forward and said, "Two sisters?"

"It's a terrible story," Aunty Em said. "Not one for children, really. You see, Annabeth, a bad woman was jealous of me, long ago, when I was young. I had a . . . a boyfriend, you know, and this bad woman was determined to break us apart. She caused a terrible accident. My sisters stayed by me. They shared my bad fortune as long as they could, but eventually they passed on. They faded away. I alone have survived, but at a price. Such a price."

I wasn't sure what she meant, but I felt bad for her. My eyelids kept getting heavier, my full stomach making me sleepy. Poor old lady. Who would want to hurt somebody so nice?

"Percy?" Annabeth was shaking me to get my attention.

"Maybe we should go. I mean, the ringmaster will be waiting."

She sounded tense. I wasn't sure why. Grover was eating the waxed paper off the tray now, but if Aunty Em found that strange, she didn't say anything.

"Such beautiful gray eyes," Aunty Em told Annabeth again. "My, yes, it has been a long time since I've seen gray eyes like those."

She reached out as if to stroke Annabeth's cheek, but Annabeth stood up abruptly.

"We really should go."

"Yes!" Grover swallowed his waxed paper and stood up. "The ringmaster is waiting! Right!"

I didn't want to leave. I felt full and content. Aunty Em was so nice. I wanted to stay with her a while.

"Please, dears," Aunty Em pleaded. "I so rarely get to be with children. Before you go, won't you at least sit for a pose?"

"A pose?" Annabeth asked warily.

"A photograph. I will use it to model a new statue set. Children are so popular, you see. Everyone loves children."

Annabeth shifted her weight from foot to foot. "I don't think we can, ma'am. Come on, Percy—"

"Sure we can," I said. I was irritated with Annabeth for being so bossy, so rude to an old lady who'd just fed us for free. "It's just a photo, Annabeth. What's the harm?"

"Yes, Annabeth," the woman purred. "No harm."

I could tell Annabeth didn't like it, but she allowed

Aunty Em to lead us back out the front door, into the garden of statues.

Aunty Em directed us to a park bench next to the stone satyr. "Now," she said, "I'll just position you correctly. The young girl in the middle, I think, and the two young gentlemen on either side."

"Not much light for a photo," I remarked.

"Oh, enough," Aunty Em said. "Enough for us to see each other, yes?"

"Where's your camera?" Grover asked.

Aunty Em stepped back, as if to admire the shot. "Now, the face is the most difficult. Can you smile for me please, everyone? A large smile?"

Grover glanced at the cement satyr next to him, and mumbled, "That sure does look like Uncle Ferdinand."

"Grover," Aunty Em chastised, "look this way, dear."

She still had no camera in her hands.

"Percy—" Annabeth said.

Some instinct warned me to listen to Annabeth, but I was fighting the sleepy feeling, the comfortable lull that came from the food and the old lady's voice.

"I will just be a moment," Aunty Em said. "You know, I can't see you very well in this cursed veil. . . ."

"Percy, something's wrong," Annabeth insisted.

"Wrong?" Aunty Em said, reaching up to undo the wrap around her head. "Not at all, dear. I have such noble company tonight. What could be wrong?"

"That *is* Uncle Ferdinand!" Grover gasped.

"Look away from her!" Annabeth shouted. She whipped

her Yankees cap onto her head and vanished. Her invisible hands pushed Grover and me both off the bench.

I was on the ground, looking at Aunt Em's sandaled feet.

I could hear Grover scrambling off in one direction, Annabeth in another. But I was too dazed to move.

Then I heard a strange, rasping sound above me. My eyes rose to Aunty Em's hands, which had turned gnarled and warty, with sharp bronze talons for fingernails.

I almost looked higher, but somewhere off to my left Annabeth screamed, "No! Don't!"

More rasping—the sound of tiny snakes, right above me, from . . . from about where Aunty Em's head would be.

"Run!" Grover bleated. I heard him racing across the gravel, yelling, *"Maia!"* to kick-start his flying sneakers.

I couldn't move. I stared at Aunty Em's gnarled claws, and tried to fight the groggy trance the old woman had put me in.

"Such a pity to destroy a handsome young face," she told me soothingly. "Stay with me, Percy. All you have to do is look up."

I fought the urge to obey. Instead I looked to one side and saw one of those glass spheres people put in gardens— a gazing ball. I could see Aunty Em's dark reflection in the orange glass; her headdress was gone, revealing her face as a shimmering pale circle. Her hair was moving, writhing like serpents.

Aunty Em.

Aunty "M."

How could I have been so stupid?

Think, I told myself. How did Medusa die in the myth?

But I couldn't think. Something told me that in the myth Medusa had been asleep when she was attacked by my namesake, Perseus. She wasn't anywhere near asleep now. If she wanted, she could take those talons right now and rake open my face.

"The Gray-Eyed One did this to me, Percy," Medusa said, and she didn't sound anything like a monster. Her voice invited me to look up, to sympathize with a poor old grandmother. "Annabeth's mother, the cursed Athena, turned me from a beautiful woman into this."

"Don't listen to her!" Annabeth's voice shouted, somewhere in the statuary. "Run, Percy!"

"Silence!" Medusa snarled. Then her voice modulated back to a comforting purr. "You see why I must destroy the girl, Percy. She is my enemy's daughter. I shall crush her statue to dust. But you, dear Percy, you need not suffer."

"No," I muttered. I tried to make my legs move.

"Do you really want to help the gods?" Medusa asked. "Do you understand what awaits you on this foolish quest, Percy? What will happen if you reach the Underworld? Do not be a pawn of the Olympians, my dear. You would be better off as a statue. Less pain. Less pain."

"Percy!" Behind me, I heard a buzzing sound, like a two-hundred-pound hummingbird in a nosedive. Grover yelled, "Duck!"

I turned, and there he was in the night sky, flying in from twelve o'clock with his winged shoes fluttering,

Grover, holding a tree branch the size of a baseball bat. His eyes were shut tight, his head twitched from side to side. He was navigating by ears and nose alone.

"Duck!" he yelled again. "I'll get her!"

That finally jolted me into action. Knowing Grover, I was sure he'd miss Medusa and nail me. I dove to one side.

Thwack!

At first I figured it was the sound of Grover hitting a tree. Then Medusa roared with rage.

"You miserable satyr," she snarled. "I'll add you to my collection!"

"That was for Uncle Ferdinand!" Grover yelled back.

I scrambled away and hid in the statuary while Grover swooped down for another pass.

Ker-whack!

"Arrgh!" Medusa yelled, her snake-hair hissing and spitting.

Right next to me, Annabeth's voice said, "Percy!"

I jumped so high my feet nearly cleared a garden gnome. "Jeez! Don't do that!"

Annabeth took off her Yankees cap and became visible. "You have to cut her head off."

"What? Are you crazy? Let's get out of here."

"Medusa is a menace. She's evil. I'd kill her myself, but . . ." Annabeth swallowed, as if she were about to make a difficult admission. "But you've got the better weapon. Besides, I'd never get close to her. She'd slice me to bits because of my mother. You—you've got a chance."

"What? I can't—"

"Look, do you want her turning more innocent people into statues?"

She pointed to a pair of statue lovers, a man and a woman with their arms around each other, turned to stone by the monster.

Annabeth grabbed a green gazing ball from a nearby pedestal. "A polished shield would be better." She studied the sphere critically. "The convexity will cause some distortion. The reflection's size should be off by a factor of—"

"Would you speak English?"

"I *am!*" She tossed me the glass ball. "Just look at her in the glass. *Never* look at her directly."

"Hey, guys!" Grover yelled somewhere above us. "I think she's unconscious!"

"*Roooaaarrr!*"

"Maybe not," Grover corrected. He went in for another pass with the tree branch.

"Hurry," Annabeth told me. "Grover's got a great nose, but he'll eventually crash."

I took out my pen and uncapped it. The bronze blade of Riptide elongated in my hand.

I followed the hissing and spitting sounds of Medusa's hair.

I kept my eyes locked on the gazing ball so I would only glimpse Medusa's reflection, not the real thing. Then, in the green tinted glass, I saw her.

Grover was coming in for another turn at bat, but this time he flew a little too low. Medusa grabbed the stick and pulled him off course. He tumbled through the air and crashed into the arms of a stone grizzly bear with a painful "Ummphh!"

Medusa was about to lunge at him when I yelled, "Hey!"

I advanced on her, which wasn't easy, holding a sword and a glass ball. If she charged, I'd have a hard time defending myself.

But she let me approach—twenty feet, ten feet.

I could see the reflection of her face now. Surely it wasn't really *that* ugly. The green swirls of the gazing ball must be distorting it, making it look worse.

"You wouldn't harm an old woman, Percy," she crooned. "I know you wouldn't."

I hesitated, fascinated by the face I saw reflected in the glass—the eyes that seemed to burn straight through the green tint, making my arms go weak.

From the cement grizzly, Grover moaned, "Percy, don't listen to her!"

Medusa cackled. "Too late."

She lunged at me with her talons.

I slashed up with my sword, heard a sickening *shlock!*, then a hiss like wind rushing out of a cavern—the sound of a monster disintegrating.

Something fell to the ground next to my foot. It took all my willpower not to look. I could feel warm ooze soaking into my sock, little dying snake heads tugging at my shoelaces.

"Oh, yuck," Grover said. His eyes were still tightly closed, but I guess he could hear the thing gurgling and steaming. "Mega-yuck."

Annabeth came up next to me, her eyes fixed on the sky. She was holding Medusa's black veil. She said, "Don't move."

Very, very carefully, without looking down, she knelt and draped the monster's head in black cloth, then picked it up. It was still dripping green juice.

"Are you okay?" she asked me, her voice trembling.

"Yeah," I decided, though I felt like throwing up my double cheeseburger. "Why didn't . . . why didn't the head evaporate?"

"Once you sever it, it becomes a spoil of war," she said. "Same as your minotaur horn. But don't unwrap the head. It can still petrify you."

Grover moaned as he climbed down from the grizzly statue. He had a big welt on his forehead. His green rasta cap hung from one of his little goat horns, and his fake feet had been knocked off his hooves. The magic sneakers were flying aimlessly around his head.

"The Red Baron," I said. "Good job, man."

He managed a bashful grin. "That really was *not* fun, though. Well, the hitting-her-with-a-stick part, that was fun. But crashing into a concrete bear? *Not* fun."

He snatched his shoes out of the air. I recapped my sword. Together, the three of us stumbled back to the warehouse.

We found some old plastic grocery bags behind the snack counter and double-wrapped Medusa's head. We plopped it on the table where we'd eaten dinner and sat around it, too exhausted to speak.

Finally I said, "So we have Athena to thank for this monster?"

Annabeth flashed me an irritated look. "Your dad, actually. Don't you remember? Medusa was Poseidon's girlfriend. They decided to meet in my mother's temple. That's why Athena turned her into a monster. Medusa and her two sisters who had helped her get into the temple, they became the three gorgons. That's why Medusa wanted to slice me up, but she wanted to preserve you as a nice statue. She's still sweet on your dad. You probably reminded her of him."

My face was burning. "Oh, so now it's *my* fault we met Medusa."

Annabeth straightened. In a bad imitation of my voice, she said: "'It's just a photo, Annabeth. What's the harm?'"

"Forget it," I said. "You're impossible."

"You're insufferable."

"You're—"

"Hey!" Grover interrupted. "You two are giving me a migraine, and satyrs don't even *get* migraines. What are we going to do with the head?"

I stared at the thing. One little snake was hanging out of a hole in the plastic. The words printed on the side of the bag said: WE APPRECIATE YOUR BUSINESS!

I was angry, not just with Annabeth or her mom, but with all the gods for this whole quest, for getting us blown off the road and in two major fights the very first day out from camp. At this rate, we'd never make it to L.A. alive, much less before the summer solstice.

What had Medusa said?

Do not be a pawn of the Olympians, my dear. You would be better off as a statue.

I got up. "I'll be back."

"Percy," Annabeth called after me. "What are you—"

I searched the back of the warehouse until I found Medusa's office. Her account book showed her six most recent sales, all shipments to the Underworld to decorate Hades and Persephone's garden. According to one freight bill, the Underworld's billing address was DOA Recording Studios, West Hollywood, California. I folded up the bill and stuffed it in my pocket.

In the cash register I found twenty dollars, a few golden drachmas, and some packing slips for Hermes Overnight Express, each with a little leather bag attached for coins. I rummaged around the rest of the office until I found the right-size box.

I went back to the picnic table, packed up Medusa's head, and filled out a delivery slip:

The Gods
Mount Olympus
600th Floor,
Empire State Building
New York, NY

With best wishes,
PERCY JACKSON

"They're not going to like that," Grover warned. "They'll think you're impertinent."

I poured some golden drachmas in the pouch. As soon as I closed it, there was a sound like a cash register. The package floated off the table and disappeared with a *pop!*

"I *am* impertinent," I said.

I looked at Annabeth, daring her to criticize.

She didn't. She seemed resigned to the fact that I had a major talent for ticking off the gods. "Come on," she muttered. "We need a new plan."

12 ⚡ WE GET ADVICE FROM A POODLE

We were pretty miserable that night.

We camped out in the woods, a hundred yards from the main road, in a marshy clearing that local kids had obviously been using for parties. The ground was littered with flattened soda cans and fast-food wrappers.

We'd taken some food and blankets from Aunty Em's, but we didn't dare light a fire to dry our damp clothes. The Furies and Medusa had provided enough excitement for one day. We didn't want to attract anything else.

We decided to sleep in shifts. I volunteered to take first watch.

Annabeth curled up on the blankets and was snoring as soon as her head hit the ground. Grover fluttered with his flying shoes to the lowest bough of a tree, put his back to the trunk, and stared at the night sky.

"Go ahead and sleep," I told him. "I'll wake you if there's trouble."

He nodded, but still didn't close his eyes. "It makes me sad, Percy."

"What does? The fact that you signed up for this stupid quest?"

"No. *This* makes me sad." He pointed at all the garbage

on the ground. "And the sky. You can't even see the stars. They've polluted the sky. This is a terrible time to be a satyr."

"Oh, yeah. I guess you'd be an environmentalist."

He glared at me. "Only a human wouldn't be. Your species is clogging up the world so fast . . . ah, never mind. It's useless to lecture a human. At the rate things are going, I'll never find Pan."

"Pam? Like the cooking spray?"

"Pan!" he cried indignantly. "P-A-N. The great god Pan! What do you think I want a searcher's license for?"

A strange breeze rustled through the clearing, temporarily overpowering the stink of trash and muck. It brought the smell of berries and wildflowers and clean rainwater, things that might've once been in these woods. Suddenly I was nostalgic for something I'd never known.

"Tell me about the search," I said.

Grover looked at me cautiously, as if he were afraid I was just making fun.

"The God of Wild Places disappeared two thousand years ago," he told me. "A sailor off the coast of Ephesos heard a mysterious voice crying out from the shore, 'Tell them that the great god Pan has died!' When humans heard the news, they believed it. They've been pillaging Pan's kingdom ever since. But for the satyrs, Pan was our lord and master. He protected us and the wild places of the earth. We refuse to believe that he died. In every generation, the bravest satyrs pledge their lives to finding Pan. They search the earth, exploring all the wildest places, hoping to find where he is hidden, and wake him from his sleep."

"And you want to be a searcher."

"It's my life's dream," he said. "My father was a searcher. And my Uncle Ferdinand . . . the statue you saw back there—"

"Oh, right, sorry."

Grover shook his head. "Uncle Ferdinand knew the risks. So did my dad. But I'll succeed. I'll be the first searcher to return alive."

"Hang on—*the first?*"

Grover took his reed pipes out of his pocket. "No searcher has ever come back. Once they set out, they disappear. They're never seen alive again."

"Not once in two thousand years?"

"No."

"And your dad? You have no idea what happened to him?"

"None."

"But you still want to go," I said, amazed. "I mean, you really think you'll be the one to find Pan?"

"I have to believe that, Percy. Every searcher does. It's the only thing that keeps us from despair when we look at what humans have done to the world. I have to believe Pan can still be awakened."

I stared at the orange haze of the sky and tried to understand how Grover could pursue a dream that seemed so hopeless. Then again, was I any better?

"How are we going to get into the Underworld?" I asked him. "I mean, what chance do we have against a god?"

"I don't know," he admitted. "But back at Medusa's,

when you were searching her office? Annabeth was telling me—"

"Oh, I forgot. Annabeth will have a plan all figured out."

"Don't be so hard on her, Percy. She's had a tough life, but she's a good person. After all, she forgave me. . . ." His voice faltered.

"What do you mean?" I asked. "Forgave you for what?"

Suddenly, Grover seemed very interested in playing notes on his pipes.

"Wait a minute," I said. "Your first keeper job was five years ago. Annabeth has been at camp five years. She wasn't . . . I mean, your first assignment that went wrong—"

"I can't talk about it," Grover said, and his quivering lower lip suggested he'd start crying if I pressed him. "But as I was saying, back at Medusa's, Annabeth and I agreed there's something strange going on with this quest. Something isn't what it seems."

"Well, duh. I'm getting blamed for stealing a thunderbolt that Hades took."

"That's not what I mean," Grover said. "The Fur—The Kindly Ones were sort of holding back. Like Mrs. Dodds at Yancy Academy . . . why did she wait so long to try to kill you? Then on the bus, they just weren't as aggressive as they could've been."

"They seemed plenty aggressive to me."

Grover shook his head. "They were screeching at us: 'Where is it? Where?'"

"Asking about me," I said.

"Maybe . . . but Annabeth and I, we both got the feeling they weren't asking about a person. They said 'Where is *it*?' They seemed to be asking about an object."

"That doesn't make sense."

"I know. But if we've misunderstood something about this quest, and we only have nine days to find the master bolt. . . ." He looked at me like he was hoping for answers, but I didn't have any.

I thought about what Medusa had said: I was being used by the gods. What lay ahead of me was worse than petrification. "I haven't been straight with you," I told Grover. "I don't care about the master bolt. I agreed to go to the Underworld so I could bring back my mother."

Grover blew a soft note on his pipes. "I know that, Percy. But are you sure that's the only reason?"

"I'm not doing it to help my father. He doesn't care about me. I don't care about him."

Grover gazed down from his tree branch. "Look, Percy, I'm not as smart as Annabeth. I'm not as brave as you. But I'm pretty good at reading emotions. You're glad your dad is alive. You feel good that he's claimed you, and part of you wants to make him proud. That's why you mailed Medusa's head to Olympus. You wanted him to notice what you'd done."

"Yeah? Well maybe satyr emotions work differently than human emotions. Because you're wrong. I don't care what he thinks."

Grover pulled his feet up onto the branch. "Okay, Percy. Whatever."

"Besides, I haven't done anything worth bragging about. We barely got out of New York and we're stuck here with no money and no way west."

Grover looked at the night sky, like he was thinking about that problem. "How about *I* take first watch, huh? You get some sleep."

I wanted to protest, but he started to play Mozart, soft and sweet, and I turned away, my eyes stinging. After a few bars of Piano Concerto no. 12, I was asleep.

In my dreams, I stood in a dark cavern before a gaping pit. Gray mist creatures churned all around me, whispering rags of smoke that I somehow knew were the spirits of the dead.

They tugged at my clothes, trying to pull me back, but I felt compelled to walk forward to the very edge of the chasm.

Looking down made me dizzy.

The pit yawned so wide and was so completely black, I knew it must be bottomless. Yet I had a feeling that something was trying to rise from the abyss, something huge and evil.

The little hero, an amused voice echoed far down in the darkness. *Too weak, too young, but perhaps you will do.*

The voice felt ancient—cold and heavy. It wrapped around me like sheets of lead.

They have misled you, boy, it said. *Barter with me. I will give you what you want.*

A shimmering image hovered over the void: my mother, frozen at the moment she'd dissolved in a shower of gold.

Her face was distorted with pain, as if the Minotaur were still squeezing her neck. Her eyes looked directly at me, pleading: *Go!*

I tried to cry out, but my voice wouldn't work.

Cold laughter echoed from the chasm.

An invisible force pulled me forward. It would drag me into the pit unless I stood firm.

Help me rise, boy. The voice became hungrier. *Bring me the bolt. Strike a blow against the treacherous gods!*

The spirits of the dead whispered around me, *No! Wake!*

The image of my mother began to fade. The thing in the pit tightened its unseen grip around me.

I realized it wasn't interested in pulling me in. It was using me to pull itself *out.*

Good, it murmured. *Good.*

Wake! the dead whispered. *Wake!*

Someone was shaking me.

My eyes opened, and it was daylight.

"Well," Annabeth said, "the zombie lives."

I was trembling from the dream. I could still feel the grip of the chasm monster around my chest. "How long was I asleep?"

"Long enough for me to cook breakfast." Annabeth tossed me a bag of nacho-flavored corn chips from Aunty Em's snack bar. "And Grover went exploring. Look, he found a friend."

My eyes had trouble focusing.

Grover was sitting cross-legged on a blanket with

something fuzzy in his lap, a dirty, unnaturally pink stuffed animal.

No. It wasn't a stuffed animal. It was a pink poodle.

The poodle yapped at me suspiciously. Grover said, "No, he's not."

I blinked. "Are you . . . talking to that thing?"

The poodle growled.

"This *thing*," Grover warned, "is our ticket west. Be nice to him."

"You can talk to animals?"

Grover ignored the question. "Percy, meet Gladiola. Gladiola, Percy."

I stared at Annabeth, figuring she'd crack up at this practical joke they were playing on me, but she looked deadly serious.

"I'm not saying hello to a pink poodle," I said. "Forget it."

"Percy," Annabeth said. "I said hello to the poodle. You say hello to the poodle."

The poodle growled.

I said hello to the poodle.

Grover explained that he'd come across Gladiola in the woods and they'd struck up a conversation. The poodle had run away from a rich local family, who'd posted a $200 reward for his return. Gladiola didn't really want to go back to his family, but he was willing to if it meant helping Grover.

"How does Gladiola know about the reward?" I asked.

"He read the signs," Grover said. "Duh."

"Of course," I said. "Silly me."

"So we turn in Gladiola," Annabeth explained in her best strategy voice, "we get money, and we buy tickets to Los Angeles. Simple."

I thought about my dream—the whispering voices of the dead, the thing in the chasm, and my mother's face, shimmering as it dissolved into gold. All that might be waiting for me in the West.

"Not another bus," I said warily.

"No," Annabeth agreed.

She pointed downhill, toward train tracks I hadn't been able to see last night in the dark. "There's an Amtrack station half a mile that way. According to Gladiola, the west-bound train leaves at noon."

13 ⚡ I PLUNGE TO MY DEATH

We spent two days on the Amtrak train, heading west through hills, over rivers, past amber waves of grain.

We weren't attacked once, but I didn't relax. I felt that we were traveling around in a display case, being watched from above and maybe from below, that something was waiting for the right opportunity.

I tried to keep a low profile because my name and picture were splattered over the front pages of several East Coast newspapers. The *Trenton Register-News* showed a photo taken by a tourist as I got off the Greyhound bus. I had a wild look in my eyes. My sword was a metallic blur in my hands. It might've been a baseball bat or a lacrosse stick.

The picture's caption read:

> *Twelve-year-old Percy Jackson, wanted for questioning in the Long Island disappearance of his mother two weeks ago, is shown here fleeing from the bus where he accosted several elderly female passengers. The bus exploded on an east New Jersey roadside shortly after Jackson fled the scene. Based on eyewitness accounts, police believe the boy may be traveling with two teenage accomplices. His stepfather, Gabe Ugliano, has offered a cash reward for information leading to his capture.*

"Don't worry," Annabeth told me. "Mortal police could never find us." But she didn't sound so sure.

The rest of the day I spent alternately pacing the length of the train (because I had a really hard time sitting still) or looking out the windows.

Once, I spotted a family of centaurs galloping across a wheat field, bows at the ready, as they hunted lunch. The little boy centaur, who was the size of a second-grader on a pony, caught my eye and waved. I looked around the passenger car, but nobody else had noticed. The adult riders all had their faces buried in laptop computers or magazines.

Another time, toward evening, I saw something huge moving through the woods. I could've sworn it was a lion, except that lions don't live wild in America, and this thing was the size of a Hummer. Its fur glinted gold in the evening light. Then it leaped through the trees and was gone.

Our reward money for returning Gladiola the poodle had only been enough to purchase tickets as far as Denver. We couldn't get berths in the sleeper car, so we dozed in our seats. My neck got stiff. I tried not to drool in my sleep, since Annabeth was sitting right next to me.

Grover kept snoring and bleating and waking me up. Once, he shuffled around and his fake foot fell off. Annabeth and I had to stick it back on before any of the other passengers noticed.

"So," Annabeth asked me, once we'd gotten Grover's sneaker readjusted. "Who wants your help?"

"What do you mean?"

"When you were asleep just now, you mumbled, 'I won't help you.' Who were you dreaming about?"

I was reluctant to say anything. It was the second time I'd dreamed about the evil voice from the pit. But it bothered me so much I finally told her.

Annabeth was quiet for a long time. "That doesn't sound like Hades. He always appears on a black throne, and he never laughs."

"He offered my mother in trade. Who else could do that?"

"I guess . . . if he meant, 'Help me rise from the Underworld.' If he wants war with the Olympians. But why ask you to bring him the master bolt if he already has it?"

I shook my head, wishing I knew the answer. I thought about what Grover had told me, that the Furies on the bus seemed to have been looking for something.

Where is it? Where?

Maybe Grover sensed my emotions. He snorted in his sleep, muttered something about vegetables, and turned his head.

Annabeth readjusted his cap so it covered his horns. "Percy, you can't barter with Hades. You know that, right? He's deceitful, heartless, and greedy. I don't care if his Kindly Ones weren't as aggressive this time—"

"This time?" I asked. "You mean you've run into them before?"

Her hand crept up to her necklace. She fingered a glazed white bead painted with the image of a pine tree, one of her clay end-of-summer tokens. "Let's just say I've got no love for the Lord of the Dead. You can't be tempted to make a deal for your mom."

"What would you do if it was your dad?"

"That's easy," she said. "I'd leave him to rot."

"You're not serious?"

Annabeth's gray eyes fixed on me. She wore the same expression she'd worn in the woods at camp, the moment she drew her sword against the hellhound. "My dad's resented me since the day I was born, Percy," she said. "He never wanted a baby. When he got me, he asked Athena to take me back and raise me on Olympus because he was too busy with his work. She wasn't happy about that. She told him heroes had to be raised by their mortal parent."

"But how . . . I mean, I guess you weren't born in a hospital. . . ."

"I appeared on my father's doorstep, in a golden cradle, carried down from Olympus by Zephyr the West Wind. You'd think my dad would remember that as a miracle, right? Like, maybe he'd take some digital photos or something. But he always talked about my arrival as if it were the most inconvenient thing that had ever happened to him. When I was five he got married and totally forgot about Athena. He got a 'regular' mortal wife, and had two 'regular' mortal kids, and tried to pretend I didn't exist."

I stared out the train window. The lights of a sleeping town were drifting by. I wanted to make Annabeth feel better, but I didn't know how.

"My mom married a really awful guy," I told her. "Grover said she did it to protect me, to hide me in the scent of a human family. Maybe that's what your dad was thinking."

Annabeth kept worrying at her necklace. She was pinching the gold college ring that hung with the beads. It occurred to me that the ring must be her father's. I wondered why she wore it if she hated him so much.

"He doesn't care about me," she said. "His wife—my stepmom—treated me like a freak. She wouldn't let me play with her children. My dad went along with her. Whenever something dangerous happened—you know, something with monsters—they would both look at me resentfully, like, 'How dare you put our family at risk.' Finally, I took the hint. I wasn't wanted. I ran away."

"How old were you?"

"Same age as when I started camp. Seven."

"But . . . you couldn't have gotten all the way to Half-Blood Hill by yourself."

"Not alone, no. Athena watched over me, guided me toward help. I made a couple of unexpected friends who took care of me, for a short time, anyway."

I wanted to ask what happened, but Annabeth seemed lost in sad memories. So I listened to the sound of Grover snoring and gazed out the train windows as the dark fields of Ohio raced by.

Toward the end of our second day on the train, June 13, eight days before the summer solstice, we passed through some golden hills and over the Mississippi River into St. Louis.

Annabeth craned her neck to see the Gateway Arch, which looked to me like a huge shopping bag handle stuck on the city.

"I want to do that," she sighed.

"What?" I asked.

"Build something like that. You ever see the Parthenon, Percy?"

"Only in pictures."

"Someday, I'm going to see it in person. I'm going to build the greatest monument to the gods, ever. Something that'll last a thousand years."

I laughed. "You? An architect?"

I don't know why, but I found it funny. Just the idea of Annabeth trying to sit quietly and draw all day.

Her cheeks flushed. "Yes, an architect. Athena expects her children to create things, not just tear them down, like a certain god of earthquakes I could mention."

I watched the churning brown water of the Mississippi below.

"Sorry," Annabeth said. "That was mean."

"Can't we work together a little?" I pleaded. "I mean, didn't Athena and Poseidon ever cooperate?"

Annabeth had to think about it. "I guess . . . the chariot," she said tentatively. "My mom invented it, but Poseidon created horses out of the crests of waves. So they had to work together to make it complete."

"Then we can cooperate, too. Right?"

We rode into the city, Annabeth watching as the Arch disappeared behind a hotel.

"I suppose," she said at last.

We pulled into the Amtrak station downtown. The intercom told us we'd have a three-hour layover before departing for Denver.

Grover stretched. Before he was even fully awake, he said, "Food."

"Come on, goat boy," Annabeth said. "Sightseeing."

"Sightseeing?"

"The Gateway Arch," she said. "This may be my only chance to ride to the top. Are you coming or not?"

Grover and I exchanged looks.

I wanted to say no, but I figured that if Annabeth was going, we couldn't very well let her go alone.

Grover shrugged. "As long as there's a snack bar without monsters."

The Arch was about a mile from the train station. Late in the day the lines to get in weren't that long. We threaded our way through the underground museum, looking at covered wagons and other junk from the 1800s. It wasn't all that thrilling, but Annabeth kept telling us interesting facts about how the Arch was built, and Grover kept passing me jelly beans, so I was okay.

I kept looking around, though, at the other people in line. "You smell anything?" I murmured to Grover.

He took his nose out of the jelly-bean bag long enough to sniff. "Underground," he said distastefully. "Underground air always smells like monsters. Probably doesn't mean anything."

But something felt wrong to me. I had a feeling we shouldn't be here.

"Guys," I said. "You know the gods' symbols of power?"

Annabeth had been in the middle of reading about the construction equipment used to build the Arch, but she looked over. "Yeah?"

"Well, Hade—"

Grover cleared his throat. "We're in a public place. . . . You mean, our friend downstairs?"

"Um, right," I said. "Our friend *way* downstairs. Doesn't he have a hat like Annabeth's?"

"You mean the Helm of Darkness," Annabeth said. "Yeah, that's his symbol of power. I saw it next to his seat during the winter solstice council meeting."

"He was there?" I asked.

She nodded. "It's the only time he's allowed to visit Olympus—the darkest day of the year. But his helm is a lot more powerful than my invisibility hat, if what I've heard is true. . . ."

"It allows him to become darkness," Grover confirmed. "He can melt into shadow or pass through walls. He can't be touched, or seen, or heard. And he can radiate fear so intense it can drive you insane or stop your heart. Why do you think all rational creatures fear the dark?"

"But then . . . how do we know he's not here right now, watching us?" I asked.

Annabeth and Grover exchanged looks.

"We don't," Grover said.

"Thanks, that makes me feel a lot better," I said. "Got any blue jelly beans left?"

I'd almost mastered my jumpy nerves when I saw the tiny little elevator car we were going to ride to the top of the Arch, and I knew I was in trouble. I hate confined places. They make me nuts.

We got shoehorned into the car with this big fat lady and her dog, a Chihuahua with a rhinestone collar. I figured maybe the dog was a seeing-eye Chihuahua, because none of the guards said a word about it.

We started going up, inside the Arch. I'd never been in an elevator that went in a curve, and my stomach wasn't too happy about it.

"No parents?" the fat lady asked us.

She had beady eyes; pointy, coffee-stained teeth; a floppy denim hat, and a denim dress that bulged so much, she looked like a blue-jean blimp.

"They're below," Annabeth told her. "Scared of heights."

"Oh, the poor darlings."

The Chihuahua growled. The woman said, "Now, now, sonny. Behave." The dog had beady eyes like its owner, intelligent and vicious.

I said, "Sonny. Is that his name?"

"No," the lady told me.

She smiled, as if that cleared everything up.

At the top of the Arch, the observation deck reminded me of a tin can with carpeting. Rows of tiny windows looked out over the city on one side and the river on the other. The view was okay, but if there's anything I like less than a confined space, it's a confined space six hundred feet in the air. I was ready to go pretty quick.

Annabeth kept talking about structural supports, and how she would've made the windows bigger, and designed a see-through floor. She probably could've stayed up there for hours, but luckily for me the park ranger announced that the observation deck would be closing in a few minutes.

I steered Grover and Annabeth toward the exit, loaded them into the elevator, and I was about to get in myself when I realized there were already two other tourists inside. No room for me.

The park ranger said, "Next car, sir."

"We'll get out," Annabeth said. "We'll wait with you."

But that was going to mess everybody up and take even more time, so I said, "Naw, it's okay. I'll see you guys at the bottom."

Grover and Annabeth both looked nervous, but they let the elevator door slide shut. Their car disappeared down the ramp.

Now the only people left on the observation deck were me, a little boy with his parents, the park ranger, and the fat lady with her Chihuahua.

I smiled uneasily at the fat lady. She smiled back, her forked tongue flickering between her teeth.

Wait a minute.

Forked tongue?

Before I could decide if I'd really seen that, her Chihuahua jumped down and started yapping at me.

"Now, now, sonny," the lady said. "Does this look like a good time? We have all these nice people here."

"Doggie!" said the little boy. "Look, a doggie!"

His parents pulled him back.

The Chihuahua bared his teeth at me, foam dripping from his black lips.

"Well, son," the fat lady sighed. "If you insist."

Ice started forming in my stomach. "Um, did you just call that Chihuahua your son?"

"*Chimera*, dear," the fat lady corrected. "Not a Chihuahua. It's an easy mistake to make."

She rolled up her denim sleeves, revealing that the skin of her arms was scaly and green. When she smiled, I saw that her teeth were fangs. The pupils of her eyes were sideways slits, like a reptile's.

The Chihuahua barked louder, and with each bark, it grew. First to the size of a Doberman, then to a lion. The bark became a roar.

The little boy screamed. His parents pulled him back toward the exit, straight into the park ranger, who stood, paralyzed, gaping at the monster.

The Chimera was now so tall its back rubbed against the roof. It had the head of a lion with a blood-caked mane, the body and hooves of a giant goat, and a serpent for a tail, a ten-foot-long diamondback growing right out of its shaggy behind. The rhinestone dog collar still hung around its neck, and the plate-sized dog tag was now easy to read: CHIMERA—RABID, FIRE-BREATHING, POISONOUS—IF FOUND, PLEASE CALL TARTARUS—EXT. 954.

I realized I hadn't even uncapped my sword. My hands were numb. I was ten feet away from the Chimera's bloody maw, and I knew that as soon as I moved, the creature would lunge.

The snake lady made a hissing noise that might've been laughter. "Be honored, Percy Jackson. Lord Zeus rarely allows me to test a hero with one of my brood. For I am the Mother of Monsters, the terrible Echidna!"

I stared at her. All I could think to say was: "Isn't that a kind of anteater?"

She howled, her reptilian face turning brown and green with rage. "I hate it when people say that! I hate Australia! Naming that ridiculous animal after me. For that, Percy Jackson, my son shall destroy you!"

The Chimera charged, its lion teeth gnashing. I managed to leap aside and dodge the bite.

I ended up next to the family and the park ranger, who were all screaming now, trying to pry open the emergency exit doors.

I couldn't let them get hurt. I uncapped my sword, ran to the other side of the deck, and yelled, "Hey, Chihuahua!"

The Chimera turned faster than I would've thought possible.

Before I could swing my sword, it opened its mouth, emitting a stench like the world's largest barbecue pit, and shot a column of flame straight at me.

I dove through the explosion. The carpet burst into flames; the heat was so intense, it nearly seared off my eyebrows.

Where I had been standing a moment before was a ragged hole in the side of the Arch, with melted metal steaming around the edges.

Great, I thought. We just blowtorched a national monument.

Riptide was now a shining bronze blade in my hands, and as the Chimera turned, I slashed at its neck.

That was my fatal mistake. The blade sparked harmlessly off the dog collar. I tried to regain my balance, but I was so worried about defending myself against the fiery lion's mouth, I completely forgot about the serpent tail until it whipped around and sank its fangs into my calf.

My whole leg was on fire. I tried to jab Riptide into the Chimera's mouth, but the serpent tail wrapped around my ankles and pulled me off balance, and my blade flew out of my hand, spinning out of the hole in the Arch and down toward the Mississippi River.

I managed to get to my feet, but I knew I had lost. I was weaponless. I could feel deadly poison racing up to my chest. I remembered Chiron saying that Anaklusmos would always return to me, but there was no pen in my pocket. Maybe it had fallen too far away. Maybe it only returned when it was in pen form. I didn't know, and I wasn't going to live long enough to figure it out.

I backed into the hole in the wall. The Chimera advanced, growling, smoke curling from its lips. The snake lady, Echidna, cackled. "They don't make heroes like they used to, eh, son?"

The monster growled. It seemed in no hurry to finish

me off now that I was beaten.

I glanced at the park ranger and the family. The little boy was hiding behind his father's legs. I had to protect these people. I couldn't just . . . die. I tried to think, but my whole body was on fire. My head felt dizzy. I had no sword. I was facing a massive, fire-breathing monster and its mother. And I was scared.

There was no place else to go, so I stepped to the edge of the hole. Far, far below, the river glittered.

If I died, would the monsters go away? Would they leave the humans alone?

"If you are the son of Poseidon," Echidna hissed, "you would not fear water. Jump, Percy Jackson. Show me that water will not harm you. Jump and retrieve your sword. Prove your bloodline."

Yeah, right, I thought. I'd read somewhere that jumping into water from a couple of stories up was like jumping onto solid asphalt. From here, I'd splatter on impact.

The Chimera's mouth glowed red, heating up for another blast.

"You have no faith," Echidna told me. "You do not trust the gods. I cannot blame you, little coward. Better you die now. The gods are faithless. The poison is in your heart."

She was right: I was dying. I could feel my breath slowing down. Nobody could save me, not even the gods.

I backed up and looked down at the water. I remembered the warm glow of my father's smile when I was a baby. He must have seen me. He must have visited me when I was in my cradle.

I remembered the swirling green trident that had appeared above my head the night of capture the flag, when Poseidon had claimed me as his son.

But this wasn't the sea. This was the Mississippi, dead center of the USA. There was no Sea God here.

"Die, faithless one," Echidna rasped, and the Chimera sent a column of flame toward my face.

"Father, help me," I prayed.

I turned and jumped. My clothes on fire, poison coursing through my veins, I plummeted toward the river.

14 I BECOME A KNOWN FUGITIVE

I'd love to tell you I had some deep revelation on my way down, that I came to terms with my own mortality, laughed in the face of death, et cetera.

The truth? My only thought was: Aaaaggghhhhh!

The river raced toward me at the speed of a truck. Wind ripped the breath from my lungs. Steeples and skyscrapers and bridges tumbled in and out of my vision.

And then: *Flaaa-boooom!*

A whiteout of bubbles. I sank through the murk, sure that I was about to end up embedded in a hundred feet of mud and lost forever.

But my impact with the water hadn't hurt. I was falling slowly now, bubbles trickling up through my fingers. I settled on the river bottom soundlessly. A catfish the size of my stepfather lurched away into the gloom. Clouds of silt and disgusting garbage—beer bottles, old shoes, plastic bags—swirled up all around me.

At that point, I realized a few things: first, I had not been flattened into a pancake. I had not been barbecued. I couldn't even feel the Chimera poison boiling in my veins anymore. I was alive, which was good.

Second realization: I wasn't wet. I mean, I could feel the

coolness of the water. I could see where the fire on my clothes had been quenched. But when I touched my own shirt, it felt perfectly dry.

I looked at the garbage floating by and snatched an old cigarette lighter.

No way, I thought.

I flicked the lighter. It sparked. A tiny flame appeared, right there at the bottom of the Mississippi.

I grabbed a soggy hamburger wrapper out of the current and immediately the paper turned dry. I lit it with no problem. As soon as I let it go, the flames sputtered out. The wrapper turned back into a slimy rag. Weird.

But the strangest thought occurred to me only last: I was breathing. I was underwater, and I was breathing normally.

I stood up, thigh-deep in mud. My legs felt shaky. My hands trembled. I should've been dead. The fact that I wasn't seemed like . . . well, a miracle. I imagined a woman's voice, a voice that sounded a bit like my mother: *Percy, what do you say?*

"Um . . . thanks." Underwater, I sounded like I did on recordings, like a much older kid. "Thank you . . . Father."

No response. Just the dark drift of garbage downriver, the enormous catfish gliding by, the flash of sunset on the water's surface far above, turning everything the color of butterscotch.

Why had Poseidon saved me? The more I thought about it, the more ashamed I felt. So I'd gotten lucky a few times before. Against a thing like the Chimera, I had never stood a chance. Those poor people in the Arch were probably toast. I couldn't protect them. I was no hero. Maybe I should just stay down here with the catfish, join the bottom feeders.

Fump-fump-fump. A riverboat's paddlewheel churned above me, swirling the silt around.

There, not five feet in front of me, was my sword, its gleaming bronze hilt sticking up in the mud.

I heard that woman's voice again: *Percy, take the sword. Your father believes in you.* This time, I knew the voice wasn't in my head. I wasn't imagining it. Her words seemed to come from everywhere, rippling through the water like dolphin sonar.

"Where are you?" I called aloud.

Then, through the gloom, I saw her—a woman the color of the water, a ghost in the current, floating just above the sword. She had long billowing hair, and her eyes, barely visible, were green like mine.

A lump formed in my throat. I said, "Mom?"

No, child, only a messenger, though your mother's fate is not as hopeless as you believe. Go to the beach in Santa Monica.

"What?"

It is your father's will. Before you descend into the Underworld, you must go to Santa Monica. Please, Percy, I cannot stay long. The river here is too foul for my presence.

"But . . ." I was sure this woman was my mother, or a vision of her, anyway. "Who—how did you—"

There was so much I wanted to ask, the words jammed up in my throat.

I cannot stay, brave one, the woman said. She reached out, and I felt the current brush my face like a caress. *You must go to Santa Monica! And, Percy, do not trust the gifts. . . .*

Her voice faded.

"Gifts?" I asked. "What gifts? Wait!"

She made one more attempt to speak, but the sound was gone. Her image melted away. If it was my mother, I had lost her again.

I felt like drowning myself. The only problem: I was immune to drowning.

Your father believes in you, she had said.

She'd also called me brave . . . unless she was talking to the catfish.

I waded toward Riptide and grabbed it by the hilt. The Chimera might still be up there with its snaky, fat mother, waiting to finish me off. At the very least, the mortal police would be arriving, trying to figure out who had blown a hole in the Arch. If they found me, they'd have some questions.

I capped my sword, stuck the ballpoint pen in my pocket. "Thank you, Father," I said again to the dark water.

Then I kicked up through the muck and swam for the surface.

I came ashore next to a floating McDonald's.

A block away, every emergency vehicle in St. Louis was surrounding the Arch. Police helicopters circled overhead. The crowd of onlookers reminded me of Times Square on New Year's Eve.

A little girl said, "Mama! That boy walked out of the river."

"That's nice, dear," her mother said, craning her neck to watch the ambulances.

"But he's dry!"

"That's nice, dear."

A news lady was talking for the camera: "Probably not a terrorist attack, we're told, but it's still very early in the investigation. The damage, as you can see, is very serious. We're trying to get to some of the survivors, to question them about eyewitness reports of someone falling from the Arch."

Survivors. I felt a surge of relief. Maybe the park ranger and that family made it out safely. I hoped Annabeth and Grover were okay.

I tried to push through the crowd to see what was going on inside the police line.

". . . an adolescent boy," another reporter was saying. "Channel Five has learned that surveillance cameras show an adolescent boy going wild on the observation deck, somehow setting off this freak explosion. Hard to believe, John, but that's what we're hearing. Again, no confirmed fatalities . . ."

I backed away, trying to keep my head down. I had to go a long way around the police perimeter. Uniformed officers and news reporters were everywhere.

I'd almost lost hope of ever finding Annabeth and Grover when a familiar voice bleated, "Perrr-cy!"

I turned and got tackled by Grover's bear hug—or goat hug. He said, "We thought you'd gone to Hades the hard way!"

Annabeth stood behind him, trying to look angry, but even she seemed relieved to see me. "We can't leave you alone for five minutes! What happened?"

"I sort of fell."

"Percy! Six hundred and thirty feet?"

Behind us, a cop shouted, "Gangway!" The crowd parted, and a couple of paramedics hustled out, rolling a woman on a stretcher. I recognized her immediately as the mother of the little boy who'd been on the observation deck. She was saying, "And then this huge dog, this huge fire-breathing Chihuahua—"

"Okay, ma'am," the paramedic said. "Just calm down. Your family is fine. The medication is starting to kick in."

"I'm not crazy! This boy jumped out of the hole and the monster disappeared." Then she saw me. "There he is! That's the boy!"

I turned quickly and pulled Annabeth and Grover after me. We disappeared into the crowd.

"What's going on?" Annabeth demanded. "Was she talking about the Chihuahua on the elevator?"

I told them the whole story of the Chimera, Echidna, my high-dive act, and the underwater lady's message.

"Whoa," said Grover. "We've got to get you to Santa Monica! You can't ignore a summons from your dad."

Before Annabeth could respond, we passed another reporter doing a news break, and I almost froze in my tracks when he said, "Percy Jackson. That's right, Dan. Channel Twelve has learned that the boy who may have caused this explosion fits the description of a young man wanted by authorities for a serious New Jersey bus accident three days ago. *And* the boy is believed to be traveling west. For our viewers at home, here is a photo of Percy Jackson."

We ducked around the news van and slipped into an alley.

"First things first," I told Grover. "We've got to get out of town!"

Somehow, we made it back to the Amtrak station without getting spotted. We got on board the train just before it pulled out for Denver. The train trundled west as darkness fell, police lights still pulsing against the St. Louis skyline behind us.

15 ⚡ A GOD BUYS US CHEESEBURGERS

The next afternoon, June 14, seven days before the solstice, our train rolled into Denver. We hadn't eaten since the night before in the dining car, somewhere in Kansas. We hadn't taken a shower since Half-Blood Hill, and I was sure that was obvious.

"Let's try to contact Chiron," Annabeth said. "I want to tell him about your talk with the river spirit."

"We can't use phones, right?"

"I'm not talking about phones."

We wandered through downtown for about half an hour, though I wasn't sure what Annabeth was looking for. The air was dry and hot, which felt weird after the humidity of St. Louis. Everywhere we turned, the Rocky Mountains seemed to be staring at me, like a tidal wave about to crash into the city.

Finally we found an empty do-it-yourself car wash. We veered toward the stall farthest from the street, keeping our eyes open for patrol cars. We were three adolescents hanging out at a car wash without a car; any cop worth his doughnuts would figure we were up to no good.

"What exactly are we doing?" I asked, as Grover took out the spray gun.

"It's seventy-five cents," he grumbled. "I've only got two quarters left. Annabeth?"

"Don't look at me," she said. "The dining car wiped me out."

I fished out my last bit of change and passed Grover a quarter, which left me two nickels and one drachma from Medusa's place.

"Excellent," Grover said. "We could do it with a spray bottle, of course, but the connection isn't as good, and my arm gets tired of pumping."

"What are you talking about?"

He fed in the quarters and set the knob to FINE MIST. "I-M'ing."

"Instant messaging?"

"*Iris*-messaging," Annabeth corrected. "The rainbow goddess Iris carries messages for the gods. If you know how to ask, and she's not too busy, she'll do the same for half-bloods."

"You summon the goddess with a spray gun?"

Grover pointed the nozzle in the air and water hissed out in a thick white mist. "Unless you know an easier way to make a rainbow."

Sure enough, late afternoon light filtered through the vapor and broke into colors.

Annabeth held her palm out to me. "Drachma, please."

I handed it over.

She raised the coin over her head. "O goddess, accept our offering."

She threw the drachma into the rainbow. It disappeared in a golden shimmer.

"Half-Blood Hill," Annabeth requested.

For a moment, nothing happened.

Then I was looking through the mist at strawberry fields, and the Long Island Sound in the distance. We seemed to be on the porch of the Big House. Standing with his back to us at the railing was a sandy-haired guy in shorts and an orange tank top. He was holding a bronze sword and seemed to be staring intently at something down in the meadow.

"Luke!" I called.

He turned, eyes wide. I could swear he was standing three feet in front of me through a screen of mist, except I could only see the part of him that appeared in the rainbow.

"Percy!" His scarred face broke into a grin. "Is that Annabeth, too? Thank the gods! Are you guys okay?"

"We're . . . uh . . . fine," Annabeth stammered. She was madly straightening her dirty T-shirt, trying to comb the loose hair out of her face. "We thought—Chiron—I mean—"

"He's down at the cabins." Luke's smile faded. "We're having some issues with the campers. Listen, is everything cool with you? Is Grover all right?"

"I'm right here," Grover called. He held the nozzle out to one side and stepped into Luke's line of vision. "What kind of issues?"

Just then a big Lincoln Continental pulled into the car wash with its stereo turned to maximum hip-hop. As the car slid into the next stall, the bass from the subwoofers vibrated so much, it shook the pavement.

"Chiron had to—what's that noise?" Luke yelled.

"I'll take care of it!" Annabeth yelled back, looking very relieved to have an excuse to get out of sight. "Grover, come on!"

"What?" Grover said. "But—"

"Give Percy the nozzle and come on!" she ordered.

Grover muttered something about girls being harder to understand than the Oracle at Delphi, then he handed me the spray gun and followed Annabeth.

I readjusted the hose so I could keep the rainbow going and still see Luke.

"Chiron had to break up a fight," Luke shouted to me over the music. "Things are pretty tense here, Percy. Word leaked out about the Zeus–Poseidon standoff. We're still not sure how—probably the same scumbag who summoned the hellhound. Now the campers are starting to take sides. It's shaping up like the Trojan War all over again. Aphrodite, Ares, and Apollo are backing Poseidon, more or less. Athena is backing Zeus."

I shuddered to think that Clarisse's cabin would ever be on my dad's side for anything. In the next stall, I heard Annabeth and some guy arguing with each other, then the music's volume decreased drastically.

"So what's your status?" Luke asked me. "Chiron will be sorry he missed you."

I told him pretty much everything, including my dreams. It felt so good to see him, to feel like I was back at camp even for a few minutes, that I didn't realize how long I had talked until the beeper went off on the spray machine, and I realized I only had one more minute before the water shut off.

"I wish I could be there," Luke told me. "We can't help much from here, I'm afraid, but listen . . . it had to be Hades who took the master bolt. He was there at Olympus at the winter solstice. I was chaperoning a field trip and we saw him."

"But Chiron said the gods can't take each other's magic items directly."

"That's true," Luke said, looking troubled. "Still . . . Hades has the helm of darkness. How could anybody else sneak into the throne room and steal the master bolt? You'd have to be invisible."

We were both silent, until Luke seemed to realize what he'd said.

"Oh, hey," he protested. "I didn't mean Annabeth. She and I have known each other forever. She would never . . . I mean, she's like a little sister to me."

I wondered if Annabeth would like that description. In the stall next to us, the music stopped completely. A man screamed in terror, car doors slammed, and the Lincoln peeled out of the car wash.

"You'd better go see what that was," Luke said. "Listen, are you wearing the flying shoes? I'll feel better if I know they've done you some good."

"Oh . . . uh, yeah!" I tried not to sound like a guilty liar. "Yeah, they've come in handy."

"Really?" He grinned. "They fit and everything?"

The water shut off. The mist started to evaporate.

"Well, take care of yourself out there in Denver," Luke

called, his voice getting fainter. "And tell Grover it'll be better this time! Nobody will get turned into a pine tree if he just—"

But the mist was gone, and Luke's image faded to nothing. I was alone in a wet, empty car wash stall.

Annabeth and Grover came around the corner, laughing, but stopped when they saw my face. Annabeth's smile faded. "What happened, Percy? What did Luke say?"

"Not much," I lied, my stomach feeling as empty as a Big Three cabin. "Come on, let's find some dinner."

A few minutes later, we were sitting at a booth in a gleaming chrome diner. All around us, families were eating burgers and drinking malts and sodas.

Finally the waitress came over. She raised her eyebrow skeptically. "Well?"

I said, "We, um, want to order dinner."

"You kids have money to pay for it?"

Grover's lower lip quivered. I was afraid he would start bleating, or worse, start eating the linoleum. Annabeth looked ready to pass out from hunger.

I was trying to think up a sob story for the waitress when a rumble shook the whole building; a motorcycle the size of a baby elephant had pulled up to the curb.

All conversation in the diner stopped. The motorcycle's headlight glared red. Its gas tank had flames painted on it, and a shotgun holster riveted to either side, complete with shotguns. The seat was leather—but leather that looked like . . . well, Caucasian human skin.

The guy on the bike would've made pro wrestlers run for Mama. He was dressed in a red muscle shirt and black jeans and a black leather duster, with a hunting knife strapped to his thigh. He wore red wraparound shades, and he had the cruelest, most brutal face I'd ever seen— handsome, I guess, but wicked—with an oily black crew cut and cheeks that were scarred from many, many fights. The weird thing was, I felt like I'd seen his face somewhere before.

As he walked into the diner, a hot, dry wind blew through the place. All the people rose, as if they were hyp- notized, but the biker waved his hand dismissively and they all sat down again. Everybody went back to their conversa- tions. The waitress blinked, as if somebody had just pressed the rewind button on her brain. She asked us again, "You kids have money to pay for it?"

The biker said, "It's on me." He slid into our booth, which was way too small for him, and crowded Annabeth against the window.

He looked up at the waitress, who was gaping at him, and said, "Are you still here?"

He pointed at her, and she stiffened. She turned as if she'd been spun around, then marched back toward the kitchen.

The biker looked at me. I couldn't see his eyes behind the red shades, but bad feelings started boiling in my stom- ach. Anger, resentment, bitterness. I wanted to hit a wall. I wanted to pick a fight with somebody. Who did this guy think he was?

He gave me a wicked grin. "So you're old Seaweed's kid, huh?"

I should've been surprised, or scared, but instead I felt like I was looking at my stepdad, Gabe. I wanted to rip this guy's head off. "What's it to you?"

Annabeth's eyes flashed me a warning. "Percy, this is—"

The biker raised his hand.

"S'okay," he said. "I don't mind a little attitude. Long as you remember who's the boss. You know who I am, little cousin?"

Then it struck me why this guy looked familiar. He had the same vicious sneer as some of the kids at Camp Half-Blood, the ones from cabin five.

"You're Clarisse's dad," I said. "Ares, god of war."

Ares grinned and took off his shades. Where his eyes should've been, there was only fire, empty sockets glowing with miniature nuclear explosions. "That's right, punk. I heard you broke Clarisse's spear."

"She was asking for it."

"Probably. That's cool. I don't fight my kids' fights, you know? What I'm here for—I heard you were in town. I got a little proposition for you."

The waitress came back with heaping trays of food—cheeseburgers, fries, onion rings, and chocolate shakes.

Ares handed her a few gold drachmas.

She looked nervously at the coins. "But, these aren't . . ."

Ares pulled out his huge knife and started cleaning his fingernails. "Problem, sweetheart?"

The waitress swallowed, then left with the gold.

"You can't do that," I told Ares. "You can't just threaten people with a knife."

Ares laughed. "Are you kidding? I love this country. Best place since Sparta. Don't you carry a weapon, punk? You should. Dangerous world out there. Which brings me to my proposition. I need you to do me a favor."

"What favor could I do for a god?"

"Something a god doesn't have time to do himself. It's nothing much. I left my shield at an abandoned water park here in town. I was going on a little . . . date with my girl-friend. We were interrupted. I left my shield behind. I want you to fetch it for me."

"Why don't you go back and get it yourself?"

The fire in his eye sockets glowed a little hotter.

"Why don't I turn you into prairie dog and run you over with my Harley? Because I don't feel like it. A god is giving you an opportunity to prove yourself, Percy Jackson. Will you prove yourself a coward?" He leaned forward. "Or maybe you only fight when there's a river to dive into, so your daddy can protect you."

I wanted to punch this guy, but somehow, I knew he was waiting for that. Ares's power was causing my anger. He'd love it if I attacked. I didn't want to give him the satisfac-tion.

"We're not interested," I said. "We've already got a quest."

Ares's fiery eyes made me see things I didn't want to see—blood and smoke and corpses on the battlefield. "I know all about your quest, punk. When that *item* was first stolen, Zeus sent his best out looking for it: Apollo, Athena, Artemis, and me, naturally. If I couldn't sniff out a weapon that powerful . . ." He licked his lips, as if the very thought of the master bolt made him hungry. "Well . . . if I couldn't find it, you got no hope. Nevertheless, I'm trying to give you the benefit of the doubt. Your dad and I go way back. After all, I'm the one who told him my suspicions about old Corpse Breath."

"You told him Hades stole the bolt?"

"Sure. Framing somebody to start a war. Oldest trick in the book. I recognized it immediately. In a way, you got me to thank for your little quest."

"Thanks," I grumbled.

"Hey, I'm a generous guy. Just do my little job, and I'll help you on your way. I'll arrange a ride west for you and your friends."

"We're doing fine on our own."

"Yeah, right. No money. No wheels. No clue what you're up against. Help me out, and maybe I'll tell you something you need to know. Something about your mom."

"My mom?"

He grinned. "That got your attention. The water park is a mile west on Delancy. You can't miss it. Look for the Tunnel of Love ride."

"What interrupted your date?" I asked. "Something scare you off?"

Ares bared his teeth, but I'd seen his threatening look before on Clarisse. There was something false about it, almost like he was nervous.

"You're lucky you met me, punk, and not one of the other Olympians. They're not as forgiving of rudeness as I am. I'll meet you back here when you're done. Don't disappoint me."

After that I must have fainted, or fallen into a trance, because when I opened my eyes again, Ares was gone. I might've thought the conversation had been a dream, but Annabeth and Grover's expressions told me otherwise.

"Not good," Grover said. "Ares sought you out, Percy. This is not good."

I stared out the window. The motorcycle had disappeared.

Did Ares really know something about my mom, or was he just playing with me? Now that he was gone, all the anger had drained out of me. I realized Ares must love to mess with people's emotions. That was his power—cranking up the passions so badly, they clouded your ability to think.

"It's probably some kind of trick," I said. "Forget Ares. Let's just go."

"We can't," Annabeth said. "Look, I hate Ares as much as anybody, but you don't ignore the gods unless you want serious bad fortune. He wasn't kidding about turning you into a rodent."

I looked down at my cheeseburger, which suddenly didn't seem so appetizing. "Why does he need us?"

"Maybe it's a problem that requires brains," Annabeth said. "Ares has strength. That's all he has. Even strength has to bow to wisdom sometimes."

"But this water park . . . he acted almost scared. What would make a war god run away like that?"

Annabeth and Grover glanced nervously at each other.

Annabeth said, "I'm afraid we'll have to find out."

The sun was sinking behind the mountains by the time we found the water park. Judging from the sign, it once had been called WATERLAND, but now some of the letters were smashed out, so it read WAT R A D.

The main gate was padlocked and topped with barbed wire. Inside, huge dry waterslides and tubes and pipes curled everywhere, leading to empty pools. Old tickets and advertisements fluttered around the asphalt. With night coming on, the place looked sad and creepy.

"If Ares brings his girlfriend here for a date," I said, staring up at the barbed wire, "I'd hate to see what she looks like."

"Percy," Annabeth warned. "Be more respectful."

"Why? I thought you hated Ares."

"He's still a god. And his girlfriend is very temperamental."

"You don't want to insult her looks," Grover added.

"Who is she? Echidna?"

"No, Aphrodite," Grover said, a little dreamily. "Goddess of love."

"I thought she was married to somebody," I said. "Hephaestus."

"What's your point?" he asked.

"Oh." I suddenly felt the need to change the subject. "So how do we get in?"

"Maia!" Grover's shoes sprouted wings.

He flew over the fence, did an unintended somersault in midair, then stumbled to a landing on the opposite side. He dusted off his jeans, as if he'd planned the whole thing. "You guys coming?"

Annabeth and I had to climb the old-fashioned way, holding down the barbed wire for each other as we crawled over the top.

The shadows grew long as we walked through the park, checking out the attractions. There was Ankle Biter Island, Head Over Wedgie, and Dude, Where's My Swimsuit?

No monsters came to get us. Nothing made the slightest noise.

We found a souvenir shop that had been left open. Merchandise still lined the shelves: snow globes, pencils, postcards, and racks of—

"Clothes," Annabeth said. "Fresh clothes."

"Yeah," I said. "But you can't just—"

"Watch me."

She snatched an entire row of stuff of the racks and disappeared into the changing room. A few minutes later she came out in Waterland flower-print shorts, a big red Waterland T-shirt, and commemorative Waterland surf shoes. A Waterland backpack was slung over her shoulder, obviously stuffed with more goodies.

"What the heck." Grover shrugged. Soon, all three of us were decked out like walking advertisements for the defunct theme park.

We continued searching for the Tunnel of Love. I got

the feeling that the whole park was holding its breath. "So Ares and Aphrodite," I said, to keep my mind off the growing dark, "they have a thing going?"

"That's old gossip, Percy," Annabeth told me. "Three-thousand-year-old gossip."

"What about Aphrodite's husband?"

"Well, you know," she said. "Hephaestus. The blacksmith. He was crippled when he was a baby, thrown off Mount Olympus by Zeus. So he isn't exactly handsome. Clever with his hands, and all, but Aphrodite isn't into brains and talent, you know?"

"She likes bikers."

"Whatever."

"Hephaestus knows?"

"Oh sure," Annabeth said. "He caught them together once. I mean, literally caught them, in a golden net, and invited all the gods to come and laugh at them. Hephaestus is always trying to embarrass them. That's why they meet in out-of-the-way places, like . . ."

She stopped, looking straight ahead. "Like that."

In front of us was an empty pool that would've been awesome for skateboarding. It was at least fifty yards across and shaped like a bowl.

Around the rim, a dozen bronze statues of Cupid stood guard with wings spread and bows ready to fire. On the opposite side from us, a tunnel opened up, probably where the water flowed into when the pool was full. The sign above it read, THRILL RIDE O' LOVE: THIS IS NOT YOUR PARENTS' TUNNEL OF LOVE!

Grover crept toward the edge. "Guys, look."

Marooned at the bottom of the pool was a pink-and-white two-seater boat with a canopy over the top and little hearts painted all over it. In the left seat, glinting in the fading light, was Ares's shield, a polished circle of bronze.

"This is too easy," I said. "So we just walk down there and get it?"

Annabeth ran her fingers along the base of the nearest Cupid statue.

"There's a Greek letter carved here," she said. "Eta. I wonder . . ."

"Grover," I said, "you smell any monsters?"

He sniffed the wind. "Nothing."

"Nothing—like, in-the-Arch-and-you-didn't-smell-Echidna nothing, or really nothing?"

Grover looked hurt. "I told you, that was underground."

"Okay, I'm sorry." I took a deep breath. "I'm going down there."

"I'll go with you." Grover didn't sound too enthusiastic, but I got the feeling he was trying to make up for what had happened in St. Louis.

"No," I told him. "I want you to stay up top with the flying shoes. You're the Red Baron, a flying ace, remember? I'll be counting on you for backup, in case something goes wrong."

Grover puffed up his chest a little. "Sure. But what could go wrong?"

"I don't know. Just a feeling. Annabeth, come with me—"

"Are you kidding?" She looked at me as if I'd just dropped from the moon. Her cheeks were bright red.

"What's the problem now?" I demanded.

"Me, go with you to the . . . the 'Thrill Ride of Love'? How embarrassing is that? What if somebody saw me?"

"Who's going to see you?" But my face was burning now, too. Leave it to a girl to make everything complicated. "Fine," I told her. "I'll do it myself." But when I started down the side of the pool, she followed me, muttering about how boys always messed things up.

We reached the boat. The shield was propped on one seat, and next to it was a lady's silk scarf. I tried to imagine Ares and Aphrodite here, a couple of gods meeting in a junked-out amusement-park ride. Why? Then I noticed something I hadn't seen from up top: mirrors all the way around the rim of the pool, facing this spot. We could see ourselves no matter which direction we looked. That must be it. While Ares and Aphrodite were smooching with each other they could look at their favorite people: themselves.

I picked up the scarf. It shimmered pink, and the perfume was indescribable—rose, or mountain laurel. Something good. I smiled, a little dreamy, and was about to rub the scarf against my cheek when Annabeth ripped it out of my hand and stuffed it in her pocket. "Oh, no you don't. Stay away from that love magic."

"What?"

"Just get the shield, Seaweed Brain, and let's get out of here."

The moment I touched the shield, I knew we were in trouble. My hand broke through something that had been connecting it to the dashboard. A cobweb, I thought, but then I looked at a strand of it on my palm and saw it was some kind of metal filament, so fine it was almost invisible. A trip wire.

"Wait," Annabeth said.

"Too late."

"There's another Greek letter on the side of the boat, another Eta. This is a trap."

Noise erupted all around us, of a million gears grinding, as if the whole pool were turning into one giant machine.

Grover yelled, "Guys!"

Up on the rim, the Cupid statues were drawing their bows into firing position. Before I could suggest taking cover, they shot, but not at us. They fired at each other, across the rim of the pool. Silky cables trailed from the arrows, arcing over the pool and anchoring where they landed to form a huge golden asterisk. Then smaller metallic threads started weaving together magically between the main strands, making a net.

"We have to get out," I said.

"Duh!" Annabeth said.

I grabbed the shield and we ran, but going up the slope of the pool was not as easy as going down.

"Come on!" Grover shouted.

He was trying to hold open a section of the net for us, but wherever he touched it, the golden threads started to wrap around his hands.

The Cupids' heads popped open. Out came video cameras. Spotlights rose up all around the pool, blinding us with illumination, and a loudspeaker voice boomed: "Live to Olympus in one minute . . . Fifty-nine seconds, fifty-eight . . ."

"Hephaestus!" Annabeth screamed. "I'm so stupid! Eta is 'H.' He made this trap to catch his wife with Ares. Now we're going to be broadcast live to Olympus and look like absolute fools!"

We'd almost made it to the rim when the row of mirrors opened like hatches and thousands of tiny metallic . . . things poured out.

Annabeth screamed.

It was an army of wind-up creepy-crawlies: bronze-gear bodies, spindly legs, little pincer mouths, all scuttling toward us in a wave of clacking, whirring metal.

"Spiders!" Annabeth said. "Sp—sp—aaaah!"

I'd never seen her like this before. She fell backward in terror and almost got overwhelmed by the spider robots before I pulled her up and dragged her back toward the boat.

The things were coming out from all around the rim now, millions of them, flooding toward the center of the pool, completely surrounding us. I told myself they probably weren't programmed to kill, just corral us and bite us and make us look stupid. Then again, this was a trap meant for gods. And we weren't gods.

Annabeth and I climbed into the boat. I started kicking away the spiders as they swarmed aboard. I yelled at

Annabeth to help me, but she was too paralyzed to do much more than scream.

"Thirty, twenty-nine," called the loudspeaker.

The spiders started spitting out strands of metal thread, trying to tie us down. The strands were easy enough to break at first, but there were so many of them, and the spiders just kept coming. I kicked one away from Annabeth's leg and its pincers took a chunk out of my new surf shoe.

Grover hovered above the pool in his flying sneakers, trying to pull the net loose, but it wouldn't budge.

Think, I told myself. Think.

The Tunnel of Love entrance was under the net. We could use it as an exit, except that it was blocked by a million robot spiders.

"Fifteen, fourteen," the loudspeaker called.

Water, I thought. Where does the ride's water come from?

Then I saw them: huge water pipes behind the mirrors, where the spiders had come from. And up above the net, next to one of the Cupids, a glass-windowed booth that must be the controller's station.

"Grover!" I yelled. "Get into that booth! Find the 'on' switch!"

"But—"

"Do it!" It was a crazy hope, but it was our only chance. The spiders were all over the prow of the boat now. Annabeth was screaming her head off. I had to get us out of there.

Grover was in the controller's booth now, slamming away at the buttons.

"Five, four—"

Grover looked up at me hopelessly, raising his hands. He was letting me know that he'd pushed every button, but still nothing was happening.

I closed my eyes and thought about waves, rushing water, the Mississippi River. I felt a familiar tug in my gut. I tried to imagine that I was dragging the ocean all the way to Denver.

"Two, one, *zero!*"

Water exploded out of the pipes. It roared into the pool, sweeping away the spiders. I pulled Annabeth into the seat next to me and fastened her seat belt just as the tidal wave slammed into our boat, over the top, whisking the spiders away and dousing us completely, but not capsizing us. The boat turned, lifted in the flood, and spun in circles around the whirlpool.

The water was full of short-circuiting spiders, some of them smashing against the pool's concrete wall with such force they burst.

Spotlights glared down at us. The Cupid-cams were rolling, live to Olympus.

But I could only concentrate on controlling the boat. I willed it to ride the current, to keep away from the wall. Maybe it was my imagination, but the boat seemed to respond. At least, it didn't break into a million pieces. We spun around one last time, the water level now almost high enough to shred us against the metal net. Then the boat's nose turned toward the tunnel and we rocketed through into the darkness.

Annabeth and I held tight, both of us screaming as the boat shot curls and hugged corners and took forty-five-degree plunges past pictures of Romeo and Juliet and a bunch of other Valentine's Day stuff.

Then we were out of the tunnel, the night air whistling through our hair as the boat barreled straight toward the exit.

If the ride had been in working order, we would've sailed off a ramp between the golden Gates of Love and splashed down safely in the exit pool. But there was a problem. The Gates of Love were chained. Two boats that had been washed out of the tunnel before us were now piled against the barricade—one submerged, the other cracked in half.

"Unfasten your seat belt," I yelled to Annabeth.

"Are you crazy?"

"Unless you want to get smashed to death." I strapped Ares's shield to my arm. "We're going to have to jump for it." My idea was simple and insane. As the boat struck, we would use its force like a springboard to jump the gate. I'd heard of people surviving car crashes that way, getting thrown thirty or forty feet away from an accident. With luck, we would land in the pool.

Annabeth seemed to understand. She gripped my hand as the gates got closer.

"On my mark," I said.

"No! On my mark!"

"What?"

"Simple physics!" she yelled. "Force times the trajectory angle—"

"Fine!" I shouted. "On *your* mark!"

She hesitated . . . hesitated . . . then yelled, "Now!"

Crack!

Annabeth was right. If we'd jumped when I thought we should've, we would've crashed into the gates. She got us maximum lift.

Unfortunately, that was a little more than we needed. Our boat smashed into the pileup and we were thrown into the air, straight over the gates, over the pool, and down toward solid asphalt.

Something grabbed me from behind.

Annabeth yelled, "Ouch!"

Grover!

In midair, he had grabbed me by the shirt, and Annabeth by the arm, and was trying to pull us out of a crash landing, but Annabeth and I had all the momentum.

"You're too heavy!" Grover said. "We're going down!"

We spiraled toward the ground, Grover doing his best to slow the fall.

We smashed into a photo-board, Grover's head going straight into the hole where tourists would put their faces, pretending to be Noo-Noo the Friendly Whale. Annabeth and I tumbled to the ground, banged up but alive. Ares's shield was still on my arm.

Once we caught our breath, Annabeth and I got Grover out of the photo-board and thanked him for saving our lives. I looked back at the Thrill Ride of Love. The water was subsiding. Our boat had been smashed to pieces against the gates.

A hundred yards away, at the entrance pool, the Cupids were still filming. The statues had swiveled so that their cameras were trained straight on us, the spotlights in our faces.

"Show's over!" I yelled. "Thank you! Good night!"

The Cupids turned back to their original positions. The lights shut off. The park went quiet and dark again, except for the gentle trickle of water into the Thrill Ride of Love's exit pool. I wondered if Olympus had gone to a commercial break, or if our ratings had been any good.

I hated being teased. I hated being tricked. And I had plenty of experience handling bullies who liked to do that stuff to me. I hefted the shield on my arm and turned to my friends. "We need to have a little talk with Ares."

The war god was waiting for us in the diner parking lot.

"Well, well," he said. "You didn't get yourself killed."

"You knew it was a trap," I said.

Ares gave me a wicked grin. "Bet that crippled black-smith was surprised when he netted a couple of stupid kids. You looked good on TV."

I shoved his shield at him. "You're a jerk."

Annabeth and Grover caught their breath.

Ares grabbed the shield and spun it in the air like pizza dough. It changed form, melting into a bulletproof vest. He slung it across his back.

"See that truck over there?" He pointed to an eighteen-wheeler parked across the street from the diner. "That's your ride. Take you straight to L.A., with one stop in Vegas."

The eighteen-wheeler had a sign on the back, which I could read only because it was reverse-printed white on black, a good combination for dyslexia: KINDNESS INTER-NATIONAL: HUMANE ZOO TRANSPORT. WARNING: LIVE WILD ANIMALS.

I said, "You're kidding."

Ares snapped his fingers. The back door of the truck

unlatched. "Free ride west, punk. Stop complaining. And here's a little something for doing the job."

He slung a blue nylon backpack off his handlebars and tossed it to me.

Inside were fresh clothes for all of us, twenty bucks in cash, a pouch full of golden drachmas, and a bag of Double Stuf Oreos.

I said, "I don't want your lousy—"

"Thank you, Lord Ares," Grover interrupted, giving me his best red-alert warning look. "Thanks a lot."

I gritted my teeth. It was probably a deadly insult to refuse something from a god, but I didn't want anything that Ares had touched. Reluctantly, I slung the backpack over my shoulder. I knew my anger was being caused by the war god's presence, but I was still itching to punch him in the nose. He reminded me of every bully I'd ever faced: Nancy Bobofit, Clarisse, Smelly Gabe, sarcastic teachers—every jerk who'd called me stupid in school or laughed at me when I'd gotten expelled.

I looked back at the diner, which had only a couple of customers now. The waitress who'd served us dinner was watching nervously out the window, like she was afraid Ares might hurt us. She dragged the fry cook out from the kitchen to see. She said something to him. He nodded, held up a little disposable camera and snapped a picture of us.

Great, I thought. We'll make the papers again tomorrow.

I imagined the headline: TWELVE-YEAR-OLD OUTLAW BEATS UP DEFENSELESS BIKER.

"You owe me one more thing," I told Ares, trying to

keep my voice level. "You promised me information about my mother."

"You sure you can handle the news?" He kick-started his motorcycle. "She's not dead."

The ground seemed to spin beneath me. "What do you mean?"

"I mean she was taken away from the Minotaur before she could die. She was turned into a shower of gold, right? That's metamorphosis. Not death. She's being kept."

"Kept. Why?"

"You need to study war, punk. Hostages. You take somebody to control somebody else."

"Nobody's controlling me."

He laughed. "Oh yeah? See you around, kid."

I balled up my fists. "You're pretty smug, Lord Ares, for a guy who runs from Cupid statues."

Behind his sunglasses, fire glowed. I felt a hot wind in my hair. "We'll meet again, Percy Jackson. Next time you're in a fight, watch your back."

He revved his Harley, then roared off down Delancy Street.

Annabeth said, "That was not smart, Percy."

"I don't care."

"You don't want a god as your enemy. Especially not that god."

"Hey, guys," Grover said. "I hate to interrupt, but . . ."

He pointed toward the diner. At the register, the last two customers were paying their check, two men in identical black coveralls, with a white logo on their backs that matched the one on the KINDNESS INTERNATIONAL truck.

"If we're taking the zoo express," Grover said, "we need to hurry."

I didn't like it, but we had no better option. Besides, I'd seen enough of Denver.

We ran across the street and climbed in the back of the big rig, closing the doors behind us.

The first thing that hit me was the smell. It was like the world's biggest pan of kitty litter.

The trailer was dark inside until I uncapped Anaklusmos. The blade cast a faint bronze light over a very sad scene. Sitting in a row of filthy metal cages were three of the most pathetic zoo animals I'd ever beheld: a zebra, a male albino lion, and some weird antelope thing I didn't know the name for.

Someone had thrown the lion a sack of turnips, which he obviously didn't want to eat. The zebra and the antelope had each gotten a Styrofoam tray of hamburger meat. The zebra's mane was matted with chewing gum, like somebody had been spitting on it in their spare time. The antelope had a stupid silver birthday balloon tied to one of his horns that read OVER THE HILL!

Apparently, nobody had wanted to get close enough to the lion to mess with him, but the poor thing was pacing around on soiled blankets, in a space way too small for him, panting from the stuffy heat of the trailer. He had flies buzzing around his pink eyes and his ribs showed through his white fur.

"This is kindness?" Grover yelled. "Humane zoo transport?"

He probably would've gone right back outside to beat up the truckers with his reed pipes, and I would've helped him, but just then the truck's engine roared to life, the trailer started shaking, and we were forced to sit down or fall down.

We huddled in the corner on some mildewed feed sacks, trying to ignore the smell and the heat and the flies. Grover talked to the animals in a series of goat bleats, but they just stared at him sadly. Annabeth was in favor of breaking the cages and freeing them on the spot, but I pointed out it wouldn't do much good until the truck stopped moving. Besides, I had a feeling we might look a lot better to the lion than those turnips.

I found a water jug and refilled their bowls, then used Anaklusmos to drag the mismatched food out of their cages. I gave the meat to the lion and the turnips to the zebra and the antelope.

Grover calmed the antelope down, while Annabeth used her knife to cut the balloon off his horn. She wanted to cut the gum out of the zebra's mane, too, but we decided that would be too risky with the truck bumping around. We told Grover to promise the animals we'd help them more in the morning, then we settled in for night.

Grover curled up on a turnip sack; Annabeth opened our bag of Double Stuf Oreos and nibbled on one half-heartedly; I tried to cheer myself up by concentrating on the fact that we were halfway to Los Angeles. Halfway to our destination. It was only June fourteenth. The solstice wasn't until the twenty-first. We could make it in plenty of time.

On the other hand, I had no idea what to expect next. The gods kept toying with me. At least Hephaestus had the decency to be honest about it—he'd put up cameras and advertised me as entertainment. But even when the cameras weren't rolling, I had a feeling my quest was being watched. I was a source of amusement for the gods.

"Hey," Annabeth said, "I'm sorry for freaking out back at the water park, Percy."

"That's okay."

"It's just . . ." She shuddered. "Spiders."

"Because of the Arachne story," I guessed. "She got turned into a spider for challenging your mom to a weaving contest, right?"

Annabeth nodded. "Arachne's children have been taking revenge on the children of Athena ever since. If there's a spider within a mile of me, it'll find me. I hate the creepy little things. Anyway, I owe you."

"We're a team, remember?" I said. "Besides, Grover did the fancy flying."

I thought he was asleep, but he mumbled from the corner, "I was pretty amazing, wasn't I?"

Annabeth and I laughed.

She pulled apart an Oreo, handed me half. "In the Iris message . . . did Luke really say nothing?"

I munched my cookie and thought about how to answer. The conversation via rainbow had bothered me all evening. "Luke said you and he go way back. He also said Grover wouldn't fail this time. Nobody would turn into a pine tree."

In the dim bronze light of the sword blade, it was hard to read their expressions.

Grover let out a mournful bray.

"I should've told you the truth from the beginning." His voice trembled. "I thought if you knew what a failure I was, you wouldn't want me along."

"You were the satyr who tried to rescue Thalia, the daughter of Zeus."

He nodded glumly.

"And the other two half-bloods Thalia befriended, the ones who got safely to camp . . ." I looked at Annabeth. "That was you and Luke, wasn't it?"

She put down her Oreo, uneaten. "Like you said, Percy, a seven-year-old half-blood wouldn't have made it very far alone. Athena guided me toward help. Thalia was twelve. Luke was fourteen. They'd both run away from home, like me. They were happy to take me with them. They were . . . amazing monster-fighters, even without training. We traveled north from Virginia without any real plans, fending off monsters for about two weeks before Grover found us."

"I was supposed to escort Thalia to camp," he said, sniffling. "Only Thalia. I had strict orders from Chiron: don't do anything that would slow down the rescue. We knew Hades was after her, see, but I couldn't just leave Luke and Annabeth by themselves. I thought . . . I thought I could lead all three of them to safety. It was my fault the Kindly Ones caught up with us. I froze. I got scared on the way back to camp and took some wrong turns. If I'd just been a little quicker . . ."

"Stop it," Annabeth said. "No one blames you. Thalia didn't blame you either."

"She sacrificed herself to save us," he said miserably. "Her death was my fault. The Council of Cloven Elders said so."

"Because you wouldn't leave two other half-bloods behind?" I said. "That's not fair."

"Percy's right," Annabeth said. "I wouldn't be here today if it weren't for you, Grover. Neither would Luke. We don't care what the council says."

Grover kept sniffling in the dark. "It's just my luck. I'm the lamest satyr ever, and I find the two most powerful half-bloods of the century, Thalia and Percy."

"You're not lame," Annabeth insisted. "You've got more courage than any satyr I've ever met. Name one other who would dare go to the Underworld. I bet Percy is really glad you're here right now."

She kicked me in the shin.

"Yeah," I said, which I would've done even without the kick. "It's not luck that you found Thalia and me, Grover. You've got the biggest heart of any satyr ever. You're a natural searcher. That's why you'll be the one who finds Pan."

I heard a deep, satisfied sigh. I waited for Grover to say something, but his breathing only got heavier. When the sound turned to snoring, I realized he'd fallen sleep.

"How does he do that?" I marveled.

"I don't know," Annabeth said. "But that was really a nice thing you told him."

"I meant it."

We rode in silence for a few miles, bumping around on the feed sacks. The zebra munched a turnip. The lion licked the last of the hamburger meat off his lips and looked at me hopefully.

Annabeth rubbed her necklace like she was thinking deep, strategic thoughts.

"That pine-tree bead," I said. "Is that from your first year?"

She looked. She hadn't realized what she was doing.

"Yeah," she said. "Every August, the counselors pick the most important event of the summer, and they paint it on that year's beads. I've got Thalia's pine tree, a Greek trireme on fire, a centaur in a prom dress—now *that* was a weird summer. . . ."

"And the college ring is your father's?"

"That's none of your—" She stopped herself. "Yeah. Yeah, it is."

"You don't have to tell me."

"No . . . it's okay." She took a shaky breath. "My dad sent it to me folded up in a letter, two summers ago. The ring was, like, his main keepsake from Athena. He wouldn't have gotten through his doctoral program at Harvard without her. . . . That's a long story. Anyway, he said he wanted me to have it. He apologized for being a jerk, said he loved me and missed me. He wanted me to come home and live with him."

"That doesn't sound so bad."

"Yeah, well . . . the problem was, I believed him. I tried

to go home for that school year, but my stepmom was the same as ever. She didn't want her kids put in danger by living with a freak. Monsters attacked. We argued. Monsters attacked. We argued. I didn't even make it through winter break. I called Chiron and came right back to Camp Half-Blood."

"You think you'll ever try living with your dad again?"

She wouldn't meet my eyes. "Please. I'm not into self-inflicted pain."

"You shouldn't give up," I told her. "You should write him a letter or something."

"Thanks for the advice," she said coldly, "but my father's made his choice about who he wants to live with."

We passed another few miles of silence.

"So if the gods fight," I said, "will things line up the way they did with the Trojan War? Will it be Athena versus Poseidon?"

She put her head against the backpack Ares had given us, and closed her eyes. "I don't know what my mom will do. I just know I'll fight next to you."

"Why?"

"Because you're my friend, Seaweed Brain. Any more stupid questions?"

I couldn't think of an answer for that. Fortunately I didn't have to. Annabeth was asleep.

I had trouble following her example, with Grover snoring and an albino lion staring hungrily at me, but eventually I closed my eyes.

* * *

My nightmare started out as something I'd dreamed a million times before: I was being forced to take a standardized test while wearing a straitjacket. All the other kids were going out to recess, and the teacher kept saying, *Come on, Percy. You're not stupid, are you? Pick up your pencil.*

Then the dream strayed from the usual.

I looked over at the next desk and saw a girl sitting there, also wearing a straitjacket. She was my age, with unruly black, punk-style hair, dark eyeliner around her stormy green eyes, and freckles across her nose. Somehow, I knew who she was. She was Thalia, daughter of Zeus.

She struggled against the straitjacket, glared at me in frustration, and snapped, *Well, Seaweed Brain? One of us has to get out of here.*

She's right, my dream-self thought. I'm going back to that cavern. I'm going to give Hades a piece of my mind.

The straitjacket melted off me. I fell through the classroom floor. The teacher's voice changed until it was cold and evil, echoing from the depths of a great chasm.

Percy Jackson, it said. *Yes, the exchange went well, I see.*

I was back in the dark cavern, spirits of the dead drifting around me. Unseen in the pit, the monstrous thing was speaking, but this time it wasn't addressing me. The numbing power of its voice seemed directed somewhere else.

And he suspects nothing? it asked.

Another voice, one I almost recognized, answered at my shoulder. *Nothing, my lord. He is as ignorant as the rest.*

I looked over, but no one was there. The speaker was invisible.

Deception upon deception, the thing in the pit mused aloud. *Excellent.*

Truly, my lord, said the voice next to me, *you are well-named the Crooked One. But was it really necessary? I could have brought you what I stole directly —*

You? the monster said in scorn. *You have already shown your limits. You would have failed me completely had I not intervened.*

But, my lord—

Peace, little servant. Our six months have bought us much. Zeus's anger has grown. Poseidon has played his most desperate card. Now we shall use it against him. Shortly you shall have the reward you wish, and your revenge. As soon as both items are delivered into my hands . . . but wait. He is here.

What? The invisible servant suddenly sounded tense. *You summoned him, my lord?*

No. The full force of the monster's attention was now pouring over me, freezing me in place. *Blast his father's blood—he is too changeable, too unpredictable. The boy brought himself hither.*

Impossible! the servant cried.

For a weakling such as you, perhaps, the voice snarled. Then its cold power turned back on me. *So . . . you wish to dream of your quest, young half-blood? Then I will oblige.*

The scene changed.

I was standing in a vast throne room with black marble walls and bronze floors. The empty, horrid throne was made from human bones fused together. Standing at the foot of the dais was my mother, frozen in shimmering golden light, her arms outstretched.

I tried to step toward her, but my legs wouldn't move. I reached for her, only to realize that my hands were withering to bones. Grinning skeletons in Greek armor crowded around me, draping me with silk robes, wreathing my head with laurels that smoked with Chimera poison, burning into my scalp.

The evil voice began to laugh. *Hail, the conquering hero!*

I woke with a start.

Grover was shaking my shoulder. "The truck's stopped," he said. "We think they're coming to check on the animals."

"Hide!" Annabeth hissed.

She had it easy. She just put on her magic cap and disappeared. Grover and I had to dive behind feed sacks and hope we looked like turnips.

The trailer doors creaked open. Sunlight and heat poured in.

"Man!" one of the truckers said, waving his hand in front of his ugly nose. "I wish I hauled appliances." He climbed inside and poured some water from a jug into the animals' dishes.

"You hot, big boy?" he asked the lion, then splashed the rest of the bucket right in the lion's face.

The lion roared in indignation.

"Yeah, yeah, yeah," the man said.

Next to me, under the turnip sacks, Grover tensed. For a peace-loving herbivore, he looked downright murderous.

The trucker threw the antelope a squashed-looking Happy Meal bag. He smirked at the zebra. "How ya doin', Stripes? Least we'll be getting rid of *you* this stop. You like magic shows? You're gonna love this one. They're gonna saw you in half!"

The zebra, wild-eyed with fear, looked straight at me.

There was no sound, but as clear as day, I heard it say: *Free me, lord. Please.*

I was too stunned to react.

There was a loud *knock, knock, knock* on the side of the trailer.

The trucker inside with us yelled, "What do you want, Eddie?"

A voice outside—it must've been Eddie's—shouted back, "Maurice? What'd ya say?"

"What are you banging for?"

Knock, knock, knock.

Outside, Eddie yelled, "What banging?"

Our guy Maurice rolled his eyes and went back outside, cursing at Eddie for being an idiot.

A second later, Annabeth appeared next to me. She must've done the banging to get Maurice out of the trailer. She said, "This transport business can't be legal."

"No kidding," Grover said. He paused, as if listening. "The lion says these guys are animal smugglers!"

That's right, the zebra's voice said in my mind.

"We've got to free them!" Grover said. He and Annabeth both looked at me, waiting for my lead.

I'd heard the zebra talk, but not the lion. Why? Maybe

it was another learning disability . . . I could only understand zebras? Then I thought: horses. What had Annabeth
said about Poseidon creating horses? Was a zebra close
enough to a horse? Was that why I could understand it?

The zebra said, *Open my cage, lord. Please. I'll be fine after that.*

Outside, Eddie and Maurice were still yelling at each
other, but I knew they'd be coming inside to torment the
animals again any minute. I grabbed Riptide and slashed the
lock off the zebra's cage.

The zebra burst out. It turned to me and bowed. *Thank
you, lord.*

Grover held up his hands and said something to the
zebra in goat talk, like a blessing.

Just as Maurice was poking his head back inside to check
out the noise, the zebra leaped over him and into the street.
There was yelling and screaming and cars honking. We
rushed to the doors of the trailer in time to see the zebra galloping down a wide boulevard lined with hotels and casinos
and neon signs. We'd just released a zebra in Las Vegas.

Maurice and Eddie ran after it, with a few policemen
running after them, shouting, "Hey! You need a permit for
that!"

"Now would be a good time to leave," Annabeth said.

"The other animals first," Grover said.

I cut the locks with my sword. Grover raised his hands
and spoke the same goat-blessing he'd used for the zebra.

"Good luck," I told the animals. The antelope and the
lion burst out of their cages and went off together into the
streets.

Some tourists screamed. Most just backed off and took pictures, probably thinking it was some kind of stunt by one of the casinos.

"Will the animals be okay?" I asked Grover. "I mean, the desert and all——"

"Don't worry," he said. "I placed a satyr's sanctuary on them."

"Meaning?"

"Meaning they'll reach the wild safely," he said. "They'll find water, food, shade, whatever they need until they find a safe place to live."

"Why can't you place a blessing like that on us?" I asked.

"It only works on wild animals."

"So it would only affect Percy," Annabeth reasoned.

"Hey!" I protested.

"Kidding," she said. "Come on. Let's get out of this filthy truck."

We stumbled out into the desert afternoon. It was a hundred and ten degrees, easy, and we must've looked like deep-fried vagrants, but everybody was too interested in the wild animals to pay us much attention.

We passed the Monte Carlo and the MGM. We passed pyramids, a pirate ship, and the Statue of Liberty, which was a pretty small replica, but still made me homesick.

I wasn't sure what we were looking for. Maybe just a place to get out of the heat for a few minutes, find a sandwich and a glass of lemonade, make a new plan for getting west.

We must have taken a wrong turn, because we found

ourselves at a dead end, standing in front of the Lotus Hotel and Casino. The entrance was a huge neon flower, the petals lighting up and blinking. No one was going in or out, but the glittering chrome doors were open, spilling out air-conditioning that smelled like flowers—lotus blossom, maybe. I'd never smelled one, so I wasn't sure.

The doorman smiled at us. "Hey, kids. You look tired. You want to come in and sit down?"

I'd learned to be suspicious, the last week or so. I figured anybody might be a monster or a god. You just couldn't tell. But this guy was normal. One look at him, and I could see. Besides, I was so relieved to hear somebody who sounded sympathetic that I nodded and said we'd love to come in. Inside, we took one look around, and Grover said, "Whoa."

The whole lobby was a giant game room. And I'm not talking about cheesy old Pac-Man games or slot machines. There was an indoor waterslide snaking around the glass elevator, which went straight up at least forty floors. There was a climbing wall on the side of one building, and an indoor bungee-jumping bridge. There were virtual-reality suits with working laser guns. And hundreds of video games, each one the size of a widescreen TV. Basically, you name it, this place had it. There were a few other kids play-ing, but not that many. No waiting for any of the games. There were waitresses and snack bars all around, serving every kind of food you can imagine.

"Hey!" a bellhop said. At least I guessed he was a bell-hop. He wore a white-and-yellow Hawaiian shirt with lotus designs, shorts, and flip-flops. "Welcome to the Lotus Casino. Here's your room key."

I stammered, "Um, but . . ."

"No, no," he said, laughing. "The bill's taken care of. No extra charges, no tips. Just go on up to the top floor, room 4001. If you need anything, like extra bubbles for the hot tub, or skeet targets for the shooting range, or whatever, just call the front desk. Here are your LotusCash cards. They work in the restaurants and on all the games and rides."

He handed us each a green plastic credit card.

I knew there must be some mistake. Obviously he thought we were some millionaire's kids. But I took the card and said, "How much is on here?"

His eyebrows knit together. "What do you mean?"

"I mean, when does it run out of cash?"

He laughed. "Oh, you're making a joke. Hey, that's cool. Enjoy your stay."

We took the elevator upstairs and checked out our room. It was a suite with three separate bedrooms and a bar stocked with candy, sodas, and chips. A hotline to room service. Fluffy towels and water beds with feather pillows. A big-screen television with satellite and high-speed Internet. The balcony had its own hot tub, and sure enough, there was a skeet-shooting machine and a shotgun, so you could launch clay pigeons right out over the Las Vegas skyline and plug them with your gun. I didn't see how that could be legal, but I thought it was pretty cool. The view over the Strip and the desert was amazing, though I doubted we'd ever find time to look at the view with a room like this.

"Oh, goodness," Annabeth said. "This place is . . ."

"Sweet," Grover said. "Absolutely sweet."

There were clothes in the closet, and they fit me. I frowned, thinking that this was a little strange.

I threw Ares's backpack in the trash can. Wouldn't need that anymore. When we left, I could just charge a new one at the hotel store.

I took a shower, which felt awesome after a week of grimy travel. I changed clothes, ate a bag of chips, drank three Cokes, and came out feeling better than I had in a long time. In the back of my mind, some small problem kept nagging me. I'd had a dream or something . . . I needed to talk to my friends. But I was sure it could wait.

I came out of the bedroom and found that Annabeth and Grover had also showered and changed clothes. Grover was eating potato chips to his heart's content, while Annabeth cranked up the National Geographic Channel.

"All those stations," I told her, "and you turn on National Geographic. Are you insane?"

"It's interesting."

"I feel good," Grover said. "I love this place."

Without his even realizing it, the wings sprouted out of his shoes and lifted him a foot off the ground, then back down again.

"So what now?" Annabeth asked. "Sleep?"

Grover and I looked at each other and grinned. We both held up our green plastic LotusCash cards.

"Play time," I said.

I couldn't remember the last time I had so much fun. I came from a relatively poor family. Our idea of a splurge was eating out at Burger King and renting a video. A five-star Vegas hotel? Forget it.

I bungee-jumped the lobby five or six times, did the waterslide, snowboarded the artificial ski slope, and played virtual-reality laser tag and FBI sharpshooter. I saw Grover a few times, going from game to game. He really liked the reverse hunter thing—where the deer go out and shoot the rednecks. I saw Annabeth playing trivia games and other brainiac stuff. They had this huge 3-D sim game where you build your own city, and you could actually see the holographic buildings rise on the display board. I didn't think much of it, but Annabeth loved it.

I'm not sure when I first realized something was wrong.

Probably, it was when I noticed the guy standing next to me at VR sharpshooters. He was about thirteen, I guess, but his clothes were weird. I thought he was some Elvis impersonator's son. He wore bell-bottom jeans and a red T-shirt with black piping, and his hair was permed and gelled like a New Jersey girl's on homecoming night.

We played a game of sharpshooters together and he said, "Groovy, man. Been here two weeks, and the games keep getting better and better."

Groovy?

Later, while we were talking, I said something was "sick," and he looked at me kind of startled, as if he'd never heard the word used that way before.

He said his name was Darrin, but as soon as I started asking him questions he got bored with me and started to go back to the computer screen.

I said, "Hey, Darrin?"

"What?"

"What year is it?"

He frowned at me. "In the game?"

"No. In real life."

He had to think about it. "1977."

"No," I said, getting a little scared. "Really."

"Hey, man. Bad vibes. I got a game happening."

After that he totally ignored me.

I started talking to people, and I found it wasn't easy. They were glued to the TV screen, or the video game, or their food, or whatever. I found a guy who told me it was 1985. Another guy told me it was 1993. They all claimed they hadn't been in here very long, a few days, a few weeks at most. They didn't really know and they didn't care.

Then it occurred to me: how long had I been here? It seemed like only a couple of hours, but was it?

I tried to remember why we were here. We were going to Los Angeles. We were supposed to find the entrance to the Underworld. My mother . . . for a scary second, I had trouble remembering her name. Sally. Sally Jackson. I had to find her. I had to stop Hades from causing World War III.

I found Annabeth still building her city.

"Come on," I told her. "We've got to get out of here."

No response.

I shook her. "Annabeth?"

She looked up, annoyed. "What?"

"We need to leave."

"Leave? What are you talking about? I've just got the towers—"

"This place is a trap."

She didn't respond until I shook her again. "What?"

"Listen. The Underworld. Our quest!"

"Oh, come on, Percy. Just a few more minutes."

"Annabeth, there are people here from 1977. Kids who have never aged. You check in, and you stay forever."

"So?" she asked. "Can you imagine a better place?"

I grabbed her wrist and yanked her away from the game.

"Hey!" She screamed and hit me, but nobody else even bothered looking at us. They were too busy.

I made her look directly in my eyes. I said, "Spiders. Large, hairy spiders."

That jarred her. Her vision cleared. "Oh my gods," she said. "How long have we—"

"I don't know, but we've got to find Grover."

We went searching, and found him still playing Virtual Deer Hunter.

"Grover!" we both shouted.

He said, "Die, human! Die, silly polluting nasty person!"

"Grover!"

He turned the plastic gun on me and started clicking, as if I were just another image from the screen.

I looked at Annabeth, and together we took Grover by the arms and dragged him away. His flying shoes sprang to life and started tugging his legs in the other direction as he shouted, "No! I just got to a new level! No!"

The Lotus bellhop hurried up to us. "Well, now, are you ready for your platinum cards?"

"We're leaving," I told him.

"Such a shame," he said, and I got the feeling that he really meant it, that we'd be breaking his heart if we went. "We just added an entire new floor full of games for platinum-card members."

He held out the cards, and I wanted one. I knew that if I took one, I'd never leave. I'd stay here, happy forever, playing games forever, and soon I'd forget my mom, and my quest, and maybe even my own name. I'd be playing virtual rifleman with groovy Disco Darrin forever.

Grover reached for the card, but Annabeth yanked back his arm and said, "No, thanks."

We walked toward the door, and as we did, the smell of the food and the sounds of the games seemed to get more and more inviting. I thought about our room upstairs. We could just stay the night, sleep in a real bed for once. . . .

Then we burst through the doors of the Lotus Casino and ran down the sidewalk. It felt like afternoon, about the same time of day we'd gone into the casino, but something was wrong. The weather had completely changed. It was stormy, with heat lightning flashing out in the desert.

Ares's backpack was slung over my shoulder, which was odd, because I was sure I had thrown it in the trash can in room 4001, but at the moment I had other problems to worry about.

I ran to the nearest newspaper stand and read the year first. Thank the gods, it was the same year it had been when we went in. Then I noticed the date: June twentieth.

We had been in the Lotus Casino for five days.

We had only one day left until the summer solstice. One day to complete our quest.

17 ⚡ WE SHOP FOR WATER BEDS

It was Annabeth's idea.

She loaded us into the back of a Vegas taxi as if we actually had money, and told the driver, "Los Angeles, please."

The cabbie chewed his cigar and sized us up. "That's three hundred miles. For that, you gotta pay up front."

"You accept casino debit cards?" Annabeth asked.

He shrugged. "Some of 'em. Same as credit cards. I gotta swipe 'em through first."

Annabeth handed him her green LotusCash card.

He looked at it skeptically.

"Swipe it," Annabeth invited.

He did.

His meter machine started rattling. The lights flashed. Finally an infinity symbol came up next to the dollar sign.

The cigar fell out of the driver's mouth. He looked back at us, his eyes wide. "Where to in Los Angeles. . . uh, Your Highness?"

"The Santa Monica Pier." Annabeth sat up a little straighter. I could tell she liked the "Your Highness" thing. "Get us there fast, and you can keep the change."

Maybe she shouldn't have told him that.

The cab's speedometer never dipped below ninety-five the whole way through the Mojave Desert.

On the road, we had plenty of time to talk. I told Annabeth and Grover about my latest dream, but the details got sketchier the more I tried to remember them. The Lotus Casino seemed to have short-circuited my memory. I couldn't recall what the invisible servant's voice had sounded like, though I was sure it was somebody I knew. The servant had called the monster in the pit something other than "my lord" . . . some special name or title. . . .

"The Silent One?" Annabeth suggested. "The Rich One? Both of those are nicknames for Hades."

"Maybe . . ." I said, though neither sounded quite right.

"That throne room sounds like Hades's," Grover said. "That's the way it's usually described."

I shook my head. "Something's wrong. The throne room wasn't the main part of the dream. And that voice from the pit . . . I don't know. It just didn't feel like a god's voice."

Annabeth's eyes widened.

"What?" I asked.

"Oh . . . nothing. I was just—No, it *has* to be Hades. Maybe he sent this thief, this invisible person, to get the master bolt, and something went wrong—"

"Like what?"

"I—I don't know," she said. "But if he stole Zeus's symbol of power from Olympus, and the gods were hunting him, I mean, a lot of things could go wrong. So this thief had to hide the bolt, or he lost it somehow. Anyway, he failed to bring it to Hades. That's what the voice said in your dream, right? The guy failed. That would explain what the Furies were searching for when they came after us on the bus. Maybe they thought we had retrieved the bolt."

I wasn't sure what was wrong with her. She looked pale.

"But if I'd already retrieved the bolt," I said, "why would I be traveling to the Underworld?"

"To threaten Hades," Grover suggested. "To bribe or blackmail him into getting your mom back."

I whistled. "You have evil thoughts for a goat."

"Why, thank you."

"But the thing in the pit said it was waiting for *two* items," I said. "If the master bolt is one, what's the other?"

Grover shook his head, clearly mystified.

Annabeth was looking at me as if she knew my next question, and was silently willing me not to ask it.

"You have an idea what might be in that pit, don't you?" I asked her. "I mean, if it isn't Hades?"

"Percy . . . let's not talk about it. Because if it isn't Hades . . . No. It has to be Hades."

Wasteland rolled by. We passed a sign that said CALIFORNIA STATE LINE, 12 MILES.

I got the feeling I was missing one simple, critical piece of information. It was like when I stared at a common word I should know, but I couldn't make sense of it because one or two letters were floating around. The more I thought about my quest, the more I was sure that confronting Hades wasn't the real answer. There was something else going on, something even more dangerous.

The problem was: we were hurtling toward the Underworld at ninety-five miles an hour, betting that Hades had the master bolt. If we got there and found out we were wrong, we wouldn't have time to correct ourselves. The solstice deadline would pass and war would begin.

"The answer is in the Underworld," Annabeth assured me. "You saw spirits of the dead, Percy. There's only one place that could be. We're doing the right thing."

She tried to boost our morale by suggesting clever strategies for getting into the Land of the Dead, but my heart wasn't in it. There were just too many unknown factors. It was like cramming for a test without knowing the subject. And believe me, I'd done *that* enough times.

The cab sped west. Every gust of wind through Death Valley sounded like a spirit of the dead. Every time the brakes hissed on an eighteen-wheeler, it reminded me of Echidna's reptilian voice.

At sunset, the taxi dropped us at the beach in Santa Monica. It looked exactly the way L.A. beaches do in the movies, only it smelled worse. There were carnival rides lining the Pier, palm trees lining the sidewalks, homeless guys sleeping in the sand dunes, and surfer dudes waiting for the perfect wave.

Grover, Annabeth, and I walked down to the edge of the surf.

"What now?" Annabeth asked.

The Pacific was turning gold in the setting sun. I thought about how long it had been since I'd stood on the beach at Montauk, on the opposite side of the country, looking out at a different sea.

How could there be a god who could control all that? What did my science teacher used to say—two-thirds of the earth's surface was covered in water? How could I be the son of someone that powerful?

I stepped into the surf.

"Percy?" Annabeth said. "What are you doing?"

I kept walking, up to my waist, then my chest.

She called after me, "You know how polluted that water is? There're all kinds of toxic—"

That's when my head went under.

I held my breath at first. It's difficult to intentionally inhale water. Finally I couldn't stand it anymore. I gasped. Sure enough, I could breathe normally.

I walked down into the shoals. I shouldn't have been able to see through the murk, but somehow I could tell where everything was. I could sense the rolling texture of the bottom. I could make out sand-dollar colonies dotting the sandbars. I could even see the currents, warm and cold streams swirling together.

I felt something rub against my leg. I looked down and almost shot out of the water like a ballistic missile. Sliding along beside me was a five-foot-long mako shark.

But the thing wasn't attacking. It was nuzzling me. Heeling like a dog. Tentatively, I touched its dorsal fin. It bucked a little, as if inviting me to hold tighter. I grabbed the fin with both hands. It took off, pulling me along. The shark carried me down into the darkness. It deposited me at the edge of the ocean proper, where the sand bank dropped off into a huge chasm. It was like standing on the rim of the Grand Canyon at midnight, not being able to see much, but knowing the void was right there.

The surface shimmered maybe a hundred and fifty feet above. I knew I should've been crushed by the pressure. Then again, I shouldn't have been able to breathe. I wondered if there was a limit to how deep I could go, if I could sink straight to the bottom of the Pacific.

Then I saw something glimmering in the darkness below, growing bigger and brighter as it rose toward me. A woman's voice, like my mother's, called: "Percy Jackson."

As she got closer, her shape became clearer. She had flowing black hair, a dress made of green silk. Light flickered around her, and her eyes were so distractingly beautiful I hardly noticed the stallion-sized sea horse she was riding.

She dismounted. The sea horse and the mako shark whisked off and started playing something that looked like tag. The underwater lady smiled at me. "You've come far, Percy Jackson. Well done."

I wasn't quite sure what to do, so I bowed. "You're the woman who spoke to me in the Mississippi River."

"Yes, child. I am a Nereid, a spirit of the sea. It was not easy to appear so far upriver, but the naiads, my freshwater cousins, helped sustain my life force. They honor Lord Poseidon, though they do not serve in his court."

"And . . . you serve in Poseidon's court?"

She nodded. "It has been many years since a child of the Sea God has been born. We have watched you with great interest."

Suddenly I remembered faces in the waves off Montauk Beach when I was a little boy, reflections of smiling women. Like so many of the weird things in my life, I'd never given it much thought before.

"If my father is so interested in me," I said, "why isn't he here? Why doesn't he speak to me?"

A cold current rose out of the depths.

"Do not judge the Lord of the Sea too harshly," the Nereid told me. "He stands at the brink of an unwanted war. He has much to occupy his time. Besides, he is forbidden to help you directly. The gods may not show such favoritism."

"Even to their own children?"

"Especially to them. The gods can work by indirect influence only. That is why I give you a warning, and a gift."

She held out her hand. Three white pearls flashed in her palm.

"I know you journey to Hades's realm," she said. "Few mortals have ever done this and survived: Orpheus, who had great music skill; Hercules, who had great strength; Houdini, who could escape even the depths of Tartarus. Do you have these talents?"

"Um . . . no, ma'am."

"Ah, but you have something else, Percy. You have gifts you have only begun to know. The oracles have foretold a great and terrible future for you, should you survive to manhood. Poseidon would not have you die before your time. Therefore take these, and when you are in need, smash a pearl at your feet."

"What will happen?"

"That," she said, "depends on the need. But remember: what belongs to the sea will always return to the sea."

"What about the warning?"

Her eyes flickered with green light. "Go with what your heart tells you, or you will lose all. Hades feeds on doubt and hopelessness. He will trick you if he can, make you mistrust your own judgment. Once you are in his realm, he will never willingly let you leave. Keep faith. Good luck, Percy Jackson."

She summoned her sea horse and rode toward the void.

"Wait!" I called. "At the river, you said not to trust the gifts. What gifts?"

"Good-bye, young hero," she called back, her voice fading into the depths. "You must listen to your heart." She became a speck of glowing green, and then she was gone.

I wanted to follow her down into the darkness. I wanted to see the court of Poseidon. But I looked up at the sunset darkening on the surface. My friends were waiting. We had so little time. . . .

I kicked upward toward the shore.

When I reached the beach, my clothes dried instantly. I told Grover and Annabeth what had happened, and showed them the pearls.

Annabeth grimaced. "No gift comes without a price."

"They were free."

"No." She shook her head. "'There is no such thing as a free lunch.' That's an ancient Greek saying that translated pretty well into American. There will be a price. You wait."

On that happy thought, we turned our backs on the sea.

With some spare change from Ares's backpack, we took the bus into West Hollywood. I showed the driver the Underworld address slip I'd taken from Aunty Em's Garden Gnome Emporium, but he'd never heard of DOA Recording Studios.

"You remind me of somebody I saw on TV," he told me. "You a child actor or something?"

"Uh . . . I'm a stunt double . . . for a lot of child actors."

"Oh! That explains it."

We thanked him and got off quickly at the next stop.

We wandered for miles on foot, looking for DOA. Nobody seemed to know where it was. It didn't appear in the phone book.

Twice, we ducked into alleys to avoid cop cars.

I froze in front of an appliance-store window because a television was playing an interview with somebody who looked very familiar—my stepdad, Smelly Gabe. He was talking to Barbara Walters—I mean, as if he were some kind of huge celebrity. She was interviewing him in our apartment, in the middle of a poker game, and there was a young blond lady sitting next to him, patting his hand.

A fake tear glistened on his cheek. He was saying, "Honest, Ms. Walters, if it wasn't for Sugar here, my grief counselor, I'd be a wreck. My stepson took everything I cared about. My wife . . . my Camaro . . . I—I'm sorry. I have trouble talking about it."

"There you have it, America." Barbara Walters turned to the camera. "A man torn apart. An adolescent boy with serious issues. Let me show you, again, the last known photo of this troubled young fugitive, taken a week ago in Denver."

The screen cut to a grainy shot of me, Annabeth, and Grover standing outside the Colorado diner, talking to Ares.

"Who are the other children in this photo?" Barbara Walters asked dramatically. "Who is the man with them? Is Percy Jackson a delinquent, a terrorist, or perhaps the brainwashed victim of a frightening new cult? When we come back, we chat with a leading child psychologist. Stay tuned, America."

"C'mon," Grover told me. He hauled me away before I could punch a hole in the appliance-store window.

It got dark, and hungry-looking characters started coming out on the streets to play. Now, don't get me wrong. I'm a New Yorker. I don't scare easy. But L.A. had a totally different feel from New York. Back home, everything seemed close. It didn't matter how big the city was, you could get anywhere without getting lost. The street pattern and the subway made sense. There was a system to how things worked. A kid could be safe as long as he wasn't stupid.

L.A. wasn't like that. It was spread out, chaotic, hard to move around. It reminded me of Ares. It wasn't enough for

L.A. to be big; it had to prove it was big by being loud and strange and difficult to navigate, too. I didn't know how we were ever going to find the entrance to the Underworld by tomorrow, the summer solstice.

We walked past gangbangers, bums, and street hawkers, who looked at us like they were trying to figure if we were worth the trouble of mugging.

As we hurried passed the entrance of an alley, a voice from the darkness said, "Hey, you."

Like an idiot, I stopped.

Before I knew it, we were surrounded. A gang of kids had circled us. Six of them in all—white kids with expensive clothes and mean faces. Like the kids at Yancy Academy: rich brats playing at being bad boys.

Instinctively, I uncapped Riptide.

When the sword appeared out of nowhere, the kids backed off, but their leader was either really stupid or really brave, because he kept coming at me with a switchblade.

I made the mistake of swinging.

The kid yelped. But he must've been one hundred percent mortal, because the blade passed harmlessly right through his chest. He looked down. "What the . . ."

I figured I had about three seconds before his shock turned to anger. "Run!" I screamed at Annabeth and Grover.

We pushed two kids out of the way and raced down the street, not knowing where we were going. We turned a sharp corner.

"There!" Annabeth shouted.

Only one store on the block looked open, its windows glaring with neon. The sign above the door said something like CRSTUY'S WATRE BDE ALPACE.

"Crusty's Water Bed Palace?" Grover translated.

It didn't sound like a place I'd ever go except in an emergency, but this definitely qualified.

We burst through the doors, ran behind a water bed, and ducked. A split second later, the gang kids ran past outside.

"I think we lost them," Grover panted.

A voice behind us boomed, "Lost who?"

We all jumped.

Standing behind us was a guy who looked like a raptor in a leisure suit. He was at least seven feet tall, with absolutely no hair. He had gray, leathery skin, thick-lidded eyes, and a cold, reptilian smile. He moved toward us slowly, but I got the feeling he could move fast if he needed to.

His suit might've come from the Lotus Casino. It belonged back in the seventies, big-time. The shirt was silk paisley, unbuttoned halfway down his hairless chest. The lapels on his velvet jacket were as wide as landing strips. The silver chains around his neck—I couldn't even count them.

"I'm Crusty," he said, with a tartar-yellow smile.

I resisted the urge to say, *Yes, you are.*

"Sorry to barge in," I told him. "We were just, um, browsing."

"You mean hiding from those no-good kids," he grumbled. "They hang around every night. I get a lot of people in here, thanks to them. Say, you want to look at a water bed?"

I was about to say *No, thanks,* when he put a huge paw on my shoulder and steered me deeper into the showroom.

There was every kind of water bed you could imagine: different kinds of wood, different patterns of sheets; queen-size, king-size, emperor-of-the-universe-size.

"This is my most popular model." Crusty spread his hands proudly over a bed covered with black satin sheets, with built-in Lava Lamps on the headboard. The mattress vibrated, so it looked like oil-flavored Jell-O.

"Million-hand massage," Crusty told us. "Go on, try it out. Shoot, take a nap. I don't care. No business today, anyway."

"Um," I said, "I don't think . . ."

"Million-hand massage!" Grover cried, and dove in. "Oh, you guys! This is cool."

"Hmm," Crusty said, stroking his leathery chin. "Almost, almost."

"Almost what?" I asked.

He looked at Annabeth. "Do me a favor and try this one over here, honey. Might fit."

Annabeth said, "But what—"

He patted her reassuringly on the shoulder and led her over to the Safari Deluxe model with teakwood lions carved into the frame and a leopard-patterned comforter. When Annabeth didn't want to lie down, Crusty pushed her.

"Hey!" she protested.

Crusty snapped his fingers. *"Ergo!"*

Ropes sprang from the sides of the bed, lashing around Annabeth, holding her to the mattress.

Grover tried to get up, but ropes sprang from his black-satin bed, too, and lashed him down.

"N-not c-c-cool!" he yelled, his voice vibrating from the million-hand massage. "N-not c-cool a-at all!"

The giant looked at Annabeth, then turned toward me and grinned. "Almost, darn it."

I tried to step away, but his hand shot out and clamped around the back of my neck. "Whoa, kid. Don't worry. We'll find you one in a sec."

"Let my friends go."

"Oh, sure I will. But I got to make them fit, first."

"What do you mean?"

"All the beds are exactly six feet, see? Your friends are too short. Got to make them fit."

Annabeth and Grover kept struggling.

"Can't stand imperfect measurements," Crusty muttered. *"Ergo!"*

A new set of ropes leaped out from the top and bottom of the beds, wrapping around Grover and Annabeth's ankles, then around their armpits. The ropes started tightening, pulling my friends from both ends.

"Don't worry," Crusty told me. "These are stretching jobs. Maybe three extra inches on their spines. They might even live. Now why don't we find a bed you like, huh?"

"Percy!" Grover yelled.

My mind was racing. I knew I couldn't take on this giant water-bed salesman alone. He would snap my neck before I ever got my sword out.

"Your real name's not Crusty, is it?" I asked.

"Legally, it's Procrustes," he admitted.

"The Stretcher," I said. I remembered the story: the giant who'd tried to kill Theseus with excess hospitality on his way to Athens.

"Yeah," the salesman said. "But who can pronounce *Procrustes*? Bad for business. Now 'Crusty,' anybody can say that."

"You're right. It's got a good ring to it."

His eyes lit up. "You think so?"

"Oh, absolutely," I said. "And the workmanship on these beds? Fabulous!"

He grinned hugely, but his fingers didn't loosen on my neck. "I tell my customers that. Every time. Nobody bothers to look at the workmanship. How many built-in Lava Lamp headboards have you seen?"

"Not too many."

"That's right!"

"Percy!" Annabeth yelled. "What are you doing?"

"Don't mind her," I told Procrustes. "She's impossible."

The giant laughed. "All my customers are. Never six feet exactly. So inconsiderate. And then they complain about the fitting."

"What do you do if they're longer than six feet?"

"Oh, that happens all the time. It's a simple fix."

He let go of my neck, but before I could react, he reached behind a nearby sales desk and brought out a huge double-bladed brass axe. He said, "I just center the subject as best I can and lop off whatever hangs over on either end."

"Ah," I said, swallowing hard. "Sensible."

"I'm so glad to come across an intelligent customer!"

The ropes were really stretching my friends now. Annabeth was turning pale. Grover made gurgling sounds, like a strangled goose.

"So, Crusty . . ." I said, trying to keep my voice light. I glanced at the sales tag on the valentine-shaped Honeymoon Special. "Does this one really have dynamic stabilizers to stop wave motion?"

"Absolutely. Try it out."

"Yeah, maybe I will. But would it work even for a big guy like you? No waves at all?"

"Guaranteed."

"No way."

"Way."

"Show me."

He sat down eagerly on the bed, patted the mattress. "No waves. See?"

I snapped my fingers. *"Ergo."*

Ropes lashed around Crusty and flattened him against the mattress.

"Hey!" he yelled.

"Center him just right," I said.

The ropes readjusted themselves at my command. Crusty's whole head stuck out the top. His feet stuck out the bottom.

"No!" he said. "Wait! This is just a demo."

I uncapped Riptide. "A few simple adjustments . . ."

I had no qualms about what I was about to do. If

Crusty were human, I couldn't hurt him anyway. If he was a monster, he deserved to turn into dust for a while.

"You drive a hard bargain," he told me. "I'll give you thirty percent off on selected floor models!"

"I think I'll start with the top." I raised my sword.

"No money down! No interest for six months!"

I swung the sword. Crusty stopped making offers.

I cut the ropes on the other beds. Annabeth and Grover got to their feet, groaning and wincing and cursing me a lot.

"You look taller," I said.

"Very funny," Annabeth said. "Be faster next time."

I looked at the bulletin board behind Crusty's sales desk. There was an advertisement for Hermes Delivery Service, and another for the All-New Compendium of L.A. Area Monsters—"The only Monstrous Yellow Pages you'll ever need!" Under that, a bright orange flier for DOA Recording Studios, offering commissions for heroes' souls. "We are always looking for new talent!" DOA's address was right underneath with a map.

"Come on," I told my friends.

"Give us a minute," Grover complained. "We were almost stretched to death!"

"Then you're ready for the Underworld," I said. "It's only a block from here."

18 ⚡ ANNABETH DOES OBEDIENCE SCHOOL

We stood in the shadows of Valencia Boulevard, looking up at gold letters etched in black marble: DOA RECORDING STUDIOS.

Underneath, stenciled on the glass doors: NO SOLICITORS. NO LOITERING. NO LIVING.

It was almost midnight, but the lobby was brightly lit and full of people. Behind the security desk sat a tough-looking guard with sunglasses and an earpiece.

I turned to my friends. "Okay. You remember the plan."

"The plan," Grover gulped. "Yeah. I love the plan."

Annabeth said, "What happens if the plan doesn't work?"

"Don't think negative."

"Right," she said. "We're entering the Land of the Dead, and I shouldn't think negative."

I took the pearls out of my pocket, the three milky spheres the Nereid had given me in Santa Monica. They didn't seem like much of a backup in case something went wrong.

Annabeth put her hand on my shoulder. "I'm sorry, Percy. You're right, we'll make it. It'll be fine."

She gave Grover a nudge.

"Oh, right!" he chimed in. "We got this far. We'll find the master bolt and save your mom. No problem."

I looked at them both, and felt really grateful. Only a few minutes before, I'd almost gotten them stretched to death on deluxe water beds, and now they were trying to be brave for my sake, trying to make me feel better.

I slipped the pearls back in my pocket. "Let's whup some Underworld butt."

We walked inside the DOA lobby.

Muzak played softly on hidden speakers. The carpet and walls were steel gray. Pencil cactuses grew in the corners like skeleton hands. The furniture was black leather, and every seat was taken. There were people sitting on couches, people standing up, people staring out the windows or waiting for the elevator. Nobody moved, or talked, or did much of anything. Out of the corner of my eye, I could see them all just fine, but if I focused on any one of them in particular, they started looking . . . transparent. I could see right through their bodies.

The security guard's desk was a raised podium, so we had to look up at him.

He was tall and elegant, with chocolate-colored skin and bleached-blond hair shaved military style. He wore tortoiseshell shades and a silk Italian suit that matched his hair. A black rose was pinned to his lapel under a silver name tag.

I read the name tag, then looked at him in bewilderment. "Your name is Chiron?"

He leaned across the desk. I couldn't see anything in his

glasses except my own reflection, but his smile was sweet and cold, like a python's, right before it eats you.

"What a precious young lad." He had a strange accent—British, maybe, but also as if he had learned English as a second language. "Tell me, mate, do I look like a centaur?"

"N-no."

"Sir," he added smoothly.

"Sir," I said.

He pinched the name tag and ran his finger under the letters. "Can you read this, mate? It says C-H-*A*-R-O-N. Say it with me: CARE-ON."

"Charon."

"Amazing! Now: *Mr.* Charon."

"Mr. Charon," I said.

"Well done." He sat back. "I *hate* being confused with that old horse-man. And now, how may I help you little dead ones?"

His question caught in my stomach like a fastball. I looked at Annabeth for support.

"We want to go the Underworld," she said.

Charon's mouth twitched. "Well, that's refreshing."

"It is?" she asked.

"Straightforward and honest. No screaming. No 'There must be a mistake, Mr. Charon.'" He looked us over. "How did you die, then?"

I nudged Grover.

"Oh," he said. "Um . . . drowned . . . in the bathtub."

"All three of you?" Charon asked.

We nodded.

"Big bathtub." Charon looked mildly impressed. "I don't suppose you have coins for passage. Normally, with adults, you see, I could charge your American Express, or add the ferry price to your last cable bill. But with children . . . alas, you never die prepared. Suppose you'll have to take a seat for a few centuries."

"Oh, but we have coins." I set three golden drachmas on the counter, part of the stash I'd found in Crusty's office desk.

"Well, now . . ." Charon moistened his lips. "Real drachmas. Real golden drachmas. I haven't seen these in . . ."

His fingers hovered greedily over the coins.

We were so close.

Then Charon looked at me. That cold stare behind his glasses seemed to bore a hole through my chest. "Here now," he said. "You couldn't read my name correctly. Are you dyslexic, lad?"

"No," I said. "I'm dead."

Charon leaned forward and took a sniff. "You're not dead. I should've known. You're a godling."

"We have to get to the Underworld," I insisted.

Charon made a growling sound deep in his throat.

Immediately, all the people in the waiting room got up and started pacing, agitated, lighting cigarettes, running hands through their hair, or checking their wristwatches.

"Leave while you can," Charon told us. "I'll just take these and forget I saw you."

He started to go for the coins, but I snatched them back.

"No service, no tip." I tried to sound braver than I felt.

Charon growled again—a deep, blood-chilling sound. The spirits of the dead started pounding on the elevator doors.

"It's a shame, too," I sighed. "We had more to offer."

I held up the entire bag from Crusty's stash. I took out a fistful of drachmas and let the coins spill through my fingers.

Charon's growl changed into something more like a lion's purr. "Do you think I can be bought, godling? Eh . . . just out of curiosity, how much have you got there?"

"A lot," I said. "I bet Hades doesn't pay you well enough for such hard work."

"Oh, you don't know the half of it. How would you like to babysit these spirits all day? Always 'Please don't let me be dead' or 'Please let me across for free.' I haven't had a pay raise in three thousand years. Do you imagine suits like this come cheap?"

"You deserve better," I agreed. "A little appreciation. Respect. Good pay."

With each word, I stacked another gold coin on the counter.

Charon glanced down at his silk Italian jacket, as if imagining himself in something even better. "I must say, lad, you're making some sense now. Just a little."

I stacked another few coins. "I could mention a pay raise while I'm talking to Hades."

He sighed. "The boat's almost full, anyway. I might as well add you three and be off."

He stood, scooped up our money, and said, "Come along."

We pushed through the crowd of waiting spirits, who started grabbing at our clothes like the wind, their voices whispering things I couldn't make out. Charon shoved them out of the way, grumbling, "Freeloaders."

He escorted us into the elevator, which was already crowded with souls of the dead, each one holding a green boarding pass. Charon grabbed two spirits who were trying to get on with us and pushed them back into the lobby.

"Right. Now, no one get any ideas while I'm gone," he announced to the waiting room. "And if anyone moves the dial off my easy-listening station again, I'll make sure you're here for another thousand years. Understand?"

He shut the doors. He put a key card into a slot in the elevator panel and we started to descend.

"What happens to the spirits waiting in the lobby?" Annabeth asked.

"Nothing," Charon said.

"For how long?"

"Forever, or until I'm feeling generous."

"Oh," she said. "That's . . . fair."

Charon raised an eyebrow. "Whoever said death was fair, young miss? Wait until it's your turn. You'll die soon enough, where you're going."

"We'll get out alive," I said.

"Ha."

I got a sudden dizzy feeling. We weren't going down

anymore, but forward. The air turned misty. Spirits around me started changing shape. Their modern clothes flickered, turning into gray hooded robes. The floor of the elevator began swaying.

I blinked hard. When I opened my eyes, Charon's creamy Italian suit had been replaced by a long black robe. His tortoiseshell glasses were gone. Where his eyes should've been were empty sockets—like Ares's eyes, except Charon's were totally dark, full of night and death and despair.

He saw me looking, and said, "Well?"

"Nothing," I managed.

I thought he was grinning, but that wasn't it. The flesh of his face was becoming transparent, letting me see straight through to his skull.

The floor kept swaying.

Grover said, "I think I'm getting seasick."

When I blinked again, the elevator wasn't an elevator anymore. We were standing in a wooden barge. Charon was poling us across a dark, oily river, swirling with bones, dead fish, and other, stranger things—plastic dolls, crushed carnations, soggy diplomas with gilt edges.

"The River Styx," Annabeth murmured. "It's so . . ."

"Polluted," Charon said. "For thousands of years, you humans have been throwing in everything as you come across—hopes, dreams, wishes that never came true. Irresponsible waste management, if you ask me."

Mist curled off the filthy water. Above us, almost lost in the gloom, was a ceiling of stalactites. Ahead, the far shore glimmered with greenish light, the color of poison.

Panic closed up my throat. What was I doing here? These people around me . . . they were dead.

Annabeth grabbed hold of my hand. Under normal circumstances, this would've embarrassed me, but I understood how she felt. She wanted reassurance that somebody else was alive on this boat.

I found myself muttering a prayer, though I wasn't quite sure who I was praying to. Down here, only one god mattered, and he was the one I had come to confront.

The shoreline of the Underworld came into view. Craggy rocks and black volcanic sand stretched inland about a hundred yards to the base of a high stone wall, which marched off in either direction as far as we could see. A sound came from somewhere nearby in the green gloom, echoing off the stones—the howl of a large animal.

"Old Three-Face is hungry," Charon said. His smile turned skeletal in the greenish light. "Bad luck for you, godlings."

The bottom of our boat slid onto the black sand. The dead began to disembark. A woman holding a little girl's hand. An old man and an old woman hobbling along arm in arm. A boy no older than I was, shuffling silently along in his gray robe.

Charon said, "I'd wish you luck, mate, but there isn't any down here. Mind you, don't forget to mention my pay raise."

He counted our golden coins into his pouch, then took

up his pole. He warbled something that sounded like a Barry Manilow song as he ferried the empty barge back across the river.

We followed the spirits up a well-worn path.

I'm not sure what I was expecting—Pearly Gates, or a big black portcullis, or something. But the entrance to the Underworld looked like a cross between airport security and the Jersey Turnpike.

There were three separate entrances under one huge black archway that said YOU ARE NOW ENTERING EREBUS. Each entrance had a pass-through metal detector with security cameras mounted on top. Beyond this were tollbooths manned by black-robed ghouls like Charon.

The howling of the hungry animal was really loud now, but I couldn't see where it was coming from. The three-headed dog, Cerberus, who was supposed to guard Hades's door, was nowhere to be seen.

The dead queued up in the three lines, two marked ATTENDANT ON DUTY, and one marked EZ DEATH. The EZ DEATH line was moving right along. The other two were crawling.

"What do you figure?" I asked Annabeth.

"The fast line must go straight to the Asphodel Fields," she said. "No contest. They don't want to risk judgment from the court, because it might go against them."

"There's a court for dead people?"

"Yeah. Three judges. They switch around who sits on the bench. King Minos, Thomas Jefferson, Shakespeare—

people like that. Sometimes they look at a life and decide that person needs a special reward—the Fields of Elysium. Sometimes they decide on punishment. But most people, well, they just lived. Nothing special, good or bad. So they go to the Asphodel Fields."

"And do what?"

Grover said, "Imagine standing in a wheat field in Kansas. Forever."

"Harsh," I said.

"Not as harsh as that," Grover muttered. "Look."

A couple of black-robed ghouls had pulled aside one spirit and were frisking him at the security desk. The face of the dead man looked vaguely familiar.

"He's that preacher who made the news, remember?" Grover asked.

"Oh, yeah." I did remember now. We'd seen him on TV a couple of times at the Yancy Academy dorm. He was this annoying televangelist from upstate New York who'd raised millions of dollars for orphanages and then got caught spending the money on stuff for his mansion, like gold-plated toilet seats, and an indoor putt-putt golf course. He'd died in a police chase when his "Lamborghini for the Lord" went off a cliff.

I said, "What're they doing to him?"

"Special punishment from Hades," Grover guessed. "The really bad people get his personal attention as soon as they arrive. The Fur—the Kindly Ones will set up an eternal torture for him."

The thought of the Furies made me shudder. I realized

I was in their home territory now. Old Mrs. Dodds would be licking her lips with anticipation.

"But if he's a preacher," I said, "and he believes in a different hell. . . ."

Grover shrugged. "Who says he's seeing this place the way we're seeing it? Humans see what they want to see. You're very stubborn—er, persistent, that way."

We got closer to the gates. The howling was so loud now it shook the ground at my feet, but I still couldn't figure out where it was coming from.

Then, about fifty feet in front of us, the green mist shimmered. Standing just where the path split into three lanes was an enormous shadowy monster.

I hadn't seen it before because it was half transparent, like the dead. Until it moved, it blended with whatever was behind it. Only its eyes and teeth looked solid. And it was staring straight at me.

My jaw hung open. All I could think to say was, "He's a Rottweiler."

I'd always imagined Cerberus as a big black mastiff. But he was obviously a purebred Rottweiler, except of course that he was twice the size of a woolly mammoth, mostly invisible, and had three heads.

The dead walked right up to him—no fear at all. The ATTENDANT ON DUTY lines parted on either side of him. The EZ DEATH spirits walked right between his front paws and under his belly, which they could do without even crouching.

"I'm starting to see him better," I muttered. "Why is that?"

"I think . . ." Annabeth moistened her lips. "I'm afraid it's because we're getting closer to being dead."

The dog's middle head craned toward us. It sniffed the air and growled.

"It can smell the living," I said.

"But that's okay," Grover said, trembling next to me. "Because we have a plan."

"Right," Annabeth said. I'd never heard her voice sound quite so small. "A plan."

We moved toward the monster.

The middle head snarled at us, then barked so loud my eyeballs rattled.

"Can you understand it?" I asked Grover.

"Oh yeah," he said. "I can understand it."

"What's it saying?"

"I don't think humans have a four-letter word that translates, exactly."

I took the big stick out of my backpack—a bedpost I'd broken off Crusty's Safari Deluxe floor model. I held it up, and tried to channel happy dog thoughts toward Cerberus—Alpo commercials, cute little puppies, fire hydrants. I tried to smile, like I wasn't about to die.

"Hey, Big Fella," I called up. "I bet they don't play with you much."

"GROWWWLLLL!"

"Good boy," I said weakly.

I waved the stick. The dog's middle head followed the movement. The other two heads trained their eyes on me, completely ignoring the spirits. I had Cerberus's undivided attention. I wasn't sure that was a good thing.

"Fetch!" I threw the stick into the gloom, a good solid throw. I heard it go *ker-sploosh* in the River Styx.

Cerberus glared at me, unimpressed. His eyes were baleful and cold.

So much for the plan.

Cerberus was now making a new kind of growl, deeper down in his three throats.

"Um," Grover said. "Percy?"

"Yeah?"

"I just thought you'd want to know."

"Yeah?"

"Cerberus? He's saying we've got ten seconds to pray to the god of our choice. After that . . . well . . . he's hungry."

"Wait!" Annabeth said. She started rifling through her pack.

Uh-oh, I thought.

"Five seconds," Grover said. "Do we run now?"

Annabeth produced a red rubber ball the size of a grapefruit. It was labeled WATERLAND, DENVER, CO. Before I could stop her, she raised the ball and marched straight up to Cerberus.

She shouted, "See the ball? You want the ball, Cerberus? Sit!"

Cerberus looked as stunned as we were.

All three of his heads cocked sideways. Six nostrils dilated.

"Sit!" Annabeth called again.

I was sure that any moment she would become the world's largest Milkbone dog biscuit.

But instead, Cerberus licked his three sets of lips, shifted on his haunches, and sat, immediately crushing a dozen spirits who'd been passing underneath him in the EZ DEATH line. The spirits made muffled hisses as they dissipated, like the air let out of tires.

Annabeth said, "Good boy!"

She threw Cerberus the ball.

He caught it in his middle mouth. It was barely big enough for him to chew, and the other heads started snapping at the middle, trying to get the new toy.

"Drop it!" Annabeth ordered.

Cerberus's heads stopped fighting and looked at her. The ball was wedged between two of his teeth like a tiny piece of gum. He made a loud, scary whimper, then dropped the ball, now slimy and bitten nearly in half, at Annabeth's feet.

"Good boy." She picked up the ball, ignoring the monster spit all over it.

She turned toward us. "Go now. EZ DEATH line—it's faster."

I said, "But—"

"Now!" She ordered, in the same tone she was using on the dog.

Grover and I inched forward warily.

Cerberus started to growl.

"Stay!" Annabeth ordered the monster. "If you want the ball, stay!"

Cerberus whimpered, but he stayed where he was.

"What about you?" I asked Annabeth as we passed her.

"I know what I'm doing, Percy," she muttered. "At least, I'm pretty sure. . . ."

Grover and I walked between the monster's legs.

Please, Annabeth, I prayed. Don't tell him to sit again.

We made it through. Cerberus wasn't any less scary-looking from the back.

Annabeth said, "Good dog!"

She held up the tattered red ball, and probably came to the same conclusion I did—if she rewarded Cerberus, there'd be nothing left for another trick.

She threw the ball anyway. The monster's left mouth immediately snatched it up, only to be attacked by the middle head, while the right head moaned in protest.

While the monster was distracted, Annabeth walked briskly under its belly and joined us at the metal detector.

"How did you do that?" I asked her, amazed.

"Obedience school," she said breathlessly, and I was surprised to see there were tears in her eyes. "When I was little, at my dad's house, we had a Doberman. . . ."

"Never mind that," Grover said, tugging at my shirt. "Come on!"

We were about to bolt through the EZ DEATH line when Cerberus moaned pitifully from all three mouths. Annabeth stopped.

She turned to face the dog, which had done a one-eighty to look at us.

Cerberus panted expectantly, the tiny red ball in pieces in a puddle of drool at its feet.

"Good boy," Annabeth said, but her voice sounded melancholy and uncertain.

The monster's heads turned sideways, as if worried about her.

"I'll bring you another ball soon," Annabeth promised faintly. "Would you like that?"

The monster whimpered. I didn't need to speak dog to know Cerberus was still waiting for the ball.

"Good dog. I'll come visit you soon. I—I promise." Annabeth turned to us. "Let's go."

Grover and I pushed through the metal detector, which immediately screamed and set off flashing red lights. "Unauthorized possessions! Magic detected!"

Cerberus started to bark.

We burst through the EZ DEATH gate, which started even more alarms blaring, and raced into the Underworld.

A few minutes later, we were hiding, out of breath, in the rotten trunk of an immense black tree as security ghouls scuttled past, yelling for backup from the Furies.

Grover murmured, "Well, Percy, what have we learned today?"

"That three-headed dogs prefer red rubber balls over sticks?"

"No," Grover told me. "We've learned that your plans really, really bite!"

I wasn't sure about that. I thought maybe Annabeth and I had both had the right idea. Even here in the Underworld, everybody—even monsters—needed a little attention once in a while.

I thought about that as we waited for the ghouls to pass. I pretended not to see Annabeth wipe a tear from her cheek as she listened to the mournful keening of Cerberus in the distance, longing for his new friend.

19 ⚡ WE FIND OUT THE TRUTH, SORT OF

Imagine the largest concert crowd you've ever seen, a football field packed with a million fans.

Now imagine a field a million times that big, packed with people, and imagine the electricity has gone out, and there is no noise, no light, no beach ball bouncing around over the crowd. Something tragic has happened backstage. Whispering masses of people are just milling around in the shadows, waiting for a concert that will never start.

If you can picture that, you have a pretty good idea what the Fields of Asphodel looked like. The black grass had been trampled by eons of dead feet. A warm, moist wind blew like the breath of a swamp. Black trees—Grover told me they were poplars—grew in clumps here and there.

The cavern ceiling was so high above us it might've been a bank of storm clouds, except for the stalactites, which glowed faint gray and looked wickedly pointed. I tried not to imagine they'd fall on us at any moment, but dotted around the fields were several that had fallen and impaled themselves in the black grass. I guess the dead didn't have to worry about little hazards like being speared by stalactites the size of booster rockets.

Annabeth, Grover, and I tried to blend into the crowd,

keeping an eye out for security ghouls. I couldn't help looking for familiar faces among the spirits of Asphodel, but the
dead are hard to look at. Their faces shimmer. They all look
slightly angry or confused. They will come up to you and
speak, but their voices sound like chatter, like bats twitter-
ing. Once they realize you can't understand them, they
frown and move away.

The dead aren't scary. They're just sad.

We crept along, following the line of new arrivals that
snaked from the main gates toward a black-tented pavilion
with a banner that read:

JUDGMENTS FOR ELYSIUM AND ETERNAL DAMNATION
Welcome, Newly Deceased!

Out the back of the tent came two much smaller lines.

To the left, spirits flanked by security ghouls were
marched down a rocky path toward the Fields of Punishment, which glowed and smoked in the distance, a vast,
cracked wasteland with rivers of lava and minefields and
miles of barbed wire separating the different torture areas.
Even from far away, I could see people being chased by
hellhounds, burned at the stake, forced to run naked
through cactus patches or listen to opera music. I could just
make out a tiny hill, with the ant-size figure of Sisyphus
struggling to move his boulder to the top. And I saw worse
tortures, too—things I don't want to describe.

The line coming from the right side of the judgment
pavilion was much better. This one led down toward a small
valley surrounded by walls—a gated community, which

seemed to be the only happy part of the Underworld. Beyond the security gate were neighborhoods of beautiful houses from every time period in history, Roman villas and medieval castles and Victorian mansions. Silver and gold flowers bloomed on the lawns. The grass rippled in rainbow colors. I could hear laughter and smell barbecue cooking.

Elysium.

In the middle of that valley was a glittering blue lake, with three small islands like a vacation resort in the Bahamas. The Isles of the Blest, for people who had chosen to be reborn three times, and three times achieved Elysium. Immediately I knew that's where I wanted to go when I died.

"That's what it's all about," Annabeth said, like she was reading my thoughts. "That's the place for heroes."

But I thought of how few people there were in Elysium, how tiny it was compared to the Fields of Asphodel or even the Fields of Punishment. So few people did good in their lives. It was depressing.

We left the judgment pavilion and moved deeper into the Asphodel Fields. It got darker. The colors faded from our clothes. The crowds of chattering spirits began to thin.

After a few miles of walking, we began to hear a familiar screech in the distance. Looming on the horizon was a palace of glittering black obsidian. Above the parapets swirled three dark batlike creatures: the Furies. I got the feeling they were waiting for us.

"I suppose it's too late to turn back," Grover said wistfully.

"We'll be okay." I tried to sound confident.

"Maybe we should search some of the other places first," Grover suggested. "Like, Elysium, for instance . . ."

"Come on, goat boy." Annabeth grabbed his arm.

Grover yelped. His sneakers sprouted wings and his legs shot forward, pulling him away from Annabeth. He landed flat on his back in the grass.

"Grover," Annabeth chided. "Stop messing around."

"But I didn't—"

He yelped again. His shoes were flapping like crazy now. They levitated off the ground and started dragging him away from us.

"Maia!" he yelled, but the magic word seemed to have no effect. *"Maia,* already! Nine-one-one! Help!"

I got over being stunned and made a grab for Grover's hand, but too late. He was picking up speed, skidding downhill like a bobsled.

We ran after him.

Annabeth shouted, "Untie the shoes!"

It was a smart idea, but I guess it's not so easy when your shoes are pulling you along feetfirst at full speed. Grover tried to sit up, but he couldn't get close to the laces.

We kept after him, trying to keep him in sight as he zipped between the legs of spirits who chattered at him in annoyance.

I was sure Grover was going to barrel straight through the gates of Hades's palace, but his shoes veered sharply to the right and dragged him in the opposite direction.

The slope got steeper. Grover picked up speed. Annabeth

and I had to sprint to keep up. The cavern walls narrowed on either side, and I realized we'd entered some kind of side tunnel. No black grass or trees now, just rock underfoot, and the dim light of the stalactites above.

"Grover!" I yelled, my voice echoing. "Hold on to something!"

"What?" he yelled back.

He was grabbing at gravel, but there was nothing big enough to slow him down.

The tunnel got darker and colder. The hairs on my arms bristled. It smelled evil down here. It made me think of things I shouldn't even know about—blood spilled on an ancient stone altar, the foul breath of a murderer.

Then I saw what was ahead of us, and I stopped dead in my tracks.

The tunnel widened into a huge dark cavern, and in the middle was a chasm the size of a city block.

Grover was sliding straight toward the edge.

"Come on, Percy!" Annabeth yelled, tugging at my wrist.

"But that's—"

"I know!" she shouted. "The place you described in your dream! But Grover's going to fall if we don't catch him." She was right, of course. Grover's predicament got me moving again.

He was yelling, clawing at the ground, but the winged shoes kept dragging him toward the pit, and it didn't look like we could possibly get to him in time.

What saved him were his hooves.

The flying sneakers had always been a loose fit on him,

and finally Grover hit a big rock and the left shoe came flying off. It sped into the darkness, down into the chasm. The right shoe kept tugging him along, but not as fast. Grover was able to slow himself down by grabbing on to the big rock and using it like an anchor.

He was ten feet from the edge of the pit when we caught him and hauled him back up the slope. The other winged shoe tugged itself off, circled around us angrily and kicked our heads in protest before flying off into the chasm to join its twin.

We all collapsed, exhausted, on the obsidian gravel. My limbs felt like lead. Even my backpack seemed heavier, as if somebody had filled it with rocks.

Grover was scratched up pretty bad. His hands were bleeding. His eyes had gone slit-pupiled, goat style, the way they did whenever he was terrified.

"I don't know how . . ." he panted. "I didn't . . ."

"Wait," I said. "Listen."

I heard something—a deep whisper in the darkness.

Another few seconds, and Annabeth said, "Percy, this place—"

"Shh." I stood.

The sound was getting louder, a muttering, evil voice from far, far below us. Coming from the pit.

Grover sat up. "Wh—what's that noise?"

Annabeth heard it too, now. I could see it in her eyes. "Tartarus. The entrance to Tartarus."

I uncapped Anaklusmos.

The bronze sword expanded, gleaming in the darkness,

and the evil voice seemed to falter, just for a moment, before resuming its chant.

I could almost make out words now, ancient, ancient words, older even than Greek. As if . . .

"Magic," I said.

"We have to get out of here," Annabeth said.

Together, we dragged Grover to his hooves and started back up the tunnel. My legs wouldn't move fast enough. My backpack weighed me down. The voice got louder and angrier behind us, and we broke into a run.

Not a moment too soon.

A cold blast of wind pulled at our backs, as if the entire pit were inhaling. For a terrifying moment, I lost ground, my feet slipping in the gravel. If we'd been any closer to the edge, we would've been sucked in.

We kept struggling forward, and finally reached the top of the tunnel, where the cavern widened out into the Fields of Asphodel. The wind died. A wail of outrage echoed from deep in the tunnel. Something was not happy we'd gotten away.

"What *was* that?" Grover panted, when we'd collapsed in the relative safety of a black poplar grove. "One of Hades's pets?"

Annabeth and I looked at each other. I could tell she was nursing an idea, probably the same one she'd gotten during the taxi ride to L.A., but she was too scared to share it. That was enough to terrify me.

I capped my sword, put the pen back in my pocket. "Let's keep going." I looked at Grover. "Can you walk?"

He swallowed. "Yeah, sure. I never liked those shoes, anyway."

He tried to sound brave about it, but he was trembling as badly as Annabeth and I were. Whatever was in that pit was nobody's pet. It was unspeakably old and powerful. Even Echidna hadn't given me that feeling. I was almost relieved to turn my back on that tunnel and head toward the palace of Hades.

Almost.

The Furies circled the parapets, high in the gloom. The outer walls of the fortress glittered black, and the two-story-tall bronze gates stood wide open.

Up close, I saw that the engravings on the gates were scenes of death. Some were from modern times—an atomic bomb exploding over a city, a trench filled with gas mask–wearing soldiers, a line of African famine victims waiting with empty bowls—but all of them looked as if they'd been etched into the bronze thousands of years ago. I wondered if I was looking at prophecies that had come true.

Inside the courtyard was the strangest garden I'd ever seen. Multicolored mushrooms, poisonous shrubs, and weird luminous plants grew without sunlight. Precious jewels made up for the lack of flowers, piles of rubies as big as my fist, clumps of raw diamonds. Standing here and there like frozen party guests were Medusa's garden statues— petrified children, satyrs, and centaurs—all smiling grotesquely.

In the center of the garden was an orchard of

pomegranate trees, their orange blooms neon bright in the dark. "The garden of Persephone," Annabeth said. "Keep walking."

I understood why she wanted to move on. The tart smell of those pomegranates was almost overwhelming. I had a sudden desire to eat them, but then I remembered the story of Persephone. One bite of Underworld food, and we would never be able to leave. I pulled Grover away to keep him from picking a big juicy one.

We walked up the steps of the palace, between black columns, through a black marble portico, and into the house of Hades. The entry hall had a polished bronze floor, which seemed to boil in the reflected torchlight. There was no ceiling, just the cavern roof, far above. I guess they never had to worry about rain down here.

Every side doorway was guarded by a skeleton in military gear. Some wore Greek armor, some British redcoat uniforms, some camouflage with tattered American flags on the shoulders. They carried spears or muskets or M-16s. None of them bothered us, but their hollow eye sockets followed us as we walked down the hall, toward the big set of doors at the opposite end.

Two U.S. Marine skeletons guarded the doors. They grinned down at us, rocket-propelled grenade launchers held across their chests.

"You know," Grover mumbled, "I bet Hades doesn't have trouble with door-to-door salesmen."

My backpack weighed a ton now. I couldn't figure out why. I wanted to open it, check to see if I had somehow picked up a stray bowling ball, but this wasn't the time.

"Well, guys," I said. "I suppose we should . . . knock?"

A hot wind blew down the corridor, and the doors swung open. The guards stepped aside.

"I guess that means *entrez-vous*," Annabeth said.

The room inside looked just like in my dream, except this time the throne of Hades was occupied.

He was the third god I'd met, but the first who really struck me as godlike.

He was at least ten feet tall, for one thing, and dressed in black silk robes and a crown of braided gold. His skin was albino white, his hair shoulder-length and jet black. He wasn't bulked up like Ares, but he radiated power. He lounged on his throne of fused human bones, looking lithe, graceful, and dangerous as a panther.

I immediately felt like he should be giving the orders. He knew more than I did. He should be my master. Then I told myself to snap out of it.

Hades's aura was affecting me, just as Ares's had. The Lord of the Dead resembled pictures I'd seen of Adolph Hitler, or Napoleon, or the terrorist leaders who direct suicide bombers. Hades had the same intense eyes, the same kind of mesmerizing, evil charisma.

"You are brave to come here, Son of Poseidon," he said in an oily voice. "After what you have done to me, very brave indeed. Or perhaps you are simply very foolish."

Numbness crept into my joints, tempting me to lie

down and just take a little nap at Hades's feet. Curl up here and sleep forever.

I fought the feeling and stepped forward. I knew what I had to say. "Lord and Uncle, I come with two requests."

Hades raised an eyebrow. When he sat forward in his throne, shadowy faces appeared in the folds of his black robes, faces of torment, as if the garment were stitched of trapped souls from the Fields of Punishment, trying to get out. The ADHD part of me wondered, off-task, whether the rest of his clothes were made the same way. What horrible things would you have to do in your life to get woven into Hades's underwear?

"Only two requests?" Hades said. "Arrogant child. As if you have not already taken enough. Speak, then. It amuses me not to strike you dead yet."

I swallowed. This was going about as well as I'd feared.

I glanced at the empty, smaller throne next to Hades's. It was shaped like a black flower, gilded with gold. I wished Queen Persephone were here. I recalled something in the myths about how she could calm her husband's moods. But it was summer. Of course, Persephone would be above in the world of light with her mother, the goddess of agriculture, Demeter. Her visits, not the tilt of the planet, create the seasons.

Annabeth cleared her throat. Her finger prodded me in the back.

"Lord Hades," I said. "Look, sir, there can't be a war among the gods. It would be . . . bad."

"Really bad," Grover added helpfully.

"Return Zeus's master bolt to me," I said. "Please, sir. Let me carry it to Olympus."

Hades's eyes grew dangerously bright. "You dare keep up this pretense, after what you have done?"

I glanced back at my friends. They looked as confused as I was.

"Um . . . Uncle," I said. "You keep saying 'after what you've done.' What exactly have I done?"

The throne room shook with a tremor so strong, they probably felt it upstairs in Los Angeles. Debris fell from the cavern ceiling. Doors burst open all along the walls, and skeletal warriors marched in, hundreds of them, from every time period and nation in Western civilization. They lined the perimeter of the room, blocking the exits.

Hades bellowed, "Do you think I *want* war, godling?"

I wanted to say, *Well, these guys don't look like peace activists.* But I thought that might be a dangerous answer.

"You are the Lord of the Dead," I said carefully. "A war would expand your kingdom, right?"

"A typical thing for my brothers to say! Do you think I need more subjects? Did you not see the sprawl of the Asphodel Fields?"

"Well . . ."

"Have you any idea how much my kingdom has swollen in this past century alone, how many subdivisions I've had to open?"

I opened my mouth to respond, but Hades was on a roll now.

"More security ghouls," he moaned. "Traffic problems

at the judgment pavilion. Double overtime for the staff. I used to be a rich god, Percy Jackson. I control all the precious metals under the earth. But my expenses!"

"Charon wants a pay raise," I blurted, just remembering the fact. As soon as I said it, I wished I could sew up my mouth.

"Don't get me started on Charon!" Hades yelled. "He's been impossible ever since he discovered Italian suits! Problems everywhere, and I've got to handle all of them personally. The commute time alone from the palace to the gates is enough to drive me insane! And the dead just keep arriving. *No*, godling. I need no help getting subjects! *I* did not ask for this war."

"But you took Zeus's master bolt."

"Lies!" More rumbling. Hades rose from his throne, towering to the height of a football goalpost. "Your father may fool Zeus, boy, but I am not so stupid. I see his plan."

"His plan?"

"*You* were the thief on the winter solstice," he said. "Your father thought to keep you his little secret. He directed you into the throne room on Olympus. You took the master bolt *and* my helm. Had I not sent my Fury to discover you at Yancy Academy, Poseidon might have succeeded in hiding his scheme to start a war. But now you have been forced into the open. You will be exposed as Poseidon's thief, and I will have my helm back!"

"But . . ." Annabeth spoke. I could tell her mind was going a million miles an hour. "Lord Hades, your helm of darkness is missing, too?"

"Do not play innocent with me, girl. You and the satyr have been helping this hero—coming here to threaten me in Poseidon's name, no doubt—to bring me an ultimatum. Does Poseidon think I can be blackmailed into supporting him?"

"No!" I said. "Poseidon didn't—I didn't—"

"I have said nothing of the helm's disappearance," Hades snarled, "because I had no illusions that anyone on Olympus would offer me the slightest justice, the slightest help. I can ill afford for word to get out that my most powerful weapon of fear is missing. So I searched for you myself, and when it was clear you were coming to me to deliver your threat, I did not try to stop you."

"You didn't try to stop us? But—"

"Return my helm now, or I will stop death," Hades threatened. "That is my counterproposal. I will open the earth and have the dead pour back into the world. I will make your lands a nightmare. And you, Percy Jackson—*your* skeleton will lead my army out of Hades."

The skeletal soldiers all took one step forward, making their weapons ready.

At that point, I probably should have been terrified. The strange thing was, I felt offended. Nothing gets me angrier than being accused of something I didn't do. I've had a lot of experience with that.

"You're as bad as Zeus," I said. "You think I stole from you? That's why you sent the Furies after me?"

"Of course," Hades said.

"And the other monsters?"

Hades curled his lip. "I had nothing to do with them. I

wanted no quick death for you—I wanted you brought before me alive so you might face every torture in the Fields of Punishment. Why do you think I let you enter my kingdom so easily?"

"Easily?"

"Return my property!"

"But I don't have your helm. I came for the master bolt."

"Which you already possess!" Hades shouted. "You came here with it, little fool, thinking you could you threaten me!"

"But I didn't!"

"Open your pack, then."

A horrible feeling struck me. The weight in my backpack, like a bowling ball. It couldn't be. . . .

I slung it off my shoulder and unzipped it. Inside was a two-foot-long metal cylinder, spiked on both ends, humming with energy.

"Percy," Annabeth said. "How—"

"I—I don't know. I don't understand."

"You heroes are always the same," Hades said. "Your pride makes you foolish, thinking you could bring such a weapon before me. I did not ask for Zeus's master bolt, but since it is here, you will yield it to me. I am sure it will make an excellent bargaining tool. And now . . . my helm. Where is it?"

I was speechless. I had no helm. I had no idea how the master bolt had gotten into my backpack. I wanted to think Hades was pulling some kind of trick. Hades was the bad guy. But suddenly the world turned sideways. I realized I'd been played with. Zeus, Poseidon, and Hades had been set at each other's throats by someone else. The master bolt had been in the backpack, and I'd gotten the backpack from . . .

"Lord Hades, wait," I said. "This is all a mistake."

"A mistake?" Hades roared.

The skeletons aimed their weapons. From high above, there was a fluttering of leathery wings, and the three Furies swooped down to perch on the back of their master's throne. The one with Mrs. Dodds's face grinned at me eagerly and flicked her whip.

"There is no mistake," Hades said. "I know why you have come—I know the *real* reason you brought the bolt. You came to bargain for *her.*"

Hades loosed a ball of gold fire from his palm. It exploded on the steps in front of me, and there was my mother, frozen in a shower of gold, just as she was at the moment when the Minotaur began to squeeze her to death.

I couldn't speak. I reached out to touch her, but the light was as hot as a bonfire.

"Yes," Hades said with satisfaction. "I took her. I knew, Percy Jackson, that you would come to bargain with me eventually. Return my helm, and perhaps I will let her go. She is not dead, you know. Not yet. But if you displease me, that will change."

I thought about the pearls in my pocket. Maybe they could get me out of this. If I could just get my mom free . . .

"Ah, the pearls," Hades said, and my blood froze. "Yes, my brother and his little tricks. Bring them forth, Percy Jackson."

My hand moved against my will and brought out the pearls.

"Only three," Hades said. "What a shame. You do realize each only protects a single person. Try to take your mother, then, little godling. And which of your friends will you leave behind to spend eternity with me? Go on. Choose. Or give me the backpack and accept my terms."

I looked at Annabeth and Grover. Their faces were grim.

"We were tricked," I told them. "Set up."

"Yes, but why?" Annabeth asked. "And the voice in the pit—"

"I don't know yet," I said. "But I intend to ask."

"Decide, boy!" Hades yelled.

"Percy." Grover put his hand on my shoulder. "You can't give him the bolt."

"I know that."

"Leave me here," he said. "Use the third pearl on your mom."

"No!"

"I'm a satyr," Grover said. "We don't have souls like humans do. He can torture me until I die, but he won't get me forever. I'll just be reincarnated as a flower or something. It's the best way."

"No." Annabeth drew her bronze knife. "You two go on. Grover, you have to protect Percy. You have to get your searcher's license and start your quest for Pan. Get his mom out of here. I'll cover you. I plan to go down fighting."

"No way," Grover said. "I'm staying behind."

"Think again, goat boy," Annabeth said.

"Stop it, both of you!" I felt like my heart was being ripped in two. They had both been with me through so much. I remembered Grover dive-bombing Medusa in the statue garden, and Annabeth saving us from Cerberus; we'd survived Hephaestus's Waterland ride, the St. Louis Arch, the Lotus Casino. I had spent thousands of miles worried that I'd be betrayed by a friend, but these friends would never do that. They had done nothing but save me, over and over, and now they wanted to sacrifice their lives for my mom.

"I know what to do," I said. "Take these."

I handed them each a pearl.

Annabeth said, "But, Percy . . ."

I turned and faced my mother. I desperately wanted to sacrifice myself and use the last pearl on her, but I knew what she would say. She would never allow it. I had to get the bolt back to Olympus and tell Zeus the truth. I had to stop the war. She would never forgive me if I saved her instead. I thought about the prophecy made at Half-Blood Hill, what seemed like a million years ago. *You will fail to save what matters most in the end.*

"I'm sorry," I told her. "I'll be back. I'll find a way."

The smug look on Hades's face faded. He said, "Godling . . . ?"

"I'll find your helm, Uncle," I told him. "I'll return it. Remember about Charon's pay raise."

"Do not defy me—"

"And it wouldn't hurt to play with Cerberus once in a while. He likes red rubber balls."

"Percy Jackson, you will not—"

I shouted, "Now, guys!"

We smashed the pearls at our feet. For a scary moment, nothing happened.

Hades yelled, "Destroy them!"

The army of skeletons rushed forward, swords out, guns clicking to full automatic. The Furies lunged, their whips bursting into flame.

Just as the skeletons opened fire, the pearl fragments at my feet exploded with a burst of green light and a gust of fresh sea wind. I was encased in a milky white sphere, which was starting to float off the ground.

Annabeth and Grover were right behind me. Spears and bullets sparked harmlessly off the pearl bubbles as we floated up. Hades yelled with such rage, the entire fortress shook and I knew it was not going to be a peaceful night in L.A.

"Look up!" Grover yelled. "We're going to crash!"

Sure enough, we were racing right toward the stalactites, which I figured would pop our bubbles and skewer us.

"How do you control these things?" Annabeth shouted.

"I don't think you do!" I shouted back.

We screamed as the bubbles slammed into the ceiling and . . . Darkness.

Were we dead?

No, I could still feel the racing sensation. We were going up, right through solid rock as easily as an air bubble in water. That was the power of the pearls, I realized—*What belongs to the sea will always return to the sea.*

For a few moments, I couldn't see anything outside the

smooth walls of my sphere, then my pearl broke through on the ocean floor. The two other milky spheres, Annabeth and Grover, kept pace with me as we soared upward through the water. And—*ker-blam!*

We exploded on the surface, in the middle of the Santa Monica Bay, knocking a surfer off his board with an indignant, "Dude!"

I grabbed Grover and hauled him over to a life buoy. I caught Annabeth and dragged her over too. A curious shark was circling us, a great white about eleven feet long.

I said, "Beat it."

The shark turned and raced away.

The surfer screamed something about bad mushrooms and paddled away from us as fast as he could.

Somehow, I knew what time it was: early morning, June 21, the day of the summer solstice.

In the distance, Los Angeles was on fire, plumes of smoke rising from neighborhoods all over the city. There had been an earthquake, all right, and it was Hades's fault. He was probably sending an army of the dead after me right now.

But at the moment, the Underworld wasn't my biggest problem.

I had to get to shore. I had to get Zeus's thunderbolt back to Olympus. Most of all, I had to have a serious conversation with the god who'd tricked me.

20 I BATTLE MY
JERK RELATIVE

A Coast Guard boat picked us up, but they were too busy to keep us for long, or to wonder how three kids in street clothes had gotten out into the middle of the bay. There was a disaster to mop up. Their radios were jammed with distress calls.

They dropped us off at the Santa Monica Pier with towels around our shoulders and water bottles that said I'M A JUNIOR COAST GUARD! and sped off to save more people.

Our clothes were sopping wet, even mine. When the Coast Guard boat had appeared, I'd silently prayed they wouldn't pick me out of the water and find me perfectly dry, which might've raised some eyebrows. So I'd willed myself to get soaked. Sure enough, my usual waterproof magic had abandoned me. I was also barefoot, because I'd given my shoes to Grover. Better the Coast Guard wonder why one of us was barefoot than wonder why one of us had hooves.

After reaching dry land, we stumbled down the beach, watching the city burn against a beautiful sunrise. I felt as if I'd just come back from the dead—which I had. My backpack was heavy with Zeus's master bolt. My heart was even heavier from seeing my mother.

"I don't believe it," Annabeth said. "We went all that way—"

"It was a trick," I said. "A strategy worthy of Athena."

"Hey," she warned.

"You get it, don't you?"

She dropped her eyes, her anger fading. "Yeah. I get it."

"Well, I don't!" Grover complained. "Would some-body—"

"Percy . . ." Annabeth said. "I'm sorry about your mother. I'm so sorry. . . ."

I pretended not to hear her. If I talked about my mother, I was going to start crying like a little kid.

"The prophecy was right," I said. "'You shall go west and face the god who has turned.' But it wasn't Hades. Hades didn't want war among the Big Three. Someone else pulled off the theft. Someone stole Zeus's master bolt, and Hades's helm, and framed me because I'm Poseidon's kid. Poseidon will get blamed by both sides. By sundown today, there will be a three-way war. And I'll have caused it."

Grover shook his head, mystified. "But who would be that sneaky? Who would want war that bad?"

I stopped in my tracks, looking down the beach. "Gee, let me think."

There he was, waiting for us, in his black leather duster and his sunglasses, an aluminum baseball bat propped on his shoulder. His motorcycle rumbled beside him, its head-light turning the sand red.

"Hey, kid," Ares said, seeming genuinely pleased to see me. "You were supposed to die."

"You tricked me," I said. "*You* stole the helm and the master bolt."

Ares grinned. "Well, now, I didn't steal them personally. Gods taking each other's symbols of power—that's a big no-no. But you're not the only hero in the world who can run errands."

"Who did you use? Clarisse? She was there at the winter solstice."

The idea seemed to amuse him. "Doesn't matter. The point is, kid, you're impeding the war effort. See, you've got to die in the Underworld. Then Old Seaweed will be mad at Hades for killing you. Corpse Breath will have Zeus's master bolt, so Zeus'll be mad at *him*. And Hades is still looking for this . . ."

From his pocket he took out a ski cap—the kind bank robbers wear—and placed it between the handlebars of his bike. Immediately, the cap transformed into an elaborate bronze war helmet.

"The helm of darkness," Grover gasped.

"Exactly," Ares said. "Now where was I? Oh yeah, Hades will be mad at both Zeus and Poseidon, because he doesn't know who took this. Pretty soon, we got a nice little three-way slugfest going."

"But they're your family!" Annabeth protested.

Ares shrugged. "Best kind of war. Always the bloodiest. Nothing like watching your relatives fight, I always say."

"You gave me the backpack in Denver," I said. "The master bolt was in there the whole time."

"Yes and no," Ares said. "It's probably too complicated for your little mortal brain to follow, but the backpack is the master bolt's sheath, just morphed a bit. The bolt is connected to it, sort of like that sword you got, kid. It always returns to your pocket, right?"

I wasn't sure how Ares knew about that, but I guess a god of war had to make it his business to know about weapons.

"Anyway," Ares continued, "I tinkered with the magic a bit, so the bolt would only return to the sheath once you reached the Underworld. You get close to Hades. . . . Bingo, you got mail. If you died along the way—no loss. I still had the weapon."

"But why not just keep the master bolt for yourself?" I said. "Why send it to Hades?"

Ares got a twitch in his jaw. For a moment, it was almost as if he were listening to another voice, deep inside his head. "Why didn't I . . . yeah . . . with that kind of fire-power . . ."

He held the trance for one second . . . two seconds. . . .

I exchanged nervous looks with Annabeth.

Ares's face cleared. "I didn't want the trouble. Better to have you caught redhanded, holding the thing."

"You're lying," I said. "Sending the bolt to the Underworld wasn't your idea, was it?"

"Of course it was!" Smoke drifted up from his sunglasses, as if they were about to catch fire.

"You didn't order the theft," I guessed. "Someone else sent a hero to steal the two items. Then, when Zeus sent you to hunt him down, you caught the thief. But you didn't turn him over to Zeus. Something convinced you to let him go.

You kept the items until another hero could come along and complete the delivery. That thing in the pit is ordering you around."

"I am the god of war! I take orders from no one! I don't have dreams!"

I hesitated. "Who said anything about dreams?"

Ares looked agitated, but he tried to cover it with a smirk.

"Let's get back to the problem at hand, kid. You're alive. I can't have you taking that bolt to Olympus. You just might get those hardheaded idiots to listen to you. So I've got to kill you. Nothing personal."

He snapped his fingers. The sand exploded at his feet and out charged a wild boar, even larger and uglier than the one whose head hung above the door of cabin seven at Camp Half-Blood. The beast pawed the sand, glaring at me with beady eyes as it lowered its razor-sharp tusks and waited for the command to kill.

I stepped into the surf. "Fight me yourself, Ares."

He laughed, but I heard a little edge to his laughter . . . an uneasiness. "You've only got one talent, kid, running away. You ran from the Chimera. You ran from the Underworld. You don't have what it takes."

"Scared?"

"In your adolescent dreams." But his sunglasses were starting to melt from the heat of his eyes. "No direct involvement. Sorry, kid. You're not at my level."

Annabeth said, "Percy, run!"

The giant boar charged.

But I was done running from monsters. Or Hades, or Ares, or anybody.

As the boar rushed me, I uncapped my pen and side-stepped. Riptide appeared in my hands. I slashed upward. The boar's severed right tusk fell at my feet, while the disoriented animal charged into the sea.

I shouted, "Wave!"

Immediately, a wave surged up from nowhere and engulfed the boar, wrapping around it like a blanket. The beast squealed once in terror. Then it was gone, swallowed by the sea.

I turned back to Ares. "Are you going to fight me now?" I asked. "Or are you going to hide behind another pet pig?"

Ares's face was purple with rage. "Watch it, kid. I could turn you into—"

"A cockroach," I said. "Or a tapeworm. Yeah, I'm sure. That'd save you from getting your godly hide whipped, wouldn't it?"

Flames danced along the top of his glasses. "Oh, man, you are really asking to be smashed into a grease spot."

"If I lose, turn me into anything you want. Take the bolt. If I win, the helm and the bolt are mine and *you* have to go away."

Ares sneered.

He swung the baseball bat off his shoulder. "How would you like to get smashed: classic or modern?"

I showed him my sword.

"That's cool, dead boy," he said. "Classic it is." The

baseball bat changed into a huge, two-handed sword. The hilt was a large silver skull with a ruby in its mouth.

"Percy," Annabeth said. "Don't do this. He's a god."

"He's a coward," I told her.

She swallowed. "Wear this, at least. For luck."

She took off her necklace, with her five years' worth of camp beads and the ring from her father, and tied it around my neck.

"Reconciliation," she said. "Athena and Poseidon together."

My face felt a little warm, but I managed a smile. "Thanks."

"And take this," Grover said. He handed me a flattened tin can that he'd probably been saving in his pocket for a thousand miles. "The satyrs stand behind you."

"Grover . . . I don't know what to say."

He patted me on the shoulder. I stuffed the tin can in my back pocket.

"You all done saying good-bye?" Ares came toward me, his black leather duster trailing behind him, his sword glinting like fire in the sunrise. "I've been fighting for eternity, kid. My strength is unlimited and I cannot die. What have you got?"

A smaller ego, I thought, but I said nothing. I kept my feet in the surf, backing into the water up to my ankles. I thought back to what Annabeth had said at the Denver diner, so long ago: *Ares has strength. That's all he has. Even strength has to bow to wisdom sometimes.*

He cleaved downward at my head, but I wasn't there.

My body thought for me. The water seemed to push me into the air and I catapulted over him, slashing as I came down. But Ares was just as quick. He twisted, and the strike that should've caught him directly in the spine was deflected off the end of his sword hilt.

He grinned. "Not bad, not bad."

He slashed again and I was forced to jump onto dry land. I tried to sidestep, to get back to the water, but Ares seemed to know what I wanted. He outmaneuvered me, pressing so hard I had to put all my concentration on not getting sliced into pieces. I kept backing away from the surf. I couldn't find any openings to attack. His sword had a reach several feet longer than Anaklusmos.

Get in close, Luke had told me once, back in our sword class. *When you've got the shorter blade, get in close.*

I stepped inside with a thrust, but Ares was waiting for that. He knocked my blade out of my hands and kicked me in the chest. I went airborne—twenty, maybe thirty feet. I would've broken my back if I hadn't crashed into the soft sand of a dune.

"Percy!" Annabeth yelled. "Cops!"

I was seeing double. My chest felt like it had just been hit with a battering ram, but I managed to get to my feet.

I couldn't look away from Ares for fear he'd slice me in half, but out of the corner of my eye I saw red lights flashing on the shoreline boulevard. Car doors were slamming.

"There, officer!" somebody yelled. "See?"

A gruff cop voice: "Looks like that kid on TV . . . what the heck . . ."

"That guy's armed," another cop said. "Call for backup."

I rolled to one side as Ares's blade slashed the sand.

I ran for my sword, scooped it up, and launched a swipe at Ares's face, only to find my blade deflected again.

Ares seemed to know exactly what I was going to do the moment before I did it.

I stepped back toward the surf, forcing him to follow.

"Admit it, kid," Ares said. "You got no hope. I'm just toying with you."

My senses were working overtime. I now understood what Annabeth had said about ADHD keeping you alive in battle. I was wide awake, noticing every little detail.

I could see where Ares was tensing. I could tell which way he would strike. At the same time, I was aware of Annabeth and Grover, thirty feet to my left. I saw a second cop car pulling up, siren wailing. Spectators, people who had been wandering the streets because of the earthquake, were starting to gather. Among the crowd, I thought I saw a few who were walking with the strange, trotting gait of disguised satyrs. There were shimmering forms of spirits, too, as if the dead had risen from Hades to watch the battle. I heard the flap of leathery wings circling somewhere above.

More sirens.

I stepped farther into the water, but Ares was fast. The tip of his blade ripped my sleeve and grazed my forearm.

A police voice on a megaphone said, "Drop the guns! Set them on the ground. Now!"

Guns?

I looked at Ares's weapon, and it seemed to be flickering; sometimes it looked like a shotgun, sometimes a two-handed sword. I didn't know what the humans were seeing in my hands, but I was pretty sure it wouldn't make them like me.

Ares turned to glare at our spectators, which gave me a moment to breathe. There were five police cars now, and a line of officers crouching behind them, pistols trained on us.

"This is a private matter!" Ares bellowed. "Be gone!"

He swept his hand, and a wall of red flame rolled across the patrol cars. The police barely had time to dive for cover before their vehicles exploded. The crowd behind them scattered, screaming.

Ares roared with laughter. "Now, little hero. Let's add you to the barbecue."

He slashed. I deflected his blade. I got close enough to strike, tried to fake him out with a feint, but my blow was knocked aside. The waves were hitting me in the back now. Ares was up to his thighs, wading in after me.

I felt the rhythm of the sea, the waves growing larger as the tide rolled in, and suddenly I had an idea. *Little waves*, I thought. And the water behind me seemed to recede. I was holding back the tide by force of will, but tension was building, like carbonation behind a cork.

Ares came toward, grinning confidently. I lowered my blade, as if I were too exhausted to go on. *Wait for it*, I told the sea. The pressure now was almost lifting me off my feet. Ares raised his sword. I released the tide and jumped, rocketing straight over Ares on a wave.

A six-foot wall of water smashed him full in the face, leaving him cursing and sputtering with a mouth full of seaweed. I landed behind him with a splash and feinted toward his head, as I'd done before. He turned in time to raise his sword, but this time he was disoriented, he didn't anticipate the trick. I changed direction, lunged to the side, and stabbed Riptide straight down into the water, sending the point through the god's heel.

The roar that followed made Hades's earthquake look like a minor event. The very sea was blasted back from Ares, leaving a wet circle of sand fifty feet wide.

Ichor, the golden blood of the gods, flowed from a gash in the war god's boot. The expression on his face was beyond hatred. It was pain, shock, complete disbelief that he'd been wounded.

He limped toward me, muttering ancient Greek curses.

Something stopped him.

It was as if a cloud covered the sun, but worse. Light faded. Sound and color drained away. A cold, heavy presence passed over the beach, slowing time, dropping the temperature to freezing, and making me feel like life was hopeless, fighting was useless.

The darkness lifted.

Ares looked stunned.

Police cars were burning behind us. The crowd of spectators had fled. Annabeth and Grover stood on the beach, in shock, watching the water flood back around Ares's feet, his glowing golden ichor dissipating in the tide.

Ares lowered his sword.

"You have made an enemy, godling," he told me. "You have sealed your fate. Every time you raise your blade in battle, every time you hope for success, you will feel my curse. Beware, Perseus Jackson. Beware."

His body began to glow.

"Percy!" Annabeth shouted. "Don't watch!"

I turned away as the god Ares revealed his true immortal form. I somehow knew that if I looked, I would disintegrate into ashes.

The light died.

I looked back. Ares was gone. The tide rolled out to reveal Hades's bronze helm of darkness. I picked it up and walked toward my friends.

But before I got there, I heard the flapping of leathery wings. Three evil-looking grandmothers with lace hats and fiery whips drifted down from the sky and landed in front of me.

The middle Fury, the one who had been Mrs. Dodds, stepped forward. Her fangs were bared, but for once she didn't look threatening. She looked more disappointed, as if she'd been planning to have me for supper, but had decided I might give her indigestion.

"We saw the whole thing," she hissed. "So . . . it truly was not you?"

I tossed her the helmet, which she caught in surprise.

"Return that to Lord Hades," I said. "Tell him the truth. Tell him to call off the war."

She hesitated, then ran a forked tongue over her green, leathery lips. "Live well, Percy Jackson. Become a true hero.

Because if you do not, if you ever come into my clutches again . . ."

She cackled, savoring the idea. Then she and her sisters rose on their bats' wings, fluttered into the smoke-filled sky, and disappeared.

I joined Grover and Annabeth, who were staring at me in amazement.

"Percy . . ." Grover said. "That was so incredibly . . ."

"Terrifying," said Annabeth.

"Cool!" Grover corrected.

I didn't feel terrified. I certainly didn't feel cool. I was tired and sore and completely drained of energy.

"Did you guys feel that . . . whatever it was?" I asked.

They both nodded uneasily.

"Must've been the Furies overhead," Grover said.

But I wasn't so sure. Something had stopped Ares from killing me, and whatever could do that was a lot stronger than the Furies.

I looked at Annabeth, and an understanding passed between us. I knew now what was in that pit, what had spoken from the entrance of Tartarus.

I reclaimed my backpack from Grover and looked inside. The master bolt was still there. Such a small thing to almost cause World War III.

"We have to get back to New York," I said. "By tonight."

"That's impossible," Annabeth said, "unless we—"

"Fly," I agreed.

She stared at me. "Fly, like, in an airplane, which you

were warned never to do lest Zeus strike you out of the sky, *and* carrying a weapon that has more destructive power than a nuclear bomb?"

"Yeah," I said. "Pretty much exactly like that. Come on."

It's funny how humans can wrap their mind around things and fit them into their version of reality. Chiron had told me that long ago. As usual, I didn't appreciate his wisdom until much later.

According to the L.A. news, the explosion at the Santa Monica beach had been caused when a crazy kidnapper fired a shotgun at a police car. He accidentally hit a gas main that had ruptured during the earthquake.

This crazy kidnapper (a.k.a. Ares) was the same man who had abducted me and two other adolescents in New York and brought us across country on a ten-day odyssey of terror.

Poor little Percy Jackson wasn't an international criminal after all. He'd caused a commotion on that Greyhound bus in New Jersey trying to get away from his captor (and afterward, witnesses would even swear they had seen the leather-clad man on the bus—"Why didn't I remember him before?"). The crazy man had caused the explosion in the St. Louis Arch. After all, no kid could've done that. A concerned waitress in Denver had seen the man threatening his abductees outside her diner, gotten a friend to take a photo, and notified the police. Finally, brave Percy Jackson (I was beginning to like this kid) had stolen a gun from his captor in Los Angeles and battled him shotgun-to-rifle on the beach. Police had arrived just in time. But in the spectacular explosion, five police cars had been destroyed and the captor had fled. No fatalities had occurred. Percy Jackson and his two friends were safely in police custody.

The reporters fed us this whole story. We just nodded and acted tearful and exhausted (which wasn't hard), and played victimized kids for the cameras.

"All I want," I said, choking back my tears, "is to see my loving stepfather again. Every time I saw him on TV, calling me a delinquent punk, I knew . . . somehow . . . we would be okay. And I know he'll want to reward each and every person in this beautiful city of Los Angeles with a free major appliance from his store. Here's the phone number." The police and reporters were so moved that they passed around the hat and raised money for three tickets on the next plane to New York.

I knew there was no choice but to fly. I hoped Zeus would cut me some slack, considering the circumstances. But it was still hard to force myself on board the flight.

Takeoff was a nightmare. Every spot of turbulence was scarier than a Greek monster. I didn't unclench my hands from the armrests until we touched down safely at La Guardia. The local press was waiting for us outside security, but we managed to evade them thanks to Annabeth, who lured them away in her invisible Yankees cap, shouting, "They're over by the frozen yogurt! Come on!," then rejoined us at baggage claim.

We split up at the taxi stand. I told Annabeth and Grover to get back to Half-Blood Hill and let Chiron know what had happened. They protested, and it was hard to let them go after all we'd been through, but I knew I had to do this last part of the quest by myself. If things went wrong, if the gods didn't believe me . . . I wanted Annabeth and Grover to survive to tell Chiron the truth.

I hopped in a taxi and headed into Manhattan.

Thirty minutes later, I walked into the lobby of the Empire State Building.

I must have looked like a homeless kid, with my tattered clothes and my scraped-up face. I hadn't slept in at least twenty-four hours.

I went up to the guard at the front desk and said, "Six hundredth floor."

He was reading a huge book with a picture of a wizard on the front. I wasn't much into fantasy, but the book must've been good, because the guard took a while to look up. "No such floor, kiddo."

"I need an audience with Zeus."

He gave me a vacant smile. "Sorry?"

"You heard me."

I was about to decide this guy was just a regular mortal, and I'd better run for it before he called the straitjacket patrol, when he said, "No appointment, no audience, kiddo. Lord Zeus doesn't see anyone unannounced."

"Oh, I think he'll make an exception." I slipped off my backpack and unzipped the top.

The guard looked inside at the metal cylinder, not getting what it was for a few seconds. Then his face went pale. "That isn't . . ."

"Yes, it is," I promised. "You want me take it out and—"

"No! No!" He scrambled out of his seat, fumbled around his desk for a key card, then handed it to me. "Insert this in the security slot. Make sure nobody else is in the elevator with you."

I did as he told me. As soon as the elevator doors closed, I slipped the key into the slot. The card disappeared and a new button appeared on the console, a red one that said 600.

I pressed it and waited, and waited.

Muzak played. "Raindrops keep falling on my head. . . ."

Finally, *ding*. The doors slid open. I stepped out and almost had a heart attack.

I was standing on a narrow stone walkway in the middle of the air. Below me was Manhattan, from the height of an airplane. In front of me, white marble steps wound up the spine of a cloud, into the sky. My eyes followed the stairway to its end, where my brain just could not accept what I saw.

Look again, my brain said.

We're looking, my eyes insisted. It's really there.

From the top of the clouds rose the decapitated peak of a mountain, its summit covered with snow. Clinging to the mountainside were dozens of multileveled palaces—a city of mansions—all with white-columned porticos, gilded terraces, and bronze braziers glowing with a thousand fires.

Roads wound crazily up to the peak, where the largest palace gleamed against the snow. Precariously perched gardens bloomed with olive trees and rosebushes. I could make out an open-air market filled with colorful tents, a stone amphitheater built on one side of the mountain, a hippodrome and a coliseum on the other. It was an Ancient Greek city, except it wasn't in ruins. It was new, and clean, and colorful, the way Athens must've looked twenty-five hundred years ago.

This place can't be here, I told myself. The tip of a mountain hanging over New York City like a billion-ton asteroid? How could something like that be anchored above the Empire State Building, in plain sight of millions of people, and not get noticed?

But here it was. And here I was.

My trip through Olympus was a daze. I passed some giggling wood nymphs who threw olives at me from their garden. Hawkers in the market offered to sell me ambrosia-on-a-stick, and a new shield, and a genuine glitter-weave replica of the Golden Fleece, as seen on Hephaestus-TV. The nine muses were tuning their instruments for a concert in the park while a small crowd gathered—satyrs and naiads and a bunch of good-looking teenagers who might've been minor gods and goddesses. Nobody seemed worried about an impending civil war. In fact, everybody seemed in a festive mood. Several of them turned to watch me pass, and whispered to themselves.

I climbed the main road, toward the big palace at the peak. It was a reverse copy of the palace in the Underworld.

There, everything had been black and bronze. Here, everything glittered white and silver.

I realized Hades must've built his palace to resemble this one. He wasn't welcomed in Olympus except on the winter solstice, so he'd built his own Olympus underground. Despite my bad experience with him, I felt a little sorry for the guy. To be banished from this place seemed really unfair. It would make anybody bitter.

Steps led up to a central courtyard. Past that, the throne room.

Room really isn't the right word. The place made Grand Central Station look like a broom closet. Massive columns rose to a domed ceiling, which was gilded with moving constellations.

Twelve thrones, built for beings the size of Hades, were arranged in an inverted U, just like the cabins at Camp Half-Blood. An enormous fire crackled in the central hearth pit. The thrones were empty except for two at the end: the head throne on the right, and the one to its immediate left. I didn't have to be told who the two gods were that were sitting there, waiting for me to approach. I came toward them, my legs trembling.

The gods were in giant human form, as Hades had been, but I could barely look at them without feeling a tingle, as if my body were starting to burn. Zeus, the Lord of the Gods, wore a dark blue pinstriped suit. He sat on a simple throne of solid platinum. He had a well-trimmed beard, marbled gray and black like a storm cloud. His face was proud and handsome and grim, his eyes rainy gray.

As I got nearer to him, the air crackled and smelled of ozone.

The god sitting next to him was his brother, without a doubt, but he was dressed very differently. He reminded me of a beachcomber from Key West. He wore leather sandals, khaki Bermuda shorts, and a Tommy Bahama shirt with coconuts and parrots all over it. His skin was deeply tanned, his hands scarred like an old-time fisherman's. His hair was black, like mine. His face had that same brooding look that had always gotten me branded a rebel. But his eyes, sea-green like mine, were surrounded by sun-crinkles that told me he smiled a lot, too.

His throne was a deep-sea fisherman's chair. It was the simple swiveling kind, with a black leather seat and a built-in holster for a fishing pole. Instead of a pole, the holster held a bronze trident, flickering with green light around the tips.

The gods weren't moving or speaking, but there was tension in the air, as if they'd just finished an argument.

I approached the fisherman's throne and knelt at his feet. "Father." I dared not look up. My heart was racing. I could feel the energy emanating from the two gods. If I said the wrong thing, I had no doubt they could blast me into dust.

To my left, Zeus spoke. "Should you not address the master of this house first, boy?"

I kept my head down, and waited.

"Peace, brother," Poseidon finally said. His voice stirred my oldest memories: that warm glow I remembered as a baby, the sensation of this god's hand on my forehead. "The boy defers to his father. This is only right."

"You still claim him then?" Zeus asked, menacingly. "You claim this child whom you sired against our sacred oath?"

"I have admitted my wrongdoing," Poseidon said. "Now I would hear him speak."

Wrongdoing.

A lump welled up in my throat. Was that all I was? A wrongdoing? The result of a god's mistake?

"I have spared him once already," Zeus grumbled. "Daring to fly through my domain . . . pah! I should have blasted him out of the sky for his impudence."

"And risk destroying your own master bolt?" Poseidon asked calmly. "Let us hear him out, brother."

Zeus grumbled some more. "I shall listen," he decided. "Then I shall make up my mind whether or not to cast this boy down from Olympus."

"Perseus," Poseidon said. "Look at me."

I did, and I wasn't sure what I saw in his face. There was no clear sign of love or approval. Nothing to encourage me. It was like looking at the ocean: some days, you could tell what mood it was in. Most days, though, it was unreadable, mysterious.

I got the feeling Poseidon really didn't know what to think of me. He didn't know whether he was happy to have me as a son or not. In a strange way, I was glad that Poseidon was so distant. If he'd tried to apologize, or told me he loved me, or even smiled, it would've felt fake. Like a human dad, making some lame excuse for not being around. I could live with that. After all, I wasn't sure about him yet, either.

"Address Lord Zeus, boy," Poseidon told me. "Tell him your story."

So I told Zeus everything, just as it had happened. I took out the metal cylinder, which began sparking in the Sky God's presence, and laid it at his feet.

There was a long silence, broken only by the crackle of the hearth fire.

Zeus opened his palm. The lightning bolt flew into it. As he closed his fist, the metallic points flared with electricity, until he was holding what looked more like the classic thunderbolt, a twenty-foot javelin of arcing, hissing energy that made the hairs on my scalp rise.

"I sense the boy tells the truth," Zeus muttered. "But that Ares would do such a thing . . . it is most unlike him."

"He is proud and impulsive," Poseidon said. "It runs in the family."

"Lord?" I asked.

They both said, "Yes?"

"Ares didn't act alone. Someone else—something else— came up with the idea."

I described my dreams, and the feeling I'd had on the beach, that momentary breath of evil that had seemed to stop the world, and made Ares back off from killing me.

"In the dreams," I said, "the voice told me to bring the bolt to the Underworld. Ares hinted that he'd been having dreams, too. I think he was being used, just as I was, to start a war."

"You are accusing Hades, after all?" Zeus asked.

"No," I said. "I mean, Lord Zeus, I've been in the presence of Hades. This feeling on the beach was different. It was the same thing I felt when I got close to that pit. That was the entrance to Tartarus, wasn't it? Something powerful and evil is stirring down there . . . something even older than the gods."

Poseidon and Zeus looked at each other. They had a quick, intense discussion in Ancient Greek. I only caught one word. *Father.*

Poseidon made some kind of suggestion, but Zeus cut him off. Poseidon tried to argue. Zeus held up his hand angrily. "We will speak of this no more," Zeus said. "I must go personally to purify this thunderbolt in the waters of Lemnos, to remove the human taint from its metal."

He rose and looked at me. His expression softened just a fraction of a degree. "You have done me a service, boy. Few heroes could have accomplished as much."

"I had help, sir," I said. "Grover Underwood and Annabeth Chase—"

"To show you my thanks, I shall spare your life. I do not trust you, Perseus Jackson. I do not like what your arrival means for the future of Olympus. But for the sake of peace in the family, I shall let you live."

"Um . . . thank you, sir."

"Do not presume to fly again. Do not let me find you

here when I return. Otherwise you shall taste this bolt. And it shall be your last sensation."

Thunder shook the palace. With a blinding flash of lightning, Zeus was gone.

I was alone in the throne room with my father.

"Your uncle," Poseidon sighed, "has always had a flair for dramatic exits. I think he would've done well as the god of theater."

An uncomfortable silence.

"Sir," I said, "what was in that pit?"

Poseidon regarded me. "Have you not guessed?"

"Kronos," I said. "The king of the Titans."

Even in the throne room of Olympus, far away from Tartarus, the name *Kronos* darkened the room, made the hearth fire seem not quite so warm on my back.

Poseidon gripped his trident. "In the First War, Percy, Zeus cut our father Kronos into a thousand pieces, just as Kronos had done to his own father, Ouranos. Zeus cast Kronos's remains into the darkest pit of Tartarus. The Titan army was scattered, their mountain fortress on Etna destroyed, their monstrous allies driven to the farthest corners of the earth. And yet Titans cannot die, any more than we gods can. Whatever is left of Kronos is still alive in some hideous way, still conscious in his eternal pain, still hungering for power."

"He's healing," I said. "He's coming back."

Poseidon shook his head. "From time to time, over the eons, Kronos has stirred. He enters men's nightmares and breathes evil thoughts. He wakens restless monsters from the depths. But to suggest he could rise from the pit is another thing."

"That's what he intends, Father. That's what he said."

Poseidon was silent for a long time.

"Lord Zeus has closed discussion on this matter. He will not allow talk of Kronos. You have completed your quest, child. That is all you need to do."

"But—" I stopped myself. Arguing would do no good. It would very possibly anger the only god who I had on my side. "As . . . as you wish, Father."

A faint smile played on his lips. "Obedience does not come naturally to you, does it?"

"No . . . sir."

"I must take some blame for that, I suppose. The sea does not like to be restrained." He rose to his full height and took up his trident. Then he shimmered and became the size of a regular man, standing directly in front of me. "You must go, child. But first, know that your mother has returned."

I stared at him, completely stunned. "My mother?"

"You will find her at home. Hades sent her when you recovered his helm. Even the Lord of Death pays his debts."

My heart was pounding. I couldn't believe it. "Do you . . . would you . . ."

I wanted to ask if Poseidon would come with me to see her, but then I realized that was ridiculous. I imagined loading the God of the Sea into a taxi and taking him to the Upper East Side. If he'd wanted to see my mom all these years, he would have. And there was Smelly Gabe to think about.

Poseidon's eyes took on a little sadness. "When you return home, Percy, you must make an important choice. You will find a package waiting in your room."

"A package?"

"You will understand when you see it. No one can choose your path, Percy. You must decide."

I nodded, though I didn't know what he meant.

"Your mother is a queen among women," Poseidon said wistfully. "I had not met such a mortal woman in a thousand years. Still . . . I am sorry you were born, child. I have brought you a hero's fate, and a hero's fate is never happy. It is never anything but tragic."

I tried not to feel hurt. Here was my own dad, telling me he was sorry I'd been born. "I don't mind, Father."

"Not yet, perhaps," he said. "Not yet. But it was an unforgivable mistake on my part."

"I'll leave you then." I bowed awkwardly. "I—I won't bother you again."

I was five steps away when he called, "Perseus."

I turned.

There was a different light in his eyes, a fiery kind of pride. "You did well, Perseus. Do not misunderstand me. Whatever else you do, know that you are mine. You are a true son of the Sea God."

As I walked back through the city of the gods, conversations stopped. The muses paused their concert. People and satyrs and naiads all turned toward me, their faces filled with respect and gratitude, and as I passed, they knelt, as if I were some kind of hero.

* * *

Fifteen minutes later, still in a trance, I was back on the streets of Manhattan.

I caught a taxi to my mom's apartment, rang the doorbell, and there she was—my beautiful mother, smelling of peppermint and licorice, the weariness and worry evaporating from her face as soon as she saw me.

"Percy! Oh, thank goodness. Oh, my baby."

She crushed the air right out of me. We stood in the hallway as she cried and ran her hands through my hair.

I'll admit it—my eyes were a little misty, too. I was shaking, I was so relieved to see her.

She told me she'd just appeared at the apartment that morning, scaring Gabe half out of his wits. She didn't remember anything since the Minotaur, and couldn't believe it when Gabe told her I was a wanted criminal, traveling across the country, blowing up national monuments. She'd been going out of her mind with worry all day because she hadn't heard the news. Gabe had forced her to go into work, saying she had a month's salary to make up and she'd better get started.

I swallowed back my anger and told her my own story. I tried to make it sound less scary than it had been, but that wasn't easy. I was just getting to the fight with Ares when Gabe's voice interrupted from the living room. "Hey, Sally! That meat loaf done yet or what?"

She closed her eyes. "He isn't going to be happy to see you, Percy. The store got half a million phone calls today from Los Angeles . . . something about free appliances."

"Oh, yeah. About that . . ."

She managed a weak smile. "Just don't make him angrier, all right? Come on."

In the month I'd been gone, the apartment had turned into Gabeland. Garbage was ankle deep on the carpet. The sofa had been reupholstered in beer cans. Dirty socks and underwear hung off the lampshades.

Gabe and three of his big goony friends were playing poker at the table.

When Gabe saw me, his cigar dropped out of his mouth. His face got redder than lava. "You got nerve coming here, you little punk. I thought the police—"

"He's not a fugitive after all," my mom interjected. "Isn't that wonderful, Gabe?"

Gabe looked back and forth between us. He didn't seem to think my homecoming was so wonderful.

"Bad enough I had to give back your life insurance money, Sally," he growled. "Get me the phone. I'll call the cops."

"Gabe, no!"

He raised his eyebrows. "Did you just say 'no'? You think I'm gonna put up with this punk again? I can still press charges against him for ruining my Camaro."

"But—"

He raised his hand, and my mother flinched.

For the first time, I realized something. Gabe had hit my mother. I didn't know when, or how much. But I was sure he'd done it. Maybe it had been going on for years, when I wasn't around.

A balloon of anger started expanding in my chest. I came toward Gabe, instinctively taking my pen out of my pocket.

He just laughed. "What, punk? You gonna write on me? You touch me, and you are going to jail forever, you understand?"

"Hey, Gabe," his friend Eddie interrupted. "He's just a kid."

Gabe looked at him resentfully and mimicked in a falsetto voice: *"Just a kid."*

His other friends laughed like idiots.

"I'll be nice to you, punk." Gabe showed me his tobacco-stained teeth. "I'll give you five minutes to get your stuff and clear out. After that, I call the police."

"Gabe!" my mother pleaded.

"He ran away," Gabe told her. "Let him stay gone."

I was itching to uncap Riptide, but even if I did, the blade wouldn't hurt humans. And Gabe, by the loosest definition, was human.

My mother took my arm. "Please, Percy. Come on. We'll go to your room."

I let her pull me away, my hands still trembling with rage.

My room had been completely filled with Gabe's junk. There were stacks of used car batteries, a rotting bouquet of sympathy flowers with a card from somebody who'd seen his Barbara Walters interview.

"Gabe is just upset, honey," my mother told me. "I'll talk to him later. I'm sure it will work out."

"Mom, it'll never work out. Not as long as Gabe's here."

She wrung her hands nervously. "I can . . . I'll take you to work with me for the rest of the summer. In the fall, maybe there's another boarding school—"

"Mom."

She lowered her eyes. "I'm trying, Percy. I just . . . I need some time."

A package appeared on my bed. At least, I could've sworn it hadn't been there a moment before.

It was a battered cardboard box about the right size to fit a basketball. The address on the mailing slip was in my own handwriting:

The Gods
Mount Olympus
600th Floor,
Empire State Building
New York, NY

With best wishes,
PERCY JACKSON

Over the top in black marker, in a man's clear, bold print, was the address of our apartment, and the words: RETURN TO SENDER.

Suddenly I understood what Poseidon had told me on Olympus.

A package. A decision.

Whatever else you do, know that you are mine. You are a true son of the Sea God.

I looked at my mother. "Mom, do you want Gabe gone?"

"Percy, it isn't that simple. I—"

"Mom, just tell me. That jerk has been hitting you. Do you want him gone or not?"

She hesitated, then nodded almost imperceptibly. "Yes, Percy. I do. And I'm trying to get up my courage to tell him. But you can't do this for me. You can't solve my problems."

I looked at the box.

I *could* solve her problem. I wanted to slice that package open, plop it on the poker table, and take out what was inside. I could start my very own statue garden, right there in the living room.

That's what a Greek hero would do in the stories, I thought. That's what Gabe deserves.

But a hero's story always ended in tragedy. Poseidon had told me that.

I remembered the Underworld. I thought about Gabe's spirit drifting forever in the Fields of Asphodel, or condemned to some hideous torture behind the barbed wire of the Fields of Punishment—an eternal poker game, sitting up to his waist in boiling oil listening to opera music. Did I have the right to send someone there? Even Gabe?

A month ago, I wouldn't have hesitated. Now . . .

"I can do it," I told my mom. "One look inside this box, and he'll never bother you again."

She glanced at the package, and seemed to understand immediately. "No, Percy," she said, stepping away. "You can't."

"Poseidon called you a queen," I told her. "He said he hadn't met a woman like you in a thousand years."

Her cheeks flushed. "Percy—"

"You deserve better than this, Mom. You should go to college, get your degree. You can write your novel, meet a nice guy maybe, live in a nice house. You don't need to protect me anymore by staying with Gabe. Let me get rid of him."

She wiped a tear off her cheek. "You sound so much like your father," she said. "He offered to stop the tide for me once. He offered to build me a palace at the bottom of the sea. He thought he could solve all my problems with a wave of his hand."

"What's wrong with that?"

Her multicolored eyes seemed to search inside me. "I think you know, Percy. I think you're enough like me to understand. If my life is going to mean anything, I have to live it myself. I can't let a god take care of me . . . or my son. I have to . . . find the courage on my own. Your quest has reminded me of that."

We listened to the sound of poker chips and swearing, ESPN from the living room television.

"I'll leave the box," I said. "If he threatens you . . ."

She looked pale, but she nodded. "Where will you go, Percy?"

"Half-Blood Hill."

"For the summer . . . or forever?"

"I guess that depends."

We locked eyes, and I sensed that we had an agreement.

We would see how things stood at the end of the summer.

She kissed my forehead. "You'll be a hero, Percy. You'll be the greatest of all."

I took one last look around my bedroom. I had a feeling I'd never see it again. Then I walked with my mother to the front door.

"Leaving so soon, punk?" Gabe called after me. "Good riddance."

I had one last twinge of doubt. How could I turn down the perfect chance to take revenge on him? I was leaving here without saving my mother.

"Hey, Sally," he yelled. "What about that meat loaf, huh?"

A steely look of anger flared in my mother's eyes, and I thought, just maybe, I was leaving her in good hands after all. Her own.

"The meat loaf is coming right up, dear," she told Gabe. "Meat loaf surprise."

She looked at me, and winked.

The last thing I saw as the door swung closed was my mother staring at Gabe, as if she were contemplating how he would look as a garden statue.

22 ⚡ THE PROPHECY COMES TRUE

We were the first heroes to return alive to Half-Blood Hill since Luke, so of course everybody treated us as if we'd won some reality-TV contest. According to camp tradition, we wore laurel wreaths to a big feast prepared in our honor, then led a procession down to the bonfire, where we got to burn the burial shrouds our cabins had made for us in our absence.

Annabeth's shroud was so beautiful—gray silk with embroidered owls—I told her it seemed a shame not to bury her in it. She punched me and told me to shut up.

Being the son of Poseidon, I didn't have any cabin mates, so the Ares cabin had volunteered to make my shroud. They'd taken an old bedsheet and painted smiley faces with X'ed-out eyes around the border, and the word LOSER painted really big in the middle.

It was fun to burn.

As Apollo's cabin led the sing-along and passed out s'mores, I was surrounded by my old Hermes cabinmates, Annabeth's friends from Athena, and Grover's satyr buddies, who were admiring the brand-new searcher's license he'd received from the Council of Cloven Elders. The council had called Grover's performance on the quest "Brave to the point of indigestion. Horns-and-whiskers above anything we have seen in the past."

The only ones not in a party mood were Clarisse and her cabinmates, whose poisonous looks told me they'd never forgive me for disgracing their dad.

That was okay with me.

Even Dionysus's welcome-home speech wasn't enough to dampen my spirits. "Yes, yes, so the little brat didn't get himself killed and now he'll have an even bigger head. Well, huzzah for that. In other announcements, there will be *no* canoe races this Saturday. . . ."

I moved back into cabin three, but it didn't feel so lonely anymore. I had my friends to train with during the day. At night, I lay awake and listened to the sea, knowing my father was out there. Maybe he wasn't quite sure about me yet, maybe he hadn't even wanted me born, but he was watching. And so far, he was proud of what I'd done.

As for my mother, she had a chance at a new life. Her letter arrived a week after I got back to camp. She told me Gabe had left mysteriously—disappeared off the face of the planet, in fact. She'd reported him missing to the police, but she had a funny feeling they would never find him.

On a completely unrelated subject, she'd sold her first life-size concrete sculpture, entitled *The Poker Player*, to a collector, through an art gallery in Soho. She'd gotten so much money for it, she'd put a deposit down on a new apartment and made a payment on her first semester's tuition at NYU. The Soho gallery was clamoring for more of her work, which they called "a huge step forward in super-ugly neorealism."

But don't worry, my mom wrote. *I'm done with sculpture. I've disposed of that box of tools you left me. It's time for me to turn to writing.*

At the bottom, she wrote a P.S.: *Percy, I've found a good private school here in the city. I've put a deposit down to hold you a spot, in case you want to enroll for seventh grade. You could live at home. But if you want to go year-round at Half-Blood Hill, I'll understand.*

I folded the note carefully and set it on my bedside table. Every night before I went to sleep, I read it again, and I tried to decide how to answer her.

On the Fourth of July, the whole camp gathered at the beach for a fireworks display by cabin nine. Being Hephaestus's kids, they weren't going to settle for a few lame red-white-and-blue explosions. They'd anchored a barge offshore and loaded it with rockets the size of Patriot missiles. According to Annabeth, who'd seen the show before, the blasts would be sequenced so tightly they'd look like frames of animation across the sky. The finale was supposed to be a couple of hundred-foot-tall Spartan warriors who would crackle to life above the ocean, fight a battle, then explode into a million colors.

As Annabeth and I were spreading a picnic blanket, Grover showed up to tell us good-bye. He was dressed in his usual jeans and T-shirt and sneakers, but in the last few weeks he'd started to look older, almost high-school age. His goatee had gotten thicker. He'd put on weight. His horns had grown at least an inch, so he now had to wear his rasta cap all the time to pass as human.

"I'm off," he said. "I just came to say . . . well, you know."

I tried to feel happy for him. After all, it wasn't every day a satyr got permission to go look for the great god Pan. But it was hard saying good-bye. I'd only known Grover a year, yet he was my oldest friend.

Annabeth gave him a hug. She told him to keep his fake feet on.

I asked him where he was going to search first.

"Kind of a secret," he said, looking embarrassed. "I wish you could come with me, guys, but humans and Pan . . ."

"We understand," Annabeth said. "You got enough tin cans for the trip?"

"Yeah."

"And you remembered your reed pipes?"

"Jeez, Annabeth," he grumbled. "You're like an old mama goat."

But he didn't really sound annoyed.

He gripped his walking stick and slung a backpack over his shoulder. He looked like any hitchhiker you might see on an American highway—nothing like the little runty boy I used to defend from bullies at Yancy Academy.

"Well," he said, "wish me luck."

He gave Annabeth another hug. He clapped me on the shoulder, then headed back through the dunes.

Fireworks exploded to life overhead: Hercules killing

the Nemean lion, Artemis chasing the boar, George Washington (who, by the way, was a son of Athena) crossing the Delaware.

"Hey, Grover," I called.

He turned at the edge of the woods.

"Wherever you're going—I hope they make good enchiladas."

Grover grinned, and then he was gone, the trees closing around him.

"We'll see him again," Annabeth said.

I tried to believe it. The fact that no searcher had ever come back in two thousand years . . . well, I decided not to think about that. Grover would be the first. He had to be.

July passed.

I spent my days devising new strategies for capture-the-flag and making alliances with the other cabins to keep the banner out of Ares's hands. I got to the top of the climbing wall for the first time without getting scorched by lava.

From time to time, I'd walk past the Big House, glance up at the attic windows, and think about the Oracle. I tried to convince myself that its prophecy had come to completion.

You shall go west, and face the god who has turned.

Been there, done that—even though the traitor god had turned out to be Ares rather than Hades.

You shall find what was stolen, and see it safe returned.

Check. One master bolt delivered. One helm of darkness back on Hades's oily head.

You shall be betrayed by one who calls you a friend.

This line still bothered me. Ares had pretended to be my friend, then betrayed me. That must be what the Oracle meant. . . .

And you shall fail to save what matters most, in the end.

I *had* failed to save my mom, but only because I'd let her save herself, and I knew that was the right thing.

So why was I still uneasy?

The last night of the summer session came all too quickly.

The campers had one last meal together. We burned part of our dinner for the gods. At the bonfire, the senior counselors awarded the end-of-summer beads.

I got my own leather necklace, and when I saw the bead for my first summer, I was glad the firelight covered my blushing. The design was pitch black, with a sea-green trident shimmering in the center.

"The choice was unanimous," Luke announced. "This bead commemorates the first Son of the Sea God at this camp, and the quest he undertook into the darkest part of the Underworld to stop a war!"

The entire camp got to their feet and cheered. Even Ares's cabin felt obliged to stand. Athena's cabin steered Annabeth to the front so she could share in the applause.

I'm not sure I'd ever felt as happy or sad as I did at that moment. I'd finally found a family, people who cared about me and thought I'd done something right. And in the morning, most of them would be leaving for the year.

* * *

The next morning, I found a form letter on my bedside table.

I knew Dionysus must've filled it out, because he stubbornly insisted on getting my name wrong:

Dear _____ Peter Johnson _____,

    If you intend to stay at Camp Half-Blood year-round, you must inform the Big House by noon today. If you do not announce your intentions, we will assume you have vacated your cabin or died a horrible death. Cleaning harpies will begin work at sundown. They will be authorized to eat any unregistered campers. All personal articles left behind will be incinerated in the lava pit.

    Have a nice day!

    Mr. D (Dionysus)

    Camp Director, Olympian Council #12

That's another thing about ADHD. Deadlines just aren't real to me until I'm staring one in the face. Summer was over, and I still hadn't answered my mother, or the camp, about whether I'd be staying. Now I had only a few hours to decide.

The decision should have been easy. I mean, nine months of hero training or nine months of sitting in a classroom—duh.

But there was my mom to consider. For the first time, I had the chance to live with her for a whole year, without Gabe. I had a chance be at home and knock around the city in my free time. I remembered what Annabeth had said so long ago on our quest: *The real world is where the monsters are. That's where you learn whether you're any good or not.*

I thought about the fate of Thalia, daughter of Zeus. I wondered how many monsters would attack me if I left Half-Blood Hill. If I stayed in one place for a whole school year, without Chiron or my friends around to help me, would my mother and I even survive until the next summer? That was assuming the spelling tests and five-paragraph essays didn't kill me. I decided I'd go down to the arena and do some sword practice. Maybe that would clear my head.

The campgrounds were mostly deserted, shimmering in the August heat. All the campers were in their cabins packing up, or running around with brooms and mops, getting ready for final inspection. Argus was helping some of the Aphrodite kids haul their Gucci suitcases and makeup kits over the hill, where the camp's shuttle bus would be waiting to take them to the airport.

Don't think about leaving yet, I told myself. Just train.

I got to the sword-fighters arena and found that Luke had had the same idea. His gym bag was plopped at the edge of the stage. He was working solo, whaling on battle dummies with a sword I'd never seen before. It must've been a regular steel blade, because he was slashing the dummies' heads right off, stabbing through their straw-stuffed guts. His orange counselor's shirt was dripping with sweat. His expression was so intense, his life might've really been in danger. I watched, fascinated, as he disemboweled the whole row of dummies, hacking off limbs and basically reducing them to a pile of straw and armor.

They were only dummies, but I still couldn't help being awed by Luke's skill. The guy was an incredible fighter. It made me wonder, again, how he possibly could've failed at his quest.

Finally, he saw me, and stopped mid-swing. "Percy."

"Um, sorry," I said, embarrassed. "I just—"

"It's okay," he said, lowering his sword. "Just doing some last-minute practice."

"Those dummies won't be bothering anybody anymore."

Luke shrugged. "We build new ones every summer."

Now that his sword wasn't swirling around, I could see something odd about it. The blade was two different types of metal—one edge bronze, the other steel.

Luke noticed me looking at it. "Oh, this? New toy. This is Backbiter."

"Backbiter?"

Luke turned the blade in the light so it glinted wickedly. "One side is celestial bronze. The other is tempered steel. Works on mortals and immortals both."

I thought about what Chiron had told me when I started my quest—that a hero should never harm mortals unless absolutely necessary.

"I didn't know they could make weapons like that."

"*They* probably can't," Luke agreed. "It's one of a kind."

He gave me a tiny smile, then slid the sword into its scabbard. "Listen, I was going to come looking for you.

What do you say we go down to the woods one last time, look for something to fight?"

I don't know why I hesitated. I should've felt relieved that Luke was being so friendly. Ever since I'd gotten back from the quest, he'd been acting a little distant. I was afraid he might resent me for all the attention I'd gotten.

"You think it's a good idea?" I asked. "I mean—"

"Aw, come on." He rummaged in his gym bag and pulled out a six-pack of Cokes. "Drinks are on me."

I stared at the Cokes, wondering where the heck he'd gotten them. There were no regular mortal sodas at the camp store. No way to smuggle them in unless you talked to a satyr, maybe.

Of course, the magic dinner goblets would fill with anything you want, but it just didn't taste the same as a real Coke, straight out of the can.

Sugar and caffeine. My willpower crumbled.

"Sure," I decided. "Why not?"

We walked down to the woods and kicked around for some kind of monster to fight, but it was too hot. All the monsters with any sense must've been taking siestas in their nice cool caves.

We found a shady spot by the creek where I'd broken Clarisse's spear during my first capture the flag game. We sat on a big rock, drank our Cokes, and watched the sunlight in the woods.

After a while Luke said, "You miss being on a quest?"

"With monsters attacking me every three feet? Are you kidding?"

Luke raised an eyebrow.

"Yeah, I miss it," I admitted. "You?"

A shadow passed over his face.

I was used to hearing from the girls how good-looking Luke was, but at the moment, he looked weary, and angry, and not at all handsome. His blond hair was gray in the sunlight. The scar on his face looked deeper than usual. I could imagine him as an old man.

"I've lived at Half-Blood Hill year-round since I was fourteen," he told me. "Ever since Thalia . . . well, you know. I trained, and trained, and trained. I never got to be a normal teenager, out there in the real world. Then they threw me one quest, and when I came back, it was like, 'Okay, ride's over. Have a nice life.'"

He crumpled his Coke can and threw into the creek, which really shocked me. One of the first things you learn at Camp Half-Blood is: Don't litter. You'll hear from the nymphs and the naiads. They'll get even. You'll crawl into bed one night and find your sheets filled with centipedes and mud.

"The heck with laurel wreaths," Luke said. "I'm not going to end up like those dusty trophies in the Big House attic."

"You make it sound like you're leaving."

Luke gave me a twisted smile. "Oh, I'm leaving, all right, Percy. I brought you down here to say good-bye."

He snapped his fingers. A small fire burned a hole in the ground at my feet. Out crawled something glistening black, about the size of my hand. A scorpion.

I started to go for my pen.

"I wouldn't," Luke cautioned. "Pit scorpions can jump up to fifteen feet. Its stinger can pierce right through your clothes. You'll be dead in sixty seconds."

"Luke, what—"

Then it hit me.

You will be betrayed by one who calls you a friend.

"You," I said.

He stood calmly and brushed off his jeans.

The scorpion paid him no attention. It kept its beady black eyes on me, clamping its pincers as it crawled onto my shoe.

"I saw a lot out there in the world, Percy," Luke said. "Didn't you feel it—the darkness gathering, the monsters growing stronger? Didn't you realize how useless it all is? All the heroics—being pawns of the gods. They should've been overthrown thousands of years ago, but they've hung on, thanks to us half-bloods."

I couldn't believe this was happening.

"Luke . . . you're talking about our parents," I said.

He laughed. "That's supposed to make me love them? Their precious 'Western civilization' is a disease, Percy. It's killing the world. The only way to stop it is to burn it to the ground, start over with something more honest."

"You're as crazy as Ares."

His eyes flared. "Ares is a fool. He never realized the true master he was serving. If I had time, Percy, I could explain. But I'm afraid you won't live that long."

The scorpion crawled onto my pants leg.

There had to be a way out of this. I needed time to think.

"Kronos," I said. "That's who you serve."

The air got colder.

"You should be careful with names," Luke warned.

"Kronos got you to steal the master bolt and the helm. He spoke to you in your dreams."

Luke's eye twitched. "He spoke to you, too, Percy. You should've listened."

"He's brainwashing you, Luke."

"You're wrong. He showed me that my talents are being wasted. You know what my quest was two years ago, Percy? My father, Hermes, wanted me to steal a golden apple from the Garden of the Hesperides and return it to Olympus. After all the training I'd done, *that* was the best he could think up."

"That's not an easy quest," I said. "Hercules did it."

"Exactly," Luke said. "Where's the glory in repeating what others have done? All the gods know how to do is replay their past. My heart wasn't in it. The dragon in the garden gave me this"—he pointed angrily at his scar—"and when I came back, all I got was pity. I wanted to pull Olympus down stone by stone right then, but I bided my time. I began to dream of Kronos. He convinced me to steal something worthwhile, something no hero had ever had the courage to take. When we went on that winter-solstice field trip, while the other campers were asleep, I snuck into the throne room and took Zeus's master bolt right from his chair. Hades's helm of darkness, too. You wouldn't believe how easy it was. The Olympians are so arrogant; they never dreamed someone would dare steal from them. Their security is horrible. I was halfway across New Jersey before I heard the storms rumbling, and I knew they'd discovered my theft."

The scorpion was sitting on my knee now, staring at me with its glittering eyes. I tried to keep my voice level. "So why didn't you bring the items to Kronos?"

Luke's smile wavered. "I . . . I got overconfident. Zeus sent out his sons and daughters to find the stolen bolt—Artemis, Apollo, my father, Hermes. But it was Ares who caught me. I could have beaten him, but I wasn't careful enough. He disarmed me, took the items of power, threatened to return them to Olympus and burn me alive. Then Kronos's voice came to me and told me what to say. I put the idea in Ares's head about a great war between the gods. I said all he had to do was hide the items away for a while and watch the others fight. Ares got a wicked gleam in his eyes. I knew he was hooked. He let me go, and I returned to Olympus before anyone noticed my absence." Luke drew his new sword. He ran his thumb down the flat of the blade, as if he were hypnotized by its beauty. "Afterward, the Lord of the Titans . . . h-he punished me with nightmares. I swore not to fail again. Back at Camp Half-Blood, in my dreams, I was told that a second hero would arrive, one who could be tricked into taking the bolt and the helm the rest of the way—from Ares down to Tartarus."

"*You* summoned the hellhound, that night in the forest."

"We had to make Chiron think the camp wasn't safe for

you, so he would start you on your quest. We had to confirm his fears that Hades was after you. And it worked."

"The flying shoes were cursed," I said. "They were supposed to drag me and the backpack into Tartarus."

"And they would have, if you'd been wearing them. But you gave them to the satyr, which wasn't part of the plan. Grover messes up everything he touches. He even confused the curse."

Luke looked down at the scorpion, which was now sitting on my thigh. "You should have died in Tartarus, Percy. But don't worry, I'll leave you with my little friend to set things right."

"Thalia gave her life to save you," I said, gritting my teeth. "And this is how you repay her?"

"Don't speak of Thalia!" he shouted. "The gods *let* her die! That's one of the many things they will pay for."

"You're being used, Luke. You and Ares both. Don't listen to Kronos."

"*I've* been used?" Luke's voice turned shrill. "Look at yourself. What has your dad ever done for you? Kronos will rise. You've only delayed his plans. He will cast the Olympians into Tartarus and drive humanity back to their caves. All except the strongest—the ones who serve him."

"Call off the bug," I said. "If you're so strong, fight me yourself."

Luke smiled. "Nice try, Percy. But I'm not Ares. You can't bait me. My lord is waiting, and he's got plenty of quests for me to undertake."

"Luke—"

"Good-bye, Percy. There is a new Golden Age coming. You won't be part of it."

He slashed his sword in an arc and disappeared in a ripple of darkness.

The scorpion lunged.

I swatted it away with my hand and uncapped my sword. The thing jumped at me and I cut it in half in midair.

I was about to congratulate myself until I looked down at my hand. My palm had a huge red welt, oozing and smoking with yellow guck. The thing had gotten me after all.

My ears pounded. My vision went foggy. The water, I thought. It healed me before.

I stumbled to the creek and submerged my hand, but nothing seemed to happen. The poison was too strong. My vision was getting dark. I could barely stand up.

Sixty seconds, Luke had told me.

I had to get back to camp. If I collapsed out here, my body would be dinner for a monster. Nobody would ever know what had happened.

My legs felt like lead. My forehead was burning. I stumbled toward the camp, and the nymphs stirred from their trees.

"Help," I croaked. "Please . . ."

Two of them took my arms, pulling me along. I remember making it to the clearing, a counselor shouting for help, a centaur blowing a conch horn.

Then everything went black.

* * *

I woke with a drinking straw in my mouth. I was sipping something that tasted like liquid chocolate-chip cookies. Nectar.

I opened my eyes.

I was propped up in bed in the sickroom of the Big House, my right hand bandaged like a club. Argus stood guard in the corner. Annabeth sat next to me, holding my nectar glass and dabbing a washcloth on my forehead.

"Here we are again," I said.

"You idiot," Annabeth said, which is how I knew she was overjoyed to see me conscious. "You were green and turning gray when we found you. If it weren't for Chiron's healing . . ."

"Now, now," Chiron's voice said. "Percy's constitution deserves some of the credit."

He was sitting near the foot of my bed in human form, which was why I hadn't noticed him yet. His lower half was magically compacted into the wheelchair, his upper half dressed in a coat and tie. He smiled, but his face looked weary and pale, the way it did when he'd been up all night grading Latin papers.

"How are you feeling?" he asked.

"Like my insides have been frozen, then microwaved."

"Apt, considering that was pit scorpion venom. Now you must tell me, if you can, exactly what happened."

Between sips of nectar, I told them the story.

The room was quiet for a long time.

"I can't believe that Luke . . ." Annabeth's voice faltered. Her expression turned angry and sad. "Yes. Yes, I *can* believe it. May the gods curse him. . . . He was never the same after his quest."

"This must be reported to Olympus," Chiron murmured. "I will go at once."

"Luke is out there right now," I said. "I have to go after him."

Chiron shook his head. "No, Percy. The gods—"

"Won't even *talk* about Kronos," I snapped. "Zeus declared the matter closed!"

"Percy, I know this is hard. But you must not rush out for vengeance. You aren't ready."

I didn't like it, but part of me suspected Chiron was right. One look at my hand, and I knew I wasn't going to be sword fighting any time soon. "Chiron . . . your prophecy from the Oracle . . . it was about Kronos, wasn't it? Was I in it? And Annabeth?"

Chiron glanced nervously at the ceiling. "Percy, it isn't my place—"

"You've been ordered not to talk to me about it, haven't you?"

His eyes were sympathetic, but sad. "You will be a great hero, child. I will do my best to prepare you. But if I'm right about the path ahead of you . . ."

Thunder boomed overhead, rattling the windows.

"All right!" Chiron shouted. "Fine!"

He sighed in frustration. "The gods have their reasons, Percy. Knowing too much of your future is never a good thing."

"We can't just sit back and do nothing," I said.

"*We* will not sit back," Chiron promised. "But *you* must be careful. Kronos wants you to come unraveled. He wants your life disrupted, your thoughts clouded with fear and anger. Do not give him what he wants. Train patiently. Your time will come."

"Assuming I live that long."

Chiron put his hand on my ankle. "You'll have to trust me, Percy. You will live. But first you must decide your path for the coming year. I cannot tell you the right choice. . . ." I got the feeling that he had a very definite opinion, and it was taking all his willpower not to advise me. "But you must decide whether to stay at Camp Half-Blood year-round, or return to the mortal world for seventh grade and be a summer camper. Think on that. When I get back from Olympus, you must tell me your decision."

I wanted to protest. I wanted to ask him more questions. But his expression told me there could be no more discussion; he had said as much as he could.

"I'll be back as soon as I can," Chiron promised. "Argus will watch over you."

He glanced at Annabeth. "Oh, and, my dear . . . whenever you're ready, they're here."

"Who's here?" I asked.

Nobody answered.

Chiron rolled himself out of the room. I heard the wheels of his chair clunk carefully down the front steps, two at a time.

Annabeth studied the ice in my drink.

"What's wrong?" I asked her.

"Nothing." She set the glass on the table. "I . . . just took your advice about something. You . . . um . . . need anything?"

"Yeah. Help me up. I want to go outside."

"Percy, that isn't a good idea."

I slid my legs out of bed. Annabeth caught me before I could crumple to the floor. A wave of nausea rolled over me.

Annabeth said, "I told you . . ."

"I'm fine," I insisted. I didn't want to lie in bed like an invalid while Luke was out there planning to destroy the Western world.

I managed a step forward. Then another, still leaning heavily on Annabeth. Argus followed us outside, but he kept his distance.

By the time we reached the porch, my face was beaded with sweat. My stomach had twisted into knots. But I had managed to make it all the way to the railing.

It was dusk. The camp looked completely deserted. The cabins were dark and the volleyball pit silent. No canoes cut the surface of the lake. Beyond the woods and the strawberry fields, the Long Island Sound glittered in the last light of the sun.

"What are you going to do?" Annabeth asked me.

"I don't know."

I told her I got the feeling Chiron wanted me to stay year-round, to put in more individual training time, but I wasn't sure that's what I wanted. I admitted I'd feel bad about leaving her alone, though, with only Clarisse for company. . . .

Annabeth pursed her lips, then said quietly, "I'm going home for the year, Percy."

I stared at her. "You mean, to your dad's?"

She pointed toward the crest of Half-Blood Hill. Next to Thalia's pine tree, at the very edge of the camp's magical boundaries, a family stood silhouetted—two little children, a woman, and a tall man with blond hair. They seemed to be waiting. The man was holding a backpack that looked like the one Annabeth had gotten from Waterland in Denver.

"I wrote him a letter when we got back," Annabeth said. "Just like you suggested. I told him . . . I was sorry. I'd come home for the school year if he still wanted me. He wrote back immediately. We decided . . . we'd give it another try."

"That took guts."

She pursed her lips. "You won't try anything stupid during the school year, will you? At least . . . not without sending me an Iris-message?"

I managed a smile. "I won't go looking for trouble. I usually don't have to."

"When I get back next summer," she said, "we'll hunt down Luke. We'll ask for a quest, but if we don't get approval, we'll sneak off and do it anyway. Agreed?"

"Sounds like a plan worthy of Athena."

She held out her hand. I shook it.

"Take care, Seaweed Brain," Annabeth told me. "Keep your eyes open."

"You too, Wise Girl."

I watched her walk up the hill and join her family. She

gave her father an awkward hug and looked back at the valley one last time. She touched Thalia's pine tree, then allowed herself to be led over the crest and into the mortal world.

For the first time at camp, I felt truly alone. I looked out at Long Island Sound and I remembered my father saying, *The sea does not like to be restrained.*

I made my decision.

I wondered, if Poseidon were watching, would he approve of my choice?

"I'll be back next summer," I promised him. "I'll survive until then. After all, I am your son." I asked Argus to take me down to cabin three, so I could pack my bags for home.

ACKNOWLEDGMENTS

Without the assistance of numerous valiant helpers, I would have been slain by monsters many times over as I endeavored to bring this story to print. Thanks to my elder son, Haley Michael, who heard the story first; my younger son, Patrick John, who at the age of six is the level-headed one in the family; and my wife, Becky, who puts up with my many long hours at Camp Half-Blood. Thanks also to my cadre of middle-school beta testers: Travis Stoll, clever and quick as Hermes; C. C. Kellogg, beloved as Athena; Allison Bauer, clear-eyed as Artemis the Huntress; and Mrs. Margaret Floyd, the wise and kindly seer of middle-school English. My appreciation also to Professor Egbert J. Bakker, classicist extraordinaire; Nancy Gallt, agent *summa cum laude*; Jonathan Burnham, Jennifer Besser, and Sarah Hughes for believing in Percy.

Literature Circle Questions

Use the questions and the activities that follow to get more out of the experience of reading *The Lightning Thief* by Rick Riordan.

1. Describe what kind of student Percy Jackson is. What troubles does he have in school?

2. What is Percy's relationship with his mother? Why does he think she has bad luck?

3. What does Percy discover about the Greek gods at Camp Half-Blood? What do they have to do with the camp?

4. Why is Percy more excited than scared about his upcoming quest to the Underworld? What other feelings does he have about his assignment?

5. What clues do Percy and his friends have that all is not right with "Auntie Em"? Why do you think they overlook the clues?

6. What does Percy's fight with Echidna reveal about his character? What new things does he discover about himself?

7. The god Ares says he loves America. He calls it "the best place since Sparta." What does he mean? Do you agree with his assessment of America? Why? Why not?

8. At the Lotus Casino, Percy realizes that unless he gets out quickly, he will "...stay here, happy forever, playing games forever, and soon I'd forget my mom, and my quest, and maybe my own name. I'd be playing Virtual Rifleman with groovy Disco Darrin forever." What critique is the author offering of modern life? Do you agree with it?

9. When describing the effects of Mist, Chiron says, "Remarkable, really, the lengths humans will go to fit things into their version of reality." How is this true in the novel? In Greek mythology?

10. When Percy finally meets his father, Poseidon seems distant and hard to read. Percy says that he is actually glad about this. "If he'd tried to apologize, or told me he loved me, or even smiled—that would have felt fake. Like a human dad, making some lame excuse for not being around." Do you agree with Percy?

11. How does the last line of the prophecy—*you shall fail to save what matters most in the end*—come true? What do you think of this ending? Did Percy make the right choice?

12. Throughout the story, Percy is troubled by frightening dreams. In what ways do those dreams increase the tension in the story? Is their menace completely resolved by the end of the story?

13. After her return from the quest, Annabeth resolves to try again to live with her father and her stepfamily. Do you think they will all get along better now? Why? Why not? What do you predict will happen?

14. In the end of the book, do you sympathize at all with Luke's feelings of betrayal? Is there anything you can relate to about his point of view?

15. Percy's learning difficulties become strengths in a different context. What seem to be attention problems enable him to be aware of all sides of attack during a battle. While he struggles to read English, he masters ancient Greek almost effortlessly. What skills are valued most in today's society? How might students who struggle today have been successful in a different moment in history?

Note: These Literature Circle questions are keyed to Bloom's Taxonomy *as follows: Knowledge: 1–3; Comprehension: 4–6; Application: 7–8; Analysis: 9–11; Synthesis: 12–13; Evaluation: 14–15.*

Activities

1. Imagine you have just discovered you are a half-blood. What cabin do you think you will end up in at Camp Half-Blood? What are the possibilities? Write a fictional essay describing your arrival and the discovery of your true parentage.

2. This book is the first in a series. Luke is still at large, Cronos is growing stronger, and Percy is about to step out into the world as the acknowledged son of Poseidon. What will happen next? Like the Oracle, make four predictions about the next book. What will happen in it? Share your predictions and the clues that support them, and create a chart showing what you think are the most likely upcoming events.

3. World War II is revealed in the book to actually have been triggered by an epic battle between the gods. How can a modern event be explained by the gods? Pick a current event—an earthquake, a battle, or even a surprising celebrity love affair—and explain how the gods were really behind it. You can present your explanations as a television newscast!

PERCY JACKSON & THE OLYMPIANS

BOOK TWO

THE SEA OF MONSTERS

RICK RIORDAN

SCHOLASTIC INC.

New York Toronto London Auckland
Sydney Mexico City New Delhi Hong Kong

ISBN 978-0-439-02702-1

7 6 5 4 3 2 1   13 14 15/0

Printed in the U.S.A.   40

First Scholastic printing, January 2007

This book is set in 13-point Centaur MT.

Lexile is a registered trademark of MetaMetrics, Inc.

To Patrick John Riordan,
the best storyteller in the family

CONTENTS

ONE

MY BEST FRIEND SHOPS FOR A WEDDING DRESS

My nightmare started like this.

I was standing on a deserted street in some little beach town. It was the middle of the night. A storm was blowing. Wind and rain ripped at the palm trees along the sidewalk. Pink and yellow stucco buildings lined the street, their windows boarded up. A block away, past a line of hibiscus bushes, the ocean churned.

Florida, I thought. Though I wasn't sure how I knew that. I'd never been to Florida.

Then I heard hooves clattering against the pavement. I turned and saw my friend Grover running for his life.

Yeah, I said *hooves*.

Grover is a satyr. From the waist up, he looks like a typical gangly teenager with a peach-fuzz goatee and a bad case of acne. He walks with a strange limp, but unless you happen to catch him without his pants on (which I don't recommend), you'd never know there was anything unhuman about him. Baggy jeans and fake feet hide the fact that he's got furry hindquarters and hooves.

Grover had been my best friend in sixth grade. He'd gone on this adventure with me and a girl named Annabeth to save the world, but I hadn't seen him since last July, when he set off alone on a dangerous quest—a quest no satyr had ever returned from.

Anyway, in my dream, Grover was hauling goat tail, holding his human shoes in his hands the way he does when he needs to move fast. He clopped past the little tourist shops and surfboard rental places. The wind bent the palm trees almost to the ground.

Grover was terrified of something behind him. He must've just come from the beach. Wet sand was caked in his fur. He'd escaped from somewhere. He was trying to get away from . . . something.

A bone-rattling growl cut through the storm. Behind Grover, at the far end of the block, a shadowy figure loomed. It swatted aside a street lamp, which burst in a shower of sparks.

Grover stumbled, whimpering in fear. He muttered to himself, *Have to get away. Have to warn them!*

I couldn't see what was chasing him, but I could hear it muttering and cursing. The ground shook as it got closer. Grover dashed around a street corner and faltered. He'd run into a dead-end courtyard full of shops. No time to back up. The nearest door had been blown open by the storm. The sign above the darkened display window read: ST. AUGUSTINE BRIDAL BOUTIQUE.

Grover dashed inside. He dove behind a rack of wedding dresses.

The monster's shadow passed in front of the shop. I could smell the thing—a sickening combination of wet sheep wool and rotten meat and that weird sour body odor only monsters have, like a skunk that's been living off Mexican food.

Grover trembled behind the wedding dresses. The monster's shadow passed on.

Silence except for the rain. Grover took a deep breath. Maybe the thing was gone.

Then lightning flashed. The entire front of the store exploded, and a monstrous voice bellowed: "MIIIIINE!"

I sat bolt upright, shivering in my bed.

There was no storm. No monster.

Morning sunlight filtered through my bedroom window.

I thought I saw a shadow flicker across the glass—a humanlike shape. But then there was a knock on my bedroom door—my mom called: "Percy, you're going to be late"—and the shadow at the window disappeared.

It must've been my imagination. A fifth-story window with a rickety old fire escape . . . there couldn't have been anyone out there.

"Come on, dear," my mother called again. "Last day of school. You should be excited! You've almost made it!"

"Coming," I managed.

I felt under my pillow. My fingers closed reassuringly around the ballpoint pen I always slept with. I brought it out, studied the Ancient Greek writing engraved on the side: *Anaklusmos*. Riptide.

I thought about uncapping it, but something held me

back. I hadn't used Riptide for so long. . . .

Besides, my mom had made me promise not to use deadly weapons in the apartment after I'd swung a javelin the wrong way and taken out her china cabinet. I put Anaklusmos on my nightstand and dragged myself out of bed.

I got dressed as quickly as I could. I tried not to think about my nightmare or monsters or the shadow at my window.

Have to get away. Have to warn them!

What had Grover meant?

I made a three-fingered claw over my heart and pushed outward—an ancient gesture Grover had once taught me for warding off evil.

The dream couldn't have been real.

Last day of school. My mom was right, I should have been excited. For the first time in my life, I'd almost made it an entire year without getting expelled. No weird accidents. No fights in the classroom. No teachers turning into monsters and trying to kill me with poisoned cafeteria food or exploding homework. Tomorrow, I'd be on my way to my favorite place in the world—Camp Half-Blood.

Only one more day to go. Surely even I couldn't mess that up.

As usual, I didn't have a clue how wrong I was.

My mom made blue waffles and blue eggs for breakfast. She's funny that way, celebrating special occasions with blue food. I think it's her way of saying anything is possible. Percy can pass seventh grade. Waffles can be blue. Little miracles like that.

I ate at the kitchen table while my mom washed dishes. She was dressed in her work uniform—a starry blue skirt and a red-and-white striped blouse she wore to sell candy at Sweet on America. Her long brown hair was pulled back in a ponytail.

The waffles tasted great, but I guess I wasn't digging in like I usually did. My mom looked over and frowned. "Percy, are you all right?"

"Yeah . . . fine."

But she could always tell when something was bothering me. She dried her hands and sat down across from me. "School, or . . ."

She didn't need to finish. I knew what she was asking.

"I think Grover's in trouble," I said, and I told her about my dream.

She pursed her lips. We didn't talk much about the *other* part of my life. We tried to live as normally as possible, but my mom knew all about Grover.

"I wouldn't be too worried, dear," she said. "Grover is a big satyr now. If there were a problem, I'm sure we would've heard from . . . from camp. . . ." Her shoulders tensed as she said the word *camp*.

"What is it?" I asked.

"Nothing," she said. "I'll tell you what. This afternoon we'll celebrate the end of school. I'll take you and Tyson to Rockefeller Center—to that skateboard shop you like."

Oh, man, that was tempting. We were always struggling with money. Between my mom's night classes and my private school tuition, we could never afford to do special stuff like shop for a skateboard. But something in her voice bothered me.

"Wait a minute," I said. "I thought we were packing me up for camp tonight."

She twisted her dishrag. "Ah, dear, about that . . . I got a message from Chiron last night."

My heart sank. Chiron was the activities director at Camp Half-Blood. He wouldn't contact us unless something serious was going on. "What did he say?"

"He thinks . . . it might not be safe for you to come to camp just yet. We might have to postpone."

"*Postpone?* Mom, how could it not be *safe*? I'm a half-blood! It's like the only safe place on earth for me!"

"Usually, dear. But with the problems they're having—"

"*What* problems?"

"Percy . . . I'm very, very sorry. I was hoping to talk to you about it this afternoon. I can't explain it all now. I'm not even sure Chiron can. Everything happened so suddenly."

My mind was reeling. How could I *not* go to camp? I wanted to ask a million questions, but just then the kitchen clock chimed the half-hour.

My mom looked almost relieved. "Seven-thirty, dear. You should go. Tyson will be waiting."

"But—"

"Percy, we'll talk this afternoon. Go on to school."

That was the last thing I wanted to do, but my mom had this fragile look in her eyes—a kind of warning, like if I pushed her too hard she'd start to cry. Besides, she was right about my friend Tyson. I had to meet him at the subway station on time or he'd get upset. He was scared of traveling underground alone.

I gathered up my stuff, but I stopped in the doorway. "Mom, this problem at camp. Does it . . . could it have anything to do with my dream about Grover?"

She wouldn't meet my eyes. "We'll talk this afternoon, dear. I'll explain . . . as much as I can."

Reluctantly, I told her good-bye. I jogged downstairs to catch the Number Two train.

I didn't know it at the time, but my mom and I would never get to have our afternoon talk.

In fact, I wouldn't be seeing home for a long, long time.

As I stepped outside, I glanced at the brownstone building across the street. Just for a second I saw a dark shape in the morning sunlight—a human silhouette against the brick wall, a shadow that belonged to no one.

Then it rippled and vanished.

TWO

I PLAY DODGEBALL WITH CANNIBALS

My day started normal. Or as normal as it ever gets at Meriwether College Prep.

See, it's this "progressive" school in downtown Manhattan, which means we sit on beanbag chairs instead of at desks, and we don't get grades, and the teachers wear jeans and rock concert T-shirts to work.

That's all cool with me. I mean, I'm ADHD and dyslexic, like most half-bloods, so I'd never done that great in regular schools even before they kicked me out. The only bad thing about Meriwether was that the teachers always looked on the bright side of things, and the kids weren't always . . . well, bright.

Take my first class today: English. The whole middle school had read this book called *Lord of the Flies*, where all these kids get marooned on an island and go psycho. So for our final exam, our teachers sent us into the break yard to spend an hour with no adult supervision to see what would happen. What happened was a massive wedgie contest between the seventh and eighth graders, two pebble fights, and a full-tackle basketball game. The school bully, Matt Sloan, led most of those activities.

Sloan wasn't big or strong, but he acted like he was. He had eyes like a pit bull, and shaggy black hair, and he always dressed in expensive but sloppy clothes, like he wanted everybody to see how little he cared about his family's money. One of his front teeth was chipped from the time he'd taken his daddy's Porsche for a joyride and run into a PLEASE SLOW DOWN FOR CHILDREN sign.

Anyway, Sloan was giving everybody wedgies until he made the mistake of trying it on my friend Tyson.

Tyson was the only homeless kid at Meriwether College Prep. As near as my mom and I could figure, he'd been abandoned by his parents when he was very young, probably because he was so . . . different. He was six-foot-three and built like the Abominable Snowman, but he cried a lot and was scared of just about everything, including his own reflection. His face was kind of misshapen and brutal-looking. I couldn't tell you what color his eyes were, because I could never make myself look higher than his crooked teeth. His voice was deep, but he talked funny, like a much younger kid—I guess because he'd never gone to school before coming to Meriwether. He wore tattered jeans, grimy size-twenty sneakers, and a plaid flannel shirt with holes in it. He smelled like a New York City alleyway, because that's where he lived, in a cardboard refrigerator box off 72nd Street.

Meriwether Prep had adopted him as a community service project so all the students could feel good about themselves. Unfortunately, most of them couldn't stand Tyson. Once they discovered he was a big softie, despite his massive strength and his scary looks, they made themselves feel good by picking on him. I was pretty much his only friend, which meant he was *my* only friend.

My mom had complained to the school a million times that they weren't doing enough to help him. She'd called social services, but nothing ever seemed to happen. The social workers claimed Tyson didn't exist. They swore up and down that they'd visited the alley we described and couldn't find him, though how you miss a giant kid living in a refrigerator box, I don't know.

Anyway, Matt Sloan snuck up behind him and tried to give him a wedgie, and Tyson panicked. He swatted Sloan away a little too hard. Sloan flew fifteen feet and got tangled in the little kids' tire swing.

"You freak!" Sloan yelled. "Why don't you go back to your cardboard box!"

Tyson started sobbing. He sat down on the jungle gym so hard he bent the bar, and buried his head in his hands.

"Take it back, Sloan!" I shouted.

Sloan just sneered at me. "Why do you even bother, Jackson? You might have *friends* if you weren't always sticking up for that freak."

I balled my fists. I hoped my face wasn't as red as it felt. "He's *not* a freak. He's just . . ."

I tried to think of the right thing to say, but Sloan wasn't listening. He and his big ugly friends were too busy laughing. I wondered if it were my imagination, or if Sloan had more goons hanging around him than usual. I was used to seeing him with two or three, but today he had like, half a dozen more, and I was pretty sure I'd never seen them before.

"Just wait till PE, Jackson," Sloan called. "You are *so* dead."

When first period ended, our English teacher Mr. de Milo came outside to inspect the carnage. He pronounced that we'd understood *Lord of the Flies* perfectly. We all passed his course, and we should never, never grow up to be violent people. Matt Sloan nodded earnestly, then gave me a chip-toothed grin.

I had to promise to buy Tyson an extra peanut butter sandwich at lunch to get him to stop sobbing.

"I . . . I am a freak?" he asked me.

"No," I promised, gritting my teeth. "Matt Sloan is the freak."

Tyson sniffled. "You are a good friend. Miss you next year if . . . if I can't . . ."

His voice trembled. I realized he didn't know if he'd be invited back next year for the community service project. I wondered if the headmaster had even bothered talking to him about it.

"Don't worry, big guy," I managed. "Everything's going to be fine."

Tyson gave me such a grateful look I felt like a big liar. How could I promise a kid like him that *anything* would be fine?

Our next exam was science. Mrs. Tesla told us that we had to mix chemicals until we succeeded in making something explode. Tyson was my lab partner. His hands were way too big for the tiny vials we were supposed to use. He accidentally knocked a tray of chemicals off the counter and made an orange mushroom cloud in the trash can.

After Mrs. Tesla evacuated the lab and called the hazardous waste removal squad, she praised Tyson and me for being natural chemists. We were the first ones who'd ever aced her exam in under thirty seconds.

I was glad the morning went fast, because it kept me from thinking too much about my problems. I couldn't stand the idea that something might be wrong at camp. Even worse, I couldn't shake the memory of my bad dream. I had a terrible feeling that Grover was in danger.

In social studies, while we were drawing latitude/longitude maps, I opened my notebook and stared at the photo inside—my friend Annabeth on vacation in Washington, D.C. She was wearing jeans and a denim jacket over her orange Camp Half-Blood T-shirt. Her blond hair was pulled back in a bandanna. She was standing in front of the Lincoln Memorial with her arms crossed, looking extremely pleased with herself, like she'd personally designed the place. See, Annabeth wants to be an architect when she grows up, so she's always visiting famous monuments and stuff. She's weird that way. She'd e-mailed me the picture after spring break, and every once in a while I'd look at it just to remind myself she was real and Camp Half-Blood hadn't just been my imagination.

I wished Annabeth were here. She'd know what to make of my dream. I'd never admit it to her, but she was smarter than me, even if she was annoying sometimes.

I was about to close my notebook when Matt

Sloan reached over and ripped the photo out of the rings.

"Hey!" I protested.

Sloan checked out the picture and his eyes got wide. "No way, Jackson. Who is that? She is *not* your—"

"Give it back!" My ears felt hot.

Sloan handed the photo to his ugly buddies, who snickered and started ripping it up to make spit wads. They were new kids who must've been visiting, because they were all wearing those stupid HI! MY NAME IS: tags from the admissions office. They must've had a weird sense of humor, too, because they'd all filled in strange names like: MARROW SUCKER, SKULL EATER, and JOE BOB. No human beings had names like that.

"These guys are moving here next year," Sloan bragged, like that was supposed to scare me. "I bet they can *pay* the tuition, too, unlike your retard friend."

"He's *not* retarded." I had to try really, really hard not to punch Sloan the face.

"You're such a loser, Jackson. Good thing I'm gonna put you out of your misery next period."

His huge buddies chewed up my photo. I wanted to pulverize them, but I was under strict orders from Chiron never to take my anger out on regular mortals, no matter how obnoxious they were. I had to save my fighting for monsters.

Still, part of me thought, if Sloan only knew who I really was . . .

The bell rang.

As Tyson and I were leaving class, a girl's voice whispered, "Percy!"

I looked around the locker area, but nobody was paying me any attention. Like any girl at Meriwether would ever be caught dead calling my name.

Before I had time to consider whether or not I'd been imagining things, a crowd of kids rushed for the gym, carrying Tyson and me along with them. It was time for PE. Our coach had promised us a free-for-all dodgeball game, and Matt Sloan had promised to kill me.

The gym uniform at Meriwether is sky blue shorts and tie-dyed T-shirts. Fortunately, we did most of our athletic stuff inside, so we didn't have to jog through Tribeca looking like a bunch of boot-camp hippie children.

I changed as quickly as I could in the locker room because I didn't want to deal with Sloan. I was about to leave when Tyson called, "Percy?"

He hadn't changed yet. He was standing by the weight room door, clutching his gym clothes. "Will you . . . uh . . ."

"Oh. Yeah." I tried not to sound aggravated about it. "Yeah, sure, man."

Tyson ducked inside the weight room. I stood guard outside the door while he changed. I felt kind of awkward doing this, but he asked me to most days. I think it's because he's completely hairy and he's got weird scars on his back that I've never had the courage to ask him about.

Anyway, I'd learned the hard way that if people teased Tyson while he was dressing out, he'd get upset and start ripping the doors off lockers.

When we got into the gym, Coach Nunley was sitting

at his little desk reading *Sports Illustrated*. Nunley was about a million years old, with bifocals and no teeth and a greasy wave of gray hair. He reminded me of the Oracle at Camp Half-Blood—which was a shriveled-up mummy—except Coach Nunley moved a lot less and he never billowed green smoke. Well, at least not that I'd observed.

Matt Sloan said, "Coach, can I be captain?"

"Eh?" Coach Nunley looked up from his magazine. "Yeah," he mumbled. "Mm-hmm."

Sloan grinned and took charge of the picking. He made me the other team's captain, but it didn't matter who I picked, because all the jocks and the popular kids moved over to Sloan's side. So did the big group of visitors.

On my side I had Tyson, Corey Bailer the computer geek, Raj Mandali the calculus whiz, and a half dozen other kids who always got harassed by Sloan and his gang. Normally I would've been okay with just Tyson—he was worth half a team all by himself—but the visitors on Sloan's team were almost as tall and strong-looking as Tyson, and there were six of them.

Matt Sloan spilled a cage full of balls in the middle of the gym.

"Scared," Tyson mumbled. "Smell funny."

I looked at him. "What smells funny?" Because I didn't figure he was talking about himself.

"Them." Tyson pointed at Sloan's new friends. "Smell funny."

The visitors were cracking their knuckles, eyeing us like it was slaughter time. I couldn't help wondering where they were from. Someplace where they fed kids raw meat and beat them with sticks.

Sloan blew the coach's whistle and the game began. Sloan's team ran for the center line. On my side, Raj Mandali yelled something in Urdu, probably "I have to go potty!" and ran for the exit. Corey Bailer tried to crawl behind the wall mat and hide. The rest of my team did their best to cower in fear and not look like targets.

"Tyson," I said. "Let's g—"

A ball slammed into my gut. I sat down hard in the middle of the gym floor. The other team exploded in laughter.

My eyesight was fuzzy. I felt like I'd just gotten the Heimlich maneuver from a gorilla. I couldn't believe anybody could throw that hard.

Tyson yelled, "Percy, duck!"

I rolled as another dodgeball whistled past my ear at the speed of sound.

Whooom!

It hit the wall mat, and Corey Bailer yelped.

"Hey!" I yelled at Sloan's team. "You could kill somebody!"

The visitor named Joe Bob grinned at me evilly. Somehow, he looked a lot bigger now . . . even taller than Tyson. His biceps bulged beneath his T-shirt. "I hope so, Perseus Jackson! I hope so!"

The way he said my name sent a chill down my back. Nobody called me Perseus except those who knew my true identity. Friends . . . and enemies.

What had Tyson said? *They smell funny.*

Monsters.

All around Matt Sloan, the visitors were growing in size. They were no longer kids. They were eight-foot-tall giants with wild eyes, pointy teeth, and hairy arms tattooed with snakes and hula women and Valentine hearts.

Matt Sloan dropped his ball. "Whoa! You're not from Detroit! Who . . ."

The other kids on his team started screaming and backing toward the exit, but the giant named Marrow Sucker threw a ball with deadly accuracy. It streaked past Raj Mandali just as he was about to leave and hit the door, slamming it shut like magic. Raj and some of the other kids banged on it desperately but it wouldn't budge.

"Let them go!" I yelled at the giants.

The one called Joe Bob growled at me. He had a tattoo on his biceps that said: *JB luvs Babycakes*. "And lose our tasty morsels? No, Son of the Sea God. We Laistrygonians aren't just playing for your death. We want lunch!"

He waved his hand and a new batch of dodgeballs appeared on the center line—but these balls weren't made of red rubber. They were bronze, the size of cannon balls, perforated like wiffle balls with fire bubbling out the holes. They must've been searing hot, but the giants picked them up with their bare hands.

"Coach!" I yelled.

Nunley looked up sleepily, but if he saw anything abnormal about the dodgeball game, he didn't let on. That's the problem with mortals. A magical force called the Mist obscures the true appearance of monsters and gods from their vision, so mortals tend to see only what they can understand. Maybe the coach saw a few eighth graders pounding the younger kids like usual. Maybe the other kids saw Matt Sloan's thugs getting ready to toss Molotov cocktails around. (It wouldn't have been the first time.) At any rate, I was pretty sure nobody else realized we were dealing with genuine man-eating bloodthirsty monsters.

"Yeah. Mm-hmm," Coach muttered. "Play nice."

And he went back to his magazine.

The giant named Skull Eater threw his ball. I dove aside as the fiery bronze comet sailed past my shoulder.

"Corey!" I screamed.

Tyson pulled him out from behind the exercise mat just as the ball exploded against it, blasting the mat to smoking shreds.

"Run!" I told my teammates. "The other exit!"

They ran for the locker room, but with another wave of Joe Bob's hand, that door also slammed shut.

"No one leaves unless you're out!" Joe Bob roared. "And you're not out until we eat you!"

He launched his own fireball. My teammates scattered as it blasted a crater in the gym floor.

I reached for Riptide, which I always kept in my pocket, but then I realized I was wearing gym shorts. I *had* no pockets. Riptide was tucked in my jeans inside my gym locker. And the locker room door was sealed. I was completely defenseless.

Another fireball came streaking toward me. Tyson pushed me out of the way, but the explosion still blew me head over heels. I found myself sprawled on the gym floor, dazed from smoke, my tie-dyed T-shirt peppered with sizzling holes. Just across the center line, two hungry giants were glaring down at me.

"Flesh!" they bellowed. "Hero flesh for lunch!" They both took aim.

"Percy needs help!" Tyson yelled, and he jumped in front of me just as they threw their balls.

"Tyson!" I screamed, but it was too late.

Both balls slammed into him . . . but no . . . he'd caught them. Somehow Tyson, who was so clumsy he knocked over lab equipment and broke playground structures on a regular basis, had caught two fiery metal balls speeding toward him at a zillion miles an hour. He sent them hurtling back toward their surprised owners, who screamed, "BAAAAAD!" as the bronze spheres exploded against their chests.

The giants disintegrated in twin columns of flame—a sure sign they were monsters, all right. Monsters don't die. They just dissipate into smoke and dust, which saves heroes a lot of trouble cleaning up after a fight.

"My brothers!" Joe Bob the Cannibal wailed. He flexed his muscles and his *Babycakes* tattoo rippled. "You will pay for their destruction!"

"Tyson!" I said. "Look out!"

Another comet hurtled toward us. Tyson just had time to swat it aside. It flew straight over Coach Nunley's head and landed in the bleachers with a huge KA-BOOM!

Kids were running around screaming, trying to avoid the sizzling craters in the floor. Others were banging on the door, calling for help. Sloan himself stood petrified in the middle of the court, watching in disbelief as balls of death flew around him.

Coach Nunley still wasn't seeing anything. He tapped his hearing aid like the explosions were giving him interference, but he kept his eyes on his magazine.

Surely the whole school could hear the noise. The headmaster, the police, somebody would come help us.

"Victory will be ours!" roared Joe Bob the Cannibal. "We will feast on your bones!"

I wanted to tell him he was taking the dodgeball game way too seriously, but before I could, he hefted another ball. The other three giants followed his lead.

I knew we were dead. Tyson couldn't deflect all those balls at once. His hands *had* to be seriously burned from blocking the first volley. Without my sword . . .

I had a crazy idea.

I ran toward the locker room.

"Move!" I told my teammates. "Away from the door."

Explosions behind me. Tyson had batted two of the balls back toward their owners and blasted them to ashes.

That left two giants still standing.

A third ball hurtled straight at me. I forced myself to wait—one Mississippi, two Mississippi—then dove aside as the fiery sphere demolished the locker room door.

Now, I figured that the built-up gas in most boys' locker rooms was enough to cause an explosion, so I wasn't surprised when the flaming dodgeball ignited a huge *WHOOOOOOOM!*

The wall blew apart. Locker doors, socks, athletic supporters, and other various nasty personal belongings rained all over the gym.

I turned just in time to see Tyson punch Skull Eater in the face. The giant crumpled. But the last giant, Joe Bob, had wisely held on to his own ball, waiting for an opportunity. He threw just as Tyson was turning to face him.

"No!" I yelled.

The ball caught Tyson square in the chest. He slid the length of the court and slammed into the back wall, which cracked and partially crumbled on top of him, making a hole right onto Church Street. I didn't see how Tyson could still be alive, but he only looked dazed. The bronze ball was smoking at his feet. Tyson tried to pick it up, but he fell back, stunned, into a pile of cinder blocks.

"Well!" Joe Bob gloated. "I'm the last one standing! I'll have enough meat to bring Babycakes a doggie bag!"

He picked up another ball and aimed it at Tyson.

"Stop!" I yelled. "It's me you want!"

The giant grinned. "You wish to die first, young hero?"

I had to do something. Riptide had to be around here somewhere.

Then I spotted my jeans in a smoking heap of clothes right by the giant's feet. If I could only get there. . . . I knew it was hopeless, but I charged.

The giant laughed. "My lunch approaches." He raised his arm to throw. I braced myself to die.

Suddenly the giant's body went rigid. His expression changed from gloating to surprise. Right where his belly button should've been, his T-shirt ripped open and he grew something like a horn—no, not a horn—the glowing tip of a blade.

The ball dropped out of his hand. The monster stared down at the knife that had just run him through from behind.

He muttered, "Ow," and burst into a cloud of green flame, which I figured was going to make Babycakes pretty upset.

Standing in the smoke was my friend Annabeth. Her face was grimy and scratched. She had a ragged backpack slung over her shoulder, her baseball cap tucked in her pocket, a bronze knife in her hand, and a wild look in her storm-gray eyes, like she'd just been chased a thousand miles by ghosts.

Matt Sloan, who'd been standing there dumbfounded the whole time, finally came to his senses. He blinked at Annabeth, as if he dimly recognized her from my notebook picture. "That's the girl . . . That's the girl—"

Annabeth punched him in the nose and knocked him flat. "And *you*," she told him, "lay off my friend."

The gym was in flames. Kids were still running around screaming. I heard sirens wailing and a garbled voice over the intercom. Through the glass windows of the exit doors, I could see the headmaster, Mr. Bonsai, wrestling with the lock, a crowd of teachers piling up behind him.

"Annabeth . . ." I stammered. "How did you . . . how long have you . . ."

"Pretty much all morning." She sheathed her bronze knife. "I've been trying to find a good time to talk to you, but you were never alone."

"The shadow I saw this morning—that was—" My face felt hot. "Oh my gods, you were looking in my bedroom window?"

"There's no time to explain!" she snapped, though she looked a little red-faced herself. "I just didn't want to—"

"There!" a woman screamed. The doors burst open and the adults came pouring in.

"Meet me outside," Annabeth told me. "And him." She pointed to Tyson, who was still sitting dazed against the wall. Annabeth gave him a look of distaste that I didn't quite understand. "You'd better bring him."

"*What?*"

"No time!" she said. "Hurry!"

She put on her Yankees baseball cap, which was a magic gift from her mom, and instantly vanished.

That left me standing alone in the middle of the burning gymnasium when the headmaster came charging in with half the faculty and a couple of police officers.

"Percy Jackson?" Mr. Bonsai said. "What . . . how . . ."

Over by the broken wall, Tyson groaned and stood up from the pile of cinder blocks. "Head hurts."

Matt Sloan was coming around, too. He focused on me with a look of terror. "Percy did it, Mr. Bonsai! He set the whole building on fire. Coach Nunley will tell you! He saw it all!"

Coach Nunley had been dutifully reading his magazine, but just my luck—he chose that moment to look up when Sloan said his name. "Eh? Yeah. Mm-hmm."

The other adults turned toward me. I knew they would never believe me, even if I could tell them the truth.

I grabbed Riptide out of my ruined jeans, told Tyson, "Come on!" and jumped through the gaping hole in the side of the building.

THREE

WE HAIL THE TAXI
OF ETERNAL TORMENT

Annabeth was waiting for us in an alley down Church Street. She pulled Tyson and me off the sidewalk just as a fire truck screamed past, heading for Meriwether Prep.

"Where'd you find *him*?" she demanded, pointing at Tyson.

Now, under different circumstances, I would've been really happy to see her. We'd made our peace last summer, despite the fact that her mom was Athena and didn't get along with my dad. I'd missed Annabeth probably more than I wanted to admit.

But I'd just been attacked by cannibal giants, Tyson had saved my life three or four times, and all Annabeth could do was glare at him like *he* was the problem.

"He's my friend," I told her.

"Is he homeless?"

"What does that have to do with anything? He can hear you, you know. Why don't you ask him?"

She looked surprised. "He can talk?"

"I talk," Tyson admitted. "You are pretty."

"Ah! Gross!" Annabeth stepped away from him.

I couldn't believe she was being so rude. I examined

Tyson's hands, which I was sure must've been badly scorched by the flaming dodge balls, but they looked fine—grimy and scarred, with dirty fingernails the size of potato chips—but they always looked like that. "Tyson," I said in disbelief. "Your hands aren't even burned."

"Of course not," Annabeth muttered. "I'm surprised the Laistrygonians had the guts to attack you with him around."

Tyson seemed fascinated by Annabeth's blond hair. He tried to touch it, but she smacked his hand away.

"Annabeth," I said, "what are you talking about? Laistry-what?"

"Laistrygonians. The monsters in the gym. They're a race of giant cannibals who live in the far north. Odysseus ran into them once, but I've never seen them as far south as New York before."

"Laistry—I can't even say that. What would you call them in English?"

She thought about it for a moment. "Canadians," she decided. "Now come on, we have to get out of here."

"The police'll be after me."

"That's the least of our problems," she said. "Have you been having the dreams?"

"The dreams . . . about Grover?"

Her face turned pale. "Grover? No, what about Grover?"

I told her my dream. "Why? What were *you* dreaming about?"

Her eyes looked stormy, like her mind was racing a million miles an hour.

"Camp," she said at last. "Big trouble at camp."

"My mom was saying the same thing! But what *kind* of trouble?"

"I don't know exactly. Something's wrong. We have to get there right away. Monsters have been chasing me all the way from Virginia, trying to stop me. Have you had a lot of attacks?"

I shook my head. "None all year . . . until today."

"None? But how . . ." Her eyes drifted to Tyson. "Oh."

"What do mean, 'oh'?"

Tyson raised his hand like he was still in class. "Canadians in the gym called Percy something . . . Son of the Sea God?"

Annabeth and I exchanged looks.

I didn't know how I could explain, but I figured Tyson deserved the truth after almost getting killed.

"Big guy," I said, "you ever hear those old stories about the Greek gods? Like Zeus, Poseidon, Athena—"

"Yes," Tyson said.

"Well . . . those gods are still alive. They kind of follow Western Civilization around, living in the strongest countries, so like now they're in the U.S. And sometimes they have kids with mortals. Kids called half-bloods."

"Yes," Tyson said, like he was still waiting for me to get to the point.

"Uh, well, Annabeth and I are half-bloods," I said. "We're like . . . heroes-in-training. And whenever monsters pick up our scent, they attack us. That's what those giants were in the gym. Monsters."

"Yes."

I stared at him. He didn't seem surprised or confused by what I was telling him, which surprised and confused me. "So . . . you believe me?"

Tyson nodded. "But you are . . . Son of the Sea God?"

"Yeah," I admitted. "My dad is Poseidon."

Tyson frowned. *Now* he looked confused. "But then . . ."

A siren wailed. A police car raced past our alley.

"We don't have time for this," Annabeth said. "We'll talk in the taxi."

"A taxi all the way to camp?" I said. "You know how much money—"

"Trust me."

I hesitated. "What about Tyson?"

I imagined escorting my giant friend into Camp Half-Blood. If he freaked out on a regular playground with regular bullies, how would he act at a training camp for demigods? On the other hand, the cops would be looking for us.

"We can't just leave him," I decided. "He'll be in trouble, too."

"Yeah." Annabeth looked grim. "We definitely need to take him. Now come on."

I didn't like the way she said that, as if Tyson were a big disease we needed to get to the hospital, but I followed her down the alley. Together the three of us sneaked through the side streets of downtown while a huge column of smoke billowed up behind us from my school gymnasium.

"Here." Annabeth stopped us on the corner of Thomas and Trimble. She fished around in her backpack. "I hope I have one left."

She looked even worse than I'd realized at first. Her chin was cut. Twigs and grass were tangled in her ponytail, as if she'd slept several nights in the open. The slashes on the hems of her jeans looked suspiciously like claw marks.

"What are you looking for?" I asked.

All around us, sirens wailed. I figured it wouldn't be long before more cops cruised by, looking for juvenile delinquent gym-bombers. No doubt Matt Sloan had given them a statement by now. He'd probably twisted the story around so that Tyson and I were the bloodthirsty cannibals.

"Found one. Thank the gods." Annabeth pulled out a gold coin that I recognized as a drachma, the currency of Mount Olympus. It had Zeus's likeness stamped on one side and the Empire State Building on the other.

"Annabeth," I said, "New York taxi drivers won't take that."

"*Anakoche,*" she shouted in Ancient Greek. "*Harma epitribeios!*"

As usual, the moment she spoke in the language of Olympus, I somehow understood it. She'd said: *Stop, Chariot of Damnation!*

That didn't exactly make me feel real excited about whatever her plan was.

She threw her coin into the street, but instead of clattering on the asphalt, the drachma sank right through and disappeared.

For a moment, nothing happened.

Then, just where the coin had fallen, the asphalt darkened. It melted into a rectangular pool about the size of a parking space—bubbling red liquid like blood. Then a car erupted from the ooze.

It was a taxi, all right, but unlike every other taxi in New York, it wasn't yellow. It was smoky gray. I mean it looked like it was *woven* out of smoke, like you could walk right through it. There were words printed on the door—something like GYAR SSIRES—but my dyslexia made it hard for me to decipher what it said.

The passenger window rolled down, and an old woman stuck her head out. She had a mop of grizzled hair covering her eyes, and she spoke in a weird mumbling way, like she'd just had a shot of Novocain. "Passage? Passage?"

"Three to Camp Half-Blood," Annabeth said. She opened the cab's back door and waved at me to get in, like this was all completely normal.

"Ach!" the old woman screeched. "We don't take *his* kind!"

She pointed a bony finger at Tyson.

What was it? Pick-on-Big-and-Ugly-Kids Day?

"Extra pay," Annabeth promised. "Three more drachma on arrival."

"Done!" the woman screamed.

Reluctantly I got in the cab. Tyson squeezed in the middle. Annabeth crawled in last.

The interior was also smoky gray, but it felt solid enough. The seat was cracked and lumpy—no different than most taxis. There was no Plexiglas screen separating us from the old lady driving . . . Wait a minute. There wasn't just one old lady. There were three, all crammed in the front seat, each with stringy hair covering her eyes, bony hands, and a charcoal-colored sackcloth dress.

The one driving said, "Long Island! Out-of-metro fare bonus! Ha!"

She floored the accelerator, and my head slammed against the backrest. A prerecorded voice came on over the speaker: *Hi, this is Ganymede, cup-bearer to Zeus, and when I'm out buying wine for the Lord of the Skies, I always buckle up!*

I looked down and found a large black chain instead of a seat belt. I decided I wasn't that desperate . . . yet.

The cab sped around the corner of West Broadway, and the gray lady sitting in the middle screeched, "Look out! Go left!"

"Well, if you'd give me the eye, Tempest, I could *see* that!" the driver complained.

Wait a minute. *Give her the eye?*

I didn't have time to ask questions because the driver swerved to avoid an oncoming delivery truck, ran over the curb with a jaw-rattling *thump*, and flew into the next block.

"Wasp!" the third lady said to the driver. "Give me the girl's coin! I want to bite it."

"You bit it last time, Anger!" said the driver, whose name must've been Wasp. "It's my turn!"

"Is not!" yelled the one called Anger.

The middle one, Tempest, screamed, "Red light!"

"Brake!" yelled Anger.

Instead, Wasp floored the accelerator and rode up on the curb, screeching around another corner, and knocking over a newspaper box. She left my stomach somewhere back on Broome Street.

"Excuse me," I said. "But . . . can you see?"

"No!" screamed Wasp from behind the wheel.

"No!" screamed Tempest from the middle.

"Of course!" screamed Anger by the shotgun window.

I looked at Annabeth. "They're blind?"

"Not completely," Annabeth said. "They have an eye."

"One eye?"

"Yeah."

"Each?"

"No. One eye total."

Next to me, Tyson groaned and grabbed the seat. "Not feeling so good."

"Oh, man," I said, because I'd seen Tyson get carsick on school field trips and it was *not* something you wanted to be within fifty feet of. "Hang in there, big guy. Anybody got a garbage bag or something?"

The three gray ladies were too busy squabbling to pay me any attention. I looked over at Annabeth, who was hanging on for dear life, and I gave her a *why-did-you-do-this-to-me* look.

"Hey," she said, "Gray Sisters Taxi is the fastest way to camp."

"Then why didn't you take it from Virginia?"

"That's outside their service area," she said, like that

should be obvious. "They only serve Greater New York and surrounding communities."

"We've had famous people in this cab!" Anger exclaimed. "Jason! You remember him?"

"Don't remind me!" Wasp wailed. "And we didn't have a cab back then, you old bat. That was three thousand years ago!"

"Give me the tooth!" Anger tried to grab at Wasp's mouth, but Wasp swatted her hand away.

"Only if Tempest gives me the eye!"

"No!" Tempest screeched. "You had it yesterday!"

"But I'm driving, you old hag!"

"Excuses! Turn! That was your turn!"

Wasp swerved hard onto Delancey Street, squishing me between Tyson and the door. She punched the gas and we shot up the Williamsburg Bridge at seventy miles an hour.

The three sisters were fighting for real now, slapping each other as Anger tried to grab at Wasp's face and Wasp tried to grab at Tempest's. With their hair flying and their mouths open, screaming at each other, I realized that none of the sisters had any teeth except for Wasp, who had one mossy yellow incisor. Instead of eyes, they just had closed, sunken eyelids, except for Anger, who had one bloodshot green eye that stared at everything hungrily, as if it couldn't get enough of anything it saw.

Finally Anger, who had the advantage of sight, managed to yank the tooth out of her sister Wasp's mouth. This made Wasp so mad she swerved toward the edge of the Williamsburg Bridge, yelling, "'Ivit back! 'Ivit back!"

Tyson groaned and clutched his stomach.

"Uh, if anybody's interested," I said, "we're going to die!"

"Don't worry," Annabeth told me, sounding pretty worried. "The Gray Sisters know what they're doing. They're really very wise."

This coming from the daughter of Athena, but I wasn't exactly reassured. We were skimming along the edge of a bridge a hundred and thirty feet above the East River.

"Yes, wise!" Anger grinned in the rearview mirror, showing off her newly acquired tooth. "We know things!"

"Every street in Manhattan!" Wasp bragged, still hitting her sister. "The capital of Nepal!"

"The location you seek!" Tempest added.

Immediately her sisters pummeled her from either side, screaming, "Be quiet! Be quiet! He didn't even ask yet!"

"What?" I said. "What location? I'm not seeking any—"

"Nothing!" Tempest said. "You're right, boy. It's nothing!"

"Tell me."

"No!" they all screamed.

"The last time we told, it was horrible!" Tempest said.

"Eye tossed in a lake!" Anger agreed.

"Years to find it again!" Wasp moaned. "And speaking of that—give it back!"

"No!" yelled Anger.

"Eye!" Wasp yelled. "Gimme!"

She whacked her sister Anger on the back. There was a sickening *pop* and something flew out of Anger's face. Anger fumbled for it, trying to catch it, but she only managed to bat it with the back of her hand. The slimy green orb sailed over her shoulder, into the backseat, and straight into my lap.

I jumped so hard, my head hit the ceiling and the eyeball rolled away.

"I can't see!" all three sisters yelled.

"Give me the eye!" Wasp wailed.

"Give her the eye!" Annabeth screamed.

"I don't have it!" I said.

"There, by your foot," Annabeth said. "Don't step on it! Get it!"

"I'm not picking that up!"

The taxi slammed against the guardrail and skidded along with a horrible grinding noise. The whole car shuddered, billowing gray smoke as if it were about to dissolve from the strain.

"Going to be sick!" Tyson warned.

"Annabeth," I yelled, "let Tyson use your backpack!"

"Are you crazy? Get the eye!"

Wasp yanked the wheel, and the taxi swerved away from the rail. We hurtled down the bridge toward Brooklyn, going faster than any human taxi. The Gray Sisters screeched and pummeled each other and cried out for their eye.

At last I steeled my nerves. I ripped off a chunk of my tie-dyed T-shirt, which was already falling apart from all the burn marks, and used it to pick the eyeball off the floor.

"Nice boy!" Anger cried, as if she somehow knew I had her missing peeper. "Give it back!"

"Not until you explain," I told her. "What were you talking about, the location I seek?"

"No time!" Tempest cried. "Accelerating!"

I looked out the window. Sure enough, trees and cars and whole neighborhoods were now zipping by in a gray blur. We were already out of Brooklyn, heading through the middle of Long Island.

"Percy," Annabeth warned, "they can't find our destination without the eye. We'll just keep accelerating until we break into a million pieces."

"First they have to tell me," I said. "Or I'll open the window and throw the eye into oncoming traffic."

"No!" the Gray Sisters wailed. "Too dangerous!"

"I'm rolling down the window."

"Wait!" the Gray Sisters screamed. "30, 31, 75, 12!"

They belted it out like a quarterback calling a play.

"What do you mean?" I said. "That makes no sense!"

"30, 31, 75, 12!" Anger wailed. "That's all we can tell you. Now give us the eye! Almost to camp!"

We were off the highway now, zipping through the countryside of northern Long Island. I could see Half-Blood Hill ahead of us, with its giant pine tree at the crest—Thalia's tree, which contained the life force of a fallen hero.

"Percy!" Annabeth said more urgently. "Give them the eye *now*!"

I decided not to argue. I threw the eye into Wasp's lap.

The old lady snatched it up, pushed it into her eye

socket like somebody putting in a contact lens, and blinked. "Whoa!"

She slammed on the brakes. The taxi spun four or five times in a cloud of smoke and squealed to a halt in the middle of the farm road at the base of Half-Blood Hill.

Tyson let loose a huge belch. "Better now."

"All right," I told the Gray Sisters. "Now tell me what those numbers mean."

"No time!" Annabeth opened her door. "We have to get out *now*."

I was about to ask why, when I looked up at Half-Blood Hill and understood.

At the crest of the hill was a group of campers. And they were under attack.

FOUR

TYSON PLAYS WITH FIRE

Mythologically speaking, if there's anything I hate worse than trios of old ladies, it's bulls. Last summer, I fought the Minotaur on top of Half-Blood Hill. This time what I saw up there was even worse: two bulls. And not just regular bulls—bronze ones the size of elephants. And even *that* wasn't bad enough. Naturally they had to breathe fire, too.

As soon as we exited the taxi, the Gray Sisters peeled out, heading back to New York, where life was safer. They didn't even wait for their extra three-drachma payment. They just left us on the side of the road, Annabeth with nothing but her backpack and knife, Tyson and me still in our burned-up tie-dyed gym clothes.

"Oh, man," said Annabeth, looking at the battle raging on the hill.

What worried me most weren't the bulls themselves. Or the ten heroes in full battle armor who were getting their bronze-plated booties whooped. What worried me was that the bulls were ranging all over the hill, even around the back side of the pine tree. That shouldn't have been possible. The camp's magic boundaries didn't allow monsters to cross past Thalia's tree. But the metal bulls were doing it anyway.

One of the heroes shouted, "Border patrol, to me!" A girl's voice—gruff and familiar.

Border patrol? I thought. The camp didn't *have* a border patrol.

"It's Clarisse," Annabeth said. "Come on, we have to help her."

Normally, rushing to Clarisse's aid would not have been high on my "to do" list. She was one of the biggest bullies at camp. The first time we'd met she tried to introduce my head to a toilet. She was also a daughter of Ares, and I'd had a very serious disagreement with her father last summer, so now the god of war and all his children basically hated my guts.

Still, she *was* in trouble. Her fellow warriors were scattering, running in panic as the bulls charged. The grass was burning in huge swathes around the pine tree. One hero screamed and waved his arms as he ran in circles, the horsehair plume on his helmet blazing like a fiery Mohawk. Clarisse's own armor was charred. She was fighting with a broken spear shaft, the other end embedded uselessly in the metal joint of one bull's shoulder.

I uncapped my ballpoint pen. It shimmered, growing longer and heavier until I held the bronze sword Anaklusmos in my hands. "Tyson, stay here. I don't want you taking any more chances."

"No!" Annabeth said. "We need him."

I stared at her. "He's mortal. He got lucky with the dodge balls but he can't—"

"Percy, do you know what those are up there? The

Colchis bulls, made by Hephaestus himself. We can't fight them without Medea's Sunscreen SPF 50,000. We'll get burned to a crisp."

"Medea's *what?*"

Annabeth rummaged through her backpack and cursed. "I had a jar of tropical coconut scent sitting on my nightstand at home. Why didn't I bring it?"

I'd learned a long time ago not to question Annabeth too much. It just made me more confused. "Look, I don't know what you're talking about, but I'm *not* going to let Tyson get fried."

"Percy—"

"Tyson, stay back." I raised my sword. "I'm going in."

Tyson tried to protest, but I was already running up the hill toward Clarisse, who was yelling at her patrol, trying to get them into phalanx formation. It was a good idea. The few who were listening lined up shoulder-to-shoulder, locking their shields to form an ox-hide–and-bronze wall, their spears bristling over the top like porcupine quills.

Unfortunately, Clarisse could only muster six campers. The other four were still running around with their helmets on fire. Annabeth ran toward them, trying to help. She taunted one of the bulls into chasing her, then turned invisible, completely confusing the monster. The other bull charged Clarisse's line.

I was halfway up the hill—not close enough to help. Clarisse hadn't even seen me yet.

The bull moved deadly fast for something so big. Its metal hide gleamed in the sun. It had fist-sized rubies for eyes and horns of polished silver. When it opened its hinged mouth, a column of white-hot flame blasted out.

"Hold the line!" Clarisse ordered her warriors.

Whatever else you could say about Clarisse, she was brave. She was a big girl with cruel eyes like her father's. She looked like she was born to wear Greek battle armor, but I didn't see how even she could stand against that bull's charge.

Unfortunately, at that moment, the other bull lost interest in finding Annabeth. It turned, wheeling around behind Clarisse on her unprotected side.

"Behind you!" I yelled. "Look out!"

I shouldn't have said anything, because all I did was startle her. Bull Number One crashed into her shield, and the phalanx broke. Clarisse went flying backward and landed in a smoldering patch of grass. The bull charged past her, but not before blasting the other heroes with its fiery breath. Their shields melted right off their arms. They dropped their weapons and ran as Bull Number Two closed in on Clarisse for the kill.

I lunged forward and grabbed Clarisse by the straps of her armor. I dragged her out of the way just as Bull Number Two freight-trained past. I gave it a good swipe with Riptide and cut a huge gash in its flank, but the monster just creaked and groaned and kept on going.

It hadn't touched me, but I could feel the heat of its metal skin. Its body temperature could've microwaved a frozen burrito.

"Let me go!" Clarisse pummeled my hand. "Percy, curse you!"

I dropped her in a heap next to the pine tree and turned to face the bulls. We were on the inside slope of the hill now, the valley of Camp Half-Blood directly below us—the cabins, the training facilities, the Big House—all of it at risk if these bulls got past us.

Annabeth shouted orders to the other heroes, telling them to spread out and keep the bulls distracted.

Bull Number One ran a wide arc, making its way back toward me. As it passed the middle of the hill, where the invisible boundary line should've kept it out, it slowed down a little, as if it were struggling against a strong wind; but then it broke through and kept coming. Bull Number Two turned to face me, fire sputtering from the gash I'd cut in its side. I couldn't tell if it felt any pain, but its ruby eyes seemed to glare at me like I'd just made things personal.

I couldn't fight both bulls at the same time. I'd have to take down Bull Number Two first, cut its head off before Bull Number One charged back into range. My arms already felt tired. I realized how long it had been since I'd worked out with Riptide, how out of practice I was.

I lunged but Bull Number Two blew flames at me. I rolled aside as the air turned to pure heat. All the oxygen was sucked out of my lungs. My foot caught on something—a tree root, maybe—and pain shot up my ankle. Still, I managed to slash with my sword and lop off part of the monster's snout. It galloped away, wild and disoriented. But before I could feel too good about that, I tried to stand, and my left leg buckled underneath me. My ankle was sprained, maybe broken.

Bull Number One charged straight toward me. No way could I crawl out of its path.

Annabeth shouted: "Tyson, help him!"

Somewhere near, toward the crest of the hill, Tyson wailed, "Can't—get—through!"

"I, Annabeth Chase, give you permission to enter camp!"

Thunder shook the hillside. Suddenly Tyson was there, barreling toward me, yelling: "Percy needs help!"

Before I could tell him no, he dove between me and the bull just as it unleashed a nuclear firestorm.

"Tyson!" I yelled.

The blast swirled around him like a red tornado. I could only see the black silhouette of his body. I knew with horrible certainty that my friend had just been turned into a column of ashes.

But when the fire died, Tyson was still standing there, completely unharmed. Not even his grungy clothes were scorched. The bull must've been as surprised as I was, because before it could unleash a second blast, Tyson balled his fists and slammed them into the bull's face. "BAD COW!"

His fists made a crater where the bronze bull's snout used to be. Two small columns of flame shot out of its ears. Tyson hit it again, and the bronze crumpled under his hands like aluminum foil. The bull's face now looked like a sock puppet pulled inside out.

"Down!" Tyson yelled.

The bull staggered and fell on its back. Its legs moved

feebly in the air, steam coming out of its ruined head in odd places.

Annabeth ran over to check on me.

My ankle felt like it was filled with acid, but she gave me some Olympian nectar to drink from her canteen, and I immediately started to feel better. There was a burning smell that I later learned was me. The hair on my arms had been completely singed off.

"The other bull?" I asked.

Annabeth pointed down the hill. Clarisse had taken care of Bad Cow Number Two. She'd impaled it through the back leg with a celestial bronze spear. Now, with its snout half gone and a huge gash in its side, it was trying to run in slow motion, going in circles like some kind of merry-go-round animal.

Clarisse pulled off her helmet and marched toward us. A strand of her stringy brown hair was smoldering, but she didn't seem to notice. "You—ruin—everything!" she yelled at me. "I had it under control!"

I was too stunned to answer. Annabeth grumbled, "Good to see you too, Clarisse."

"Argh!" Clarisse screamed. "Don't ever, EVER try saving me again!"

"Clarisse," Annabeth said, "you've got wounded campers."

That sobered her up. Even Clarisse cared about the soldiers under her command.

"I'll be back," she growled, then trudged off to assess the damage.

I stared at Tyson. "You didn't die."

Tyson looked down like he was embarrassed. "I am sorry. Came to help. Disobeyed you."

"My fault," Annabeth said. "I had no choice. I had to let Tyson cross the boundary line to save you. Otherwise, you would've died."

"*Let* him cross the boundary line?'" I asked. "But—"

"Percy," she said, "have you ever looked at Tyson closely? I mean . . . in the face. Ignore the Mist, and *really* look at him."

The Mist makes humans see only what their brains can process . . . I knew it could fool demigods too, but . . .

I looked Tyson in the face. It wasn't easy. I'd always had trouble looking directly at him, though I'd never quite understood why. I'd thought it was just because he always had peanut butter in his crooked teeth. I forced myself to focus at his big lumpy nose, then a little higher at his eyes.

No, not *eyes*.

One eye. One large, calf-brown eye, right in the middle of his forehead, with thick lashes and big tears trickling down his cheeks on either side.

"Tyson," I stammered. "You're a . . ."

"Cyclops," Annabeth offered. "A baby, by the looks of him. Probably why he couldn't get past the boundary line as easily as the bulls. Tyson's one of the homeless orphans."

"One of the what?"

"They're in almost all the big cities," Annabeth said distastefully. "They're . . . *mistakes*, Percy. Children of nature spirits and gods . . . Well, one god in particular, usually . . . and they don't always come out right. No one wants them. They get tossed aside. They grow up wild on the streets. I don't know how this one found you, but he obviously likes you. We should take him to Chiron, let him decide what to do."

"But the fire. How—"

"He's a Cyclops." Annabeth paused, as if she were remembering something unpleasant. "They work the forges of the gods. They *have* to be immune to fire. That's what I was trying to tell you."

I was completely shocked. How had I never realized what Tyson was?

But I didn't have much time to think about it just then. The whole side of the hill was burning. Wounded heroes needed attention. And there were still two banged-up bronze bulls to dispose of, which I didn't figure would fit in our normal recycling bins.

Clarisse came back over and wiped the soot off her forehead. "Jackson, if you can stand, get up. We need to carry the wounded back to the Big House, let Tantalus know what's happened."

"Tantalus?" I asked.

"The activities director," Clarisse said impatiently.

"Chiron is the activities director. And where's Argus? He's head of security. He should be here."

Clarisse made a sour face. "Argus got fired. You two have been gone too long. Things are changing."

"But Chiron . . . He's trained kids to fight monsters for

over three thousand years. He can't just be *gone*. What happened?"

"*That* happened," Clarisse snapped.

She pointed to Thalia's tree.

Every camper knew the story behind the tree. Six years ago, Grover, Annabeth, and two other demigods named Thalia and Luke had come to Camp Half-Blood chased by an army of monsters. When they got cornered on top of this hill, Thalia, a daughter of Zeus, had made her last stand here to give her friends time to reach safety. As she was dying, her father Zeus took pity on her and changed her into a pine tree. Her spirit had reinforced the magic borders of the camp, protecting it from monsters. The pine had been here ever since, strong and healthy.

But now, its needles were yellow. A huge pile of dead ones littered the base of the tree. In the center of the trunk, three feet from the ground, was a puncture mark the size of a bullet hole, oozing green sap.

A sliver of ice ran through my chest. Now I understood why the camp was in danger. The magical borders were failing because Thalia's tree was dying.

Someone had poisoned it.

FIVE

I GET A NEW CABIN MATE

Ever come home and found your room messed up? Like some helpful person (hi, Mom) has tried to "clean" it, and suddenly you can't find anything? And even if nothing is missing, you get that creepy feeling like somebody's been looking through your private stuff and dusting everything with lemon furniture polish?

That's kind of the way I felt seeing Camp Half-Blood again.

On the surface, things didn't look all that different. The Big House was still there with its blue gabled roof and its wraparound porch. The strawberry fields still baked in the sun. The same white-columned Greek buildings were scattered around the valley—the amphitheater, the combat arena, the dining pavilion overlooking Long Island Sound. And nestled between the woods and the creek were the same cabins—a crazy assortment of twelve buildings, each representing a different Olympian god.

But there was an air of danger now. You could tell something was wrong. Instead of playing volleyball in the sandpit, counselors and satyrs were stockpiling weapons in the tool shed. Dryads armed with bows and arrows talked nervously at the edge of the woods. The forest looked sickly, the grass in the meadow was pale yellow, and the fire marks on Half-Blood Hill stood out like ugly scars.

Somebody had messed with my favorite place in the world, and I was not . . . well, a happy camper.

As we made our way to the Big House, I recognized a lot of kids from last summer. Nobody stopped to talk. Nobody said, "Welcome back." Some did double takes when they saw Tyson, but most just walked grimly past and carried on with their duties—running messages, toting swords to sharpen on the grinding wheels. The camp felt like a military school. And believe me, I know. I've been kicked out of a couple.

None of that mattered to Tyson. He was absolutely fascinated by everything he saw. "Whasthat!" he gasped.

"The stables for pegasi," I said. "The winged horses."

"Whasthat!"

"Um . . . those are the toilets."

"Whasthat!"

"The cabins for the campers. If they don't know who your Olympian parent is, they put you in the Hermes cabin—that brown one over there—until you're determined. Then, once they know, they put you in your dad or mom's group."

He looked at me in awe. "You . . . have a *cabin*?"

"Number three." I pointed to a low gray building made of sea stone.

"You live with friends in the cabin?"

"No. No, just me." I didn't feel like explaining. The

embarrassing truth: I was the only one who stayed in that cabin because I wasn't supposed to be alive. The "Big Three" gods—Zeus, Poseidon, and Hades—had made a pact after World War II not to have any more children with mortals. We were more powerful than regular half-bloods. We were too unpredictable. When we got mad we tended to cause problems . . . like World War II, for instance. The "Big Three" pact had only been broken twice—once when Zeus sired Thalia, once when Poseidon sired me. Neither of us should've been born.

Thalia had gotten herself turned into a pine tree when she was twelve. Me . . . well, I was doing my best not to follow her example. I had nightmares about what Poseidon might turn me into if I were ever on the verge of death—plankton, maybe. Or a floating patch of kelp.

When we got to the Big House, we found Chiron in his apartment, listening to his favorite 1960s lounge music while he packed his saddlebags. I guess I should mention—Chiron is a centaur. From the waist up he looks like a regular middle-aged guy with curly brown hair and a scraggly beard. From the waist down, he's a white stallion. He can pass for human by compacting his lower half into a magic wheelchair. In fact, he'd passed himself off as my Latin teacher during my sixth-grade year. But most of the time, if the ceilings are high enough, he prefers hanging out in full centaur form.

As soon as we saw him, Tyson froze. "Pony!" he cried in total rapture.

Chiron turned, looking offended. "I beg your pardon?"

Annabeth ran up and hugged him. "Chiron, what's happening? You're not . . . leaving?" Her voice was shaky. Chiron was like a second father to her.

Chiron ruffled her hair and gave her a kindly smile. "Hello, child. And Percy, my goodness. You've grown over the year!"

I swallowed. "Clarisse said you were . . . you were . . ."

"Fired." Chiron's eyes glinted with dark humor. "Ah, well, someone had to take the blame. Lord Zeus was most upset. The tree he'd created from the spirit of his daughter, poisoned! Mr. D had to punish someone."

"Besides himself, you mean," I growled. Just the thought of the camp director, Mr. D, made me angry.

"But this is crazy!" Annabeth cried. "Chiron, you couldn't have had anything to do with poisoning Thalia's tree!"

"Nevertheless," Chiron sighed, "some in Olympus do not trust me now, under the circumstances."

"What circumstances?" I asked.

Chiron's face darkened. He stuffed a Latin-English dictionary into his saddlebag while the Frank Sinatra music oozed from his boom box.

Tyson was still staring at Chiron in amazement. He whimpered like he wanted to pat Chiron's flank but was afraid to come closer. "Pony?"

Chiron sniffed. "My dear young Cyclops! I am a *centaur*."

"Chiron," I said. "What about the tree? What happened?"

He shook his head sadly. "The poison used on Thalia's

pine is something from the Underworld, Percy. Some venom even I have never seen. It must have come from a monster quite deep in the pits of Tartarus."

"Then we know who's responsible. Kro—"

"Do not invoke the titan lord's name, Percy. Especially not here, not now."

"But last summer he tried to cause a civil war in Olympus! This *has* to be his idea. He'd get Luke to do it, that traitor."

"Perhaps," Chiron said. "But I fear I am being held responsible because I did not prevent it and I cannot cure it. The tree has only a few weeks of life left unless . . ."

"Unless what?" Annabeth asked.

"No," Chiron said. "A foolish thought. The whole valley is feeling the shock of the poison. The magical borders are deteriorating. The camp itself is dying. Only one source of magic would be strong enough to reverse the poison, and it was lost centuries ago."

"What *is* it?" I asked. "We'll go find it!"

Chiron closed his saddlebag. He pressed the stop button on his boom box. Then he turned and rested his hand on my shoulder, looking me straight in the eyes. "Percy, you must promise me that you will *not* act rashly. I told your mother I did not want you to come here at all this summer. It's much too dangerous. But now that you are here, *stay* here. Train hard. Learn to fight. But do not leave."

"Why?" I asked. "I want to do something! I can't just let the borders fail. The whole camp will be—"

"Overrun by monsters," Chiron said. "Yes, I fear so. But

you must not let yourself be baited into hasty action! This could be a trap of the titan lord. Remember last summer! He almost took your life."

It was true, but still, I wanted to help so badly. I also wanted to make Kronos pay. I mean, you'd think the titan lord would've learned his lesson eons ago when he was overthrown by the gods. You'd think getting chopped into a million pieces and cast into the darkest part of the Underworld would give him a subtle clue that nobody wanted him around. But no. Because he was immortal, he was still alive down there in Tartarus—suffering in eternal pain, hungering to return and take revenge on Olympus. He couldn't act on his own, but he was great at twisting the minds of mortals and even gods to do his dirty work.

The poisoning *had* to be his doing. Who else would be so low as to attack Thalia's tree, the only thing left of a hero who'd given her life to save her friends?

Annabeth was trying hard not to cry. Chiron brushed a tear from her cheek. "Stay with Percy, child," he told her. "Keep him safe. The prophecy—remember it!"

"I—I will."

"Um . . ." I said. "Would this be the super-dangerous prophecy that has me in it, but the gods have forbidden you to tell me about?"

Nobody answered.

"Right," I muttered. "Just checking."

"Chiron . . ." Annabeth said. "You told me the gods made you immortal only so long as you were needed to train heroes. If they dismiss you from camp—"

"Swear you will do your best to keep Percy from danger," he insisted. "Swear upon the River Styx."

"I—I swear it upon the River Styx," Annabeth said.

Thunder rumbled outside.

"Very well," Chiron said. He seemed to relax just a little. "Perhaps my name will be cleared and I shall return. Until then, I go to visit my wild kinsmen in the Everglades. It's possible they know of some cure for the poisoned tree that I have forgotten. In any event, I will stay in exile until this matter is resolved . . . one way or another."

Annabeth stifled a sob. Chiron patted her shoulder awkwardly. "There, now, child. I must entrust your safety to Mr. D and the new activities director. We must hope . . . well, perhaps they won't destroy the camp quite as quickly as I fear."

"Who is this Tantalus guy, anyway?" I demanded. "Where does he get off taking your job?"

A conch horn blew across the valley. I hadn't realized how late it was. It was time for the campers to assemble for dinner.

"Go," Chiron said. "You will meet him at the pavilion. I will contact your mother, Percy, and let her know you're safe. No doubt she'll be worried by now. Just remember my warning! You are in grave danger. Do not think for a moment that the titan lord has forgotten you!"

With that, he clopped out of the apartment and down the hall, Tyson calling after him, "Pony! Don't go!"

I realized I'd forgotten to tell Chiron about my dream of Grover. Now it was too late. The best teacher I'd ever had was gone, maybe for good.

Tyson started bawling almost as bad as Annabeth.

I tried to tell them that things would be okay, but I didn't believe it.

The sun was setting behind the dining pavilion as the campers came up from their cabins. We stood in the shadow of a marble column and watched them file in. Annabeth was still pretty shaken up, but she promised she'd talk to us later. Then she went off to join her siblings from the Athena cabin—a dozen boys and girls with blond hair and gray eyes like hers. Annabeth wasn't the oldest, but she'd been at camp more summers than just about anybody. You could tell that by looking at her camp necklace—one bead for every summer, and Annabeth had six. No one questioned her right to lead the line.

Next came Clarisse, leading the Ares cabin. She had one arm in a sling and a nasty-looking gash on her cheek, but otherwise her encounter with the bronze bulls didn't seem to have fazed her. Someone had taped a piece of paper to her back that said, YOU MOO, GIRL! But nobody in her cabin was bothering to tell her about it.

After the Ares kids came the Hephaestus cabin—six guys led by Charles Beckendorf, a big fifteen-year-old African American kid. He had hands the size of catchers' mitts and a face that was hard and squinty from looking into a blacksmith's forge all day. He was nice enough once you got to know him, but no one ever called him Charlie or Chuck or Charles. Most just called him Beckendorf. Rumor was he could make anything. Give him a chunk of metal and he could create a razor-sharp sword or a robotic warrior or a singing birdbath for your grandmother's garden. Whatever you wanted.

The other cabins filed in: Demeter, Apollo, Aphrodite, Dionysus. Naiads came up from the canoe lake. Dryads melted out of the trees. From the meadow came a dozen satyrs, who reminded me painfully of Grover.

I'd always had a soft spot for the satyrs. When they were at camp, they had to do all kinds of odd jobs for Mr. D, the director, but their most important work was out in the real world. They were the camp's seekers. They went undercover into schools all over the world, looking for potential half-bloods and escorting them back to camp. That's how I'd met Grover. He had been the first one to recognize I was a demigod.

After the satyrs filed in to dinner, the Hermes cabin brought up the rear. They were always the biggest cabin. Last summer, it had been led by Luke, the guy who'd fought with Thalia and Annabeth on top of Half-Blood Hill. For a while, before Poseidon had claimed me, I'd lodged in the Hermes cabin. Luke had befriended me . . . and then he'd tried to kill me.

Now the Hermes cabin was led by Travis and Connor Stoll. They weren't twins, but they looked so much alike it didn't matter. I could never remember which one was older. They were both tall and skinny, with mops of brown hair that hung in their eyes. They wore orange CAMP HALF-BLOOD T-shirts untucked over baggy shorts, and they had those elfish features all Hermes's kids had: upturned eyebrows, sarcastic smiles, a gleam in their eyes whenever they looked at you—like they were about to drop a firecracker down your shirt. I'd always thought it was funny that the god of thieves would have kids with the last name "Stoll," but the only time I mentioned it to Travis and Connor, they both stared at me blankly like they didn't get the joke.

As soon as the last campers had filed in, I led Tyson into the middle of the pavilion. Conversations faltered. Heads turned. "Who invited *that*?" somebody at the Apollo table murmured.

I glared in their direction, but I couldn't figure out who'd spoken.

From the head table a familiar voice drawled, "Well, well, if it isn't Peter Johnson. My millennium is complete."

I gritted my teeth. "*Percy Jackson* . . . sir."

Mr. D sipped his Diet Coke. "Yes. Well, as you young people say these days: *Whatever.*"

He was wearing his usual leopard-pattern Hawaiian shirt, walking shorts, and tennis shoes with black socks. With his pudgy belly and his blotchy red face, he looked like a Las Vegas tourist who'd stayed up too late in the casinos. Behind him, a nervous-looking satyr was peeling the skins off grapes and handing them to Mr. D one at a time.

Mr. D's real name is Dionysus. The god of wine. Zeus appointed him director of Camp Half-Blood to dry out for a hundred years—a punishment for chasing some off-limits wood nymph.

Next to him, where Chiron usually sat (or stood, in centaur form), was someone I'd never seen before—a pale, horribly thin man in a threadbare orange prisoner's jump-suit. The number over his pocket read 0001. He had blue shadows under his eyes, dirty fingernails, and badly cut gray hair, like his last haircut had been done with a weed whacker. He stared at me; his eyes made me nervous. He looked . . . fractured. Angry and frustrated and hungry all at the same time.

"This boy," Dionysus told him, "you need to watch. Poseidon's child, you know."

"Ah!" the prisoner said. "That one."

His tone made it obvious that he and Dionysus had already discussed me at length.

"I am Tantalus," the prisoner said, smiling coldly. "On special assignment here until, well, until my Lord Dionysus decides otherwise. And you, Perseus Jackson, I *do* expect you to refrain from causing any more trouble."

"Trouble?" I demanded.

Dionysus snapped his fingers. A newspaper appeared on the table—the front page of today's *New York Post*. There was my yearbook picture from Meriwether Prep. It was hard for me to make out the headline, but I had a pretty good guess what it said. Something like: *Thirteen-Year-Old Lunatic Torches Gymnasium.*

"Yes, trouble," Tantalus said with satisfaction. "You caused plenty of it last summer, I understand."

I was too mad to speak. Like it was *my* fault the gods had almost gotten into a civil war?

A satyr inched forward nervously and set a plate of bar-becue in front of Tantalus. The new activities director licked his lips. He looked at his empty goblet and said, "Root beer. Barq's special stock. 1967."

The glass filled itself with foamy soda. Tantalus stretched out his hand hesitantly, as if he were afraid the goblet was hot.

"Go on, then, old fellow," Dionysus said, a strange sparkle in his eyes. "Perhaps now it will work."

Tantalus grabbed for the glass, but it scooted away before he could touch it. A few drops of root beer spilled, and Tantalus tried to dab them up with his fingers, but the drops rolled away like quicksilver before he could touch them. He growled and turned toward the plate of barbecue. He picked up a fork and tried to stab a piece of brisket, but the plate skittered down the table and flew off the end, straight into the coals of the brazier.

"Blast!" Tantalus muttered.

"Ah, well," Dionysus said, his voice dripping with false sympathy. "Perhaps a few more days. Believe me, old chap, working at this camp will be torture enough. I'm sure your old curse will fade eventually."

"Eventually," muttered Tantalus, staring at Dionysus's Diet Coke. "Do you have any idea how dry one's throat gets after three thousand years?"

"You're that spirit from the Fields of Punishment," I said. "The one who stands in the lake with the fruit tree hanging over you, but you can't eat or drink."

Tantalus sneered at me. "A real scholar, aren't you, boy?"

"You must've done something really horrible when you were alive," I said, mildly impressed. "What was it?"

Tantalus's eyes narrowed. Behind him, the satyrs were shaking their heads vigorously, trying to warn me.

"I'll be watching you, Percy Jackson," Tantalus said. "I don't want any problems at my camp."

"*Your* camp has problems already . . . sir."

"Oh, go sit down, Johnson," Dionysus sighed. "I believe that table over there is yours—the one where no one else ever wants to sit."

My face was burning, but I knew better than to talk back. Dionysus was an overgrown brat, but he was an immortal, superpowerful overgrown brat. I said, "Come on, Tyson."

"Oh, no," Tantalus said. "The monster stays here. We must decide what to do with it."

"*Him*," I snapped. "His name is Tyson."

The new activities director raised an eyebrow.

"Tyson saved the camp," I insisted. "He pounded those bronze bulls. Otherwise they would've burned down this whole place."

"Yes," Tantalus sighed, "and *what* a pity that would've been."

Dionysus snickered.

"Leave us," Tantalus ordered, "while we decide this creature's fate."

Tyson looked at me with fear in his one big eye, but I knew I couldn't disobey a direct order from the camp directors. Not openly, anyway.

"I'll be right over here, big guy," I promised. "Don't worry. We'll find you a good place to sleep tonight."

Tyson nodded. "I believe you. You are my friend."

Which made me feel a whole lot guiltier.

I trudged over to the Poseidon table and slumped onto the bench. A wood nymph brought me a plate of Olympian olive-and-pepperoni pizza, but I wasn't hungry. I'd been almost killed twice today. I'd managed to end my school year with a complete disaster. Camp Half-Blood was in serious trouble and Chiron had told me not to do anything about it.

I didn't feel very thankful, but I took my dinner, as was customary, up to the bronze brazier and scraped part of it into the flames.

"Poseidon," I murmured, "accept my offering."

And send me some help while you're at it, I prayed silently. *Please.*

The smoke from the burning pizza changed into something fragrant—the smell of a clean sea breeze with wildflowers mixed in—but I had no idea if that meant my father was really listening.

I went back to my seat. I didn't think things could get much worse. But then Tantalus had one of the satyrs blow the conch horn to get our attention for announcements.

"Yes, well," Tantalus said, once the talking had died down. "Another fine meal! Or so I am told." As he spoke, he inched his hand toward his refilled dinner plate, as if maybe the food wouldn't notice what he was doing, but it did. It shot away down the table as soon as he got within six inches.

"And here on my first day of authority," he continued, "I'd like to say what a pleasant form of punishment it is to be here. Over the course of the summer, I hope to torture, er, interact with each and every one of you children. You all look good enough to eat."

Dionysus clapped politely, leading to some halfhearted applause from the satyrs. Tyson was still standing at the head table, looking uncomfortable, but every time he tried to scoot out of the limelight, Tantalus pulled him back.

"And now some changes!" Tantalus gave the campers a crooked smile. "We are reinstituting the chariot races!"

Murmuring broke out at all the tables—excitement, fear, disbelief.

"Now I know," Tantalus continued, raising his voice, "that these races were discontinued some years ago due to, ah, technical problems."

"Three deaths and twenty-six mutilations," someone at the Apollo table called.

"Yes, yes!" Tantalus said. "But I know that you will all join me in welcoming the return of this camp tradition. Golden laurels will go to the winning charioteers each month. Teams may register in the morning! The first race will be held in three days time. We will release you from most of your regular activities to prepare your chariots and choose your horses. Oh, and did I mention, the victorious team's cabin will have no chores for the month in which they win?"

An explosion of excited conversation—no KP for a whole month? No stable cleaning? Was he serious?

Then the last person I expected to object did so.

"But, sir!" Clarisse said. She looked nervous, but she stood up to speak from the Ares table. Some of the campers snickered when they saw the YOU MOO, GIRL! sign on her back. "What about patrol duty? I mean, if we drop everything to ready our chariots—"

"Ah, the hero of the day," Tantalus exclaimed. "Brave Clarisse, who single-handedly bested the bronze bulls!"

Clarisse blinked, then blushed. "Um, I didn't—"

"And modest, too." Tantalus grinned. "Not to worry, my dear! This is a summer camp. We are here to enjoy ourselves, yes?"

"But the tree—"

"And now," Tantalus said, as several of Clarisse's cabin mates pulled her back into her seat, "before we proceed to the campfire and sing-along, one slight housekeeping issue. Percy Jackson and Annabeth Chase have seen fit, for some reason, to bring *this* here." Tantalus waved a hand toward Tyson.

Uneasy murmuring spread among the campers. A lot of sideways looks at me. I wanted to kill Tantalus.

"Now, of course," he said, "Cyclopes have a reputation for being bloodthirsty monsters with a very small brain capacity. Under normal circumstances, I would release this beast into the woods and have you hunt it down with torches and pointed sticks. But who knows? Perhaps this Cyclops is not as horrible as most of its brethren. Until it proves worthy of destruction, we need a place to keep it! I've thought about the stables, but that will make the horses nervous. Hermes's cabin, possibly?"

Silence at the Hermes table. Travis and Connor Stoll developed a sudden interest in the tablecloth. I couldn't blame them. The Hermes cabin was always full to bursting. There was no way they could take in a six-foot-three Cyclops.

"Come now," Tantalus chided. "The monster may be able to do some menial chores. Any suggestions as to where such a beast should be kenneled?"

Suddenly everybody gasped.

Tantalus scooted away from Tyson in surprise. All I could do was stare in disbelief at the brilliant green light that was about to change my life—a dazzling holographic image that had appeared above Tyson's head.

With a sickening twist in my stomach, I remembered what Annabeth had said about Cyclopes, *They're the children of nature spirits and gods . . . Well, one god in particular, usually . . .*

Swirling over Tyson was a glowing green trident—the same symbol that had appeared above me the day Poseidon had claimed me as his son.

There was a moment of awed silence.

Being claimed was a rare event. Some campers waited in vain for it their whole lives. When I'd been claimed by Poseidon last summer, everyone had reverently knelt. But now, they followed Tantalus's lead, and Tantalus roared with laughter. "Well! I think we know where to put the beast now. By the gods, I can see the family resemblance!"

Everybody laughed except Annabeth and a few of my other friends.

Tyson didn't seem to notice. He was too mystified, trying to swat the glowing trident that was now fading over his head. He was too innocent to understand how much they were making fun of him, how cruel people were.

But I got it.

I had a new cabin mate. I had a monster for a half-brother.

SIX

DEMON PIGEONS
ATTACK

The next few days were torture, just like Tantalus wanted.

First there was Tyson moving into the Poseidon cabin, giggling to himself every fifteen seconds and saying, "Percy is my brother?" like he'd just won the lottery.

"Aw, Tyson," I'd say. "It's not that simple."

But there was no explaining it to him. He was in heaven. And me . . . as much as I liked the big guy, I couldn't help feeling embarrassed. Ashamed. There, I said it.

My father, the all-powerful Poseidon, had gotten moony-eyed for some nature spirit, and Tyson had been the result. I mean, I'd read the myths about Cyclopes. I even remembered that they were often Poseidon's children. But I'd never really processed that this made them my . . . family. Until I had Tyson living with me in the next bunk.

And then there were the comments from the other campers. Suddenly, I wasn't Percy Jackson, the cool guy who'd retrieved Zeus's lightning bolt last summer. Now I was Percy Jackson, the poor schmuck with the ugly monster for a brother.

"He's not my *real* brother!" I protested whenever Tyson

wasn't around. "He's more like a half-brother on the monstrous side of the family. Like . . . a half-brother twice removed, or something."

Nobody bought it.

I admit—I was angry at my dad. I felt like being his son was now a joke.

Annabeth tried to make me feel better. She suggested we team up for the chariot race to take our minds off our problems. Don't get me wrong—we both hated Tantalus and we were worried sick about camp—but we didn't know what to do about it. Until we could come up with some brilliant plan to save Thalia's tree, we figured we might as well go along with the races. After all, Annabeth's mom, Athena, had invented the chariot, and my dad had created horses. Together we would *own* that track.

One morning Annabeth and I were sitting by the canoe lake sketching chariot designs when some jokers from Aphrodite's cabin walked by and asked me if I needed to borrow some eyeliner for my eye . . . "Oh sorry, *eyes.*"

As they walked away laughing, Annabeth grumbled, "Just ignore them, Percy. It isn't your fault you have a monster for a brother."

"He's *not* my brother!" I snapped. "And he's not a monster, either!"

Annabeth raised her eyebrows. "Hey, don't get mad at me! And technically, he *is* a monster."

"Well *you* gave him permission to enter the camp."

"Because it was the only way to save your life! I

mean . . . I'm sorry, Percy, I didn't expect Poseidon to *claim* him. Cyclopes are the most deceitful, treacherous—"

"He is not! What have you got against Cyclopes, anyway?"

Annabeth's ears turned pink. I got the feeling there was something she wasn't telling me—something bad.

"Just forget it," she said. "Now, the axle for this chariot—"

"You're treating him like he's this horrible thing," I said. "He saved my life."

Annabeth threw down her pencil and stood. "Then maybe you should design a chariot with *him*."

"Maybe I should."

"Fine!"

"Fine!"

She stormed off and left me feeling even worse than before.

The next couple of days, I tried to keep my mind off my problems.

Silena Beauregard, one of the nicer girls from Aphrodite's cabin, gave me my first riding lesson on a pegasus. She explained that there was only one immortal winged horse named Pegasus, who still wandered free somewhere in the skies, but over the eons he'd sired a lot of children, none quite so fast or heroic, but all named after the first and greatest.

Being the son of the sea god, I never liked going into the air. My dad had this rivalry with Zeus, so I tried to stay out of the lord of the sky's domain as much as possible. But riding a winged horse felt different. It didn't make me nearly as nervous as being in an airplane. Maybe that was because my dad had created horses out of sea foam, so the pegasi were sort of . . . neutral territory. I could understand their thoughts. I wasn't surprised when my pegasus went galloping over the treetops or chased a flock of seagulls into a cloud.

The problem was that Tyson wanted to ride the "chicken ponies," too, but the pegasi got skittish whenever he approached. I told them telepathically that Tyson wouldn't hurt them, but they didn't seem to believe me. That made Tyson cry.

The only person at camp who had *no* problem with Tyson was Beckendorf from the Hephaestus cabin. The blacksmith god had always worked with Cyclopes in his forges, so Beckendorf took Tyson down to the armory to teach him metalworking. He said he'd have Tyson crafting magic items like a master in no time.

After lunch, I worked out in the arena with Apollo's cabin. Swordplay had always been my strength. People said I was better at it than any camper in the last hundred years, except maybe Luke. People always compared me to Luke.

I thrashed the Apollo guys easily. I should've been testing myself against the Ares and Athena cabins, since they had the best sword fighters, but I didn't get along with Clarisse and her siblings, and after my argument with Annabeth, I just didn't want to see her.

I went to archery class, even though I was terrible at it, and it wasn't the same without Chiron teaching. In arts and crafts, I started a marble bust of Poseidon, but it started looking like Sylvester Stallone, so I ditched it. I scaled the climbing wall in full lava-and-earthquake mode. And in the evenings, I did border patrol. Even though Tantalus had insisted we forget trying to protect the camp, some of the campers had quietly kept it up, working out a schedule during our free times.

I sat at the top of Half-Blood Hill and watched the dryads come and go, singing to the dying pine tree. Satyrs brought their reed pipes and played nature magic songs, and for a while the pine needles seemed to get fuller. The flowers on the hill smelled a little sweeter and the grass looked greener. But as soon as the music stopped, the sickness crept back into the air. The whole hill seemed to be infected, dying from the poison that had sunk into the tree's roots. The longer I sat there, the angrier I got.

Luke had done this. I remembered his sly smile, the dragon-claw scar across his face. He'd pretended to be my friend, and the whole time he'd been Kronos's number-one servant.

I opened the palm of my hand. The scar Luke had given me last summer was fading, but I could still see it—a white asterisk-shaped wound where his pit scorpion had stung me.

I thought about what Luke had told me right before he'd tried to kill me: *Good-bye, Percy. There is a new Golden Age coming. You won't be part of it.*

* * *

At night, I had more dreams of Grover. Sometimes, I just heard snatches of his voice. Once, I heard him say: *It's here.* Another time: *He likes sheep.*

I thought about telling Annabeth about my dreams, but I would've felt stupid. I mean, *He likes sheep?* She would've thought I was crazy.

The night before the race, Tyson and I finished our chariot. It was wicked cool. Tyson had made the metal parts in the armory's forges. I'd sanded the wood and put the carriage together. It was blue and white, with wave designs on the sides and a trident painted on the front. After all that work, it seemed only fair that Tyson would ride shotgun with me, though I knew the horses wouldn't like it, and Tyson's extra weight would slow us down.

As we were turning in for bed, Tyson said, "You are mad?"

I realized I'd been scowling. "Nah. I'm not mad."

He lay down in his bunk and was quiet in the dark. His body was way too long for his bed. When he pulled up the covers, his feet stuck out the bottom. "I am a monster."

"Don't say that."

"It is okay. I will be a *good* monster. Then you will not have to be mad."

I didn't know what to say. I stared at the ceiling and felt like I was dying slowly, right along with Thalia's tree.

"It's just . . . I never had a half-brother before." I tried to keep my voice from cracking. "It's really different for me. And I'm worried about the camp. And another friend of mine, Grover . . . he might be in trouble. I keep feeling like

I should be doing something to help, but I don't know what."

Tyson said nothing.

"I'm sorry," I told him. "It's not your fault. I'm mad at Poseidon. I feel like he's trying to embarrass me, like he's trying to compare us or something, and I don't understand why."

I heard a deep rumbling sound. Tyson was snoring.

I sighed. "Good night, big guy."

And I closed my eyes, too.

In my dream, Grover was wearing a wedding dress.

It didn't fit him very well. The gown was too long and the hem was caked with dried mud. The neckline kept falling off his shoulders. A tattered veil covered his face.

He was standing in a dank cave, lit only by torches. There was a cot in one corner and an old-fashioned loom in the other, a length of white cloth half woven on the frame. And he was staring right at me, like I was a TV program he'd been waiting for. "Thank the gods!" he yelped. "Can you hear me?"

My dream-self was slow to respond. I was still looking around, taking in the stalactite ceiling, the stench of sheep and goats, the growling and grumbling and bleating sounds that seemed to echo from behind a refrigerator-sized boulder, which was blocking the room's only exit, as if there were a much larger cavern beyond it.

"Percy?" Grover said. "Please, I don't have the strength to project any better. You *have* to hear me!"

"I hear you," I said. "Grover, what's going on?"

From behind the boulder, a monstrous voice yelled, "Honeypie! Are you done yet?"

Grover flinched. He called out in falsetto, "Not quite, dearest! A few more days!"

"Bah! Hasn't it been two weeks yet?"

"N-no, dearest. Just five days. That leaves twelve more to go."

The monster was silent, maybe trying to do the math. He must've been worse at arithmetic than I was, because he said, "All right, but hurry! I want to SEEEEE under that veil, heh-heh-heh."

Grover turned back to me. "You have to help me! No time! I'm stuck in this cave. On an island in the sea."

"*Where?*"

"I don't know exactly! I went to Florida and turned left."

"What? How did you—"

"It's a trap!" Grover said. "It's the reason no satyr has ever returned from this quest. He's a shepherd, Percy! And he *has* it. Its nature magic is *so* powerful it smells just like the great god Pan! The satyrs come here thinking they've found Pan, and they get trapped and eaten by Polyphemus!"

"Poly-who?"

"The Cyclops!" Grover said, exasperated. "I almost got away. I made it all the way to St. Augustine."

"But he followed you," I said, remembering my first dream. "And trapped you in a bridal boutique."

"That's right," Grover said. "My first empathy link

must've worked then. Look, this bridal dress is the only thing keeping me alive. He thinks I smell good, but I told him it was just goat-scented perfume. Thank goodness he can't see very well. His eye is still half blind from the last time somebody poked it out. But soon he'll realize what I am. He's only giving me two weeks to finish the bridal train, and he's getting impatient!"

"Wait a minute. This Cyclops thinks you're—"

"Yes!" Grover wailed. "He thinks I'm a lady Cyclops and he wants to marry me!"

Under different circumstances, I might've busted out laughing, but Grover's voice was deadly serious. He was shaking with fear.

"I'll come rescue you," I promised. "Where are you?"

"The Sea of Monsters, of course!"

"The sea of *what*?"

"I told you! I don't know exactly where! And look, Percy . . . um, I'm really sorry about this, but this empathy link . . . well, I had no choice. Our emotions are connected now. If I die . . ."

"Don't tell me, I'll die too."

"Oh, well, perhaps not. You might live for years in a vegetative state. But, uh, it would be a lot better if you got me out of here."

"Honeypie!" the monster bellowed. "Dinnertime! Yummy yummy sheep meat!"

Grover whimpered. "I have to go. Hurry!"

"Wait! You said 'it' was here. What?"

But Grover's voice was already growing fainter. "Sweet dreams. Don't let me die!"

The dream faded and I woke with a start. It was early morning. Tyson was staring down at me, his one big brown eye full of concern.

"Are you okay?" he asked.

His voice sent a chill down my back, because he sounded almost exactly like the monster I'd heard in my dream.

The morning of the race was hot and humid. Fog lay low on the ground like sauna steam. Millions of birds were roosting in the trees—fat gray-and-white pigeons, except they didn't coo like regular pigeons. They made this annoying metallic screeching sound that reminded me of submarine radar.

The racetrack had been built in a grassy field between the archery range and the woods. Hephaestus's cabin had used the bronze bulls, which were completely tame since they'd had their heads smashed in, to plow an oval track in a matter of minutes.

There were rows of stone steps for the spectators—Tantalus, the satyrs, a few dryads, and all of the campers who weren't participating. Mr. D didn't show. He never got up before ten o'clock.

"Right!" Tantalus announced as the teams began to assemble. A naiad had brought him a big platter of pastries, and as Tantalus spoke, his right hand chased a chocolate éclair across the judge's table. "You all know the rules. A quarter-mile track. Twice around to win. Two horses per chariot. Each team will consist of a driver and a fighter. Weapons are allowed. Dirty tricks are expected. But try not to kill anybody!" Tantalus smiled at us like we were all naughty children. "Any killing will result in harsh punishment. No s'mores at the campfire for a week! Now ready your chariots!"

Beckendorf led the Hephaestus team onto the track. They had a sweet ride made of bronze and iron—even the horses, which were magical automatons like the Colchis bulls. I had no doubt that their chariot had all kinds of mechanical traps and more fancy options than a fully loaded Maserati.

The Ares chariot was bloodred, and pulled by two grisly horse skeletons. Clarisse climbed aboard with a batch of javelins, spiked balls, caltrops, and a bunch of other nasty toys.

Apollo's chariot was trim and graceful and completely gold, pulled by two beautiful palominos. Their fighter was armed with a bow, though he had promised not to shoot regular pointed arrows at the opposing drivers.

Hermes's chariot was green and kind of old-looking, as if it hadn't been out of the garage in years. It didn't look like anything special, but it was manned by the Stoll brothers, and I shuddered to think what dirty tricks they'd schemed up.

That left two chariots: one driven by Annabeth, and the other by me.

Before the race began, I tried to approach Annabeth and tell her about my dream.

She perked up when I mentioned Grover, but when I told her what he'd said, she seemed to get distant again, suspicious.

"You're trying to distract me," she decided.

"What? No I'm not!"

"Oh, right! Like Grover would just happen to stumble across the *one* thing that could save the camp."

"What do you mean?"

She rolled her eyes. "Go back to your chariot, Percy."

"I'm not making this up. He's in trouble, Annabeth."

She hesitated. I could tell she was trying to decide whether or not to trust me. Despite our occasional fights, we'd been through a lot together. And I knew she would never want anything bad to happen to Grover.

"Percy, an empathy link is so hard to do. I mean, it's more likely you really were dreaming."

"The Oracle," I said. "We could consult the Oracle."

Annabeth frowned.

Last summer, before my quest, I'd visited the strange spirit that lived in the Big House attic and it had given me a prophecy that came true in ways I'd never expected. The experience had freaked me out for months. Annabeth knew I'd never suggest going back there if I wasn't completely serious.

Before she could answer, the conch horn sounded.

"Charioteers!" Tantalus called. "To your mark!"

"We'll talk later," Annabeth told me, "*after* I win."

As I was walking back to my own chariot, I noticed how many more pigeons were in the trees now—screeching like crazy, making the whole forest rustle. Nobody else seemed to be paying them much attention, but they made me nervous. Their beaks glinted strangely. Their eyes seemed shinier than regular birds.

Tyson was having trouble getting our horses under control. I had to talk to them a long time before they would settle down.

He's a monster, lord! they complained to me.

He's a son of Poseidon, I told them. *Just like . . . well, just like me.*

No! they insisted. *Monster! Horse-eater! Not trusted!*

I'll give you sugar cubes at the end of the race, I said.

Sugar cubes?

Very big sugar cubes. And apples. Did I mention the apples?

Finally they agreed to let me harness them.

Now, if you've never seen a Greek chariot, it's built for speed, not safety or comfort. It's basically a wooden basket, open at the back, mounted on an axle between two wheels. The driver stands up the whole time, and you can feel every bump in the road. The carriage is made of such light wood that if you wipe out making the hairpin turns at either end of the track, you'll probably tip over and crush both the chariot and yourself. It's an even better rush than skateboarding.

I took the reins and maneuvered the chariot to the starting line. I gave Tyson a ten-foot pole and told him that his job was to push the other chariots away if they got too close, and to deflect anything they might try to throw at us.

"No hitting ponies with the stick," he insisted.

"No," I agreed. "Or people, either, if you can help it. We're going to run a clean race. Just keep the distractions away and let me concentrate on driving."

"We will win!" He beamed.

We are *so* going to lose, I thought to myself, but I *had* to try. I wanted to show the others . . . well, I wasn't sure what, exactly. That Tyson wasn't such a bad guy? That I wasn't ashamed of being seen with him in public? Maybe that they hadn't hurt me with all their jokes and name-calling?

As the chariots lined up, more shiny-eyed pigeons gathered in the woods. They were screeching so loudly the campers in the stands were starting to take notice, glancing nervously at the trees, which shivered under the weight of the birds. Tantalus didn't look concerned, but he did have to speak up to be heard over the noise.

"Charioteers!" he shouted. "Attend your mark!"

He waved his hand and the starting signal dropped. The chariots roared to life. Hooves thundered against the dirt. The crowd cheered.

Almost immediately there was a loud nasty *crack!* I looked back in time to see the Apollo chariot flip over. The Hermes chariot had rammed into it—maybe by mistake, maybe not. The riders were thrown free, but their panicked horses dragged the golden chariot diagonally across the track. The Hermes team, Travis and Connor Stoll, were laughing at their good luck, but not for long. The Apollo horses crashed into theirs, and the Hermes chariot flipped too, leaving a pile of broken wood and four rearing horses in the dust.

Two chariots down in the first twenty feet. I loved this sport.

I turned my attention back to the front. We were making good time, pulling ahead of Ares, but Annabeth's chariot was way ahead of us. She was already making her turn around the first post, her javelin man grinning and waving at us, shouting: "See ya!"

The Hephaestus chariot was starting to gain on us, too.

Beckendorf pressed a button, and a panel slid open on the side of his chariot.

"Sorry, Percy!" he yelled. Three sets of balls and chains shot straight toward our wheels. They would've wrecked us completely if Tyson hadn't whacked them aside with a quick swipe of his pole. He gave the Hephaestus chariot a good shove and sent them skittering sideways while we pulled ahead.

"Nice work, Tyson!" I yelled.

"Birds!" he cried.

"What?"

We were whipping along so fast it was hard to hear or see anything, but Tyson pointed toward the woods and I saw what he was worried about. The pigeons had risen from the trees. They were spiraling like a huge tornado, heading toward the track.

No big deal, I told myself. *They're just pigeons.*

I tried to concentrate on the race.

We made our first turn, the wheels creaking under us, the chariot threatening to tip, but we were now only ten feet behind Annabeth. If I could just get a little closer, Tyson could use his pole. . . .

Annabeth's fighter wasn't smiling now. He pulled a javelin from his collection and took aim at me. He was about to throw when we heard the screaming.

The pigeons were swarming—thousands of them dive-bombing the spectators in the stands, attacking the other chariots. Beckendorf was mobbed. His fighter tried to bat the birds away but he couldn't see anything. The chariot veered off course and plowed through the strawberry fields, the mechanical horses steaming.

In the Ares chariot, Clarisse barked an order to her fighter, who quickly threw a screen of camouflage netting over their basket. The birds swarmed around it, pecking and clawing at the fighter's hands as he tried to hold up the net, but Clarisse just gritted her teeth and kept driving. Her skeletal horses seemed immune to the distraction. The pigeons pecked uselessly at their empty eye sockets and flew through their rib cages, but the stallions kept right on running.

The spectators weren't so lucky. The birds were slashing at any bit of exposed flesh, driving everyone into a panic. Now that the birds were closer, it was clear they weren't normal pigeons. Their eyes were beady and evil-looking. Their beaks were made of bronze, and judging from the yelps of the campers, they must've been razor sharp.

"Stymphalian birds!" Annabeth yelled. She slowed down and pulled her chariot alongside mine. "They'll strip everyone to bones if we don't drive them away!"

"Tyson," I said, "we're turning around!"

"Going the wrong way?" he asked.

"Always," I grumbled, but I steered the chariot toward the stands.

Annabeth rode right next to me. She shouted, "Heroes, to arms!" But I wasn't sure anyone could hear her over the screeching of the birds and the general chaos.

I held my reins in one hand and managed to draw Riptide as a wave of birds dived at my face, their metal beaks snapping. I slashed them out of the air and they exploded into dust and feathers, but there were still millions of them left. One nailed me in the back end and I almost jumped straight out of the chariot.

Annabeth wasn't having much better luck. The closer we got to the stands, the thicker the cloud of birds became.

Some of the spectators were trying to fight back. The Athena campers were calling for shields. The archers from Apollo's cabin brought out their bows and arrows, ready to slay the menace, but with so many campers mixed in with the birds, it wasn't safe to shoot.

"Too many!" I yelled to Annabeth. "How do you get rid of them?"

She stabbed at a pigeon with her knife. "Hercules used noise! Brass bells! He scared them away with the most horrible sound he could—"

Her eyes got wide. "Percy . . . Chiron's collection!"

I understood instantly. "You think it'll work?"

She handed her fighter the reins and leaped from her chariot into mine like it was the easiest thing in the world. "To the Big House! It's our only chance!"

Clarisse has just pulled across the finish line, completely

unopposed, and seemed to notice for the first time how serious the bird problem was.

When she saw us driving away, she yelled, "You're *running*? The fight is here, cowards!" She drew her sword and charged for the stands.

I urged our horses into a gallop. The chariot rumbled through the strawberry fields, across the volleyball pit, and lurched to a halt in front of the Big House. Annabeth and I ran inside, tearing down the hallway to Chiron's apartment.

His boom box was still on his nightstand. So were his favorite CDs. I grabbed the most repulsive one I could find, Annabeth snatched the boom box, and together we ran back outside.

Down at the track, the chariots were in flames. Wounded campers ran in every direction, with birds shredding their clothes and pulling out their hair, while Tantalus chased breakfast pastries around the stands, every once in a while yelling, "Everything's under control! Not to worry!"

We pulled up to the finish line. Annabeth got the boom box ready. I prayed the batteries weren't dead.

I pressed PLAY and started up Chiron's favorite—the *All-Time Greatest Hits of Dean Martin*. Suddenly the air was filled with violins and a bunch of guys moaning in Italian.

The demon pigeons went nuts. They started flying in circles, running into each other like they wanted to bash their own brains out. Then they abandoned the track altogether and flew skyward in a huge dark wave.

"Now!" shouted Annabeth. "Archers!"

With clear targets, Apollo's archers had flawless aim. Most of them could nock five or six arrows at once. Within minutes, the ground was littered with dead bronze-beaked pigeons, and the survivors were a distant trail of smoke on the horizon.

The camp was saved, but the wreckage wasn't pretty. Most of the chariots had been completely destroyed. Almost everyone was wounded, bleeding from multiple bird pecks. The kids from Aphrodite's cabin were screaming because their hairdos had been ruined and their clothes pooped on.

"Bravo!" Tantalus said, but he wasn't looking at me or Annabeth. "We have our first winner!" He walked to the finish line and awarded the golden laurels for the race to a stunned-looking Clarisse.

Then he turned and smiled at me. "And now to punish the troublemakers who disrupted this race."

SEVEN

I ACCEPT GIFTS
FROM A STRANGER

The way Tantalus saw it, the Stymphalian birds had simply been minding their own business in the woods and would not have attacked if Annabeth, Tyson, and I hadn't disturbed them with our bad chariot driving.

This was so completely unfair, I told Tantalus to go chase a doughnut, which didn't help his mood. He sentenced us to kitchen patrol—scrubbing pots and platters all afternoon in the underground kitchen with the cleaning harpies. The harpies washed with lava instead of water, to get that extra-clean sparkle and kill ninety-nine point nine percent of all germs, so Annabeth and I had to wear asbestos gloves and aprons.

Tyson didn't mind. He plunged his bare hands right in and started scrubbing, but Annabeth and I had to suffer through hours of hot, dangerous work, especially since there were tons of extra plates. Tantalus had ordered a special luncheon banquet to celebrate Clarisse's chariot victory—a full-course meal featuring country-fried Stymphalian death-bird.

The only good thing about our punishment was that it gave Annabeth and me a common enemy and lots of time to talk. After listening to my dream about Grover again, she looked like she might be starting to believe me.

"If he's really found it," she murmured, "and if we could retrieve it—"

"Hold on," I said. "You act like this . . . whatever-it-is Grover found is the only thing in the world that could save the camp. What *is* it?"

"I'll give you a hint. What do you get when you skin a ram?"

"Messy?"

She sighed. "A *fleece*. The coat of a ram is called a fleece. And if that ram happens to have golden wool—"

"The Golden Fleece. Are you serious?"

Annabeth scrapped a plateful of death-bird bones into the lava. "Percy, remember the Gray Sisters? They said they knew the location of the thing you seek. And they mentioned Jason. Three thousand years ago, they told *him* how to find the Golden Fleece. You *do* know the story of Jason and the Argonauts?"

"Yeah," I said. "That old movie with the clay skeletons."

Annabeth rolled her eyes. "Oh my gods, Percy! You are so hopeless."

"*What?*" I demanded.

"Just listen. The real story of the Fleece: there were these two children of Zeus, Cadmus and Europa, okay? They were about to get offered up as human sacrifices, when they prayed to Zeus to save them. So Zeus sent this magical flying ram with golden wool, which picked them up in Greece and carried them all the way to Colchis in Asia Minor. Well, actually it carried Cadmus. Europa fell off and died along the way, but that's not important."

"It was probably important to her."

"The *point* is, when Cadmus got to Colchis, he sacrificed the golden ram to the gods and hung the Fleece in a tree in the middle of the kingdom. The Fleece brought prosperity to the land. Animals stopped getting sick. Plants grew better. Farmers had bumper crops. Plagues never visited. That's why Jason wanted the Fleece. It can revitalize any land where it's placed. It cures sickness, strengthens nature, cleans up pollution—"

"It could cure Thalia's tree."

Annabeth nodded. "And it would totally strengthen the borders of Camp Half-Blood. But Percy, the Fleece has been missing for centuries. Tons of heroes have searched for it with no luck."

"But Grover found it," I said. "He went looking for Pan and he found the Fleece instead because they both radiate nature magic. It makes sense, Annabeth. We can rescue him and save the camp at the same time. It's perfect!"

Annabeth hesitated. "A little *too* perfect, don't you think? What if it's a trap?"

I remembered last summer, how Kronos had manipulated our quest. He'd almost fooled us into helping him start a war that would've destroyed Western Civilization.

"What choice do we have?" I asked. "Are you going to help me rescue Grover or not?"

She glanced at Tyson, who'd lost interest in our conversation and was happily making toy boats out of cups and spoons in the lava.

"Percy," she said under her breath, "we'll have to fight a Cyclops. Polyphemus, the *worst* of the Cyclopes. And there's only one place his island could be. The Sea of Monsters."

"Where's that?"

She stared at me like she thought I was playing dumb. "The Sea of Monsters. The same sea Odysseus sailed through, and Jason, and Aeneas, and all the others."

"You mean the Mediterranean?"

"No. Well, yes . . . but no."

"Another straight answer. Thanks."

"Look, Percy, the Sea of Monsters is the sea all heroes sail through on their adventures. It used to be in the Mediterranean, yes. But like everything else, it shifts locations as the West's center of power shifts."

"Like Mount Olympus being above the Empire State Building," I said. "And Hades being under Los Angeles."

"Right."

"But a whole sea full of monsters—how could you hide something like that? Wouldn't the mortals notice weird things happening . . . like, ships getting eaten and stuff?"

"Of course they notice. They don't understand, but they know something is strange about that part of the ocean. The Sea of Monsters is off the east coast of the U.S. now, just northeast of Florida. The mortals even have a name for it."

"The Bermuda Triangle?"

"Exactly."

I let that sink in. I guess it wasn't stranger than anything else I'd learned since coming to Camp Half-Blood. "Okay . . . so at least we know where to look."

"It's still a huge area, Percy. Searching for one tiny island in monster-infested waters—"

"Hey, I'm the son of the sea god. This is my home turf. How hard can it be?"

Annabeth knit her eyebrows. "We'll have to talk to Tantalus, get approval for a quest. He'll say no."

"Not if we tell him tonight at the campfire in front of everybody. The whole camp will hear. They'll pressure him. He won't be able to refuse."

"Maybe." A little bit of hope crept into Annabeth's voice. "We'd better get these dishes done. Hand me the lava spray gun, will you?"

That night at the campfire, Apollo's cabin led the sing-along. They tried to get everybody's spirits up, but it wasn't easy after that afternoon's bird attack. We all sat around a semicircle of stone steps, singing halfheartedly and watching the bonfire blaze while the Apollo guys strummed their guitars and picked their lyres.

We did all the standard camp numbers: "Down by the Aegean," "I Am My Own Great-Great-Great-Great-Grandpa," "This Land is Minos's Land." The bonfire was enchanted, so the louder you sang, the higher it rose, changing color and heat with the mood of the crowd. On a good night, I'd seen it twenty feet high, bright purple, and so hot the whole front row's marshmallows burst into the flames. Tonight, the fire was only five feet high, barely warm, and the flames were the color of lint.

Dionysus left early. After suffering through a few songs,

he muttered something about how even pinochle with Chiron had been more exciting than this. Then he gave Tantalus a distasteful look and headed back toward the Big House.

When the last song was over, Tantalus said, "Well, that was lovely!"

He came forward with a toasted marshmallow on a stick and tried to pluck it off, real casual-like. But before he could touch it, the marshmallow flew off the stick. Tantalus made a wild grab, but the marshmallow committed suicide, diving into the flames.

Tantalus turned back toward us, smiling coldly. "Now then! Some announcements about tomorrow's schedule."

"Sir," I said.

Tantalus's eye twitched. "Our kitchen boy has something to say?"

Some of the Ares campers snickered, but I wasn't going to let anybody embarrass me into silence. I stood and looked at Annabeth. Thank the gods, she stood up with me.

I said, "We have an idea to save the camp."

Dead silence, but I could tell I'd gotten everybody's interest, because the campfire flared bright yellow.

"Indeed," Tantalus said blandly. "Well, if it has anything to do with chariots—"

"The Golden Fleece," I said. "We know where it is."

The flames burned orange. Before Tantalus could stop me, I blurted out my dream about Grover and Polyphemus's island. Annabeth stepped in and reminded everybody what the Fleece could do. It sounded more convincing coming from her.

"The Fleece can save the camp," she concluded. "I'm certain of it."

"Nonsense," said Tantalus. "We don't need saving."

Everybody stared at him until Tantalus started looking uncomfortable.

"Besides," he added quickly, "the Sea of Monsters? That's hardly an exact location. You wouldn't even know where to look."

"Yes, I would," I said.

Annabeth leaned toward me and whispered, "You would?"

I nodded, because Annabeth had jogged something in my memory when she reminded me about our taxi drive with the Gray Sisters. At the time, the information they'd given me made no sense. But now . . .

"30, 31, 75, 12," I said.

"Ooo-kay," Tantalus said. "Thank you for sharing those meaningless numbers."

"They're sailing coordinates," I said. "Latitude and longitude. I, uh, learned about it in social studies."

Even Annabeth looked impressed. "30 degrees, 31 minutes north, 75 degrees, 12 minutes west. He's right! The Gray Sisters gave us those coordinates. That'd be somewhere in the Atlantic, off the coast of Florida. The Sea of Monsters. We need a quest!"

"Wait just a minute," Tantalus said.

But the campers took up the chant. "We need a quest! We need a quest!"

The flames rose higher.

"It isn't necessary!" Tantalus insisted.

"WE NEED A QUEST! WE NEED A QUEST!"

"Fine!" Tantalus shouted, his eyes blazing with anger. "You brats want me to assign a quest?"

"YES!"

"Very well," he agreed. "I shall authorize a champion to undertake this perilous journey, to retrieve the Golden Fleece and bring it back to camp. Or die trying."

My heart filled with excitement. I wasn't going to let Tantalus scare me. This was what I needed to do. I was going to save Grover and the camp. Nothing would stop me.

"I will allow our champion to consult the Oracle!" Tantalus announced. "And choose two companions for the journey. And I think the choice of champions is obvious."

Tantalus looked at Annabeth and me as if he wanted to flay us alive. "The champion should be one who has earned the camp's respect, who has proven resourceful in the chariot races and courageous in the defense of the camp. *You* shall lead this quest . . . Clarisse!"

The fire flickered a thousand different colors. The Ares cabin started stomping and cheering, "CLARISSE! CLARISSE!"

Clarisse stood up, looking stunned. Then she swallowed, and her chest swelled with pride. "I accept the quest!"

"Wait!" I shouted. "Grover is my friend. The dream came to *me*."

"Sit down!" yelled one of the Ares campers. "You had your chance last summer!"

"Yeah, he just wants to be in the spotlight again!" another said.

Clarisse glared at me. "I accept the quest!" she repeated. "I, Clarisse, daughter of Ares, will save the camp!"

The Ares campers cheered even louder. Annabeth protested, and the other Athena campers joined in. Everybody else started taking sides—shouting and arguing and throwing marshmallows. I thought it was going to turn into a full-fledged s'more war until Tantalus shouted, "Silence, you brats!"

His tone stunned even me.

"Sit down!" he ordered. "And I will tell you a ghost story."

I didn't know what he was up to, but we all moved reluctantly back to our seats. The evil aura radiating from Tantalus was as strong as any monster I'd ever faced.

"Once upon a time there was a mortal king who was beloved of the Gods!" Tantalus put his hand on his chest, and I got the feeling he was talking about himself.

"This king," he said, "was even allowed to feast on Mount Olympus. But when he tried to take some ambrosia and nectar back to earth to figure out the recipe—just one little doggie bag, mind you—the gods punished him. They banned him from their halls forever! His own people mocked him! His children scolded him! And, oh yes, campers, he had horrible children. Children—just—like—you!"

He pointed a crooked finger at several people in the audience, including me.

"Do you know what he did to his ungrateful children?" Tantalus asked softly. "Do you know how he paid back the gods for their cruel punishment? He invited the Olympians to a feast at his palace, just to show there were no hard feelings. No one noticed that his children were missing. And when he served the gods dinner, my dear campers, can you guess what was in the stew?"

No one dared answer. The firelight glowed dark blue, reflecting evilly on Tantalus's crooked face.

"Oh, the gods punished him in the afterlife," Tantalus croaked. "They did indeed. But he'd had his moment of satisfaction, hadn't he? His children never again spoke back to him or questioned his authority. And do you know what? Rumor has it that the king's spirit now dwells at this very camp, waiting for a chance to take revenge on ungrateful, rebellious children. And so . . . are there any more complaints, before we send Clarisse off on her quest?"

Silence.

Tantalus nodded at Clarisse. "The Oracle, my dear. Go on."

She shifted uncomfortably, like even *she* didn't want glory at the price of being Tantalus's pet. "Sir—"

"Go!" he snarled.

She bowed awkwardly and hurried off toward the Big House.

"What about you, Percy Jackson?" Tantalus asked. "No comments from our dishwasher?"

I didn't say anything. I wasn't going to give him the satisfaction of punishing me again.

"Good," Tantalus said. "And let me remind everyone—no one leaves this camp without my permission. Anyone who tries . . . well, if they survive the attempt, they will be expelled forever, but it won't come to that. The harpies will be enforcing curfew from now on, and they are always hungry! Good night, my dear campers. Sleep well."

With a wave of Tantalus's hand, the fire was extinguished, and the campers trailed off toward their cabins in the dark.

I couldn't explain things to Tyson. He knew I was sad. He knew I wanted to go on a trip and Tantalus wouldn't let me.

"You will go anyway?" he asked.

"I don't know," I admitted. "It would be hard. Very hard."

"I will help."

"No. I—uh, I couldn't ask you to do that, big guy. Too dangerous."

Tyson looked down at the pieces of metal he was assembling in his lap—springs and gears and tiny wires. Beckendorf had given him some tools and spare parts, and now Tyson spent every night tinkering, though I wasn't sure how his huge hands could handle such delicate little pieces.

"What are you building?" I asked.

Tyson didn't answer. Instead he made a whimpering sound in the back of his throat. "Annabeth doesn't like Cyclopes. You . . . don't want me along?"

"Oh, that's not it," I said halfheartedly. "Annabeth likes you. Really."

He had tears in the corners of his eye.

I remembered that Grover, like all satyrs, could read human emotions. I wondered if Cyclopes had the same ability.

Tyson folded up his tinkering project in an oilcloth. He lay down on his bunk bed and hugged his bundle like a teddy bear. When he turned toward the wall, I could see the weird scars on his back, like somebody had plowed over him with a tractor. I wondered for the millionth time how he'd gotten hurt.

"Daddy always cared for m-me," he sniffled. "Now . . . I think he was mean to have a Cyclops boy. I should not have been born."

"Don't talk that way! Poseidon claimed you, didn't he? So . . . he must care about you . . . a lot. . . ."

My voice trailed off as I thought about all those years Tyson had lived on the streets of New York in a cardboard refrigerator box. How could Tyson think that Poseidon had cared for him? What kind of dad let that happen to his kid, even if his kid was a monster?

"Tyson . . . camp will be a good home for you. The others will get used to you. I promise."

Tyson sighed. I waited for him to say something. Then I realized he was already asleep.

I lay back on my bed and tried to close my eyes, but I just couldn't. I was afraid I might have another dream about Grover. If the empathy link was real . . . if something happened to Grover . . . would I ever wake up?

The full moon shone through my window. The sound of the surf rumbled in the distance. I could smell the warm scent of the strawberry fields, and hear the laughter of the dryads as they chased owls through the forest. But something felt wrong about the night—the sickness of Thalia's tree, spreading across the valley.

Could Clarisse save Half-Blood Hill? I thought the odds were better of me getting a "Best Camper" award from Tantalus.

I got out of bed and pulled on some clothes. I grabbed a beach blanket and a six-pack of Coke from under my bunk. The Cokes were against the rules. No outside snacks or drinks were allowed, but if you talked to the right guy in Hermes's cabin and paid him a few golden drachma, he could smuggle in almost anything from the nearest convenience store.

Sneaking out after curfew was against the rules, too. If I got caught I'd either get in big trouble or be eaten by the harpies. But I wanted to see the ocean. I always felt better there. My thoughts were clearer. I left the cabin and headed for the beach.

I spread my blanket near the surf and popped open a Coke. For some reason sugar and caffeine always calmed down my hyperactive brain. I tried to decide what to do to save the camp, but nothing came to me. I wished Poseidon would talk to me, give me some advice or something.

The sky was clear and starry. I was checking out the constellations Annabeth had taught me—Sagittarius, Hercules, Corona Borealis—when somebody said, "Beautiful, aren't they?"

I almost spewed soda.

Standing right next to me was a guy in nylon running shorts and a New York City Marathon T-shirt. He was slim and fit, with salt-and-pepper hair and a sly smile. He looked kind of familiar, but I couldn't figure out why.

My first thought was that he must've been taking a mid-night jog down the beach and strayed inside the camp bor-ders. That wasn't supposed to happen. Regular mortals couldn't enter the valley. But maybe with the tree's magic weakening he'd managed to slip in. But in the middle of the night? And there was nothing around except farmland and state preserves. Where would this guy have jogged from?

"May I join you?" he asked. "I haven't sat down in ages."

Now, I know—a strange guy in the middle of the night. Common sense: I was supposed to run away, yell for help, etc. But the guy acted so calm about the whole thing that I found it hard to be afraid.

I said, "Uh, sure."

He smiled. "Your hospitality does you credit. Oh, and Coca-Cola! May I?'

He sat at the other end of the blanket, popped a soda and took a drink. "Ah . . . that hits the spot. Peace and quiet at—"

A cell phone went off in his pocket.

The jogger sighed. He pulled out his phone and my eyes got big, because it glowed with a bluish light. When he extended the antenna, two creatures began writhing around it—green snakes, no bigger than earthworms.

The jogger didn't seem to notice. He checked his LCD

display and cursed. "I've got to take this. Just a sec . . ." Then into the phone: "Hello?"

He listened. The mini-snakes writhed up and down the antenna right next to his ear.

"Yeah," the jogger said. "Listen—I know, but . . . I don't care if he *is* chained to a rock with vultures pecking at his liver, if he doesn't have a tracking number, we can't locate his package. . . . A gift to humankind, great . . . You know how many of those we deliver—Oh, never mind. Listen, just refer him to Eris in customer service. I gotta go."

He hung up. "Sorry. The overnight express business is just booming. Now, as I was saying—"

"You have snakes on your phone."

"What? Oh, they don't bite. Say hello, George and Martha."

Hello, George and Martha, a raspy male voice said inside my head.

Don't be sarcastic, said a female voice.

Why not? George demanded. *I do all the* real *work.*

"Oh, let's not go into that again!" The jogger slipped his phone back into his pocket. "Now, where were we . . . Ah, yes. Peace and quiet."

He crossed his ankles and stared up at the stars. "Been a long time since I've gotten to relax. Ever since the telegraph—rush, rush, rush. Do you have a favorite constellation, Percy?"

I was still kind of wondering about the little green snakes he'd shoved into his jogging shorts, but I said, "Uh, I like Hercules."

"Why?"

"Well . . . because he had rotten luck. Even worse than mine. It makes me feel better."

The jogger chuckled. "Not because he was strong and famous and all that?"

"No."

"You're an interesting young man. And so, what now?"

I knew immediately what he was asking. What did I intend to do about the Fleece?

Before I could answer, Martha the snake's muffled voice came from his pocket: *I have Demeter on line two.*

"Not now," the jogger said. "Tell her to leave a message."

She's not going to like that. The last time you put her off, all the flowers in the floral delivery division wilted.

"Just tell her I'm in a meeting!" The jogger rolled his eyes. "Sorry again, Percy. You were saying . . ."

"Um . . . who are you, exactly?"

"Haven't you guessed by now, a smart boy like you?"

Show him! Martha pleaded. *I haven't been full-size for months.*

Don't listen to her! George said. *She just wants to show off!*

The man took out his phone again. "Original form, please."

The phone glowed a brilliant blue. It stretched into a three-foot-long wooden staff with dove wings sprouting out the top. George and Martha, now full-sized green snakes, coiled together around the middle. It was a caduceus, the symbol of Cabin Eleven.

My throat tightened. I realized who the jogger

reminded me of with his elfish features, the mischievous twinkle in his eyes. . . .

"You're Luke's father," I said. "Hermes."

The god pursed his lips. He stuck his caduceus in the sand like an umbrella pole. " 'Luke's father.' Normally, that's not the first way people introduce me. God of thieves, yes. God of messengers and travelers, if they wish to be kind."

God of thieves works, George said.

Oh, don't mind George. Martha flicked her tongue at me. *He's just bitter because Hermes likes me best.*

He does not!

Does too!

"Behave, you two," Hermes warned, "or I'll turn you back into a cell phone and set you on vibrate! Now, Percy, you still haven't answered my question. What do you intend to do about the quest?"

"I—I don't have permission to go."

"No, indeed. Will that stop you?"

"I want to go. I have to save Grover."

Hermes smiled. "I knew a boy once . . . oh, younger than you by far. A mere baby, really."

Here we go again, George said. *Always talking about himself.*

Quiet! Martha snapped. *Do you want to get set on vibrate?*

Hermes ignored them. "One night, when this boy's mother wasn't watching, he sneaked out of their cave and stole some cattle that belong to Apollo."

"Did he get blasted to tiny pieces?" I asked.

"Hmm . . . no. Actually, everything turned out quite well. To make up for his theft, the boy gave Apollo an instrument he'd invented—a lyre. Apollo was so enchanted with the music that he forgot all about being angry."

"So what's the moral?"

"The moral?" Hermes asked. "Goodness, you act like it's a fable. It's a true story. Does truth have a moral?"

"Um . . ."

"How about this: stealing is not always bad?"

"I don't think my mom would like that moral."

Rats are delicious, suggested George.

What does that have to do with the story? Martha demanded.

Nothing, George said. *But I'm hungry.*

"I've got it," Hermes said. "Young people don't always do what they're told, but if they can pull it off and do something wonderful, sometimes they escape punishment. How's that?"

"You're saying I should go anyway," I said, "even without permission."

Hermes's eyes twinkled. "Martha, may I have the first package, please?"

Martha opened her mouth . . . and kept opening it until it was as wide as my arm. She belched out a stainless steel canister—an old-fashioned lunch box thermos with a black plastic top. The sides of the thermos were enameled with red and yellow Ancient Greek scenes—a hero killing a lion; a hero lifting up Cerberus, the three-headed dog.

"That's Hercules," I said. "But how—"

"Never question a gift," Hermes chided. "This is a collector's item from *Hercules Busts Heads*. The first season."

"*Hercules Busts Heads?*"

"Great show." Hermes sighed. "Back before Hephaestus-TV was all reality programming. Of course, the thermos would be worth much more if I had the whole lunch box—"

Or if it hadn't been in Martha's mouth, George added.

I'll get you for that. Martha began chasing him around the caduceus.

"Wait a minute," I said. "This is a gift?"

"One of two," Hermes said. "Go on, pick it up."

I almost dropped it because it was freezing cold on one side and burning hot on the other. The weird thing was, when I turned the thermos, the side facing the ocean—north—was always the cold side. . . .

"It's a compass!" I said.

Hermes looked surprised. "Very clever. I never thought of that. But its intended use is a bit more dramatic. Uncap it, and you will release the winds from the four corners of the earth to speed you on your way. Not now! And please, when the time comes, only unscrew the lid a tiny bit. The winds are a bit like me—always restless. Should all four escape at once . . . ah, but I'm sure you'll be careful. And now my second gift. George?"

She's touching me, George complained as he and Martha slithered around the pole.

"She's *always* touching you," Hermes said. "You're intertwined. And if you don't stop that, you'll get knotted again!"

The snakes stopped wrestling.

George unhinged his jaw and coughed up a little plastic bottle filled with chewable vitamins.

"You're kidding," I said. "Are those Minotaur-shaped?"

Hermes picked up the bottle and rattled it. "The lemon ones, yes. The grape ones are Furies, I think. Or are they hydras? At any rate, these are potent. Don't take one unless you really, really need it."

"How will I know if I really, really need it?"

"You'll know, believe me. Nine essential vitamins, minerals, amino acids . . . oh, everything you need to feel yourself again."

He tossed me the bottle.

"Um, thanks," I said. "But Lord Hermes, why are you helping me?"

He gave me a melancholy smile. "Perhaps because I hope that you can save many people on this quest, Percy. Not just your friend Grover."

I stared at him. "You don't mean . . . *Luke?*"

Hermes didn't answer.

"Look," I said. "Lord Hermes, I mean, thanks and everything, but you might as well take back your gifts. Luke can't be saved. Even if I could find him . . . he told me he wanted to tear down Olympus stone by stone. He betrayed everybody he knew. He—he hates you especially."

Hermes gazed up at the stars. "My dear young cousin, if there's one thing I've learned over the eons, it's that you *can't* give up on your family, no matter how tempting they make it. It doesn't matter if they hate you, or embarrass you, or simply don't appreciate your genius for inventing the Internet—"

"You invented the Internet?"

It was my idea, Martha said.

Rats are delicious, George said.

"It was *my* idea!" Hermes said. "I mean the Internet, not the rats. But that's not the point. Percy, do you understand what I'm saying about family?"

"I—I'm not sure."

"You will some day." Hermes got up and brushed the sand off his legs. "In the meantime, I must be going."

You have sixty calls to return, Martha said.

And one thousand-thirty-eight e-mails, George added. *Not counting the offers for online discount ambrosia.*

"And you, Percy," Hermes said, "have a shorter deadline than you realize to complete your quest. Your friends should be coming right about . . . now."

I heard Annabeth's voice calling my name from the sand dunes. Tyson, too, was shouting from a little bit farther away.

"I hope I packed well for you," Hermes said. "I do have some experience with travel."

He snapped his fingers and three yellow duffel bags appeared at my feet. "Waterproof, of course. If you ask nicely, your father should be able to help you reach the ship."

"Ship?"

Hermes pointed. Sure enough, a big cruise ship was cutting across Long Island Sound, its white-and-gold lights glowing against the dark water.

"Wait," I said. "I don't understand any of this. I haven't even agreed to go!"

"I'd make up your mind in the next five minutes, if I were you," Hermes advised. "That's when the harpies will come to eat you. Now, good night, cousin, and dare I say it? May the gods go with you."

He opened his hand and the caduceus flew into it.

Good luck, Martha told me.

Bring me back a rat, George said.

The caduceus changed into a cell phone and Hermes slipped it into his pocket.

He jogged off down the beach. Twenty paces away, he shimmered and vanished, leaving me alone with a thermos, a bottle of chewable vitamins, and five minutes to make an impossible decision.

EIGHT

WE BOARD THE
PRINCESS ANDROMEDA

I was staring at the waves when Annabeth and Tyson found me.

"What's going on?" Annabeth asked. "I heard you calling for help!"

"Me, too!" Tyson said. "Heard you yell, 'Bad things are attacking!'"

"I didn't call you guys," I said. "I'm fine."

"But then who . . ." Annabeth noticed the three yellow duffel bags, then the thermos and the bottle of vitamins I was holding. "What—"

"Just listen," I said. "We don't have much time."

I told them about my conversation with Hermes. By the time I was finished, I could hear screeching in the distance—patrol harpies picking up our scent.

"Percy," Annabeth said, "we have to do the quest."

"We'll get expelled, you know. Trust me, I'm an expert at getting expelled."

"So? If we fail, there won't be any camp to come back to."

"Yeah, but you promised Chiron—"

"I promised I'd keep you from danger. I can only do that by coming with you! Tyson can stay behind and tell them—"

"I want to go," Tyson said.

"No!" Annabeth's voice sounded close to panic. "I mean . . . Percy, come on. You know that's impossible."

I wondered again why she had such a grudge against Cyclopes. There was something she wasn't telling me.

She and Tyson both looked at me, waiting for an answer. Meanwhile, the cruise ship was getting farther and farther away.

The thing was, part of me didn't want Tyson along. I'd spent the last three days in close quarters with the guy, getting razzed by the other campers and embarrassed a million times a day, constantly reminded that I was related to him. I needed some space.

Plus, I didn't know how much help he'd be, or how I'd keep him safe. Sure, he was strong, but Tyson was a little kid in Cyclops terms, maybe seven or eight years old, mentally. I could see him freaking out and starting to cry while we were trying to sneak past a monster or something. He'd get us all killed.

On the other hand, the sound of the harpies was getting closer. . . .

"We can't leave him," I decided. "Tantalus will punish him for us being gone."

"Percy," Annabeth said, trying to keep her cool, "we're going to Polyphemus's island! Polyphemus is an S-i-k . . . a C-y-k . . . ." She stamped her foot in frustration. As smart as she was, Annabeth was dyslexic, too. We could've been there all night while she tried to spell Cyclops. "You know what I mean!"

"Tyson can go," I insisted, "if he wants to."

Tyson clapped his hands. "Want to!"

Annabeth gave me the evil eye, but I guess she could tell I wasn't going to change my mind. Or maybe she just knew we didn't have time to argue.

"All right," she said. "How do we get to that ship?"

"Hermes said my father would help."

"Well then, Seaweed Brain? What are you waiting for?"

I'd always had a hard time calling on my father, or praying, or whatever you want to call it, but I stepped into the waves.

"Um, Dad?" I called. "How's it going?"

"Percy!" Annabeth whispered. "We're in a hurry!"

"We need your help," I called a little louder. "We need to get to that ship, like, before we get eaten and stuff, so . . ."

At first, nothing happened. Waves crashed against the shore like normal. The harpies sounded like they were right behind the sand dunes. Then, about a hundred yards out to sea, three white lines appeared on the surface. They moved fast toward the shore, like claws ripping through the ocean.

As they neared the beach, the surf burst apart and the heads of three white stallions reared out of the waves.

Tyson caught his breath. "Fish ponies!"

He was right. As the creatures pulled themselves onto the sand, I saw that they were only horses in the front; their back halves were silvery fish bodies, with glistening scales and rainbow–tail fins.

"Hippocampi!" Annabeth said. "They're beautiful."

The nearest one whinnied in appreciation and nuzzled Annabeth.

"We'll admire them later," I said. "Come on!"

"There!" a voice screeched behind us. "Bad children out of cabins! Snack time for lucky harpies!"

Five of them were fluttering over the top of the dunes—plump little hags with pinched faces and talons and feathery wings too small for their bodies. They reminded me of miniature cafeteria ladies who'd been crossbred with dodo birds. They weren't very fast, thank the gods, but they were vicious if they caught you.

"Tyson!" I said. "Grab a duffel bag!"

He was still staring at the hippocampi with his mouth hanging open.

"Tyson!"

"Uh?"

"Come on!"

With Annabeth's help I got him moving. We gathered the bags and mounted our steeds. Poseidon must've known Tyson was one of the passengers, because one hippocampus was much larger than the other two—just right for carrying a Cyclops.

"Giddyup!" I said. My hippocampus turned and plunged into the waves. Annabeth's and Tyson's followed right behind.

The harpies cursed at us, wailing for their snacks to come back, but the hippocampi raced over the water at the speed of Jet Skis. The harpies fell behind, and soon the shore of Camp Half-Blood was nothing but a dark smudge.

I wondered if I'd ever see the place again. But right then I had other problems.

The cruise ship was now looming in front of us—our ride toward Florida and the Sea of Monsters.

Riding the hippocampus was even easier than riding a pegasus. We zipped along with the wind in our faces, speeding through the waves so smooth and steady I hardly needed to hold on at all.

As we got closer to the cruise ship, I realized just how huge it was. I felt as though I were looking up at a building in Manhattan. The white hull was at least ten stories tall, topped with another dozen levels of decks with brightly lit balconies and portholes. The ship's name was painted just above the bow line in black letters, lit with a spotlight. It took me a few seconds to decipher it:

PRINCESS ANDROMEDA

Attached to the bow was a huge masthead—a three-story-tall woman wearing a white Greek chiton, sculpted to look as if she were chained to the front of the ship. She was young and beautiful, with flowing black hair, but her expression was one of absolute terror. Why anybody would want a screaming princess on the front of their vacation ship, I had no idea.

I remembered the myth about Andromeda and how she had been chained to a rock by her own parents as a sacrifice to a sea monster. Maybe she'd gotten too many F's on her report card or something. Anyway, my namesake, Perseus, had saved her just in time and turned the sea monster to stone using the head of Medusa.

That Perseus always won. That's why my mom had named me after him, even though he was a son of Zeus and I was a son of Poseidon. The original Perseus was one of the only heroes in the Greek myths who got a happy ending. The others died—betrayed, mauled, mutilated, poisoned, or cursed by the gods. My mom hoped I would inherit Perseus's luck. Judging by how my life was going so far, I wasn't real optimistic.

"How do we get aboard?" Annabeth shouted over the noise of the waves, but the hippocampi seemed to know what we needed. They skimmed along the starboard side of the ship, riding easily through its huge wake, and pulled up next to a service ladder riveted to the side of the hull.

"You first," I told Annabeth.

She slung her duffel bag over her shoulder and grabbed the bottom rung. Once she'd hoisted herself onto the ladder, her hippocampus whinnied a farewell and dove underwater. Annabeth began to climb. I let her get a few rungs up, then followed her.

Finally it was just Tyson in the water. His hippocampus was treating him to 360° aerials and backward ollies, and Tyson was laughing so hysterically, the sound echoed up the side of the ship.

"Tyson, shhh!" I said. "Come on, big guy!"

"Can't we take Rainbow?" he asked, his smile fading.

I stared at him. "*Rainbow?*"

The hippocampus whinnied as if he liked his new name.

"Um, we have to go," I said. "Rainbow . . . well, he can't climb ladders."

Tyson sniffled. He buried his face in the hippocampus's mane. "I will miss you, Rainbow!"

The hippocampus made a neighing sound I could've sworn was crying.

"Maybe we'll see him again sometime," I suggested.

"Oh, please!" Tyson said, perking up immediately. "Tomorrow!"

I didn't make any promises, but I finally convinced Tyson to say his farewells and grab hold of the ladder. With a final sad whinny, Rainbow the hippocampus did a backflip and dove into the sea.

The ladder led to a maintenance deck stacked with yellow lifeboats. There was a set of locked double doors, which Annabeth managed to pry open with her knife and a fair amount of cursing in Ancient Greek.

I figured we'd have to sneak around, being stowaways and all, but after checking a few corridors and peering over a balcony into a huge central promenade lined with closed shops, I began to realize there was nobody to hide from. I mean, sure it was the middle of the night, but we walked half the length of the boat and met no one. We passed forty or fifty cabin doors and heard no sound behind any of them.

"It's a ghost ship," I murmured.

"No," Tyson said, fiddling with the strap of his duffel bag. "Bad smell."

Annabeth frowned. "I don't smell anything."

"Cyclopes are like satyrs," I said. "They can smell monsters. Isn't that right, Tyson?"

He nodded nervously. Now that we were away from Camp Half-Blood, the Mist had distorted his face again. Unless I concentrated very hard, it seemed that he had two eyes instead of one.

"Okay," Annabeth said. "So what exactly do you smell?"

"Something bad," Tyson answered.

"Great," Annabeth grumbled. "That clears it up."

We came outside on the swimming pool level. There were rows of empty deck chairs and a bar closed off with a chain curtain. The water in the pool glowed eerily, sloshing back and forth from the motion of the ship.

Above us fore and aft were more levels—a climbing wall, a putt-putt golf course, a revolving restaurant, but no sign of life.

And yet . . . I sensed something familiar. Something dangerous. I had the feeling that if I weren't so tired and burned out on adrenaline from our long night, I might be able to put a name to what was wrong.

"We need a hiding place," I said. "Somewhere safe to sleep."

"Sleep," Annabeth agreed wearily.

We explored a few more corridors until we found an empty suite on the ninth level. The door was open, which struck me as weird. There was a basket of chocolate goodies on the table, an iced-down bottle of sparkling cider on the nightstand, and a mint on the pillow with a hand-written note that said: *Enjoy your cruise!*

We opened our duffel bags for the first time and found

that Hermes really had thought of everything—extra clothes, toiletries, camp rations, a Ziploc bag full of cash, a leather pouch full of golden drachmas. He'd even managed to pack Tyson's oilcloth with his tools and metal bits, and Annabeth's cap of invisibility, which made them both feel a lot better.

"I'll be next door," Annabeth said. "You guys *don't* drink or eat anything."

"You think this place is enchanted?"

She frowned. "I don't know. Something isn't right. Just . . . be careful."

We locked our doors.

Tyson crashed on the couch. He tinkered for a few minutes on his metalworking project—which he still wouldn't show me—but soon enough he was yawning. He wrapped up his oilcloth and passed out.

I lay on the bed and stared out the porthole. I thought I heard voices out in the hallway, like whispering. I knew that couldn't be. We'd walked all over the ship and had seen nobody. But the voices kept me awake. They reminded me of my trip to the Underworld—the way the spirits of the dead sounded as they drifted past.

Finally my weariness got the best of me. I fell asleep . . . and had my worst dream yet.

I was standing in a cavern at the edge of an enormous pit. I knew the place too well. The entrance to Tartarus. And I recognized the cold laugh that echoed from the darkness below.

If it isn't the young hero. The voice was like a knife blade scraping across stone. *On his way to another great victory.*

I wanted to shout at Kronos to leave me alone. I wanted to draw Riptide and strike him down. But I couldn't move. And even if I could, how could I kill something that had already been destroyed—chopped to pieces and cast into eternal darkness?

Don't let me stop you, the titan said. *Perhaps this time, when you fail, you'll wonder if it's worthwhile slaving for the gods. How exactly has your father shown his appreciation lately?*

His laughter filled the cavern, and suddenly the scene changed.

It was a different cave—Grover's bedroom prison in the Cyclops's lair.

Grover was sitting at the loom in his soiled wedding dress, madly unraveling the threads of the unfinished bridal train.

"Honeypie!" the monster shouted from behind the boulder.

Grover yelped and began weaving the threads back together.

The room shook as the boulder was pushed aside. Looming in the doorway was a Cyclops so huge he made Tyson look vertically challenged. He had jagged yellow teeth and gnarled hands as big as my whole body. He wore a faded purple T-shirt that said WORLD SHEEP EXPO 2001. He must've been at least fifteen feet tall, but the most startling thing was his enormous milky eye, scarred and webbed with cataracts. If he wasn't completely blind, he had to be pretty darn close.

"What are you doing?" the monster demanded.

"Nothing!" Grover said in his falsetto voice. "Just weaving my bridal train, as you can see."

The Cyclops stuck one hand into the room and groped around until he found the loom. He pawed at the cloth. "It hasn't gotten any longer!"

"Oh, um, yes it has, dearest. See? I've added at least an inch."

"Too many delays!" the monster bellowed. Then he sniffed the air. "You smell good! Like goats!"

"Oh." Grover forced a weak giggle. "Do you like it? It's *Eau de Chévre.* I wore it just for you."

"Mmmm!" The Cyclopes bared his pointed teeth. "Good enough to eat!"

"Oh, you're such a flirt!"

"No more delays!"

"But dear, I'm not done!"

"Tomorrow!"

"No, no. Ten more days."

"Five!"

"Oh, well, seven then. If you insist."

"Seven! That is less than five, right?"

"Certainly. Oh yes."

The monster grumbled, still not happy with his deal, but he left Grover to his weaving and rolled the boulder back into place.

Grover closed his eyes and took a shaky breath, trying to calm his nerves.

"Hurry, Percy," he muttered. "Please, please, please!"

I woke to a ship's whistle and a voice on the intercom—some guy with an Australian accent who sounded way too happy.

"Good morning, passengers! We'll be at sea all day today. Excellent weather for the poolside mambo party! Don't forget million-dollar bingo in the Kraken Lounge at one o'clock, and for our *special guests*, disemboweling practice on the Promenade!"

I sat up in bed. "What did he say?"

Tyson groaned, still half asleep. He was lying facedown on the couch, his feet so far over the edge they were in the bathroom. "The happy man said . . . bowling practice?"

I hoped he was right, but then there was an urgent knock on the suite's interior door. Annabeth stuck her head in—her blond hair in a rat's nest. "*Disemboweling* practice?"

Once we were all dressed, we ventured out into the ship and were surprised to see other people. A dozen senior citizens were heading to breakfast. A dad was taking his kids to the pool for a morning swim. Crew members in crisp white uniforms strolled the deck, tipping their hats to the passengers.

Nobody asked who we were. Nobody paid us much attention. But there was something wrong.

As the family of swimmers passed us, the dad told his kids: "We are on a cruise. We are having fun."

"Yes," his three kids said in unison, their expressions blank. "We are having a blast. We will swim in the pool."

They wandered off.

"Good morning," a crew member told us, his eyes glazed. "We are all enjoying ourselves aboard the *Princess Andromeda*. Have a nice day." He drifted away.

"Percy, this is weird," Annabeth whispered. "They're all in some kind of trance."

Then we passed a cafeteria and saw our first monster. It was a hellhound—a black mastiff with its front paws up on the buffet line and its muzzle buried in the scrambled eggs. It must've been young, because it was small compared to most—no bigger than a grizzly bear. Still, my blood turned cold. I'd almost gotten killed by one of those before.

The weird thing was: a middle-aged couple was standing in the buffet line right behind the devil dog, patiently waiting their turn for the eggs. They didn't seem to notice anything out of the ordinary.

"Not hungry anymore," Tyson murmured.

Before Annabeth or I could reply, a reptilian voice came from down the corridor, "Ssssix more joined yesssterday."

Annabeth gestured frantically toward the nearest hiding place—the women's room—and all three of us ducked inside. I was so freaked out it didn't even occur to me to be embarrassed.

Something—or more like *two* somethings—slithered past the bathroom door, making sounds like sandpaper against the carpet.

"Yesss," a second reptilian voice said. "He drawssss them. Ssssoon we will be ssssstrong."

The things slithered into the cafeteria with a cold hissing that might have been snake laughter.

Annabeth looked at me. "We have to get out of here."

"You think I *want* to be in the girls' restroom?"

"I mean the ship, Percy! We have to get off the ship."

"Smells bad," Tyson agreed. "And dogs eat all the eggs. Annabeth is right. We must leave the restroom and ship."

I shuddered. If Annabeth and Tyson were actually *agreeing* about something, I figured I'd better listen.

Then I heard another voice outside—one that chilled me worse than any monster's.

"—only a matter of time. Don't push me, Agrius!"

It was Luke, beyond a doubt. I could never forget his voice.

"I'm not pushing you!" another guy growled. His voice was deeper and even angrier than Luke's. "I'm just saying, if this gamble doesn't pay off—"

"It'll pay off," Luke snapped. "They'll take the bait. Now, come, we've got to get to the admiralty suite and check on the casket."

Their voices receded down the corridor.

Tyson whimpered. "Leave now?"

Annabeth and I exchanged looks and came to a silent agreement.

"We can't," I told Tyson.

"We have to find out what Luke is up to," Annabeth agreed. "And if possible, we're going to beat him up, bind him in chains, and drag him to Mount Olympus."

NINE

I HAVE THE WORST
FAMILY REUNION EVER

Annabeth volunteered to go alone since she had the cap of invisibility, but I convinced her it was too dangerous. Either we all went together, or nobody went.

"Nobody!" Tyson voted. "Please?"

But in the end he came along, nervously chewing on his huge fingernails. We stopped at our cabin long enough to gather our stuff. We figured whatever happened, we would *not* be staying another night aboard the zombie cruise ship, even if they did have million-dollar bingo. I made sure Riptide was in my pocket and the vitamins and thermos from Hermes were at the top of my bag. I didn't want Tyson to carry everything, but he insisted, and Annabeth told me not to worry about it. Tyson could carry three full duffel bags over his shoulder as easily as I could carry a backpack.

We sneaked through the corridors, following the ship's YOU ARE HERE signs toward the admiralty suite. Annabeth scouted ahead invisibly. We hid whenever someone passed by, but most of the people we saw were just glassy-eyed zombie passengers.

As we came up the stairs to deck thirteen, where the admiralty suite was supposed to be, Annabeth hissed,

"Hide!" and shoved us into a supply closet.

I heard a couple of guys coming down the hall.

"You see that Aethiopian drakon in the cargo hold?" one of them said.

The other laughed. "Yeah, it's awesome."

Annabeth was still invisible, but she squeezed my arm hard. I got a feeling I should know that second guy's voice.

"I hear they got two more coming," the familiar voice said. "They keep arriving at this rate, oh, man—no contest!"

The voices faded down the corridor.

"That was Chris Rodriguez!" Annabeth took off her cap and turned visible. "You remember—from Cabin Eleven."

I sort of recalled Chris from the summer before. He was one of those undetermined campers who got stuck in the Hermes cabin because his Olympian dad or mom never claimed him. Now that I thought about it, I realized I hadn't seen Chris at camp this summer. "What's another half-blood doing here?"

Annabeth shook her head, clearly troubled.

We kept going down the corridor. I didn't need maps anymore to know I was getting close to Luke. I sensed something cold and unpleasant—the presence of evil.

"Percy." Annabeth stopped suddenly. "Look."

She stood in front of a glass wall looking down into the multistory canyon that ran through the middle of the ship. At the bottom was the Promenade—a mall full of shops— but that's not what had caught Annabeth's attention.

A group of monsters had assembled in front of the

candy store: a dozen Laistrygonian giants like the ones who'd attacked me with dodge balls, two hellhounds, and a few even stranger creatures—humanoid females with twin serpent tails instead of legs.

"Scythian Dracaenae," Annabeth whispered. "Dragon women."

The monsters made a semicircle around a young guy in Greek armor who was hacking on a straw dummy. A lump formed in my throat when I realized the dummy was wearing an orange Camp Half-Blood T-shirt. As we watched, the guy in armor stabbed the dummy through its belly and ripped upward. Straw flew everywhere. The monsters cheered and howled.

Annabeth stepped away from the window. Her face was ashen.

"Come on," I told her, trying to sound braver than I felt. "The sooner we find Luke the better."

At the end of the hallway were double oak doors that looked like they must lead somewhere important. When we were thirty feet away, Tyson stopped. "Voices inside."

"You can hear that far?" I asked.

Tyson closed his eye like he was concentrating hard. Then his voice changed, becoming a husky approximation of Luke's. "—the prophecy ourselves. The fools won't know which way to turn."

Before I could react, Tyson's voice changed again, becoming deeper and gruffer, like the other guy we'd heard talking to Luke outside the cafeteria. "You really think the old horseman is gone for good?"

Tyson laughed Luke's laugh. "They can't trust him. Not with the skeletons in *his* closet. The poisoning of the tree was the final straw."

Annabeth shivered. "Stop that, Tyson! How do you do that? It's creepy."

Tyson opened his eye and looked puzzled. "Just listening."

"Keep going," I said. "What else are they saying?"

Tyson closed his eye again.

He hissed in the gruff man's voice: "Quiet!" Then Luke's voice, whispering: "Are you sure?"

"Yes," Tyson said in the gruff voice. "Right outside."

Too late, I realized what was happening.

I just had time to say, "Run!" when the doors of the stateroom burst open and there was Luke, flanked by two hairy giants armed with javelins, their bronze tips aimed right at our chests.

"Well," Luke said with a crooked smile. "If it isn't my two favorite cousins. Come right in."

The stateroom was beautiful, and it was horrible.

The beautiful part: Huge windows curved along the back wall, looking out over the stern of the ship. Green sea and blue sky stretched all the way to the horizon. A Persian rug covered the floor. Two plush sofas occupied the middle of the room, with a canopied bed in one corner and a mahogany dining table in the other. The table was loaded with food—pizza boxes, bottles of soda, and a stack of roast beef sandwiches on a silver platter.

The horrible part: On a velvet dais at the back of the room lay a ten-foot-long golden casket. A sarcophagus, engraved with Ancient Greek scenes of cities in flames and heroes dying grisly deaths. Despite the sunlight streaming through the windows, the casket made the whole room feel cold.

"Well," Luke said, spreading his arms proudly. "A little nicer than Cabin Eleven, huh?"

He'd changed since the last summer. Instead of Bermuda shorts and a T-shirt, he wore a button-down shirt, khaki pants, and leather loafers. His sandy hair, which used to be so unruly, was now clipped short. He looked like an evil male model, showing off what the fashionable college-age villain was wearing to Harvard this year.

He still had the scar under his eye—a jagged white line from his battle with a dragon. And propped against the sofa was his magical sword, Backbiter, glinting strangely with its half-steel, half-Celestial bronze blade that could kill both mortals and monsters.

"Sit," he told us. He waved his hand and three dining chairs scooted themselves into the center of the room.

None of us sat.

Luke's large friends were still pointing their javelins at us. They looked like twins, but they weren't human. They stood about eight feet tall, for one thing, and wore only blue jeans, probably because their enormous chests were already shag-carpeted with thick brown fur. They had claws for fingernails, feet like paws. Their noses were snoutlike, and their teeth were all pointed canines.

"Where are my manners?" Luke said smoothly. "These are my assistants, Agrius and Oreius. Perhaps you've heard of them."

I said nothing. Despite the javelins pointed at me, it wasn't the bear twins who scared me.

I'd imagined meeting Luke again many times since he'd tried to kill me last summer. I'd pictured myself boldly standing up to him, challenging him to a duel. But now that we were face-to-face, I could barely stop my hands from shaking.

"You don't know Agrius and Oreius's story?" Luke asked. "Their mother . . . well, it's sad, really. Aphrodite ordered the young woman to fall in love. She refused and ran to Artemis for help. Artemis let her become one of her maiden huntresses, but Aphrodite got her revenge. She bewitched the young woman into falling in love with a bear. When Artemis found out, she abandoned the girl in disgust. Typical of the gods, wouldn't you say? They fight with one another and the poor humans get caught in the middle. The girl's twin sons here, Agrius and Oreius, have no love for Olympus. They like half-bloods well enough, though . . ."

"For lunch," Agrius growled. His gruff voice was the one I'd heard talking with Luke earlier.

"Hehe! Hehe!" His brother Oreius laughed, licking his fur-lined lips. He kept laughing like he was having an asthmatic fit until Luke and Agrius both stared at him.

"Shut up, you idiot!" Agrius growled. "Go punish yourself!"

Oreius whimpered. He trudged over to the corner of the room, slumped onto a stool, and banged his forehead against the dining table, making the silver plates rattle.

Luke acted like this was perfectly normal behavior. He made himself comfortable on the sofa and propped his feet up on the coffee table. "Well, Percy, we let you survive another year. I hope you appreciated it. How's your mom? How's school?"

"You poisoned Thalia's tree."

Luke sighed. "Right to the point, eh? Okay, sure I poisoned the tree. So what?"

"How could you?" Annabeth sounded so angry I thought she'd explode. "Thalia saved your life! *Our* lives! How could you dishonor her—"

"I didn't dishonor her!" Luke snapped. "The gods dishonored her, Annabeth! If Thalia were alive, she'd be on my side."

"Liar!"

"If you knew what was coming, you'd understand—"

"I understand you want to destroy the camp!" she yelled. "You're a monster!"

Luke shook his head. "The gods have blinded you. Can't you imagine a world without them, Annabeth? What good is that ancient history you study? Three thousand years of baggage! The West is rotten to the core. It has to be destroyed. Join me! We can start the world anew. We could use your intelligence, Annabeth."

"Because you have none of your own!"

His eyes narrowed. "I know you, Annabeth. You deserve

better than tagging along on some hopeless quest to save the camp. Half-Blood Hill will be overrun by monsters within the month. The heroes who survive will have no choice but to join us or be hunted to extinction. You really want to be on a losing team . . . with company like this?" Luke pointed at Tyson.

"Hey!" I said.

"Traveling with a *Cyclops*," Luke chided. "Talk about dishonoring Thalia's memory! I'm surprised at you, Annabeth. You of all people—"

"Stop it!" she shouted.

I didn't know what Luke was talking about, but Annabeth buried her head in her hands like she was about to cry.

"Leave her alone," I said. "And leave Tyson out this."

Luke laughed. "Oh, yeah, I heard. Your father claimed him."

I must have looked surprised, because Luke smiled. "Yes, Percy, I know all about that. And about your plan to find the Fleece. What were those coordinates, again . . . 30, 31, 75, 12? You see, I still have friends at camp who keep me posted."

"Spies, you mean."

He shrugged. "How many insults from your father can you stand, Percy? You think he's grateful to you? You think Poseidon cares for you any more than he cares for this monster?"

Tyson clenched his fists and made a rumbling sound down in his throat.

Luke just chuckled. "The gods are *so* using you, Percy. Do you have any idea what's in store for you if you reach your sixteenth birthday? Has Chiron even *told* you the prophecy?"

I wanted to get in Luke's face and tell him off, but as usual, he knew just how to throw me off balance.

Sixteenth birthday?

I mean, I knew Chiron had received a prophecy from the Oracle many years ago. I knew part of it was about me. But, *if* I reached my sixteenth birthday? I didn't like the sound of that.

"I know what I need to know," I managed. "Like, who my enemies are."

"Then you're a fool."

Tyson smashed the nearest dining chair to splinters. "Percy is not a fool!"

Before I could stop him, he charged Luke. His fists came down toward Luke's head—a double overhead blow that would've knocked a hole in titanium—but the bear twins intercepted. They each caught one of Tyson's arms and stopped him cold. They pushed him back and Tyson stumbled. He fell to the carpet so hard the deck shook.

"Too bad, Cyclops," Luke said. "Looks like my grizzly friends together are more than a match for your strength. Maybe I should let them—"

"Luke," I cut in. "Listen to me. Your father sent us."

His face turned the color of pepperoni. "Don't—*even*—mention him."

"He told us to take this boat. I thought it was just for

a ride, but he sent us here to find you. He told me he won't give up on you, no matter how angry you are."

"*Angry?*" Luke roared. "*Give up on me?* He abandoned me, Percy! I want Olympus destroyed! Every throne crushed to rubble! You tell Hermes it's going to happen, too. Each time a half-blood joins us, the Olympians grow weaker and we grow stronger. *He* grows stronger." Luke pointed to the gold sarcophagus.

The box creeped me out, but I was determined not to show it. "So?" I demanded. "What's so special . . ."

Then it hit me, what might be inside the sarcophagus. The temperature in the room seemed to drop twenty degrees. "Whoa, you don't mean—"

"He is re-forming," Luke said. "Little by little, we're calling his life force out of the pit. With every recruit who pledges our cause, another small piece appears—"

"That's disgusting!" Annabeth said.

Luke sneered at her. "Your mother was born from Zeus's split skull, Annabeth. I wouldn't talk. Soon there will be enough of the titan lord so that we can make him whole again. We will piece together a new body for him, a work worthy of the forges of Hephaestus."

"You're insane," Annabeth said.

"Join us and you'll be rewarded. We have powerful friends, sponsors rich enough to buy this cruise ship and much more. Percy, your mother will never have to work again. You can buy her a mansion. You can have power, fame—whatever you want. Annabeth, you can realize your dream of being an architect. You can build a monument to last a thousand years. A temple to the lords of the next age!"

"Go to Tartarus," she said.

Luke sighed. "A shame."

He picked up something that looked like a TV remote and pressed a red button. Within seconds the door of the stateroom opened and two uniformed crew members came in, armed with nightsticks. They had the same glassy-eyed look as the other mortals I'd seen, but I had a feeling this wouldn't make them any less dangerous in a fight.

"Ah, good, security," Luke said, "I'm afraid we have some stowaways."

"Yes, sir," they said dreamily.

Luke turned to Oreius. "It's time to feed the Aethiopian drakon. Take these fools below and show them how it's done."

Oreius grinned stupidly. "Hehe! Hehe!"

"Let me go, too," Agrius grumbled. "My brother is worthless. That Cyclops—"

"Is no threat," Luke said. He glanced back at the golden casket, as if something were troubling him. "Agrius, stay here. We have important matters to discuss."

"But—"

"Oreius, don't fail me. Stay in the hold to make sure the drakon is properly fed."

Oreius prodded us with his javelin and herded us out of the stateroom, followed by the two human security guards.

As I walked down the corridor with Oreius's javelin poking me in the back, I thought about what Luke had said—that the bear twins *together* were a match for Tyson's strength. But maybe separately . . .

We exited the corridor amidships and walked across an open deck lined with lifeboats. I knew the ship well enough to realize this would be our last look at sunlight. Once we got to the other side, we'd take the elevator down into the hold, and that would be it.

I looked at Tyson and said, "Now."

Thank the gods, he understood. He turned and smacked Oreius thirty feet backward into the swimming pool, right into the middle of the zombie tourist family.

"Ah!" the kids yelled in unison. "We are *not* having a blast in the pool!"

One of the security guards drew his nightstick, but Annabeth knocked the wind out of him with a well-placed kick. The other guard ran for the nearest alarm box.

"Stop him!" Annabeth yelled, but it was too late.

Just before I banged him on head with a deck chair, he hit the alarm.

Red lights flashed. Sirens wailed.

"Lifeboat!" I yelled.

We ran for the nearest one.

By the time we got the cover off, monsters and more security men were swarming the deck, pushing aside tourists and waiters with trays of tropical drinks. A guy in Greek armor drew his sword and charged, but slipped in a puddle of piña colada. Laistrygonian archers assembled on the deck above us, notching arrows in their enormous bows.

"How do you launch this thing?" screamed Annabeth.

A hellhound leaped at me, but Tyson slammed it aside with a fire extinguisher.

"Get in!" I yelled. I uncapped Riptide and slashed the first volley of arrows out of the air. Any second we would be overwhelmed.

The lifeboat was hanging over the side of the ship, high above the water. Annabeth and Tyson were having no luck with the release pulley.

I jumped in beside them.

"Hold on!" I yelled, and I cut the ropes.

A shower of arrows whistled over our heads as we free-fell toward the ocean.

TEN

WE HITCH A RIDE WITH DEAD CONFEDERATES

"Thermos!" I screamed as we hurtled toward the water.

"*What?*" Annabeth must've thought I'd lost my mind. She was holding on to the boat straps for dear life, her hair flying straight up like a torch.

But Tyson understood. He managed to open my duffel bag and take out Hermes's magical thermos without losing his grip on it or the boat.

Arrows and javelins whistled past us.

I grabbed the thermos and hoped I was doing the right thing. "Hang on!"

"I *am* hanging on!" Annabeth yelled.

"Tighter!"

I hooked my feet under the boat's inflatable bench, and as Tyson grabbed Annabeth and me by the backs of our shirts, I gave the thermos cap a quarter turn.

Instantly, a white sheet of wind jetted out of the thermos and propelled us sideways, turning our downward plummet into a forty-five-degree crash landing.

The wind seemed to laugh as it shot from the thermos, like it was glad to be free. As we hit the ocean, we bumped once, twice, skipping like a stone, then we were whizzing along like a speed boat, salt spray in our faces and nothing but sea ahead.

I heard a wail of outrage from the ship behind us, but we were already out of weapon range. The *Princess Andromeda* faded to the size of a white toy boat in the distance, and then it was gone.

As we raced over the sea, Annabeth and I tried to send an Iris-message to Chiron. We figured it was important we let somebody know what Luke was doing, and we didn't know who else to trust.

The wind from the thermos stirred up a nice sea spray that made a rainbow in the sunlight—perfect for an Iris-message—but our connection was still poor. When Annabeth threw a gold drachma into the mist and prayed for the rainbow goddess to show us Chiron, his face appeared all right, but there was some kind of weird strobe light flashing in the background and rock music blaring, like he was at a dance club.

We told him about sneaking away from camp, and Luke and the *Princess Andromeda* and the golden box for Kronos's remains, but between the noise on his end and the rushing wind and water on our end, I'm not sure how much he heard.

"Percy," Chiron yelled, "you have to watch out for—"

His voice was drowned out by loud shouting behind him—a bunch of voices whooping it up like Comanche warriors.

"What?" I yelled.

"Curse my relatives!" Chiron ducked as a plate flew over his head and shattered somewhere out of sight. "Annabeth, you shouldn't have let Percy leave camp! But if you *do* get the Fleece—"

"Yeah, baby!" somebody behind Chiron yelled. "Woo-hoooooo!"

The music got cranked up, subwoofers so loud it made our boat vibrate.

"—Miami," Chiron was yelling. "I'll try to keep watch—"

Our misty screen smashed apart like someone on the other side had thrown a bottle at it, and Chiron was gone.

An hour later we spotted land—a long stretch of beach lined with high-rise hotels. The water became crowded with fishing boats and tankers. A coast guard cruiser passed on our starboard side, then turned like it wanted a second look. I guess it isn't every day they see a yellow lifeboat with no engine going a hundred knots an hour, manned by three kids.

"That's Virginia Beach!" Annabeth said as we approached the shoreline. "Oh my gods, how did the *Princess Andromeda* travel so far overnight? That's like—"

"Five hundred and thirty nautical miles," I said.

She stared at me. "How did you know that?"

"I—I'm not sure."

Annabeth thought for a moment. "Percy, what's our position?"

"36 degrees, 44 minutes north, 76 degrees, 2 minutes west," I said immediately. Then I shook my head. "Whoa. How did I know that?"

"Because of your dad," Annabeth guessed. "When you're at sea, you have perfect bearings. That is *so* cool."

I wasn't sure about that. I didn't want to be a human GPS unit. But before I could say anything, Tyson tapped my shoulder. "Other boat is coming."

I looked back. The coast guard vessel was definitely on our tail now. Its lights were flashing and it was gaining speed.

"We can't let them catch us," I said. "They'll ask too many questions."

"Keep going into Chesapeake Bay," Annabeth said. "I know a place we can hide."

I didn't ask what she meant, or how she knew the area so well. I risked loosening the thermos cap a little more, and a fresh burst of wind sent us rocketing around the northern tip of Virginia Beach into Chesapeake Bay. The coast guard boat fell farther and farther behind. We didn't slow down until the shores of the bay narrowed on either side, and I realized we'd entered the mouth of a river.

I could feel the change from salt water to fresh water. Suddenly I was tired and frazzled, like I was coming down off a sugar high. I didn't know where I was anymore, or which way to steer the boat. It was a good thing Annabeth was directing me.

"There," she said. "Past that sandbar."

We veered into a swampy area choked with marsh grass. I beached the lifeboat at the foot of a giant cypress.

Vine-covered trees loomed above us. Insects chirred in the woods. The air was muggy and hot, and steam curled off the river. Basically, it wasn't Manhattan, and I didn't like it.

"Come on," Annabeth said. "It's just down the bank."

"What is?" I asked.

"Just follow." She grabbed a duffel bag. "And we'd better cover the boat. We don't want to draw attention."

After burying the lifeboat with branches, Tyson and I followed Annabeth along the shore, our feet sinking in red mud. A snake slithered past my shoe and disappeared into the grass.

"Not a good place," Tyson said. He swatted the mosquitoes that were forming a buffet line on his arm.

After another few minutes, Annabeth said, "Here."

All I saw was a patch of brambles. Then Annabeth moved aside a woven circle of branches, like a door, and I realized I was looking into a camouflaged shelter.

The inside was big enough for three, even with Tyson being the third. The walls were woven from plant material, like a Native American hut, but they looked pretty waterproof. Stacked in the corner was everything you could want for a campout—sleeping bags, blankets, an ice chest, and a kerosene lamp. There were demigod provisions, too— bronze javelin tips, a quiver full of arrows, an extra sword, and a box of ambrosia. The place smelled musty, like it had been vacant for a long time.

"A half-blood hideout." I looked at Annabeth in awe. "You *made* this place?"

"Thalia and I," she said quietly. "And Luke."

That shouldn't have bothered me. I mean, I knew Thalia and Luke had taken care of Annabeth when she was little. I knew the three of them had been runaways together, hiding from monsters, surviving on their own before Grover found them and tried to get them to Half-Blood Hill. But whenever Annabeth talked about the time she'd spent with them, I kind of felt . . . I don't know. Uncomfortable?

No. That's not the word.

The word was *jealous*.

"So . . ." I said. "You don't think Luke will look for us here?"

She shook her head. "We made a dozen safe houses like this. I doubt Luke even remembers where they are. Or cares."

She threw herself down on the blankets and started going through her duffel bag. Her body language made it pretty clear she didn't want to talk.

"Um, Tyson?" I said. "Would you mind scouting around outside? Like, look for a wilderness convenience store or something?"

"Convenience store?"

"Yeah, for snacks. Powdered donuts or something. Just don't go too far."

"Powdered donuts," Tyson said earnestly. "I will look for powdered donuts in the wilderness." He headed outside and started calling, "Here, donuts!"

Once he was gone, I sat down across from Annabeth. "Hey, I'm sorry about, you know, seeing Luke."

"It's not your fault." She unsheathed her knife and started cleaning the blade with a rag.

"He let us go too easily," I said.

I hoped I'd been imagining it, but Annabeth nodded. "I was thinking the same thing. What we overheard him say about a gamble, and 'they'll take the bait' . . . I think he was talking about us."

"The Fleece is the bait? Or Grover?"

She studied the edge of her knife. "I don't know, Percy. Maybe he wants the Fleece for himself. Maybe he's hoping we'll do the hard work and then he can steal it from us. I just can't believe he would poison the tree."

"What did he mean," I asked, "that Thalia would've been on his side?"

"He's wrong."

"You don't sound sure."

Annabeth glared at me, and I started to wish I hadn't asked her about this while she was holding a knife.

"Percy, you know who you remind me of most? *Thalia.* You guys are so much alike it's scary. I mean, either you would've been best friends or you would've strangled each other."

"Let's go with 'best friends.' "

"Thalia got angry with her dad sometimes. So do you. Would *you* turn against Olympus because of that?"

I stared at the quiver of arrows in the corner. "No."

"Okay, then. Neither would she. Luke's wrong." Annabeth stuck her knife blade into the dirt.

I wanted to ask her about the prophecy Luke had mentioned and what it had to do with my sixteenth birthday. But I figured she wouldn't tell me. Chiron had made it pretty clear that I wasn't allowed to hear it until the gods decided otherwise.

"So what did Luke mean about Cyclopes?" I asked. "He said you of all people—"

"I know what he said. He . . . he was talking about the *real* reason Thalia died."

I waited, not sure what to say.

Annabeth drew a shaky breath. "You can never trust a Cyclops, Percy. Six years ago, on the night Grover was leading us to Half-Blood Hill—"

She was interrupted when the door of the hut creaked open. Tyson crawled in.

"Powdered donuts!" he said proudly, holding up a pastry box.

Annabeth stared at him. "Where did you get that? We're in the middle of the wilderness. There's nothing around for—"

"Fifty feet," Tyson said. "Monster Donut shop—just over the hill!"

"This is bad," Annabeth muttered.

We were crouching behind a tree, staring at the donut shop in the middle of the woods. It looked brand new, with brightly lit windows, a parking area, and a little road leading off into the forest, but there was nothing else around, and no cars parked in the lot. We could see one employee reading a magazine behind the cash register. That was it. On the store's marquis, in huge black letters that even I could read, it said:

MONSTER DONUT

A cartoon ogre was taking a bite out of the *O* in *MONSTER*. The place smelled good, like fresh-baked chocolate donuts.

"This shouldn't be here," Annabeth whispered. "It's wrong."

"What?" I asked. "It's a donut shop."

"Shhh!"

"Why are we whispering? Tyson went in and bought a dozen. Nothing happened to him."

"*He's* a monster."

"Aw, c'mon, Annabeth. Monster Donut doesn't mean monsters! It's a chain. We've got them in New York."

"A chain," she agreed. "And don't you think it's strange that one appeared immediately after you told Tyson to get donuts? Right here in the middle of the woods?"

I thought about it. It did seem a little weird, but, I mean, donut shops weren't real high on my list of sinister forces.

"It could be a nest," Annabeth explained.

Tyson whimpered. I doubt he understood what Annabeth was saying any better than I did, but her tone was making him nervous. He'd plowed through half a dozen donuts from his box and was getting powdered sugar all over his face.

"A nest for what?" I asked.

"Haven't you ever wondered how franchise stores pop up so fast?" she asked. "One day there's nothing and then the next day—*boom*, there's a new burger place or a coffee shop or whatever? First a single store, then two, then four—exact replicas spreading across the country?"

"Um, no. Never thought about it."

"Percy, some of the chains multiply so fast because all their locations are magically linked to the life force of a monster. Some children of Hermes figured out how to do it back in the 1950s. They breed—"

She froze.

"What?" I demanded. "They breed what?"

"No—sudden—moves," Annabeth said, like her life depended on it. "Very slowly, turn around."

Then I heard it: a scraping noise, like something large dragging its belly through the leaves.

I turned and saw a rhino-size *thing* moving through the shadows of the trees. It was hissing, its front half writhing in all different directions. I couldn't understand what I was seeing at first. Then I realized the thing had multiple necks—at least seven, each topped with a hissing reptilian head. Its skin was leathery, and under each neck it wore a plastic bib that read: I'M A MONSTER DONUT KID!

I took out my ballpoint pen, but Annabeth locked eyes with me—a silent warning. *Not yet.*

I understood. A lot of monsters have terrible eyesight. It was possible the Hydra might pass us by. But if I uncapped my sword now, the bronze glow would certainly get its attention.

We waited.

The Hydra was only a few feet away. It seemed to be sniffing the ground and the trees like it was hunting for something. Then I noticed that two of the heads were ripping apart a piece of yellow canvas—one of our duffel bags. The thing had already been to our campsite. It was following our scent.

My heart pounded. I'd seen a stuffed Hydra-head trophy at camp before, but that did nothing to prepare me for the real thing. Each head was diamond-shaped, like a rattlesnake's, but the mouths were lined with jagged rows of sharklike teeth.

Tyson was trembling. He stepped back and accidentally snapped a twig. Immediately, all seven heads turned toward us and hissed.

"Scatter!" Annabeth yelled. She dove to the right.

I rolled to the left. One of the Hydra heads spat an arc of green liquid that shot past my shoulder and splashed against an elm. The trunk smoked and began to disintegrate. The whole tree toppled straight toward Tyson, who still hadn't moved, petrified by the monster that was now right in front of him.

"Tyson!" I tackled him with all my might, knocking him aside just as the Hydra lunged and the tree crashed on top of two of its heads.

The Hydra stumbled backward, yanking its heads free then wailing in outrage at the fallen tree. All seven heads shot acid, and the elm melted into a steaming pool of muck.

"Move!" I told Tyson. I ran to one side and uncapped Riptide, hoping to draw the monster's attention.

It worked.

The sight of celestial bronze is hateful to most monsters. As soon as my glowing blade appeared, the Hydra whipped toward it with all its heads, hissing and baring its teeth.

The good news: Tyson was momentarily out of danger. The bad news: I was about to be melted into a puddle of goo.

One of the heads snapped at me experimentally. Without thinking, I swung my sword.

"No!" Annabeth yelled.

Too late. I sliced the Hydra's head clean off. It rolled away into the grass, leaving a flailing stump, which immediately stopped bleeding and began to swell like a balloon.

In a matter of seconds the wounded neck split into two necks, each of which grew a full-size head. Now I was looking at an eight-headed Hydra.

"Percy!" Annabeth scolded. "You just opened another Monster Donut shop somewhere!"

I dodged a spray of acid. "I'm about to die and you're worried about *that*? How do we kill it?"

"Fire!" Annabeth said. "We have to have fire!"

As soon as she said that, I remembered the story. The Hydra's heads would only stop multiplying if we burned the stumps before they regrew. That's what Heracles had done, anyway. But we had no fire.

I backed up toward river. The Hydra followed.

Annabeth moved in on my left and tried to distract one of the heads, parrying its teeth with her knife, but another head swung sideways like a club and knocked her into the muck.

"No hitting my friends!" Tyson charged in, putting

himself between the Hydra and Annabeth. As Annabeth got to her feet, Tyson started smashing at the monster heads with his fists so fast it reminded me of the whack-a-mole game at the arcade. But even Tyson couldn't fend off the Hydra forever.

We kept inching backward, dodging acid splashes and deflecting snapping heads without cutting them off, but I knew we were only postponing our deaths. Eventually, we would make a mistake and the thing would kill us.

Then I heard a strange sound—a chug-chug-chug that at first I thought was my heartbeat. It was so powerful it made the riverbank shake.

"What's that noise?" Annabeth shouted, keeping her eyes on the Hydra.

"Steam engine," Tyson said.

"*What?*" I ducked as the Hydra spat acid over my head.

Then from the river behind us, a familiar female voice shouted: "There! Prepare the thirty-two-pounder!"

I didn't dare look away from the Hydra, but if that was who I thought it was behind us, I figured we now had enemies on two fronts.

A gravelly male voice said, "They're too close, m'lady!"

"Damn the heroes!" the girl said. "Full steam ahead!"

"Aye, m'lady."

"Fire at will, Captain!"

Annabeth understood what was happening a split second before I did. She yelled, "Hit the dirt!" and we dove for the ground as an earth-shattering *BOOM* echoed from the river. There was a flash of light, a column of smoke, and the Hydra exploded right in front of us, showering us with nasty green slime that vaporized as soon as it hit, the way monster guts tend to do.

"Gross!" screamed Annabeth.

"Steamship!" yelled Tyson.

I stood, coughing from the cloud of gunpowder smoke that was rolling across the banks.

Chugging toward us down the river was the strangest ship I'd ever seen. It rode low in the water like a submarine, its deck plated with iron. In the middle was a trapezoid-shaped casemate with slats on each side for cannons. A flag waved from the top—a wild boar and spear on a bloodred field. Lining the deck were zombies in gray uniforms— dead soldiers with shimmering faces that only partially covered their skulls, like the ghouls I'd seen in the Underworld guarding Hades's palace.

The ship was an ironclad. A Civil War battle cruiser. I could just make out the name along the prow in moss-covered letters: CSS *Birmingham*.

And standing next to the smoking cannon that had almost killed us, wearing full Greek battle armor, was Clarisse.

"Losers," she sneered. "But I suppose I have to rescue you. Come aboard."

ELEVEN

CLARISSE BLOWS UP
EVERYTHING

"You are in *so* much trouble," Clarisse said.

We'd just finished a ship tour we didn't want, through dark rooms overcrowded with dead sailors. We'd seen the coal bunker, the boilers and engine, which huffed and groaned like it would explode any minute. We'd seen the pilothouse and the powder magazine and gunnery deck (Clarisse's favorite) with two Dahlgren smoothbore cannons on the port and starboard sides and a Brooke nine-inch rifled gun fore and aft—all specially refitted to fire celestial bronze cannon balls.

Everywhere we went, dead Confederate sailors stared at us, their ghostly bearded faces shimmering over their skulls. They approved of Annabeth because she told them she was from Virginia. They were interested in me, too, because my name was Jackson—like the Southern general—but then I ruined it by telling them I was from New York. They all hissed and muttered curses about Yankees.

Tyson was terrified of them. All through the tour, he insisted Annabeth hold his hand, which she didn't look too thrilled about.

Finally, we were escorted to dinner. The CSS *Birmingham*

captain's quarters were about the size of a walk-in closet, but still much bigger than any other room on board. The table was set with white linen and china. Peanut butter and jelly sandwiches, potato chips, and Dr. Peppers were served by skeletal crewmen. I didn't want to eat anything served by ghosts, but my hunger overruled my fear.

"Tantalus expelled you for eternity," Clarisse told us smugly. "Mr. D said if any of you show your face at camp again, he'll turn you into squirrels and run you over with his SUV."

"Did *they* give you this ship?" I asked.

"'Course not. My father did."

"*Ares?*"

Clarisse sneered. "You think your daddy is the only one with sea power? The spirits on the losing side of every war owe a tribute to Ares. That's their curse for being defeated. I prayed to my father for a naval transport and here it is. These guys will do anything I tell them. Won't you, Captain?"

The captain stood behind her looking stiff and angry. His glowing green eyes fixed me with a hungry stare. "If it means an end to this infernal war, ma'am, peace at last, we'll do anything. Destroy anyone."

Clarisse smiled. "Destroy anyone. I like that."

Tyson gulped.

"Clarisse," Annabeth said, "Luke might be after the Fleece, too. We saw him. He's got the coordinates and he's heading south. He has a cruise ship full of monsters—"

"Good! I'll blow him out of the water."

"You don't understand," Annabeth said. "We have to combine forces. Let us help you—"

"No!" Clarisse pounded the table. "This is *my* quest, smart girl! Finally *I* get to be the hero, and you two will *not* steal my chance."

"Where are your cabin mates?" I asked. "You were allowed to take two friends with you, weren't you?"

"They didn't . . . I let them stay behind. To protect the camp."

"You mean even the people in your own cabin wouldn't help you?"

"Shut up, Prissy! I don't need them! Or you!"

"Clarisse," I said, "Tantalus is using you. He doesn't care about the camp. He'd love to see it destroyed. He's setting you up to fail."

"No! I don't care what the Oracle—" She stopped herself.

"What?" I said. "What did the Oracle tell you?"

"Nothing." Clarisse's ears turned pink. "All you need to know is that I'm finishing this quest and you're *not* helping. On the other hand, I can't let you go . . ."

"So we're prisoners?" Annabeth asked.

"Guests. For now." Clarisse propped her feet up on the white linen tablecloth and opened another Dr Pepper. "Captain, take them below. Assign them hammocks on the berth deck. If they don't mind their manners, show them how we deal with enemy spies."

The dream came as soon as I fell asleep.

Grover was sitting at his loom, desperately unraveling his wedding train, when the boulder door rolled aside and the Cyclops bellowed, "Aha!"

Grover yelped. "Dear! I didn't—you were so quiet!"

"Unraveling!" Polyphemus roared. "So that's the problem!"

"Oh, no. I—I wasn't—"

"Come!" Polyphemus grabbed Grover around the waist and half carried, half dragged him through the tunnels of the cave. Grover struggled to keep his high heels on his hooves. His veil kept tilting on his head, threatening to come off.

The Cyclops pulled him into a warehouse-size cavern decorated with sheep junk. There was a wool-covered Lay-Z-Boy recliner and a wool-covered television set, crude bookshelves loaded with sheep collectibles—coffee mugs shaped like sheep faces, plaster figurines of sheep, sheep board games, and picture books and action figures. The floor was littered with piles of sheep bones, and other bones that didn't look exactly like sheep—the bones of satyrs who'd come to the island looking for Pan.

Polyphemus set Grover down only long enough to move another huge boulder. Daylight streamed into the cave, and Grover whimpered with longing. Fresh air!

The Cyclops dragged him outside to a hilltop overlooking the most beautiful island I'd ever seen.

It was shaped kind of like a saddle cut in half by an ax. There were lush green hills on either side and a wide valley in the middle, split by a deep chasm that was spanned by a rope bridge. Beautiful streams rolled to the edge of the canyon and dropped off in rainbow-colored waterfalls. Parrots fluttered in the trees. Pink and purple flowers bloomed on the bushes. Hundreds of sheep grazed in the meadows, their wool glinting strangely like copper and silver coins.

And at the center of the island, right next to the rope bridge, was an enormous twisted oak tree with something glittering in its lowest bough.

The Golden Fleece.

Even in a dream, I could feel its power radiating across the island, making the grass greener, the flowers more beautiful. I could almost smell the nature magic at work. I could only imagine how powerful the scent would be for a satyr.

Grover whimpered.

"Yes," Polyphemus said proudly. "See over there? Fleece is the prize of my collection! Stole it from heroes long ago, and ever since—free food! Satyrs come from all over the world, like moths to flame. Satyrs good eating! And now—"

Polyphemus scooped up a wicked set of bronze shears.

Grover yelped, but Polyphemus just picked up the nearest sheep like it was a stuffed animal and shaved off its wool. He handed a fluffy mass of it to Grover.

"Put that on the spinning wheel!" he said proudly. "Magic. Cannot be unraveled."

"Oh . . . well . . ."

"Poor Honeypie!" Polyphemus grinned. "Bad weaver. Ha-ha! Not to worry. That thread will solve problem. Finish wedding train by tomorrow!"

"Isn't that . . . thoughtful of you!"

"Hehe."

"But—but, dear," Grover gulped, "what if someone were to rescue—I mean attack this island?" Grover looked straight at me, and I knew he was asking for my benefit. "What would keep them from marching right up here to your cave?"

"Wifey scared! So cute! Not to worry. Polyphemus has state-of-the-art security system. Have to get through my pets."

"Pets?"

Grover looked across the island, but there was nothing to see except sheep grazing peacefully in the meadows.

"And then," Polyphemus growled, "they would have to get through me!"

He pounded his fist against the nearest rock, which cracked and split in half. "Now, come!" he shouted. "Back to the cave."

Grover looked about ready to cry—so close to freedom, but so hopelessly far. Tears welled in his eyes as the boulder door rolled shut, sealing him once again in the stinky torch-lit dankness of the Cyclops's cave.

I woke to alarm bells ringing throughout the ship.

The captain's gravelly voice: "All hands on deck! Find Lady Clarisse! Where is that girl?"

Then his ghostly face appeared above me. "Get up, Yankee. Your friends are already above. We are approaching the entrance."

"The entrance to what?"

He gave me a skeletal smile. "The Sea of Monsters, of course."

I stuffed my few belongings that had survived the Hydra into a sailor's canvas knapsack and slung it over my shoulder. I had a sneaking suspicion that one way or another I would not be spending another night aboard the CSS *Birmingham*.

I was on my way upstairs when something made me freeze. A presence nearby—something familiar and unpleasant. For no particular reason, I felt like picking a fight. I wanted to punch a dead Confederate. The last time I'd felt like that kind of anger . . .

Instead of going up, I crept to the edge of the ventilation grate and peered down into the boiler deck.

Clarisse was standing right below me, talking to an image that shimmered in the steam from the boilers—a muscular man in black leather biker clothes, with a military haircut, red-tinted sunglasses, and a knife strapped to his side.

My fists clenched. It was my least favorite Olympian: Ares, the god of war.

"I don't want excuses, little girl!" he growled.

"Y-yes, father," Clarisse mumbled.

"You don't want to see me mad, do you?"

"No, father."

"*No, father,*" Ares mimicked. "You're pathetic. I should've let one of my *sons* take this quest."

"I'll succeed!" Clarisse promised, her voice trembling. "I'll make you proud."

"You'd better," he warned. "You asked me for this quest, girl. If you let that slimeball Jackson kid steal it from you—"

"But the Oracle said—"

"I DON'T CARE WHAT IT SAID!" Ares bellowed with such force that his image shimmered. "You *will* succeed. And if you don't . . ."

He raised his fist. Even though he was only a figure in the steam, Clarisse flinched.

"Do we understand each other?" Ares growled.

The alarm bells rang again. I heard voices coming toward me, officers yelling orders to ready the cannons.

I crept back from the ventilation grate and made my way upstairs to join Annabeth and Tyson on the spar deck.

"What's wrong?" Annabeth asked me. "Another dream?"

I nodded, but I didn't say anything. I didn't know what to think about what I'd seen downstairs. It bothered me almost as much as the dream about Grover.

Clarisse came up the stairs right after me. I tried not to look at her.

She grabbed a pair of binoculars from a zombie officer and peered toward the horizon. "At last. Captain, full steam ahead!"

I looked in the same direction as she was, but I couldn't see much. The sky was overcast. The air was hazy and humid, like steam from an iron. If I squinted real hard, I could just make out a couple of dark fuzzy splotches in the distance.

My nautical senses told me we were somewhere off the coast of northern Florida, so we'd come a long way overnight, farther than any mortal ship should've been able to travel.

The engine groaned as we increased speed.

Tyson muttered nervously, "Too much strain on the pistons. Not meant for deep water."

I wasn't sure how he knew that, but it made me nervous.

After a few more minutes, the dark splotches ahead of us came into focus. To the north, a huge mass of rock rose out of the sea—an island with cliffs at least a hundred feet tall. About half a mile south of that, the other patch of darkness was a storm brewing. The sky and sea boiled together in a roaring mass.

"Hurricane?" Annabeth asked.

"No," Clarisse said. "Charybdis."

Annabeth paled. "Are you crazy?"

"Only way into the Sea of Monsters. Straight between Charybdis and her sister Scylla." Clarisse pointed to the top of the cliffs, and I got the feeling something lived up there that I did not want to meet.

"What do you mean the only way?" I asked. "The sea is wide open! Just sail around them."

Clarisse rolled her eyes. "Don't you know anything? If I tried to sail around them, they would just appear in my path again. If you want to get into the Sea of Monsters, you *have* to sail through them."

"What about the Clashing Rocks?" Annabeth said. "That's another gateway. Jason used it."

"I can't blow apart rocks with my cannons," Clarisse said. "Monsters, on the other hand . . ."

"You *are* crazy," Annabeth decided.

"Watch and learn, Wise Girl." Clarisse turned to the captain. "Set course for Charybdis!"

"Aye, m'lady."

The engine groaned, the iron plating rattled, and the ship began to pick up speed.

"Clarisse," I said, "Charybdis sucks up the sea. Isn't that the story?"

"And spits it back out again, yeah."

"What about Scylla?"

"She lives in a cave, up on those cliffs. If we get too close, her snaky heads will come down and start plucking sailors off the ship."

"Choose Scylla then," I said. "Everybody goes below deck and we chug right past."

"No!" Clarisse insisted. "If Scylla doesn't get her easy meat, she might pick up the whole ship. Besides, she's too high to make a good target. My cannons can't shoot straight up. Charybdis just sits there at the center of her whirlwind. We're going to steam straight toward her, train our guns on her, and blow her to Tartarus!"

She said it with such relish I almost wanted to believe her.

The engine hummed. The boilers were heating up so much I could feel the deck getting warm beneath my feet. The smokestacks billowed. The red Ares flag whipped in the wind.

As we got closer to the monsters, the sound of Charybdis got louder and louder—a horrible wet roar like the galaxy's biggest toilet being flushed. Every time Charybdis inhaled, the ship shuddered and lurched forward. Every time she exhaled, we rose in the water and were buffeted by ten-foot waves.

I tried to time the whirlpool. As near as I could figure, it took Charybdis about three minutes to suck up and destroy everything within a half-mile radius. To avoid her, we would have to skirt right next to Scylla's cliffs. And as bad as Scylla might be, those cliffs were looking awfully good to me.

Undead sailors calmly went about their business on the spar deck. I guess they'd fought a losing cause before, so this didn't bother them. Or maybe they didn't care about getting destroyed because they were already deceased. Neither thought made me feel any better.

Annabeth stood next to me, gripping the rail. "You still have your thermos full of wind?"

I nodded. "But it's too dangerous to use with a whirlpool like that. More wind might just make things worse."

"What about controlling the water?" she asked. "You're Poseidon's son. You've done it before."

She was right. I closed my eyes and tried to calm the sea, but I couldn't concentrate. Charybdis was too loud and powerful. The waves wouldn't respond.

"I—I can't," I said miserably.

"We need a backup plan," Annabeth said. "This isn't going to work."

"Annabeth is right," Tyson said. "Engine's no good."

"What do you mean?" she asked.

"Pressure. Pistons need fixing."

Before he could explain, the cosmic toilet flushed with a mighty *roaaar!* The ship lurched forward and I was thrown to the deck. We were in the whirlpool.

"Full reverse!" Clarisse screamed above the noise. The sea churned around us, waves crashing over the deck. The iron plating was now so hot it steamed. "Get us within firing range! Make ready starboard cannons!"

Dead Confederates rushed back and forth. The propeller grinded into reverse, trying to slow the ship, but we kept sliding toward the center of the vortex.

A zombie sailor burst out of the hold and ran to Clarisse. His gray uniform was smoking. His beard was on fire. "Boiler room overheating, ma'am! She's going to blow!"

"Well, get down there and fix it!"

"Can't!" the sailor yelled. "We're vaporizing in the heat."

Clarisse pounded the side of the casemate. "All I need is a few more minutes! Just enough to get in range!"

"We're going in too fast," the captain said grimly. "Prepare yourself for death."

"No!" Tyson bellowed. "I can fix it."

Clarisse looked at him incredulously. "You?"

"He's a Cyclops," Annabeth said. "He's immune to fire. And he knows mechanics."

"Go!" yelled Clarisse.

"Tyson, no!" I grabbed his arm. "It's too dangerous!"

He patted my hand. "Only way, brother." His expression was determined—confident, even. I'd never seen him look like this before. "I will fix it. Be right back."

As I watched him follow the smoldering sailor down the hatch, I had a terrible feeling. I wanted to run after him, but the ship lurched again—and then I saw Charybdis.

She appeared only a few hundred yards away, through a swirl of mist and smoke and water. The first thing I noticed was the reef—a black crag of coral with a fig tree clinging to the top, an oddly peaceful thing in the middle of a maelstrom. All around it, water curved into a funnel, like light around a black hole. Then I saw the horrible thing anchored to the reef just below the waterline—an enormous mouth with slimy lips and mossy teeth the size of rowboats. And worse, the teeth had braces, bands of corroded scummy metal with pieces of fish and driftwood and floating garbage stuck between them.

Charybdis was an orthodontist's nightmare. She was nothing but a huge black maw with bad teeth alignment and a serious overbite, and she'd done nothing for centuries but eat without brushing after meals. As I watched, the entire sea around her was sucked into the void—sharks, schools of fish, a giant squid. And I realized that in a few seconds, the CSS *Birmingham* would be next.

"Lady Clarisse," the captain shouted. "Starboard and forward guns are in range!"

"Fire!" Clarisse ordered.

Three rounds were blasted into the monster's maw. One blew off the edge of an incisor. Another disappeared into her gullet. The third hit one of Charybdis's retaining bands and shot back at us, snapping the Ares flag off its pole.

"Again!" Clarisse ordered. The gunners reloaded, but I knew it was hopeless. We would have to pound the monster a hundred more times to do any real damage, and we didn't have that long. We were being sucked in too fast.

Then the vibrations in the deck changed. The hum of the engine got stronger and steadier. The ship shuddered and we started pulling away from the mouth.

"Tyson did it!" Annabeth said.

"Wait!" Clarisse said. "We need to stay close!"

"We'll die!" I said. "We *have* to move away."

I gripped the rail as the ship fought against the suction. The broken Ares flag raced past us and lodged in Charybdis's braces. We weren't making much progress, but at least we were holding our own. Tyson had somehow given us just enough juice to keep the ship from being sucked in.

Suddenly, the mouth snapped shut. The sea died to absolute calm. Water washed over Charybdis.

Then, just as quickly as it had closed, the mouth exploded open, spitting out a wall of water, ejecting everything inedible, including our cannonballs, one of which slammed into the side of the CSS *Birmingham* with a *ding* like the bell on a carnival game.

We were thrown backward on a wave that must've been forty feet high. I used all of my willpower to keep the ship from capsizing, but we were still spinning out of control, hurtling toward the cliffs on the opposite side of the strait.

Another smoldering sailor burst out of the hold. He

stumbled into Clarisse, almost knocking them both over-board. "The engine is about to blow!"

"Where's Tyson?" I demanded.

"Still down there," the sailor said. "Holding it together somehow, though I don't know for how much longer."

The captain said, "We have to abandon ship."

"No!" Clarisse yelled.

"We have no choice, m'lady. The hull is already crack-ing apart! She can't—"

He never finished his sentence. Quick as lightning, something brown and green shot from the sky, snatched up the captain, and lifted him away. All that was left were his leather boots.

"Scylla!" a sailor yelled, as another column of reptilian flesh shot from the cliffs and snapped him up. It happened so fast it was like watching a laser beam rather than a mon-ster. I couldn't even make out the thing's face, just a flash of teeth and scales.

I uncapped Riptide and tried to swipe at the monster as it carried off another deckhand, but I was way too slow.

"Everyone get below!" I yelled.

"We can't!" Clarisse drew her own sword. "Below deck is in flames."

"Lifeboats!" Annabeth said. "Quick!"

"They'll never get clear of the cliffs," Clarisse said. "We'll all be eaten."

"We have to try. Percy, the thermos."

"I can't leave Tyson!"

"We have to get the boats ready!"

Clarisse took Annabeth's command. She and a few of her undead sailors uncovered one of the two emergency rowboats while Scylla's heads rained from the sky like a meteor shower with teeth, picking off Confederate sailors one after another.

"Get the other boat." I threw Annabeth the thermos. "I'll get Tyson."

"You can't!" she said. "The heat will kill you!"

I didn't listen. I ran for the boiler room hatch, when suddenly my feet weren't touching the deck anymore. I was flying straight up, the wind whistling in my ears, the side of the cliff only inches from my face.

Scylla had somehow caught me by the knapsack, and was lifting me up toward her lair. Without thinking, I swung my sword behind me and managed to jab the thing in her beady yellow eye. She grunted and dropped me.

The fall would've been bad enough, considering I was a hundred feet in the air. But as I fell, the CSS *Birmingham* exploded below me.

KAROOM!

The engine room blew, sending chunks of ironclad flying in either direction like a fiery set of wings.

"Tyson!" I yelled.

The lifeboats had managed to get away from the ship, but not very far. Flaming wreckage was raining down. Clarisse and Annabeth would either be smashed or burned or pulled to the bottom by the force of the sinking hull, and that was thinking optimistically, assuming they got away from Scylla.

Then I heard a different kind of explosion—the sound of Hermes's magic thermos being opened a little too far. White sheets of wind blasted in every direction, scattering the lifeboats, lifting me out of my free fall and propelling me across the ocean.

I couldn't see anything. I spun in the air, got clonked on the head by something hard, and hit the water with a crash that would've broken every bone in my body if I hadn't been the son of the Sea God.

The last thing I remembered was sinking in a burning sea, knowing that Tyson was gone forever, and wishing I were able to drown.

TWELVE

WE CHECK IN TO
C.C.'S SPA & RESORT

I woke up in a rowboat with a makeshift sail stitched of gray uniform fabric. Annabeth sat next to me, tacking into the wind.

I tried to sit up and immediately felt woozy.

"Rest," she said. "You're going to need it."

"Tyson . . . ?"

She shook her head. "Percy, I'm really sorry."

We were silent while the waves tossed us up and down.

"He may have survived," she said halfheartedly. "I mean, fire can't kill him."

I nodded, but I had no reason to feel hopeful. I'd seen that explosion rip through solid iron. If Tyson had been down in the boiler room, there was no way he could've lived.

He'd given his life for us, and all I could think about were the times I'd felt embarrassed by him and had denied that the two of us were related.

Waves lapped at the boat. Annabeth showed me some things she'd salvaged from the wreckage—Hermes's thermos (now empty), a Ziploc bag full of ambrosia, a couple of sailors' shirts, and a bottle of Dr Pepper. She'd fished me out of the water and found my knapsack, bitten in half by Scylla's teeth. Most of my stuff had floated away, but I still had Hermes's bottle of multivitamins, and of course I had Riptide. The ballpoint pen always appeared back in my pocket no matter where I lost it.

We sailed for hours. Now that we were in the Sea of Monsters, the water glittered a more brilliant green, like Hydra acid. The wind smelled fresh and salty, but it carried a strange metallic scent, too—as if a thunderstorm were coming. Or something even more dangerous. I knew what direction we needed to go. I knew we were exactly one hundred thirteen nautical miles west by northwest of our destination. But that didn't make me feel any less lost.

No matter which way we turned, the sun seemed to shine straight into my eyes. We took turns sipping from the Dr Pepper, shading ourselves with the sail as best we could. And we talked about my latest dream of Grover.

By Annabeth's estimate, we had less than twenty-four hours to find Grover, assuming my dream was accurate, and assuming the Cyclops Polyphemus didn't change his mind and try to marry Grover earlier.

"Yeah," I said bitterly. "You can never trust a Cyclops."

Annabeth stared across the water. "I'm sorry, Percy. I was wrong about Tyson, okay? I wish I could tell him that."

I tried to stay mad at her, but it wasn't easy. We'd been through a lot together. She'd saved my life plenty of times. It was stupid of me to resent her.

I looked down at our measly possessions—the empty wind thermos, the bottle of multivitamins. I thought about Luke's look of rage when I'd tried to talk to him about his dad.

"Annabeth, what's Chiron's prophecy?"

She pursed her lips. "Percy, I shouldn't—"

"I know Chiron promised the gods he wouldn't tell me. But *you* didn't promise, did you?"

"Knowledge isn't always good for you."

"Your mom is the wisdom goddess!"

"I know! But every time heroes learn the future, they try to change it, and it never works."

"The gods are worried about something I'll do when I get older," I guessed. "Something when I turn sixteen."

Annabeth twisted her Yankees cap in her hands. "Percy, I don't know the full prophecy, but it warns about a half-blood child of the Big Three—the next one who lives to the age of sixteen. That's the real reason Zeus, Poseidon, and Hades swore a pact after World War II not to have any more kids. The next child of the Big Three who reaches sixteen will be a dangerous weapon."

"Why?"

"Because that hero will decide the fate of Olympus. He or she will make a decision that either saves the Age of the Gods, or destroys it."

I let that sink in. I don't get seasick, but suddenly I felt ill. "That's why Kronos didn't kill me last summer."

She nodded. "You could be very useful to him. If he can get you on his side, the gods will be in serious trouble."

"But if it's *me* in the prophecy—"

"We'll only know that if you survive three more years. That can be a long time for a half-blood. When Chiron first learned about Thalia, he assumed *she* was the one in the prophecy. That's why he was so desperate to get her safely to camp. Then she went down fighting and got turned into a pine tree and none of us knew what to think. Until you came along."

On our port side, a spiky green dorsal fin about fifteen feet long curled out of the water and disappeared.

"This kid in the prophecy . . . he or she couldn't be like, a Cyclops?" I asked. "The Big Three have lots of monster children."

Annabeth shook her head. "The Oracle said 'half-blood.' That always means half-human, half-god. There's really nobody alive who it could be, except you."

"Then why do the gods even let me live? It would be safer to kill me."

"You're right."

"Thanks a lot."

"Percy, I don't know. I guess some of the gods *would* like to kill you, but they're probably afraid of offending Poseidon. Other gods . . . maybe they're still watching you, trying to decide what kind of hero you're going be. You could be a weapon for their survival, after all. The real question is . . . what will you do in three years? What decision will you make?"

"Did the prophecy give any hints?"

Annabeth hesitated.

Maybe she would've told me more, but just then a sea-gull swooped down out of nowhere and landed on our makeshift mast. Annabeth looked startled as the bird dropped a small cluster of leaves into her lap.

"Land," she said. "There's land nearby!"

I sat up. Sure enough, there was a line of blue and brown in the distance. Another minute and I could make out an island with a small mountain in the center, a dazzling white collection of buildings, a beach dotted with palm trees, and a harbor filled with a strange assortment of boats.

The current was pulling our rowboat toward what looked like a tropical paradise.

"Welcome!" said the lady with the clipboard.

She looked like a flight attendant—blue business suit, perfect makeup, hair pulled back in a ponytail. She shook our hands as we stepped onto the dock. With the dazzling smile she gave us, you would've thought we'd just gotten off the *Princess Andromeda* rather than a banged-up rowboat.

Then again, our rowboat wasn't the weirdest ship in port. Along with a bunch of pleasure yachts, there was a U.S. Navy submarine, several dugout canoes, and an old-fashioned three-masted sailing ship. There was a helipad with a "Channel Five Fort Lauderdale" helicopter on it, and a short runway with a Learjet and a propeller plane that looked like a World War II fighter. Maybe they were replicas for tourists to look at or something.

"Is this your first time with us?" the clipboard lady inquired.

Annabeth and I exchanged looks. Annabeth said, "Umm . . ."

"First—time—at—spa," the lady said as she wrote on her clipboard. "Let's see . . ."

She looked us up and down critically. "Mmm. An herbal wrap to start for the young lady. And of course, a complete makeover for the young gentleman."

"A what?" I asked.

She was too busy jotting down notes to answer.

"Right!" She said with a breezy smile. "Well, I'm sure C.C. will want to speak with you personally before the luau. Come, please."

Now here's the thing. Annabeth and I were used to traps, and usually those traps looked good at first. So I expected the clipboard lady to turn into a snake or a demon, or something, any minute. But on the other hand, we'd been floating in a rowboat for most of the day. I was hot, tired, and hungry, and when this lady mentioned a luau, my stomach sat up on its hind legs and begged like a dog.

"I guess it couldn't hurt," Annabeth muttered.

Of course it could, but we followed the lady anyway. I kept my hands in my pockets where I'd stashed my only magic defenses—Hermes's multivitamins and Riptide—but the farther we wandered into the resort, the more I forgot about them.

The place was amazing. There was white marble and blue water everywhere I looked. Terraces climbed up the side of the mountain, with swimming pools on every level, connected by waterslides and waterfalls and underwater tubes you could swim through. Fountains sprayed water into the air, forming impossible shapes, like flying eagles and galloping horses.

Tyson loved horses, and I knew he'd love those

fountains. I almost turned around to see the expression on his face before I remembered: Tyson was gone.

"You okay?" Annabeth asked me. "You look pale."

"I'm okay," I lied. "Just . . . let's keep walking."

We passed all kinds of tame animals. A sea turtle napped in a stack of beach towels. A leopard stretched out asleep on the diving board. The resort guests—only young women, as far as I could see—lounged in deck chairs, drinking fruit smoothies or reading magazines while herbal gunk dried on their faces and manicurists in white uniforms did their nails.

As we headed up a staircase toward what looked like the main building, I heard a woman singing. Her voice drifted through the air like a lullaby. Her words were in some language other than Ancient Greek, but just as old—Minoan, maybe, or something like that. I could understand what she sang about—moonlight in the olive groves, the colors of the sunrise. And magic. Something about magic. Her voice seemed to lift me off the steps and carry me toward her.

We came into a big room where the whole front wall was windows. The back wall was covered in mirrors, so the room seemed to go on forever. There was a bunch of expensive-looking white furniture, and on a table in one corner was a large wire pet cage. The cage seemed out of place, but I didn't think about it too much, because just then I saw the lady who'd been singing . . . and whoa.

She sat at a loom the size of a big screen TV, her hands weaving colored thread back and forth with amazing skill. The tapestry shimmered like it was three dimensional—a waterfall scene so real I could see the water moving and clouds drifting across a fabric sky.

Annabeth caught her breath. "It's beautiful."

The woman turned. She was even prettier than her fabric. Her long dark hair was braided with threads of gold. She had piercing green eyes and she wore a silky black dress with shapes that seemed to move in the fabric: animal shadows, black upon black, like deer running through a forest at night.

"You appreciate weaving, my dear?" the woman asked.

"Oh, yes, ma'am!" Annabeth said. "My mother is—"

She stopped herself. You couldn't just go around announcing that your mom was Athena, the goddess who invented the loom. Most people would lock you in a rubber room.

Our hostess just smiled. "You have good taste, my dear. I'm so glad you've come. My name is C.C."

The animals in the corner cage started squealing. They must've been guinea pigs, from the sound of them.

We introduced ourselves to C.C. She looked me over with a twinge of disapproval, as if I'd failed some kind of test. Immediately, I felt bad. For some reason, I really wanted to please this lady.

"Oh, dear," she sighed. "You *do* need my help."

"Ma'am?" I asked.

C.C. called to the lady in the business suit. "Hylla, take Annabeth on a tour, will you? Show her what we have available. The clothing will need to change. And the hair, my goodness. We will do a full image consultation after I've spoken with this young gentleman."

"But . . ." Annabeth's voice sounded hurt. "What's wrong with my hair?"

C.C. smiled benevolently. "My dear, you are lovely. Really! But you're not showing off yourself or your talents at all. So much wasted potential!"

"Wasted?"

"Well, surely you're not happy the way you are! My goodness, there's not a single person who is. But don't worry. We can improve anyone here at the spa. Hylla will show you what I mean. You, my dear, need to unlock your true self!"

Annabeth's eyes glowed with longing. I'd never seen her so much at a loss for words. "But . . . what about Percy?"

"Oh, definitely," C.C. said, giving me a sad look. "Percy requires my personal attention. He needs *much* more work than you."

Normally if somebody had told me that, I would've gotten angry, but when C.C. said it, I felt sad. I'd disappointed her. I had to figure out how to do better.

The guinea pigs squealed like they were hungry.

"Well . . ." Annabeth said. "I suppose . . ."

"Right this way, dear," Hylla said. And Annabeth allowed herself to be led away into the waterfall-laced gardens of the spa.

C.C. took my arm and guided me toward the mirrored wall. "You see, Percy . . . to unlock your potential, you'll need serious help. The first step is admitting that you're not happy the way you are."

I fidgeted in the front of the mirror. I hated thinking about my appearance—like the first zit that had cropped up on my nose at the beginning of the school year, or the fact that my two front teeth weren't perfectly even, or that my hair never stayed down straight.

C.C.'s voice brought all of these things to mind, as if she were passing me under a microscope. And my clothes were not cool. I knew that.

Who cares? Part of me thought. But standing in front of C.C.'s mirror, it was hard to see anything good in myself.

"There, there," C.C. consoled. "How about we try . . . this."

She snapped her fingers and a sky-blue curtain rolled down over the mirror. It shimmered like the fabric on her loom.

"What do you see?" C.C. asked.

I looked at the blue cloth, not sure what she meant. "I don't—"

Then it changed colors. I saw myself—a reflection, but not a reflection. Shimmering there on the cloth was a cooler version of Percy Jackson—with just the right clothes, a confident smile on my face. My teeth were straight. No zits. A perfect tan. More athletic. Maybe a couple of inches taller. It was me, without the faults.

"Whoa," I managed.

"Do you want that?" C.C. asked. "Or shall I try a different—"

"No," I said. "That's . . . that's amazing. Can you really—"

"I can give you a full makeover," C.C. promised.

"What's the catch?" I said. "I have to like . . . eat a special diet?"

"Oh, it's quite easy," C.C. said. "Plenty of fresh fruit, a mild exercise program, and of course . . . this."

She stepped over to her wet bar and filled a glass with water. Then she ripped open a drink-mix packet and poured in some red powder. The mixture began to glow. When it faded, the drink looked just like a strawberry milk shake.

"One of these, substituted for a regular meal," C.C. said. "I guarantee you'll see results immediately."

"How is that possible?"

She laughed. "Why question it? I mean, don't you want the perfect you right away?"

Something nagged at the back of my mind. "Why are there no guys at this spa?"

"Oh, but there are," C.C. assured me. "You'll meet them quite soon. Just try the mixture. You'll see."

I looked at the blue tapestry, at the reflection of me, but not me.

"Now, Percy," C.C. chided. "The hardest part of the makeover process is giving up control. You have to decide: do you want to trust *your* judgment about what you should be, or *my* judgment?"

My throat felt dry. I heard myself say, "Your judgment."

C.C. smiled and handed me the glass. I lifted it to my lips.

It tasted just like it looked—like a strawberry milk shake. Almost immediately a warm feeling spread through my gut: pleasant at first, then painfully hot, searing, as if the mixture were coming to a boil inside of me.

I doubled over and dropped the cup. "What have you . . . what's happening?"

"Don't worry, Percy," C.C. said. "The pain will pass. Look! As I promised. Immediate results."

Something was horribly wrong.

The curtain dropped away, and in the mirror I saw my hands shriveling, curling, growing long delicate claws. Fur sprouted on my face, under my shirt, in every uncomfortable place you can imagine. My teeth felt too heavy in my mouth. My clothes were getting too big, or C.C. was getting too tall—no, I was shrinking.

In one awful flash, I sank into a cavern of dark cloth. I was buried in my own shirt. I tried to run but hands grabbed me—hands as big as I was. I tried to scream for help, but all that came out of my mouth was, *"Reeet, reeet, reeet!"*

The giant hands squeezed me around the middle, lifting me into the air. I struggled and kicked with legs and arms that seemed much too stubby, and then I was staring, horrified, into the enormous face of C.C.

"Perfect!" her voice boomed. I squirmed in alarm, but she only tightened her grip around my furry belly. "See, Percy? You've unlocked your true self!"

She held me up to the mirror, and what I saw made me scream in terror, *"Reeet, reeet, reeet!"* There was C.C., beautiful and smiling, holding a fluffy, bucktoothed creature with tiny claws and white and orange fur. When I twisted, so did the furry critter in the mirror. I was . . . I was . . .

"A guinea pig," C.C. said. "Lovely, aren't you? Men are pigs, Percy Jackson. I used to turn them into *real* pigs, but they were so smelly and large and difficult to keep. Not much different than they were before, really. Guinea pigs are much more convenient! Now come, and meet the other men."

"*Reeet!*" I protested, trying to scratch her, but C.C. squeezed me so tight I almost blacked out.

"None of that, little one," she scolded, "or I'll feed you to the owls. Go into the cage like a good little pet. Tomorrow, if you behave, you'll be on your way. There is always a classroom in need of a new guinea pig."

My mind was racing as fast as my tiny little heart. I needed to get back to my clothes, which were lying in a heap on the floor. If I could do that, I could get Riptide out of my pocket and . . . And what? I couldn't uncap the pen. Even if I did, I couldn't hold the sword.

I squirmed helplessly as C.C. brought me over to the guinea pig cage and opened the wire door.

"Meet my discipline problems, Percy," she warned. "They'll never make good classroom pets, but they might teach you some manners. Most of them have been in this cage for three hundred years. If you don't want to stay with them permanently, I'd suggest you—"

Annabeth's voice called: "Miss C.C.?"

C.C. cursed in Ancient Greek. She plopped me into the cage and closed the door. I squealed and clawed at the bars, but it was no good. I watched as C.C. hurriedly kicked my clothes under the loom just as Annabeth came in.

I almost didn't recognize her. She was wearing a sleeveless silk dress like C.C.'s, only white. Her blond hair was newly washed and combed and braided with gold. Worst of all, she was wearing makeup, which I never thought Annabeth would be caught dead in. I mean, she looked good. Really good. I probably would've been tongue-tied if I could've said anything except *reet, reet, reet*. But there was also something totally wrong about it. It just wasn't Annabeth.

She looked around the room and frowned. "Where's Percy?"

I squealed up a storm, but she didn't seem to hear me.

C.C. smiled. "He's having one of our treatments, my dear. Not to worry. You look wonderful! What did you think of your tour?"

Annabeth's eyes brightened. "Your library is amazing!"

"Yes, indeed," C.C. said. "The best knowledge of the past three millennia. Anything you want to study, anything you want to *be*, my dear."

"An architect?"

"Pah!" C.C. said. "You, my dear, have the makings of a sorceress. Like me."

Annabeth took a step back. "A sorceress?"

"Yes, my dear." C.C. held up her hand. A flame appeared in her palm and danced across her fingertips. "My mother is Hecate, the goddess of magic. I know a daughter of Athena when I see one. We are not so different, you and I. We both seek knowledge. We both admire greatness. Neither of us needs to stand in the shadow of men."

"I—I don't understand."

Again, I squealed my best, trying to get Annabeth's attention, but she either couldn't hear me or didn't think the noises were important. Meanwhile, the other guinea pigs were emerging from their hutch to check me out. I didn't think it was possible for guinea pigs to look mean, but these did. There were half a dozen, with dirty fur and cracked teeth and beady red eyes. They were covered with shavings and smelled like they really had been in here for three hundred years, without getting their cage cleaned.

"Stay with me," C.C. was telling Annabeth. "Study with me. You can join our staff, become a sorceress, learn to bend others to your will. You will become immortal!"

"But—"

"You are too intelligent, my dear," C.C. said. "You know better than to trust that silly camp for heroes. How many great female half-blood heroes can you name?"

"Um, Atalanta, Amelia Earhart—"

"Bah! Men get all the glory." C.C. closed her fist and extinguished the magic flame. "The only way to power for women is sorcery. Medea, Calypso, now there were powerful women! And me, of course. The greatest of all."

"You . . . C.C. . . . . Circe!"

"Yes, my dear."

Annabeth backed up, and Circe laughed. "You need not worry. I mean you no harm."

"What have you done to Percy?"

"Only helped him realize his true form."

Annabeth scanned the room. Finally she saw the cage,

and me scratching at the bars, all the other guinea pigs crowding around me. Her eyes went wide.

"Forget him," Circe said. "Join me and learn the ways of sorcery."

"But—"

"Your friend will be well cared for. He'll be shipped to a wonderful new home on the mainland. The kindergartners will adore him. Meanwhile, you will be wise and powerful. You will have all you ever wanted."

Annabeth was still staring at me, but she had a dreamy expression on her face. She looked the same way I had when Circe enchanted me into drinking the guinea pig milk shake. I squealed and scratched, trying to warn her to snap out of it, but I was absolutely powerless.

"Let me think about it," Annabeth murmured. "Just . . . give me a minute alone. To say good-bye."

"Of course, my dear," Circe cooed. "One minute. Oh . . . and so you have absolute privacy . . ." She waved her hand and iron bars slammed down over the windows. She swept out of the room and I heard the locks on the door click shut behind her.

The dreamy look melted off Annabeth's face.

She rushed over to my cage. "All right, which one is you?"

I squealed, but so did all the other guinea pigs. Annabeth looked desperate. She scanned the room and spotted the cuff of my jeans sticking out from under the loom.

Yes!

She rushed over and rummaged through my pockets.

But instead of bringing out Riptide, she found the bottle of Hermes multivitamins and started struggling with the cap.

I wanted to scream at her that this wasn't the time for taking supplements! She had to draw the sword!

She popped a lemon chewable in her mouth just as the door flew open and Circe came back in, flanked by two of her business-suited attendants.

"Well," Circe sighed, "how fast a minute passes. What is your answer, my dear?"

"This," Annabeth said, and she drew her bronze knife.

The sorceress stepped back, but her surprise quickly passed. She sneered. "Really, little girl, a knife against *my* magic? Is that wise?"

Circe looked back at her attendants, who smiled. They raised their hands as if preparing to cast a spell.

Run! I wanted to tell Annabeth, but all I could make were rodent noises. The other guinea pigs squealed in terror and scuttled around the cage. I had the urge to panic and hide, too, but I had to think of something! I couldn't stand to lose Annabeth the way I'd lost Tyson.

"What will Annabeth's makeover be?" Circe mused. "Something small and ill-tempered. I know . . . a shrew!"

Blue fire coiled from her fingers curling like serpents around Annabeth.

I watched, horror-struck, but nothing happened. Annabeth was still Annabeth, only angrier. She leaped forward and stuck the point of her knife against Circe's neck.

"How about turning me into a panther instead? One that has her claws at your throat!"

"How!" Circe yelped.

Annabeth held up my bottle of vitamins for the sorceress to see.

Circe howled in frustration. "Curse Hermes and his multivitamins! Those are such a fad! They do *nothing* for you."

"Turn Percy back to a human or else!" Annabeth said.

"I can't!"

"Then you asked for it."

Circe's attendants stepped forward, but their mistress said, "Get back! She's immune to magic until that cursed vitamin wears off."

Annabeth dragged Circe over to the guinea pig cage, knocked the top off, and poured the rest of the vitamins inside.

"No!" Circe screamed.

I was the first to get a vitamin, but all the other guinea pigs scuttled out, too, and checked out this new food.

The first nibble, and I felt all fiery inside. I gnawed at the vitamin until it stopped looking so huge, and the cage got smaller, and then suddenly, *bang!* The cage exploded. I was sitting on the floor, a human again—somehow back in my regular clothes, thank the gods—with six other guys who all looked disoriented, blinking and shaking wood shavings out of their hair.

"No!" Circe screamed. "You don't understand! Those are the worst!"

One of the men stood up—a huge guy with a long tangled pitch-black beard and teeth the same color. He wore mismatched clothes of wool and leather, knee-length boots, and a floppy felt hat. The other men were dressed more simply—in breeches and stained white shirts. All of them were barefoot.

"Argggh!" bellowed the big man. "What's the witch done t'me!"

"No!" Circe moaned.

Annabeth gasped. "I recognize you! Edward Teach, son of Ares?"

"Aye, lass," the big man growled. "Though most call me Blackbeard! And there's the sorceress what captured us, lads. Run her through, and then I mean to find me a big bowl of celery! Argggh!"

Circe screamed. She and her attendants ran from the room, chased by the pirates.

Annabeth sheathed her knife and glared at me.

"Thanks . . ." I faltered. "I'm really sorry—"

Before I could figure out how to apologize for being such an idiot, she tackled me with a hug, then pulled away just as quickly. "I'm glad you're not a guinea pig."

"Me, too." I hoped my face wasn't as red as it felt.

She undid the golden braids in her hair.

"Come on, Seaweed Brain," she said. "We have to get away while Circe's distracted."

We ran down the hillside through the terraces, past screaming spa workers and pirates ransacking the resort. Blackbeard's men broke the tiki torches for the luau, threw herbal wraps into the swimming pool, and kicked over tables of sauna towels.

I almost felt bad letting the unruly pirates out, but I guessed they deserved something more entertaining than the exercise wheel after being cooped up in a cage for three centuries.

"Which ship?" Annabeth said as we reached the docks.

I looked around desperately. We couldn't very well take our rowboat. We had to get off the island fast, but what else could we use? A sub? A fighter jet? I couldn't pilot any of those things. And then I saw it.

"There," I said.

Annabeth blinked. "But—"

"I can make it work."

"How?"

I couldn't explain. I just somehow knew an old sailing vessel was the best bet for me. I grabbed Annabeth's hand and pulled her toward the three-mast ship. Painted on its prow was the name that I would only decipher later: *Queen Anne's Revenge*.

"Argggh!" Blackbeard yelled somewhere behind us. "Those scalawags are a-boarding me vessel! Get 'em, lads!"

"We'll never get going in time!" Annabeth yelled as we climbed aboard.

I looked around at the hopeless maze of sail and ropes. The ship was in great condition for a three-hundred-year-old vessel, but it would still take a crew of fifty several hours to get underway. We didn't have several hours. I could see the pirates running down the stairs, waving tiki torches and sticks of celery.

I closed my eyes and concentrated on the waves lapping against the hull, the ocean currents, the winds all around me. Suddenly, the right word appeared in my mind. "Mizzenmast!" I yelled.

Annabeth looked at me like I was nuts, but in the next second, the air was filled with whistling sounds of ropes being snapped taut, canvases unfurling, and wooden pulleys creaking.

Annabeth ducked as a cable flew over her head and wrapped itself around the bowsprit. "Percy, how . . ."

I didn't have an answer, but I could feel the ship responding to me as if it were part of my body. I willed the sails to rise as easily as if I were flexing my arm. I willed the rudder to turn.

The *Queen Anne's Revenge* lurched away from the dock, and by the time the pirates arrived at the water's edge, we were already underway, sailing into the Sea of Monsters.

THIRTEEN

ANNABETH TRIES
TO SWIM HOME

I'd finally found something I was really good at.

The *Queen Anne's Revenge* responded to my every command. I knew which ropes to hoist, which sails to raise, which direction to steer. We plowed through the waves at what I figured was about ten knots. I even understood how fast that was. For a sailing ship, pretty darn fast.

It all felt perfect—the wind in my face, the waves breaking over the prow.

But now that we were out of danger, all I could think about was how much I missed Tyson, and how worried I was about Grover.

I couldn't get over how badly I'd messed up on Circe's Island. If it hadn't been for Annabeth, I'd still be a rodent, hiding in a hutch with a bunch of cute furry pirates. I thought about what Circe had said: *See, Percy? You've unlocked your true self!*

I still felt changed. Not just because I had a sudden desire to eat lettuce. I felt jumpy, like the instinct to be a scared little animal was now a part of me. Or maybe it had always been there. That's what really worried me.

We sailed through the night.

Annabeth tried to help me keep lookout, but sailing didn't agree with her. After a few hours rocking back and forth, her face turned the color of guacamole and she went below to lie in a hammock.

I watched the horizon. More than once I spotted monsters. A plume of water as tall as a skyscraper spewed into the moonlight. A row of green spines slithered across the waves—something maybe a hundred feet long, reptilian. I didn't really want to know.

Once I saw Nereids, the glowing lady spirits of the sea. I tried to wave at them, but they disappeared into the depths, leaving me unsure whether they'd seen me or not.

Sometime after midnight, Annabeth came up on deck. We were just passing a smoking volcano island. The sea bubbled and steamed around the shore.

"One of the forges of Hephaestus," Annabeth said. "Where he makes his metal monsters."

"Like the bronze bulls?"

She nodded. "Go around. Far around."

I didn't need to be told twice. We steered clear of the island, and soon it was just a red patch of haze behind us.

I looked at Annabeth: "The reason you hate Cyclopes so much . . . the story about how Thalia really died. What happened?"

It was hard to see her expression in the dark.

"I guess you deserve to know," she said finally. "The night Grover was escorting us to camp, he got confused, took some wrong turns. You remember he told you that once?"

I nodded.

"Well, the worst wrong turn was into a Cyclops's lair in Brooklyn."

"They've got Cyclopes in Brooklyn?" I asked.

"You wouldn't believe how many, but that's not the point. This Cyclops, he tricked us. He managed to split us up inside this maze of corridors in an old house in Flatbush. And he could sound like anyone, Percy. Just the way Tyson did aboard the *Princess Andromeda*. He lured us, one at time. Thalia thought she was running to save Luke. Luke thought he heard me scream for help. And me . . . I was alone in the dark. I was seven years old. I couldn't even find the exit."

She brushed the hair out of her face. "I remember finding the main room. There were bones all over the floor. And there were Thalia and Luke and Grover, tied up and gagged, hanging from the ceiling like smoked hams. The Cyclops was starting a fire in the middle of the floor. I drew my knife, but he heard me. He turned and smiled. He spoke, and somehow he knew my dad's voice. I guess he just plucked it out of my mind. He said, 'Now, Annabeth, don't you worry. I love you. You can stay here with me. You can stay forever.'"

I shivered. The way she told it—even now, six years later—freaked me out worse than any ghost story I'd ever heard. "What did you do?"

"I stabbed him in the foot."

I stared at her. "Are you kidding? You were seven years old and you stabbed a grown Cyclops in the foot?"

"Oh, he would've killed me. But I surprised him. It gave

me just enough time to run to Thalia and cut the ropes on her hands. She took it from there."

"Yeah, but still . . . that was pretty brave, Annabeth."

She shook her head. "We barely got out alive. I still have nightmares, Percy. The way that Cyclops talked in my father's voice. It was his fault we took so long getting to camp. All the monsters who'd been chasing us had time to catch up. That's really why Thalia died. If it hadn't been for that Cyclops, she'd still be alive today."

We sat on the deck, watching the Hercules constellation rise in the night sky.

"Go below," Annabeth told me at last. "You need some rest."

I nodded. My eyes were heavy. But when I got below and found a hammock, it took me a long time to fall asleep. I kept thinking about Annabeth's story. I wondered, if I were her, would I have had enough courage to go on this quest, to sail straight toward the lair of another Cyclops?

I didn't dream about Grover.

Instead I found myself back in Luke's stateroom aboard the *Princess Andromeda*. The curtains were open. It was nighttime outside. The air swirled with shadows. Voices whispered all around me—spirits of the dead.

Beware, they whispered. *Traps. Trickery.*

Kronos's golden sarcophagus glowed faintly—the only source of light in the room.

A cold laugh startled me. It seemed to come from miles below the ship. *You don't have the courage, young one. You can't stop me.*

I knew what I had to do. I had to open that coffin.

I uncapped Riptide. Ghosts whirled around me like a tornado. *Beware!*

My heart pounded. I couldn't make my feet move, but I had to stop Kronos. I had to destroy whatever was in that box.

Then a girl spoke right next to me: "Well, Seaweed Brain?"

I looked over, expecting to see Annabeth, but the girl wasn't Annabeth. She wore punk-style clothes with silver chains on her wrists. She had spiky black hair, dark eyeliner around her stormy blue eyes, and a spray of freckles across her nose. She looked familiar, but I wasn't sure why.

"Well?" she asked. "Are we going to stop him or not?"

I couldn't answer. I couldn't move.

The girl rolled her eyes. "Fine. Leave it to me and Aegis."

She tapped her wrist and her silver chains transformed— flattening and expanding into a huge shield. It was silver and bronze, with the monstrous face of Medusa protruding from the center. It looked like a death mask, as if the gorgon's real head had been pressed into the metal. I didn't know if that was true, or if the shield could really petrify me, but I looked away. Just being near it made me cold with fear. I got a feeling that in a real fight, the bearer of that shield would be almost impossible to beat. Any sane enemy would turn and run.

The girl drew her sword and advanced on the sarcophagus. The shadowy ghosts parted for her, scattering before the terrible aura of her shield.

"No," I tried to warn her.

But she didn't listen. She marched straight up to the sarcophagus and pushed aside the golden lid.

For a moment she stood there, gazing down at whatever was in the box.

The coffin began to glow.

"No." The girl's voice trembled. "It can't be."

From the depths of the ocean, Kronos laughed so loudly the whole ship trembled.

"No!" The girl screamed as the sarcophagus engulfed her in a blast of a golden light.

"Ah!" I sat bolt upright in my hammock.

Annabeth was shaking me. "Percy, you were having a nightmare. You need to get up."

"Wh—what is it?" I rubbed my eyes. "What's wrong?"

"Land," she said grimly. "We're approaching the island of the Sirens."

I could barely make out the island ahead of us—just a dark spot in the mist.

"I want you to do me a favor," Annabeth said. "The Sirens . . . we'll be in range of their singing soon."

I remembered stories about the Sirens. They sang so sweetly their voices enchanted sailors and lured them to their death.

"No problem," I assured her. "We can just stop up our ears. There's a big tub of candle wax below deck—"

"I want to hear them."

I blinked. "Why?"

"They say the Sirens sing the truth about what you desire. They tell you things about yourself you didn't even realize. That's what's so enchanting. If you survive . . . you become wiser. I want to hear them. How often will I get that chance?"

Coming from most people, this would've made no sense. But Annabeth being who she was—well, if she could struggle through Ancient Greek architecture books and enjoy documentaries on the History Channel, I guessed the Sirens would appeal to her, too.

She told me her plan. Reluctantly, I helped her get ready.

As soon as the rocky coastline of the island came into view, I ordered one of the ropes to wrap around Annabeth's waist, tying her to the foremast.

"Don't untie me," she said, "no matter what happens or how much I plead. I'll want to go straight over the edge and drown myself."

"Are you trying to tempt me?"

"Ha-ha."

I promised I'd keep her secure. Then I took two large wads of candle wax, kneaded them into earplugs, and stuffed my ears.

Annabeth nodded sarcastically, letting me know the earplugs were a real fashion statement. I made a face at her and turned to the pilot's wheel.

The silence was eerie. I couldn't hear anything but the rush of blood in my head. As we approached the island, jagged rocks loomed out of the fog. I willed the *Queen Anne's*

Revenge to skirt around them. If we sailed any closer, those rocks would shred our hull like blender blades.

I glanced back. At first, Annabeth seemed totally normal. Then she got a puzzled look on her face. Her eyes widened.

She strained against the ropes. She called my name—I could tell just from reading her lips. Her expression was clear: She had to get out. This was life or death. I had to let her out of the ropes *right now*.

She seemed so miserable it was hard not to cut her free.

I forced myself to look away. I urged the *Queen Anne's Revenge* to go faster.

I still couldn't see much of the island—just mist and rocks—but floating in the water were pieces of wood and fiberglass, the wreckage of old ships, even some flotation cushions from airplanes.

How could music cause so many lives to veer off course? I mean, sure, there were some Top Forty songs that made me want to take a fiery nosedive, but still . . . What could the Sirens possibly sing about?

For one dangerous moment, I understood Annabeth's curiosity. I was tempted to take out the earplugs, just to get a taste of the song. I could feel the Sirens' voices vibrating in the timbers of the ship, pulsing along with the roar of blood in my ears.

Annabeth was pleading with me. Tears streamed down her cheeks. She strained against the ropes, as if they were holding her back from everything she cared about.

How could you be so cruel? She seemed to be asking me. *I thought you were my friend.*

I glared at the misty island. I wanted to uncap my sword, but there was nothing to fight. How do you fight a song?

I tried hard not to look at Annabeth. I managed it for about five minutes.

That was my big mistake.

When I couldn't stand it any longer, I looked back and found . . . a heap of cut ropes. An empty mast. Annabeth's bronze knife lay on the deck. Somehow, she'd managed to wriggle it into her hand. I'd totally forgotten to disarm her.

I rushed to the side of the boat and saw her, paddling madly for the island, the waves carrying her straight toward the jagged rocks.

I screamed her name, but if she heard me, it didn't do any good. She was entranced, swimming toward her death.

I looked back at the pilot's wheel and yelled, "Stay!"

Then I jumped over the side.

I sliced into the water and willed the currents to bend around me, making a jet stream that shot me forward.

I came to the surface and spotted Annabeth, but a wave caught her, sweeping her between two razor-sharp fangs of rock.

I had no choice. I plunged after her.

I dove under the wrecked hull of a yacht, wove through a collection of floating metal balls on chains that I realized afterward were mines. I had to use all my power over water to avoid getting smashed against the rocks or tangled in the nets of barbed wire strung just below the surface.

I jetted between the two rock fangs and found myself in

a half-moon-shaped bay. The water was choked with more rocks and ship wreckage and floating mines. The beach was black volcanic sand.

I looked around desperately for Annabeth.

There she was.

Luckily or unluckily, she was a strong swimmer. She'd made it past the mines and the rocks. She was almost to the black beach.

Then the mist cleared and I saw them—the Sirens.

Imagine a flock of vultures the size of people—with dirty black plumage, gray talons, and wrinkled pink necks. Now imagine human heads on top of those necks, but the human heads keep changing.

I couldn't hear them, but I could see they were singing. As their mouths moved, their faces morphed into people I knew—my mom, Poseidon, Grover, Tyson, Chiron. All the people I most wanted to see. They smiled reassuringly, inviting me forward. But no matter what shape they took, their mouths were greasy and caked with the remnants of old meals. Like vultures, they'd been eating with their faces, and it didn't look like they'd been feasting on Monster Donuts.

Annabeth swam toward them.

I knew I couldn't let her get out of the water. The sea was my only advantage. It had always protected me one way or another. I propelled myself forward and grabbed her ankle.

The moment I touched her, a shock went through my body, and I saw the Sirens the way Annabeth must've been seeing them.

Three people sat on a picnic blanket in Central Park. A feast was spread out before them. I recognized Annabeth's dad from photos she'd shown me—an athletic-looking, sandy-haired guy in his forties. He was holding hands with a beautiful woman who looked a lot like Annabeth. She was dressed casually—in blue jeans and a denim shirt and hiking boots—but something about the woman radiated power. I knew that I was looking at the goddess Athena. Next to them sat a young man . . . Luke.

The whole scene glowed in a warm, buttery light. The three of them were talking and laughing, and when they saw Annabeth, their faces lit up with delight. Annabeth's mom and dad held out their arms invitingly. Luke grinned and gestured for Annabeth to sit next to him—as if he'd never betrayed her, as if he were still her friend.

Behind the trees of Central Park, a city skyline rose. I caught my breath, because it was Manhattan, but *not* Manhattan. It had been totally rebuilt from dazzling white marble, bigger and grander than ever—with golden windows and rooftop gardens. It was better than New York. Better than Mount Olympus.

I knew immediately that Annabeth had designed it all. She was the architect for a whole new world. She had reunited her parents. She had saved Luke. She had done everything she'd ever wanted.

I blinked hard. When I opened my eyes, all I saw were the Sirens—ragged vultures with human faces, ready to feed on another victim.

I pulled Annabeth back into the surf. I couldn't hear

her, but I could tell she was screaming. She kicked me in the face, but I held on.

I willed the currents to carry us out into the bay. Annabeth pummeled and kicked me, making it hard to concentrate. She thrashed so much we almost collided with a floating mine. I didn't know what to do. I'd never get back to the ship alive if she kept fighting.

We went under and Annabeth stopped struggling. Her expression became confused. Then our heads broke the surface and she started to fight again.

The water! Sound didn't travel well underwater. If I could submerge her long enough, I could break the spell of the music. Of course, Annabeth wouldn't be able to breathe, but at the moment, that seemed like a minor problem.

I grabbed her around the waist and ordered the waves to push us down.

We shot into the depths—ten feet, twenty feet. I knew I had to be careful because I could withstand a lot more pressure than Annabeth. She fought and struggled for breath as bubbles rose around us.

Bubbles.

I was desperate. I had to keep Annabeth alive. I imagined all the bubbles in the sea—always churning, rising. I imagined them coming together, being pulled toward me.

The sea obeyed. There was a flurry of white, a tickling sensation all around me, and when my vision cleared, Annabeth and I had a huge bubble of air around us. Only our legs stuck into the water.

She gasped and coughed. Her whole body shuddered, but

when she looked at me, I knew the spell had been broken.

She started to sob—I mean horrible, heartbroken sobbing. She put her head on my shoulder and I held her.

Fish gathered to look at us—a school of barracudas, some curious marlins.

Scram! I told them.

They swam off, but I could tell they went reluctantly. I swear I understood their intentions. They were about to start rumors flying around the sea about the son of Poseidon and some girl at the bottom of Siren Bay.

"I'll get us back to the ship," I told her. "It's okay. Just hang on."

Annabeth nodded to let me know she was better now, then she murmured something I couldn't hear because of the wax in my ears.

I made the current steer our weird little air submarine through the rocks and barbed wire and back toward the hull of the *Queen Anne's Revenge*, which was maintaining a slow and steady course away from the island.

We stayed underwater, following the ship, until I judged we had moved out of earshot of the Sirens. Then I surfaced and our air bubble popped.

I ordered a rope ladder to drop over the side of the ship, and we climbed aboard.

I kept my earplugs in, just to be sure. We sailed until the island was completely out of sight. Annabeth sat huddled in a blanket on the forward deck. Finally she looked up, dazed and sad, and mouthed, *safe.*

I took out the earplugs. No singing. The afternoon was

quiet except for the sound of the waves against the hull. The fog had burned away to a blue sky, as if the island of the Sirens had never existed.

"You okay?" I asked. The moment I said it, I realized how lame that sounded. Of course she wasn't okay.

"I didn't realize," she murmured.

"What?"

Her eyes were the same color as the mist over the Sirens' island. "How powerful the temptation would be."

I didn't want to admit that I'd seen what the Sirens had promised her. I felt like a trespasser. But I figured I owed it to Annabeth.

"I saw the way you rebuilt Manhattan," I told her. "And Luke and your parents."

She blushed. "You saw that?"

"What Luke told you back on the *Princess Andromeda*, about starting the world from scratch . . . that really got to you, huh?"

She pulled her blanket around her. "My fatal flaw. That's what the Sirens showed me. My fatal flaw is hubris."

I blinked. "That brown stuff they spread on veggie sandwiches?"

She rolled her eyes. "No, Seaweed Brain. That's *hummus*. Hubris is worse."

"What could be worse than hummus?"

"Hubris means deadly pride, Percy. Thinking you can do things better than anyone else . . . even the gods."

"You feel that way?"

She looked down. "Don't you ever feel like, what if the

[199]

world really *is* messed up? What if we *could* do it all over again from scratch? No more war. Nobody homeless. No more summer reading homework."

"I'm listening."

"I mean, the West represents a lot of the best things mankind ever did—that's why the fire is still burning. That's why Olympus is still around. But sometimes you just see the bad stuff, you know? And you start thinking the way Luke does: 'If I could tear this all down, I would do it better.' Don't you ever feel that way? Like *you* could do a better job if you ran the world?"

"Um . . . no. Me running the world would kind of be a nightmare."

"Then you're lucky. Hubris isn't your fatal flaw."

"What is?"

"I don't know, Percy, but every hero has one. If you don't find it and learn to control it . . . well, they don't call it 'fatal' for nothing."

I thought about that. It didn't exactly cheer me up.

I also noticed Annabeth hadn't said much about the *personal* things she would change—like getting her parents back together, or saving Luke. I understood. I didn't want to admit how many times I'd dreamed of getting my own parents back together.

I pictured my mom, alone in our little apartment on the Upper East Side. I tried to remember the smell of her blue waffles in the kitchen. It seemed so far away.

"So was it worth it?" I asked Annabeth. "Do you feel . . . wiser?"

She gazed into the distance. "I'm not sure. But we *have* to save the camp. If we don't stop Luke . . ."

She didn't need to finish. If Luke's way of thinking could even tempt Annabeth, there was no telling how many other half-bloods might join him.

I thought about my dream of the girl and the golden sarcophagus. I wasn't sure what it meant, but I got the feeling I was missing something. Something terrible that Kronos was planning. What had the girl seen when she opened that coffin lid?

Suddenly Annabeth's eyes widened. "Percy."

I turned.

Up ahead was another blotch of land—a saddle-shaped island with forested hills and white beaches and green meadows—just like I'd seen in my dreams.

My nautical senses confirmed it. 30 degrees, 31 minutes north, 75 degrees, 12 minutes west.

We had reached the home of the Cyclops.

FOURTEEN

WE MEET THE SHEEP
OF DOOM

When you think "monster island," you think craggy rocks and bones scattered on the beach like the island of the Sirens.

The Cyclops's island was nothing like that. I mean, okay, it had a rope bridge across a chasm, which was not a good sign. You might as well put up a billboard that said, SOMETHING EVIL LIVES HERE. But except for that, the place looked like a Caribbean postcard. It had green fields and tropical fruit trees and white beaches. As we sailed toward the shore, Annabeth breathed in the sweet air. "The Fleece," she said.

I nodded. I couldn't see the Fleece yet, but I could feel its power. I could believe it would heal anything, even Thalia's poisoned tree. "If we take it away, will the island die?"

Annabeth shook her head. "It'll fade. Go back to what it would be normally, whatever that is."

I felt a little guilty about ruining this paradise, but I reminded myself we had no choice. Camp Half-Blood was in trouble. And Tyson . . . Tyson would still be with us if it wasn't for this quest.

In the meadow at the base of the ravine, several dozen

sheep were milling around. They looked peaceful enough, but they were huge—the size of hippos. Just past them was a path that led up into the hills. At the top of the path, near the edge of the canyon, was the massive oak tree I'd seen in my dreams. Something gold glittered in its branches.

"This is too easy," I said. "We could just hike up there and take it?"

Annabeth's eyes narrowed. "There's supposed be a guardian. A dragon or . . ."

That's when a deer emerged from the bushes. It trotted into the meadow, probably looking for grass to eat, when the sheep all bleated at once and rushed the animal. It happened so fast that the deer stumbled and was lost in a sea of wool and trampling hooves.

Grass and tufts of fur flew into the air.

A second later the sheep all moved away, back to their regular peaceful wanderings. Where the deer had been was a pile of clean white bones.

Annabeth and I exchanged looks.

"They're like piranhas," she said.

"Piranhas with wool. How will we—"

"Percy!" Annabeth gasped, grabbing my arm. "Look."

She pointed down the beach, to just below the sheep meadow, where a small boat had been run aground . . . the other lifeboat from the CSS *Birmingham*.

We decided there was no way we could get past the man-eating sheep. Annabeth wanted to sneak up the path invisibly and grab the Fleece, but in the end I convinced her that something would go wrong. The sheep would smell her. Another guardian would appear. Something. And if that happened, I'd be too far away to help.

Besides, our first job was to find Grover and whoever had come ashore in that lifeboat—assuming they'd gotten past the sheep. I was too nervous to say what I was secretly hoping . . . that Tyson might still be alive.

We moored the *Queen Anne's Revenge* on the back side of the island where the cliffs rose straight up a good two hundred feet. I figured the ship was less likely to be seen there.

The cliffs looked climbable, barely—about as difficult as the lava wall back at camp. At least it was free of sheep. I hoped that Polyphemus did not also keep carnivorous mountain goats.

We rowed a lifeboat to the edge of the rocks and made our way up, very slowly. Annabeth went first because she was the better climber.

We only came close to dying six or seven times, which I thought was pretty good. Once, I lost my grip and I found myself dangling by one hand from a ledge fifty feet above the rocky surf. But I found another handhold and kept climbing. A minute later Annabeth hit a slippery patch of moss and her foot slipped. Fortunately, she found something else to put it against. Unfortunately, that something was my face.

"Sorry," she murmured.

"S'okay," I grunted, though I'd never really wanted to know what Annabeth's sneaker tasted like.

Finally, when my fingers felt like molten lead and my

arm muscles were shaking from exhaustion, we hauled ourselves over the top of the cliff and collapsed.

"Ugh," I said.

"Ouch," moaned Annabeth.

"Garrr!" bellowed another voice.

If I hadn't been so tired, I would've leaped another two hundred feet. I whirled around, but I couldn't see who'd spoken.

Annabeth clamped her hand over my mouth. She pointed.

The ledge we were sitting on was narrower than I'd realized. It dropped off on the opposite side, and that's where the voice was coming from—right below us.

"You're a feisty one!" the deep voice bellowed.

"Challenge me!" Clarisse's voice, no doubt about it. "Give me back my sword and I'll fight you!"

The monster roared with laughter.

Annabeth and I crept to the edge. We were right above the entrance of the Cyclops's cave. Below us stood Polyphemus and Grover, still in his wedding dress. Clarisse was tied up, hanging upside down over a pot of boiling water. I was half hoping to see Tyson down there, too. Even if he'd been in danger, at least I would've known he was alive. But there was no sign of him.

"Hmm," Polyphemus pondered. "Eat loudmouth girl now or wait for wedding feast? What does my bride think?"

He turned to Grover, who backed up and almost tripped over his completed bridal train. "Oh, um, I'm not hungry right now, dear. Perhaps—"

"Did you say *bride*?" Clarisse demanded. "Who—Grover?"

Next to me, Annabeth muttered, "Shut up. She has to shut up."

Polyphemus glowered. "What 'Grover'?"

"The satyr!" Clarisse yelled.

"Oh!" Grover yelped. "The poor thing's brain is boiling from that hot water. Pull her down, dear!"

Polyphemus's eyelids narrowed over his baleful milky eye, as if he were trying to see Clarisse more clearly.

The Cyclops was an even more horrible sight than he had been in my dreams. Partly because his rancid smell was now up close and personal. Partly because he was dressed in his wedding outfit—a crude kilt and shoulder-wrap, stitched together from baby-blue tuxedoes, as if the he'd skinned an entire wedding party.

"What satyr?" asked Polyphemus. "Satyrs are good eating. You bring me a satyr?"

"No, you big idiot!" bellowed Clarisse. "*That* satyr! Grover! The one in the wedding dress!"

I wanted to wring Clarisse's neck, but it was too late. All I could do was watch as Polyphemus turned and ripped off Grover's wedding veil—revealing his curly hair, his scruffy adolescent beard, his tiny horns.

Polyphemus breathed heavily, trying to contain his anger. "I don't see very well," he growled. "Not since many years ago when the other hero stabbed me in eye. But YOU'RE—NO—LADY—CYCLOPS!"

The Cyclops grabbed Grover's dress and tore it away.

Underneath, the old Grover reappeared in his jeans and T-shirt. He yelped and ducked as the monster swiped over his head.

"Stop!" Grover pleaded. "Don't eat me raw! I—I have a good recipe!"

I reached for my sword, but Annabeth hissed, "Wait!"

Polyphemus was hesitating, a boulder in his hand, ready to smash his would-be bride.

"Recipe?" he asked Grover.

"Oh y-yes! You don't want to eat me raw. You'll get E coli and botulism and all sorts of horrible things. I'll taste much better grilled over a slow fire. With mango chutney! You could go get some mangos right now, down there in the woods. I'll just wait here."

The monster pondered this. My heart hammered against my ribs. I figured I'd die if I charged. But I couldn't let the monster kill Grover.

"Grilled satyr with mango chutney," Polyphemus mused. He looked back at Clarisse, still hanging over the pot of boiling water. "You a satyr, too?"

"No, you overgrown pile of dung!" she yelled. "I'm a girl! The daughter of Ares! Now untie me so I can rip your arms off!"

"Rip my arms off," Polyphemus repeated.

"And stuff them down your throat!"

"You got spunk."

"Let me down!"

Polyphemus snatched up Grover as if he were a wayward puppy. "Have to graze sheep now. Wedding postponed until tonight. Then we'll eat satyr for the main course!"

"But . . . you're still getting married?" Grover sounded hurt. "Who's the bride?"

Polyphemus looked toward the boiling pot.

Clarisse made a strangled sound. "Oh, no! You can't be serious. I'm not—"

Before Annabeth or I could do anything, Polyphemus plucked her off the rope like she was a ripe apple, and tossed her and Grover deep into the cave. "Make yourself comfortable! I come back at sundown for big event!"

Then the Cyclops whistled, and a mixed flock of goats and sheep—smaller than the man-eaters—flooded out of the cave and past their master. As they went to pasture, Polyphemus patted some on the back and called them by name—Beltbuster, Tammany, Lockhart, etc.

When the last sheep had waddled out, Polyphemus rolled a boulder in front of the doorway as easily as I would close a refrigerator door, shutting off the sound of Clarisse and Grover screaming inside.

"Mangos," Polyphemus grumbled to himself. "What are mangos?"

He strolled off down the mountain in his baby-blue groom's outfit, leaving us alone with a pot of boiling water and a six-ton boulder.

We tried for what seemed like hours, but it was no good. The boulder wouldn't move. We yelled into the cracks, tapped on the rock, did everything we could think of to get a signal to Grover, but if he heard us, we couldn't tell.

Even if by some miracle we managed to kill Polyphemus, it wouldn't do us any good. Grover and Clarisse would die inside that sealed cave. The only way to move the rock was to have the Cyclops do it.

In total frustration, I stabbed Riptide against the boulder. Sparks flew, but nothing else happened. A large rock is not the kind of enemy you can fight with a magic sword.

Annabeth and I sat on the ridge in despair and watched the distant baby-blue shape of the Cyclops as he moved among his flocks. He had wisely divided his regular animals from his man-eating sheep, putting each group on either side of the huge crevice that divided the island. The only way across was the rope bridge, and the planks were much too far apart for sheep hooves.

We watched as Polyphemus visited his carnivorous flock on the far side. Unfortunately, they didn't eat him. In fact, they didn't seem to bother him at all. He fed them chunks of mystery meat from a great wicker basket, which only reinforced the feelings I'd been having since Circe turned me into a guinea pig—that maybe it was time I joined Grover and became a vegetarian.

"Trickery," Annabeth decided. "We can't beat him by force, so we'll have to use trickery."

"Okay," I said. "What trick?'

"I haven't figured that part out yet."

"Great."

"Polyphemus will have to move the rock to let the sheep inside."

"At sunset," I said. "Which is when he'll marry

Clarisse and have Grover for dinner. I'm not sure which is grosser."

"I could get inside," she said, "invisibly."

"What about me?"

"The sheep," Annabeth mused. She gave me one of those sly looks that always made me wary. "How much do you like sheep?"

"Just don't let go!" Annabeth said, standing invisibly somewhere off to my right. That was easy for her to say. She wasn't hanging upside down from the belly of a sheep.

Now, I'll admit it wasn't as hard as I'd thought. I'd crawled under a car before to change my mom's oil, and this wasn't too different. The sheep didn't care. Even the Cyclops's smallest sheep were big enough to support my weight, and they had thick wool. I just twirled the stuff into handles for my hands, hooked my feet against the sheep's thigh bones, and presto—I felt like a baby wallaby, riding around against the sheep's chest, trying to keep the wool out of my mouth and my nose.

In case you're wondering, the underside of a sheep doesn't smell that great. Imagine a winter sweater that's been dragged through the mud and left in the laundry hamper for a week. Something like that.

The sun was going down.

No sooner was I in position than the Cyclops roared, "Oy! Goaties! Sheepies!"

The flock dutifully began trudging back up the slopes toward the cave.

"This is it!" Annabeth whispered. "I'll be close by. Don't worry."

I made a silent promise to the gods that if we survived this, I'd tell Annabeth she was a genius. The frightening thing was, I knew the gods would hold me to it.

My sheep taxi started plodding up the hill. After a hundred yards, my hands and feet started to hurt from holding on. I gripped the sheep's wool more tightly, and the animal made a grumbling sound. I didn't blame it. I wouldn't want anybody rock climbing in my hair either. But if I didn't hold on, I was sure I'd fall off right there in front of the monster.

"Hasenpfeffer!" the Cyclops said, patting one of the sheep in front of me. "Einstein! Widget—eh there, Widget!"

Polyphemus patted my sheep and nearly knocked me to the ground. "Putting on some extra mutton there?"

Uh-oh, I thought. *Here it comes.*

But Polyphemus just laughed and swatted the sheep's rear end, propelling us forward. "Go on, fatty! Soon Polyphemus will eat you for breakfast!"

And just like that, I was in the cave.

I could see the last of the sheep coming inside. If Annabeth didn't pull off her distraction soon . . .

The Cyclops was about to roll the stone back into place, when from somewhere outside Annabeth shouted, "Hello, ugly!"

Polyphemus stiffened. "Who said that?"

"Nobody!" Annabeth yelled.

That got exactly the reaction she'd been hoping for. The monster's face turned red with rage.

"Nobody!" Polyphemus yelled back. "I remember you!"

"You're too stupid to remember anybody," Annabeth taunted. "Much less Nobody."

I hoped to the gods she was already moving when she said that, because Polyphemus bellowed furiously, grabbed the nearest boulder (which happened to be his front door) and threw it toward the sound of Annabeth's voice. I heard the rock smash into a thousand fragments.

For a terrible moment, there was silence. Then Annabeth shouted, "You haven't learned to throw any better, either!"

Polyphemus howled. "Come here! Let me kill you, Nobody!"

"You can't kill Nobody, you stupid oaf," she taunted. "Come find me!"

Polyphemus barreled down the hill toward her voice.

Now, the "Nobody" thing wouldn't have made sense to anybody, but Annabeth had explained to me that it was the name Odysseus had used to trick Polyphemus centuries ago, right before he poked the Cyclops's eye out with a large hot stick. Annabeth had figured Polyphemus would still have a grudge about that name, and she was right. In his frenzy to find his old enemy, he forgot about resealing the cave entrance. Apparently, he didn't even stop to consider that Annabeth's voice was female, whereas the first Nobody had been male. On the other hand, he'd wanted to marry Grover, so he couldn't have been all that bright about the whole male/female thing.

I just hoped Annabeth could stay alive and keep distracting him long enough for me to find Grover and Clarisse.

I dropped off my ride, patted Widget on the head, and apologized. I searched the main room, but there was no sign of Grover or Clarisse. I pushed through the crowd of sheep and goats toward the back of the cave.

Even though I'd dreamed about this place, I had a hard time finding my way through the maze. I ran down corridors littered with bones, past rooms full of sheepskin rugs and life-size cement sheep that I recognized as the work of Medusa. There were collections of sheep T-shirts; large tubs of lanolin cream; and wooly coats, socks, and hats with ram's horns. Finally, I found the spinning room, where Grover was huddled in the corner, trying to cut Clarisse's bonds with a pair of safety scissors.

"It's no good," Clarisse said. "This rope is like iron!"

"Just a few more minutes!"

"Grover," she cried, exasperated. "You've been working at it for hours!"

And then they saw me.

"*Percy?*" Clarisse said. "You're supposed to be blown up!"

"Good to see you, too. Now hold still while I—"

"Perrrrrcy!" Grover bleated and tackled me with a goat-hug. "You heard me! You came!"

"Yeah, buddy," I said. "Of course I came."

"Where's Annabeth?"

"Outside," I said. "But there's no time to talk. Clarisse, hold still."

I uncapped Riptide and sliced off her ropes. She stood stiffly, rubbing her wrists. She glared at me for a moment, then looked at the ground and mumbled, "Thanks."

"You're welcome," I said. "Now, was anyone else on board your lifeboat?"

Clarisse looked surprised. "No. Just me. Everybody else aboard the *Birmingham* . . . well, I didn't even know you guys made it out."

I looked down, trying not to believe that my last hope of seeing Tyson alive had just been crushed. "Okay. Come on, then. We have to help—"

An explosion echoed through the cave, followed by a scream that told me we might be too late. It was Annabeth crying out in fear.

FIFTEEN

NOBODY GETS
THE FLEECE

"I got Nobody!" Polyphemus gloated.

We crept to the cave entrance and saw the Cyclops, grinning wickedly, holding up empty air. The monster shook his fist, and a baseball cap fluttered to the ground. There was Annabeth, hanging upside down by her legs.

"Hah!" the Cyclops said. "Nasty invisible girl! Already got feisty one for wife. Means you gotta be grilled with mango chutney!"

Annabeth struggled, but she looked dazed. She had a nasty cut on her forehead. Her eyes were glassy.

"I'll rush him," I whispered to Clarisse. "Our ship is around the back of the island. You and Grover—"

"No way," they said at the same time. Clarisse had armed herself with a highly collectible ram's-horn spear from the Cyclops's cave. Grover had found a sheep's thigh bone, which he didn't look too happy about, but he was gripping it like a club, ready to attack.

"We'll take him together," Clarisse growled.

"Yeah," Grover said. Then he blinked, like he couldn't believe he'd just agreed with Clarisse about something.

"All right," I said. "Attack plan Macedonia."

They nodded. We'd all taken the same training courses at Camp Half-Blood. They knew what I was talking about. They would sneak around either side and attack the Cyclops from the flanks while I held his attention in the front. Probably what this meant was that we'd *all* die instead of just me, but I was grateful for the help.

I hefted my sword and shouted, "Hey, Ugly!"

The giant whirled toward me. "*Another* one? Who are you?"

"Put down my friend. *I'm* the one who insulted you."

"*You* are Nobody?"

"That's right, you smelly bucket of nose drool!" It didn't sound quite as good as Annabeth's insults, but it was all I could think of. "I'm Nobody and I'm proud of it! Now, put her down and get over here. I want to stab your eye out again."

"RAAAR!" he bellowed.

The good news: he dropped Annabeth. The bad news: he dropped her headfirst onto the rocks, where she lay motionless as a rag doll.

The other bad news: Polyphemus barreled toward me, a thousand smelly pounds of Cyclops that I would have to fight with a very small sword.

"For Pan!" Grover rushed in from the right. He threw his sheep bone, which bounced harmlessly off the monster's forehead. Clarisse ran in from the left and set her spear against the ground just in time for the Cyclops to step on it. He wailed in pain, and Clarisse dove out of the way to avoid getting trampled. But the Cyclops just plucked out the shaft like a large splinter and kept advancing on me.

I moved in with Riptide.

The monster made a grab for me. I rolled aside and stabbed him in the thigh.

I was hoping to see him disintegrate, but this monster was much too big and powerful.

"Get Annabeth!" I yelled at Grover.

He rushed over, grabbed her invisibility cap, and picked her up while Clarisse and I tried to keep Polyphemus distracted.

I have to admit, Clarisse was brave. She charged the Cyclops again and again. He pounded the ground, stomped at her, grabbed at her, but she was too quick. And as soon as she made an attack, I followed up by stabbing the monster in the toe or the ankle or the hand.

But we couldn't keep this up forever. Eventually we would tire or the monster would get in a lucky shot. It would only take one hit to kill us.

Out of the corner of my eye, I saw Grover carrying Annabeth across the rope bridge. It wouldn't have been my first choice, given the man-eating sheep on the other side, but at the moment that looked better than *this* side of the chasm, and it gave me an idea.

"Fall back!" I told Clarisse.

She rolled away as the Cyclops's fist smashed the olive tree beside her.

We ran for the bridge, Polyphemus right behind us. He was cut up and hobbling from so many wounds, but all we'd done was slow him down and make him mad.

"Grind you into sheep chow!" he promised. "A thousand curses on Nobody!"

"Faster!" I told Clarisse.

We tore down the hill. The bridge was our only chance. Grover had just made it to the other side and was setting Annabeth down. We had to make it across, too, before the giant caught us.

"Grover!" I yelled. "Get Annabeth's knife!"

His eyes widened when he saw the Cyclops behind us, but he nodded like he understood. As Clarisse and I scrambled across the bridge, Grover began sawing at the ropes.

The first strand went *snap!*

Polyphemus bounded after us, making the bridge sway wildly.

The ropes were now half cut. Clarisse and I dove for solid ground, landing beside Grover. I made a wild slash with my sword and cut the remaining ropes.

The bridge fell away into the chasm, and the Cyclops howled . . . with delight, because he was standing right next to us.

"Failed!" he yelled gleefully. "Nobody failed!"

Clarisse and Grover tried to charge him, but the monster swatted them aside like flies.

My anger swelled. I couldn't believe I'd come this far, lost Tyson, suffered through so much, only to fail—stopped by a big stupid monster in a baby-blue tuxedo kilt. Nobody was going to swat down my friends like that! I mean . . . *nobody*, not Nobody. Ah, you know what I mean.

Strength coursed through my body. I raised my sword and attacked, forgetting that I was hopelessly outmatched. I jabbed the Cyclops in the belly. When he doubled over I smacked him in the nose with the hilt of my sword. I slashed and kicked and bashed until the next thing I knew, Polyphemus was sprawled on his back, dazed and groaning, and I was standing above him, the tip of my sword hovering over his eye.

"Uhhhhhhhh," Polyphemus moaned.

"Percy!" Grover gasped. "How did you—"

"Please, noooo!" the Cyclops moaned, pitifully staring up at me. His nose was bleeding. A tear welled in the corner of his half-blind eye. "M-m-my sheepies need me. Only trying to protect my sheep!"

He began to sob.

I had won. All I had to do was stab—one quick strike.

"Kill him!" Clarisse yelled. "What are you waiting for?"

The Cyclops sounded so heartbroken, just like . . . like Tyson.

"He's a Cyclops!" Grover warned. "Don't trust him!"

I knew he was right. I knew Annabeth would've said the same thing.

But Polyphemus sobbed . . . and for the first time it sank in that *he* was a son of Poseidon, too. Like Tyson. Like me. How could I just kill him in cold blood?

"We only want the Fleece," I told the monster. "Will you agree to let us take it?"

"No!" Clarisse shouted. "Kill him!"

The monster sniffed. "My beautiful Fleece. Prize of my collection. Take it, cruel human. Take it and go in peace."

"I'm going to step back slowly," I told the monster. "One false move . . ."

Polyphemus nodded like he understood.

I stepped back . . . and as fast as a cobra, Polyphemus smacked me to the edge of the cliff.

"Foolish mortal!" he bellowed, rising to his feet. "Take my Fleece? Ha! I eat you first."

He opened his enormous mouth, and I knew that his rotten molars were the last things I would ever see.

Then something went *whoosh* over my head and *thump!*

A rock the size of a basketball sailed into Polyphemus's throat—a beautiful three-pointer, nothing but net. The Cyclops choked, trying to swallow the unexpected pill. He staggered backward, but there was no place to stagger. His heel slipped, the edge of the cliff crumbled, and the great Polyphemus made chicken wing motions that did nothing to help him fly as he tumbled into the chasm.

I turned.

Halfway down the path to the beach, standing completely unharmed in the midst of a flock of killer sheep, was an old friend.

"Bad Polyphemus," Tyson said. "Not all Cyclopes as nice as we look."

Tyson gave us the short version: Rainbow the hippocampus—who'd apparently been following us ever since the Long Island Sound, waiting for Tyson to play with him—had found Tyson sinking beneath the wreckage of the CSS *Birmingham* and pulled him to safety. He and Tyson had been searching the Sea of Monsters ever since, trying to find us, until Tyson caught the scent of sheep and found this island.

I wanted to hug the big oaf, except he was standing in the middle of killer sheep. "Tyson, thank the gods. Annabeth is hurt!"

"You thank the gods she is hurt?" he asked, puzzled.

"No!" I knelt beside Annabeth and was worried sick by what I saw. The gash on her forehead was worse than I'd realized. Her hairline was sticky with blood. Her skin was pale and clammy.

Grover and I exchanged nervous looks. Then an idea came to me. "Tyson, the Fleece. Can you get it for me?"

"Which one?" Tyson said, looking around at the hundreds of sheep.

"In the tree!" I said. "The gold one!"

"Oh. Pretty. Yes."

Tyson lumbered over, careful not to step on the sheep. If any of us had tried to approach the Fleece, we would've been eaten alive, but I guess Tyson smelled like Polyphemus, because the flock didn't bother him at all. They just cuddled up to him and bleated affectionately, as though they expected to get sheep treats from the big wicker basket. Tyson reached up and lifted the Fleece off its branch. Immediately the leaves on the oak tree turned yellow. Tyson started wading back toward me, but I yelled, "No time! Throw it!"

The gold ram skin sailed through the air like a glittering shag Frisbee. I caught it with a grunt. It was heavier than I'd expected—sixty or seventy pounds of precious gold wool.

I spread it over Annabeth, covering everything but her face, and prayed silently to all the gods I could think of, even the ones I didn't like.

Please. Please.

The color returned to her face. Her eyelids fluttered open. The cut on her forehead began to close. She saw Grover and said weakly, "You're not . . . married?"

Grover grinned. "No. My friends talked me out of it."

"Annabeth," I said, "just lay still."

But despite our protests she sat up, and I noticed that the cut on her face was almost completely healed. She looked a lot better. In fact, she shimmered with health, as if someone had injected her with glitter.

Meanwhile, Tyson was starting to have trouble with the sheep. "Down!" he told them as they tried to climb him, looking for food. A few were sniffing in our direction. "No, sheepies. This way! Come here!"

They heeded him, but it was obvious they were hungry, and they were starting to realize Tyson didn't have any treats for them. They wouldn't hold out forever with so much fresh meat nearby.

"We have to go," I said. "Our ship is. . ." The *Queen Anne's Revenge* was a very long way away. The shortest route was across the chasm, and we'd just destroyed the only bridge. The only other possibility was through the sheep.

"Tyson," I called, "can you lead the flock as far away as possible?"

"The sheep want food."

"I know! They want people food! Just lead them away

from the path. Give us time to get to the beach. Then join us there."

Tyson looked doubtful, but he whistled. "Come, sheepies! Um, people food this way!"

He jogged off into the meadow, the sheep in pursuit.

"Keep the Fleece around you," I told Annabeth. "Just in case you're not fully healed yet. Can you stand?"

She tried, but her face turned pale again. "Ohh. *Not* fully healed."

Clarisse dropped next to her and felt her chest, which made Annabeth gasp.

"Ribs broken," Clarisse said. "They're mending, but definitely broken."

"How can you tell?" I asked.

Clarisse glared at me. "Because I've broken a few, runt! I'll have to carry her."

Before I could argue, Clarisse picked up Annabeth like a sack of flour and lugged her down to the beach. Grover and I followed.

As soon as we got to the edge of the water, I concentrated on the *Queen Anne's Revenge*. I willed it to raise anchor and come to me. After a few anxious minutes, I saw the ship rounding the tip of the island.

"Incoming!" Tyson yelled. He was bounding down the path to join us, the sheep about fifty yards behind, bleating in frustration as their Cyclops friend ran away without feeding them.

"They probably won't follow us into the water," I told the others. "All we have to do is swim for the ship."

"With Annabeth like this?" Clarisse protested.

"We can do it," I insisted. I was starting to feel confident again. I was back in my home turf—the sea. "Once we get to the ship, we're home free."

We almost made it, too.

We were just wading past the entrance to the ravine, when we heard a tremendous roar and saw Polyphemus, scraped up and bruised but still very much alive, his baby-blue wedding outfit in tatters, splashing toward us with a boulder in each hand.

SIXTEEN

I GO DOWN
WITH THE SHIP

"You'd think he'd run out of rocks," I muttered.

"Swim for it!" Grover said.

He and Clarisse plunged into the surf. Annabeth hung on to Clarisse's neck and tried to paddle with one hand, the wet Fleece weighing her down.

But the monster's attention wasn't on the Fleece.

"You, young Cyclops!" Polyphemus roared. "Traitor to your kind!"

Tyson froze.

"Don't listen to him!" I pleaded. "Come on."

I pulled Tyson's arm, but I might as well have been pulling a mountain. He turned and faced the older Cyclops. "I am not a traitor."

"You serve mortals!" Polyphemus shouted. "Thieving humans!"

Polyphemus threw his first boulder. Tyson swatted it aside with his fist.

"Not a traitor," Tyson said. "And you are *not* my kind."

"Death or victory!" Polyphemus charged into the surf, but his foot was still wounded. He immediately stumbled and fell on his face. That would've been funny, except he started to get up again, spitting salt water and growling.

"Percy!" Clarisse yelled. "Come on!"

They were almost to the ship with the Fleece. If I could just keep the monster distracted a little longer . . .

"Go," Tyson told me. "I will hold Big Ugly."

"No! He'll kill you." I'd already lost Tyson once. I wasn't going to lose him again. "We'll fight him together."

"Together," Tyson agreed.

I drew my sword.

Polyphemus advanced carefully, limping worse than ever. But there was nothing wrong with his throwing arm. He chucked his second boulder. I dove to one side, but I still would've been squashed if Tyson's fist hadn't blasted the rock to rubble.

I willed the sea to rise. A twenty-foot wave surged up, lifting me on its crest. I rode toward the Cyclops and kicked him in the eye, leaping over his head as the water blasted him onto the beach.

"Destroy you!" Polyphemus spluttered. "Fleece stealer!"

"*You* stole the Fleece!" I yelled. "You've been using it to lure satyrs to their deaths!"

"So? Satyrs good eating!"

"The Fleece should be used to heal! It belongs to the children of the gods!"

"*I* am a child of the gods!" Polyphemus swiped at me, but I sidestepped. "Father Poseidon, curse this thief!" He was blinking hard now, like he could barely see, and

I realized he was targeting by the sound of my voice.

"Poseidon won't curse me," I said, backing up as the Cyclops grabbed air. "I'm his son, too. He won't play favorites."

Polyphemus roared. He ripped an olive tree out of the side of the cliff and smashed it where I'd been standing a moment before. "Humans not the same! Nasty, tricky, lying!"

Grover was helping Annabeth aboard the ship. Clarisse was waving frantically at me, telling me to come on.

Tyson worked his way around Polyphemus, trying to get behind him.

"Young one!" the older Cyclops called. "Where are you? Help me!"

Tyson stopped.

"You weren't raised right!" Polyphemus wailed, shaking his olive tree club. "Poor orphaned brother! Help me!"

No one moved. No sound but the ocean and my own heartbeat. Then Tyson stepped forward, raising his hands defensively. "Don't fight, Cyclops brother. Put down the—"

Polyphemus spun toward his voice.

"Tyson!" I shouted.

The tree struck him with such force it would've flattened me into a Percy pizza with extra olives. Tyson flew backward, plowing a trench in the sand. Polyphemus charged after him, but I shouted, "No!" and lunged as far as I could with Riptide. I'd hoped to sting Polyphemus in the back of the thigh, but I managed to leap a little bit higher.

"Blaaaaah!" Polyphemus bleated just like his sheep, and swung at me with his tree.

I dove, but still got raked across the back by a dozen jagged branches. I was bleeding and bruised and exhausted. The guinea pig inside me wanted to bolt. But I swallowed down my fear.

Polyphemus swung the tree again, but this time I was ready. I grabbed a branch as it passed, ignoring the pain in my hands as I was jerked skyward, and let the Cyclops lift me into the air. At the top of the arc I let go and fell straight against the giant's face—landing with both feet on his already damaged eye.

Polyphemus yowled in pain. Tyson tackled him, pulling him down. I landed next to them—sword in hand, within striking distance of the monster's heart. But I locked eyes with Tyson, and I knew I couldn't do it. It just wasn't right.

"Let him go," I told Tyson. "Run."

With one last mighty effort, Tyson pushed the cursing older Cyclops away, and we ran for the surf.

"I will smash you!" Polyphemus yelled, doubling over in pain. His enormous hands cupped over his eye.

Tyson and I plunged into the waves.

"Where are you?" Polyphemus screamed. He picked up his tree club and threw it into the water. It splashed off to our right.

I summoned up a current to carry us, and we started gaining speed. I was beginning to think we might make it to the ship, when Clarisse shouted from the deck, "Yeah, Jackson! In your face, Cyclops!"

Shut up, I wanted to yell.

"Rarrr!" Polyphemus picked up a boulder. He threw it toward the sound of Clarisse's voice, but it fell short, narrowly missing Tyson and me.

"Yeah, yeah!" Clarisse taunted. "You throw like a wimp! Teach you to try marrying me, you idiot!"

"Clarisse!" I yelled, unable to stand it. "Shut up!"

Too late. Polyphemus threw another boulder, and this time I watched helplessly as it sailed over my head and crashed through the hull of the *Queen Anne's Revenge.*

You wouldn't believe how fast a ship can sink. The *Queen Anne's Revenge* creaked and groaned and listed forward like it was going down a playground slide.

I cursed, willing the sea to push us faster, but the ship's masts were already going under.

"Dive!" I told Tyson. And as another rock sailed over our heads, we plunged underwater.

My friends were sinking fast, trying to swim, without luck, in the bubbly trail of the ship's wreckage.

Not many people realize that when a ship goes down, it acts like a sinkhole, pulling down everything around it. Clarisse was strong swimmer, but even she wasn't making any progress. Grover frantically kicked with his hooves. Annabeth was hanging on to the Fleece, which flashed in the water like a wave of new pennies.

I swam toward them, knowing that I might not have the strength to pull my friends out. Worse, pieces of timber were swirling around them; none of my power with water would help if I got whacked on the head by a beam.

We need help, I thought.

Yes. Tyson's voice, loud and clear in my head.

I looked over at him, startled. I'd heard Nereids and other water spirits speak to me underwater before, but it never occurred to me . . . Tyson was a son of Poseidon. We could communicate with each other.

Rainbow, Tyson said.

I nodded, then closed my eyes and concentrated, adding my voice to Tyson's: *RAINBOW! We need you!*

Immediately, shapes shimmered in the darkness below—three horses with fish tails, galloping upward faster than dolphins. Rainbow and his friends glanced in our direction and seemed to read our thoughts. They whisked into the wreckage, and a moment later burst upward in a cloud of bubbles—Grover, Annabeth, and Clarisse each clinging to the neck of a hippocampus.

Rainbow, the largest, had Clarisse. He raced over to us and allowed Tyson to grab hold of his mane. His friend who bore Annabeth did the same for me.

We broke the surface of the water and raced away from Polyphemus's island. Behind us, I could hear the Cyclops roaring in triumph, "I did it! I finally sank Nobody!"

I hoped he never found out he was wrong.

We skimmed across the sea as the island shrank to a dot and then disappeared.

"Did it," Annabeth muttered in exhaustion. "We . . ."

She slumped against the neck of the hippocampus and instantly fell asleep.

I didn't know how far the hippocampi could take us. I didn't know where we were going. I just propped up Annabeth so she wouldn't fall off, covered her in the Golden Fleece that we'd been through so much to get, and said a silent prayer of thanks.

Which reminded me . . . I still owed the gods a debt.

"You're a genius," I told Annabeth quietly.

Then I put my head against the Fleece, and before I knew it, I was asleep, too.

SEVENTEEN

WE GET A SURPRISE
ON MIAMI BEACH

"Percy, wake up."

Salt water splashed my face. Annabeth was shaking my shoulder.

In the distance, the sun was setting behind a city skyline. I could see a beachside highway lined with palm trees, storefronts glowing with red and blue neon, a harbor filled with sailboats and cruise ships.

"Miami, I think," Annabeth said. "But the hippocampi are acting funny."

Sure enough, our fishy friends had slowed down and were whinnying and swimming in circles, sniffing the water. They didn't look happy. One of them sneezed. I could tell what they were thinking.

"This is as far as they'll take us," I said. "Too many humans. Too much pollution. We'll have to swim to shore on our own."

None of us was very psyched about that, but we thanked Rainbow and his friends for the ride. Tyson cried a little. He unfastened the makeshift saddle pack he'd made, which contained his tool kit and a couple of other things he'd salvaged from the *Birmingham* wreck.

He hugged Rainbow around the neck, gave him a soggy mango he'd picked up on the island, and said good-bye.

Once the hippocampi's white manes disappeared into the sea, we swam for shore. The waves pushed us forward, and in no time we were back in the mortal world. We wandered along the cruise line docks, pushing through crowds of people arriving for vacations. Porters bustled around with carts of luggage. Taxi drivers yelled at each other in Spanish and tried to cut in line for customers. If anybody noticed us—five kids dripping wet and looking like they'd just had a fight with a monster—they didn't let on.

Now that we were back among mortals, Tyson's single eye had blurred from the Mist. Grover had put on his cap and sneakers. Even the Fleece had transformed from a sheepskin to a red-and-gold high school letter jacket with a large glittery Omega on the pocket.

Annabeth ran to the nearest newspaper box and checked the date on the *Miami Herald.* She cursed. "June eighteenth! We've been away from camp ten days!"

"That's impossible!" Clarisse said.

But I knew it wasn't. Time traveled differently in monstrous places.

"Thalia's tree must be almost dead," Grover wailed. "We have to get the Fleece back *tonight.*"

Clarisse slumped down on the pavement. "How are we supposed to do that?" Her voice trembled. "We're hundreds of miles away. No money. No ride. This is just like the Oracle said. It's *your* fault, Jackson! If you hadn't interfered—"

"Percy's fault?!" Annabeth exploded. "Clarisse, how can you say that? You are the biggest—"

"Stop it!" I said.

Clarisse put her head in hands. Annabeth stomped her foot in frustration.

The thing was: I'd almost forgotten this quest was supposed to be Clarisse's. For a scary moment, I saw things from her point of view. How would I feel if a bunch of other heroes had butted in and made me look bad?

I thought about what I'd overheard in the boiler room of the CSS *Birmingham*—Ares yelling at Clarisse, warning her that she'd better not fail. Ares couldn't care less about the camp, but if Clarisse made him look bad . . .

"Clarisse," I said, "what did the Oracle tell you exactly?"

She looked up. I thought she was going to tell me off, but instead she took a deep breath and recited her prophecy:

> *"You shall sail the iron ship with warriors of bone,*
> *You shall find what you seek and make it your own,*
> *But despair for your life entombed within stone,*
> *And fail without friends, to fly home alone."*

"Ouch," Grover mumbled.

"No," I said. "No . . . wait a minute. I've got it."

I searched my pockets for money, and found nothing but a golden drachma. "Does anybody have any cash?"

Annabeth and Grover shook their heads morosely. Clarisse pulled a wet Confederate dollar from her pocket and sighed.

"Cash?" Tyson asked hesitantly. "Like . . . green paper?"

I looked at him. "Yeah."

"Like the kind in duffel bags?"

"Yeah, but we lost those bags days a-g-g—"

I stuttered to a halt as Tyson rummaged in his saddle pack and pulled out the Ziploc bag full of cash that Hermes had included in our supplies.

"Tyson!" I said. "How did you—"

"Thought it was a feed bag for Rainbow," he said. "Found it floating in sea, but only paper inside. Sorry."

He handed me the cash. Fives and tens, at least three hundred dollars.

I ran to the curb and grabbed a taxi that was just letting out a family of cruise passengers. "Clarisse," I yelled. "Come on. You're going to the airport. Annabeth, give her the Fleece."

I'm not sure which of them looked more stunned as I took the Fleece letter jacket from Annabeth, tucked the cash into its pocket, and put it in Clarisse's arms.

Clarisse said, "You'd let me—"

"It's your quest," I said. "We only have enough money for one flight. Besides, I can't travel by air. Zeus would blast me into a million pieces. That's what the prophecy meant: you'd fail without friends, meaning you'd need our help, but you'd have to fly home alone. You have to get the Fleece back safely."

I could see her mind working—suspicious at first, wondering what trick I was playing, then finally deciding I meant what I said.

She jumped in the cab. "You can count on me. I won't fail."

"Not failing would be good."

The cab peeled out in a cloud of exhaust. The Fleece was on its way.

"Percy," Annabeth said, "that was so—"

"Generous?" Grover offered.

"*Insane,*" Annabeth corrected. "You're betting the lives of everybody at camp that Clarisse will get the Fleece safely back by tonight?"

"It's her quest," I said. "She deserves a chance."

"Percy is nice," Tyson said.

"Percy is *too* nice," Annabeth grumbled, but I couldn't help thinking that maybe, just maybe, she was a little impressed. I'd surprised her, anyway. And that wasn't easy to do.

"Come on," I told my friends. "Let's find another way home."

That's when I turned and found a sword's point at my throat.

"Hey, cuz," said Luke. "Welcome back to the States."

His bear-man thugs appeared on either of side of us. One grabbed Annabeth and Grover by their T-shirt collars. The other tried to grab Tyson, but Tyson knocked him into a pile of luggage and roared at Luke.

"Percy," Luke said calmly, "tell your giant to back down or I'll have Oreius bash your friends' heads together."

Oreius grinned and raised Annabeth and Grover off the ground, kicking and screaming.

"What do you want, Luke?" I growled.

He smiled, the scar rippling on the side of his face.

He gestured toward the end of the dock, and I noticed what should've been obvious. The biggest boat in port was the *Princess Andromeda*.

"Why, Percy," Luke said, "I want to extend my hospitality, of course."

The bear twins herded us aboard the *Princess Andromeda*. They threw us down on the aft deck in front of a swimming pool with sparkling fountains that sprayed into the air. A dozen of Luke's assorted goons—snake people, Laistrygonians, demigods in battle armor—had gathered to watch us get some "hospitality."

"And so, the Fleece," Luke mused. "Where is it?"

He looked us over, prodding my shirt with the tip of his sword, poking Grover's jeans.

"Hey!" Grover yelled. "That's real goat fur under there!"

"Sorry, old friend." Luke smiled. "Just give me the Fleece and I'll leave you to return to your, ah, little nature quest."

"Blaa-ha-ha!" Grover protested. "Some old friend!"

"Maybe you didn't hear me." Luke's voice was dangerously calm. "Where—is—the—Fleece?"

"Not here," I said. I probably shouldn't have told him anything, but it felt good to throw the truth in his face. "We sent it on ahead of us. You messed up."

Luke's eyes narrowed. "You're lying. You couldn't have . . ." His face reddened as a horrible possibility occurred to him. "Clarisse?"

I nodded.

"You trusted . . . you gave . . ."

"Yeah."

"Agrius!"

The bear giant flinched. "Y-yes?"

"Get below and prepare my steed. Bring it to the deck. I need to fly to the Miami Airport, fast!"

"But boss—"

"Do it!" Luke screamed. "Or I'll feed you to the drakon!"

The bear-man gulped and lumbered down the stairs. Luke paced in front of the swimming pool, cursing in Ancient Greek, gripping his sword so tight his knuckles turned white.

The rest of Luke's crew looked uneasy. Maybe they'd never seen their boss so unhinged before.

I started thinking . . . If I could use Luke's anger, get him to talk so everybody could hear how crazy his plans were . . .

I looked at the swimming pool, at the fountains spraying mist into the air, making a rainbow in the sunset. And suddenly I had an idea.

"You've been toying with us all along," I said. "You wanted us to bring you the Fleece and save you the trouble of getting it."

Luke scowled. "Of course, you idiot! And you've messed everything up!"

"Traitor!" I dug my last gold drachma out of my pocket and threw it at Luke. As I expected, he dodged it easily.

The coin sailed into the spray of rainbow-colored water.

I hoped my prayer would be accepted in silence. I thought with all my heart: *O goddess, accept my offering.*

"You tricked all of us!" I yelled at Luke. "Even DIONYSUS at CAMP HALF-BLOOD!"

Behind Luke, the fountain began to shimmer, but I needed everyone's attention on me, so I uncapped Riptide.

Luke just sneered. "This is no time for heroics, Percy. Drop your puny little sword, or I'll have you killed sooner rather than later."

"Who poisoned Thalia's tree, Luke?"

"I did, of course," he snarled. "I already told you that. I used elder python venom, straight from the depths of Tartarus."

"Chiron had nothing to do with it?"

"Ha! You know he would never do that. The old fool wouldn't have the guts."

"You call it guts? Betraying your friends? Endangering the whole camp?"

Luke raised his sword. "You don't understand the half of it. I was going to let you take the Fleece . . . once I was done with it."

That made me hesitate. Why would he let me take the Fleece? He must've been lying. But I couldn't afford to lose his attention.

"You were going to heal Kronos," I said.

"Yes! The Fleece's magic would've sped his mending process by tenfold. But you haven't stopped us, Percy. You've only slowed us down a little."

"And so you poisoned the tree, you betrayed Thalia, you set us up—all to help Kronos destroy the gods."

Luke gritted his teeth. "You know that! Why do you keep asking me?"

"Because I want everybody in the audience to hear you."

"*What* audience?"

Then his eyes narrowed. He looked behind him and his goons did the same. They gasped and stumbled back.

Above the pool, shimmering in the rainbow mist, was an Iris-message vision of Dionysus, Tantalus, and the whole camp in the dining pavilion. They sat in stunned silence, watching us.

"Well," said Dionysus dryly, "some unplanned dinner entertainment."

"Mr. D, you heard him," I said. "You all heard Luke. The poisoning of the tree wasn't Chiron's fault."

Mr. D sighed. "I suppose not."

"The Iris-message could be a trick," Tantalus suggested, but his attention was mostly on his cheeseburger, which he was trying to corner with both hands.

"I fear not," Mr. D said, looking with distaste at Tantalus. "It appears I shall have to reinstate Chiron as activities director. I suppose I do miss the old horse's pinochle games."

Tantalus grabbed the cheeseburger. It didn't bolt away from him. He lifted it from the plate and stared at it in amazement, as if it were the largest diamond in the world. "I got it!" he cackled.

"We are no longer in need of your services, Tantalus," Mr. D announced.

Tantalus looked stunned. "What? But—"

"You may return to the Underworld. You are dismissed."

"No! But—Noooooooooooo!"

As he dissolved into mist, his fingers clutched at the cheeseburger, trying to bring it to his mouth. But it was too late. He disappeared and the cheeseburger fell back onto its plate. The campers exploded into cheering.

Luke bellowed with rage. He slashed his sword through the fountain and the Iris-message dissolved, but the deed was done.

I was feeling pretty good about myself, until Luke turned and gave me a murderous look.

"Kronos was right, Percy. You're an unreliable weapon. You need to be replaced."

I wasn't sure what he meant, but I didn't have time to think about it. One of his men blew a brass whistle, and the deck doors flew open. A dozen more warriors poured out, making a circle around us, the brass tips of their spears bristling.

Luke smiled at me. "You'll never leave this boat alive."

EIGHTEEN

THE PARTY PONIES
INVADE

"One on one," I challenged Luke. "What are you afraid of?"

Luke curled his lip. The soldiers who were about to kill us hesitated, waiting for his order.

Before he could saying anything, Agrius, the bear-man, burst onto the deck leading a flying horse. It was the first pure-black pegasus I'd ever seen, with wings like a giant raven. The pegasus mare bucked and whinnied. I could understand her thoughts. She was calling Agrius and Luke some names so bad Chiron would've washed her muzzle out with saddle soap.

"Sir!" Agrius called, dodging a pegasus hoof. "Your steed is ready!"

Luke kept his eyes on me.

"I told you last summer, Percy," he said. "You can't bait me into a fight."

"And you keep avoiding one," I noticed. "Scared your warriors will see you get whipped?"

Luke glanced at his men, and he saw I'd trapped him. If he backed down now, he would look weak. If he fought me, he'd lose valuable time chasing after Clarisse. For my part, the best I could hope for was to distract him, giving my friends a chance to escape. If anybody could think of a plan to get them out of there, Annabeth could. On the downside, I knew how good Luke was at sword-fighting.

"I'll kill you quickly," he decided, and raised his weapon. Backbiter was a foot longer than my own sword. Its blade glinted with an evil gray-and-gold light where the human steel had been melded with celestial bronze. I could almost feel the blade fighting against itself, like two opposing magnets bound together. I didn't know how the blade had been made, but I sensed a tragedy. Someone had died in the process. Luke whistled to one of his men, who threw him a round leather-and-bronze shield.

He grinned at me wickedly.

"Luke," Annabeth said, "at least give him a shield."

"Sorry, Annabeth," he said. "You bring your own equipment to this party."

The shield was a problem. Fighting two-handed with just a sword gives you more power, but fighting one-handed with a shield gives you better defense and versatility. There are more moves, more options, more ways to kill. I thought back to Chiron, who'd told me to stay at camp no matter what, and learn to fight. Now I was going to pay for not listening to him.

Luke lunged and almost killed me on the first try. His sword went under my arm, slashing through my shirt and grazing my ribs.

I jumped back, then counterattacked with Riptide, but Luke slammed my blade away with his shield.

"My, Percy," Luke chided. "You're out of practice."

He came at me again with a swipe to the head. I parried, returned with a thrust. He sidestepped easily.

The cut on my ribs stung. My heart was racing. When Luke lunged again, I jumped backward into the swimming pool and felt a surge of strength. I spun underwater, creating a funnel cloud, and blasted out of the deep end, straight at Luke's face.

The force of the water knocked him down, spluttering and blinded. But before I could strike, he rolled aside and was on his feet again.

I attacked and sliced off the edge of his shield, but that didn't even faze him. He dropped to a crouch and jabbed at my legs. Suddenly my thigh was on fire, with a pain so intense I collapsed. My jeans were ripped above the knee. I was hurt. I didn't know how badly. Luke hacked downward and I rolled behind a deck chair. I tried to stand, but my leg wouldn't take the weight.

"Perrrrrcy!" Grover bleated.

I rolled again as Luke's sword slashed the deck chair in half, metal pipes and all.

I clawed toward the swimming pool, trying hard not to black out. I'd never make it. Luke knew it, too. He advanced slowly, smiling. The edge of his sword was tinged with red.

"One thing I want you to watch before you die, Percy." He looked at the bear-man Oreius, who was still holding Annabeth and Grover by the necks. "You can eat your dinner now, Oreius. Bon appetit."

"He-he! He-he!" The bear-man lifted my friends and bared his teeth.

That's when all Hades broke loose.

Whish!

A red-feathered arrow sprouted from Oreius's mouth. With a surprised look on his hairy face, he crumpled to the deck.

"Brother!" Agrius wailed. He let the pegasus's reins go slack just long enough for the black steed to kick him in the head and fly away free over Miami Bay.

For a split second, Luke's guards were too stunned to do anything except watch the bear twins' bodies dissolve into smoke.

Then there was a wild chorus of war cries and hooves thundering against metal. A dozen centaurs charged out of the main stairwell.

"Ponies!" Tyson cried with delight.

My mind had trouble processing everything I saw. Chiron was among the crowd, but his relatives were almost nothing like him. There were centaurs with black Arabian stallion bodies, others with gold palomino coats, others with orange-and-white spots like paint horses. Some wore brightly colored T-shirts with Day-Glo letters that said PARTY PONIES: SOUTH FLORIDA CHAPTER. Some were armed with bows, some with baseball bats, some with paintball guns. One had his face painted like a Comanche warrior and was waving a large orange Styrofoam hand making a big Number 1. Another was bare-chested and painted entirely green. A third had googly-eye glasses with the eyeballs bouncing around on Slinky coils, and one of those baseball caps with soda-can-and-straw attachments on either side.

They exploded onto the deck with such ferocity and color that for a moment even Luke was stunned. I couldn't tell whether they had come to celebrate or attack.

Apparently both. As Luke was raising his sword to rally his troops, a centaur shot a custom-made arrow with a leather boxing glove on the end. It smacked Luke in the face and sent him crashing into the swimming pool.

His warriors scattered. I couldn't blame them. Facing the hooves of a rearing stallion is scary enough, but when it's a centaur, armed with a bow and whooping it up in a soda-drinking hat, even the bravest warrior would retreat.

"Come get some!" yelled one of the party ponies.

They let loose with their paintball guns. A wave of blue and yellow exploded against Luke's warriors, blinding them and splattering them from head to toe. They tried to run, only to slip and fall.

Chiron galloped toward Annabeth and Grover, neatly plucked them off the deck, and deposited them on his back.

I tried to get up, but my wounded leg still felt like it was on fire.

Luke was crawling out of the pool.

"Attack, you fools!" he ordered his troops. Somewhere down below deck, a large alarm bell thrummed.

I knew any second we would be swamped by Luke's reinforcements. Already, his warriors were getting over their surprise, coming at the centaurs with swords and spears drawn.

Tyson slapped half a dozen of them aside, knocking

them over the guardrail into Miami Bay. But more warriors were coming up the stairs.

"Withdraw, brethren!" Chiron said.

"You won't get away with this, horse man!" Luke shouted. He raised his sword, but got smacked in the face with another boxing glove arrow, and sat down hard in a deck chair.

A palomino centaur hoisted me onto his back. "Dude, get your big friend!"

"Tyson!" I yelled. "Come on!"

Tyson dropped the two warriors he was about to tie into a knot and jogged after us. He jumped on the centaur's back.

"Dude!" the centaur groaned, almost buckling under Tyson's weight. "Do the words 'low-carb diet' mean anything to you?"

Luke's warriors were organizing themselves into a phalanx. But by the time they were ready to advance, the centaurs had galloped to the edge of the deck and fearlessly jumped the guardrail, as if it were a steeplechase and not ten stories above the ground. I was sure we were going to die. We plummeted toward the docks, but the centaurs hit the asphalt with hardly a jolt and galloped off, whooping and yelling taunts at the *Princess Andromeda* as we raced into the streets of downtown Miami.

I have no idea what the Miamians thought as we galloped by.

Streets and buildings began to blur as the centaurs

picked up speed. It felt as if space were compacting—as if each centaur step took us miles and miles. In no time, we'd left the city behind. We raced through marshy fields of high grass and ponds and stunted trees.

Finally, we found ourselves in a trailer park at the edge of a lake. The trailers were all horse trailers, tricked out with televisions and mini-refrigerators and mosquito netting. We were in a centaur camp.

"Dude!" said a party pony as he unloaded his gear. "Did you see that bear guy? He was all like: 'Whoa, I have an arrow in my mouth!'"

The centaur with the googly-eye glasses laughed. "That was awesome! Head slam!"

The two centaurs charged at each other full-force and knocked heads, then went staggering off in different directions with crazy grins on their faces.

Chiron sighed. He set Annabeth and Grover down on a picnic blanket next to me. "I really wish my cousins wouldn't slam their heads together. They don't have the brain cells to spare."

"Chiron," I said, still stunned by the fact that he was here. "You saved us."

He gave me a dry smile. "Well now, I couldn't very well let you die, especially since you've cleared my name."

"But how did you know where we were?" Annabeth asked.

"Advanced planning, my dear. I figured you would wash up near Miami if you made it out of the Sea of Monsters alive. Almost everything strange washes up near Miami."

"Gee, thanks," Grover mumbled.

"No, no," Chiron said. "I didn't mean . . . Oh, never mind. I *am* glad to see you, my young satyr. The point is, I was able to eavesdrop on Percy's Iris-message and trace the signal. Iris and I have been friends for centuries. I asked her to alert me to any important communications in this area. It then took no effort to convince my cousins to ride to your aid. As you see, centaurs can travel quite fast when we wish to. Distance for us is not the same as distance for humans."

I looked over at the campfire, where three party ponies were teaching Tyson to operate a paintball gun. I hoped they knew what they were getting into.

"So what now?" I asked Chiron. "We just let Luke sail away? He's got Kronos aboard that ship. Or parts of him, anyway."

Chiron knelt, carefully folding his front legs underneath him. He opened the medicine pouch on his belt and started to treat my wounds. "I'm afraid, Percy, that today has been something of a draw. We didn't have the strength of numbers to take that ship. Luke was not organized enough to pursue us. Nobody won."

"But we got the Fleece!" Annabeth said. "Clarisse is on her way back to camp with it right now."

Chiron nodded, though he still looked uneasy. "You are all true heroes. And as soon as we get Percy fixed up, you must return to Half-Blood Hill. The centaurs shall carry you."

"You're coming, too?" I asked.

"Oh yes, Percy. I'll be relieved to get home. My brethren here simply do not appreciate Dean Martin's music. Besides, I must have some words with Mr. D. There's the rest of the summer to plan. So much training to do. And I want to see . . . I'm curious about the Fleece."

I didn't know exactly what he meant, but it made me worried about what Luke had said: *I was going to let you take the Fleece . . . once I was done with it.*

Had he just been lying? I'd learned with Kronos there was usually a plan within a plan. The titan lord wasn't called the Crooked One for nothing. He had ways of getting people to do what he wanted without them ever realizing his true intentions.

Over by the campfire, Tyson let loose with his paintball gun. A blue projectile splattered against one of the centaurs, hurling him backward into the lake. The centaur came up grinning, covered in swamp muck and blue paint, and gave Tyson two thumbs up.

"Annabeth," Chiron said, "perhaps you and Grover would go supervise Tyson and my cousins before they, ah, teach each other too many bad habits?"

Annabeth met his eyes. Some kind of understanding passed between them.

"Sure, Chiron," Annabeth said. "Come on, goat boy."

"But I don't like paintball."

"Yes, you do." She hoisted Grover to his hooves and led him off toward the campfire.

Chiron finished bandaging my leg. "Percy, I had a talk with Annabeth on the way here. A talk about the prophecy."

Uh-oh, I thought.

"It wasn't her fault," I said. "I made her tell me."

His eyes flickered with irritation. I was sure he was going to chew me out, but then his look turned to weariness. "I suppose I could not expect to keep it secret forever."

"So *am* I the one in the prophecy?"

Chiron tucked his bandages back into his pouch. "I wish I knew, Percy. You're not yet sixteen. For now we must simply train you as best we can, and leave the future to the Fates."

The Fates. I hadn't thought about those old ladies in a long time, but as soon as Chiron mentioned them, something clicked.

"That's what it meant," I said.

Chiron frowned. "That's what *what* meant?"

"Last summer. The omen from the Fates, when I saw them snip somebody's life string. I thought it meant I was going to die right away, but it's worse than that. It's got something to do with your prophecy. The death they foretold—it's going to happen when I'm sixteen."

Chiron's tail whisked nervously in the grass. "My boy, you can't be sure of that. We don't even know if the prophecy is about you."

"But there isn't any other half-blood child of the Big Three!"

"That we know of."

"And Kronos is rising. He's going to destroy Mount Olympus!"

"He will try," Chiron agreed. "And Western Civilization along with it, if we don't stop him. But we *will* stop him. You will not be alone in that fight."

I knew he was trying to make me feel better, but I remembered what Annabeth had told me. It would come down to one hero. One decision that would save or destroy the West. And I felt sure the Fates had been giving me some kind of warning about that. Something terrible was going to happen, either to me or to somebody I was close to.

"I'm just a *kid*, Chiron," I said miserably. "What good is one lousy hero against something like Kronos?"

Chiron managed a smile. "'What good is one lousy hero? Joshua Lawrence Chamberlain said something like that to me once, just before he single-handedly changed the course of your Civil War."

He pulled an arrow from his quiver and turned the razor-sharp tip so it glinted in the firelight. "Celestial bronze, Percy. An immortal weapon. What would happen if you shot this at a human?"

"Nothing," I said. "It would pass right through."

"That's right," he said. "Humans don't exist on the same level as the immortals. They can't even be hurt by our weapons. But you, Percy—you are part god, part human. You live in both worlds. You can be harmed by both, and you can affect both. *That's* what makes heroes so special. You carry the hopes of humanity into the realm of the eternal. Monsters never die. They are reborn from the chaos and barbarism that is always bubbling underneath civilization, the very stuff that makes Kronos stronger. They must be defeated again and again, kept at bay. Heroes embody that struggle. You fight the battles humanity must win, every generation, in order to stay human. Do you understand?"

"I . . . I don't know."

"You must try, Percy. Because whether or not you are the child of the prophecy, Kronos thinks you might be. And after today, he will finally despair of turning you to his side. That *is* the only reason he hasn't killed you yet, you know. As soon as he's sure he can't use you, he will destroy you."

"You talk like you know him."

Chiron pursed his lips. "I *do* know him."

I stared at him. I sometimes forgot just how old Chiron was. "Is that why Mr. D blamed you when the tree was poisoned? Why you said some people don't trust you?"

"Indeed."

"But Chiron . . . I mean, come on! Why would they think you'd ever betray the camp for Kronos?"

Chiron's eyes were deep brown, full of thousands of years of sadness. "Percy, remember your training. Remember your study of mythology. What is my connection to the titan lord?"

I tried to think, but I'd always gotten my mythology mixed up. Even now, when it was so real, so important to my own life, I had trouble keeping all the names and facts straight. I shook my head. "You, uh, owe Kronos a favor or something? He spared your life?"

"Percy," Chiron said, his voice impossibly soft. "The titan Kronos is my father."

NINETEEN

THE CHARIOT RACE
ENDS WITH A BANG

We arrived in Long Island just after Clarisse, thanks to the centaurs' travel powers. I rode on Chiron's back, but we didn't talk much, especially not about Kronos. I knew it had been difficult for Chiron to tell me. I didn't want to push him with more questions. I mean, I've met plenty of embarrassing parents, but Kronos, the evil titan lord who wanted to destroy Western Civilization? Not the kind of dad you invited to school for career day.

When we got to camp, the centaurs were anxious to meet Dionysus. They'd heard he threw some really wild parties, but they were disappointed. The wine god was in no mood to celebrate as the whole camp gathered at the top of Half-Blood Hill.

The camp had been through a hard two weeks. The arts and crafts cabin had burned to the ground from an attack by a *Draco Aionius* (which as near as I could figure was Latin for "really-big-lizard-with-breath-that-blows-stuff-up"). The Big House's rooms were overflowing with wounded. The kids in the Apollo cabin, who were the best healers, had been working overtime performing first aid. Everybody looked weary and battered as we crowded around Thalia's tree.

The moment Clarisse draped the Golden Fleece over the lowest bough, the moonlight seemed to brighten, turning from gray to liquid silver. A cool breeze rustled in the branches and rippled through the grass, all the way into the valley. Everything came into sharper focus—the glow of the fireflies down in the woods, the smell of the strawberry fields, the sound of the waves on the beach.

Gradually, the needles on the pine tree started turning from brown to green.

Everybody cheered. It was happening slowly, but there could be no doubt—the Fleece's magic was seeping into the tree, filling it with new power and expelling the poison.

Chiron ordered a twenty-four/seven guard duty on the hilltop, at least until he could find an appropriate monster to protect the Fleece. He said he'd place an ad in *Olympus Weekly* right away.

In the meantime, Clarisse was carried on her cabin mates' shoulders down to the amphitheater, where she was honored with a laurel wreath and a lot of celebrating around the campfire.

Nobody gave Annabeth or me a second look. It was as if we'd never left. In a way, I guess that was the best thank-you anyone could give us, because if they admitted we'd snuck out of camp to do the quest, they'd have to expel us. And really, I didn't want any more attention. It felt good to be just one of the campers for once.

Later that night, as we were roasting s'mores and listening to the Stoll brothers tell us a ghost story about an evil king who was eaten alive by demonic breakfast pastries,

Clarisse shoved me from behind and whispered in my ear, "Just because you were cool one time, Jackson, don't think you're off the hook with Ares. I'm still waiting for the right opportunity to pulverize you."

I gave her a grudging smile.

"What?" she demanded.

"Nothing," I said. "Just good to be home."

The next morning, after the party ponies headed back to Florida, Chiron made a surprise announcement: the chariot races would go ahead as scheduled. We'd all figured they were history now that Tantalus was gone, but completing them did feel like the right thing to do, especially now that Chiron was back and the camp was safe.

Tyson wasn't too keen on the idea of getting back in a chariot after our first experience, but he was happy to let me team-up with Annabeth. I would drive, Annabeth would defend, and Tyson would act as our pit crew. While I worked with the horses, Tyson fixed up Athena's chariot and added a whole bunch of special modifications.

We spent the next two days training like crazy. Annabeth and I agreed that if we won, the prize of no chores for the rest of the month would be split between our two cabins. Since Athena had more campers, they would get most of the time off, which was fine by me. I didn't care about the prize. I just wanted to win.

The night before the race, I stayed late at the stables. I was talking to our horses, giving them one final brushing, when somebody right behind me said, "Fine animals, horses. Wish I'd thought of them."

A middle-aged guy in a postal carrier outfit was leaning against the stable door. He was slim, with curly black hair under his white pith helmet, and he had a mailbag slung over his shoulder.

"Hermes?" I stammered.

"Hello, Percy. Didn't recognize me without my jogging clothes?"

"Uh . . ." I wasn't sure whether I was supposed to kneel or buy stamps from him or what. Then it occurred to me why he must be here. "Oh, listen, Lord Hermes, about Luke . . ."

The god arched his eyebrows.

"Uh, we saw him, all right," I said, "but—"

"You weren't able to talk sense into him?"

"Well, we kind of tried to kill each other in a duel to the death."

"I see. You tried the diplomatic approach."

"I'm really sorry. I mean, you gave us those awesome gifts and everything. And I know you wanted Luke to come back. But . . . he's turned bad. *Really* bad. He said he feels like you abandoned him."

I waited for Hermes to get angry. I figured he'd turn me into a hamster or something, and I did *not* want to spend any more time as a rodent.

Instead, he just sighed. "Do you ever feel your father abandoned *you*, Percy?"

Oh, man.

I wanted to say, "Only a few hundred times a day." I hadn't spoken to Poseidon since last summer. I'd never even been to his underwater palace. And then there was the whole thing with Tyson—no warning, no explanation. Just *boom*, you have a brother. You'd think that deserved a little heads-up phone call or something.

The more I thought about it, the angrier I got. I realized I *did* want recognition for the quest I'd completed, but not from the other campers. I wanted my dad to say something. To notice me.

Hermes readjusted the mailbag on his shoulder. "Percy, the hardest part about being a god is that you must often act indirectly, especially when it comes to your own children. If we were to intervene every time our children had a problem . . . well, that would only create more problems and more resentment. But I believe if you give it some thought, you will see that Poseidon *has* been paying attention to you. He has answered your prayers. I can only hope that some day, Luke may realize the same about me. Whether you feel like you succeeded or not, you reminded Luke who he was. You spoke to him."

"I tried to kill him."

Hermes shrugged. "Families are messy. Immortal families are eternally messy. Sometimes the best we can do is to remind each other that we're related, for better or worse . . . and try to keep the maiming and killing to a minimum."

It didn't sound like much of a recipe for the perfect family. Then again, as I thought about my quest, I realized maybe Hermes was right. Poseidon had sent the hippocampi to help us. He'd given me powers over the sea that I'd never known about before. And there was Tyson. Had Poseidon brought us together on purpose? How many times had Tyson saved my life this summer?

In the distance, the conch horn sounded, signaling curfew.

"You should get to bed," Hermes said. "I've helped you get into quite enough trouble this summer already. I really only came to make this delivery."

"A delivery?"

"I *am* the messenger of the gods, Percy." He took an electronic signature pad from his mailbag and handed it to me. "Sign there, please."

I picked up the stylus before realizing it was entwined with a pair of tiny green snakes. "Ah!" I dropped the pad.

Ouch, said George.

Really, Percy, Martha scolded. *Would you want to be dropped on the floor of a horse stable?*

"Oh, uh, sorry." I didn't much like touching snakes, but I picked up the pad and the stylus again. Martha and George wriggled under my fingers, forming a kind of pencil grip like the ones my special ed teacher made me use in second grade.

Did you bring me a rat? George asked.

"No . . ." I said. "Uh, we didn't find any."

What about a guinea pig?

George! Martha chided. *Don't tease the boy.*

I signed my name and gave the pad back to Hermes.

In exchange, he handed me a sea-blue envelope.

My fingers trembled. Even before I opened it, I could tell it was from my father. I could sense his power in the cool blue paper, as if the envelope itself had been folded out of an ocean wave.

"Good luck tomorrow," Hermes said. "Fine team of horses you have there, though you'll excuse me if I root for the Hermes cabin."

And don't be too discouraged when you read it, dear, Martha told me. *He* does *have your interests at heart*.

"What do you mean?" I asked.

Don't mind her, George said. *And next time, remember, snakes work for tips.*

"Enough, you two," Hermes said. "Good-bye, Percy. For now."

Small white wings sprouted from his pith helmet. He began to glow, and I knew enough about the gods to avert my eyes before he revealed his true divine form. With a brilliant white flash he was gone, and I was alone with the horses.

I stared at the blue envelope in my hands. It was addressed in strong but elegant handwriting that I'd seen once before, on a package Poseidon had sent me last summer.

Percy Jackson
c/o Camp Half-Blood
Farm Road 3.141
Long Island, New York 11954

An actual letter from my father. Maybe he would tell me

I'd done a good job getting the Fleece. He'd explain about Tyson, or apologize for not talking to me sooner. There were so many things that I wanted that letter to say.

I opened the envelope and unfolded the paper.

Two simple words were printed in the middle of the page:

Brace Yourself

The next morning, everybody was buzzing about the chariot race, though they kept glancing nervously toward the sky like they expected to see Stymphalian birds gathering. None did. It was a beautiful summer day with blue sky and plenty of sunshine. The camp had started to look the way it should look: the meadows were green and lush; the white columns gleamed on the Greek buildings; dryads played happily in the woods.

And I was miserable. I'd been lying awake all night, thinking about Poseidon's warning.

Brace yourself.

I mean, he goes to the trouble of writing a letter, and he writes two words?

Martha the snake had told me not to feel disappointed. Maybe Poseidon had a reason for being so vague. Maybe he didn't know exactly what he was warning me about, but he sensed something big was about to happen—something that could completely knock me off my feet unless I was prepared. It was hard, but I tried to turn my thoughts to the race.

As Annabeth and I drove onto the track, I couldn't help admiring the work Tyson had done on the Athena chariot. The carriage gleamed with bronze reinforcements. The wheels were realigned with magical suspension so we glided along with hardly a bump. The rigging for the horses was so perfectly balanced that the team turned at the slightest tug of the reins.

Tyson had also made us two javelins, each with three buttons on the shaft. The first button primed the javelin to explode on impact, releasing razor wire that would tangle and shred an opponent's wheels. The second button produced a blunt (but still very painful) bronze spearhead designed to knock a driver out of his carriage. The third button brought up a grappling hook that could be used to lock onto an enemy's chariot or push it away.

I figured we were in pretty good shape for the race, but Tyson still warned me to be careful. The other chariot teams had plenty of tricks up their togas.

"Here," he said, just before the race began.

He handed me a wristwatch. There wasn't anything special about it—just a white-and-silver clock face, a black leather strap—but as soon as I saw it I realized that this is what I'd seen him tinkering on all summer.

I didn't usually like to wear watches. Who cared what time it was? But I couldn't say no to Tyson.

"Thanks, man." I put it on and found it was surprisingly light and comfortable. I could hardly tell I was wearing it.

"Didn't finish in time for the trip," Tyson mumbled. "Sorry, sorry."

"Hey, man. No big deal."

"If you need protection in race," he advised, "hit the button."

"Ah, okay." I didn't see how keeping time was going to help a whole lot, but I was touched that Tyson was concerned. I promised him I'd remember the watch. "And, hey, um, Tyson . . ."

He looked at me.

"I wanted to say, well . . ." I tried to figure out how to apologize for getting embarrassed about him before the quest, for telling everyone he wasn't my real brother. It wasn't easy to find the words.

"I know what you will tell me," Tyson said, looking ashamed. "Poseidon did care for me after all."

"Uh, well—"

"He sent you to help me. Just what I asked for."

I blinked. "You asked Poseidon for . . . me?"

"For a friend," Tyson said, twisting his shirt in his hands. "Young Cyclopes grow up alone on the streets, learn to make things out of scraps. Learn to survive."

"But that's so cruel!"

He shook his head earnestly. "Makes us appreciate blessings, not be greedy and mean and fat like Polyphemus. But I got scared. Monsters chased me so much, clawed me sometimes—"

"The scars on your back?"

A tear welled in his eye. "Sphinx on Seventy-second Street. Big bully. I prayed to Daddy for help. Soon the people at Meriwether found me. Met you. Biggest blessing ever.

Sorry I said Poseidon was mean. He sent me a brother."

I stared at the watch that Tyson had made me.

"Percy!" Annabeth called. "Come on!"

Chiron was at the starting line, ready to blow the conch.

"Tyson . . ." I said.

"Go," Tyson said. "You will win!"

"I—yeah, okay, big guy. We'll win this one for you." I climbed on board the chariot and got into position just as Chiron blew the starting signal.

The horses knew what to do. We shot down the track so fast I would've fallen out if my arms hadn't been wrapped in the leather reins. Annabeth held on tight to the rail. The wheels glided beautifully. We took the first turn a full chariot-length ahead of Clarisse, who was busy trying to fight off a javelin attack from the Stoll brothers in the Hermes chariot.

"We've got 'em!" I yelled, but I spoke too soon.

"Incoming!" Annabeth yelled. She threw her first javelin in grappling hook mode, knocking away a lead-weighted net that would have entangled us both. Apollo's chariot had come up on our flank. Before Annabeth could rearm herself, the Apollo warrior threw a javelin into our right wheel. The javelin shattered, but not before snapping some of our spokes. Our chariot lurched and wobbled. I was sure the wheel would collapse altogether, but we somehow kept going.

I urged the horses to keep up the speed. We were now neck and neck with Apollo. Hephaestus was coming up close behind. Ares and Hermes were falling behind, riding side by side as Clarisse went sword-on-javelin with Connor Stoll.

If we took one more hit to our wheel, I knew we would capsize.

"You're mine!" the driver from Apollo yelled. He was a first-year camper. I didn't remember his name, but he sure was confident.

"Yeah, right!" Annabeth yelled back.

She picked up her second javelin—a real risk considering we still had one full lap to go—and threw it at the Apollo driver.

Her aim was perfect. The javelin grew a heavy spear point just as it caught the driver in the chest, knocking him against his teammate and sending them both toppling out of their chariot in a backward somersault. The horses felt the reins go slack and went crazy, riding straight for the crowd. Campers scrambled for cover as the horses leaped the corner of the bleachers and the golden chariot flipped over. The horses galloped back toward their stable, dragging the upside-down chariot behind them.

I held our own chariot together through the second turn, despite the groaning of the right wheel. We passed the starting line and thundered into our final lap.

The axle creaked and moaned. The wobbling wheel was making us lose speed, even though the horses were responding to my every command, running like a well-oiled machine.

The Hephaestus team was still gaining.

Beckendorf grinned as he pressed a button on his command console. Steel cables shot out of the front of his mechanical horses, wrapping around our back rail. Our chariot shuddered as Beckendorf's winch system started working—pulling us backward while Beckendorf pulled himself forward.

Annabeth cursed and drew her knife. She hacked at the cables but they were too thick.

"Can't cut them!" she yelled.

The Hephaestus chariot was now dangerously close, their horses about to trample us underfoot.

"Switch with me!" I told Annabeth. "Take the reins!"

"But—"

"Trust me!"

She pulled herself to the front and grabbed the reins. I turned, trying hard to keep my footing, and uncapped Riptide.

I slashed down and the cables snapped like kite string. We lurched forward, but Beckendorf's driver just swung his chariot to our left and pulled up next to us. Beckendorf drew his sword. He slashed at Annabeth and I parried the blade away.

We were coming up on the last turn. We'd never make it. I needed to disable the Hephaestus chariot and get it out of the way, but I had to protect Annabeth, too. Just because Beckendorf was a nice guy didn't mean he wouldn't send us both to the infirmary if we let our guard down.

We were neck and neck now, Clarisse coming up from behind, making up for lost time.

"See ya, Percy!" Beckendorf yelled. "Here's a little parting gift!"

He threw a leather pouch into our chariot. It stuck to the floor immediately and began billowing green smoke.

"Greek fire!" Annabeth yelled.

I cursed. I'd heard stories about what Greek fire could do. I figured we had maybe ten seconds before it exploded.

"Get rid of it!" Annabeth shouted, but I couldn't. Hephaestus's chariot was still alongside, waiting until the last second to make sure their little present blew up. Beckendorf was keeping me busy with his sword. If I let my guard down long enough to deal with the Greek fire, Annabeth would get sliced and we'd crash anyway. I tried to kick the leather pouch away with my foot, but I couldn't. It was stuck fast.

Then I remembered the watch.

I didn't know how it could help, but I managed to punch the stopwatch button. Instantly, the watch changed. It expanded, the metal rim spiraling outward like an old-fashioned camera shutter, a leather strap wrapping around my forearm until I was holding a round war shield four feet wide, the inside soft leather, the outside polished bronze engraved with designs I didn't have time to examine.

All I knew: Tyson had come through. I raised the shield and Beckendorf's sword clanged against it. His blade shattered.

"What?" he shouted. "How—"

He didn't have time to say more because I knocked him in the chest with my new shield and sent him flying out of his chariot, tumbling in the dirt.

I was about use Riptide to slash at the driver when Annabeth yelled, "Percy!"

The Greek fire was shooting sparks. I shoved the tip of my sword under the leather pouch and flipped it up like a spatula. The firebomb dislodged and flew into the Hephaestus chariot at the driver's feet. He yelped.

In a split second the driver made the right choice: he dove out of the chariot, which careened away and exploded in green flames. The metal horses seemed to short-circuit. They turned and dragged the burning wreckage back toward Clarisse and the Stoll brothers, who had to swerve to avoid it.

Annabeth pulled the reins for the last turn. I held on, sure we would capsize, but somehow she brought us through and spurred the horses across the finish line. The crowd roared.

Once the chariot stopped, our friends mobbed us. They started chanting our names, but Annabeth yelled over the noise: "Hold up! Listen! It wasn't just us!"

The crowd didn't want to be quiet, but Annabeth made herself heard: "We couldn't have done it without somebody else! We couldn't have won this race or gotten the Fleece or saved Grover or anything! We owe our lives to Tyson, Percy's . . ."

"Brother!" I said, loud enough for everybody to hear. "Tyson, my baby brother."

Tyson blushed. The crowd cheered. Annabeth planted a kiss on my cheek. The roaring got a lot louder after that.

The entire Athena cabin lifted me and Annabeth and Tyson onto their shoulders and carried us toward the winner's platform, where Chiron was waiting to bestow the laurel wreaths.

TWENTY

THE FLEECE WORKS
ITS MAGIC TOO WELL

That afternoon was one of the happiest I'd ever spent at camp, which maybe goes to show, you never know when your world is about to be rocked to pieces.

Grover announced that he'd be able to spend the rest of the summer with us before resuming his quest for Pan. His bosses at the Council of Cloven Elders were so impressed that he hadn't gotten himself killed and had cleared the way for future searchers, that they granted him a two-month furlough and a new set of reed pipes. The only bad news: Grover insisted on playing those pipes all afternoon long, and his musical skills hadn't improved much. He played "YMCA," and the strawberry plants started going crazy, wrapping around our feet like they were trying to strangle us. I guess I couldn't blame them.

Grover told me he could dissolve the empathy link between us, now that we were face to face, but I told him I'd just as soon keep it if that was okay with him. He put down his reed pipes and stared at me. "But, if I get in trouble again, you'll be in danger, Percy! You could die!"

"If you get in trouble again, I want to know about it.

And I'll come help you again, G-man. I wouldn't have it any other way."

In the end he agreed not to break the link. He went back to playing "YMCA" for the strawberry plants. I didn't need an empathy link with the plants to know how they felt about it.

Later on during archery class, Chiron pulled me aside and told me he'd fixed my problems with Meriwether Prep. The school no longer blamed me for destroying their gymnasium. The police were no longer looking for me.

"How did you manage that?" I asked.

Chiron's eyes twinkled. "I merely suggested that the mortals had seen something different on that day—a furnace explosion that was not your fault."

"You just said that and they bought it?"

"I manipulated the Mist. Some day, when you're ready, I'll show how it's done."

"You mean, I can go back to Meriwether next year?"

Chiron raised his eyebrows. "Oh, no, they've still expelled you. Your headmaster, Mr. Bonsai, said you had—how did he put it?—un-groovy karma that disrupted the school's educational aura. But you're not in any legal trouble, which was a relief to your mother. Oh, and speaking of your mother . . ."

He unclipped his cell phone from his quiver and handed it to me. "It's high time you called her."

The worst part was the beginning—the "Percy-Jackson-what-were-you-thinking-do-you-have-any-idea-how-worried-I-was-sneaking-off-to-camp-without-permission-going-on-dangerous-quests-and-scaring-me-half-to-death" part.

But finally she paused to catch her breath. "Oh, I'm just glad you're safe!"

That's the great thing about my mom. She's no good at staying angry. She tries, but it just isn't in her nature.

"I'm sorry, Mom," I told her. "I won't scare you again."

"Don't promise me that, Percy. You know very well it will only get worse." She tried to sound casual about it, but I could tell she was pretty shaken up.

I wanted to say something to make her feel better, but I knew she was right. Being a half-blood, I would always be doing things that scared her. And as I got older, the dangers would just get greater.

"I could come home for a while," I offered.

"No, no. Stay at camp. Train. Do what you need to do. But you *will* come home for the next school year?"

"Yeah, of course. Uh, if there's any school that will take me."

"Oh, we'll find something, dear," my mother sighed. "Some place where they don't know us yet."

As for Tyson, the campers treated him like a hero. I would've been happy to have him as my cabin mate forever, but that evening, as we were sitting on a sand dune overlooking the Long Island Sound, he made an announcement that completely took me by surprise.

"Dream came from Daddy last night," he said. "He wants me to visit."

I wondered if he was kidding, but Tyson really didn't know how to kid. "Poseidon sent you a dream message?"

Tyson nodded. "Wants me to go underwater for the rest of the summer. Learn to work at Cyclopes' forges. He called it an inter—an intern—"

"An internship?"

"Yes."

I let that sink in. I'll admit, I felt a little jealous. Poseidon had never invited *me* underwater. But then I thought, Tyson was *going*? Just like that?

"When would you leave?" I asked.

"Now."

"Now. Like . . . *now* now?"

"Now."

I stared out at the waves in the Long Island Sound. The water was glistening red in the sunset.

"I'm happy for you, big guy," I managed. "Seriously."

"Hard to leave my new brother," he said with a tremble in his voice. "But I want to make things. Weapons for the camp. You will need them."

Unfortunately, I knew he was right. The Fleece hadn't solved all the camp's problems. Luke was still out there, gathering an army aboard the *Princess Andromeda*. Kronos was still re-forming in his golden coffin. Eventually, we would have to fight them.

"You'll make the best weapons ever," I told Tyson. I held up my watch proudly. "I bet they'll tell good time, too."

Tyson sniffled. "Brothers help each other."

"You're my brother," I said. "No doubt about it."

He patted me on the back so hard he almost knocked me down the sand dune. Then he wiped a tear from his cheek and stood to go. "Use the shield well."

"I will, big guy."

"Save your life some day."

The way he said it, so matter-of-fact, I wondered if that Cyclops eye of his could see into the future.

He headed down to the beach and whistled. Rainbow, the hippocampus, burst out of the waves. I watched the two of them ride off together into the realm of Poseidon.

Once they were gone, I looked down at my new wristwatch. I pressed the button and the shield spiraled out to full size. Hammered into the bronze were pictures in Ancient Greek style, scenes from our adventures this summer. There was Annabeth slaying a Laistrygonian dodgeball player, me fighting the bronze bulls on Half-Blood Hill, Tyson riding Rainbow toward the *Princess Andromeda*, the CSS *Birmingham* blasting its cannons at Charybdis. I ran my hand across a picture of Tyson, battling the Hydra as he held aloft a box of Monster Donuts.

I couldn't help feeling sad. I knew Tyson would have an awesome time under the ocean. But I'd miss everything about him—his fascination with horses, the way he could fix chariots or crumple metal with his bare hands, or tie bad guys into knots. I'd even miss him snoring like an earthquake in the next bunk all night.

"Hey, Percy."

I turned.

Annabeth and Grover were standing at the top of the sand dune. I guess maybe I had some sand in my eyes, because I was blinking a lot.

"Tyson . . ." I told them. "He had to . . ."

"We know," Annabeth said softly. "Chiron told us."

"Cyclopes forges." Grover shuddered. "I hear the cafeteria food there is terrible! Like, no enchiladas *at all*."

Annabeth held out her hand. "Come on, Seaweed Brain. Time for dinner."

We walked back toward the dining pavilion together, just the three of us, like old times.

A storm raged that night, but it parted around Camp Half-Blood as storms usually did. Lightning flashed against the horizon, waves pounded the shore, but not a drop fell in our valley. We were protected again thanks to the Fleece, sealed inside our magical borders.

Still, my dreams were restless. I heard Kronos taunting me from the depths of Tartarus: *Polyphemus sits blindly in his cave, young hero, believing he has won a great victory. Are you any less deluded?* The titan's cold laughter filled the darkness.

Then my dream changed. I was following Tyson to the bottom of the sea, into the court of Poseidon. It was a radiant hall filled with blue light, the floor cobbled with pearls. And there, on a throne of coral, sat my father, dressed like a simple fisherman in khaki shorts and a sun-bleached T-shirt. I looked up into his tan weathered face, his deep green eyes, and he spoke two words: *Brace yourself.*

I woke with a start.

There was a banging on the door. Grover flew inside without waiting for permission. "Percy!" he stammered. "Annabeth . . . on the hill . . . she . . ."

The look in his eyes told me something was terribly wrong. Annabeth had been on guard duty that night, protecting the Fleece. If something had happened—

I ripped off the covers, my blood like ice water in my veins. I threw on some clothes while Grover tried to make a complete sentence, but he was too stunned, too out of breath. "She's lying there . . . just lying there . . ."

I ran outside and raced across the central yard, Grover right behind me. Dawn was just breaking, but the whole camp seemed to be stirring. Word was spreading. Something huge had happened. A few campers were already making their way toward the hill, satyrs and nymphs and heroes in a weird mix of armor and pajamas.

I heard the clop of horse hooves, and Chiron galloped up behind us, looking grim.

"Is it true?" he asked Grover.

Grover could only nod, his expression dazed.

I tried to ask what was going on, but Chiron grabbed me by the arm and effortlessly lifted me onto his back. Together we thundered up Half-Blood Hill, where a small crowd had started to gather.

I expected to see the Fleece missing from the pine tree, but it was still there, glittering in the first light of dawn. The storm had broken and the sky was bloodred.

"Curse the Titan Lord," Chiron said. "He's tricked

us again, given himself another chance to control the prophecy."

"What do you mean?" I asked.

"The Fleece," he said. "The Fleece did its work too well."

We galloped forward, everyone moving out of our way. There at the base of the tree, a girl was lying unconscious. Another girl in Greek armor was kneeling next to her.

Blood roared in my ears. I couldn't think straight. Annabeth had been attacked? But why was the Fleece still there?

The tree itself looked perfectly fine, whole and healthy, suffused with the essence of the Golden Fleece.

"It healed the tree," Chiron said, his voice ragged. "And poison was not the only thing it purged."

Then I realized Annabeth wasn't the one lying on the ground. She was the one in armor, kneeling next to the unconscious girl. When Annabeth saw us, she ran to Chiron. "It . . . she . . . just suddenly there . . ."

Her eyes were streaming with tears, but I still didn't understand. I was too freaked out to make sense of it all. I leaped off Chiron's back and ran toward the unconscious girl. Chiron said: "Percy, wait!"

I knelt by her side. She had short black hair and freckles across her nose. She was built like a long-distance runner, lithe and strong, and she wore clothes that were somewhere between punk and Goth—a black T-shirt, black tattered jeans, and a leather jacket with buttons from a bunch of bands I'd never heard of.

She wasn't a camper. I didn't recognize her from any of

the cabins. And yet I had the strangest feeling I'd seen her before. . . .

"It's true," Grover said, panting from his run up the hill. "I can't believe . . ."

Nobody else came close to the girl.

I put my hand on her forehead. Her skin was cold, but my fingertips tingled as if they were burning.

"She needs nectar and ambrosia," I said. She was clearly a half-blood, whether she was a camper or not. I could sense that just from one touch. I didn't understand why everyone was acting so scared.

I took her by the shoulders and lifted her into sitting position, resting her head on my shoulder.

"Come on!" I yelled to the others. "What's wrong with you people? Let's get her to the Big House."

No one moved, not even Chiron. They were all too stunned.

Then the girl took a shaky breath. She coughed and opened her eyes.

Her irises were startlingly blue—electric blue.

The girl stared at me in bewilderment, shivering and wild-eyed. "Who—"

"I'm Percy," I said. "You're safe now."

"Strangest dream . . ."

"It's okay."

"Dying."

"No," I assured her. "You're okay. What's your name?"

That's when I knew. Even before she said it.

The girl's blue eyes stared into mine, and I understood

what the Golden Fleece quest had been about. The poisoning of the tree. Everything. Kronos had done it to bring another chess piece into play—*another chance to control the prophecy.*

Even Chiron, Annabeth, and Grover, who should've been celebrating this moment, were too shocked, thinking about what it might mean for the future. And I was holding someone who was destined to be my best friend, or possibly my worst enemy.

"I am Thalia," the girl said. "Daughter of Zeus."

ACKNOWLEDGMENTS

Many thanks to my young beta testers, Geoffrey Cole and Travis Stoll, for reading the manuscript and making good suggestions; Egbert Bakker of Yale University for his help with Ancient Greek; Nancy Gallt for her able representation; my editor, Jennifer Besser, for her guidance and perseverance; the students at the many schools I've visited for their enthusiastic support; and of course Becky, Haley, and Patrick Riordan, who make my trips to Camp Half-Blood possible.

Literature Circle Questions

Use the following questions and activities to get more out of the experience of reading *The Sea of Monsters* by Rick Riordan.

1. What does Percy Jackson say is his favorite place in the world?

2. In the first chapter, Percy dreams that his friend Grover is hiding from a monster. Based on what you learn later in the story, who or what is this monster?

3. During gym class, what magical force prevents Coach Nunley from noticing when the visitors turn into monsters?

4. The letters Percy sees on the door of the taxi in Chapter Three appear jumbled. Why is this? What do these letters probably spell out if arranged properly?

5. Who are the "Big Three" gods and what pact did they make after World War II? According to Percy, why was this pact made?

6. List three items that Hermes gives to Percy for his journey and explain one way in which each of these items helps the heroes on their quest.

7. Late in the book, Chiron tells Percy, Tyson, and Annabeth that they are "all true heroes." Choose one moment from the quest when you think Percy, Tyson, or Annabeth acts heroically and explain why you think the character is heroic at this moment.

8. In the story, Percy is able to command the sea, while Tyson has great strength and keen senses of smell and hearing. Imagine you are the son or daughter of a god and possess an extraordinary ability. Describe the ability you would choose for yourself and how you might use it on the quest.

9. On page 199, Annabeth tells Percy that her fatal flaw is hubris. What does she say "hubris" means? Briefly describe one time when you or someone you know acted with hubris.

10. Reread the description of Annabeth's vision on page 196. What do you think this vision reveals about Annabeth's true desires?

11. Choose two father–son or father–daughter relationships from the story to compare and contrast. Describe one way in which these relationships are similar and one way in which they are different.

12. How do Percy's feelings about Tyson at the end of the story differ from his feelings about Tyson at the beginning of the story? What do you think is the reason for this change?

13. On page 167, Annabeth tells Percy about Chiron's prophecy and warns, "Knowledge isn't always good for you." Do you agree with Annabeth? If there was a prophecy about something that might happen to you in the future, would you want to know about it?

14. After Circe turns Percy into a guinea pig, she tells him he has unlocked his true self. Do you agree with Circe? If so, explain why. If not, when in the book — if ever — do you think Percy *does* unlock his true self?

15. Think about the quest the heroes undertake in this story. First, state the purpose of the quest. Then, using evidence from the text to support your argument, explain whether you think the quest was a success. Be sure to read the final pages of the book carefully before you answer.

Note: These questions are keyed to Bloom's Taxonomy as follows: Knowledge: 1–3; Comprehension: 4–5; Application: 6–8; Analysis: 9–10; Synthesis: 11–12; Evaluation: 13–15.

Activities

1. Percy encounters many mythical creatures on his quest. Examples include hippocampi, harpies, hydra, and Charybdis. Using the descriptions in the text, draw one of these creatures on a blank piece of paper. If there is another creature from the book you prefer to draw, you can do that, too.

2. Draw a map of the East Coast of the United States. Be sure to include real places like New York City and Miami *and* mythical ones like Camp Half-Blood and the Sea of Monsters. Then label your map with a legend using symbols to represent the important events that occurred at each location. For example, for Cyclops Island, you might want to draw a golden fleece.

3. Look at the list of names below. On the blank line next to each half-blood's name, write the name of his or her immortal parent. See how many you can remember before looking in the book.

Percy   _____

Annabeth   _____

Luke   _____

Clarisse   _____

Chiron   _____

Thalia   _____

Other Books by Rick Riordan

Percy Jackson & the Olympians, Book One: The Lightning Thief

PERCY JACKSON & THE OLYMPIANS

BOOK THREE

THE TITAN'S CURSE

RICK RIORDAN

SCHOLASTIC INC.

New York Toronto London Auckland Sydney
Mexico City New Delhi Hong Kong Buenos Aires

ISBN-13: 978-0-545-05704-2
ISBN-10: 0-545-05704-3

Copyright © 2007 by Rick Riordan. All rights reserved. Published by Scholastic Inc., 557 Broadway, New York, NY 10012, by arrangement with Hyperion Books for Children, an imprint of Disney Children's Book Group, LLC. SCHOLASTIC and associated logos are trademarks and/or registered trademarks of Scholastic Inc.

35 34 33 32 31 30 29 28   13/0

Printed in the U.S.A.   40

First Scholastic printing, January 2008

This book is set in 13-point Centaur MT.

To Topher Bradfield
A camper who has made a world of difference

CONTENTS

MY RESCUE OPERATION GOES VERY WRONG

The Friday before winter break, my mom packed me an overnight bag and a few deadly weapons and took me to a new boarding school. We picked up my friends Annabeth and Thalia on the way.

It was an eight-hour drive from New York to Bar Harbor, Maine. Sleet and snow pounded the highway. Annabeth, Thalia, and I hadn't seen each other in months, but between the blizzard and the thought of what we were about to do, we were too nervous to talk much. Except for my mom. She talks *more* when she's nervous. By the time we finally got to Westover Hall, it was getting dark, and she'd told Annabeth and Thalia every embarrassing baby story there was to tell about me.

Thalia wiped the fog off the car window and peered outside. "Oh, yeah. This'll be fun."

Westover Hall looked like an evil knight's castle. It was all black stone, with towers and slit windows and a big set of wooden double doors. It stood on a snowy cliff overlooking this big frosty forest on one side and the gray churning ocean on the other.

"Are you sure you don't want me to wait?" my mother asked.

"No, thanks, Mom," I said. "I don't know how long it will take. We'll be okay."

"But how will you get back? I'm worried, Percy."

I hoped I wasn't blushing. It was bad enough I had to depend on my mom to drive me to my battles.

"It's okay, Ms. Jackson." Annabeth smiled reassuringly. Her blond hair was tucked into a ski cap and her gray eyes were the same color as the ocean. "We'll keep him out of trouble."

My mom seemed to relax a little. She thinks Annabeth is the most levelheaded demigod ever to hit eighth grade. She's sure Annabeth often keeps me from getting killed. She's right, but that doesn't mean I have to like it.

"All right, dears," my mom said. "Do you have everything you need?"

"Yes, Ms. Jackson," Thalia said. "Thanks for the ride."

"Extra sweaters? You have my cell phone number?"

"Mom—"

"Your ambrosia and nectar, Percy? And a golden drachma in case you need to contact camp?"

"Mom, seriously! We'll be fine. Come on, guys."

She looked a little hurt, and I was sorry about that, but I was ready to be out of that car. If my mom told one more story about how cute I looked in the bathtub when I was three years old, I was going to burrow into the snow and freeze myself to death.

Annabeth and Thalia followed me outside. The wind blew straight through my coat like ice daggers.

Once my mother's car was out of sight, Thalia said, "Your mom is so cool, Percy."

"She's pretty okay," I admitted. "What about you? You ever get in touch with your mom?"

As soon as I said it, I wished I hadn't. Thalia was great at giving evil looks, what with the punk clothes she always wears—the ripped-up army jacket, black leather pants and chain jewelry, the black eyeliner and those intense blue eyes. But the look she gave me now was a perfect evil "ten." "If that was any of your business, Percy—"

"We'd better get inside," Annabeth interrupted. "Grover will be waiting."

Thalia looked at the castle and shivered. "You're right. I wonder what he found here that made him send the distress call."

I stared up at the dark towers of Westover Hall. "Nothing good," I guessed.

The oak doors groaned open, and the three of us stepped into the entry hall in a swirl of snow.

All I could say was, "Whoa."

The place was huge. The walls were lined with battle flags and weapon displays: antique rifles, battle axes, and a bunch of other stuff. I mean, I knew Westover was a military school and all, but the decorations seemed like overkill. Literally.

My hand went to my pocket, where I kept my lethal ballpoint pen, Riptide. I could already sense something wrong in this place. Something dangerous. Thalia was rubbing her silver bracelet, her favorite magic item. I knew we were thinking the same thing. A fight was coming.

Annabeth started to say, "I wonder where—"

The doors slammed shut behind us.

"Oo-kay," I mumbled. "Guess we'll stay awhile."

I could hear music echoing from the other end of the hall. It sounded like dance music.

We stashed our overnight bags behind a pillar and started down the hall. We hadn't gone very far when I heard footsteps on the stone floor, and a man and woman marched out of the shadows to intercept us.

They both had short gray hair and black military-style uniforms with red trim. The woman had a wispy mustache, and the guy was clean-shaven, which seemed kind of backward to me. They both walked stiffly, like they had broomsticks taped to their spines.

"Well?" the woman demanded. "What are you doing here?"

"Um . . ." I realized I hadn't planned for this. I'd been so focused on getting to Grover and finding out what was wrong, I hadn't considered that someone might question three kids sneaking into the school at night. We hadn't talked at all in the car about how we would get inside. I said, "Ma'am, we're just—"

"Ha!" the man snapped, which made me jump. "Visitors are not allowed at the dance! You shall be *eee-jected*!"

He had an accent—French, maybe. He pronounced his *J* like in *Jacques*. He was tall, with a hawkish face. His nostrils flared when he spoke, which made it really hard not to stare up his nose, and his eyes were two different colors—one brown, one blue—like an alley cat's.

I figured he was about to toss us into the snow, but then Thalia stepped forward and did something very weird.

She snapped her fingers. The sound was sharp and loud. Maybe it was just my imagination, but I felt a gust of wind ripple out from her hand, across the room. It washed over all of us, making the banners rustle on the walls.

"Oh, but we're not visitors, sir," Thalia said. "We go to school here. You remember: I'm Thalia. And this is Annabeth and Percy. We're in the eighth grade."

The male teacher narrowed his two-colored eyes. I didn't know what Thalia was thinking. Now we'd probably get punished for lying *and* thrown into the snow. But the man seemed to be hesitating.

He looked at his colleague. "Ms. Gottschalk, do you know these students?"

Despite the danger we were in, I had to bite my tongue to keep from laughing. A teacher named *Got Chalk*? He had to be kidding.

The woman blinked, like someone had just woken her up from a trance. "I . . . yes. I believe I do, sir." She frowned at us. "Annabeth. Thalia. Percy. What are you doing away from the gymnasium?"

Before we could answer, I heard more footsteps, and Grover ran up, breathless. "You made it! You—"

He stopped short when he saw the teachers. "Oh, Mrs. Gottschalk. Dr. Thorn! I, uh—"

"What *is* it, Mr. Underwood?" said the man. His tone made it clear that he detested Grover. "What do you mean, they made it? These students live here."

Grover swallowed. "Yes, sir. Of course, Dr. Thorn. I just meant, I'm so glad they made . . . the punch for the dance! The punch is great. And they made it!"

Dr. Thorn glared at us. I decided one of his eyes had to be fake. The brown one? The blue one? He looked like he wanted to pitch us off the castle's highest tower, but then Mrs. Gottschalk said dreamily, "Yes, the punch is excellent. Now run along, all of you. You are not to leave the gymnasium again!"

We didn't wait to be told twice. We left with a lot of "Yes, ma'ams" and "Yes, sirs" and a couple of salutes, just because it seemed like the thing to do.

Grover hustled us down the hall in the direction of the music.

I could feel the teachers' eyes on my back, but I walked closely to Thalia and asked in a low voice, "How did you do that finger-snap thing?"

"You mean the Mist? Hasn't Chiron shown you how to do that yet?"

An uncomfortable lump formed in my throat. Chiron was our head trainer at camp, but he'd never shown me anything like that. Why had he shown Thalia and not me?

Grover hurried us to a door that had GYM written on the glass. Even with my dyslexia, I could read that much.

"That was close!" Grover said. "Thank the gods you got here!"

Annabeth and Thalia both hugged Grover. I gave him a big high five.

It was good to see him after so many months. He'd

gotten a little taller and had sprouted a few more whiskers, but otherwise he looked like he always did when he passed for human—a red cap on his curly brown hair to hide his goat horns, baggy jeans and sneakers with fake feet to hide his furry legs and hooves. He was wearing a black T-shirt that took me a few seconds to read. It said WESTOVER HALL: GRUNT. I wasn't sure whether that was, like, Grover's rank or maybe just the school motto.

"So what's the emergency?" I asked.

Grover took a deep breath. "I found two."

"Two half-bloods?" Thalia asked, amazed. "Here?"

Grover nodded.

Finding one half-blood was rare enough. This year, Chiron had put the satyrs on emergency overtime and sent them all over the country, scouring schools from fourth grade through high school for possible recruits. These were desperate times. We were losing campers. We needed all the new fighters we could find. The problem was, there just weren't that many demigods out there.

"A brother and a sister," he said. "They're ten and twelve. I don't know their parentage, but they're strong. We're running out of time, though. I need help."

"Monsters?"

"One." Grover looked nervous. "He suspects. I don't think he's positive yet, but this is the last day of term. I'm sure he won't let them leave campus without finding out. It may be our last chance! Every time I try to get close to them, he's always there, blocking me. I don't know what to do!"

Grover looked at Thalia desperately. I tried not to feel upset by that. Used to be, Grover looked to me for answers, but Thalia had seniority. Not just because her dad was Zeus. Thalia had more experience than any of us with fending off monsters in the real world.

"Right," she said. "These half-bloods are at the dance?"

Grover nodded.

"Then let's dance," Thalia said. "Who's the monster?"

"Oh," Grover said, and looked around nervously. "You just met him. The vice principal, Dr. Thorn."

Weird thing about military schools: the kids go absolutely nuts when there's a special event and they get to be out of uniform. I guess it's because everything's so strict the rest of the time, they feel like they've got to overcompensate or something.

There were black and red balloons all over the gym floor, and guys were kicking them in each other's faces, or trying to strangle each other with the crepe-paper streamers taped to the walls. Girls moved around in football huddles, the way they always do, wearing lots of makeup and spaghetti-strap tops and brightly colored pants and shoes that looked like torture devices. Every once in a while they'd surround some poor guy like a pack of piranhas, shrieking and giggling, and when they finally moved on, the guy would have ribbons in his hair and a bunch of lipstick graffiti all over his face. Some of the older guys looked more like me—uncomfortable, hanging out at the edges of the gym and trying to hide, like any minute they might have to fight for their lives. Of course, in my case, it was true. . . .

"There they are." Grover nodded toward a couple of younger kids arguing in the bleachers. "Bianca and Nico di Angelo."

The girl wore a floppy green cap, like she was trying to hide her face. The boy was obviously her little brother. They both had dark silky hair and olive skin, and they used their hands a lot as they talked. The boy was shuffling some kind of trading cards. His sister seemed to be scolding him about something. She kept looking around like she sensed something was wrong.

Annabeth said, "Do they . . . I mean, have you told them?"

Grover shook his head. "You know how it is. That could put them in more danger. Once they realize who they are, their scent becomes stronger."

He looked at me, and I nodded. I'd never really understood what half-bloods "smell" like to monsters and satyrs, but I knew that your scent could get you killed. And the more powerful a demigod you became, the more you smelled like a monster's lunch.

"So let's grab them and get out of here," I said.

I started forward, but Thalia put her hand on my shoulder. The vice principal, Dr. Thorn, had slipped out of a doorway near the bleachers and was standing near the di Angelo siblings. He nodded coldly in our direction. His blue eye seemed to glow.

Judging from his expression, I guessed Thorn hadn't been fooled by Thalia's trick with the Mist after all. He suspected who we were. He was just waiting to see why we were here.

"Don't look at the kids," Thalia ordered. "We have to wait for a chance to get them. We need to pretend we're not interested in them. Throw him off the scent."

"How?"

"We're three powerful half-bloods. Our presence should confuse him. Mingle. Act natural. Do some dancing. But keep an eye on those kids."

"Dancing?" Annabeth asked.

Thalia nodded. She cocked her ear to the music and made a face. "Ugh. Who chose the Jesse McCartney?"

Grover looked hurt. "I did."

"Oh my gods, Grover. That is so lame. Can't you play, like, Green Day or something?"

"Green who?"

"Never mind. Let's dance."

"But I can't dance!"

"You can if I'm leading," Thalia said. "Come on, goat boy."

Grover yelped as Thalia grabbed his hand and led him onto the dance floor.

Annabeth smiled.

"What?" I asked.

"Nothing. It's just cool to have Thalia back."

Annabeth had grown taller than me since last summer, which I found kind of disturbing. She used to wear no jewelry except for her Camp Half-Blood bead necklace, but now she wore little silver earrings shaped like owls—the symbol of her mother, Athena. She pulled off her ski cap, and her long blond hair tumbled down her shoulders. It made her look older, for some reason.

"So . . ." I tried to think of something to say. *Act natural*, Thalia had told us. When you're a half-blood on a dangerous mission, what the heck is natural? "Um, design any good buildings lately?"

Annabeth's eyes lit up, the way they always did when she talked about architecture. "Oh my gods, Percy. At my new school, I get to take 3-D design as an elective, and there's this cool computer program . . ."

She went on to explain how she'd designed this huge monument that she wanted to build at Ground Zero in Manhattan. She talked about structural supports and facades and stuff, and I tried to listen. I knew she wanted to be a super architect when she grew up—she loves math and historical buildings and all that—but I hardly understood a word she was saying.

The truth was I was kind of disappointed to hear that she liked her new school so much. It was the first time she'd gone to school in New York. I'd been hoping to see her more often. It was a boarding school in Brooklyn, and she and Thalia were both attending, close enough to Camp Half-Blood that Chiron could help if they got in any trouble. Because it was an all-girls school, and I was going to MS-54 in Manhattan, I hardly ever saw them.

"Yeah, uh, cool," I said. "So you're staying there the rest of the year, huh?"

Her face got dark. "Well, maybe, if I don't—"

"Hey!" Thalia called to us. She was slow dancing with Grover, who was tripping all over himself, kicking Thalia in the shins, and looking like he wanted to die. At least his feet were fake. Unlike me, he had an excuse for being clumsy.

"Dance, you guys!" Thalia ordered. "You look stupid just standing there."

I looked nervously at Annabeth, then at the groups of girls who were roaming the gym.

"Well?" Annabeth said.

"Um, who should I ask?"

She punched me in the gut. "*Me*, Seaweed Brain."

"Oh. Oh, right."

So we went onto the dance floor, and I looked over to see how Thalia and Grover were doing things. I put one hand on Annabeth's hip, and she clasped my other hand like she was about to judo throw me.

"I'm not going to bite," she told me. "Honestly, Percy. Don't you guys have dances at your school?"

I didn't answer. The truth was we did. But I'd never, like, actually *danced* at one. I was usually one of the guys playing basketball in the corner.

We shuffled around for a few minutes. I tried to concentrate on little things, like the crepe-paper streamers and the punch bowl—anything but the fact that Annabeth was taller than me, and my hands were sweaty and probably gross, and I kept stepping on her toes.

"What were you saying earlier?" I asked. "Are you having trouble at school or something?"

She pursed her lips. "It's not that. It's my dad."

"Uh-oh." I knew Annabeth had a rocky relationship with her father. "I thought it was getting better with you two. Is it your stepmom again?"

Annabeth sighed. "He decided to move. Just when I was getting settled in New York, he took this stupid new job researching for a World War I book. In *San Francisco*."

She said this the same way she might say *Fields of Punishment* or *Hades's gym shorts*.

"So he wants you to move out there with him?" I asked.

"To the other side of the country," she said miserably. "And half-bloods can't live in San Francisco. He should know that."

"What? Why not?"

Annabeth rolled her eyes. Maybe she thought I was kidding. "You know. It's right *there*."

"Oh," I said. I had no idea what she was talking about, but I didn't want to sound stupid. "So . . . you'll go back to living at camp or what?"

"It's more serious than that, Percy. I . . . I probably should tell you something."

Suddenly she froze. "They're gone."

"What?"

I followed her gaze. The bleachers. The two half-blood kids, Bianca and Nico, were no longer there. The door next to the bleachers was wide open. Dr. Thorn was nowhere in sight.

"We have to get Thalia and Grover!" Annabeth looked around frantically. "Oh, where'd they dance off to? Come on!"

She ran through the crowd. I was about to follow when a mob of girls got in my way. I maneuvered around them to avoid getting the ribbon-and-lipstick treatment, and by the time I was free, Annabeth had disappeared. I turned a full circle, looking for her or Thalia and Grover. Instead, I saw something that chilled my blood.

About fifty feet away, lying on the gym floor, was a floppy green cap just like the one Bianca di Angelo had been wearing. Near it were a few scattered trading cards. Then I caught a glimpse of Dr. Thorn. He was hurrying out a door at the opposite end of the gym, steering the di Angelo kids by the scruffs of their necks, like kittens.

I still couldn't see Annabeth, but I knew she'd be heading the other way, looking for Thalia and Grover.

I almost ran after her, and then I thought, *Wait.*

I remembered what Thalia had said to me in the entry hall, looking at me all puzzled when I asked about the finger-snap trick: *Hasn't Chiron shown you how to do that yet?* I thought about the way Grover had turned to her, expecting her to save the day.

Not that I resented Thalia. She was cool. It wasn't her fault her dad was Zeus and she got all the attention. . . . Still, I didn't need to run after her to solve every problem. Besides, there wasn't time. The di Angelos were in danger. They might be long gone by the time I found my friends. I knew monsters. I could handle this myself.

I took Riptide out of my pocket and ran after Dr. Thorn.

* * *

The door led into a dark hallway. I heard sounds of scuffling up ahead, then a painful grunt. I uncapped Riptide.

The pen grew in my hands until I held a bronze Greek sword about three feet long with a leather-bound grip. The blade glowed faintly, casting a golden light on the rows of lockers.

I jogged down the corridor, but when I got to the other end, no one was there. I opened a door and found myself back in the main entry hall. I was completely turned around. I didn't see Dr. Thorn anywhere, but there on the opposite side of the room were the di Angelo kids. They stood frozen in horror, staring right at me.

I advanced slowly, lowering the tip of my sword. "It's okay. I'm not going to hurt you."

They didn't answer. Their eyes were full of fear. What was wrong with them? Where was Dr. Thorn? Maybe he'd sensed the presence of Riptide and retreated. Monsters hated celestial bronze weapons.

"My name's Percy," I said, trying to keep my voice level. "I'm going to take you out of here, get you somewhere safe."

Bianca's eyes widened. Her fists clenched. Only too late did I realize what her look meant. She wasn't afraid of me. She was trying to warn me.

I whirled around and something went *WHIIISH!* Pain exploded in my shoulder. A force like a huge hand yanked me backward and slammed me to the wall.

I slashed with my sword but there was nothing to hit.

A cold laugh echoed through the hall.

"Yes, Perseus *Jackson,*" Dr. Thorn said. His accent

mangled the *J* in my last name. "I know who you are."

I tried to free my shoulder. My coat and shirt were pinned to the wall by some kind of spike—a black dagger-like projectile about a foot long. It had grazed the skin of my shoulder as it passed through my clothes, and the cut burned. I'd felt something like this before. Poison.

I forced myself to concentrate. I would *not* pass out.

A dark silhouette now moved toward us. Dr. Thorn stepped into the dim light. He still looked human, but his face was ghoulish. He had perfect white teeth and his brown/blue eyes reflected the light of my sword.

"Thank you for coming out of the gym," he said. "I hate middle school dances."

I tried to swing my sword again, but he was just out of reach.

WHIIIISH! A second projectile shot from somewhere behind Dr. Thorn. He didn't appear to move. It was as if someone invisible were standing behind him, throwing knives.

Next to me, Bianca yelped. The second thorn impaled itself in the stone wall, half an inch from her face.

"All three of you will come with me," Dr. Thorn said. "Quietly. Obediently. If you make a single noise, if you call out for help or try to fight, I will show you just how accurately I can throw."

TWO

THE VICE PRINCIPAL GETS A MISSILE LAUNCHER

I didn't know what kind of monster Dr. Thorn was, but he was fast.

Maybe I could defend myself if I could get my shield activated. All that it would take was a touch of my wristwatch. But defending the di Angelo kids was another matter. I needed help, and there was only one way I could think to get it.

I closed my eyes.

"What are you doing, Jackson?" hissed Dr. Thorn. "Keep moving!"

I opened my eyes and kept shuffling forward. "It's my shoulder," I lied, trying to sound miserable, which wasn't hard. "It burns."

"Bah! My poison causes pain. It will not kill you. Walk!"

Thorn herded us outside, and I tried to concentrate. I pictured Grover's face. I focused on my feelings of fear and danger. Last summer, Grover had created an empathy link between us. He'd sent me visions in my dreams to let me know when he was in trouble. As far as I knew, we were still linked, but I'd never tried to contact Grover before. I didn't even know if it would work while Grover was awake.

Hey, Grover! I thought. *Thorn's kidnapping us! He's a poisonous spike-throwing maniac! Help!*

Thorn marched us into the woods. We took a snowy path dimly lit by old-fashioned lamplights. My shoulder ached. The wind blowing through my ripped clothes was so cold that I felt like a Percysicle.

"There is a clearing ahead," Thorn said. "We will summon your ride."

"What ride?" Bianca demanded. "Where are you taking us?"

"Silence, you insufferable girl!"

"Don't talk to my sister that way!" Nico said. His voice quivered, but I was impressed that he had the guts to say anything at all.

Dr. Thorn made a growling sound that definitely wasn't human. It made the hairs stand up on the back of my neck, but I forced myself to keep walking and pretend I was being a good little captive. Meanwhile, I projected my thoughts like crazy—anything to get Grover's attention: *Grover! Apples! Tin cans! Get your furry goat behind out here and bring some heavily armed friends!*

"Halt," Thorn said.

The woods had opened up. We'd reached a cliff overlooking the sea. At least, I *sensed* the sea was down there, hundreds of feet below. I could hear the waves churning and I could smell the cold salty froth. But all I could see was mist and darkness.

Dr. Thorn pushed us toward the edge. I stumbled, and Bianca caught me.

"Thanks," I murmured.

"What *is* he?" she whispered. "How do we fight him?"

"I . . . I'm working on it."

"I'm scared," Nico mumbled. He was fiddling with something—a little metal toy soldier of some kind.

"Stop talking!" Dr. Thorn said. "Face me!"

We turned.

Thorn's two-tone eyes glittered hungrily. He pulled something from under his coat. At first I thought it was a switchblade, but it was only a phone. He pressed the side button and said, "The package—it is ready to deliver."

There was a garbled reply, and I realized Thorn was in walkie-talkie mode. This seemed way too modern and creepy—a monster using a mobile phone.

I glanced behind me, wondering how far the drop was.

Dr. Thorn laughed. "By all means, Son of Poseidon. *Jump!* There is the sea. Save yourself."

"What did he call you?" Bianca muttered.

"I'll explain later," I said.

"You do have a plan, right?"

Grover! I thought desperately. *Come to me!*

Maybe I could get both the di Angelos to jump with me into the ocean. If we survived the fall, I could use the water to protect us. I'd done things like that before. If my dad was in a good mood, and listening, he might help. Maybe.

"I would kill you before you ever reached the water," Dr. Thorn said, as if reading my thoughts. "You do not realize who I am, do you?"

A flicker of movement behind him, and another missile whistled so close to me that it nicked my ear. Something had sprung up behind Dr. Thorn—like a catapult, but more flexible . . . almost like a tail.

"Unfortunately," Thorn said, "you are wanted alive, if possible. Otherwise you would already be dead."

"Who wants us?" Bianca demanded. "Because if you think you'll get a ransom, you're wrong. We don't have any family. Nico and I . . ." Her voice broke a little. "We've got no one but each other."

"Aww," Dr. Thorn said. "Do not worry, little brats. You will be meeting my employer soon enough. Then you will have a brand-new family."

"Luke," I said. "You work for Luke."

Dr. Thorn's mouth twisted with distaste when I said the name of my old enemy—a former friend who'd tried to kill me several times. "You have no idea what is happening, Perseus Jackson. I will let the General enlighten you. You are going to do him a great service tonight. He is looking forward to meeting you."

"The General?" I asked. Then I realized I'd said it with a French accent. "I mean . . . who's the General?"

Thorn looked toward the horizon. "Ah, here we are. Your transportation."

I turned and saw a light in the distance, a searchlight over the sea. Then I heard the chopping of helicopter blades getting louder and closer.

"Where are you taking us?" Nico said.

"You should be honored, my boy. You will have the

opportunity to join a great army! Just like that silly game you play with cards and dolls."

"They're not dolls! They're figurines! And you can take your great army and—"

"Now, now," Dr. Thorn warned. "You will change your mind about joining us, my boy. And if you do not, well . . . there are other uses for half-bloods. We have many monstrous mouths to feed. The Great Stirring is underway."

"The Great what?" I asked. Anything to keep him talking while I tried to figure out a plan.

"The stirring of monsters." Dr. Thorn smiled evilly. "The worst of them, the most powerful, are now waking. Monsters that have not been seen in thousands of years. They will cause death and destruction the likes of which mortals have never known. And soon we shall have the most important monster of all—the one that shall bring about the downfall of Olympus!"

"Okay," Bianca whispered to me. "He's completely nuts."

"We have to jump off the cliff," I told her quietly. "Into the sea."

"Oh, super idea. You're completely nuts, too."

I never got the chance to argue with her, because just then an invisible force slammed into me.

Looking back on it, Annabeth's move was brilliant. Wearing her cap of invisibility, she plowed into the di Angelos and me, knocking us to the ground. For a split second, Dr. Thorn was taken by surprise, so his first volley of missiles zipped harmlessly over our heads. This gave Thalia and Grover a chance to advance from behind—Thalia wielding her magic shield, Aegis.

If you've never seen Thalia run into battle, you have never been truly frightened. She uses a huge spear that expands from this collapsible Mace canister she carries in her pocket, but that's not the scary part. Her shield is modeled after one her dad Zeus uses—also called Aegis—a gift from Athena. The shield has the head of the gorgon Medusa molded into the bronze, and even though it won't turn you to stone, it's so horrible, most people will panic and run at the sight of it.

Even Dr. Thorn winced and growled when he saw it.

Thalia moved in with her spear. "For Zeus!"

I thought Dr. Thorn was a goner. Thalia jabbed at his head, but he snarled and swatted the spear aside. His hand changed into an orange paw, with enormous claws that sparked against Thalia's shield as he slashed. If it hadn't been for Aegis, Thalia would've been sliced like a loaf of bread. As it was, she managed to roll backward and land on her feet.

The sound of the helicopter was getting louder behind me, but I didn't dare look.

Dr. Thorn launched another volley of missiles at Thalia, and this time I could see how he did it. He had a tail—a leathery, scorpionlike tail that bristled with spikes at the tip. The missiles deflected off Aegis, but the force of their impact knocked Thalia down.

Grover sprang forward. He put his reed pipes to his lips

and began to play—a frantic jig that sounded like something pirates would dance to. Grass broke through the snow. Within seconds, rope-thick weeds were wrapping around Dr. Thorn's legs, entangling him.

Dr. Thorn roared and began to change. He grew larger until he was in his true form—his face still human, but his body that of a huge lion. His leathery, spiky tail whipped deadly thorns in all directions.

"A manticore!" Annabeth said, now visible. Her magical New York Yankees cap had come off when she'd plowed into us.

"Who *are* you people?" Bianca di Angelo demanded. "And what is *that*?"

"A manticore?" Nico gasped. "He's got three thousand attack power and plus five to saving throws!"

I didn't know what he was talking about, but I didn't have time to worry about it. The manticore clawed Grover's magic weeds to shreds then turned toward us with a snarl.

"Get down!" Annabeth pushed the di Angelos flat into the snow. At the last second, I remembered my own shield. I hit my wristwatch, and metal plating spiraled out into a thick bronze shield. Not a moment too soon. The thorns impacted against it with such force they dented the metal. The beautiful shield, a gift from my brother, was badly damaged. I wasn't sure it would even stop a second volley.

I heard a *thwack* and a yelp, and Grover landed next to me with a thud.

"Yield!" the monster roared.

"Never!" Thalia yelled from across the field. She

charged the monster, and for a second, I thought she would run him through. But then there was a thunderous noise and a blaze of light from behind us. The helicopter appeared out of the mist, hovering just beyond the cliffs. It was a sleek black military-style gunship, with attachments on the sides that looked like laser-guided rockets. The helicopter had to be manned by mortals, but what was it doing here? How could mortals be working with a monster? The searchlights blinded Thalia, and the manticore swatted her away with its tail. Her shield flew off into the snow. Her spear flew in the other direction.

"No!" I ran out to help her. I parried away a spike just before it would've hit her chest. I raised my shield over us, but I knew it wouldn't be enough.

Dr. Thorn laughed. "Now do you see how hopeless it is? Yield, little heroes."

We were trapped between a monster and a fully armed helicopter. We had no chance.

Then I heard a clear, piercing sound: the call of a hunting horn blowing in the woods.

The manticore froze. For a moment, no one moved. There was only the swirl of snow and wind and the chopping of the helicopter blades.

"No," Dr. Thorn said. "It cannot be——"

His sentence was cut short when something shot past me like a streak of moonlight. A glowing silver arrow sprouted from Dr. Thorn's shoulder.

He staggered backward, wailing in agony.

[24]

"Curse you!" Thorn cried. He unleashed his spikes, dozens of them at once, into the woods where the arrow had come from, but just as fast, silvery arrows shot back in reply. It almost looked like the arrows had intercepted the thorns in midair and sliced them in two, but my eyes must've been playing tricks on me. No one, not even Apollo's kids at camp, could shoot with that much accuracy.

The manticore pulled the arrow out of his shoulder with a howl of pain. His breathing was heavy. I tried to swipe at him with my sword, but he wasn't as injured as he looked. He dodged my attack and slammed his tail into my shield, knocking me aside.

Then the archers came from the woods. They were girls, about a dozen of them. The youngest was maybe ten. The oldest, about fourteen, like me. They wore silvery ski parkas and jeans, and they were all armed with bows. They advanced on the manticore with determined expressions.

"The Hunters!" Annabeth cried.

Next to me, Thalia muttered, "Oh, wonderful."

I didn't have a chance to ask what she meant.

One of the older archers stepped forward with her bow drawn. She was tall and graceful with coppery colored skin. Unlike the other girls, she had a silver circlet braided into the top of her long dark hair, so she looked like some kind of Persian princess. "Permission to kill, my lady?"

I couldn't tell who she was talking to, because she kept her eyes on the manticore.

The monster wailed. "This is not fair! Direct interference! It is against the Ancient Laws."

"Not so," another girl said. This one was a little younger than me, maybe twelve or thirteen. She had auburn hair gathered back in a ponytail and strange eyes, silvery yellow like the moon. Her face was so beautiful it made me catch my breath, but her expression was stern and dangerous. "The hunting of all wild beasts is within my sphere. And you, foul creature, are a wild beast." She looked at the older girl with the circlet. "Zoë, permission granted."

The manticore growled. "If I cannot have these alive, I shall have them dead!"

He lunged at Thalia and me, knowing we were weak and dazed.

"No!" Annabeth yelled, and she charged at the monster.

"Get back, half-blood!" the girl with the circlet said. "Get out of the line of fire!"

But Annabeth leaped onto the monster's back and drove her knife into his mane. The manticore howled, turning in circles with his tail flailing as Annabeth hung on for dear life.

"Fire!" Zoë ordered.

"No!" I screamed.

But the Hunters let their arrows fly. The first caught the manticore in the neck. Another hit his chest. The manticore staggered backward, wailing, "This is not the end, Huntress! You shall pay!"

And before anyone could react, the monster, with Annabeth still on his back, leaped over the cliff and tumbled into the darkness.

"Annabeth!" I yelled.

I started to run after her, but our enemies weren't done with us. There was a *snap-snap-snap* from the helicopter—the sound of gunfire.

Most of the Hunters scattered as tiny holes appeared in the snow at their feet, but the girl with auburn hair just looked up calmly at the helicopter.

"Mortals," she announced, "are not allowed to witness my hunt."

She thrust out her hand, and the helicopter exploded into dust—no, not dust. The black metal dissolved into a flock of birds—ravens, which scattered into the night.

The Hunters advanced on us.

The one called Zoë stopped short when she saw Thalia. "You," she said with distaste.

"Zoë Nightshade." Thalia's voice trembled with anger. "Perfect timing, as usual."

Zoë scanned the rest of us. "Four half-bloods and a satyr, my lady."

"Yes," the younger girl said. "Some of Chiron's campers, I see."

"Annabeth!" I yelled. "You have to let us save her!"

The auburn-haired girl turned toward me. "I'm sorry, Percy Jackson, but your friend is beyond help."

I tried to struggle to my feet, but a couple of the girls held me down.

"You are in no condition to be hurling yourself off cliffs," the auburn-haired girl said.

"Let me go!" I demanded. "Who do you think you are?"

Zoë stepped forward as if to smack me.

"No," the other girl ordered. "I sense no disrespect, Zoë. He is simply distraught. He does not understand."

The young girl looked at me, her eyes colder and brighter than the winter moon. "I am Artemis," she said. "Goddess of the Hunt."

THREE

BIANCA DI ANGELO
MAKES A CHOICE

After seeing Dr. Thorn turn into a monster and plummet off the edge of a cliff with Annabeth, you'd think nothing else could shock me. But when this twelve-year-old girl told me she was the goddess Artemis, I said something real intelligent like, "Um . . . okay."

That was nothing compared to Grover. He gasped, then knelt hastily in the snow and started yammering, "Thank you, Lady Artemis! You're so . . . you're so . . . Wow!"

"Get up, goat boy!" Thalia snapped. "We have other things to worry about. Annabeth is gone!"

"Whoa," Bianca di Angelo said. "Hold up. Time out."

Everybody looked at her. She pointed her finger at all of us in turn, like she was trying to connect the dots. "Who . . . who are you people?"

Artemis's expression softened. "It might be a better question, my dear girl, to ask who are *you?* Who are your parents?"

Bianca glanced nervously at her brother, who was still staring in awe at Artemis.

"Our parents are dead," Bianca said. "We're orphans. There's a bank trust that pays for our school, but . . ."

She faltered. I guess she could tell from our faces that we didn't believe her.

"What?" she demanded. "I'm telling the truth."

"You are a half-blood," Zoë Nightshade said. Her accent was hard to place. It sounded old-fashioned, like she was reading from a really old book. "One of thy parents was mortal. The other was an Olympian."

"An Olympian . . . athlete?"

"No," Zoë said. "One of the gods."

"Cool!" said Nico.

"No!" Bianca's voice quavered. "This is not cool!"

Nico danced around like he needed to use the restroom. "Does Zeus really have lightning bolts that do six hundred damage? Does he get extra movement points for—"

"Nico, shut up!" Bianca put her hands to her face. "This is not your stupid Mythomagic game, okay? There are no gods!"

As anxious as I felt about Annabeth—all I wanted to do was search for her—I couldn't help feeling sorry for the di Angelos. I remembered what it was like for me when I first learned I was a demigod.

Thalia must've been feeling something similar, because the anger in her eyes subsided a little bit. "Bianca, I know it's hard to believe. But the gods are still around. Trust me. They're immortal. And whenever they have kids with regular humans, kids like us, well . . . Our lives are dangerous."

"Dangerous," Bianca said, "like the girl who fell."

Thalia turned away. Even Artemis looked pained.

"Do not despair for Annabeth," the goddess said. "She was a brave maiden. If she can be found, I shall find her."

"Then why won't you let us go look for her?" I asked.

"She is gone. Can't you sense it, Son of Poseidon? Some magic is at work. I do not know exactly how or why, but your friend has vanished."

I still wanted to jump off the cliff and search for her, but I had a feeling that Artemis was right. Annabeth was gone. If she'd been down there in the sea, I thought, I'd be able to feel her presence.

"Oo!" Nico raised his hand. "What about Dr. Thorn? That was awesome how you shot him with arrows! Is he dead?"

"He was a manticore," Artemis said. "Hopefully he is destroyed for now, but monsters never truly die. They re-form over and over again, and they must be hunted whenever they reappear."

"Or they'll hunt us," Thalia said.

Bianca di Angelo shivered. "That explains . . . Nico, you remember last summer, those guys who tried to attack us in the alley in D.C.?"

"And that bus driver," Nico said. "The one with the ram's horns. I *told* you that was real."

"That's why Grover has been watching you," I said. "To keep you safe, if you turned out to be half-bloods."

"Grover?" Bianca stared at him. "You're a demigod?"

"Well, a satyr, actually." He kicked off his shoes and displayed his goat hooves. I thought Bianca was going to faint right there.

"Grover, put your shoes back on," Thalia said. "You're freaking her out."

"Hey, my hooves are clean!"

"Bianca," I said, "we came here to help you. You and Nico need training to survive. Dr. Thorn won't be the last monster you meet. You need to come to camp."

"Camp?" she asked.

"Camp Half-Blood," I said. "It's where half-bloods learn to survive and stuff. You can join us, stay there year-round if you like."

"Sweet, let's go!" said Nico.

"Wait." Bianca shook her head. "I don't—"

"There *is* another option," Zoë said.

"No, there isn't!" Thalia said.

Thalia and Zoë glared at each other. I didn't know what they were talking about, but I could tell there was bad history between them. For some reason, they seriously hated each other.

"We've burdened these children enough," Artemis announced. "Zoë, we will rest here for a few hours. Raise the tents. Treat the wounded. Retrieve our guests' belongings from the school."

"Yes, my lady."

"And, Bianca, come with me. I would like to speak with you."

"What about me?" Nico asked.

Artemis considered the boy. "Perhaps you can show Grover how to play that card game you enjoy. I'm sure Grover would be happy to entertain you for a while . . . as a favor to me?"

[32]

Grover just about tripped over himself getting up. "You bet! Come on, Nico!"

Nico and Grover walked off toward the woods, talking about hit points and armor ratings and a bunch of other geeky stuff. Artemis led a confused-looking Bianca along the cliff. The Hunters began unpacking their knapsacks and making camp.

Zoë gave Thalia one more evil look, then left to oversee things.

As soon as she was gone, Thalia stamped her foot in frustration. "The nerve of those Hunters! They think they're so . . . Argh!"

"I'm with you," I said. "I don't trust—"

"Oh, you're with me?" Thalia turned on me furiously. "What were you thinking back there in the gym, Percy? You'd take on Dr. Thorn all by yourself? You *knew* he was a monster!"

"I—"

"If we'd stuck together, we could've taken him without the Hunters getting involved. Annabeth might still be here. Did you think of that?"

My jaw clenched. I thought of some harsh things to say, and I might've said them too, but then I looked down and saw something navy blue lying in the snow at my feet. Annabeth's New York Yankees baseball cap.

Thalia didn't say another word. She wiped a tear from her cheek, turned, and marched off, leaving me alone with a trampled cap in the snow.

* * *

The Hunters set up their camping site in a matter of minutes. Seven large tents, all of silver silk, curved in a crescent around one side of a bonfire. One of the girls blew a silver dog whistle, and a dozen white wolves appeared out of the woods. They began circling the camp like guard dogs. The Hunters walked among them and fed them treats, completely unafraid, but I decided I would stick close to the tents. Falcons watched us from the trees, their eyes flashing in the firelight, and I got the feeling they were on guard duty, too. Even the weather seemed to bend to the goddess's will. The air was still cold, but the wind died down and the snow stopped falling, so it was almost pleasant sitting by the fire.

Almost . . . except for the pain in my shoulder and the guilt weighing me down. I couldn't believe Annabeth was gone. And as angry as I was at Thalia, I had a sinking feeling that she was right. It *was* my fault.

What had Annabeth wanted to tell me in the gym? *Something serious*, she'd said. Now I might never find out. I thought about how we'd danced together for half a song, and my heart felt even heavier.

I watched Thalia pacing in the snow at the edge of camp, walking among the wolves without fear. She stopped and looked back at Westover Hall, which was now completely dark, looming on the hillside beyond the woods. I wondered what she was thinking.

Seven years ago, Thalia had been turned into a pine tree by her father, to prevent her from dying. She'd stood her ground against an army of monsters on top of Half-Blood Hill in order to give her friends Luke and Annabeth time to escape. She'd only been back as a human for a few months now, and once in a while she would stand so motionless you'd think she was still a tree.

Finally, one of the Hunters brought me my backpack. Grover and Nico came back from their walk, and Grover helped me fix up my wounded arm.

"It's green!" Nico said with delight.

"Hold still," Grover told me. "Here, eat some ambrosia while I clean that out."

I winced as he dressed the wound, but the ambrosia square helped. It tasted like homemade brownie, dissolving in my mouth and sending a warm feeling through my whole body. Between that and the magic salve Grover used, my shoulder felt better within a couple of minutes.

Nico rummaged through his own bag, which the Hunters had apparently packed for him, though how they'd snuck into Westover Hall unseen, I didn't know. Nico laid out a bunch of figurines in the snow—little battle replicas of Greek gods and heroes. I recognized Zeus with a lightning bolt, Ares with a spear, Apollo with his sun chariot.

"Big collection," I said.

Nico grinned. "I've got almost all of them, plus their holographic cards! Well, except for a few really rare ones."

"You've been playing this game a long time?"

"Just this year. Before that . . ." He knit his eyebrows.

"What?" I asked.

"I forget. That's weird."

He looked unsettled, but it didn't last long. "Hey, can I see that sword you were using?"

I showed him Riptide, and explained how it turned from a pen into a sword just by uncapping it.

"Cool! Does it ever run out of ink?"

"Um, well, I don't actually write with it."

"Are you really the son of Poseidon?"

"Well, yeah."

"Can you surf really well, then?"

I looked at Grover, who was trying hard not to laugh.

"Jeez, Nico," I said. "I've never really tried."

He went on asking questions. Did I fight a lot with Thalia, since she was a daughter of Zeus? (I didn't answer that one.) If Annabeth's mother was Athena, the goddess of wisdom, then why didn't Annabeth know better than to fall off a cliff? (I tried not to strangle Nico for asking that one.) Was Annabeth my girlfriend? (At this point, I was ready to stick the kid in a meat-flavored sack and throw him to the wolves.)

I figured any second he was going to ask me how many hit points I had, and I'd lose my cool completely, but then Zoë Nightshade came up to us.

"Percy Jackson."

She had dark brown eyes and a slightly upturned nose. With her silver circlet and her proud expression, she looked so much like royalty that I had to resist the urge to sit up straight and say "Yes, ma'am." She studied me distastefully, like I was a bag of dirty laundry she'd been sent to fetch.

"Come with me," she said. "Lady Artemis wishes to speak with thee."

* * *

Zoë led me to the last tent, which looked no different from the others, and waved me inside. Bianca di Angelo was seated next to the auburn-haired girl, who I still had trouble thinking of as Artemis.

The inside of the tent was warm and comfortable. Silk rugs and pillows covered the floor. In the center, a golden brazier of fire seemed to burn without fuel or smoke. Behind the goddess, on a polished oak display stand, was her huge silver bow, carved to resemble gazelle horns. The walls were hung with animal pelts: black bear, tiger, and several others I didn't recognize. I figured an animal rights activist would've had a heart attack looking at all those rare skins, but maybe since Artemis was the goddess of the hunt, she could replenish whatever she shot. I thought she had another animal pelt lying next to her, and then I realized it was a live animal—a deer with glittering fur and silver horns, its head resting contentedly in Artemis's lap.

"Join us, Percy Jackson," the goddess said.

I sat across from her on the tent floor. The goddess studied me, which made me uncomfortable. She had such old eyes for a young girl.

"Are you surprised by my age?" she asked.

"Uh . . . a little."

"I could appear as a grown woman, or a blazing fire, or anything else I want, but this is what I prefer. This is the average age of my Hunters, and all young maidens for whom I am patron, before they go astray."

"Go astray?" I asked.

[37]

"Grow up. Become smitten with boys. Become silly, preoccupied, insecure. Forget themselves."

"Oh."

Zoë sat down at Artemis's right. She glared at me as if all the stuff Artemis had just said was my fault, like I'd invented the idea of being a guy.

"You must forgive my Hunters if they do not welcome you," Artemis said. "It is very rare that we would have boys in this camp. Boys are usually forbidden to have any contact with the Hunters. The last one to see this camp . . ." She looked at Zoë. "Which one was it?"

"That boy in Colorado," Zoë said. "You turned him into a jackalope."

"Ah, yes." Artemis nodded, satisfied. "I enjoy making jackalopes. At any rate, Percy, I've asked you here so that you might tell me more of the manticore. Bianca has reported some of the . . . mmm, disturbing things the monster said. But she may not have understood them. I'd like to hear them from you."

And so I told her.

When I was done, Artemis put her hand thoughtfully on her silver bow. "I feared this was the answer."

Zoë sat forward. "The scent, my lady?"

"Yes."

"What scent?" I asked.

"Things are stirring that I have not hunted in millennia," Artemis murmured. "Prey so old I have nearly forgotten."

She stared at me intently. "We came here tonight

sensing the manticore, but he was not the one I seek. Tell me again, exactly what Dr. Thorn said."

"Um, 'I hate middle school dances.'"

"No, no. After that."

"He said somebody called the General was going to explain things to me."

Zoë's face paled. She turned to Artemis and started to say something, but Artemis raised her hand.

"Go on, Percy," the goddess said.

"Well, then Thorn was talking about the Great Stir Pot—"

"Stirring," Bianca corrected.

"Yeah. And he said, 'Soon we shall have the most important monster of all—the one that shall bring about the downfall of Olympus.'"

The goddess was so still she could've been a statue.

"Maybe he was lying," I said.

Artemis shook her head. "No. He was not. I've been too slow to see the signs. I must hunt this monster."

Zoë looked like she was trying very hard not to be afraid, but she nodded. "We will leave right away, my lady."

"No, Zoë. I must do this alone."

"But, Artemis—"

"This task is too dangerous even for the Hunters. You know where I must start my search. You cannot go there with me."

"As . . . as you wish, my lady."

"I will find this creature," Artemis vowed. "And I shall bring it back to Olympus by winter solstice. It will be all the proof I need to convince the Council of the Gods of how much danger we are in."

"You know what the monster is?" I asked.

Artemis gripped her bow. "Let us pray I am wrong."

"Can goddesses pray?" I asked, because I'd never really thought about that.

A flicker of a smile played across Artemis's lips. "Before I go, Percy Jackson, I have a small task for you."

"Does it involve getting turned into a jackalope?"

"Sadly, no. I want you to escort the Hunters back to Camp Half-Blood. They can stay there in safety until I return."

"What?" Zoë blurted out. "But, Artemis, we hate that place. The last time we stayed there—"

"Yes, I know," Artemis said. "But I'm sure Dionysus will not hold a grudge just because of a little, ah, misunderstanding. It's your right to use Cabin Eight whenever you are in need. Besides, I hear they rebuilt the cabins you burned down."

Zoë muttered something about foolish campers.

"And now there is one last decision to make." Artemis turned to Bianca. "Have you made up your mind, my girl?"

Bianca hesitated. "I'm still thinking about it."

"Wait," I said. "Thinking about what?"

"They . . . they've invited me to join the Hunt."

"What? But you can't! You have to come to Camp Half-Blood so Chiron can train you. It's the only way you can learn to survive."

"It is *not* the only way for a girl," Zoë said.

I couldn't believe I was hearing this. "Bianca, camp is cool! It's got a pegasus stable and a sword-fighting arena and . . . I mean, what do you get by joining the Hunters?"

"To begin with," Zoë said, "immortality."

I stared at her, then at Artemis. "She's kidding, right?"

"Zoë rarely kids about anything," Artemis said. "My Hunters follow me on my adventures. They are my maidservants, my companions, my sisters-in-arms. Once they swear loyalty to me, they are indeed immortal . . . unless they fall in battle, which is unlikely. Or break their oath."

"What oath?" I said.

"To foreswear romantic love forever," Artemis said. "To never grow up, never get married. To be a maiden eternally."

"Like you?"

The goddess nodded.

I tried to imagine what she was saying. Being immortal. Hanging out with only middle-school girls forever. I couldn't get my mind around it. "So you just go around the country recruiting half-bloods—"

"Not just half-bloods," Zoë interrupted. "Lady Artemis does not discriminate by birth. All who honor the goddess may join. Half-bloods, nymphs, mortals—"

"Which are you, then?"

Anger flashed in Zoë's eyes. "That is not thy concern, boy. The point is Bianca may join if she wishes. It is her choice."

"Bianca, this is crazy," I said. "What about your brother? Nico can't be a Hunter."

"Certainly not," Artemis agreed. "He will go to camp. Unfortunately, that's the best boys can do."

"Hey!" I protested.

"You can see him from time to time," Artemis assured Bianca. "But you will be free of responsibility. He will have the camp counselors to take care of him. And you will have a new family. Us."

"A new family," Bianca repeated dreamily. "Free of responsibility."

"Bianca, you can't do this," I said. "It's nuts."

She looked at Zoë. "Is it worth it?"

Zoë nodded. "It is."

"What do I have to do?"

"Say this," Zoë told her, "'I pledge myself to the goddess Artemis.'"

"I . . . I pledge myself to the goddess Artemis."

"'I turn my back on the company of men, accept eternal maidenhood, and join the Hunt.'"

Bianca repeated the lines. "That's it?"

Zoë nodded. "If Lady Artemis accepts thy pledge, then it is binding."

"I accept it," Artemis said.

The flames in the brazier brightened, casting a silver glow over the room. Bianca looked no different, but she took a deep breath and opened her eyes wide. "I feel . . . stronger."

"Welcome, sister," Zoë said.

"Remember your pledge," Artemis said. "It is now your life."

I couldn't speak. I felt like a trespasser. And a complete failure. I couldn't believe I'd come all this way and suffered so much only to lose Bianca to some eternal girls' club.

"Do not despair, Percy Jackson," Artemis said. "You will still get to show the di Angelos your camp. And if Nico so chooses, he can stay there."

"Great," I said, trying not to sound surly. "How are we supposed to get there?"

Artemis closed her eyes. "Dawn is approaching. Zoë, break camp. You must get to Long Island quickly and safely. I shall summon a ride from my brother."

Zoë didn't look real happy about this idea, but she nodded and told Bianca to follow her. As she was leaving, Bianca paused in front of me. "I'm sorry, Percy. But I want this. I really, really do."

Then she was gone, and I was left alone with the twelve-year-old goddess.

"So," I said glumly. "We're going to get a ride from your brother, huh?"

Artemis's silver eyes gleamed. "Yes, boy. You see, Bianca di Angelo is not the only one with an annoying brother. It's time for you to meet my irresponsible twin, Apollo."

FOUR

THALIA TORCHES
NEW ENGLAND

Artemis assured us that dawn was coming, but you could've fooled me. It was colder and darker and snowier than ever. Up on the hill, Westover Hall's windows were completely lightless. I wondered if the teachers had even noticed the di Angelos and Dr. Thorn were missing yet. I didn't want to be around when they did. With my luck, the only name Mrs. Gottschalk would remember was "Percy Jackson," and then I'd be the subject of a nationwide manhunt . . . again.

The Hunters broke camp as quickly as they'd set it up. I stood shivering in the snow (unlike the Hunters, who didn't seem to feel at all uncomfortable), and Artemis stared into the east like she was expecting something. Bianca sat off to one side, talking with Nico. I could tell from his gloomy face that she was explaining her decision to join the Hunt. I couldn't help thinking how selfish it was of her, abandoning her brother like that.

Thalia and Grover came up and huddled around me, anxious to hear what had happened in my audience with the goddess.

When I told them, Grover turned pale. "The last time the Hunters visited camp, it didn't go well."

"How'd they even show up here?" I wondered. "I mean, they just appeared out of nowhere."

"And Bianca *joined* them," Thalia said, disgusted. "It's all Zoë's fault. That stuck-up, no good—"

"Who can blame her?" Grover said. "Eternity with Artemis?" He heaved a big sigh.

Thalia rolled her eyes. "You satyrs. You're all in love with Artemis. Don't you get that she'll never love you back?"

"But she's so . . . into nature," Grover swooned.

"You're nuts," said Thalia.

"Nuts and berries," Grover said dreamily. "Yeah."

Finally the sky began to lighten. Artemis muttered, "About time. He's so-o-o lazy during the winter."

"You're, um, waiting for sunrise?" I asked.

"For my brother. Yes."

I didn't want to be rude. I mean, I knew the legends about Apollo—or sometimes Helios—driving a big sun chariot across the sky. But I also knew that the sun was really a star about a zillion miles away. I'd gotten used to some of the Greek myths being true, but still . . . I didn't see how Apollo could drive the sun.

"It's not exactly as you think," Artemis said, like she was reading my mind.

"Oh, okay." I started to relax. "So, it's not like he'll be pulling up in a—"

There was a sudden burst of light on the horizon. A blast of warmth.

"Don't look," Artemis advised. "Not until he parks."

Parks?

I averted my eyes, and saw that the other kids were doing the same. The light and warmth intensified until my winter coat felt like it was melting off of me. Then suddenly the light died.

I looked. And I couldn't believe it. It was *my* car. Well, the car I wanted, anyway. A red convertible Maserati Spyder. It was so awesome it glowed. Then I realized it was glowing because the metal was hot. The snow had melted around the Maserati in a perfect circle, which explained why I was now standing on green grass and my shoes were wet.

The driver got out, smiling. He looked about seventeen or eighteen, and for a second, I had the uneasy feeling it was Luke, my old enemy. This guy had the same sandy hair and outdoorsy good looks. But it wasn't Luke. This guy was taller, with no scar on his face like Luke's. His smile was brighter and more playful. (Luke didn't do much more than scowl and sneer these days.) The Maserati driver wore jeans and loafers and a sleeveless T-shirt.

"Wow," Thalia muttered. "Apollo is hot."

"He's the sun god," I said.

"That's not what I meant."

"Little sister!" Apollo called. If his teeth were any whiter he could've blinded us without the sun car. "What's up? You never call. You never write. I was getting worried!"

Artemis sighed. "I'm fine, Apollo. And I am not your *little* sister."

"Hey, I was born first."

"We're twins! How many millennia do we have to argue—"

"So what's up?" he interrupted. "Got the girls with you, I see. You all need some tips on archery?"

Artemis grit her teeth. "I need a favor. I have some hunting to do, *alone.* I need you to take my companions to Camp Half-Blood."

"Sure, sis!" Then he raised his hands in a *stop everything* gesture. "I feel a haiku coming on."

The Hunters all groaned. Apparently they'd met Apollo before.

He cleared his throat and held up one hand dramatically.

"Green grass breaks through snow.
Artemis pleads for my help.
I am so cool."

He grinned at us, waiting for applause.

"That last line was only four syllables," Artemis said.

Apollo frowned. "Was it?"

"Yes. What about *I am so big-headed?*"

"No, no, that's six syllables. Hmm." He started muttering to himself.

Zoë Nightshade turned to us. "Lord Apollo has been going through this haiku phase ever since he visited Japan. 'Tis not as bad as the time he visited Limerick. If I'd had to hear one more poem that started with, *There once was a goddess from Sparta—*"

"I've got it!" Apollo announced. "*I am so awesome.* That's five syllables!" He bowed, looking very pleased with himself.

"And now, sis. Transportation for the Hunters, you say? Good timing. I was just about ready to roll."

"These demigods will also need a ride," Artemis said, pointing to us. "Some of Chiron's campers."

"No problem!" Apollo checked us out. "Let's see . . . Thalia, right? I've heard all about you."

Thalia blushed. "Hi, Lord Apollo."

"Zeus's girl, yes? Makes you my half sister. Used to be a tree, didn't you? Glad you're back. I hate it when pretty girls turn into trees. Man, I remember one time—"

"Brother," Artemis said. "You should get going."

"Oh, right." Then he looked at me, and his eyes narrowed. "Percy Jackson?"

"Yeah. I mean . . . yes, sir."

It seemed weird calling a teenager "sir," but I'd learned to be careful with immortals. They tended to get offended easily. Then they blew stuff up.

Apollo studied me, but he didn't say anything, which I found a little creepy.

"Well!" he said at last. "We'd better load up, huh? Ride only goes one way—west. And if you miss it, you miss it."

I looked at the Maserati, which would seat two people max. There were about twenty of us.

"Cool car," Nico said.

"Thanks, kid," Apollo said.

"But how will we all fit?"

"Oh." Apollo seemed to notice the problem for the first time. "Well, yeah. I hate to change out of sports-car mode, but I suppose . . ."

He took out his car keys and beeped the security alarm button. *Chirp, chirp.*

For a moment, the car glowed brightly again. When the glare died, the Maserati had been replaced by one of those Turtle Top shuttle buses like we used for school basketball games.

"Right," he said. "Everybody in."

Zoë ordered the Hunters to start loading. She picked up her camping pack, and Apollo said, "Here, sweetheart. Let me get that."

Zoë recoiled. Her eyes flashed murderously.

"Brother," Artemis chided. "You do not help my Hunters. You do not look at, talk to, or flirt with my Hunters. And you do *not* call them sweetheart."

Apollo spread his hands. "Sorry. I forgot. Hey, sis, where are you off to, anyway?"

"Hunting," Artemis said. "It's none of your business."

"I'll find out. I see all. Know all."

Artemis snorted. "Just drop them off, Apollo. And no messing around!"

"No, no! I never mess around."

Artemis rolled her eyes, then looked at us. "I will see you by winter solstice. Zoë, you are in charge of the Hunters. Do well. Do as I would do."

Zoë straightened. "Yes, my lady."

Artemis knelt and touched the ground as if looking for tracks. When she rose, she looked troubled. "So much danger. The beast must be found."

She sprinted toward the woods and melted into the snow and shadows.

Apollo turned and grinned, jangling the car keys on his finger. "So," he said. "Who wants to drive?"

The Hunters piled into the van. They all crammed into the back so they'd be as far away as possible from Apollo and the rest of us highly infectious males. Bianca sat with them, leaving her little brother to hang in the front with us, which seemed cold to me, but Nico didn't seem to mind.

"This is so cool!" Nico said, jumping up and down in the driver's seat. "Is this really the sun? I thought Helios and Selene were the sun and moon gods. How come sometimes it's them and sometimes it's you and Artemis?"

"Downsizing," Apollo said. "The Romans started it. They couldn't afford all those temple sacrifices, so they laid off Helios and Selene and folded their duties into our job descriptions. My sis got the moon. I got the sun. It was pretty annoying at first, but at least I got this cool car."

"But how does it work?" Nico asked. "I thought the sun was a big fiery ball of gas!"

Apollo chuckled and ruffled Nico's hair. "That rumor probably got started because Artemis used to call me a big fiery ball of gas. Seriously, kid, it depends on whether you're talking astronomy or philosophy. You want to talk astronomy? Bah, what fun is that? You want to talk about how humans *think* about the sun? Ah, now that's more interesting. They've got a lot riding on the sun . . . er, so to speak. It keeps them warm, grows their crops, powers engines, makes everything look, well, sunnier. This chariot is built out of human *dreams* about the sun, kid. It's as old as Western

Civilization. Every day, it drives across the sky from east to west, lighting up all those puny little mortal lives. The chariot is a manifestation of the sun's power, the way mortals perceive it. Make sense?"

Nico shook his head. "No."

"Well then, just think of it as a really powerful, really dangerous solar car."

"Can I drive?"

"No. Too young."

"Oo! Oo!" Grover raised his hand.

"Mm, no," Apollo said. "Too furry." He looked past me and focused on Thalia.

"Daughter of Zeus!" he said. "Lord of the sky. Perfect."

"Oh, no." Thalia shook her head. "No, thanks."

"C'mon," Apollo said. "How old are you?"

Thalia hesitated. "I don't know."

It was sad, but true. She'd been turned into a tree when she was twelve, but that had been seven years ago. So she should be nineteen, if you went by years. But she still felt like she was twelve, and if you looked at her, she seemed somewhere in between. The best Chiron could figure, she had kept aging while in tree form, but much more slowly.

Apollo tapped his finger to his lips. "You're fifteen, almost sixteen."

"How do you know that?"

"Hey, I'm the god of prophecy. I know stuff. You'll turn sixteen in about a week."

"That's my birthday! December twenty-second."

"Which means you're old enough now to drive with a learner's permit!"

Thalia shifted her feet nervously. "Uh—"

"I know what you're going to say," Apollo said. "You don't deserve an honor like driving the sun chariot."

"That's not what I was going to say."

"Don't sweat it! Maine to Long Island is a really short trip, and don't worry about what happened to the last kid I trained. You're Zeus's daughter. He's not going to blast *you* out of the sky."

Apollo laughed good-naturedly. The rest of us didn't join him.

Thalia tried to protest, but Apollo was absolutely not going to take "no" for an answer. He hit a button on the dashboard, and a sign popped up along the top of the windshield. I had to read it backward (which, for a dyslexic, really isn't that different than reading forward). I was pretty sure it said WARNING: STUDENT DRIVER.

"Take it away!" Apollo told Thalia. "You're gonna be a natural!"

I'll admit I was jealous. I couldn't wait to start driving. A couple of times that fall, my mom had taken me out to Montauk when the beach road was empty, and she'd let me try out her Mazda. I mean, yeah, that was a Japanese compact, and this was the sun chariot, but how different could it be?

"Speed equals heat," Apollo advised. "So start slowly, and make sure you've got good altitude before you really open her up."

Thalia gripped the wheel so tight her knuckles turned white. She looked like she was going to be sick.

"What's wrong?" I asked her.

"Nothing," she said shakily. "N-nothing is wrong."

She pulled back on the wheel. It tilted, and the bus lurched upward so fast I fell back and crashed against something soft.

"Ow," Grover said.

"Sorry."

"Slower!" Apollo said.

"Sorry!" Thalia said. "I've got it under control!"

I managed to get to my feet. Looking out the window, I saw a smoking ring of trees from the clearing where we'd taken off.

"Thalia," I said, "lighten up on the accelerator."

"I've *got* it, Percy," she said, gritting her teeth. But she kept it floored.

"Loosen up," I told her.

"I'm loose!" Thalia said. She was so stiff she looked like she was made out of plywood.

"We need to veer south for Long Island," Apollo said. "Hang a left."

Thalia jerked the wheel and again threw me into Grover, who yelped.

"The other left," Apollo suggested.

I made the mistake of looking out the window again. We were at airplane height now—so high the sky was starting to look black.

"Ah . . ." Apollo said, and I got the feeling he was

forcing himself to sound calm. "A little lower, sweetheart. Cape Cod is freezing over."

Thalia tilted the wheel. Her face was chalk white, her forehead beaded with sweat. Something was definitely wrong. I'd never seen her like this.

The bus pitched down and somebody screamed. Maybe it was me. Now we were heading straight toward the Atlantic Ocean at a thousand miles an hour, the New England coastline off to our right. And it was getting hot in the bus.

Apollo had been thrown somewhere in the back of the bus, but he started climbing up the rows of seats.

"Take the wheel!" Grover begged him.

"No worries," Apollo said. He looked plenty worried. "She just has to learn to—WHOA!"

I saw what he was seeing. Down below us was a little snow-covered New England town. At least, it used to be snow-covered. As I watched, the snow melted off the trees and the roofs and the lawns. The white steeple on a church turned brown and started to smolder. Little plumes of smoke, like birthday candles, were popping up all over the town. Trees and rooftops were catching fire.

"Pull up!" I yelled.

There was a wild light in Thalia's eyes. She yanked back on the wheel, and I held on this time. As we zoomed up, I could see through the back window that the fires in the town were being snuffed out by the sudden blast of cold.

"There!" Apollo pointed. "Long Island, dead ahead. Let's slow down, dear. 'Dead' is only an expression."

Thalia was thundering toward the coastline of northern Long Island. There was Camp Half-Blood: the valley, the woods, the beach. I could see the dining pavilion and cabins and the amphitheater.

"I'm under control," Thalia muttered. "I'm under control."

We were only a few hundred yards away now.

"Brake," Apollo said.

"I can do this."

"BRAKE!"

Thalia slammed her foot on the brake, and the sun bus pitched forward at a forty-five-degree angle, slamming into the Camp Half-Blood canoe lake with a huge *FLOOOOOOSH!* Steam billowed up, sending several frightened naiads scrambling out of the water with half-woven wicker baskets.

The bus bobbed to the surface, along with a couple of capsized, half-melted canoes.

"Well," said Apollo with a brave smile. "You were right, my dear. You had everything under control! Let's go see if we boiled anyone important, shall we?"

FIVE

I PLACE AN UNDERWATER
PHONE CALL

I'd never seen Camp Half-Blood in winter before, and the snow surprised me.

See, the camp has the ultimate magic climate control. Nothing gets inside the borders unless the director, Mr. D, wants it to. I thought it would be warm and sunny, but instead the snow had been allowed to fall lightly. Frost covered the chariot track and the strawberry fields. The cabins were decorated with tiny flickering lights, like Christmas lights, except they seemed to be balls of real fire. More lights glowed in the woods, and weirdest of all, a fire flickered in the attic window of the Big House, where the Oracle dwelt, imprisoned in an old mummified body. I wondered if the spirit of Delphi was roasting marshmallows up there or something.

"Whoa," Nico said as he climbed off the bus. "Is that a climbing wall?"

"Yeah," I said.

"Why is there lava pouring down it?"

"Little extra challenge. Come on. I'll introduce you to Chiron. Zoë, have you met—"

"I know Chiron," Zoë said stiffly. "Tell him we will be in Cabin Eight. Hunters, follow me."

"I'll show you the way," Grover offered.

"We know the way."

"Oh, really, it's no trouble. It's easy to get lost here, if you don't"—he tripped over a canoe and came up still talking—"like my old daddy goat used to say! Come on!"

Zoë rolled her eyes, but I guess she figured there was no getting rid of Grover. The Hunters shouldered their packs and their bows and headed off toward the cabins. As Bianca di Angelo was leaving, she leaned over and whispered something in her brother's ear. She looked at him for an answer, but Nico just scowled and turned away.

"Take care, sweethearts!" Apollo called after the Hunters. He winked at me. "Watch out for those prophecies, Percy. I'll see you soon."

"What do you mean?"

Instead of answering, he hopped back in the bus. "Later, Thalia," he called. "And, uh, be good!"

He gave her a wicked smile, as if he knew something she didn't. Then he closed the doors and revved the engine. I turned aside as the sun chariot took off in a blast of heat. When I looked back, the lake was steaming. A red Maserati soared over the woods, glowing brighter and climbing higher until it disappeared in a ray of sunlight.

Nico was still looking grumpy. I wondered what his sister had told him.

"Who's Chiron?" he asked. "I don't have his figurine."

"Our activities director," I said. "He's . . . well, you'll see."

"If those Hunter girls don't like him," Nico grumbled, "that's good enough for me. Let's go."

The second thing that surprised me about camp was how empty it was. I mean, I knew most half-bloods only trained during the summer. Just the year-rounders would be here— the ones who didn't have homes to go to, or would get attacked by monsters too much if they left. But there didn't even seem to be many of them, either.

I spotted Charles Beckendorf from the Hephaestus cabin stoking the forge outside the camp armory. The Stoll brothers, Travis and Connor, from the Hermes cabin, were picking the lock on the camp store. A few kids from the Ares cabin were having a snowball fight with the wood nymphs at the edge of the forest. That was about it. Even my old rival from the Ares cabin, Clarisse, didn't seem to be around.

The Big House was decorated with strings of red and yellow fireballs that warmed the porch but didn't seem to catch anything on fire. Inside, flames crackled in the hearth. The air smelled like hot chocolate. Mr. D, the camp director, and Chiron were playing a quiet game of cards in the parlor.

Chiron's brown beard was shaggier for the winter. His curly hair had grown a little longer. He wasn't posing as a teacher this year, so I guess he could afford to be casual. He wore a fuzzy sweater with a hoofprint design on it, and he had a blanket on his lap that almost hid his wheelchair completely.

He smiled when he saw us. "Percy! Thalia! Ah, and this must be—"

"Nico di Angelo," I said. "He and his sister are half-bloods."

Chiron breathed a sigh of relief. "You succeeded, then."

"Well . . ."

His smile melted. "What's wrong? And where is Annabeth?"

"Oh, dear," Mr. D said in a bored voice. "Not another one lost."

I'd been trying not to pay attention to Mr. D, but he was kind of hard to ignore in his neon orange leopard-skin warm-up suit and his purple running shoes. (Like Mr. D had ever run a day in his immortal life.) A golden laurel wreath was tilted sideways on his curly black hair, which must've meant he'd won the last hand of cards.

"What do you mean?" Thalia asked. "Who else is lost?"

Just then, Grover trotted into the room, grinning like crazy. He had a black eye and red lines on his face that looked like a slap mark. "The Hunters are all moved in!"

Chiron frowned. "The Hunters, eh? I see we have much to talk about." He glanced at Nico. "Grover, perhaps you should take our young friend to the den and show him our orientation film."

"But . . . Oh, right. Yes, sir."

"Orientation film?" Nico asked. "Is it G or PG? 'Cause Bianca is kinda strict—"

"It's PG-13," Grover said.

"Cool!" Nico happily followed him out of the room.

"Now," Chiron said to Thalia and me, "perhaps you two should sit down and tell us the whole story."

When we were done, Chiron turned to Mr. D. "We should launch a search for Annabeth immediately."

"I'll go," Thalia and I said at the same time.

Mr. D sniffed. "Certainly not!"

Thalia and I both started complaining, but Mr. D held up his hand. He had that purplish angry fire in his eyes that usually meant something bad and godly was going to happen if we didn't shut up.

"From what you have told me," Mr. D said, "we have broken even on this escapade. We have, ah, regrettably lost Annie Bell—"

"Annabeth," I snapped. She'd gone to camp since she was seven, and still Mr. D pretended not to know her name.

"Yes, yes," he said. "And you procured a small annoying boy to replace her. So I see no point risking further half-bloods on a ridiculous rescue. The possibility is very great that this Annie girl is dead."

I wanted to strangle Mr. D. It wasn't fair Zeus had sent him here to dry out as camp director for a hundred years. It was meant to be a punishment for Mr. D's bad behavior on Olympus, but it ended up being a punishment for all of us.

"Annabeth may be alive," Chiron said, but I could tell he was having trouble sounding upbeat. He'd practically raised Annabeth all those years she was a year-round camper, before she'd given living with her dad and stepmom a second try. "She's very bright. If . . . if our enemies have her,

[60]

she will try to play for time. She may even pretend to cooperate."

"That's right," Thalia said. "Luke would want her alive."

"In which case," said Mr. D, "I'm afraid she will have to be smart enough to escape on her own."

I got up from the table.

"Percy." Chiron's tone was full of warning. In the back of my mind, I knew Mr. D was not somebody to mess with. Even if you were an impulsive ADHD kid like me, he wouldn't give you any slack. But I was so angry I didn't care.

"You're glad to lose another camper," I said. "You'd like it if we all disappeared!"

Mr. D stifled a yawn. "You have a point?"

"Yeah," I growled. "Just because you were sent here as a punishment doesn't mean you have to be a lazy jerk! This is your civilization, too. Maybe you could try helping out a little!"

For a second, there was no sound except the crackle of the fire. The light reflected in Mr. D's eyes, giving him a sinister look. He opened his mouth to say something—probably a curse that would blast me to smithereens—when Nico burst into the room, followed by Grover.

"SO COOL!" Nico yelled, holding his hands out to Chiron. "You're . . . you're a centaur!"

Chiron managed a nervous smile. "Yes, Mr. di Angelo, if you please. Though, I prefer to stay in human form in this wheelchair for, ah, first encounters."

"And, whoa!" He looked at Mr. D. "You're the wine dude? No way!"

Mr. D turned his eyes away from me and gave Nico a look of loathing. "The wine dude?"

"Dionysus, right? Oh, wow! I've got your figurine."

"My figurine."

"In my game, Mythomagic. And a holofoil card, too! And even though you've only got like five hundred attack points and everybody thinks you're the lamest god card, I totally think your powers are sweet!"

"Ah." Mr. D seemed truly perplexed, which probably saved my life. "Well, that's . . . gratifying."

"Percy," Chiron said quickly, "you and Thalia go down to the cabins. Inform the campers we'll be playing capture the flag tomorrow evening."

"Capture the flag?" I asked. "But we don't have enough—"

"It is a tradition," Chiron said. "A friendly match, whenever the Hunters visit."

"Yeah," Thalia muttered. "I bet it's real friendly."

Chiron jerked his head toward Mr. D, who was still frowning as Nico talked about how many defense points all the gods had in his game. "Run along now," Chiron told us.

"Oh, right," Thalia said. "Come on, Percy."

She hauled me out of the Big House before Dionysus could remember that he wanted to kill me.

"You've already got Ares on your bad side," Thalia reminded me as we trudged toward the cabins. "You need another immortal enemy?"

She was right. My first summer as a camper, I'd gotten

in a fight with Ares, and now he and all his children wanted to kill me. I didn't need to make Dionysus mad, too.

"Sorry," I said. "I couldn't help it. It's just so unfair."

She stopped by the armory and looked out across the valley, toward the top of Half-Blood Hill. Her pine tree was still there, the Golden Fleece glittering in its lowest branch. The tree's magic still protected the borders of camp, but it no longer used Thalia's spirit for power.

"Percy, everything is unfair," Thalia muttered. "Sometimes I wish . . ."

She didn't finish, but her tone was so sad I felt sorry for her. With her ragged black hair and her black punk clothes, an old wool overcoat wrapped around her, she looked like some kind of huge raven, completely out of place in the white landscape.

"We'll get Annabeth back," I promised. "I just don't know how yet."

"First I found out that Luke is lost," she said. "Now Annabeth—"

"Don't think like that."

"You're right." She straightened up. "We'll find a way."

Over at the basketball court, a few of the Hunters were shooting hoops. One of them was arguing with a guy from the Ares cabin. The Ares kid had his hand on his sword and the Hunter girl looked like she was going to exchange her basketball for a bow and arrow any second.

"I'll break that up," Thalia said. "You circulate around the cabins. Tell everybody about capture the flag tomorrow."

"All right. You should be team captain."

"No, no," she said. "You've been at camp longer. You do it."

"We can, uh . . . co-captain or something."

She looked about as comfortable with that as I felt, but she nodded.

As she headed for the court, I said, "Hey, Thalia."

"Yeah?"

"I'm sorry about what happened at Westover. I should've waited for you guys."

"'S okay, Percy. I probably would've done the same thing." She shifted from foot to foot, like she was trying to decide whether or not to say more. "You know, you asked about my mom and I kinda snapped at you. It's just . . . I went back to find her after seven years, and I found out she died in Los Angeles. She, um . . . she was a heavy drinker, and apparently she was out driving late one night about two years ago, and . . ." Thalia blinked hard.

"I'm sorry."

"Yeah, well. It's . . . it's not like we were ever close. I ran away when I was ten. Best two years of my life were when I was running around with Luke and Annabeth. But still—"

"That's why you had trouble with the sun van."

She gave me a wary look. "What do you mean?"

"The way you stiffened up. You must've been thinking about your mom, not wanting to get behind the wheel."

I was sorry I'd said anything. Thalia's expression was dangerously close to Zeus's, the one time I'd seen him get angry—like any minute, her eyes would shoot a million volts.

"Yeah," she muttered. "Yeah, that must've been it."

She trudged off toward the court, where the Ares camper and the Hunter were trying to kill each other with a sword and a basketball.

The cabins were the weirdest collection of buildings you've ever seen. Zeus and Hera's big white-columned buildings, Cabins One and Two, stood in the middle, with five gods' cabins on the left and five goddesses' cabins on the right, so they all made a U around the central green and the barbecue hearth.

I made the rounds, telling everybody about capture the flag. I woke up some Ares kid from his midday nap and he yelled at me to go away. When I asked him where Clarisse was he said, "Went on a quest for Chiron. Top secret!"

"Is she okay?"

"Haven't heard from her in a month. She's missing in action. Like your butt's gonna be if you don't get outta here!"

I decided to let him go back to sleep.

Finally I got to Cabin Three, the cabin of Poseidon. It was a low gray building hewn from sea stone, with shells and coral fossils imprinted in the rock. Inside, it was just as empty as always, except for my bunk. A Minotaur horn hung on the wall next to my pillow.

I took Annabeth's baseball cap out of my backpack and set it on my nightstand. I'd give it to her when I found her. And I *would* find her.

I took off my wristwatch and activated the shield. It creaked noisily as it spiraled out. Dr. Thorn's spikes had dented the brass in a dozen places. One gash kept the shield from opening all the way, so it looked like a pizza with two slices missing. The beautiful metal pictures that my brother had crafted were all banged up. In the picture of me and Annabeth fighting the Hydra, it looked like a meteor had made a crater in my head. I hung the shield on its hook, next to the Minotaur horn, but it was painful to look at now. Maybe Beckendorf from the Hephaestus cabin could fix it for me. He was the best armorsmith in the camp. I'd ask him at dinner.

I was staring at the shield when I noticed a strange sound—water gurgling—and I realized there was something new in the room. At the back of the cabin was a big basin of gray sea rock, with a spout like the head of a fish carved in stone. Out of its mouth burst a stream of water, a saltwater spring that trickled into the pool. The water must've been hot, because it sent mist into the cold winter air like a sauna. It made the room feel warm and summery, fresh with the smell of the sea.

I stepped up to the pool. There was no note attached or anything, but I knew it could only be a gift from Poseidon.

I looked into the water and said, "Thanks, Dad."

The surface rippled. At the bottom of the pool, coins shimmered—a dozen or so golden drachma. I realized what the fountain was for. It was a reminder to keep in touch with my family.

I opened the nearest window, and the wintry sunlight made a rainbow in the mist. Then I fished a coin out of the hot water.

"Iris, O Goddess of the Rainbow," I said, "accept my offering."

I tossed a coin into the mist and it disappeared. Then I realized I didn't know who to contact first.

My mom? That would've been the "good son" thing to do, but she wouldn't be worried about me yet. She was used to me disappearing for days or weeks at a time.

My father? It had been way too long, almost two years, since I'd actually talked to him. But could you even send an Iris-message to a god? I'd never tried. Would it make them mad, like a sales call or something?

I hesitated. Then I made up my mind.

"Show me Tyson," I requested. "At the forges of the Cyclopes."

The mist shimmered, and the image of my half brother appeared. He was surrounded in fire, which would've been a problem if he weren't a Cyclops. He was bent over an anvil, hammering a red-hot sword blade. Sparks flew and flames swirled around his body. There was a marble-framed window behind him, and it looked out onto dark blue water— the bottom of the ocean.

"Tyson!" I yelled.

He didn't hear me at first because of the hammering and the roar of the flames.

"TYSON!"

He turned, and his one enormous eye widened. His face broke into a crooked yellow grin. "Percy!"

He dropped the sword blade and ran at me, trying to give me a hug. The vision blurred and I instinctively lurched back. "Tyson, it's an Iris-message. I'm not really here."

"Oh." He came back into view, looking embarrassed. "Oh, I knew that. Yes."

"How are you?" I asked. "How's the job?"

His eye lit up. "Love the job! Look!" He picked up the hot sword blade with his bare hands. "I made this!"

"That's really cool."

"I wrote my name on it. Right there."

"Awesome. Listen, do you talk to Dad much?"

Tyson's smile faded. "Not much. Daddy is busy. He is worried about the war."

"What do you mean?"

Tyson sighed. He stuck the sword blade out the window, where it made a cloud of boiling bubbles. When Tyson brought it back in, the metal was cool. "Old sea spirits making trouble. Aigaios. Oceanus. Those guys."

I sort of knew what he was talking about. He meant the immortals who ruled the oceans back in the days of the Titans. Before the Olympians took over. The fact that they were back now, with the Titan Lord Kronos and his allies gaining strength, was not good.

"Is there anything I can do?" I asked.

Tyson shook his head sadly. "We are arming the mermaids. They need a thousand more swords by tomorrow." He looked at his sword blade and sighed. "Old spirits are protecting the bad boat."

"The *Princess Andromeda*?" I said. "Luke's boat?"

"Yes. They make it hard to find. Protect it from Daddy's storms. Otherwise he would smash it."

"Smashing it would be good."

Tyson perked up, as if he'd just had another thought. "Annabeth! Is she there?"

"Oh, well . . ." My heart felt like a bowling ball. Tyson thought Annabeth was just about the coolest thing since peanut butter (and he seriously loved peanut butter). I didn't have the heart to tell him she was missing. He'd start crying so bad he'd probably put out his fires. "Well, no . . . she's not here right now."

"Tell her hello!" He beamed. "Hello to Annabeth!"

"Okay." I fought back a lump in my throat. "I'll do that."

"And, Percy, don't worry about the bad boat. It is going away."

"What do you mean?"

"Panama Canal! Very far away."

I frowned. Why would Luke take his demon-infested cruise ship all the way down there? The last time we'd seen him, he'd been cruising along the East Coast, recruiting half-bloods and training his monstrous army.

"All right," I said, not feeling reassured. "That's . . . good. I guess."

In the forges, a deep voice bellowed something I couldn't make out. Tyson flinched. "Got to get back to work! Boss will get mad. Good luck, Brother!"

"Okay, tell Dad—"

But before I could finish, the vision shimmered and faded. I was alone again in my cabin, feeling even lonelier than before.

* * *

I was pretty miserable at dinner that night.

I mean, the food was excellent as usual. You can't go wrong with barbecue, pizza, and never-empty soda goblets. The torches and braziers kept the outdoor pavilion warm, but we all had to sit with our cabin mates, which meant I was alone at the Poseidon table. Thalia sat alone at the Zeus table, but we couldn't sit together. Camp rules. At least the Hephaestus, Ares, and Hermes cabins had a few people each. Nico sat with the Stoll brothers, since new campers always got stuck in the Hermes cabin if their Olympian parent was unknown. The Stoll brothers seemed to be trying to convince Nico that poker was a much better game than Mythomagic. I hoped Nico didn't have any money to lose.

The only table that really seemed to be having a good time was the Artemis table. The Hunters drank and ate and laughed like one big happy family. Zoë sat at the head like she was the mama. She didn't laugh as much as the others, but she did smile from time to time. Her silver lieutenant's band glittered in the dark braids of her hair. I thought she looked a lot nicer when she smiled. Bianca di Angelo seemed to be having a great time. She was trying to learn how to arm wrestle from the big girl who'd picked a fight with the Ares kid on the basketball court. The bigger girl was beating her every time, but Bianca didn't seem to mind.

When we'd finished eating, Chiron made the customary toast to the gods and formally welcomed the Hunters of Artemis. The clapping was pretty halfhearted. Then he announced the "good will" capture-the-flag game for tomorrow night, which got a lot better reception.

Afterward, we all trailed back to our cabins for an early, winter lights out. I was exhausted, which meant I fell asleep easily. That was the good part. The bad part was, I had a nightmare, and even by my standards it was a whopper.

Annabeth was on a dark hillside, shrouded in fog. It almost seemed like the Underworld, because I immediately felt claustrophobic and I couldn't see the sky above—just a close, heavy darkness, as if I were in a cave.

Annabeth struggled up the hill. Old broken Greek columns of black marble were scattered around, as though something had blasted a huge building to ruins.

"Thorn!" Annabeth cried. "Where are you? Why did you bring me here?" She scrambled over a section of broken wall and came to the crest of the hill.

She gasped.

There was Luke. And he was in pain.

He was crumpled on the rocky ground, trying to rise. The blackness seemed to be thicker around him, fog swirling hungrily. His clothes were in tatters and his face was scratched and drenched with sweat.

"Annabeth!" he called. "Help me! Please!"

She ran forward.

I tried to cry out: *He's a traitor! Don't trust him!*

But my voice didn't work in the dream.

Annabeth had tears in her eyes. She reached down like she wanted to touch Luke's face, but at the last second she hesitated.

"What happened?" she asked.

"They left me here," Luke groaned. "Please. It's killing me."

I couldn't see what was wrong with him. He seemed to be struggling against some invisible curse, as though the fog were squeezing him to death.

"Why should I trust you?" Annabeth asked. Her voice was filled with hurt.

"You shouldn't," Luke said. "I've been terrible to you. But if you don't help me, I'll die."

Let him die, I wanted to scream. Luke had tried to kill us in cold blood too many times. He didn't deserve anything from Annabeth.

Then the darkness above Luke began to crumble, like a cavern roof in an earthquake. Huge chunks of black rock began falling. Annabeth rushed in just as a crack appeared, and the whole ceiling dropped. She held it somehow—tons of rock. She kept it from collapsing on her and Luke just with her own strength. It was impossible. She shouldn't have been able to do that.

Luke rolled free, gasping. "Thanks," he managed.

"Help me hold it," Annabeth groaned.

Luke caught his breath. His face was covered in grime and sweat. He rose unsteadily.

"I knew I could count on you." He began to walk away as the trembling blackness threatened to crush Annabeth.

"HELP ME!" she pleaded.

"Oh, don't worry," Luke said. "Your help is on the way. It's all part of the plan. In the meantime, try not to die."

The ceiling of darkness began to crumble again, pushing Annabeth against the ground.

I sat bolt upright in bed, clawing at the sheets. There was no sound in my cabin except the gurgle of the saltwater spring. The clock on my nightstand read just after midnight.

Only a dream, but I was sure of two things: Annabeth was in terrible danger. And Luke was responsible.

SIX

AN OLD DEAD FRIEND COMES TO VISIT

The next morning after breakfast, I told Grover about my dream. We sat in the meadow watching the satyrs chase the wood nymphs through the snow. The nymphs had promised to kiss the satyrs if they got caught, but they hardly ever did. Usually the nymph would let the satyr get up a full head of steam, then she'd turn into a snow-covered tree and the poor satyr would slam into it headfirst and get a pile of snow dumped on him.

When I told Grover my nightmare, he started twirling his finger in his shaggy leg fur.

"A cave ceiling collapsed on her?" he asked.

"Yeah. What the heck does that mean?"

Grover shook his head. "I don't know. But after what Zoë dreamed—"

"Whoa. What do you mean? Zoë had a dream like that?"

"I . . . I don't know, exactly. About three in the morning she came to the Big House and demanded to talk to Chiron. She looked really panicked."

"Wait, how do you know this?"

Grover blushed. "I was sort of camped outside the Artemis cabin."

"What for?"

"Just to be, you know, near them."

"You're a stalker with hooves."

"I am not! Anyway, I followed her to the Big House and hid in a bush and watched the whole thing. She got real upset when Argus wouldn't let her in. It was kind of a dangerous scene."

I tried to imagine that. Argus was the head of security for camp—a big blond dude with eyes all over his body. He rarely showed himself unless something serious was going on. I wouldn't want to place bets on a fight between him and Zoë Nightshade.

"What did she say?" I asked.

Grover grimaced. "Well, she starts talking really old-fashioned when she gets upset, so it was kind of hard to understand. But something about Artemis being in trouble and needing the Hunters. And then she called Argus a boil-brained lout . . . I think that's a bad thing. And then he called her—"

"Whoa, wait. How could Artemis be in trouble?"

"I . . . well, finally Chiron came out in his pajamas and his horse tail in curlers and—"

"He wears curlers in his tail?"

Grover covered his mouth.

"Sorry," I said. "Go on."

"Well, Zoë said she needed permission to leave camp immediately. Chiron refused. He reminded Zoë that the Hunters were supposed to stay here until they received orders from Artemis. And she said . . ." Grover gulped. "She said 'How are we to get orders from Artemis if Artemis is lost?'"

"What do you mean lost? Like she needs directions?"

"No. I think she meant gone. Taken. Kidnapped."

"Kidnapped?" I tried to get my mind around that idea. "How would you kidnap an immortal goddess? Is that even possible?"

"Well, yeah. I mean, it happened to Persephone."

"But she was like, the goddess of *flowers*."

Grover looked offended. "Springtime."

"Whatever. Artemis is a lot more powerful than that. Who could kidnap her? And why?"

Grover shook his head miserably. "I don't know. Kronos?"

"He can't be that powerful already. Can he?"

The last time we'd seen Kronos, he'd been in tiny pieces. Well . . . we hadn't actually *seen* him. Thousands of years ago, after the big Titan–God war, the gods had sliced him to bits with his own scythe and scattered his remains in Tartarus, which is like the gods' bottomless recycling bin for their enemies. Two summers ago, Kronos had tricked us to the very edge of the pit and almost pulled us in. Then last summer, on board Luke's demon cruise ship, we'd seen a golden coffin, where Luke claimed he was summoning the Titan Lord out of the abyss, bit by bit, every time someone new joined their cause. Kronos could influence people with dreams and trick them, but I didn't see how he could physically overcome Artemis if he was still like a pile of evil bark mulch.

"I don't know," Grover said. "I think somebody would know if Kronos had re-formed. The gods would be more nervous. But still, it's weird, you having a nightmare the same night as Zoë. It's almost like—"

"They're connected," I said.

Over in the frozen meadow, a satyr skidded on his hooves as he chased after a redheaded tree nymph. She giggled and held out her arms as he ran toward her. *Pop!* She turned into a Scotch pine and he kissed the trunk at top speed.

"Ah, love," Grover said dreamily.

I thought about Zoë's nightmare, which she'd had only a few hours after mine.

"I've got to talk to Zoë," I said.

"Um, before you do . . ." Grover took something out of his coat pocket. It was a three-fold display like a travel brochure. "You remember what you said—about how it was weird the Hunters just happened to show up at Westover Hall? I think they might've been scouting us."

"Scouting us? What do you mean?"

He gave me the brochure. It was about the Hunters of Artemis. The front read, A WISE CHOICE FOR YOUR FUTURE! Inside were pictures of young maidens doing hunter stuff, chasing monsters, shooting bows. There were captions like: HEALTH BENEFITS: IMMORTALITY AND WHAT IT MEANS FOR YOU! and A BOY-FREE TOMORROW!

"I found that in Annabeth's backpack," Grover said.

I stared at him. "I don't understand."

"Well, it seems to me . . . maybe Annabeth was thinking about joining."

* * *

I'd like to say I took the news well.

The truth was, I wanted to strangle the Hunters of Artemis one eternal maiden at a time. The rest of the day I tried to keep busy, but I was worried sick about Annabeth. I went to javelin-throwing class, but the Ares camper in charge chewed me out after I got distracted and threw the javelin at the target before he got out of the way. I apologized for the hole in his pants, but he still sent me packing.

I visited the pegasus stables, but Silena Beauregard from the Aphrodite cabin was having an argument with one of the Hunters, and I decided I'd better not get involved.

After that, I sat in the empty chariot stands and sulked. Down at the archery fields, Chiron was conducting target practice. I knew he'd be the best person to talk to. Maybe he could give me some advice, but something held me back. I had a feeling Chiron would try to protect me, like he always did. He might not tell me everything he knew.

I looked the other direction. At the top of Half-Blood Hill, Mr. D and Argus were feeding the baby dragon that guarded the Golden Fleece.

Then it occurred to me: no one would be in the Big House. There was someone else . . . some*thing* else I could ask for guidance.

My blood was humming in my ears as I ran into the house and took the stairs. I'd only done this once before, and I still had nightmares about it. I opened the trap door and stepped into the attic.

The room was dark and dusty and cluttered with junk, just like I remembered. There were shields with monster bites out of them, and swords bent in the shapes of daemon heads, and a bunch of taxidermy, like a stuffed harpy and a bright orange python.

Over by the window, sitting on a three-legged stool, was the shriveled-up mummy of an old lady in a tie-dyed hippie dress. The Oracle.

I made myself walk toward her. I waited for green mist to billow from the mummy's mouth, like it had before, but nothing happened.

"Hi," I said. "Uh, what's up?"

I winced at how stupid that sounded. Not much could be "up" when you're dead and stuck in the attic. But I knew the spirit of the Oracle was in there somewhere. I could feel a cold presence in the room, like a coiled sleeping snake.

"I have a question," I said a little louder. "I need to know about Annabeth. How can I save her?"

No answer. The sun slanted through the dirty attic window, lighting the dust motes dancing in the air.

I waited longer.

Then I got angry. I was being stonewalled by a corpse.

"All right," I said. "Fine. I'll figure it out myself."

I turned and bumped into a big table full of souvenirs. It seemed more cluttered than the last time I was here. Heroes stored all kinds of stuff in the attic: quest trophies they no longer wanted to keep in their cabins, or stuff that held painful memories. I knew Luke had stored a dragon claw somewhere up here—the one that had scarred his face.

There was a broken sword hilt labeled: *This broke and Leroy got killed. 1999.*

Then I noticed a pink silk scarf with a label attached to it. I picked up the tag and tried to read it:

SCARF OF THE GODDESS APHRODITE

RECOVERED AT WATERLAND, DENVER, CO.,

BY ANNABETH CHASE AND PERCY JACKSON

I stared at the scarf. I'd totally forgotten about it. Two years ago, Annabeth had ripped this scarf out of my hands and said something like, *Oh, no. No love magic for you!*

I'd just assumed she'd thrown it away. And yet here it was. She'd kept it all this time? And why had she stashed it in the attic?

I turned to the mummy. She hadn't moved, but the shadows across her face made it look like she was smiling gruesomely.

I dropped the scarf and tried not to run toward the exit.

That night after dinner, I was seriously ready to beat the Hunters at capture the flag. It was going to be a small game: only thirteen Hunters, including Bianca di Angelo, and about the same number of campers.

Zoë Nightshade looked pretty upset. She kept glancing resentfully at Chiron, like she couldn't believe he was making her do this. The other Hunters didn't look too happy, either. Unlike last night, they weren't laughing or joking around. They just huddled together in the dining pavilion, whispering nervously to each other as they strapped on their armor. Some of them even looked like they'd been crying. I guess Zoë had told them about her nightmare.

On our team, we had Beckendorf and two other Hephaestus guys, a few from the Ares cabin (though it still seemed strange that Clarisse wasn't around), the Stoll brothers and Nico from Hermes cabin, and a few Aphrodite kids. It was weird that the Aphrodite cabin wanted to play. Usually they sat on the sidelines, chatted, and checked their reflections in the river and stuff, but when they heard we were fighting the Hunters, they were raring to go.

"I'll show them 'love is worthless,'" Silena Beauregard grumbled as she strapped on her armor. "I'll pulverize them!"

That left Thalia and me.

"I'll take the offense," Thalia volunteered. "You take defense."

"Oh." I hesitated, because I'd been about to say the exact same thing, only reversed. "Don't you think with your shield and all, you'd be better defense?"

Thalia already had Aegis on her arm, and even our own teammates were giving her a wide berth, trying not to cower before the bronze head of Medusa.

"Well, I was thinking it would make better offense," Thalia said. "Besides, you've had more practice at defense."

I wasn't sure if she was teasing me. I'd had some pretty bad experiences with defense on capture the flag. My first year, Annabeth had put me out as a kind of bait, and I'd almost been gored to death with spears and killed by a hellhound.

"Yeah, no problem," I lied.

"Cool." Thalia turned to help some of the Aphrodite kids, who were having trouble suiting up their armor without breaking their nails. Nico di Angelo ran up to me with a big grin on his face.

"Percy, this is awesome!" His blue-feathered bronze helmet was falling in his eyes, and his breastplate was about six sizes too big. I wondered if there was any way I'd looked that ridiculous when I'd first arrived. Unfortunately, I probably had.

Nico lifted his sword with effort. "Do we get to kill the other team?"

"Well . . . no."

"But the Hunters are immortal, right?"

"That's only if they don't fall in battle. Besides——"

"It would be awesome if we just, like, resurrected as soon as we were killed, so we could keep fighting, and——"

"Nico, this is serious. Real swords. These can hurt."

He stared at me, a little disappointed, and I realized that I'd just sounded like my mother. Whoa. Not a good sign.

I patted Nico on the shoulder. "Hey, it's cool. Just follow the team. Stay out of Zoë's way. We'll have a blast."

Chiron's hoof thundered on the pavilion floor.

"Heroes!" he called. "You know the rules! The creek is the boundary line. Blue team—Camp Half-Blood—shall take the west woods. Hunters of Artemis—red team—shall take the east woods. I will serve as referee and battlefield medic. No intentional maiming, please! All magic items are allowed. To your positions!"

"Sweet," Nico whispered next to me. "What kind of magic items? Do I get one?"

I was about to break it to him that he didn't, when Thalia said, "Blue team! Follow me!"

They cheered and followed. I had to run to catch up, and tripped over somebody's shield, so I didn't look much like a co-captain. More like an idiot.

We set our flag at the top of Zeus's Fist. It's this cluster of boulders in the middle of the west woods that, if you look at it just the right way, looks like a huge fist sticking out of the ground. If you look at it from any other side, it looks like a pile of enormous deer droppings, but Chiron wouldn't let us call the place the Poop Pile, especially after it had been named for Zeus, who doesn't have much of a sense of humor.

Anyway, it was a good place to set the flag. The top boulder was twenty feet tall and really hard to climb, so the flag was clearly visible, like the rules said it had to be, and it didn't matter that the guards weren't allowed to stand within ten yards of it.

I set Nico on guard duty with Beckendorf and the Stoll brothers, figuring he'd be safely out of the way.

"We'll send out a decoy to the left," Thalia told the team. "Silena, you lead that."

"Got it!"

"Take Laurel and Jason. They're good runners. Make a wide arc around the Hunters, attract as many as you can. I'll take the main raiding party around to the right and catch them by surprise."

Everybody nodded. It sounded good, and Thalia said it with such confidence you couldn't help but believe it would work.

Thalia looked at me. "Anything to add, Percy?"

"Um, yeah. Keep sharp on defense. We've got four guards, two scouts. That's not much for a big forest. I'll be roving. Yell if you need help."

"And don't leave your post!" Thalia said.

"Unless you see a golden opportunity," I added.

Thalia scowled. "Just don't leave your post."

"Right, unless—"

"Percy!" She touched my arm and shocked me. I mean, everybody can give static shocks in the winter, but when Thalia does, it hurts. I guess it's because her dad is the god of lightning. She's been known to fry off people's eyebrows.

"Sorry," Thalia said, though she didn't sound particularly sorry. "Now, is everybody clear?"

Everybody nodded. We broke into our smaller groups. The horn sounded, and the game began.

Silena's group disappeared into the woods on the left. Thalia's group gave it a few seconds, then darted off toward the right.

I waited for something to happen. I climbed Zeus's Fist and had a good view over the forest. I remembered how the Hunters had stormed out of the woods when they fought the manticore, and I was prepared for something like that— one huge charge that could overwhelm us. But nothing happened.

I caught a glimpse of Silena and her two scouts. They

ran through a clearing, followed by five of the Hunters, leading them deep into the woods and away from Thalia. The plan seemed to be working. Then I spotted another clump of Hunters heading to the right, bows ready. They must've spotted Thalia.

"What's happening?" Nico demanded, trying to climb up next to me.

My mind was racing. Thalia would never get through, but the Hunters were divided. With that many on either flank, their center had to be wide open. If I moved fast . . .

I looked at Beckendorf. "Can you guys hold the fort?"

Beckendorf snorted. "Of course."

"I'm going in."

The Stoll brothers and Nico cheered as I raced toward the boundary line.

I was running at top speed and I felt great. I leaped over the creek into enemy territory. I could see their silver flag up ahead, only one guard, who wasn't even looking in my direction. I heard fighting to my left and right, somewhere in the woods. I had it made.

The guard turned at the last minute. It was Bianca di Angelo. Her eyes widened as I slammed into her and she went sprawling in the snow.

"Sorry!" I yelled. I ripped down the silver silk flag from the tree and took off.

I was ten yards away before Bianca managed to yell for help. I thought I was home free.

ZIP! A silvery cord raced across my ankles and fastened to the tree next to me. A trip wire, fired from a bow! Before

I could even think about stopping, I went down hard, sprawling in the snow.

"Percy!" Thalia yelled, off to my left. "What are you *doing?*"

Before she reached me, an arrow exploded at her feet and a cloud of yellow smoke billowed around her team. They started coughing and gagging. I could smell the gas from across the woods—the horrible smell of sulfur.

"No fair!" Thalia gasped. "Fart arrows are unsportsmanlike!"

I got up and started running again. Only a few more yards to the creek and I had the game. More arrows whizzed past my ears. A Hunter came out of nowhere and slashed at me with her knife, but I parried and kept running.

I heard yelling from our side of the creek. Beckendorf and Nico were running toward me. I thought they were coming to welcome me back, but then I saw they were chasing someone—Zoë Nightshade, racing toward me like a cheetah, dodging campers with no trouble. And she had our flag in her hands.

"No!" I yelled, and poured on the speed.

I was two feet from the water when Zoë bolted across to her own side, slamming into me for good measure. The Hunters cheered as both sides converged on the creek. Chiron appeared out of the woods, looking grim. He had the Stoll brothers on his back, and it looked as if both of them had taken some nasty whacks to the head. Connor Stoll had two arrows sticking out of his helmet like antennae.

"The Hunters win!" Chiron announced without pleasure. Then he muttered, "For the fifty-sixth time in a row."

"Perseus Jackson!" Thalia yelled, storming toward me. She smelled like rotten eggs, and she was so mad that blue sparks flickered on her armor. Everybody cringed and backed up because of Aegis. It took all my willpower not to cower.

"What in the name of the gods were you THINK-ING?" she bellowed.

I balled my fists. I'd had enough bad stuff happen to me for one day. I didn't need this. "I got the flag, Thalia!" I shook it in her face. "I saw a chance and I took it!"

"I WAS AT THEIR BASE!" Thalia yelled. "But the flag was gone. If you hadn't butted in, we would've won."

"You had too many on you!"

"Oh, so it's my fault?"

"I didn't say that."

"Argh!" Thalia pushed me, and a shock went through my body that blew me backward ten feet into the water. Some of the campers gasped. A couple of the Hunters stifled laughs.

"Sorry!" Thalia said, turning pale. "I didn't mean to—"

Anger roared in my ears. A wave erupted from the creek, blasting into Thalia's face and dousing her from head to toe.

I stood up. "Yeah," I growled. "I didn't mean to, either."

Thalia was breathing heavily.

"Enough!" Chiron ordered.

But Thalia held out her spear. "You want some, Seaweed Brain?"

Somehow, it was okay when Annabeth called me that—at least, I'd gotten used to it—but hearing it from Thalia was not cool.

"Bring it on, Pinecone Face!"

I raised Riptide, but before I could even defend myself, Thalia yelled, and a blast of lightning came down from the sky, hit her spear like a lightning rod, and slammed into my chest.

I sat down hard. There was a burning smell; I had a feeling it was my clothes.

"Thalia!" Chiron said. "That is *enough!*"

I got to my feet and willed the entire creek to rise. It swirled up, hundreds of gallons of water in a massive icy funnel cloud.

"Percy!" Chiron pleaded.

I was about to hurl it at Thalia when I saw something in the woods. I lost my anger and my concentration all at once. The water splashed back into the creekbed. Thalia was so surprised she turned to see what I was looking at.

Someone . . . something was approaching. It was shrouded in a murky green mist, but as it got closer, the campers and Hunters gasped.

"This is impossible," Chiron said. I'd never heard him sound so nervous. "It . . . she has never left the attic. Never."

And yet, the withered mummy that held the Oracle shuffled forward until she stood in the center of the group. Mist curled around our feet, turning the snow a sickly shade of green.

None of us dared move. Then her voice hissed inside

my head. Apparently everyone could hear it, because several clutched their hands over the ears.

I am the spirit of Delphi, the voice said. *Speaker of the prophecies of Phoebus Apollo, slayer of the mighty Python.*

The Oracle regarded me with its cold, dead eyes. Then she turned unmistakably toward Zoë Nightshade. *Approach, Seeker, and ask.*

Zoë swallowed. "What must I do to help my goddess?"

The Oracle's mouth opened, and green mist poured out. I saw the vague image of a mountain, and a girl standing at the barren peak. It was Artemis, but she was wrapped in chains, fettered to the rocks. She was kneeling, her hands raised as if to fend off an attacker, and it looked like she was in pain. The Oracle spoke:

> *Five shall go west to the goddess in chains,*
> *One shall be lost in the land without rain,*
> *The bane of Olympus shows the trail,*
> *Campers and Hunters combined prevail,*
> *The Titan's curse must one withstand,*
> *And one shall perish by a parent's hand.*

Then, as we were watching, the mist swirled and retreated like a great green serpent into the mummy's mouth. The Oracle sat down on a rock and became as still as she'd been in the attic, as if she might sit by this creek for a hundred years.

SEVEN

EVERYBODY HATES ME
BUT THE HORSE

The least the Oracle could've done was walk back to the attic by herself.

Instead, Grover and I were elected to carry her. I didn't figure that was because we were the most popular.

"Watch her head!" Grover warned as we went up the stairs. But it was too late.

Bonk! I whacked her mummified face against the trap-door frame and dust flew.

"Ah, man." I set her down and checked for damage. "Did I break anything?"

"I can't tell," Grover admitted.

We hauled her up and set her on her tripod stool, both of us huffing and sweating. Who knew a mummy could weigh so much?

I assumed she wouldn't talk to me, and I was right. I was relieved when we finally got out of there and slammed the attic door shut.

"Well," Grover said, "that was gross."

I knew he was trying to keep things light for my sake, but I still felt really down. The whole camp would be mad at me for losing the game to the Hunters, and then there was the new prophecy from the Oracle. It was like the spirit of Delphi had gone out of her way to exclude me. She'd ignored my question and walked half a mile to talk to Zoë. *And* she'd said nothing, not even a hint, about Annabeth.

"What will Chiron do?" I asked Grover.

"I wish I knew." He looked wistfully out the second-floor window at the rolling hills covered in snow. "I want to be out there."

"Searching for Annabeth?"

He had a little trouble focusing on me. Then he blushed. "Oh, right. That too. Of course."

"Why?" I asked. "What were you thinking?"

He clopped his hooves uneasily. "Just something the manticore said, about the Great Stirring. I can't help but wonder . . . if all those ancient powers are waking up, maybe . . . maybe not all of them are evil."

"You mean Pan."

I felt kind of selfish, because I'd totally forgotten about Grover's life ambition. The nature god had gone missing two thousand years ago. He was rumored to have died, but the satyrs didn't believe that. They were determined to find him. They'd been searching in vain for centuries, and Grover was convinced he'd be the one to succeed. This year, with Chiron putting all the satyrs on emergency duty to find half-bloods, Grover hadn't been able to continue his search. It must've been driving him nuts.

"I've let the trail go cold," he said. "I feel restless, like I'm missing something really important. He's out there somewhere. I can just feel it."

I didn't know what to say. I wanted to encourage him, but I didn't know how. My optimism had pretty much been trampled into the snow out there in the woods, along with our capture-the-flag hopes.

Before I could respond, Thalia tromped up the stairs. She was officially not talking to me now, but she looked at Grover and said, "Tell Percy to get his butt downstairs."

"Why?" I asked.

"Did he say something?" Thalia asked Grover.

"Um, he asked why."

"Dionysus is calling a council of cabin leaders to discuss the prophecy," she said. "Unfortunately, that includes Percy."

The council was held around a Ping-Pong table in the rec room. Dionysus waved his hand and supplied snacks: Cheez Whiz, crackers, and several bottles of red wine. Then Chiron reminded him that wine was against his restrictions and most of us were underage. Mr. D sighed. With a snap of his fingers the wine turned to Diet Coke. Nobody drank that either.

Mr. D and Chiron (in wheelchair form) sat at one end of the table. Zoë and Bianca di Angelo (who had kind of become Zoë's personal assistant) took the other end. Thalia and Grover and I sat along the right, and the other head councilors—Beckendorf, Silena Beauregard, and the Stoll brothers—sat on the left. The Ares kids were supposed to send a representative, too, but all of them had gotten broken limbs (accidentally) during capture the flag, courtesy of the Hunters. They were resting up in the infirmary.

Zoë started the meeting off on a positive note. "This is pointless."

"Cheez Whiz!" Grover gasped. He began scooping up crackers and Ping-Pong balls and spraying them with topping.

"There is no time for talk," Zoë continued. "Our goddess needs us. The Hunters must leave immediately."

"And go where?" Chiron asked.

"West!" Bianca said. I was amazed at how different she looked after just a few days with the Hunters. Her dark hair was braided like Zoë's now, so you could actually see her face. She had a splash of freckles across her nose, and her dark eyes vaguely reminded me of someone famous, but I couldn't think who. She looked like she'd been working out, and her skin glowed faintly, like the other Hunters, as if she'd been taking showers in liquid moonlight. "You heard the prophecy. *Five shall go west to the goddess in chains.* We can get five hunters and go."

"Yes," Zoë agreed. "Artemis is being held hostage! We must find her and free her."

"You're missing something, as usual," Thalia said. "*Campers and Hunters combined prevail.* We're supposed to do this together."

"No!" Zoë said. "The Hunters do not need thy help."

"*Your,*" Thalia grumbled. "Nobody has said *thy* in, like, three hundred years, Zoë. Get with the times."

Zoë hesitated, like she was trying to form the word correctly. "*Yerrr.* We do not need *yerrr* help."

Thalia rolled her eyes. "Forget it."

"I fear the prophecy says you *do* need our help," Chiron said. "Campers and Hunters must cooperate."

"Or do they?" Mr. D mused, swirling his Diet Coke under his nose like it had a fine bouquet. "*One shall be lost. One shall perish.* That sounds rather nasty, doesn't it? What if you fail *because* you try to cooperate?"

"Mr. D," Chiron sighed, "with all due respect, whose side are you on?"

Dionysus raised his eyebrows. "Sorry, my dear centaur. Just trying to be helpful."

"We're supposed to work together," Thalia said stubbornly. "I don't like it either, Zoë, but you know prophecies. You want to fight against one?"

Zoë grimaced, but I could tell Thalia had scored a point.

"We must not delay," Chiron warned. "Today is Sunday. This very Friday, December twenty-first, is the winter solstice."

"Oh, joy," Dionysus muttered. "Another dull annual meeting."

"Artemis must be present at the solstice," Zoë said. "She has been one of the most vocal on the council arguing for action against Kronos's minions. If she is absent, the gods will decide nothing. We will lose another year of war preparations."

"Are you suggesting that the gods have trouble acting together, young lady?" Dionysus asked.

"Yes, Lord Dionysus."

Mr. D nodded. "Just checking. You're right, of course. Carry on."

"I must agree with Zoë," said Chiron. "Artemis's presence at the winter council is critical. We have only a week to find her. And possibly even more important: to locate the monster she was hunting. Now, we must decide who goes on this quest."

"Three and two," I said.

Everybody looked at me. Thalia even forgot to ignore me.

"We're supposed to have five," I said, feeling self-conscious. "Three Hunters, two from Camp Half-Blood. That's more than fair."

Thalia and Zoë exchanged looks.

"Well," Thalia said. "It does make sense."

Zoë grunted. "I would prefer to take *all* the Hunters. We will need strength of numbers."

"You'll be retracing the goddess's path," Chiron reminded her. "Moving quickly. No doubt Artemis tracked the scent of this rare monster, whatever it is, as she moved west. You will have to do the same. The prophecy was clear: *The bane of Olympus shows the trail.* What would your mistress say? 'Too many Hunters spoil the scent.' A small group is best."

Zoë picked up a Ping-Pong paddle and studied it like she was deciding who she wanted to whack first. "This monster—the bane of Olympus. I have hunted at Lady Artemis's side for many years, yet I have no idea what this beast might be."

Everybody looked at Dionysus, I guess because he was

the only god present and gods are supposed to know things. He was flipping through a wine magazine, but when everyone got silent he glanced up. "Well, don't look at me. I'm a *young* god, remember? I don't keep track of all those ancient monsters and dusty titans. They make for terrible party conversation."

"Chiron," I said, "you don't have any ideas about the monster?"

Chiron pursed his lips. "I have several ideas, none of them good. And none of them quite make sense. Typhon, for instance, could fit this description. He was truly a bane of Olympus. Or the sea monster Keto. But if either of these were stirring, we would know it. They are ocean monsters the size of skyscrapers. Your father, Poseidon, would already have sounded the alarm. I fear this monster may be more elusive. Perhaps even more powerful."

"That's some serious danger you're facing," Connor Stoll said. (I liked how he said *you* and not *we*.) "It sounds like at least two of the five are going to die."

"One shall be lost in the land without rain," Beckendorf said. "If I were you, I'd stay out of the desert."

There was a muttering of agreement.

"And *the Titan's curse must one withstand,"* Silena said. "What could that mean?"

I saw Chiron and Zoë exchange a nervous look, but whatever they were thinking, they didn't share it.

"One shall perish by a parent's hand," Grover said in between bites of Cheez Whiz and Ping-Pong balls. "How is that possible? Whose parent would kill them?"

There was heavy silence around the table.

I glanced at Thalia and wondered if she was thinking the same thing I was. Years ago, Chiron had had a prophecy about the next child of the Big Three—Zeus, Poseidon, or Hades—who turned sixteen. Supposedly, that kid would make a decision that would save or destroy the gods forever. Because of that, the Big Three had taken an oath after World War II not to have any more kids. But Thalia and I had been born anyway, and now we were both getting close to sixteen.

I remembered a conversation I'd had last year with Annabeth. I'd asked her, if I was so potentially dangerous, why the gods didn't just kill me.

Some of the gods would like to kill you, she'd said. *But they're afraid of offending Poseidon.*

Could an Olympian parent turn against his half-blood child? Would it sometimes be easier just to let them die? If there were ever any half-bloods who needed to worry about that, it was Thalia and me. I wondered if maybe I should've sent Poseidon that seashell pattern tie for Father's Day after all.

"There will be deaths," Chiron decided. "That much we know."

"Oh, goody!" Dionysus said.

Everyone looked at him. He glanced up innocently from the pages of *Wine Connoisseur* magazine. "Ah, pinot noir is making a comeback. Don't mind me."

"Percy is right," Silena Beauregard said. "Two campers should go."

"Oh, I see," Zoë said sarcastically. "And I suppose you wish to volunteer?"

Silena blushed. "I'm not going anywhere with the Hunters. Don't look at me!"

"A daughter of Aphrodite does not wish to be looked at," Zoë scoffed. "What would thy mother say?"

Silena started to get out of her chair, but the Stoll brothers pulled her back.

"Stop it," Beckendorf said. He was a big guy with a bigger voice. He didn't talk much, but when he did, people tended to listen. "Let's start with the Hunters. Which three of you will go?"

Zoë stood. "I shall go, of course, and I will take Phoebe. She is our best tracker."

"The big girl who likes to hit people on the head?" Travis Stoll asked cautiously.

Zoë nodded.

"The one who put the arrows in my helmet?" Connor added.

"Yes," Zoë snapped. "Why?"

"Oh, nothing," Travis said. "Just that we have a T-shirt for her from the camp store." He held up a big silver T-shirt that said ARTEMIS THE MOON GODDESS, FALL HUNTING TOUR 2002, with a huge list of national parks and stuff underneath. "It's a collector's item. She was admiring it. You want to give it to her?"

I knew the Stolls were up to something. They always were. But I guess Zoë didn't know them as well as I did. She just sighed and took the T-shirt. "As I was saying, I will take Phoebe. And I wish Bianca to go."

Bianca looked stunned. "Me? But . . . I'm so new. I wouldn't be any good."

"You will do fine," Zoë insisted. "There is no better way to prove thyself."

Bianca closed her mouth. I felt kind of sorry for her. I remembered my first quest when I was twelve. I had felt totally unprepared. A little honored, maybe, but a lot resentful and plenty scared. I figured the same things were running around in Bianca's head right now.

"And for campers?" Chiron asked. His eyes met mine, but I couldn't tell what he was thinking.

"Me!" Grover stood up so fast he bumped the Ping-Pong table. He brushed cracker crumbs and Ping-Pong ball scraps off his lap. "Anything to help Artemis!"

Zoë wrinkled her nose. "I think not, satyr. You are not even a half-blood."

"But he *is* a camper," Thalia said. "And he's got a satyr's senses and woodland magic. Can you play a tracker's song yet, Grover?"

"Absolutely!"

Zoë wavered. I didn't know what a tracker's song was, but apparently Zoë thought it was a good thing.

"Very well," Zoë said. "And the second camper?"

"I'll go." Thalia stood and looked around, daring anyone to question her.

Now, okay, maybe my math skills weren't the best, but it suddenly occurred to me that we'd reached the number five, and I wasn't in the group. "Whoa, wait a sec," I said. "I want to go too."

Thalia said nothing. Chiron was still studying me, his eyes sad.

"Oh," Grover said, suddenly aware of the problem. "Whoa, yeah, I forgot! Percy has to go. I didn't mean . . . I'll stay. Percy should go in my place."

"He cannot," Zoë said. "He is a boy. I won't have Hunters traveling with a boy."

"You traveled here with me," I reminded her.

"That was a short-term emergency, and it was ordered by the goddess. I will not go across country and fight many dangers in the company of a boy."

"What about Grover?" I demanded.

Zoë shook her head. "He does not count. He's a satyr. He is not technically a boy."

"Hey!" Grover protested.

"I *have* to go," I said. "I need to be on this quest."

"Why?" Zoë asked. "Because of thy friend Annabeth?"

I felt myself blushing. I hated that everyone was looking at me. "No! I mean, partly. I just feel like I'm supposed to go!"

Nobody rose to my defense. Mr. D looked bored, still reading his magazine. Silena, the Stoll brothers, and Beckendorf were staring at the table. Bianca gave me a look of pity.

"No," Zoë said flatly. "I insist upon this. I will take a satyr if I must, but not a male hero."

Chiron sighed. "The quest is for Artemis. The Hunters should be allowed to approve their companions."

My ears were ringing as I sat down. I knew Grover and some of the others were looking at me sympathetically, but

I couldn't meet their eyes. I just sat there as Chiron concluded the council.

"So be it," he said. "Thalia and Grover will accompany Zoë, Bianca, and Phoebe. You shall leave at first light. And may the gods"—he glanced at Dionysus—"present company included, we hope—be with you."

I didn't show up for dinner that night, which was a mistake, because Chiron and Grover came looking for me.

"Percy, I'm so sorry!" Grover said, sitting next to me on the bunk. "I didn't know they'd—that you'd—Honest!"

He started to sniffle, and I figured if I didn't cheer him up he'd either start bawling or chewing up my mattress. He tends to eat household objects whenever he gets upset.

"It's okay," I lied. "Really. It's fine."

Grover's lower lip trembled. "I wasn't even thinking . . . I was so focused on helping Artemis. But I promise, I'll look everywhere for Annabeth. If I can find her, I will."

I nodded and tried to ignore the big crater that was opening in my chest.

"Grover," Chiron said, "perhaps you'd let me have a word with Percy?"

"Sure," he sniffled.

Chiron waited.

"Oh," Grover said. "You mean alone. Sure, Chiron." He looked at me miserably. "See? Nobody needs a goat."

He trotted out the door, blowing his nose on his sleeve.

Chiron sighed and knelt on his horse legs. "Percy, I don't pretend to understand prophecies."

"Yeah," I said. "Well, maybe that's because they don't make any sense."

Chiron gazed at the saltwater spring gurgling in the corner of the room. "Thalia would not have been my first choice to go on this quest. She's too impetuous. She acts without thinking. She is too sure of herself."

"Would you have chosen me?"

"Frankly, no," he said. "You and Thalia are much alike."

"Thanks a lot."

He smiled. "The difference is that you are less sure of yourself than Thalia. That could be good or bad. But one thing I can say: both of you together would be a dangerous thing."

"We could handle it."

"The way you handled it at the creek tonight?"

I didn't answer. He'd nailed me.

"Perhaps it is for the best," Chiron mused. "You can go home to your mother for the holidays. If we need you, we can call."

"Yeah," I said. "Maybe."

I pulled Riptide out of my pocket and set it on my nightstand. It didn't seem that I'd be using it for anything but writing Christmas cards.

When he saw the pen, Chiron grimaced. "It's no wonder Zoë doesn't want you along, I suppose. Not while you're carrying that particular weapon."

I didn't understand what he meant. Then I remembered something he'd told me a long time ago, when he first gave me the magic sword: *It has a long and tragic history, which we need not go into.*

I wanted to ask him about that, but then he pulled a golden drachma from his saddlebag and tossed it to me. "Call your mother, Percy. Let her know you're coming home in the morning. And, ah, for what it's worth . . . I almost volunteered for this quest myself. I would have gone, if not for the last line."

"*One shall perish by a parent's hand.* Yeah."

I didn't need to ask. I knew Chiron's dad was Kronos, the evil Titan Lord himself. The line would make perfect sense if Chiron went on the quest. Kronos didn't care for anyone, including his own children.

"Chiron," I said. "You know what this Titan's curse is, don't you?"

His face darkened. He made a claw over his heart and pushed outward—an ancient gesture for warding off evil. "Let us hope the prophecy does not mean what I think. Now, good night, Percy. And your time will come. I'm convinced of that. There's no need to rush."

He said *your time* the way people did when they meant *your death*. I didn't know if Chiron meant it that way, but the look in his eyes made me scared to ask.

I stood at the saltwater spring, rubbing Chiron's coin in my hand and trying to figure out what to say to my mom. I really wasn't in the mood to have one more adult tell me that doing nothing was the greatest thing I could do, but I figured my mom deserved an update.

Finally, I took a deep breath and threw in the coin. "O goddess, accept my offering."

The mist shimmered. The light from the bathroom was just enough to make a faint rainbow.

"Show me Sally Jackson," I said. "Upper East Side, Manhattan."

And there in the mist was a scene I did not expect. My mom was sitting at our kitchen table with some . . . guy. They were laughing hysterically. There was a big stack of textbooks between them. The man was, I don't know, thirty-something, with longish salt-and-pepper hair and a brown jacket over a black T-shirt. He looked like an actor—like a guy who might play an undercover cop on television.

I was too stunned to say anything, and fortunately, my mom and the guy were too busy laughing to notice my Iris-message.

The guy said, "Sally, you're a riot. You want some more wine?"

"Ah, I shouldn't. You go ahead if you want."

"Actually, I'd better use your bathroom. May I?"

"Down the hall," she said, trying not to laugh.

The actor dude smiled and got up and left.

"Mom!" I said.

She jumped so hard she almost knocked her textbooks off the table. Finally she focused on me. "Percy! Oh, honey! Is everything okay?"

"What are you doing?" I demanded.

She blinked. "Homework." Then she seemed to understand the look on my face. "Oh, honey, that's just Paul—um, Mr. Blofis. He's in my writing seminar."

"Mr. Blowfish?"

[104]

"*Blofis*. He'll be back in a minute, Percy. Tell me what's wrong."

She always knew when something was wrong. I told her about Annabeth. The other stuff too, but mostly it boiled down to Annabeth.

My mother's eyes teared up. I could tell she was trying hard to keep it together for my sake. "Oh, Percy . . ."

"Yeah. So they tell me there's nothing I can do. I guess I'll be coming home."

She turned her pencil around in her fingers. "Percy, as much as I want you to come home"—she sighed like she was mad at herself—"as much as I want you to be safe, I want you to understand something. You need to do whatever you think you have to."

I stared at her. "What do you mean?"

"I mean, do you really, deep down, believe that you have to help save her? Do you think it's the right thing to do? Because I know one thing about you, Percy. Your heart is always in the right place. Listen to it."

"You're . . . you're telling me to go?"

My mother pursed her lips. "I'm telling you that . . . you're getting too old for me to tell you what to do. I'm telling you that I'll support you, even if what you decide to do is dangerous. I can't believe I'm saying this."

"Mom—"

The toilet flushed down the hall in our apartment.

"I don't have much time," my mom said. "Percy, whatever you decide, I love you. And I *know* you'll do what's best for Annabeth."

"How can you be sure?"

"Because she'd do the same for you."

And with that, my mother waved her hand over the mist, and the connection dissolved, leaving me with one final image of her new friend, Mr. Blowfish, smiling down at her.

I don't remember falling asleep, but I remember the dream.

I was back in that barren cave, the ceiling heavy and low above me. Annabeth was kneeling under the weight of a dark mass that looked like a pile of boulders. She was too tired even to cry out. Her legs trembled. Any second, I knew she would run out of strength and the cavern ceiling would collapse on top of her.

"How is our mortal guest?" a male voice boomed.

It wasn't Kronos. Kronos's voice was raspy and metallic, like a knife scraped across stone. I'd heard it taunting me many times before in my dreams. But *this* voice was deeper and lower, like a bass guitar. Its force made the ground vibrate.

Luke emerged from the shadows. He ran to Annabeth, knelt beside her, then looked back at the unseen man. "She's fading. We must hurry."

The hypocrite. Like he really cared what happened to her.

The deep voice chuckled. It belonged to someone in the shadows, at the edge of my dream. Then a meaty hand thrust someone forward into the light—Artemis—her hands and feet bound in celestial bronze chains.

I gasped. Her silvery dress was torn and tattered. Her

face and arms were cut in several places, and she was bleeding ichor, the golden blood of the gods.

"You heard the boy," said the man in the shadows. "Decide!"

Artemis's eyes flashed with anger. I didn't know why she just didn't will the chains to burst, or make herself disappear, but she didn't seem able to. Maybe the chains prevented her, or some magic about this dark, horrible place.

The goddess looked at Annabeth and her expression changed to concern and outrage. "How dare you torture a maiden like this!"

"She will die soon," Luke said. "You can save her."

Annabeth made a weak sound of protest. My heart felt like it was being twisted into a knot. I wanted to run to her, but I couldn't move.

"Free my hands," Artemis said.

Luke brought out his sword, Backbiter. With one expert strike, he broke the goddess's handcuffs.

Artemis ran to Annabeth and took the burden from her shoulders. Annabeth collapsed on the ground and lay there shivering. Artemis staggered, trying to support the weight of the black rocks.

The man in the shadows chuckled. "You are as predictable as you were easy to beat, Artemis."

"You surprised me," the goddess said, straining under her burden. "It will not happen again."

"Indeed it will not," the man said. "Now you are out of the way for good! I knew you could not resist helping a young maiden. That is, after all, your specialty, my dear."

Artemis groaned. "You know nothing of mercy, you swine."

"On that," the man said, "we can agree. Luke, you may kill the girl now."

"No!" Artemis shouted.

Luke hesitated. "She—she may yet be useful, sir. Further bait."

"Bah! You truly believe that?"

"Yes, General. They will come for her. I'm sure."

The man considered. "Then the dracaenae can guard her here. Assuming she does not die from her injuries, you may keep her alive until winter solstice. After that, if our sacrifice goes as planned, her life will be meaningless. The lives of *all* mortals will be meaningless."

Luke gathered up Annabeth's listless body and carried her away from the goddess.

"You will never find the monster you seek," Artemis said. "Your plan will fail."

"How little you know, my young goddess," the man in the shadows said. "Even now, your darling attendants begin their quest to find you. They shall play directly into my hands. Now, if you'll excuse us, we have a long journey to make. We must greet your Hunters and make sure their quest is . . . challenging."

The man's laughter echoed in the darkness, shaking the ground until it seemed the whole cavern ceiling would collapse.

I woke with a start. I was sure I'd heard a loud banging.

I looked around the cabin. It was dark outside. The salt

spring still gurgled. No other sounds but the hoot of an owl in the woods and the distant surf on the beach. In the moonlight, on my nightstand, was Annabeth's New York Yankees cap. I stared at it for a second, and then: *BANG. BANG.*

Someone, or something, was pounding on my door.

I grabbed Riptide and got out of bed.

"Hello?" I called.

THUMP. THUMP.

I crept to the door.

I uncapped the blade, flung open the door, and found myself face-to-face with a black pegasus.

Whoa, boss! Its voice spoke in my mind as it clopped away from the sword blade. *I don't wanna be a horse-ke-bob!*

Its black wings spread in alarm, and the wind buffeted me back a step.

"Blackjack," I said, relieved but a little irritated. "It's the middle of the night!"

Blackjack huffed. *Ain't either, boss. It's five in the morning. What you still sleeping for?*

"How many times have I told you? Don't call me boss."

Whatever you say, boss. You're the man. You're my number one.

I rubbed the sleep out of my eyes and tried not to let the pegasus read my thoughts. That's the problem with being Poseidon's son: since he created horses out of sea foam, I can understand most equestrian animals, but they can understand me, too. Sometimes, like in Blackjack's case, they kind of adopt me.

See, Blackjack had been a captive on board Luke's ship

last summer, until we'd caused a little distraction that allowed him to escape. I'd really had very little to do with it, seriously, but Blackjack credited me with saving him.

"Blackjack," I said, "you're supposed to stay in the stables."

Meh, the stables. You see Chiron staying in the stables?

"Well . . . no."

Exactly. Listen, we got another little sea friend needs your help.

"Again?"

Yeah. I told the hippocampi I'd come get you.

I groaned. Anytime I was anywhere near the beach, the hippocampi would ask me to help them with their problems. And they had a lot of problems. Beached whales, porpoises caught in fishing nets, mermaids with hangnails—they'd call me to come underwater and help.

"All right," I said. "I'm coming."

You're the best, boss.

"And don't call me boss!"

Blackjack whinnied softly. It might've been a laugh.

I looked back at my comfortable bed. My bronze shield still hung on the wall, dented and unusable. And on my nightstand was Annabeth's magic Yankees cap. On an impulse, I stuck the cap in my pocket. I guess I had a feeling, even then, that I wasn't coming back to my cabin for a long, long time.

EIGHT

I MAKE A DANGEROUS PROMISE

Blackjack gave me a ride down the beach, and I have to admit it was cool. Being on a flying horse, skimming over the waves at a hundred miles an hour with the wind in my hair and the sea spray in my face—hey, it beats waterskiing any day.

Here. Blackjack slowed and turned in a circle. *Straight down.*

"Thanks." I tumbled off his back and plunged into the icy sea.

I'd gotten more comfortable doing stunts like that the past couple of years. I could pretty much move however I wanted to underwater, just by willing the ocean currents to change around me and propel me along. I could breathe underwater, no problem, and my clothes never got wet unless I wanted them to.

I shot down into the darkness.

Twenty, thirty, forty feet. The pressure wasn't uncomfortable. I'd never tried to push it—to see if there was a limit to how deep I could dive. I knew most regular humans couldn't go past two hundred feet without crumpling like an aluminum can. I should've been blind, too, this deep in the water at night, but I could see the heat from living forms, and the cold of the currents. It's hard to describe. It wasn't like regular seeing, but I could tell where everything was.

As I got closer to the bottom, I saw three hippocampi—fish-tailed horses—swimming in a circle around an overturned boat. The hippocampi were beautiful to watch. Their fish tails shimmered in rainbow colors, glowing phosphorescent. Their manes were white, and they were galloping through the water the way nervous horses do in a thunderstorm. Something was upsetting them.

I got closer and saw the problem. A dark shape—some kind of animal—was wedged halfway under the boat and tangled in a fishing net, one of those big nets they use on trawlers to catch everything at once. I hated those things. It was bad enough they drowned porpoises and dolphins, but they also occasionally caught mythological animals. When the nets got tangled, some lazy fishermen would just cut them loose and let the trapped animals die.

Apparently this poor creature had been mucking around on the bottom of Long Island Sound and had somehow gotten itself tangled in the net of this sunken fishing boat. It had tried to get out and managed to get even more hopelessly stuck, shifting the boat in the process. Now the wreckage of the hull, which was resting against a big rock, was teetering and threatening to collapse on top of the tangled animal.

The hippocampi were swimming around frantically, wanting to help but not sure how. One was trying to chew the net, but hippocampi teeth just aren't meant for cutting rope. Hippocampi are really strong, but they don't have hands, and they're not (shhh) all that smart.

Free it, lord! A hippocampus said when it saw me. The others joined in, asking the same thing.

I swam in for a closer look at the tangled creature. At first I thought it was a young hippocampus. I'd rescued several of them before. But then I heard a strange sound, something that did not belong underwater:

"Mooooooo!"

I got next to the thing and saw that it was a cow. I mean . . . I'd heard of sea cows, like manatees and stuff, but this really was a cow with the back end of a serpent. The front half was a calf—a baby, with black fur and big, sad brown eyes and a white muzzle—and its back half was a black-and-brown snaky tail with fins running down the top and bottom, like an enormous eel.

"Whoa, little one," I said. "Where did you come from?"

The creature looked at me sadly. "Moooo!"

But I couldn't understand its thoughts. I only speak horse.

We don't know what it is, lord, one of the hippocampi said. *Many strange things are stirring.*

"Yeah," I murmured. "So I've heard."

I uncapped Riptide, and the sword grew to full length in my hands, its bronze blade gleaming in the dark.

The cow serpent freaked out and started struggling against the net, its eyes full of terror. "Whoa!" I said. "I'm not going to hurt you! Just let me cut the net."

But the cow serpent thrashed around and got even more

tangled. The boat started to tilt, stirring up the muck on the sea bottom and threatening to topple onto the cow serpent. The hippocampi whinnied in a panic and thrashed in the water, which didn't help.

"Okay, okay!" I said. I put away the sword and started speaking as calmly as I could so the hippocampi and the cow serpent would stop panicking. I didn't know if it was possible to get stampeded underwater, but I didn't really want to find out. "It's cool. No sword. See? No sword. Calm thoughts. Sea grass. Mama cows. Vegetarianism."

I doubted the cow serpent understood what I was saying, but it responded to the tone of my voice. The hippocampi were still skittish, but they stopped swirling around me quite so fast.

Free it, lord! they pleaded.

"Yeah," I said. "I got that part. I'm thinking."

But how could I free the cow serpent when she (I decided it was probably a "she") panicked at the sight of a blade? It was like she'd seen swords before and knew how dangerous they were.

"All right," I told the hippocampi. "I need all of you to push exactly the way I tell you."

First we started with the boat. It wasn't easy, but with the strength of three horsepower, we managed to shift the wreckage so it was no longer threatening to collapse on the baby cow serpent. Then I went to work on the net, untangling it section by section, getting lead weights and fishing hooks straightened out, yanking out knots around the cow serpent's hooves. It took forever—I mean, it was worse than the time I'd had to untangle all my video game controller wires. The whole time, I kept talking to the cow fish, telling her everything was okay while she mooed and moaned.

"It's okay, Bessie," I said. Don't ask me why I started calling her that. It just seemed like a good cow name. "Good cow. Nice cow."

Finally, the net came off and the cow serpent zipped through the water and did a happy somersault.

The hippocampi whinnied with joy. *Thank you, lord!*

"Moooo!" The cow serpent nuzzled me and gave me the big brown eyes.

"Yeah," I said. "That's okay. Nice cow. Well . . . stay out of trouble."

Which reminded me, I'd been underwater how long? An hour, at least. I had to get back to my cabin before Argus or the harpies discovered I was breaking curfew.

I shot to the surface and broke through. Immediately, Blackjack zoomed down and let me catch hold of his neck. He lifted me into the air and took me back toward the shore.

Success, boss?

"Yeah. We rescued a baby . . . something or other. Took forever. Almost got stampeded."

Good deeds are always dangerous, boss. You saved my sorry mane, didn't you?

I couldn't help thinking about my dream, with Annabeth crumpled and lifeless in Luke's arms. Here I was rescuing baby monsters, but I couldn't save my friend.

As Blackjack flew back toward my cabin, I happened to glance at the dining pavilion. I saw a figure—a boy hunkered down behind a Greek column, like he was hiding from someone.

It was Nico, but it wasn't even dawn yet. Nowhere near time for breakfast. What was he doing up there?

I hesitated. The last thing I wanted was more time for Nico to tell me about his Mythomagic game. But something was wrong. I could tell by the way he was crouching.

"Blackjack," I said, "set me down over there, will you? Behind that column."

I almost blew it.

I was coming up the steps behind Nico. He didn't see me at all. He was behind a column, peeking around the corner, all his attention focused on the dining area. I was five feet away from him, and I was about to say *What are you doing?* real loud, when it occurred to me that he was pulling a Grover: he was spying on the Hunters.

There were voices—two girls talking at one of the dining tables. At this ungodly hour of the morning? Well, unless you're the goddess of dawn, I guess.

I took Annabeth's magic cap out of my pocket and put it on.

I didn't feel any different, but when I raised my arms I couldn't see them. I was invisible.

I crept up to Nico and sneaked around him. I couldn't see the girls very well in the dark, but I knew their voices: Zoë and Bianca. It sounded like they were arguing.

"It *cannot* be cured," Zoë was saying. "Not quickly, at any rate."

"But how did it happen?" Bianca asked.

"A foolish prank," Zoë growled. "Those Stoll boys from the Hermes cabin. Centaur blood is like acid. Everyone knows that. They sprayed the inside of that Artemis Hunting Tour T-shirt with it."

"That's terrible!"

"She will live," Zoë said. "But she'll be bedridden for weeks with horrible hives. There is no way she can go. It's up to me . . . and thee."

"But the prophecy," Bianca said. "If Phoebe can't go, we only have four. We'll have to pick another."

"There is no time," Zoë said. "We must leave at first light. That's immediately. Besides, the prophecy said we would lose one."

"In the land without rain," Bianca said, "but that can't be here."

"It might be," Zoë said, though she didn't sound convinced. "The camp has magic borders. Nothing, not even weather, is allowed in without permission. It *could* be a land without rain."

"But—"

"Bianca, hear me." Zoë's voice was strained. "I . . . I can't explain, but I have a sense that we should *not* pick someone else. It would be too dangerous. They would meet an end worse than Phoebe's. I don't want Chiron choosing a camper as our fifth companion. And . . . I don't want to risk another Hunter."

Bianca was silent. "You should tell Thalia the rest of your dream."

"No. It would not help."

"But if your suspicions are correct, about the General—"

"I have thy word not to talk about that," Zoë said. She sounded really anguished. "We will find out soon enough. Now come. Dawn is breaking."

Nico scooted out of their way. He was faster than me.

As the girls sprinted down the steps, Zoë almost ran into me. She froze, her eyes narrowing. Her hand crept toward her bow, but then Bianca said, "The lights of the Big House are on. Hurry!"

And Zoë followed her out of the pavilion.

I could tell what Nico was thinking. He took a deep breath and was about to run after his sister when I took off the invisibility cap and said, "Wait."

He almost slipped on the icy steps as he spun around to find me. "Where did you come from?"

"I've been here the whole time. Invisible."

He mouthed the word *invisible*. "Wow. Cool."

"How did you know Zoë and your sister were here?"

He blushed. "I heard them walk by the Hermes cabin. I don't . . . I don't sleep too well at camp. So I heard footsteps, and them whispering. And so I kind of followed."

"And now you're thinking about following them on the quest," I guessed.

"How did you know that?"

"Because if it was my sister, I'd probably be thinking the same thing. But you can't."

He looked defiant. "Because I'm too young?"

"Because they won't let you. They'll catch you and send you back here. And . . . yeah, because you're too young. You remember the manticore? There will be lots more like that. More dangerous. Some of the heroes will die."

He shoulders sagged. He shifted from foot to foot. "Maybe you're right. But, but *you* can go for me."

"Say what?"

"You can turn invisible. You can go!"

"The Hunters don't like boys," I reminded him. "If they find out—"

"Don't let them find out. Follow them invisibly. Keep an eye on my sister! You have to. Please?"

"Nico—"

"You're planning to go anyway, aren't you?"

I wanted to say no. But he looked me in the eyes, and I somehow couldn't lie to him.

"Yeah," I said. "I have to find Annabeth. I have to help, even if they don't want me to."

"I won't tell on you," he said. "But you have to promise to keep my sister safe."

"I . . . that's a big thing to promise, Nico, on a trip like this. Besides, she's got Zoë, Grover, and Thalia—"

"Promise," he insisted.

"I'll do my best. I promise that."

"Get going, then!" he said. "Good luck!"

It was crazy. I wasn't packed. I had nothing but the cap and the sword and the clothes I was wearing. I was supposed to be going home to Manhattan this morning. "Tell Chiron—"

"I'll make something up." Nico smiled crookedly. "I'm good at that. Go on!"

I ran, putting on Annabeth's cap. As the sun came up, I turned invisible. I hit the top of Half-Blood Hill in time to see the camp's van disappearing down the farm road, probably Argus taking the quest group into the city. After that they would be on their own.

I felt a twinge of guilt, and stupidity, too. How was I supposed to keep up with them. Run?

Then I heard the beating of huge wings. Blackjack landed next to me. He began casually nuzzling a few tufts of grass that stuck through the ice.

If I was guessing, boss, I'd say you need a getaway horse. You interested?

A lump of gratitude stuck in my throat, but I managed to say, "Yeah. Let's fly."

NINE

I LEARN HOW
TO GROW ZOMBIES

The thing about flying on a pegasus during the daytime is that if you're not careful, you can cause a serious traffic accident on the Long Island Expressway. I had to keep Blackjack up in the clouds, which were, fortunately, pretty low in the winter. We darted around, trying to keep the white Camp Half-Blood van in sight. And if it was cold on the ground, it was seriously cold in the air, with icy rain stinging my skin.

I was wishing I'd brought some of that Camp Half-Blood orange thermal underwear they sold in the camp store, but after the story about Phoebe and the centaur-blood T-shirt, I wasn't sure I trusted their products anymore.

We lost the van twice, but I had a pretty good sense that they would go into Manhattan first, so it wasn't too difficult to pick up their trail again.

Traffic was bad with the holidays and all. It was mid morning before they got into the city. I landed Blackjack near the top of the Chrysler Building and watched the white camp van, thinking it would pull into the bus station, but it just kept driving.

"Where's Argus taking them?" I muttered.

Oh, Argus ain't driving, boss, Blackjack told me. *That girl is.*

"Which girl?"

The Hunter girl. With the silver crown thing in her hair.

"Zoë?"

That's the one. Hey, look! There's a donut shop. Can we get something to go?

I tried explaining to Blackjack that taking a flying horse to a donut shop would give every cop in there a heart attack, but he didn't seem to get it. Meanwhile, the van kept snaking its way toward the Lincoln Tunnel. It had never even occurred to me that Zoë could drive. I mean, she didn't look sixteen. Then again, she was immortal. I wondered if she had a New York license, and if so, what her birth date said.

"Well," I said. "Let's get after them."

We were about to leap off the Chrysler Building when Blackjack whinnied in alarm and almost threw me. Something was curling around my leg like a snake. I reached for my sword, but when I looked down, there was no snake. Vines—grape vines—had sprouted from the cracks between the stones of the building. They were wrapping around Blackjack's legs, lashing down my ankles so we couldn't move.

"Going somewhere?" Mr. D asked.

He was leaning against the building with his feet levitating in the air, his leopard-skin warm-up suit and black hair whipping around in the wind.

God alert! Blackjack yelled. *It's the wine dude!*

Mr. D sighed in exasperation. "The next person, *or horse,* who calls me the 'wine dude' will end up in a bottle of Merlot!"

"Mr. D." I tried to keep my voice calm as the grape vines continued to wrap around my legs. "What do you want?"

"Oh, what do *I* want? You thought, perhaps, that the immortal, all-powerful director of camp would not notice you leaving without permission?"

"Well . . . maybe."

"I should throw you off this building, minus the flying horse, and see how heroic you sound on the way down."

I balled my fists. I knew I should keep my mouth shut, but Mr. D was about to kill me or haul me back to camp in shame, and I couldn't stand either idea. "Why do you hate me so much? What did I ever do to you?"

Purple flames flickered in his eyes. "You're a hero, boy. I need no other reason."

"I *have* to go on this quest! I've got to help my friends. That's something you wouldn't understand!"

Um, boss, Blackjack said nervously. *Seeing as how we're wrapped in vines nine hundred feet in the air, you might want to talk nice.*

The grape vines coiled tighter around me. Below us, the white van was getting farther and farther away. Soon it would be out of sight.

"Did I ever tell you about Ariadne?" Mr. D asked. "Beautiful young princess of Crete? She liked helping her friends, too. In fact, she helped a young hero named Theseus, also a son of Poseidon. She gave him a ball of magical yarn that let him find his way out of the Labyrinth.

And do you know how Theseus rewarded her?"

The answer I wanted to give was *I don't care!* But I didn't figure that would make Mr. D finish his story any faster.

"They got married," I said. "Happily ever after. The end."

Mr. D sneered. "Not quite. Theseus *said* he would marry her. He took her aboard his ship and sailed for Athens. Halfway back, on a little island called Naxos, he . . . What's the word you mortals use today? . . . he *dumped* her. I found her there, you know. Alone. Heartbroken. Crying her eyes out. She had given up everything, left everything she knew behind, to help a dashing young hero who tossed her away like a broken sandal."

"That's wrong," I said. "But that was thousands of years ago. What's that got to do with me?"

Mr. D regarded me coldly. "I fell in love with Ariadne, boy. I healed her broken heart. And when she died, I made her my immortal wife on Olympus. She waits for me even now. I shall go back to her when I am done with this infernal century of punishment at your ridiculous camp."

I stared at him. "You're . . . you're married? But I thought you got in trouble for chasing a wood nymph—"

"My *point* is you heroes never change. You accuse us gods of being vain. You should look at yourselves. You take what you want, use whoever you have to, and then you betray everyone around you. So you'll excuse me if I have no love for heroes. They are a selfish, ungrateful lot. Ask Ariadne. Or Medea. For that matter, ask Zoë Nightshade."

"What do you mean, ask Zoë?"

He waved his hand dismissively. "Go. Follow your silly friends."

The vines uncurled around my legs.

I blinked in disbelief. "You're . . . you're letting me go? Just like that?"

"The prophecy says at least two of you will die. Perhaps I'll get lucky and you'll be one of them. But mark my words, Son of Poseidon, live or die, you will prove no better than the other heroes."

With that, Dionysus snapped his fingers. His image folded up like a paper display. There was a *pop* and he was gone, leaving a faint scent of grapes that was quickly blown away by the wind.

Too close, Blackjack said.

I nodded, though I almost would have been less worried if Mr. D had hauled me back to camp. The fact that he'd let me go meant he really believed we stood a fair chance of crashing and burning on this quest.

"Come on, Blackjack," I said, trying to sound upbeat. "I'll buy you some donuts in New Jersey."

As it turned out, I didn't buy Blackjack donuts in New Jersey. Zoë drove south like a crazy person, and we were into Maryland before she finally pulled over at a rest stop. Blackjack darn near tumbled out of the sky, he was so tired.

I'll be okay, boss, he panted. *Just . . . just catching my breath.*

"Stay here," I told him. "I'm going to scout."

'Stay here' I can handle. I can do that.

I put on my cap of invisibility and walked over to the

convenience store. It was difficult not to sneak. I had to keep reminding myself that nobody could see me. It was hard, too, because I had to remember to get out of people's way so they wouldn't slam into me.

I thought I'd go inside and warm up, maybe get a cup of hot chocolate or something. I had a little change in my pocket. I could leave it on the counter. I was wondering if the cup would turn invisible when I picked it up, or if I'd have to deal with a floating hot chocolate problem, when my whole plan was ruined by Zoë, Thalia, Bianca, and Grover all coming out of the store.

"Grover, are you sure?" Thalia was saying.

"Well . . . pretty sure. Ninety-nine percent. Okay, eighty-five percent."

"And you did this with acorns?" Bianca asked, like she couldn't believe it.

Grover looked offended. "It's a time-honored tracking spell. I mean, I'm pretty sure I did it right."

"D.C. is about sixty miles from here," Bianca said. "Nico and I . . ." She frowned. "We used to live there. That's . . . that's strange. I'd forgotten."

"I dislike this," Zoë said. "We should go straight west. The prophecy said west."

"Oh, like your tracking skills are better?" Thalia growled.

Zoë stepped toward her. "You challenge my skills, you scullion? You know *nothing* of being a Hunter!"

"Oh, *scullion*? You're calling *me* a scullion? What the heck is a scullion?"

"Whoa, you two," Grover said nervously. "Come on. Not again!"

"Grover's right," Bianca said. "D.C. is our best bet."

Zoë didn't look convinced, but she nodded reluctantly. "Very well. Let us keep moving."

"You're going to get us arrested, driving," Thalia grumbled. "I look closer to sixteen than you do."

"Perhaps," Zoë snapped. "But I have been driving since automobiles were invented. Let us go."

As Blackjack and I continued south, following the van, I wondered whether Zoë had been kidding. I didn't know exactly when cars were invented, but I figured that was like prehistoric times—back when people watched black-and-white TV and hunted dinosaurs.

How old *was* Zoë? And what had Mr. D been talking about? What bad experience had she had with heroes?

As we got closer to Washington, Blackjack started slowing down and dropping altitude. He was breathing heavily.

"You okay?" I asked him.

Fine, boss. I could . . . I could take on an army.

"You don't sound so good." And suddenly I felt guilty, because I'd been running the pegasus for half a day, nonstop, trying to keep up with highway traffic. Even for a flying horse, that had to be rough.

Don't worry about me, boss! I'm a tough one.

I figured he was right, but I also figured Blackjack would run himself into the ground before he complained, and I didn't want that.

Fortunately, the van started to slow down. It crossed the Potomac River into central Washington. I started thinking about air patrols and missiles and stuff like that. I didn't know exactly how all those defenses worked, and wasn't sure if pegasi even showed up on your typical military radar, but I didn't want to find out by getting shot out of the sky.

"Set me down there," I told Blackjack. "That's close enough."

Blackjack was so tired he didn't complain. He dropped toward the Washington Monument and set me on the grass.

The van was only a few blocks away. Zoë had parked at the curb.

I looked at Blackjack. "I want you to go back to camp. Get some rest. Graze. I'll be fine."

Blackjack cocked his head skeptically. *You sure, boss?*

"You've done enough already," I said. "I'll be fine. And thanks a ton."

A ton of hay, maybe, Blackjack mused. *That sounds good. All right, but be careful, boss. I got a feeling they didn't come here to meet anything friendly and handsome like me.*

I promised to be careful. Then Blackjack took off, circling twice around the monument before disappearing into the clouds.

I looked over at the white van. Everybody was getting out. Grover pointed toward one of the big buildings lining the Mall. Thalia nodded, and the four of them trudged off into the cold wind.

I started to follow. But then I froze.

A block away, the door of a black sedan opened. A man

with gray hair and a military buzz cut got out. He was wearing dark shades and a black overcoat. Now, maybe in Washington, you'd expected guys like that to be everywhere. But it dawned on me that I'd seen this same car a couple of times on the highway, going south. It had been following the van.

The guy took out his mobile phone and said something into it. Then he looked around, like he was making sure the coast was clear, and started walking down the Mall in the direction of my friends.

The worst of it was: when he turned toward me, I recognized his face. It was Dr. Thorn, the manticore from Westover Hall.

Invisibility cap on, I followed Thorn from a distance. My heart was pounding. If *he* had survived that fall from the cliff, then Annabeth must have too. My dreams had been right. She was alive and being held prisoner.

Thorn kept well back from my friends, careful not to be seen.

Finally, Grover stopped in front of a big building that said NATIONAL AIR AND SPACE MUSEUM. The Smithsonian! I'd been here a million years ago with my mom, but everything had looked so much bigger then.

Thalia checked the door. It was open, but there weren't many people going in. Too cold, and school was out of session. They slipped inside.

Dr. Thorn hesitated. I wasn't sure why, but he didn't go into the museum. He turned and headed across the

Mall. I made a split-second decision and followed him.

Thorn crossed the street and climbed the steps of the Museum of Natural History. There was a big sign on the door. At first I thought it said CLOSED FOR PIRATE EVENT. Then I realized PIRATE must be PRIVATE.

I followed Dr. Thorn inside, through a huge chamber full of mastodons and dinosaur skeletons. There were voices up ahead, coming from behind a set of closed doors. Two guards stood outside. They opened the doors for Thorn, and I had to sprint to get inside before they closed them again.

Inside, what I saw was so terrible I almost gasped out loud, which probably would've gotten me killed.

I was in a huge round room with a balcony ringing the second level. At least a dozen mortal guards stood on the balcony, plus two monsters—reptilian women with double-snake trunks instead of legs. I'd seen them before. Annabeth had called them Scythian dracaenae.

But that wasn't the worse of it. Standing between the snake women—I could swear he was looking straight down at me—was my old enemy Luke. He looked terrible. His skin was pale and his blond hair looked almost gray, as if he'd aged ten years in just a few months. The angry light in his eyes was still there, and so was the scar down the side of his face, where a dragon had once scratched him. But the scar was now ugly red, as though it had recently been reopened.

Next to him, sitting down so that the shadows covered him, was another man. All I could see were his knuckles on the gilded arms of his chair, like a throne.

"Well?" asked the man in the chair. His voice was just like the one I'd heard in my dream—not as creepy as Kronos's, but deeper and stronger, like the earth itself was talking. It filled the whole room even though he wasn't yelling.

Dr. Thorn took off his shades. His two-colored eyes, brown and blue, glittered with excitement. He made a stiff bow, then spoke in his weird French accent: "They are here, General."

"I know that, you fool," boomed the man. "But where?"

"In the rocket museum."

"The Air and Space Museum," Luke corrected irritably.

Dr. Thorn glared at Luke. "As you say, *sir*."

I got the feeling Thorn would just as soon impale Luke with one of his spikes as call him sir.

"How many?" Luke asked.

Thorn pretended not to hear.

"How many?" the General demanded.

"Four, General," Thorn said. "The satyr, Grover Underwood. And the girl with the spiky black hair and the—how do you say—*punk* clothes and the horrible shield."

"Thalia," Luke said.

"And two other girls—Hunters. One wears a silver circlet."

"*That* one I know," the General growled.

Everyone in the room shifted uncomfortably.

"Let me take them," Luke said to the General. "We have more than enough—"

"Patience," the General said. "They'll have their hands

full already. I've sent a little playmate to keep them occupied."

"But—"

"We cannot risk you, my boy."

"Yes, *boy*," Dr. Thorn said with a cruel smile. "You are much too fragile to risk. Let *me* finish them off."

"No." The General rose from his chair, and I got my first look at him.

He was tall and muscular, with light brown skin and slicked-back dark hair. He wore an expensive brown silk suit like the guys on Wall Street wear, but you'd never mistake this dude for a broker. He had a brutal face, huge shoulders, and hands that could snap a flagpole in half. His eyes were like stone. I felt as if I were looking at a living statue. It was amazing he could even move.

"You have already failed me, Thorn," he said.

"But, General—"

"No excuses!"

Thorn flinched. I'd thought Thorn was scary when I first saw him in his black uniform at the military academy. But now, standing before the General, Thorn looked like a silly wannabe soldier. The General was the real deal. He didn't need a uniform. He was a born commander.

"I should throw you into the pits of Tartarus for your incompetence," the General said. "I send you to capture a child of the three elder gods, and you bring me a scrawny daughter of Athena."

"But you promised me revenge!" Thorn protested. "A command of my own!"

"*I* am Lord Kronos's senior commander," the General said. "And I will choose lieutenants who get me results! It was only thanks to Luke that we salvaged our plan at all. Now get out of my sight, Thorn, until I find some other menial task for you."

Thorn's face turned purple with rage. I thought he was going to start frothing at the mouth or shooting spines, but he just bowed awkwardly and left the room.

"Now, my boy." The General turned to Luke. "The first thing we must do is isolate the half-blood Thalia. The monster we seek will then come to her."

"The Hunters will be difficult to dispose of," Luke said. "Zoë Nightshade—"

"Do not speak her name!"

Luke swallowed. "S—sorry, General. I just—"

The General silenced him with a wave of his hand. "Let me show you, my boy, how we will bring the Hunters down."

He pointed to a guard on the ground level. "Do you have the teeth?"

The guy stumbled forward with a ceramic pot. "Yes, General!"

"Plant them," he said.

In the center of the room was a big circle of dirt, where I guess a dinosaur exhibit was supposed to go. I watched nervously as the guard took sharp white teeth out of the pot and pushed them into the soil. He smoothed them over while the General smiled coldly.

The guard stepped back from the dirt and wiped his hands. "Ready, General!"

"Excellent! Water them, and we will let them scent their prey."

The guard picked up a little tin watering can with daisies painted on it, which was kind of bizarre, because what he poured out wasn't water. It was dark red liquid, and I got the feeling it wasn't Hawaiian Punch.

The soil began to bubble.

"Soon," the General said, "I will show you, Luke, soldiers that will make your army from that little boat look insignificant."

Luke clenched his fists. "I've spent a year training my forces! When the *Princess Andromeda* arrives at the mountain, they'll be the best—"

"Ha!" the General said. "I don't deny your troops will make a fine honor guard for Lord Kronos. And you, of course, will have a role to play—"

I thought Luke turned paler when the General said that.

"—but under my leadership, the forces of Lord Kronos will increase a hundredfold. We will be unstoppable. Behold, my ultimate killing machines."

The soil erupted. I stepped back nervously.

In each spot where a tooth had been planted, a creature was struggling out of the dirt. The first of them said:

"Mew?"

It was a kitten. A little orange tabby with stripes like a tiger. Then another appeared, until there were a dozen, rolling around and playing in the dirt.

Everyone stared at them in disbelief. The General roared, *"What is this? Cute cuddly kittens? Where did you find those teeth?"*

The guard who'd brought the teeth cowered in fear. "From the exhibit, sir! Just like you said. The saber-toothed tiger—"

"No, you idiot! I said the tyrannosaurus! Gather up those . . . those infernal fuzzy little beasts and take them outside. And never let me see your face again."

The terrified guard dropped his watering can. He gathered up the kittens and scampered out of the room.

"You!" The General pointed to another guard. "Get me the *right teeth. NOW!*"

The new guard ran off to carry out his orders.

"Imbeciles," muttered the General.

"This is why I don't use mortals," Luke said. "They are unreliable."

"They are weak-minded, easily bought, and violent," the General said. "I love them."

A minute later, the guard hustled into the room with his hands full of large pointy teeth.

"Excellent," the General said. He climbed onto the balcony railing and jumped down, twenty feet.

Where he landed, the marble floor cracked under his leather shoes. He stood, wincing, and rubbed his shoulders. "Curse my stiff neck."

"Another hot pad, sir?" a guard asked. "More Tylenol?"

"No! It will pass." The General brushed off his silk suit, then snatched up the teeth. "I shall do this myself."

He held up one of the teeth and smiled. "Dinosaur teeth—ha! Those foolish mortals don't even know when they have dragon teeth in their possession. And not just *any* dragon teeth. These come from the ancient Sybaris herself! They shall do nicely."

He planted them in the dirt, twelve in all. Then he scooped up the watering can. He sprinkled the soil with red liquid, tossed the can away, and held his arms out wide. "Rise!"

The dirt trembled. A single, skeletal hand shot out of the ground, grasping at the air.

The General looked up at the balcony. "Quickly, do you have the scent?"

"Yesssss, lord," one of the snake ladies said. She took out a sash of silvery fabric, like the kind the Hunters wore.

"Excellent," the General said. "Once my warriors catch its scent, they will pursue its owner relentlessly. Nothing can stop them, no weapons known to half-blood or Hunter. They will tear the Hunters and their allies to shreds. Toss it here!"

As he said that, skeletons erupted from the ground. There were twelve of them, one for each tooth the General had planted. They were nothing like Halloween skeletons, or the kind you might see in cheesy movies. These were growing flesh as I watched, turning into men, but men with dull gray skin, yellow eyes, and modern clothes—gray muscle shirts, camo pants, and combat boots. If you didn't look too closely, you could almost believe they were human, but their flesh was transparent and their bones shimmered underneath, like X-ray images.

One of them looked straight at me, regarding me coldly, and I knew that no cap of invisibility would fool it.

The snake lady released the scarf and it fluttered down toward the General's hand. As soon as he gave it to the warriors, they would hunt Zoë and the others until they were extinct.

I didn't have time to think. I ran and jumped with all my might, plowing into the warriors and snatching the scarf out of the air.

"What's this?" bellowed the General.

I landed at the feet of a skeleton warrior, who hissed.

"An intruder," the General growled. "One cloaked in darkness. Seal the doors!"

"It's Percy Jackson!" Luke yelled. "It has to be."

I sprinted for the exit, but heard a ripping sound and realized the skeleton warrior had taken a chunk out of my sleeve. When I glanced back, he was holding the fabric up to his nose, sniffing the scent, handing it around to his friends. I wanted to scream, but I couldn't. I squeezed through the door just as the guards slammed it shut behind me.

And then I ran.

I BREAK A FEW
ROCKET SHIPS

I tore across the Mall, not daring to look behind me. I burst into the Air and Space Museum and took off my invisibility cap once I was through the admissions area.

The main part of the museum was one huge room with rockets and airplanes hanging from the ceiling. Three levels of balconies curled around, so you could look at the exhibits from all different heights. The place wasn't crowded, just a few families and a couple of tour groups of kids, probably doing one of those holiday school trips. I wanted to yell at them all to leave, but I figured that would only get me arrested. I had to find Thalia and Grover and the Hunters. Any minute, the skeleton dudes were going to invade the museum, and I didn't think they would settle for an audio tour.

I ran into Thalia—literally. I was barreling up the ramp to the top-floor balcony and slammed into her, knocking her into an Apollo space capsule.

Grover yelped in surprise.

Before I could regain my balance, Zoë and Bianca had arrows notched, aimed at my chest. Their bows had just appeared out of nowhere.

When Zoë realized who I was, she didn't seem anxious to lower her bow. "You! How dare you show thy face here?"

"Percy!" Grover said. "Thank goodness."

Zoë glared at him, and he blushed. "I mean, um, gosh. You're not supposed to be here!"

"Luke," I said, trying to catch my breath. "He's here."

The anger in Thalia's eyes immediately melted. She put her hand on her silver bracelet. "Where?"

I told them about the Natural History Museum, Dr. Thorn, Luke, and the General.

"The General is *here*?" Zoë looked stunned. "That is impossible! You lie."

"Why would I lie? Look, there's no time. Skeleton warriors—"

"What?" Thalia demanded. "How many?"

"Twelve," I said. "And that's not all. That guy, the General, he said he was sending something, a 'playmate,' to distract you over here. A monster."

Thalia and Grover exchanged looks.

"We were following Artemis's trail," Grover said. "I was pretty sure it led here. Some powerful monster scent . . . She must've stopped here looking for the mystery monster. But we haven't found anything yet."

"Zoë," Bianca said nervously, "if it *is* the General—"

"It *cannot* be!" Zoë snapped. "Percy must have seen an Iris-message or some other illusion."

"Illusions don't crack marble floors," I told her.

Zoë took a deep breath, trying to calm herself. I didn't know why she was taking it so personally, or how she knew this General guy, but I figured now wasn't the time to ask.

"If Percy is telling the truth about the skeleton warriors," she said, "we have no time to argue. They are the worst, the most horrible . . . We must leave now."

"Good idea," I said.

"I was *not* including thee, boy," Zoë said. "You are not part of this quest."

"Hey, I'm trying to save your lives!"

"You shouldn't have come, Percy," Thalia said grimly. "But you're here now. Come on. Let's get back to the van."

"That is not thy decision!" Zoë snapped.

Thalia scowled at her. "You're not the boss here, Zoë. I don't care how old you are! You're still a conceited little brat!"

"You never had any wisdom when it came to boys," Zoë growled. "You never could leave them behind!"

Thalia looked like she was about to hit Zoë. Then everyone froze. I heard a growl so loud I thought one of the rocket engines was starting up.

Below us, a few adults screamed. A little kid's voice screeched with delight: "Kitty!"

Something enormous bounded up the ramp. It was the size of a pick-up truck, with silver claws and golden glittering fur. I'd seen this monster once before. Two years ago, I'd glimpsed it briefly from a train. Now, up close and personal, it looked even bigger.

"The Nemean Lion," Thalia said. "Don't move."

The lion roared so loud it parted my hair. Its fangs gleamed like stainless steel.

"Separate on my mark," Zoë said. "Try to keep it distracted."

"Until when?" Grover asked.

"Until I think of a way to kill it. Go!"

I uncapped Riptide and rolled to the left. Arrows whistled past me, and Grover played a sharp *tweet-tweet* cadence on his reed pipes. I turned and saw Zoë and Bianca climbing the Apollo capsule. They were firing arrows, one after another, all shattering harmlessly against the lion's metallic fur. The lion swiped the capsule and tipped it on its side, spilling the Hunters off the back. Grover played a frantic, horrible tune, and the lion turned toward him, but Thalia stepped into its path, holding up Aegis, and the lion recoiled. *"ROOOAAAR!"*

"Hi-yah!" Thalia said. "Back!"

The lion growled and clawed the air, but it retreated as if the shield were a blazing fire.

For a second, I thought Thalia had it under control. Then I saw the lion crouching, its leg muscles tensing. I'd seen enough cat fights in the alleys around my apartment in New York. I knew the lion was going to pounce.

"Hey!" I yelled. I don't know what I was thinking, but I charged the beast. I just wanted to get it away from my friends. I slashed with Riptide, a good strike to the flank that should've cut the monster into Meow Mix, but the blade just clanged against its fur in a burst of sparks.

The lion raked me with its claws, ripping off a chunk of my coat. I backed against the railing. It sprang at me, one thousand pounds of monster, and I had no choice but to turn and jump.

I landed on the wing of an old-fashioned silver airplane, which pitched and almost spilled me to the floor, three stories below.

An arrow whizzed past my head. The lion jumped onto the aircraft, and the cords holding the plane began to groan.

The lion swiped at me, and I dropped onto the next exhibit, a weird-looking spacecraft with blades like a helicopter. I looked up and saw the lion roar—inside its maw, a pink tongue and throat.

Its mouth, I thought. Its fur was completely invulnerable, but if I could strike it in the mouth . . . The only problem was, the monster moved too quickly. Between its claws and fangs, I couldn't get close without getting sliced to pieces.

"Zoë!" I shouted. "Target the mouth!"

The monster lunged. An arrow zipped past it, missing completely, and I dropped from the spaceship onto the top of a floor exhibit, a huge model of the earth. I slid down Russia and dropped off the equator.

The Nemean Lion growled and steadied itself on the spacecraft, but its weight was too much. One of the cords snapped. As the display swung down like a pendulum, the lion leaped off onto the model earth's North Pole.

"Grover!" I yelled. "Clear the area!"

Groups of kids were running around screaming. Grover tried to corral them away from the monster just as the other cord on the spaceship snapped and the exhibit crashed to the floor. Thalia dropped off the second-floor railing and landed across from me, on the other side of the globe. The lion regarded us both, trying to decide which of us to kill first.

Zoë and Bianca were above us, bows ready, but they kept having to move around to get a good angle.

"No clear shot!" Zoë yelled. "Get it to open its mouth more!"

The lion snarled from the top of the globe.

I looked around. *Options.* I needed . . .

The gift shop. I had a vague memory from my trip here as a little kid. Something I'd made my mom buy me, and I'd regretted it. If they still sold that stuff . . .

"Thalia," I said, "keep it occupied."

She nodded grimly.

"Hi-yah!" She pointed her spear and a spidery arc of blue electricity shot out, zapping the lion in the tail.

"ROOOOOOOAR!" The lion turned and pounced. Thalia rolled out of its way, holding up Aegis to keep the monster at bay, and I ran for the gift shop.

"This is no time for souvenirs, boy!" Zoë yelled.

I dashed into the shop, knocking over rows of T-shirts, jumping over tables full of glow-in-the-dark planets and space ooze. The sales lady didn't protest. She was too busy cowering behind her cash register.

There! On the far wall—glittery silver packets. Whole racks of them. I scooped up every kind I could find and ran out of the shop with an armful.

Zoë and Bianca were still showering arrows on the monster, but it was no good. The lion seemed to know better than to open its mouth too much. It snapped at Thalia, slashing with its claws. It even kept its eyes narrowed to tiny slits.

Thalia jabbed at the monster and backed up. The lion pressed her.

"Percy," she called, "whatever you're going to do——"

The lion roared and swatted her like a cat toy, sending her flying into the side of a Titan rocket. Her head hit the metal and she slid to the floor.

"Hey!" I yelled at the lion. I was too far away to strike, so I took a risk: I hurled Riptide like a throwing knife. It bounced off the lion's side, but that was enough to get the monster's attention. It turned toward me and snarled.

There was only one way to get close enough. I charged, and as the lion leaped to intercept me, I chunked a space food pouch into its maw—a chunk of cellophane-wrapped, freeze-dried strawberry parfait.

The lion's eyes got wide and it gagged like a cat with a hairball.

I couldn't blame it. I remembered feeling the same way when I'd tried to eat space food as a kid. The stuff was just plain nasty.

"Zoë, get ready!" I yelled.

Behind me, I could hear people screaming. Grover was playing another horrible song on his pipes.

I scrambled away from the lion. It managed to choke down the space food packet and looked at me with pure hate.

"Snack time!" I yelled.

It made the mistake of roaring at me, and I got an

ice-cream sandwich in its throat. Fortunately, I had always been a pretty good pitcher, even though baseball wasn't my game. Before the lion could stop gagging, I shot in two more flavors of ice cream and a freeze-dried spaghetti dinner.

The lion's eyes bugged. It opened its mouth wide and reared up on its back paws, trying to get away from me.

"Now!" I yelled.

Immediately, arrows pierced the lion's maw—two, four, six. The lion thrashed wildly, turned, and fell backward. And then it was still.

Alarms wailed throughout the museum. People were flocking to the exits. Security guards were running around in a panic with no idea what was going on.

Grover knelt at Thalia's side and helped her up. She seemed okay, just a little dazed. Zoë and Bianca dropped from the balcony and landed next to me.

Zoë eyed me cautiously. "That was . . . an interesting strategy."

"Hey, it worked."

She didn't argue.

The lion seemed to be melting, the way dead monsters do sometimes, until there was nothing left but its glittering fur coat, and even that seemed to be shrinking to the size of a normal lion's pelt.

"Take it," Zoë told me.

I stared at her. "What, the lion's fur? Isn't that, like, an animal rights violation or something?"

"It is a spoil of war," she told me. "It is rightly thine."

"You killed it," I said.

She shook her head, almost smiling. "I think thy ice-cream sandwich did that. Fair is fair, Percy Jackson. Take the fur."

I lifted it up; it was surprisingly light. The fur was smooth and soft. It didn't feel at all like something that could stop a blade. As I watched, the pelt shifted and changed into a coat—a full-length golden-brown duster.

"Not exactly my style," I murmured.

"We have to get out of here," Grover said. "The security guards won't stay confused for long."

I noticed for the first time how strange it was that the guards hadn't rushed forward to arrest us. They were scrambling in all directions except ours, like they were madly searching for something. A few were running into the walls or each other.

"You did that?" I asked Grover.

He nodded, looking a little embarrassed. "A minor confusion song. I played some Barry Manilow. It works every time. But it'll only last a few seconds."

"The security guards are not our biggest worry," Zoë said. "Look."

Through the glass walls of the museum, I could see a group of men walking across the lawn. Gray men in gray camouflage outfits. They were too far away for us to see their eyes, but I could feel their gaze aimed straight at me.

"Go," I said. "They'll be hunting me. I'll distract them."

"No," Zoë said. "We go together."

I stared at her. "But, you said—"

"You are part of this quest now," Zoë said grudgingly. "I do not like it, but there is no changing fate. *You* are the fifth quest member. And we are not leaving anyone behind."

GROVER GETS A
LAMBORGHINI

We were crossing the Potomac when we spotted the helicopter. It was a sleek, black military model just like the one
we'd seen at Westover Hall. And it was coming straight
toward us.

"They know the van," I said. "We have to ditch it."

Zoë swerved into the fast lane. The helicopter was gaining.

"Maybe the military will shoot it down," Grover said
hopefully.

"The military probably thinks it's one of theirs," I said.
"How can the General use mortals, anyway?"

"Mercenaries," Zoë said bitterly. "It is distasteful, but
many mortals will fight for any cause as long as they are paid."

"But don't these mortals see who they're working for?"
I asked. "Don't they notice all the monsters around them?"

Zoë shook her head. "I do not know how much they see
through the Mist. I doubt it would matter to them if they
knew the truth. Sometimes mortals can be more horrible
than monsters."

The helicopter kept coming, making a lot better time
than we were through D.C. traffic.

Thalia closed her eyes and prayed hard. "Hey, Dad. A lightning bolt would be nice about now. Please?"

But the sky stayed gray and snowy. No sign of a helpful thunderstorm.

"There!" Bianca said. "That parking lot!"

"We'll be trapped," Zoë said.

"Trust me," Bianca said.

Zoë shot across two lanes of traffic and into a mall parking lot on the south bank of the river. We left the van and followed Bianca down some steps.

"Subway entrance," Bianca said. "Let's go south. Alexandria."

"Anything," Thalia agreed.

We bought tickets and got through the turnstiles, looking behind us for any signs of pursuit. A few minutes later we were safely aboard a southbound train, riding away from D.C. As our train came above ground, we could see the helicopter circling the parking lot, but it didn't come after us.

Grover let out a sigh. "Nice job, Bianca, thinking of the subway."

Bianca looked pleased. "Yeah, well. I saw that station when Nico and I came through last summer. I remember being really surprised to see it, because it wasn't here when we used to live in D.C."

Grover frowned. "New? But that station looked really old."

"I guess," Bianca said. "But trust me, when we lived here as little kids, there was no subway."

Thalia sat forward. "Wait a minute. No subway at all?"

Bianca nodded.

Now, I knew nothing about D.C., but I didn't see how their whole subway system could be less than twelve years old. I guess everyone else was thinking the same thing, because they looked pretty confused.

"Bianca," Zoë said. "How long ago . . ." Her voice faltered. The sound of the helicopter was getting louder again.

"We need to change trains," I said. "Next station."

Over the next half hour, all we thought about was getting away safely. We changed trains twice. I had no idea where we were going, but after a while we lost the helicopter.

Unfortunately, when we finally got off the train we found ourselves at the end of the line, in an industrial area with nothing but warehouses and railway tracks. And snow. Lots of snow. It seemed much colder here. I was glad for my new lion's fur coat.

We wandered through the railway yard, thinking there might be another passenger train somewhere, but there were just rows and rows of freight cars, most of which were covered in snow, like they hadn't moved in years.

A homeless guy was standing at a trash-can fire. We must've looked pretty pathetic, because he gave us a toothless grin and said, "Y'all need to get warmed up? Come on over!"

We huddled around his fire. Thalia's teeth were chattering. She said, "Well this is g-g-g-great."

"My hooves are frozen," Grover complained.

"Feet," I corrected, for the sake of the homeless guy.

"Maybe we should contact camp," Bianca said. "Chiron—"

"No," Zoë said. "They cannot help us anymore. We must finish this quest ourselves."

I gazed miserably around the rail yard. Somewhere, far to the west, Annabeth was in danger. Artemis was in chains. A doomsday monster was on the loose. And we were stuck on the outskirts of D.C., sharing a homeless person's fire.

"You know," the homeless man said, "you're never completely without friends." His face was grimy and his beard tangled, but his expression seemed kindly. "You kids need a train going west?"

"Yes, sir," I said. "You know of any?"

He pointed one greasy hand.

Suddenly I noticed a freight train, gleaming and free of snow. It was one of those automobile-carrier trains, with steel mesh curtains and a triple-deck of cars inside. The side of the freight train said SUN WEST LINE.

"That's . . . convenient," Thalia said. "Thanks, uh . . ."

She turned to the homeless guy, but he was gone. The trash can in front of us was cold and empty, as if he'd taken the flames with him.

An hour later we were rumbling west. There was no problem about who would drive now, because we all got our own luxury car. Zoë and Bianca were crashed out in a Lexus on the top deck. Grover was playing race car driver behind the wheel of a Lamborghini. And Thalia had hot-wired the radio in a black Mercedes SLK so she could pick up the alt-rock stations from D.C.

"Join you?" I asked her.

She shrugged, so I climbed into the shotgun seat.

The radio was playing the White Stripes. I knew the song because it was one of the only CDs I owned that my mom liked. She said it reminded her of Led Zeppelin. Thinking about my mom made me sad, because it didn't seem likely I'd be home for Christmas. I might not live that long.

"Nice coat," Thalia told me.

I pulled the brown duster around me, thankful for the warmth. "Yeah, but the Nemean Lion wasn't the monster we're looking for."

"Not even close. We've got a long way to go."

"Whatever this mystery monster is, the General said it would come for you. They wanted to isolate you from the group, so the monster will appear and battle you one-on-one."

"He said that?"

"Well, something like that. Yeah."

"That's great. I love being used as bait."

"No idea what the monster might be?"

She shook her head morosely. "But you know where we're going, don't you? San Francisco. That's where Artemis was heading."

I remembered something Annabeth had said at the dance: how her dad was moving to San Francisco, and there was no way she could go. Half-bloods couldn't live there.

"Why?" I asked. "What's so bad about San Francisco?"

"The Mist is really thick there because the Mountain of Despair is so near. Titan magic—what's left of it—still lingers. Monsters are attracted to that area like you wouldn't believe."

"What's the Mountain of Despair?"

Thalia raised an eyebrow. "You really don't know? Ask stupid Zoë. She's the expert."

She glared out the windshield. I wanted to ask her what she was talking about, but I also didn't want to sound like an idiot. I hated feeling like Thalia knew more than I did, so I kept my mouth shut.

The afternoon sun shone through the steel-mesh side of the freight car, casting a shadow across Thalia's face. I thought about how different she was from Zoë—Zoë all formal and aloof like a princess, Thalia with her ratty clothes and her rebel attitude. But there was something similar about them, too. The same kind of toughness. Right now, sitting in the shadows with a gloomy expression, Thalia looked a lot like one of the Hunters.

Then suddenly, it hit me: "That's why you don't get along with Zoë."

Thalia frowned. "What?"

"The Hunters tried to recruit you," I guessed.

Her eyes got dangerously bright. I thought she was going to zap me out of the Mercedes, but she just sighed.

"I almost joined them," she admitted. "Luke, Annabeth, and I ran into them once, and Zoë tried to convince me. She almost did, but . . ."

"But?"

Thalia's fingers gripped the wheel. "I would've had to leave Luke."

"Oh."

"Zoë and I got into a fight. She told me I was being stupid. She said I'd regret my choice. She said Luke would let me down someday."

I watched the sun through the metal curtain. We seemed to be traveling faster each second—shadows flickering like an old movie projector.

"That's harsh," I said. "Hard to admit Zoë was right."

"She *wasn't* right! Luke *never* let me down. Never."

"We'll have to fight him," I said. "There's no way around it."

Thalia didn't answer.

"You haven't seen him lately," I warned. "I know it's hard to believe, but—"

"I'll do what I have to."

"Even if that means killing him?"

"Do me a favor," she said. "Get out of my car."

I felt so bad for her I didn't argue.

As I was about to leave, she said, "Percy."

When I looked back, her eyes were red, but I couldn't tell if it was from anger or sadness. "Annabeth wanted to join the Hunters, too. Maybe you should think about why."

Before I could respond, she raised the power windows and shut me out.

❊ ❊ ❊

I sat in the driver's seat of Grover's Lamborghini. Grover was asleep in the back. He'd finally given up trying to impress Zoë and Bianca with his pipe music after he played "Poison Ivy" and caused that very stuff to sprout from their Lexus's air conditioner.

As I watched the sun go down, I thought of Annabeth. I was afraid to go to sleep. I was worried what I might dream.

"Oh, don't be afraid of dreams," a voice said right next to me.

I looked over. Somehow, I wasn't surprised to find the homeless guy from the rail yard sitting in the shot-gun seat. His jeans were so worn out they were almost white. His coat was ripped, with stuffing coming out. He looked kind of like a teddy bear that had been run over by a truck.

"If it weren't for dreams," he said, "I wouldn't know half the things I know about the future. They're better than Olympus tabloids." He cleared his throat, then held up his hands dramatically:

> "Dreams like a podcast,
> Downloading truth in my ears.
> They tell me cool stuff."

"Apollo?" I guessed, because I figured nobody else could make a haiku that bad.

He put his finger to his lips. "I'm incognito. Call me Fred."

"A god named Fred?"

"Eh, well . . . Zeus insists on certain rules. Hands off, when there's a human quest. Even when something really major is wrong. But nobody messes with my baby sister. *Nobody.*"

"Can you help us, then?"

"Shhh. I already have. Haven't you been looking outside?"

"The train. How fast are we moving?"

Apollo chuckled. "Fast enough. Unfortunately, we're running out of time. It's almost sunset. But I imagine we'll get you across a good chunk of America, at least."

"But where is Artemis?"

His face darkened. "I know a lot, and I see a lot. But even I don't know that. She's . . . clouded from me. I don't like it."

"And Annabeth?"

He frowned. "Oh, you mean that girl you lost? Hmm. I don't know."

I tried not to feel mad. I knew the gods had a hard time taking mortals seriously, even half-bloods. We lived such short lives, compared to the gods.

"What about the monster Artemis was seeking?" I asked. "Do you know what it is?"

"No," Apollo said. "But there is one who might. If you haven't yet found the monster when you reach San Francisco, seek out Nereus, the Old Man of the Sea. He has a long memory and a sharp eye. He has the gift of knowledge sometimes kept obscure from my Oracle."

"But it's *your* Oracle," I protested. "Can't you tell us what the prophecy means?"

Apollo sighed. "You might as well ask an artist to explain his art, or ask a poet to explain his poem. It defeats the purpose. The meaning is only clear through the search."

"In other words, you don't know."

Apollo checked his watch. "Ah, look at the time! I have to run. I doubt I can risk helping you again, Percy, but remember what I said! Get some sleep! And when you return, I expect a good haiku about your journey!"

I wanted to protest that I wasn't tired and I'd never made up a haiku in my life, but Apollo snapped his fingers, and the next thing I knew I was closing my eyes.

In my dream, I was somebody else. I was wearing an old-fashioned Greek tunic, which was a little too breezy downstairs, and laced leather sandals. The Nemean Lion's skin was wrapped around my back like a cape, and I was running somewhere, being pulled along by a girl who was tightly gripping my hand.

"Hurry!" she said. It was too dark to see her face clearly, but I could hear the fear in her voice. "He will find us!"

It was nighttime. A million stars blazed above. We were running through tall grass, and the scent of a thousand different flowers made the air intoxicating. It was a beautiful garden, and yet the girl was leading me through it, as if we were about to die.

"I'm not afraid," I tried to tell her.

"You should be!" she said, pulling me along. She had

long dark hair braided down her back. Her silk robes glowed faintly in the starlight.

We raced up the side of the hill. She pulled me behind a thorn bush and we collapsed, both breathing heavily. I didn't know why the girl was scared. The garden seemed so peaceful. And I felt strong. Stronger than I'd ever felt before.

"There is no need to run," I told her. My voice sounded deeper, much more confident. "I have bested a thousand monsters with my bare hands."

"Not this one," the girl said. "Ladon is too strong. You must go around, up the mountain to my father. It is the only way."

The hurt in her voice surprised me. She was really concerned, almost like she cared about me.

"I don't trust your father," I said.

"You should not," the girl agreed. "You will have to trick him. But you cannot take the prize directly. You will die!"

I chuckled. "Then why don't you help me, pretty one?"

"I . . . I am afraid. Ladon will stop me. My sisters, if they found out . . . they would disown me."

"Then there's nothing for it." I stood up, rubbing my hands together.

"Wait!" the girl said.

She seemed to be agonizing over a decision. Then, her fingers trembling, she reached up and plucked a long white brooch from her hair. "If you must fight, take this. My mother, Pleione, gave it to me. She was a daughter of the ocean, and the ocean's power is within it. *My* immortal power."

The girl breathed on the pin and it glowed faintly. It gleamed in the starlight like polished abalone.

"Take it," she told me. "And make of it a weapon."

I laughed. "A hairpin? How will this slay Ladon, pretty one?"

"It may not," she admitted. "But it is all I can offer, if you insist on being stubborn."

The girl's voice softened my heart. I reached down and took the hairpin, and as I did, it grew longer and heavier in my hand, until I held a familiar bronze sword.

"Well balanced," I said. "Though I usually prefer to use my bare hands. What shall I name this blade?"

"Anaklusmos," the girl said sadly. "The current that takes one by surprise. And before you know it, you have been swept out to sea."

Before I could thank her, there was a trampling sound in the grass, a hiss like air escaping a tire, and the girl said, "Too late! He is here!"

I sat bolt upright in the Lamborghini's driver's seat. Grover was shaking my arm.

"Percy," he said. "It's morning. The train's stopped. Come on!"

I tried to shake off my drowsiness. Thalia, Zoë, and Bianca had already rolled up the metal curtains. Outside were snowy mountains dotted with pine trees, the sun rising red between two peaks.

I fished my pen out of my pocket and stared at it. *Anaklusmos*, the Ancient Greek name for Riptide. A different form, but I was sure it was the same blade I'd seen in my dream.

And I was sure of something else, too. The girl I had seen was Zoë Nightshade.

TWELVE

I GO SNOWBOARDING
WITH A PIG

We'd arrived on the outskirts of a little ski town nestled in the mountains. The sign said WELCOME TO CLOUDCROFT, NEW MEXICO. The air was cold and thin. The roofs of the cabins were heaped with snow, and dirty mounds of it were piled up on the sides of the streets. Tall pine trees loomed over the valley, casting pitch-black shadows, though the morning was sunny.

Even with my lion-skin coat, I was freezing by the time we got to Main Street, which was about half a mile from the train tracks. As we walked, I told Grover about my conversation with Apollo the night before—how he'd told me to seek out Nereus in San Francisco.

Grover looked uneasy. "That's good, I guess. But we've got to get there first."

I tried not to get too depressed about our chances. I didn't want to send Grover into a panic, but I knew we had another huge deadline looming, aside from saving Artemis in time for her council of the gods. The General had said Annabeth would only be kept alive until the winter solstice. That was Friday, only four days away. And he'd said something about a sacrifice. I didn't like the sound of that at all.

We stopped in the middle of town. You could pretty much see everything from there: a school, a bunch of tourist stores and cafes, some ski cabins, and a grocery store.

"Great," Thalia said, looking around. "No bus station. No taxis. No car rental. No way out."

"There's a coffee shop!" said Grover.

"Yes," Zoë said. "Coffee is good."

"And pastries," Grover said dreamily. "And wax paper."

Thalia sighed. "Fine. How about you two go get us some food. Percy, Bianca, and I will check in the grocery store. Maybe they can give us directions."

We agreed to meet back in front of the grocery store in fifteen minutes. Bianca looked a little uncomfortable coming with us, but she did.

Inside the store, we found out a few valuable things about Cloudcroft: there wasn't enough snow for skiing, the grocery store sold rubber rats for a dollar each, and there was no easy way in or out of town unless you had your own car.

"You could call for a taxi from Alamogordo," the clerk said doubtfully. "That's down at the bottom of the mountains, but it would take at least an hour to get here. Cost several hundred dollars."

The clerk looked so lonely, I bought a rubber rat. Then we headed back outside and stood on the porch.

"Wonderful," Thalia grumped. "I'm going to walk down the street, see if anybody in the other shops has a suggestion."

"But the clerk said—"

"I know," she told me. "I'm checking anyway."

I let her go. I knew how it felt to be restless. All half-bloods had attention deficit problems because of our inborn battlefield reflexes. We couldn't stand just waiting around. Also, I had a feeling Thalia was still upset over our conversation last night about Luke.

Bianca and I stood together awkwardly. I mean . . . I was never very comfortable talking one-on-one with girls anyway, and I'd never been alone with Bianca before. I wasn't sure what to say, especially now that she was a Hunter and everything.

"Nice rat," she said at last.

I set it on the porch railing. Maybe it would attract more business for the store.

"So . . . how do you like being a Hunter so far?" I asked.

She pursed her lips. "You're not still mad at me for joining, are you?"

"Nah. Long as, you know . . . you're happy."

"I'm not sure 'happy' is the right word, with Lady Artemis gone. But being a Hunter is definitely cool. I feel calmer somehow. Everything seems to have slowed down around me. I guess that's the immortality."

I stared at her, trying to see the difference. She did seem more confident than before, more at peace. She didn't hide her face under a green cap anymore. She kept her hair tied back, and she looked me right in the eyes when she spoke. With a shiver, I realized that five hundred or a thousand years from now, Bianca di Angelo would look exactly the same as she did today. She might be having a conversation like this with some other half-blood long after I was dead, but Bianca would still look twelve years old.

"Nico didn't understand my decision," Bianca murmured. She looked at me like she wanted assurance it was okay.

"He'll be all right," I said. "Camp Half-Blood takes in a lot of young kids. They did that for Annabeth."

Bianca nodded. "I hope we find her. Annabeth, I mean. She's lucky to have a friend like you."

"Lot of good it did her."

"Don't blame yourself, Percy. You risked your life to save my brother and me. I mean, that was seriously brave. If I hadn't met you, I wouldn't have felt okay about leaving Nico at the camp. I figured if there were people like you there, Nico would be fine. You're a good guy."

The compliment took me by surprise. "Even though I knocked you down in capture the flag?"

She laughed. "Okay. Except for that, you're a good guy."

A couple hundred yards away, Grover and Zoë came out of the coffee shop loaded down with pastry bags and drinks. I kind of didn't want them to come back yet. It was weird, but I realized I liked talking to Bianca. She wasn't so bad. A lot easier to hang out with than Zoë Nightshade, anyway.

"So what's the story with you and Nico?" I asked her. "Where did you go to school before Westover?"

She frowned. "I think it was a boarding school in D.C. It seems like so long ago."

"You never lived with your parents? I mean, your mortal parent?"

"We were told our parents were dead. There was a bank trust for us. A lot of money, I think. A lawyer would come by once in a while to check on us. Then Nico and I had to leave that school."

"Why?"

She knit her eyebrows. "We had to go somewhere. I remember it was important. We traveled a long way. And we stayed in this hotel for a few weeks. And then . . . I don't know. One day a different lawyer came to get us out. He said it was time for us to leave. He drove us back east, through D.C. Then up into Maine. And we started going to Westover."

It was a strange story. Then again, Bianca and Nico were half-bloods. Nothing would be normal for them.

"So you've been raising Nico pretty much all your life?" I asked. "Just the two of you?"

She nodded. "That's why I wanted to join the Hunters so bad. I mean, I know it's selfish, but I wanted my own life and friends. I love Nico—don't get me wrong—I just needed to find out what it would be like not to be a big sister twenty-four hours a day."

I thought about last summer, the way I'd felt when I found out I had a Cyclops for a baby brother. I could relate to what Bianca was saying.

"Zoë seems to trust you," I said. "What were you guys talking about, anyway—something dangerous about the quest?"

"When?"

"Yesterday morning on the pavilion," I said, before I could stop myself. "Something about the General."

Her face darkened. "How did you . . . The invisibility hat. Were you eavesdropping?"

"No! I mean, not really. I just—"

I was saved from trying to explain when Zoë and Grover arrived with the drinks and pastries. Hot chocolate for Bianca and me. Coffee for them. I got a blueberry muffin, and it was so good I could almost ignore the outraged look Bianca was giving me.

"We should do the tracking spell," Zoë said. "Grover, do you have any acorns left?"

"Umm," Grover mumbled. He was chewing on a bran muffin, wrapper and all. "I think so. I just need to—"

He froze.

I was about to ask what was wrong, when a warm breeze rustled past, like a gust of springtime had gotten lost in the middle of winter. Fresh air seasoned with wildflowers and sunshine. And something else—almost like a voice, trying to say something. A warning.

Zoë gasped. "Grover, thy cup."

Grover dropped his coffee cup, which was decorated with pictures of birds. Suddenly the birds peeled off the cup and flew away—a flock of tiny doves. My rubber rat squeaked. It scampered off the railing and into the trees— real fur, real whiskers.

Grover collapsed next to his coffee, which steamed against the snow. We gathered around him and tried to wake him up. He groaned, his eyes fluttering.

"Hey!" Thalia said, running up from the street. "I just . . . What's wrong with Grover?"

"I don't know," I said. "He collapsed."

"Uuuuuhhhh," Grover groaned.

"Well, get him up!" Thalia said. She had her spear in her hand. She looked behind her as if she were being followed. "We have to get out of here."

We made it to the edge of the town before the first two skeleton warriors appeared. They stepped from the trees on either side of the road. Instead of gray camouflage, they were now wearing blue New Mexico State Police uniforms, but they had the same transparent gray skin and yellow eyes.

They drew their handguns. I'll admit I used to think it would be kind of cool to learn how to shoot a gun, but I changed my mind as soon as the skeleton warriors pointed theirs at me.

Thalia tapped her bracelet. Aegis spiraled to life on her arm, but the warriors didn't flinch. Their glowing yellow eyes bored right into me.

I drew Riptide, though I wasn't sure what good it would do against guns.

Zoë and Bianca drew their bows, but Bianca was having trouble because Grover kept swooning and leaning against her.

"Back up," Thalia said.

We started to—but then I heard a rustling of branches. Two more skeletons appeared on the road behind us. We were surrounded.

I wondered where the other skeletons were. I'd seen a

dozen at the Smithsonian. Then one of the warriors raised a cell phone to his mouth and spoke into it.

Except he wasn't speaking. He made a clattering, clicking sound, like dry teeth on bone. Suddenly I understood what was going on. The skeletons had split up to look for us. These skeletons were now calling their brethren. Soon we'd have a full party on our hands.

"It's near," Grover moaned.

"It's here," I said.

"No," he insisted. "The gift. The gift from the Wild."

I didn't know what he was talking about, but I was worried about his condition. He was in no shape to walk, much less fight.

"We'll have to go one-on-one," Thalia said. "Four of them. Four of us. Maybe they'll ignore Grover that way."

"Agreed," said Zoë.

"The Wild!" Grover moaned.

A warm wind blew through the canyon, rustling the trees, but I kept my eyes on the skeletons. I remembered the General gloating over Annabeth's fate. I remembered the way Luke had betrayed her.

And I charged.

The first skeleton fired. Time slowed down. I won't say I could see the bullet, but I could feel its path, the same way I felt water currents in the ocean. I deflected it off the edge of my blade and kept charging.

The skeleton drew a baton and I sliced off his arms at the elbows. Then I swung Riptide through his waist and cut him in half.

His bones unknit and clattered to the asphalt in a heap. Almost immediately, they began to move, reassembling themselves. The second skeleton clattered his teeth at me and tried to fire, but I knocked his gun into the snow.

I thought I was doing pretty well, until the other two skeletons shot me in the back.

"Percy!" Thalia screamed.

I landed facedown in the street. Then I realized something . . . I wasn't dead. The impact of the bullets had been dull, like a push from behind, but they hadn't hurt me.

The Nemean Lion's fur! My coat was bulletproof.

Thalia charged the second skeleton. Zoë and Bianca started firing arrows at the third and fourth. Grover stood there and held his hands out to the trees, looking like he wanted to hug them.

There was a crashing sound in the forest to our left, like a bulldozer. Maybe the skeletons' reinforcements were arriving. I got to my feet and ducked a police baton. The skeleton I'd cut in half was already fully re-formed, coming after me.

There was no way to stop them. Zoë and Bianca fired at their heads point-blank, but the arrows just whistled straight through their empty skulls. One lunged at Bianca, and I thought she was a goner, but she whipped out her hunting knife and stabbed the warrior in the chest. The whole skeleton erupted into flames, leaving a little pile of ashes and a police badge.

"How did you do that?" Zoë asked.

"I don't know," Bianca said nervously. "Lucky stab?"

"Well, do it again!"

Bianca tried, but the remaining three skeletons were wary of her now. They pressed us back, keeping us at baton's length.

"Plan?" I said as we retreated.

Nobody answered. The trees behind the skeletons were shivering. Branches were cracking.

"A gift," Grover muttered.

And then, with a mighty roar, the largest pig I'd ever seen came crashing into the road. It was a wild boar, thirty feet high, with a snotty pink snout and tusks the size of canoes. Its back bristled with brown hair, and its eyes were wild and angry.

"REEEEEEEEET!" it squealed, and raked the three skeletons aside with its tusks. The force was so great, they went flying over the trees and into the side of the mountain, where they smashed to pieces, thigh bones and arm bones twirling everywhere.

Then the pig turned on us.

Thalia raised her spear, but Grover yelled, "Don't kill it!"

The boar grunted and pawed the ground, ready to charge.

"That's the Erymanthian Boar," Zoë said, trying to stay calm. "I don't think we *can* kill it."

"It's a gift," Grover said. "A blessing from the Wild!"

The boar said "REEEEEET!" and swung its tusk. Zoë and Bianca dived out of the way. I had to push Grover so he wouldn't get launched into the mountain on the Boar Tusk Express.

"Yeah, I feel blessed!" I said. "Scatter!"

We ran in different directions, and for a moment the boar was confused.

"It wants to kill us!" Thalia said.

"Of course," Grover said. "It's wild!"

"So how is that a blessing?" Bianca asked.

It seemed a fair question to me, but the pig was offended and charged her. She was faster than I'd realized. She rolled out of the way of its hooves and came up behind the beast. It lashed out with its tusks and pulverized the WELCOME TO CLOUDCROFT sign.

I racked my brain, trying to remember the myth of the boar. I was pretty sure Hercules had fought this thing once, but I couldn't remember how he'd beaten it. I had a vague memory of the boar plowing down several Greek cities before Hercules managed to subdue it. I hoped Cloudcroft was insured against giant wild boar attacks.

"Keep moving!" Zoë yelled. She and Bianca ran in opposite directions. Grover danced around the boar, playing his pipes while the boar snorted and tried to gouge him. But Thalia and I won the prize for bad luck. When the boar turned on us, Thalia made the mistake of raising Aegis in defense. The sight of the Medusa head made the boar squeal in outrage. Maybe it looked too much like one of his relatives. The boar charged us.

We only managed to keep ahead of it because we ran uphill, and we could dodge in and out of trees while the boar had to plow through them.

On the other side of the hill, I found an old stretch of train tracks, half buried in the snow.

"This way!" I grabbed Thalia's arm and we ran along the rails while the boar roared behind us, slipping and sliding as it tried to navigate the steep hillside. Its hooves just were not made for this, thank the gods.

Ahead of us, I saw a covered tunnel. Past that, an old trestle bridge spanning a gorge. I had a crazy idea.

"Follow me!"

Thalia slowed down—I didn't have time to ask why—but I pulled her along and she reluctantly followed. Behind us, a ten-ton pig tank was knocking down pine trees and crushing boulders under its hooves as it chased us.

Thalia and I ran into the tunnel and came out on the other side.

"No!" Thalia screamed.

She'd turned as white as ice. We were at the edge of the bridge. Below, the mountain dropped away into a snow-filled gorge about seventy feet below.

The boar was right behind us.

"Come on!" I said. "It'll hold our weight, probably."

"I can't!" Thalia yelled. Her eyes were wild with fear.

The boar smashed into the covered tunnel, tearing through at full speed.

"Now!" I yelled at Thalia.

She looked down and swallowed. I swear she was turning green.

I didn't have time to process why. The boar was charging through the tunnel, straight toward us. Plan B. I tackled Thalia and sent us both sideways off the edge of the bridge, into the side of the mountain. We slid on Aegis like a snowboard, over rocks and mud and snow, racing downhill. The boar was less fortunate; it couldn't turn that fast, so all ten tons of the monster charged out onto the tiny trestle, which buckled under its weight. The boar free-fell into the gorge with a mighty squeal and landed in a snowdrift with a huge *POOOOOF!*

Thalia and I skidded to a stop. We were both breathing hard. I was cut up and bleeding. Thalia had pine needles in her hair. Next to us, the wild boar was squealing and struggling. All I could see was the bristly tip of its back. It was wedged completely in the snow like Styrofoam packing. It didn't seem to be hurt, but it wasn't going anywhere, either.

I looked at Thalia. "You're afraid of heights."

Now that we were safely down the mountain, her eyes had their usual angry look. "Don't be stupid."

"That explains why you freaked out on Apollo's bus. Why you didn't want to talk about it."

She took a deep breath. Then she brushed the pine needles out of her hair. "If you tell anyone, I swear—"

"No, no," I said. "That's cool. It's just . . . the daughter of Zeus, the Lord of the Sky, afraid of heights?"

She was about to knock me into the snow when, above us, Grover's voice called, "Helloooooo?"

"Down here!" I shouted.

A few minutes later, Zoë, Bianca, and Grover joined us. We stood watching the wild boar struggle in the snow.

"A blessing of the Wild," Grover said, though he now looked agitated.

"I agree," Zoë said. "We must use it."

"Hold up," Thalia said irritably. She still looked like she'd just lost a fight with a Christmas tree. "Explain to me why you're so sure this pig is a blessing."

Grover looked over, distracted. "It's our ride west. Do you have any idea how fast this boar can travel?"

"Fun," I said. "Like . . . pig cowboys."

Grover nodded. "We need to get aboard. I wish . . . I wish I had more time to look around. But it's gone now."

"What's gone?"

Grover didn't seem to hear me. He walked over to the boar and jumped onto its back. Already the boar was starting to make some headway through the drift. Once it broke free, there'd be no stopping it. Grover took out his pipes. He started playing a snappy tune and tossed an apple in front of the boar. The apple floated and spun right above the boar's nose, and the boar went nuts, straining to get it.

"Automatic steering," Thalia murmured. "Great."

She trudged over and jumped on behind Grover, which still left plenty of room for the rest of us.

Zoë and Bianca walked toward the boar.

"Wait a second," I said. "Do you two know what Grover is talking about—this wild blessing?"

"Of course," Zoë said. "Did you not feel it in the wind? It was so strong . . . I never thought I would sense that presence again."

"What presence?"

She stared at me like I was an idiot. "The Lord of the Wild, of course. Just for a moment, in the arrival of the boar, I felt the presence of Pan."

THIRTEEN

※

WE VISIT THE JUNKYARD
OF THE GODS

We rode the boar until sunset, which was about as much as my back end could take. Imagine riding a giant steel brush over a bed of gravel all day. That's about how comfortable boar-riding was.

I have no idea how many miles we covered, but the mountains faded into the distance and were replaced by miles of flat, dry land. The grass and scrub brush got sparser until we were galloping (do boars gallop?) across the desert.

As night fell, the boar came to a stop at a creek bed and snorted. He started drinking the muddy water, then ripped a saguaro cactus out of the ground and chewed it, needles and all.

"This is as far as he'll go," Grover said. "We need to get off while he's eating."

Nobody needed convincing. We slipped off the boar's back while he was busy ripping up cacti. Then we waddled away as best we could with our saddle sores.

After its third saguaro and another drink of muddy water, the boar squealed and belched, then whirled around and galloped back toward the east.

"It likes the mountains better," I guessed.

"I can't blame it," Thalia said. "Look."

Ahead of us was a two-lane road half covered with sand. On the other side of the road was a cluster of buildings too small to be a town: a boarded-up house, a taco shop that looked like it hadn't been open since before Zoë Nightshade was born, and a white stucco post office with a sign that said GILA CLAW, ARIZONA hanging crooked above the door. Beyond that was a range of hills . . . but then I noticed they weren't regular hills. The countryside was way too flat for that. The hills were enormous mounds of old cars, appliances, and other scrap metal. It was a junkyard that seemed to go on forever.

"Whoa," I said.

"Something tells me we're not going to find a car rental here," Thalia said. She looked at Grover. "I don't suppose you got another wild boar up your sleeve?"

Grover was sniffing the wind, looking nervous. He fished out his acorns and threw them into the sand, then played his pipes. They rearranged themselves in a pattern that made no sense to me, but Grover looked concerned.

"That's us," he said. "Those five nuts right there."

"Which one is me?" I asked.

"The little deformed one," Zoë suggested.

"Oh, shut up."

"That cluster right there," Grover said, pointing to the left, "that's trouble."

"A monster?" Thalia asked.

Grover looked uneasy. "I don't smell anything, which

doesn't make sense. But the acorns don't lie. Our next challenge . . ."

He pointed straight toward the junkyard. With the sunlight almost gone now, the hills of metal looked like something on an alien planet.

We decided to camp for the night and try the junkyard in the morning. None of us wanted to go Dumpster-diving in the dark.

Zoë and Bianca produced five sleeping bags and foam mattresses out of their backpacks. I don't know how they did it, because the packs were tiny, but must've been enchanted to hold so much stuff. I'd noticed their bows and quivers were also magic. I never really thought about it, but when the Hunters needed them, they just appeared slung over their backs. And when they didn't, they were gone.

The night got chilly fast, so Grover and I collected old boards from the ruined house, and Thalia zapped them with an electric shock to start a campfire. Pretty soon we were about as comfy as you can get in a rundown ghost town in the middle of nowhere.

"The stars are out," Zoë said.

She was right. There were millions of them, with no city lights to turn the sky orange.

"Amazing," Bianca said. "I've never actually seen the Milky Way."

"This is nothing," Zoë said. "In the old days, there were more. Whole constellations have disappeared because of human light pollution."

"You talk like you're not human," I said.

Zoë raised an eyebrow. "I am a Hunter. I care what happens to the wild places of the world. Can the same be said for thee?"

"For *you*," Thalia corrected. "Not *thee*."

"But you use *you* for the beginning of a sentence."

"And for the end," Thalia said. "No *thou*. No *thee*. Just *you*."

Zoë threw up her hands in exasperation. "I *hate* this language. It changes too often!"

Grover sighed. He was still looking up at the stars like he was thinking about the light pollution problem. "If only Pan were here, he would set things right."

Zoë nodded sadly.

"Maybe it was the coffee," Grover said. "I was drinking coffee, and the wind came. Maybe if I drank more coffee . . ."

I was pretty sure coffee had nothing to do with what had happened in Cloudcroft, but I didn't have the heart to tell Grover. I thought about the rubber rat and the tiny birds that had suddenly come alive when the wind blew. "Grover, do you really think that was Pan? I mean, I know you *want* it to be."

"He sent us help," Grover insisted. "I don't know how or why. But it was his presence. After this quest is done, I'm going back to New Mexico and drinking a lot of coffee. It's the best lead we've gotten in two thousand years. I was *so close*."

I didn't answer. I didn't want to squash Grover's hopes.

"What I want to know," Thalia said, looking at Bianca, "is how you destroyed one of the zombies. There are a lot more out there somewhere. We need to figure out how to fight them."

Bianca shook her head. "I don't know. I just stabbed it and it went up in flames."

"Maybe there's something special about your knife," I said.

"It is the same as mine," Zoë said. "Celestial bronze, yes. But mine did not affect the warriors that way."

"Maybe you have to hit the skeleton in a certain spot," I said.

Bianca looked uncomfortable with everybody paying attention to her.

"Never mind," Zoë told her. "We will find the answer. In the meantime, we should plan our next move. When we get through this junkyard, we must continue west. If we can find a road, we can hitchhike to the nearest city. I think that would be Las Vegas."

I was about to protest that Grover and I had had bad experiences in that town, but Bianca beat us to it.

"No!" she said. "Not there!"

She looked really freaked out, like she'd just been dropped off the steep end of a roller coaster.

Zoë frowned. "Why?"

Bianca took a shaky breath. "I . . . I think we stayed there for a while. Nico and I. When we were traveling. And then, I can't remember . . ."

Suddenly I had a really bad thought. I remembered what

Bianca had told me about Nico and her staying in a hotel for a while. I met Grover's eyes, and I got the feeling he was thinking the same thing.

"Bianca," I said. "That hotel you stayed at. Was it possibly called the Lotus Hotel and Casino?"

Her eyes widened. "How could you know that?"

"Oh, great," I said.

"Wait," Thalia said. "What is the Lotus Casino?"

"A couple of years ago," I said, "Grover, Annabeth, and I got trapped there. It's designed so you never want to leave. We stayed for about an hour. When we came out, five days had passed. It makes time speed up."

"No," Bianca said. "No, that's not possible."

"You said somebody came and got you out," I remembered.

"Yes."

"What did he look like? What did he say?"

"I . . . I don't remember. Please, I really don't want to talk about this."

Zoë sat forward, her eyebrows knit with concern. "You said that Washington, D.C., had changed when you went back last summer. You didn't remember the subway being there."

"Yes, but—"

"Bianca," Zoë said, "can you tell me the name of the president of the United States right now?"

"Don't be silly," Bianca said. She told us the correct name of the president.

"And who was the president before that?" Zoë asked.

Bianca thought for a while. "Roosevelt."

Zoë swallowed. "Theodore or Franklin?"

"Franklin," Bianca said. "F.D.R."

"Like FDR Drive?" I asked. Because seriously, that's about all I knew about F.D.R.

"Bianca," Zoë said. "F.D.R. was not the last president. That was about seventy years ago."

"That's impossible," Bianca said. "I . . . I'm not that old."

She stared at her hands as if to make sure they weren't wrinkled.

Thalia's eyes turned sad. I guess she knew what it was like to get pulled out of time for a while. "It's okay, Bianca. The important thing is you and Nico are safe. You made it out."

"But how?" I said. "We were only in there for an hour and we barely escaped. How could you have escaped after being there for so long?"

"I told you." Bianca looked about ready to cry. "A man came and said it was time to leave. And—"

"But who? Why did he do it?"

Before she could answer, we were hit with a blazing light from down the road. The headlights of a car appeared out of nowhere. I was half hoping it was Apollo, come to give us a ride again, but the engine was way too silent for the sun chariot, and besides, it was nighttime. We grabbed our sleeping bags and got out of the way as a deathly white limousine slid to a stop in front of us.

* * *

The back door of the limo opened right next to me. Before I could step away, the point of a sword touched my throat.

I heard the sound of Zoë and Bianca drawing their bows. As the owner of the sword got out of the car, I moved back very slowly. I had to, because he was pushing the point under my chin.

He smiled cruelly. "Not so fast now, are you, punk?"

He was a big man with a crew cut, a black leather biker's jacket, black jeans, a white muscle shirt, and combat boots. Wraparound shades hid his eyes, but I knew what was behind those glasses—hollow sockets filled with flames.

"Ares," I growled.

The war god glanced at my friends. "At ease, people."

He snapped his fingers, and their weapons fell to the ground.

"This is a friendly meeting." He dug the point of his blade a little farther under my chin. "Of course I'd *like* to take your head for a trophy, but someone wants to see you. And I never behead my enemies in front of a lady."

"What lady?" Thalia asked.

Ares looked over at her. "Well, well. I heard you were back."

He lowered his sword and pushed me away.

"Thalia, daughter of Zeus," Ares mused. "You're not hanging out with very good company."

"What's your business, Ares?" she said. "Who's in the car?"

Ares smiled, enjoying the attention. "Oh, I doubt she wants to meet the rest of you. Particularly not *them*." He jutted his chin toward Zoë and Bianca. "Why don't you all go get some tacos while you wait? Only take Percy a few minutes."

"We will not leave him alone with thee, Lord Ares," Zoë said.

"Besides," Grover managed, "the taco place is closed."

Ares snapped his fingers again. The lights inside the taqueria suddenly blazed to life. The boards flew off the door and the CLOSED sign flipped to OPEN. "You were saying, goat boy?"

"Go on," I told my friends. "I'll handle this."

I tried to sound more confident than I felt. I don't think Ares was fooled.

"You heard the boy," Ares said. "He's big and strong. He's got things under control."

My friends reluctantly headed over to the taco restaurant. Ares regarded me with loathing, then opened the limousine door like a chauffeur.

"Get inside, punk," he said. "And mind your manners. She's not as forgiving of rudeness as I am."

When I saw her, my jaw dropped.

I forgot my name. I forgot where I was. I forgot how to speak in complete sentences.

She was wearing a red satin dress and her hair was curled in a cascade of ringlets. Her face was the most beautiful I'd ever seen: perfect makeup, dazzling eyes, a smile that would've lit up the dark side of the moon.

Thinking back on it, I can't tell you who she looked like.

Or even what color her hair or her eyes were. Pick the most beautiful actress you can think of. The goddess was ten times more beautiful than that. Pick your favorite hair color, eye color, whatever. The goddess had that.

When she smiled at me, just for a moment she looked a little like Annabeth. Then like this television actress I used to have a crush on in fifth grade. Then . . . well, you get the idea.

"Ah, there you are, Percy," the goddess said. "I am Aphrodite."

I slipped into the seat across from her and said something like, "Um uh gah."

She smiled. "Aren't you sweet. Hold this, please."

She handed me a polished mirror the size of a dinner plate and had me hold it up for her. She leaned forward and dabbed at her lipstick, though I couldn't see anything wrong with it.

"Do you know why you're here?" she asked.

I wanted to respond. Why couldn't I form a complete sentence? She was only a lady. A seriously beautiful lady. With eyes like pools of spring water . . . Whoa.

I pinched my own arm, hard.

"I . . . I don't know," I managed.

"Oh, dear," Aphrodite said. "Still in denial?"

Outside the car, I could hear Ares chuckling. I had a feeling he could hear every word we said. The idea of him being out there made me angry, and that helped clear my mind.

"I don't know what you're talking about," I said.

"Well then, why are you on this quest?"

"Artemis has been captured!"

Aphrodite rolled her eyes. "Oh, Artemis. *Please.* Talk about a hopeless case. I mean, if they were going to kidnap a goddess, she should be breathtakingly beautiful, don't you think? I pity the poor dears who have to imprison Artemis. Bo-ring!"

"But she was chasing a monster," I protested. "A really, really bad monster. We have to find it!"

Aphrodite made me hold the mirror a little higher. She seemed to have found a microscopic problem at the corner of her eye and dabbed at her mascara. "Always some monster. But my dear Percy, that is why the *others* are on this quest. I'm more interested in *you.*"

My heart pounded. I didn't want to answer, but her eyes drew an answer right out of my mouth. "Annabeth is in trouble."

Aphrodite beamed. "Exactly!"

"I have to help her," I said. "I've been having these dreams."

"Ah, you even dream about her! That's *so cute!*"

"No! I mean . . . that's not what I meant."

She made a *tsk-tsk* sound. "Percy, I'm on your side. I'm the reason you're here, after all."

I stared at her. "What?"

"The poisoned T-shirt the Stoll brothers gave Phoebe," she said. "Did you think that was an accident? Sending Blackjack to find you? Helping you sneak out of the camp?"

"*You* did that?"

"Of course! Because really, how boring these Hunters are! A quest for some monster, blah blah blah. Saving Artemis. Let her stay lost, I say. But a quest for true love—"

"Wait a second, I never said—"

"Oh, my dear. You don't need to say it. You *do* know Annabeth was close to joining the Hunters, don't you?"

I blushed. "I wasn't sure—"

"She was about to throw her life away! And you, my dear, you can save her from that. It's so romantic!"

"Uh . . ."

"Oh, put the mirror down," Aphrodite ordered. "I look fine."

I hadn't realized I was still holding it, but as soon as I put it down, I noticed my arms were sore.

"Now listen, Percy," Aphrodite said. "The Hunters are your enemies. Forget them and Artemis and the monster. That's not important. You just concentrate on finding and saving Annabeth."

"Do you know where she is?"

Aphrodite waved her hand irritably. "No, no. I leave the details to you. But it's been ages since we've had a good tragic love story."

"Whoa, first of all, I never said anything about love. And second, what's up with *tragic*?"

"Love conquers all," Aphrodite promised. "Look at Helen and Paris. Did they let anything come between them?"

"Didn't they start the Trojan War and get thousands of people killed?"

"Pfft. That's not the point. Follow your heart."

"But . . . I don't know where it's going. My heart, I mean."

She smiled sympathetically. She really was beautiful. And not just because she had a pretty face or anything. She believed in love so much, it was impossible not to feel giddy when she talked about it.

"Not knowing is half the fun," Aphrodite said. "Exquisitely painful, isn't it? Not being sure who you love and who loves you? Oh, you kids! It's so cute I'm going to cry."

"No, no," I said. "Don't do that."

"And don't worry," she said. "I'm not going to let this be easy and boring for you. No, I have some wonderful surprises in store. Anguish. Indecision. Oh, you just wait."

"That's really okay," I told her. "Don't go to any trouble."

"You're *so* cute. I wish all my daughters could break the heart of a boy as nice as you." Aphrodite's eyes were tearing up. "Now, you'd better go. And do be careful in my husband's territory, Percy. Don't take anything. He is awfully fussy about his trinkets and trash."

"What?" I asked. "You mean Hephaestus?"

But the car door opened and Ares grabbed my shoulder, pulling me out of the car and back into the desert night.

My audience with the goddess of love was over.

"You're lucky, punk." Ares pushed me away from the limo. "Be grateful."

"For what?"

"That we're being so nice. If it was up to me—"

"So why haven't you killed me?" I shot back. It was a stupid thing to say to the god of war, but being around him always made me feel angry and reckless.

Ares nodded, like I'd finally said something intelligent.

"I'd love to kill you, seriously," he said. "But see, I got a situation. Word on Olympus is that you might start the biggest war in history. I can't risk messing that up. Besides, Aphrodite thinks you're some kinda soap-opera star or something. I kill you, that makes me look bad with her. But don't worry. I haven't forgotten my promise. Some day soon, kid—*real* soon—you're going to raise your sword to fight, and you're going to remember the wrath of Ares."

I balled my fists. "Why wait? I beat you once. How's that ankle healing up?"

He grinned crookedly. "Not bad, punk. But you got nothing on the master of taunts. I'll start the fight when I'm good and ready. Until then . . . Get lost."

He snapped his fingers and the world did a three-sixty, spinning in a cloud of red dust. I fell to the ground.

When I stood up again, the limousine was gone. The road, the taco restaurant, the whole town of Gila Claw was gone. My friends and I were standing in the middle of the junkyard, mountains of scrap metal stretched out in every direction.

"What did she *want* with you?" Bianca asked, once I'd told them about Aphrodite.

"Oh, uh, not sure," I lied. "She said to be careful in her

husband's junkyard. She said not to pick anything up."

Zoë narrowed her eyes. "The goddess of love would not make a special trip to tell thee that. Be careful, Percy. Aphrodite has led many heroes astray."

"For once I agree with Zoë," Thalia said. "You can't trust Aphrodite."

Grover was looking at me funny. Being empathic and all, he could usually read my emotions, and I got the feeling he knew exactly what Aphrodite had talked to me about.

"So," I said, anxious to change the subject, "how do we get out of here?"

"That way," Zoë said. "That is west."

"How can you tell?"

In the light of the full moon, I was surprised how well I could see her roll her eyes at me. "Ursa Major is in the north," she said, "which means *that* must be west."

She pointed west, then at the northern constellation, which was hard to make out because there were so many other stars.

"Oh, yeah," I said. "The bear thing."

Zoë looked offended. "Show some respect. It was a fine bear. A worthy opponent."

"You act like it was real."

"Guys," Grover broke in. "Look!"

We'd reached the crest of a junk mountain. Piles of metal objects glinted in the moonlight: broken heads of bronze horses, metal legs from human statues, smashed chariots, tons of shields and swords and other weapons, along with more modern stuff, like cars that gleamed gold and silver, refrigerators, washing machines, and computer monitors.

"Whoa," Bianca said. "That stuff . . . some of it looks like real gold."

"It is," Thalia said grimly. "Like Percy said, don't touch anything. This is the junkyard of the gods."

"Junk?" Grover picked up a beautiful crown made of gold, silver, and jewels. It was broken on one side, as if it had been split by an axe. "You call this junk?"

He bit off a point and began to chew. "It's delicious!"

Thalia swatted the crown out of his hands. "I'm serious!"

"Look!" Bianca said. She raced down the hill, tripping over bronze coils and golden plates. She picked up a bow that glowed silver in moonlight. "A Hunter's bow!"

She yelped in surprise as the bow began to shrink, and became a hair clip shaped like a crescent moon. "It's just like Percy's sword!"

Zoë's face was grim. "Leave it, Bianca."

"But—"

"It is here for a reason. Anything thrown away in this junkyard must stay in this yard. It is defective. Or cursed."

Bianca reluctantly set the hair clip down.

"I don't like this place," Thalia said. She gripped the shaft of her spear.

"You think we're going to get attacked by killer refrigerators?" I asked.

She gave me a hard look. "Zoë is right, Percy. Things get thrown away here for a reason. Now come on, let's get across the yard."

"That's the second time you've agreed with Zoë," I muttered, but Thalia ignored me.

We started picking our way through the hills and valleys of junk. The stuff seemed to go on forever, and if it hadn't been for Ursa Major, we would've gotten lost. All the hills pretty much looked the same.

I'd like to say we left the stuff alone, but there was too much cool junk not to check out some of it. I found an electric guitar shaped like Apollo's lyre that was so sweet I had to pick it up. Grover found a broken tree made out of metal. It had been chopped to pieces, but some of the branches still had golden birds in them, and they whirred around when Grover picked them up, trying to flap their wings.

Finally, we saw the edge of the junkyard about half a mile ahead of us, the lights of a highway stretching through the desert. But between us and the road . . .

"What is that?" Bianca gasped.

Ahead of us was a hill much bigger and longer than the others. It was like a metal mesa, the length of a football field and as tall as goalposts. At one end of the mesa was a row of ten thick metal columns, wedged tightly together.

Bianca frowned. "They look like—"

"Toes," Grover said.

Bianca nodded. "Really, really large toes."

Zoë and Thalia exchanged nervous looks.

"Let's go around," Thalia said. "*Far* around."

"But the road is right over there," I protested. "Quicker to climb over."

Ping.

Thalia hefted her spear and Zoë drew her bow, but then I realized it was only Grover. He had thrown a piece of scrap metal at the toes and hit one, making a deep echo, as if the column were hollow.

"Why did you do that?" Zoë demanded.

Grover cringed. "I don't know. I, uh, don't like fake feet?"

"Come on." Thalia looked at me. *"Around."*

I didn't argue. The toes were starting to freak me out, too. I mean, who sculpts ten-foot-tall metal toes and sticks them in a junkyard?

After several minutes of walking, we finally stepped onto the highway, an abandoned but well-lit stretch of black asphalt.

"We made it out," Zoë said. "Thank the gods."

But apparently the gods didn't want to be thanked. At that moment, I heard a sound like a thousand trash compactors crushing metal.

I whirled around. Behind us, the scrap mountain was boiling, rising up. The ten toes tilted over, and I realized why they looked like toes. They *were* toes. The thing that rose up from the metal was a bronze giant in full Greek battle armor. He was impossibly tall—a skyscraper with legs and arms. He gleamed wickedly in the moonlight. He looked down at us, and his face was deformed. The left side was partially melted off. His joints creaked with rust, and across his armored chest, written in thick dust by some giant finger, were the words WASH ME.

"Talos!" Zoë gasped.

"Who—who's Talos?" I stuttered.

"One of Hephaestus's creations," Thalia said. "But that can't be the original. It's too small. A prototype, maybe. A defective model."

The metal giant didn't like the word *defective*.

He moved one hand to his sword belt and drew his weapon. The sound of it coming out of its sheath was horrible, metal screeching against metal. The blade was a hundred feet long, easy. It looked rusty and dull, but I didn't figure that mattered. Getting hit with that thing would be like getting hit with a battleship.

"Someone took something," Zoë said. "Who took something?"

She stared accusingly at me.

I shook my head. "I'm a lot of things, but I'm not a thief."

Bianca didn't say anything. I could swear she looked guilty, but I didn't have much time to think about it, because the giant defective Talos took one step toward us, closing half the distance and making the ground shake.

"Run!" Grover yelped.

Great advice, except that it was hopeless. At a leisurely stroll, this thing could outdistance us easily.

We split up, the way we'd done with the Nemean Lion. Thalia drew her shield and held it up as she ran down the highway. The giant swung his sword and took out a row of power lines, which exploded in sparks and scattered across Thalia's path.

Zoë's arrows whistled toward the creature's face but

shattered harmlessly against the metal. Grover brayed like a baby goat and went climbing up a mountain of metal.

Bianca and I ended up next to each other, hiding behind a broken chariot.

"You took something," I said. "That bow."

"No!" she said, but her voice was quivering.

"Give it back!" I said. "Throw it down!"

"I . . . I didn't take the bow! Besides, it's too late."

"What did you take?"

Before she could answer, I heard a massive creaking noise, and a shadow blotted out the sky.

"Move!" I tore down the hill, Bianca right behind me, as the giant's foot smashed a crater in the ground where we'd been hiding.

"Hey, Talos!" Grover yelled, but the monster raised his sword, looking down at Bianca and me.

Grover played a quick melody on his pipes. Over at the highway, the downed power lines began to dance. I understood what Grover was going to do a split second before it happened. One of the poles with power lines still attached flew toward Talos's back leg and wrapped around his calf. The lines sparked and sent a jolt of electricity up the giant's backside.

Talos whirled around, creaking and sparking. Grover had bought us a few seconds.

"Come on!" I told Bianca. But she stayed frozen. From her pocket, she brought out a small metal figurine, a statue of a god. "It . . . it was for Nico. It was the only statue he didn't have."

"How can you think of Mythomagic at a time like this?" I said.

There were tears in her eyes.

"Throw it down," I said. "Maybe the giant will leave us alone."

She dropped it reluctantly, but nothing happened.

The giant kept coming after Grover. It stabbed its sword into a junk hill, missing Grover by a few feet, but scrap metal made an avalanche over him, and then I couldn't see him anymore.

"No!" Thalia yelled. She pointed her spear, and a blue arc of lightning shot out, hitting the monster in his rusty knee, which buckled. The giant collapsed, but immediately started to rise again. It was hard to tell if it could feel anything. There weren't any emotions in its half-melted face, but I got the sense that it was about as ticked off as a twenty-story-tall metal warrior could be.

He raised his foot to stomp and I saw that his sole was treaded like the bottom of a sneaker. There was a hole in his heel, like a large manhole, and there were red words painted around it, which I deciphered only after the foot came down: FOR MAINTENANCE ONLY.

"Crazy-idea time," I said.

Bianca looked at me nervously. "Anything."

I told her about the maintenance hatch. "There may be a way to control the thing. Switches or something. I'm going to get inside."

"How? You'll have to stand under its foot! You'll be crushed."

"Distract it," I said. "I'll just have to time it right."

Bianca's jaw tightened. "No. I'll go."

"You can't. You're new at this! You'll die."

"It's my fault the monster came after us," she said. "It's my responsibility. Here." She picked up the little god statue and pressed it into my hand. "If anything happens, give that to Nico. Tell him . . . tell him I'm sorry."

"Bianca, no!"

But she wasn't waiting for me. She charged at the monster's left foot.

Thalia had its attention for the moment. She'd learned that the giant was big but slow. If you could stay close to it and not get smashed, you could run around it and stay alive. At least, it was working so far.

Bianca got right next to the giant's foot, trying to balance herself on the metal scraps that swayed and shifted with his weight.

Zoë yelled, "What are you doing?"

"Get it to raise its foot!" she said.

Zoë shot an arrow toward the monster's face and it flew straight into one nostril. The giant straightened and shook its head.

"Hey, Junk Boy!" I yelled. "Down here."

I ran up to its big toe and stabbed it with Riptide. The magic blade cut a gash in the bronze.

Unfortunately, my plan worked. Talos looked down at me and raised his foot to squash me like a bug. I didn't see what Bianca was doing. I had to turn and run. The foot came down about two inches behind me and I was knocked into the air. I hit something hard and sat up, dazed. I'd been thrown into an Olympus-Air refrigerator.

The monster was about to finish me off, but Grover somehow dug himself out of the junk pile. He played his pipes frantically, and his music sent another power line pole whacking against Talos's thigh. The monster turned. Grover should've run, but he must've been too exhausted from the effort of so much magic. He took two steps, fell, and didn't get back up.

"Grover!" Thalia and I both ran toward him, but I knew we'd be too late.

The monster raised his sword to smash Grover. Then he froze.

Talos cocked his head to one side, like he was hearing strange new music. He started moving his arms and legs in weird ways, doing the Funky Chicken. Then he made a fist and punched himself in the face.

"Go, Bianca!" I yelled.

Zoë looked horrified. "She is *inside?*"

The monster staggered around, and I realized we were still in danger. Thalia and I grabbed Grover and ran with him toward the highway. Zoë was already ahead of us. She yelled, "How will Bianca get out?"

The giant hit itself in the head again and dropped his sword. A shudder ran through his whole body and he staggered toward the power lines.

"Look out!" I yelled, but it was too late.

The giant's ankle snared the lines, and blue flickers of electricity shot up his body. I hoped the inside was insulated. I had no idea what was going on in there. The giant careened back into the junkyard, and his right hand fell off, landing in the scrap metal with a horrible *CLANG!*

His left arm came loose, too. He was falling apart at the joints.

Talos began to run.

"Wait!" Zoë yelled. We ran after him, but there was no way we could keep up. Pieces of the robot kept falling off, getting in our way.

The giant crumbled from the top down: his head, his chest, and finally, his legs collapsed. When we reached the wreckage we searched frantically, yelling Bianca's name. We crawled around in the vast hollow pieces and the legs and the head. We searched until the sun started to rise, but no luck.

Zoë sat down and wept. I was stunned to see her cry.

Thalia yelled in rage and impaled her sword in the giant's smashed face.

"We can keep searching," I said. "It's light now. We'll find her."

"No we won't," Grover said miserably. "It happened just as it was supposed to."

"What are you talking about?" I demanded.

He looked up at me with big watery eyes. "The prophecy. *One shall be lost in the land without rain.*"

Why hadn't I seen it? Why had I let her go instead of me?

Here we were in the desert. And Bianca di Angelo was gone.

FOURTEEN
ᘑᛏᘔ

I HAVE A
DAM PROBLEM

At the edge of the dump, we found a tow truck so old it might've been thrown away itself. But the engine started, and it had a full tank of gas, so we decided to borrow it.

Thalia drove. She didn't seem as stunned as Zoë or Grover or me.

"The skeletons are still out there," she reminded us. "We need to keep moving."

She navigated us through the desert, under clear blue skies, the sand so bright it hurt to look at. Zoë sat up front with Thalia. Grover and I sat in the pickup bed, leaning against the tow wench. The air was cool and dry, but the nice weather just seemed like an insult after losing Bianca.

My hand closed around the little figurine that had cost her life. I still couldn't even tell what god it was supposed to be. Nico would know.

Oh, gods . . . what was I going to tell Nico?

I wanted to believe that Bianca was still alive somewhere. But I had a bad feeling that she was gone for good.

"It should've been me," I said. "I should've gone into the giant."

"Don't say that!" Grover panicked. "It's bad enough

Annabeth is gone, and now Bianca. Do you think I could stand it if . . ." He sniffled. "Do you think anybody *else* would be my best friend?"

"Ah, Grover . . ."

He wiped under his eyes with an oily cloth that left his face grimy, like he had on war paint. "I'm . . . I'm okay."

But he wasn't okay. Ever since the encounter in New Mexico—whatever had happened when that wild wind blew through—he seemed really fragile, even more emotional than usual. I was afraid to talk to him about it, because he might start bawling.

At least there's one good thing about having a friend who gets freaked out more than you do. I realized I couldn't stay depressed. I had to set aside thinking about Bianca and keep us going forward, the way Thalia was doing. I wondered what she and Zoë were talking about in the front of the truck.

The tow truck ran out of gas at the edge of a river canyon. That was just as well, because the road dead-ended.

Thalia got out and slammed the door. Immediately, one of the tires blew. "Great. What now?"

I scanned the horizon. There wasn't much to see. Desert in all directions, occasional clumps of barren mountains plopped here and there. The canyon was the only thing interesting. The river itself wasn't very big, maybe fifty yards across, green water with a few rapids, but it carved a huge scar out of the desert. The rock cliffs dropped away below us.

"There's a path," Grover said. "We could get to the river."

I tried to see what he was talking about, and finally noticed a tiny ledge winding down the cliff face. "That's a goat path," I said.

"So?" he asked.

"The rest of us aren't goats."

"We can make it," Grover said. "I think."

I thought about that. I'd done cliffs before, but I didn't like them. Then I looked over at Thalia and saw how pale she'd gotten. Her problem with heights . . . she'd never be able to do it.

"No," I said. "I, uh, think we should go farther upstream."

Grover said, "But—"

"Come on," I said. "A walk won't hurt us."

I glanced at Thalia. Her eyes said a quick *Thank you.*

We followed the river about half a mile before coming to an easier slope that led down to the water. On the shore was a canoe rental operation that was closed for the season, but I left a stack of golden drachmas on the counter and a note saying *IOU two canoes.*

"We need to go upstream," Zoë said. It was the first time I'd heard her speak since the junkyard, and I was worried about how bad she sounded, like somebody with the flu. "The rapids are too swift."

"Leave that to me," I said. We put the canoes in the water.

Thalia pulled me aside as we were getting the oars. "Thanks for back there."

"Don't mention it."

"Can you really . . ." She nodded to the rapids. "You know."

"I think so. Usually I'm good with water."

"Would you take Zoë?" she asked. "I think, ah, maybe you can talk to her."

"She's not going to like that."

"Please? I don't know if I can stand being in the same boat with her. She's . . . she's starting to worry me."

It was about the last thing I wanted to do, but I nodded.

Thalia's shoulders relaxed. "I owe you one."

"Two."

"One and a half," Thalia said.

She smiled, and for a second, I remembered that I actually liked her when she wasn't yelling at me. She turned and helped Grover get their canoe into the water.

As it turned out, I didn't even need to control the currents. As soon as we got in the river, I looked over the edge of the boat and found a couple of naiads staring at me.

They looked like regular teenage girls, the kind you'd see in any mall, except for the fact that they were underwater.

Hey, I said.

They made a bubbling sound that may have been giggling. I wasn't sure. I had a hard time understanding naiads.

We're heading upstream, I told them. *Do you think you could—*

Before I could even finish, the naiads each chose a canoe and began pushing us up the river. We started so fast

Grover fell into his canoe with his hooves sticking up in the air.

"I hate naiads," Zoë grumbled.

A stream of water squirted up from the back of the boat and hit Zoë in the face.

"She-devils!" Zoë went for her bow.

"Whoa," I said. "They're just playing."

"Cursed water spirits. They've never forgiven me."

"Forgiven you for what?"

She slung her bow back over her shoulder. "It was a long time ago. Never mind."

We sped up the river, the cliffs looming up on either side of us.

"What happened to Bianca wasn't your fault," I told her. "It was my fault. I let her go."

I figured this would give Zoë an excuse to start yelling at me. At least that might shake her out of feeling depressed.

Instead, her shoulders slumped. "No, Percy. I pushed her into going on the quest. I was too anxious. She was a powerful half-blood. She had a kind heart, as well. I . . . I thought she would be the next lieutenant."

"But you're the lieutenant."

She gripped the strap of her quiver. She looked more tired than I'd ever seen her. "Nothing can last forever, Percy. Over two thousand years I have led the Hunt, and my wisdom has not improved. Now Artemis herself is in danger."

"Look, you can't blame yourself for that."

"If I had insisted on going with her—"

"You think you could've fought something powerful

enough to kidnap Artemis? There's nothing you could have done."

Zoë didn't answer.

The cliffs along the river were getting taller. Long shadows fell across the water, making it a lot colder, even though the day was bright.

Without thinking about it, I took Riptide out of my pocket. Zoë looked at the pen, and her expression was pained.

"You made this," I said.

"Who told thee?"

"I had a dream about it."

She studied me. I was sure she was going to call me crazy, but she just sighed. "It was a gift. And a mistake."

"Who was the hero?" I asked.

Zoë shook her head. "Do not make me say his name. I swore never to speak it again."

"You act like I should know him."

"I am sure you do, hero. Don't all you boys want to be just like him?"

Her voice was so bitter, I decided not to ask what she meant. I looked down at Riptide, and for the first time, I wondered if it was cursed.

"Your mother was a water goddess?" I asked.

"Yes, Pleione. She had five daughters. My sisters and I. The Hesperides."

"Those were the girls who lived in a garden at the edge of the West. With the golden apple tree and a dragon guarding it."

"Yes," Zoë said wistfully. "Ladon."

"But weren't there only four sisters?"

"There are now. I was exiled. Forgotten. Blotted out as if I never existed."

"Why?"

Zoë pointed to my pen. "Because I betrayed my family and helped a hero. You won't find that in the legend either. He never spoke of me. After his direct assault on Ladon failed, I gave him the idea of how to steal the apples, how to trick my father, but *he* took all the credit."

"But—"

Gurgle, gurgle, the naiad spoke in my mind. The canoe was slowing down.

I looked ahead, and I saw why.

This was as far as they could take us. The river was blocked. A dam the size of a football stadium stood in our path.

"Hoover Dam," Thalia said. "It's huge."

We stood at the river's edge, looking up at a curve of concrete that loomed between the cliffs. People were walking along the top of the dam. They were so tiny they looked like fleas.

The naiads had left with a lot of grumbling—not in words I could understand, but it was obvious they hated this dam blocking up their nice river. Our canoes floated back downstream, swirling in the wake from the dam's discharge vents.

"Seven hundred feet tall," I said. "Built in the 1930s."

"Five million cubic acres of water," Thalia said.

Grover sighed. "Largest construction project in the United States."

Zoë stared at us. "How do you know all that?"

"Annabeth," I said. "She liked architecture."

"She was nuts about monuments," Thalia said.

"Spouted facts all the time." Grover sniffled. "So annoying."

"I wish she were here," I said.

The others nodded. Zoë was still looking at us strangely, but I didn't care. It seemed like cruel fate that we'd come to Hoover Dam, one of Annabeth's personal favorites, and she wasn't here to see it.

"We should go up there," I said. "For her sake. Just to say we've been."

"You are mad," Zoë decided. "But that's where the road is." She pointed to a huge parking garage next to the top of the dam. "And so, sightseeing it is."

We had to walk for almost an hour before we found a path that led up to the road. It came up on the east side of the river. Then we straggled back toward the dam. It was cold and windy on top. On one side, a big lake spread out, ringed by barren desert mountains. On the other side, the dam dropped away like the world's most dangerous skateboard ramp, down to the river seven hundred feet below, and water that churned from the dam's vents.

Thalia walked in the middle of the road, far away from the edges. Grover kept sniffing the wind and looking nervous. He didn't say anything, but I knew he smelled monsters.

"How close are they?" I asked him.

He shook his head. "Maybe not close. The wind on the dam, the desert all around us . . . the scent can probably carry for miles. But it's coming from several directions. I don't like that."

I didn't either. It was already Wednesday, only two days until winter solstice, and we still had a long way to go. We didn't need any more monsters.

"There's a snack bar in the visitor center," Thalia said.

"You've been here before?" I asked.

"Once. To see the guardians." She pointed to the far end of the dam. Carved into the side of the cliff was a little plaza with two big bronze statues. They looked kind of like Oscar statues with wings.

"They were dedicated to Zeus when the dam was built," Thalia said. "A gift from Athena."

Tourists were clustered all around them. They seemed to be looking at the statues' feet.

"What are they doing?" I asked.

"Rubbing the toes," Thalia said. "They think it's good luck."

"Why?"

She shook her head. "Mortals get crazy ideas. They don't know the statues are sacred to Zeus, but they know there's something special about them."

"When you were here last, did they talk to you or anything?"

Thalia's expression darkened. I could tell that she'd come here before hoping for exactly that—some kind of sign from her dad. Some connection. "No. They don't do anything. They're just big metal statues."

I thought about the last big metal statue we'd run into. That hadn't gone so well. But I decided not to bring it up.

"Let us find the dam snack bar," Zoë said. "We should eat while we can."

Grover cracked a smile. "The dam snack bar?"

Zoë blinked. "Yes. What is funny?"

"Nothing," Grover said, trying to keep a straight face. "I could use some dam french fries."

Even Thalia smiled at that. "And I need to use the dam restroom."

Maybe it was the fact that we were so tired and strung out emotionally, but I started cracking up, and Thalia and Grover joined in, while Zoë just looked at us. "I do not understand."

"I want to use the dam water fountain," Grover said.

"And . . ." Thalia tried to catch her breath. "I want to buy a dam T-shirt."

I busted up, and I probably would've kept laughing all day, but then I heard a noise:

"Moooo."

The smile melted off my face. I wondered if the noise was just in my head, but Grover had stopped laughing too. He was looking around, confused. "Did I just hear a cow?"

"A dam cow?" Thalia laughed.

"No," Grover said. "I'm serious."

Zoë listened. "I hear nothing."

Thalia was looking at me. "Percy, are you okay?"

"Yeah," I said. "You guys go ahead. I'll be right in."

"What's wrong?" Grover asked.

"Nothing," I said. "I . . . I just need a minute. To think."

They hesitated, but I guess I must've looked upset, because they finally went into the visitor center without me. As soon as they were gone, I jogged to the north edge of the dam and looked over.

"Moo."

She was about thirty feet below in the lake, but I could see her clearly: my friend from Long Island Sound, Bessie the cow serpent.

I looked around. There were groups of kids running along the dam. A lot of senior citizens. Some families. But nobody seemed to be paying Bessie any attention yet.

"What are you doing here?" I asked her.

"Moo!"

Her voice was urgent, like she was trying to warn me of something.

"How did you get here?" I asked. We were thousands of miles from Long Island, hundreds of miles inland. There was no way she could've swum all the way here. And yet, here she was.

Bessie swam in a circle and butted her head against the side of the dam. "Moo!"

She wanted me to come with her. She was telling me to hurry.

"I can't," I told her. "My friends are inside."

[209]

She looked at me with her sad brown eyes. Then she gave one more urgent "Mooo!," did a flip, and disappeared into the water.

I hesitated. Something was wrong. She was trying to tell me that. I considered jumping over the side and following her, but then I tensed. The hairs on my arms bristled. I looked down the dam road to the east and I saw two men walking slowly toward me. They wore gray camouflage outfits that flickered over skeletal bodies.

They passed through a group of kids and pushed them aside. A kid yelled, "Hey!" One of the warriors turned, his face changing momentarily into a skull.

"Ah!" the kid yelled, and his whole group backed away.

I ran for the visitor center.

I was almost to the stairs when I heard tires squeal. On the west side of the dam, a black van swerved to a stop in the middle of the road, nearly plowing into some old people.

The van doors opened and more skeleton warriors piled out. I was surrounded.

I bolted down the stairs and through the museum entrance. The security guard at the metal detector yelled, "Hey, kid!" But I didn't stop.

I ran through the exhibits and ducked behind a tour group. I looked for my friends, but I couldn't see them anywhere. Where was the dam snack bar?

"Stop!" The metal-detector guy yelled.

There was no place to go but into an elevator with the tour group. I ducked inside just as the door closed.

"We'll be going down seven hundred feet," our tour guide said cheerfully. She was a park ranger, with long black hair pulled back in a ponytail and tinted glasses. I guess she hadn't noticed that I was being chased. "Don't worry, ladies and gentlemen, the elevator hardly ever breaks."

"Does this go to the snack bar?" I asked her.

A few people behind me chuckled. The tour guide looked at me. Something about her gaze made my skin tingle.

"To the turbines, young man," the lady said. "Weren't you listening to my fascinating presentation upstairs?"

"Oh, uh, sure. Is there another way out of the dam?"

"It's a dead end," a tourist behind me said. "For heaven's sake. The only way out is the other elevator."

The doors opened.

"Go right ahead, folks," the tour guide told us. "Another ranger is waiting for you at the end of the corridor."

I didn't have much choice but to go out with the group.

"And young man," the tour guide called. I looked back. She'd taken off her glasses. Her eyes were startlingly gray, like storm clouds. "There is always a way out for those clever enough to find it."

The doors closed with the tour guide still inside, leaving me alone.

Before I could think too much about the woman in the elevator, a *ding* came from around the corner. The second elevator was opening, and I heard an unmistakable sound— the clattering of skeleton teeth.

I ran after the tour group, through a tunnel carved out

of solid rock. It seemed to run forever. The walls were moist, and the air hummed with electricity and the roar of water. I came out on a U-shaped balcony that overlooked this huge warehouse area. Fifty feet below, enormous turbines were running. It was a big room, but I didn't see any other exit, unless I wanted to jump into the turbines and get churned up to make electricity. I didn't.

Another tour guide was talking over the microphone, telling the tourists about water supplies in Nevada. I prayed that Thalia, Zoë, and Grover were okay. They might already be captured, or eating at the snack bar, completely unaware that we were being surrounded. And stupid me: I had trapped myself in a hole hundreds of feet below the surface.

I worked my way around the crowd, trying not to be too obvious about it. There was a hallway at the other side of the balcony—maybe some place I could hide. I kept my hand on Riptide, ready to strike.

By the time I got to the opposite side of the balcony, my nerves were shot. I backed into the little hallway and watched the tunnel I'd come from.

Then right behind me I heard a sharp *Chhh!* like the voice of a skeleton.

Without thinking, I uncapped Riptide and spun, slashing with my sword.

The girl I'd just tried to slice in half yelped and dropped her Kleenex.

"Oh my god!" she shouted. "Do you always kill people when they blow their nose?"

The first thing that went through my head was that the

sword hadn't hurt her. It had passed clean through her body, harmlessly. "You're mortal!"

She looked at me in disbelief. "What's *that* supposed to mean? Of course I'm mortal! How did you get that sword past security?"

"I didn't— Wait, you can see it's a sword?"

The girl rolled her eyes, which were green like mine. She had frizzy reddish-brown hair. Her nose was also red, like she had a cold. She wore a big maroon Harvard sweatshirt and jeans that were covered with marker stains and little holes, like she spent her free time poking them with a fork.

"Well, it's either a sword or the biggest toothpick in the world," she said. "And why didn't it hurt me? I mean, not that I'm complaining. Who are you? And whoa, what is that you're wearing? Is that made of lion fur?"

She asked so many questions so fast, it was like she was throwing rocks at me. I couldn't think of what to say. I looked at my sleeves to see if the Nemean Lion pelt had somehow changed back to fur, but it still looked like a brown winter coat to me.

I knew the skeleton warriors were still chasing me. I had no time to waste. But I just stared at the redheaded girl. Then I remembered what Thalia had done at Westover Hall to fool the teachers. Maybe I could manipulate the Mist.

I concentrated hard and snapped my fingers. "You don't see a sword," I told the girl. "It's just a ballpoint pen."

She blinked. "Um . . . no. It's a sword, weirdo."

"Who *are* you?" I demanded.

She huffed indignantly. "Rachel Elizabeth Dare. Now, are you going to answer *my* questions or should I scream for security?"

"No!" I said. "I mean, I'm kind of in a hurry. I'm in trouble."

"In a hurry or in trouble?"

"Um, sort of both."

She looked over my shoulder and her eyes widened. "Bathroom!"

"What?"

"Bathroom! Behind me! Now!"

I don't know why, but I listened to her. I slipped inside the boys' bathroom and left Rachel Elizabeth Dare standing outside. Later, that seemed cowardly to me. I'm also pretty sure it saved my life.

I heard the clattering, hissing sounds of skeletons as they came closer.

My grip tightened on Riptide. What was I thinking? I'd left a mortal girl out there to die. I was preparing to burst out and fight when Rachel Elizabeth Dare started talking in that rapid-fire machine gun way of hers.

"Oh my god! Did you *see* that kid? It's about time you got here. He tried to kill me! He had a sword, for god's sake. You security guys let a sword-swinging lunatic inside a national landmark? I mean, jeez! He ran that way toward those turbine thingies. I think he went over the side or something. Maybe he fell."

The skeletons clattered excitedly. I heard them moving off.

Rachel opened the door. "All clear. But you'd better hurry."

She looked shaken. Her face was gray and sweaty.

I peeked around the corner. Three skeleton warriors were running toward the other end of the balcony. The way to the elevator was clear for a few seconds.

"I owe you one, Rachel Elizabeth Dare."

"What are those things?" she asked. "They looked like—"

"Skeletons?"

She nodded uneasily.

"Do yourself a favor," I said. "Forget it. Forget you ever saw me."

"Forget you tried to kill me?"

"Yeah. That, too."

"But who are you?"

"Percy—" I started to say. Then the skeletons turned around. "Gotta go!"

"What kind of name is Percy Gotta-go?"

I bolted for the exit.

The café was packed with kids enjoying the best part of the tour—the dam lunch. Thalia, Zoë, and Grover were just sitting down with their food.

"We need to leave," I gasped. "Now!"

"But we just got our burritos!" Thalia said.

Zoë stood up, muttering an Ancient Greek curse. "He's right! Look."

The café windows wrapped all the way around the

observation floor, which gave us a beautiful panoramic view of the skeletal army that had come to kill us.

I counted two on the east side of the dam road, blocking the way to Arizona. Three more on the west side, guarding Nevada. All of them were armed with batons and pistols.

But our immediate problem was a lot closer. The three skeletal warriors who'd been chasing me in the turbine room now appeared on the stairs. They saw me from across the cafeteria and clattered their teeth.

"Elevator!" Grover said. We bolted that direction, but the doors opened with a pleasant *ding*, and three more warriors stepped out. Every warrior was accounted for, minus the one Bianca had blasted to flames in New Mexico. We were completely surrounded.

Then Grover had a brilliant, totally Grover-like idea.

"Burrito fight!" he yelled, and flung his Guacamole Grande at the nearest skeleton.

Now, if you have never been hit by a flying burrito, count yourself lucky. In terms of deadly projectiles, it's right up there with grenades and cannonballs. Grover's lunch hit the skeleton and knocked his skull clean off his shoulders. I'm not sure what the other kids in the café saw, but they went crazy and started throwing their burritos and baskets of chips and sodas at each other, shrieking and screaming.

The skeletons tried to aim their guns, but it was hopeless. Bodies and food and drinks were flying everywhere.

In the chaos, Thalia and I tackled the other two

skeletons on the stairs and sent them flying into the condiment table. Then we all raced downstairs, Guacamole Grandes whizzing past our heads.

"What now?" Grover asked as we burst outside.

I didn't have an answer. The warriors on the road were closing in from either direction. We ran across the street to the pavilion with the winged bronze statues, but that just put our backs to the mountain.

The skeletons moved forward, forming a crescent around us. Their brethren from the café were running up to join them. One was still putting its skull back on its shoulders. Another was covered in ketchup and mustard. Two more had burritos lodged in their rib cages. They didn't look happy about it. They drew batons and advanced.

"Four against eleven," Zoë muttered. "And *they* cannot die."

"It's been nice adventuring with you guys," Grover said, his voice trembling.

Something shiny caught the corner of my eye. I glanced behind me at the statue's feet. "Whoa," I said. "Their toes really are bright."

"Percy!" Thalia said. "This isn't the time."

But I couldn't help staring at the two giant bronze guys with tall bladed wings like letter openers. They were weathered brown except for their toes, which shone like new pennies from all the times people had rubbed them for good luck.

Good luck. The blessing of Zeus.

I thought about the tour guide in the elevator. Her gray

eyes and her smile. What had she said? *There is always a way for those clever enough to find it.*

"Thalia," I said. "Pray to your dad."

She glared at me. "He never answers."

"Just this once," I pleaded. "Ask for help. I think . . . I think the statues can give us some luck."

Six skeletons raised their guns. The other five came forward with batons. Fifty feet away. Forty feet.

"Do it!" I yelled.

"No!" Thalia said. "He won't answer me."

"This time is different!"

"Who says?"

I hesitated. "Athena, I think."

Thalia scowled like she was sure I'd gone crazy.

"Try it," Grover pleaded.

Thalia closed her eyes. Her lips moved in a silent prayer. I put in my own prayer to Annabeth's mom, hoping I was right that it had been her in that elevator—that she was trying to help us save her daughter.

And nothing happened.

The skeletons closed in. I raised Riptide to defend myself. Thalia held up her shield. Zoë pushed Grover behind her and aimed an arrow at a skeleton's head.

A shadow fell over me. I thought maybe it was the shadow of death. Then I realized it was the shadow of an enormous wing. The skeletons looked up too late. A flash of bronze, and all five of the baton-wielders were swept aside.

The other skeletons opened fire. I raised my lion coat

for protection, but I didn't need it. The bronze angels stepped in front of us and folded their wings like shields. Bullets pinged off of them like rain off a corrugated roof. Both angels slashed outward, and the skeletons went flying across the road.

"Man, it feels good to stand up!" the first angel said. His voice sounded tinny and rusty, like he hadn't had a drink since he'd been built.

"Will ya look at my toes?" the other said. "Holy Zeus, what were those tourists thinking?"

As stunned as I was by the angels, I was more concerned with the skeletons. A few of them were getting up again, reassembling, bony hands groping for their weapons.

"Trouble!" I said.

"Get us out of here!" Thalia yelled.

Both angels looked down at her. "Zeus's kid?"

"Yes!"

"Could I get a *please*, Miss Zeus's Kid?" an angel asked.

"Please!"

The angels looked at each other and shrugged.

"Could use a stretch," one decided.

And the next thing I knew, one of them grabbed Thalia and me, the other grabbed Zoë and Grover, and we flew straight up, over the dam and the river, the skeleton warriors shrinking to tiny specks below us and the sound of gunfire echoing off the sides of the mountains.

FIFTEEN
⚔

I WRESTLE SANTA'S
EVIL TWIN

"Tell me when it's over," Thalia said. Her eyes were shut tight. The statue was holding on to us so we couldn't fall, but still Thalia clutched his arm like it was the most important thing in the world.

"Everything's fine," I promised.

"Are . . . are we very high?"

I looked down. Below us, a range of snowy mountains zipped by. I stretched out my foot and kicked snow off one of the peaks.

"Nah," I said. "Not that high."

"We are in the Sierras!" Zoë yelled. She and Grover were hanging from the arms of the other statue. "I have hunted here before. At this speed, we should be in San Francisco in a few hours."

"Hey, hey, Frisco!" our angel said. "Yo, Chuck! We could visit those guys at the Mechanics Monument again! They know how to party!"

"Oh, man," the other angel said. "I am *so* there!"

"You guys have visited San Francisco?" I asked.

"We automatons gotta have some fun once in a while, right?" our statue said. "Those mechanics took us over to the de Young Museum and introduced us to these marble lady statues, see. And—"

"Hank!" the other statue Chuck cut in. "They're kids, man."

"Oh, right." If bronze statues could blush, I swear Hank did. "Back to flying."

We sped up, so I could tell the angels were excited. The mountains fell away into hills, and then we were zipping along over farmland and towns and highways.

Grover played his pipes to pass the time. Zoë got bored and started shooting arrows at random billboards as we flew by. Every time she saw a Target department store—and we passed dozens of them—she would peg the store's sign with a few bulls-eyes at a hundred miles an hour.

Thalia kept her eyes closed the whole way. She muttered to herself a lot, like she was praying.

"You did good back there," I told her. "Zeus listened."

It was hard to tell what she was thinking with her eyes closed.

"Maybe," she said. "How did you get away from the skeletons in the generator room, anyway? You said they cornered you."

I told her about the weird mortal girl, Rachel Elizabeth Dare, who seemed to be able to see right through the Mist. I thought Thalia was going to call me crazy, but she just nodded.

"Some mortals are like that," she said. "Nobody knows why."

Suddenly I flashed on something I'd never considered.

My *mom* was like that. She had seen the Minotaur on Half-Blood Hill and known exactly what it was. She hadn't been surprised at all last year when I'd told her my friend Tyson was really a Cyclops. Maybe she'd known all along. No wonder she'd been so scared for me as I was growing up. She saw through the Mist even better than I did.

"Well, the girl was annoying," I said. "But I'm glad I didn't vaporize her. That would've been bad."

Thalia nodded. "Must be nice to be a regular mortal."

She said that as if she'd given it a lot of thought.

"Where you guys want to land?" Hank asked, waking me up from a nap.

I looked down and said, "Whoa."

I'd seen San Francisco in pictures before, but never in real life. It was probably the most beautiful city I'd ever seen: kind of like a smaller, cleaner Manhattan, if Manhattan had been surrounded by green hills and fog. There was a huge bay and ships, islands and sailboats, and the Golden Gate Bridge sticking up out of the fog. I felt like I should take a picture or something. *Greetings from Frisco. Haven't Died Yet. Wish You Were Here.*

"There," Zoë suggested. "By the Embarcadero Building."

"Good thinking," Chuck said. "Me and Hank can blend in with the pigeons."

We all looked at him.

"Kidding," he said. "Sheesh, can't statues have a sense of humor?"

As it turned out, there wasn't much need to blend in. It

was early morning and not many people were around. We freaked out a homeless guy on the ferry dock when we landed. He screamed when he saw Hank and Chuck and ran off yelling something about metal angels from Mars.

We said our good-byes to the angels, who flew off to party with their statue friends. That's when I realized I had no idea what we were going to do next.

We'd made it to the West Coast. Artemis was here somewhere. Annabeth too, I hoped. But I had no idea how to find them, and tomorrow was the winter solstice. Nor did I have any clue what monster Artemis had been hunting. It was supposed to find *us* on the quest. It was supposed to "show the trail," but it never had. Now we were stuck on the ferry dock with not much money, no friends, and no luck.

After a brief discussion, we agreed that we needed to figure out just what this mystery monster was.

"But how?" I asked.

"Nereus," Grover said.

I looked at him. "What?"

"Isn't that what Apollo told you to do? Find Nereus?"

I nodded. I'd completely forgotten my last conversation with the sun god.

"The old man of the sea," I remembered. "I'm supposed to find him and force him to tell us what he knows. But how do I find him?"

Zoë made a face. "Old Nereus, eh?"

"You know him?" Thalia asked.

"My mother was a sea goddess. Yes, I know him.

Unfortunately, he is never very hard to find. Just follow the smell."

"What do you mean?" I asked.

"Come," she said without enthusiasm. "I will show thee."

I knew I was in trouble when we stopped at the Goodwill drop box. Five minutes later, Zoë had me outfitted in a ragged flannel shirt and jeans three sizes too big, bright red sneakers, and a floppy rainbow hat.

"Oh, yeah," Grover said, trying not to bust out laughing, "you look completely inconspicuous now."

Zoë nodded with satisfaction. "A typical male vagrant."

"Thanks a lot," I grumbled. "Why am I doing this again?"

"I told thee. To blend in."

She led the way back down to the waterfront. After a long time spent searching the docks, Zoë finally stopped in her tracks. She pointed down a pier where a bunch of homeless guys were huddled together in blankets, waiting for the soup kitchen to open for lunch.

"He will be down there somewhere," Zoë said. "He never travels very far from the water. He likes to sun himself during the day."

"How do I know which one is him?"

"Sneak up," she said. "Act homeless. You will know him. He will smell . . . different."

"Great." I didn't want to ask for particulars. "And once I find him?"

"Grab him," she said. "And hold on. He will try anything to get rid of thee. Whatever he does, do not let go. Force him to tell thee about the monster."

"We've got your back," Thalia said. She picked something off the back of my shirt—a big clump of fuzz that came from who-knows-where. "Eww. On second thought . . . I don't want your back. But we'll be rooting for you."

Grover gave me a big thumbs-up.

I grumbled how nice it was to have super-powerful friends. Then I headed toward the dock.

I pulled my hat down and stumbled like I was about to pass out, which wasn't hard considering how tired I was. I passed our homeless friend from the Embarcadero, who was still trying to warn the other guys about the metal angels from Mars.

He didn't smell good, but he didn't smell . . . different. I kept walking.

A couple of grimy dudes with plastic grocery bags for hats checked me out as I came close.

"Beat it, kid!" one of them muttered.

I moved away. They smelled pretty bad, but just regular old bad. Nothing unusual.

There was a lady with a bunch of plastic flamingos sticking out of a shopping cart. She glared at me like I was going to steal her birds.

At the end of the pier, a guy who looked about a million years old was passed out in a patch of sunlight. He wore pajamas and a fuzzy bathrobe that probably used to be white. He was fat, with a white beard that had turned yellow, kind of like Santa Claus, if Santa had been rolled out of bed and dragged through a landfill.

And his smell?

As I got closer, I froze. He smelled bad, all right—but *ocean* bad. Like hot seaweed and dead fish and brine. If the ocean had an ugly side . . . this guy was it.

I tried not to gag as I sat down near him like I was tired. Santa opened one eye suspiciously. I could feel him staring at me, but I didn't look. I muttered something about stupid school and stupid parents, figuring that might sound reasonable.

Santa Claus went back to sleep.

I tensed. I knew this was going to look strange. I didn't know how the other homeless people would react. But I jumped Santa Claus.

"Ahhhhh!" he screamed. I meant to grab him, but he seemed to grab me instead. It was as if he'd never been asleep at all. He certainly didn't act like a weak old man. He had a grip like steel. "Help me!" he screamed as he squeezed me to death.

"That's a crime!" one of the other homeless guys yelled. "Kid rolling an old man like that!"

I rolled, all right—straight down the pier until my head slammed into a post. I was dazed for a second, and Nereus's grip slackened. He was making a break for it. Before he could, I regained my senses and tackled him from behind.

"I don't have any money!" He tried to get up and run, but I locked my arms around his chest. His rotten fish smell was awful, but I held on.

"I don't want money," I said as he fought. "I'm a half-blood! I want information!"

That just made him struggle harder. "Heroes! Why do you always pick on me?"

"Because you know everything!"

He growled and tried to shake me off his back. It was like holding on to a roller coaster. He thrashed around, making it impossible for me to keep on my feet, but I gritted my teeth and squeezed tighter. We staggered toward the edge of the pier and I got an idea.

"Oh, no!" I said. "Not the water!"

The plan worked. Immediately, Nereus yelled in triumph and jumped off the edge. Together, we plunged into San Francisco Bay.

He must've been surprised when I tightened my grip, the ocean filling me with extra strength. But Nereus had a few tricks left, too. He changed shape until I was holding a sleek black seal.

I've heard people make jokes about trying to hold a greased pig, but I'm telling you, holding on to a seal in the water is harder. Nereus plunged straight down, wriggling and thrashing and spiraling through the dark water. If I hadn't been Poseidon's son, there's no way I could've stayed with him.

Nereus spun and expanded, turning into a killer whale, but I grabbed his dorsal fin as he burst out of the water.

A whole bunch of tourists went, "Whoa!"

I managed to wave at the crowd. *Yeah, we do this every day here in San Francisco.*

Nereus plunged into the water and turned into a slimy eel. I started to tie him into a knot until he realized what was going on and changed back to human form. "Why won't you drown?" he wailed, pummeling me with his fists.

"I'm Poseidon's son," I said.

"Curse that upstart! I was here first!"

Finally he collapsed on the edge of the boat dock. Above us was one of those tourist piers lined with shops, like a mall on water. Nereus was heaving and gasping. I was feeling great. I could've gone on all day, but I didn't tell him that. I wanted him to feel like he'd put up a good fight.

My friends ran down the steps from the pier.

"You got him!" Zoë said.

"You don't have to sound so amazed," I said.

Nereus moaned. "Oh, wonderful. An audience for my humiliation! The normal deal, I suppose? You'll let me go if I answer your question?"

"I've got more than one question," I said.

"Only one question per capture! That's the rule."

I looked at my friends.

This wasn't good. I needed to find Artemis, and I needed to figure out what the doomsday creature was. I also needed to know if Annabeth was still alive, and how to rescue her. How could I ask that all in one question?

A voice inside me was screaming *Ask about Annabeth!* That's what I cared about most.

But then I imagined what Annabeth might say. She would never forgive me if I saved her and didn't save Olympus. Zoë would want me to ask about Artemis, but

Chiron had told us the monster was even more important.

I sighed. "All right, Nereus. Tell me where to find this terrible monster that could bring an end to the gods. The one Artemis was hunting."

The Old Man of the Sea smiled, showing off his mossy green teeth.

"Oh, that's too easy," he said evilly. "He's right there."

Nereus pointed to the water at my feet.

"Where?" I said.

"The deal is complete!" Nereus gloated. With a pop, he turned into a goldfish and did a backflip into the sea.

"You tricked me!" I yelled.

"Wait." Thalia's eyes widened. "What is *that*?"

"MOOOOOOOO!"

I looked down, and there was my friend the cow serpent, swimming next to the dock. She nudged my shoe and gave me the sad brown eyes.

"Ah, Bessie," I said. "Not now."

"Mooo!"

Grover gasped. "He says his name isn't Bessie."

"You can understand her . . . er, him?"

Grover nodded. "It's a very old form of animal speech. But he says his name is the Ophiotaurus."

"The Ophi-what?"

"It means serpent bull in Greek," Thalia said. "But what's it doing here?"

"Moooooooo!"

"He says Percy is his protector," Grover announced.

"And he's running from the bad people. He says they are close."

I was wondering how you got all that out of a single *moooooo*.

"Wait," Zoë said, looking at me. "You know this cow?"

I was feeling impatient, but I told them the story.

Thalia shook her head in disbelief. "And you just forgot to mention this before?"

"Well . . . yeah." It seemed silly, now that she said it, but things had been happening so fast. Bessie, the Ophiotaurus, seemed like a minor detail.

"I am a fool," Zoë said suddenly. "I know this story!"

"What story?"

"From the War of the Titans," she said. "My . . . my father told me this tale, thousands of years ago. This is the beast we are looking for."

"Bessie?" I looked down at the bull serpent. "But . . . he's too cute. He couldn't destroy the world."

"That is how we were wrong," Zoë said. "We've been anticipating a huge dangerous monster, but the Ophiotaurus does not bring down the gods that way. He must be sacrificed."

"MMMM," Bessie lowed.

"I don't think he likes the S-word," Grover said.

I patted Bessie on the head, trying to calm him down. He let me scratch his ear, but he was trembling.

"How could anyone hurt him?" I said. "He's harmless."

Zoë nodded. "But there is power in killing innocence.

Terrible power. The Fates ordained a prophecy eons ago, when this creature was born. They said that whoever killed the Ophiotaurus and sacrificed its entrails to fire would have the power to destroy the gods."

"MMMMMM!"

"Um," Grover said. "Maybe we could avoid talking about *entrails*, too."

Thalia stared at the cow serpent with wonder. "The power to destroy the gods . . . how? I mean, what would happen?"

"No one knows," Zoë said. "The first time, during the Titan war, the Ophiotaurus was in fact slain by a giant ally of the Titans, but thy father, Zeus, sent an eagle to snatch the entrails away before they could be tossed into the fire. It was a close call. Now, after three thousand years, the Ophiotaurus is reborn."

Thalia sat down on the dock. She stretched out her hand. Bessie went right to her. Thalia placed her hand on his head. Bessie shivered.

Thalia's expression bothered me. She almost looked . . . hungry.

"We have to protect him," I told her. "If Luke gets hold of him—"

"Luke wouldn't hesitate," Thalia muttered. "The power to overthrow Olympus. That's . . . that's huge."

"Yes, it is, my dear," said a man's voice in a heavy French accent. "And it is a power *you* shall unleash."

The Ophiotaurus made a whimpering sound and submerged.

I looked up. We'd been so busy talking, we'd allowed ourselves to be ambushed.

Standing behind us, his two-color eyes gleaming wickedly, was Dr. Thorn, the manticore himself.

"This is just pairrr-fect," the manticore gloated.

He was wearing a ratty black trench coat over his Westover Hall uniform, which was torn and stained. His military haircut had grown out spiky and greasy. He hadn't shaved recently, so his face was covered in silver stubble. Basically he didn't look much better than the guys down at the soup kitchen.

"Long ago, the gods banished me to Persia," the manticore said. "I was forced to scrounge for food on the edges of the world, hiding in forests, devouring insignificant human farmers for my meals. I never got to fight any great heroes. I was not feared and admired in the old stories! But now that will change. The Titans shall honor me, and I shall feast on the flesh of half-bloods!"

On either side of him stood two armed security guys, some of the mortal mercenaries I'd seen in D.C. Two more stood on the next boat dock over, just in case we tried to escape that way. There were tourists all around— walking down the waterfront, shopping at the pier above us—but I knew that wouldn't stop the manticore from acting.

"Where . . . where are the skeletons?" I asked the manticore.

He sneered. "I do not need those foolish undead! The

General thinks I am worthless? He will change his mind when I defeat you myself!"

I needed time to think. I had to save Bessie. I could dive into the sea, but how could I make a quick getaway with a five-hundred-pound cow serpent? And what about my friends?

"We beat you once before," I said.

"Ha! You could barely fight me with a goddess on your side. And, alas . . . that goddess is preoccupied at the moment. There will be no help for you now."

Zoë notched an arrow and aimed it straight at the manticore's head. The guards on either side of us raised their guns.

"Wait!" I said. "Zoë, don't!"

The manticore smiled. "The boy is right, Zoë Nightshade. Put away your bow. It would be a shame to kill you before you witnessed Thalia's great victory."

"What are you talking about?" Thalia growled. She had her shield and spear ready.

"Surely it is clear," the manticore said. "This is your moment. This is why Lord Kronos brought you back to life. You will sacrifice the Ophiotaurus. You will bring its entrails to the sacred fire on the mountain. You will gain unlimited power. And for your sixteenth birthday, you will overthrow Olympus."

No one spoke. It made terrible sense. Thalia was only two days away from turning sixteen. She was a child of the Big Three. And here was a choice, a terrible choice that could mean the end of the gods. It was just like the prophecy said. I wasn't sure if I felt relieved, horrified, or disappointed. I wasn't the prophecy kid after all. Doomsday was happening right now.

I waited for Thalia to tell the manticore off, but she hesitated. She looked completely stunned.

"You know it is the right choice," the manticore told her. "Your friend Luke recognized it. You shall be reunited with him. You shall rule this world together under the auspices of the Titans. Your father abandoned you, Thalia. He cares nothing for you. And now you shall gain power over him. Crush the Olympians underfoot, as they deserve. Call the beast! It will come to you. Use your spear."

"Thalia," I said, "snap out of it!"

She looked at me the same way she had the morning she woke up on Half-Blood Hill, dazed and uncertain. It was almost like she didn't know me. "I . . . I don't—"

"Your father helped you," I said. "He sent the metal angels. He turned you into a tree to preserve you."

Her hand tightened on the shaft of her spear.

I looked at Grover desperately. Thank the gods, he understood what I needed. He raised his pipes to his mouth and played a quick riff.

The manticore yelled, "Stop him!"

The guards had been targeting Zoë, and before they could figure out that the kid with the pipes was the bigger problem, the wooden planks at their feet sprouted new branches and tangled their legs. Zoë let loose two quick arrows that exploded at their feet in clouds of sulfurous yellow smoke. Fart arrows!

The guards started coughing. The manticore shot spines in our direction, but they ricocheted off my lion's coat.

"Grover," I said, "tell Bessie to dive deep and stay down!"

"Moooooo!" Grover translated. I could only hope that Bessie got the message.

"The cow . . ." Thalia muttered, still in a daze.

"Come on!" I pulled her along as we ran up the stairs to the shopping center on the pier. We dashed around the corner of the nearest store. I heard the manticore shouting at his minions, "Get them!" Tourists screamed as the guards shot blindly into the air.

We scrambled to the end of the pier. We hid behind a little kiosk filled with souvenir crystals—wind chimes and dream catchers and stuff like that, glittering in the sunlight. There was a water fountain next to us. Down below, a bunch of sea lions were sunning themselves on the rocks. The whole of San Francisco Bay spread out before us: the Golden Gate Bridge, Alcatraz Island, and the green hills and fog beyond that to the north. A picture-perfect moment, except for the fact that we were about to die and the world was going to end.

"Go over the side!" Zoë told me. "You can escape in the sea, Percy. Call on thy father for help. Maybe you can save the Ophiotaurus."

She was right, but I couldn't do it.

"I won't leave you guys," I said. "We fight together."

"You have to get word to camp!" Grover said. "At least let them know what's going on!"

Then I noticed the crystals making rainbows in the sunlight. There was a drinking fountain next to me . . .

"Get word to camp," I muttered. "Good idea."

I uncapped Riptide and slashed off the top of the water fountain. Water burst out of the busted pipe and sprayed all over us.

Thalia gasped as the water hit her. The fog seemed to clear from her eyes. "Are you crazy?" she asked.

But Grover understood. He was already fishing around in his pockets for a coin. He threw a golden drachma into the rainbows created by the mist and yelled, "O goddess, accept my offering!"

The mist rippled.

"Camp Half-Blood!" I said.

And there, shimmering in the Mist right next to us, was the last person I wanted to see: Mr. D, wearing his leopard-skin jogging suit and rummaging through the refrigerator.

He looked up lazily. "Do you mind?"

"Where's Chiron!" I shouted.

"How rude." Mr. D took a swig from a jug of grape juice. "Is that how you say hello?"

"Hello," I amended. "We're about to die! Where's Chiron?"

Mr. D considered that. I wanted to scream at him to hurry up, but I knew that wouldn't work. Behind us, footsteps and shouting—the manticore's troops were closing in.

"About to die," Mr. D mused. "How exciting. I'm afraid Chiron isn't here. Would you like me to take a message?"

I looked at my friends. "We're dead."

Thalia gripped her spear. She looked like her old angry self again. "Then we'll die fighting."

"How noble," Mr. D said, stifling a yawn. "So what is the problem, exactly?"

I didn't see that it would make any difference, but I told him about the Ophiotaurus.

"Mmm." He studied the contents of the fridge. "So that's it. I see."

"You don't even care!" I screamed. "You'd just as soon watch us die!"

"Let's see. I think I'm in the mood for pizza tonight."

I wanted to slash through the rainbow and disconnect, but I didn't have time. The manticore screamed, "There!" And we were surrounded. Two of the guards stood behind him. The other two appeared on the roofs of the pier shops above us. The manticore threw off his coat and transformed into his true self, his lion claws extended and his spiky tail bristling with poison barbs.

"Excellent," he said. He glanced at the apparition in the mist and snorted. "Alone, without any *real* help. Wonderful."

"You could *ask* for help," Mr. D murmured to me, as if this were an amusing thought. "You could say please."

When wild boars fly, I thought. There was no way I was going to die begging a slob like Mr. D, just so he could laugh as we all got gunned down.

Zoë readied her arrows. Grover lifted his pipes. Thalia raised her shield, and I noticed a tear running down her cheek. Suddenly it occurred to me: this had happened to her before. She had been cornered on Half-Blood Hill. She'd willingly given her life for her friends. But this time, she couldn't save us.

How could I let that happen to her?

"Please, Mr. D," I muttered. "Help."

Of course, nothing happened.

The manticore grinned. "Spare the daughter of Zeus. She will join us soon enough. Kill the others."

The men raised their guns, and something strange happened. You know how you feel when all the blood rushes to your head, like if you hang upside down and turn right-side up too quickly? There was a rush like that all around me, and a sound like a huge sigh. The sunlight tinged with purple. I smelled grapes and something more sour—wine.

SNAP!

It was the sound of many minds breaking at the same time. The sound of madness. One guard put his pistol between his teeth like it was a bone and ran around on all fours. Two others dropped their guns and started waltzing with each other. The fourth began doing what looked like an Irish clogging dance. It would have been funny if it hadn't been so terrifying.

"No!" screamed the manticore. "I will deal with you myself!"

His tail bristled, but the planks under his paws erupted into grape vines, which immediately began wrapping around the monster's body, sprouting new leaves and clusters of green baby grapes that ripened in seconds as the manticore shrieked, until he was engulfed in a huge mass of vines, leaves, and full clusters of purple grapes. Finally the grapes stopped shivering, and I had a feeling that somewhere inside there, the manticore was no more.

"Well," said Dionysus, closing his refrigerator. "That was fun."

I stared at him, horrified. "How could you . . . How did you—"

"Such gratitude," he muttered. "The mortals will come out of it. Too much explaining to do if I made their condition permanent. I hate writing reports to Father."

He stared resentfully at Thalia. "I hope you learned your lesson, girl. It isn't easy to resist power, is it?"

Thalia blushed as if she were ashamed.

"Mr. D," Grover said in amazement. "You . . . you saved us."

"Mmm. Don't make me regret it, satyr. Now get going, Percy Jackson. I've bought you a few hours at most."

"The Ophiotaurus," I said. "Can you get it to camp?"

Mr. D sniffed. "I do not transport livestock. That's your problem."

"But where do we go?"

Dionysus looked at Zoë. "Oh, I think the huntress knows. You must enter at sunset today, you know, or all is lost. Now good-bye. My pizza is waiting."

"Mr. D," I said.

He raised his eyebrow.

"You called me by my right name," I said. "You called me Percy Jackson."

"I most certainly did not, Peter Johnson. Now off with you!"

He waved his hand, and his image disappeared in the mist.

All around us, the manticore's minions were still acting completely nuts. One of them had found our friend the homeless guy, and they were having a serious conversation about metal angels from Mars. Several other guards were harassing the tourists, making animal noises and trying to steal their shoes.

I looked at Zoë. "What did he mean . . . 'You know where to go'?"

Her face was the color of the fog. She pointed across the bay, past the Golden Gate. In the distance, a single mountain rose up above the cloud layer.

"The garden of my sisters," she said. "I must go home."

WE MEET THE DRAGON OF
ETERNAL BAD BREATH

"We will never make it," Zoë said. "We are moving too slow. But we cannot leave the Ophiotaurus."

"Mooo," Bessie said. He swam next to me as we jogged along the waterfront. We'd left the shopping center pier far behind. We were heading toward the Golden Gate Bridge, but it was a lot farther than I'd realized. The sun was already dipping in the west.

"I don't get it," I said. "Why do we have to get there at sunset?"

"The Hesperides are the nymphs of the sunset," Zoë said. "We can only enter their garden as day changes to night."

"What happens if we miss it?"

"Tomorrow is winter solstice. If we miss sunset tonight, we would have to wait until tomorrow evening. And by then, the Olympian Council will be over. We must free Lady Artemis tonight."

Or Annabeth will be dead, I thought, but I didn't say that.

"We need a car," Thalia said.

"But what about Bessie?" I asked.

Grover stopped in his tracks. "I've got an idea! The

Ophiotaurus can appear in different bodies of water, right?"

"Well, yeah," I said. "I mean, he was in Long Island Sound. Then he just popped into the water at Hoover Dam. And now he's here."

"So maybe we could coax him back to Long Island Sound," Grover said. "Then Chiron could help us get him to Olympus."

"But he was following *me*," I said. "If I'm not there, would he know where he's going?"

"Moo," Bessie said forlornly.

"I . . . I can show him," Grover said. "I'll go with him."

I stared at him. Grover was no fan of the water. He'd almost drowned last summer in the Sea of Monsters, and he couldn't swim very well with his goat hooves.

"I'm the only one who can talk to him," Grover said. "It makes sense."

He bent down and said something in Bessie's ear. Bessie shivered, then made a contented, lowing sound.

"The blessing of the Wild," Grover said. "That should help with safe passage. Percy, pray to your dad, too. See if he will grant us safe passage through the seas."

I didn't understand how they could possibly swim back to Long Island from California. Then again, monsters didn't travel the same way as humans. I'd seen plenty evidence of that.

I tried to concentrate on the waves, the smell of the ocean, the sound of the tide.

"Dad," I said. "Help us. Get the Ophiotaurus and Grover safely to camp. Protect them at sea."

"A prayer like that needs a sacrifice," Thalia said. "Something big."

I thought for a second. Then I took off my coat.

"Percy," Grover said. "Are you sure? That lion skin . . . that's really helpful. Hercules used it!"

As soon as he said that, I realized something.

I glanced at Zoë, who was watching me carefully. I realized I *did* know who Zoë's hero had been—the one who'd ruined her life, gotten her kicked out of her family, and never even mentioned how she'd helped him: Hercules, a hero I'd admired all my life.

"If I'm going to survive," I said, "it won't be because I've got a lion-skin cloak. I'm not Hercules."

I threw the coat into the bay. It turned back into a golden lion skin, flashing in the light. Then, as it began to sink beneath the waves, it seemed to dissolve into sunlight on the water.

The sea breeze picked up.

Grover took a deep breath. "Well, no time to lose."

He jumped in the water and immediately began to sink. Bessie glided next to him and let Grover take hold of his neck.

"Be careful," I told them.

"We will," Grover said. "Okay, um . . . Bessie? We're going to Long Island. It's east. Over that way."

"Moooo?" Bessie said.

"Yes," Grover answered. "Long Island. It's this island. And . . . it's long. Oh, let's just start."

"Mooo!"

Bessie lurched forward. He started to submerge and Grover said, "I can't breathe underwater! Just thought I'd mention—" *Glub!*

Under they went, and I hoped my father's protection would extend to little things, like breathing.

"Well, that is one problem addressed," Zoë said. "But how can we get to my sisters' garden?"

"Thalia's right," I said. "We need a car. But there's nobody to help us here. Unless we, uh, borrowed one."

I didn't like that option. I mean, sure this was a life-or-death situation, but still, it was stealing, and it was bound to get us noticed.

"Wait," Thalia said. She started rifling through her backpack. "There *is* somebody in San Francisco who can help us. I've got the address here somewhere."

"Who?" I asked.

Thalia pulled out a crumpled piece of notebook paper and held it up. "Professor Chase. Annabeth's dad."

After hearing Annabeth gripe about her dad for two years, I was expecting him to have devil horns and fangs. I was *not* expecting him to be wearing an old-fashioned aviator's cap and goggles. He looked so weird, with his eyes bugging out through the glasses, that we all took a step back on the front porch.

"Hello," he said in a friendly voice. "Are you delivering my airplanes?"

Thalia, Zoë, and I looked at each other warily.

"Um, no, sir," I said.

"Drat," he said. "I need three more Sopwith Camels."

"Right," I said, though I had no clue what he was talking about. "We're friends of Annabeth."

"Annabeth?" He straightened as if I'd just given him an electric shock. "Is she all right? Has something happened?"

None of us answered, but our faces must've told him that something was very wrong. He took off his cap and goggles. He had sandy-colored hair like Annabeth and intense brown eyes. He was handsome, I guess, for an older guy, but it looked like he hadn't shaved in a couple of days, and his shirt was buttoned wrong, so one side of his collar stuck up higher than the other side.

"You'd better come in," he said.

It didn't look like a house they'd just moved into. There were LEGO robots on the stairs and two cats sleeping on the sofa in the living room. The coffee table was stacked with magazines, and a little kid's winter coat was spread on the floor. The whole house smelled like fresh-baked chocolate-chip cookies. There was jazz music coming from the kitchen. It seemed like a messy, happy kind of home—the kind of place that had been lived in forever.

"Dad!" a little boy screamed. "He's taking apart my robots!"

"Bobby," Dr. Chase called absently, "don't take apart your brother's robots."

"*I'm* Bobby," the little boy protested. "He's Matthew!"

"Matthew," Dr. Chase called, "don't take apart your brother's robots!"

"Okay, Dad!"

Dr. Chase turned to us. "We'll go upstairs to my study. This way."

"Honey?" a woman called. Annabeth's stepmom appeared in the living room, wiping her hands on a dish towel. She was a pretty Asian woman with red highlighted hair tied in a bun.

"Who are our guests?" she asked.

"Oh," Dr. Chase said. "This is . . ."

He stared at us blankly.

"Frederick," she chided. "You forgot to ask them their names?"

We introduced ourselves a little uneasily, but Mrs. Chase seemed really nice. She asked if we were hungry. We admitted we were, and she told us she'd bring us some cookies and sandwiches and sodas.

"Dear," Dr. Chase said. "They came about Annabeth."

I half expected Mrs. Chase to turn into a raving lunatic at the mention of her stepdaughter, but she just pursed her lips and looked concerned. "All right. Go on up to the study and I'll bring you some food." She smiled at me. "Nice meeting you, Percy. I've heard a lot about you."

Upstairs, we walked into Dr. Chase's study and I said, "Whoa!"

The room was wall-to-wall books, but what really caught my attention were the war toys. There was a huge table with miniature tanks and soldiers fighting along a blue painted river, with hills and fake trees and stuff. Old-fashioned biplanes hung on strings from the ceiling, tilted at crazy angles like they were in the middle of a dogfight.

Dr. Chase smiled. "Yes. The Third Battle of Ypres. I'm writing a paper, you see, on the use of Sopwith Camels to strafe enemy lines. I believe they played a much greater role than they've been given credit for."

He plucked a biplane from its string and swept it across the battlefield, making airplane engine noises as he knocked down little German soldiers.

"Oh, right," I said. I knew Annabeth's dad was a professor of military history. She'd never mentioned he played with toy soldiers.

Zoë came over and studied the battlefield. "The German lines were farther from the river."

Dr. Chase stared at her. "How do you know that?"

"I was there," she said matter-of-factly. "Artemis wanted to show us how horrible war was, the way mortal men fight each other. And how foolish, too. The battle was a complete waste."

Dr. Chase opened his mouth in shock. "You—"

"She's a Hunter, sir," Thalia said. "But that's not why we're here. We need—"

"You saw the Sopwith Camels?" Dr. Chase said. "How many were there? What formations did they fly?"

"Sir," Thalia broke in again. "Annabeth is in danger."

That got his attention. He set the biplane down.

"Of course," he said. "Tell me everything."

It wasn't easy, but we tried. Meanwhile, the afternoon light was fading outside. We were running out of time.

When we'd finished, Dr. Chase collapsed in his leather recliner. He laced his hands. "My poor brave Annabeth. We must hurry."

"Sir, we need transportation to Mount Tamalpais," Zoë said. "And we need it immediately."

"I'll drive you. Hmm, it would be faster to fly in my Camel, but it only seats two."

"Whoa, you have an actual biplane?" I said.

"Down at Crissy Field," Dr. Chase said proudly. "That's the reason I had to move here. My sponsor is a private collector with some of the finest World War I relics in the world. He let me restore the Sopwith Camel—"

"Sir," Thalia said. "Just a car would be great. And it might be better if we went without you. It's too dangerous."

Dr. Chase frowned uncomfortably. "Now wait a minute, young lady. Annabeth is my daughter. Dangerous or not, I . . . I can't just—"

"Snacks," Mrs. Chase announced. She pushed through the door with a tray full of peanut-butter-and-jelly sandwiches and Cokes and cookies fresh out of the oven, the chocolate chips still gooey. Thalia and I inhaled a few cookies while Zoë said, "I can drive, sir. I'm not as young as I look. I promise not to destroy your car."

Mrs. Chase knit her eyebrows. "What's this about?"

"Annabeth is in danger," Dr. Chase said. "On Mount Tam. I would drive them, but . . . apparently it's no place for mortals."

It sounded like it was really hard for him to get that last part out.

I waited for Mrs. Chase to say no. I mean, what mortal parent would allow three underage teenagers to borrow their car? To my surprise, Mrs. Chase nodded. "Then they'd better get going."

"Right!" Dr. Chase jumped up and started patting his pockets. "My keys . . ."

His wife sighed. "Frederick, honestly. You'd lose your head if it weren't wrapped inside your aviator hat. The keys are hanging on the peg by the front door."

"Right!" Dr. Chase said.

Zoë grabbed a sandwich. "Thank you both. We should go. *Now.*"

We hustled out the door and down the stairs, the Chases right behind us.

"Percy," Mrs. Chase called as I was leaving, "tell Annabeth . . . Tell her she still has a home here, will you? Remind her of that."

I took one last look at the messy living room, Annabeth's half brothers spilling LEGOs and arguing, the smell of cookies filling the air. Not a bad place, I thought.

"I'll tell her," I promised.

We ran out to the yellow VW convertible parked in the driveway. The sun was going down. I figured we had less than an hour to save Annabeth.

"Can't this thing go any faster?" Thalia demanded.

Zoë glared at her. "I cannot control traffic."

"You both sound like my mother," I said.

"Shut up!" they said in unison.

Zoë weaved in and out of traffic on the Golden Gate Bridge. The sun was sinking on the horizon when we finally got into Marin County and exited the highway.

The roads were insanely narrow, winding through forests and up the sides of hills and around the edges of steep ravines. Zoë didn't slow down at all.

"Why does everything smell like cough drops?" I asked.

"Eucalyptus." Zoë pointed to the huge trees all around us.

"The stuff koala bears eat?"

"And monsters," she said. "They love chewing the leaves. Especially dragons."

"Dragons chew eucalyptus leaves?"

"Believe me," Zoë said, "if you had dragon breath, you would chew eucalyptus too."

I didn't question her, but I did keep my eyes peeled more closely as we drove. Ahead of us loomed Mount Tamalpais. I guess, in terms of mountains, it was a small one, but it looked plenty huge as we were driving toward it.

"So that's the Mountain of Despair?" I asked.

"Yes," Zoë said tightly.

"Why do they call it that?"

She was silent for almost a mile before answering. "After the war between the Titans and the gods, many of the Titans were punished and imprisoned. Kronos was sliced to pieces and thrown into Tartarus. Kronos's right-hand man, the general of his forces, was imprisoned up there, on the summit, just beyond the Garden of the Hesperides."

"The General," I said. Clouds seemed to be swirling

around its peak, as though the mountain was drawing them in, spinning them like a top. "What's going on up there? A storm?"

Zoë didn't answer. I got the feeling she knew exactly what the clouds meant, and she didn't like it.

"We have to concentrate," Thalia said. "The Mist is really strong here."

"The magical kind or the natural kind?" I asked.

"Both."

The gray clouds swirled even thicker over the mountain, and we kept driving straight toward them. We were out of the forest now, into wide open spaces of cliffs and grass and rocks and fog.

I happened to glance down at the ocean as we passed a scenic curve, and I saw something that made me jump out of my seat.

"Look!" But we turned a corner and the ocean disappeared behind the hills.

"What?" Thalia asked.

"A big white ship," I said. "Docked near the beach. It looked like a cruise ship."

Her eyes widened. "Luke's ship?"

I wanted to say I wasn't sure. It might be a coincidence. But I knew better. The *Princess Andromeda*, Luke's demon cruise ship, was docked at that beach. That's why he'd sent his ship all the way down to the Panama Canal. It was the only way to sail it from the East Coast to California.

"We will have company, then," Zoë said grimly. "Kronos's army."

I was about to answer, when suddenly the hairs on the back of my neck stood up. Thalia shouted, "Stop the car. NOW!"

Zoë must've sensed something was wrong, because she slammed on the brakes without question. The yellow VW spun twice before coming to a stop at the edge of the cliff.

"Out!" Thalia opened the door and pushed me hard. We both rolled onto the pavement. The next second: *BOOOM!*

Lightning flashed, and Dr. Chase's Volkswagen erupted like a canary-yellow grenade. I probably would've been killed by shrapnel except for Thalia's shield, which appeared over me. I heard a sound like metal rain, and when I opened my eyes, we were surrounded by wreckage. Part of the VW's fender had impaled itself in the street. The smoking hood was spinning in circles. Pieces of yellow metal were strewn across the road.

I swallowed the taste of smoke out of my mouth, and looked at Thalia. "You saved my life."

"*One shall perish by a parent's hand,*" she muttered. "Curse him. He would destroy me? *Me?*"

It took me a second to realize she was talking about her dad. "Oh, hey, that couldn't have been Zeus's lightning bolt. No way."

"Whose, then?" Thalia demanded.

"I don't know. Zoë said Kronos's name. Maybe he—"

Thalia shook her head, looking angry and stunned. "No. That wasn't it."

"Wait," I said. "Where's Zoë? Zoë!"

We both got up and ran around the blasted VW. Nothing inside. Nothing either direction down the road. I looked down the cliff. No sign of her.

"Zoë!" I shouted.

Then she was standing right next to me, pulling me by my arm. "Silence, fool! Do you want to wake Ladon?"

"You mean we're here?"

"Very close," she said. "Follow me."

Sheets of fog were drifting right across the road. Zoë stepped into one of them, and when the fog passed, she was no longer there. Thalia and I looked at each other.

"Concentrate on Zoë," Thalia advised. "We are following her. Go straight into the fog and keep that in mind."

"Wait, Thalia. About what happened back on the pier . . . I mean, with the manticore and the sacrifice—"

"I don't want to talk about it."

"You wouldn't actually have . . . you know?"

She hesitated. "I was just shocked. That's all."

"Zeus didn't send that lighting bolt at the car. It was Kronos. He's trying to manipulate you, make you angry at your dad."

She took a deep breath. "Percy, I know you're trying to make me feel better. Thanks. But come on. We need to go."

She stepped into the fog, into the Mist, and I followed.

When the fog cleared, I was still on the side of the mountain, but the road was dirt. The grass was thicker. The sunset made a bloodred slash across the sea. The summit of the mountain seemed closer now, swirling with storm clouds and raw power. There was only one path to the top, directly in front of us. And it led through a lush meadow of shadows and flowers: the garden of twilight, just like I'd seen in my dream.

If it hadn't been for the enormous dragon, the garden would've been the most beautiful place I'd ever seen. The grass shimmered with silvery evening light, and the flowers were such brilliant colors they almost glowed in the dark. Stepping stones of polished black marble led around either side of a five-story-tall apple tree, every bough glittering with golden apples, and I don't mean *yellow* golden apples like in the grocery store. I mean *real* golden apples. I can't describe why they were so appealing, but as soon as I smelled their fragrance, I knew that one bite would be the most delicious thing I'd ever tasted.

"The apples of immortality," Thalia said. "Hera's wedding gift from Zeus."

I wanted to step right up and pluck one, except for the dragon coiled around the tree.

Now, I don't know what you think of when I say *dragon*. Whatever it is, it's not scary enough. The serpent's body was as thick as a booster rocket, glinting with coppery scales. He had more heads than I could count, as if a hundred deadly pythons had been fused together. He appeared to be asleep. The heads lay curled in a big spaghetti-like mound on the grass, all the eyes closed.

Then the shadows in front of us began to move. There was a beautiful, eerie singing, like voices from the bottom of a well. I reached for Riptide, but Zoë stopped my hand.

Four figures shimmered into existence, four young women who looked very much like Zoë. They all wore white Greek chitons. Their skin was like caramel. Silky black hair tumbled loose around their shoulders. It was strange, but I'd never realized how beautiful Zoë was until I saw her siblings, the Hesperides. They looked just like Zoë—gorgeous, and probably very dangerous.

"Sisters," Zoë said.

"We do not see any sister," one of the girls said coldly. "We see two half-bloods and a Hunter. All of whom shall soon die."

"You've got it wrong." I stepped forward. "Nobody is going to die."

The girls studied me. They had eyes like volcanic rock, glassy and completely black.

"Perseus Jackson," one of them said.

"Yes," mused another. "I do not see why he is a threat."

"Who said I was a threat?"

The first Hesperid glanced behind her, toward the top of the mountain. "They fear thee. They are unhappy that *this* one has not yet killed thee."

She pointed at Thalia.

"Tempting sometimes," Thalia admitted. "But no, thanks. He's my friend."

"There are no friends here, daughter of Zeus," the girl said. "Only enemies. Go back."

"Not without Annabeth," Thalia said.

"And Artemis," Zoë said. "We must approach the mountain."

"You know he will kill thee," the girl said. "You are no match for him."

"Artemis must be freed," Zoë insisted. "Let us pass."

The girl shook her head. "You have no rights here anymore. We have only to raise our voices and Ladon will wake."

"He will not hurt me," Zoë said.

"No? And what about thy so-called friends?"

Then Zoë did the last thing I expected. She shouted, "Ladon! Wake!"

The dragon stirred, glittering like a mountain of pennies. The Hesperides yelped and scattered. The lead girl said to Zoë, "Are you mad?"

"You never had any courage, sister," Zoë said. "That is thy problem."

The dragon Ladon was writhing now, a hundred heads whipping around, tongues flickering and tasting the air. Zoë took a step forward, her arms raised.

"Zoë, don't," Thalia said. "You're not a Hesperid anymore. He'll kill you."

"Ladon is trained to protect the tree," Zoë said. "Skirt around the edges of the garden. Go up the mountain. As long as I am a bigger threat, he should ignore thee."

"*Should*," I said. "Not exactly reassuring."

"It is the only way," she said. "Even the three of us together cannot fight him."

Ladon opened his mouths. The sound of a hundred heads hissing at once sent a shiver down my back, and that was before his breath hit me. The smell was like acid. It made my eyes burn, my skin crawl, and my hair stand on end. I remembered the time a rat had died inside our apartment wall in New York in the middle of the summer. This stench was like that, except a hundred times stronger, and mixed with the smell of chewed eucalyptus. I promised myself right then that I would *never* ask a school nurse for another cough drop.

I wanted to draw my sword. But then I remembered my dream of Zoë and Hercules, and how Hercules had failed in a head-on assault. I decided to trust Zoë's judgment.

Thalia went left. I went right. Zoë walked straight toward the monster.

"It's me, my little dragon," Zoë said. "Zoë has come back."

Ladon shifted forward, then back. Some of the mouths closed. Some kept hissing. Dragon confusion. Meanwhile, the Hesperides shimmered and turned into shadows. The voice of the eldest whispered, "Fool."

"I used to feed thee by hand," Zoë continued, speaking in a soothing voice as she stepped toward the golden tree. "Do you still like lamb's meat?"

The dragon's eyes glinted.

Thalia and I were about halfway around the garden. Ahead, I could see a single rocky trail leading up to the black peak of the mountain. The storm swirled above it, spinning on the summit like it was the axis for the whole world.

We'd almost made it out of the meadow when something went wrong. I felt the dragon's mood shift. Maybe

Zoë got too close. Maybe the dragon realized he was hungry. Whatever the reason, he lunged at Zoë.

Two thousand years of training kept her alive. She dodged one set of slashing fangs and tumbled under another, weaving through the dragon's heads as she ran in our direction, gagging from the monster's horrible breath.

I drew Riptide to help.

"No!" Zoë panted. "Run!"

The dragon snapped at her side, and Zoë cried out. Thalia uncovered Aegis, and the dragon hissed. In his moment of indecision, Zoë sprinted past us up the mountain, and we followed.

The dragon didn't try to pursue. He hissed and stomped the ground, but I guess he was well trained to guard that tree. He wasn't going to be lured off, even by the tasty prospect of eating some heroes.

We ran up the mountain as the Hesperides resumed their song in the shadows behind us. The music didn't sound so beautiful to me now—more like the sound track for a funeral.

At the top of mountain were ruins, blocks of black granite and marble as big as houses. Broken columns. Statues of bronze that looked as though they'd been half melted.

"The ruins of Mount Othrys," Thalia whispered in awe.

"Yes," Zoë said. "It was not here before. This is bad."

"What's Mount Othrys?" I asked, feeling like a fool as usual.

"The mountain fortress of the Titans," Zoë said. "In the first war, Olympus and Othrys were the two rival capitals of the world. Othrys was—" She winced and held her side.

"You're hurt," I said. "Let me see."

"No! It is nothing. I was saying . . . in the first war, Othrys was blasted to pieces."

"But . . . how is it here?"

Thalia looked around cautiously as we picked our way through the rubble, past blocks of marble and broken archways. "It moves in the same way that Olympus moves. It always exists on the edges of civilization. But the fact that it is here, on *this* mountain, is not good."

"Why?"

"This is Atlas's mountain," Zoë said. "Where he holds—" She froze. Her voice was ragged with despair. "Where he used to hold up the sky."

We had reached the summit. A few yards ahead of us, gray clouds swirled in a heavy vortex, making a funnel cloud that almost touched the mountaintop, but instead rested on the shoulders of a twelve-year-old girl with auburn hair and a tattered silvery dress: Artemis, her legs bound to the rock with celestial bronze chains. This is what I had seen in my dream. It hadn't been a cavern roof that Artemis was forced to hold. It was the roof of the world.

"My lady!" Zoë rushed forward, but Artemis said, "Stop! It is a trap. You must leave now."

Her voice was strained. She was drenched in sweat. I had never seen a goddess in pain before, but the weight of the sky was clearly too much for Artemis.

Zoë was crying. She ran forward despite Artemis's protests, and tugged at the chains.

A booming voice spoke behind us: "Ah, how touching."

We turned. The General was standing there in his brown silk suit. At his side were Luke and half a dozen dracaenae bearing the golden sarcophagus of Kronos. Annabeth stood at Luke's side. She had her hands cuffed behind her back, a gag in her mouth, and Luke was holding the point of his sword to her throat.

I met her eyes, trying to ask her a thousand questions. There was just one message she was sending me, though: *RUN.*

"Luke," Thalia snarled. "Let her go."

Luke's smile was weak and pale. He looked even worse than he had three days ago in D.C. "That is the General's decision, Thalia. But it's good to see you again."

Thalia spat at him.

The General chuckled. "So much for old friends. And you, Zoë. It's been a long time. How is my little traitor? I will enjoy killing you."

"Do not respond," Artemis groaned. "Do not challenge him."

"Wait a second," I said. "You're Atlas?"

The General glanced at me. "So, even the stupidest of heroes can finally figure something out. Yes, I am Atlas, the general of the Titans and terror of the gods. Congratulations. I will kill you presently, as soon as I deal with this wretched girl."

"You're not going to hurt Zoë," I said. "I won't let you."

The General sneered. "You have no right to interfere, little hero. This is a family matter."

I frowned. "A family matter?"

"Yes," Zoë said bleakly. "Atlas is my father."

SEVENTEEN

I PUT ON A FEW MILLION EXTRA POUNDS

The horrible thing was: I could see the family resemblance. Atlas had the same regal expression as Zoë, the same cold proud look in his eyes that Zoë sometimes got when she was mad, though on him it looked a thousand times more evil. He was all the things I'd originally disliked about Zoë, with none of the good I'd come to appreciate.

"Let Artemis go," Zoë demanded.

Atlas walked closer to the chained goddess. "Perhaps you'd like to take the sky for her, then? Be my guest."

Zoë opened her mouth to speak, but Artemis said, "No! Do not offer, Zoë! I forbid you."

Atlas smirked. He knelt next to Artemis and tried to touch her face, but the goddess bit at him, almost taking off his fingers.

"Hoo-hoo," Atlas chuckled. "You see, daughter? Lady Artemis likes her new job. I think I will have all the Olympians take turns carrying my burden, once Lord Kronos rules again, and this is the center of our palace. It will teach those weaklings some humility."

I looked at Annabeth. She was desperately trying to tell me something. She motioned her head toward Luke. But all

I could do was stare at her. I hadn't noticed before, but something about her had changed. Her blond hair was now streaked with gray.

"From holding the sky," Thalia muttered, as if she'd read my mind. "The weight should've killed her."

"I don't understand," I said. "Why can't Artemis just let go of the sky?"

Atlas laughed. "How little you understand, young one. This is the point where the sky and the earth first met, where Ouranos and Gaia first brought forth their mighty children, the Titans. The sky still yearns to embrace the earth. Someone must hold it at bay, or else it would crush down upon this place, instantly flattening the mountain and everything within a hundred leagues. Once you have taken the burden, there is no escape." Atlas smiled. "Unless someone else takes it from you."

He approached us, studying Thalia and me. "So these are the best heroes of the age, eh? Not much of a challenge."

"Fight us," I said. "And let's see."

"Have the gods taught you nothing? An immortal does not fight a mere mortal directly. It is beneath our dignity. I will have Luke crush you instead."

"So you're another coward," I said.

Atlas's eyes glowed with hatred. With difficulty, he turned his attention to Thalia.

"As for you, daughter of Zeus, it seems Luke was wrong about you."

"I wasn't wrong," Luke managed. He looked terribly weak, and he spoke every word as if it were painful. If I didn't hate his guts so much, I almost would've felt sorry for him. "Thalia, you still can join us. Call the Ophiotaurus. It will come to you. Look!"

He waved his hand, and next to us a pool of water appeared: a pond ringed in black marble, big enough for the Ophiotaurus. I could imagine Bessie in that pool. In fact, the more I thought about it, the more I was sure I could hear Bessie mooing.

Don't think about him! Suddenly Grover's voice was inside my mind—the empathy link. I could feel his emotions. He was on the verge of panic. *I'm losing Bessie. Block the thoughts!*

I tried to make my mind go blank. I tried to think about basketball players, skateboards, the different kinds of candy in my mom's shop. Anything but Bessie.

"Thalia, call the Ophiotaurus," Luke persisted. "And you will be more powerful than the gods."

"Luke . . ." Her voice was full of pain. "What happened to you?"

"Don't you remember all those times we talked? All those times we cursed the gods? Our fathers have done nothing for us. They have no right to rule the world!"

Thalia shook her head. "Free Annabeth. Let her go."

"If you join me," Luke promised, "it can be like old times. The three of us together. Fighting for a better world. Please, Thalia, if you don't agree . . ."

His voice faltered. "It's my last chance. He will use the other way if you don't agree. Please."

I didn't know what he meant, but the fear in his voice sounded real enough. I believed that Luke was in danger.

His life depended on Thalia's joining his cause. And I was afraid Thalia might believe it, too.

"Do not, Thalia," Zoë warned. "We must fight them."

Luke waved his hand again, and a fire appeared. A bronze brazier, just like the one at camp. A sacrificial flame.

"Thalia," I said. "No."

Behind Luke, the golden sarcophagus began to glow. As it did, I saw images in the mist all around us: black marble walls rising, the ruins becoming whole, a terrible and beautiful palace rising around us, made of fear and shadow.

"We will raise Mount Othrys right here," Luke promised, in a voice so strained it was hardly his. "Once more, it will be stronger and greater than Olympus. Look, Thalia. We are not weak."

He pointed toward the ocean, and my heart fell. Marching up the side of the mountain, from the beach where the *Princess Andromeda* was docked, was a great army. Dracaenae and Laestrygonians, monsters and half-bloods, hell hounds, harpies, and other things I couldn't even name. The whole ship must've been emptied, because there were hundreds, many more than I'd seen on board last summer. And they were marching toward us. In a few minutes, they would be here.

"This is only a taste of what is to come," Luke said. "Soon we will be ready to storm Camp Half-Blood. And after that, Olympus itself. All we need is your help."

For a terrible moment, Thalia hesitated. She gazed at Luke, her eyes full of pain, as if the only thing she wanted in the world was to believe him. Then she leveled her spear. "You aren't Luke. I don't know you anymore."

"Yes, you do, Thalia," he pleaded. "Please. Don't make me . . . Don't make *him* destroy you."

There was no time. If that army got to the top of the hill, we would be overwhelmed. I met Annabeth's eyes again. She nodded.

I looked at Thalia and Zoë, and I decided it wouldn't be the worst thing in the world to die fighting with friends like this.

"Now," I said.

Together, we charged.

Thalia went straight for Luke. The power of her shield was so great that his dragon-women bodyguards fled in a panic, dropping the golden coffin and leaving him alone. But despite his sickly appearance, Luke was still quick with his sword. He snarled like a wild animal and counterattacked. When his sword, Backbiter, met Thalia's shield, a ball of lightning erupted between them, frying the air with yellow tendrils of power.

As for me, I did the stupidest thing in my life, which is saying a lot. I attacked the Titan Lord Atlas.

He laughed as I approached. A huge javelin appeared in his hands. His silk suit melted into full Greek battle armor. "Go on, then!"

"Percy!" Zoë said. "Beware!"

I knew what she was warning me about. Chiron had told me long ago: *Immortals are constrained by ancient rules. But a hero can go anywhere, challenge anyone, as long as he has the nerve. Once*

I attacked, however, Atlas was free to attack back directly, with all his might.

I swung my sword, and Atlas knocked me aside with the shaft of his javelin. I flew through the air and slammed into a black wall. It wasn't Mist anymore. The palace was rising, brick by brick. It was becoming real.

"Fool!" Atlas screamed gleefully, swatting aside one of Zoë's arrows. "Did you think, simply because you could challenge that petty war god, that you could stand up to *me?*"

The mention of Ares sent a jolt through me. I shook off my daze and charged again. If I could get to that pool of water, I could double my strength.

The javelin's point slashed toward me like a scythe. I raised Riptide, planning to cut off his weapon at the shaft, but my arm felt like lead. My sword suddenly weighed a ton.

And I remembered Ares's warning, spoken on the beach in Los Angeles so long ago: *When you need it most, your sword will fail you.*

Not now! I pleaded. But it was no good. I tried to dodge, but the javelin caught me in the chest and sent me flying like a rag doll. I slammed into the ground, my head spinning. I looked up and found I was at the feet of Artemis, still straining under the weight of the sky.

"Run, boy," she told me. "You must run!"

Atlas was taking his time coming toward me. My sword was gone. It had skittered away over the edge of the cliff. It might reappear in my pocket—maybe in a few seconds—but it didn't matter. I'd be dead by then. Luke and Thalia were fighting like demons, lightning crackling around them. Annabeth was on the ground, desperately struggling to free her hands.

"Die, little hero," Atlas said.

He raised his javelin to impale me.

"No!" Zoë yelled, and a volley of silver arrows sprouted from the armpit chink in Atlas's armor.

"ARGH!" He bellowed and turned toward his daughter.

I reached down and felt Riptide back in my pocket. I couldn't fight Atlas, even with a sword. And then a chill went down my back. I remembered the words of the prophecy: *The Titan's curse must one withstand.* I couldn't hope to beat Atlas. But there was someone else who might stand a chance.

"The sky," I told the goddess. "Give it to me."

"No, boy," Artemis said. Her forehead was beaded with metallic sweat, like quicksilver. "You don't know what you're asking. It will crush you!"

"Annabeth took it!"

"She barely survived. She had the spirit of a true huntress. You will not last so long."

"I'll die anyway," I said. "Give me the weight of the sky!"

I didn't wait for her answer. I took out Riptide and slashed through her chains. Then I stepped next to her and braced myself on one knee—holding up my hands—and touched the cold, heavy clouds. For a moment, Artemis and I bore the weight together. It was the heaviest thing I'd ever felt, as if I were being crushed under a thousand trucks. I wanted to black out from the pain, but I breathed deeply. *I can do this.*

Then Artemis slipped out from under the burden, and I held it alone.

Afterward, I tried many times to explain what it felt like. I couldn't.

Every muscle in my body turned to fire. My bones felt like they were melting. I wanted to scream, but I didn't have the strength to open my mouth. I began to sink, lower and lower to the ground, the sky's weight crushing me.

Fight back! Grover's voice said inside my head. *Don't give up.*

I concentrated on breathing. If I could just keep the sky aloft a few more seconds. I thought about Bianca, who had given her life so we could get here. If she could do that, I could hold the sky.

My vision turned fuzzy. Everything was tinged with red. I caught glimpses of the battle, but I wasn't sure if I was seeing clearly. There was Atlas in full battle armor, jabbing with his javelin, laughing insanely as he fought. And Artemis, a blur of silver. She had two wicked hunting knives, each as long as her arm, and she slashed wildly at the Titan, dodging and leaping with unbelievable grace. She seemed to change form as she maneuvered. She was a tiger, a gazelle, a bear, a falcon. Or perhaps that was just my fevered brain. Zoë shot arrows at her father, aiming for the chinks in his armor. He roared in pain each time one found its mark, but they affected him like bee stings. He just got madder and kept fighting.

Thalia and Luke went spear on sword, lightning still

flashing around them. Thalia pressed Luke back with the aura of her shield. Even he was not immune to it. He retreated, wincing and growling in frustration.

"Yield!" Thalia yelled. "You never could beat me, Luke."

He bared his teeth. "We'll see, my old friend."

Sweat poured down my face. My hands were slippery. My shoulders would've screamed with agony if they could. I felt like the vertebrae in my spine were being welded together by a blowtorch.

Atlas advanced, pressing Artemis. She was fast, but his strength was unstoppable. His javelin slammed into the earth where Artemis had been a split second before, and a fissure opened in the rocks. He leaped over it and kept pursuing her. She was leading him back toward me.

Get ready, she spoke in my mind.

I was losing the ability to think through the pain. My response was something like *Agggghh-owwwwwwww.*

"You fight well for a girl." Atlas laughed. "But you are no match for me."

He feinted with the tip of his javelin and Artemis dodged. I saw the trick coming. Atlas's javelin swept around and knocked Artemis's legs off the ground. She fell, and Atlas brought up his javelin tip for the kill.

"No!" Zoë screamed. She leaped between her father and Artemis and shot an arrow straight into the Titan's forehead, where it lodged like a unicorn's horn. Atlas bellowed in rage. He swept aside his daughter with the back of his hand, sending her flying into the black rocks.

I wanted to shout her name, run to her aid, but I couldn't speak or move. I couldn't even see where Zoë had landed. Then Atlas turned on Artemis with a look of triumph in his face. Artemis seemed to be wounded. She didn't get up.

"The first blood in a new war," Atlas gloated. And he stabbed downward.

As fast as thought, Artemis grabbed his javelin shaft. It hit the earth right next to her and she pulled backward, using the javelin like a lever, kicking the Titan Lord and sending him flying over her. I saw him coming down on top of me and I realized what would happen. I loosened my grip on the sky, and as Atlas slammed into me I didn't try to hold on. I let myself be pushed out of the way and rolled for all I was worth.

The weight of the sky dropped onto Atlas's back, almost smashing him flat until he managed to get to his knees, struggling to get out from under the crushing weight of the sky. But it was too late.

"Noooooo!" He bellowed so hard it shook the mountain. "Not again!"

Atlas was trapped under his old burden.

I tried to stand and fell back again, dazed from pain. My body felt like it was burning up.

Thalia backed Luke to the edge of a cliff, but still they fought on, next to the golden coffin. Thalia had tears in her eyes. Luke had a bloody slash across his chest and his pale face glistened with sweat.

He lunged at Thalia and she slammed him with her

shield. Luke's sword spun out of his hands and clattered to the rocks. Thalia put her spear point to his throat.

For a moment, there was silence.

"Well?" Luke asked. He tried to hide it, but I could hear fear in his voice.

Thalia trembled with fury.

Behind her, Annabeth came scrambling, finally free from her bonds. Her face was bruised and streaked with dirt. "Don't kill him!"

"He's a traitor," Thalia said. "A traitor!"

In my daze, I realized that Artemis was no longer with me. She had run off toward the black rocks where Zoë had fallen.

"We'll bring Luke back," Annabeth pleaded. "To Olympus. He . . . he'll be useful."

"Is that what you want, Thalia?" Luke sneered. "To go back to Olympus in triumph? To please your dad?"

Thalia hesitated, and Luke made a desperate grab for her spear.

"No!" Annabeth shouted. But it was too late. Without thinking, Thalia kicked Luke away. He lost his balance, terror on his face, and then he fell.

"Luke!" Annabeth screamed.

We rushed to the cliff's edge. Below us, the army from the *Princess Andromeda* had stopped in amazement. They were staring at Luke's broken form on the rocks. Despite how much I hated him, I couldn't stand to see it. I wanted to believe he was still alive, but that was impossible. The fall was fifty feet at least, and he wasn't moving.

One of the giants looked up and growled, "Kill them!"

Thalia was stiff with grief, tears streaming down her cheeks. I pulled her back as a wave of javelins sailed over our heads. We ran for the rocks, ignoring the curses and threats of Atlas as we passed.

"Artemis!" I yelled.

The goddess looked up, her face almost as grief-stricken as Thalia's. Zoë lay in the goddess's arms. She was breathing. Her eyes were open. But still . . .

"The wound is poisoned," Artemis said.

"Atlas poisoned her?" I asked.

"No," the goddess said. "Not Atlas."

She showed us the wound in Zoë's side. I'd almost forgotten her scrape with Ladon the dragon. The bite was much worse than Zoë had let on. I could barely look at the wound. She had charged into battle against her father with a horrible cut already sapping her strength.

"The stars," Zoë murmured. "I cannot see them."

"Nectar and ambrosia," I said. "Come on! We have to get her some."

No one moved. Grief hung in air. The army of Kronos was just below the rise. Even Artemis was too shocked to stir. We might've met our doom right there, but then I heard a strange buzzing noise.

Just as the army of monsters came over the hill, a Sopwith Camel swooped down out of the sky.

"Get away from my daughter!" Dr. Chase called down, and his machine guns burst to life, peppering the ground with bullet holes and startling the whole group of monsters into scattering.

"Dad?" yelled Annabeth in disbelief.

"Run!" he called back, his voice growing fainter as the biplane swooped by.

This shook Artemis out of her grief. She stared up at the antique plane, which was now banking around for another strafe.

"A brave man," Artemis said with grudging approval. "Come. We must get Zoë away from here."

She raised her hunting horn to her lips, and its clear sound echoed down the valleys of Marin. Zoë's eyes were fluttering.

"Hang in there!" I told her. "It'll be all right!"

The Sopwith Camel swooped down again. A few giants threw javelins, and one flew straight between the wings of the plane, but the machine guns blazed. I realized with amazement that somehow Dr. Chase must've gotten hold of celestial bronze to fashion his bullets. The first row of snake women wailed as the machine gun's volley blew them into sulfurous yellow powder.

"That's . . . my dad!" Annabeth said in amazement.

We didn't have time to admire his flying. The giants and snake women were already recovering from their surprise. Dr. Chase would be in trouble soon.

Just then, the moonlight brightened, and a silver chariot appeared from the sky, drawn by the most beautiful deer I had ever seen. It landed right next to us.

"Get in," Artemis said.

Annabeth helped me get Thalia on board. Then I helped Artemis with Zoë. We wrapped Zoë in a blanket as Artemis pulled the reins and the chariot sped away from the mountain, straight into the air.

"Like Santa Claus's sleigh," I murmured, still dazed with pain.

Artemis took time to look back at me. "Indeed, young half-blood. And where do you think that legend came from?"

Seeing us safely away, Dr. Chase turned his biplane and followed us like an honor guard. It must have been one of the strangest sights ever, even for the Bay Area: a silver flying chariot pulled by deer, escorted by a Sopwith Camel.

Behind us, the army of Kronos roared in anger as they gathered on the summit of Mount Tamalpais, but the loudest sound was the voice of Atlas, bellowing curses against the gods as he struggled under the weight of the sky.

A FRIEND SAYS
GOOD-BYE

We landed at Crissy Field after nightfall.

As soon as Dr. Chase stepped out of his Sopwith Camel, Annabeth ran to him and gave him a huge hug. "Dad! You flew . . . you shot . . . oh my gods! That was the most amazing thing I've ever seen!"

Her father blushed. "Well, not bad for a middle-aged mortal, I suppose."

"But the celestial bronze bullets! How did you *get* those?"

"Ah, well. You did leave quite a few half-blood weapons in your room in Virginia, the last time you . . . left."

Annabeth looked down, embarrassed. I noticed Dr. Chase was very careful not to say *ran away*.

"I decided to try melting some down to make bullet casings," he continued. "Just a little experiment."

He said it like it was no big deal, but he had a gleam in his eye. I could understand all of a sudden why Athena, Goddess of Crafts and Wisdom, had taken a liking to him. He was an excellent mad scientist at heart.

"Dad . . ." Annabeth faltered.

"Annabeth, Percy," Thalia interrupted. Her voice was

urgent. She and Artemis were kneeling at Zoë's side, binding the huntress's wounds.

Annabeth and I ran over to help, but there wasn't much we could do. We had no ambrosia or nectar. No regular medicine would help. It was dark, but I could see that Zoë didn't look good. She was shivering, and the faint glow that usually hung around her was fading.

"Can't you heal her with magic?" I asked Artemis. "I mean . . . you're a goddess."

Artemis looked troubled. "Life is a fragile thing, Percy. If the Fates will the string to be cut, there is little I can do. But I can try."

She tried to set her hand on Zoë's side, but Zoë gripped her wrist. She looked into the goddess's eyes, and some kind of understanding passed between them.

"Have I . . . served thee well?" Zoë whispered.

"With great honor," Artemis said softly. "The finest of my attendants."

Zoë's face relaxed. "Rest. At last."

"I can try to heal the poison, my brave one."

But in that moment, I knew it wasn't just the poison that was killing her. It was her father's final blow. Zoë had known all along that the Oracle's prophecy was about her: she would die by a parent's hand. And yet she'd taken the quest anyway. She had chosen to save me, and Atlas's fury had broken her inside.

She saw Thalia, and took her hand.

"I am sorry we argued," Zoë said. "We could have been sisters."

"It's my fault," Thalia said, blinking hard. "You were right about Luke, about heroes, men—everything."

"Perhaps not all men," Zoë murmured. She smiled weakly at me. "Do you still have the sword, Percy?"

I couldn't speak, but I brought out Riptide and put the pen in her hand. She grasped it contentedly. "You spoke the truth, Percy Jackson. You are nothing like . . . like Hercules. I am honored that you carry this sword."

A shudder ran through her body.

"Zoë—" I said.

"Stars," she whispered. "I can see the stars again, my lady."

A tear trickled down Artemis's cheek. "Yes, my brave one. They are beautiful tonight."

"Stars," Zoë repeated. Her eyes fixed on the night sky. And she did not move again.

Thalia lowered her head. Annabeth gulped down a sob, and her father put his hands on her shoulders. I watched as Artemis cupped her hand above Zoë's mouth and spoke a few words in Ancient Greek. A silvery wisp of smoke exhaled from Zoë's lips and was caught in the hand of the goddess. Zoë's body shimmered and disappeared.

Artemis stood, said a kind of blessing, breathed into her cupped hand and released the silver dust to the sky. It flew up, sparkling, and vanished.

For a moment I didn't see anything different. Then Annabeth gasped. Looking up in the sky, I saw that the stars were brighter now. They made a pattern I had never noticed before—a gleaming constellation that looked a lot like a girl's figure—a girl with a bow, running across the sky.

"Let the world honor you, my Huntress," Artemis said. "Live forever in the stars."

It wasn't easy saying our good-byes. The thunder and lightning were still boiling over Mount Tamalpais in the north. Artemis was so upset she flickered with silver light. This made me nervous, because if she suddenly lost control and appeared in her fully divine form, we would disintegrate by looking at her.

"I must go to Olympus immediately," Artemis said. "I will not be able to take you, but I will send help."

The goddess set her hand on Annabeth's shoulder. "You are brave beyond measure, my girl. You will do what is right."

Then she looked quizzically at Thalia, as if she weren't sure what to make of this younger daughter of Zeus. Thalia seemed reluctant to look up, but something made her, and she held the goddess's eyes. I wasn't sure what passed between them, but Artemis's gaze softened with sympathy. Then she turned to me.

"You did well," she said. "For a man."

I wanted to protest. But then I realized it was the first time she hadn't called me a boy.

She mounted her chariot, which began to glow. We averted our eyes. There was a flash of silver, and the goddess was gone.

"Well," Dr. Chase sighed. "She was impressive; though I must say I still prefer Athena."

Annabeth turned toward him. "Dad, I . . . I'm sorry that—"

"Shh." He hugged her. "Do what you must, my dear. I know this isn't easy for you."

His voice was a little shaky, but he gave Annabeth a brave smile.

Then I heard the whoosh of large wings. Three pegasi descended through the fog: two white winged horses and one pure black one.

"Blackjack!" I called.

Yo, boss! he called. *You manage to stay alive okay without me?*

"It was rough," I admitted.

I brought Guido and Porkpie with me.

How ya doin? The other two pegasi spoke in my mind.

Blackjack looked me over with concern, then checked out Dr. Chase, Thalia, and Annabeth. *Any of these goons you want us to stampede?*

"Nah," I said aloud. "These are my friends. We need to get to Olympus pretty fast."

No problem, Blackjack said. *Except for the mortal over there. Hope he's not going.*

I assured him Dr. Chase was not. The professor was staring openmouthed at the pegasi.

"Fascinating," he said. "Such maneuverability! How does the wingspan compensate for the weight of the horse's body, I wonder?"

Blackjack cocked his head. *Whaaaat?*

"Why, if the British had had these pegasi in the cavalry

charges on the Crimea," Dr. Chase said, "the charge of the light brigade—"

"Dad!" Annabeth interrupted.

Dr. Chase blinked. He looked at his daughter and managed a smile. "I'm sorry, my dear. I know you must go."

He gave her one last awkward, well-meaning hug. As she turned to climb aboard the pegasus Guido, Dr. Chase called, "Annabeth. I know . . . I know San Francisco is a dangerous place for you. But please remember, you always have a home with us. We will keep you safe."

Annabeth didn't answer, but her eyes were red as she turned away. Dr. Chase started to say more, then apparently thought better of it. He raised his hand in a sad farewell and trudged away across the dark field.

Thalia and Annabeth and I mounted our pegasi. Together we soared over the bay and flew toward the eastern hills. Soon San Francisco was only a glittering crescent behind us, with an occasional flicker of lightning in the north.

Thalia was so exhausted she fell asleep on Porkpie's back. I knew she had to be really tired to sleep in the air, despite her fear of heights, but she didn't have much to worry about. Her pegasus flew with ease, adjusting himself every once in a while so Thalia stayed safely on his back.

Annabeth and I flew along side by side.

"Your dad seems cool," I told her.

It was too dark to see her expression. She looked back, even though California was far behind us now.

"I guess so," she said. "We've been arguing for so many years."

"Yeah, you said."

"You think I was lying about that?" It sounded like a challenge, but a pretty halfhearted one, like she was asking it of herself.

"I didn't say you were lying. It's just . . . he seems okay. Your stepmom, too. Maybe they've, uh, gotten cooler since you saw them last."

She hesitated. "They're still in San Francisco, Percy. I can't live so far from camp."

I didn't want to ask my next question. I was scared to know the answer. But I asked it anyway. "So what are you going to do now?"

We flew over a town, an island of lights in the middle of the dark. It whisked by so fast we might've been in an airplane.

"I don't know," she admitted. "But thank you for rescuing me."

"Hey, no big deal. We're friends."

"You didn't believe I was dead?"

"Never."

She hesitated. "Neither is Luke, you know. I mean . . . he isn't dead."

I stared at her. I didn't know if she was cracking under the stress or what. "Annabeth, that fall was pretty bad. There's no way—"

"He isn't dead," she insisted. "I know it. The same way you knew about me."

That comparison didn't make me too happy.

The towns were zipping by faster now, islands of light thicker together, until the whole landscape below was a glittering carpet. Dawn was close. The eastern sky was turning gray. And up ahead, a huge white-and-yellow glow spread out before us—the lights of New York.

How's that for speedy, boss? Blackjack bragged. *We get extra hay for breakfast or what?*

"You're the man, Blackjack," I told him. "Er, the horse, I mean."

"You don't believe me about Luke," Annabeth said, "but we'll see him again. He's in trouble, Percy. He's under Kronos's spell."

I didn't feel like arguing, though it made me mad. How could she still have any feelings for that creep? How could she possibly make excuses for him? He deserved that fall. He deserved . . . okay, I'll say it. He deserved to die. Unlike Bianca. Unlike Zoë. Luke couldn't be alive. It wouldn't be fair.

"There it is." Thalia's voice; she'd woken up. She was pointing toward Manhattan, which was quickly zooming into view. "It's started."

"What's started?" I asked.

Then I looked where she was pointing. High above the Empire State Building, Olympus was its own island of light, a floating mountain ablaze with torches and braziers, white marble palaces gleaming in the early morning air.

"The winter solstice," Thalia said. "The Council of the Gods."

NINETEEN

THE GODS VOTE HOW
TO KILL US

Flying was bad enough for a son of Poseidon, but flying straight up to Zeus's palace, with thunder and lightning swirling around it, was even worse.

We circled over midtown Manhattan, making one complete orbit around Mount Olympus. I'd only been there once before, traveling by elevator up to the secret six hundredth floor of the Empire State Building. This time, if it was possible, Olympus amazed me even more.

In the early-morning darkness, torches and fires made the mountainside palaces glow twenty different colors, from bloodred to indigo. Apparently no one ever slept on Olympus. The twisting streets were full of demigods and nature spirits and minor godlings bustling about, riding chariots or sedan chairs carried by Cyclopes. Winter didn't seem to exist here. I caught the scent of the gardens in full bloom, jasmine and roses and even sweeter things I couldn't name. Music drifted up from many windows, the soft sounds of lyres and reed pipes.

Towering at the peak of the mountain was the greatest palace of all, the glowing white hall of the gods.

Our pegasi set us down in the outer courtyard, in front

of huge silver gates. Before I could even think to knock, the gates opened by themselves.

Good luck, boss, Blackjack said.

"Yeah." I didn't know why, but I had a sense of doom. I'd never seen all the gods together. I knew any one of them could blast me to dust, and a few of them would like to.

Hey, if ya don't come back, can I have your cabin for my stable?

I looked at the pegasus.

Just a thought, he said. *Sorry.*

Blackjack and his friends flew off, leaving Thalia, Annabeth, and me alone. For a minute we stood there regarding the palace, the way we'd stood together in front of Westover Hall, what seemed like a million years ago.

And then, side by side, we walked into the throne room.

Twelve enormous thrones made a U around a central hearth, just like the placement of the cabins at camp. The ceiling above glittered with constellations—even the newest one, Zoë the Huntress, making her way across the heavens with her bow drawn.

All of the seats were occupied. Each god and goddess was about fifteen feet tall, and I'm telling you, if you've ever had a dozen all-powerful super-huge beings turn their eyes on you at once . . . Well, suddenly, facing monsters seemed like a picnic.

"Welcome, heroes," Artemis said.

"Mooo!"

That's when I noticed Bessie and Grover.

A sphere of water was hovering in the center of the

room, next to the hearth fire. Bessie was swimming happily around, swishing his serpent tail and poking his head out the sides and bottom of the sphere. He seemed to be enjoying the novelty of swimming in a magic bubble. Grover was kneeling at Zeus's throne, as if he'd just been giving a report, but when he saw us, he cried, "You made it!"

He started to run toward me, then remembered he was turning his back on Zeus, and looked for permission.

"Go on," Zeus said. But he wasn't really paying attention to Grover. The lord of the sky was staring intently at Thalia.

Grover trotted over. None of the gods spoke. Every clop of Grover's hooves echoed on the marble floor. Bessie splashed in his bubble of water. The hearth fire crackled.

I looked nervously at my father, Poseidon. He was dressed similar to the last time I'd seen him: beach shorts, a Hawaiian shirt, and sandals. He had a weathered, suntanned face with a dark beard and deep green eyes. I wasn't sure how he would feel about seeing me again, but the corners of his eyes crinkled with smile lines. He nodded as if to say *It's okay.*

Grover gave Annabeth and Thalia big hugs. Then he grasped my arms. "Percy, Bessie and I made it! But you have to convince them! They can't do it!"

"Do what?" I asked.

"Heroes," Artemis called.

The goddess slid down from her throne and turned to human size, a young auburn-haired girl, perfectly at ease in the midst of the giant Olympians. She walked toward us, her silver robes shimmering. There was no emotion in her

[286]

face. She seemed to walk in a column of moonlight.

"The Council has been informed of your deeds," Artemis told us. "They know that Mount Othrys is rising in the West. They know of Atlas's attempt for freedom, and the gathering armies of Kronos. We have voted to act."

There was some mumbling and shuffling among the gods, as if they weren't all happy with this plan, but nobody protested.

"At my Lord Zeus's command," Artemis said, "my brother Apollo and I shall hunt the most powerful monsters, seeking to strike them down before they can join the Titans' cause. Lady Athena shall personally check on the other Titans to make sure they do not escape their various prisons. Lord Poseidon has been given permission to unleash his full fury on the cruise ship *Princess Andromeda* and send it to the bottom of the sea. And as for you, my heroes . . ."

She turned to face the other immortals. "These half-bloods have done Olympus a great service. Would any here deny that?"

She looked around at the assembled gods, meeting their faces individually. Zeus in his dark pin-striped suit, his black beard neatly trimmed, and his eyes sparking with energy. Next to him sat a beautiful woman with silver hair braided over one shoulder and a dress that shimmered colors like peacock feathers. The Lady Hera.

On Zeus's right, my father Poseidon. Next to him, a huge lump of a man with a leg in a steel brace, a misshapen head, and a wild brown beard, fire flickering through his whiskers. The Lord of the Forges, Hephaestus.

Hermes winked at me. He was wearing a business suit today, checking messages on his caduceus mobile phone. Apollo leaned back in his golden throne with his shades on. He had iPod headphones on, so I wasn't sure he was even listening, but he gave me a thumbs-up. Dionysus looked bored, twirling a grape vine between his fingers. And Ares, well, he sat on his chrome-and-leather throne, glowering at me while he sharpened a knife.

On the ladies' side of the throne room, a dark-haired goddess in green robes sat next to Hera on a throne woven of apple-tree branches. Demeter, Goddess of the Harvest. Next to her sat a beautiful gray-eyed woman in an elegant white dress. She could only be Annabeth's mother, Athena. Then there was Aphrodite, who smiled at me knowingly and made me blush in spite of myself.

All the Olympians in one place. So much power in this room it was a miracle the whole palace didn't blow apart.

"I gotta say"—Apollo broke the silence—"these kids did okay." He cleared his throat and began to recite: *"Heroes win laurels—"*

"Um, yes, first class," Hermes interrupted, like he was anxious to avoid Apollo's poetry. "All in favor of not disintegrating them?"

A few tentative hands went up—Demeter, Aphrodite.

"Wait just a minute," Ares growled. He pointed at Thalia and me. "These two are dangerous. It'd be much safer, while we've got them here—"

"Ares," Poseidon interrupted, "they are worthy heroes. We will not blast my son to bits."

"Nor my daughter," Zeus grumbled. "She has done well."

Thalia blushed. She studied the floor. I knew how she felt. I'd hardly ever talked to my father, much less gotten a compliment.

The goddess Athena cleared her throat and sat forward. "I am proud of my daughter as well. But there is a security risk here with the other two."

"Mother!" Annabeth said. "How can you—"

Athena cut her off with a calm but firm look. "It is unfortunate that my father, Zeus, and my uncle, Poseidon, chose to break their oath not to have more children. Only Hades kept his word, a fact that I find ironic. As we know from the Great Prophecy, children of the three elder gods . . . such as Thalia and Percy . . . are dangerous. As thick-headed as he is, Ares has a point."

"Right!" Ares said. "Hey, wait a minute. Who you callin'—"

He started to get up, but a grape vine grew around his waist like a seat belt and pulled him back down.

"Oh, please, Ares," Dionysus sighed. "Save the fighting for later."

Ares cursed and ripped away the vine. "You're one to talk, you old drunk. You seriously want to protect these brats?"

Dionysus gazed down at us wearily. "I have no love for them. Athena, do you truly think it safest to destroy them?"

"I do not pass judgment," Athena said. "I only point out the risk. What we do, the Council must decide."

"I will not have them punished," Artemis said. "I will

have them rewarded. If we destroy heroes who do us a great favor, then we are no better than the Titans. If this is Olympian justice, I will have none of it."

"Calm down, sis," Apollo said. "Jeez, you need to lighten up."

"Don't call me *sis!* I will reward them."

"Well," Zeus grumbled. "Perhaps. But the monster at least must be destroyed. We have agreement on that?"

A lot of nodding heads.

It took me a second to realize what they were saying. Then my heart turned to lead. "Bessie? You want to destroy Bessie?"

"Mooooooo!" Bessie protested.

My father frowned. "You have named the Ophiotaurus Bessie?"

"Dad," I said, "he's just a sea creature. A really *nice* sea creature. You can't destroy him."

Poseidon shifted uncomfortably. "Percy, the monster's power is considerable. If the Titans were to steal it, or—"

"You can't," I insisted. I looked at Zeus. I probably should have been afraid of him, but I stared him right in the eye. "Controlling the prophecies never works. Isn't that true? Besides, Bess— the Ophiotaurus is innocent. Killing something like that is wrong. It's just as wrong as . . . as Kronos eating his children, just because of something they *might* do. It's wrong!"

Zeus seemed to consider this. His eyes drifted to his daughter Thalia. "And what of the risk? Kronos knows full well, if one of you were to sacrifice the beast's entrails, you would have the power to destroy us. Do you think we can let that possibility remain? You, my daughter, will turn sixteen on the morrow, just as the prophecy says."

"You have to trust them," Annabeth spoke up. "Sir, you have to trust them."

Zeus scowled. "Trust a hero?"

"Annabeth is right," Artemis said. "Which is why I must first make a reward. My faithful companion, Zoë Nightshade, has passed into the stars. I must have a new lieutenant. And I intend to choose one. But first, Father Zeus, I must speak to you privately."

Zeus beckoned Artemis forward. He leaned down and listened as she spoke in his ear.

A feeling of panic seized me. "Annabeth," I said under my breath. "Don't."

She frowned at me. "What?"

"Look, I need to tell you something," I continued. The words came stumbling out of me. "I couldn't stand it if . . . I don't want you to—"

"Percy?" she said. "You look like you're going to be sick."

And that's how I felt. I wanted to say more, but my tongue betrayed me. It wouldn't move because of the fear in my stomach. And then Artemis turned.

"I shall have a new lieutenant," she announced. "If she will accept it."

"No," I murmured.

"Thalia," Artemis said. "Daughter of Zeus. Will you join the Hunt?"

Stunned silence filled the room. I stared at Thalia, unable to believe what I was hearing. Annabeth smiled. She squeezed Thalia's hand and let it go, as if she'd been expecting this all along.

"I will," Thalia said firmly.

Zeus rose, his eyes full of concern. "My daughter, consider well—"

"Father," she said. "I will not turn sixteen tomorrow. I will never turn sixteen. I won't let this prophecy be mine. I stand with my sister Artemis. Kronos will never tempt me again."

She knelt before the goddess and began the words I remembered from Bianca's oath, what seemed like so long ago. "I pledge myself to the goddess Artemis. I turn my back on the company of men . . ."

Afterward, Thalia did something that surprised me almost as much as the pledge. She came over to me, smiled, and in front of the whole assembly, she gave me a big hug.

I blushed.

When she pulled away and gripped my shoulders, I said, "Um . . . aren't you supposed to not do that anymore? Hug boys, I mean?"

"I'm honoring a friend," she corrected. "I *must* join the Hunt, Percy. I haven't known peace since . . . since Half-Blood Hill. I finally feel like I have a home. But you're a hero. You will be the one of the prophecy."

"Great," I muttered.

"I'm proud to be your friend."

She hugged Annabeth, who was trying hard not to cry. Then she even hugged Grover, who looked ready to pass out, like somebody had just given him an all-you-can-eat enchilada coupon.

Then Thalia went to stand by Artemis's side.

"Now for the Ophiotaurus," Artemis said.

"This boy is still dangerous," Dionysus warned. "The beast is a temptation to great power. Even if we spare the boy—"

"No." I looked around at all the gods. "Please. Keep the Ophiotaurus safe. My dad can hide him under the sea somewhere, or keep him in an aquarium here in Olympus. But you have to protect him."

"And why should we trust you?" rumbled Hephaestus.

"I'm only fourteen," I said. "If this prophecy is about me, that's two more years."

"Two years for Kronos to deceive you," Athena said. "Much can change in two years, my young hero."

"Mother!" Annabeth said, exasperated.

"It is only the truth, child. It is bad strategy to keep the animal alive. Or the boy."

My father stood. "I will not have a sea creature destroyed, if I can help it. And I *can* help it."

He held out his hand, and a trident appeared in it: a twenty foot long bronze shaft with three spear tips that shimmered with blue, watery light. "I will vouch for the boy and the safety of the Ophiotaurus."

"You won't take it under the sea!" Zeus stood suddenly. "I won't have that kind of bargaining chip in your possession."

"Brother, please," Poseidon sighed.

Zeus's lightning bolt appeared in his hand, a shaft of electricity that filled the whole room with the smell of ozone.

"Fine," Poseidon said. "I will build an aquarium for the creature here. Hephaestus can help me. The creature will be safe. We shall protect it with all our powers. The boy will not betray us. I vouch for this on my honor."

Zeus thought about this. "All in favor?"

To my surprise, a lot of hands went up. Dionysus abstained. So did Ares and Athena. But everybody else . . .

"We have a majority," Zeus decreed. "And so, since we will not be destroying these heroes . . . I imagine we should honor them. Let the triumph celebration begin!"

There are parties, and then there are huge, major, blowout parties. And then there are Olympian parties. If you ever get a choice, go for the Olympian.

The Nine Muses cranked up the tunes, and I realized the music was whatever you wanted it to be: the gods could listen to classical and the younger demigods heard hip-hop or whatever, and it was all the same sound track. No arguments. No fights to change the radio station. Just requests to crank it up.

Dionysus went around growing refreshment stands out of the ground, and a beautiful woman walked with him arm in arm—his wife, Ariadne. Dionysus looked happy for the first time. Nectar and ambrosia overflowed from golden fountains, and platters of mortal snack food crowded the banquet tables. Golden goblets filled with whatever drink you wanted. Grover trotted around with a full plate of tin cans and enchiladas, and his goblet was full of double-espresso latte, which he kept muttering over like an incantation: "Pan! Pan!"

Gods kept coming over to congratulate me. Thankfully, they had reduced themselves to human size, so they didn't accidentally trample partygoers under their feet. Hermes started chatting with me, and he was so cheerful I hated to tell him what had happened to his least-favorite son, Luke, but before I could even get up the courage, Hermes got a call on his caduceus and walked away.

Apollo told me I could drive his sun chariot any time, and if I ever wanted archery lessons—

"Thanks," I told him. "But seriously, I'm no good at archery."

"Ah, nonsense," he said. "Target practice from the chariot as we fly over the U.S.? Best fun there is!"

I made some excuses and wove through the crowds that were dancing in the palace courtyards. I was looking for Annabeth. Last I saw her, she'd been dancing with some minor godling.

Then a man's voice behind me said, "You won't let me down, I hope."

I turned and found Poseidon smiling at me.

"Dad . . . hi."

"Hello, Percy. You've done well."

His praise made me uneasy. I mean, it felt good, but I knew just how much he'd put himself on the line, vouching for me. It would've been a lot easier to let the others disintegrate me.

"I won't let you down," I promised.

He nodded. I had trouble reading gods' emotions, but I wondered if he had some doubts.

"Your friend Luke—"

"He's not my friend," I blurted out. Then I realized it was probably rude to interrupt. "Sorry."

"Your *former* friend Luke," Poseidon corrected. "He once promised things like that. He was Hermes's pride and joy. Just bear that in mind, Percy. Even the bravest can fall."

"Luke fell pretty hard," I agreed. "He's dead."

Poseidon shook his head. "No, Percy. He is not."

I stared at him. "What?"

"I believe Annabeth told you this. Luke still lives. I have seen it. His boat sails from San Francisco with the remains of Kronos even now. He will retreat and regroup before assaulting you again. I will do my best to destroy his boat with storms, but he is making alliances with my enemies, the older spirits of the ocean. They will fight to protect him."

"How can he be alive?" I said. "That fall should've killed him!"

Poseidon looked troubled. "I don't know, Percy, but beware of him. He is more dangerous than ever. And the golden coffin is still with him, still growing in strength."

"What about Atlas?" I said. "What's to prevent him from escaping again? Couldn't he just force some giant or something to take the sky for him?"

My father snorted in derision. "If it were so easy, he

would have escaped long ago. No, my son. The curse of the sky can only be forced upon a Titan, one of the children of Gaia and Ouranous. Anyone else must *choose* to take the burden of their own free will. Only a hero, someone with strength, a true heart, and great courage, would do such a thing. No one in Kronos's army would dare try to bear that weight, even upon pain of death."

"Luke did it," I said. "He let Atlas go. Then he tricked Annabeth into saving him and used her to convince Artemis to take the sky."

"Yes," Poseidon said. "Luke is . . . an interesting case."

I think he wanted to say more, but just then, Bessie started mooing from across the courtyard. Some demigods were playing with his water sphere, joyously pushing it back and forth over the top of the crowd.

"I'd better take care of that," Poseidon grumbled. "We can't have the Ophiotaurus tossed around like a beach ball. Be good, my son. We may not speak again for some time."

And just like that he was gone.

I was about to keep searching the crowd when another voice spoke. "Your father takes a great risk, you know."

I found myself face-to-face with a gray-eyed woman who looked so much like Annabeth I almost called her that.

"Athena." I tried not to sound resentful, after the way she'd written me off in the council, but I guess I didn't hide it very well.

She smiled dryly. "Do not judge me too harshly, half-blood. Wise counsel is not always popular, but I spoke the truth. You are dangerous."

"You never take risks?"

She nodded. "I concede the point. You may perhaps be useful. And yet . . . your fatal flaw may destroy us as well as yourself."

My heart crept into my throat. A year ago, Annabeth and I had had a talk about fatal flaws. Every hero had one. Hers, she said, was pride. She believed she could do anything . . . like holding up the world, for instance. Or saving Luke. But I didn't really know what mine was.

Athena looked almost sorry for me. "Kronos knows your flaw, even if you do not. He knows how to study his enemies. Think, Percy. How has he manipulated you? First, your mother was taken from you. Then your best friend, Grover. Now my daughter, Annabeth." She paused, disapproving. "In each case, your loved ones have been used to lure you into Kronos's traps. Your fatal flaw is personal loyalty, Percy. You do not know when it is time to cut your losses. To save a friend, you would sacrifice the world. In a hero of the prophecy, that is very, very dangerous."

I balled my fists. "That's not a flaw. Just because I want to help my friends—"

"The most dangerous flaws are those which are good in moderation," she said. "Evil is easy to fight. Lack of wisdom . . . that is very hard indeed."

I wanted to argue, but I found I couldn't. Athena was pretty darn smart.

"I hope the Council's decisions prove wise," Athena said. "But I will be watching, Percy Jackson. I do not approve of your friendship with my daughter. I do not think it wise for either of you. And should you begin to waver in your loyalties . . ."

She fixed me with her cold gray stare, and I realized what a terrible enemy Athena would make, ten times worse than Ares or Dionysus or maybe even my father. Athena would never give up. She would never do something rash or stupid just because she hated you, and if she made a plan to destroy you, it would not fail.

"Percy!" Annabeth said, running through the crowd. She stopped short when she saw who I was talking to. "Oh . . . Mom."

"I will leave you," Athena said. "For now."

She turned and strode through the crowds, which parted before her as if she were carrying Aegis.

"Was she giving you a hard time?" Annabeth asked.

"No," I said. "It's . . . fine."

She studied me with concern. She touched the new streak of gray in my hair that matched hers exactly—our painful souvenir from holding Atlas's burden. There was a lot I'd wanted to say to Annabeth, but Athena had taken the confidence out of me. I felt like I'd been punched in the gut.

I do not approve of your friendship with my daughter.

"So," Annabeth said. "What did you want to tell me earlier?"

The music was playing. People were dancing in the streets. I said, "I, uh, was thinking we got interrupted at Westover Hall. And . . . I think I owe you a dance."

She smiled slowly. "All right, Seaweed Brain."

So I took her hand, and I don't know what everybody else heard, but to me it sounded like a slow dance: a little sad, but maybe a little hopeful, too.

TWENTY.

I GET A NEW ENEMY
FOR CHRISTMAS

Before I left Olympus, I decided to make a few calls. It wasn't easy, but I finally found a quiet fountain in a corner garden and sent an Iris-message to my brother, Tyson, under the sea. I told him about our adventures, and Bessie—he wanted to hear every detail about the cute baby cow serpent—and I assured him that Annabeth was safe. Finally I got around to explaining how the shield he'd made me last summer had been damaged in the manticore attack.

"Yay!" Tyson said. "That means it was good! It saved your life!"

"It sure did, big guy," I said. "But now it's ruined."

"Not ruined!" Tyson promised. "I will visit and fix it next summer."

The idea picked me up instantly. I guess I hadn't realized how much I missed having Tyson around.

"Seriously?" I asked. "They'll let you take time off?"

"Yes! I have made two thousand seven hundred and forty-one magic swords," Tyson said proudly, showing me the newest blade. "The boss says 'good work'! He will let me take the whole summer off. I will visit camp!"

We talked for a while about war preparations and our

dad's fight with the old sea gods, and all the cool things we could do together next summer, but then Tyson's boss started yelling at him and he had to get back to work.

I dug out my last golden drachma and made one more Iris-message.

"Sally Jackson," I said. "Upper East Side, Manhattan."

The mist shimmered, and there was my mom at our kitchen table, laughing and holding hands with her friend Mr. Blowfish.

I felt so embarrassed, I was about to wave my hand through the mist and cut the connection, but before I could, my mom saw me.

Her eyes got wide. She let go of Mr. Blowfish's hand real quick. "Oh, Paul! You know what? I left my writing journal in the living room. Would you mind getting it for me?"

"Sure, Sally. No problem."

He left the room, and instantly my mom leaned toward the Iris-message. "Percy! Are you all right?"

"I'm, uh, fine. How's that writing seminar going?"

She pursed her lips. "It's fine. But that's not important. Tell me what's happened!"

I filled her in as quickly as I could. She sighed with relief when she heard that Annabeth was safe.

"I knew you could do it!" she said. "I'm so proud."

"Yeah, well, I'd better let you get back to your home-work."

"Percy, I . . . Paul and I—"

"Mom, are you happy?"

The question seemed to take her by surprise. She

[302]

thought for a moment. "Yes. I really am, Percy. Being around him makes me happy."

"Then it's cool. Seriously. Don't worry about me."

The funny thing was, I meant it. Considering the quest I'd just had, maybe I should have been worried for my mom. I'd seen just how mean people could be to each other, like Hercules was to Zoë Nightshade, like Luke was to Thalia. I'd met Aphrodite, Goddess of Love, in person, and her powers had scared me worse than Ares. But seeing my mother laughing and smiling, after all the years she'd suffered with my nasty ex-stepfather, Gabe Ugliano, I couldn't help feeling happy for her.

"You promise not to call him Mr. Blowfish?" she asked.

I shrugged. "Well, maybe not to his face, anyway."

"Sally?" Mr. Blofis called from our living room. "You need the green binder or the red one?"

"I'd better go," she told me. "See you for Christmas?"

"Are you putting blue candy in my stocking?"

She smiled. "If you're not too old for that."

"I'm never too old for candy."

"I'll see you then."

She waved her hand across the mist. Her image disappeared, and I thought to myself that Thalia had been right, so many days ago at Westover Hall: my mom really was pretty cool.

Compared to Mount Olympus, Manhattan was quiet. Friday before Christmas, but it was early in the morning, and hardly anyone was on Fifth Avenue. Argus, the many-eyed security chief, picked up Annabeth, Grover, and me at the Empire State Building and ferried us back to camp through a light snowstorm. The Long Island Expressway was almost deserted.

As we trudged back up Half-Blood Hill to the pine tree where the Golden Fleece glittered, I half expected to see Thalia there, waiting for us. But she wasn't. She was long gone with Artemis and the rest of the Hunters, off on their next adventure.

Chiron greeted us at the Big House with hot chocolate and toasted cheese sandwiches. Grover went off with his satyr friends to spread the word about our strange encounter with the magic of Pan. Within an hour, the satyrs were all running around agitated, asking where the nearest espresso bar was.

Annabeth and I sat with Chiron and some of the other senior campers—Beckendorf, Silena Beauregard, and the Stoll brothers. Even Clarisse from the Ares cabin was there, back from her secretive scouting mission. I knew she must've had a difficult quest, because she didn't even try to pulverize me. She had a new scar on her chin, and her dirty blond hair had been cut short and ragged, like someone had attacked it with a pair of safety scissors.

"I got news," she mumbled uneasily. "*Bad* news."

"I'll fill you in later," Chiron said with forced cheerfulness. "The important thing is you have prevailed. And you saved Annabeth!"

Annabeth smiled at me gratefully, which made me look away.

For some strange reason, I found myself thinking about Hoover Dam, and the odd mortal girl I'd run into there, Rachel Elizabeth Dare. I didn't know why, but her annoying comments kept coming back to me. *Do you always kill people when they blow their nose?* I was only alive because so many people had helped me, even a random mortal girl like that. I'd never even explained to her who I was.

"Luke is alive," I said. "Annabeth was right."

Annabeth sat up. "How do you know?"

I tried not to feel annoyed by her interest. I told her what my dad had said about the *Princess Andromeda*.

"Well." Annabeth shifted uncomfortably in her chair. "If the final battle does come when Percy is sixteen, at least we have two more years to figure something out."

I had a feeling that when she said "figure something out," she meant "get Luke to change his ways," which annoyed me even more.

Chiron's expression was gloomy. Sitting by the fire in his wheelchair, he looked really old. I mean . . . he *was* really old, but he usually didn't look it.

"Two years may seem like a long time," he said. "But it is the blink of an eye. I still hope you are not the child of the prophecy, Percy. But if you are, then the second Titan war is almost upon us. Kronos's first strike will be here."

"How do you know?" I asked. "Why would he care about camp?"

"Because the gods use heroes as their tools," Chiron said simply. "Destroy the tools, and the gods will be crippled. Luke's forces will come here. Mortal, demigod, monstrous . . . We must be prepared. Clarisse's news may give us a clue as to how they will attack, but—"

There was a knock on the door, and Nico di Angelo came huffing into the parlor, his cheeks bright red from the cold.

He was smiling, but he looked around anxiously. "Hey! Where's . . . where's my sister?"

Dead silence. I stared at Chiron. I couldn't believe nobody had told him yet. And then I realized why. They'd been waiting for us to appear, to tell Nico in person.

That was the last thing I wanted to do. But I owed it to Bianca.

"Hey, Nico." I got up from my comfortable chair. "Let's take a walk, okay? We need to talk."

He took the news in silence, which somehow made it worse. I kept talking, trying to explain how it had happened, how Bianca had sacrificed herself to save the quest. But I felt like I was only making things worse.

"She wanted you to have this." I brought out the little god figurine Bianca had found in the junkyard. Nico held it in his palm and stared at it.

We were standing at the dining pavilion, just where we'd last spoken before I went on the quest. The wind was bitter cold, even with the camp's magical weather protection. Snow fell lightly against the marble steps. I figured outside the camp borders, there must be a blizzard happening.

"You promised you would protect her," Nico said.

He might as well have stabbed me with a rusty dagger.

It would've hurt less than reminding me of my promise.

"Nico," I said. "I tried. But Bianca gave herself up to save the rest of us. I told her not to. But she—"

"You promised!"

He glared at me, his eyes rimmed with red. He closed his small fist around the god statue.

"I shouldn't have trusted you." His voice broke. "You lied to me. My nightmares were right!"

"Wait. What nightmares?"

He flung the god statue to the ground. It clattered across the icy marble. "I hate you!"

"She might be alive," I said desperately. "I don't know for sure—"

"She's dead." He closed his eyes. His whole body trembled with rage. "I should've known it earlier. She's in the Fields of Asphodel, standing before the judges right now, being evaluated. I can feel it."

"What do you mean, you can feel it?"

Before he could answer, I heard a new sound behind me. A hissing, clattering noise I recognized all too well.

I drew my sword and Nico gasped. I whirled and found myself facing four skeleton warriors. They grinned fleshless grins and advanced with swords drawn. I wasn't sure how they'd made it inside the camp, but it didn't matter. I'd never get help in time.

"You're trying to kill me!" Nico screamed. "You brought these . . . these things?"

"No! I mean, yes, they followed me, but *no!* Nico, run. They can't be destroyed."

"I don't trust you!"

The first skeleton charged. I knocked aside its blade, but the other three kept coming. I sliced one in half, but immediately it began to knit back together. I knocked another's head off but it just kept fighting.

"Run, Nico!" I yelled. "Get help!"

"No!" He pressed his hands to his ears.

I couldn't fight four at once, not if they wouldn't die. I slashed, whirled, blocked, jabbed, but they just kept advancing. It was only a matter of seconds before the zombies overpowered me.

"No!" Nico shouted louder. *"Go away!"*

The ground rumbled beneath me. The skeletons froze. I rolled out of the way just as a crack opened at the feet of the four warriors. The ground ripped apart like a snapping mouth. Flames erupted from the fissure, and the earth swallowed the skeletons in one loud *CRUNCH!*

Silence.

In the place where the skeletons had stood, a twenty-foot-long scar wove across the marble floor of the pavilion. Otherwise there was no sign of the warriors.

Awestruck, I looked to Nico. "How did you—"

"Go away!" he yelled. "I hate you! I wish you were dead!"

The ground didn't swallow *me* up, but Nico ran down the steps, heading toward the woods. I started to follow but slipped and fell to the icy steps. When I got up, I noticed what I'd slipped on.

I picked up the god statue Bianca had retrieved from the

junkyard for Nico. *The only statue he didn't have,* she'd said. A last gift from his sister.

I stared at it with dread, because now I understood why the face looked familiar. I'd seen it before.

It was a statue of Hades, Lord of the Dead.

Annabeth and Grover helped me search the woods for hours, but there was no sign of Nico di Angelo.

"We have to tell Chiron," Annabeth said, out of breath.

"No," I said.

She and Grover both stared at me.

"Um," Grover said nervously, "what do you mean . . . no?"

I was still trying to figure out why I'd said that, but the words spilled out of me. "We can't let anyone know. I don't think anyone realizes that Nico is a—"

"A son of Hades," Annabeth said. "Percy, do you have *any idea* how serious this is? Even Hades broke the oath! This is horrible!"

"I don't think so," I said. "I don't think Hades broke the oath."

"What?"

"He's their dad," I said, "but Bianca and Nico have been out of commission for a long time, since even before World War II."

"The Lotus Casino!" Grover said, and he told Annabeth about the conversations we'd had with Bianca on the quest. "She and Nico were stuck there for decades. They were born before the oath was made."

I nodded.

"But how did they get out?" Annabeth protested.

"I don't know," I admitted. "Bianca said a lawyer came and got them and drove them to Westover Hall. I don't know who that could've been, or why. Maybe it's part of this Great Stirring thing. I don't think Nico understands who he is. But we can't go telling anyone. Not even Chiron. If the Olympians find out—"

"It might start them fighting among each other again," Annabeth said. "That's the last thing we need."

Grover looked worried. "But you can't hide things from the gods. Not forever."

"I don't need forever," I said. "Just two years. Until I'm sixteen."

Annabeth paled. "But, Percy, this means the prophecy might *not* be about you. It might be about Nico. We have to—"

"No," I said. "I choose the prophecy. It will be about me."

"Why are you saying that?" she cried. "You want to be responsible for the whole world?"

It was the last thing I wanted, but I didn't say that. I knew I had to step up and claim it.

"I can't let Nico be in any more danger," I said. "I owe that much to his sister. I . . . let them both down. I'm not going to let that poor kid suffer any more."

"The poor kid who hates you and wants to see you dead," Grover reminded me.

"Maybe we can find him," I said. "We can convince him it's okay, hide him someplace safe."

Annabeth shivered. "If Luke gets hold of him—"

"Luke won't," I said. "I'll make sure he's got other things to worry about. Namely, me."

I wasn't sure Chiron believed the story Annabeth and I told him. I think he could tell I was holding something back about Nico's disappearance, but in the end, he accepted it. Unfortunately, Nico wasn't the first half-blood to disappear.

"So young," Chiron sighed, his hands on the rail of the front porch. "Alas, I hope he was eaten by monsters. Much better than being recruited into the Titans' army."

That idea made me really uneasy. I almost changed my mind about telling Chiron, but I didn't.

"You really think the first attack will be here?" I asked.

Chiron stared at the snow falling on the hills. I could see smoke from the dragon guardian at the pine tree, the glitter of the distant Fleece.

"It will not be until summer, at least," Chiron said. "This winter will be hard . . . the hardest for many centuries. It's best that you go home to the city, Percy; try to keep your mind on school. And rest. You will need rest."

I looked at Annabeth. "What about you?"

Her cheeks flushed. "I'm going to try San Francisco after all. Maybe I can keep an eye on Mount Tam, make sure the Titans don't try anything else."

"You'll send an Iris-message if anything goes wrong?"

She nodded. "But I think Chiron's right. It won't be until the summer. Luke will need time to regain his strength."

I didn't like the idea of waiting. Then again, next August I would be turning fifteen. So close to sixteen I didn't want to think about it.

"All right," I said. "Just take care of yourself. And no crazy stunts in the Sopwith Camel."

She smiled tentatively. "Deal. And, Percy—"

Whatever she was going to say was interrupted by Grover, who stumbled out of the Big House, tripping over tin cans. His face was haggard and pale, like he'd seen a specter.

"He spoke!" Grover cried.

"Calm down, my young satyr," Chiron said, frowning. "What is the matter?"

"I . . . I was playing music in the parlor," he stammered, "and drinking coffee. Lots and lots of coffee! And he spoke in my mind!"

"Who?" Annabeth demanded.

"Pan!" Grover wailed. "The Lord of the Wild himself. I heard him! I have to . . . I have to find a suitcase."

"Whoa, whoa, whoa," I said. "What did he say?"

Grover stared at me. "Just three words. He said, *'I await you.'*"

PERCY JACKSON & THE OLYMPIANS

BOOK FOUR

THE BATTLE OF THE LABYRINTH

RICK RIORDAN

SCHOLASTIC INC.

New York Toronto London Auckland Sydney
Mexico City New Delhi Hong Kong Buenos Aires

ISBN-13: 978-0-545-17481-7
ISBN-10: 0-545-17481-3

20 19 18 17 16   13 14/0

Printed in the U.S.A.   40

First Scholastic printing, September 2009

This book is set in 13-point Centaur MT.

To Becky, who always leads me through the maze

CONTENTS

I BATTLE THE
CHEERLEADING SQUAD

The last thing I wanted to do on my summer break was blow up another school. But there I was Monday morning, the first week of June, sitting in my mom's car in front of Goode High School on East 81st.

Goode was this big brownstone building overlooking the East River. A bunch of BMWs and Lincoln Town Cars were parked out front. Staring up at the fancy stone archway, I wondered how long it would take me to get kicked out of this place.

"Just relax." My mom didn't sound relaxed. "It's only an orientation tour. And remember, dear, this is Paul's school. So try not to . . . you know."

"Destroy it?"

"Yes."

Paul Blofis, my mom's boyfriend, was standing out front, greeting future ninth graders as they came up the steps. With his salt-and-pepper hair, denim clothes, and leather jacket, he reminded me of a TV actor, but he was just an English teacher. He'd managed to convince Goode High School to accept me for ninth grade, despite the fact that I'd gotten kicked out of every school I'd ever attended.

I'd tried to warn him it wasn't a good idea, but he wouldn't listen.

I looked at my mom. "You haven't told him the truth about me, have you?"

She tapped her fingers nervously on the wheel. She was dressed up for a job interview—her best blue dress and high-heeled shoes.

"I thought we should wait," she admitted.

"So we don't scare him away."

"I'm sure orientation will be fine, Percy. It's only one morning."

"Great," I mumbled. "I can get expelled before I even start the school year."

"Think positive. Tomorrow you're off to camp! After orientation, you've got your date—"

"It's not a date!" I protested. "It's just Annabeth, Mom. Jeez!"

"She's coming all the way from camp to meet you."

"Well, yeah."

"You're going to the movies."

"Yeah."

"Just the two of you."

"Mom!"

She held up her hands in surrender, but I could tell she was trying hard not to smile. "You'd better get inside, dear. I'll see you tonight."

I was about to get out of the car when I looked over at the steps of the school. Paul Blofis was greeting a girl with frizzy red hair. She wore a maroon T-shirt and ratty jeans decorated with marker drawings. When she turned, I caught a glimpse of her face, and the hairs on my arms stood straight up.

"Percy?" my mom asked. "What's wrong?"

"N-nothing," I stammered. "Does the school have a side entrance?"

"Down the block on the right. Why?"

"I'll see you later."

My mom started to say something, but I got out of the car and ran, hoping the redheaded girl wouldn't see me.

What was *she* doing here? Not even *my* luck could be this bad.

Yeah, right. I was about to find out my luck could get a whole lot worse.

Sneaking into orientation didn't work out too well. Two cheerleaders in purple-and-white uniforms were standing at the side entrance, waiting to ambush freshmen.

"Hi!" They smiled, which I figured was the first and last time any cheerleaders would be that friendly to me. One was blond with icy blue eyes. The other was African American with dark curly hair like Medusa's (and believe me, I know what I'm talking about). Both girls had their names stitched in cursive on their uniforms, but with my dyslexia, the words looked like meaningless spaghetti.

"Welcome to Goode," the blond girl said. "You are *so* going to love it."

But as she looked me up and down, her expression said something more like, *Eww, who is this loser?*

The other girl stepped uncomfortably close to me. I studied the stitching on her uniform and made out *Kelli*. She smelled like roses and something else I recognized from riding lessons at camp—the scent of freshly washed horses. It was a weird smell for a cheerleader. Maybe she owned a horse or something. Anyway, she stood so close I got the feeling she was going to try to push me down the steps. "What's your name, fish?"

"Fish?"

"Freshman."

"Uh, Percy."

The girls exchanged looks.

"Oh, Percy Jackson," the blond one said. "We've been waiting for you."

That sent a major *Uh-oh* chill down my back. They were blocking the entrance, smiling in a not-very-friendly way. My hand crept instinctively toward my pocket, where I kept my lethal ballpoint pen, Riptide.

Then another voice came from inside the building: "Percy?" It was Paul Blofis, somewhere down the hallway. I'd never been so glad to hear his voice.

The cheerleaders backed off. I was so anxious to get past them I accidentally kneed Kelli in the thigh.

Clang.

Her leg made a hollow, metallic sound, like I'd just hit a flagpole.

"Ow," she muttered. "Watch it, *fish*."

I glanced down, but her leg looked like a regular old leg. I was too freaked out to ask questions. I dashed into

[4]

the hall, the cheerleaders laughing behind me.

"There you are!" Paul told me. "Welcome to Goode!"

"Hey, Paul—uh, Mr. Blofis." I glanced back, but the weird cheerleaders had disappeared.

"Percy, you look like you've seen a ghost."

"Yeah, uh—"

Paul clapped me on the back. "Listen, I know you're nervous, but don't worry. We get a lot of kids here with ADHD and dyslexia. The teachers know how to help."

I almost wanted to laugh. If only ADHD and dyslexia were my biggest worries. I mean, I knew Paul was trying to help, but if I told him the truth about me, he'd either think I was crazy or he'd run away screaming. Those cheerleaders, for instance. I had a bad feeling about them. . . .

Then I looked down the hall, and I remembered I had another problem. The redheaded girl I'd seen on the front steps was just coming in the main entrance.

Don't notice me, I prayed.

She noticed me. Her eyes widened.

"Where's the orientation?" I asked Paul.

"The gym. That way. But—"

"Bye."

"Percy?" he called, but I was already running.

I thought I'd lost her.

A bunch of kids were heading for the gym, and soon I was just one of three hundred fourteen-year-olds all crammed into the bleachers. A marching band played an out-of-tune fight song that sounded like somebody hitting a bag of cats with a metal baseball bat. Older kids, probably student council members, stood up front modeling the Goode school uniform and looking all, *Hey, we're cool.* Teachers milled around, smiling and shaking hands with students. The walls of the gym were plastered with big purple-and-white banners that said WELCOME FUTURE FRESHMEN, GOODE IS GOOD, WE'RE ALL FAMILY, and a bunch of other happy slogans that pretty much made me want to throw up.

None of the other freshmen looked thrilled to be here, either. I mean, coming to orientation in June, when school doesn't even start until September, is not cool. But at Goode, "We prepare to excel early!" At least that's what the brochure said.

The marching band stopped playing. A guy in a pinstripe suit came to the microphone and started talking, but the sound echoed around the gym so I had no idea what he was saying. He might've been gargling.

Someone grabbed my shoulder. "What are you doing here?"

It was her: my redheaded nightmare.

"Rachel Elizabeth Dare," I said.

Her jaw dropped like she couldn't believe I had the nerve to remember her name. "And you're Percy somebody. I didn't get your full name last December when you tried to *kill* me."

"Look, I wasn't—I didn't—What are *you* doing here?"

"Same as you, I guess. Orientation."

"You live in New York?"

"What, you thought I lived at Hoover Dam?"

It had never occurred to me. Whenever I thought about her (and I'm *not* saying I *thought* about her; she just like crossed my mind from time to time, okay?), I always figured she lived in the Hoover Dam area, since that's where I'd met her. We'd spent maybe ten minutes together, during which time I'd accidentally swung a sword at her, she'd saved my life, and I'd run away chased by a band of supernatural killing machines. You know, your typical chance meeting.

Some guy behind us whispered, "Hey, shut up. The cheerleaders are talking!"

"Hi, guys!" a girl bubbled into the microphone. It was the blonde I'd seen at the entrance. "My name is Tammi, and this is, like, Kelli." Kelli did a cartwheel.

Next to me, Rachel yelped like someone had stuck her with a pin. A few kids looked over and snickered, but Rachel just stared at the cheerleaders in horror. Tammi didn't seem to notice the outburst. She started talking about all the great ways we could get involved during our freshman year.

"Run," Rachel told me. "Now."

"Why?"

Rachel didn't explain. She pushed her way to the edge of the bleachers, ignoring the frowning teachers and grumbling kids she was stepping on.

I hesitated. Tammi was explaining how we were about to break into small groups and tour the school. Kelli caught my eye and gave me an amused smile, like she was waiting to see what I'd do. It would look bad if I left right now. Paul Blofis was down there with the rest of the teachers. He'd wonder what was wrong.

Then I thought about Rachel Elizabeth Dare, and the special ability she'd shown last winter at Hoover Dam. She'd been able to see a group of security guards who weren't guards at all, who weren't even human. My heart pounding, I got up and followed her out of the gym.

I found Rachel in the band room. She was hiding behind a bass drum in the percussion section.

"Get over here!" she said. "Keep your head down!"

I felt pretty silly hiding behind a bunch of bongos, but I crouched beside her.

"Did they follow you?" Rachel asked.

"You mean the cheerleaders?"

She nodded nervously.

"I don't think so," I said. "What are they? What did you see?"

Her green eyes were bright with fear. She had a sprinkle of freckles on her face that reminded me of constellations. Her maroon T-shirt read HARVARD ART DEPT. "You . . . you wouldn't believe me."

"Oh, yeah, I would," I promised. "I know you can see through the Mist."

"The what?"

"The Mist. It's . . . well, it's like this veil that hides the way things really are. Some mortals are born with the ability to see through it. Like you."

She studied me carefully. "You did that at Hoover Dam. You called me a mortal. Like you're not."

I felt like punching a bongo. What was I thinking?

I could never explain. I shouldn't even try.

"Tell me," she begged. "You know what it means. All these horrible things I see?"

"Look, this is going to sound weird. Do you know anything about Greek myths?"

"Like . . . the Minotaur and the Hydra?"

"Yeah, just try not to say those names when I'm around, okay?"

"And the Furies," she said, warming up. "And the Sirens, and—"

"Okay!" I looked around the band hall, sure that Rachel was going to make a bunch of bloodthirsty nasties pop out of the walls; but we were still alone. Down the hallway, I heard a mob of kids coming out of the gymnasium. They were starting the group tours. We didn't have long to talk.

"All those monsters," I said, "all the Greek gods— they're real."

"I knew it!"

I would've been more comfortable if she'd called me a liar, but Rachel looked like I'd just confirmed her worst suspicion.

"You don't know how hard it's been," she said. "For years I thought I was going crazy. I couldn't tell anybody. I couldn't—" Her eyes narrowed. "Wait. Who are you? I mean *really*?"

"I'm not a monster."

"Well, I know that. I could *see* if you were. You look like . . . you. But you're not human, are you?"

I swallowed. Even though I'd had three years to get used

to who I was, I'd never talked about it with a regular mortal before—I mean, except for my mom, but she already knew. I don't know why, but I took the plunge.

"I'm a half-blood," I said. "I'm half human."

"And half what?"

Just then Tammi and Kelli stepped into the band room. The doors slammed shut behind them.

"There you are, Percy Jackson," Tammi said. "It's time for your orientation."

"They're horrible!" Rachel gasped.

Tammi and Kelli were still wearing their purple-and-white cheerleader costumes, holding pom-poms from the rally.

"What do they really look like?" I asked, but Rachel seemed too stunned to answer.

"Oh, forget her." Tammi gave me a brilliant smile and started walking toward us. Kelli stayed by the doors, blocking our exit.

They'd trapped us. I knew we'd have to fight our way out, but Tammi's smile was so dazzling it distracted me. Her blue eyes were beautiful, and the way her hair swept over her shoulders . . .

"Percy," Rachel warned.

I said something really intelligent like, "Uhhh?"

Tammi was getting closer. She held out her pom-poms.

"Percy!" Rachel's voice seemed to be coming from a long way away. "Snap out of it!"

It took all my willpower, but I got my pen out of my

pocket and uncapped it. Riptide grew into a three-foot-long bronze sword, its blade glowing with a faint golden light. Tammi's smile turned to a sneer.

"Oh, come on," she protested. "You don't need that. How about a kiss instead?"

She smelled like roses and clean animal fur—a weird but somehow intoxicating smell.

Rachel pinched my arm, hard. "Percy, she wants to bite you! Look at her!"

"She's just jealous." Tammi looked back at Kelli. "May I, mistress?"

Kelli was still blocking the door, licking her lips hungrily. "Go ahead, Tammi. You're doing fine."

Tammi took another step forward, but I leveled the tip of my sword at her chest. "Get back."

She snarled. "Freshmen," she said with disgust. "This is *our* school, half-blood. We feed on whom we choose!"

Then she began to change. The color drained out of her face and arms. Her skin turned as white as chalk, her eyes completely red. Her teeth grew into fangs.

"A vampire!" I stammered. Then I noticed her legs. Below the cheerleader skirt, her left leg was brown and shaggy with a donkey's hoof. Her right leg was shaped like a human leg, but it was made of bronze. "Uhh, a vampire with—"

"Don't mention the legs!" Tammi snapped. "It's rude to make fun!"

She advanced on her weird, mismatched legs. She looked totally bizarre, especially with the pom-poms, but I couldn't laugh—not facing those red eyes and sharp fangs.

"A vampire, you say?" Kelli laughed. "That silly legend was based on *us*, you fool. We are *empousai*, servants of Hecate."

"Mmmm." Tammi edged closer to me. "Dark magic formed us from animal, bronze, and ghost! We exist to feed on the blood of young men. Now come, give me that kiss!"

She bared her fangs. I was so paralyzed I couldn't move, but Rachel threw a snare drum at the *empousa*'s head.

The demon hissed and batted the drum away. It went rolling along the aisles between music stands, its springs rattling against the drumhead. Rachel threw a xylophone, but the demon just swatted that away, too.

"I don't usually kill girls," Tammi growled. "But for you, mortal, I'll make an exception. Your eyesight is a little *too* good!"

She lunged at Rachel.

"No!" I slashed with Riptide. Tammi tried to dodge my blade, but I sliced straight through her cheerleader uniform, and with a horrible wail she exploded into dust all over Rachel.

Rachel coughed. She looked like she'd just had a sack of flour dumped on her head. "Gross!"

"Monsters do that," I said. "Sorry."

"You killed my trainee!" Kelli yelled. "You need a lesson in school spirit, half-blood!"

Then she too began to change. Her wiry hair turned to flickering flames. Her eyes turned red. She grew fangs. She loped toward us, her brass foot and hoof clopping unevenly on the band-room floor.

"I am senior *empousa*," she growled. "No hero has bested me in a thousand years."

"Yeah?" I said. "Then you're overdue!"

Kelli was a lot faster than Tammi. She dodged my first strike and rolled into the brass section, knocking over a row of trombones with a mighty crash. Rachel scrambled out of the way. I put myself between her and the *empousa*. Kelli circled us, her eyes going from me to the sword.

"Such a pretty little blade," she said. "What a shame it stands between us."

Her form shimmered—sometimes a demon, sometimes a pretty cheerleader. I tried to keep my mind focused, but it was really distracting.

"Poor dear." Kelli chuckled. "You don't even know what's happening, do you? Soon, your pretty little camp in flames, your friends made slaves to the Lord of Time, and there's nothing you can do to stop it. It would be merciful to end your life now, before you have to see that."

From down the hall, I heard voices. A tour group was approaching. A man was saying something about locker combinations.

The *empousa*'s eyes lit up. "Excellent! We're about to have company!"

She picked up a tuba and threw it at me. Rachel and I ducked. The tuba sailed over our heads and crashed through the window.

The voices in the hall died down.

"Percy!" Kelli shouted, pretending to be scared, "why did you throw that?"

I was too surprised to answer. Kelli picked up a music stand and swiped a row of clarinets and flutes. Chairs and musical instruments crashed to the floor.

"Stop it!" I said.

People were tromping down the hall now, coming in our direction.

"Time to greet our visitors!" Kelli bared her fangs and ran for the doors. I charged after her with Riptide. I had to stop her from hurting the mortals.

"Percy, don't!" Rachel shouted. But I hadn't realized what Kelli was up to until it was too late.

Kelli flung open the doors. Paul Blofis and a bunch of freshmen stepped back in shock. I raised my sword.

At the last second, the *empousa* turned toward me like a cowering victim. "Oh no, please!" she cried. I couldn't stop my blade. It was already in motion.

Just before the celestial bronze hit her, Kelli exploded into flames like a Molotov cocktail. Waves of fire splashed over everything. I'd never seen a monster do that before, but I didn't have time to wonder about it. I backed into the band room as flames engulfed the doorway.

"Percy?" Paul Blofis looked completely stunned, staring at me from across the fire. "What have you done?"

Kids screamed and ran down the hall. The fire alarm wailed. Ceiling sprinklers hissed to life.

In the chaos, Rachel tugged on my sleeve. "You have to get out of here!"

She was right. The school was in flames and I'd be held responsible. Mortals couldn't see through the Mist properly. To them it would look like I'd just attacked a help-less cheerleader in front of a group of witnesses. There was no way I could explain it. I turned from Paul and sprinted for the broken band room window.

I burst out of the alley onto East 81st and ran straight into Annabeth.

"Hey, you're out early!" She laughed, grabbing my shoulders to keep me from tumbling into the street. "Watch where you're going, Seaweed Brain."

For a split second she was in a good mood and every-thing was fine. She was wearing jeans and an orange camp T-shirt and her clay bead necklace. Her blond hair was pulled back in a ponytail. Her gray eyes sparkled. She looked like she was ready to catch a movie, have a cool after-noon hanging out together.

Then Rachel Elizabeth Dare, still covered in monster dust, came charging out of the alley, yelling, "Percy, wait up!"

Annabeth's smile melted. She stared at Rachel, then at the school. For the first time, she seemed to notice the black smoke and the ringing fire alarms.

She frowned at me. "What did you do this time? And who is this?"

"Oh, Rachel—Annabeth. Annabeth—Rachel. Um, she's a friend. I guess."

I wasn't sure what else to call Rachel. I mean, I barely knew her, but after being in two life-or-death situations together, I couldn't just call her nobody.

"Hi," Rachel said. Then she turned to me. "You are in *so* much trouble. And you still owe me an explanation!"

Police sirens wailed on FDR Drive.

"Percy," Annabeth said coldly. "We should go."

"I want to know more about half-bloods," Rachel insisted. "And monsters. And this stuff about the gods." She grabbed my arm, whipped out a permanent marker, and wrote a phone number on my hand. "You're going to call me and explain, okay? You owe me that. Now get going."

"But—"

"I'll make up some story," Rachel said. "I'll tell them it wasn't your fault. Just go!"

She ran back toward the school, leaving Annabeth and me in the street.

Annabeth stared at me for a second. Then she turned and took off.

"Hey!" I jogged after her. "There were these two *empousai*," I tried to explain. "They were cheerleaders, see, and they said camp was going to burn, and—"

"You told a mortal girl about half-bloods?"

"She can see through the Mist. She saw the monsters before I did."

"So you told her the truth."

"She recognized me from Hoover Dam, so—"

"You've met her *before*?"

"Um, last winter. But seriously, I barely know her."

"She's kind of cute."

"I—I never thought about it."

Annabeth kept walking toward York Avenue.

"I'll deal with the school," I promised, anxious to change the subject. "Honest, it'll be fine."

Annabeth wouldn't even look at me. "I guess our afternoon is off. We should get you out of here, now that the police will be searching for you."

Behind us, smoke billowed up from Goode High School. In the dark column of ashes, I thought I could almost see a face—a she-demon with red eyes, laughing at me.

Your pretty little camp in flames, Kelli had said. *Your friends made slaves to the Lord of Time.*

"You're right," I told Annabeth, my heart sinking. "We have to get to Camp Half-Blood. *Now.*"

TWO

THE UNDERWORLD SENDS
ME A PRANK CALL

Nothing caps off the perfect morning like a long taxi ride with an angry girl.

I tried to talk to Annabeth, but she was acting like I'd just punched her grandmother. All I managed to get out of her was that she'd had a monster-infested spring in San Francisco; she'd come back to camp twice since Christmas but wouldn't tell me why (which kind of ticked me off, because she hadn't even told me she was in New York); and she'd learned nothing about the whereabouts of Nico di Angelo (long story).

"Any word on Luke?" I asked.

She shook her head. I knew this was a touchy subject for her. Annabeth had always admired Luke, the former head counselor for Hermes who had betrayed us and joined the evil Titan Lord Kronos. She wouldn't admit it, but I knew she still liked him. When we'd fought Luke on Mount Tamalpais last winter, he'd somehow survived a fifty-foot fall off a cliff. Now, as far as I knew, he was still sailing around on his demon-infested cruise ship while his chopped-up Lord Kronos re-formed, bit by bit, in a golden sarcophagus, biding his time until he had enough power to challenge the Olympian gods. In demigod-speak, we call this a "problem."

"Mount Tam is still overrun with monsters," Annabeth said. "I didn't dare go close, but I don't think Luke is up there. I think I would know if he was."

That didn't make me feel much better. "What about Grover?"

"He's at camp," she said. "We'll see him today."

"Did he have any luck? I mean, with the search for Pan?"

Annabeth fingered her bead necklace, the way she does when she's worried.

"You'll see," she said. But she didn't explain.

As we headed through Brooklyn, I used Annabeth's phone to call my mom. Half-bloods try not to use cell phones if we can avoid it, because broadcasting our voices is like sending up a flare to the monsters: *Here I am! Please eat me now!* But I figured this call was important. I left a message on our home voice mail, trying to explain what had happened at Goode. I probably didn't do a very good job. I told my mom I was fine, she shouldn't worry, but I was going to stay at camp until things cooled down. I asked her to tell Paul Blofis I was sorry.

We rode in silence after that. The city melted away until we were off the expressway and rolling through the countryside of northern Long Island, past orchards and wineries and fresh produce stands.

I stared at the phone number Rachel Elizabeth Dare had scrawled on my hand. I knew it was crazy, but I was tempted to call her. Maybe she could help me understand what the *empousa* had been talking about—the camp burning, my friends imprisoned. And why had Kelli exploded into flames?

I knew monsters never truly died. Eventually—maybe weeks, months, or years from now—Kelli would re-form out of the primordial nastiness seething in the Underworld. But still, monsters didn't usually let themselves get destroyed so easily. If she really *was* destroyed.

The taxi exited on Route 25A. We headed through the woods along the North Shore until a low ridge of hills appeared on our left. Annabeth told the driver to pull over on Farm Road 3.141, at the base of Half-Blood Hill.

The driver frowned. "There ain't nothing here, miss. You sure you want out?"

"Yes, please." Annabeth handed him a roll of mortal cash, and the driver decided not to argue.

Annabeth and I hiked to the crest of the hill. The young guardian dragon was dozing, coiled around the pine tree, but he lifted his coppery head as we approached and let Annabeth scratch under his chin. Steam hissed out his nostrils like from a teakettle, and he went cross-eyed with pleasure.

"Hey, Peleus," Annabeth said. "Keeping everything safe?"

The last time I'd seen the dragon he'd been six feet long. Now he was at least twice that, and as thick around as the tree itself. Above his head, on the lowest branch of the pine tree, the Golden Fleece shimmered, its magic protecting the camp's borders from invasion. The dragon seemed relaxed, like everything was okay. Below us, Camp Half-Blood looked peaceful—green fields, forest, shiny white Greek buildings. The four-story farmhouse we called the Big House sat proudly in the midst of the strawberry fields. To the north, past the beach, the Long Island Sound glittered in the sunlight.

Still . . . something felt wrong. There was tension in the air, as if the hill itself were holding its breath, waiting for something bad to happen.

We walked down into the valley and found the summer session in full swing. Most of the campers had arrived last Friday, so I already felt out of it. The satyrs were playing their pipes in the strawberry fields, making the plants grow with woodland magic. Campers were having flying horse-back lessons, swooping over the woods on their pegasi. Smoke rose from the forges, and hammers rang as kids made their own weapons for Arts & Crafts. The Athena and Demeter teams were having a chariot race around the track, and over at the canoe lake some kids in a Greek trireme were fighting a large orange sea serpent. A typical day at camp.

"I need to talk to Clarisse," Annabeth said.

I stared at her as if she'd just said *I need to eat a large, smelly boot.* "What for?"

Clarisse from the Ares cabin was one of my least favorite people. She was a mean, ungrateful bully. Her dad, the war god, wanted to kill me. She tried to beat me to a pulp on a regular basis. Other than that, she was just great.

"We've been working on something," Annabeth said. "I'll see you later."

"Working on what?"

Annabeth glanced toward the forest.

"I'll tell Chiron you're here," she said. "He'll want to talk to you before the hearing."

"What hearing?"

But she jogged down the path toward the archery field without looking back.

"Yeah," I muttered. "Great talking with you, too."

As I made my way through camp, I said hi to some of my friends. In the Big House's driveway, Connor and Travis Stoll from the Hermes cabin were hot-wiring the camp's SUV. Silena Beauregard, the head counselor for Aphrodite, waved at me from her pegasus as she flew past. I looked for Grover, but I didn't see him. Finally I wandered into the sword arena, where I usually go when I'm in a bad mood. Practicing always calms me down. Maybe that's because swordplay is one thing I actually understand.

I walked into the amphitheater and my heart almost stopped. In the middle of the arena floor, with its back to me, was the biggest hellhound I'd ever seen.

I mean, I've seen some pretty big hellhounds. One the size of a rhino tried to kill me when I was twelve. But *this* hellhound was bigger than a tank. I had no idea how it had gotten past the camp's magic boundaries. It looked right at home, lying on its belly, growling contentedly as it chewed the head off a combat dummy. It hadn't noticed me yet, but if I made a sound, I knew it would sense me. There was no time to go for help. I pulled out Riptide and uncapped it.

"Yaaaaah!" I charged. I brought down the blade on the

monster's enormous backside when out of nowhere another sword blocked my strike.

CLANG!

The hellhound pricked up its ears. *"WOOF!"*

I jumped back and instinctively struck at the swordsman—a gray-haired man in Greek armor. He parried my attack with no problem.

"Whoa there!" he said. "Truce!"

"WOOF!" The hellhound's bark shook the arena.

"That's a hellhound!" I shouted.

"She's harmless," the man said. "That's Mrs. O'Leary."

I blinked. "Mrs. O'Leary?"

At the sound of her name, the hellhound barked again. I realized she wasn't angry. She was excited. She nudged the soggy, badly chewed target dummy toward the swordsman.

"Good girl," the man said. With his free hand he grabbed the armored manikin by the neck and heaved it toward the bleachers. "Get the Greek! Get the Greek!"

Mrs. O'Leary bounded after her prey and pounced on the dummy, flattening its armor. She began chewing on its helmet.

The swordsman smiled dryly. He was in his fifties, I guess, with short gray hair and a clipped gray beard. He was in good shape for an older guy. He wore black mountain-climbing pants and a bronze breastplate strapped over an orange camp T-shirt. At the base of his neck was a strange mark, a purplish blotch like a birthmark or a tattoo, but before I could make out what it was, he shifted his armor straps and the mark disappeared under his collar.

"Mrs. O'Leary is my pet," he explained. "I couldn't let

you stick a sword in her rump, now, could I? That might have scared her."

"Who are you?"

"Promise not to kill me if I put my sword away?"

"I guess."

He sheathed his sword and held out his hand. "Quintus."

I shook his hand. It was as rough as sandpaper.

"Percy Jackson," I said. "Sorry about—How did you, um—"

"Get a hellhound for a pet? Long story, involving many close calls with death and quite a few giant chew toys. I'm the new sword instructor, by the way. Helping out Chiron while Mr. D is away."

"Oh." I tried not to stare as Mrs. O'Leary ripped off the target dummy's shield with the arm still attached and shook it like a Frisbee. "Wait, Mr. D is away?"

"Yes, well . . . busy times. Even Dionysus must help out. He's gone to visit some old friends. Make sure they're on the right side. I probably shouldn't say more than that."

If Dionysus was gone, that was the best news I'd had all day. He was only our camp director because Zeus had sent him here as a punishment for chasing some off-limits wood nymph. He hated the campers and tried to make our lives miserable. With him away, this summer might actually be cool. On the other hand, if Dionysus had gotten off his butt and actually started helping the gods recruit against the Titan threat, things must be looking pretty bad.

Off to my left, there was a loud *BUMP*. Six wooden

crates the size of picnic tables were stacked nearby, and they were rattling. Mrs. O'Leary cocked her head and bounded toward them.

"Whoa, girl!" Quintus said. "Those aren't for you." He distracted her with the bronze shield Frisbee.

The crates thumped and shook. There were words printed on the sides, but with my dyslexia they took me a few minutes to decipher:

TRIPLE G RANCH
FRAGILE
THIS END UP

Along the bottom, in smaller letters: OPEN WITH CARE. TRIPLE G RANCH IS NOT RESPONSIBLE FOR PROPERTY DAMAGE, MAIMING, OR EXCRUCIATINGLY PAINFUL DEATHS.

"What's in the boxes?" I asked.

"A little surprise," Quintus said. "Training activity for tomorrow night. You'll love it."

"Uh, okay," I said, though I wasn't sure about the "excruciatingly painful death" part.

Quintus threw the bronze shield, and Mrs. O'Leary lumbered after it. "You young ones need more challenges. They didn't have camps like this when I was a boy."

"You—you're a half-blood?" I didn't mean to sound so surprised, but I'd never seen an old demigod before.

Quintus chuckled. "Some of us *do* survive into adulthood, you know. Not all of us are the subject of terrible prophecies."

"You know about my prophecy?"

"I've heard a few things."

I wanted to ask *what* few things, but just then Chiron clip-clopped into the arena. "Percy, there you are!"

He must've just come from teaching archery. He had a quiver and bow slung over his #1 CENTAUR T-shirt. He'd trimmed his curly brown hair and beard for the summer, and his lower half, which was a white stallion, was flecked with mud and grass.

"I see you've met our new instructor." Chiron's tone was light, but there was an uneasy look in his eyes. "Quintus, do you mind if I borrow Percy?"

"Not at all, Master Chiron."

"No need to call me 'Master,'" Chiron said, though he sounded sort of pleased. "Come, Percy. We have much to discuss."

I took one more glance at Mrs. O'Leary, who was now chewing off the target dummy's legs.

"Well, see you," I told Quintus.

As we were walking away, I whispered to Chiron, "Quintus seems kind of—"

"Mysterious?" Chiron suggested. "Hard to read?"

"Yeah."

Chiron nodded. "A very qualified half-blood. Excellent swordsman. I just wish I understood . . ."

Whatever he was going to say, he apparently changed his mind. "First things first, Percy. Annabeth told me you met some *empousai*."

"Yeah." I told him about the fight at Goode, and

how Kelli had exploded into flames.

"Mm," Chiron said. "The more powerful ones can do that. She did not die, Percy. She simply escaped. It is not good that the she-demons are stirring."

"What were they doing there?" I asked. "Waiting for me?"

"Possibly." Chiron frowned. "It is amazing you survived. Their powers of deception . . . almost any male hero would've fallen under their spell and been devoured."

"I would've been," I admitted. "Except for Rachel."

Chiron nodded. "Ironic to be saved by a mortal, yet we owe her a debt. What the *empousa* said about an attack on camp—we must speak of this further. But for now, come, we should get to the woods. Grover will want you there."

"Where?"

"At his formal hearing," Chiron said grimly. "The Council of Cloven Elders is meeting now to decide his fate."

Chiron said we needed to hurry, so I let him give me a ride on his back. As we galloped past the cabins, I glanced at the dining hall—an open-air Greek pavilion on a hill overlooking the sea. It was the first time I'd seen the place since last summer, and it brought back bad memories.

Chiron plunged into the woods. Nymphs peeked out of the trees to watch us pass. Large shapes rustled in the shadows—monsters that were stocked in here as a challenge to the campers.

I thought I knew the forest pretty well after playing capture the flag here for two summers, but Chiron took me a way I didn't recognize, through a tunnel of old willow trees, past a little waterfall, and into a glade blanketed with wildflowers.

A bunch of satyrs were sitting in a circle in the grass. Grover stood in the middle, facing three really old, really fat satyrs who sat on topiary thrones shaped out of rose bushes. I'd never seen the three old satyrs before, but I guessed they must be the Council of Cloven Elders.

Grover seemed to be telling them a story. He twisted the bottom of his T-shirt, shifting nervously on his goat hooves. He hadn't changed much since last winter, maybe because satyrs age half as fast as humans. His acne had flared up. His horns had gotten a little bigger so they just stuck out over his curly hair. I realized with a start that I was taller than he was now.

Standing off to one side of the circle were Annabeth, another girl I'd never seen before, and Clarisse. Chiron dropped me next to them.

Clarisse's stringy brown hair was tied back with a camouflage bandanna. If possible, she looked even buffer, like she'd been working out. She glared at me and muttered, "Punk," which must've meant she was in a good mood. Usually she says hello by trying to kill me.

Annabeth had her arm around the other girl, who looked like she'd been crying. She was small—petite, I guess you'd call it—with wispy hair the color of amber and a pretty, elfish face. She wore a green chiton and laced sandals, and she was dabbing her eyes with a handkerchief. "It's going terribly," she sniffled.

"No, no." Annabeth patted her shoulder. "He'll be fine, Juniper."

Annabeth looked at me and mouthed the words *Grover's girlfriend.*

At least I thought that's what she said, but that made no sense. Grover with a girlfriend? Then I looked at Juniper more closely, and I realized her ears were slightly pointed. Her eyes, instead of being red from crying, were tinged green, the color of chlorophyll. She was a tree nymph—a dryad.

"Master Underwood!" the council member on the right shouted, cutting off whatever Grover was trying to say. "Do you seriously expect us to believe this?"

"B-but, Silenus," Grover stammered. "It's the truth!"

The Council guy, Silenus, turned to his colleagues and muttered something. Chiron cantered up to the front and stood next to them. I remembered he was an honorary member of the council, but I'd never thought about it much. The elders didn't look very impressive. They reminded me of the goats in a petting zoo—huge bellies, sleepy expressions, and glazed eyes that couldn't see past the next handful of goat chow. I wasn't sure why Grover looked so nervous.

Silenus tugged his yellow polo shirt over his belly and adjusted himself on his rosebush throne. "Master Underwood, for six months—*six months*—we have been hearing these scandalous claims that you heard the wild god Pan speak."

"But I did!"

"Impudence!" said the elder on the left.

"Now, Maron," Chiron said. "Patience."

"Patience, indeed!" Maron said. "I've had it up to my horns with this nonsense. As if the wild god would speak to . . . to *him*."

Juniper looked like she wanted to charge the old satyr and beat him up, but Annabeth and Clarisse held her back. "Wrong fight, girlie," Clarisse muttered. "Wait."

I don't know what surprised me more: Clarisse holding somebody back from a fight, or the fact that she and Annabeth, who despised each other, almost seemed like they were working together.

"For six months," Silenus continued, "we have indulged you, Master Underwood. We let you travel. We allowed you to keep your searcher's license. We waited for you to bring proof of your preposterous claim. And what have you found in six months of travel?"

"I just need more time," Grover pleaded.

"Nothing!" the elder in the middle chimed in. "You have found nothing."

"But, Leneus—"

Silenus raised his hand. Chiron leaned in and said something to the satyrs. The satyrs didn't look happy. They muttered and argued among themselves, but Chiron said something else, and Silenus sighed. He nodded reluctantly.

"Master Underwood," Silenus announced, "we will give you one more chance."

Grover brightened. "Thank you!"

"One more week."

"What? But, sir! That's impossible!"

"One more week, Master Underwood. And then, if you cannot prove your claims, it will be time for you to pursue another career. Something to suit your dramatic talents. Puppet theater, perhaps. Or tap dancing."

"But, sir, I—I can't lose my searcher's license. My whole life—"

"This meeting of the council is adjourned," Silenus said. "And now let us enjoy our noonday meal!"

The old satyr clapped his hands, and a bunch of nymphs melted out of the trees with platters of vegetables, fruits, tin cans, and other goat delicacies. The circle of satyrs broke and charged the food. Grover walked dejectedly toward us. His faded blue T-shirt had a picture of a satyr on it. It read GOT HOOVES?

"Hi, Percy," he said, so depressed he didn't even offer to shake my hand. "That went well, huh?"

"Those old goats!" Juniper said. "Oh, Grover, they don't know how hard you've tried!"

"There is another option," Clarisse said darkly.

"No. No." Juniper shook her head. "Grover, I won't let you."

His face was ashen. "I—I'll have to think about it. But we don't even know where to look."

"What are you talking about?" I asked.

In the distance, a conch horn sounded.

Annabeth pursed her lips. "I'll fill you in later, Percy. We'd better get back to our cabins. Inspection is starting."

* * *

It didn't seem fair that I'd have to do cabin inspection when I just got to camp, but that's the way it worked. Every afternoon, one of the senior counselors came around with a papyrus scroll checklist. Best cabin got first shower hour, which meant hot water guaranteed. Worst cabin got kitchen patrol after dinner.

The problem for me: I was usually the only one in the Poseidon cabin, and I'm not exactly what you would call neat. The cleaning harpies only came through on the last day of summer, so my cabin was probably just the way I'd left it on winter break: my candy wrappers and chip bags still on my bunk, my armor for capture the flag lying in pieces all around the cabin.

I raced toward the commons area, where the twelve cabins—one for each Olympian god—made a U around the central green. The Demeter kids were sweeping out theirs and making fresh flowers grow in their window boxes. Just by snapping their fingers they could make honeysuckle vines bloom over their doorway and daisies cover their roof, which was totally unfair. I don't think they ever got last place in inspection. The guys in the Hermes cabin were scrambling around in a panic, stashing dirty laundry under their beds and accusing each other of taking stuff. They were slobs, but they still had a head start on me.

Over at the Aphrodite cabin, Silena Beauregard was just coming out, checking items off the inspection scroll. I cursed under my breath. Silena was nice, but she was an absolute neat freak, the worst inspector. She liked things to be pretty. I didn't do "pretty." I could almost feel my arms getting heavy from all the dishes I would have to scrub tonight.

The Poseidon cabin was at the end of the row of "male god" cabins on the right side of the green. It was made of gray shell-encrusted sea rock, long and low like a bunker, but it had windows that faced the sea and it always had a good breeze blowing through it.

I dashed inside, wondering if maybe I could do a quick under-the-bed cleaning job like the Hermes guys, and I found my half-brother Tyson sweeping the floor.

"Percy!" he bellowed. He dropped his broom and ran at me. If you've never been charged by an enthusiastic Cyclops wearing a flowered apron and rubber cleaning gloves, I'm telling you, it'll wake you up quick.

"Hey, big guy!" I said. "Ow, watch the ribs. The ribs."

I managed to survive his bear hug. He put me down, grinning like crazy, his single calf-brown eye full of excitement. His teeth were as yellow and crooked as ever, and his hair was a rat's nest. He wore ragged XXXL jeans and a tattered flannel shirt under his flowered apron, but he was still a sight for sore eyes. I hadn't seen him in almost a year, since he'd gone under the sea to work at the Cyclopes' forges.

"You are okay?" he asked. "Not eaten by monsters?"

"Not even a little bit." I showed him that I still had both arms and both legs, and Tyson clapped happily.

"Yay!" he said. "Now we can eat peanut butter sandwiches and ride fish ponies! We can fight monsters and see Annabeth and make things go BOOM!"

I hoped he didn't mean all at the same time, but I told

him absolutely, we'd have a lot of fun this summer. I couldn't help smiling, he was so enthusiastic about everything.

"But first," I said, "we've gotta worry about inspection. We should . . ."

Then I looked around and realized Tyson had been busy. The floor was swept. The bunk beds were made. The saltwater fountain in the corner had been freshly scrubbed so the coral gleamed. On the windowsills, Tyson had set out water-filled vases with sea anemones and strange glowing plants from the bottom of the ocean, more beautiful than any flower bouquets the Demeter kids could whip up.

"Tyson, the cabin looks . . . amazing!"

He beamed. "See the fish ponies? I put them on the ceiling!"

A herd of miniature bronze hippocampi hung on wires from the ceiling, so it looked like they were swimming through the air. I couldn't believe Tyson, with his huge hands, could make things so delicate. Then I looked over at my bunk, and I saw my old shield hanging on the wall.

"You fixed it!"

The shield had been badly damaged in a manticore attack last winter, but now it was perfect again—not a scratch. All the bronze pictures of my adventures with Tyson and Annabeth in the Sea of Monsters were polished and gleaming.

I looked at Tyson. I didn't know how to thank him.

Then somebody behind me said, "Oh, my."

Silena Beauregard was standing in the doorway with her inspection scroll. She stepped into the cabin, did a quick twirl, then raised her eyebrows at me. "Well, I had my doubts. But you clean up nicely, Percy. I'll remember that."

She winked at me and left the room.

Tyson and I spent the afternoon catching up and just hanging out, which was nice after a morning of getting attacked by demon cheerleaders.

We went down to the forge and helped Beckendorf from the Hephaestus cabin with his metalworking. Tyson showed us how he'd learned to craft magic weapons. He fashioned a flaming double-bladed war axe so fast even Beckendorf was impressed.

While he worked, Tyson told us about his year under the sea. His eye lit up when he described the Cyclopes' forges and the palace of Poseidon, but he also told us how tense things were. The old gods of the sea, who'd ruled during Titan times, were starting to make war on our father. When Tyson had left, battles had been raging all over the Atlantic. Hearing that made me feel anxious, like I should be helping out, but Tyson assured me that Dad wanted us both at camp.

"Lots of bad people above the sea, too," Tyson said. "We can make them go boom."

After the forges, we spent some time at the canoe lake with Annabeth. She was really glad to see Tyson, but I could tell she was distracted. She kept looking over at the forest, like she was thinking about Grover's problem with the council. I couldn't blame her. Grover was nowhere to be seen, and I felt really bad for him. Finding the lost god Pan had been his lifelong goal. His father and his uncle had both disappeared following the same dream. Last winter, Grover had heard a voice in his head: *I await you*—a voice he was sure belonged to Pan—but apparently his search had led nowhere. If the council took away his searcher's license now, it would crush him.

"What's this 'other way'?" I asked Annabeth. "The thing Clarisse mentioned?"

She picked up a stone and skipped it across the lake. "Something Clarisse scouted out. I helped her a little this spring. But it would be dangerous. Especially for Grover."

"Goat boy scares me," Tyson murmured.

I stared at him. Tyson had faced down fire-breathing bulls and sea monsters and cannibal giants. "Why would you be scared of Grover?"

"Hooves and horns," Tyson muttered nervously. "And goat fur makes my nose itchy."

And that pretty much ended our Grover conversation.

Before dinner, Tyson and I went down to the sword arena. Quintus was glad to have company. He still wouldn't tell me what was in the wooden crates, but he did teach me a few sword moves. The guy was good. He fought the way some people play chess—like he was putting all the moves together and you couldn't see the pattern until he made the last stroke and won with a sword at your throat.

"Good try," he told me. "But your guard is too low."

He lunged and I blocked.

"Have you always been a swordsman?" I asked.

He parried my overhead cut. "I've been many things."

He jabbed and I sidestepped. His shoulder strap slipped down, and I saw that mark on his neck—the purple blotch. But it wasn't a random mark. It had a definite shape—a bird with folded wings, like a quail or something.

"What's that on your neck?" I asked, which was probably a rude question, but you can blame my ADHD. I tend to just blurt things out.

Quintus lost his rhythm. I hit his sword hilt and knocked the blade out of his hand.

He rubbed his fingers. Then he shifted his armor to hide the mark. It wasn't a tattoo, I realized. It was an old burn . . . like he'd been branded.

"A reminder." He picked up his sword and forced a smile. "Now, shall we go again?"

He pressed me hard, not giving me time for any more questions.

While he and I fought, Tyson played with Mrs. O'Leary, who he called the "little doggie." They had a great time wrestling for the bronze shield and playing Get the Greek. By sunset, Quintus hadn't even broken a sweat, which seemed kind of strange; but Tyson and I were hot and sticky, so we hit the showers and got ready for dinner.

I was feeling good. It was almost like a normal day at camp. Then dinner came, and all the campers lined up by cabin and marched into the dining pavilion. Most of them ignored the sealed fissure in the marble floor at the entrance—a ten-foot-long jagged scar that hadn't been there last summer—but I was careful to step over it.

"Big crack," Tyson said when we were at our table. "Earthquake, maybe?"

"No," I said. "Not an earthquake."

I wasn't sure I should tell him. It was a secret only Annabeth and Grover and I knew. But looking in Tyson's big eye, I knew I couldn't hide anything from him.

"Nico di Angelo," I said, lowering my voice. "He's this half-blood kid we brought to camp last winter. He, uh . . . he asked me to guard his sister on a quest, and I failed. She died. Now he blames me."

Tyson frowned. "So he put a crack in the floor?"

"These skeletons attacked us," I said. "Nico told them to go away, and the ground just opened up and swallowed them. Nico . . ." I looked around to make sure no one was listening. "Nico is a son of Hades."

Tyson nodded thoughtfully. "The god of dead people."

"Yeah."

"So the Nico boy is gone now?"

"I—I guess. I tried to search for him this spring. So did Annabeth. But we didn't have any luck. This is secret, Tyson. Okay? If anyone found out he was a son of Hades, he would be in danger. You can't even tell Chiron."

"The bad prophecy," Tyson said. "Titans might use him if they knew."

I stared at him. Sometimes it was easy to forget that as big and childlike as he was, Tyson was pretty smart. He knew that the next child of the Big Three gods—Zeus, Poseidon, or Hades—who turned sixteen was prophesied to either save or destroy Mount Olympus. Most people assumed that meant me, but if I died before I turned six-teen, the prophecy could just as easily apply to Nico.

"Exactly," I said. "So—"

"Mouth sealed," Tyson promised. "Like the crack in the ground."

I had trouble falling asleep that night. I lay in bed listening to the waves on the beach, and the owls and monsters in the woods. I was afraid once I drifted off I'd have nightmares.

See, for half-bloods, dreams are hardly ever just dreams. We get messages. We glimpse things that are happening to our friends or enemies. Sometimes we even glimpse the past or the future. And at camp, my dreams were always more frequent and vivid.

So I was still awake around midnight, staring at the bunk bed mattress above me, when I realized there was a strange light in the room. The saltwater fountain was glowing.

I threw off the covers and walked cautiously toward it. Steam rose from the hot salt water. Rainbow colors shimmered through it, though there was no light in the room except for the moon outside. Then a pleasant female voice spoke from the steam: *Please deposit one drachma.*

I looked over at Tyson, but he was still snoring. He sleeps about as heavily as a tranquilized elephant.

I didn't know what to think. I'd never gotten a collect Iris-message before. One golden drachma gleamed at the bottom of the fountain. I scooped it up and tossed it through the mist. The coin vanished.

"O, Iris, Goddess of the Rainbow," I whispered. "Show me . . . Uh, whatever you need to show me."

The mist shimmered. I saw the dark shore of a river. Wisps of fog drifted across black water. The beach was strewn with jagged volcanic rock. A young boy squatted at the riverbank, tending a campfire. The flames burned an unnatural blue color. Then I saw the boy's face. It was Nico di Angelo. He was throwing pieces of paper into the fire— Mythomagic trading cards, part of the game he'd been obsessed with last winter.

Nico was only ten, or maybe eleven by now, but he looked older. His hair had grown longer. It was shaggy and almost touched his shoulders. His eyes were dark. His olive skin had turned paler. He wore ripped black jeans and a battered aviator's jacket that was several sizes too big, unzipped over a black shirt. His face was grimy, his eyes a little wild. He looked like a kid who'd been living on the streets.

I waited for him to look at me. No doubt he'd get crazy angry, start accusing me of letting his sister die. But he didn't seem to notice me.

I stayed quiet, not daring to move. If he hadn't sent this Iris-message, who had?

Nico tossed another trading card into the blue flames. "Useless," he muttered. "I can't believe I ever liked this stuff."

"A childish game, master," another voice agreed. It seemed to come from near the fire, but I couldn't see who was talking.

Nico stared across the river. On the far shore was black

beach shrouded in haze. I recognized it: the Underworld. Nico was camping at the edge of the River Styx.

"I've failed," he muttered. "There's no way to get her back."

The other voice kept silent.

Nico turned toward it doubtfully. "Is there? Speak."

Something shimmered. I thought it was just firelight. Then I realized it was the form of a man—a wisp of blue smoke, a shadow. If you looked at him head-on, he wasn't there. But if you looked out of the corner of your eye, you could make out his shape. A ghost.

"It has never been done," the ghost said. "But there may be a way."

"Tell me," Nico commanded. His eyes shined with a fierce light.

"An exchange," the ghost said. "A soul for a soul."

"I've offered!"

"Not yours," the ghost said. "You cannot offer your father a soul he will eventually collect anyway. Nor will he be anxious for the death of his son. I mean a soul that should have died already. Someone who has cheated death."

Nico's face darkened. "Not that again. You're talking about murder."

"I'm talking about justice," the ghost said. "Vengeance."

"Those are not the same thing."

The ghost laughed dryly. "You will learn differently as you get older."

Nico stared at the flames. "Why can't I at least summon her? I want to talk to her. She would . . . she would help me."

"*I* will help you," the ghost promised. "Have I not saved you many times? Did I not lead you through the maze and teach you to use your powers? Do you want revenge for your sister or not?"

I didn't like the ghost's tone of voice. He reminded me of a kid at my old school, a bully who used to convince other kids to do stupid things like steal lab equipment and vandalize the teachers' cars. The bully never got in trouble himself, but he got tons of other kids suspended.

Nico turned from the fire so the ghost couldn't see him, but I could. A tear traced its way down his face. "Very well. You have a plan?"

"Oh, yes," the ghost said, sounding quite pleased. "We have many dark roads to travel. We must start—"

The image shimmered. Nico vanished. The woman's voice from the mist said, *Please deposit one drachma for another five minutes.*

There were no other coins in the fountain. I grabbed for my pockets, but I was wearing pajamas. I lunged for the nightstand to check for spare change, but the Iris-message had already blinked out, and the room went dark again. The connection was broken.

I stood in the middle of the cabin, listening to the gurgle of the saltwater fountain and the ocean waves outside.

Nico was alive. He was trying to bring his sister back from the dead. And I had a feeling I knew what soul he wanted to exchange—someone who had cheated death. Vengeance.

Nico di Angelo would come looking for me.

WE PLAY TAG WITH SCORPIONS

The next morning there was a lot of excitement at breakfast.

Apparently around three in the morning an Aethiopian drakon had been spotted at the borders of camp. I was so exhausted I slept right through the noise. The magical boundaries had kept the monster out, but it prowled the hills, looking for weak spots in our defenses, and it didn't seem anxious to go away until Lee Fletcher from Apollo's cabin led a couple of his siblings in pursuit. After a few dozen arrows lodged in the chinks of the drakon's armor, it got the message and withdrew.

"It's still out there," Lee warned us during announcements. "Twenty arrows in its hide, and we just made it mad. The thing was thirty feet long and bright green. Its eyes—" He shuddered.

"You did well, Lee." Chiron patted him on the shoulder. "Everyone stay alert, but stay calm. This has happened before."

"Aye," Quintus said from the head table. "And it will happen again. More and more frequently."

The campers murmured among themselves.

Everyone knew the rumors: Luke and his army of monsters were planning an invasion of the camp. Most of us expected it to happen this summer, but no one knew how or when. It didn't help that our attendance was down. We only had about eighty campers. Three years ago, when I'd started, there had been more than a hundred. Some had died. Some had joined Luke. Some had just disappeared.

"This is a good reason for new war games," Quintus continued, a glint in his eyes. "We'll see how you all do with that tonight."

"Yes . . ." Chiron said. "Well, enough announcements. Let us bless this meal and eat." He raised his goblet. "To the gods!"

We all raised our glasses and repeated the blessing.

Tyson and I took our plates to the bronze brazier and scraped a portion of our food into the flames. I hoped the gods liked raisin toast and Froot Loops.

"Poseidon," I said. Then I whispered, "Help me with Nico, and Luke, and Grover's problem . . ."

There was so much to worry about I could've stood there all morning, but I headed back to my table.

Once everyone was eating, Chiron and Grover came over to visit. Grover was bleary-eyed. His shirt was inside out. He slid his plate onto the table and slumped next to me.

Tyson shifted uncomfortably. "I will go . . . um . . . polish my fish ponies."

He lumbered off, leaving his breakfast half eaten.

Chiron tried for a smile. He probably wanted to look reassuring, but in centaur form he towered over me, casting a shadow across the table. "Well, Percy, how did you sleep?"

"Uh, fine." I wondered why he asked that. Was it possible he knew something about the weird Iris-message I'd gotten?

"I brought Grover over," Chiron said, "because I thought you two might want to, ah, discuss matters. Now if you'll excuse me, I have some Iris-messages to send. I'll see you later in the day." He gave Grover a meaningful look, then trotted out of the pavilion.

"What's he talking about?" I asked Grover.

Grover chewed his eggs. I could tell he was distracted, because he bit off the tines of his fork and chewed those down, too. "He wants you to convince me," he mumbled.

Somebody else slid next to me on the bench: Annabeth.

"I'll tell you what it's about," she said. "The Labyrinth."

It was hard to concentrate on what she was saying, because everybody in the dining pavilion was stealing glances at us and whispering. And Annabeth was right next to me. I mean *right* next to me.

"You're not supposed to be here," I said.

"We need to talk," she insisted.

"But the rules . . ."

She knew as well as I did that campers weren't allowed to switch tables. Satyrs were different. They weren't really demigods. But the half-bloods had to sit with their cabins. I wasn't even sure what the punishment was for switching tables. I'd never seen it happen. If Mr. D had been here, he probably would've strangled Annabeth with magical grapevines or something, but Mr. D wasn't here. Chiron had already left the pavilion. Quintus looked over and raised an eyebrow, but he didn't say anything.

"Look," Annabeth said, "Grover is in trouble. There's only one way we can figure to help him. It's the Labyrinth. That's what Clarisse and I have been investigating."

I shifted my weight, trying to think clearly. "You mean the maze where they kept the Minotaur, back in the old days?"

"Exactly," Annabeth said.

"So . . . it's not under the king's palace in Crete any-more," I guessed. "The Labyrinth is under some building in America."

See? It only took me a few years to figure things out. I knew that important places moved around with Western Civilization, like Mount Olympus being over the Empire State Building, and the Underworld entrance being in Los Angeles. I was feeling pretty proud of myself.

Annabeth rolled her eyes. "Under a building? Please, Percy. The Labyrinth is *huge*. It wouldn't fit under a single city, much less a single building."

I thought about my dream of Nico at the River Styx. "So . . . is the Labyrinth part of the Underworld?"

"No." Annabeth frowned. "Well, there may be passages from the Labyrinth down *into* the Underworld. I'm not sure. But the Underworld is way, way down. The Labyrinth is right under the surface of the mortal world, kind of like a second skin. It's been growing for thousands of years, lac-ing its way under Western cities, connecting everything together underground. You can get anywhere through the Labyrinth."

"If you don't get lost," Grover muttered. "And die a horrible death."

"Grover, there has to be a way," Annabeth said. I got the feeling they'd had this conversation before. "Clarisse lived."

"Barely!" Grover said. "And the other guy—"

"He was driven insane. He didn't die."

"Oh, joy." Grover's lower lip quivered. "That makes me feel much better."

"Whoa," I said. "Back up. What's this about Clarisse and a crazy guy?"

Annabeth glanced over toward the Ares table. Clarisse was watching us like she knew what we were talking about, but then she fixed her eyes on her breakfast plate.

"Last year," Annabeth said, lowering her voice, "Clarisse went on a mission for Chiron."

"I remember," I said. "It was secret."

Annabeth nodded. Despite how serious she was acting, I was happy she wasn't mad at me anymore. And I kind of liked the fact that she'd broken the rules to come sit next to me.

"It was secret," Annabeth agreed, "because she found Chris Rodriguez."

"The guy from the Hermes cabin?" I remembered him from two years ago. We'd eavesdropped on Chris Rodriguez aboard Luke's ship, the *Princess Andromeda*. Chris was one of the half-bloods who'd abandoned camp and joined the Titan army.

"Yeah," Annabeth said. "Last summer he just appeared in Phoenix, Arizona, near Clarisse's mom's house."

"What do you mean he just appeared?"

"He was wandering around the desert, in a hundred and twenty degrees, in full Greek armor, babbling about string."

"String," I said.

"He'd been driven completely insane. Clarisse brought him back to her mom's house so the mortals wouldn't institutionalize him. She tried to nurse him back to health. Chiron came out and interviewed him, but it wasn't much good. The only thing they got out of him: Luke's men have been exploring the Labyrinth."

I shivered, though I wasn't sure exactly why. Poor Chris . . . he hadn't been that bad a guy. What could've driven him mad? I looked at Grover, who was chewing up the rest of his fork.

"Okay," I asked. "Why were they exploring the Labyrinth?"

"We weren't sure," Annabeth said. "That's why Clarisse went on a scouting expedition. Chiron kept things hushed up because he didn't want anyone panicking. He got me involved because . . . well, the Labyrinth has always been one of my favorite subjects. The architecture involved—" Her expression turned a little dreamy. "The builder, Daedalus, was a genius. But the point is, the Labyrinth has entrances everywhere. If Luke could figure out how to navigate it, he could move his army around with incredible speed."

"Except it's a maze, right?"

"Full of horrible traps," Grover agreed. "Dead ends. Illusions. Psychotic goat-killing monsters."

"But not if you had Ariadne's string," Annabeth said.

"In the old days, Ariadne's string guided Theseus out of the maze. It was a navigation instrument of some kind, invented by Daedalus. And Chris Rodriguez was mumbling about string."

"So Luke is trying to find Ariadne's string," I said. "Why? What's he planning?"

Annabeth shook her head. "I don't know. I thought maybe he wanted to invade camp through the maze, but that doesn't make any sense. The closest entrances Clarisse found were in Manhattan, which wouldn't help Luke get past our borders. Clarisse explored a little way into the tunnels, but . . . it was very dangerous. She had some close calls. I researched everything I could find about Daedalus. I'm afraid it didn't help much. I don't understand exactly what Luke's planning, but I do know this: the Labyrinth might be the key to Grover's problem."

I blinked. "You think Pan is underground?"

"It would explain why he's been impossible to find."

Grover shuddered. "Satyrs hate going underground. No searcher would ever try going in *that* place. No flowers. No sunshine. No coffee shops!"

"But," Annabeth said, "the Labyrinth can lead you almost anywhere. It reads your thoughts. It was designed to fool you, to trick you and kill you; but if you can make the Labyrinth work *for* you—"

"It could lead you to the wild god," I said.

"I can't do it." Grover hugged his stomach. "Just thinking about it makes me want to throw up my silverware."

"Grover, it may be your last chance," Annabeth said.

"The council is serious. *One* week or you learn to tap dance!"

Over at the head table, Quintus cleared his throat. I got the feeling he didn't want to make a scene, but Annabeth was really pushing it, sitting at my table so long.

"We'll talk later." Annabeth squeezed my arm a little too hard. "Convince him, will you?"

She returned to the Athena table, ignoring all the people who were staring at her.

Grover buried his head in his hands. "I can't do it, Percy. My searcher's license. Pan. I'm going to lose it all. I'll have to start a puppet theater."

"Don't say that! We'll figure something out."

He looked at me teary-eyed. "Percy, you're my best friend. You've seen me underground. In that Cyclops's cave. Do you really think I could . . ."

His voice faltered. I remembered the Sea of Monsters, when he'd been stuck in a Cyclops's cave. He'd never liked underground places to begin with, but now Grover really hated them. Cyclopes gave him the creeps, too. Even Tyson . . . Grover tried to hide it, but Grover and I could sort of read each other's emotions because of this empathy link Grover had made between us. I knew how he felt. Grover was terrified of the big guy.

"I have to leave," Grover said miserably. "Juniper's waiting for me. It's a good thing she finds cowards attractive."

After he was gone, I looked over at Quintus. He nodded gravely, like we were sharing some dark secret. Then he went back to cutting his sausage with a dagger.

In the afternoon, I went down to the pegasus stables to visit my friend Blackjack.

Yo, boss! He capered around in his stall, his black wings buffeting the air. *Ya bring me some sugar cubes?*

"You know those aren't good for you, Blackjack."

Yeah, so you brought me some, huh?

I smiled and fed him a handful. Blackjack and I went back a long way. I sort of helped rescue him from Luke's demon cruise ship a few years ago, and ever since, he insisted on repaying me with favors.

So we got any quests coming up? Blackjack asked. *I'm ready to fly, boss!*

I patted his nose. "Not sure, man. Everybody keeps talking about underground mazes."

Blackjack whinnied nervously. *Nuh-uh. Not for this horse! You ain't gonna be crazy enough to go in no maze, boss. Are ya? You'll end up in the glue factory!*

"You may be right, Blackjack. We'll see."

Blackjack crunched down his sugar cubes. He shook his mane like he was having a sugar seizure. *Whoa! Good stuff! Well, boss, you come to your senses and want to fly somewhere, just give a whistle. Ole Blackjack and his buddies, we'll stampede anybody for ya!*

I told him I'd keep it in mind. Then a group of younger campers came into the stables to start their riding lessons, and I decided it was time to leave. I had a bad feeling I wasn't going to see Blackjack for a long time.

That night after dinner, Quintus had us suit up in combat

armor like we were getting ready for capture the flag, but the mood among the campers was a lot more serious. Sometime during the day the crates in the arena had disappeared, and I had a feeling whatever was in them had been emptied into the woods.

"Right," Quintus said, standing on the head dining table. "Gather 'round."

He was dressed in black leather and bronze. In the torchlight, his gray hair made him look like a ghost. Mrs. O'Leary bounded happily around him, foraging for dinner scraps.

"You will be in teams of two," Quintus announced. When everybody started talking and trying to grab their friends, he yelled: "Which have already been chosen!"

"AWWWWW!" everybody complained.

"Your goal is simple: collect the gold laurels without dying. The wreath is wrapped in a silk package, tied to the back of one of the monsters. There are six monsters. Each has a silk package. Only one holds the laurels. You must find the wreath before the other teams. And, of course . . . you will have to slay the monster to get it, and stay alive."

The crowd started murmuring excitedly. The task sounded pretty straightforward. Hey, we'd all slain monsters before. That's what we trained for.

"I will now announce your partners," Quintus said. "There will be no trading. No switching. No complaining."

"*Aroooof!*" Mrs. O'Leary buried her face in a plate of pizza.

Quintus produced a big scroll and started reading off

names. Beckendorf would be with Silena Beauregard, which Beckendorf looked pretty happy about. The Stoll brothers, Travis and Connor, would be together. No surprise. They did everything together. Clarisse was with Lee Fletcher from the Apollo cabin—melee and ranged combat combined, they would be a tough combo to beat. Quintus kept rattling off the names until he said, "Percy Jackson with Annabeth Chase."

"Nice." I grinned at Annabeth.

"Your armor is crooked" was her only comment, and she redid my straps for me.

"Grover Underwood," Quintus said, "with Tyson."

Grover just about jumped out of his goat fur. "What? B-but—"

"No, no," Tyson whimpered. "Must be a mistake. Goat boy—"

"No complaining!" Quintus ordered. "Get with your partner. You have two minutes to prepare!"

Tyson and Grover both looked at me pleadingly. I tried to give them an encouraging nod, and gestured that they should move together. Tyson sneezed. Grover started chewing nervously on his wooden club.

"They'll be fine," Annabeth said. "Come on. Let's worry about how we're going to stay alive."

It was still light when we got into the woods, but the shadows from the trees made it feel like midnight. It was cold, too, even in summer. Annabeth and I found tracks almost immediately—scuttling marks made by something with a lot of legs. We began to follow the trail.

We jumped a creek and heard some twigs snapping nearby. We crouched behind a boulder, but it was only the Stoll brothers tripping through the woods and cursing. Their dad was the god of thieves, but they were about as stealthy as water buffaloes.

Once the Stolls had passed, we forged deeper into the west woods where the monsters were wilder. We were standing on a ledge overlooking a marshy pond when Annabeth tensed. "This is where we stopped looking."

It took me a second to realize what she meant. Last winter, when we'd been searching for Nico di Angelo, this is where we'd given up hope of finding him. Grover, Annabeth, and I had stood on this rock, and I'd convinced them not to tell Chiron the truth: that Nico was a son of Hades. At the time it seemed the right thing to do. I wanted to protect his identity. I wanted to be the one to find him and make things right for what had happened to his sister. Now, six months later, I hadn't even come close to finding him. It left a bitter taste in my mouth.

"I saw him last night," I said.

Annabeth knit her eyebrows. "What do you mean?"

I told her about the Iris-message. When I was done, she stared into the shadows of the woods. "He's summoning the dead? That's not good."

"The ghost was giving him bad advice," I said. "Telling him to take revenge."

"Yeah . . . spirits are never good advisers. They've got their own agendas. Old grudges. And they resent the living."

"He's going to come after me," I said. "The spirit mentioned a maze."

She nodded. "That settles it. We *have* to figure out the Labyrinth."

"Maybe," I said uncomfortably. "But who sent the Iris-message? If Nico didn't know I was there—"

A branch snapped in the woods. Dry leaves rustled. Something large was moving in the trees, just beyond the ridge.

"That's not the Stoll brothers," Annabeth whispered.

Together we drew our swords.

We got to Zeus's Fist, a huge pile of boulders in the middle of the west woods. It was a natural landmark where campers often rendezvoused on hunting expeditions, but now there was nobody around.

"Over there," Annabeth whispered.

"No, wait," I said. "Behind us."

It was weird. Scuttling noises seemed to be coming from several different directions. We were circling the boulders, our swords drawn, when someone right behind us said, "Hi."

We whirled around, and the tree nymph Juniper yelped.

"Put those down!" she protested. "Dryads don't like sharp blades, okay?"

"Juniper," Annabeth exhaled. "What are you doing here?"

"I live here."

I lowered my sword. "In the boulders?"

She pointed toward the edge of the clearing. "In the juniper. Duh."

It made sense, and I felt kind of stupid. I'd been hanging around dryads for years, but I never really talked to them much. I knew they couldn't go very far from their tree, which was their source of life. But I didn't know much else.

"Are you guys busy?" Juniper asked.

"Well," I said, "we're in the middle of this game against a bunch of monsters and we're trying not to die."

"We're not busy," Annabeth said. "What's wrong, Juniper?"

Juniper sniffled. She wiped her silky sleeve under her eyes. "It's Grover. He seems so distraught. All year he's been out looking for Pan. And every time he comes back, it's worse. I thought maybe, at first, he was seeing another tree."

"No," Annabeth said, as Juniper started crying. "I'm sure that's not it."

"He had a crush on a blueberry bush once," Juniper said miserably.

"Juniper," Annabeth said, "Grover would never even *look* at another tree. He's just stressed out about his searcher's license."

"He can't go underground!" she protested. "You can't let him."

Annabeth looked uncomfortable. "It might be the only way to help him; if we just knew where to start."

"Ah." Juniper wiped a green tear off her cheek. "About that . . ."

Another rustle in the woods, and Juniper yelled, "Hide!"

Before I could ask why, she went *poof* into green mist.

Annabeth and I turned. Coming out of the woods was a glistening amber insect, ten feet long, with jagged pincers, an armored tail, and a stinger as long as my sword. A scorpion. Tied to its back was a red silk package.

"One of us gets behind it," Annabeth said, as the thing clattered toward us. "Cuts off its tail while the other distracts it in front."

"I'll take point," I said. "You've got the invisibility hat."

She nodded. We'd fought together so many times we knew each other's moves. We could do this, easy. But it all went wrong when the other two scorpions appeared from the woods.

"Three?" Annabeth said. "That's not possible! The whole woods, and half the monsters come at us?"

I swallowed. One, we could take. Two, with a little luck. Three? Doubtful.

The scorpions scurried toward us, whipping their barbed tails like they'd come here just to kill us. Annabeth and I put our backs against the nearest boulder.

"Climb?" I said.

"No time," she said.

She was right. The scorpions were already surrounding us. They were so close I could see their hideous mouths foaming, anticipating a nice juicy meal of demigods.

"Look out!" Annabeth parried away a stinger with the flat of her blade. I stabbed with Riptide, but the scorpion backed out of range. We clambered sideways along the boulders, but the scorpions followed us. I slashed at another one, but going on the offensive was too dangerous. If I went for the body, the tail stabbed downward. If I went for the tail, the thing's pincers came from either side and tried to grab me. All we could do was defend, and we wouldn't be able to keep that up for very long.

I took another step sideways, and suddenly there was nothing behind me. It was a crack between two of the largest boulders, something I'd probably passed by a million times, but . . .

"In here," I said.

Annabeth sliced at a scorpion then looked at me like I was crazy. "*In there?* It's too narrow."

"I'll cover you. Go!"

She ducked behind me and started squeezing between the two boulders. Then she yelped and grabbed my armor straps, and suddenly I was tumbling into a pit that hadn't been there a moment before. I could see the scorpions above us, the purple evening sky and the trees, and then the hole shut like the lens of a camera, and we were in complete darkness.

Our breathing echoed against stone. It was wet and cold. I was sitting on a bumpy floor that seemed to be made of bricks.

I lifted Riptide. The faint glow of the blade was just enough to illuminate Annabeth's frightened face and the mossy stone walls on either side of us.

"Wh-where are we?" Annabeth said.

"Safe from scorpions, anyway." I tried to sound calm, but I was freaking out. The crack between the boulders couldn't have led into a cave. I would've known if there was a cave here; I was sure of it. It was like the ground had opened up and swallowed us. All I could think of was the fissure in the dining room pavilion, where those skeletons had been consumed last summer. I wondered if the same thing had happened to us.

I lifted my sword again for light.

"It's a long room," I muttered.

Annabeth gripped my arm. "It's not a room. It's a corridor."

She was right. The darkness felt . . . emptier in front of us. There was a warm breeze, like in subway tunnels, only it felt older, more dangerous somehow.

I started forward, but Annabeth stopped me. "Don't take another step," she warned. "We need to find the exit."

She sounded really scared now.

"It's okay," I promised. "It's right—"

I looked up and realized I couldn't see where we'd fallen in. The ceiling was solid stone. The corridor seemed to stretch endlessly in both directions.

Annabeth's hand slipped into mine. Under different circumstances I would've been embarrassed, but here in the dark I was glad to know where she was. It was about the only thing I was sure of.

"Two steps back," she advised.

We stepped backward together like we were in a minefield.

"Okay," she said. "Help me examine the walls."

"What for?"

[59]

"The mark of Daedalus," she said, as if that was supposed to make sense.

"Uh, okay. What kind of—"

"Got it!" she said with relief. She set her hand on the wall and pressed against a tiny fissure, which began to glow blue. A Greek symbol appeared: Δ, the Ancient Greek Delta.

The roof slid open and we saw night sky, stars blazing. It was a lot darker than it should've been. Metal ladder rungs appeared in the side of the wall, leading up, and I could hear people yelling our names.

"Percy! Annabeth!" Tyson's voice bellowed the loudest, but others were calling out too.

I looked nervously at Annabeth. Then we began to climb.

We made our way around the rocks and ran into Clarisse and a bunch of other campers carrying torches.

"Where have you two been?" Clarisse demanded. "We've been looking forever."

"But we were only gone a few minutes," I said.

Chiron trotted up, followed by Tyson and Grover.

"Percy!" Tyson said. "You are okay?"

"We're fine," I said. "We fell in a hole."

The others looked at me skeptically, then at Annabeth.

"Honest!" I said. "There were three scorpions after us, so we ran and hid in the rocks. But we were only gone a minute."

"You've been missing for almost an hour," Chiron said. "The game is over."

"Yeah," Grover muttered. "We would've won, but a Cyclops sat on me."

"Was an accident!" Tyson protested, and then he sneezed.

Clarisse was wearing the gold laurels, but she didn't even brag about winning them, which wasn't like her. "A hole?" she said suspiciously.

Annabeth took a deep breath. She looked around at the other campers. "Chiron . . . maybe we should talk about this at the Big House."

Clarisse gasped. "You found it, didn't you?"

Annabeth bit her lip. "I—Yeah. Yeah, we did."

A bunch of campers started asking questions, looking about as confused as I was, but Chiron raised his hand for silence. "Tonight is not the right time, and this is not the right place." He stared at the boulders as if he'd just noticed how dangerous they were. "All of you, back to your cabins. Get some sleep. A game well played, but curfew is past!"

There was a lot of mumbling and complaints, but the campers drifted off, talking among themselves and giving me suspicious looks.

"This explains a lot," Clarisse said. "It explains what Luke is after."

"Wait a second," I said. "What do you mean? What did we find?"

Annabeth turned toward me, her eyes dark with worry. "An entrance to the Labyrinth. An invasion route straight into the heart of the camp."

ANNABETH BREAKS
THE RULES

Chiron had insisted we talk about it in the morning, which was kind of like, *Hey, your life's in mortal danger. Sleep tight!* It was hard to fall asleep, but when I finally did, I dreamed of a prison.

I saw a boy in a Greek tunic and sandals crouching alone in a massive stone room. The ceiling was open to the night sky, but the walls were twenty feet high and polished marble, completely smooth. Scattered around the room were wooden crates. Some were cracked and tipped over, as if they'd been flung in there. Bronze tools spilled out of one—a compass, a saw, and a bunch of other things I didn't recognize.

The boy huddled in the corner, shivering from cold, or maybe fear. He was spattered in mud. His legs, arms, and face were scraped up as if he'd been dragged here along with the boxes.

Then the double oak doors moaned open. Two guards in bronze armor marched in, holding an old man between them. They flung him to the floor in a battered heap.

"Father!" The boy ran to him. The man's robes were in tatters. His hair was streaked with gray, and his beard was long and curly. His nose had been broken. His lips were bloody.

The boy took the old man's head in his arms. "What did they do to you?" Then he yelled at the guards, "I'll kill you!"

"There will be no killing today," a voice said.

The guards moved aside. Behind them stood a tall man in white robes. He wore a thin circlet of gold on his head. His beard was pointed like a spear blade. His eyes glittered cruelly. "You helped the Athenian kill my Minotaur, Daedalus. You turned my own daughter against me."

"You did that yourself, Your Majesty," the old man croaked.

A guard planted a kick in the old man's ribs. He groaned in agony. The young boy cried, "Stop!"

"You love your maze so much," the king said, "I have decided to let you stay here. This will be your workshop. Make me new wonders. Amuse me. Every maze needs a monster. You shall be mine!"

"I don't fear you," the old man groaned.

The king smiled coldly. He locked his eyes on the boy. "But a man cares about his son, eh? Displease me, old man, and the next time my guards inflict a punishment, it will be on him!"

The king swept out of the room with his guards, and the doors slammed shut, leaving the boy and his father alone in the darkness.

"What will we do?" the boy moaned. "Father, they will kill you!"

The old man swallowed with difficulty. He tried to smile, but it was a gruesome sight with his bloody mouth.

"Take heart, my son." He gazed up at the stars. "I—I will find a way."

A bar lowered across the doors with a fatal *BOOM*, and I woke in a cold sweat.

I was still feeling shaky the next morning when Chiron called a war council. We met in the sword arena, which I thought was pretty strange—trying to discuss the fate of the camp while Mrs. O'Leary chewed on a life-size squeaky pink rubber yak.

Chiron and Quintus stood at the front by the weapon racks. Clarisse and Annabeth sat next to each other and led the briefing. Tyson and Grover sat as far away from each other as possible. Also present around the table: Juniper the tree nymph, Silena Beauregard, Travis and Connor Stoll, Beckendorf, Lee Fletcher, even Argus, our hundred-eyed security chief. That's how I knew it was serious. Argus hardly ever shows up unless something really major is going on. The whole time Annabeth spoke, he kept his hundred blue eyes trained on her so hard his whole body turned bloodshot.

"Luke must have known about the Labyrinth entrance," Annabeth said. "He knew everything about camp."

I thought I heard a little pride in her voice, like she still respected the guy, as evil as he was.

Juniper cleared her throat. "That's what I was trying to tell you last night. The cave entrance has been there a long time. Luke used to use it."

Silena Beauregard frowned. "You knew about the Labyrinth entrance, and you didn't say anything?"

Juniper's face turned green. "I didn't know it was important. Just a cave. I don't like yucky old caves."

"She has good taste," Grover said.

"I wouldn't have paid any attention except . . . well, it was Luke." She blushed a little greener.

Grover huffed. "Forget what I said about good taste."

"Interesting." Quintus polished his sword as he spoke. "And you believe this young man, Luke, would dare use the Labyrinth as an invasion route?"

"Definitely," Clarisse said. "If he could get an army of monsters inside Camp Half-Blood, just pop up in the middle of the woods without having to worry about our magical boundaries, we wouldn't stand a chance. He could wipe us out easy. He must've been planning this for months."

"He's been sending scouts into the maze," Annabeth said. "We know because . . . because we found one."

"Chris Rodriguez," Chiron said. He gave Quintus a meaningful look.

"Ah," Quintus said. "The one in the . . . Yes. I understand."

"The one in the what?" I asked.

Clarisse glared at me. "The point is, Luke has been looking for a way to navigate the maze. He's searching for Daedalus's workshop."

I remembered my dream the night before—the bloody old man in tattered robes. "The guy who created the maze."

"Yes," Annabeth said. "The greatest architect, the greatest inventor of all time. If the legends are true, his workshop is in the center of the Labyrinth. He's the only one who knew how to navigate the maze perfectly. If Luke managed to find the workshop and convince Daedalus to help him, Luke wouldn't have to fumble around searching for paths, or risk losing his army in the maze's traps. He could navigate anywhere he wanted—quickly and safely. First to Camp Half-Blood to wipe us out. Then . . . to Olympus."

The arena was silent except for Mrs. O'Leary's toy yak getting disemboweled: *SQUEAK! SQUEAK!*

Finally Beckendorf put his huge hands on the table. "Back up a sec. Annabeth, you said 'convince Daedalus'? Isn't Daedalus dead?"

Quintus grunted. "I would hope so. He lived, what, three thousand years ago? And even if he were alive, don't the old stories say he fled from the Labyrinth?"

Chiron clopped restlessly on his hooves. "That's the problem, my dear Quintus. No one knows. There are rumors . . . well, there are *many* disturbing rumors about Daedalus, but one is that he disappeared back into the Labyrinth toward the end of his life. He might still be down there."

I thought about the old man I'd seen in my dream. He'd looked so frail, it was hard to believe he'd last another week, much less three thousand years.

"We need to go in," Annabeth announced. "We have to find the workshop before Luke does. If Daedalus is alive, we convince him to help us, not Luke. If Ariadne's string still exists, we make sure it never falls into Luke's hands."

"Wait a second," I said. "If we're worried about an attack, why not just blow up the entrance? Seal the tunnel?"

"Great idea!" Grover said. "I'll get the dynamite!"

"It's not so easy, stupid," Clarisse growled. "We tried that at the entrance we found in Phoenix. It didn't go well."

Annabeth nodded. "The Labyrinth is magical architecture, Percy. It would take huge power to seal even one of its entrances. In Phoenix, Clarisse demolished a whole building with a wrecking ball, and the maze entrance just shifted a few feet. The best we can do is prevent Luke from learning to navigate the Labyrinth."

"We could fight," Lee Fletcher said. "We know where the entrance is now. We can set up a defensive line and wait for them. If an army tries to come through, they'll find us waiting with our bows."

"We will certainly set up defenses," Chiron agreed. "But I fear Clarisse is right. The magical borders have kept this camp safe for hundreds of years. If Luke manages to get a large army of monsters into the center of camp, bypassing our boundaries . . . we may not have the strength to defeat them."

Nobody looked real happy about that news. Chiron usually tried to be upbeat and optimistic. If he was predicting we couldn't hold off an attack, that wasn't good.

"We have to get to Daedalus's workshop first," Annabeth insisted. "Find Ariadne's string and prevent Luke from using it."

"But if nobody can navigate in there," I said, "what chance do we have?"

"I've been studying architecture for years," she said. "I know Daedalus's Labyrinth better than anybody."

"From reading about it."

"Well, yes."

"That's not enough."

"It has to be!"

"It isn't!"

"Are you going to help me or not?"

I realized everyone was watching Annabeth and me like a tennis match. Mrs. O'Leary's squeaky yak went *EEK!* as she ripped off its pink rubber head.

Chiron cleared his throat. "First things first. We need a quest. Someone must enter the Labyrinth, find the workshop of Daedalus, and prevent Luke from using the maze to invade this camp."

"We all know who should lead this," Clarisse said. "Annabeth."

There was a murmur of agreement. I knew Annabeth had been waiting for her own quest since she was a little kid, but she looked uncomfortable.

"You've done as much as I have, Clarisse," she said. "You should go, too."

Clarisse shook her head. "I'm not going back in there."

Travis Stoll laughed. "Don't tell me you're scared. Clarisse, chicken?"

Clarisse got to her feet. I thought she was going to pulverize Travis, but she said in a shaky voice: "You don't understand anything, punk. I'm never going in there again. Never!"

She stormed out of the arena.

Travis looked around sheepishly. "I didn't mean to—"

Chiron raised his hand. "The poor girl has had a difficult year. Now, do we have agreement that Annabeth should lead the quest?"

We all nodded except Quintus. He folded his arms and stared at the table, but I wasn't sure anyone else noticed.

"Very well." Chiron turned to Annabeth. "My dear, it's your time to visit the Oracle. Assuming you return to us in one piece, we shall discuss what to do next."

Waiting for Annabeth was harder than visiting the Oracle myself.

I'd heard it speak prophecies twice before. The first time had been in the dusty attic of the Big House, where the spirit of Delphi slept inside the body of a mummified hippie lady. The second time, the Oracle had come out for a little stroll in the woods. I still had nightmares about that.

I'd never felt threatened by the Oracle's presence, but I'd heard stories: campers who'd gone insane, or who'd seen visions so real they died of fear.

I paced the arena, waiting. Mrs. O'Leary ate her lunch, which consisted of a hundred pounds of ground beef and several dog biscuits the size of trash-can lids. I wondered where Quintus got dog biscuits that size. I didn't figure you could just walk into Pet Zone and put those in your shopping cart.

Chiron was deep in conversation with Quintus and

Argus. It looked to me like they were disagreeing about something. Quintus kept shaking his head.

On the other side of the arena, Tyson and the Stoll brothers were racing miniature bronze chariots that Tyson had made out of armor scraps.

I gave up on pacing and left the arena. I stared across the fields at the Big House's attic window, dark and still. What was taking Annabeth so long? I was pretty sure it hadn't taken me this long to get my quest.

"Percy," a girl whispered.

Juniper was standing in the bushes. It was weird how she almost turned invisible when she was surrounded by plants.

She gestured me over urgently. "You need to know: Luke wasn't the only one I saw around that cave."

"What do you mean?"

She glanced back at the arena. "I was trying to say something, but he was right there."

"Who?"

"The sword master," she said. "He was poking around the rocks."

My stomach clenched. "Quintus? When?"

"I don't know. I don't pay attention to time. Maybe a week ago, when he first showed up."

"What was he doing? Did he go in?"

"I—I'm not sure. He's creepy, Percy. I didn't even see him come into the glade. Suddenly he was just *there*. You have to tell Grover it's too dangerous—"

"Juniper?" Grover called from inside the arena. "Where'd you go?"

Juniper sighed. "I'd better go in. Just remember what I said. Don't trust that man!"

She ran into the arena.

I stared at the Big House, feeling more uneasy than ever. If Quintus was up to something . . . I needed Annabeth's advice. She might know what to make of Juniper's news. But where the heck was she? Whatever was happening with the Oracle, it shouldn't be taking this long.

Finally I couldn't stand it anymore.

It was against the rules, but then again, nobody was watching. I ran down the hill and headed across the fields.

The front parlor of the Big House was strangely quiet. I was used to seeing Dionysus by the fireplace, playing cards and eating grapes and griping at satyrs, but Mr. D was still away.

I walked down the hallway, floorboards creaking under my feet. When I got to the base of the stairs, I hesitated. Four floors above would be a little trapdoor leading to the attic. Annabeth would be up there somewhere. I stood quietly and listened. But what I heard wasn't what I had expected.

Sobbing. And it was coming from below me.

I crept around the back of the stairs. The basement door was open. I didn't even know the Big House *had* a basement. I peered inside and saw two figures in the far corner, sitting amid a bunch of stockpiled cases of ambrosia and strawberry preserves. One was Clarisse. The other was a teenage Hispanic guy in tattered camouflage pants and a dirty black T-shirt. His hair was greasy and matted. He was hugging his shoulders and sobbing. It was Chris Rodriguez, the half-blood who'd gone to work for Luke.

"It's okay," Clarisse was telling him. "Try a little more nectar."

"You're an illusion, Mary!" Chris backed farther into the corner. "G-get away."

"My name's not Mary." Clarisse's voice was gentle but really sad. I never knew Clarisse could sound that way. "My name is Clarisse. Remember. Please."

"It's dark!" Chris yelled. "So dark!"

"Come outside," Clarisse coaxed. "The sunlight will help you."

"A . . . a thousand skulls. The earth keeps healing him."

"Chris," Clarisse pleaded. It sounded like she was close to tears. "You have to get better. Please. Mr. D will be back soon. He's an expert in madness. Just hang on."

Chris's eyes were like a cornered rat's—wild and desperate. "There's no way out, Mary. No way out."

Then he caught a glimpse of me and made a strangled, terrified sound. "The son of Poseidon! He's horrible!"

I backed away, hoping Clarisse hadn't seen me. I listened for her to come charging out and yell at me, but instead she just kept talking to Chris in a sad pleading voice, trying to get him to drink the nectar. Maybe she thought it was part of Chris's hallucination, but . . . *son of Poseidon?* Chris had been looking at me, and yet why did I get the feeling he hadn't been talking about me at all?

And Clarisse's tenderness—it had never even occurred to me that she might like someone; but the way she said

Chris's name . . . She'd known him before he changed sides. She'd known him a lot better than I realized. And now he was shivering in a dark basement, afraid to come out, and mumbling about someone named Mary. No wonder Clarisse didn't want anything to do with the Labyrinth. What had happened to Chris in there?

I heard a creak from above—like the attic door opening—and I ran for the front door. I needed to get out of that house.

"My dear," Chiron said. "You made it."

Annabeth walked into the arena. She sat on a stone bench and stared at the floor.

"Well?" Quintus asked.

Annabeth looked at me first. I couldn't tell if she was trying to warn me, or if the look in her eyes was just plain fear. Then she focused on Quintus. "I got the prophecy. I will lead the quest to find Daedalus's workshop."

Nobody cheered. I mean, we all liked Annabeth, and we wanted her to have a quest, but this one seemed insanely dangerous. After what I'd seen of Chris Rodriguez, I didn't even want to think about Annabeth descending into that weird maze again.

Chiron scraped a hoof on the dirt floor. "What did the prophecy say exactly, my dear? The wording is important."

Annabeth took a deep breath. "I, ah . . . well, it said, *You shall delve in the darkness of the endless maze . . .*"

We waited.

"The dead, the traitor, and the lost one raise."

Grover perked up. "The lost one! That must mean Pan! That's great!"

"With the dead and the traitor," I added. "Not so great."

"And?" Chiron asked. "What is the rest?"

"You shall rise or fall by the ghost king's hand," Annabeth said, *"the child of Athena's final stand."*

Everyone looked around uncomfortably. Annabeth was a daughter of Athena, and a final stand didn't sound good.

"Hey . . . we shouldn't jump to conclusions," Silena said. "Annabeth isn't the only child of Athena, right?"

"But who's this ghost king?" Beckendorf asked.

No one answered. I thought about the Iris-message I'd seen of Nico summoning spirits. I had a bad feeling the prophecy was connected to that.

"Are there more lines?" Chiron asked. "The prophecy does not sound complete."

Annabeth hesitated. "I don't remember exactly."

Chiron raised an eyebrow. Annabeth was known for her memory. She never forgot something she heard.

Annabeth shifted on her bench. "Something about . . . *Destroy with a hero's final breath.*"

"And?" Chiron asked.

She stood. "Look, the point is, I have to go in. I'll find the workshop and stop Luke. And . . . I need help." She turned to me. "Will you come?"

I didn't even hesitate. "I'm in."

She smiled for the first time in days, and that made it all worthwhile. "Grover, you too? The wild god is waiting."

Grover seemed to forget how much he hated the underground. The line about the "lost one" had completely energized him. "I'll pack extra recyclables for snacks!"

"And Tyson," Annabeth said. "I'll need you too."

"Yay! Blow-things-up time!" Tyson clapped so hard he woke up Mrs. O'Leary, who was dozing in the corner.

"Wait, Annabeth," Chiron said. "This goes against the ancient laws. A hero is allowed only two companions."

"I need them all," she insisted. "Chiron, it's important."

I didn't know why she was so certain, but I was happy she'd included Tyson. I couldn't imagine leaving him behind. He was huge and strong and great at figuring out mechanical things. Unlike satyrs, Cyclopes had no problem underground.

"Annabeth." Chiron flicked his tail nervously. "Consider well. You would be breaking the ancient laws, and there are always consequences. Last winter, five went on a quest to save Artemis. Only three came back. Think on that. Three is a sacred number. There are three Fates, three Furies, three Olympian sons of Kronos. It is a good strong number that stands against many dangers. Four . . . this is risky."

Annabeth took a deep breath. "I know. But we have to. Please."

I could tell Chiron didn't like it. Quintus was studying us, like he was trying to decide which of us would come back alive.

Chiron sighed. "Very well. Let us adjourn. The members of the quest must prepare themselves. Tomorrow at dawn, we send you into the Labyrinth."

* * *

Quintus pulled me aside as the council was breaking up.

"I have a bad feeling about this," he told me.

Mrs. O'Leary came over, wagging her tail happily. She dropped her shield at my feet, and I threw it for her. Quintus watched her romp after it. I remembered what Juniper had said about him scouting out the maze. I didn't trust him, but when he looked at me, I saw real concern in his eyes.

"I don't like the idea of you going down there," he said. "Any of you. But if you must, I want you to remember something. The Labyrinth exists to fool you. It will distract you. That's dangerous for half-bloods. We are easily distracted."

"You've been in there?"

"Long ago." His voice was ragged. "I barely escaped with my life. Most who enter aren't that lucky."

He gripped my shoulder. "Percy, keep your mind on what matters most. If you can do that, you might find the way. And here, I wanted to give you something."

He handed me a little silver tube. It was so cold I almost dropped it.

"A whistle?" I asked.

"A dog whistle," Quintus said. "For Mrs. O'Leary."

"Um, thanks, but—"

"How will it work in the maze? I'm not a hundred percent certain it will. But Mrs. O'Leary is a hellhound. She can appear when called, no matter how far away she is. I'd feel better knowing you had this. If you really need help, use it; but be careful, the whistle is made of Stygian ice."

"*What* ice?"

"From the River Styx. Very hard to craft. Very delicate. It cannot melt, but it will shatter when you blow it, so you can only use it once."

I thought about Luke, my old enemy. Right before I'd gone on my first quest, Luke had given me a gift, too—magic shoes that had been designed to drag me to my death. Quintus seemed so nice. So concerned. And Mrs. O'Leary liked him, which had to count for something. She dropped the slimy shield at my feet and barked excitedly.

I felt ashamed that I could even think about mistrusting Quintus. But then again, I'd trusted Luke once.

"Thanks," I told Quintus. I slipped the freezing whistle into my pocket, promising myself that I would never use it, and I dashed off to find Annabeth.

As long as I'd been at camp, I'd never been inside the Athena cabin.

It was a silvery building, nothing fancy, with plain white curtains and a carved stone owl over the doorway. The owl's onyx eyes seemed to follow me as I walked closer.

"Hello?" I called inside.

Nobody answered. I stepped in and caught my breath. The place was a workshop for brainiac kids. The bunks were all pushed against one wall as if sleeping didn't matter very much. Most of the room was filled with workbenches and tables and sets of tools and weapons. The back of the room was a huge library crammed with old scrolls and leather-bound books and paperbacks. There was an architect's drafting table with a bunch of rulers and protractors, and some 3-D models of buildings. Huge old war maps were plastered to the ceiling. Sets of armor hung under the windows, their bronze plates glinting in the sun.

Annabeth stood in the back of the room, rifling through old scrolls.

"Knock, knock?" I said.

She turned with a start. "Oh . . . hi. Didn't hear you."

"You okay?"

She frowned at the scroll in her hands. "Just trying to do some research. Daedalus's Labyrinth is so huge. None of the stories agree about anything. The maps just lead from nowhere to nowhere."

I thought about what Quintus had said, how the maze tries to distract you. I wondered if Annabeth knew that already.

"We'll figure it out," I promised.

Her hair had come loose and was hanging in a tangled blond curtain all around her face. Her gray eyes looked almost black.

"I've wanted to lead a quest since I was seven," she said.

"You're going to do awesome."

She looked at me gratefully, but then stared down at all the books and scrolls she'd pulled from the shelves. "I'm worried, Percy. Maybe I shouldn't have asked you to do this. Or Tyson and Grover."

"Hey, we're your friends. We wouldn't miss it."

"But . . ." She stopped herself.

[78]

"What is it?" I asked. "The prophecy?"

"I'm sure it's fine," she said in a small voice.

"What was the last line?"

Then she did something that really surprised me. She blinked back tears and put out her arms.

I stepped forward and hugged her. Butterflies started turning my stomach into a mosh pit.

"Hey, it's . . . it's okay." I patted her back.

I was aware of everything in the room. I felt like I could read the tiniest print on any book on the shelves. Annabeth's hair smelled like lemon soap. She was shivering.

"Chiron might be right," she muttered. "I'm breaking the rules. But I don't know what else to do. I need you three. It just feels right."

"Then don't worry about it," I managed. "We've had plenty of problems before, and we solved them."

"This is different. I don't want anything happening to . . . any of you."

Behind me, somebody cleared his throat.

It was one of Annabeth's half-brothers, Malcolm. His face was bright red. "Um, sorry," he said. "Archery practice is starting, Annabeth. Chiron said to come find you."

I stepped away from Annabeth. "We were just looking at maps," I said stupidly.

Malcolm stared at me. "Okay."

"Tell Chiron I'll be right there," Annabeth said, and Malcolm left in a hurry.

Annabeth rubbed her eyes. "You go ahead, Percy. I'd better get ready for archery."

I nodded, feeling more confused than I ever had in my life. I wanted to run from the cabin . . . but then again I didn't.

"Annabeth?" I said. "About your prophecy. The line about a hero's last breath—"

"You're wondering which hero? I don't know."

"No. Something else. I was thinking the last line usually rhymes with the one before it. Was it something about—did it end in the word *death*?"

Annabeth stared down at her scrolls. "You'd better go, Percy. Get ready for the quest. I'll—I'll see you in the morning."

I left her there, staring at maps that led from nowhere to nowhere; but I couldn't shake the feeling that one of us wasn't going to come back from this quest alive.

FIVE

NICO BUYS HAPPY MEALS
FOR THE DEAD

At least I got a good night's sleep before the quest, right?

Wrong.

That night in my dreams, I was in the stateroom of the *Princess Andromeda*. The windows were open on a moonlit sea. Cold wind rustled the velvet drapes.

Luke knelt on a Persian rug in front of the golden sarcophagus of Kronos. In the moonlight, Luke's blond hair looked pure white. He wore an ancient Greek *chiton* and a white *himation*, a kind of cape that flowed down his shoulders. The white clothes made him look timeless and a little unreal, like one of the minor gods on Mount Olympus. The last time I'd seen him, he'd been broken and unconscious after a nasty fall from Mount Tam. Now he looked perfectly fine. Almost *too* healthy.

"Our spies report success, my lord," he said. "Camp Half-Blood is sending a quest, as you predicted. Our side of the bargain is almost complete."

Excellent. The voice of Kronos didn't so much speak as pierce my mind like a dagger. It was freezing with cruelty. *Once we have the means to navigate, I will lead the vanguard through myself.*

Luke closed his eyes as if collecting his thoughts. "My lord, perhaps it is too soon. Perhaps Krios or Hyperion should lead—"

No. The voice was quiet but absolutely firm. *I will lead. One more heart shall join our cause, and that will be sufficient. At last I shall rise fully from Tartarus.*

"But the form, my lord . . ." Luke's voice started shaking.

Show me your sword, Luke Castellan.

A jolt went through me. I realized I'd never heard Luke's last name before. It had never even occurred to me.

Luke drew his sword. Backbiter's double edge glowed wickedly—half steel, half celestial bronze. I'd almost been killed several times by that sword. It was an evil weapon, able to kill both mortals and monsters. It was the only blade I really feared.

You pledged yourself to me, Kronos reminded him. *You took this sword as proof of your oath.*

"Yes, my lord. It's just—"

You wanted power. I gave you that. You are now beyond harm. Soon you will rule the world of gods and mortals. Do you not wish to avenge yourself? To see Olympus destroyed?

A shiver ran through Luke's body. "Yes."

The coffin glowed, golden light filling the room. *Then make ready the strike force. As soon as the bargain is done, we shall move forward. First, Camp Half-Blood will be reduced to ashes. Once those bothersome heroes are eliminated, we will march on Olympus.*

There was a knock on the stateroom doors. The light of the coffin faded. Luke rose. He sheathed his sword, adjusted his white clothes, and took a deep breath.

"Come in."

The doors opened. Two *dracaenae* slithered in—snake women with double serpent trunks instead of legs. Between them walked Kelli, the *empousa* cheerleader from my freshman orientation.

"Hello, Luke." Kelli smiled. She was wearing a red dress and she looked awesome, but I'd seen her real form. I knew what she was hiding: mismatched legs, red eyes, fangs, and flaming hair.

"What is it, demon?" Luke's voice was cold. "I told you not to disturb me."

Kelli pouted. "That's not very nice. You look tense. How about a nice shoulder massage?"

Luke stepped back. "If you have something to report, say it. Otherwise leave!"

"I don't know why you're so huffy these days. You *used* to be fun to hang around."

"That was before I saw what you did to that boy in Seattle."

"Oh, he meant nothing to me," Kelli said. "Just a snack, really. You know my heart belongs to you, Luke."

"Thanks, but no thanks. Now report or get out."

Kelli shrugged. "Fine. The advance team is ready, as you requested. We can leave—" She frowned.

"What is it?" Luke asked.

"A presence," Kelli said. "Your senses are getting dull, Luke. We're being watched."

She scanned the stateroom. Her eyes focused right on me. Her face withered into a hag's. She bared her fangs and lunged.

* * *

I woke with a start, my heart pounding. I could've sworn the *empousa*'s fangs were an inch from my throat.

Tyson was snoring in the next bunk. The sound calmed me down a little.

I didn't know how Kelli could sense me in a dream, but I'd heard more than I wanted to know. An army was ready. Kronos would lead it personally. All they needed was a way to navigate the Labyrinth so they could invade and destroy Camp Half-Blood, and Luke apparently thought that was going to happen very soon.

I was tempted to go wake up Annabeth and tell her, middle of the night or not. Then I realized the room was lighter than it should have been. A blue-and-green glow was coming from the saltwater fountain, brighter and more urgent than the night before. It was almost like the water was humming.

I got out of bed and approached.

No voice spoke out of the water this time, asking for a deposit. I got the feeling the fountain was waiting for me to make the first move.

I probably should've gone back to bed. Instead I thought about what I'd seen last night—the weird image of Nico at the banks of the River Styx.

"You're trying to tell me something," I said.

No response from the fountain.

"All right," I said. "Show me Nico di Angelo."

I didn't even throw a coin in, but this time it didn't matter. It was like some other force had control of the water

[84]

besides Iris the messenger goddess. The water shimmered. Nico appeared, but he was no longer in the Underworld. He was standing in a graveyard under a starry sky. Giant willow trees loomed all around him.

He was watching some gravediggers at work. I heard shovels and saw dirt flying out of a hole. Nico was dressed in a black cloak. The night was foggy. It was warm and humid, and frogs were croaking. A large Wal-Mart bag sat next to Nico's feet.

"Is it deep enough yet?" Nico asked. He sounded irritated.

"Nearly, my lord." It was the same ghost I'd seen Nico with before, the faint shimmering image of a man. "But, my lord, I tell you, this is unnecessary. You already have me for advice."

"I want a second opinion!" Nico snapped his fingers, and the digging stopped. Two figures climbed out of the hole. They weren't people. They were skeletons in ragged clothes.

"You are dismissed," Nico said. "Thank you."

The skeletons collapsed into piles of bones.

"You might as well thank the shovels," the ghost complained. "They have as much sense."

Nico ignored him. He reached into his Wal-Mart bag and pulled out a twelve-pack of Coke. He popped open a can. Instead of drinking it, he poured it into the grave.

"Let the dead taste again," he murmured. "Let them rise and take this offering. Let them remember."

He dropped the rest of the Cokes into the grave and

pulled out a white paper bag decorated with cartoons. I hadn't seen one in years, but I recognized it—a McDonald's Happy Meal.

He turned it upside down and shook the fries and hamburger into the grave.

"In my day, we used animal blood," the ghost mumbled. "It's perfectly good enough. They can't taste the difference."

"I will treat them with respect," Nico said.

"At least let me keep the toy," the ghost said.

"Be quiet!" Nico ordered. He emptied another twelve-pack of soda and three more Happy Meals into the grave, then began chanting in Ancient Greek. I caught only some of the words—a lot about the dead and memories and returning from the grave. Real happy stuff.

The grave started to bubble. Frothy brown liquid rose to the top like the whole thing was filling with soda. The fog thickened. The frogs stopped croaking. Dozens of figures began to appear among the gravestones: bluish, vaguely human shapes. Nico had summoned the dead with Coke and cheeseburgers.

"There are too many," the ghost said nervously. "You don't know your own powers."

"I've got it under control," Nico said, though his voice sounded fragile. He drew his sword—a short blade made of solid black metal. I'd never seen anything like it. It wasn't celestial bronze or steel. Iron, maybe? The crowd of shades retreated at the sight of it.

"One at a time," Nico commanded.

A single figure floated forward and knelt at the pool.

It made slurping sounds as it drank. Its ghostly hands scooped french fries out of the pool. When it stood again, I could see it much more clearly—a teenage guy in Greek armor. He had curly hair and green eyes, a clasp shaped like a seashell on his cloak.

"Who are you?" Nico said. "Speak."

The young man frowned as if trying to remember. Then he spoke in a voice like dry, crumpling paper: "I am Theseus."

No way, I thought. This couldn't be *the* Theseus. He was just a kid. I'd grown up hearing stories about him fighting the Minotaur and stuff, but I'd always pictured him as this huge, buff guy. The ghost I was looking at wasn't strong or tall. And he wasn't any older than I was.

"How can I retrieve my sister?" Nico asked.

Theseus's eyes were lifeless as glass. "Do not try. It is madness."

"Just tell me!"

"My stepfather died," Theseus remembered. "He threw himself into the sea because he thought I was dead in the Labyrinth. I wanted to bring him back, but I could not."

Nico's ghost hissed, "My lord, the soul exchange! Ask him about that!"

Theseus scowled. "That voice. I know that voice."

"No you don't, fool!" the ghost said. "Answer the lord's questions and nothing more!"

"I know you," Theseus insisted, as if struggling to recall.

"I want to hear about my sister," Nico said. "Will this quest into the Labyrinth help me win her back?"

Theseus was looking for the ghost, but apparently couldn't see him. Slowly he turned his eyes back on Nico. "The Labyrinth is treacherous. There is only one thing that saw me through: the love of a mortal girl. The string was only part of the answer. It was the princess who guided me."

"We don't need any of that," the ghost said. "I will guide you, my lord. Ask him if it is true about an exchange of souls. He will tell you."

"A soul for a soul," Nico asked. "Is it true?"

"I—I must say yes. But the specter—"

"Just answer the questions, knave!" the ghost said.

Suddenly, around the edges of the pool, the other ghosts became restless. They stirred, whispering in nervous tones.

"I want to see my sister!" Nico demanded. "Where is she?"

"He is coming," Theseus said fearfully. "He has sensed your summons. He comes."

"Who?" Nico demanded.

"He comes to find the source of this power," Theseus said. "You must release us!"

The water in my fountain began to tremble, humming with power. I realized the whole cabin was shaking. The noise grew louder. The image of Nico in the graveyard started to glow until it was painful to watch.

"Stop," I said out loud. "Stop it!"

The fountain began to crack. Tyson muttered in his sleep and turned over. Purple light threw horrible, ghostly shadows on the cabin walls, as if the specters were escaping right out of the fountain.

In desperation I uncapped Riptide and slashed at the fountain, cleaving it in two. Salt water spilled everywhere, and the great stone font crashed to the floor in pieces. Tyson snorted and muttered, but he kept sleeping.

I sank to the ground, shivering from what I'd seen. Tyson found me there in the morning, still staring at the shattered remains of the saltwater fountain.

Just after dawn, the quest group met at Zeus's Fist. I'd packed my knapsack—thermos with nectar, baggie of ambrosia, bedroll, rope, clothes, flashlights, and lots of extra batteries. I had Riptide in my pocket. The magic shield/wristwatch Tyson had made for me was on my wrist.

It was a clear morning. The fog had burned off and the sky was blue. Campers would be having their lessons today, flying pegasi and practicing archery and scaling the lava wall. Meanwhile, we would be heading underground.

Juniper and Grover stood apart from the group. Juniper had been crying again, but she was trying to keep it together for Grover's sake. She kept fussing with his clothes, straightening his rasta cap and brushing goat fur off his shirt. Since we had no idea what we would encounter, he was dressed as a human, with the cap to hide his horns, and jeans, fake feet, and sneakers to hide his goat legs.

Chiron, Quintus, and Mrs. O'Leary stood with the other campers who'd come to wish us well, but there was too much activity for it to feel like a happy send-off. A couple of tents had been set up by the rocks for guard duty. Beckendorf and his siblings were working on a line of defensive spikes and trenches. Chiron had decided we needed to guard the Labyrinth exit at all times, just in case.

Annabeth was doing one last check on her supply pack. When Tyson and I came over, she frowned. "Percy, you look terrible."

"He killed the water fountain last night," Tyson confided.

"What?" she asked.

Before I could explain, Chiron trotted over. "Well, it appears you are ready!"

He tried to sound upbeat, but I could tell he was anxious. I didn't want to freak him out any more, but I thought about last night's dream, and before I could change my mind, I said, "Hey, uh, Chiron, can I ask you a favor while I'm gone?"

"Of course, my boy."

"Be right back, guys." I nodded toward the woods. Chiron raised an eyebrow, but he followed me out of earshot.

"Last night," I said, "I dreamed about Luke and Kronos." I told him the details. The news seemed to weigh on his shoulders.

"I feared this," Chiron said. "Against my father, Kronos, we would stand no chance in a fight."

Chiron rarely called Kronos his father. I mean, we all knew it was true. Everybody in the Greek world—god, monster, or Titan—was related to one another somehow. But it wasn't exactly something Chiron liked to brag about. *Oh, my dad is the all-powerful evil Titan lord who wants to destroy Western Civilization. I want to be just like him when I grow up!*

"Do you know what he meant about a bargain?" I asked.

"I am not sure, but I fear they seek to make a deal with Daedalus. If the old inventor is truly alive, if he has not been driven insane by millennia in the Labyrinth . . . well, Kronos can find ways to twist anyone to his will."

"Not anyone," I promised.

Chiron managed a smile. "No. Perhaps not anyone. But, Percy, you must beware. I have worried for some time that Kronos may be looking for Daedalus for a different reason, not just passage through the maze."

"What else would he want?"

"Something Annabeth and I were discussing. Do you remember what you told me about your first trip to the *Princess Andromeda*, the first time you saw the golden coffin?"

I nodded. "Luke was talking about raising Kronos, little pieces of him appearing in the coffin every time someone new joined his cause."

"And what did Luke say they would do when Kronos had risen completely?"

A chill went down my spine. "He said they would make Kronos a new body, worthy of the forges of Hephaestus."

"Indeed," Chiron said. "Daedalus was the world's greatest inventor. He created the Labyrinth, but much more. Automatons, thinking machines . . . What if Kronos wishes Daedalus to make him a new form?"

That was a real pleasant thought.

"We've got to get to Daedalus first," I said, "and convince him not to."

Chiron stared off into the trees. "One other thing I do

not understand . . . this talk of a last soul joining their cause. That does not bode well."

I kept my mouth shut, but I felt guilty. I'd made the decision not to tell Chiron about Nico being a son of Hades. The mention of souls, though—What if Kronos knew about Nico? What if he managed to turn him evil? It was almost enough to make me want to tell Chiron, but I didn't. For one thing, I wasn't sure Chiron could do anything about it. I had to find Nico myself. I had to explain things to him, make him listen.

"I don't know," I said at last. "But, uh, something Juniper said, maybe you should hear." I told him how the tree nymph had seen Quintus poking around the rocks.

Chiron's jaw tightened. "That does not surprise me."

"It doesn't sur— you mean you knew?"

"Percy, when Quintus showed up at camp offering his services . . . well, I would have to be a fool not to be suspicious."

"Then why did you let him in?"

"Because sometimes it is better to have someone you mistrust close to you, so that you can keep an eye on him. He may be just what he says: a half-blood in search of a home. Certainly he has done nothing openly that would make me question his loyalty. But believe me, I will keep an eye—"

Annabeth trudged over, probably curious why we were taking so long.

"Percy, you ready?"

I nodded. My hand slipped into my pocket, where I

kept the ice whistle Quintus had given me. I looked over and saw Quintus watching me carefully. He raised his hand in farewell.

Our spies report success, Luke had said. The same day we decided to send a quest, Luke had known about it.

"Take care," Chiron told us. "And good hunting."

"You too," I said.

We walked over to the rocks, where Tyson and Grover were waiting. I stared at the crack between the boulders—the entrance that was about to swallow us.

"Well," Grover said nervously, "good-bye sunshine."

"Hello rocks," Tyson agreed.

And together, the four of us descended into darkness.

SIX

WE MEET THE GOD WITH TWO FACES

We made it a hundred feet before we were hopelessly lost.

The tunnel looked nothing like the one Annabeth and I had stumbled into before. Now it was round like a sewer, constructed of red brick with iron-barred portholes every ten feet. I shined a light through one of the portholes out of curiosity, but I couldn't see anything. It opened into infinite darkness. I thought I heard voices on the other side, but it may have been just the cold wind.

Annabeth tried her best to guide us. She had this idea that we should stick to the left wall.

"If we keep one hand on the left wall and follow it," she said, "we should be able to find our way out again by reversing course."

Unfortunately, as soon as she said that, the left wall disappeared. We found ourselves in the middle of a circular chamber with eight tunnels leading out, and no idea how we'd gotten there.

"Um, which way did we come in?" Grover said nervously.

"Just turn around," Annabeth said.

We each turned toward a different tunnel. It was ridiculous. None of us could decide which way led back to camp.

"Left walls are mean," Tyson said. "Which way now?"

Annabeth swept her flashlight beam over the archways of the eight tunnels. As far as I could tell, they were identical. "That way," she said.

"How do you know?" I asked.

"Deductive reasoning."

"So . . . you're guessing."

"Just come on," she said.

The tunnel she'd chosen narrowed quickly. The walls turned to gray cement, and the ceiling got so low that pretty soon we were hunching over. Tyson was forced to crawl.

Grover's hyperventilating was the loudest noise in the maze. "I can't stand it anymore," he whispered. "Are we there yet?"

"We've been down here maybe five minutes," Annabeth told him.

"It's been longer than that," Grover insisted. "And why would Pan be down here? This is the opposite of the wild!"

We kept shuffling forward. Just when I was sure the tunnel would get so narrow it would squish us, it opened into a huge room. I shined my light around the walls and said, "Whoa."

The whole room was covered in mosaic tiles. The pictures were grimy and faded, but I could still make out the colors—red, blue, green, gold. The frieze showed the Olympian gods at a feast. There was my dad, Poseidon, with his trident, holding out grapes for Dionysus to turn into wine. Zeus was partying with satyrs, and Hermes was flying through the air on his winged sandals. The pictures were beautiful, but they weren't very accurate. I'd seen the gods. Dionysus was not that handsome, and Hermes's nose wasn't that big.

In the middle of the room was a three-tiered fountain. It looked like it hadn't held water in a long time.

"What is this place?" I muttered. "It looks—"

"Roman," Annabeth said. "Those mosaics are about two thousand years old."

"But how can they be Roman?" I wasn't that great on ancient history, but I was pretty sure the Roman Empire never made it as far as Long Island.

"The Labyrinth is a patchwork," Annabeth said. "I told you, it's always expanding, adding pieces. It's the only work of architecture that grows by itself."

"You make it sound like it's alive."

A groaning noise echoed from the tunnel in front of us.

"Let's not talk about it being alive," Grover whimpered. "Please?"

"All right," Annabeth said. "Forward."

"Down the hall with the bad sounds?" Tyson said. Even he looked nervous.

"Yeah," Annabeth said. "The architecture is getting older. That's a good sign. Daedalus's workshop would be in the oldest part."

That made sense. But soon the maze was toying with us—we went fifty feet and the tunnel turned back to cement, with brass pipes running down the sides. The walls were spray-painted with graffiti. A neon tagger sign read MOZ RULZ.

"I'm thinking this is not Roman," I said helpfully.

Annabeth took a deep breath, then forged ahead.

Every few feet the tunnels twisted and turned and branched off. The floor beneath us changed from cement to mud to bricks and back again. There was no sense to any of it. We stumbled into a wine cellar—a bunch of dusty bottles in wooden racks—like we were walking through somebody's basement, only there was no exit above us, just more tunnels leading on.

Later the ceiling turned to wooden planks, and I could hear voices above us and the creaking of footsteps, as if we were walking under some kind of bar. It was reassuring to hear people, but then again, we couldn't get to them. We were stuck down here with no way out. Then we found our first skeleton.

He was dressed in white clothes, like some kind of uniform. A wooden crate of glass bottles sat next to him.

"A milkman," Annabeth said.

"What?" I asked.

"They used to deliver milk."

"Yeah, I know what they are, but . . . that was when my mom was little, like a million years ago. What's he doing here?"

"Some people wander in by mistake," Annabeth said. "Some come exploring on purpose and never make it back. A long time ago, the Cretans even sent people in here as human sacrifices."

Grover gulped. "He's been down here a long time." He pointed to the skeleton's bottles, which were coated with white dust. The skeleton's fingers were clawing at the brick wall, like he had died trying to get out.

"Only bones," Tyson said. "Don't worry, goat boy. The milkman is dead."

"The milkman doesn't bother me," Grover said. "It's the smell. Monsters. Can't you smell it?"

Tyson nodded. "Lots of monsters. But underground smells like that. Monsters and dead milk people."

"Oh, good," Grover whimpered. "I thought maybe I was wrong."

"We have to get deeper into the maze," Annabeth said. "There has to be a way to the center."

She led us to the right, then the left, through a corridor of stainless steel like some kind of air shaft, and we arrived back in the Roman tile room with the fountain.

This time, we weren't alone.

What I noticed first were his faces. Both of them. They jutted out from either side of his head, staring over his shoulders, so his head was much wider than it should've been, kind of like a hammerhead shark's. Looking straight at him, all I saw were two overlapping ears and mirror-image sideburns.

He was dressed like a New York City doorman: a long black overcoat, shiny shoes, and a black top-hat that somehow managed to stay on his double-wide head.

"Well, Annabeth?" said his left face. "Hurry up!"

"Don't mind him," said the right face. "He's terribly rude. Right this way, miss."

Annabeth's jaw dropped. "Uh . . . I don't . . ."

Tyson frowned. "That funny man has two faces."

"The funny man has ears, you know!" the left face scolded. "Now come along, miss."

"No, no," the right face said. "This way, miss. Talk to *me*, please."

The two-faced man regarded Annabeth as best he could out of the corners of his eyes. It was impossible to look at him straight on without focusing on one side or the other. And suddenly I realized that's what he was asking—he wanted Annabeth to choose.

Behind him were two exits, blocked by wooden doors with huge iron locks. They hadn't been there our first time through the room. The two-faced doorman held a silver key, which he kept passing from his left hand to his right hand. I wondered if this was a different room completely, but the frieze of the gods looked exactly the same.

Behind us, the doorway we'd come through had disappeared, replaced by more mosaics. We wouldn't be going back the way we came.

"The exits are closed," Annabeth said.

"Duh!" the man's left face said.

"Where do they lead?" she asked.

"One probably leads the way you wish to go," the right face said encouragingly. "The other leads to certain death."

"I—I know who you are," Annabeth said.

"Oh, you're a smart one!" The left face sneered. "But do you know which way to choose? I don't have all day."

"Why are you trying to confuse me?" Annabeth asked.

The right face smiled. "You're in charge now, my dear. All the decisions are on your shoulders. That's what you wanted, isn't it?"

"I—"

"We know you, Annabeth," the left face said. "We know what you wrestle with every day. We know your indecision. You will have to make your choice sooner or later. And the choice may kill you."

I didn't know what they were talking about, but it sounded like it was about more than a choice between doors.

The color drained out of Annabeth's face. "No . . . I don't—"

"Leave her alone," I said. "Who are you, anyway?"

"I'm your best friend," the right face said.

"I'm your worst enemy," the left face said.

"I'm Janus," both faces said in harmony. "God of Doorways. Beginnings. Endings. Choices."

"I'll see you soon enough, Perseus Jackson," said the right face. "But for now it's Annabeth's turn." He laughed giddily. "Such fun!"

"Shut up!" his left face said. "This is serious. One bad choice can ruin your whole life. It can kill you and all your friends. But no pressure, Annabeth. Choose!"

With a sudden chill, I remembered the words of the prophecy: *the child of Athena's final stand.*

"Don't do it," I said.

"I'm afraid she has to," the right face said cheerfully.

Annabeth moistened her lips. "I—I choose—"

Before she could point to a door, a brilliant light flooded the room.

Janus raised his hands to either side of his head to cover his eyes. When the light died, a woman was standing at the fountain.

She was tall and graceful with long hair the color of chocolate, braided in plaits with gold ribbons. She wore a simple white dress, but when she moved, the fabric shimmered with colors like oil on water.

"Janus," she said, "are we causing trouble again?"

"N-no, milady!" Janus's right face stammered.

"Yes!" the left face said.

"Shut up!" the right face said.

"Excuse me?" the woman asked.

"Not you, milady! I was talking to myself."

"I see," the lady said. "You know very well your visit is premature. The girl's time has not yet come. So I give *you* a choice: leave these heroes to me, or I shall turn *you* into a door and break you down."

"What kind of door?" the left face asked.

"Shut up!" the right face said.

"Because French doors are nice," the left face mused. "Lots of natural light."

"Shut up!" the right face wailed. "Not you, milady! Of course I'll leave. I was just having a bit of fun. Doing my job. Offering choices."

"Causing indecision," the woman corrected. "Now be gone!"

The left face muttered, "Party pooper," then he raised

his silver key, inserted it into the air, and disappeared.

The woman turned toward us, and fear closed around my heart. Her eyes shined with power. *Leave these heroes to me.* That didn't sound good. For a second, I almost wished we could've taken our chances with Janus. But then the woman smiled.

"You must be hungry," she said. "Sit with me and talk."

She waved her hand, and the old Roman fountain began to flow. Jets of clear water sprayed into the air. A marble table appeared, laden with platters of sandwiches and pitchers of lemonade.

"Who . . . who are you?" I asked.

"I am Hera." The woman smiled. "Queen of Heaven."

I'd seen Hera once before at a Council of the Gods, but I hadn't paid much attention to her. At the time I'd been surrounded by a bunch of other gods who were debating whether or not to kill me.

I didn't remember her looking so normal. Of course, gods are usually twenty feet tall when they're on Olympus, so that makes them look a lot less normal. But now, Hera looked like a regular mom.

She served us sandwiches and poured lemonade.

"Grover, dear," she said, "use your napkin. Don't eat it."

"Yes, ma'am," Grover said.

"Tyson, you're wasting away. Would you like another peanut butter sandwich?"

Tyson stifled a belch. "Yes, nice lady."

"Queen Hera," Annabeth said. "I can't believe it. What are you doing in the Labyrinth?"

Hera smiled. She flicked one finger and Annabeth's hair combed itself. All the dirt and grime disappeared from her face.

"I came to see you, naturally," the goddess said.

Grover and I exchanged nervous looks. Usually when gods come looking for you, it's not out of the goodness of their hearts. It's because they want something.

Still, that didn't keep me from chowing down on turkey-and-Swiss sandwiches and chips and lemonade. I hadn't realized how hungry I was. Tyson was inhaling one peanut butter sandwich after another, and Grover was loving the lemonade, crunching the Styrofoam cup like an ice-cream cone.

"I didn't think—" Annabeth faltered. "Well, I didn't think you liked heroes."

Hera smiled indulgently. "Because of that little spat I had with Hercules? Honestly, I got so much bad press because of one disagreement."

"Didn't you try to kill him, like, a lot of times?" Annabeth asked.

Hera waved her hand dismissively. "Water under the bridge, my dear. Besides, he was one of my loving husband's children by *another* woman. My patience wore thin, I'll admit it. But Zeus and I have had some excellent marriage counseling sessions since then. We've aired our feelings and come to an understanding—especially after that last little incident."

"You mean when he sired Thalia?" I guessed, but

immediately wished I hadn't. As soon as I said the name of our friend, the half-blood daughter of Zeus, Hera's eyes turned toward me frostily.

"Percy Jackson, isn't it? One of Poseidon's . . . children." I got the feeling she was thinking of another word besides *children*. "As I recall, I voted to let you live at the winter solstice. I hope I voted correctly."

She turned back to Annabeth with a sunny smile. "At any rate, I certainly bear you no ill will, my girl. I appreciate the difficulty of your quest. Especially when you have troublemakers like Janus to deal with."

Annabeth lowered her gaze. "Why was he here? He was driving me crazy."

"Trying to," Hera agreed. "You must understand, the minor gods like Janus have always been frustrated by the small parts they play in the universe. Some, I fear, have little love for Olympus, and could easily be swayed to support the rise of my father."

"Your father?" I said. "Oh. Right."

I'd forgotten that Kronos was Hera's dad, too, along with being father to Zeus, Poseidon, and all the eldest Olympians. I guess that made Kronos my grandfather, but that thought was so weird I put it out of my mind.

"We must watch the minor gods," Hera said. "Janus. Hecate. Morpheus. They give lip service to Olympus, and yet—"

"That's where Dionysus went," I remembered. "He was checking on the minor gods."

"Indeed." Hera stared at the fading mosaics of the

Olympians. "You see, in times of trouble, even gods can lose faith. They start putting their trust in the wrong things, petty things. They stop looking at the big picture and start being selfish. But I'm the goddess of marriage, you see. I'm used to perseverance. You have to rise above the squabbling and chaos, and keep believing. You have to always keep your goals in mind."

"What are your goals?" Annabeth asked.

She smiled. "To keep my family, the Olympians, together, of course. At the moment, the best way I can do that is by helping you. Zeus does not allow me to interfere much, I am afraid. But once every century or so, for a quest I care deeply about, he allows me to grant a wish."

"A wish?"

"Before you ask it, let me give you some advice, which I can do for free. I know you seek Daedalus. His Labyrinth is as much a mystery to me as it is to you. But if you want to know his fate, I would visit my son Hephaestus at his forge. Daedalus was a great inventor, a mortal after Hephaestus's heart. There has never been a mortal Hephaestus admired more. If anyone would have kept up with Daedalus and could tell you his fate, it is Hephaestus."

"But how do we get there?" Annabeth asked. "That's my wish. I want a way to navigate the Labyrinth."

Hera looked disappointed. "So be it. You wish for something, however, that you have already been given."

"I don't understand."

"The means is already within your grasp." She looked at me. "Percy knows the answer."

"I do?"

"But that's not fair," Annabeth said. "You're not telling us what it is!"

Hera shook her head. "Getting something and having the wits to use it . . . those are two different things. I'm sure your mother Athena would agree."

The room rumbled like distant thunder. Hera stood. "That would be my cue. Zeus grows impatient. Think on what I have said, Annabeth. Seek out Hephaestus. You will have to pass through the ranch, I imagine. But keep going. And use all the means at your disposal, however common they may seem."

She pointed toward the two doors and they melted away, revealing twin corridors, open and dark. "One last thing, Annabeth. I have postponed your day of choice. I have not prevented it. Soon, as Janus said, you *will* have to make a decision. Farewell!"

She waved a hand and turned into white smoke. So did the food, just as Tyson chomped down on a sandwich that turned to mist in his mouth. The fountain trickled to a stop. The mosaic walls dimmed and turned grungy and faded again. The room was no longer any place you'd want to have a picnic.

Annabeth stamped her foot. "What sort of help was that? 'Here, have a sandwich. Make a wish. Oops, I can't help you!' Poof!"

"Poof," Tyson agreed sadly, looking at his empty plate.

"Well," Grover sighed, "she said Percy knows the answer. That's something."

They all looked at me.

"But I don't," I said. "I don't know what she was talking about."

Annabeth sighed. "All right. Then we'll just keep going."

"Which way?" I asked. I really wanted to ask what Hera had meant—about the choice Annabeth needed to make. But then Grover and Tyson both tensed. They stood up together, like they'd rehearsed it. "Left," they both said.

Annabeth frowned. "How can you be sure?"

"Because something is coming from the right," Grover said.

"Something big," Tyson agreed. "In a hurry."

"Left is sounding pretty good," I decided. Together we plunged into the dark corridor.

SEVEN

TYSON LEADS
A JAILBREAK

The good news: the left tunnel was straight with no side exits, twists, or turns. The bad news: it was a dead end. After sprinting a hundred yards, we ran into an enormous boulder that completely blocked our path. Behind us, the sounds of dragging footsteps and heavy breathing echoed down the corridor. Something—definitely not human—was on our tail.

"Tyson," I said, "can you—"

"Yes!" He slammed his shoulder against the rock so hard the whole tunnel shook. Dust trickled from the stone ceiling.

"Hurry!" Grover said. "Don't bring the roof down, but hurry!"

The boulder finally gave way with a horrible grinding noise. Tyson pushed it into a small room and we dashed through behind it.

"Close the entrance!" Annabeth said.

We all got on the other side of the boulder and pushed. Whatever was chasing us wailed in frustration as we heaved the rock back into place and sealed the corridor.

"We trapped it," I said.

"Or trapped ourselves," Grover said.

I turned. We were in a twenty-foot-square cement room, and the opposite wall was covered with metal bars. We'd tunneled straight into a cell.

"What in Hades?" Annabeth tugged on the bars. They didn't budge. Through the bars we could see rows of cells in a ring around a dark courtyard—at least three stories of metal doors and metal catwalks.

"A prison," I said. "Maybe Tyson can break—"

"Shh," said Grover. "Listen."

Somewhere above us, deep sobbing echoed through the building. There was another sound, too—a raspy voice muttering something that I couldn't make out. The words were strange, like rocks in a tumbler.

"What's that language?" I whispered.

Tyson's eye widened. "Can't be."

"What?" I asked.

He grabbed two bars on our cell door and bent them wide enough for even a Cyclops to slip through.

"Wait!" Grover called.

But Tyson wasn't about to wait. We ran after him. The prison was dark, only a few dim fluorescent lights flickering above.

"I know this place," Annabeth told me. "This is Alcatraz."

"You mean that island near San Francisco?"

She nodded. "My school took a field trip here. It's like a museum."

It didn't seem possible that we could've popped out of the Labyrinth on the other side of the country, but Annabeth had been living in San Francisco all year, keeping an eye on Mount Tamalpais just across the bay. She probably knew what she was talking about.

"Freeze," Grover warned.

But Tyson kept going. Grover grabbed his arm and pulled him back with all his strength. "Stop, Tyson!" he whispered. "Can't you see it?"

I looked where he was pointing, and my stomach did a somersault. On the second-floor balcony, across the courtyard, was a monster more horrible than anything I'd ever seen before.

It was sort of like a centaur, with a woman's body from the waist up. But instead of a horse's lower body, it had the body of a dragon—at least twenty feet long, black and scaly with enormous claws and a barbed tail. Her legs looked like they were tangled in vines, but then I realized they were sprouting snakes, hundreds of vipers darting around, constantly looking for something to bite. The woman's hair was also made of snakes, like Medusa's. Weirdest of all, around her waist, where the woman part met the dragon part, her skin bubbled and morphed, occasionally producing the heads of animals—a vicious wolf, a bear, a lion, as if she were wearing a belt of ever-changing creatures. I got the feeling I was looking at something half formed, a monster so old it was from the beginning of time, before shapes had been fully defined.

"It's her," Tyson whimpered.

"Get down!" Grover said.

We crouched in the shadows, but the monster wasn't paying us any attention. It seemed to be talking to someone inside a cell on the second floor. That's where the sobbing was coming from. The dragon woman said something in her weird rumbling language.

"What's she saying?" I muttered. "What's that language?"

"The tongue of the old times." Tyson shivered. "What Mother Earth spoke to Titans and . . . her other children. Before the gods."

"You understand it?" I asked. "Can you translate?"

Tyson closed his eyes and began to speak in a horrible, raspy woman's voice. "You will work for the master or suffer."

Annabeth shuddered. "I hate it when he does that."

Like all Cyclopes, Tyson had superhuman hearing and an uncanny ability to mimic voices. It was almost like he entered a trance when he spoke in other voices.

"I will not serve," Tyson said in a deep, wounded voice.

He switched to the monster's voice: "Then I shall enjoy your pain, Briares." Tyson faltered when he said that name. I'd never heard him break character when he was mimicking somebody, but he let out a strangled gulp. Then he continued in the monster's voice. "If you thought your first imprisonment was unbearable, you have yet to feel true torment. Think on this until I return."

The dragon lady tromped toward the stairwell, vipers hissing around her legs like grass skirts. She spread wings that I hadn't noticed before—huge bat wings she kept folded against her dragon back. She leaped off the catwalk and soared across the courtyard. We crouched lower in the shadows. A hot sulfurous wind blasted my face as the monster flew over. Then she disappeared around the corner.

"H-h-horrible," Grover said. "I've never smelled any monster that strong."

"Cyclopes' worst nightmare," Tyson murmured. "Kampê."

"Who?" I asked.

Tyson swallowed. "Every Cyclops knows about her. Stories about her scare us when we're babies. She was our jailer in the bad years."

Annabeth nodded. "I remember now. When the Titans ruled, they imprisoned Gaea and Ouranos's earlier children— the Cyclopes and the Hekatonkheires."

"The Heka-what?" I asked.

"The Hundred-Handed Ones," she said. "They called them that because . . . well, they had a hundred hands. They were elder brothers of the Cyclopes."

"Very powerful," Tyson said. "Wonderful! As tall as the sky. So strong they could break mountains!"

"Cool," I said. "Unless you're a mountain."

"Kampê was the jailer," he said. "She worked for Kronos. She kept our brothers locked up in Tartarus, tortured them always, until Zeus came. He killed Kampê and freed Cyclopes and Hundred-Handed Ones to help fight against the Titans in the big war."

"And now Kampê is back," I said.

"Bad," Tyson summed up.

"So who's in that cell?" I asked. "You said a name—"

"Briares!" Tyson perked up. "He is a Hundred-Handed One. They are as tall as the sky and—"

"Yeah," I said. "They break mountains."

I looked up at the cells above us, wondering how something as tall as the sky could fit in a tiny cell, and why he was crying.

"I guess we should check it out," Annabeth said, "before Kampê comes back."

As we approached the cell, the weeping got louder. When I first saw the creature inside, I wasn't sure what I was looking at. He was human-size and his skin was very pale, the color of milk. He wore a loincloth like a big diaper. His feet seemed too big for his body, with cracked dirty toenails, eight toes on each foot. But the top half of his body was the weird part. He made Janus look downright normal. His chest sprouted more arms than I could count, in rows, all around his body. The arms looked like normal arms, but there were so many of them, all tangled together, that his chest looked kind of like a forkful of spaghetti somebody had twirled together. Several of his hands were covering his face as he sobbed.

"Either the sky isn't as tall as it used to be," I muttered, "or he's short."

Tyson didn't pay any attention. He fell to his knees.

"Briares!" he called.

The sobbing stopped.

"Great Hundred-Handed One!" Tyson said. "Help us!"

Briares looked up. His face was long and sad, with a crooked nose and bad teeth. He had deep brown eyes—I mean completely brown with no whites or black pupils, like eyes formed out of clay.

"Run while you can, Cyclops," Briares said miserably. "I cannot even help myself."

"You are a Hundred-Handed One!" Tyson insisted. "You can do anything!"

Briares wiped his nose with five or six hands. Several others were fidgeting with little pieces of metal and wood from a broken bed, the way Tyson always played with spare parts. It was amazing to watch. The hands seemed to have a mind of their own. They built a toy boat out of wood, then disassembled it just as fast. Other hands were scratching at the cement floor for no apparent reason. Others were playing rock, paper, scissors. A few others were making ducky and doggie shadow puppets against the wall.

"I cannot," Briares moaned. "Kampê is back! The Titans will rise and throw us back into Tartarus."

"Put on your brave face!" Tyson said.

Immediately Briares's face morphed into something else. Same brown eyes, but otherwise totally different features. He had an upturned nose, arched eyebrows, and a weird smile, like he was trying to act brave. But then his face turned back to what it had been before.

"No good," he said. "My scared face keeps coming back."

"How did you do that?" I asked.

Annabeth elbowed me. "Don't be rude. The Hundred-Handed Ones have fifty different faces."

"Must make it hard to get a yearbook picture," I said.

Tyson was still entranced. "It will be okay, Briares! We will help you! Can I have your autograph?"

Briares sniffled. "Do you have one hundred pens?"

"Guys," Grover interrupted. "We have to get out of here. Kampê will be back. She'll sense us sooner or later."

"Break the bars," Annabeth said.

"Yes!" Tyson said, smiling proudly. "Briares can do it. He is very strong. Stronger than Cyclopes, even! Watch!"

Briares whimpered. A dozen of his hands started playing patty-cake, but none of them made any attempt to break the bars.

"If he's so strong," I said, "why is he stuck in jail?"

Annabeth ribbed me again. "He's terrified," she whispered. "Kampê imprisoned him in Tartarus for thousands of years. How would you feel?"

The Hundred-Handed One covered his face again.

"Briares?" Tyson asked. "What . . . what is wrong? Show us your great strength!"

"Tyson," Annabeth said, "I think you'd better break the bars."

Tyson's smile melted slowly.

"I will break the bars," he repeated. He grabbed the cell door and ripped it off its hinges like it was made of wet clay.

"Come on, Briares," Annabeth said. "Let's get you out of here."

She held out her hand. For a second, Briares's face morphed to a hopeful expression. Several of his arms reached out, but twice as many slapped them away.

"I cannot," he said. "She will punish me."

"It's all right," Annabeth promised. "You fought the Titans before, and you won, remember?"

"I remember the war." Briares's face morphed again—furrowed brow and a pouting mouth. His brooding face, I guess. "Lightning shook the world. We threw many rocks. The Titans and the monsters almost won. Now they are getting strong again. Kampê said so."

"Don't listen to her," I said. "Come on!"

He didn't move. I knew Grover was right. We didn't have much time before Kampê returned. But I couldn't just leave him here. Tyson would cry for weeks.

"One game of rock, paper, scissors," I blurted out. "If I win, you come with us. If I lose, we'll leave you in jail."

Annabeth looked at me like I was crazy.

Briares's face morphed to doubtful. "I always win rock, paper, scissors."

"Then let's do it!" I pounded my fist in my palm three times.

Briares did the same with all one hundred hands, which sounded like an army marching three steps forward. He came up with a whole avalanche of rocks, a classroom set of scissors, and enough paper to make a fleet of airplanes.

"I told you," he said sadly. "I always—" His face morphed to confusion. "What is that you made?"

"A gun," I told him, showing him my finger gun. It was

a trick Paul Blofis had pulled on me, but I wasn't going to tell him that. "A gun beats anything."

"That's not fair."

"I didn't say anything about fair. Kampê's not going to be fair if we hang around. She's going to blame you for ripping off the bars. Now come on!"

Briares sniffled. "Demigods are cheaters." But he slowly rose to his feet and followed us out of the cell.

I started to feel hopeful. All we had to do was get downstairs and find the Labyrinth entrance. But then Tyson froze.

On the ground floor right below, Kampê was snarling at us.

"The other way," I said.

We bolted down the catwalk. This time Briares was happy to follow us. In fact he sprinted out front, a hundred arms waving in panic.

Behind us, I heard the sound of giant wings as Kampê took to the air. She hissed and growled in her ancient language, but I didn't need a translation to know she was planning to kill us.

We scrambled down the stairs, through a corridor, and past a guard's station—out into another block of prison cells.

"Left," Annabeth said. "I remember this from the tour."

We burst outside and found ourselves in the prison yard, ringed by security towers and barbed wire. After being inside so long, the daylight almost blinded me. Tourists were milling around, taking pictures. The wind whipped cold off the bay. In the south, San Francisco gleamed all white and beautiful, but in the north, over Mount Tamalpais, huge storm clouds swirled. The whole sky seemed like a black top spinning from the mountain where Atlas was imprisoned, and where the Titan palace of Mount Othrys was rising anew. It was hard to believe the tourists couldn't see the supernatural storm brewing, but they didn't give any hint that anything was wrong.

"It's even worse," Annabeth said, gazing to the north. "The storms have been bad all year, but that—"

"Keep moving," Briares wailed. "She is behind us!"

We ran to the far end of the yard, as far from the cell-block as possible.

"Kampê's too big to get through the doors," I said hopefully.

Then the wall exploded.

Tourists screamed as Kampê appeared from the dust and rubble, her wings spread out as wide as the yard. She was holding two swords—long bronze scimitars that glowed with a weird greenish aura, boiling wisps of vapor that smelled sour and hot even across the yard.

"Poison!" Grover yelped. "Don't let those things touch you or . . ."

"Or we'll die?" I guessed.

"Well . . . after you shrivel slowly to dust, yes."

"Let's avoid the swords," I decided.

"Briares, fight!" Tyson urged. "Grow to full size!"

Instead, Briares looked like he was trying to shrink even smaller. He appeared to be wearing his *absolutely terrified* face.

Kampê thundered toward us on her dragon legs, hundreds of snakes slithering around her body.

For a second I thought about drawing Riptide and facing her, but my heart crawled into my throat. Then Annabeth said what I was thinking: "Run."

That was the end of the debate. There was no fighting this thing. We ran through the jail yard and out the gates of the prison, the monster right behind us. Mortals screamed and ran. Emergency sirens began to blare.

We hit the wharf just as a tour boat was unloading. The new group of visitors froze as they saw us charging toward them, followed by a mob of frightened tourists, followed by . . . I don't know what they saw through the Mist, but it could not have been good.

"The boat?" Grover asked.

"Too slow," Tyson said. "Back into the maze. Only chance."

"We need a diversion," Annabeth said.

Tyson ripped a metal lamppost out of the ground. "I will distract Kampê. You run ahead."

"I'll help you," I said.

"No," Tyson said. "You go. Poison will hurt Cyclopes. A lot of pain. But it won't kill."

"Are you sure?"

"Go, brother. I will meet you inside."

I hated the idea. I'd almost lost Tyson once before, and I didn't want to ever risk that again. But there was no time to argue, and I had no better idea. Annabeth, Grover, and I each took one of Briares's hands and dragged him toward the concession stands while Tyson bellowed, lowered his pole, and charged Kampê like a jousting knight.

She'd been glaring at Briares, but Tyson got her attention as soon as he nailed her in the chest with the pole, pushing her back into the wall. She shrieked and slashed with her swords, slicing the pole to shreds. Poison dripped in pools all around her, sizzling into the cement.

Tyson jumped back as Kampê's hair lashed and hissed, and the vipers around her legs darted their tongues in every direction. A lion popped out of the weird half-formed faces around her waist and roared.

As we sprinted for the cellblocks, the last thing I saw was Tyson picking up a Dippin' Dots stand and throwing it at Kampê. Ice cream and poison exploded everywhere, all the little snakes in Kampê's hair dotted with tutti-frutti. We dashed back into the jail yard.

"Can't make it," Briares huffed.

"Tyson is risking his life to help you!" I yelled at him. "You *will* make it."

As we reached the door of the cellblock, I heard an angry roar. I glanced back and saw Tyson running toward us at full speed, Kampê right behind him. She was plastered in ice cream and T-shirts. One of the bear heads on her waist was now wearing a pair of crooked plastic Alcatraz sunglasses.

"Hurry!" Annabeth said, like I needed to be told that.

We finally found the cell where we'd come in, but the back wall was completely smooth—no sign of a boulder or anything.

"Look for the mark!" Annabeth said.

"There!" Grover touched a tiny scratch, and it became a Greek Δ. The mark of Daedalus glowed blue, and the stone wall grinded open.

Too slowly. Tyson was coming through the cellblock, Kampê's swords lashing out behind him, slicing indiscriminately through cell bars and stone walls.

I pushed Briares inside the maze, then Annabeth and Grover.

"You can do it!" I told Tyson. But immediately I knew he couldn't. Kampê was gaining. She raised her swords. I needed a distraction—something big. I slapped my wristwatch and it spiraled into a bronze shield. Desperately, I threw it at the monster's face.

SMACK! The shield hit her in the face and she faltered just long enough for Tyson to dive past me into the maze. I was right behind him.

Kampê charged, but she was too late. The stone door closed and its magic sealed us in. I could feel the whole tunnel shake as Kampê pounded against it, roaring furiously. We didn't stick around to play knock, knock with her, though. We raced into the darkness, and for the first time (and the last) I was glad to be back in the Labyrinth.

EIGHT

ɔʈɔ

WE VISIT THE DEMON
DUDE RANCH

We finally stopped in a room full of waterfalls. The floor was one big pit, ringed by a slippery stone walkway. Around us, on all four walls, water tumbled from huge pipes. The water spilled down into the pit, and even when I shined a light, I couldn't see the bottom.

Briares slumped against the wall. He scooped up water in a dozen hands and washed his face. "This pit goes straight to Tartarus," he murmured. "I should jump in and save you trouble."

"Don't talk that way," Annabeth told him. "You can come back to camp with us. You can help us prepare. You know more about fighting Titans than anybody."

"I have nothing to offer," Briares said. "I have lost everything."

"What about your brothers?" Tyson asked. "The other two must still stand tall as mountains! We can take you to them."

Briares's expression morphed to something even sadder: his grieving face. "They are no more. They faded."

The waterfalls thundered. Tyson stared into the pit and blinked tears out of his eye.

"What exactly do you mean, *they faded?*" I asked. "I

thought monsters were immortal, like the gods."

"Percy," Grover said weakly, "even immortality has limits. Sometimes . . . sometimes monsters get forgotten and they lose their will to stay immortal."

Looking at Grover's face, I wondered if he was thinking of Pan. I remembered something Medusa had told us once: how her sisters, the other two gorgons, had passed on and left her alone. Then last year Apollo said something about the old god Helios disappearing and leaving him with the duties of the sun god. I'd never thought about it too much, but now, looking at Briares, I realized how terrible it would be to be so old—thousands and thousands of years old— and totally alone.

"I must go," Briares said.

"Kronos's army will invade camp," Tyson said. "We need help."

Briares hung his head. "I cannot, Cyclops."

"You are strong."

"Not anymore." Briares rose.

"Hey." I grabbed one of his arms and pulled him aside, where the roar of the water would hide our words. "Briares, we need you. In case you haven't noticed, Tyson believes in you. He risked his life for you."

I told him about everything—Luke's invasion plan, the Labyrinth entrance at camp, Daedalus's workshop, Kronos's golden coffin.

Briares just shook his head. "I cannot, demigod. I do not have a finger gun to win this game." To prove his point, he made one hundred finger guns.

"Maybe that's why monsters fade," I said. "Maybe it's not about what the mortals believe. Maybe it's because *you* give up on yourself."

His pure brown eyes regarded me. His face morphed into an expression I recognized—shame. Then he turned and trudged off down the corridor until he was lost in the shadows.

Tyson sobbed.

"It's okay." Grover hesitantly patted his shoulder, which must've taken all his courage.

Tyson sneezed. "It is not okay, goat boy. He was my hero."

I wanted to make him feel better, but I wasn't sure what to say.

Finally, Annabeth stood and shouldered her backpack. "Come on, guys. This pit is making me nervous. Let's find a better place to camp for the night."

We settled in a corridor made of huge marble blocks. It looked like it could've been part of a Greek tomb, with bronze torch holders fastened to the walls. It had to be an older part of the maze, and Annabeth decided this was a good sign.

"We must be close to Daedalus's workshop," she said. "Get some rest, everybody. We'll keep going in the morning."

"How do we know when it's morning?" Grover asked.

"Just rest," she insisted.

Grover didn't need to be told twice. He pulled a heap of

straw out of his pack, ate some of it, made a pillow out of the rest, and was snoring in no time. Tyson took longer getting to sleep. He tinkered with some metal scraps from his building kit for a while, but whatever he was making, he wasn't happy with it. He kept disassembling the pieces.

"I'm sorry I lost the shield," I told him. "You worked so hard to repair it."

Tyson looked up. His eye was bloodshot from crying. "Do not worry, brother. You saved me. You wouldn't have had to if Briares had helped."

"He was just scared," I said. "I'm sure he'll get over it."

"He is not strong," Tyson said. "He is not important anymore."

He heaved a big sad sigh, then closed his eye. The metal pieces fell out of his hand, still unassembled, and Tyson began to snore.

I tried to fall asleep myself, but I couldn't. Something about getting chased by a large dragon lady with poison swords made it real hard to relax. I picked up my bedroll and dragged it over to where Annabeth was sitting, keeping watch.

I sat down next to her.

"You should sleep," she said.

"Can't. You doing all right?"

"Sure. First day leading the quest. Just great."

"We'll get there," I said. "We'll find the workshop before Luke does."

She brushed her hair out of her face. She had a smudge of dirt on her chin, and I imagined what she must've looked like when she was little, wandering around the country with Thalia and Luke. Once she'd saved them from the mansion of the evil Cyclops when she was only seven. Even when she looked scared, like now, I knew she had a lot of guts.

"I just wish the quest was *logical*," she complained. "I mean, we're traveling but we have no idea where we'll end up. How can you walk from New York to California in a day?"

"Space isn't the same in the maze."

"I know, I know. It's just . . ." She looked at me hesitantly. "Percy, I was kidding myself. All that planning and reading, I don't have a clue where we're going."

"You're doing great. Besides, we *never* know what we're doing. It always works out. Remember Circe's island?"

She snorted. "You made a cute guinea pig."

"And Waterland, how you got us thrown off that ride?"

"*I* got us thrown off? That was totally your fault!"

"See? It'll be fine."

She smiled, which I was glad to see, but the smile faded quickly.

"Percy, what did Hera mean when she said you knew the way to get through the maze?"

"I don't know," I admitted. "Honestly."

"You'd tell me if you did?"

"Sure. Maybe . . ."

"Maybe what?"

"Maybe if you told me the last line of the prophecy, it would help."

Annabeth shivered. "Not here. Not in the dark."

"What about the choice Janus mentioned? Hera said—"

"Stop," Annabeth snapped. Then she took a shaky breath. "I'm sorry, Percy. I'm just stressed. But I don't . . . I've got to think about it."

We sat in silence, listening to strange creaks and groans in the maze, the echo of stones grinding together as tunnels changed, grew, and expanded. The dark made me think about the visions I'd seen of Nico di Angelo, and suddenly I realized something.

"Nico is down here somewhere," I said. "That's how he disappeared from camp. He found the Labyrinth. Then he found a path that led down even farther—to the Underworld. But now he's back in the maze. He's coming after me."

Annabeth was quiet for a long time. "Percy, I hope you're wrong. But if you're right . . ." She stared at the flashlight beam, casting a dim circle on the stone wall. I had a feeling she was thinking about her prophecy. I'd never seen her look more tired.

"How about I take first watch?" I said. "I'll wake you if anything happens."

Annabeth looked like she wanted to protest, but she just nodded, slumped onto her bedroll, and closed her eyes.

When it was my turn to sleep, I dreamed I was back in the old man's Labyrinth prison.

It looked more like a workshop now. Tables were littered with measuring instruments. A forge burned red hot in the corner. The boy I'd seen in the last dream was stoking the bellows, except he was taller now, almost my age. A weird funnel device was attached to the forge's chimney, trapping the smoke and heat and channeling it through a pipe into the floor, next to a big bronze manhole cover.

It was daytime. The sky above was blue, but the walls of the maze cast deep shadows across the workshop. After being in tunnels so long, I found it weird that part of the Labyrinth could be open to the sky. Somehow that made the maze seem like an even crueler place.

The old man looked sickly. He was terribly thin, his hands raw and red from working. White hair covered his eyes, and his tunic was smudged with grease. He was bent over a table, working on some kind of long metal patch-work—like a swath of chain mail. He picked up a delicate curl of bronze and fitted it into place.

"Done," he announced. "It's done."

He picked up his project. It was so beautiful, my heart leaped—metal wings constructed from thousands of inter-locking bronze feathers. There were two sets. One still lay on the table. Daedalus stretched the frame, and the wings expanded to twenty feet. Part of me knew it could never fly. It was too heavy, and there'd be no way to get off the ground. But the craftsmanship was amazing. Metal feathers caught the light and flashed thirty different shades of gold.

The boy left the bellows and ran over to see. He grinned, despite the fact that he was grimy and sweaty. "Father, you're a genius!"

The old man smiled. "Tell me something I don't know,

Icarus. Now hurry. It will take at least an hour to attach them. Come."

"You first," Icarus said.

The old man protested, but Icarus insisted. "You made them, Father. You should get the honor of wearing them first."

The boy attached a leather harness to his father's chest, like climbing gear, with straps that ran from his shoulders to his wrists. Then he began fastening on the wings, using a metal canister that looked like an enormous hot-glue gun.

"The wax compound should hold for several hours," Daedalus said nervously as his son worked. "But we must let it set first. And we would do well to avoid flying too high or too low. The sea would wet the wax seals—"

"And the sun's heat would loosen them," the boy finished. "Yes, Father. We've been through this a million times!"

"One cannot be too careful."

"I have complete faith in your inventions, Father! No one has ever been as smart as you."

The old man's eyes shone. It was obvious he loved his son more than anything in the world. "Now I will do your wings, and give mine a chance to set properly. Come!"

It was slow going. The old man's hands fumbled with the straps. He had a hard time keeping the wings in position while he sealed them. His own metal wings seemed to weigh him down, getting in his way while he tried to work.

"Too slow," the old man muttered. "I am too slow."

"Take your time, Father," the boy said. "The guards aren't due until—"

BOOM!

The workshop doors shuddered. Daedalus had barred them from the inside with a wooden brace, but still they shook on their hinges.

"Hurry!" Icarus said.

BOOM! BOOM!

Something heavy was slamming into the doors. The brace held, but a crack appeared in the left door.

Daedalus worked furiously. A drop of hot wax spilled onto Icarus's shoulder. The boy winced but did not cry out. When his left wing was sealed to the straps, Daedalus began working on the right.

"We must have more time," Daedalus murmured. "They are too early! We need more time for the seal to hold."

"It'll be fine," Icarus said, as his father finished the right wing. "Help me with the manhole—"

CRASH! The doors splintered and the head of a bronze battering ram emerged through the breach. Axes cleared the debris, and two armed guards entered the room, followed by the king with the golden crown and the spear-shaped beard.

"Well, well," the king said with a cruel smile. "Going somewhere?"

Daedalus and his son froze, their metal wings glimmering on their backs.

"We're leaving, Minos," the old man said.

King Minos chuckled. "I was curious to see how far you'd get on this little project before I dashed your hopes. I must say I'm impressed."

The king admired their wings. "You look like metal chickens," he decided. "Perhaps we should pluck you and make a soup."

The guards laughed stupidly.

"Metal chickens," one repeated. "Soup."

"Shut up," the king said. Then he turned again to Daedalus. "You let my daughter escape, old man. You drove my wife to madness. You killed my monster and made me the laughingstock of the Mediterranean. You will never escape me!"

Icarus grabbed the wax gun and sprayed it at the king, who stepped back in surprise. The guards rushed forward, but each got a stream of hot wax in his face.

"The vent!" Icarus yelled to his father.

"Get them!" King Minos raged.

Together, the old man and his son pried open the man-hole cover, and a column of hot air blasted out of the ground. The king watched, incredulous, as the inventor and son shot into the sky on their bronze wings, carried by the updraft.

"Shoot them!" the king yelled, but his guards had brought no bows. One threw his sword in desperation, but Daedalus and Icarus were already out of reach. They wheeled above the maze and the king's palace, then zoomed across the city of Knossos and out past the rocky shores of Crete.

Icarus laughed. "Free, Father! You did it."

The boy spread his wings to their full limit and soared away on the wind.

"Wait!" Daedalus called. "Be careful!"

But Icarus was already out over the open sea, heading north and delighting in their good luck. He soared up and scared an eagle out of its flight path, then plummeted toward the sea like he was born to fly, pulling out of a nose-dive at the last second. His sandals skimmed the waves.

"Stop that!" Daedalus called. But the wind carried his voice away. His son was drunk on his own freedom.

The old man struggled to catch up, gliding clumsily after his son.

They were miles from Crete, over deep sea, when Icarus looked back and saw his father's worried expression.

Icarus smiled. "Don't worry, Father! You're a genius! I trust your handiwork—"

The first metal feather shook loose from his wings and fluttered away. Then another. Icarus wobbled in midair. Suddenly he was shedding bronze feathers, which twirled away from him like a flock of frightened birds.

"Icarus!" his father cried. "Glide! Extend the wings. Stay as still as possible!"

But Icarus flapped his arms, desperately trying to reassert control.

The left wing went first—ripping away from the straps.

"Father!" Icarus cried. And then he fell, the wings stripped away until he was just a boy in a climbing harness and a white tunic, his arms extended in a useless attempt to glide.

I woke with a start, feeling like I was falling. The corridor was dark. In the constant moaning of the Labyrinth, I thought I could hear the anguished cry of Daedalus calling his son's name, as Icarus, his only joy, plummeted toward the sea, three hundred feet below.

There was no morning in the maze, but once everyone woke up and had a fabulous breakfast of granola bars and juice boxes, we kept traveling. I didn't mention my dream. Something about it had really freaked me out, and I didn't think the others needed to know that.

The old stone tunnels changed to dirt with cedar beams, like a gold mine or something. Annabeth started getting agitated.

"This isn't right," she said. "It should still be stone."

We came to a cave where stalactites hung low from the ceiling. In the center of the dirt floor was a rectangular pit, like a grave.

Grover shivered. "It smells like the Underworld in here."

Then I saw something glinting at the edge of the pit—a foil wrapper. I shined my flashlight into the hole and saw a half-chewed cheeseburger floating in brown carbonated muck.

"Nico," I said. "He was summoning the dead again."

Tyson whimpered. "Ghosts were here. I don't like ghosts."

"We've got to find him." I don't know why, but standing at the edge of that pit gave me a sense of urgency. Nico was close. I could feel it. I couldn't let him wander around down here, alone except for the dead. I started to run.

"Percy!" Annabeth called.

I ducked into a tunnel and saw light up ahead. By the time Annabeth, Tyson, and Grover caught up with me, I was staring at daylight streaming through a set of bars above my head. We were under a steel grate made out of metal pipes. I could see trees and blue sky.

"Where are we?" I wondered.

Then a shadow fell across the grate and a cow stared down at me. It looked like a normal cow except it was a weird color—bright red, like a cherry. I didn't know cows came in that color.

The cow mooed, put one hoof tentatively on the bars, then backed away.

"It's a cattle guard," Grover said.

"A what?" I asked.

"They put them at the gates of ranches so cows can't get out. They can't walk on them."

"How do you know that?"

Grover huffed indignantly. "Believe me, if *you* had hooves, you'd know about cattle guards. They're annoying!"

I turned to Annabeth. "Didn't Hera say something about a ranch? We need to check it out. Nico might be up there."

She hesitated. "All right. But how do we get out?"

Tyson solved that problem by hitting the cattle guard with both hands. It popped off and went flying out of sight. We heard a *CLANG!* and a startled *Moo!* Tyson blushed.

"Sorry, cow!" he called.

Then he gave us a boost out of the tunnel.

We were on a ranch, all right. Rolling hills stretched to the horizon, dotted with oak trees and cactuses and boulders. A barbed wire fence ran from the gate in either direction. Cherry-colored cows roamed around, grazing on clumps of grass.

"Red cattle," Annabeth said. "The cattle of the sun."

"What?" I asked.

"They're sacred to Apollo."

"Holy cows?"

"Exactly. But what are they doing—"

"Wait," Grover said. "Listen."

At first everything seemed quiet . . . but then I heard it: the distant baying of dogs. The sound got louder. Then the underbrush rustled, and two dogs broke through. Except it wasn't two dogs. It was *one* dog with two heads. It looked like a greyhound, long and snaky and sleek brown, but its neck V'd into two heads, both of them snapping and snarling and generally not very glad to see us.

"Bad Janus dog!" Tyson cried.

"*Arf!*" Grover told it, and raised a hand in greeting.

The two-headed dog bared its teeth. I guess it wasn't impressed that Grover could speak animal. Then its master lumbered out of the woods, and I realized the dog was the least of our problems.

He was a huge guy with stark white hair, a straw cowboy hat, and a braided white beard—kind of like Father Time, if Father Time went redneck and got totally jacked. He was wearing jeans, a DON'T MESS WITH TEXAS T-shirt, and a denim jacket with the sleeves ripped off so you could see his muscles. On his right bicep was a crossed-swords tattoo. He held a wooden club about the size of a nuclear warhead, with six-inch spikes bristling at the business end.

"Heel, Orthus," he told the dog.

The dog growled at us once more, just to make his feelings clear, then circled back to his master's feet. The man looked us up and down, keeping his club ready.

"What've we got here?" he asked. "Cattle rustlers?"

"Just travelers," Annabeth said. "We're on a quest."

The man's eye twitched. "Half-bloods, eh?"

I started to say, "How did you know—"

Annabeth put her hand on my arm. "I'm Annabeth, daughter of Athena. This is Percy, son of Poseidon. Grover the satyr. Tyson the—"

"Cyclops," the man finished. "Yes, I can see that." He glowered at me. "And I know half-bloods because I *am* one, sonny. I'm Eurytion, the cowherd for this here ranch. Son of Ares. You came through the Labyrinth like the other one, I reckon."

"The other one?" I asked. "You mean Nico di Angelo?"

"We get a load of visitors from the Labyrinth," Eurytion said darkly. "Not many ever leave."

"Wow," I said. "I feel welcome."

The cowherd glanced behind him like someone was watching. Then he lowered his voice. "I'm only going to say this once, demigods. Get back in the maze now. Before it's too late."

"We're not leaving," Annabeth insisted. "Not until we see this other demigod. Please."

Eurytion grunted. "Then you leave me no choice, missy. I've got to take you to see the boss."

I didn't feel like we were hostages or anything. Eurytion walked alongside us with his club across his shoulder. Orthus the two-headed dog growled a lot and sniffed at Grover's legs and shot into the bushes once in a while to chase animals, but Eurytion kept him more or less under control.

We walked down a dirt path that seemed to go on forever. It must've been close to a hundred degrees, which was a shock after San Francisco. Heat shimmered off the ground. Insects buzzed in the trees. Before we'd gone very far, I was sweating like crazy. Flies swarmed us. Every so often we'd see a pen full of red cows or even stranger animals. Once we passed a corral where the fence was coated in asbestos. Inside, a herd of fire-breathing horses milled around. The hay in their feeding trough was on fire. The ground smoked around their feet, but the horses seemed tame enough. One big stallion looked at me and whinnied, columns of red flame billowing out his nostrils. I wondered if it hurt his sinuses.

"What are *they* for?" I asked.

Eurytion scowled. "We raise animals for lots of clients. Apollo, Diomedes, and . . . others."

"Like who?"

"No more questions."

Finally we came out of the woods. Perched on a hill above us was a big ranch house—all white stone and wood and big windows.

"It looks like a Frank Lloyd Wright!" Annabeth said.

I guess she was talking about some architectural thing. To me it just looked like the kind of place where a few demigods could get into serious trouble. We hiked up the hill.

"Don't break the rules," Eurytion warned as we walked up the steps to the front porch. "No fighting. No drawing weapons. And don't make any comments about the boss's appearance."

"Why?" I asked. "What does he look like?"

Before Eurytion could reply, a new voice said, "Welcome to the Triple G Ranch."

The man on the porch had a normal head, which was a relief. His face was weathered and brown from years in the sun. He had slick black hair and a black pencil moustache like villains have in old movies. He smiled at us, but the smile wasn't friendly; more amused, like *Oh boy, more people to torture!*

I didn't ponder that very long, though, because then I noticed his body . . . or bodies. He had three of them. Now, you'd think I would've gotten used to weird anatomy after Janus and Briares, but this guy was three complete people. His neck connected to the middle chest like normal, but he had two more chests, one to either side, connected at the shoulders, with a few inches in between. His left arm grew out of his left chest, and the same on the right, so he had two arms, but four armpits, if that makes any sense. The chests all connected into one enormous torso, with two regular but very beefy legs, and he wore the most oversized pair of Levis I'd ever seen. His chests each wore a different color Western shirt—green, yellow, red, like a stoplight. I wondered how he dressed the middle chest, since it had no arms.

The cowherd Eurytion nudged me. "Say hello to Mr. Geryon."

"Hi," I said. "Nice chests—uh, ranch! Nice ranch you have."

Before the three-bodied man could respond, Nico di Angelo came out of the glass doors onto the porch. "Geryon, I won't wait for—"

He froze when he saw us. Then he drew his sword. The blade was just like I'd seen in my dream: short, sharp, and dark as midnight.

Geryon snarled when he saw it. "Put that away, Mr. di Angelo. I ain't gonna have my guests killin' each other."

"But that's—"

"Percy Jackson," Geryon supplied. "Annabeth Chase. And a couple of their monster friends. Yes, I know."

"Monster friends?" Grover said indignantly.

"That man is wearing three shirts," Tyson said, like he was just realizing this.

"They let my sister die!" Nico's voice trembled with rage. "They're here to kill me!"

"Nico, we're not here to kill you." I raised my hands. "What happened to Bianca was—"

"Don't speak her name! You're not worthy to even talk about her!"

"Wait a minute." Annabeth pointed at Geryon. "How do you know our names?"

The three-bodied man winked. "I make it my business to keep informed, darlin'. Everybody pops into the ranch from time to time. Everyone needs something from ole Geryon. Now, Mr. di Angelo, put that ugly sword away before I have Eurytion take it from you."

Eurytion sighed, but he hefted his spiked club. At his feet, Orthus growled.

Nico hesitated. He looked thinner and paler than he had in the Iris-messages. I wondered if he'd eaten in the last week. His black clothes were dusty from traveling in the Labyrinth, and his dark eyes were full of hate. He was too young to look so angry. I still remembered him as the cheerful little kid who played with Mythomagic cards.

Reluctantly, he sheathed his sword. "If you come near me, Percy, I'll summon help. You don't want to meet my helpers, I promise."

"I believe you," I said.

Geryon patted Nico's shoulder. "There, we've all made nice. Now come along, folks. I want to give you a tour of the ranch."

Geryon had a trolley thing—like one of those kiddie trains that take you around zoos. It was painted black and white in a cowhide pattern. The driver's car had a set of longhorns stuck to the hood, and the horn sounded like a cowbell. I figured maybe this was how he tortured people. He embarrassed them to death riding around in the moo-mobile.

Nico sat in the very back, probably so he could keep an eye on us. Eurytion crawled in next to him with his spiked club and pulled his cowboy hat over his eyes like he was going to take a nap. Orthus jumped in the front seat next to Geryon and began barking happily in two-part harmony.

Annabeth, Tyson, Grover, and I took the middle two cars.

"We have a huge operation!" Geryon boasted as the moo-mobile lurched forward. "Horses and cattle mostly, but all sorts of exotic varieties, too."

We came over a hill, and Annabeth gasped. "Hippalektryons? I thought they were extinct!"

At the bottom of the hill was a fenced-in pasture with a dozen of the weirdest animals I'd ever seen. Each had the front half of a horse and the back half of a rooster. Their rear feet were huge yellow claws. They had feathery tails and red wings. As I watched, two of them got in a fight over a pile of seed. They reared up on their back legs and whinnied and flapped their wings at each other until the smaller one galloped away, its rear bird legs putting a little hop in its step.

"Rooster ponies," Tyson said in amazement. "Do they lay eggs?"

"Once a year!" Geryon grinned in the rearview mirror. "Very much in demand for omelettes!"

"That's horrible!" Annabeth said. "They must be an endangered species!"

Geryon waved his hand. "Gold is gold, darling. And you haven't tasted the omelettes."

"That's not right," Grover murmured, but Geryon just kept narrating the tour.

"Now, over here," he said, "we have our fire-breathing horses, which you may have seen on your way in. They're bred for war, naturally."

"What war?" I asked.

Geryon grinned slyly. "Oh, whichever one comes along. And over yonder, of course, are our prize red cows."

Sure enough, hundreds of the cherry-colored cattle were grazing the side of a hill.

"So many," Grover said.

"Yes, well, Apollo is too busy to see to them," Geryon explained, "so he subcontracts to us. We breed them vigorously because there's such a demand."

"For what?" I asked.

Geryon raised an eyebrow. "Meat, of course! Armies have to eat."

"You kill the sacred cows of the sun god for hamburger meat?" Grover said. "That's against the ancient laws!"

"Oh, don't get so worked up, satyr. They're just animals."

"Just animals!"

"Yes, and if Apollo cared, I'm sure he would tell us."

"If he knew," I muttered.

Nico sat forward. "I don't care about any of this, Geryon. We had business to discuss, and this wasn't it!"

"All in good time, Mr. di Angelo. Look over here; some of my exotic game."

The next field was ringed in barbed wire. The whole area was crawling with giant scorpions.

"Triple G Ranch," I said, suddenly remembering. "Your mark was on the crates at camp. Quintus got his scorpions from you."

"Quintus . . ." Geryon mused. "Short gray hair, muscular, swordsman?"

"Yeah."

"Never heard of him," Geryon said. "Now, over here are my prize stables! You must see them."

I didn't need to see them, because as soon as we got within three hundred yards I started to smell them. Near the banks of a green river was a horse corral the size of a football field. Stables lined one side of it. About a hundred horses were milling around in the muck—and when I say muck, I mean horse poop. It was the most disgusting thing I'd ever seen, like a poop blizzard had come through and dumped four feet of the stuff overnight. The horses were really gross from wading through it, and the stables were just as bad. It reeked like you would not believe—worse than the garbage boats on the East River.

Even Nico gagged. "What *is* that?"

"My stables!" Geryon said. "Well, actually they belong to Aegeas, but we watch over them for a small monthly fee. Aren't they lovely?"

"They're disgusting!" Annabeth said.

"Lots of poop," Tyson observed.

"How can you keep animals like that?" Grover cried.

"Y'all gettin' on my nerves," Geryon said. "These are

flesh-eating horses, see? They like these conditions."

"Plus, you're too cheap to have them cleaned," Eurytion mumbled from under his hat.

"Quiet!" Geryon snapped. "All right, perhaps the stables are a bit challenging to clean. Perhaps they do make me nauseous when the wind blows the wrong way. But so what? My clients still pay me well."

"What clients?" I demanded.

"Oh, you'd be surprised how many people will pay for a flesh-eating horse. They make great garbage disposals. Wonderful way to terrify your enemies. Great at birthday parties! We rent them out all the time."

"You're a monster," Annabeth decided.

Geryon stopped the moo-mobile and turned to look at her. "What gave it away? Was it the three bodies?"

"You have to let these animals go," Grover said. "It's not right!"

"And the clients you keep talking about," Annabeth said. "You work for Kronos, don't you? You're supplying his army with horses, food, whatever they need."

Geryon shrugged, which was very weird since he had three sets of shoulders. It looked like he was doing the wave all by himself. "I work for anyone with gold, young lady. I'm a businessman. And I sell them anything I have to offer."

He climbed out of the moo-mobile and strolled toward the stables as if enjoying the fresh air. It would've been a nice view, with the river and the trees and hills and all, except for the quagmire of horse muck.

Nico got out of the back car and stormed over to

Geryon. The cowherd Eurytion wasn't as sleepy as he looked. He hefted his club and walked after Nico.

"I came here for business, Geryon," Nico said. "And you haven't answered me."

"Mmm." Geryon examined a cactus. His left arm reached over and scratched his middle chest. "Yes, you'll get a deal, all right."

"My ghost told me you could help. He said you could guide us to the soul we need."

"Wait a second," I said. "I thought *I* was the soul you wanted."

Nico looked at me like I was crazy. "You? Why would I want you? Bianca's soul is worth a thousand of yours! Now, can you help me, Geryon, or not?"

"Oh, I imagine I could," the rancher said. "Your ghost friend, by the way, where is he?"

Nico looked uneasy. "He can't form in broad daylight. It's hard for him. But he's around somewhere."

Geryon smiled. "I'm sure. Minos likes to disappear when things get . . . difficult."

"Minos?" I remembered the man I'd seen in my dreams, with the golden crown, the pointed beard, and the cruel eyes. "You mean that evil king? *That's* the ghost who's been giving you advice?"

"It's none of your business, Percy!" Nico turned back to Geryon. "And what do you mean about things getting difficult?"

The three-bodied man sighed. "Well you see, Nico— can I call you Nico?"

"No."

"You see, Nico, Luke Castellan is offering very good money for half-bloods. Especially powerful half-bloods. And I'm sure when he learns your little secret, who you really are, he'll pay very, very well indeed."

Nico drew his sword, but Eurytion knocked it out of his hand. Before I could get up, Orthus pounced on my chest and growled, his faces an inch away from mine.

"I would stay in the car, all of you," Geryon warned. "Or Orthus will tear Mr. Jackson's throat out. Now, Eurytion, if would be so kind, secure Nico."

The cowherd spit into the grass. "Do I have to?"

"Yes, you fool!"

Eurytion looked bored, but he wrapped one huge arm around Nico and lifted him up like a wrestler.

"Pick up the sword, too," Geryon said with distaste. "There's nothing I hate worse than Stygian iron."

Eurytion picked up the sword, careful not to touch the blade.

"Now," Geryon said cheerfully, "we've had the tour. Let's go back to the lodge, have some lunch, and send an Iris-message to our friends in the Titan army."

"You fiend!" Annabeth cried.

Geryon smiled at her. "Don't worry, my dear. Once I've delivered Mr. di Angelo, you and your party can go. I don't interfere with quests. Besides, I've been paid well to give you safe passage, which does not, I'm afraid, include Mr. di Angelo."

"Paid by whom?" Annabeth said. "What do you mean?"

"Never you mind, darlin'. Let's be off, shall we?"

"Wait!" I said, and Orthus growled. I stayed perfectly still so he wouldn't tear my throat out. "Geryon, you said you're a businessman. Make me a deal."

Geryon narrowed his eyes. "What sort of deal? Do you have gold?"

"I've got something better. Barter."

"But Mr. Jackson, you've got nothing."

"You could have him clean the stables," Eurytion suggested innocently.

"I'll do it!" I said. "If I fail, you get all of us. Trade us all to Luke for gold."

"Assuming the horses don't eat you," Geryon observed.

"Either way, you get my friends," I said. "But if I succeed, you've got to let all of us go, including Nico."

"No!" Nico screamed. "Don't do me any favors, Percy. I don't want your help!"

Geryon chuckled. "Percy Jackson, those stables haven't been cleaned in a thousand years . . . though it's true I might be able to sell more stable space if all that poop was cleared away."

"So what have you got to lose?"

The rancher hesitated. "All right, I'll accept your offer, but you have to get it done by sunset. If you fail, your friends get sold, and I get rich."

"Deal."

He nodded. "I'm going to take your friends with me, back to the lodge. We'll wait for you there."

Eurytion gave me a funny look. It might have been

sympathy. He whistled, and the dog jumped off me and onto Annabeth's lap. She yelped. I knew Tyson and Grover would never try anything as long as Annabeth was a hostage.

I got out of the car and locked eyes with her.

"I hope you know what you're doing," she said quietly.

"I hope so, too."

Geryon got behind the driver's wheel. Eurytion hauled Nico into the backseat.

"Sunset," Geryon reminded me. "No later."

He laughed at me once more, sounded his cowbell horn, and the moo-mobile rumbled off down the trail.

I SCOOP POOP

I lost hope when I saw the horses' teeth.

As I got closer to the fence I held my shirt over my nose to block the smell. One stallion waded through the muck and whinnied angrily at me. He bared his teeth, which were pointed like a bear's.

I tried to talk to him in my mind. I can do that with most horses.

Hi, I told him. *I'm going to clean your stables. Won't that be great?*

Yes! The horse said. *Come inside! Eat you! Tasty half-blood!*

But I'm Poseidon's son, I protested. *He created horses.*

Usually this gets me VIP treatment in the equestrian world, but not this time.

Yes! The horse agreed enthusiastically. *Poseidon can come in, too! We will eat you both! Seafood!*

Seafood! The other horses chimed in as they waded through the field. Flies were buzzing everywhere, and the heat of the day didn't make the smell any better. I'd had some idea that I could do this challenge, because I remembered how Hercules had done it. He'd channeled a river into the stables and cleaned them out that way. I figured I could maybe control the water. But if I couldn't get close to the horses without getting eaten, that was a problem. And the river was downhill from the stables, a lot farther away than I'd realized, almost half a mile. The problem of the poop looked a lot bigger up close. I picked up a rusted shovel and experimentally scooped some away from the fence line. Great. Only four billion shovelfuls to go.

The sun was already sinking. I had a few hours at best. I decided the river was my only hope. At least it would be easier to think at the riverside than it was here. I set off downhill.

When I got to the river, I found a girl waiting for me. She was wearing jeans and a green T-shirt and her long brown hair was braided with river grass. She had a stern look on her face. Her arms were crossed.

"Oh no you don't," she said.

I stared at her. "Are you a naiad?"

She rolled her eyes. "Of course!"

"But you speak English. And you're out of the water."

"What, you don't think we can act human if we want to?"

I'd never thought about it. I kind of felt stupid, though, because I'd seen plenty of naiads at camp, and they'd never done much more than giggle and wave at me from the bottom of the canoe lake.

"Look," I said, "I just came to ask—"

"I know who you are," she said. "And I know what you want. And the answer is no! I'm not to going have my river used again to clean that filthy stable."

"But—"

"Oh, save it, sea boy. You ocean-god types always think

you're soooo much more important than some little river, don't you? Well let me tell you, *this* naiad is not going to be pushed around just because your daddy is Poseidon. This is freshwater territory, mister. The last guy who asked me this favor—oh, he was way better-looking than you, by the way—he convinced me, and that was the worst mistake I've ever made! Do you have any idea what all that horse manure does to my ecosystem? Do I look like a sewage treatment plant to you? My fish will die. I'll *never* get the muck out of my plants. I'll be sick for years. NO THANK YOU!"

The way she talked reminded me of my mortal friend, Rachel Elizabeth Dare—kind of like she was punching me with words. I couldn't blame the naiad. Now that I thought about it, I'd be pretty mad if somebody dumped four million pounds of manure in my home. But still . . .

"My friends are in danger," I told her.

"Well, that's too bad! But it's not my problem. And you're not going to ruin my river."

She looked like she was ready for a fight. Her fists were balled, but I thought I heard a little quiver in her voice. Suddenly I realized that despite her angry attitude, she was afraid of me. She probably thought I was going to fight her for control of the river, and she was worried she would lose.

The thought made me sad. I felt like a bully, a son of Poseidon throwing his weight around.

I sat down on a tree stump. "Okay, you win."

The naiad looked surprised. "Really?"

"I'm not going to fight you. It's your river."

She relaxed her shoulders. "Oh. Oh, good. I mean— good thing for you!"

"But my friends and I are going to get sold to the Titans if I don't clean those stables by sunset. And I don't know how."

The river gurgled along cheerfully. A snake slid through the water and ducked its head under. Finally the naiad sighed.

"I'll tell you a secret, son of the sea god. Scoop up some dirt."

"What?"

"You heard me."

I crouched down and scooped up a handful of Texas dirt. It was dry and black and spotted with tiny clumps of white rock . . . No, something besides rock.

"Those are shells," the naiad said. "Petrified seashells. Millions of years ago, even before the time of the gods, when only Gaea and Ouranos reigned, this land was under water. It was part of the sea."

Suddenly I saw what she meant. There were little pieces of ancient sea urchins in my hand, mollusk shells. Even the limestone rocks had impressions of seashells embedded in them.

"Okay," I said. "What good does that do me?"

"You're not so different from me, demigod. Even when I'm out of the water, the water is within me. It is my life source." She stepped back, put her feet in the river, and smiled. "I hope you find a way to rescue your friends."

And with that she turned to liquid and melted into the river.

* * *

The sun was touching the hills when I got back to the stables. Somebody must've come by and fed the horses, because they were tearing into huge animal carcasses. I couldn't tell what kind of animal, and I really didn't want to know. If it was possible for the stables to get more disgusting, fifty horses tearing into raw meat did it.

Seafood! one thought when he saw me. *Come in! We're still hungry.*

What was I supposed to do? I couldn't use the river. And the fact that this place had been under water a million years ago didn't exactly help me now. I looked at the little calcified seashell in my palm, then at the huge mountain of dung.

Frustrated, I threw the shell into the poop. I was about to turn my back on the horses when I heard a sound.

PFFFFFFT! Like a balloon with a leak.

I looked down where I had thrown the shell. A tiny spout of water was shooting out of the muck.

"No way," I muttered.

Hesitantly, I stepped toward the fence. "Get bigger," I told the waterspout.

SPOOOOOOOSH!

Water shot three feet into the air and kept bubbling. It was impossible, but there it was. A couple of horses came over to check it out. One put his mouth to the spring and recoiled.

Yuck! he said. *Salty!*

It was seawater in the middle of a Texas ranch. I

scooped up another handful of dirt and picked out the shell fossils. I didn't really know what I was doing, but I ran around the length of the stable, throwing shells into the dung piles. Everywhere a shell hit, a saltwater spring erupted.

Stop! The horses cried. *Meat is good! Baths are bad!*

Then I noticed the water wasn't running out of the stables or flowing downhill like water normally would. It simply bubbled around each spring and sank into the ground, taking the dung with it. The horse poop dissolved in the saltwater, leaving regular old wet dirt.

"More!" I yelled.

There was a tugging sensation in my gut, and the waterspouts exploded like the world's largest carwash. Salt water shot twenty feet into the air. The horses went crazy, running back and forth as the geysers sprayed them from all directions. Mountains of poop began to melt like ice.

The tugging sensation became more intense, painful even, but there was something exhilarating about seeing all that salt water. I had made this. I had brought the ocean to this hillside.

Stop, lord! a horse cried. *Stop, please!*

Water was sloshing everywhere now. The horses were drenched, and some were panicking and slipping in the mud. The poop was completely gone, tons of it just dissolved into the earth, and the water was now starting to pool, trickling out of the stable, making a hundred little streams down toward the river.

"Stop," I told the water.

Nothing happened. The pain in my gut was building. If I didn't shut off the geysers soon, the salt water would run into the river and poison the fish and plants.

"Stop!" I concentrated all my might on shutting off the force of the sea.

Suddenly the geysers shut down. I collapsed to my knees, exhausted. In front of me was a shiny clean horse stable, a field of wet salty mud, and fifty horses that had been scoured so thoroughly their coats gleamed. Even the meat scraps between their teeth had been washed out.

We won't eat you! the horses wailed. *Please, lord! No more salty baths!*

"On one condition," I said. "You only eat the food your handlers give you from now on. Not people. Or I'll be back with more seashells!"

The horses whinnied and made me a whole lot of promises that they would be good flesh-eating horses from now on, but I didn't stick around to chat. The sun was going down. I turned and ran full speed toward the ranch house.

I smelled barbecue before I reached the house, and that made me madder than ever, because I really love barbecue.

The deck was set up for a party. Streamers and balloons decorated the railing. Geryon was flipping burgers on a huge barbecue cooker made from an oil drum. Eurytion lounged at a picnic table, picking his fingernails with a knife. The two-headed dog sniffed the ribs and burgers that were frying on the grill. And then I saw my friends: Tyson, Grover, Annabeth, and Nico all tossed in a corner, tied up like rodeo animals, with their ankles and wrists roped together and their mouths gagged.

"Let them go!" I yelled, still out of breath from running up the steps. "I cleaned the stables!"

Geryon turned. He wore an apron on each chest, with one word on each, so together they spelled out: KISS—THE—CHEF. "Did you, now? How'd you manage it?"

I was pretty impatient, but I told him.

He nodded appreciatively. "Very ingenious. It would've been better if you'd poisoned that pesky naiad, but no matter."

"Let my friends go," I said. "We had a deal."

"Ah, I've been thinking about that. The problem is, if I let them go, I don't get paid."

"You promised!"

Geryon made a *tsk-tsk* noise. "But did you make me swear on the River Styx? No you didn't. So it's not binding. When you're conducting business, sonny, you should always get a binding oath."

I drew my sword. Orthus growled. One head leaned down next to Grover's ear and bared its fangs.

"Eurytion," Geryon said, "the boy is starting to annoy me. Kill him."

Eurytion studied me. I didn't like my odds against him and that huge club.

"Kill him yourself," Eurytion said.

Geryon raised his eyebrows. "Excuse me?"

"You heard me," Eurytion grumbled. "You keep sending me out to do your dirty work. You pick fights for no good reason, and I'm tired of dying for you. You want to fight the kid, do it yourself."

It was the most un-Areslike thing I'd ever heard a son of Ares say.

Geryon threw down his spatula. "You dare defy me? I should fire you right now!"

"And who'd take care of your cattle? Orthus, heel."

The dog immediately stopped growling at Grover and came to sit by the cowherd's feet.

"Fine!" Geryon snarled. "I'll deal with you later, after the boy is dead!"

He picked up two carving knives and threw them at me. I deflected one with my sword. The other impaled itself in the picnic table an inch from Eurytion's hand.

I went on the attack. Geryon parried my first strike with a pair of red-hot tongs and lunged at my face with a barbecue fork. I got inside his next thrust and stabbed him right through the middle chest.

"Aghhh!" He crumpled to his knees. I waited for him to disintegrate, the way monsters usually do. But instead he just grimaced and began to stand up. The wound in his chef's apron started to heal.

"Nice try, sonny," he said. "Thing is, I have three hearts. The perfect backup system."

He tipped over the barbecue, and coals spilled everywhere. One landed next to Annabeth's face, and she let out a muffled scream. Tyson strained against his bonds, but even his strength wasn't enough to break them. I had to end this fight before my friends got hurt.

I jabbed Geryon in left chest, but he only laughed. I stuck him in the right stomach. No good. I might as well have been sticking a sword in a teddy bear for all the reaction he showed.

Three hearts. The perfect backup system. Stabbing one at a time was no good. . . .

I ran into the house.

"Coward!" he cried. "Come back and die right!"

The living room walls were decorated with a bunch of gruesome hunting trophies—stuffed deer and dragon heads, a gun case, a sword display, and a bow with a quiver.

Geryon threw his barbecue fork, and it thudded into the wall right next to my head. He drew two swords from the wall display. "Your head's gonna go right there, Jackson! Next to the grizzly bear!"

I had a crazy idea. I dropped Riptide and grabbed the bow off the wall.

I was the worst archery shot in the world. I couldn't hit the targets at camp, much less a bull's-eye. But I had no choice. I couldn't win this fight with a sword. I prayed to Artemis and Apollo, the twin archers, hoping they might take pity on me for once. *Please, guys. Just one shot. Please.*

I notched an arrow.

Geryon laughed. "You fool! One arrow is no better than one sword."

He raised his swords and charged. I dove sideways. Before he could turn, I shot my arrow into the side of his right chest. I heard *THUMP, THUMP, THUMP,* as the arrow passed clean through each of his chests and flew out his left side, embedding itself in the forehead of the grizzly bear trophy.

Geryon dropped his swords. He turned and stared at me. "You can't shoot. They told me you couldn't . . ."

His face turned a sickly shade of green. He collapsed to his knees and began crumbling into sand, until all that was left were three cooking aprons and an oversized pair of cowboy boots.

I got my friends untied. Eurytion didn't try to stop me. Then I stoked up the barbecue and threw the food into the flames as a burnt offering for Artemis and Apollo.

"Thanks, guys," I said. "I owe you one."

The sky thundered in the distance, so I figured maybe the burgers smelled okay.

"Yay for Percy!" Tyson said.

"Can we tie up this cowherd now?" Nico asked.

"Yeah!" Grover agreed. "And that dog almost killed me!"

I looked at Eurytion, who still was sitting relaxed at the picnic table. Orthus had both his heads on the cowherd's knees.

"How long will it take Geryon to re-form?" I asked him.

Eurytion shrugged. "Hundred years? He's not one of those fast re-formers, thank the gods. You've done me a favor."

"You said you'd died for him before," I remembered. "How?"

"I've worked for that creep for thousands of years.

Started as a regular half-blood, but I chose immortality when my dad offered it. Worst mistake I ever made. Now I'm stuck here at this ranch. I can't leave. I can't quit. I just tend the cows and fight Geryon's fights. We're kinda tied together."

"Maybe you can change things," I said.

Eurytion narrowed his eyes. "How?"

"Be nice to the animals. Take care of them. Stop selling them for food. And stop dealing with the Titans."

Eurytion thought about that. "That'd be all right."

"Get the animals on your side, and they'll help you. Once Geryon gets back, maybe he'll be working for you this time."

Eurytion grinned. "Now, *that* I could live with."

"You won't try to stop us leaving?"

"Shoot, no."

Annabeth rubbed her bruised wrists. She was still looking at Eurytion suspiciously. "Your boss said that somebody paid for our safe passage. Who?"

The cowherd shrugged. "Maybe he was just saying that to fool you."

"What about the Titans?" I asked. "Did you Iris-message them about Nico yet?"

"Nope. Geryon was waiting until after the barbecue. They don't know anything about him."

Nico was glaring at me. I wasn't sure what to do about him. I doubted he would agree to come with us. On the other hand, I couldn't just let him roam around on his own.

"You could stay here until we're done with our quest," I told him. "It would be safe."

"Safe?" Nico said. "What do you care if I'm safe? You got my sister killed!"

"Nico," Annabeth said, "that wasn't Percy fault. And Geryon wasn't lying about Kronos wanting to capture you. If he knew who you were, he'd do anything to get you on his side."

"I'm not on anyone's side. And I'm not afraid!"

"You should be," Annabeth said. "Your sister wouldn't want—"

"If you cared for my sister, you'd help me bring her back!"

"A soul for a soul?" I said.

"Yes!"

"But if you didn't want my soul—"

"I'm not explaining anything to you!" He blinked tears out of his eyes. "And I *will* bring her back."

"Bianca wouldn't want to be brought back," I said. "Not like that."

"You didn't know her!" he shouted. "How do you know what she'd want?"

I stared at the flames in the barbecue pit. I thought about the line in Annabeth's prophecy: *You shall rise or fall by the ghost king's hand.* That had to be Minos, and I *had* to convince Nico not to listen to him. "Let's ask Bianca."

The sky seemed to grow darker all of the sudden.

"I've tried," Nico's said miserably. "She won't answer."

"Try again. I've got a feeling she'll answer with me here."

"Why would she?"

"Because she's been sending me Iris-messages," I said, suddenly sure of it. "She's been trying to warn me what you're up to, so I can protect you."

Nico shook his head. "That's impossible."

"One way to find out. You said you're not afraid." I turned to Eurytion. "We're going to need a pit, like a grave. And food and drinks."

"Percy," Annabeth warned. "I don't think this is a good—"

"All right," Nico said. "I'll try."

Eurytion scratched his beard. "There's a hole dug out back for a septic tank. We could use that. Cyclops boy, fetch my ice chest from the kitchen. I hope the dead like root beer."

TEN

WE PLAY THE GAME SHOW
OF DEATH

We did our summons after dark, at a twenty-foot-long pit in front of the septic tank. The tank was bright yellow, with a smiley face and red words painted on the side: HAPPY FLUSH DISPOSAL CO. It didn't quite go with the mood of summoning the dead.

The moon was full. Silver clouds drifted across the sky.

"Minos should be here by now," Nico said, frowning. "It's full dark."

"Maybe he got lost," I said hopefully.

Nico poured root beer and tossed barbecue into the pit, then began chanting in Ancient Greek. Immediately the bugs in the woods stopped chirping. In my pocket, the Stygian ice dog whistle started to grow colder, freezing against the side of my leg.

"Make him stop," Tyson whispered to me.

Part of me agreed. This was unnatural. The night air felt cold and menacing. But before I could say anything, the first spirits appeared. Sulfurous mist seeped out of the ground. Shadows thickened into human forms. One blue shade drifted to the edge of the pit and knelt to drink.

"Stop him!" Nico said, momentarily breaking his chant. "Only Bianca may drink!"

I drew Riptide. The ghosts retreated with a collective hiss at the sight of my celestial bronze blade. But it was too late to stop the first spirit. He had already solidified into the shape of a bearded man in white robes. A circlet of gold wreathed his head, and even in death his eyes were alive with malice.

"Minos!" Nico said. "What are you doing?"

"My apologies, master," the ghost said, though he didn't sound very sorry. "The sacrifice smelled so good, I couldn't resist." He examined his own hands and smiled. "It is good to see myself again. Almost in solid form—"

"You are disrupting the ritual!" Nico protested. "Get—"

The spirits of the dead began shimmering dangerously bright, and Nico had to take up the chant again to keep them at bay.

"Yes, quite right, master," Minos said with amusement. "You keep chanting. I've only come to protect you from these *liars* who would deceive you."

He turned to me as if I were some kind of cockroach. "Percy Jackson . . . my, my. The sons of Poseidon haven't improved over the centuries, have they?"

I wanted to punch him, but I figured my fist would go right through his face. "We're looking for Bianca di Angelo," I said. "Get lost."

The ghost chuckled. "I understand you once killed my Minotaur with your bare hands. But worse things await you in the maze. Do you really believe Daedalus will help you?"

The other spirits stirred in agitation. Annabeth drew her knife and helped me keep them away from the pit. Grover got so nervous he clung to Tyson's shoulder.

"Daedalus cares nothing for you, half-bloods," Minos warned. "You can't trust him. He is old beyond counting, and crafty. He is bitter from the guilt of murder and is cursed by the gods."

"The guilt of murder?" I asked. "Who did he kill?"

"Do not change the subject!" the ghost growled. "You are hindering Nico. You try to persuade him to give up his goal. *I* would make him a lord!"

"Enough, Minos," Nico commanded.

The ghost sneered. "Master, these are your enemies. You must not listen to them! Let me protect you. I will turn their minds to madness, as I did the others."

"The others?" Annabeth gasped. "You mean Chris Rodriguez? That was *you*?"

"The maze is my property," the ghost said, "not Daedalus's! Those who intrude deserve madness."

"Be gone, Minos!" Nico demanded. "I want to see my sister!"

The ghost bit back his rage. "As you wish, master. But I warn you. You cannot trust these heroes."

With that, he faded into mist.

Other spirits rushed forward, but Annabeth and I kept them back.

"Bianca, appear!" Nico intoned. He started chanting faster, and the spirits shifted restlessly.

"Any time now," Grover muttered.

Then a silvery light flickered in the trees—a spirit that seemed brighter and stronger than the others. It came closer, and something told me to let it pass. It knelt to drink at the pit. When it arose, it was the ghostly form of Bianca di Angelo.

Nico's chanting faltered. I lowered my sword. The other spirits started to crowd forward, but Bianca raised her arms and they retreated into the woods.

"Hello, Percy," she said.

She looked the same as she had in life: a green cap set sideways on her thick black hair, dark eyes and olive skin like her brother. She wore jeans and a silvery jacket, the outfit of a Hunter of Artemis. A bow was slung over her shoulder. She smiled faintly, and her whole form flickered.

"Bianca," I said. My voice was thick. I'd felt guilty about her death for a long time, but seeing her in front of me was five times as bad, like her death was fresh and new. I remembered searching through the wreckage of the giant bronze warrior she'd sacrificed her life to defeat, and not finding any sign of her.

"I'm so sorry," I said.

"You have nothing to apologize for, Percy. I made my own choice. I don't regret it."

"Bianca!" Nico stumbled forward like he was just coming out of a daze.

She turned toward her brother. Her expression was sad, as if she'd been dreading this moment. "Hello, Nico. You've gotten so tall."

"Why didn't you answer me sooner?" he cried. "I've been trying for months!"

"I was hoping you would give up."

"Give up?" He sounded heartbroken. "How can you say that? I'm trying to save you!"

"You can't, Nico. Don't do this. Percy is right."

"No! He let you die! He's not your friend."

Bianca stretched out a hand as if to touch her brother's face, but she was made of mist. Her hand evaporated as it got close to living skin.

"You must listen to me," she said. "Holding grudges is dangerous for a child of Hades. It is our fatal flaw. You have to forgive. You have to promise me this."

"I can't. Never."

"Percy has been worried about you, Nico. He can help. I let him see what you were up to, hoping he would find you."

"So it *was* you," I said. "You sent those Iris-messages."

Bianca nodded.

"Why are you helping him and not me?" Nico screamed. "It's not fair!"

"You are close to the truth now," Bianca told him. "It's not Percy you're mad at, Nico. It's me."

"No."

"You're mad because I left you to become a Hunter of Artemis. You're mad because I died and left you alone. I'm sorry for that, Nico. I truly am. But you must overcome the anger. And stop blaming Percy for my choices. It will be your doom."

"She's right," Annabeth broke in. "Kronos is rising, Nico. He'll twist anyone he can to his cause."

"I don't care about Kronos," Nico said. "I just want my sister back."

"You can't have that, Nico," Bianca told him gently.

"I'm the son of Hades! I *can*."

"Don't try," she said. "If you love me, don't . . ."

Her voice trailed off. Spirits had started to gather around us again, and they seemed agitated. Their shadows shifted. Their voices whispered, *Danger!*

"Tartarus stirs," Bianca said. "Your power draws the attention of Kronos. The dead must return to the Underworld. It is not safe for us to remain."

"Wait," Nico said. "Please—"

"Good-bye, Nico," Bianca said. "I love you. Remember what I said."

Her form shivered and the ghosts disappeared, leaving us alone with a pit, a *Happy Flush* septic tank, and a cold full moon.

None of us were anxious to travel that night, so we decided to wait until morning. Grover and I crashed on the leather couches in Geryon's living room, which was a lot more comfortable than a bedroll in the maze; but it didn't make my nightmares any better.

I dreamed I was with Luke, walking through the dark palace on top of Mount Tam. It was a real building now—not some half-finished illusion like I'd seen last winter. Green fires burned in braziers along the walls. The floor was polished black marble. A cold wind blew down the hallway, and above us through the open ceiling, the sky swirled with gray storm clouds.

Luke was dressed for battle. He wore camouflage pants,

a white T-shirt, and a bronze breastplate, but his sword, Backbiter, wasn't at his side—only an empty scabbard. We walked into a large courtyard where dozens of warriors and *dracaenae* were preparing for war. When they saw him, the demigods rose to attention. They beat their swords against their shields.

"Issss it time, my lord?" a *dracaena* asked.

"Soon," Luke promised. "Continue your work."

"My lord," a voice said behind him. Kelli the *empousa* was smiling at him. She wore a blue dress tonight, and looked wickedly beautiful. Her eyes flickered—sometimes dark brown, sometimes pure red. Her hair was braided down her back and seemed to catch the light of the torches, as if it were anxious to turn back into pure flame.

My heart was pounding. I waited for Kelli to see me, to chase me out of the dream as she did before, but this time she didn't seem to notice me.

"You have a visitor," she told Luke. She stepped aside, and even Luke seemed stunned by what he saw.

The monster Kampê towered above him. Her snakes hissed around her legs. Animal heads growled at her waist. Her swords were drawn, shimmering with poison, and with her bat wings extended, she took up the entire corridor.

"You." Luke's voice sounded a little shaky. "I told you to stay on Alcatraz."

Kampê's eyelids blinked sideways like a reptile's. She spoke in that weird rumbling language, but this time I understood, somewhere in the back of my mind: *I come to serve. Give me revenge.*

"You're a jailor," Luke said. "Your job—"

I will have them dead. No one escapes me.

Luke hesitated. A line of sweat trickled down the side of his face. "Very well," he said. "You will go with us. You may carry Ariadne's string. It is a position of great honor."

Kampê hissed at the stars. She sheathed her swords and turned, pounding down the hallway on her enormous dragon legs.

"We should have left that one in Tartarus," Luke mumbled. "She is too chaotic. Too powerful."

Kelli laughed softly. "You should not fear power, Luke. Use it!"

"The sooner we leave, the better," Luke said. "I want this over with."

"Aww," Kelli sympathized, running a finger down his arm. "You find it unpleasant to destroy your old camp?"

"I didn't say that."

"You're not having second thoughts about your own, ah, special part?"

Luke's face turned stony. "I know my duty."

"That is good," the demon said. "Is our strike force sufficient, do you think? Or will I need to call Mother Hecate for help?"

"We have more than enough," Luke said grimly. "The deal is almost complete. All I need now is to negotiate safe passage through the arena."

"Mmm," Kelli said. "That should be interesting. I would hate to see your handsome head on a spike if you fail."

"I will not fail. And you, demon, don't you have other matters to attend to?"

"Oh, yes." Kelli smiled. "I am bringing despair to our eavesdropping enemies. I am doing that right now."

She turned her eyes directly on me, exposed her talons, and ripped through my dream.

Suddenly I was in a different place.

I stood at the top of a stone tower, overlooking rocky cliffs and the ocean below. The old man Daedalus was hunched over a worktable, wrestling with some kind of navigational instrument, like a huge compass. He looked years older than when I'd last seen him. He was stooped and his hands were gnarled. He cursed in Ancient Greek and squinted as if he couldn't see his work, even though it was a sunny day.

"Uncle!" a voice called.

A smiling boy about Nico's age came bounding up the steps, carrying a wooden box.

"Hello, Perdix," the old man said, though his tone sounded cold. "Done with your projects already?"

"Yes, Uncle. They were easy!"

Daedalus scowled. "Easy? The problem of moving water uphill without a pump was easy?"

"Oh, yes! Look!"

The boy dumped his box and rummaged through the junk. He came up with a strip of papyrus and showed the old inventor some diagrams and notes. They didn't make any sense to me, but Daedalus nodded grudgingly. "I see. Not bad."

"The king loved it!" Perdix said. "He said I might be even smarter than you!"

"Did he now?"

"But I don't believe that. I'm so glad Mother sent me to study with you! I want to know everything you do."

"Yes," Daedalus muttered. "So when I die, you can take my place, eh?"

The boy's eyes widened. "Oh no, Uncle! But I've been thinking . . . why does a man have to die, anyway?"

The inventor scowled. "It is the way of things, lad. Everything dies but the gods."

"But *why?*" the boy insisted. "If you could capture the *animus*, the soul in another form . . . Well, you've told me about your automatons, Uncle. Bulls, eagles, dragons, horses of bronze. Why not a bronze form for a man?"

"No, my boy," Daedalus said sharply. "You are naïve. Such a thing is impossible."

"I don't think so," Perdix insisted. "With the use of a little magic—"

"Magic? Bah!"

"Yes, Uncle! Magic and mechanics together—with a little work, one could make a body that would look exactly human, only better. I've made some notes."

He handed the old man a thick scroll. Daedalus unfurled it. He read for a long time. His eyes narrowed. He glanced at the boy, then closed the scroll and cleared his throat. "It would never work, my boy. When you're older, you'll see."

"Can I fix that astrolabe, then, Uncle? Are your joints swelling up again?"

The old man's jaw clenched. "No. Thank you. Now why don't you run along?"

Perdix didn't seem to notice the old man's anger. He snatched a bronze beetle from his mound of stuff and ran to the edge of the tower. A low sill ringed the rim, coming just up to the boy's knees. The wind was strong.

Move back, I wanted to tell him. But my voice didn't work.

Perdix wound up the beetle and tossed it into the sky. It spread its wings and hummed away. Perdix laughed with delight.

"Smarter than me," Daedalus mumbled, too soft for the boy to hear.

"Is it true your son died flying, Uncle? I heard you made him enormous wings, but they failed."

Daedalus's hands clenched. "Take my place," he muttered.

The wind whipped around the boy, tugging at his clothes, making his hair ripple.

"I would like to fly," Perdix said. "I'd make my own wings that wouldn't fail. Do you think I could?"

Maybe it was a dream within my dream, but suddenly I imagined the two-headed god Janus shimmering in the air next to Daedalus, smiling as he tossed a silver key from hand to hand. *Choose*, he whispered to the old inventor. *Choose.*

Daedalus picked up another one of the boy's metal bugs. The inventor's old eyes were red with anger.

"Perdix," he called. "Catch."

He tossed the bronze beetle toward the boy. Delighted,

Perdix tried to catch it, but the throw was too long. The beetle sailed into open sky, and Perdix reached a little too far. The wind caught him.

Somehow he managed to grab the rim of the tower with his fingers as he fell. "Uncle!" he screamed. "Help me!"

The old man's face was a mask. He did not move from his spot.

"Go on, Perdix," Daedalus said softly. "Make your own wings. Be quick about it."

"Uncle!" the boy cried as he lost his grip. He tumbled toward the sea.

There was a moment of deadly silence. The god Janus flickered and disappeared. Then thunder shook the sky. A woman's stern voice spoke from above: *You will pay the price for that, Daedalus.*

I'd heard that voice before. It was Annabeth's mother: Athena.

Daedalus scowled up at the heavens. "I have always honored you, Mother. I have sacrificed everything to follow your way."

Yet the boy had my blessing as well. And you have killed him. For that, you must pay.

"I've paid and paid!" Daedalus growled. "I've lost everything. I'll suffer in the Underworld, no doubt. But in the meantime . . ."

He picked up the boy's scroll, studied it for a moment, and slipped it into his sleeve.

You do not understand, Athena said coldly. *You will pay now and forever.*

Suddenly Daedalus collapsed in agony. I felt what he felt. A searing pain closed around my neck like a molten-hot collar—cutting off my breath, making everything go black.

I woke in the dark, my hands clutching at my throat.

"Percy?" Grover called from the other sofa. "Are you okay?"

I steadied my breathing. I wasn't sure how to answer. I'd just watched the guy we were looking for, Daedalus, murder his own nephew. How could I be okay? The television was going. Blue light flickered through the room.

"What—what time is it?" I croaked.

"Two in morning," Grover said. "I couldn't sleep. I was watching the Nature Channel." He sniffled. "I miss Juniper."

I rubbed the sleep out of my eyes. "Yeah, well . . . you'll see her again soon."

Grover shook his head sadly. "Do you know what day it is, Percy? I just saw it on TV. It's June thirteenth. Seven days since we left camp."

"What?" I said. "That can't be right."

"Time is faster in the Labyrinth," Grover reminded me. "The first time you and Annabeth went down there, you thought you were only gone a few minutes, right? But it was an hour."

"Oh," I said. "Right." Then it dawned on me what he was saying, and my throat felt searing hot again. "Your deadline with the Council of Cloven Elders."

Grover put the TV remote in his mouth and crunched

off the end of it. "I'm out of time," he said with a mouth-ful of plastic. "As soon as I go back, they'll take away my searcher's license. I'll never be allowed to go out again."

"We'll talk to them," I promised. "Make them give you more time."

Grover swallowed. "They'll never go for it. The world is dying, Percy. Every day it gets worse. The wild . . . I can just feel it fading. I *have* to find Pan."

"You will, man. No doubt."

Grover looked at me with sad goat eyes. "You've always been a good friend, Percy. What you did today—saving the ranch animals from Geryon—that was amazing. I—I wish I could be more like you."

"Hey," I said. "Don't say that. You're just as much a hero—"

"No I'm not. I keep trying, but . . ." He sighed. "Percy, I can't go back to camp without finding Pan. I just can't. You understand that, don't you? I can't face Juniper if I fail. I can't even face myself."

His voice was so unhappy it hurt to hear. We'd been through a lot together, but I'd never heard him sound this down.

"We'll figure out something," I said. "You haven't failed. You're the champion goat boy, all right? Juniper knows that. So do I."

Grover closed his eyes. "Champion goat boy," he mut-tered dejectedly.

A long time after he dozed off, I was still awake,

watching the blue light of the Nature Channel wash over the stuffed trophy heads on Geryon's walls.

The next morning we walked down to the cattle guard and said our good-byes.

"Nico, you could come with us," I blurted out. I guess I was thinking about my dream, and how much the young boy Perdix reminded me of Nico.

He shook his head. I don't think any of us had slept well in the demon ranch house, but Nico looked worse than anybody else. His eyes were red and his face chalky. He was wrapped in a black robe that must've belonged to Geryon, because it was three sizes too big even for a grown man.

"I need time to think." His eyes wouldn't meet mine, but I could tell from his tone he was still angry. The fact that his sister had come out of the Underworld for me and not for him didn't seem to sit well with him.

"Nico," Annabeth said. "Bianca just wants you to be okay."

She put her hand on his shoulder, but he pulled away and trudged up the road toward the ranch house. Maybe it was my imagination, but the morning mist seemed to cling to him as he walked.

"I'm worried about him," Annabeth told me. "If he starts talking to Minos's ghost again—"

"He'll be all right," Eurytion promised. The cowherd had cleaned up nicely. He was wearing new jeans and a clean Western shirt and he'd even trimmed his beard. He'd put on Geryon's boots. "The boy can stay here and gather his thoughts as long as he wants. He'll be safe, I promise."

"What about you?" I asked.

Eurytion scratched Orthus behind one chin, then the other. "Things are going to be run a little different on this ranch from now on. No more sacred cattle meat. I'm thinking about soybean patties. And I'm going to befriend those flesh-eating horses. Might just sign up for the next rodeo."

The idea made me shudder. "Well, good luck."

"Yep." Eurytion spit into the grass. "I reckon you'll be looking for Daedalus's workshop now?"

Annabeth's eyes lit up. "Can you help us?"

Eurytion studied the cattle guard, and I got the feeling the subject of Daedalus's workshop made him uncomfortable. "Don't know where it is. But Hephaestus probably would."

"That's what Hera said," Annabeth agreed. "But how do we find *Hephaestus*?"

Eurytion pulled something from under the collar of his shirt. It was a necklace—a smooth silver disk on a silver chain. The disk had a depression on the middle, like a thumbprint. He handed it to Annabeth.

"Hephaestus comes here from time to time," Eurytion said. "Studies the animals and such so he can make bronze automaton copies. Last time, I—uh—did him a favor. A little trick he wanted to play on my dad, Ares, and Aphrodite. He gave me that chain in gratitude. Said if I ever needed to find him, the disk would lead me to his forges. But only once."

"And you're giving it to me?" Annabeth asked.

Eurytion blushed. "I don't need to see the forges, miss. Got enough to do here. Just press the button and you'll be on your way."

Annabeth pressed the button and the disk sprang to life. It grew eight metallic legs. Annabeth shrieked and dropped it, much to Eurytion's confusion.

"Spider!" she screamed.

"She's, um, a little scared of spiders," Grover explained. "That old grudge between Athena and Arachne."

"Oh." Eurytion looked embarrassed. "Sorry, miss."

The spider scrambled to the cattle guard and disappeared between the bars.

"Hurry," I said. "That thing's not going to wait for us."

Annabeth wasn't anxious to follow, but we didn't have much choice. We said our good-byes to Eurytion, Tyson pulled the cattle guard off the hole, and we dropped back into the maze.

I wish I could've put the mechanical spider on a leash. It scuttled along the tunnels so fast, most of time I couldn't even see it. If it hadn't been for Tyson's and Grover's excellent hearing, we never would've known which way it was going.

We ran down a marble tunnel, then dashed to the left and almost fell into an abyss. Tyson grabbed me and hauled me back before I could fall. The tunnel continued in front of us, but there was no floor for about a hundred feet, just gaping darkness and a series of iron rungs in the ceiling. The mechanical spider was about halfway across, swinging from bar to bar by shooting out metal web fiber.

"Monkey bars," Annabeth said. "I'm great at these."

She leaped onto the first rung and started swinging her way across. She was scared of tiny spiders, but not of plummeting to her death from a set of monkey bars. Go figure.

Annabeth got to the opposite side and ran after the spider. I followed. When I got across, I looked back and saw Tyson giving Grover a piggyback ride (or was it a goatyback ride?). The big guy made it across in three swings, which was a good thing since, just as he landed, the last iron bar ripped free under his weight.

We kept moving and passed a skeleton crumpled in the tunnel. It wore the remains of a dress shirt, slacks, and a tie. The spider didn't slow down. I slipped on a pile of wood scraps, but when I shined a light on them I realized they were pencils—hundreds of them, all broken in half.

The tunnel opened up onto a large room. A blazing light hit us. Once my eyes adjusted, the first thing I noticed were the skeletons. Dozens littered the floor around us. Some were old and bleached white. Others were more recent and a lot grosser. They didn't smell quite as bad as Geryon's stables, but almost.

Then I saw the monster. She stood on a glittery dais on the opposite side of the room. She had the body of a huge lion and the head of a woman. She would've been pretty, but her hair was tied back in a tight bun and she wore too much makeup, so she kind of reminded me of my third-grade choir teacher. She had a blue ribbon badge pinned to her chest that took me a moment to read: THIS MONSTER HAS BEEN RATED **EXEMPLARY!**

Tyson whimpered. "Sphinx."

I knew exactly why he was scared. When he was small, Tyson had been attacked by a Sphinx in New York. He still had the scars on his back to prove it.

Spotlights blazed on either side of the creature. The only exit was a tunnel right behind the dais. The mechanical spider scuttled between the Sphinx's paws and disappeared.

Annabeth started forward, but the Sphinx roared, showing fangs in her otherwise human face. Bars came down on both tunnel exits, behind us and in front.

Immediately the monster's snarl turned into a brilliant smile.

"Welcome, lucky contestants!" she announced. "Get ready to play . . . ANSWER THAT RIDDLE!"

Canned applause blasted from the ceiling, as if there were invisible loudspeakers. Spotlights swept across the room and reflected off the dais, throwing disco glitter over the skeletons on the floor.

"Fabulous prizes!" the Sphinx said. "Pass the test, and you get to advance! Fail, and I get to eat you! Who will be our contestant?"

Annabeth grabbed my arm. "I've got this," she whispered. "I know what she's going to ask."

I didn't argue too hard. I didn't want Annabeth getting devoured by a monster, but I figured if the Sphinx was going to ask riddles, Annabeth was the best one of us to try.

She stepped forward to the contestant's podium, which had a skeleton in a school uniform hunched over it. She pushed the skeleton out of the way, and it clattered to the floor.

"Sorry," Annabeth told it.

"Welcome, Annabeth Chase!" the monster cried, though Annabeth hadn't said her name. "Are you ready for your test?"

"Yes," she said. "Ask your riddle."

"Twenty riddles, actually!" the Sphinx said gleefully.

"What? But back in the old days—"

"Oh, we've raised our standards! To pass, you must show proficiency in all twenty. Isn't that great?"

Applause switched on and off like somebody turning a faucet.

Annabeth glanced at me nervously. I gave her an encouraging nod.

"Okay," she told the Sphinx. "I'm ready."

A drumroll sounded from above. The Sphinx's eyes glittered with excitement. "What . . . is the capital of Bulgaria?"

Annabeth frowned. For a terrible moment, I thought she was stumped.

"Sofia," she said, "but—"

"Correct!" More canned applause. The Sphinx smiled so wide her fangs showed. "Please be sure to mark your answer clearly on your test sheet with a number 2 pencil."

"What?" Annabeth looked mystified. Then a test booklet appeared on the podium in front of her, along with a sharpened pencil.

"Make sure you bubble each answer clearly and stay inside the circle," the Sphinx said. "If you have to erase, erase completely or the machine will not be able to read your answers."

"What machine?" Annabeth asked.

The Sphinx pointed with her paw. Over by the spotlight was a bronze box with a bunch of gears and levers and a big Greek letter Êta on the side, the mark of Hephaestus.

"Now," said the Sphinx, "next question—"

"Wait a second," Annabeth protested. "What about 'What walks on four legs in the morning'?"

"I beg your pardon?" the Sphinx said, clearly annoyed now.

"The riddle about man. He walks on four legs in the morning, like a baby, two legs in the afternoon, like an adult, and three legs in the evening, as an old man with a cane. That's the riddle you used to ask."

"Exactly why we changed the test!" the Sphinx exclaimed. "You already knew the answer. Now second question, what is the square root of sixteen?"

"Four," Annabeth said, "but—"

"Correct! Which U.S. president signed the Emancipation Proclamation?"

"Abraham Lincoln, but—"

"Correct! Riddle number four. How much—"

"Hold up!" Annabeth shouted.

I wanted to tell her to stop complaining. She was doing great! She should just answer the questions so we could leave.

"These aren't riddles," Annabeth said.

"What do you mean?" the Sphinx snapped. "Of course they are. This test material is specially designed—"

"It's just a bunch of dumb, random facts," Annabeth insisted. "Riddles are supposed to make you think."

"Think?" The Sphinx frowned. "How am I supposed to test whether you can think? That's ridiculous! Now, how much force is required—"

"Stop!" Annabeth insisted. "This is a stupid test."

"Um, Annabeth," Grover cut in nervously. "Maybe you should just, you know, finish first and complain later?"

"I'm a child of Athena," she insisted. "And this is an insult to my intelligence. I won't answer these questions."

Part of me was impressed with her for standing up like that. But part of me thought her pride was going to get us all killed.

The spotlights glared. The Sphinx's eyes glittered pure black.

"Why then, my dear," the monster said calmly. "If you won't pass, you fail. And since we can't allow any children to be held back, you'll be EATEN!"

The Sphinx bared her claws, which gleamed like stainless steel. She pounced at the podium.

"No!" Tyson charged. He hates it when people threaten Annabeth, but I couldn't believe he was being so brave, especially since he'd had such a bad experience with a Sphinx before.

He tackled the Sphinx midair and they crashed sideways into a pile of bones. This gave Annabeth just enough time to gather her wits and draw her knife. Tyson got up, his shirt clawed to shreds. The Sphinx growled, looking for an opening.

I drew Riptide and stepped in front of Annabeth.

"Turn invisible," I told her.

"I can fight!"

"No!" I yelled. "The Sphinx is after *you!* Let us get it."

As if to prove my point, the Sphinx knocked Tyson aside and tried to charge past me. Grover poked her in the eye with somebody's leg bone. She screeched in pain. Annabeth put on her cap and vanished. The Sphinx pounced right where she'd been standing, but came up with empty paws.

"No fair!" the Sphinx wailed. "Cheater!"

With Annabeth no longer in sight, the Sphinx turned on me. I raised my sword, but before I could strike, Tyson ripped the monster's grading machine out of the floor and threw it at the Sphinx's head, ruining her hair bun. It landed in pieces all around her.

"My grading machine!" she cried. "I can't be exemplary without my test scores!"

The bars lifted from the exits. We all dashed for the far tunnel. I could only hope Annabeth was doing the same.

The Sphinx started to follow, but Grover raised his reed pipes and began to play. Suddenly the pencils remembered they used to be parts of trees. They collected around the Sphinx's paws, grew roots and branches, and began wrapping around the monster's legs. The Sphinx ripped through them, but it bought us just enough time.

Tyson pulled Grover into the tunnel, and the bars slammed shut behind us.

"Annabeth!" I yelled.

"Here!" she said, right next to me. "Keep moving!"

We ran through the dark tunnels, listening to the roar of the Sphinx behind us as she complained about all the tests she would have to grade by hand.

ELEVEN

I SET MYSELF ON FIRE

I thought we'd lost the spider until Tyson heard a faint pinging sound. We made a few turns, backtracked a few times, and eventually found the spider banging its tiny head on a metal door.

The door looked like one of those old-fashioned submarine hatches—oval, with metal rivets around the edges and a wheel for a doorknob. Where the portal should've been was a big brass plaque, green with age, with a Greek Êta inscribed in the middle.

We all looked at each other.

"Ready to meet Hephaestus?" Grover said nervously.

"No," I admitted.

"Yes!" Tyson said gleefully, and he turned the wheel.

As soon as the door opened, the spider scuttled inside with Tyson right behind it. The rest of us followed, not quite as anxious.

The room was enormous. It looked like a mechanic's garage, with several hydraulic lifts. Some had cars on them, but others had stranger things: a bronze hippalektryon with its horse head off and a bunch of wires hanging out its rooster tail, a metal lion that seemed to be hooked up to a battery charger, and a Greek war chariot made entirely of flames.

Smaller projects cluttered a dozen worktables. Tools hung along the walls. Each had its own outline on a Peg-Board, but nothing seemed to be in the right place. The hammer was over the screwdriver place. The staple gun was where the hacksaw was supposed to go.

Under the nearest hydraulic lift, which was holding a '98 Toyota Corolla, a pair of legs stuck out—the lower half of a huge man in grubby gray pants and shoes even bigger than Tyson's. One leg was in a metal brace.

The spider scuttled straight under the car, and the sounds of banging stopped.

"Well, well," a deep voice boomed from under the Corolla. "What have we here?"

The mechanic pushed out on a back trolley and sat up. I'd seen Hephaestus once before, briefly on Olympus, so I thought I was prepared, but his appearance made me gulp.

I guess he'd cleaned up when I saw him on Olympus, or used magic to make his form seem a little less hideous. Here in his own workshop, he apparently didn't care how he looked. He wore a jumpsuit smeared with oil and grime. *Hephaestus*, was embroidered over the chest pocket. His leg creaked and clicked in its metal brace as he stood, and his left shoulder was lower than his right, so he seemed to be leaning even when he was standing up straight. His head was misshapen and bulging. He wore a permanent scowl. His black beard smoked and hissed. Every once in a while a small wildfire would erupt in his whiskers then die out. His hands were the size of catcher's mitts, but he handled the spider with amazing skill. He disassembled it in two seconds, then put it back together.

"There," he muttered to himself. "Much better."

The spider did a happy flip in his palm, shot a metallic web at the ceiling, and went swinging away.

Hephaestus glowered up at us. "I didn't make you, did I?"

"Uh," Annabeth said, "no, sir."

"Good," the god grumbled. "Shoddy workmanship."

He studied Annabeth and me. "Half-bloods," he grunted. "Could be automatons, of course, but probably not."

"We've met, sir," I told him.

"Have we?" the god asked absently. I got the feeling he didn't care one way or the other. He was just trying to figure out how my jaw worked, whether it was a hinge or lever or what. "Well then, if I didn't smash you to a pulp the first time we met, I suppose I won't have to do it now."

He looked at Grover and frowned. "Satyr." Then he looked at Tyson, and his eyes twinkled. "Well, a Cyclops. Good, good. What are you doing traveling with this lot?"

"Uh . . ." said Tyson, staring in wonder at the god.

"Yes, well said," Hephaestus agreed. "So, there'd better be a good reason you're disturbing me. The suspension on this Corolla is no small matter, you know."

"Sir," Annabeth said hesitantly, "we're looking for Daedalus. We thought—"

"*Daedalus?*" the god roared. "You want that old scoundrel? You dare to seek him out!"

His beard burst into flames and his black eyes glowed.

"Uh, yes, sir, please," Annabeth said.

"Humph. You're wasting your time." He frowned at something on his worktable and limped over to it. He picked up a lump of springs and metal plates and tinkered with them. In a few seconds he was holding a bronze and silver falcon. It spread its metal wings, blinked its obsidian eyes, and flew around the room.

Tyson laughed and clapped his hands. The bird landed on Tyson's shoulder and nipped his ear affectionately.

Hephaestus regarded him. The god's scowl didn't change, but I thought I saw a kinder twinkle in his eyes. "I sense you have something to tell me, Cyclops."

Tyson's smile faded. "Y-yes, lord. We met a Hundred-Handed One."

Hephaestus nodded, looking unsurprised. "Briares?"

"Yes. He—he was scared. He would not help us."

"And that bothered you."

"Yes!" Tyson's voice wavered. "Briares should be strong! He is older and greater than Cyclopes. But he ran away."

Hephaestus grunted. "There was a time I admired the Hundred-Handed Ones. Back in the days of the first war. But people, monsters, even gods change, young Cyclops. You can't trust 'em. Look at my loving mother, Hera. You met her, didn't you? She'll smile to your face and talk about how important family is, eh? Didn't stop her from pitching me off Mount Olympus when she saw my ugly face."

"But I thought Zeus did that to you," I said.

Hephaestus cleared his throat and spat into a bronze spittoon. He snapped his fingers, and the robotic falcon flew back to the worktable.

"Mother likes telling that version of the story," he grumbled. "Makes her seem more likable, doesn't it? Blaming it all on my dad. The truth is, my mother likes families, but she likes a certain kind of family. *Perfect* families. She took one look at me and . . . well, I don't fit the image, do I?"

He pulled a feather from the falcon's back, and the whole automaton fell apart.

"Believe me, young Cyclops," Hephaestus said, "you can't trust others. All you can trust is the work of your own hands."

It seemed like a pretty lonely way to live. Plus, I didn't exactly trust the work of Hephaestus. One time in Denver, his mechanical spiders had almost killed Annabeth and me. And last year, it had been a defective Talos statue that cost Bianca her life—another one of Hephaestus's little projects.

He focused on me and narrowed his eyes, as if he were reading my thoughts. "Oh, this one doesn't like me," he mused. "No worries, I'm used to that. What would you ask of me, little demigod?"

"We told you," I said. "We need to find Daedalus. There's this guy Luke, and he's working for Kronos. He's trying to find a way to navigate the Labyrinth so he can invade our camp. If we don't get to Daedalus first—"

"And I told *you*, boy. Looking for Daedalus is a waste of time. He won't help you."

"Why not?"

Hephaestus shrugged. "Some of us get thrown off mountainsides. Some of us . . . the way we learn not to trust people is even more painful. Ask me for gold. Or a flaming sword. Or a magical steed. These I can grant you easily. But a way to Daedalus? That's an expensive favor."

"You know where he is, then," Annabeth pressed.

"It isn't wise to go looking, girl."

"My mother says looking is the nature of wisdom."

Hephaestus narrowed his eyes. "Who's your mother, then?"

"Athena."

"Figures." He sighed. "Fine goddess, Athena. A shame she pledged never to marry. All right, half-blood. I can tell you what you want to know. But there is a price. I need a favor done."

"Name it," Annabeth said.

Hephaestus actually laughed—a booming sound like a huge bellows stoking a fire. "You heroes," he said, "always making rash promises. How refreshing!"

He pressed a button on his workbench, and metal shutters opened along the wall. It was either a huge window or a big-screen TV, I couldn't tell which. We were looking at a gray mountain ringed in forests. It must've been a volcano, because smoke rose from its crest.

"One of my forges," Hephaestus said. "I have many, but that used to be my favorite."

"That's Mount St. Helens," Grover said. "Great forests around there."

"You've been there?" I asked.

"Looking for . . . you know. Pan."

"Wait," Annabeth said, looking at Hephaestus. "You

said it *used to be* your favorite. What happened?"

Hephaestus scratched his smoldering beard. "Well, that's where the monster Typhon is trapped, you know. Used to be under Mount Etna, but when we moved to America, his force got pinned under Mount St. Helens instead. Great source of fire, but a bit dangerous. There's always a chance he will escape. Lots of eruptions these days, smoldering all the time. He's restless with the Titan rebellion."

"What do you want us to do?" I said. "Fight him?"

Hephaestus snorted. "That would be suicide. The gods themselves ran from Typhon when he was free. No, pray you never have to see him, much less fight him. But lately I have sensed intruders in my mountain. Someone or something is using my forges. When I go there, it is empty, but I can tell it is being used. They sense me coming, and they disappear. I send my automatons to investigate, but they do not return. Something . . . ancient is there. Evil. I want to know who dares invade my territory, and if they mean to loose Typhon."

"You want us to find out who it is," I said.

"Aye," Hephaestus said. "Go there. They may not sense you coming. You are not gods."

"Glad you noticed," I muttered.

"Go and find out what you can," Hephaestus said. "Report back to me, and I will tell you what you need to know about Daedalus."

"All right," Annabeth said. "How do we get there?"

Hephaestus clapped his hands. The spider came

swinging down from the rafters. Annabeth flinched when it landed at her feet.

"My creation will show you the way," Hephaestus said. "It is not far through the Labyrinth. And try to stay alive, will you? Humans are much more fragile than automatons."

We were doing okay until we hit the tree roots. The spider raced along and we were keeping up, but then we spotted a tunnel off to the side that was dug from raw earth, and wrapped in thick roots. Grover stopped dead in his tracks.

"What is it?" I said.

He didn't move. He stared openmouthed into the dark tunnel. His curly hair rustled in the breeze.

"Come on!" Annabeth said. "We have to keep moving."

"This is the way," Grover muttered in awe. "This is it."

"What way?" I asked. "You mean . . . to Pan?"

Grover looked at Tyson. "Don't you smell it?"

"Dirt," Tyson said. "And plants."

"Yes! This is the way. I'm sure of it!"

Up ahead, the spider was getting farther down the stone corridor. A few more seconds and we'd lose it.

"We'll come back," Annabeth promised. "On our way back to Hephaestus."

"The tunnel will be gone by then," Grover said. "I have to follow it. A door like this won't stay open!"

"But we can't," Annabeth said. "The forges!"

Grover looked at her sadly. "I have to, Annabeth. Don't you understand?"

She looked desperate, like she didn't understand at all.

The spider was almost out of sight. But I thought about my conversation with Grover last night, and I knew what we had to do.

"We'll split up," I said.

"No!" Annabeth said. "That's way too dangerous. How will we ever find each other again? And Grover can't go alone."

Tyson put his hand on Grover's shoulder. "I—I will go with him."

I couldn't believe I was hearing this. "Tyson, are you sure?"

The big guy nodded. "Goat boy needs help. We will find the god person. I am not like Hephaestus. I trust friends."

Grover took a deep breath. "Percy, we'll find each other again. We've still got the empathy link. I just . . . have to."

I didn't blame him. This was his life's goal. If he didn't find Pan on this journey, the council would never give him another chance.

"I hope you're right," I said.

"I know I am." I'd never heard him sound so confident about anything, except maybe that cheese enchiladas were better than chicken enchiladas.

"Be careful," I told him. Then I looked at Tyson. He gulped back a sob and gave me a hug that just about squeezed my eyes out of their sockets. Then he and Grover disappeared through the tunnel of tree roots and were lost in the darkness.

"This is bad," Annabeth said. "Splitting up is a really, really bad idea."

"We'll see them again," I said, trying to sound confident. "Now come on. The spider is getting away!"

It wasn't long before the tunnel started to get hot.

The stone walls glowed. The air felt as if we were walking through an oven. The tunnel sloped down and I could hear a loud roar, like a river of metal. The spider skittered along, with Annabeth right behind.

"Hey, wait up," I called to her.

She glanced back at me. "Yeah?"

"Something Hephaestus said back there . . . about Athena."

"She swore never to marry," Annabeth said. "Like Artemis and Hestia. She's one of the maiden goddesses."

I blinked. I'd never heard that about Athena before. "But then—"

"How come she has demigod children?"

I nodded. I was probably blushing, but hopefully it was so hot anyway that Annabeth didn't notice.

"Percy, you know how Athena was born?"

"She sprung from the head of Zeus in full battle armor or something."

"Exactly. She wasn't born in the normal way. She was literally born from thoughts. Her children are born the same way. When Athena falls in love with a mortal man, it's purely intellectual, the way she loved Odysseus in the old stories. It's a meeting of minds. She would tell you that's the purest kind of love."

"So your dad and Athena . . . so you weren't . . ."

"I was a brain child," Annabeth said. "Literally. Children of Athena are sprung from the divine thoughts of our mother and the mortal ingenuity of our father. We are supposed to be a gift, a blessing from Athena on the men she favors."

"But—"

"Percy, the spider's getting away. Do you really want me to explain the exact details of how I was born?"

"Um . . . no. That's okay."

She smirked. "I thought not." And she ran ahead. I followed, but I wasn't sure I would ever look at Annabeth the same way again. I decided some things were better left as mysteries.

The roaring got louder. After another half mile or so, we emerged in a cavern the size of a Super Bowl stadium. Our spider escort stopped and curled into a ball. We had arrived at the forge of Hephaestus.

There was no floor, just bubbling lava hundreds of feet below. We stood on a rock ridge that circled the cavern. A network of metal bridges spanned across it. At the center was a huge platform with all sorts of machines, cauldrons, forges, and the largest anvil I'd ever seen—a block of iron the size of a house. Creatures moved around the platform—several strange, dark shapes, but they were too far away to make out details.

"We'll never be able to sneak up on them," I said.

Annabeth picked up the metal spider and slipped it into her pocket. "I can. Wait here."

"Hold it!" I said, but before I could argue, she put on her Yankees cap and turned invisible.

I didn't dare call after her, but I didn't like the idea of her approaching the forge on her own. If those things out there could sense a god coming, would Annabeth be safe?

I looked back at the Labyrinth tunnel. I missed Grover and Tyson already. Finally I decided I couldn't stay put. I crept along the outer rim of the lava lake, hoping I could get a better angle to see what was happening in the middle.

The heat was horrible. Geryon's ranch had been a winter wonderland compared to this. In no time I was drenched with sweat. My eyes stung from the smoke. I moved along, trying to keep away from the edge, until I found my way blocked by a cart on metal wheels, like the kind they use in mine shafts. I lifted up the tarp and found it was half full of scrap metal. I was about to squeeze my way around it when I heard voices from up ahead, probably from a side tunnel.

"Bring it in?" one asked.

"Yeah," another said. "Movie's just about done."

I panicked. I didn't have time to back up. There was nowhere to hide except . . . the cart. I scrambled inside and pulled the tarp over me, hoping no one had seen me. I curled my fingers around Riptide, just in case I had to fight.

The cart lurched forward.

"Oi," a gruff voice said. "Thing weighs a ton."

"It's celestial bronze," the other said. "What did you expect?"

I got pulled along. We turned a corner, and from the sound of the wheels echoing against the walls I guessed we had passed down a tunnel and into a smaller room.

Hopefully I was not about to be dumped into a smelting pot. If they started to tip me over, I'd have to fight my way out quick. I heard lots of talking, chattering voices that didn't sound human—somewhere between a seal's bark and a dog's growl. There were other sounds too—like an old-fashioned film projector and a tinny voice narrating.

"Just set it in the back," a new voice ordered from across the room. "Now, younglings, please attend to the film. There will be time for questions afterward."

The voices quieted down, and I could hear the film.

As a young sea demon matures, the narrator said, *changes happen in the monster's body. You may notice your fangs getting longer and you may have a sudden desire to devour human beings. These changes are perfectly normal and happen to all young monsters.*

Excited snarling filled the room. The teacher—I guess it must have been a teacher—told the younglings to be quiet, and the film continued. I didn't understand most of it, and I didn't dare look. The film kept talking about growth spurts and acne problems caused by working in the forges, and proper flipper hygiene, and finally it was over.

"Now, younglings," the instructor said, "what is the proper name of our kind?"

"Sea demons!" one of them barked.

"No. Anyone else?"

"Telekhines!" another monster growled.

"Very good," the instructor said. "And why are we here?"

"Revenge!" several shouted.

"Yes, yes, but why?"

"Zeus is evil!" one monster said. "He cast us into Tartarus just because we used magic!"

"Indeed," the instructor said. "After we made so many of the gods' finest weapons. The trident of Poseidon, for one. And of course—we made the greatest weapon of the Titans! Nevertheless, Zeus cast us away and relied on those fumbling Cyclopes. That is why we are taking over the forges of the usurper Hephaestus. And soon we will control the undersea furnaces, our ancestral home!"

I clutched my pen-sword. These snarling things had created Poseidon's trident? What were they talking about? I'd never even heard of a telekhine.

"And so, younglings," the instructor continued, "who do we serve?"

"Kronos!" they shouted.

"And when you grow to be big telekhines, will you make weapons for his army?"

"Yes!"

"Excellent. Now, we've brought in some scraps for you to practice with. Let's see how ingenious you are."

There was a rush of movement and excited voices coming toward the cart. I got ready to uncap Riptide. The tarp was thrown back. I jumped up, my bronze sword springing to life in my hands, and found myself facing a bunch of . . . dogs.

Well, their faces were dogs, anyway, with black snouts, brown eyes, and pointy ears. Their bodies were sleek and black like sea mammals, with stubby legs that were half flipper, half foot, and humanlike hands with sharp claws. If you blended together a kid, a Doberman pinscher, and a sea lion, you'd get something like what I was looking at.

"A demigod!" one snarled.

"Eat it!" yelled another.

But that's as far as they got before I slashed a wide arc with Riptide and vaporized the entire front row of monsters.

"Back off!" I yelled at the rest, trying to sound fierce. Behind them stood their instructor—a six-foot-tall telekhine with Doberman fangs snarling at me. I did my best to stare him down.

"New lesson, class," I announced. "Most monsters will vaporize when sliced with a celestial bronze sword. This change is perfectly normal, and will happen to you *right now* if you don't BACK OFF!"

To my surprise, it worked. The monsters backed up, but there were at least twenty of them. My fear factor wasn't going to last long.

I jumped out of the cart, yelled, "CLASS DISMISSED!" and ran for the exit.

The monsters charged after me, barking and growling. I hoped they couldn't run very fast with those stubby little legs and flippers, but they waddled along pretty well. Thank the gods there was a door on the tunnel leading out to the main cavern. I slammed it shut and turned the wheel handle to lock it, but I doubted it would keep them long.

I didn't know what to do. Annabeth was out here somewhere, invisible. Our chance for a subtle reconnaissance mission had just been blown. I ran toward the platform at the center of the lava lake.

"Annabeth!" I yelled.

"Shhh!" An invisible hand clamped over my mouth and wrestled me down behind a big bronze cauldron. "You want to get us killed?"

I found her head and took off her Yankees cap. She shimmered into existence in front of me, scowling, her face streaked with ash and grime. "Percy, what is your problem?"

"We're going to have company!" I explained quickly about the monster orientation class. Her eyes widened.

"So that's what they are," she said. "Telekhines. I should've known. And they're making . . . Well, look."

We peeked over the cauldron. In the center of the platform stood four sea demons, but these were fully grown, at least eight feet tall. Their black skin glistened in the firelight as they worked, sparks flying as they took turns hammering on a long piece of glowing hot metal.

"The blade is almost complete," one said. "It needs another cooling in blood to fuse the metals."

"Aye," a second said. "It shall be even sharper than before."

"What *is* that?" I whispered.

Annabeth shook her head. "They keep talking about fusing metals. I wonder—"

"They were talking about the greatest Titan weapon," I said. "And they . . . they said they made my father's trident."

"The telekhines betrayed the gods," Annabeth said.

"They were practicing dark magic. I don't know what, exactly, but Zeus banished them to Tartarus."

"With Kronos."

She nodded. "We have to get out—"

No sooner had she said that than the door to the classroom exploded and young telekhines came pouring out. They stumbled over each other, trying to figure out which way to charge.

"Put your cap back on," I said. "Get out!"

"What?" Annabeth shrieked. "No! I'm not leaving you."

"I've got a plan. I'll distract them. You can use the metal spider—maybe it'll lead you back to Hephaestus. You have to tell him what's going on."

"But you'll be killed!"

"I'll be fine. Besides, we've got no choice."

Annabeth glared at me like she was going to punch me. And then she did something that surprised me even more. She kissed me.

"Be careful, Seaweed Brain." She put on her hat and vanished.

I probably would've sat there for the rest of the day, staring at the lava and trying to remember what my name was, but the sea demons jarred me back to reality.

"There!" one yelled. The entire class of telekhines charged across the bridge toward me. I ran for the middle of the platform, surprising the four elder sea demons so much they dropped the red-hot blade. It was about six feet long and curved like a crescent moon. I'd seen a lot of terrifying things, but this unfinished whatever-it-was scared me worse.

The elder demons got over their surprise quickly. There were four ramps leading off the platform, and before I could dash in any direction, each of them had covered an exit.

The tallest one snarled. "What do we have here? A son of Poseidon?'

"Yes," another growled. "I can smell the sea in his blood."

I raised Riptide. My heart was pounding.

"Strike down one of us, demigod," the third demon said, "and the rest of us shall tear you to shreds. Your father betrayed us. He took our gift and said nothing as we were cast into the pit. We will see *him* sliced to pieces. He and all the other Olympians."

I wished I had a plan. I wished I hadn't been lying to Annabeth. I'd wanted her to get out safely, and I hoped she'd been sensible enough to do it. But now it was dawning on me that this might be the place I would die. No prophecies for me. I would get overrun in the heart of a volcano by a pack of dog-faced sea-lion people. The young telekhines were at the platform now, too, snarling and waiting to see how their four elders would deal with me.

I felt something burning against the side of my leg. The ice whistle in my pocket was getting colder. If I ever needed help, now was the time. But I hesitated. I didn't trust Quintus's gift.

Before I could make up my mind, the tallest telekhine said, "Let us see how strong he is. Let us see how long it takes him to burn!"

He scooped some lava out of the nearest furnace. It set his fingers ablaze, but this didn't seem to bother him at all. The other elder telekhines did the same. The first one threw a glop of molten rock at me and set my pants on fire. Two more splattered across my chest. I dropped my sword in sheer terror and swatted at my clothes. Fire was engulfing me. Strangely, it felt only warm at first, but it was getting hotter by the instant.

"Your father's nature protects you," one said. "Makes you hard to burn. But not impossible, youngling. Not impossible."

They threw more lava at me, and I remember screaming. My whole body was on fire. The pain was worse than anything I'd ever felt. I was being consumed. I crumpled to the metal floor and heard the sea demon children howling in delight.

Then I remembered the voice of the river naiad at the ranch: *The water is within me.*

I needed the sea. I felt a tugging sensation in my gut, but I had nothing around to help me. Not a faucet or a river. Not even a petrified seashell this time. And besides, the last time I'd unleashed my power at the stables, there'd been that scary moment when it had almost gotten away from me.

I had no choice. I called to the sea. I reached inside myself and remembered the waves and the currents, the endless power of the ocean. And I let it loose in one horrible scream.

Afterward, I could never describe what happened. An explosion, a tidal wave, a whirlwind of power simultaneously catching me up and blasting me downward into the lava. Fire and water collided, superheated steam, and I shot upward from the heart of the volcano in a huge explosion, just one piece of flotsam thrown free by a million pounds of pressure. The last thing I remember before losing consciousness was flying, flying so high Zeus would never have forgiven me, and then beginning to fall, smoke and fire and water streaming from me. I was a comet hurtling toward the earth.

TWELVE

I TAKE A PERMANENT VACATION

I woke up feeling like I was still on fire. My skin stung. My throat felt as dry as sand.

I saw blue sky and trees above me. I heard a fountain gurgling, and smelled juniper and cedar and a bunch of other sweet-scented plants. I heard waves, too, gently lapping on a rocky shore. I wondered if I was dead, but I knew better. I'd been to the Land of the Dead, and there was no blue sky.

I tried to sit up. My muscles felt like they were melting.

"Stay still," a girl's voice said. "You're too weak to rise."

She laid a cool cloth across my forehead. A bronze spoon hovered over me and liquid was dribbled into my mouth. The drink soothed my throat and left a warm chocolaty aftertaste. Nectar of the gods. Then the girl's face appeared above me.

She had almond eyes and caramel-color hair braided over one shoulder. She was . . . fifteen? Sixteen? It was hard to tell. She had one of those faces that just seemed timeless. She began singing, and my pain dissolved. She was working magic. I could feel her music sinking into my skin, healing and repairing my burns.

"Who?" I croaked.

"Shhh, brave one," she said. "Rest and heal. No harm will come to you here. I am Calypso."

The next time I woke I was in a cave, but as far as caves go, I'd been in a lot worse. The ceiling glittered with different-color crystal formations—white and purple and green, like I was inside one of those cut geodes you see in souvenir shops. I was lying on a comfortable bed with feather pillows and white cotton sheets. The cave was divided into sections by white silk curtains. Against one wall stood a large loom and a harp. Against the other wall were shelves neatly stacked with jars of fruit preserves. Dried herbs hung from the ceiling: rosemary, thyme, and a bunch of other stuff. My mother could've named them all.

There was a fireplace built into the cave wall, and a pot bubbling over the flames. It smelled great, like beef stew.

I sat up, trying to ignore the throbbing pain in my head. I looked at my arms, sure that they would be hideously scarred, but they seemed fine. A little pinker than usual, but not bad. I was wearing a white cotton T-shirt and cotton drawstring pants that weren't mine. My feet were bare. In a moment of panic, I wondered what happened to Riptide, but I felt my pocket and there was my pen, right where it always reappeared.

Not only that but the Stygian ice dog whistle was back in my pocket, too. Somehow it had followed me. And that didn't exactly reassure me.

With difficulty, I stood. The stone floor was freezing

under my feet. I turned and found myself staring into a polished bronze mirror.

"Holy Poseidon," I muttered. I looked as if I'd lost
twenty pounds I couldn't afford to lose. My hair was a rat's
nest. It was singed at the edges like Hephaestus's beard. If I
saw that face on somebody walking down a highway inter-
section asking for money, I would've locked the car doors.

I turned away from the mirror. The cave entrance was to
my left. I headed toward the daylight.

The cave opened onto a green meadow. On the left was
a grove of cedar trees and on the right a huge flower garden.
Four fountains gurgled in the meadow, each shooting water
from the pipes of stone satyrs. Straight ahead, the grass
sloped down to a rocky beach. The waves of a lake lapped
against the stones. I could tell it was a lake because . . . well,
I just could. Fresh water. Not salt. The sun sparkled on the
water, and the sky was pure blue. It seemed like a paradise,
which immediately made me nervous. You deal with mythological stuff for a few years, you learn that paradises are
usually places where you get killed.

The girl with the braided caramel hair, the one who'd
called herself Calypso, was standing at the beach, talking to
someone. I couldn't see him very well in the shimmer from
the sunlight off the water, but they appeared to be arguing.
I tried to remember what I knew about Calypso from the
old myths. I'd heard the name before, but . . . I couldn't
remember. Was she a monster? Did she trap heroes and kill
them? But if she was evil, why was I still alive?

I walked toward her slowly because my legs were still

stiff. When the grass changed to gravel, I looked down to keep my balance, and when I looked up again, the girl was alone. She wore a white sleeveless Greek dress with a low circular neckline trimmed in gold. She brushed at her eyes like she'd just been crying.

"Well," she said, trying for a smile, "the sleeper finally awakes."

"Who were you talking to?" My voice sounded like a frog that had spent time in a microwave.

"Oh . . . just a messenger," she said. "How do you feel?"

"How long have I been out?"

"Time," Calypso mused. "Time is always difficult here. I honestly don't know, Percy."

"You know my name?"

"You talk in your sleep."

I blushed. "Yeah. I've been . . . uh, told that before."

"Yes. Who is Annabeth?"

"Oh, uh. A friend. We were together when—wait, how did I get here? Where am I?"

Calypso reached up and ran her fingers through my mangled hair. I stepped back nervously.

"I'm sorry," she said. "I've just grown used to caring for you. As to how you got here, you fell from the sky. You landed in the water, just there." She pointed across the beach. "I do not know how you survived. The water seemed to cushion your fall. As to where you are, you are in Ogygia."

She pronounced it like *oh-jee-jee-ah*.

"Is that near Mount St. Helens?" I asked, because my geography was pretty terrible.

Calypso laughed. It was a small restrained laugh, like she found me really funny but didn't want to embarrass me. She was cute when she laughed.

"It isn't near anything, brave one," she said. "Ogygia is my phantom island. It exists by itself, anywhere and nowhere. You can heal here in safety. Never fear."

"But my friends——"

"Annabeth," she said. "And Grover and Tyson?"

"Yes!" I said. "I have to get back to them. They're in danger."

She touched my face, and I didn't back away this time. "Rest first. You are no good to your friends until you heal."

As soon as she said it, I realized how tired I was. "You're not . . . you're not an evil sorceress, are you?"

She smiled coyly. "Why would you think that?"

"Well, I met Circe once, and she had a pretty nice island, too. Except she liked to turn men into guinea pigs."

Calypso gave me that laugh again. "I promise I will not turn you into a guinea pig."

"Or anything else?"

"I am no evil sorceress," Calypso said. "And I am not your enemy, brave one. Now rest. Your eyes are already closing."

She was right. My knees buckled, and I would've landed face-first in the gravel if Calypso hadn't caught me. Her hair smelled like cinnamon. She was very strong, or maybe I was just really weak and thin. She walked me back to a cushioned bench by the fountain and helped me lie down.

"Rest," she ordered. And I fell asleep to the sound of the fountains and the smell of cinnamon and juniper.

The next time I awoke it was night, but I wasn't sure if it was the same night or many nights later. I was in the bed in the cave, but I rose and wrapped a robe around myself and padded outside. The stars were brilliant—thousands of them, like you only see way out in the country. I could make out all the constellations Annabeth had taught me: Capricorn, Pegasus, Sagittarius. And there, near the southern horizon, was a new constellation: the Huntress, a tribute to a friend of ours who had died last winter.

"Percy, what do you see?"

I brought my eyes back to earth. However amazing the stars were, Calypso was twice as brilliant. I mean, I've seen the goddess of love herself, Aphrodite, and I would never say this out loud or she'd blast me to ashes, but for my money, Calypso was a lot more beautiful, because she just seemed so natural, like she wasn't trying to be beautiful and didn't even care about that. She just *was*. With her braided hair and white dress, she seemed to glow in the moonlight. She was holding a tiny plant in her hands. Its flowers were silver and delicate.

"I was just looking at . . ." I found myself staring at her face. "Uh . . . I forgot."

She laughed gently. "Well, as long as you're up, you can help me plant these."

She handed me a plant, which had a clump of dirt and roots at the base. The flowers glowed as I held them.

Calypso picked up her gardening spade and directed me to the edge of the garden, where she began to dig.

"That's moonlace," Calypso explained. "It can only be planted at night."

I watched the silvery light flicker around the petals. "What does it do?"

"Do?" Calypso mused. "It doesn't really *do* anything, I suppose. It lives, it gives light, it provides beauty. Does it have to do anything else?"

"I suppose not," I said.

She took the plant, and our hands met. Her fingers were warm. She planted the moonlace and stepped back, surveying her work. "I love my garden."

"It's awesome," I agreed. I mean, I wasn't exactly a gardening type, but Calypso had arbors covered with six different colors of roses, lattices filled with honeysuckle, rows of grapevines bursting with red and purple grapes that would've made Dionysus sit up and beg.

"Back home," I said, "my mom always wanted a garden."

"Why did she not plant one?"

"Well, we live in Manhattan. In an apartment."

"Manhattan? Apartment?"

I stared at her. "You don't know what I'm talking about, do you?"

"I fear not. I haven't left Ogygia in . . . a long time."

"Well, Manhattan's a big city, with not much gardening space."

Calypso frowned. "That is sad. Hermes visits from time to time. He tells me the world outside has changed greatly.

I did not realize it had changed so much you cannot have gardens."

"Why haven't you left your island?"

She looked down. "It is my punishment."

"Why? What did you do?"

"I? Nothing. But I'm afraid my father did a great deal. His name is Atlas."

The name sent a shiver down my back. I'd met the Titan Atlas last winter, and it had not been a happy time. He'd tried to kill pretty much everyone I cared about.

"Still," I said hesitantly, "it's not fair to punish you for what your father's done. I knew another daughter of Atlas. Her name was Zoë. She was one of the bravest people I've ever met."

Calypso studied me for a long time. Her eyes were sad.

"What is it?" I asked.

"Are—are you healed yet, my brave one? Do you think you'll be ready to leave soon?"

"What?" I asked. "I don't know." I moved my legs. They were still stiff. I was already getting dizzy from standing up so long. "You want me to go?"

"I . . ." Her voice broke. "I'll see you in the morning. Sleep well."

She ran off toward the beach. I was too confused to do anything but watch until she disappeared in the dark.

I don't know exactly how much time passed. Like Calypso said, it was hard to keep track on the island. I knew I should be leaving. At the very least, my friends would be worried.

At worst, they could be in serious danger. I didn't even know if Annabeth had made it out of the volcano. I tried to use my empathy link with Grover several times, but I couldn't make contact. I hated not knowing if they were all right.

On the other hand, I really was weak. I couldn't stay on my feet more than a few hours. Whatever I'd done in Mount St. Helens had drained me like nothing else I'd ever experienced.

I didn't feel like a prisoner or anything. I remembered the Lotus Hotel and Casino in Vegas, where I'd been lured into this amazing game world until I almost forgot everything I cared about. But the island of Ogygia wasn't like that at all. I thought about Annabeth, Grover, and Tyson constantly. I remembered exactly why I needed to leave. I just . . . couldn't. And then there was Calypso herself.

She never talked much about herself, but that just made me want to know more. I would sit in the meadow, sipping nectar, and I would try to concentrate on the flowers or the clouds or the reflections on the lake, but I was really staring at Calypso as she worked, the way she brushed her hair over her shoulder, and the little strand that fell in her face whenever she knelt to dig in the garden. Sometimes she would hold out her hand and birds would fly out of the woods to settle on her arm—lorikeets, parrots, doves. She would tell them good morning, ask how it was going back at the nest, and they would chirp for a while, then fly off cheerfully. Calypso's eyes gleamed. She would look at me and we'd share a smile, but almost immediately she'd get that sad expression again and turn away. I didn't understand what was bothering her.

One night we were eating dinner together at the beach. Invisible servants had set up a table with beef stew and apple cider, which may not sound all that exciting, but that's because you haven't tasted it. I hadn't even noticed the invisible servants when I first got to the island, but after a while I became aware of the beds making themselves, meals cooking on their own, clothes being washed and folded by unseen hands.

Anyway, Calypso and I were sitting at dinner, and she looked beautiful in the candlelight. I was telling her about New York and Camp Half-Blood, and then I starting telling her about the time Grover had eaten an apple while we were playing Hacky Sack with it. She laughed, showing off her amazing smile, and our eyes met. Then she dropped her gaze.

"There it is again," I said.

"What?"

"You keep pulling away, like you're trying not to enjoy yourself."

She kept her eyes on her glass of cider. "As I told you, Percy, I have been punished. Cursed, you might say."

"How? Tell me. I want to help."

"Don't say that. Please don't say that."

"Tell me what the punishment is."

She covered her half-finished stew with a napkin, and immediately an invisible servant whisked the bowl away. "Percy, this island, Ogygia, is my home, my birthplace. But it is also my prison. I am under . . . house arrest, I guess you would call it. I will never visit this Manhattan of yours. Or anywhere else. I am alone here."

"Because your father was Atlas."

She nodded. "The gods do not trust their enemies. And rightly so. I should not complain. Some of the prisons are not nearly as nice as mine."

"But that's not fair," I said. "Just because you're related doesn't mean you support him. This other daughter I knew, Zoë Nightshade—she fought against him. She wasn't imprisoned."

"But, Percy," Calypso said gently, "I *did* support him in the first war. He is my father."

"*What?* But the Titans are evil!"

"Are they? All of them? All the time?" She pursed her lips. "Tell me, Percy. I have no wish to argue with you. But do you support the gods because they are good, or because they are your family?"

I didn't answer. She had a point. Last winter, after Annabeth and I had saved Olympus, the gods had had a debate about whether or not they should kill me. That hadn't been exactly good. But still, I felt like I supported them because Poseidon was my dad.

"Perhaps I was wrong in the war," Calypso said. "And in fairness, the gods have treated me well. They visit me from time to time. They bring me word of the outside world. But they can leave. And I cannot."

"You don't have any friends?" I asked. "I mean . . . wouldn't anyone else live here with you? It's a nice place."

A tear trickled down her cheek. "I . . . I promised myself I wouldn't speak of this. But—"

She was interrupted by a rumbling sound somewhere out on the lake. A glow appeared on the horizon. It got brighter and brighter, until I could see a column of fire moving across the surface of the water, coming toward us.

I stood and reached for my sword. "What is that?"

Calypso sighed. "A visitor."

As the column of fire reached the beach, Calypso stood and bowed to it formally. The flames dissipated, and standing before us was a tall man in gray overalls and a metal leg brace, his beard and hair smoldering with fire.

"Lord Hephaestus," Calypso said. "This is a rare honor."

The fire god grunted. "Calypso. Beautiful as always. Would you excuse us, please, my dear? I need to have a word with our young Percy Jackson."

Hephaestus sat down clumsily at the dinner table and ordered a Pepsi. The invisible servant brought him one, opened it too suddenly, and sprayed soda all over the god's work clothes. Hephaestus roared and spat a few curses and swatted the can away.

"Stupid servants," he muttered. "Good automatons are what she needs. They never act up!"

"Hephaestus," I said, "what's going on? Is Annabeth—"

"She's fine," he said. "Resourceful girl, that one. Found her way back, told me the whole story. She's worried sick, you know."

"You haven't told her I'm okay?"

"That's not for me to say," Hephaestus said. "Everyone thinks you're dead. I had to be sure you were coming back before I started telling everyone where you were."

"What do you mean?" I said. "Of course I'm coming back!"

Hephaestus studied me skeptically. He fished something out of his pocket—a metal disk the size of an iPod. He clicked a button and it expanded into a miniature bronze TV. On the screen was news footage of Mount St. Helens, a huge plume of fire and ash trailing into the sky.

"*Still uncertain about further eruptions,*" the newscaster was saying. "*Authorities have ordered the evacuation of almost half a million people as a precaution. Meanwhile, ash has fallen as far away as Lake Tahoe and Vancouver, and the entire Mount St. Helens area is closed to traffic within a hundred-mile radius. While no deaths have been reported, minor injuries and illnesses include—*"

Hephaestus switched it off. "You caused quite an explosion."

I stared at the blank bronze screen. Half a million people evacuated? Injuries. Illness. What had I done?

"The telekhines were scattered," the god told me. "Some vaporized. Some got away, no doubt. I don't think they'll be using my forge any time soon. On the other hand, neither will I. The explosion caused Typhon to stir in his sleep. We'll have to wait and see—"

"I couldn't release him, could I? I mean, I'm not that powerful!"

The god grunted. "Not that powerful, eh? Could have fooled me. You're the son of the Earthshaker, lad. You don't know your own strength."

That's the last thing I wanted him to say. I hadn't been in control of myself in that mountain. I'd released so much energy I'd almost vaporized myself, drained all the life out of me. Now I found out I'd nearly destroyed the Northwest U.S. and almost woken the most horrible monster ever imprisoned by the gods. Maybe I was too dangerous. Maybe it was safer for my friends to think I was dead.

"What about Grover and Tyson?" I asked.

Hephaestus shook his head. "No word, I'm afraid. I suppose the Labyrinth has them."

"So what am I supposed to do?"

Hephaestus winced. "Don't ever ask an old cripple for advice, lad. But I'll tell you this. You've met my wife?"

"Aphrodite."

"That's her. She's a tricky one, lad. Be careful of love. It'll twist your brain around and leave you thinking up is down and right is wrong."

I thought about my meeting with Aphrodite, in the back of a white Cadillac in the desert last winter. She'd told me that she had taken a special interest in me, and she'd be making things hard for me in the romance department, just because she liked me.

"Is this part of her plan?" I asked. "Did she land me here?"

"Possibly. Hard to say with her. But if you decide to leave this place—and I don't say what's right or wrong—then I promised you an answer to your quest. I promised you the way to Daedalus. Well now, here's the thing. It has nothing to do with Ariadne's string. Not really. Sure, the string works. That's what the Titan's army will be after. But the best way through the maze . . . Theseus had the princess's help. And the princess was a regular mortal. Not a drop of god blood in her. But she was clever, and she could see, lad. She could see very clearly. So what I'm saying—I think you know how to navigate the maze."

It finally sank in. Why hadn't I seen it before? Hera had been right. The answer was there all the time.

"Yeah," I said. "Yeah, I know."

"Then you'll need to decide whether or not you're leaving."

"I . . ." I wanted to say yes. Of course I would. But the words stuck in my throat. I found myself looking out at the lake, and suddenly the idea of leaving seemed very hard.

"Don't decide yet," Hephaestus advised. "Wait until daybreak. Daybreak is a good time for decisions."

"Will Daedalus even help us?" I asked. "I mean, if he gives Luke a way to navigate the Labyrinth, we're dead. I saw dreams about . . . Daedalus killed his nephew. He turned bitter and angry and—"

"It isn't easy being a brilliant inventor," Hephaestus rumbled. "Always alone. Always misunderstood. Easy to turn bitter, make horrible mistakes. People are more difficult to work with than machines. And when you break a person, he can't be fixed."

Hephaestus brushed the last drops of Pepsi off his work clothes. "Daedalus started well enough. He helped the Princess Ariadne and Theseus because he felt sorry for them. He tried to do a good deed. And everything in his life went bad because of it. Was that fair?" The god shrugged. "I don't know if Daedalus will help you, lad, but don't judge someone until you've stood at his forge and worked with his hammer, eh?"

"I'll—I'll try."

Hephaestus stood. "Good-bye, lad. You did well, destroying the telekhines. I'll always remember you for that."

It sounded very final, that good-bye. Then he erupted into a column of flame, and the fire moved over the water, heading back to the world outside.

I walked along the beach for several hours. When I finally came back to the meadow, it was very late, maybe four or five in the morning, but Calypso was still in her garden, tending the flowers by starlight. Her moonlace glowed silver, and the other plants responded to the magic, glowing red and yellow and blue.

"He has ordered you to return," Calypso guessed.

"Well, not ordered. He gave me a choice."

Her eyes met mine. "I promised I would not offer."

"Offer what?"

"For you to stay."

"Stay," I said. "Like . . . forever?"

"You would be immortal on this island," she said quietly. "You would never age or die. You could leave the fight to others, Percy Jackson. You could escape your prophecy."

I stared at her, stunned. "Just like that?"

She nodded. "Just like that."

"But . . . my friends."

Calypso rose and took my hand. Her touch sent a warm current through my body. "You asked about my curse, Percy. I did not want to tell you. The truth is the gods send me companionship from time to time. Every thousand years or so, they allow a hero to wash up on my shores, someone who needs my help. I tend to him and befriend him, but it is never random. The Fates make sure that the sort of hero they send . . ."

Her voice trembled, and she had to stop.

I squeezed her hand tighter. "What? What have I done to make you sad?"

"They send a person who can never stay," she whispered. "Who can never accept my offer of companionship for more than a little while. They send me a hero I can't help . . . just the sort of person I can't help falling in love with."

The night was quiet except for the gurgle of the fountains and waves lapping on the shore. It took me a long time to realize what she was saying.

"Me?" I asked.

"If you could see your face." She suppressed a smile, though her eyes were still teary. "Of course, you."

"That's why you've been pulling away all this time?"

"I tried very hard. But I can't help it. The Fates are cruel. They sent you to me, my brave one, knowing that you would break my heart."

"But . . . I'm just . . . I mean, I'm just *me*."

"That is enough," Calypso promised. "I told myself I would not even speak of this. I would let you go without even offering. But I can't. I suppose the Fates knew that, too. You could stay with me, Percy. I'm afraid that is the only way you could help me."

I stared at the horizon. The first red streaks of dawn were lightening the sky. I could stay here forever, disappear from the earth. I could live with Calypso, with invisible servants tending to my every need. We could grow flowers in the garden and talk to songbirds and walk on the beach under perfect blue skies. No war. No prophecy. No more taking sides.

"I can't," I told her.

She looked down sadly.

"I would never do anything to hurt you," I said, "but my friends need me. I know how to help them now. I have to get back."

She picked a flower from her garden—a sprig of silver moonlace. Its glow faded as the sunrise came up. *Daybreak is a good time for decisions*, Hephaestus had said. Calypso tucked the flower into my T-shirt pocket.

She stood on her tiptoes and kissed me on the forehead, like a blessing. "Then come to the beach, my hero. And we will send you on your way."

The raft was a ten-foot square of logs lashed together with a pole for a mast and a simple white linen sail. It didn't look like it would be very seaworthy, or lakeworthy.

"This will take you wherever you desire," Calypso promised. "It is quite safe."

I took her hand, but she let it slip out of mine.

"Maybe I can visit you," I said.

She shook her head. "No man ever finds Ogygia twice, Percy. When you leave, I will never see you again."

"But—"

"Go, please." Her voice broke. "The Fates are cruel, Percy. Just remember me." Then a little trace of her smile returned. "Plant a garden in Manhattan for me, will you?"

"I promise." I stepped onto the raft. Immediately it began to sail from the shore.

As I sailed into the lake I realized the Fates really were cruel. They sent Calypso someone she couldn't help but love. But it worked both ways. For the rest of my life I would be thinking about her. She would always be my biggest *what if*.

Within minutes the island of Ogygia was lost in the mist. I was sailing alone over the water toward the sunrise.

Then I told the raft what to do. I said the only place I could think of, because I needed comfort and friends.

"Camp Half-Blood," I said. "Sail me home."

THIRTEEN

WE HIRE A NEW GUIDE

Hours later, my raft washed up at Camp Half-Blood. How I got there, I have no idea. At some point the lake water just changed to salt water. The familiar shoreline of Long Island appeared up ahead, and a couple of friendly great white sharks surfaced and steered me toward the beach.

When I landed, the camp seemed deserted. It was late afternoon, but the archery range was empty. The climbing wall poured lava and rumbled all by itself. Pavilion: nothing. Cabins: all vacant. Then I noticed smoke rising from the amphitheater. Too early for a campfire, and I didn't figure they were roasting marshmallows. I ran toward it.

Before I even got there I heard Chiron making an announcement. When I realized what he was saying, I stopped in my tracks.

"—assume he is dead," Chiron said. "After so long a silence, it is unlikely our prayers will be answered. I have asked his best surviving friend to do the final honors."

I came up on the back of the amphitheater. Nobody noticed me. They were all looking forward, watching as Annabeth took a long green silk burial cloth, embroidered with a trident, and set it on the flames. They were burning my shroud.

Annabeth turned to face the audience. She looked terrible. Her eyes were puffy from crying, but she managed to say, "He was probably the bravest friend I've ever had. He . . ." Then she saw me. Her face went blood red. "He's right there!"

Heads turned. People gasped.

"Percy!" Beckendorf grinned. A bunch of other kids crowded around me and clapped me on the back. I heard a few curses from the Ares cabin, but Clarisse just rolled her eyes, like she couldn't believe I'd had the nerve to survive. Chiron cantered over and everyone made way for him.

"Well," he sighed with obvious relief. "I don't believe I've ever been happier to see a camper return. But you must tell me—"

"WHERE HAVE YOU BEEN?" Annabeth interrupted, shoving aside the other campers. I thought she was going to punch me, but instead she hugged me so fiercely she nearly cracked my ribs. The other campers fell silent. Annabeth seemed to realize she was making a scene and pushed me away. "I—we thought you were dead, Seaweed Brain!"

"I'm sorry," I said. "I got lost."

"LOST?" she yelled. "Two weeks, Percy? Where in the world—"

"Annabeth," Chiron interrupted. "Perhaps we should discuss this somewhere more private, shall we? The rest of you, back to your normal activities!"

Without waiting for us to protest, he picked up Annabeth and me as easily as if we were kittens, slung us both onto his back, and galloped off toward the Big House.

* * *

I didn't tell them the whole story. I just couldn't bring myself to talk about Calypso. I explained how I'd caused the explosion at Mount St. Helens and gotten blasted out of the volcano. I told them I'd been marooned on an island. Then Hephaestus had found me and told me I could leave. A magic raft had carried me back to camp.

All that was true, but as I said it my palms felt sweaty.

"You've been gone two weeks." Annabeth's voice was steadier now, but she still looked pretty shaken up. "When I heard the explosion, I thought—"

"I know," I said. "I'm sorry. But I figured out how to get through the Labyrinth. I talked to Hephaestus."

"He told you the answer?"

"Well, he sort of told me that I already knew. And I do. I understand now."

I told them my idea.

Annabeth's jaw dropped. "Percy, that's crazy!"

Chiron sat back in his wheelchair and stroked his beard. "There is precedent, however. Theseus had the help of Ariadne. Harriet Tubman, daughter of Hermes, used many mortals on her Underground Railroad for just this reason."

"But this is *my* quest," Annabeth said. "*I* need to lead it."

Chiron looked uncomfortable. "My dear, it is your quest. But you need help."

"And *this* is supposed to help? Please! It's wrong. It's cowardly. It's—"

"Hard to admit we need a mortal's help," I said. "But it's true."

Annabeth glared at me. "You are the *single most annoying* person I have ever met!" And she stormed out of the room.

I stared at the doorway. I felt like hitting something. "So much for being the bravest friend she's ever had."

"She will calm down," Chiron promised. "She's jealous, my boy."

"That's stupid. She's not . . . it's not like . . ."

Chiron chuckled. "It hardly matters. Annabeth is very territorial about her friends, in case you haven't noticed. She was quite worried about you. And now that you're back, I think she suspects where you were marooned."

I met his eyes, and I knew Chiron had guessed about Calypso. It was hard to hide anything from a guy who's been training heroes for three thousand years. He's pretty much seen it all.

"We won't dwell on your choices," Chiron said. "You came back. That is what matters."

"Tell that to Annabeth."

Chiron smiled. "In the morning I will have Argus take the two of you into Manhattan. You might stop by your mother's, Percy. She is . . . understandably distraught."

My heart skipped a beat. All that time on Calypso's island, I'd never even thought how my mom would be feeling. She'd think I was dead. She'd be devastated. What was wrong with me that I hadn't even considered that?

"Chiron," I said, "what about Grover and Tyson? Do you think—"

"I don't know, my boy." Chiron gazed into the empty fireplace. "Juniper is quite distressed. All her branches are turning yellow. The Council of Cloven Elders has revoked Grover's searcher's license *in absentia*. Assuming he comes back alive, they will force him into a shameful exile." He sighed. "Grover and Tyson are very resourceful, however. We can still hope."

"I shouldn't have let them run off."

"Grover has his own destiny, and Tyson was brave to follow him. You would know if Grover was in mortal danger, don't you think?"

"I suppose. The empathy link. But—"

"There is something else I should tell you, Percy," he said. "Actually two unpleasant things."

"Great."

"Chris Rodriguez, our guest . . ."

I remembered what I'd seen in the basement, Clarisse trying to talk to him while he babbled about the Labyrinth. "Is he dead?"

"Not yet," Chiron said grimly. "But he's much worse. He's in the infirmary now, too weak to move. I had to order Clarisse back to her regular schedule, because she was at his bedside constantly. He doesn't respond to anything. He won't take food or drink. None of my medicines help. He has simply lost the will to live."

I shuddered. Despite all the run-ins I'd had with Clarisse, I felt horrible for her. She'd tried so hard to help him. And now that I'd been in the Labyrinth, I could understand why it had been so easy for the ghost of Minos to drive Chris mad. If I'd been wandering around down there alone, without my friends to help, I'd never have made it out.

"I'm sorry to say," Chiron continued, "the other news is less pleasant still. Quintus has disappeared."

"Disappeared? How?"

"Three nights ago he slipped into the Labyrinth. Juniper watched him go. It appears you may have been right about him."

"He's a spy for Luke." I told Chiron about the Triple G Ranch—how Quintus had bought his scorpions there and Geryon had been supplying Kronos's army. "It can't be a coincidence."

Chiron sighed heavily. "So many betrayals. I had hoped Quintus would prove a friend. It seems my judgment was bad."

"What about Mrs. O'Leary?" I asked.

"The hellhound is still in the arena. It won't let anyone approach. I did not have the heart to force it into a cage . . . or destroy it."

"Quintus wouldn't just leave her."

"As I said, Percy, we seem to have been wrong about him. Now, you should prepare yourself for the morning. You and Annabeth still have much to do."

I left him in his wheelchair, staring sadly into the fireplace. I wondered how many times he'd sat here, waiting for heroes that never came back.

Before dinner I stopped by the sword arena. Sure enough, Mrs. O'Leary was curled up in an enormous black furry mound in the middle of the stadium, chewing halfheartedly on the head of a warrior dummy.

When she saw me, she barked and came bounding toward me. I thought I was dead meat. I just had time to say, "Whoa!" before she bowled me over and started licking my face. Now usually, being the son of Poseidon and all, I only get wet if I want to, but my powers apparently did not extend to dog saliva, because I got a pretty good bath.

"Whoa, girl!" I yelled. "Can't breathe. Lemme up!"

Eventually I managed to get her off me. I scratched her ears and found her an extra-gigantic dog biscuit.

"Where's your master?" I asked her. "How could he just leave you, huh?"

She whimpered like she wanted to know that, too. I was ready to believe Quintus was an enemy, but still I couldn't understand why he'd leave Mrs. O'Leary behind. If there was one thing I was sure of, it was that he really cared for his megadog.

I was thinking about that and toweling the dog spit off my face when a girl's voice said, "You're lucky she didn't bite your head off."

Clarisse was standing at the other end of the arena with her sword and shield. "Came here to practice yesterday," she grumbled. "Dog tried to chew me up."

"She's an intelligent dog," I said.

"Funny."

She walked toward us. Mrs. O'Leary growled, but I patted her on the head and calmed her down.

"Stupid hellhound," Clarisse said. "Not going to keep me from practicing."

"I heard about Chris," I said. "I'm sorry."

Clarisse paced a circle around the arena. When she came to the nearest dummy, she attacked viciously, chopping its head off with a single blow and driving her sword through its guts. She pulled the sword out and kept walking.

"Yeah, well. Sometimes things go wrong." Her voice was shaky. "Heroes get hurt. They . . . they die, and the monsters just keep coming back."

She picked up a javelin and threw it across the arena. It nailed a dummy straight between the eyeholes of its helmet.

She had called Chris a hero, like he had never gone over to the Titans' side. It reminded me of the way Annabeth sometimes talked about Luke. I decided not to bring that up.

"Chris was brave," I said. "I hope he gets better."

She glared at me as if I were her next target. Mrs. O'Leary growled.

"Do me a favor," Clarisse told me.

"Yeah, sure."

"If you find Daedalus, don't trust him. Don't ask him for help. Just kill him."

"Clarisse—"

"Because anybody who can make something like the Labyrinth, Percy? That person is evil. Plain evil."

For a second she reminded me of Eurytion the cowherd, her much older half brother. She had the same hard look in her eyes, as if she'd been used for the past two thousand years and was getting tired of it. She sheathed her sword. "Practice time is over. From now on, it's for real."

* * *

That night I slept in my own bunk, and for the first time since Calypso's Island, dreams found me.

I was in a king's courtroom—a big white chamber with marble columns and a wooden throne. Sitting on it was a plump guy with curly red hair and a crown of laurels. At his side stood three girls who looked like his daughters. They all had his red hair and were dressed in blue robes.

The doors creaked open and a herald announced, "Minos, King of Crete!"

I tensed, but the man on the throne just smiled at his daughters. "I can't wait to see the expression on his face."

Minos, the royal creep himself, swept into the room. He was so tall and serious he made the other king look silly. Minos's pointed beard had gone gray. He looked thinner than the last time I'd dreamed of him, and his sandals were spattered with mud, but the same cruel light shined in his eyes.

He bowed stiffly to the man on the throne. "King Cocalus. I understand you have solved my little riddle?"

Cocalus smiled. "Hardly *little*, Minos. Especially when you advertise across the world that you are willing to pay a thousand gold talents to the one who can solve it. Is the offer genuine?"

Minos clapped his hands. Two buff guards walked in, struggling with a big wooden crate. They set it at Cocalus's feet and opened it. Stacks of gold bars glittered. It had to be worth like a gazillion dollars.

Cocalus whistled appreciatively. "You must have bankrupted your kingdom for such a reward, my friend."

"That is not your concern."

Cocalus shrugged. "The riddle was quite simple, really. One of my retainers solved it."

"Father," one of the girls warned. She looked like the oldest—a little taller than her sisters.

Cocalus ignored her. He took a spiral seashell from the folds of his robe. A silver string had been threaded through it, so it hung like a huge bead on a necklace.

Minos stepped forward and took the shell. "One of your retainers, you say? How did he thread the string without breaking the shell?"

"He used an ant, if you can believe it. Tied a silk string to the little creature and coaxed it through the shell by putting honey at the far end."

"Ingenious man," Minos said.

"Oh, indeed. My daughters' tutor. They are quite fond of him."

Minos's eyes turned cold. "I would be careful of that."

I wanted to warn Cocalus: *Don't trust this guy! Throw him in the dungeon with some man-eating lions or something!* But the red-headed king just chuckled. "Not to worry, Minos. My daughters are wise beyond their years. Now, about my gold—"

"Yes," Minos said. "But you see the gold is for the man who solved the riddle. And there can be only one such man. You are harboring Daedalus."

Cocalus shifted uncomfortably on his throne. "How is it that you know his name?"

"He is a thief," Minos said. "He once worked in my

court, Cocalus. He turned my own daughter against me. He helped a usurper make a fool of me in my own palace. And then he escaped justice. I have been pursuing him for ten years."

"I knew nothing of this. But I have offered the man my protection. He has been a most useful—"

"I offer you a choice," Minos said. "Turn over the fugitive to me, and this gold is yours. Or risk making me your enemy. You do not want Crete as your enemy."

Cocalus paled. I thought it was stupid for him to look so scared in the middle of his own throne room. He should've summoned his army or something. Minos only had two guards. But Cocalus just sat there sweating on his throne.

"Father," his oldest daughter said, "you can't—"

"Silence, Aelia." Cocalus twisted his beard. He looked again at the glittering gold. "This pains me, Minos. The gods do not love a man who breaks his oath of hospitality."

"The gods do not love those who harbor criminals, either."

Cocalus nodded. "Very well. You shall have your man in chains."

"Father!" Aelia said again. Then she caught herself, and changed her voice to a sweeter tone. "At—at least let us feast our guest first. After his long journey, he should be treated to a hot bath, new clothes, and a decent meal. I would be honored to draw the bath myself."

She smiled prettily at Minos, and the old king grunted. "I suppose a bath would not be amiss." He looked at

Cocalus. "I will see you at dinner, my lord. With the prisoner."

"This way, Your Majesty," said Aelia. She and her sisters led Minos out of the chamber.

I followed them into a bath chamber decorated with mosaic tiles. Steam filled the air. A running-water faucet poured hot water into the tub. Aelia and her sisters filled it with rose petals and something that must've been Ancient Greek Mr. Bubble, because soon the water was covered with multicolored foam. The girls turned aside as Minos dropped his robes and slipped into the bath.

"Ahh." He smiled. "An excellent bath. Thank you, my dears. The journey has been long indeed."

"You have been chasing your prey ten years, my lord?" Aelia asked, batting her eyelashes. "You must be very determined."

"I never forget a debt." Minos grinned. "Your father was wise to agree to my demands."

"Oh, indeed, my lord!" Aelia said. I thought she was laying on the flattery pretty thick, but the old guy was eating it up. Aelia's sisters trickled scented oil over the king's head.

"You know, my lord," Aelia said, "Daedalus thought you would come. He thought the riddle might be a trap, but he couldn't resist solving it."

Minos frowned. "Daedalus spoke to you about me?"

"Yes, my lord."

"He is a bad man, princess. My own daughter fell under his spell. Do not listen to him."

"He is a genius," Aelia said. "And he believes a woman

is just as smart as a man. He was the first to ever teach us as if we had minds of our own. Perhaps your daughter felt the same way."

Minos tried to sit up, but Aelia's sisters pushed him back into the water. Aelia came up behind him. She held three tiny orbs in her palm. At first I thought they were bath beads, but she threw them in the water and the beads sprouted bronze threads that began wrapping around the king, tying him up at the ankles, binding his wrists to his sides, circling his neck. Even though I hated Minos, it was pretty horrible to watch. He thrashed and cried out, but the girls were much stronger. Soon he was helpless, lying in the bath with his chin just above the water. The bronze strands were still wrapping around him like a cocoon, tightening across his body.

"What do you want?" Minos demanded. "Why do you do this?"

Aelia smiled. "Daedalus has been kind to us, Your Majesty. And I do not like you threatening our father."

"You tell Daedalus," Minos growled. "You tell him I will hound him even after death! If there is any justice in the Underworld, my soul will haunt him for eternity!"

"Brave words, Your Majesty," Aelia said. "I wish you luck finding your justice in the Underworld."

And with that, the bronze threads wrapped around Minos's face, making him a bronze mummy.

The door of the bathhouse opened. Daedalus stepped in, carrying a traveler's bag.

He'd trimmed his hair short. His beard was pure white.

He looked frail and sad, but he reached down and touched the mummy's forehead. The threads unraveled and sank to the bottom of the tub. There was nothing inside them. It was as if King Minos had just dissolved.

"A painless death," Daedalus mused. "More than he deserved. Thank you, my princesses."

Aelia hugged him. "You cannot stay here, teacher. When our father finds out—"

"Yes," Daedalus said. "I fear I have brought you trouble."

"Oh, do not worry for us. Father will be happy enough taking that old man's gold. And Crete is a very long way away. But he will blame you for Minos's death. You must flee to somewhere safe."

"Somewhere safe," the old man repeated. "For years I have fled from kingdom to kingdom, looking for somewhere safe. I fear Minos told the truth. Death will not stop him from hounding me. There is no place under the sun that will harbor me, once word of this crime gets out."

"Then where will you go?" Aelia said.

"A place I swore never to enter again," Daedalus said. "My prison may be my only sanctuary."

"I do not understand," Aelia said.

"It's best you did not."

"But what of the Underworld?" one her sisters asked. "Terrible judgment will await you! Every man must die."

"Perhaps," Daedalus said. Then he brought a scroll from his traveling bag—the same scroll I'd seen in my last dream, with his nephew's notes. "Or perhaps not."

He patted Aelia's shoulder, then blessed her and her sisters. He looked down once more at the coppery threads glinting in the bottom of the bath. "Find me if you dare, king of ghosts."

He turned toward the mosaic wall and touched a tile. A glowing mark appeared—a Greek Δ—and the wall slid aside. The princesses gasped.

"You never told us of secret passages!" Aelia said. "You have been busy."

"The *Labyrinth* has been busy," Daedalus corrected. "Do not try to follow me, my dears, if you value your sanity."

My dream shifted. I was underground in a stone chamber. Luke and another half-blood warrior were studying a map by flashlight.

Luke cursed. "It should've been the last turn." He crumpled up the map and tossed it aside.

"Sir!" his companion protested.

"Maps are useless here," Luke said. "Don't worry. I'll find it."

"Sir, is it true that the larger the group—"

"The more likely you'll get lost? Yes, that's true. Why do you think we sent out solo explorers to begin with? But don't worry. As soon as we have the thread, we can lead the vanguard through."

"But how will we *get* the thread?"

Luke stood, flexing his fingers. "Oh, Quintus will come through. All we have to do is reach the arena, and it's at a juncture. Impossible to get anywhere without passing it.

That's why we must have a truce with its master. We just have to stay alive until—"

"Sir!" a new voice came from the corridor. Another guy in Greek armor ran forward, carrying a torch. "The *dracaenae* found a half-blood!"

Luke scowled. "Alone? Wandering the maze?"

"Yes, sir! You'd better come quick. They're in the next chamber. They've got him cornered."

"Who is it?"

"No one I've ever seen before, sir."

Luke nodded. "A blessing from Kronos. We may be able to use this half-blood. Come!"

They ran down the corridor, and I woke with a start, staring into the dark. *A lone half-blood, wandering in the maze.* It was a long time before I got to sleep again.

The next morning I made sure Mrs. O'Leary had enough dog biscuits. I asked Beckendorf to keep an eye on her, which he didn't seem too happy about. Then I hiked over Half-Blood Hill and met Annabeth and Argus on the road.

Annabeth and I didn't talk much in the van. Argus never spoke, probably because he had eyes all over his body, including—so I'd heard—at the tip of his tongue, and he didn't like to show that off.

Annabeth looked queasy, as if she'd slept even worse than me.

"Bad dreams?" I asked at last.

She shook her head. "An Iris-message from Eurytion."

"Eurytion! Is something wrong with Nico?"

"He left the ranch last night, heading back into the maze."

"*What?* Didn't Eurytion try to stop him?"

"Nico was gone before he woke up. Orthus tracked his scent as far as the cattle guard. Eurytion said he'd been hearing Nico talk to himself the last few nights. Only now he thinks Nico was talking with the ghost again, Minos."

"He's in danger," I said.

"No kidding. Minos is one of the judges of the dead, but he's got a vicious streak a mile wide. I don't know what he wants with Nico, but—"

"That's not what I meant," I said. "I had this dream last night . . ." I told her about Luke, how he'd mentioned Quintus, and how his men had found a half-blood alone in the maze.

Annabeth's jaw clenched. "That's very, very bad."

"So what do we do?"

She raised an eyebrow. "Well, it's a good thing you have a plan to guide us, huh?"

It was Saturday, and traffic was heavy going into the city. We arrived at my mom's apartment around noon. When she answered the door, she gave me a hug only a little less overwhelming than having a hellhound jump on you.

"I *told* them you were all right," my mom said, but she sounded like the weight of the sky had just been lifted off her shoulders—and believe me, I know firsthand how that feels.

She sat us down at the kitchen table and insisted on

feeding us her special blue chocolate-chip cookies while we caught her up on the quest. As usual, I tried to water down the frightening parts (which was pretty much everything), but somehow that just made it sound more dangerous.

When I got to the part about Geryon and the stables, my mom pretended like she was going to strangle me. "I can't get him to clean his room, but he'll clean a hundred tons of horse manure out of some monster's stables?"

Annabeth laughed. It was the first time I'd heard her laugh in a long time, and it was nice to hear.

"So," my mom said when I was done with the story, "you wrecked Alcatraz Island, made Mount St. Helens explode, and displaced half a million people, but at least you're safe." That's my mom, always looking on the bright side.

"Yep," I agreed. "That pretty much covers it."

"I wish Paul were here," she said, half to herself. "He wanted to talk to you."

"Oh, right. The school."

So much had happened since then that I'd almost forgotten about the high school orientation at Goode—the fact I'd left the band hall in flames, and my mom's boyfriend had last seen me jumping though a window like a fugitive.

"What did you tell him?" I asked.

My mom shook her head. "What could I say? He knows something is different about you, Percy. He's a smart man. He believes that you're not a bad person. He doesn't know what's going on, but the school is pressuring him. After all, he got you admitted there. He needs to convince them the fire wasn't your fault. And since you ran away, that looks bad."

Annabeth was studying me. She looked pretty sympathetic. I knew she'd been in similar situations. It's never easy for a half-blood in the mortal world.

"I'll talk to him," I promised. "After we're done with the quest. I'll even tell him the truth if you want."

My mom put her hand on my shoulder. "You would do that?"

"Well, yeah. I mean, he'll think we're crazy."

"He already thinks that."

"Then there's nothing to lose."

"Thank you, Percy. I'll tell him you'll be home . . ." She frowned. "When? What happens now?"

Annabeth broke her cookie in half. "Percy has this *plan.*"

Reluctantly I told my mom.

She nodded slowly. "It sounds very dangerous. But it might work."

"You have the same abilities, don't you?" I asked. "You can see through the Mist."

My mom sighed. "Not so much now. When I was younger it was easier. But yes, I've always been able to see more than was good for me. It's one of the things that caught your father's attention, when we first met. Just be careful. Promise me you'll be safe."

"We'll try, Ms. Jackson," Annabeth said. "Keeping your son safe is a big job, though." She folded her arms and glared out the kitchen window. I picked at my napkin and tried not to say anything.

My mom frowned. "What's going on with you two? Have you been fighting?"

Neither of us said anything.

"I see," my mom said, and I wondered if she could see through more than just the Mist. It sounded like she understood what was going on with Annabeth and me, but *I* sure as heck didn't. "Well, remember," she said, "Grover and Tyson are counting on you two."

"I know," Annabeth and I said at the same time, which embarrassed me even more.

My mom smiled. "Percy, you'd better use the phone in the hall. Good luck."

I was relieved to get out of the kitchen, even though I was nervous about what I was about to do. I went to the phone and placed the call. The number had washed off my hand a long time ago, but that was okay. Without meaning to, I'd memorized it.

We arranged a meeting in Times Square. We found Rachel Elizabeth Dare in front of the Marriott Marquis, and she was completely painted gold.

I mean her face, her hair, her clothes—everything. She looked like she'd been touched by King Midas. She was standing like a statue with five other kids all painted metallic—copper, bronze, silver. They were frozen in different poses while tourists hustled past or stopped to stare. Some passersby threw money at the tarp on the sidewalk.

The sign at Rachel's feet said, URBAN ART FOR KIDS, DONATIONS APPRECIATED.

Annabeth and I stood there for like five minutes, staring at Rachel, but if she noticed us she didn't let on. She didn't move or even blink that I could see. Being ADHD and all, I could not have done that. Standing still that long would've driven me crazy. It was weird to see Rachel in gold, too. She looked like a statue of somebody famous, an actress or something. Only her eyes were normal green.

"Maybe if we push her over," Annabeth suggested.

I thought that was a little mean, but Rachel didn't respond. After another few minutes, a kid in silver walked up from the hotel taxi stand, where he'd been taking a break. He took a pose like he was lecturing the crowd, right next to Rachel. Rachel unfroze and stepped off the tarp.

"Hey, Percy." She grinned. "Good timing! Let's get some coffee."

We walked down to a place called the Java Moose on West 43rd. Rachel ordered an Espresso Extreme, the kind of stuff Grover would like. Annabeth and I got fruit smoothies and we sat at a table right under the stuffed moose. Nobody even looked twice at Rachel in her golden outfit.

"So," she said, "it's Annabell, right?"

"Annabeth," Annabeth corrected. "Do you always dress in gold?"

"Not usually," Rachel said. "We're raising money for our group. We do volunteer art projects for elementary kids 'cause they're cutting art from the schools, you know? We do this once a month, take in about five hundred dollars on a good weekend. But I'm guessing you don't want to talk about that. You're a half-blood, too?"

"Shhh!" Annabeth said, looking around. "Just announce it to the world, how about?"

"Okay." Rachel stood up and said really loud, "Hey, everybody! These two aren't human! They're half Greek god!"

Nobody even looked over. Rachel shrugged and sat down. "They don't seem to care."

"That's not funny," Annabeth said. "This isn't a joke, mortal girl."

"Hold it, you two," I said. "Just calm down."

"I'm calm," Rachel insisted. "Every time I'm around you, some monster attacks us. What's to be nervous about?"

"Look," I said. "I'm sorry about the band room. I hope they didn't kick you out or anything."

"Nah. They asked me a lot of questions about you. I played dumb."

"Was it hard?" Annabeth asked.

"Okay, stop!" I intervened. "Rachel, we've got a problem. And we need your help."

Rachel narrowed her eyes at Annabeth. "*You* need my help?"

Annabeth stirred her straw in her smoothie. "Yeah," she said sullenly. "Maybe."

I told Rachel about the Labyrinth, and how we needed to find Daedalus. I told her what had happened the last few times we'd gone in.

"So you want me to guide you," she said. "Through a place I've never been."

"You can see through the Mist," I said. "Just like

Ariadne. I'm betting you can see the right path. The Labyrinth won't be able to fool you as easily."

"And if you're wrong?"

"Then we'll get lost. Either way, it'll be dangerous. Very, very dangerous."

"I could die?"

"Yeah."

"I thought you said monsters don't care about mortals. That sword of yours—"

"Yeah," I said. "Celestial bronze doesn't hurt mortals. Most monsters would ignore you. But Luke . . . he doesn't care. He'll use mortals, demigods, monsters, whatever. And he'll kill anyone who gets in his way."

"Nice guy," Rachel said.

"He's under the influence of a Titan," Annabeth said defensively. "He's been deceived."

Rachel looked back and forth between us. "Okay," she said. "I'm in."

I blinked. I hadn't figured it would be so easy. "Are you sure?"

"Hey, my summer was going to be boring. This is the best offer I've gotten yet. So what do I look for?"

"We have to find an entrance to the Labyrinth," Annabeth said. "There's an entrance at Camp Half-Blood, but you can't go there. It's off-limits to mortals."

She said *mortals* like it was some sort of terrible condition, but Rachel just nodded. "Okay. What does an entrance to the Labyrinth look like?"

"It could be anything," Annabeth said. "A section of

wall. A boulder. A doorway. A sewer entrance. But it would have the mark of Daedalus on it. A Greek Δ, glowing in blue."

"Like this?" Rachel drew the symbol Delta in water on our table.

"That's it," Annabeth said. "You know Greek?"

"No," Rachel said. She pulled a big blue plastic hairbrush from her pocket and started brushing the gold out of her hair. "Let me get changed. You'd better come with me to the Marriott."

"Why?" Annabeth asked.

"Because there's an entrance like that in the hotel basement, where we store our costumes. It's got the mark of Daedalus."

ᴄᴛ◌

MY BROTHER DUELS ME TO
THE DEATH

The metal door was half hidden behind a laundry bin full of dirty hotel towels. I didn't see anything strange about it, but Rachel showed me where to look, and I recognized the faint blue symbol etched in the metal.

"It hasn't been used in a long time," Annabeth said.

"I tried to open it once," Rachel said, "just out of curiosity. It's rusted shut."

"No." Annabeth stepped forward. "It just needs the touch of a half-blood."

Sure enough, as soon as Annabeth put her hand on the mark, it glowed blue. The metal door unsealed and creaked open, revealing a dark staircase leading down.

"Wow." Rachel looked calm, but I couldn't tell if she was pretending or not. She'd changed into a ratty Museum of Modern Art T-shirt and her regular marker-colored jeans, her blue plastic hairbrush sticking out of her pocket. Her red hair was tied back, but she still had flecks of gold in it, and traces of the gold glitter on her face. "So . . . after you?"

"You're the guide," Annabeth said with mock politeness. "Lead on."

The stairs led down to a large brick tunnel. It was so dark I couldn't see two feet in front of us, but Annabeth and I had restocked on flashlights. As soon as we switched them on, Rachel yelped.

A skeleton was grinning at us. It wasn't human. It was huge, for one thing—at least ten feet tall. It had been strung up, chained by its wrists and ankles so it made a kind of giant X over the tunnel. But what really sent a shiver down my back was the single black eye socket in the center of its skull.

"A Cyclops," Annabeth said. "It's very old. It's not . . . anybody we know."

It wasn't Tyson, she meant. But that didn't make me feel much better. I still felt like it had been put here as a warning. Whatever could kill a grown Cyclops, I didn't want to meet.

Rachel swallowed. "You have a friend who's a Cyclops?"

"Tyson," I said. "My half brother."

"Your *half brother*?"

"Hopefully we'll find him down here," I said. "And Grover. He's a satyr."

"Oh." Her voice was small. "Well then, we'd better keep moving."

She stepped under the skeleton's left arm and kept walking. Annabeth and I exchanged looks. Annabeth shrugged. We followed Rachel deeper into the maze.

After fifty feet we came to a crossroads. Ahead, the brick tunnel continued. To the right, the walls were made of ancient marble slabs. To the left, the tunnel was dirt and tree roots.

I pointed left. "That looks like the tunnel Tyson and Grover took."

Annabeth frowned. "Yeah, but the architecture to the right—those old stones—that's more likely to lead to an ancient part of the maze, toward Daedalus's workshop."

"We need to go straight," Rachel said.

Annabeth and I both looked at her.

"That's the least likely choice," Annabeth said.

"You don't see it?" Rachel asked. "Look at the floor."

I saw nothing except well-worn bricks and mud.

"There's a brightness there," Rachel insisted. "Very faint. But forward is the correct way. To the left, farther down the tunnel, those tree roots are moving like feelers. I don't like that. To the right, there's a trap about twenty feet down. Holes in the walls, maybe for spikes. I don't think we should risk it."

I didn't see anything like she was describing, but I nodded. "Okay. Forward."

"You believe her?" Annabeth asked.

"Yeah," I said. "Don't you?"

Annabeth looked like she wanted to argue, but she waved at Rachel to lead on. Together we kept walking down the brick corridor. It twisted and turned, but there were no more side tunnels. We seemed to be angling down, heading deeper underground.

"No traps?" I asked anxiously.

"Nothing." Rachel knit her eyebrows. "Should it be this easy?"

"I don't know," I said. "It never was before."

"So, Rachel," Annabeth said, "where are you from, exactly?"

She said it like, *What planet are you from?* But Rachel didn't look offended.

"Brooklyn," she said.

"Aren't your parents going to be worried if you're out late?"

Rachel exhaled. "Not likely. I could be gone a week and they'd never notice."

"Why not?" This time Annabeth didn't sound as sarcastic. Having trouble with parents was something she understood.

Before Rachel could answer, there was a creaking noise in front of us, like huge doors opening.

"What was that?" Annabeth asked.

"I don't know," Rachel said. "Metal hinges."

"Oh, that's very helpful. I mean, *what is it?*"

Then I heard heavy footsteps shaking the corridor—coming toward us.

"Run?" I asked.

"Run," Rachel agreed.

We turned and fled the way we'd come, but we didn't make it twenty feet before we ran straight into some old friends. Two *dracaenae*—snake women in Greek armor—leveled their javelins at our chests. Standing between them was Kelli, the *empousa* cheerleader.

"Well, well," Kelli said.

I uncapped Riptide, and Annabeth pulled her knife; but before my sword was even out of pen form, Kelli pounced on Rachel. Her hand turned into a claw and she spun Rachel around, holding her tight with her talons at Rachel's neck.

"Taking your little mortal pet for a walk?" Kelli asked me. "They're such fragile things. So easy to break!"

Behind us, the footsteps came closer. A huge form appeared out of the gloom—an eight-foot-tall Laistrygonian giant with red eyes and fangs.

The giant licked his lips when he saw us. "Can I eat them?"

"No," Kelli said. "Your master will want these. They will provide a great deal of entertainment." She smiled at me. "Now march, half-bloods. Or you all die here, starting with the mortal girl."

It was pretty much my worst nightmare. And believe me, I've had plenty of nightmares. We were marched down the tunnel flanked by *dracaenae*, with Kelli and the giant in back, just in case we tried to run for it. Nobody seemed to worry about us running forward. That was the direction they wanted us to go.

Up ahead I could see bronze doors. They were about ten feet tall, emblazoned with a pair of crossed swords. From behind them came a muffled roar, like from a crowd.

"Oh, yessssss," said the snake woman on my left. "You'll be very popular with our hossssst."

I'd never gotten to look at a *dracaena* up close before, and I wasn't real thrilled to have the opportunity. She would've had a beautiful face, except her tongue was forked and her eyes were yellow with black slits for pupils. She wore bronze armor that stopped at her waist. Below that, where her legs should've been, were two massive snake trunks, mottled bronze and green. She moved by a combination of slithering and walking, as if she were on living skis.

"Who's your host?" I asked.

She hissed, which might have been a laugh. "Oh, you'll sssssee. You'll get along famousssly. He'ssss your brother, after all."

"My what?" Immediately I thought of Tyson, but that was impossible. What was she talking about?

The giant pushed past us and opened the doors. He picked up Annabeth by her shirt and said, "You stay here."

"Hey!" she protested, but the guy was twice her size and he'd already confiscated her knife and my sword.

Kelli laughed. She still had her claws at Rachel's neck. "Go on, Percy. Entertain us. We'll wait here with your friends to make sure you behave."

I looked at Rachel. "I'm sorry. I'll get you out of this."

She nodded as much as she could with a demon at her throat. "That would be nice."

The *dracaenae* prodded me toward the doorway at javelin-point, and I walked out onto the floor of an arena.

I guess it wasn't the largest arena I'd ever been in, but it seemed pretty spacious considering the whole place was underground. The dirt floor was circular, just big enough that you could drive a car around the rim if you pulled it really tight. In the center of the arena, a fight was going on between a giant and a centaur. The centaur looked panicked. He was galloping around his enemy, using sword and shield, while the giant swung a javelin the size of a telephone pole and the crowd cheered.

The first tier of seats was twelve feet above the arena floor. Plain stone benches wrapped all the way around, and every seat was full. There were giants, *dracaenae*, demigods, telekhines, and stranger things: bat-winged demons and creatures that seemed half human and half you name it— bird, reptile, insect, mammal.

But the creepiest things were the skulls. The arena was full of them. They ringed the edge of the railing. Three-foot-high piles of them decorated the steps between the benches. They grinned from pikes at the back of the stands and hung on chains from the ceiling like horrible chandeliers. Some of them looked very old—nothing but bleached-white bone. Others looked a lot fresher. I'm not going to describe them. Believe me, you don't want me to.

In the middle of all this, proudly displayed on the side of the spectator's wall, was something that made no sense to me—a green banner with the trident of Poseidon in the center. What was *that* doing in a horrible place like this?

Above the banner, sitting in a seat of honor, was an old enemy.

"Luke," I said.

I'm not sure he could hear me over the roar of the crowd, but he smiled coldly. He was wearing camouflage pants, a white T-shirt, and bronze breastplate, just like I'd seen in my dream. But he still wasn't wearing his sword, which I thought was strange. Next to him sat the largest giant I'd ever seen, much larger than the one on the floor fighting the centaur. The giant next to Luke must've been fifteen feet tall, easy, and so wide he took up three seats. He wore only a loincloth, like a sumo wrestler. His skin was dark red and tattooed with blue wave designs. I figured he must be Luke's new bodyguard or something.

There was a cry from the arena floor, and I jumped back as the centaur crashed to the dirt beside me.

He met my eyes pleadingly. "Help!"

I reached for my sword, but it had been taken from me and hadn't reappeared in my pocket yet.

The centaur struggled to get up as the giant approached, his javelin ready.

A taloned hand gripped my shoulder. "If you value your friendsss' livesss," my *dracaena* guard said, "you won't interfere. This isssn't your fight. Wait your turn."

The centaur couldn't get up. One of his legs was broken. The giant put his huge foot on the horseman's chest and raised the javelin. He looked up at Luke. The crowd cheered, "DEATH! DEATH!"

Luke didn't do anything, but the tattooed sumo dude sitting next to him rose. He smiled down at the centaur, who was whimpering, "Please! No!"

Then the sumo dude held out his hand and gave the *thumbs down* sign.

I closed my eyes as the gladiator giant thrust his javelin. When I looked again, the centaur was gone, disintegrated to ashes. All that was left was a single hoof, which the giant took up as a trophy and showed the crowd. They roared their approval.

A gate opened at the opposite end of the stadium and the giant marched out in triumph.

In the stands, the sumo dude raised his hands for silence.

"Good entertainment!" he bellowed. "But nothing I haven't seen before. What else do you have, Luke, Son of Hermes?"

Luke's jaw tightened. I could tell he didn't like being called *son of Hermes*. He hated his father. But he rose calmly to his feet. His eyes glittered. In fact, he seemed to be in a pretty good mood.

"Lord Antaeus," Luke said, loud enough for the crowd to hear. "You have been an excellent host! We would be happy to amuse you, to repay the favor of passing through your territory."

"A favor I have not yet granted," Antaeus growled. "I want entertainment!"

Luke bowed. "I believe I have something better than centaurs to fight in your arena now. I have a brother of yours." He pointed at me. "Percy Jackson, son of Poseidon."

The crowd began jeering at me and throwing stones, most of which I dodged, but one caught me on the cheek and made a good-sized cut.

Antaeus's eyes lit up. "A son of Poseidon? Then he should fight well! Or die well!"

"If his death pleases you," Luke said, "will you let our armies cross your territory?"

"Perhaps!" Antaeus said.

Luke didn't look too pleased about the "perhaps." He glared down at me, as if warning me that I'd better die in a really spectacular way or I'd be in big trouble.

"Luke!" Annabeth yelled. "Stop this. Let us go!"

Luke seemed to notice her for the first time. He looked stunned for a moment. "Annabeth?"

"Enough time for the females to fight afterward," Antaeus interrupted. "First, Percy Jackson, what weapons will you choose?"

The *dracaenae* pushed me into the middle of the arena.

I stared up at Antaeus. "How can you be a son of Poseidon?"

Antaeus laughed, and the rest of the crowd laughed too.

"I am his favorite son!" Antaeus boomed. "Behold, my temple to the Earthshaker, built from the skulls of all those I've killed in his name! Your skull shall join them!"

I stared in horror at all the skulls—hundreds of them—and the banner of Poseidon. How could this be a temple for my dad? My dad was a nice guy. He'd never asked me for a Father's Day card, much less somebody's skull.

"Percy!" Annabeth yelled at me. "His mother is Gaea! Gae—"

Her Laistrygonian captor clamped his hand over her mouth. *His mother is Gaea.* The earth goddess. Annabeth was trying to tell me that this was important, but I didn't know why. Maybe just because the guy had two godly parents. That would make him even harder to kill.

"You're crazy, Antaeus," I said. "If you think this is a

good tribute, you know nothing about Poseidon."

The crowd screamed insults at me, but Antaeus raised his hand for silence.

"Weapons," he insisted. "And then we will see how you die. Will you have axes? Shields? Nets? Flamethrowers?"

"Just my sword," I said.

Laughter erupted from the monsters, but immediately Riptide appeared in my hands, and some of the voices in the crowd turned nervous. The bronze blade glowed with a faint light.

"Round one!" Antaeus announced. The gates opened, and a *dracaena* slithered out. She had a trident in one hand and a weighted net in the other—classic gladiator style. I'd trained against those weapons at camp for years.

She jabbed at me experimentally. I stepped away. She threw her net, hoping to tangle my sword hand, but I sidestepped easily, sliced her spear in half, and stabbed Riptide through a chink in her armor. With a painful wail, she vaporized into nothing, and the cheering of the crowd died.

"No!" Antaeus bellowed. "Too fast! You must wait for the kill. Only I give that order!"

I glanced over at Annabeth and Rachel. I had to find a way to get them free, maybe distract their guards.

"Nice job, Percy." Luke smiled. "You've gotten better with the sword. I'll grant you that."

"Round two!" Antaeus yelled. "And slower this time! More entertainment! Wait for my call before killing anybody, OR ELSE!"

The gates opened again, and this time a young warrior

came out. He was a little older than me, about sixteen. He had glossy black hair, and his left eye was covered with an eye patch. He was thin and wiry so his Greek armor hung on him loosely. He stabbed his sword into the dirt, adjusted his shield straps, and pulled on his horsehair helmet.

"Who are you?" I asked.

"Ethan Nakamura," he said. "I have to kill you."

"Why are you doing this?"

"Hey!" a monster jeered from the stands. "Stop talking and fight already!" The others took up the call.

"I have to prove myself," Ethan told me. "Only way to join up."

And with that he charged. Our swords met in midair and the crowd roared. It didn't seem right. I didn't want to fight to entertain a bunch of monsters, but Ethan Nakamura wasn't giving me much choice.

He pressed forward. He was good. He'd never been at Camp Half-Blood, as far as I knew, but he'd been trained. He parried my strike and almost slammed me with his shield, but I jumped back. He slashed. I rolled to one side. We exchanged thrusts and parries, getting a feel for each other's fighting style. I tried to keep on Ethan's blind side, but it didn't help much. He'd apparently been fighting with only one eye for a long time, because he was excellent at guarding his left.

"Blood!" the monsters cried.

My opponent glanced up at the stands. That was his weakness, I realized. He needed to impress them. I didn't.

He yelled an angry battle cry and charged me, but I

parried his blade and backed away, letting him come after me.

"Booo!" Antaeus said. "Stand and fight!"

Ethan pressed me, but I had no trouble defending, even without a shield. He was dressed for defense—heavy armor and shield—which made it very tiring to play offense. I was a softer target, but I also was lighter and faster. The crowd went nuts, yelling complaints and throwing rocks. We'd been fighting for almost five minutes and there was no blood.

Finally Ethan made his mistake. He tried to jab at my stomach, and I locked his sword hilt in mine and twisted. His sword dropped into the dirt. Before he could recover, I slammed the butt of my sword into his helmet and pushed him down. His heavy armor helped me more than him. He fell on his back, dazed and tired. I put the tip of my sword on his chest.

"Get it over with," Ethan groaned.

I looked up at Antaeus. His red face was stony with displeasure, but he held up his hand and put it *thumbs down*.

"Forget it." I sheathed my sword.

"Don't be a fool," Ethan groaned. "They'll just kill us both."

I offered him my hand. Reluctantly, he took it. I helped him up.

"No one dishonors the games!" Antaeus bellowed. "Your heads shall both be tributes to Poseidon!"

I looked at Ethan. "When you see your chance, run." Then I turned back to Antaeus. "Why don't you fight me yourself? If you've got Dad's favor, come down here and prove it!"

The monsters grumbled in the stands. Antaeus looked around, and apparently realized he had no choice. He couldn't say no without looking like a coward.

"I am the greatest wrestler in the world, boy," he warned. "I have been wrestling since the first *pankration!*"

"*Pankration?*" I asked.

"He means fighting to the death," Ethan said. "No rules. No holds barred. It used to be an Olympic sport."

"Thanks for the tip," I said.

"Don't mention it."

Rachel was watching me with wide eyes. Annabeth shook her head emphatically, the Laistrygonian's hand still clamped over her mouth.

I pointed my sword at Antaeus. "Winner takes all! I win, we all go free. You win, we die. Swear upon the River Styx."

Antaeus laughed. "This shouldn't take long. I swear to your terms!"

He leaped off the railing, into the arena.

"Good luck," Ethan told me. "You'll need it." Then he backed up quickly.

Antaeus cracked his knuckles. He grinned, and I saw that even his teeth were etched in wave patterns, which must've made brushing after meals a real pain.

"Weapons?" he asked.

"I'll stick with my sword. You?"

He held up his huge hands and wiggled his fingers. "I

don't need anything else! Master Luke, you will referee this one."

Luke smiled down at me. "With pleasure."

Antaeus lunged. I rolled under his legs and stabbed him in the back of his thigh.

"Argggh!" he yelled. But where blood should've come out, there was a spout of sand, like I'd busted the side of an hourglass. It spilled into the dirt floor, and the dirt collected around his leg, almost like a cast. When the dirt fell away, the wound was gone.

He charged again. Fortunately I'd had some experience fighting giants. I dodged sideways this time and stabbed him under the arm. Riptide's blade was buried to the hilt in his ribs. That was the good news. The bad news was that it wrenched out of my hand when the giant turned, and I was thrown across the arena, weaponless.

Antaeus bellowed in pain. I waited for him to disintegrate. No monster had ever withstood a direct hit from my sword like that. The celestial bronze blade had to be destroying his essence. But Antaeus groped for the hilt, pulled out the sword, and tossed it behind him. More sand poured from the wound, but again the earth rose up to cover him. Dirt coated his body all the way to his shoulders. As soon as the dirt spilled away, Antaeus was fine.

"Now you see why I never lose, demigod!" Antaeus gloated. "Come here and let me crush you. I'll make it quick!"

Antaeus stood between me and my sword. Desperately, I glanced to either side, and I caught Annabeth's eye.

The earth, I thought. What had Annabeth been trying to tell me? Antaeus's mother was Gaea the earth mother, the most ancient goddess of all. Antaeus's father might have been Poseidon, but Gaea was keeping him alive. I couldn't hurt him as long as he was touching the ground.

I tried to skirt around him, but Antaeus anticipated my move. He blocked my path, chuckling. He was just toying with me now. He had me cornered.

I looked up at the chains hanging from the ceiling, dangling the skulls of his enemies on hooks. Suddenly I had an idea.

I feinted to the other side. Antaeus blocked me. The crowd jeered and screamed at Antaeus to finish me off, but he was having too much fun.

"Puny boy," he said. "Not a worthy son of the sea god!"

I felt my pen return to my pocket, but Antaeus wouldn't know about that. He would think Riptide was still in the dirt behind him. He would think my goal was to get my sword. It wasn't much of an advantage, but it was all I had.

I charged straight ahead, crouching low so he would think I was going to roll between his legs again. While he was stooping, ready to catch me like a grounder, I jumped for all I was worth—kicking off his forearm, scrambling up his shoulder like it was a ladder, placing my shoe on his head. He did the natural thing. He straightened up indignantly and yelled "HEY!" I pushed off, using his force to catapult me toward the ceiling. I caught the top of a chain, and the skulls and hooks jangled beneath me. I wrapped my legs around the chain, just like I used to do at the ropes course in gym class. I drew Riptide and sawed off the chain next to me.

"Come down here, coward!" Antaeus bellowed. He tried to grab me, but I was just out of reach. Hanging on for dear life, I yelled, "Come up and get me! Or are you too slow and fat?"

He howled and made another grab for me. He caught a chain and tried to pull himself up. While he was struggling, I lowered my sawed-off chain, hook first. It took me two tries, but finally I snagged Antaeus's loincloth.

"WAAA!" he yelled. Quickly I slipped the free chain through the fastening link on my own chain, pulled it taut, and secured it the best I could. Antaeus tried to slip back to the ground, but his butt stayed suspended by his loincloth. He had to hold on to the other chains with both hands to avoid getting flipped upside down. I prayed the loincloth and the chain would hold up for a few more seconds. While Antaeus cursed and flailed, I scrambled around the chains, swinging and cutting like I was some kind of crazed monkey. I made loops with hooks and metal links. I don't know how I did it. My mom always said I have a gift for getting stuff tangled up. Plus I was desperate to save my friends. Anyway, within a couple of minutes the giant was suspended above the ground, hopelessly snarled in chains and hooks.

I dropped to the floor, panting and sweaty. My hands were raw from climbing.

"Get me down!" Antaeus demanded.

"Free him!" Luke ordered. "He is our host!"

I uncapped Riptide. "I'll free him."

And I stabbed the giant in the stomach. He bellowed, and sand poured out, but he was too far up to touch the earth, and the dirt did not rise to help him. Antaeus just dissolved, pouring out bit by bit, until there was nothing left but empty swinging chains, a really big loincloth on a hook, and a bunch of grinning skulls dancing above me like they finally had something to smile about.

"Jackson!" Luke yelled. "I should have killed you long ago!"

"You tried," I reminded him. "Let us go, Luke. We had a sworn agreement with Antaeus. I'm the winner."

He did just what I expected. He said, "Antaeus is dead. His oath dies with him. But since I'm feeling merciful today, I'll have you killed quickly."

He pointed at Annabeth. "Spare the girl." His voice quavered just a little. "I would speak to her before—before our great triumph."

Every monster in the audience drew a weapon or extended its claws. We were trapped. Hopelessly outnumbered.

Then I felt something in my pocket—a freezing sensation, growing colder and colder. *The dog whistle.* My fingers closed around it. For days I'd avoided using Quintus's gift. It had to be a trap. But now . . . I had no choice. I took it out of my pocket and blew. It made no audible sound as it shattered into shards of ice, melting in my hand.

Luke laughed. "What was that supposed to do?"

From behind me came a surprised yelp. The Laistrygonian

giant who'd been guarding Annabeth flew past me and smashed into the wall.

"AROOOOF!"

Kelli the *empousa* screamed as a five-hundred-pound black mastiff picked her up like a chew toy and tossed her through the air, straight into Luke's lap. Mrs. O'Leary snarled, and the two *dracaenae* guards backed away. For a moment the monsters in the audience were caught completely by surprise.

"Let's go!" I yelled at my friends. "Heel, Mrs. O'Leary!"

"The far exit!" Rachel cried. "That's the right way!"

Ethan Nakamura took his cue. Together we raced across the arena and out the far exit, Mrs. O'Leary right behind us. As we ran, I could hear the disorganized sounds of an entire army trying to jump out of the stands and follow us.

FIFTEEN

WE STEAL SOME SLIGHTLY
USED WINGS

"This way!" Rachel yelled.

"Why should we follow you?" Annabeth demanded. "You led us straight into that death trap!"

"It was the way you needed to go," Rachel said. "And so is this. Come on!"

Annabeth didn't look happy about it, but she ran along with the rest of us. Rachel seemed to know exactly where she was going. She whipped around corners and didn't even hesitate at crossroads. Once she said, "Duck!" and we all crouched as a huge axe swung over our heads. Then we kept going as if nothing had happened.

I lost track of how many turns we made. We didn't stop to rest until we came to a room the size of a gymnasium with old marble columns holding up the roof. I stood at the doorway, listening for sounds of pursuit, but I heard nothing. Apparently, we'd lost Luke and his minions in the maze.

Then I realized something else: Mrs. O'Leary was gone. I didn't know when she'd disappeared. I didn't know if she'd gotten lost or been overrun by monsters or what. My heart turned to lead. She'd saved our lives, and I hadn't even waited to make sure she was following us.

Ethan collapsed on the floor. "You people are crazy." He pulled off his helmet. His face gleamed with sweat.

Annabeth gasped. "I remember you! You were one of the undetermined kids in the Hermes cabin, years ago."

He glared at her. "Yeah, and you're Annabeth. I remember."

"What—what happened to your eye?"

Ethan looked away, and I got the feeling that was one subject he would *not* discuss.

"You must be the half-blood from my dream," I said. "The one Luke's people cornered. It wasn't Nico after all."

"Who's Nico?"

"Never mind," Annabeth said quickly. "Why were you trying to join up with the wrong side?"

Ethan sneered. "There's no right side. The gods never cared about us. Why shouldn't I—"

"Sign up with an army that makes you fight to the death for entertainment?" Annabeth said. "Gee, I wonder."

Ethan struggled to his feet. "I'm not going to argue with you. Thanks for the help, but I'm out of here."

"We're going after Daedalus," I said. "Come with us. Once we get through, you'd be welcome back at camp."

"You really *are* crazy if you think Daedalus will help you."

"He has to," Annabeth said. "We'll make him listen."

Ethan snorted. "Yeah, well. Good luck with that."

I grabbed his arm. "You're just going to head off alone into the maze? That's suicide."

He looked at me with barely controlled anger. His eye

patch was frayed around the edges and the black cloth was faded, like he'd been wearing it a long, long time. "You shouldn't have spared me, Jackson. Mercy has no place in this war."

Then he ran off into the darkness, back the way we'd come.

Annabeth, Rachel, and I were so exhausted we made camp right there in the huge room. I found some scrap wood and we started a fire. Shadows danced off the columns rising around us like trees.

"Something was wrong with Luke," Annabeth muttered, poking at the fire with her knife. "Did you notice the way he was acting?"

"He looked pretty pleased to me," I said. "Like he'd spent a nice day torturing heroes."

"That's not true! There was something wrong with him. He looked . . . nervous. He told his monsters to spare me. He wanted to tell me something."

"Probably, *'Hi, Annabeth! Sit here with me and watch while I tear your friends apart. It'll be fun!'*"

"You're impossible," Annabeth grumbled. She sheathed her dagger and looked at Rachel. "So which way now, Sacagawea?"

Rachel didn't respond right away. She'd become quieter since the arena. Now, whenever Annabeth made a sarcastic comment, Rachel hardly bothered to answer. She'd burned the tip of a stick in the fire and was using it to draw ash figures on the floor, images of the monsters we'd seen. With a few strokes she caught the likeness of a *dracaena* perfectly.

"We'll follow the path," she said. "The brightness on the floor."

"The brightness that led us straight into a trap?" Annabeth asked.

"Lay off her, Annabeth," I said. "She's doing the best she can."

Annabeth stood. "The fire's getting low. I'll go look for some more scraps while *you* guys talk strategy." And she marched off into the shadows.

Rachel drew another figure with her stick—an ashy Antaeus dangling from his chains.

"Annabeth's usually not like this," I told her. "I don't know what her problem is."

Rachel raised her eyebrows. "Are you sure you don't know?"

"What do you mean?"

"Boys," she muttered. "Totally blind."

"Hey, don't you get on my case, too! Look, I'm sorry I got you involved in this."

"No, you were right," she said. "I can see the path. I can't explain it, but it's really clear." She pointed toward the other end of the room, into the darkness. "The workshop is that way. The heart of the maze. We're very close now. I don't know why the path led through that arena. I—I'm sorry about that. I thought you were going to die."

She sounded like she was close to crying.

"Hey, I'm usually about to die," I promised. "Don't feel bad."

She studied my face. "So you do this every summer? Fight monsters? Save the world? Don't you ever get to do just, you know, normal stuff?"

I'd never really thought about it like that. The last time I'd had something like a normal life had been . . . well, never. "Half-bloods get used to it, I guess. Or maybe not used to it, but . . ." I shifted uncomfortably. "What about you? What do you do normally?"

Rachel shrugged. "I paint. I read a lot."

Okay, I thought. So far we are scoring a zero on the similarities chart. "What about your family?"

I could sense her mental shields going up, like this was not a safe subject. "Oh . . . they're just, you know, family."

"You said they wouldn't notice if you were gone."

She set down her drawing stick. "Wow, I'm really tired. I may sleep for a while, okay?"

"Oh, sure. Sorry if . . ."

But Rachel was already curling up, using her backpack as a pillow. She closed her eyes and lay very still, but I got the feeling she wasn't really asleep.

A few minutes later, Annabeth came back. She tossed some more sticks on the fire. She looked at Rachel, then at me.

"I'll take first watch," she said. "You should sleep, too."

"You don't have to act like that."

"Like what?"

"Like . . . never mind." I lay down, feeling miserable. I was so tired I fell asleep as soon as my eyes closed.

In my dreams I heard laughter. Cold, harsh laughter, like knives being sharpened.

I was standing at the edge of a pit in the depths of Tartarus. Below me the darkness seethed like inky soup.

"So close to your own destruction, little hero," the voice of Kronos chided. "And still you are blind."

The voice was different than it had been before. It seemed almost physical now, as if it were speaking from a real body instead of . . . whatever he'd been in his chopped-up condition.

"I have much to thank you for," Kronos said. "You have assured my rise."

The shadows in the cavern became deeper and heavier. I tried to back away from the edge of the pit, but it was like swimming through oil. Time slowed down. My breathing almost stopped.

"A favor," Kronos said. "The Titan lord always pays his debts. Perhaps a glimpse of the friends you abandoned . . ."

The darkness rippled around me, and I was in a different cave.

"Hurry!" Tyson said. He came barreling into the room. Grover stumbled along behind him. There was a rumbling in the corridor they'd come from, and the head of an enormous snake burst into the cave. I mean, this thing was so big its body barely fit through the tunnel. Its scales were coppery. Its head was diamond-shaped like a rattler, and its yellow eyes glowed with hatred. When it opened its mouth, its fangs were as tall as Tyson.

It lashed at Grover, but Grover scampered out of the way. The snake got a mouthful of dirt. Tyson picked up a boulder and threw it at the monster, smacking it between the eyes, but the snake just recoiled and hissed.

"It's going to eat you!" Grover yelled at Tyson.

"How do you know?"

"It just told me! Run!"

Tyson darted to one side, but the snake used its head like a club and knocked him off his feet.

"No!" Grover yelled. But before Tyson could regain his balance, the snake wrapped around him and started to squeeze.

Tyson strained, pushing with all his immense strength, but the snake squeezed tighter. Grover frantically hit the snake with his reed pipes, but he might as well have been banging on a stone wall.

The whole room shook as the snake flexed its muscles, shuddering to overcome Tyson's strength.

Grover began to play with pipes, and stalactites rained down from the ceiling. The whole cave seemed about to collapse. . . .

I woke with Annabeth shaking my shoulder. "Percy, wake up!"

"Tyson—Tyson's in trouble!" I said. "We have to help him!"

"First things first," she said. "Earthquake!"

Sure enough, the room was rumbling. "Rachel!" I yelled. Her eyes opened instantly. She grabbed her pack, and the three of us ran. We were almost to the far tunnel when a column next to us groaned and buckled. We kept going as a hundred tons of marble crashed down behind us.

We made it to the corridor and turned just in time to see the other columns toppling. A cloud of white dust billowed over us, and we kept running.

"You know what?" Annabeth said. "I like this way after all."

It wasn't long before we saw light up ahead—like regular electric lighting.

"There," Rachel said.

We followed her into a stainless steel hallway, like I imagined they'd have on a space station or something. Fluorescent lights glowed from the ceiling. The floor was a metal grate.

I was so used to being in the darkness that I had to squint. Annabeth and Rachel both looked pale in the harsh illumination.

"This way," Rachel said, beginning to run. "We're close!"

"This is so wrong!" Annabeth said. "The workshop should be in the oldest section of the maze. This can't—"

She faltered, because we'd arrived at a set of metal double doors. Inscribed in the steel, at eye level, was a large blue Greek Δ.

"We're here," Rachel announced. "Daedalus's workshop."

* * *

Annabeth pressed the symbol on the doors and they hissed open.

"So much for ancient architecture," I said.

Annabeth scowled. Together we walked inside.

The first thing that struck me was the daylight—blazing sun coming through giant windows. Not the kind of thing you expect in the heart of a dungeon. The workshop was like an artist's studio, with thirty-foot ceilings and industrial lighting, polished stone floors, and workbenches along with windows. A spiral staircase led up to a second-story loft. Half a dozen easels displayed hand-drawn diagrams for buildings and machines that looked like Leonardo da Vinci sketches. Several laptop computers were scattered around on the tables. Glass jars of green oil—Greek fire—lined one shelf. There were inventions, too—weird metal machines I couldn't make sense of. One was a bronze chair with a bunch of electrical wires attached to it, like some kind of torture device. In another corner stood a giant metal egg about the size of a man. There was a grandfather clock that appeared to be made entirely of glass, so you could see all the gears turning. And hanging on the wall were several sets of bronze and silver wings.

"*Di immortales,*" Annabeth muttered. She ran to the nearest easel and looked at the sketch. "He's a genius. Look at the curves on this building!"

"And an artist," Rachel said in amazement. "These wings are amazing!"

The wings looked more advanced than the ones I'd seen in my dreams. The feathers were more tightly interwoven.

Instead of wax seals, self-adhesive strips ran down the sides.

I kept my hand on Riptide. Apparently Daedalus was not at home, but the workshop looked like it had been recently used. The laptops were running their screen savers. A half-eaten blueberry muffin and a coffee cup sat on a workbench.

I walked to the window. The view outside was amazing. I recognized the Rocky Mountains in the distance. We were high up in the foothills, at least five hundred feet, and down below a valley spread out, filled with a tumbled collection of red mesas and boulders and spires of stone. It looked like some huge kid had been building a toy city with sky-scraper-size blocks, and then decided to knock it over.

"Where are we?" I wondered.

"Colorado Springs," a voice said behind us. "The Garden of the Gods."

Standing on the spiral staircase above us, with his weapon drawn, was our missing sword master Quintus.

"You," Annabeth said. "What have you done with Daedalus?"

Quintus smiled faintly. "Trust me, my dear. You don't want to meet him."

"Look, Mr. Traitor," she growled, "I didn't fight a dragon woman and a three-bodied man and a psychotic Sphinx to see *you*. Now where is DAEDALUS?"

Quintus came down the stairs, holding his sword at his side. He was dressed in jeans and boots and his counselor's T-shirt from Camp Half-Blood, which seemed like an insult now that we knew he was a spy. I didn't know if I could beat him in a sword fight. He was pretty good. But I figured I would have to try.

"You think I'm an agent of Kronos," he said. "That I work for Luke."

"Well, duh," said Annabeth.

"You're an intelligent girl," he said. "But you're wrong. I work only for myself."

"Luke mentioned you," I said. "Geryon knew about you, too. You've been to his ranch."

"Of course," he said. "I've been almost everywhere. Even here."

He walked past me like I was no threat at all and stood by the window. "The view changes from day to day," he mused. "It's always some place high up. Yesterday it was from a skyscraper overlooking Manhattan. The day before that, there was a beautiful view of Lake Michigan. But it keeps coming back to the Garden of the Gods. I think the Labyrinth likes it here. A fitting name, I suppose."

"You've been here before," I said.

"Oh, yes."

"That's an illusion out there?" I asked. "A projection or something?"

"No," Rachel murmured. "It's real. We're really in Colorado."

Quintus regarded her. "You have clear vision, don't you? You remind me of another mortal girl I once knew. Another princess who came to grief."

"Enough games," I said. "What have you done with Daedalus?"

Quintus stared at me. "My boy, you need lessons from your friend on seeing clearly. I *am* Daedalus."

There were a lot of answers I might've given, from "I knew that" to "LIAR!" to "Yeah right, and I'm Zeus."

The only thing I could think to say was, "But you're not an inventor! You're a swordsman!"

"I am both," Quintus said. "And an architect. And a scholar. I also play basketball pretty well for a guy who didn't start until he was two thousand years old. A real artist must be good at many things."

"That's true," Rachel said. "Like I can paint with my feet as well as my hands."

"You see?" Quintus said. "A girl of many talents."

"But you don't even look like Daedalus," I protested. "I saw him in a dream, and . . ." Suddenly a horrible thought dawned on me.

"Yes," Quintus said. "You've finally guessed the truth."

"You're an automaton. You made yourself a new body."

"Percy," Annabeth said uneasily, "that's not possible. That—that can't be an automaton."

Quintus chuckled. "Do you know what Quintus means, my dear?"

"The fifth, in Latin. But—"

"This is my fifth body." The swordsman held out his forearm. He pressed his elbow and part of his wrist popped open—a rectangular hatch in his skin. Underneath, bronze gears whirred. Wires glowed.

"That's amazing!" Rachel said.

"That's weird," I said.

"You found a way to transfer your *animus* into a machine?" Annabeth said. "That's . . . not natural."

"Oh, I assure you, my dear, it's still me. I'm still very much Daedalus. Our mother, Athena, makes sure I never forget that." He tugged back the collar of his shirt. At the base of his neck was the mark I'd seen before—the dark shape of a bird grafted to his skin.

"A murderer's brand," Annabeth said.

"For your nephew, Perdix," I guessed. "The boy you pushed off the tower."

Quintus's face darkened. "I did not push him. I simply—"

"Made him lose his balance," I said. "Let him die."

Quintus gazed out the windows at the purple mountains. "I regret what I did, Percy. I was angry and bitter. But I cannot take it back, and Athena never lets me forget. As Perdix died, she turned him into a small bird—a partridge. She branded the bird's shape on my neck as a reminder. No matter what body I take, the brand appears on my skin."

I looked into his eyes, and I realized he was the same man I'd seen in my dreams. His face might be totally different, but the same soul was in there—the same intelligence and all the sadness.

"You really are Daedalus," I decided. "But why did you come to the camp? Why spy on us?"

"To see if your camp was worth saving. Luke had given me one story. I preferred to come to my own conclusions."

"So you *have* talked to Luke."

"Oh, yes. Several times. He is quite persuasive."

"But now you've seen the camp!" Annabeth persisted. "So you know we need your help. You can't let Luke through the maze!"

Daedalus set his sword on the workbench. "The maze is no longer mine to control, Annabeth. I created it, yes. In fact, it is tied to my life force. But I have allowed it to live and grow on its own. That is the price I paid for privacy."

"Privacy from what?" ·

"The gods," he said. "And death. I have been alive for two millennia, my dear, hiding from death."

"But how can you hide from Hades?" I asked. "I mean . . . Hades has the Furies."

"They do not know everything," he said. "Or see everything. You have encountered them, Percy. You know this is true. A clever man can hide quite a long time, and I have buried myself very deep. Only my greatest enemy has kept after me, and even him I have thwarted."

"You mean Minos," I said.

Daedalus nodded. "He hunts for me relentlessly. Now that he is a judge of the dead, he would like nothing better than for me to come before him so he can punish me for my crimes. After the daughters of Cocalus killed him, Minos's ghost began torturing me in my dreams. He promised that he would hunt me down. I did the only thing I could. I retreated from the world completely. I descended into my Labyrinth. I decided this would be my ultimate accomplishment: I would cheat death."

"And you did," Annabeth marveled, "for two thousand

years." She sounded kind of impressed, despite the horrible things Daedalus had done.

Just then a loud bark echoed from the corridor. I heard the *ba-BUMP*, *ba-BUMP*, *ba-BUMP* of huge paws, and Mrs. O'Leary bounded into the workshop. She licked my face once, then almost knocked Daedalus over with an enthusiastic leap.

"There is my old friend!" Daedalus said, scratching Mrs. O'Leary behind the ears. "My only companion all these long lonely years."

"You let her save me," I said. "That whistle actually worked."

Daedalus nodded. "Of course it did, Percy. You have a good heart. And I knew Mrs. O'Leary liked you. I wanted to help you. Perhaps I—I felt guilty, as well."

"Guilty about what?"

"That your quest would be in vain."

"What?" Annabeth said. "But you can still help us. You have to! Give us Ariadne's string so Luke can't get it."

"Yes . . . the string. I told Luke that the eyes of a clearsighted mortal are the best guide, but he did not trust me. He was so focused on the idea of a magic item. And the string works. It's not as accurate as your mortal friend here, perhaps. But good enough. Good enough."

"Where is it?" Annabeth said.

"With Luke," Daedalus said sadly. "I'm sorry, my dear. But you are several hours too late."

With a chill I realized why Luke had been in such a good mood in the arena. He'd already gotten the string from

Daedalus. His only obstacle had been the arena master, and I'd taken care of that for him by killing Antaeus.

"Kronos promised me freedom," Quintus said. "Once Hades is overthrown, he will set me over the Underworld. I will reclaim my son Icarus. I will make things right with poor young Perdix. I will see Minos's soul cast into Tartarus, where it cannot bother me again. And I will no longer have to run from death."

"That's your brilliant idea?" Annabeth yelled. "You're going to let Luke destroy our camp, kill hundreds of demigods, and then attack Olympus? You're going to bring down the entire world so you can get what you want?"

"Your cause is doomed, my dear. I saw that as soon as I began to work at your camp. There is no way you can hold back the might of Kronos."

"That's not true!" she cried.

"I am doing what I must, my dear. The offer was too sweet to refuse. I'm sorry."

Annabeth pushed over an easel. Architectural drawings scattered across the floor. "I used to respect you. You were my hero! You—you built amazing things. You solved problems. Now . . . I don't know what you are. Children of Athena are supposed to be *wise*, not just clever. Maybe you *are* just a machine. You should have died two thousand years ago."

Instead of getting mad, Daedalus hung his head. "You should go warn your camp. Now that Luke has the string—"

Suddenly Mrs. O'Leary pricked up her ears.

"Someone's coming!" Rachel warned.

The doors of the workshop burst open, and Nico was pushed inside, his hands in chains. Then Kelli and two Laistrygonians marched in behind him, followed by the ghost of Minos. He looked almost solid now—a pale bearded king with cold eyes and tendrils of Mist coiling off his robes.

He fixed his gaze on Daedalus. "There you are, my old friend."

Daedalus's jaw clenched. He looked at Kelli. "What is the meaning of this?"

"Luke sends his compliments," Kelli said. "He thought you might like to see your old employer Minos."

"This was not part of our agreement," Daedalus said.

"No indeed," Kelli said. "But we already have what we want from you, and we have other agreements to honor. Minos required something else from us, in order to turn over this fine young demigod." She ran a finger under Nico's chin. "He'll be quite useful. And all Minos asked in return was your head, old man."

Daeadalus paled. "Treachery."

"Get used to it," Kelli said.

"Nico," I said. "Are you okay?"

He nodded morosely. "I—I'm sorry, Percy. Minos told me you were in danger. He convinced me to go back into the maze."

"You were trying to *help* us?"

"I was tricked," he said. "He tricked all of us."

I glared at Kelli. "Where's Luke? Why isn't he here?"

The she-demon smiled like we were sharing a private

joke. "Luke is . . . busy. He is preparing for the assault. But don't worry. We have more friends on the way. And in the meantime, I think I'll have a wonderful snack!" Her hands changed to claws. Her hair burst into flame and her legs turned to their true form—one donkey leg, one bronze.

"Percy," Rachel whispered, "the wings. Do you think—"

"Get them," I said. "I'll try to buy you some time."

And with that, all Hades broke loose. Annabeth and I charged at Kelli. The giants came right at Daedalus, but Mrs. O'Leary leaped to his defense. Nico got pushed to the ground and struggled with his chains while the spirit of Minos wailed, "Kill the inventor! Kill him!"

Rachel grabbed the wings off the wall. Nobody paid her any attention. Kelli slashed at Annabeth. I tried to get to her, but the demon was quick and deadly. She turned over tables, smashed inventions, and wouldn't let us get close. Out of the corner of my eye, I saw Mrs. O'Leary chomp her fangs into a giant's arm. He wailed in pain and flung her around, trying to shake her. Daedalus grabbed for his sword, but the second giant smashed the workbench with his fist, and the sword went flying. A clay jar of Greek fire broke on the floor and began to burn, green flames spreading quickly.

"To me!" Minos cried. "Spirits of the dead!" He raised his ghostly hands and the air began to hum.

"No!" Nico cried. He was on his feet now. He'd somehow managed to remove his shackles.

"You do not control me, young fool." Minos sneered. "All this time, I have been controlling you! A soul for a soul, yes. But it is not your sister who will return from the dead. It is I, as soon as I slay the inventor!"

Spirits began to appear around Minos—shimmering forms that slowly multiplied, solidifying into Cretan soldiers.

"I am the son of Hades," Nico insisted. "Be gone!"

Minos laughed. "You have no power over me. I am the lord of spirits! The ghost king!"

"No." Nico drew his sword. "*I* am."

He stabbed his black blade into the floor, and it cleaved through the stone like butter.

"Never!" Minos's form rippled. "I will not—"

The ground rumbled. The windows cracked and shattered to pieces, letting in a blast of fresh air. A fissure opened in the stone floor of the workshop, and Minos and all his spirits were sucked into the void with a horrible wail.

The bad news: the fight was still going on all around us, and I let myself get distracted. Kelli pounced on me so fast I had no time to defend myself. My sword skittered away and I hit my head hard on a worktable as I fell. My eyesight went fuzzy. I couldn't raise my arms.

Kelli laughed. "You will taste wonderful!"

She bared her fangs. Then suddenly her body went rigid. Her red eyes widened. She gasped, "No . . . school . . . spirit . . ."

And Annabeth took her knife out of the *empousa*'s back. With an awful screech, Kelli dissolved into yellow vapor.

Annabeth helped me up. I still felt dizzy, but we had no time to lose. Mrs. O'Leary and Daedalus were still locked in combat with the giants, and I could hear shouting in the tunnel. More monsters were coming toward the workshop.

"We have to help Daedalus!" I said.

"No time," Rachel said. "Too many coming!"

She'd already fitted herself with wings and was working on Nico, who looked pale and sweaty from his struggle with Minos. The wings grafted instantly to his back and arms.

"Now you!" she told me.

In seconds, Nico, Annabeth, Rachel, and I had fitted ourselves with coppery wings. Already I could feel myself being lifted by the wind coming through the window. Greek fire was burning the tables and furniture, spreading up the circular stairs.

"Daedalus!" I yelled. "Come on!"

He was cut in a hundred places—but he was bleeding golden oil instead of blood. He'd found his sword and was using part of a smashed table as a shield against the giants. "I won't leave Mrs. O'Leary!" he said. "Go!"

There was no time to argue. Even if we stayed, I wasn't sure we could help.

"None of us know how to fly!" Nico protested.

"Great time to find out," I said. And together, the four of us jumped out the window into open sky.

SIXTEEN

I OPEN A COFFIN

Jumping out a window five hundred feet aboveground is not usually my idea of fun. Especially when I'm wearing bronze wings and flapping my arms like a duck.

I plummeted toward the valley and the red rocks below. I was pretty sure I was going to become a grease spot in the Garden of the Gods, as Annabeth yelled from somewhere above me, "Spread your arms! Keep them extended."

The small part of my brain that wasn't engulfed in panic heard her, and my arms responded. As soon as I spread them out, the wings stiffened, caught the wind, and my descent slowed. I soared downward, but at a controlled angle, like a kite in a dive.

Experimentally, I flapped my arms once. I arced into the sky, the wind whistling in my ears.

"Yeah!" I yelled. The feeling was unbelievable. After getting the hang of it, I felt like the wings were part of my body. I could soar and swoop and dive anywhere I wanted to.

I turned and saw my friends—Rachel, Annabeth, and Nico—spiraling above me, glinting in the sunlight. Behind them, smoke billowed from the windows of Daedalus's workshop.

"Land!" Annabeth yelled. "These wings won't last forever."

"How long?" Rachel cried.

"I don't want to find out!" Annabeth said.

We swooped down toward the Garden of the Gods. I did a complete circle around one of the rock spires and freaked out a couple of climbers. Then the four of us soared across the valley, over a road, and landed on the terrace of the visitor center. It was late afternoon and the place looked pretty empty, but we ripped off our wings as quickly as we could. Looking at them, I could see Annabeth was right. The self-adhesive seals that bound the wings to our backs were already melting, and we were shedding bronze feathers. It seemed a shame, but we couldn't fix them, and couldn't leave them around for the mortals, so we stuffed the wings in the trash bin outside the cafeteria.

I used the tourist binocular camera to look up at the hill where Daedalus's workshop had been, but it had vanished. No more smoke. No broken windows. Just the side of a hill.

"The workshop moved," Annabeth guessed. "There's no telling where."

"So what do we do now?" I asked. "How do we get back in the maze?"

Annabeth gazed at the summit of Pikes Peak in the distance. "Maybe we can't. If Daedalus died . . . he said his life force was tied to the Labyrinth. The whole thing might've been destroyed. Maybe that will stop Luke's invasion."

I thought about Grover and Tyson, still down there

somewhere. And Daedalus . . . even though he'd done some terrible things and put everybody I cared about at risk, it still seemed like a pretty horrible way to die.

"No," Nico said. "He isn't dead."

"How can you be sure?" I asked.

"I *know* when people die. It's this feeling I get, like a buzzing in my ears."

"What about Tyson and Grover, then?"

Nico shook his head. "That's harder. They're not humans or half-bloods. They don't have mortal souls."

"We have to get into town," Annabeth decided. "Our chances will be better of finding an entrance to the Labyrinth. We have to make it back to camp before Luke and his army."

"We could just take a plane," Rachel said.

I shuddered. "I don't fly."

"But you just did."

"That was low flying," I said, "and even that's risky. Flying up really high—that's Zeus's territory. I can't do it. Besides, we don't even have time for a flight. The Labyrinth is the quickest way back."

I didn't want to say it, but I was also hoping that maybe, just maybe, we would find Grover and Tyson along the way.

"So we need a car to take us into the city," Annabeth said.

Rachel looked down into the parking lot. She grimaced, as if she were about to do something she regretted. "I'll take care of it."

"How?" Annabeth asked.

"Just trust me."

Annabeth looked uneasy, but she nodded. "Okay, I'm going to buy a prism in the gift shop, try to make a rainbow, and send an Iris-message to camp."

"I'll go with you," Nico said. "I'm hungry."

"I'll stick with Rachel, then," I said. "Meet you guys in the parking lot."

Rachel frowned like she didn't want me with her. That made me feel kind of bad, but I followed her down to the parking lot anyway.

She headed toward a big black car parked at the edge of the lot. It was a chauffeured Lexus, like the kind I always saw driving around Manhattan. The driver was out front, reading a newspaper. He wore a dark suit and tie.

"What are you going to do?" I asked Rachel.

"Just wait here," she said miserably. "Please."

Rachel marched straight up to the driver and talked to him. He frowned. Rachel said something else. He turned pale and hastily folded up his magazine. He nodded and fumbled for his cell phone. After a brief call, he opened the back door of the car for Rachel to get in. She pointed back in my direction, and the driver bobbed his head some more, like *Yes, ma'am. Whatever you want.*

I couldn't figure out why he was acting so flustered.

Rachel came back to get me just as Nico and Annabeth appeared from the gift shop.

"I talked to Chiron," Annabeth said. "They're doing their best to prepare for battle, but he still wants us back. They're going to need every hero they can get. Did we find a ride?"

"The driver's ready when we are," Rachel said.

The chauffeur was now talking to another guy in khakis and a polo shirt, probably his client who'd rented the car. The client was complaining, but I could hear the driver saying, "I'm sorry, sir. Emergency. I've ordered another car for you."

"Come on," Rachel said. She led us to the car and got in without even looking at the flustered guy who'd rented it. A minute later we were cruising down the road. The seats were leather. There was plenty of legroom. The backseat had flat-panel TVs built into the headrests and a mini-fridge stocked with bottled water, sodas, and snacks. We started pigging out.

"Where to, Miss Dare?" the driver asked.

"I'm not sure yet, Robert," she said. "We just need to drive through town and, uh, look around."

"Whatever you say, miss."

I looked at Rachel. "Do you know this guy?"

"No."

"But he dropped everything to help you. Why?"

"Just keep your eyes peeled," she said. "Help me look."

Which didn't exactly answer my question.

We drove through Colorado Springs for about half an hour and saw nothing that Rachel considered a possible Labyrinth entrance. I was very aware of Rachel's shoulder pressing against mine. I kept wondering who she was exactly, and how she could walk up to some random chauffeur and immediately get a ride.

After about an hour we decided to head north toward Denver, thinking that maybe a bigger city would be more likely to have a Labyrinth entrance, but we were all getting nervous. We were losing time.

Then, right as we were leaving Colorado Springs, Rachel sat bolt upright. "Get off the highway!"

The driver glanced back. "Miss?"

"I saw something, I think. Get off here."

The driver swerved across traffic and took the exit.

"What did you see?" I asked, because we were pretty much out of the city now. There wasn't anything around except hills, grassland, and some scattered farm buildings. Rachel had the driver turn down this unpromising dirt road. We drove by a sign too fast for me to read it, but Rachel said, "Western Museum of Mining & Industry."

For a museum, it didn't look like much—a little house like an old-fashioned railroad station, some drills and pumps and old steam shovels on display outside.

"There." Rachel pointed to a hole in the side of a nearby hill—a tunnel that was boarded up and chained. "An old mine entrance."

"A door to the Labyrinth?" Annabeth asked. "How can you be sure?"

"Well, look at it!" Rachel said. "I mean . . . I can see it, okay?"

She thanked the driver and we all got out. He didn't ask for money or anything. "Are you sure you'll be all right, Miss Dare? I'd be happy to call your—"

"No!" Rachel said. "No, really. Thanks, Robert. But we're fine."

The museum seemed to be closed, so nobody bothered

us as we climbed the hill to the mine shaft. When we got to the entrance, I saw the mark of Daedalus engraved on the padlock, though how Rachel had seen something so tiny all the way from the highway I had no idea. I touched the padlock and the chains fell away. We kicked down a few boards and walked inside. For better or worse, we were back in the Labyrinth.

The dirt tunnels turned to stone. They wound around and split off and basically tried to confuse us, but Rachel had no trouble guiding us. We told her we needed to get back to New York, and she hardly even paused when the tunnels offered a choice.

To my surprise, Rachel and Annabeth started up a conversation as we walked. Annabeth asked her more about her background, but Rachel was evasive, so they started talking about architecture. It turned out that Rachel knew something about it from studying art. They talked about different facades on buildings around New York—"Have you seen this one," blah, blah, blah, so I hung back and walked next to Nico in uncomfortable silence.

"Thanks for coming after us," I told him at last.

Nico's eyes narrowed. He didn't seem as angry as he used to—just suspicious, careful. "I owed you for the ranch, Percy. Plus . . . I wanted to see Daedalus for myself. Minos was right, in a way. Daedalus *should* die. Nobody should be able to avoid death that long. It's not natural."

"That's what you were after all along," I said. "Trading Daedalus's soul for your sister's."

Nico walked for another fifty yards before answering. "It hasn't been easy, you know. Having only the dead for company. Knowing that I'll never be accepted by the living. Only the dead respect me, and they only do that out of fear."

"You could be accepted," I said. "You could have friends at camp."

He stared at me. "Do you really believe that, Percy?"

I didn't answer. The truth was, I didn't know. Nico had always been a little different, but since Bianca's death, he'd gotten almost . . . scary. He had his father's eyes—that intense, manic fire that made you suspect he was either a genius or a madman. And the way he'd banished Minos, and called *himself* the king of ghosts—it was kind of impressive, but it made me uncomfortable, too.

Before I could figure out what to tell him, I ran into Rachel, who'd stopped in front of me. We'd come to a crossroads. The tunnel continued straight ahead, but a side tunnel T'd off to the right—a circular shaft carved from black volcanic rock.

"What is it?" I asked.

Rachel stared down the dark tunnel. In the dim flash-light beam, her face looked like one of Nico's specters.

"Is that the way?" Annabeth asked.

"No," Rachel said nervously. "Not at all."

"Why are we stopping then?" I asked.

"Listen," Nico said.

I heard wind coming down the tunnel, as if the exit were close. And I smelled something vaguely familiar—something that brought back bad memories.

"Eucalyptus trees," I said. "Like in California."

Last winter, when we'd faced Luke and the Titan Atlas on the top of Mount Tamalpais, the air had smelled just like that.

"There's something evil down that tunnel," Rachel said. "Something very powerful."

"And the smell of death," Nico added, which made me feel a whole lot better.

Annabeth and I exchanged glances.

"Luke's entrance," she guessed. "The one to Mount Othrys—the Titans' palace."

"I have to check it out," I said.

"Percy, no."

"Luke could be right there," I said. "Or . . . or Kronos. I have to find out what's going on."

Annabeth hesitated. "Then we'll all go."

"No," I said. "It's too dangerous. If they got hold of Nico, or Rachel for that matter, Kronos could use them. You stay here and guard them."

What I didn't say: I was also worried about Annabeth. I didn't trust what she would do if she saw Luke again. He had fooled her and manipulated her too many times before.

"Percy, don't," Rachel said. "Don't go up there alone."

"I'll be quick," I promised. "I won't do anything stupid."

Annabeth took her Yankees cap out of her pocket. "At least take this. And be careful."

"Thanks." I remembered the last time Annabeth and I had parted ways, when she'd given me a kiss for luck in Mount St. Helens. This time, all I got was the hat.

I put it on. "Here goes nothing." And I sneaked invisibly down the dark stone tunnel.

Before I even got to the exit I heard voices: the growling, barking sounds of sea-demon smiths, the telekhines.

"At least we salvaged the blade," one said. "The master will still reward us."

"Yes! Yes!" a second shrieked. "Rewards beyond measure!"

Another voice, this one more human, said: "Um, yeah, well that's great. Now, if you're done with me—"

"No, half-blood!" a telekhine said. "You must help us make the presentation. It is a great honor!"

"Gee, thanks," the half-blood said, and I realized it was Ethan Nakamura, the guy who'd run away after I'd saved his sorry life in the arena.

I crept toward the end of the tunnel. I had to remind myself I was invisible. They shouldn't be able to see me.

A blast of cold air hit me as I emerged. I was standing near the top of Mount Tam. The Pacific Ocean spread out below, gray under a cloudy sky. About twenty feet downhill, two telekhines were placing something on a big rock—something long and thin and wrapped in black cloth. Ethan was helping them open it.

"Careful, fool," the telekhine scolded. "One touch, and the blade will sever your soul from your body."

Ethan swallowed nervously. "Maybe I'll let you unwrap it, then."

I glanced up at the mountain's peak, where a black

marble fortress loomed, just like I'd seen in my dreams. It reminded me of an oversized mausoleum, with walls fifty feet high. I had no idea how mortals could miss the fact that it was here. But then again, everything below the summit seemed fuzzy to me, as if there were a thick veil between me and the lower half of the mountain. There was magic going on here—really powerful Mist. Above me, the sky swirled into a huge funnel cloud. I couldn't see Atlas, but I could hear him groaning in the distance, still laboring under the weight of the sky, just beyond the fortress.

"There!" the telekhine said. Reverently, he lifted the weapon, and my blood turned to ice.

It was a scythe—a six-foot-long blade curved like a crescent moon, with a wooden handle wrapped in leather. The blade glinted two different colors—steel and bronze. It was the weapon of Kronos, the one he'd used to slice up his father, Ouranos, before the gods had taken it away from him and cut *Kronos* to pieces, casting him into Tartarus. Now the weapon was re-forged.

"We must sanctify it in blood," the telekhine said. "Then you, half-blood, shall help present it when the lord awakes."

I ran toward the fortress, my pulse pounding in my ears. I didn't want to get anywhere close to that horrible black mausoleum, but I knew what I had to do. I had to stop Kronos from rising. This might be my only chance.

I dashed through a dark foyer and into the main hall. The floor shined like a mahogany piano—pure black and yet full of light. Black marble statues lined the walls. I didn't recognize the faces, but I knew I was looking at images of the Titans who'd ruled before the gods. At the end of the room, between two bronze braziers, was a dais. And on the dais, the golden sarcophagus.

The room was silent except for the crackle of the fires. Luke wasn't here. No guards. Nothing.

It was too easy, but I approached the dais.

The sarcophagus was just like I remembered—about ten feet long, much too big for a human. It was carved with elaborate scenes of death and destruction, pictures of the gods being trodden under chariots, temples and famous world landmarks being smashed and burned. The whole coffin gave off an aura of extreme cold, like I was walking into a freezer. My breath began to steam.

I drew Riptide and took a little comfort from the familiar weight of the sword in my hand.

Whenever I'd approached Kronos before, his evil voice had spoken in my mind. Why was he silent now? He'd been shred into a thousand pieces, cut with his own scythe. What would I find if I opened that lid? How could they make a new body for him?

I had no answers. I just knew that if he was about rise, I had to strike him down before he got his scythe. I had to figure out a way to stop him.

I stood over the coffin. The lid was decorated even more intricately than the sides—with scenes of carnage and power. In the middle was an inscription carved in letters even older than Greek, a language of magic. I couldn't read it, exactly, but I knew what it said: KRONOS, LORD OF TIME.

My hand touched the lid. My fingertips turned blue. Frost gathered on my sword.

Then I heard noises behind me—voices approaching. It was now or never. I pushed back the golden lid and it fell to the floor with a huge *WHOOOOM!*

I lifted my sword, ready to strike. But when I looked inside, I didn't comprehend what I was seeing. Mortal legs, dressed in gray pants. A white T-shirt, hands folded over his stomach. One piece of his chest was missing—a clean black hole about the size of a bullet wound, right where his heart should've been. His eyes were closed. His skin was pale. Blond hair . . . and a scar running along the left side of his face.

The body in the coffin was Luke's.

I should have stabbed him right then. I should've brought the point of Riptide down with all my strength.

But I was too stunned. I didn't understand. As much as I hated Luke, as much as he had betrayed me, I just didn't get why he was in the coffin, and why he looked so very, very dead.

Then the voices of the telekhines were right behind me.

"What has happened!" one of the demons screamed when he saw the lid. I stumbled away from the dais, forgetting that I was invisible, and hid behind a column as they approached.

"Careful!" the other demon warned. "Perhaps he stirs. We must present the gifts now. Immediately!"

The two telekhines shuffled forward and knelt, holding

up the scythe on its wrapping cloth. "My lord," one said. "Your symbol of power is remade."

Silence. Nothing happened in the coffin.

"You fool," the other telekhine muttered. "He requires the half-blood first."

Ethan stepped back. "Whoa, what do you mean, he requires me?"

"Don't be a coward!" the first telekhine hissed. "He does not require your death. Only your allegiance. Pledge him your service. Renounce the gods. That is all."

"No!" I yelled. It was a stupid thing to do, but I charged into the room and took off the cap. "Ethan, don't!"

"Trespasser!" The telekhines bared their seal teeth. "The master will deal with you soon enough. Hurry, boy!"

"Ethan," I pleaded, "don't listen to them. Help me destroy it."

Ethan turned toward me, his eye patch blending in with the shadows on his face. His expression was something like pity. "I told you not to spare me, Percy. 'An eye for an eye.' You ever hear that saying? I learned what it means the hard way—when I discovered my godly parent. I'm the child of Nemesis, Goddess of Revenge. And this is what I was made to do."

He turned toward the dais. "I renounce the gods! What have they ever done for me? I will see them destroyed. I will serve Kronos."

The building rumbled. A wisp of blue light rose from the floor at Ethan Nakamura's feet. It drifted toward the coffin and began to shimmer, like a cloud of pure energy. Then it descended into the sarcophagus.

Luke sat bolt upright. His eyes opened, and they were no longer blue. They were golden, the same color as the coffin. The hole in his chest was gone. He was complete. He leaped out of the coffin with ease, and where his feet touched the floor, the marble froze like craters of ice.

He looked at Ethan and the telekhines with those horrible golden eyes, as if he were a newborn baby, not sure what he was seeing. Then he looked at me, and a smile of recognition crept across his mouth.

"This body has been well prepared." His voice was like a razor blade running over my skin. It was Luke's, but not Luke's. Underneath his voice was another, more horrible sound—an ancient, cold sound like metal scraping against rock. "Don't you think so, Percy Jackson?"

I couldn't move. I couldn't answer.

Kronos threw back his head and laughed. The scar on his face rippled.

"Luke feared you," the Titan's voice said. "His jealousy and hatred have been powerful tools. It has kept him obedient. For that I thank you."

Ethan collapsed in terror. He covered his face with his hands. The telekhines trembled, holding up the scythe.

Finally I found my nerve. I lunged at the thing that used to be Luke, thrusting my blade straight at his chest, but his skin deflected the blow like he was made of pure steel. He looked at me with amusement. Then he flicked his hand, and I flew across the room.

I slammed against a pillar. I struggled to my feet,

blinking the stars out of my eyes, but Kronos had already grasped the handle of his scythe.

"Ah . . . much better," he said. "Backbiter, Luke called it. An appropriate name. Now that it is re-forged completely, it shall indeed *bite back*."

"What have you done to Luke?" I groaned.

Kronos raised his scythe. "He serves me with his whole being, as I require. The difference is, he feared you, Percy Jackson. I do not."

That's when I ran. There wasn't even any thought to it. No debate in my mind about—gee, should I stand up to him and try to fight again? Nope. I simply ran.

But my feet felt like lead. Time slowed down around me, like the world was turning to Jell-O. I'd had this feeling once before, and I knew it was the power of Kronos. His presence was so strong it could bend time itself.

"Run, little hero," he laughed. "Run!"

I glanced back and saw him approaching leisurely, swinging his scythe as if he were enjoying the feel of having it in his hands again. No weapon in the world could stop him. No amount of celestial bronze.

He was ten feet away when I heard, "PERCY!"

Rachel's voice.

Something flew past me, and a blue plastic hairbrush hit Kronos in the eye.

"Ow!" he yelled. For a moment it was only Luke's voice, full of surprise and pain. My limbs were freed and I ran straight into Rachel, Nico, and Annabeth, who were standing in the entry hall, their eyes wide with dismay.

"Luke?" Annabeth called. "What—"

I grabbed her by the shirt and hauled her after me. I ran as fast as I've ever run, straight out of the fortress. We were almost back to the Labyrinth entrance when I heard the loudest bellow in the world—the voice of Kronos, coming back into control. "AFTER THEM!"

"No!" Nico yelled. He clapped his hands together, and a jagged spire of rock the size of an eighteen-wheeler erupted from the ground right in front of the fortress. The tremor it caused was so powerful the front columns of the building came crashing down. I heard muffled screams from the telekhines inside. Dust billowed everywhere.

We plunged into the Labyrinth and kept running, the howl of the Titan lord shaking the entire world behind us.

SEVENTEEN

THE LOST GOD SPEAKS

We ran until we were exhausted. Rachel steered us away from traps, but we had no destination in mind—only *away* from that dark mountain and the roar of Kronos.

We stopped in a tunnel of wet white rock, like part of a natural cave. I couldn't hear anything behind us, but I didn't feel any safer. I could still remember those unnatural golden eyes staring out of Luke's face, and the feeling that my limbs were slowly turning to stone.

"I can't go any farther," Rachel gasped, hugging her chest.

Annabeth had been crying the entire time we'd been running. Now she collapsed and put her head between her knees. Her sobs echoed in the tunnel. Nico and I sat next to each other. He dropped his sword next to mine and took a shaky breath.

"That sucked," he said, which I thought summed things up pretty well.

"You saved our lives," I said.

Nico wiped the dust off his face. "Blame the girls for dragging me along. That's the only thing they could agree on. We needed to help you or you'd mess things up."

"Nice that they trust me so much." I shined my

flashlight across the cavern. Water dripped from the stalactites like a slow-motion rain. "Nico . . . you, uh, kind of
gave yourself away."

"What do you mean?"

"That wall of black stone? That was pretty impressive.
If Kronos didn't know who you were before, he does now—
a child of the Underworld."

Nico frowned. "Big deal."

I let it drop. I figured he was just trying to hide how
scared he was, and I couldn't blame him.

Annabeth lifted her head. Her eyes were red from crying. "What . . . what was wrong with Luke? What did they
do to him?"

I told her what I'd seen in the coffin, the way the last
piece of Kronos's spirit had entered Luke's body when
Ethan Nakamura pledged his service.

"No," Annabeth said. "That's can't be true. He couldn't—"

"He gave himself over to Kronos," I said. "I'm sorry,
Annabeth. But Luke is gone."

"No!" she insisted. "You saw when Rachel hit him."

I nodded, looking at Rachel with respect. "You hit the
Lord of the Titans in the eye with a blue plastic hairbrush."

Rachel looked embarrassed. "It was the only thing I
had."

"But you *saw*," Annabeth insisted. "When it hit him, just
for a second, he was dazed. He came back to his senses."

"So maybe Kronos wasn't completely settled in the
body, or whatever," I said. "It doesn't mean Luke was in
control."

"You *want* him to be evil, is that it?" Annabeth yelled. "You didn't know him before, Percy. I did!"

"What is it with you?" I snapped. "Why do you keep defending him?"

"Whoa, you two," Rachel said. "Knock it off."

Annabeth turned on her. "Stay out of it, mortal girl! If it wasn't for you . . ."

Whatever she was going to say, her voice broke. She put her head down again and sobbed miserably. I wanted to comfort her, but I didn't know how. I still felt stunned, like Kronos's time-slow effect had affected my brain. I just couldn't comprehend what I'd seen. Kronos was alive. He was armed. And the end of the world was probably close at hand.

"We have to keep moving," Nico said. "He'll send monsters after us."

Nobody was in any shape to run, but Nico was right. I hauled myself up and helped Rachel to her feet.

"You did good back there," I told her.

She managed a weak smile. "Yeah, well. I didn't want you to die." She blushed. "I mean . . . just because, you know. You owe me too many favors. How am I going to collect if you die?"

I knelt next to Annabeth. "Hey, I'm sorry. We need to move."

"I know," she said. "I'm . . . I'm all right."

She was clearly *not* all right. But she got to her feet, and we started straggling through the Labyrinth again.

"Back to New York," I said. "Rachel, can you—"

I froze. A few feet in front of us, my flashlight beam fixed on a trampled clump of red fabric lying on the ground. It was a Rasta cap: the one Grover always wore.

My hands shook as I picked up the cap. It looked like it had been stepped on by a huge muddy boot. After all that I'd gone through today, I couldn't stand the thought that something might've happened to Grover, too.

Then I noticed something else. The cave floor was mushy and wet from the water dripping off the stalactites. There were large footprints like Tyson's, and smaller ones—goat hooves—leading off to the left.

"We have to follow them," I said. "They went that way. It must have been recently."

"What about Camp Half-Blood?" Nico said. "There's no time."

"We have to find them," Annabeth insisted. "They're our friends."

She picked up Grover's smashed cap and forged ahead.

I followed, bracing myself for the worst. The tunnel was treacherous. It sloped at weird angles and was slimy with moisture. Half the time we were slipping and sliding rather than walking.

Finally we got to the bottom of a slope and found ourselves in a large cave with huge stalagmite columns. Through the center of the room ran an underground river, and Tyson was sitting by the banks, cradling Grover in his lap. Grover's eyes were closed. He wasn't moving.

"Tyson!" I yelled.

"Percy! Come quick!"

We ran over to him. Grover wasn't dead, thank the gods, but his whole body trembled like he was freezing to death.

"What happened?" I asked.

"So many things," Tyson murmured. "Large snake. Large dogs. Men with swords. But then . . . we got close to here. Grover was excited. He ran. Then we reached this room, and he fell. Like this."

"Did he say anything?" I asked.

"He said, 'We're close.' Then he hit his head on rocks."

I knelt next to him. The only other time I'd seen Grover pass out was in New Mexico, when he'd felt the presence of Pan.

I shined my flashlight around the cavern. The rocks glittered. At the far end was the entrance to another cave, flanked by gigantic columns of crystal that looked like diamonds. And beyond that entrance . . .

"Grover," I said. "Wake up."

"Uhhhhhhhh."

Annabeth knelt next to him and splashed icy cold river water in his face.

"Splurg!" His eyelids fluttered. "Percy? Annabeth? Where . . ."

"It's okay," I said. "You passed out. The presence was too much for you."

"I—I remember. Pan."

"Yeah," I said. "Something powerful is just beyond that doorway."

✳ ✳ ✳

I made quick introductions, since Tyson and Grover had never met Rachel. Tyson told Rachel she was pretty, which made Annabeth's nostrils flare like she was going to blow fire.

"Anyway," I said. "Come on, Grover. Lean on me."

Annabeth and I helped him up, and together we waded across the underground river. The current was strong. The water came up to our waists. I willed myself to stay dry, which is a handy little ability, but that didn't help the others, and I could still feel the cold, like wading through a snowdrift.

"I think we're in Carlsbad Caverns," Annabeth said, her teeth chattering. "Maybe an unexplored section."

"How do you know?"

"Carlsbad is in New Mexico," she said. "That would explain last winter."

I nodded. Grover's swooning episode had happened when we passed through New Mexico. That's where he'd felt closest to the power of Pan.

We got out of the water and kept walking. As the crystal pillars loomed larger, I started to feel the power emanating from the next room. I'd been in the presence of gods before, but this was different. My skin tingled with living energy. My weariness fell away, as if I'd just gotten a good night's sleep. I could feel myself growing stronger, like one of those plants in a time-lapse video. And the scent coming from the cave was nothing like the dank wet underground. It smelled of trees and flowers and a warm summer day.

Grover whimpered with excitement. I was too stunned

to talk. Even Nico seemed speechless. We stepped into the cave, and Rachel said, "Oh, wow."

The walls glittered with crystals—red, green, and blue. In the strange light, beautiful plants grew—giant orchids, star-shaped flowers, vines bursting with orange and purple berries that crept among the crystals. The cave floor was covered with soft green moss. Overhead, the ceiling was higher than a cathedral, sparkling like a galaxy of stars. In the center of the cave stood a Roman-style bed, gilded wood shaped like a curly U, with velvet cushions. Animals lounged around it—but they were animals that shouldn't have been alive. There was a dodo bird, something that looked like a cross between a wolf and a tiger, a huge rodent like the mother of all guinea pigs, and roaming behind the bed, picking berries with its trunk, was a wooly mammoth.

On the bed lay an old satyr. He watched us as we approached, his eyes as blue as the sky. His curly hair was white and so was his pointed beard. Even the goat fur on his legs was frosted with gray. His horns were enormous—glossy brown and curved. There was no way he could've hidden those under a hat the way Grover did. Around his neck hung a set of reed pipes.

Grover fell to his knees in front of the bed. "Lord Pan!"

The god smiled kindly, but there was sadness in his eyes. "Grover, my dear, brave satyr. I have waited a very long time for you."

"I . . . got lost," Grover apologized.

Pan laughed. It was a wonderful sound, like the first breeze of springtime, filling the whole cavern with hope.

The tiger-wolf sighed and rested his head on the god's knee. The dodo bird pecked affectionately at the god's hooves, making a strange sound in the back of its bill. I could swear it was humming "It's a Small World."

Still, Pan looked tired. His whole form shimmered as if he were made of Mist.

I noticed my other friends were kneeling. They had awed looks on their faces. I got to my knees.

"You have a humming dodo bird," I said stupidly.

The god's eyes twinkled. "Yes, that's Dede. My little actress."

Dede the dodo looked offended. She pecked at Pan's knee and hummed something that sounded like a funeral dirge.

"This is the most beautiful place!" Annabeth said. "It's better than any building ever designed."

"I'm glad you like it, dear," Pan said. "It is one of the last wild places. My realm above is gone, I'm afraid. Only pockets remain. Tiny pieces of life. This one shall stay undisturbed . . . for a little longer."

"My lord," Grover said, "please, you must come back with me! The Elders will never believe it! They'll be overjoyed! You can save the wild!"

Pan placed his hand on Grover's head and ruffled his curly hair. "You are so young, Grover. So good and true. I think I chose well."

"Chose?" Grover said. "I—I don't understand."

Pan's image flickered, momentarily turning to smoke. The giant guinea pig scuttled under the bed with a terrified squeal. The wooly mammoth grunted nervously. Dede stuck her head under her wing. Then Pan re-formed.

"I have slept many eons," the god said forlornly. "My dreams have been dark. I wake fitfully, and each time my waking is shorter. Now we are near the end."

"What?" Grover cried. "But no! You're right here!"

"My dear satyr," Pan said. "I tried to tell the world, two thousand years ago. I announced it to Lysas, a satyr very much like you. He lived in Ephesos, and he tried to spread the word."

Annabeth's eyes widened. "The old story. A sailor passing by the coast of Ephesos heard a voice crying from the shore, 'Tell them the great god Pan is dead.'"

"But that wasn't true!" Grover said.

"Your kind never believed it," Pan said. "You sweet, stubborn satyrs refused to accept my passing. And I love you for that, but you only delayed the inevitable. You only prolonged my long, painful passing, my dark twilight sleep. It must end."

"No!" Grover's voice trembled.

"Dear Grover," Pan said. "You must accept the truth. Your companion, Nico, he understands."

Nico nodded slowly. "He's dying. He should have died long ago. This . . . this is more like a memory."

"But gods can't die," Grover said.

"They can fade," Pan said, "when everything they stood for is gone. When they cease to have power, and their sacred places disappear. The wild, my dear Grover, is so small now, so shattered, that no god can save it. My realm is gone. That is why I need you to carry a message. You must go back to the council. You must tell the satyrs, and the dryads, and the other spirits of nature, that the great god Pan *is* dead. Tell them of my passing. Because they must stop waiting for me to save them. I cannot. The only salvation you must make yourself. Each of you must—"

He stopped and frowned at the dodo bird, who had started humming again.

"Dede, what are you doing?" Pan demanded. "Are you singing *Kumbaya* again?"

Dede looked up innocently and blinked her yellow eyes.

Pan sighed. "Everybody's a cynic. But as I was saying, my dear Grover, each of you must take up my calling."

"But . . . no!" Grover whimpered.

"Be strong," Pan said. "You have found me. And now you must release me. You must carry on my spirit. It can no longer be carried by a god. It must be taken up by all of you."

Pan looked straight at me with his clear blue eyes, and I realized he wasn't just talking about the satyrs. He meant half-bloods, too, and humans. Everyone.

"Percy Jackson," the god said. "I know what you have seen today. I know your doubts. But I give you this news: when the time comes, you will not be ruled by fear."

He turned to Annabeth. "Daughter of Athena, your time is coming. You will play a great role, though it may not be the role you imagined."

Then he looked at Tyson. "Master Cyclops, do not despair. Heroes rarely live up to our expectations. But you,

Tyson—your name shall live among the Cyclopes for generations. And Miss Rachel Dare . . ."

Rachel flinched when he said her name. She backed up like she was guilty of something, but Pan only smiled. He raised his hand in a blessing.

"I know you believe you cannot make amends," he said. "But you are just as important as your father."

"I—" Rachel faltered. A tear traced her cheek.

"I know you don't believe this now," Pan said. "But look for opportunities. They will come."

Finally he turned back toward Grover. "My dear satyr," Pan said kindly, "will you carry my message?"

"I—I can't."

"You can," Pan said. "You are the strongest and bravest. Your heart is true. You have believed in me more than anyone ever has, which is why you must bring the message, and why you must be the first to release me."

"I don't want to."

"I know," the god said. "But my name, *Pan* . . . originally it meant *rustic*. Did you know that? But over the years it has come to mean *all*. The spirit of the wild must pass to all of you now. You must tell each one you meet: if you would find Pan, take up Pan's spirit. Remake the wild, a little at a time, each in your own corner of the world. You cannot wait for anyone else, even a god, to do that for you."

Grover wiped his eyes. Then slowly he stood. "I've spent my whole life looking for you. Now . . . I release you."

Pan smiled. "Thank you, dear satyr. My final blessing."

He closed his eyes, and the god dissolved. White mist

divided into wisps of energy, but this kind of energy wasn't scary like the blue power I'd seen from Kronos. It filled the room. A curl of smoke went straight into my mouth, and Grover's, and the others. But I think a little more of it went into Grover. The crystals dimmed. The animals gave us a sad look. Dede the dodo sighed. Then they all turned gray and crumbled to dust. The vines withered. And we were alone in a dark cave, with an empty bed.

I switched on my flashlight.

Grover took a deep breath.

"Are . . . are you okay?" I asked him.

He looked older and sadder. He took his cap from Annabeth, brushed off the mud, and stuck it firmly on his curly head.

"We should go now," he said, "and tell them. The great god Pan is dead."

EIGHTEEN

GROVER CAUSES A STAMPEDE

Distance was shorter in the Labyrinth. Still, by the time Rachel got us back to Times Square, I felt like we'd pretty much run all the way from New Mexico. We climbed out of the Marriott basement and stood on the sidewalk in the bright summer daylight, squinting at the traffic and crowds.

I couldn't decide which seemed less real—New York or the crystal cave where I'd watched a god die.

I led the way into an alley, where I could get a nice echo. Then I whistled as loud as I could, five times.

A minute later, Rachel gasped. "They're beautiful!"

A flock of pegasi descended from the sky, swooping between the skyscrapers. Blackjack was in the lead, followed by four of his white friends.

Yo, boss! He spoke in my mind. *You lived!*

"Yeah," I told him. "I'm lucky that way. Listen, we need a ride to camp *quick.*"

That's my specialty! Oh man, you got that Cyclops with you? Yo, Guido! How's your back holding up?

The pegasus Guido groaned and complained, but eventually he agreed to carry Tyson. Everybody started saddling up—except Rachel.

"Well," she told me, "I guess this is it."

I nodded uncomfortably. We both knew she couldn't go to camp. I glanced at Annabeth, who was pretending to be very busy with her pegasus.

"Thanks, Rachel," I said. "We couldn't have done it without you."

"I wouldn't have missed it. I mean, except for almost dying, and Pan . . ." Her voice faltered.

"He said something about your father," I remembered. "What did he mean?"

Rachel twisted the strap on her backpack. "My dad . . . My dad's job. He's kind of a famous businessman."

"You mean . . . you're *rich*?"

"Well, yeah."

"So that's how you got the chauffeur to help us? You just said your dad's name and—"

"Yes," Rachel cut me off. "Percy . . . my dad's a land developer. He flies all over the world, looking for tracts of undeveloped land." She took a shaky breath. "The wild. He—he buys it up. I hate it, but he plows it down and builds ugly subdivisions and shopping centers. And now that I've seen Pan . . . Pan's death—"

"Hey, you can't blame yourself for that."

"You don't know the worst of it. I—I don't like to talk about my family. I didn't want you to know. I'm sorry. I shouldn't have said anything."

"No," I said. "It's cool. Look, Rachel, you did awesome. You led us through the maze. You were so brave. That's the only thing I'm going to judge you on. I don't care what your dad does."

Rachel looked at me gratefully. "Well . . . if you ever feel like hanging out with a mortal again . . . you could call me or something."

"Uh, yeah. Sure."

She knit her eyebrows. I guess I sounded unenthusiastic or something, but that's not how I meant it. I just wasn't sure what to say with all my friends standing around. And I guess my feelings had gotten pretty mixed up the last couple of days.

"I mean . . . I'd like that," I said.

"My number's not in the book," she said.

"I've got it."

"Still on your hand? No way."

"No. I kinda . . . memorized it."

Her smile came back slowly, but a lot happier. "See you later, Percy Jackson. Go save the world for me, okay?"

She walked off down Seventh Avenue and disappeared into the crowds.

When I got back to the horses, Nico was having trouble. His pegasus kept shying away from him, reluctant to let him mount.

He smells like dead people! the pegasus complained.

Hey now, Blackjack said. *Come on, Porkpie. Lotsa demigods smell weird. It ain't their fault. Oh—uh, I didn't mean you, boss.*

"Go without me!" Nico said. "I don't want to go back to that camp anyway."

"Nico," I said, "we need your help."

He folded his arms and scowled. Then Annabeth put her hand on his shoulder.

"Nico," she said. "Please."

Slowly, his expression softened. "All right," he said reluctantly. "For *you*. But I'm not staying."

I raised an eyebrow at Annabeth, like, *How come all of the sudden Nico listens to you?* She stuck her tongue out at me.

At last we got everybody on a pegasus. We shot into the air, and soon we were over the East River with Long Island spread out before us.

We landed in the middle of the cabin area and were immediately met by Chiron, the potbellied satyr Silenus, and a couple of Apollo cabin archers. Chiron raised an eyebrow when he saw Nico, but if I expected him to be surprised by our latest news about Quintus being Daedalus, or Kronos rising, I was mistaken.

"I feared as much," Chiron said. "We must hurry. Hopefully you have slowed down the Titan lord, but his vanguard will still be coming through. They will be anxious for blood. Most of our defenders are already in place. Come!"

"Wait a moment," Silenus demanded. "What of the search for Pan? You are almost three weeks overdue, Grover Underwood! Your searcher's license is revoked!"

Grover took a deep breath. He stood up straight and looked Silenus in the eye. "Searcher's licenses don't matter anymore. The great god Pan is dead. He has passed on and left us his spirit."

"What?" Silenus's face turned bright red. "Sacrilege and lies! Grover Underwood, I will have you exiled for speaking thus!"

"It's true," I said. "We were there when he died. All of us."

"Impossible! You are all liars! Nature-destroyers!"

Chiron studied Grover's face. "We will speak of this later."

"We will speak of it now!" Silenus said. "We must deal with this—"

"Silenus," Chiron cut in. "My camp is under attack. The matter of Pan has waited two thousand years. I fear it will have to wait a bit longer. Assuming we are still here this evening."

And on that happy note, he readied his bow and galloped toward the woods, leaving us to follow as best we could.

It was the biggest military operation I'd ever seen at camp. Everyone was at the clearing, dressed in full battle armor, but this time it wasn't for capture the flag. The Hephaestus cabin had set up traps around the entrance to the Labyrinth—razor wire, pits filled with pots of Greek fire, rows of sharpened sticks to deflect a charge. Beckendorf was manning two catapults the size of pickup trucks, already primed and aimed at Zeus's Fist. The Ares cabin was on the front line, drilling in phalanx formation with Clarisse calling orders. Apollo's and Hermes's cabins were scattered in the woods with bows ready. Many had taken up positions in the trees. Even the dryads were armed with bows, and the satyrs trotted around with wooden cudgels and shields made of rough tree bark.

Annabeth went to join her brethren from the Athena cabin, who had set up a command tent and were directing operations. A gray banner with an owl fluttered outside the tent. Our security chief, Argus, stood guard at the door. Aphrodite's children were running around straightening everybody's armor and offering to comb the tangles out of our horsehair plumes. Even Dionysus's kids had found something to do. The god himself was still nowhere to be seen, but his two blond twin sons were running around providing all the sweaty warriors with water bottles and juice boxes.

It looked like a pretty good setup, but Chiron muttered next to me, "It isn't enough."

I thought about what I'd seen in the Labyrinth, all the monsters in Antaeus's stadium, and the power of Kronos I'd felt on Mt. Tam. My heart sank. Chiron was right, but it was all we could muster. For once I wished Dionysus was here, but even if he had been, I didn't know if he could do anything. When it came to war, gods were forbidden to interfere directly. Apparently, the Titans didn't believe in restrictions like that.

Over at the edge of the clearing, Grover was talking to Juniper. She held his hands while he told her our story. Green tears formed in her eyes as he delivered the news about Pan.

Tyson helped the Hephaestus kids prepare the defenses. He picked up boulders and piled them next to the catapults for firing.

"Stay with me, Percy," Chiron said. "When the fighting

begins, I want you to wait until we know what we're dealing with. You must go where we most need reinforcements."

"I saw Kronos," I said, still stunned by the fact. "I looked straight into his eyes. It was Luke . . . but it wasn't."

Chiron ran his fingers along his bowstring. "He had golden eyes, I would guess. And in his presence, time seemed to turn to liquid."

I nodded. "How could he take over a mortal body?"

"I do not know, Percy. Gods have assumed the shapes of mortals for ages, but to actually become one . . . to merge the divine form with the mortal. I don't know how this could be done without Luke's form turning to ashes."

"Kronos said his body had been prepared."

"I shudder to think what that means. But perhaps it will limit Kronos's power. For a time, at least, he is confined to a human form. It binds him together. Hopefully it also restricts him."

"Chiron, if he leads this attack—"

"I do not think so, my boy. I would sense if he were drawing near. No doubt he planned to, but I believe you inconvenienced him when you pulled down his throne room on top of him." He looked at me reproachfully. "You and your friend Nico, son of Hades."

A lump formed in my throat. "I'm sorry, Chiron. I know I should've told you. It's just—"

Chiron raised his hand. "I understand why you did it, Percy. You felt responsible. You sought to protect him. But, my boy, if we are to survive this, we must trust each other. We must . . ."

His voice wavered. The ground underneath us was trembling.

Everyone in the clearing stopped what they were doing. Clarisse barked a single order: "Lock shields!"

Then the Titan lord's army exploded from the Labyrinth.

I mean I'd been in fights before, but this was a full-scale battle. The first thing I saw were a dozen Laistrygonian giants erupting from the ground, yelling so loudly my ears felt like bursting. They carried shields made from flattened cars, and clubs that were tree trunks with rusty spikes bristling at the end. One of the giants bellowed at the Ares phalanx, smashed it sideways with his club, and the entire cabin was thrown aside, a dozen warriors tossed to the wind like rag dolls.

"Fire!" Beckendorf yelled. The catapults swung into action. Two boulders hurtled toward the giants. One deflected off a car shield with hardly a dent, but the other caught a Laistrygonian in the chest, and the giant went down. Apollo's archers fired a volley, dozens of arrows sticking in the thick armor of the giants like porcupine quills. Several found chinks in armor, and some of the giants vaporized at the touch of celestial bronze.

But just when it looked like the Lastrygonians were about to get overwhelmed, the next wave surged out of the maze: thirty, maybe forty *dracaenae* in full battle armor, wielding spears and nets. They dispersed in all directions. Some hit the traps the Hephaestus cabin had laid. One got stuck on the spikes and became an easy target for archers. Another triggered a trip wire, and pots of Greek fire exploded into green flames, engulfing several of the snake women. But many more kept coming. Argus and Athena's warriors rushed forward to meet them. I saw Annabeth draw a sword and engage one of them. Nearby, Tyson was riding a giant. Somehow he'd managed to climb onto the giant's back and was hitting him on the head with a bronze shield—*BONG! BONG! BONG!*

Chiron calmly aimed arrow after arrow, taking down a monster with every shot. But more enemies just kept climbing out of the maze. Finally a hellhound—not Mrs. O'Leary—leaped out of the tunnel and barreled straight toward the satyrs.

"GO!" Chiron yelled to me.

I drew Riptide and charged.

As I raced across the battlefield, I saw horrible things. An enemy half-blood was fighting with a son of Dionysus, but it wasn't much of a contest. The enemy stabbed him in the arm then clubbed him over the head with the butt of his sword, and Dionysus's son went down. Another enemy warrior shot flaming arrows into the trees, sending our archers and dryads into a panic.

A dozen *dracaenae* suddenly broke away from the main fight and slithered down the path that led toward camp, like they knew where they were going. If they got out, they could burn down the entire place, completely unopposed.

The only person anywhere near was Nico di Angelo. He stabbed a telekhine, and his black Stygian blade absorbed the monster's essence, drinking its energy until there was nothing left but dust.

"Nico!" I yelled.

He looked where I was pointing, saw the serpent women, and immediately understood.

He took a deep breath and held out his black sword. "Serve me," he called.

The earth trembled. A fissure opened in front of the *dracaenae*, and a dozen undead warriors crawled from the earth—horrible corpses in military uniforms from all different time periods—U.S. Revolutionaries, Roman centurions, Napoleonic cavalry on skeletal horses. As one, they drew their swords and engaged the *dracaenea*. Nico crumpled to his knees, but I didn't have time to make sure he was okay.

I closed on the hellhound, which was now pushing the satyrs back toward the woods. The beast snapped at one satyr, who danced out of its way, but then it pounced on another who was too slow. The satyr's tree-bark shield cracked as he fell.

"Hey!" I yelled.

The hellhound turned. It snarled at me and leaped. It would've clawed me to pieces, but as I fell backward, my fingers closed around a clay jar—one of Beckendorf's containers of Greek fire. I tossed it into the hellhound's maw, and the creature went up in flames. I scrambled away, breathing heavily.

The satyr who'd gotten trampled wasn't moving. I rushed over to check on him, but then I heard Grover's voice: "Percy!"

A forest fire had started. Flames roared within ten feet of Juniper's tree, and Juniper and Grover were going nuts trying to save it. Grover played a rain song on his pipes. Juniper desperately tried to beat out the flames with her green shawl, but it was only making things worse.

I ran toward them, jumping past duels, weaving between the legs of giants. The nearest water was the creek, half a mile away . . . but I had to do something. I concentrated. There was a pull in my gut, a roar in my ears. Then a wall of water came rushing through the trees. It doused the fire, Juniper, Grover, and pretty much everything else.

Grover blew a spout of water. "Thanks, Percy!"

"No problem!" I ran back toward the fight, and Grover and Juniper followed. Grover had a cudgel in his hand and Juniper held a stick—like an old-fashioned whipping switch. She looked really angry, like she was going to tan somebody's backside.

Just when it seemed like the battle had balanced out again—like we might stand a chance—an unearthly shriek echoed out of the Labyrinth, a sound I had heard before.

Kampê shot into the sky, her bat wings fully extended. She landed on the top of Zeus's Fist and surveyed the carnage. Her face was filled with evil glee. The mutant animal heads growled at her waist. Snakes hissed and swirled around her legs. In her right hand she held a glittering ball of thread—Ariadne's string—but she popped it into a lion's mouth at her waist and drew her curved swords. The blades glowed green with poison. Kampê screeched in triumph, and some of the campers screamed. Others tried to run and got trampled by hellhounds or giants.

"*Di Immortales!*" Chiron yelled. He quickly aimed an arrow, but Kampê seemed to sense his presence. She took flight with amazing speed, and Chiron's arrow whizzed harmlessly past her head.

Tyson untangled himself from the giant whom he'd pummeled into unconsciousness. He ran at our lines, shouting, "Stand! Do not run from her! Fight!"

But then a hellhound leaped on him, and Tyson and the hound went rolling away.

Kampê landed on the Athena command tent, smashing it flat. I ran after her and found Annabeth at my side, keeping pace, her sword in her hand.

"This might be it," she said.

"Could be."

"Nice fighting with you, Seaweed Brain."

"Ditto."

Together we leaped into the monster's path. Kampê hissed and sliced at us. I dodged, trying to distract her, while Annabeth went in for a strike, but the monster seemed able to fight with both hands independently. She blocked Annabeth's sword, and Annabeth had to jump back to avoid the cloud of poison. Just being near the thing was like standing in an acid fog. My eyes burned. My lungs couldn't get enough air. I knew we couldn't stand our ground for more than a few seconds.

"Come on!" I shouted. "We need help!"

But no help came. Everyone was either down, or fighting for their lives, or too scared to move forward. Three of

Chiron's arrows sprouted from Kampê's chest, but she just roared louder.

"Now!" Annabeth said.

Together we charged, dodged the monster's slashes, got inside her guard, and almost . . . *almost* managed to stab Kampê in the chest, but a huge bear's head lashed out from the monster's waist, and we had to stumble backward to avoid getting bitten.

Slam!

My eyesight went black. The next thing I knew, Annabeth and I were on the ground. The monster had its forelegs on our chests, holding us down. Hundreds of snakes slithered right above me, hissing like laughter. Kampê raised her green-tinged swords, and I knew Annabeth and I were out of options.

Then, behind me, something howled. A wall of darkness slammed into Kampê, sending the monster sideways. And Mrs. O'Leary was standing over us, snarling and snapping at Kampê.

"Good girl!" said a familiar voice. Daedalus was fighting his way out of the Labyrinth, slashing down enemies left and right as he made his way toward us. Next to him was someone else—a familiar giant, much taller than the Laistrygonians, with a hundred rippling arms, each holding a huge chunk of rock.

"Briares!" Tyson cried in wonder.

"Hail, little brother!" Briares bellowed. "Stand firm!"

And as Mrs. O'Leary leaped out of the way, the Hundred-Handed One launched a volley of boulders at

Kampê. The rocks seemed to enlarge as they left Briares's hands. There were so many, it looked like half the earth had learned to fly.

BOOOOOM!

Where Kampê had stood a moment before was a mountain of boulders, almost as tall as Zeus's Fist. The only sign that the monster had ever existed were two green sword points sticking through the cracks.

A cheer went up from the campers, but our enemies weren't done yet. One of the *dracaenae* yelled, "Ssssslay them! Kill them all or Kronossss will flay you alive!"

Apparently, that threat was more terrifying than we were. The giants surged forward in a last desperate attempt. One surprised Chiron with a glancing blow to the back legs, and he stumbled and fell. Six giants cried in glee and rushed forward.

"No!" I screamed, but I was too far away to help.

Then it happened. Grover opened his mouth, and the most horrible sound I'd ever heard came out. It was like a brass trumpet magnified a thousand times—the sound of pure fear.

As one, the forces of Kronos dropped their weapons and ran for their lives. The giants trampled the *dracaenae* trying to get into the Labyrinth first. Telekhines and hellhounds and enemy half-bloods scrambled after them. The tunnel rumbled shut, and the battle was over. The clearing was quiet except for fires burning in the woods, and the cries of the wounded.

I helped Annabeth to her feet. We ran to Chiron.

"Are you all right?" I asked.

He was lying on his side, trying in vain to get up. "How embarrassing," he muttered. "I think I will be fine. Fortunately, we do not shoot centaurs with broken . . . Ow! . . . broken legs."

"You need help," Annabeth said. "I'll get a medic from Apollo's cabin."

"No," Chiron insisted. "There are more serious injuries to attend to. Go! I am fine. But, Grover . . . later we must talk about how you did that."

"That was amazing," I agreed.

Grover blushed. "I don't know where it came from."

Juniper hugged him fiercely. "I do!"

Before she could say more, Tyson called, "Percy, come quick! It is Nico!"

There was smoke curling off his black clothes. His fingers were clenched, and the grass all around his body had turned yellow and died.

I rolled him over as gently as I could and put my hand against his chest. His heart was beating faintly. "Get some nectar!" I yelled.

One of the Ares campers hobbled over and handed me a canteen. I trickled some of the magic drink into Nico's mouth. He coughed and spluttered, but his eyelids fluttered open.

"Nico, what happened?" I asked. "Can you talk?"

He nodded weakly. "Never tried to summon so many before. I—I'll be fine."

We helped him sit up and gave him some more nectar.

He blinked at all of us, like he was trying to remember who we were, and then he focused on someone behind me.

"Daedalus," he croaked.

"Yes, my boy," the inventor said. "I made a very bad mistake. I came to correct it."

Daedalus had a few scratches that were bleeding golden oil, but he looked better than most of us. Apparently his automaton body healed itself quickly. Mrs. O'Leary loomed behind him, licking the wounds on his master's head so Daedalus's hair stood up funny. Briares stood next to him, surrounded by a group of awed campers and satyrs. He looked kind of bashful, but he was signing autographs on armor, shields, and T-shirts.

"I found the Hundred-Handed One as I came through the maze," Daedalus explained. "It seems he had the same idea, to come help, but he was lost. And so we fell in together. We both came to make amends."

"Yay!" Tyson jumped up and down. "Briares! I knew you would come!"

"I did not know," the Hundred-Handed One said. "But you reminded me who I am, Cyclops. You are the hero."

Tyson blushed, but I patted him on the back. "I knew that a long time ago," I said. "But, Daedalus . . . the Titan army is still down there. Even without the string, they'll be back. They'll find a way sooner or later, with Kronos leading them."

Daedalus sheathed his sword. "You are right. As long as the Labyrinth is here, your enemies can use it. Which is why the Labyrinth cannot continue."

Annabeth stared at him. "But you said the Labyrinth is tied to your life force! As long as you're alive—"

"Yes, my young architect," Daedalus agreed. "When I die, the Labyrinth will die as well. And so I have a present for you."

He slung a leather satchel off his back, unzipped it, and produced a sleek silver laptop computer—one of the ones I'd seen in the workshop. On the lid was the blue symbol Δ.

"My work is here," he said. "It's all I managed to save from the fire. Notes on projects I never started. Some of my favorite designs. I couldn't develop these over the last few millennia. I did not dare reveal my work to the mortal world. But perhaps you will find it interesting."

He handed the computer to Annabeth, who stared at it like it was solid gold. "You're giving me this? But this is priceless! This is worth . . . I don't even know how much!"

"Small compensation for the way I have acted," Daedalus said. "You were right, Annabeth, about children of Athena. We should be wise, and I was not. Someday you will be a greater architect than I ever was. Take my ideas and improve them. It is the least I can do before I pass on."

"Whoa," I said. "Pass on? But you can't just kill yourself. That's wrong!"

He shook his head. "Not as wrong as hiding from my crimes for two thousand years. Genius does not excuse evil, Percy. My time has come. I must face my punishment."

"You won't get a fair trial," Annabeth said. "The spirit of Minos sits in judgment—"

"I will take what comes," he said. "And trust in the

justice of the Underworld, such as it is. That is all we can do, isn't it?"

He looked straight at Nico, and Nico's face darkened.

"Yes," he said.

"Will you take my soul for ransom, then?" Daedalus asked. "You could use it to reclaim your sister."

"No," Nico said. "I will help you release your spirit. But Bianca has passed. She must stay where she is."

Daedalus nodded. "Well done, son of Hades. You are becoming wise." Then he turned toward me. "One last favor, Percy Jackson. I cannot leave Mrs. O'Leary alone. And she has no desire to return to the Underworld. Will you care for her?"

I looked at the massive black hound, who whimpered pitifully, still licking Daedalus's hair. I was thinking that my mom's apartment wouldn't allow dogs, especially dogs bigger than the apartment, but I said, "Yeah. Of course I will."

"Then I am ready to see my son . . . and Perdix," he said. "I must tell them how sorry I am."

Annabeth had tears in her eyes.

Daedalus turned toward Nico, who drew his sword. At first I was afraid Nico would kill the old inventor, but he simply said, "Your time is long since come. Be released and rest."

A smile of relief spread across Daedalus's face. He froze like a statue. His skin turned transparent, revealing the bronze gears and machinery whirring inside his body. Then the statue turned to gray ash and disintegrated.

Mrs. O'Leary howled. I patted her head, trying to

comfort her as best I could. The earth rumbled—an earth-quake that could probably be felt in every major city across the country—as the ancient Labyrinth collapsed. Some-where, I hoped, the remains of the Titan's strike force had been buried.

I looked around at the carnage in the clearing, and the weary faces of my friends.

"Come on," I told them. "We have work to do."

NINETEEN

THE COUNCIL GETS CLOVEN

There were too many good-byes.

That night was the first time I actually saw camp burial shrouds used on bodies, and it was not something I wanted to see again.

Among the dead, Lee Fletcher from the Apollo cabin had been downed by a giant's club. He was wrapped in a golden shroud without any decoration. The son of Dionysus who'd gone down fighting an enemy half-blood was wrapped in a deep purple shroud embroidered with grapevines. His name was Castor. I was ashamed that I'd seen him around camp for three years and never even bothered to learn his name. He'd been seventeen years old. His twin brother, Pollux, tried to say a few words, but he choked up and just took the torch. He lit the funeral pyre in the middle of the amphitheater, and within seconds the row of shrouds was engulfed in fire, sending smoke and sparks up to the stars.

We spent the next day treating the wounded, which was almost everybody. The satyrs and dryads worked to repair the damage to the woods.

At noon, the Council of Cloven Elders held an

emergency meeting in their sacred grove. The three senior satyrs were there, along with Chiron, who was in wheelchair form. His broken horse leg was still mending, so he would be confined to the chair for a few months, until the leg was strong enough to take his weight. The grove was filled with satyrs and dryads and naiads up from the water—hundreds of them, anxious to hear what would happen. Juniper, Annabeth, and I stood by Grover's side.

Silenus wanted to exile Grover immediately, but Chiron persuaded him to at least hear evidence first, so we told everyone what had happened in the crystal cavern, and what Pan had said. Then several eyewitnesses from the battle described the weird sound Grover had made, which drove the Titan's army back underground.

"It was panic," insisted Juniper. "Grover summoned the power of the wild god."

"Panic?" I asked.

"Percy," Chiron explained, "during the first war of the gods and the Titans, Lord Pan let forth a horrible cry that scared away the enemy armies. It is—it *was* his greatest power—a massive wave of fear that helped the gods win the day. The word *panic* is named after Pan, you see. And Grover used that power, calling it forth from within himself."

"Preposterous!" Silenus bellowed. "Sacrilege! Perhaps the wild god favored us with a blessing. Or perhaps Grover's music was so awful it scared the enemy away!"

"That wasn't it, sir," Grover said. He sounded a lot calmer than I would have if I'd been insulted like that. "He let his spirit pass into all of us. We must act. Each of us

[338]

must work to renew the wild, to protect what's left of it. We must spread the word. Pan is dead. There is no one but us."

"After two thousand years of searching, this is what you would have us believe?" Silenus cried. "Never! We must continue the search. Exile the traitor!"

Some of the older satyrs muttered assent.

"A vote!" Silenus demanded. "Who would believe this ridiculous young satyr, anyway?"

"I would," said a familiar voice.

Everyone turned. Striding into the grove was Dionysus. He wore a formal black suit, so I almost didn't recognize him, a deep purple tie and violet dress shirt, his curly dark hair carefully combed. His eyes were bloodshot as usual, and his pudgy face was flushed, but he looked like he was suffering from grief more than wine-withdrawal.

The satyrs all stood respectfully and bowed as he approached. Dionysus waved his hand, and a new chair grew out of the ground next to Silenus's—a throne made of grapevines.

Dionysus sat down and crossed his legs. He snapped his fingers and a satyr hurried forward with a plate of cheese and crackers and a Diet Coke.

The god of wine looked around at the assembled crowd. "Miss me?"

The satyrs fell over themselves nodding and bowing. "Oh, yes, very much, sire!"

"Well, I did not miss this place!" Dionysus snapped. "I bear bad news, my friends. Evil news. The minor gods are changing sides. Morpheus has gone over to the enemy.

Hecate, Janus, and Nemesis, as well. Zeus knows how many more."

Thunder rumbled in the distance.

"Strike that," Dionysus said. "Even *Zeus* doesn't know. Now, I want to hear Grover's story. Again, from the top."

"But, my lord," Silenus protested. "It's just nonsense!"

Dionysus's eyes flared with purple fire. "I have just learned that my son Castor is dead, Silenus. I am not in a good mood. You would do well to humor me."

Silenus gulped, and waved at Grover to start again.

When Grover was done, Mr. D nodded. "It sounds like just the sort of thing Pan would do. Grover is right. The search is tiresome. You must start thinking for yourselves." He turned to a satyr. "Bring me some peeled grapes, right away!"

"Yes, sire!" The satyr scampered off.

"We must exile the traitor!" Silenus insisted.

"I say no," Dionysus countered. "That is my vote."

"I vote no as well," Chiron put in.

Silenus set his jaw stubbornly. "All in favor of the exile?"

He and the two other old satyrs raised their hands.

"Three to two," Silenus said.

"Ah, yes," Dionysus said. "But unfortunately for you, a god's vote counts twice. And as I voted against, we are tied."

Silenus stood, indignant. "This is an outrage! The council cannot stand at an impasse."

"Then let it be dissolved!" Mr. D said. "I don't care."

Silenus bowed stiffly, along with his two friends, and

they left the grove. About twenty satyrs went with them. The rest stood around murmuring uncomfortably.

"Don't worry," Grover told them. "We don't need a council to tell us what to do. We can figure it out ourselves."

He told them again the words of Pan—how they must save the wild a little at a time. He started dividing the satyrs into groups—which ones would go to the national parks, which ones would search out the last wild places, which ones would defend the parks in big cities.

"Well," Annabeth said to me, "Grover seems to be growing up."

Later that afternoon I found Tyson at the beach, talking to Briares. Briares was building a sand castle with about fifty of his hands. He wasn't really paying attention to it, but his hands had constructed a three-story compound with fortified walls, a moat, and a drawbridge.

Tyson was drawing a map in the sand.

"Go left at the reef," he told Briares. "Straight down when you see the sunken ship. Then about one mile east, past the mermaid graveyard, you will start to see fires burning."

"You're giving him directions to the forges?" I asked.

Tyson nodded. "Briares wants to help. He will teach Cyclopes ways we have forgotten, how to make better weapons and armor."

"I want to see Cyclopes," Briares agreed. "I don't want to be lonely anymore."

"I doubt you'll be lonely down there," I said a little

wistfully, because I'd never even been in Poseidon's kingdom. "They're going to keep you really busy."

Briares's face morphed to a happy expression. "Busy sounds good! I only wish Tyson could go, too."

Tyson blushed. "I need to stay here with my brother. You will do fine, Briares. Thank you."

The Hundred-Handed One shook my hand about a hundred times. "We will meet again, Percy. I know it!"

Then he gave Tyson a big octopus hug and waded out into the ocean. We watched until his enormous head disappeared under the waves.

I clapped Tyson on the back. "You helped him a lot."

"I only talked to him."

"You believed in him. Without Briares, we never would've taken down Kampê."

Tyson grinned. "He throws good rocks!"

I laughed. "Yeah. He throws really good rocks. Come on, big guy. Let's have dinner."

It felt good to have a regular dinner at camp. Tyson sat with me at the Poseidon table. The sunset over Long Island Sound was beautiful. Things weren't back to normal by a long shot, but when I went up to the brazier and scraped part of my meal into the flames as an offering to Poseidon, I felt like I really did have a lot to be grateful for. My friends and I were alive. The camp was safe. Kronos had suffered a setback, at least for a while.

The only thing that bothered me was Nico, hanging out in the shadows at the edge of the pavilion. He'd been offered a place at the Hermes table, and even at the head table with Chiron, but he had refused.

After dinner, the campers headed toward the amphitheater, where Apollo's cabin promised an awesome sing-along to pick up our spirits, but Nico turned and disappeared into the woods. I decided I'd better follow him.

As I passed under the shadows of the trees, I realized how dark it was getting. I'd never been scared in the forest before, though I knew there were plenty of monsters. Still, I thought about yesterday's battle, and I wondered if I'd ever be able to walk in these woods again without remembering the horror of so much fighting.

I couldn't see Nico, but after a few minutes of walking I saw a glow up ahead. At first I thought Nico had lit a torch. As I got closer, I realized the glow was a ghost. The shimmering form of Bianca di Angelo stood in the clearing, smiling at her brother. She said something to him and touched his face—or tried to. Then her image faded.

Nico turned and saw me, but he didn't look mad.

"Saying good-bye," he said hoarsely.

"We missed you at dinner," I said. "You could've sat with me."

"No."

"Nico, you can't miss every meal. If you don't want to stay with Hermes, maybe they can make an exception and put you in the Big House. There've got plenty of rooms."

"I'm not staying, Percy."

"But . . . you can't just leave. It's too dangerous out there for a lone half-blood. You need to train."

"I train with the dead," he said flatly. "This camp isn't for me. There's a reason they didn't put a cabin to Hades here, Percy. He's not welcome, any more than he is on Olympus. I don't belong. I have to go."

I wanted to argue, but part of me knew he was right. I didn't like it, but Nico would have to find his own, dark way. I remembered in Pan's cave, how the wild god had addressed each one of us individually . . . except Nico.

"When will you go?" I asked.

"Right away. I've got tons of questions. Like who was my mother? Who paid for Bianca and me to go to school? Who was that lawyer guy who got us out of the Lotus Hotel? I know *nothing* about my past. I need to find out."

"Makes sense," I admitted. "But I hope we don't have to be enemies."

He lowered his gaze. "I'm sorry I was a brat. I should've listened to you about Bianca."

"By the way . . ." I fished something out of my pocket. "Tyson found this while we were cleaning the cabin. Thought you might want it." I held out a lead figurine of Hades—the little Mythomagic statue Nico had abandoned when he fled camp last winter.

Nico hesitated. "I don't play that game anymore. It's for kids."

"It's got four thousand attack power," I coaxed.

"Five thousand," Nico corrected. "But only if your opponent attacks first."

I smiled. "Maybe it's okay to still be a kid once in a while." I tossed him the statuette.

Nico studied it in his palm for a few seconds, then slipped it into his pocket. "Thanks."

I put out my hand. He shook reluctantly. His hand was as cold as ice.

"I've got a lot of things to investigate," he said. "Some of them . . . Well, if I learn anything useful, I'll let you know."

I wasn't sure what he meant, but I nodded. "Keep in touch, Nico."

He turned and trudged off into the woods. The shadows seemed to bend toward him as he walked, like they were reaching out for his attention.

A voice right behind me said, "There goes a very troubled young man."

I turned and found Dionysus standing there, still in his black suit.

"Walk with me," he said.

"Where to?" I asked suspiciously.

"Just to the campfire," he said. "I was beginning to feel better, so I thought I would talk with you a bit. You always manage to annoy me."

"Uh, thanks."

We walked through the woods in silence. I noticed that Dionysus was treading on air, his polished black shoes hovering an inch off the ground. I guess he didn't want to get them dirty.

"We have had many betrayals," he said. "Things are not looking good for Olympus. Yet you and Annabeth saved this camp. I'm not sure I should thank you for that."

"It was a group effort."

He shrugged. "Regardless, I suppose it was mildly competent, what you two did. I thought you should know—it wasn't a total loss."

We reached the amphitheater, and Dionysus pointed toward the campfire. Clarisse was sitting shoulder to shoulder with a big Hispanic kid who was telling her a joke. It was Chris Rodriguez, the half-blood who'd gone insane in the Labyrinth.

I turned to Dionysus. "You cured him?"

"Madness is my specialty. It was quite simple."

"But . . . you did something nice. Why?"

He raised an eyebrow. "I am nice! I simply ooze niceness, Perry Johansson. Haven't you noticed?"

"Uh—"

"Perhaps I felt grieved by my son's death. Perhaps I thought this Chris boy deserved a second chance. At any rate, it seems to have improved Clarisse's mood."

"Why are you telling me this?"

The wine god sighed. "Oh, Hades if I know. But remember, boy, that a kind act can sometimes be as powerful as a sword. As a mortal, I was never a great fighter or athlete or poet. I only made wine. The people in my village laughed at me. They said I would never amount to anything. Look at me now. Sometimes small things can become very large indeed."

He left me alone to think about that. And as I watched Clarisse and Chris singing a stupid campfire song together, holding hands in the darkness, where they thought nobody could see them, I had to smile.

ᴤᴛᴄ

MY BIRTHDAY PARTY
TAKES A DARK TURN

The rest of the summer seemed strange because it was so normal. The daily activities continued: archery, rock climbing, pegasus riding. We played capture the flag (though we all avoided Zeus's Fist). We sang at the campfire and raced chariots and played practical jokes on the other cabins. I spent a lot of time with Tyson, playing with Mrs. O'Leary, but she would still howl at night when she got lonely for her old master. Annabeth and I pretty much skirted around each other. I was glad to be with her, but it also kind of hurt, and it hurt when I wasn't with her, too.

I wanted to talk to her about Kronos, but I couldn't do that anymore without bringing up Luke. And that was one subject I couldn't raise. She would shut me out every time I tried.

July passed, with fireworks on the beach on the Fourth. August turned so hot the strawberries started baking in the fields. Finally, the last day of camp arrived. The standard form letter appeared on my bed after breakfast, warning me that the cleaning harpies would devour me if I stayed past noon.

At ten o'clock I stood on the top of Half-Blood Hill,

waiting for the camp van that would take me into the city. I'd made arrangements to leave Mrs. O'Leary at camp, where Chiron promised she'd be looked after. Tyson and I would take turns visiting her during the year.

I hoped Annabeth would be riding into Manhattan with me, but she only came to see me off. She said she'd arranged to stay at camp a little longer. She would tend to Chiron until his leg was fully recovered, and keep studying Daedalus's laptop, which had engrossed her for the last two months. Then she would head back to her father's place in San Francisco.

"There's a private school out there that I'll be going to," she said. "I'll probably hate it, but . . ." She shrugged.

"Yeah, well, call me, okay?"

"Sure," she said half-heartedly. "I'll keep my eyes open for . . ."

There it was again. *Luke.* She couldn't even say his name without opening up a huge box of hurt and worry and anger.

"Annabeth," I said. "What was the rest of the prophecy?"

She fixed her eyes on the woods in the distance, but she didn't say anything.

"*You shall delve in the darkness of the endless maze,*" I remembered. "*The dead, the traitor, and the lost one raise.* We raised a lot of the dead. We saved Ethan Nakamura, who turned out to be a traitor. We raised the spirit of Pan, the lost one."

Annabeth shook her head like she wanted me to stop.

"*You shall rise or fall by the ghost king's hand,*" I pressed on. "That wasn't Minos, like I'd thought. It was Nico. By choosing to be on our side, he saved us. And *the child of Athena's final stand*—that was Daedalus."

"Percy—"

"*Destroy with a hero's final breath.* That makes sense now. Daedalus died to destroy the Labyrinth. But what was the last—"

"*And lose a love to worse than death.*" Annabeth had tears in her eyes. "That was the last line, Percy. Are you happy now?"

The sun seemed colder than it had a moment ago. "Oh," I said. "So Luke—"

"Percy, I didn't know who the prophecy was talking about. I—I didn't know if . . ." She faltered helplessly. "Luke and I—for years, he was the only one who really cared about me. I thought . . ."

Before she could continue, a sparkle of light appeared next to us, like someone had opened a gold curtain in the air.

"You have nothing to apologize for, my dear." Standing on the hill was a tall woman in a white dress, her dark hair braided over her shoulder.

"Hera," Annabeth said.

The goddess smiled. "You found the answers, as I knew you would. Your quest was a success."

"*A success?*" Annabeth said. "Luke is gone. Daedalus is dead. Pan is dead. How is that—"

"Our family is safe," Hera insisted. "Those others are better gone, my dear. I am proud of you."

I balled my fists. I couldn't believe she was saying this.

"You're the one who paid Geryon to let us through the ranch, weren't you?"

Hera shrugged. Her dress shimmered in rainbow colors. "I wanted to speed you on your way."

"But you didn't care about Nico. You were happy to see him turned over to the Titans."

"Oh, please." Hera waved her hand dismissively. "The son of Hades said it himself. No one wants him around. He does not belong."

"Hephaestus was right," I growled. "You only care about your *perfect* family, not real people."

Her eyes turned dangerously bright. "Watch yourself, son of Poseidon. I guided you more than you know in the maze. I was at your side when you faced Geryon. *I* let your arrow fly straight. I sent you to Calypso's island. I opened the way to the Titan's mountain. Annabeth, my dear, surely you see how I've helped. I would welcome a sacrifice for my efforts."

Annabeth stood still as a statue. She could've said thank you. She could've promised to throw some barbecue on the brazier for Hera and forget the whole thing. But she clenched her jaw stubbornly. She looked just the way she had when she'd faced the Sphinx—like she wasn't going to accept an easy answer, even if it got her in serious trouble. I realized that was one of the things I liked best about Annabeth.

"Percy is right." She turned her back on the goddess. "*You're* the one who doesn't belong, Queen Hera. So next time, thanks . . . but no thanks."

Hera's sneer was worse than an *empousa's*. Her form began to glow. "You will regret this insult, Annabeth. You will regret this very much."

I averted my eyes as the goddess turned into her true divine form and disappeared in a blaze of light.

The hilltop was peaceful again. Over at the pine tree, Peleus the dragon dozed under the Golden Fleece as if nothing had happened.

"I'm sorry," Annabeth told me. "I—I should get back. I'll keep in touch."

"Listen, Annabeth—" I thought about Mount St. Helens, Calypso's Island, Luke and Rachel Elizabeth Dare, and how suddenly everything had gotten so complicated. I wanted to tell Annabeth that I didn't really want to be so distant from her.

Then Argus honked his horn down at the road, and I lost my chance.

"You'd better getting going," Annabeth said. "Take care, Seaweed Brain."

She jogged down the hill. I watched her until she reached the cabins. She didn't look back once.

Two days later was my birthday. I never advertised the date, because it always fell right after camp, so none of my camp friends could usually come, and I didn't have that many mortal friends. Besides, getting older didn't seem like anything to celebrate since I'd gotten the big prophecy about me destroying or saving the world when I turned sixteen. Now I was turning fifteen. I was running out of time.

My mom threw me a small party at our apartment. Paul Blofis came over, but that was okay because Chiron had manipulated the Mist to convince everyone at Goode High School that I had nothing to do with the band room explosion. Now Paul and the other witnesses were convinced that Kelli had been a crazy, firebomb-throwing cheerleader, while I had simply been an innocent bystander who'd panicked and ran from the scene. I would still be allowed to start as a freshman at Goode next month. If I wanted to keep my record of getting kicked out of school every year, I'd have to try harder.

Tyson came to my party, too, and my mother baked two extra blue cakes just for him. While Tyson helped my mom blow up party balloons, Paul Blofis asked me to help him in the kitchen.

As we were pouring punch, he said, "I hear your mom signed you up for driver's ed this fall."

"Yeah. It's cool. I can't wait."

Seriously, I'd been excited about getting my license forever, but I guess my heart wasn't in it anymore, and Paul could tell. In a weird way he reminded me of Chiron sometimes, how he could look at you and actually *see* your thoughts. I guess it was that teacher aura.

"You've had a rough summer," he said. "I'm guessing you lost someone important. And . . . girl trouble?"

I stared at him. "How do you know that? Did my mom—"

He held up his hands. "Your mom hasn't said a thing. And I won't pry. I just know there's something unusual about you, Percy. You've got a lot going on that I can't figure. But I was also fifteen once, and I'm just guessing from your expression . . . Well, you've had a rough time."

I nodded. I'd promised my mom I would tell Paul the truth about me, but now didn't seem the time. Not yet. "I lost a couple of friends at this camp I go to," I said. "I mean, not close friends, but still—"

"I'm sorry."

"Yeah. And, uh, I guess the girl stuff . . ."

"Here." Paul handed me some punch. "To your fifteenth birthday. And to a better year to come."

We tapped our paper cups together and drank.

"Percy, I kind of feel bad giving you one more thing to think about," Paul said. "But I wanted to ask you something."

"Yeah?"

"Girl stuff."

I frowned. "What do you mean?"

"Your mom," Paul said. "I'm thinking about proposing to her."

I almost dropped my cup. "You mean . . . marrying her? You and her?"

"Well, that was the general idea. Would that be okay with you?"

"You're asking my permission?"

Paul scratched his beard. "I don't know if it's permission, so much, but she's your mother. And I know you're going through a lot. I wouldn't feel right if I didn't talk to you about it first, man to man."

"Man to man," I repeated. It sounded strange, saying that. I thought about Paul and my mom, how she smiled and laughed more whenever he was around, and how Paul had gone out of his way to get me into high school. I found myself saying, "I think that's a great idea, Paul. Go for it."

He smiled really wide then. "Cheers, Percy. Let's join the party."

I was just getting ready to blow out the candles when the doorbell rang.

My mom frowned. "Who could that be?"

It was weird, because our new building had a doorman, but he hadn't called up or anything. My mom opened the door and gasped.

It was my dad. He was wearing Bermuda shorts and a Hawaiian shirt and Birkenstocks, like he usually does. His black beard was neatly trimmed and his sea-green eyes twinkled. He wore a battered cap decorated with fishing lures. It said NEPTUNE'S LUCKY FISHING HAT.

"Pos—" My mother stopped herself. She was blushing right to the roots of her hair. "Um, hello."

"Hello, Sally," Poseidon said. "You look as beautiful as ever. May I come in?"

My mother made a squeaking sound that might've been either "Yes" or "Help." Poseidon took it as a yes and came in.

Paul was looking back and forth between us, trying to read our expressions. Finally he stepped forward. "Hi, I'm Paul Blofis."

Poseidon raised his eyebrows as they shook hands. "Blowfish, did you say?"

"Ah, no. Blofis, actually."

"Oh, I see," Poseidon said. "A shame. I quite like blowfish. I am Poseidon."

"Poseidon? That's an interesting name."

"Yes, I like it. I've gone by other names, but I do prefer Poseidon."

"Like the god of the sea."

"Very much like that, yes."

"Well!" my mom interrupted. "Um, we're so glad you could drop by. Paul, this is Percy's father."

"Ah." Paul nodded, though he didn't look real pleased. "I see."

Poseidon smiled at me. "There you are, my boy. And Tyson, hello, son!"

"Daddy!" Tyson bounded across the room and gave Poseidon a big hug, which almost knocked off his fishing hat.

Paul's jaw dropped. He stared at my mom. "Tyson is . . ."

"Not mine," she promised. "It's a long story."

"I couldn't miss Percy's fifteenth birthday," Poseidon said. "Why, if this were Sparta, Percy would be a man today!"

"That's true," Paul said. "I used to teach ancient history."

Poseidon's eyes twinkled. "That's me. Ancient history. Sally, Paul, Tyson . . . would you mind if I borrowed Percy for just a moment?"

He put his arm around me and steered me into the kitchen.

Once we were alone, his smile faded.

"Are you all right, my boy?"

"Yeah. I'm fine. I guess."

"I heard stories," Poseidon said. "But I wanted to hear it directly from you. Tell me everything."

So I did. It was kind of disconcerting, because Poseidon listened so intently. His eyes never left my face. His expression didn't change the whole time I talked. When I was done, he nodded slowly.

"So Kronos is indeed back. It will not be long before full war is upon us."

"What about Luke?" I asked. "Is he really gone?"

"I don't know, Percy. It is most disturbing."

"But his body is mortal. Couldn't you just destroy him?"

Poseidon looked troubled. "Mortal, perhaps. But there is something different about Luke, my boy. I don't know how he was prepared to host the Titan's soul, but he will not be easily killed. And yet, I fear he must be killed if we are to send Kronos back to the pit. I will have to think on this. Unfortunately, I have other problems of my own."

I remembered what Tyson had told me at the beginning of the summer. "The old sea gods?"

"Indeed. The battle came first to me, Percy. In fact, I cannot stay long. Even now the ocean is at war with itself. It is all I can do to keep hurricanes and typhoons from destroying your surface world, the fighting is so intense."

"Let me come down there," I said. "Let me help."

Poseidon's eyes crinkled as he smiled. "Not yet, my boy. I sense you will be needed here. Which reminds me . . ." He brought out a sand dollar and pressed it into my hand. "Your birthday present. Spend it wisely."

"Uh, spend a sand dollar?"

"Oh, yes. In my day, you could buy quite a lot with a sand dollar. I think you will find it still buys a lot, if used in the right situation."

"What situation?"

"When the time comes," Poseidon said, "I think you'll know."

I closed my hand around the sand dollar, but something was really bothering me.

"Dad," I said, "when I was in the maze, I met Antaeus. He said . . . well, he said he was your favorite son. He decorated his arena with skulls and—"

"He dedicated them to me," Poseidon supplied. "And you are wondering how someone could do something so horrible in my name."

I nodded uncomfortably.

Poseidon put his weathered hand on my shoulder. "Percy, lesser beings do many horrible things in the name of the gods. That does not mean we gods approve. The way our sons and daughters act in our names . . . well, it usually says more about *them* than it does about us. And *you*, Percy, are my favorite son."

He smiled, and at that moment, just being in the kitchen with him was the best birthday present I ever got.

Then my mom called from the living room, "Percy? The candles are melting!"

"You'd better go," Poseidon said. "But, Percy, one last thing you should know. That incident at Mount St. Helens . . ."

For a second I thought he was talking about Annabeth kissing me, and I blushed, but then I realized he was talking about something a lot bigger.

"The eruptions are continuing," he said. "Typhon is stirring. It is very likely that soon, in a few months, perhaps a year at best, he will escape his bonds."

"I'm sorry," I said. "I didn't mean—"

Poseidon raised his hand. "It is not your fault, Percy. It would've happened sooner or later, with Kronos awakening the ancient monsters. But be aware, if Typhon stirs . . . it will be unlike anything you have faced before. The first time he appeared, all the forces of Olympus were barely enough to battle him. And when he stirs again, he will come here, to New York. He will make straight for Olympus."

That was just the kind of wonderful news I wanted to get on my birthday, but Poseidon patted me on the back like everything was fine. "I should go. Enjoy your cake."

And just like that he turned to mist and was swept out the window on a warm ocean breeze.

It took a little work to convince Paul that Poseidon had left via the fire escape, but since people can't vanish into thin air, he had no choice but to believe it.

We ate blue cake and ice cream until we couldn't eat anymore. Then we played a bunch of cheesy party games like charades and Monopoly. Tyson didn't get charades. He kept shouting out the answer he was trying to mime, but it turned out he was really good at Monopoly. He knocked me out of the game in the first five rounds and started bankrupting my mom and Paul. I left them playing and went into my bedroom.

I set an uneaten slice of blue cake on my dresser. Then I took off my Camp Half-Blood necklace and laid it on the windowsill. There were three beads now, representing my three summers at camp—a trident, the Golden Fleece, and the latest: an intricate maze, symbolizing the Battle of the Labyrinth, as the campers had started to call it. I wondered what next year's bead would be, if I was still around to get it. If the camp survived until next summer.

I looked at the telephone by my bedside. I thought about calling Rachel Elizabeth Dare. My mom had asked me if there was anyone else I wanted to have over tonight, and I'd thought about Rachel. But I didn't call. I don't know why. The idea made me almost as nervous as a door into the Labyrinth.

I patted my pockets and emptied out my stuff—Riptide, a Kleenex, my apartment key. Then I patted my shirt pocket and felt a small lump. I hadn't even realized it, but I was wearing the white cotton shirt Calypso had given me on Ogygia. I brought out a little piece of cloth, unwrapped it, and found the clipping of moonlace. It was a tiny sprig, shriveled up after two months, but I could still smell the faint scent of the enchanted garden. It made me sad.

I remembered Calypso's last request of me: *Plant a garden in Manhattan for me, will you?* I opened the window and stepped onto the fire escape.

My mom kept a planter box out there. In the spring she usually filled it with flowers, but now it was all dirt, waiting for something new. It was a clear night. The moon was full over Eighty-second Street. I planted the dried sprig of moonlace carefully in the dirt and sprinkled a little nectar on it from my camp canteen.

Nothing happened at first.

Then, as I watched, a tiny silver plant sprang out of the soil—a baby moonlace, glowing in the warm summer night.

"Nice plant," a voice said.

I jumped. Nico di Angelo was standing on the fire escape right next to me. He'd just appeared there.

"Sorry," he said. "Didn't mean to startle you."

"That's—that's okay. I mean . . . what are you doing here?"

He'd grown about an inch taller over the last couple of months. His hair was a shaggy black mess. He wore a black T-shirt, black jeans, and a new silver ring shaped like a skull. His Stygian iron sword hung at his side.

"I've done some exploring," he said. "Thought you'd like to know, Daedalus got his punishment."

"You saw him?"

Nico nodded. "Minos wanted to boil him in cheese fondue for eternity, but my father had other ideas. Daedalus will be building overpasses and exit ramps in Asphodel for all time. It'll help ease the traffic congestion. Truthfully, I think the old guy is pretty happy with that. He's still build-ing. Still creating. And he gets to see his son and Perdix on the weekends."

"That's good."

Nico tapped at his silver ring. "But that's not the real reason I've come. I've found out some things. I want to make you an offer."

"What?"

"The way to beat Luke," he said. "If I'm right, it's the *only* way you'll stand a chance."

I took a deep breath. "Okay. I'm listening."

Nico glanced inside my room. His eyebrows furrowed. "Is that . . . is that blue birthday cake?"

He sounded hungry, maybe a little wistful. I wondered if the poor kid had ever had a birthday party, or if he'd ever even been invited to one.

"Come inside for cake and ice cream," I said. "It sounds like we've got a lot to talk about."

THE
LAST
OLYMPIAN

PERCY JACKSON & THE OLYMPIANS

BOOK FIVE

THE LAST OLYMPIAN

RICK RIORDAN

SCHOLASTIC INC.

New York Toronto London Auckland
Sydney Mexico City New Delhi Hong Kong

ISBN 978-0-545-27262-9

12 11 10 9 8   13 14 15/0

Printed in the U.S.A.   40

First Scholastic printing, September 2010

This book is set in Centaur MT.
Map illustration © 2009 by Greg Call

To Mrs. Pabst, my eighth grade English teacher,
who started me on my journey as a writer

Also by RICK RIORDAN

CONTENTS

THE
LAST
OLYMPIAN

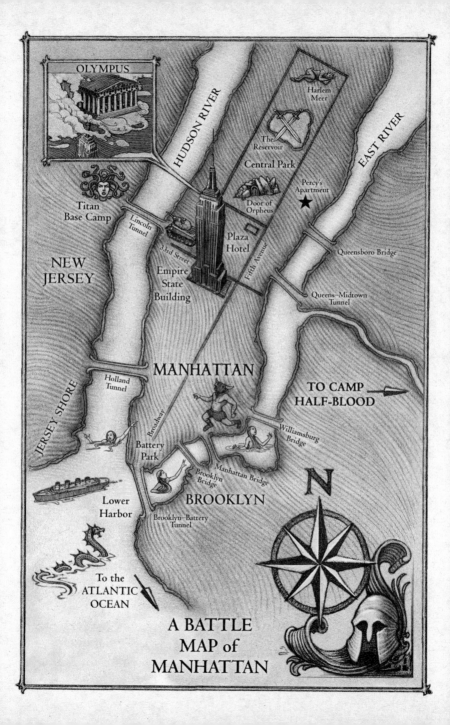

ONE

I GO CRUISING WITH EXPLOSIVES

The end of the world started when a pegasus landed on the hood of my car.

Up until then, I was having a great afternoon. Technically I wasn't supposed to be driving because I wouldn't turn sixteen for another week, but my mom and my stepdad, Paul, took my friend Rachel and me to this private stretch of beach on the South Shore, and Paul let us borrow his Prius for a short spin.

Now, I know you're thinking, *Wow, that was really irresponsible of him, blah, blah, blah,* but Paul knows me pretty well. He's seen me slice up demons and leap out of exploding school buildings, so he probably figured taking a car a few hundred yards wasn't exactly the most dangerous thing I'd ever done.

Anyway, Rachel and I were driving along. It was a hot August day. Rachel's red hair was pulled back in a ponytail and she wore a white blouse over her swimsuit. I'd never seen her in anything but ratty T-shirts and paint-splattered jeans before, and she looked like a million golden drachmas.

"Oh, pull up right there!" she told me.

We parked on a ridge overlooking the Atlantic. The sea is always one of my favorite places, but today it was especially nice—glittery green and smooth as glass, as though my dad was keeping it calm just for us.

My dad, by the way, is Poseidon. He can do stuff like that.

"So." Rachel smiled at me. "About that invitation."

"Oh . . . right." I tried to sound excited. I mean, she'd asked me to her family's vacation house on St. Thomas for three days. I didn't get a lot of offers like that. My family's idea of a fancy vacation was a weekend in a rundown cabin on Long Island with some movie rentals and a couple of frozen pizzas, and here Rachel's folks were willing to let me tag along to the Caribbean.

Besides, I seriously needed a vacation. This summer had been the hardest of my life. The idea of taking a break even for a few days was really tempting.

Still, something big was supposed to go down any day now. I was "on call" for a mission. Even worse, next week was my birthday. There was this prophecy that said when I turned sixteen, bad things would happen.

"Percy," she said, "I know the timing is bad. But it's *always* bad for you, right?"

She had a point.

"I really want to go," I promised. "It's just—"

"The war."

I nodded. I didn't like talking about it, but Rachel knew. Unlike most mortals, she could see through the Mist—the magic veil that distorts human vision. She'd seen monsters. She'd met some of the other demigods who were fighting the Titans and their allies. She'd even been there last summer when the chopped-up Lord Kronos rose out of his coffin in a terrible new form, and she'd earned my permanent respect by nailing him in the eye with a blue plastic hairbrush.

She put her hand on my arm. "Just think about it, okay? We don't leave for a couple of days. My dad . . ." Her voice faltered.

"Is he giving you a hard time?" I asked.

Rachel shook her head in disgust. "He's trying to be *nice* to me, which is almost worse. He wants me to go to Clarion Ladies Academy in the fall."

"The school where your mom went?"

"It's a stupid finishing school for society girls, all the way in New Hampshire. Can you see me in finishing school?"

I admitted the idea sounded pretty dumb. Rachel was into urban art projects and feeding the homeless and going to protest rallies to "Save the Endangered Yellow-bellied Sapsucker" and stuff like that. I'd never even seen her wear a dress. It was hard to imagine her learning to be a socialite.

She sighed. "He thinks if he does a bunch of nice stuff for me, I'll feel guilty and give in."

"Which is why he agreed to let me come with you guys on vacation?"

"Yes . . . but Percy, you'd be doing me a huge favor. It would be *so* much better if you were with us. Besides, there's something I want to talk—" She stopped abruptly.

"Something you want to talk about?" I asked. "You mean . . . so serious we'd have to go to St. Thomas to talk about it?"

She pursed her lips. "Look, just forget it for now. Let's pretend we're a couple of normal people. We're out for a drive, and we're watching the ocean, and it's nice to be together."

I could tell something was bothering her, but she put on a brave smile. The sunlight made her hair look like fire.

We'd spent a lot of time together this summer. I hadn't exactly planned it that way, but the more serious things got at camp, the more I found myself needing to call up Rachel and get away, just for some breathing room. I needed to remind myself that the mortal world was still out there, away from all the monsters using me as their personal punching bag.

"Okay," I said. "Just a normal afternoon and two normal people."

She nodded. "And so . . . hypothetically, if these two people liked each other, what would it take to get the stupid guy to kiss the girl, huh?"

"Oh . . ." I felt like one of Apollo's sacred cows—slow, dumb, and bright red. "Um . . ."

I can't pretend I hadn't thought about Rachel. She was so much easier to be around than . . . well, than some other girls I knew. I didn't have to work hard, or watch what I said, or rack my brain trying to figure out what she was thinking. Rachel didn't hide much. She let you know how she felt.

I'm not sure what I would have done next—but I was so distracted, I didn't notice the huge black form swooping down from the sky until four hooves landed on the hood of the Prius with a *WUMP-WUMP-CRUNCH!*

Hey, boss, a voice said in my head. *Nice car!*

Blackjack the pegasus was an old friend of mine, so I tried not to get too annoyed by the craters he'd just put in the hood; but I didn't think my stepdad would be real stoked.

"Blackjack," I sighed. "What are you—"

Then I saw who was riding on his back, and I knew my day was about to get a lot more complicated.

"'Sup, Percy."

Charles Beckendorf, senior counselor for the Hephaestus cabin, would make most monsters cry for their mommies. He was huge, with ripped muscles from working on the forges every summer, two years older than me, and one of the camp's best armorsmiths. He made some seriously ingenious mechanical stuff. A month before, he'd rigged a Greek firebomb in the bathroom of a tour bus that was carrying a bunch of monsters across country. The explosion took out a whole legion of Kronos's evil meanies as soon as the first harpy went *flush.*

Beckendorf was dressed for combat. He wore a bronze breastplate and war helm with black camo pants and a sword strapped to his side. His explosives bag was slung over his shoulder.

"Time?" I asked.

He nodded grimly.

A clump formed in my throat. I'd known this was coming. We'd been planning for it for weeks, but I'd half hoped it would never happen.

Rachel looked up at Beckendorf. "Hi."

"Oh, hey. I'm Beckendorf. You must be Rachel. Percy's told me . . . uh, I mean he mentioned you."

Rachel raised an eyebrow. "Really? Good." She glanced at Blackjack, who was clopping his hooves against the hood of the Prius. "So I guess you guys have to go save the world now."

"Pretty much," Beckendorf agreed.

I looked at Rachel helplessly. "Would you tell my mom—"

"I'll tell her. I'm sure she's used to it. And I'll explain to Paul about the hood."

I nodded my thanks. I figured this might be the last time Paul loaned me his car.

"Good luck." Rachel kissed me before I could even react. "Now, get going, half-blood. Go kill some monsters for me."

My last view of her was sitting in the shotgun seat of the Prius, her arms crossed, watching as Blackjack circled higher and higher, carrying Beckendorf and me into the sky. I wondered what Rachel wanted to talk to me about, and whether I'd live long enough to find out.

"So," Beckendorf said, "I'm guessing you don't want me to mention that little scene to Annabeth."

"Oh, gods," I muttered. "Don't even think about it."

Beckendorf chuckled, and together we soared out over the Atlantic.

It was almost dark by the time we spotted our target. The *Princess Andromeda* glowed on the horizon—a huge cruise ship lit up yellow and white. From a distance, you'd think it was just a party ship, not the headquarters for the Titan lord. Then as you got closer, you might notice the giant figurehead—a dark-haired maiden in a Greek chiton, wrapped in chains with a look of horror on her face, as if she could smell the stench of all the monsters she was being forced to carry.

Seeing the ship again twisted my gut into knots. I'd almost died twice on the *Princess Andromeda*. Now it was heading straight for New York.

"You know what to do?" Beckendorf yelled over the wind.

I nodded. We'd done dry runs at the dockyards in New Jersey, using abandoned ships as our targets. I knew how little time we would have. But I also knew this was our best chance to end Kronos's invasion before it ever started.

"Blackjack," I said, "set us down on the lowest stern deck."

Gotcha, boss, he said. *Man, I hate seeing that boat.*

Three years ago, Blackjack had been enslaved on the *Princess Andromeda* until he'd escaped with a little help from my friends and me. I figured he'd rather have his mane braided like My Little Pony than be back here again.

"Don't wait for us," I told him.

But, boss—

"Trust me," I said. "We'll get out by ourselves."

Blackjack folded his wings and plummeted toward the boat like a black comet. The wind whistled in my ears. I saw monsters patrolling the upper decks of the ship—*dracaenae* snake-women, hellhounds, giants, and the humanoid seal-demons known as telkhines—but we zipped by so fast, none of them raised the alarm. We shot down the stern of the boat, and Blackjack spread his wings, lightly coming to a landing on the lowest deck. I climbed off, feeling queasy.

Good luck, boss, Blackjack said. *Don't let 'em turn you into horse meat!*

With that, my old friend flew off into the night. I took my pen out of my pocket and uncapped it, and Riptide sprang to full size—three feet of deadly Celestial bronze glowing in the dusk.

Beckendorf pulled a piece of paper out of his pocket. I thought it was a map or something. Then I realized it was a photograph. He stared at it in the dim light—the smiling face of Silena Beauregard, daughter of Aphrodite. They'd started going out last summer, after years of the rest of us saying, "Duh, you guys like each other!" Even with all the dangerous missions, Beckendorf had been happier this summer than I'd ever seen him.

"We'll make it back to camp," I promised.

For a second I saw worry in his eyes. Then he put on his old confident smile.

"You bet," he said. "Let's go blow Kronos back into a million pieces."

Beckendorf led the way. We followed a narrow corridor to the service stairwell, just like we'd practiced, but we froze when we heard noises above us.

"I don't care what your nose says!" snarled a half-human,

half-dog voice—a telkhine. "The last time you smelled half-blood, it turned out to be a meat loaf sandwich!"

"Meat loaf sandwiches are good!" a second voice snarled. "But this is half-blood scent, I swear. They are on board!"

"Bah, your *brain* isn't on board!"

They continued to argue, and Beckendorf pointed downstairs. We descended as quietly as we could. Two floors down, the voices of the telkhines started to fade.

Finally we came to a metal hatch. Beckendorf mouthed the words "engine room."

It was locked, but Beckendorf pulled some chain cutters out of his bag and split the bolt like it was made of butter.

Inside, a row of yellow turbines the size of grain silos churned and hummed. Pressure gauges and computer terminals lined the opposite wall. A telkhine was hunched over a console, but he was so involved with his work, he didn't notice us. He was about five feet tall, with slick black seal fur and stubby little feet. He had the head of a Doberman, but his clawed hands were almost human. He growled and muttered as he tapped on his keyboard. Maybe he was messaging his friends on uglyface.com.

I stepped forward, and he tensed, probably smelling something was wrong. He leaped sideways toward a big red alarm button, but I blocked his path. He hissed and lunged at me, but one slice of Riptide, and he exploded into dust.

"One down," Beckendorf said. "About five thousand to go." He tossed me a jar of thick green liquid—Greek fire, one of the most dangerous magical substances in the world.

Then he threw me another essential tool of demigod heroes—duct tape.

"Slap that one on the console," he said. "I'll get the turbines."

We went to work. The room was hot and humid, and in no time we were drenched in sweat.

The boat kept chugging along. Being the son of Poseidon and all, I have perfect bearings at sea. Don't ask me how, but I could tell we were at 40.19° North, 71.90° West, making eighteen knots, which meant the ship would arrive in New York Harbor by dawn. This would be our only chance to stop it.

I had just attached a second jar of Greek fire to the control panels when I heard the pounding of feet on metal steps—so many creatures coming down the stairwell I could hear them over the engines. Not a good sign.

I locked eyes with Beckendorf. "How much longer?"

"Too long." He tapped his watch, which was our remote control detonator. "I still have to wire the receiver and prime the charges. Ten more minutes at least."

Judging from the sound of the footsteps, we had about ten seconds.

"I'll distract them," I said. "Meet you at the rendezvous point."

"Percy—"

"Wish me luck."

He looked like he wanted to argue. The whole idea had been to get in and out without being spotted. But we were going to have to improvise.

"Good luck," he said.

I charged out the door.

A half dozen telkhines were tromping down the stairs. I cut through them with Riptide faster than they could yelp. I kept climbing—past another telkhine, who was so startled he dropped his Lil' Demons lunch box. I left him alive—partly because his lunch box was cool, partly so he could raise the alarm and hopefully get his friends to follow me rather than head toward the engine room.

I burst through a door onto deck six and kept running. I'm sure the carpeted hall had once been very plush, but over the last three years of monster occupation the wallpaper, carpet, and stateroom doors had been clawed up and slimed so it looked like the inside of a dragon's throat (and yes, unfortunately, I speak from experience).

Back on my first visit to the *Princess Andromeda*, my old enemy Luke had kept some dazed tourists on board for show, shrouded in Mist so they didn't realize they were on a monster-infested ship. Now I didn't see any sign of tourists. I hated to think what had happened to them, but I kind of doubted they'd been allowed to go home with their bingo winnings.

I reached the promenade, a big shopping mall that took up the whole middle of the ship, and I stopped cold. In the middle of the courtyard stood a fountain. And in the fountain squatted a giant crab.

I'm not talking "giant" like $7.99 all-you-can-eat Alaskan king crab. I'm talking *giant* like bigger than the fountain. The monster rose ten feet out of the water. Its shell was mottled blue and green, its pincers longer than my body.

If you've ever seen a crab's mouth, all foamy and gross with whiskers and snapping bits, you can imagine this one didn't look any better blown up to billboard size. Its beady black eyes glared at me, and I could see intelligence in them—and hate. The fact that I was the son of the sea god was not going to win me any points with Mr. Crabby.

"*FFFFfffffff*," it hissed, sea foam dripping from its mouth. The smell coming off it was like a garbage can full of fish sticks that had been sitting in the sun all week.

Alarms blared. Soon I was going to have lots of company and I had to keep moving.

"Hey, crabby." I inched around the edge of the courtyard. "I'm just gonna scoot around you so—"

The crab moved with amazing speed. It scuttled out of the fountain and came straight at me, pincers snapping. I dove into a gift shop, plowing through a rack of T-shirts. A crab pincer smashed the glass walls to pieces and raked across the room. I dashed back outside, breathing heavily, but Mr. Crabby turned and followed.

"There!" a voice said from a balcony above me. "Intruder!"

If I'd wanted to create a distraction, I'd succeeded, but this was not where I wanted to fight. If I got pinned down in the center of the ship, I was crab chow.

The demonic crustacean lunged at me. I sliced with Riptide, taking off the tip of its claw. It hissed and foamed, but didn't seem very hurt.

I tried to remember anything from the old stories that might help with this thing. Annabeth had told me about a monster crab—something about Hercules crushing it under his foot? That wasn't going to work here. This crab was slightly bigger than my Reeboks.

Then a weird thought occurred to me. Last Christmas, my mom and I had brought Paul Blofis to our old cabin at Montauk, where we'd been going forever. Paul had taken me crabbing, and when he'd brought up a net full of the things, he'd shown me how crabs have a chink in their armor, right in the middle of their ugly bellies.

The only problem was getting to the ugly belly.

I glanced at the fountain, then at the marble floor, already slick from scuttling crab tracks. I held out my hand, concentrating on the water, and the fountain exploded. Water sprayed everywhere, three stories high, dousing the balconies and the elevators and the windows of the shops. The crab didn't care. It loved water. It came at me sideways, snapping and hissing, and I ran straight at it, screaming, "AHHHHHHH!"

Just before we collided, I hit the ground baseball-style and slid on the wet marble floor straight under the creature. It was like sliding under a seven-ton armored vehicle. All the crab had to do was sit and squash me, but before it realized what was going on, I jabbed Riptide into the chink in its armor, let go of the hilt, and pushed myself out the back-side.

The monster shuddered and hissed. Its eyes dissolved. Its shell turned bright red as its insides evaporated. The empty shell clattered to the floor in a massive heap.

I didn't have time to admire my handiwork. I ran for the nearest stairs while all around me monsters and demigods shouted orders and strapped on their weapons. I was empty-handed. Riptide, being magic, would appear in my pocket sooner or later, but for now it was stuck somewhere under the wreckage of the crab, and I had no time to retrieve it.

In the elevator foyer on deck eight, a couple of *dracaenae* slithered across my path. From the waist up, they were women with green scaly skin, yellow eyes, and forked tongues. From the waist down, they had double snake trunks instead of legs. They held spears and weighted nets, and I knew from experience they could use them.

"What isss thisss?" one said. "A prize for Kronosss!"

I wasn't in the mood to play break-the-snake, but in front of me was a stand with a model of the ship, like a YOU ARE HERE display. I ripped the model off the pedestal and hurled it at the first *dracaena*. The boat smacked her in the face and she went down with the ship. I jumped over her, grabbed her friend's spear, and swung her around. She slammed into the elevator, and I kept running toward the front of the ship.

"Get him!" she screamed.

Hellhounds bayed. An arrow from somewhere whizzed past my face and impaled itself in the mahogany-paneled wall of the stairwell.

I didn't care—as long as I got the monsters away from the engine room and gave Beckendorf more time.

As I was running up the stairwell, a kid charged down.

He looked like he'd just woken up from a nap. His armor was half on. He drew his sword and yelled, "Kronos!" but he sounded more scared than angry. He couldn't have been more than twelve—about the same age I was when I'd first arrived at Camp Half-Blood.

That thought depressed me. This kid was getting brainwashed—trained to hate the gods and lash out because he'd been born half Olympian. Kronos was using him, and yet the kid thought I was his enemy.

No way was I going to hurt him. I didn't need a weapon for this. I stepped inside his strike and grabbed his wrist, slamming it against the wall. His sword clattered out of his hand.

Then I did something I hadn't planned on. It was probably stupid. It definitely jeopardized our mission, but I couldn't help it.

"If you want to live," I told him, "get off this ship *now*. Tell the other demigods." Then I shoved him down the stairs and sent him tumbling to the next floor.

I kept climbing.

Bad memories: a hallway ran past the cafeteria. Annabeth, my half brother Tyson, and I had sneaked through here three years ago on my first visit.

I burst outside onto the main deck. Off the port bow, the sky was darkening from purple to black. A swimming pool glowed between two glass towers with more balconies and restaurant decks. The whole upper ship seemed eerily deserted.

All I had to do was cross to the other side. Then I could

take the staircase down to the helipad—our emergency rendezvous point. With any luck, Beckendorf would meet me there. We'd jump into the sea. My water powers would protect us both, and we'd detonate the charges from a quarter mile away.

I was halfway across the deck when the sound of a voice made me freeze. "You're late, Percy."

Luke stood on the balcony above me, a smile on his scarred face. He wore jeans, a white T-shirt, and flip-flops, like he was just a normal college-age guy, but his eyes told the truth. They were solid gold.

"We've been expecting you for days." At first he sounded normal, like Luke. But then his face twitched. A shudder passed through his body as though he'd just drunk something really nasty. His voice became heavier, ancient, and powerful—the voice of the Titan lord Kronos. The words scraped down my spine like a knife blade. "Come, bow before me."

"Yeah, that'll happen," I muttered.

Laistrygonian giants filed in on either side of the swimming pool as if they'd been waiting for a cue. Each was eight feet tall with tattooed arms, leather armor, and spiked clubs. Demigod archers appeared on the roof above Luke. Two hellhounds leaped down from the opposite balcony and snarled at me. Within seconds I was surrounded. A trap: there's no way they could've gotten into position so fast unless they'd known I was coming.

I looked up at Luke, and anger boiled inside me. I didn't know if Luke's consciousness was even still alive inside that body. Maybe, the way his voice had changed . . . or maybe it was just Kronos adapting to his new form. I told myself it didn't matter. Luke had been twisted and evil long before Kronos possessed him.

A voice in my head said: *I have to fight him eventually. Why not now?*

According to that big prophecy, I was supposed to make a choice that saved or destroyed the world when I was sixteen. That was only seven days away. Why not now? If I really had the power, what difference would a week make? I could end this threat right here by taking down Kronos. Hey, I'd fought monsters and gods before.

As if reading my thoughts, Luke smiled. No, he was *Kronos.* I had to remember that.

"Come forward," he said. "If you dare."

The crowd of monsters parted. I moved up the stairs, my heart pounding. I was sure somebody would stab me in the back, but they let me pass. I felt my pocket and found my pen waiting. I uncapped it, and Riptide grew into a sword.

Kronos's weapon appeared in his hands—a six-foot-long scythe, half Celestial bronze, half mortal steel. Just looking at the thing made my knees turn to Jell-O. But before I could change my mind, I charged.

Time slowed down. I mean *literally* slowed down, because Kronos had that power. I felt like I was moving through syrup. My arms were so heavy, I could barely raise my sword. Kronos smiled, swirling his scythe at normal speed and waiting for me to creep toward my death.

I tried to fight his magic. I concentrated on the sea

around me—the source of my power. I'd gotten better at channeling it over the years, but now nothing seemed to happen.

I took another slow step forward. Giants jeered. *Dracaenae* hissed with laughter.

Hey, ocean, I pleaded. *Any day now would be good.*

Suddenly there was a wrenching pain in my gut. The entire boat lurched sideways, throwing monsters off their feet. Four thousand gallons of salt water surged out of the swimming pool, dousing me and Kronos and everyone on the deck. The water revitalized me, breaking the time spell, and I lunged forward.

I struck at Kronos, but I was still too slow. I made the mistake of looking at his face—*Luke's face*—a guy who was once my friend. As much as I hated him, it was hard to kill him.

Kronos had no such hesitation. He sliced downward with his scythe. I leaped back, and the evil blade missed by an inch, cutting a gash in the deck right between my feet.

I kicked Kronos in the chest. He stumbled backward, but he was heavier than Luke should've been. It was like kicking a refrigerator.

Kronos swung his scythe again. I intercepted with Riptide, but his strike was so powerful, my blade could only deflect it. The edge of the scythe shaved off my shirtsleeve and grazed my arm. It shouldn't have been a serious cut, but the entire side of my body exploded with pain. I remembered what a sea demon had once said about Kronos's scythe: *Careful, fool. One touch, and the blade will sever your soul from your body.* Now I understood what he meant. I wasn't just losing blood. I could feel my strength, my will, my identity draining away.

I stumbled backward, switched my sword to my left hand, and lunged desperately. My blade should've run him through, but it deflected off his stomach like I was hitting solid marble. There was no way he should've survived that.

Kronos laughed. "A poor performance, Percy Jackson. Luke tells me you were never his match at swordplay."

My vision started to blur. I knew I didn't have much time. "Luke had a big head," I said. "But at least it was *his* head."

"A shame to kill you now," Kronos mused, "before the final plan unfolds. I would love to see the terror in your eyes when you realize how I will destroy Olympus."

"You'll never get this boat to Manhattan." My arm was throbbing. Black spots danced in my vision.

"And why would that be?" Kronos's golden eyes glittered. His face—Luke's face—seemed like a mask, unnatural and lit from behind by some evil power. "Perhaps you are counting on your friend with the explosives?"

He looked down at the pool and called, "Nakamura!"

A teenage guy in full Greek armor pushed through the crowd. His left eye was covered with a black patch. I knew him, of course: Ethan Nakamura, the son of Nemesis. I'd saved his life in the Labyrinth last summer, and in return, the little punk had helped Kronos come back to life.

"Success, my lord," Ethan called. "We found him just as we were told."

He clapped his hands, and two giants lumbered forward, dragging Charles Beckendorf between them. My heart almost stopped. Beckendorf had a swollen eye and cuts all over his face and arms. His armor was gone and his shirt was nearly torn off.

"No!" I yelled.

Beckendorf met my eyes. He glanced at his hand like he was trying to tell me something. *His watch.* They hadn't taken it yet, and that was the detonator. Was it possible the explosives were armed? Surely the monsters would've dismantled them right away.

"We found him amidships," one of the giants said, "trying to sneak to the engine room. Can we eat him now?"

"Soon." Kronos scowled at Ethan. "Are you sure he didn't set the explosives?"

"He was going *toward* the engine room, my lord."

"How do you know that?"

"Er . . ." Ethan shifted uncomfortably. "He was heading in that direction. And he told us. His bag is still full of explosives."

Slowly, I began to understand. Beckendorf had fooled them. When he'd realized he was going to be captured, he turned to make it look like he was going the other way. He'd convinced them he hadn't made it to the engine room yet. The Greek fire might still be primed! But that didn't do us any good unless we could get off the ship and detonate it.

Kronos hesitated.

Buy the story, I prayed. The pain in my arm was so bad now I could barely stand.

"Open his bag," Kronos ordered.

One of the giants ripped the explosives satchel from Beckendorf's shoulders. He peered inside, grunted, and turned it upside down. Panicked monsters surged backward. If the bag really had been full of Greek fire jars, we would've all blown up. But what fell out were a dozen cans of peaches.

I could hear Kronos breathing, trying to control his anger.

"Did you, perhaps," he said, "capture this demigod near the galley?"

Ethan turned pale. "Um—"

"And did you, perhaps, send someone to actually CHECK THE ENGINE ROOM?"

Ethan scrambled back in terror, then turned on his heels and ran.

I cursed silently. Now we had only minutes before the bombs were disarmed. I caught Beckendorf's eyes again and asked a silent question, hoping he would understand: *How long?*

He cupped his fingers and thumb, making a circle. *Zero.* There was no delay on the timer at all. If he managed to press the detonator button, the ship would blow at once. We'd never be able to get far enough away before using it. The monsters would kill us first, or disarm the explosives, or both.

Kronos turned toward me with a crooked smile. "You'll have to excuse my incompetent help, Percy Jackson. But it doesn't matter. We have you now. We've known you were coming for weeks."

He held out his hand and dangled a little silver bracelet with a scythe charm—the Titan lord's symbol.

The wound in my arm was sapping my ability to think, but I muttered, "Communication device . . . spy at camp."

Kronos chuckled. "You can't count on friends. They will always let you down. Luke learned that lesson the hard way. Now drop your sword and surrender to me, or your friend dies."

I swallowed. One of the giants had his hand around Beckendorf's neck. I was in no shape to rescue him, and even if I tried, he would die before I got there. We both would.

Beckendorf mouthed one word: *Go.*

I shook my head. I couldn't just leave him.

The second giant was still rummaging through the peach cans, which meant Beckendorf's left arm was free. He raised it slowly—toward the watch on his right wrist.

I wanted to scream, *NO!*

Then down by the swimming pool, one of the *dracaenae* hissed, "What isss he doing? What isss that on hisss wrissst?"

Beckendorf closed eyes tight and brought his hand up to his watch.

I had no choice. I threw my sword like a javelin at Kronos. It bounced harmlessly off his chest, but it did startle him. I pushed through a crowd of monsters and jumped off the side of the ship—toward the water a hundred feet below.

I heard rumbling deep in the ship. Monsters yelled at

me from above. A spear sailed past my ear. An arrow pierced my thigh, but I barely had time to register the pain. I plunged into the sea and willed the currents to take me far, far away—a hundred yards, two hundred yards.

Even from that distance, the explosion shook the world. Heat seared the back of my head. The *Princess Andromeda* blew up from both sides, a massive fireball of green flame roiling into the dark sky, consuming everything.

Beckendorf, I thought.

Then I blacked out and sank like an anchor toward the bottom of the sea.

I MEET SOME FISHY RELATIVES

Demigod dreams suck.

The thing is, they're never just *dreams*. They've got to be visions, omens, and all that other mystical stuff that makes my brain hurt.

I dreamed I was in a dark palace at the top of a mountain. Unfortunately, I recognized it: the palace of the Titans on top of Mount Othrys, otherwise known as Mount Tamalpais, in California. The main pavilion was open to the night, ringed with black Greek columns and statues of the Titans. Torchlight glowed against the black marble floor. In the center of the room, an armored giant struggled under the weight of a swirling funnel cloud—Atlas, holding up the sky.

Two other giant men stood nearby over a bronze brazier, studying images in the flames.

"Quite an explosion," one said. He wore black armor studded with silver dots like a starry night. His face was covered in a war helm with a ram's horn curling on either side.

"It doesn't matter," the other said. This Titan was dressed in gold robes, with golden eyes like Kronos. His entire body glowed. He reminded me of Apollo, God of the Sun, except the Titan's light was harsher, and his expression crueler. "The gods have answered the challenge. Soon they will be destroyed."

The images in the fire were hard to make out: storms, buildings crumbling, mortals screaming in terror.

"I will go east to marshal our forces," the golden Titan said. "Krios, you shall remain and guard Mount Othrys."

The ram horn dude grunted. "I always get the stupid jobs. Lord of the South. Lord of Constellations. Now I get to babysit Atlas while *you* have all the fun."

Under the whirlwind of clouds, Atlas bellowed in agony. "Let me out, curse you! I am your greatest warrior. Take my burden so I may fight!"

"Quiet!" the golden Titan roared. "You had your chance, Atlas. You failed. Kronos likes you just where you are. As for you, Krios, do your duty."

"And if you need more warriors?" Krios asked. "Our treacherous nephew in the tuxedo will not do you much good in a fight."

The golden Titan laughed. "Don't worry about him. Besides, the gods can barely handle our first little challenge. They have no idea how many others we have in store. Mark my words, in a few days' time, Olympus will be in ruins, and we will meet here again to celebrate the dawn of the Sixth Age!"

The golden Titan erupted into flames and disappeared.

"Oh, sure," Krios grumbled. "He gets to erupt into flames. I get to wear these stupid ram's horns."

The scene shifted. Now I was outside the pavilion, hiding in the shadows of a Greek column. A boy stood next to me, eavesdropping on the Titans. He had dark silky hair, pale skin, and dark clothes—my friend Nico di Angelo, the son of Hades.

He looked straight at me, his expression grim. "You see, Percy?" he whispered. "You're running out of time. Do you really think you can beat them without my plan?"

His words washed over me as cold as the ocean floor, and my dreams went black.

"Percy?" a deep voice said.

My head felt like it had been microwaved in aluminum foil. I opened my eyes and saw a large shadowy figure looming over me.

"Beckendorf?" I asked hopefully.

"No, brother."

My eyes refocused. I was looking at a Cyclops—a misshapen face, ratty brown hair, one big brown eye full of concern. "Tyson?"

My brother broke into a toothy grin. "Yay! Your brain works!"

I wasn't so sure. My body felt weightless and cold. My voice sounded wrong. I could hear Tyson, but it was more like I was hearing vibrations inside my skull, not the regular sounds.

I sat up, and a gossamer sheet floated away. I was on a bed made of silky woven kelp, in a room paneled with abalone shell. Glowing pearls the size of basketballs floated around the ceiling, providing light. I was under water.

Now, being the son of Poseidon and all, I was okay with this. I can breathe underwater just fine, and my clothes don't even get wet unless I want them to. But it was still a bit of a shock when a hammerhead shark drifted through the bedroom window, regarded me, and then swam calmly out the opposite side of the room.

"Where—"

"Daddy's palace," Tyson said.

Under different circumstances, I would've been excited. I'd never visited Poseidon's realm, and I'd been dreaming about it for years. But my head hurt. My shirt was still speckled with burn marks from the explosion. My arm and leg wounds had healed—just being in the ocean can do that for me, given enough time—but I still felt like I'd been trampled by a Laistrygonian soccer team in cleats.

"How long—"

"We found you last night," Tyson said, "sinking through the water."

"The *Princess Andromeda*?"

"Went ka-boom," Tyson confirmed.

"Beckendorf was on board. Did you find . . ."

Tyson's face darkened. "No sign of him. I am sorry, brother."

I stared out the window into deep blue water. Beckendorf was supposed to go to college in the fall. He had a girlfriend, lots of friends, his whole life ahead of him. He couldn't be *gone*. Maybe he'd made it off the ship like I had. Maybe he'd jumped over the side . . . and what? He couldn't have survived a hundred-foot fall into the water like I could. He couldn't have put enough distance between himself and the explosion.

I knew in my gut he was dead. He'd sacrificed himself to take out the *Princess Andromeda*, and I had abandoned him.

I thought about my dream: the Titans discussing the explosion as if it didn't matter, Nico di Angelo warning me that I would never beat Kronos without following his plan—a dangerous idea I'd been avoiding for more than a year.

A distant blast shook the room. Green light blazed outside, turning the whole sea as bright as noon.

"What was that?" I asked.

Tyson looked worried. "Daddy will explain. Come, he is blowing up monsters."

The palace might have been the most amazing place I'd ever seen if it hadn't been in the process of getting destroyed. We swam to the end of a long hallway and shot upward on a geyser. As we rose over the rooftops I caught my breath—well, if you can catch your breath underwater.

The palace was as big as the city on Mount Olympus, with wide courtyards, gardens, and columned pavilions. The gardens were sculpted with coral colonies and glowing sea plants. Twenty or thirty buildings were made of abalone, white but gleaming with rainbow colors. Fish and octopi darted in and out of the windows. The paths were lined with glowing pearls like Christmas lights.

The main courtyard was filled with warriors—mermen with fish tails from the waist down and human bodies from the waist up, except their skin was blue, which I'd never known before. Some were tending the wounded. Some were sharpening spears and swords. One passed us, swimming in a hurry. His eyes were bright green, like that stuff they put in glo-sticks, and his teeth were shark teeth. They don't show you stuff like that in *The Little Mermaid*.

Outside the main courtyard stood large fortifications—towers, walls, and antisiege weapons—but most of these had been smashed to ruins. Others were blazing with a strange green light that I knew well—Greek fire, which can burn even underwater.

Beyond this, the sea floor stretched into gloom. I could see battles raging—flashes of energy, explosions, the glint of armies clashing. A regular human would've found it too dark to see. Heck, a regular human would've been crushed by the pressure and frozen by the cold. Even my heat-sensitive eyes couldn't make out exactly what was going on.

At the edge of the palace complex, a temple with a red coral roof exploded, sending fire and debris streaming in slow motion across the farthest gardens. Out of the darkness above, an enormous form appeared—a squid larger than any skyscraper. It was surrounded by a glittering cloud of dust—at least I thought it was dust, until I realized it was a swarm of mermen trying to attack the monster. The squid descended on the palace and swatted its tentacles, smashing a whole column of warriors. Then a brilliant arc of blue light shot from the rooftop of one of the tallest buildings. The light hit the giant squid, and the monster dissolved like food coloring in water.

"Daddy," Tyson said, pointing to where the light had come from.

"*He* did that?" I suddenly felt more hopeful. My dad had unbelievable powers. He was the god of the sea. He could deal with this attack, right? Maybe he'd let me help.

"Have you been in the fight?" I asked Tyson in awe. "Like bashing heads with your awesome Cyclops strength and stuff?"

Tyson pouted, and immediately I knew I'd asked a bad question. "I have been . . . fixing weapons," he mumbled. "Come. Let's go find Daddy."

I know this might sound weird to people with, like, regular parents, but I'd only seen my dad four or five times in my life, and never for more than a few minutes. The Greek gods don't exactly show up for their kids' basketball games. Still, I thought I would recognize Poseidon on sight.

I was wrong.

The roof of the temple was a big open deck that had been set up as a command center. A mosaic on the floor showed an exact map of the palace grounds and the surrounding ocean, but the mosaic moved. Colored stone tiles representing different armies and sea monsters shifted around as the forces changed position. Buildings that collapsed in real life also collapsed in the picture.

Standing around the mosaic, grimly studying the battle, was a strange assortment of warriors, but none of them looked like my dad. I was searching for a big guy with a good tan and a black beard, wearing Bermuda shorts and a Hawaiian shirt.

There was nobody like that. One guy was a merman with two fish tails instead of one. His skin was green, his armor studded with pearls. His black hair was tied in a ponytail, and he looked young—though it's hard to tell with non-humans. They could be a thousand years old or three. Standing next to him was an old man with a bushy white beard and gray hair. His battle armor seemed to weigh him down. He had green eyes and smile wrinkles around his eyes, but he wasn't smiling now. He was studying the map and leaning on a large metal staff. To his right stood a beautiful woman in green armor with flowing black hair and strange little horns like crab claws. And there was a dolphin—just a regular dolphin, but it was staring at the map intently.

"Delphin," the old man said. "Send Palaemon and his legion of sharks to the western front. We have to neutralize those leviathans."

The dolphin spoke in a chattering voice, but I could understand it in my mind: *Yes, lord!* It sped away.

I looked in dismay at Tyson, then back at the old man.

It didn't seem possible, but . . . "Dad?" I asked.

The old man looked up. I recognized the twinkle in his eyes, but his face . . . he looked like he'd aged forty years.

"Hello, Percy."

"What—what happened to you?"

Tyson nudged me. He was shaking his head so hard I

was afraid it would fall off, but Poseidon didn't look offended.

"It's all right, Tyson," he said. "Percy, excuse my appearance. The war has been hard on me."

"But you're immortal," I said quietly. "You can look . . . any way you want."

"I reflect the state of my realm," he said. "And right now that state is quite grim. Percy, I should introduce you—I'm afraid you just missed my lieutenant Delphin, God of the Dolphins. This is my, er, wife, Amphitrite. My dear—"

The lady in green armor stared at me coldly, then crossed her arms and said, "Excuse me, my lord. I am needed in the battle."

She swam away.

I felt pretty awkward, but I guess I couldn't blame her. I'd never thought about it much, but my dad had an immortal wife. All his romances with mortals, including with my mom . . . well, Amphitrite probably didn't like that much.

Poseidon cleared his throat. "Yes, well . . . and this is my son Triton. Er, my *other* son."

"Your son and heir," the green dude corrected. His double fish tails swished back and forth. He smiled at me, but there was no friendliness in his eyes. "Hello, Perseus Jackson. Come to help at last?"

He acted like I was late or lazy. If you can blush underwater, I probably did.

"Tell me what to do," I said.

Triton smiled like that was a cute suggestion—like I

was a slightly amusing dog that had barked for him or something. He turned to Poseidon. "I will see to the front line, Father. Don't worry. *I* will not fail."

He nodded politely to Tyson. How come I didn't get that much respect? Then he shot off into the water.

Poseidon sighed. He raised his staff, and it changed into his regular weapon—a huge three-pointed trident. The tips glowed with blue light, and the water around it boiled with energy.

"I'm sorry about that," he told me.

A huge sea serpent appeared from above us and spiraled down toward the roof. It was bright orange with a fanged mouth big enough to swallow a gymnasium.

Hardly looking up, Poseidon pointed his trident at the beast and zapped it with blue energy. *Ka-boom!* The monster burst into a million goldfish, which all swam off in terror.

"My family is anxious," Poseidon continued as if nothing had happened. "The battle against Oceanus is going poorly."

He pointed to the edge of the mosaic. With the butt of his trident he tapped the image of a merman larger than the rest, with the horns of a bull. He appeared to be riding a chariot pulled by crawfish, and instead of a sword he wielded a live serpent.

"Oceanus," I said, trying to remember. "The Titan of the sea?"

Poseidon nodded. "He was neutral in the first war of gods and Titans. But Kronos has convinced him to fight. This is . . . well, it's not a good sign. Oceanus would not commit unless he was sure he could pick the winning side."

"He looks stupid," I said, trying to sound upbeat. "I mean, who fights with a snake?"

"Daddy will tie it in knots," Tyson said firmly.

Poseidon smiled, but he looked weary. "I appreciate your faith. We have been at war almost a year now. My powers are taxed. And still he finds new forces to throw at me—sea monsters so ancient I had forgotten about them."

I heard an explosion in the distance. About half a mile away, a mountain of coral disintegrated under the weight of two giant creatures. I could dimly make out their shapes. One was a lobster. The other was a giant humanoid like a Cyclops, but he was surrounded by a flurry of limbs. At first I thought he wearing a bunch of giant octopi. Then I realized they were his own arms—a hundred flailing, fighting arms.

"Briares!" I said.

I was happy to see him, but he looked like he was fighting for his life. He was the last of his kind—a Hundred-Handed One, cousin of the Cyclopes. We'd saved him from Kronos's prison last summer, and I knew he'd come to help Poseidon, but I hadn't heard of him since.

"He fights well," Poseidon said. "I wish we had a whole army like him, but he is the only one."

I watched as Briares bellowed in rage and picked up the lobster, which thrashed and snapped its pincers. He threw it off the coral mountain, and the lobster disappeared into the darkness. Briares swam after it, his hundred arms spinning like the blades of a motorboat.

"Percy, we may not have much time," my dad said. "Tell me of your mission. Did you see Kronos?"

I told him everything, though my voice choked up when I explained about Beckendorf. I looked down at the courtyards below and saw hundreds of wounded mermen lying on makeshift cots. I saw rows of coral mounds that must've been hastily made graves. I realized Beckendorf wasn't the first death. He was only one of hundreds, maybe thousands. I'd never felt so angry and helpless.

Poseidon stroked his beard. "Percy, Beckendorf chose a heroic death. You bear no blame for that. Kronos's army will be in disarray. Many were destroyed."

"But we didn't kill him, did we?"

As I said it, I knew it was a naive hope. We might blow up his ship and disintegrate his monsters, but a Titan lord wouldn't be so easy to kill.

"No," Poseidon admitted. "But you've bought our side some time."

"There were demigods on that ship," I said, thinking of the kid I'd seen in the stairwell. Somehow I'd allowed myself to concentrate on the monsters and Kronos. I'd convinced myself that destroying their ship was all right because they were evil, they were sailing to attack my city, and besides, they couldn't really be permanently killed. Monsters just vaporized and re-formed eventually. But demigods . . .

Poseidon put his hand on my shoulder. "Percy, there were only a few demigod warriors aboard that ship, and they all chose to battle for Kronos. Perhaps some heeded your warning and escaped. If they did not . . . they chose their path."

"They were brainwashed!" I said. "Now they're dead and Kronos is still alive. That's supposed to make me feel better?"

I glared at the mosaic—little tile explosions destroying tile monsters. It seemed so easy when it was just a picture.

Tyson put his arm around me. If anybody else had tried that, I would've pushed him away, but Tyson was too big and stubborn. He hugged me whether I wanted it or not. "Not your fault, brother. Kronos does not explode good. Next time we will use a big stick."

"Percy," my father said. "Beckendorf's sacrifice wasn't in vain. You have scattered the invasion force. New York will be safe for a time, which frees the other Olympians to deal with the bigger threat."

"The bigger threat?" I thought about what the golden Titan had said in my dream: *The gods have answered the challenge. Soon they will be destroyed.*

A shadow passed over my father's face. "You've had enough sorrow for one day. Ask Chiron when you return to camp."

"Return to camp? But you're in trouble here. I want to help!"

"You can't, Percy. Your job is elsewhere."

I couldn't believe I was hearing this. I looked at Tyson for backup.

My brother chewed his lip. "Daddy . . . Percy can fight with a sword. He is good."

"I know that," Poseidon said gently.

"Dad, I can help," I said. "I know I can. You're not going to hold out here much longer."

A fireball launched into the sky from behind the enemy lines. I thought Poseidon would deflect it or something, but it landed on the outer corner of the yard and exploded, sending mermen tumbling through the water. Poseidon winced as if he'd just been stabbed.

"Return to camp," he insisted. "And tell Chiron it is time."

"For what?"

"You must hear the prophecy. The *entire* prophecy."

I didn't need to ask him which prophecy. I'd been hearing about the "Great Prophecy" for years, but nobody would ever tell me the whole thing. All I knew was that I was supposed to make a decision that would decide the fate of the world—but no pressure.

"What if *this* is the decision?" I said. "Staying here to fight, or leaving? What if I leave and you . . ."

I couldn't say *die*. Gods weren't supposed to die, but I'd seen it happen. Even if they didn't die, they could be reduced to nearly nothing, exiled, imprisoned in the depths of Tartarus like Kronos had been.

"Percy, you must go," Poseidon insisted. "I don't know what your final decision will be, but your fight lies in the world above. If nothing else, you must warn your friends at camp. Kronos knew your plans. You have a spy. We will hold here. We have no choice."

Tyson gripped my hand desperately. "I will miss you, brother!"

Watching us, our father seemed to age another ten years. "Tyson, you have work to do as well, my son. They need you in the armory."

Tyson pouted some more.

"I will go," he sniffled. He hugged me so hard he almost cracked my ribs. "Percy, be careful! Do not let monsters kill you dead!"

I tried to nod confidently, but it was too much for the big guy. He sobbed and swam away toward the armory, where his cousins were fixing spears and swords.

"You should let him fight," I told my father. "He hates being stuck in the armory. Can't you tell?"

Poseidon shook his head. "It is bad enough I must send you into danger. Tyson is too young. I must protect him."

"You should trust him," I said. "Not try to protect him."

Poseidon's eyes flared. I thought I'd gone too far, but then he looked down at the mosaic and his shoulders sagged. On the tiles, the mermaid guy in the crawfish chariot was coming closer to the palace.

"Oceanus approaches," my father said. "I must meet him in battle."

I'd never been scared for a god before, but I didn't see how my dad could face this Titan and win.

"I will hold," Poseidon promised. "I will not give up my domain. Just tell me, Percy, do you still have the birthday gift I gave you last summer?"

I nodded and pulled out my camp necklace. It had a bead for every summer I'd been at Camp Half-Blood, but since last year I'd also kept a sand dollar on the cord. My father had given it to me for my fifteenth birthday. He'd told me I would know when to "spend it," but so far I hadn't figured out what he meant. All I knew was that it didn't fit the vending machines in the school cafeteria.

"The time is coming," he promised. "With luck, I will see you for your birthday next week, and we will have a proper celebration."

He smiled, and for a moment I saw the old light in his eyes.

Then the entire sea grew dark in front of us, like an inky storm was rolling in. Thunder crackled, which should've been impossible underwater. A huge icy presence was approaching. I sensed a wave of fear roll through the armies below us.

"I must assume my true godly form," Poseidon said. "Go—and good luck, my son."

I wanted to encourage him, to hug him or something, but knew better than to stick around. When a god assumes his true form, the power is so great that any mortal looking on him will disintegrate.

"Good-bye, Father," I managed.

Then I turned away. I willed the ocean currents to aid me. Water swirled around me, and I shot toward the surface at speeds that would've caused any normal human to pop like a balloon.

When I looked back, all I could see were flashes of green and blue as my father fought the Titan, and the sea itself was torn apart by the two armies.

THREE

I GET A SNEAK PEEK AT MY DEATH

If you want to be popular at Camp Half-Blood, don't come back from a mission with bad news.

Word of my arrival spread as soon as I walked out of the ocean. Our beach is on the North Shore of Long Island, and it's enchanted so most people can't even see it. People don't just *appear* on the beach unless they're demigods or gods or really, really lost pizza delivery guys. (It's happened—but that's another story.)

Anyway, that afternoon the lookout on duty was Connor Stoll from the Hermes cabin. When he spotted me, he got so excited he fell out of his tree. Then he blew the conch horn to signal the camp and ran to greet me.

Connor had a crooked smile that matched his crooked sense of humor. He's a pretty nice guy, but you should always keep one hand on your wallet when he's around, and do not, under any circumstances, give him access to shaving cream unless you want to find your sleeping bag full of it. He's got curly brown hair and is a little shorter than his brother, Travis, which is the only way I can tell them apart. They are both so unlike my old enemy Luke it's hard to believe they're all sons of Hermes.

"Percy!" he yelled. "What happened? Where's Becken-dorf?"

Then he saw my expression, and his smile melted. "Oh, no. Poor Silena. Holy Zeus, when she finds out . . ."

Together we climbed the sand dunes. A few hundred yards away, people were already streaming toward us, smiling and excited. *Percy's back*, they were probably thinking. *He's saved the day! Maybe he brought souvenirs!*

I stopped at the dining pavilion and waited for them. No sense rushing down there to tell them what a loser I was.

I gazed across the valley and tried to remember how Camp Half-Blood looked the first time I ever saw it. That seemed like a bajillion years ago.

From the dining pavilion, you could see pretty much everything. Hills ringed the valley. On the tallest, Half-Blood Hill, Thalia's pine tree stood with the Golden Fleece hanging from its branches, magically protecting the camp from its enemies. The guard dragon Peleus was so big now I could see him from here—curled around the tree trunk, sending up smoke signals as he snored.

To my right spread the woods. To my left, the canoe lake glittered and the climbing wall glowed from the lava pouring down its side. Twelve cabins—one for each Olympian god—made a horseshoe pattern around the commons area. Farther south were the strawberry fields, the armory, and the four-story Big House with its sky blue paint job and its bronze eagle weathervane.

In some ways, the camp hadn't changed. But you couldn't see the war by looking at the buildings or the fields. You could see it in the faces of the demigods and satyrs and naiads coming up the hill.

There weren't as many at camp as four summers ago. Some had left and never come back. Some had died fighting. Others—we tried not to talk about them—had gone over to the enemy.

The ones who were still here were battle-hardened and weary. There was little laughter at camp these days. Even the Hermes cabin didn't play so many pranks. It's hard to enjoy practical jokes when your whole life feels like one.

Chiron galloped into the pavilion first, which was easy for him since he's a white stallion from the waist down. His beard had grown wilder over the summer. He wore a green T-shirt that said MY OTHER CAR IS A CENTAUR and a bow slung over his back.

"Percy!" he said. "Thank the gods. But where . . ."

Annabeth ran in right behind him, and I'll admit my heart did a little relay race in my chest when I saw her. It's not that she tried to look good. We'd been doing so many combat missions lately, she hardly brushed her curly blond hair anymore, and she didn't care what clothes she was wearing—usually the same old orange camp T-shirt and jeans, and once in a while her bronze armor. Her eyes were stormy gray. Most of the time we couldn't get through a conversation without trying to strangle each other. Still, just seeing her made me feel fuzzy in the head. Last summer, before Luke had turned into Kronos and everything went sour, there had been a few times when I thought maybe . . . well, that we might get past the strangle-each-other phase.

"What happened?" She grabbed my arm. "Is Luke—"

"The ship blew up," I said. "He wasn't destroyed. I don't know where—"

Silena Beauregard pushed through the crowd. Her hair wasn't combed and she wasn't even wearing makeup, which wasn't like her.

"Where's Charlie?" she demanded, looking around like he might be hiding.

I glanced at Chiron helplessly.

The old centaur cleared his throat. "Silena, my dear, let's talk about this at the Big House—"

"No," she muttered. "No. *No.*"

She started to cry, and the rest of us stood around, too stunned to speak. We'd already lost so many people over the summer, but this was the worst. With Beckendorf gone, it felt like someone had stolen the anchor for the entire camp.

Finally Clarisse from the Ares cabin came forward. She put her arm around Silena. They had one of the strangest friendships ever—a daughter of the war god and a daughter of the love goddess—but ever since Silena had given Clarisse advice last summer about her first boyfriend, Clarisse had decided she was Silena's personal bodyguard.

Clarisse was dressed in her bloodred combat armor, her brown hair tucked into a bandana. She was as big and beefy as a rugby player, with a permanent scowl on her face, but she spoke gently to Silena.

"Come on, girl," she said. "Let's get to the Big House. I'll make you some hot chocolate."

Everyone turned and wandered off in twos and threes,

heading back to the cabins. Nobody was excited to see me now. Nobody wanted to hear about the blown-up ship.

Only Annabeth and Chiron stayed behind.

Annabeth wiped a tear from her cheek. "I'm glad you're not dead, Seaweed Brain."

"Thanks," I said. "Me too."

Chiron put a hand on my shoulder. "I'm sure you did everything you could, Percy. Will you tell us what happened?"

I didn't want to go through it again, but I told them the story, including my dream about the Titans. I left out the detail about Nico. Nico had made me promise not to tell anybody about his plan until I made up my mind, and the plan was so scary I didn't mind keeping it a secret.

Chiron gazed down at the valley. "We must call a war council immediately, to discuss this spy, and other matters."

"Poseidon mentioned another threat," I said. "Something even bigger than the *Princess Andromeda*. I thought it might be that challenge the Titan had mentioned in my dream."

Chiron and Annabeth exchanged looks, like they knew something I didn't. I hated when they did that.

"We will discuss that also," Chiron promised.

"One more thing." I took a deep breath. "When I talked to my father, he said to tell you it's time. I need to know the full prophecy."

Chiron's shoulders sagged, but he didn't look surprised. "I've dreaded this day. Very well. Annabeth, we will show Percy the truth—all of it. Let's go to the attic."

I'd been to the Big House attic three times before, which was three times more than I wanted to.

A ladder led up from the top of the staircase. I wondered how Chiron was going to get up there, being half horse and all, but he didn't try.

"You know where it is," he told Annabeth. "Bring it down, please."

Annabeth nodded. "Come on, Percy."

The sun was setting outside, so the attic was even darker and creepier than usual. Old hero trophies were stacked everywhere—dented shields, pickled heads in jars from various monsters, a pair of fuzzy dice on a bronze plaque that read: STOLEN FROM CHRYSAOR'S HONDA CIVIC, BY GUS, SON OF HERMES, 1988.

I picked up a curved bronze sword so badly bent it looked like the letter *M*. I could still see green stains on the metal from the magical poison that used to cover it. The tag was dated last summer. It read: *Scimitar of Kampê, destroyed in the Battle of the Labyrinth.*

"You remember Briares throwing those boulders?" I asked.

Annabeth gave me a grudging smile. "And Grover causing a Panic?"

We locked eyes. I thought of a different time last summer, under Mount St. Helens, when Annabeth thought I was going to die and she kissed me.

She cleared her throat and looked away. "Prophecy."

"Right." I put down the scimitar. "Prophecy."

We walked over to the window. On a three-legged stool sat the Oracle—a shriveled female mummy in a tie-dyed dress. Tufts of black hair clung to her skull. Glassy eyes stared out of her leathery face. Just looking at her made my skin crawl.

If you wanted to leave camp during the summer, it used to be you had to come up here to get a quest. This summer, that rule had been tossed. Campers left all the time on combat missions. We had no choice if we wanted to stop Kronos.

Still, I remembered too well the strange green mist—the spirit of the Oracle—that lived inside the mummy. She looked lifeless now, but whenever she spoke a prophecy, she moved. Sometimes fog gushed out of her mouth and created strange shapes. Once, she'd even left the attic and taken a little zombie stroll into the woods to deliver a message. I wasn't sure what she'd do for the "Great Prophecy." I half expected her to start tap dancing or something.

But she just sat there like she was dead—which she was.

"I never understood this," I whispered.

"What?" Annabeth asked.

"Why it's a mummy."

"Percy, she didn't used to be a mummy. For thousands of years the spirit of the Oracle lived inside a beautiful maiden. The spirit would be passed on from generation to generation. Chiron told me *she* was like that fifty years ago." Annabeth pointed at the mummy. "But she was the last."

"What happened?"

Annabeth started to say something, then apparently changed her mind. "Let's just do our job and get out of here."

I looked nervously at the Oracle's withered face. "So what now?"

Annabeth approached the mummy and held out her palms. "O Oracle, the time is at hand. I ask for the Great Prophecy."

I braced myself, but the mummy didn't move. Instead, Annabeth approached and unclasped one of its necklaces. I'd never paid too much attention to its jewelry before. I figured it was just hippie love beads and stuff. But when Annabeth turned toward me, she was holding a leather pouch—like a Native American medicine pouch on a cord braided with feathers. She opened the bag and took out a roll of parchment no bigger than her pinky.

"No way," I said. "You mean all these years, I've been asking about this stupid prophecy, and it's been right there around her neck?"

"The time wasn't right," Annabeth said. "Believe me, Percy, I read this when I was ten years old, and I still have nightmares about it."

"Great," I said. "Can I read it now?"

"Downstairs at the war council," Annabeth said. "Not in front of . . . you know."

I looked at the glassy eyes of the Oracle, and I decided not to argue. We headed downstairs to join the others. I didn't know it then, but it would be the last time I ever visited the attic.

The senior counselors had gathered around the Ping-Pong table. Don't ask me why, but the rec room had become the camp's informal headquarters for war councils. When Annabeth, Chiron, and I came in, though, it looked more like a shouting match.

Clarisse was still in full battle gear. Her electric spear was strapped to her back. (Actually, her *second* electric spear, since I'd broken the first one. She called the spear "Maimer." Behind her back, everybody else called it "Lamer.") She had her boar-shaped helmet under one arm and a knife at her belt.

She was in the midst of yelling at Michael Yew, the new head counselor for Apollo, which looked kind of funny since Clarisse was a foot taller. Michael had taken over the Apollo cabin after Lee Fletcher died in battle last summer. Michael stood four feet six, with another two feet of attitude. He reminded me of a ferret, with a pointy nose and scrunched-up features—either because he scowled so much or because he spent too much time looking down the shaft of an arrow.

"It's *our* loot!" he yelled, standing on his tiptoes so he could get in Clarisse's face. "If you don't like it, you can kiss my quiver!"

Around the table, people were trying not to laugh—the Stoll brothers, Pollux from the Dionysus cabin, Katie Gardner from Demeter. Even Jake Mason, the hastily appointed new counselor from Hephaestus, managed a faint smile. Only Silena Beauregard didn't pay any attention.

She sat beside Clarisse and stared vacantly at the Ping-Pong net. Her eyes were red and puffy. A cup of hot chocolate sat untouched in front of her. It seemed unfair that she had to be here. I couldn't believe Clarisse and Michael standing over her, arguing about something as stupid as loot, when she'd just lost Beckendorf.

"STOP IT!" I yelled. "What are you guys doing?"

Clarisse glowered at me. "Tell Michael not to be a selfish jerk."

"Oh, that's perfect, coming from you," Michael said.

"The only reason I'm here is to support Silena!" Clarisse shouted. "Otherwise I'd be back in my cabin."

"What are you talking about?" I demanded.

Pollux cleared his throat. "Clarisse has refused to speak to any us, until her, um, issue is resolved. She hasn't spoken for three days."

"It's been wonderful," Travis Stoll said wistfully.

"What issue?" I asked.

Clarisse turned to Chiron. "You're in charge, right? Does my cabin get what we want or not?"

Chiron shuffled his hooves. "My dear, as I've already explained, Michael is correct. Apollo's cabin has the best claim. Besides, we have more important matters—"

"Sure," Clarisse snapped. "Always more important matters than what Ares needs. We're just supposed to show up and fight when you need us, and not complain!"

"That would be nice," Connor Stoll muttered.

Clarisse gripped her knife. "Maybe I should ask Mr. D—"

"As you know," Chiron interrupted, his tone slightly angry now, "our director, Dionysus, is busy with the war. He can't be bothered with this."

"I see," Clarisse said. "And the senior counselors? Are *any* of you going to side with me?"

Nobody was smiling now. None of them met Clarisse's eyes.

"Fine." Clarisse turned to Silena. "I'm sorry. I didn't mean to get into this when you've just lost . . . Anyway, I apologize. To *you*. Nobody else."

Silena didn't seem to register her words.

Clarisse threw her knife on the Ping-Pong table. "All of you can fight this war without Ares. Until I get satisfaction, no one in my cabin is lifting a finger to help. Have fun dying."

The counselors were all too stunned to say anything as Clarisse stormed out of the room.

Finally Michael Yew said, "Good riddance."

"Are you kidding?" Katie Gardner protested. "This is a disaster!"

"She can't be serious," Travis said. "Can she?"

Chiron sighed. "Her pride has been wounded. She'll calm down eventually." But he didn't sound convinced.

I wanted to ask what the heck Clarisse was so mad about, but I looked at Annabeth and she mouthed the words *I'll tell you later.*

"Now," Chiron continued, "if you please, counselors. Percy has brought something I think you should hear. Percy—the Great Prophecy."

Annabeth handed me the parchment. It felt dry and old, and my fingers fumbled with the string. I uncurled the paper, trying not to rip it, and began to read:

"A half-blood of the eldest dogs . . ."

"Er, Percy?" Annabeth interrupted. "That's *gods*. Not *dogs*."

"Oh, right," I said. Being dyslexic is one mark of a demigod, but sometimes I really hate it. The more nervous I am, the worse my reading gets. *"A half-blood of the eldest gods . . . shall reach sixteen against all odds . . ."*

I hesitated, staring at the next lines. A cold feeling started in my fingers as if the paper was freezing.

"And see the world in endless sleep,
The hero's soul, cursed blade shall reap."

Suddenly Riptide seemed heavier in my pocket. A cursed blade? Chiron once told me Riptide had brought many people sorrow. Was it possible my own sword could get me killed? And how could the world fall into endless sleep, unless that meant death?

"Percy," Chiron urged. "Read the rest."

My mouth felt like it was full of sand, but I spoke the last two lines.

"A single choice shall . . . shall end his days.
Olympus to per—pursue—"

"Preserve," Annabeth said gently. "It means *to save*."

"I know what it means," I grumbled. *"Olympus to preserve or raze."*

The room was silent. Finally Connor Stoll said, "Raise is good, isn't it?"

"Not *raise*," Silena said. Her voice was hollow, but I was startled to hear her speak at all. "R-a-z-e means *destroy*."

"Obliterate," Annabeth said. "Annihilate. Turn to rubble."

"Got it." My heart felt like lead. "Thanks."

Everybody was looking at me—with concern, or pity, or maybe a little fear.

Chiron closed his eyes as if he were saying a prayer. In horse form, his head almost brushed the lights in the rec room. "You see now, Percy, why we thought it best not to tell you the whole prophecy. You've had enough on your shoulders—"

"Without realizing I was going to die in the end anyway?" I said. "Yeah, I get it."

Chiron gazed at me sadly. The guy was three thousand years old. He'd seen hundreds of heroes die. He might not like it, but he was used to it. He probably knew better than to try to reassure me.

"Percy," Annabeth said. "You know prophecies always have double meanings. It might not literally mean you die."

"Sure," I said. *"A single choice shall end his days.* That has tons of meanings, right?"

"Maybe we can stop it," Jake Mason offered. *"The hero's soul, cursed blade shall reap.* Maybe we could find this cursed blade and destroy it. Sounds like Kronos's scythe, right?"

I hadn't thought about that, but it didn't matter if the cursed blade was Riptide or Kronos's scythe. Either way, I doubted we could stop the prophecy. A blade was supposed to reap my soul. As a general rule, I preferred not to have my soul reaped.

"Perhaps we should let Percy think about these lines," Chiron said. "He needs time—"

"No." I folded up the prophecy and shoved it into my pocket. I felt defiant and angry, though I wasn't sure who I was angry with. "I don't need time. If I die, I die. I can't worry about that, right?"

Annabeth's hands were shaking a little. She wouldn't meet my eyes.

"Let's move on," I said. "We've got other problems. We've got a spy."

Michael Yew scowled. "A spy?"

I told them what had happened on the *Princess Andromeda*—how Kronos had known we were coming, how he'd shown me the silver scythe pendant he'd used to communicate with someone at camp.

Silena started to cry again, and Annabeth put an arm around her shoulders.

"Well," Connor Stoll said uncomfortably, "we've suspected there might a spy for years, right? Somebody kept passing information to Luke—like the location of the Golden Fleece a couple of years ago. It must be somebody who knew him well."

Maybe subconsciously, he glanced at Annabeth. She'd known Luke better than anyone, of course, but Connor looked away quickly. "Um, I mean, it could be anybody."

"Yes." Katie Gardner frowned at the Stoll brothers. She'd disliked them ever since they'd decorated the grass roof of the Demeter cabin with chocolate Easter bunnies. "Like one of Luke's siblings."

Travis and Connor both started arguing with her.

"Stop!" Silena banged the table so hard her hot chocolate spilled. "Charlie's dead and . . . and you're all arguing like little kids!" She put her head down and began to sob.

Hot chocolate trickled off the Ping-Pong table. Everybody looked ashamed.

"She's right," Pollux said at last. "Accusing each other doesn't help. We need to keep our eyes open for a silver necklace with a scythe charm. If Kronos had one, the spy probably does too."

Michael Yew grunted. "We need to find this spy before we plan our next operation. Blowing up the *Princess Andromeda* won't stop Kronos forever."

"No indeed," Chiron said. "In fact his next assault is already on the way."

I scowled. "You mean the 'bigger threat' Poseidon mentioned?"

He and Annabeth looked at each other like, *It's time.* Did I mention I hate it when they do that?

"Percy," Chiron said, "we didn't want to tell you until you returned to camp. You needed a break with your . . . mortal friends."

Annabeth blushed. It dawned on me that she knew I'd been hanging out with Rachel, and I felt guilty. Then I felt angry that I felt guilty. I was allowed to have friends outside camp, right? It wasn't like . . .

"Tell me what's happened," I said.

Chiron picked up a bronze goblet from the snack table. He tossed water onto the hot plate where we usually melted nacho cheese. Steam billowed up, making a rainbow in the fluorescent lights. Chiron fished a golden drachma out of his pouch, tossed it through the mist, and muttered, "O Iris, Goddess of the Rainbow, show us the threat."

The mist shimmered. I saw the familiar image of a smoldering volcano—Mount St. Helens. As I watched, the side of the mountain exploded. Fire, ash, and lava rolled out. A newscaster's voice was saying *"—even larger than last year's eruption, and geologists warn that the mountain may not be done."*

I knew all about last year's eruption. I'd caused it. But this explosion was much worse. The mountain tore itself apart, collapsing inward, and an enormous form rose out of the smoke and lava like it was emerging from a manhole. I hoped the Mist would keep the humans from seeing it clearly, because what I saw would've caused panic and riots across the entire United States.

The giant was bigger than anything I'd ever encountered. Even my demigod eyes couldn't make out its exact form through the ash and fire, but it was vaguely humanoid and so huge it could've used the Chrysler Building as a baseball bat. The mountain shook with a horrible rumbling, as if the monster were laughing.

"It's him," I said. "Typhon."

I was seriously hoping Chiron would say something good, like *No, that's our huge friend Leroy! He's going to help us!* But no such luck. He simply nodded. "The most horrible monster of all, the biggest single threat the gods ever faced. He has been freed from under the mountain at last. But this scene is from two days ago. *Here* is what is happening today."

Chiron waved his hand and the image changed. I saw a bank of storm clouds rolling across the Midwest plains. Lightning flickered. Lines of tornadoes destroyed everything in their path—ripping up houses and trailers, tossing cars around like Matchbox toys.

"Monumental floods," an announcer was saying. *"Five states declared disaster areas as the freak storm system sweeps east, continuing its path of destruction."* The cameras zoomed in on a column of storm bearing down on some Midwest city. I couldn't tell which one. Inside the storm I could see the giant—just small glimpses of his true form: a smoky arm, a dark clawed hand the size of a city block. His angry roar rolled across the plains like a nuclear blast. Other smaller forms darted through the clouds, circling the monster. I saw flashes of light, and I realized the giant was trying to swat them. I squinted and thought I saw a golden chariot flying into the blackness. Then some kind of huge bird—a monstrous owl—dived in to attack the giant.

"Are those . . . the gods?" I said.

"Yes, Percy," Chiron said. "They have been fighting him for days now, trying to slow him down. But Typhon is marching forward—toward New York. Toward Olympus."

I let that sink in. "How long until he gets here?"

"Unless the gods can stop him? Perhaps five days. Most of the Olympians are there . . . except your father, who has a war of his own to fight."

"But then who's guarding Olympus?"

Connor Stoll shook his head. "If Typhon gets to New York, it won't matter who's guarding Olympus."

I thought about Kronos's words on the ship: *I would love to see the terror in your eyes when you realize how I will destroy Olympus.*

Was this what he was talking about: an attack by Typhon? It was sure terrifying enough. But Kronos was always fooling us, misdirecting our attention. This seemed too obvious for him. And in my dream, the golden Titan had talked about several more challenges to come, as if Typhon were only the first.

"It's a trick," I said. "We have to warn the gods. Something else is going to happen."

Chiron looked at me gravely. "Something worse than Typhon? I hope not."

"We have to defend Olympus," I insisted. "Kronos has another attack planned."

"He did," Travis Stoll reminded me. "But you sunk his ship."

Everyone was looking at me. They wanted some good news. They wanted to believe that at least I'd given them a little bit of hope.

I glanced at Annabeth. I could tell we were thinking the same thing: What if the *Princess Andromeda* was a ploy? What if Kronos *let* us blow up that ship so we'd lower our guard?

But I wasn't going to say that in front of Silena. Her boyfriend had sacrificed himself for that mission.

"Maybe you're right," I said, though I didn't believe it.

I tried to imagine how things could get much worse. The gods were in the Midwest fighting a huge monster that had almost defeated them once before. Poseidon was under siege and losing a war against the sea Titan Oceanus. Kronos was still out there somewhere. Olympus was virtually undefended. The demigods of Camp Half-Blood were on our own with a spy in our midst.

Oh, and according to the ancient prophecy, I was going to die when I turned sixteen—which happened to be in five days, the exact same time Typhon was supposed to hit New York. Almost forgot that.

"Well," Chiron said, "I think that's enough for one night."

He waved his hand and the steam dissipated. The stormy battle of Typhon and the gods disappeared.

"That's an understatement," I muttered.

And the war council adjourned.

FOUR

WE BURN A METAL SHROUD

I dreamed Rachel Elizabeth Dare was throwing darts at my picture.

She was standing in her room . . . Okay, back up. I have to explain that Rachel doesn't have a room. She has the top floor of her family's mansion, which is a renovated brown-stone in Brooklyn. Her "room" is a huge loft with industrial lighting and floor-to-ceiling windows. It's about twice as big as my mom's apartment.

Some alt rock was blaring from her paint-covered Bose docking system. As far as I could tell, Rachel's only rule about music was that no two songs on her iPod could sound the same, and they all had to be strange.

She wore a kimono, and her hair was frizzy, like she'd been sleeping. Her bed was messed up. Sheets hung over a bunch of artist's easels. Dirty clothes and old energy bar wrappers were strewn around the floor, but when you've got a room that big, the mess doesn't look so bad. Out the windows you could see the entire nighttime skyline of Manhattan.

The picture she was attacking was a painting of me standing over the giant Antaeus. Rachel had painted it a couple of months ago. My expression in the picture was fierce—disturbing, even—so it was hard to tell if I was the good guy or the bad guy, but Rachel said I'd looked just like that after the battle.

"*Demigods*," Rachel muttered as she threw another dart at the canvas. "And their *stupid* quests."

Most of the darts bounced off, but a few stuck. One hung off my chin like a goatee.

Someone pounded on her bedroom door.

"Rachel!" a man shouted. "What in the world are you doing? Turn off that—"

Rachel scooped up her remote control and shut off the music. "Come in!"

Her dad walked in, scowling and blinking from the light. He had rust-colored hair a little darker than Rachel's. It was smushed on one side like he'd lost a fight with his pillow. His blue silk pajamas had "WD" monogrammed on the pocket. Seriously, who has monogrammed pajamas?

"What is going on?" he demanded. "It's three in the morning."

"Couldn't sleep," Rachel said.

On the painting, a dart fell off my face. Rachel hid the rest behind her back, but Mr. Dare noticed.

"So . . . I take it your friend isn't coming to St. Thomas?" That's what Mr. Dare called me. Never *Percy*. Just *your friend*. Or *young man* if he was talking to me, which he rarely did.

Rachel knit her eyebrows. "I don't know."

"We leave in the morning," her dad said. "If he hasn't made up his mind yet—"

"He's probably not coming," Rachel said miserably. "Happy?"

Mr. Dare put his hands behind his back. He paced the room with a stern expression. I imagined he did that in the boardroom of his land development company and made his employees nervous.

"Are you still having bad dreams?" he asked. "Headaches?"

Rachel threw her darts on the floor. "I should never have told you about that."

"I'm your father," he said. "I'm worried about you."

"Worried about the family's reputation," Rachel muttered.

Her father didn't react—maybe because he'd heard that comment before, or maybe because it was true.

"We could call Dr. Arkwright," he suggested. "He helped you get through the death of your hamster."

"I was six then," she said. "And no, Dad, I don't need a therapist. I just . . ." She shook her head helplessly.

Her father stopped in front of the windows. He gazed at the New York skyline as if he owned it—which wasn't true. He only owned part of it.

"It will be good for you to get away," he decided. "You've had some unhealthy influences."

"I'm not going to Clarion Ladies Academy," Rachel said. "And my friends are none of your business."

Mr. Dare smiled, but it wasn't a warm smile. It was more like, *Someday you'll realize how silly you sound.*

"Try to get some sleep," he urged. "We'll be at the beach by tomorrow night. It will be fun."

"Fun," Rachel repeated. "Lots of fun."

Her father exited the room. He left the door open behind him.

Rachel stared at the portrait of me. Then she walked to the easel next to it, which was covered in a sheet.

"I hope they're dreams," she said.

She uncovered the easel. On it was a hastily sketched charcoal, but Rachel was a good artist. The picture was definitely Luke as a young boy. He was about nine years old, with a wide grin and no scar on his face. I had no idea how Rachel could've known what he looked like back then, but the portrait was so good I had a feeling she wasn't guessing. From what I knew about Luke's life (which wasn't much), the picture showed him just before he'd found out he was a half-blood and had run away from home.

Rachel stared at the portrait. Then she uncovered the next easel. This picture was even more disturbing. It showed the Empire State Building with lightning all around it. In the distance a dark storm was brewing, with a huge hand coming out of the clouds. At the base of the building a crowd had gathered . . . but it wasn't a normal crowd of tourists and pedestrians. I saw spears, javelins, and banners—the trappings of an army.

"Percy," Rachel muttered, as if she knew I was listening, "what is going on?"

The dream faded, and the last thing I remember was wishing I could answer her question.

The next morning, I wanted to call her, but there were no phones at camp. Dionysus and Chiron didn't need a landline. They just called Olympus with an Iris-message whenever they needed something. And when demigods use cell phones, the signals agitate every monster within a hundred miles. It's like sending up a flare: *Here I am! Please rearrange my face!* Even within the safe borders of camp, that's not the kind of advertising we wanted to do.

Most demigods (except for Annabeth and a few others) don't even own cell phones. And I definitely couldn't tell Annabeth, "Hey, let me borrow your phone so I can call Rachel!" To make the call, I would've had to leave camp and walk several miles to the nearest convenience store. Even if Chiron let me go, by the time I got there, Rachel would've been on the plane to St. Thomas.

I ate a depressing breakfast by myself at the Poseidon table. I kept staring at the fissure in the marble floor where two years ago Nico had banished a bunch of bloodthirsty skeletons to the Underworld. The memory didn't exactly improve my appetite.

After breakfast, Annabeth and I walked down to inspect the cabins. Actually, it was Annabeth's turn for inspection. My morning chore was to sort through reports for Chiron. But since we both hated our jobs, we decided to do them together so it wouldn't be so heinous.

We started at the Poseidon cabin, which was basically just me. I'd made my bunk bed that morning (well, sort of) and straightened the Minotaur horn on the wall, so I gave myself a four out of five.

Annabeth made a face. "You're being generous." She

used the end of her pencil to pick up an old pair of running shorts.

I snatched them away. "Hey, give me a break. I don't have Tyson cleaning up after me this summer."

"Three out of five," Annabeth said. I knew better than to argue, so we moved along.

I tried to skim through Chiron's stack of reports as we walked. There were messages from demigods, nature spirits, and satyrs all around the country, writing about the latest monster activity. They were pretty depressing, and my ADHD brain did *not* like concentrating on depressing stuff.

Little battles were raging everywhere. Camp recruitment was down to zero. Satyrs were having trouble finding new demigods and bringing them to Half-Blood Hill because so many monsters were roaming the country. Our friend Thalia, who led the Hunters of Artemis, hadn't been heard from in months, and if Artemis knew what had happened to them, she wasn't sharing information.

We visited the Aphrodite cabin, which of course got a five out of five. The beds were perfectly made. The clothes in everyone's footlockers were color coordinated. Fresh flowers bloomed on the windowsills. I wanted to dock a point because the whole place reeked of designer perfume, but Annabeth ignored me.

"Great job as usual, Silena," Annabeth said.

Silena nodded listlessly. The wall behind her bed was decorated with pictures of Beckendorf. She sat on her bunk with a box of chocolates on her lap, and I remembered that her dad owned a chocolate store in the Village, which was how he'd caught the attention of Aphrodite.

"You want a bonbon?" Silena asked. "My dad sent them. He thought—he thought they might cheer me up."

"Are they any good?" I asked.

She shook her head. "They taste like cardboard."

I didn't have anything against cardboard, so I tried one. Annabeth passed. We promised to see Silena later and kept going.

As we crossed the commons area, a fight broke out between the Ares and Apollo cabins. Some Apollo campers armed with firebombs flew over the Ares cabin in a chariot pulled by two pegasi. I'd never seen the chariot before, but it looked like a pretty sweet ride. Soon, the roof of the Ares cabin was burning, and naiads from the canoe lake rushed over to blow water on it.

Then the Ares campers called down a curse, and all the Apollo kids' arrows turned to rubber. The Apollo kids kept shooting at the Ares kids, but the arrows bounced off.

Two archers ran by, chased by an angry Ares kid who was yelling in poetry: "Curse me, eh? I'll make you pay! / I don't want to rhyme all day!"

Annabeth sighed. "Not that again. Last time Apollo cursed a cabin, it took a week for the rhyming couplets to wear off."

I shuddered. Apollo was god of poetry as well as archery, and I'd heard him recite in person. I'd almost rather get shot by an arrow.

"What are they fighting about anyway?" I asked.

Annabeth ignored me while she scribbled on her inspection scroll, giving both cabins a one out of five.

I found myself staring at her, which was stupid since I'd seen her a billion times. She and I were about the same height this summer, which was a relief. Still, she seemed so much more mature. It was kind of intimidating. I mean, sure, she'd always been cute, but she was starting to be seriously beautiful.

Finally she said, "That flying chariot."

"What?"

"You asked what they were fighting about."

"Oh. Oh, right."

"They captured it in a raid in Philadelphia last week. Some of Luke's demigods were there with that flying chariot. The Apollo cabin seized it during the battle, but the Ares cabin led the raid. So they've been fighting about who gets it ever since."

We ducked as Michael Yew's chariot dive-bombed an Ares camper. The Ares camper tried to stab him and cuss him out in rhyming couplets. He was pretty creative about rhyming those cuss words.

"We're fighting for our lives," I said, "and they're bickering about some stupid chariot."

"They'll get over it," Annabeth said. "Clarisse will come to her senses."

I wasn't so sure. That didn't sound like the Clarisse I knew.

I scanned more reports and we inspected a few more cabins. Demeter got a four. Hephaestus got a three and probably should've gotten lower, but with Beckendorf being gone and all, we cut them some slack. Hermes got a two, which was no surprise. All campers who didn't know their godly parentage were shoved into the Hermes cabin, and since the gods were kind of forgetful, that cabin was always overcrowded.

Finally we got to Athena's cabin, which was orderly and clean as usual. Books were straightened on the shelves. The armor was polished. Battle maps and blueprints decorated the walls. Only Annabeth's bunk was messy. It was covered in papers, and her silver laptop was still running.

"*Vlacas*," Annabeth muttered, which was basically calling herself an idiot in Greek.

Her second-in-command, Malcolm, suppressed a smile. "Yeah, um . . . we cleaned everything else. Didn't know if it was safe to move your notes."

That was probably smart. Annabeth had a bronze knife that she reserved just for monsters and people who messed with her stuff.

Malcolm grinned at me. "We'll wait outside while you finish inspection." The Athena campers filed out the door while Annabeth cleaned up her bunk.

I shuffled uneasily and pretended to go through some more reports. Technically, even on inspection, it was against camp rules for two campers to be . . . like, *alone* in a cabin.

That rule had come up a lot when Silena and Beckendorf started dating. And I know some of you might be thinking, Aren't all demigods related on the godly side, and doesn't that make dating gross? But the thing is, the godly side of your family doesn't count, genetically speaking, since gods don't have DNA. A demigod would never think about dating someone who had the same godly parent. Like two kids from Athena cabin? No way. But a daughter of Aphrodite and a son of Hephaestus? They're not related. So it's no problem.

Anyway, for some strange reason I was thinking about this as I watched Annabeth straighten up. She closed her laptop, which had been given to her as a gift from the inventor Daedalus last summer.

I cleared my throat. "So . . . get any good info from that thing?"

"Too much," she said. "Daedalus had so many ideas, I could spend fifty years just trying to figure them all out."

"Yeah," I muttered. "That would be fun."

She shuffled her papers—mostly drawings of buildings and a bunch of handwritten notes. I knew she wanted to be an architect someday, but I'd learned the hard way not to ask what she was working on. She'd start talking about angles and load-bearing joints until my eyes glazed over.

"You know . . ." She brushed her hair behind her ear, like she does when she's nervous. "This whole thing with Beckendorf and Silena. It kind of makes you think. About . . . what's important. About losing people who are important."

I nodded. My brain started seizing on little random details, like the fact that she was still wearing those silver owl earrings from her dad, who was this brainiac military history professor in San Francisco.

"Um, yeah," I stammered. "Like . . . is everything cool with your family?"

Okay, really stupid question, but hey, I was nervous.

Annabeth looked disappointed, but she nodded.

"My dad wanted to take me to Greece this summer," she said wistfully. "I've always wanted to see—"

"The Parthenon," I remembered.

She managed a smile. "Yeah."

"That's okay. There'll be other summers, right?"

As soon as I said it, I realized it was a boneheaded comment. I was facing the *end of my days*. Within a week, Olympus might fall. If the Age of the Gods really did end, the world as we knew it would dissolve into chaos. Demigods would be hunted to extinction. There would be no more summers for us.

Annabeth stared at her inspection scroll. "Three out five," she muttered, "for a sloppy head counselor. Come on. Let's finish your reports and get back to Chiron."

On the way to the Big House, we read the last report, which was handwritten on a maple leaf from a satyr in Canada. If possible, the note made me feel even worse.

"'Dear Grover,'" I read aloud. "'Woods outside Toronto attacked by giant evil badger. Tried to do as you suggested and summon power of Pan. No effect. Many naiads' trees destroyed. Retreating to Ottawa. Please advise. Where are you? —Gleeson Hedge, protector.'"

Annabeth grimaced. "You haven't heard *anything* from him? Even with your empathy link?"

I shook my head dejectedly.

Ever since last summer when the god Pan had died, our friend Grover had been drifting farther and farther away. The Council of Cloven Elders treated him like an outcast, but Grover still traveled all over the East Coast, trying to spread the word about Pan and convince nature spirits to protect their own little bits of the wild. He'd only come back to camp a few times to see his girlfriend, Juniper.

Last I'd heard he was in Central Park organizing the dryads, but nobody had seen or heard from him in two months. We'd tried to send Iris-messages. They never got through. I had an empathy link with Grover, so I hoped I would know if anything bad happened to him. Grover had told me one time that if he died, the empathy link might kill me too. But I wasn't sure if that was still true or not.

I wondered if he was still in Manhattan. Then I thought about my dream of Rachel's sketch—dark clouds closing on the city, an army gathered around the Empire State Building.

"Annabeth." I stopped her by the tetherball court. I knew I was asking for trouble, but I didn't know who else to trust. Plus, I'd always depended on Annabeth for advice. "Listen, I had this dream about, um, Rachel . . ."

I told her the whole thing, even the weird picture of Luke as a child.

For a while she didn't say anything. Then she rolled up her inspection scroll so tight she ripped it. "What do you want me to say?"

"I'm not sure. You're the best strategist I know. If you were Kronos planning this war, what would you do next?"

"I'd use Typhon as a distraction. Then I'd hit Olympus directly, while the gods were in the West."

"Just like in Rachel's picture."

"Percy," she said, her voice tight, "Rachel is just a mortal."

"But what if her dream is true? Those other Titans— they said Olympus would be destroyed in a matter of days. They said they had plenty of other challenges. And what's with that picture of Luke as a kid—"

"We'll just have to be ready."

"How?" I said. "Look at our camp. We can't even stop fighting each other. And I'm supposed to get my stupid soul reaped."

She threw down her scroll. "I knew we shouldn't have shown you the prophecy." Her voice was angry and hurt. "All it did was scare you. You run away from things when you're scared."

I stared at her, completely stunned. "*Me?* Run away?"

She got right in my face. "Yes, you. You're a coward, Percy Jackson!"

We were nose to nose. Her eyes were red, and I suddenly realized that when she called me a coward, maybe she wasn't talking about the prophecy.

"If you don't like our chances," she said, "maybe you should go on that vacation with Rachel."

"Annabeth—"

"If you don't like our company."

"That's not fair!"

She pushed past me and stormed toward the strawberry

fields. She hit the tetherball as she passed and sent it spinning angrily around the pole.

I'd like to say my day got better from there. Of course it didn't.

That afternoon we had an assembly at the campfire to burn Beckendorf's burial shroud and say our good-byes. Even the Ares and Apollo cabins called a temporary truce to attend.

Beckendorf's shroud was made out of metal links, like chain mail. I didn't see how it would burn, but the Fates must've been helping out. The metal melted in the fire and turned to golden smoke, which rose into the sky. The campfire flames always reflected the campers' moods, and today they burned black.

I hoped Beckendorf's spirit would end up in Elysium. Maybe he'd even choose to be reborn and try for Elysium in three different lifetimes so he could reach the Isles of the Blest, which was like the Underworld's ultimate party headquarters. If anyone deserved it, Beckendorf did.

Annabeth left without a word to me. Most of the other campers drifted off to their afternoon activities. I just stood there staring at the dying fire. Silena sat nearby crying, while Clarisse and her boyfriend, Chris Rodriguez, tried to comfort her.

Finally I got up the nerve to walk over. "Hey, Silena, I'm really sorry."

She sniffled. Clarisse glared at me, but she always glares at everyone. Chris would barely look at me. He'd been one of Luke's men until Clarisse rescued him from the Labyrinth last summer, and I guess he still felt guilty about it.

I cleared my throat. "Silena, you know Beckendorf carried your picture. He looked at it right before we went into battle. You meant a lot to him. You made the last year the best of his life."

Silena sobbed.

"Good work, Percy," Clarisse muttered.

"No, it's all right," Silena said. "Thank . . . thank you, Percy. I should go."

"You want company?" Clarisse asked.

Silena shook her head and ran off.

"She's stronger than she looks," Clarisse muttered, almost to herself. "She'll survive."

"You could help with that," I suggested. "You could honor Beckendorf's memory by fighting with us."

Clarisse went for her knife, but it wasn't there anymore. She'd thrown it on the Ping-Pong table in the Big House.

"Not my problem," she growled. "My cabin doesn't get honor, I don't fight."

I noticed she wasn't speaking in rhymes. Maybe she hadn't been around when her cabinmates got cursed, or maybe she had a way of breaking the spell. With a chill, I wondered if Clarisse could be Kronos's spy at camp. Was that why she was keeping her cabin out of the fight? But as much as I disliked Clarisse, spying for the Titans didn't seem like her style.

"All right," I told her. "I didn't want to bring this up,

but you owe me one. You'd be rotting in a Cyclops's cave in the Sea of Monsters if it wasn't for me."

She clenched her jaw. "Any other favor, Percy. Not this. The Ares cabin has been dissed too many times. And don't think I don't know what people say about me behind my back."

I wanted to say, *Well, it's true.* But I bit my tongue.

"So, what—you're just going to let Kronos crush us?" I asked.

"If you want my help so bad, tell Apollo to give us the chariot."

"You're such a big baby."

She charged me, but Chris got between us. "Whoa, guys," he said. "Clarisse, you know, maybe he's got a point."

She sneered at him. "Not you too!" She trudged off with Chris at her heels.

"Hey, wait! I just meant—Clarisse, wait!"

I watched the last sparks from Beckendorf's fire curl into the afternoon sky. Then I headed toward the sword-fighting arena. I needed a break, and I wanted to see an old friend.

FIVE

I DRIVE MY DOG INTO
A TREE

Mrs. O'Leary saw me before I saw her, which was a pretty good trick considering she's the size of a garbage truck. I walked into the arena, and a wall of darkness slammed into me.

"WOOF!"

The next thing I knew I was flat on the ground with a huge paw on my chest and an oversize Brillo-pad tongue licking my face.

"Ow!" I said. "Hey, girl. Good to see you too. Ow!"

It took a few minutes for Mrs. O'Leary to calm down and get off me. By then I was pretty much drenched in dog drool. She wanted to play fetch, so I picked up a bronze shield and tossed it across the arena.

By the way, Mrs. O'Leary is the world's only friendly hellhound. I kind of inherited her when her previous owner died. She lived at camp, but Beckendorf . . . well, Beckendorf *used to* take care of her whenever I was gone. He had smelted Mrs. O'Leary's favorite bronze chewing bone. He'd forged her collar with the little smiley face and a crossbones name tag. Next to me, Beckendorf had been her best friend.

Thinking about that made me sad all over again, but I

threw the shield a few more times because Mrs. O'Leary insisted.

Soon she started barking—a sound slightly louder than an artillery gun—like she needed to go for a walk. The other campers didn't think it was funny when she went to the bathroom in the arena. It had caused more than one unfortunate slip-and-slide accident. So I opened the gates of the arena, and she bounded straight toward the woods.

I jogged after her, not too concerned that she was getting ahead. Nothing in the woods could threaten Mrs. O'Leary. Even the dragons and giant scorpions ran away when she came close.

When I finally tracked her down, she wasn't using the facilities. She was in a familiar clearing where the Council of Cloven Elders had once put Grover on trial. The place didn't look so good. The grass had turned yellow. The three topiary thrones had lost all their leaves. But that's not what surprised me. In the middle of the glade stood the weirdest trio I'd ever seen: Juniper the tree nymph, Nico di Angelo, and a very old, very fat satyr.

Nico was the only one who didn't seem freaked out by Mrs. O'Leary's appearance. He looked pretty much like I'd seen him in my dream—an aviator's jacket, black jeans, and a T-shirt with dancing skeletons on it, like one of those Day of the Dead pictures. His Stygian iron sword hung at his side. He was only twelve, but he looked much older and sadder.

He nodded when he saw me, then went back to scratching Mrs. O'Leary's ears. She sniffed his legs like he was the most interesting thing since rib-eye steaks. Being the son of Hades, he'd probably been traveling in all sorts of hellhound-friendly places.

The old satyr didn't look nearly so happy. "Will someone—what is this *underworld* creature doing in my forest!" He waved his arms and trotted on his hooves as if the grass were hot. "You there, Percy Jackson! Is this your beast?"

"Sorry, Leneus," I said. "That's your name, right?"

The satyr rolled his eyes. His fur was dust-bunny gray, and a spiderweb grew between his horns. His belly would've made him an invincible bumper car. "Well, of course I'm Leneus. Don't tell me you've forgotten a member of the Council so quickly. Now, call off your beast!"

"*WOOF!*" Mrs. O'Leary said happily.

The old satyr gulped. "Make it go away! Juniper, I will not help you under these circumstances!"

Juniper turned toward me. She was pretty in a dryad-y way, with her purple gossamer dress and her elfish face, but her eyes were green-tinted with chlorophyll from crying.

"Percy," she sniffled. "I was just asking about Grover. I *know* something's happened. He wouldn't stay gone this long if he wasn't in trouble. I was hoping that Leneus—"

"I told you!" the satyr protested. "You are better off without that traitor."

Juniper stamped her foot. "He is not a traitor! He's the bravest satyr ever, and I want to know where he is!"

"*WOOF!*"

Leneus's knees started knocking. "I . . . I won't answer

questions with this hellhound sniffing my tail!"

Nico looked like he was trying to not crack up. "I'll walk the dog," he volunteered.

He whistled, and Mrs. O'Leary bounded after him to the far end of the grove.

Leneus huffed indignantly and brushed the twigs off his shirt. "Now, as I was trying to explain, young lady, your boyfriend has not sent *any* reports since we voted him into exile."

"You *tried* to vote him into exile," I corrected. "Chiron and Dionysus stopped you."

"Bah! They are *honorary* Council members. It wasn't a proper vote."

"I'll tell Dionysus you said that."

Leneus paled. "I only meant . . . Now see here, Jackson. This is none of your business."

"Grover's my friend," I said. "He wasn't lying to you about Pan's death. I saw it myself. You were just too scared to accept the truth."

Leneus's lips quivered. "No! Grover's a liar and good riddance. We're better off without him."

I pointed at the withered thrones. "If things are going so well, where are your friends? Looks like your Council hasn't been meeting lately."

"Maron and Silenus . . . I . . . I'm sure they'll be back," he said, but I could hear the panic in his voice. "They're just taking some time off to think. It's been a very unsettling year."

"It's going to get a lot more unsettling," I promised.

"Leneus, we *need* Grover. There's got to be a way you can find him with your magic."

The old satyr's eye twitched. "I'm telling you, I've heard nothing. Perhaps he's dead."

Juniper choked back a sob.

"He's not dead," I said. "I can feel that much."

"Empathy links," Leneus said disdainfully. "Very unreliable."

"So ask around," I insisted. "Find him. There's a war coming. Grover was preparing the nature spirits."

"Without my permission! And it's not *our* war."

I grabbed him by the shirt, which seriously wasn't like me, but the stupid old goat was making me mad. "Listen, Leneus. When Kronos attacks, he's going to have *packs* of hellhounds. He's going to destroy everything in his path—mortals, gods, demigods. Do you think he'll let the satyrs go free? You're supposed to be a leader. So LEAD. Get out there and see what's happening. Find Grover and bring Juniper some news. Now, GO!"

I didn't push him very hard, but he was kind of top-heavy. He fell on his furry rump, then scrambled to his hooves and ran away with his belly jiggling. "Grover will never be accepted! He will die an outcast!"

When he'd disappeared into the bushes, Juniper wiped her eyes. "I'm sorry, Percy. I didn't mean to get you involved. Leneus is still a lord of the Wild. You don't want to make an enemy of him."

"No problem," I said. "I've got worse enemies than overweight satyrs."

Nico walked back to us. "Good job, Percy. Judging from the trail of goat pellets, I'd say you shook him up pretty well."

I was afraid I knew why Nico was here, but I tried for a smile. "Welcome back. Did you come by just to see Juniper?"

He blushed. "Um, no. That was an accident. I kind of . . . dropped into the middle of their conversation."

"He scared us to death!" Juniper said. "Right out of the shadows. But, Nico, you *are* the son of Hades and all. Are you sure you haven't heard anything about Grover?"

Nico shifted his weight. "Juniper, like I tried to tell you . . . even if Grover died, he would reincarnate into something else in nature. I can't sense things like that, only mortal souls."

"But if you *do* hear anything?" she pleaded, putting her hand on his arm. "Anything at all?"

Nico's cheeks got even brighter red. "Uh, you bet. I'll keep my ears open."

"We'll find him, Juniper," I promised. "Grover's alive, I'm sure. There must be a simple reason why he hasn't contacted us."

She nodded glumly. "I hate not being able to leave the forest. He could be anywhere, and I'm stuck here waiting. Oh, if that silly goat has gotten himself hurt—"

Mrs. O'Leary bounded back over and took an interest in Juniper's dress.

Juniper yelped. "Oh, no you don't! I know about dogs and trees. I'm gone!"

She went *poof* into green mist. Mrs. O'Leary looked disappointed, but she lumbered off to find another target, leaving Nico and me alone.

Nico tapped his sword on the ground. A tiny mound of animal bones erupted from the dirt. They knit themselves together into a skeletal field mouse and scampered off. "I was sorry to hear about Beckendorf."

A lump formed in my throat. "How did you—"

"I talked to his ghost."

"Oh . . . right." I'd never get used to the fact that this twelve-year-old kid spent more time talking with the dead than the living. "Did he say anything?"

"He doesn't blame you. He figured you'd be beating yourself up, and he said you shouldn't."

"Is he going to try for rebirth?"

Nico shook his head. "He's staying in Elysium. Said he's waiting for someone. Not sure what he meant, but he seems okay with death."

It wasn't much comfort, but it was something.

"I had a vision you were on Mount Tam," I told Nico. "Was that—"

"Real," he said. "I didn't mean to be spying on the Titans, but I was in the neighborhood."

"Doing what?"

Nico tugged at his sword belt. "Following a lead on . . . you know, my family."

I nodded. I knew his past was a painful subject. Until two years ago, he and his sister Bianca had been frozen in time at a place called the Lotus Hotel and Casino. They'd been there for like seventy years. Eventually a mysterious lawyer rescued them and checked them into a boarding school, but Nico had no memories of his life before the casino. He didn't know anything about his mother. He didn't know who the lawyer was, or why they'd been frozen in time or allowed to go free. After Bianca died and left Nico alone, he'd been obsessed with finding answers.

"So how did it go?" I asked. "Any luck?"

"No," he murmured. "But I may have a new lead soon."

"What's the lead?"

Nico chewed his lip. "That's not important right now. You know why I'm here."

A feeling of dread started to build in my chest. Ever since Nico first proposed his plan for beating Kronos last summer, I'd had nightmares about it. He would show up occasionally and press me for an answer, but I kept putting him off.

"Nico, I don't know," I said. "It seems pretty extreme."

"You've got Typhon coming in, what . . . a week? Most of the other Titans are unleashed now and on Kronos's side. Maybe it's time to think extreme."

I looked back toward the camp. Even from this distance I could hear the Ares and Apollo campers fighting again, yelling curses and spouting bad poetry.

"They're no match for the Titan army," Nico said. "You know that. This comes down to you and Luke. And there's only one way you can beat Luke."

I remembered the fight on the *Princess Andromeda*. I'd been hopelessly outmatched. Kronos had almost killed me with a single cut to my arm, and I couldn't even wound him. Riptide had glanced right off his skin.

"We can give you the same power," Nico urged. "You heard the Great Prophecy. Unless you want to have your soul reaped by a cursed blade . . ."

I wondered how Nico had heard the prophecy—probably from some ghost.

"You can't prevent a prophecy," I said.

"But you can fight it." Nico had a strange, hungry light in his eyes. "You can become invincible."

"Maybe we should wait. Try to fight without—"

"No!" Nico snarled. "It has to be now!"

I stared at him. I hadn't seen his temper flare like that in a long time. "Um, you sure you're okay?"

He took a deep breath. "Percy, all I mean . . . when the fighting starts, we won't be able to make the journey. This is our last chance. I'm sorry if I'm being too pushy, but two years ago my sister gave her life to protect you. I want you to honor that. Do whatever it takes to stay alive and defeat Kronos."

I didn't like the idea. Then I thought about Annabeth calling me a coward, and I got angry.

Nico had a point. If Kronos attacked New York, the campers would be no match for his forces. I had to do something. Nico's way was dangerous—maybe even deadly. But it might give me a fighting edge.

"All right," I decided. "What do we do first?"

His cold creepy smile made me sorry I'd agreed. "First we'll need to retrace Luke's steps. We need to know more about his past, his childhood."

I shuddered, thinking about Rachel's picture from my dream—a smiling nine-year-old Luke. "Why do we need to know about that?"

"I'll explain when we get there," Nico said. "I've already tracked down his mother. She lives in Connecticut."

I stared at him. I'd never thought much about Luke's mortal parent. I'd met his dad, Hermes, but his mom . . .

"Luke ran away when he was really young," I said. "I didn't think his mom was alive."

"Oh, she's alive." The way he said it made me wonder what was wrong with her. What kind of horrible person could she be?

"Okay . . ." I said. "So how do we get to Connecticut? I can call Blackjack—"

"No." Nico scowled. "Pegasi don't like me, and the feeling is mutual. But there's no need for flying." He whistled, and Mrs. O'Leary came loping out of the woods.

"Your friend here can help." Nico patted her head. "You haven't tried shadow travel yet?"

"Shadow travel?"

Nico whispered in Mrs. O'Leary's ear. She tilted her head, suddenly alert.

"Hop on board," Nico told me.

I'd never considered riding a dog before, but Mrs. O'Leary was certainly big enough. I climbed onto her back and held her collar.

"This will make her very tired," Nico warned, "so you can't do it often. And it works best at night. But all shadows are part of the same substance. There is only one darkness, and creatures of the Underworld can use it as a road, or a door."

"I don't understand," I said.

"No," Nico said. "It took me a long time to learn. But Mrs. O'Leary knows. Tell her where to go. Tell her Westport, the home of May Castellan."

"You're not coming?"

"Don't worry," he said. "I'll meet you there."

I was a little nervous, but I leaned down to Mrs. O'Leary's ear. "Okay, girl. Uh, can you take me to Westport, Connecticut? May Castellan's place?"

Mrs. O'Leary sniffed the air. She looked into the gloom of the forest. Then she bounded forward, straight into an oak tree.

Just before we hit, we passed into shadows as cold as the dark side of the moon.

MY COOKIES GET SCORCHED

I don't recommend shadow travel if you're scared of:

a) The dark
b) Cold shivers up your spine
c) Strange noises
d) Going so fast you feel like your face is peeling off

In other words, I thought it was awesome. One minute I couldn't see anything. I could only feel Mrs. O'Leary's fur and my fingers wrapped around the bronze links of her dog collar.

The next minute the shadows melted into a new scene. We were on a cliff in the woods of Connecticut. At least, it looked like Connecticut from the few times I'd been there: lots of trees, low stone walls, big houses. Down one side of the cliff, a highway cut through a ravine. Down the other side was someone's backyard. The property was huge—more wilderness than lawn. The house was a two-story white Colonial. Despite the fact that it was right on the other side of the hill from a highway, it felt like it was in the middle of nowhere. I could see a light glowing in the kitchen window. A rusty old swing set stood under an apple tree.

I couldn't imagine living in a house like this, with an

actual yard and everything. I'd lived in a tiny apartment or a school dorm my whole life. If this was Luke's home, I wondered why he'd ever wanted to leave.

Mrs. O'Leary staggered. I remembered what Nico had said about shadow travel draining her, so I slipped off her back. She let out a huge toothy yawn that would've scared a T. rex, then turned in a circle and flopped down so hard the ground shook.

Nico appeared right next to me, as if the shadows had darkened and created him. He stumbled, but I caught his arm.

"I'm okay," he managed, rubbing his eyes.

"How did you do that?"

"Practice. A few times running into walls. A few accidental trips to China."

Mrs. O'Leary started snoring. If it hadn't been for the roar of traffic behind us, I'm sure she would've woken up the whole neighborhood.

"Are you going to take a nap too?" I asked Nico.

He shook his head. "The first time I shadow traveled, I passed out for a week. Now it just makes me a little drowsy, but I can't do it more than once or twice a night. Mrs. O'Leary won't be going anywhere for a while."

"So we've got some quality time in Connecticut." I gazed at the white Colonial house. "What now?"

"We ring the doorbell," Nico said.

If I were Luke's mom, I would not have opened my door at night for two strange kids. But I wasn't *anything* like Luke's mom.

I knew that even before we reached the front door. The sidewalk was lined with those little stuffed beanbag animals you see in gift shops. There were miniature lions, pigs, dragons, hydras, even a teeny Minotaur in a little Minotaur diaper. Judging from their sad shape, the beanbag creatures had been sitting out here a long time—since the snow melted last spring at least. One of the hydras had a tree sapling sprouting between its necks.

The front porch was infested with wind chimes. Shiny bits of glass and metal clinked in the breeze. Brass ribbons tinkled like water and made me realize I needed to use the bathroom. I didn't know how Ms. Castellan could stand all the noise.

The front door was painted turquoise. The name CASTELLAN was written in English, and below in Greek: Διοικητής φρουρίου.

Nico looked at me. "Ready?"

He'd barely tapped the door when it swung open.

"Luke!" the old lady cried happily.

She looked like someone who enjoyed sticking her fingers in electrical sockets. Her white hair stuck out in tufts all over her head. Her pink housedress was covered in scorch marks and smears of ash. When she smiled, her face looked unnaturally stretched, and the high-voltage light in her eyes made me wonder if she was blind.

"Oh, my dear boy!" She hugged Nico. I was trying to figure out why she thought Nico was Luke (they looked absolutely nothing alike), when she smiled at me and said, "Luke!"

She forgot all about Nico and gave me a hug. She smelled like burned cookies. She was as thin as a scarecrow, but that didn't stop her from almost crushing me.

"Come in!" she insisted. "I have your lunch ready!"

She ushered us inside. The living room was even weirder than the front lawn. Mirrors and candles filled every available space. I couldn't look anywhere without seeing my own reflection. Above the mantel, a little bronze Hermes flew around the second hand of a ticking clock. I tried to imagine the god of messengers ever falling in love with this old woman, but the idea was too bizarre.

Then I noticed the framed picture on the mantel, and I froze. It was exactly like Rachel's sketch—Luke around nine years old, with blond hair and a big smile and two missing teeth. The lack of a scar on his face made him look like a different person—carefree and happy. How could Rachel have known about that picture?

"This way, my dear!" Ms. Castellan steered me toward the back of the house. "Oh, I told them you would come back. I knew it!"

She sat us down at the kitchen table. Stacked on the counter were hundreds—I mean hundreds—of Tupperware boxes with peanut butter and jelly sandwiches inside. The ones on the bottom were green and fuzzy, like they'd been there for a long time. The smell reminded me of my sixth grade locker—and that's not a good thing.

On top of the oven was a stack of cookie sheets. Each one had a dozen burned cookies on it. In the sink was a mountain of empty plastic Kool-Aid pitchers. A beanbag

Medusa sat by the faucet like she was guarding the mess.

Ms. Castellan started humming as she got out peanut butter and jelly and started making a new sandwich. Something was burning in the oven. I got the feeling more cookies were on the way.

Above the sink, taped all around the window, were dozens of little pictures cut from magazines and newspaper ads—pictures of Hermes from the FTD Flowers logo and Quickie Cleaners, pictures of the caduceus from medical ads.

My heart sank. I wanted to get out of that room, but Ms. Castellan kept smiling at me as she made the sandwich, like she was making sure I didn't bolt.

Nico coughed. "Um, Ms. Castellan?"

"Mm?"

"We need to ask you about your son."

"Oh, yes! They told me he would never come back. But I knew better." She patted my cheek affectionately, giving me peanut butter racing stripes.

"When did you last see him?" Nico asked.

Her eyes lost focus.

"He was so young when he left," she said wistfully. "Third grade. That's too young to run away! He said he'd be back for lunch. And I waited. He likes peanut butter sandwiches and cookies and Kool-Aid. He'll be back for lunch very soon. . . ." Then she looked at me and smiled. "Why, Luke, there you are! You look so handsome. You have your father's eyes."

She turned toward the pictures of Hermes above the

sink. "Now, there's a good man. Yes, indeed. He comes to visit me, you know."

The clock kept ticking in the other room. I wiped the peanut butter off my face and looked at Nico pleadingly, like *Can we get out of here now?*

"Ma'am," Nico said. "What, uh . . . what happened to your eyes?"

Her gaze seemed fractured—like she was trying to focus on him through a kaleidoscope. "Why, Luke, you know the story. It was right before you were born, wasn't it? I'd always been special, able to see through the . . . whatever-they-call-it."

"The Mist?" I said.

"Yes, dear." She nodded encouragingly. "And they offered me an important job. That's how special I was!"

I glanced at Nico, but he looked as confused as I was.

"What sort of job?" I asked. "What happened?"

Ms. Castellan frowned. Her knife hovered over the sandwich bread. "Dear me, it didn't work out, did it? Your father warned me not to try. He said it was too dangerous. But I had to. It was my destiny! And now . . . I still can't get the images out of my head. They make everything seem so fuzzy. Would you like some cookies?"

She pulled a tray out of the oven and dumped a dozen lumps of chocolate chip charcoal on the table.

"Luke was so kind," Ms. Castellan murmured. "He left to protect me, you know. He said if he went away, the monsters wouldn't threaten me. But I told him the monsters are no threat! They sit outside on the sidewalk all day, and they never come in." She picked up the little stuffed Medusa from the windowsill. "Do they, Mrs. Medusa? No, no threat at all." She beamed at me. "I'm so glad you came home. I knew you weren't ashamed of me!"

I shifted in my seat. I imagined being Luke sitting at this table, eight or nine years old, and just beginning to realize that my mother wasn't all there.

"Ms. Castellan," I said.

"Mom," she corrected.

"Um, yeah. Have you seen Luke since he left home?"

"Well, of course!"

I didn't know if she was imagining that or not. For all I knew, every time the mailman came to the door he was Luke. But Nico sat forward expectantly.

"When?" he asked. "When did Luke visit you last?"

"Well, it was . . . Oh goodness . . ." A shadow passed across her face. "The last time, he looked so different. A scar. A terrible scar, and his voice so full of pain . . ."

"His eyes," I said. "Were they gold?"

"Gold?" She blinked. "No. How silly. Luke has blue eyes. Beautiful blue eyes!"

So Luke really had been here, and this had happened before last summer—before he'd turned into Kronos.

"Ms. Castellan?" Nico put his hand on the old woman's arm. "This is very important. Did he ask you for anything?"

She frowned as if trying to remember. "My—my blessing. Isn't that sweet?" She looked at us uncertainly. "He was going to a river, and he said he needed my blessing. I gave it to him. Of course I did."

Nico looked at me triumphantly. "Thank you, ma'am. That's all the information we—"

Ms. Castellan gasped. She doubled over, and her cookie tray clattered to the floor. Nico and I jumped to our feet.

"Ms. Castellan?" I said.

"AHHHH." She straightened. I scrambled away and almost fell over the kitchen table, because her eyes—her eyes were glowing green.

"My child," she rasped in a much deeper voice. *"Must protect him! Hermes, help! Not my child! Not his fate—no!"*

She grabbed Nico by the shoulders and began to shake him as if to make him understand. *"Not his fate!"*

Nico made a strangled scream and pushed her away. He gripped the hilt of his sword. "Percy, we need to get out—"

Suddenly Ms. Castellan collapsed. I lurched forward and caught her before she could hit the edge of the table. I managed to get her into a chair.

"Ms. C?" I asked.

She muttered something incomprehensible and shook her head. "Goodness. I . . . I dropped the cookies. How silly of me."

She blinked, and her eyes were back to normal—or at least, what they had been before. The green glow was gone.

"Are you okay?" I asked.

"Well, of course, dear. I'm fine. Why do you ask?"

I glanced at Nico, who mouthed the word *Leave*.

"Ms. C, you were telling us something," I said. "Something about your son."

"Was I?" she said dreamily. "Yes, his blue eyes. We were

talking about his blue eyes. Such a handsome boy!"

"We have to go," Nico said urgently. "We'll tell Luke . . . uh, we'll tell him you said hello."

"But you can't leave!" Ms. Castellan got shakily to her feet, and I backed away. I felt silly being scared of a frail old woman, but the way her voice had changed, the way she'd grabbed Nico . . .

"Hermes will be here soon," she promised. "He'll want to see his boy!"

"Maybe next time," I said. "Thank you for—" I looked down at the burned cookies scattered on the floor. "Thanks for everything."

She tried to stop us, to offer us Kool-Aid, but I had to get out of that house. On the front porch, she grabbed my wrist and I almost jumped out of my skin. "Luke, at least be safe. Promise me you'll be safe."

"I will . . . Mom."

That made her smile. She released my wrist, and as she closed the front door I could hear her talking to the candles: "You hear that? He will be safe. I told you he would be!"

As the door shut, Nico and I ran. The little beanbag animals on the sidewalk seemed to grin at us as we passed.

Back at the cliff, Mrs. O'Leary had found a friend.

A cozy campfire crackled in a ring of stones. A girl about eight years old was sitting cross-legged next to Mrs. O'Leary, scratching the hellhound's ears.

The girl had mousy brown hair and a simple brown dress. She wore a scarf over her head so she looked like a pioneer kid—like the ghost of *Little House on the Prairie* or something. She poked the fire with a stick, and it seemed to glow more richly red than a normal fire.

"Hello," she said.

My first thought was: monster. When you're a demigod and you find a sweet little girl alone in the woods—that's typically a good time to draw your sword and attack. Plus, the encounter with Ms. Castellan had rattled me pretty bad.

But Nico bowed to the little girl. "Hello again, Lady."

She studied me with eyes as red as the firelight. I decided it was safest to bow.

"Sit, Percy Jackson," she said. "Would you like some dinner?"

After staring at moldy peanut butter sandwiches and burned cookies, I didn't have much of an appetite, but the girl waved her hand and a picnic appeared at the edge of the fire. There were plates of roast beef, baked potatoes, buttered carrots, fresh bread, and a whole bunch of other foods I hadn't had in a long time. My stomach started to rumble. It was the kind of home-cooked meal people are supposed to have but never do. The girl made a five-foot-long dog biscuit appear for Mrs. O'Leary, who happily began tearing it to shreds.

I sat next to Nico. We picked up our food, and I was about to dig in when I thought better of it.

I scraped part of my meal into the flames, the way we do at camp. "For the gods," I said.

The little girl smiled. "Thank you. As tender of the flame, I get a share of every sacrifice, you know."

"I recognize you now," I said. "The first time I came to camp, you were sitting by the fire, in the middle of the commons area."

"You did not stop to talk," the girl recalled sadly. "Alas, most never do. Nico talked to me. He was the first in many years. Everyone rushes about. No time for visiting family."

"You're Hestia," I said. "Goddess of the Hearth."

She nodded.

Okay . . . so she looked eight years old. I didn't ask. I'd learned that gods could look any way they pleased.

"My lady," Nico asked, "why aren't you with the other Olympians, fighting Typhon?"

"I'm not much for fighting." Her red eyes flickered. I realized they weren't just reflecting the flames. They were filled with flames—but not like Ares's eyes. Hestia's eyes were warm and cozy.

"Besides," she said, "someone has to keep the home fires burning while the other gods are away."

"So you're guarding Mount Olympus?" I asked.

"'Guard' may be too strong a word. But if you ever need a warm place to sit and a home-cooked meal, you are welcome to visit. Now eat."

My plate was empty before I knew it. Nico scarfed his down just as fast.

"That was great," I said. "Thank you, Hestia."

She nodded. "Did you have a good visit with May Castellan?"

For a moment I'd almost forgotten the old lady with her

bright eyes and her maniacal smile, the way she'd suddenly seemed possessed.

"What's wrong with her, exactly?" I asked.

"She was born with a gift," Hestia said. "She could see through the Mist."

"Like my mother," I said. And I was also thinking, *Like Rachel.* "But the glowing eyes thing—"

"Some bear the curse of sight better than others," the goddess said sadly. "For a while, May Castellan had many talents. She attracted the attention of Hermes himself. They had a beautiful baby boy. For a brief time, she was happy. And then she went too far."

I remembered what Ms. Castellan had said: *They offered me an important job . . . It didn't work out.* I wondered what kind of job left you like that.

"One minute she was all happy," I said. "And then she was freaking out about her son's fate, like she knew he'd turned into Kronos. What happened to . . . to divide her like that?"

The goddess's face darkened. "That is a story I do not like to tell. But May Castellan saw too much. If you are to understand your enemy Luke, you must understand his family."

I thought about the sad little pictures of Hermes taped above May Castellan's sink. I wondered if Ms. Castellan had been so crazy when Luke was little. That green-eyed fit could've seriously scared a nine-year-old kid. And if Hermes never visited, if he'd left Luke alone with his mom all those years . . .

"No wonder Luke ran away," I said. "I mean, it wasn't right to leave his mom like that, but still—he was just a kid. Hermes shouldn't have abandoned them."

Hestia scratched behind Mrs. O'Leary's ears. The hellhound wagged her tail and accidentally knocked over a tree.

"It's easy to judge others," Hestia warned. "But will you follow Luke's path? Seek the same powers?"

Nico set down his plate. "We have no choice, my lady. It's the only way Percy stands a chance."

"Mmm." Hestia opened her hand and the fire roared. Flames shot thirty feet into the air. Heat slapped me in the face. Then the fire died back down to normal.

"Not all powers are spectacular." Hestia looked at me. "Sometimes the hardest power to master is the power of yielding. Do you believe me?"

"Uh-huh," I said. Anything to keep her from messing with her flame powers again.

The goddess smiled. "You are a good hero, Percy Jackson. Not too proud. I like that. But you have much to learn. When Dionysus was made a god, I gave up my throne for him. It was the only way to avoid a civil war among the gods."

"It unbalanced the Council," I remembered. "Suddenly there were seven guys and five girls."

Hestia shrugged. "It was the best solution, not a perfect one. Now I tend the fire. I fade slowly into the background. No one will ever write epic poems about the deeds of Hestia. Most demigods don't even stop to talk to me. But that is no matter. I keep the peace. I yield when necessary. Can you do this?"

"I don't know what you mean."

She studied me. "Perhaps not yet. But soon. Will you continue your quest?"

"Is that why you're here—to warn me against going?"

Hestia shook her head. "I am here because when all else fails, when all the other mighty gods have gone off to war, I am all that's left. Home. Hearth. I am the last Olympian. You must remember me when you face your final decision."

I didn't like the way she said *final*.

I looked at Nico, then back at Hestia's warm glowing eyes. "I have to continue, my lady. I have to stop Luke . . . I mean Kronos."

Hestia nodded. "Very well. I cannot be of much assistance, beyond what I have already told you. But since you sacrificed to me, I can return you to your own hearth. I will see you again, Percy, on Olympus."

Her tone was ominous, as though our next meeting would not be happy.

The goddess waved her hand, and everything faded.

Suddenly I was home. Nico and I were sitting on the couch in my mom's apartment on the Upper East Side. That was the good news. The bad news was that the rest of the living room was occupied by Mrs. O'Leary.

I heard a muffled yell from the bedroom. Paul's voice said, "Who put this wall of fur in the doorway?"

"Percy?" my mom called out. "Are you here? Are you all right?"

"I'm here!" I shouted back.

"*WOOF!*" Mrs. O'Leary tried to turn in a circle to find my mom, knocking all the pictures off the walls. She's only met my mom once before (long story), but she loves her.

It took a few minutes, but we finally got things worked out. After destroying most of the furniture in the living room and probably making our neighbors really mad, we got my parents out of the bedroom and into the kitchen, where we sat around the kitchen table. Mrs. O'Leary still took up the entire living room, but she'd settled her head in the kitchen doorway so she could see us, which made her happy. My mom tossed her a ten-pound family-size tube of ground beef, which disappeared down her gullet. Paul poured lemonade for the rest of us while I explained about our visit to Connecticut.

"So it's true." Paul stared at me like he'd never seen me before. He was wearing his white bathrobe, now covered in hellhound fur, and his salt-and-pepper hair was sticking up in every direction. "All the talk about monsters, and being a demigod . . . it's really true."

I nodded. Last fall I'd explained to Paul who I was. My mom had backed me up. But until this moment, I don't think he really believed us.

"Sorry about Mrs. O'Leary," I said, "destroying the living room and all."

Paul laughed like he was delighted. "Are you kidding? This is awesome! I mean, when I saw the hoofprints on the Prius, I thought maybe. But this!"

He patted Mrs. O'Leary's snout. The living room shook—*BOOM, BOOM, BOOM*—which either meant a SWAT team was breaking down the door or Mrs. O'Leary was wagging her tail.

I couldn't help but smile. Paul was a pretty cool guy, even if he was my English teacher as well as my stepdad.

"Thanks for not freaking out," I said.

"Oh, I'm freaking out," he promised, his eyes wide. "I just think it's awesome!"

"Yeah, well," I said, "you may not be so excited when you hear what's happening."

I told Paul and my mom about Typhon, and the gods, and the battle that was sure to come. Then I told them Nico's plan.

My mom laced her fingers around her lemonade glass. She was wearing her old blue flannel bathrobe, and her hair was tied back. Recently she'd started writing a novel, like she'd wanted to do for years, and I could tell she'd been working on it late into the night, because the circles under her eyes were darker than usual.

Behind her at the kitchen window, silvery moon lace glowed in the flower box. I'd brought the magical plant back from Calypso's island last summer, and it bloomed like crazy under my mother's care. The scent always calmed me down, but it also made me sad because it reminded me of lost friends.

My mom took a deep breath, like she was thinking how to tell me no.

"Percy, it's dangerous," she said. "Even for you."

"Mom, I know. I could die. Nico explained that. But if we don't try—"

"We'll all die," Nico said. He hadn't touched his lemonade. "Ms. Jackson, we don't stand a chance against an invasion. And there *will* be an invasion."

"An invasion of New York?" Paul said. "Is that even possible? How could we not see the . . . the monsters?"

He said the word like he still couldn't believe this was real.

"I don't know," I admitted. "I don't see how Kronos could just march into Manhattan, but the Mist is strong. Typhon is trampling across the country right now, and mortals think he's a storm system."

"Ms. Jackson," Nico said, "Percy needs your blessing. The process *has* to start that way. I wasn't sure until we met Luke's mom, but now I'm positive. This has only been done successfully twice before. Both times, the mother had to give her blessing. She had to be willing to let her son take the risk."

"You want me to bless this?" She shook her head. "It's crazy. Percy, please—"

"Mom, I can't do it without you."

"And if you survive this . . . this *process?*"

"Then I go to war," I said. "Me against Kronos. And only one of us will survive."

I didn't tell her the whole prophecy—about the soul reaping and the end of my days. She didn't need to know that I was probably doomed. I could only hope I'd stop Kronos and save the rest of the world before I died.

"You're my son," she said miserably. "I can't just . . ."

I could tell I'd have to push her harder if I wanted her to agree, but I didn't want to. I remembered poor Ms. Castellan in her kitchen, waiting for her son to come home. And I realized how lucky I was. My mom had always been there for me, always tried to make things normal for me, even with the gods and monsters and stuff. She put up with me going off on adventures, but now I was asking her blessing to do something that would probably get me killed.

I locked eyes with Paul, and some kind of understanding passed between us.

"Sally." He put his hand over my mother's hands. "I can't claim to know what you and Percy have been going through all these years. But it sounds to me . . . it sounds like Percy is doing something noble. I wish I had that much courage."

I got a lump in my throat. I didn't get compliments like that too much.

My mom stared at her lemonade. She looked like she was trying not to cry. I thought about what Hestia had said, about how hard it was to yield, and I figured maybe my mom was finding that out.

"Percy," she said, "I give you my blessing."

I didn't feel any different. No magic glow lit the kitchen or anything.

I glanced at Nico.

He looked more anxious than ever, but he nodded. "It's time."

"Percy," my mom said. "One last thing. If you . . . if you

survive this fight with Kronos, send me a sign." She rummaged through her purse and handed me her cell phone.

"Mom," I said, "you know demigods and phones—"

"I know," she said. "But just in case. If you're not able to call . . . maybe a sign that I could see from anywhere in Manhattan. To let me know you're okay."

"Like Theseus," Paul suggested. "He was supposed to raise white sails when he came home to Athens."

"Except he forgot," Nico muttered. "And his father jumped off the palace roof in despair. But other than that, it was a great idea."

"What about a flag or a flare?" my mom said. "From Olympus—the Empire State Building."

"Something blue," I said.

We'd had a running joke for years about blue food. It was my favorite color, and my mom went out of her way to humor me. Every year my birthday cake, my Easter basket, my Christmas candy canes always had to be blue.

"Yes," my mom agreed. "I'll watch for a blue signal. And I'll try to avoid jumping off palace roofs."

She gave me one last hug. I tried not to feel like I was saying good-bye. I shook hands with Paul. Then Nico and I walked to the kitchen doorway and looked at Mrs. O'Leary.

"Sorry, girl," I said. "Shadow travel time again."

She whimpered and crossed her paws over her snout.

"Where now?" I asked Nico. "Los Angeles?"

"No need," he said. "There's a closer entrance to the Underworld."

SEVEN

MY MATH TEACHER
GIVES ME A LIFT

We emerged in Central Park just north of the Pond. Mrs. O'Leary looked pretty tired as she limped over to a cluster of boulders. She started sniffing around, and I was afraid she might mark her territory, but Nico said, "It's okay. She just smells the way home."

I frowned. "Through the rocks?"

"The Underworld has two major entrances," Nico said. "You know the one in L.A."

"Charon's ferry."

Nico nodded. "Most souls go that way, but there's a smaller path, harder to find. The Door of Orpheus."

"The dude with the harp."

"Dude with the lyre," Nico corrected. "But yeah, him. He used his music to charm the earth and open a new path into the Underworld. He sang his way right into Hades's palace and almost got away with his wife's soul."

I remembered the story. Orpheus wasn't supposed to look behind him when he was leading his wife back to the world, but of course he did. It was one of those typical "and-so-they-died/the-end" stories that always made us demigods feel warm and fuzzy.

"So this is the Door of Orpheus." I tried to be impressed, but it still looked like a pile of rocks to me. "How does it open?"

"We need music," Nico said. "How's your singing?"

"Um, no. Can't you just, like, tell it to open? You're the son of Hades and all."

"It's not so easy. We need music."

I was pretty sure if I tried to sing, all I would cause was an avalanche.

"I have a better idea." I turned and called, "GROVER!"

We waited for a long time. Mrs. O'Leary curled up and took a nap. I could hear the crickets in the woods and an owl hooting. Traffic hummed along Central Park West. Horse hooves clopped down a nearby path, maybe a mounted police patrol. I was sure they'd love to find two kids hanging out in the park at one in the morning.

"It's no good," Nico said at last.

But I had a feeling. My empathy link was really tingling for the first time in months, which either meant a whole lot of people had suddenly switched on the Nature Channel, or Grover was close.

I shut my eyes and concentrated. *Grover.*

I knew he was somewhere in the park. Why couldn't I sense his emotions? All I got was a faint hum in the base of my skull.

Grover, I thought more insistently.

Hmm-hmmmm, something said.

An image came into my head. I saw a giant elm tree deep

in the woods, well off the main paths. Gnarled roots laced the ground, making a kind of bed. Lying in it with his arms crossed and his eyes closed was a satyr. At first I couldn't be sure it was Grover. He was covered in twigs and leaves, like he'd been sleeping there a long time. The roots seemed to be shaping themselves around him, slowly pulling him into the earth.

Grover, I said. *Wake up.*

Unnnh—zzzzz.

Dude, you're covered in dirt. Wake up!

Sleepy, his mind murmured.

FOOD, I suggested. *PANCAKES!*

His eyes shot open. A blur of thoughts filled my head like he was suddenly on fast-forward. The image shattered, and I almost fell over.

"What happened?" Nico asked.

"I got through. He's . . . yeah. He's on his way."

A minute later, the tree next to us shivered. Grover fell out of the branches, right on his head.

"Grover!" I yelled.

"Woof!" Mrs. O'Leary looked up, probably wondering if we were going to play fetch with the satyr.

"Blah-haa-haa!" Grover bleated.

"You okay, man?"

"Oh, I'm fine." He rubbed his head. His horns had grown so much they poked an inch above his curly hair. "I was at the other end of the park. The dryads had this great idea of passing me through the trees to get me here. They don't understand *height* very well."

He grinned and got to his feet—well, his *hooves*, actually. Since last summer, Grover had stopped trying to disguise himself as human. He never wore a cap or fake feet anymore. He didn't even wear jeans, since he had furry goat legs from the waist down. His T-shirt had a picture from that book *Where the Wild Things Are*. It was covered with dirt and tree sap. His goatee looked fuller, almost manly (or goatly?), and he was as tall as me now.

"Good to see you, G-man," I said. "You remember Nico."

Grover nodded at Nico, then he gave me a big hug. He smelled like fresh-mown lawns.

"Perrrrcy!" he bleated. "I missed you! I miss camp. They don't serve very good enchiladas in the wilderness."

"I was worried," I said. "Where've you been the last two months?"

"The last two—" Grover's smile faded. "The last *two months*? What are you talking about?"

"We haven't heard from you," I said. "Juniper's worried. We sent Iris-messages, but—"

"Hold on." He looked up at the stars like he was trying to calculate his position. "What month is this?"

"August."

The color drained from his face. "That's impossible. It's June. I just lay down to take a nap and . . ." He grabbed my arms. "I remember now! He knocked me out. Percy, we have to stop him!"

"Whoa," I said. "Slow down. Tell me what happened."

He took a deep breath. "I was . . . I was walking in the

woods up by Harlem Meer. And I felt this tremble in the ground, like something powerful was near."

"You can sense stuff like that?" Nico asked.

Grover nodded. "Since Pan's death, I can feel when something is wrong in nature. It's like my ears and eyes are sharper when I'm in the Wild. Anyway, I started following the scent. This man in a long black coat was walking through the park, and I noticed he didn't cast a shadow. Middle of a sunny day, and he cast no shadow. He kind of shimmered as he moved."

"Like a mirage?" Nico asked.

"Yes," Grover said. "And whenever he passed humans—"

"The humans would pass out," Nico said. "Curl up and go to sleep."

"That's right! Then after he was gone, they'd get up and go about their business like nothing happened."

I stared at Nico. "You know this guy in black?"

"Afraid so," Nico said. "Grover, what happened?"

"I followed the guy. He kept looking up at the buildings around the park like he was making estimates or something. This lady jogger ran by, and she curled up on the sidewalk and started snoring. The guy in black put his hand on her forehead like he was checking her temperature. Then he kept walking. By this time, I knew he was a monster or something even worse. I followed him into this grove, to the base of a big elm tree. I was about to summon some dryads to help me capture him when he turned and . . ."

Grover swallowed. "Percy, his face. I couldn't make out his face because it kept shifting. Just looking at him made me sleepy. I said, 'What are you doing?' He said, 'Just having a look around. You should always scout a battlefield before the battle.' I said something really smart like, 'This forest is under my protection. You won't start any battles here!' And he laughed. He said, 'You're lucky I'm saving my energy for the main event, little satyr. I'll just grant you a short nap. Pleasant dreams.' And that's the last thing I remember."

Nico exhaled. "Grover, you met Morpheus, the God of Dreams. You're lucky you *ever* woke up."

"Two months," Grover moaned. "He put me to sleep for two months!"

I tried to wrap my mind around what this meant. Now it made sense why we hadn't been able to contact Grover all this time.

"Why didn't the nymphs try to wake you?" I asked.

Grover shrugged. "Most nymphs aren't good with time. Two months for a tree—that's nothing. They probably didn't think anything was wrong."

"We've got to figure out what Morpheus was doing in the park," I said. "I don't like this 'main event' thing he mentioned."

"He's working for Kronos," Nico said. "We know that already. A lot of the minor gods are. This just proves there's going to be an invasion. Percy, we have to get on with our plan."

"Wait," Grover said. "What plan?"

We told him, and Grover started tugging at his leg fur. "You're not serious," he said. "Not the Underworld again."

"I'm not asking you to come, man," I promised. "I know you just woke up. But we need some music to open the door. Can you do it?"

Grover took out his reed pipes. "I guess I could try. I know a few Nirvana tunes that can split rocks. But, Percy, are you sure you want to do this?"

"Please, man," I said. "It would mean a lot. For old times' sake?"

He whimpered. "As I recall, in the old times we almost died a lot. But okay, here goes nothing."

He put his pipes to his lips and played a shrill, lively tune. The boulders trembled. A few more stanzas, and they cracked open, revealing a triangular crevice.

I peered inside. Steps led down into the darkness. The air smelled of mildew and death. It brought back bad memories of my trip through the Labyrinth last year, but this tunnel felt even more dangerous. It led straight to the land of Hades, and that was almost always a one-way trip.

I turned to Grover. "Thanks . . . I think."

"Perrrrcy, is Kronos really going to invade?"

"I wish I could tell you better, but yeah. He will."

I thought Grover might chew up his reed pipes in anxiety, but he straightened up and brushed off his T-shirt. I couldn't help thinking how different he looked from fat old Leneus. "I've got to rally the nature spirits, then. Maybe we can help. I'll see if we can find this Morpheus!"

"Better tell Juniper you're okay, too."

His eyes widened. "Juniper! Oh, she's going to kill me!"

He started to run off, then scrambled back and gave me

another hug. "Be careful down there! Come back alive!"

Once he was gone, Nico and I roused Mrs. O'Leary from her nap.

When she smelled the tunnel, she got excited and led the way down the steps. It was a pretty tight fit. I hoped she wouldn't get stuck. I couldn't imagine how much Drano we'd need to un-stick a hellhound wedged halfway down a tunnel to the Underworld.

"Ready?" Nico asked me. "It'll be fine. Don't worry."

He sounded like he was trying to convince himself.

I glanced up at the stars, wondering if I would ever see them again. Then we plunged into darkness.

The stairs went on forever—narrow, steep, and slippery. It was completely dark except for the light of my sword. I tried to go slow, but Mrs. O'Leary had other ideas. She bounded ahead, barking happily. The sound echoed through the tunnel like cannon shots, and I figured we would not be catching anybody by surprise once we reached the bottom.

Nico lagged behind, which I thought was strange.

"You okay?" I asked him.

"Fine." What was that expression on his face . . . doubt? "Just keep moving," he said.

I didn't have much choice. I followed Mrs. O'Leary into the depths. After another hour, I started to hear the roar of a river.

We emerged at the base of a cliff, on a plain of black volcanic sand. To our right, the River Styx gushed from the rocks and roared off in a cascade of rapids. To our left, far away in the gloom, fires burned on the ramparts of Erebos, the great black walls of Hades's kingdom.

I shuddered. I'd first been here when I was twelve, and only Annabeth and Grover's company had given me the courage to keep going. Nico wasn't going to be quite as helpful with the "courage" thing. He looked pale and worried himself.

Only Mrs. O'Leary acted happy. She ran along the beach, picked up a random human leg bone, and romped back toward me. She dropped the bone at my feet and waited for me to throw it.

"Um, maybe later, girl." I stared at the dark waters, trying to get up my nerve. "So, Nico . . . how do we do this?"

"We have to go inside the gates first," he said.

"But the river's right here."

"I have to get something," he said. "It's the only way."

He marched off without waiting.

I frowned. Nico hadn't mentioned anything about going inside the gates. But now that we were here, I didn't know what else to do. Reluctantly, I followed him down the beach toward the big black gates.

Lines of the dead stood outside waiting to get in. It must've been a heavy day for funerals, because even the EZ-DEATH line was backed up.

"Woof!" Mrs. O'Leary said. Before I could stop her she bounded toward the security checkpoint. Cerberus, the guard dog of Hades, appeared out of the gloom—a three-headed rottweiler so big he made Mrs. O'Leary look like a toy poodle. Cerberus was half transparent, so he's really

hard to see until he's close enough to kill you, but he acted like he didn't care about us. He was too busy saying hello to Mrs. O'Leary.

"Mrs. O'Leary, no!" I shouted at her. "Don't sniff . . . Oh, man."

Nico smiled. Then he looked at me and his expression turned all serious again, like he'd remembered something unpleasant. "Come on. They won't give us any trouble in the line. You're with me."

I didn't like it, but we slipped through the security ghouls and into the Fields of Asphodel. I had to whistle for Mrs. O'Leary three times before she left Cerberus alone and ran after us.

We hiked over black fields of grass dotted with black poplar trees. If I really died in a few days like the prophecy said, I might end up here forever, but I tried not to think about that.

Nico trudged ahead, bringing us closer and closer to the palace of Hades.

"Hey," I said, "we're inside the gates already. Where are we—"

Mrs. O'Leary growled. A shadow appeared overhead— something dark, cold, and stinking of death. It swooped down and landed in the top of a poplar tree.

Unfortunately, I recognized her. She had a shriveled face, a horrible blue knit hat, and a crumpled velvet dress. Leathery bat wings sprang from her back. Her feet had sharp talons, and in her brass-clawed hands she held a flaming whip and a paisley handbag.

"Mrs. Dodds," I said.

She bared her fangs. "Welcome back, honey."

Her two sisters—the other Furies—swooped down and settled next to her in the branches of the poplar.

"You know Alecto?" Nico asked me.

"If you mean the hag in the middle, yeah," I said. "She was my math teacher."

Nico nodded, like this didn't surprise him. He looked up at the Furies and took a deep breath. "I've done what my father asked. Take us to the palace."

I tensed. "Wait a second, Nico. What do you—"

"I'm afraid this is my new lead, Percy. My father promised me information about my family, but he wants to see you before we try the river. I'm sorry."

"You *tricked* me?" I was so mad I couldn't think. I lunged at him, but the Furies were fast. Two of them swooped down and plucked me up by the arms. My sword fell out of my hand, and before I knew it, I was dangling sixty feet in the air.

"Oh, don't struggle, honey," my old math teacher cackled in my ear. "I'd hate to drop you."

Mrs. O'Leary barked angrily and jumped, trying to reach me, but we were too high.

"Tell Mrs. O'Leary to behave," Nico warned. He was hovering near me in the clutches of the third Fury. "I don't want her to get hurt, Percy. My father is waiting. He just wants to talk."

I wanted to tell Mrs. O'Leary to attack Nico, but it wouldn't have done any good, and Nico was right about one thing: my dog could get hurt if she tried to pick a fight with the Furies.

I gritted my teeth. "Mrs. O'Leary, down! It's okay, girl."

She whimpered and turned in circles, looking up at me.

"All right, traitor," I growled at Nico. "You've got your prize. Take me to the stupid palace."

Alecto dropped me like a sack of turnips in the middle of the palace garden.

It was beautiful in a creepy way. Skeletal white trees grew from marble basins. Flower beds overflowed with golden plants and gemstones. A pair of thrones, one bone and one silver, sat on the balcony with a view of the Fields of Asphodel. It would've been a nice place to spend a Saturday morning except for the sulfurous smell and the cries of tortured souls in the distance.

Skeletal warriors guarded the only exit. They wore tattered U.S. Army desert combat fatigues and carried M16s.

The third Fury deposited Nico next to me. Then all three of them settled on the top of the skeletal throne. I resisted the urge to strangle Nico. They'd only stop me. I'd have to wait for my revenge.

I stared at the empty thrones, waiting for something to happen. Then the air shimmered. Three figures appeared—Hades and Persephone on their thrones, and an older woman standing between them. They seemed to be in the middle of an argument.

"—told you he was a bum!" the older woman said.

"Mother!" Persephone replied.

"We have visitors!" Hades barked. "Please!"

Hades, one of my least favorite gods, smoothed his black robes, which were covered with the terrified faces of the damned. He had pale skin and the intense eyes of a madman.

"Percy Jackson," he said with satisfaction. "At last."

Queen Persephone studied me curiously. I'd seen her once before in the winter, but now in the summer she looked like a totally different goddess. She had lustrous black hair and warm brown eyes. Her dress shimmered with colors. Flower patterns in the fabric changed and bloomed—roses, tulips, honeysuckle.

The woman standing between them was obviously Persephone's mother. She had the same hair and eyes, but looked older and sterner. Her dress was golden, the color of a wheat field. Her hair was woven with dried grasses so it reminded me of a wicker basket. I figured if somebody lit a match next to her, she'd be in serious trouble.

"Hmmph," the older woman said. "Demigods. Just what we need."

Next to me, Nico knelt. I wished I had my sword so I could cut his stupid head off. Unfortunately, Riptide was still out in the fields somewhere.

"Father," Nico said. "I have done as you asked."

"Took you long enough," Hades grumbled. "Your sister would've done a better job."

Nico lowered his head. If I hadn't been so mad at the little creep, I might've felt sorry for him.

I glared up at the god of the dead. "What do you want, Hades?"

"To talk, of course." The god twisted his mouth in a cruel smile. "Didn't Nico tell you?"

"So this whole quest was a lie. Nico brought me down here to get me killed."

"Oh, no," Hades said. "I'm afraid Nico was quite sincere about wanting to help you. The boy is as honest as he is dense. I simply convinced him to take a small detour and bring you here first."

"Father," Nico said, "you promised that Percy would not be harmed. You said if I brought him, you would tell me about my past—about my mother."

Queen Persephone sighed dramatically. "Can we *please* not talk about *that woman* in my presence?"

"I'm sorry, my dove," Hades said. "I had to promise the boy something."

The older lady harrumphed. "I warned you, daughter. This scoundrel Hades is no good. You could've married the god of doctors or the god of lawyers, but *noooo*. You had to eat the pomegranate."

"Mother—"

"And get stuck in the Underworld!"

"Mother, please—"

"And here it is August, and do you come home like you're supposed to? Do you ever think about your poor lonely mother?"

"DEMETER!" Hades shouted. "That is enough. You are a guest in my house."

"Oh, a house is it?" she said. "You call this dump a house? Make my daughter live in this dark, damp—"

"I told you," Hades said, grinding his teeth, "there's a *war* in the world above. You and Persephone are better off here with me."

"Excuse me," I broke in. "But if you're going to kill me, could you just get on with it?"

All three gods looked at me.

"Well, this one has an attitude," Demeter observed.

"Indeed," Hades agreed. "I'd love to kill him."

"Father!" Nico said. "You promised!"

"Husband, we talked about this," Persephone chided. "You can't go around incinerating every hero. Besides, he's brave. I like that."

Hades rolled his eyes. "You liked that Orpheus fellow too. Look how well that turned out. Let me kill him, just a little bit."

"Father, you promised!" Nico said. "You said you only wanted to talk to him. You said if I brought him, you'd explain."

Hades glowered, smoothing the folds of his robes. "And so I shall. Your mother—what can I tell you? She was a wonderful woman." He glanced uncomfortably at Persephone. "Forgive me, my dear. I mean for a mortal, of course. Her name was Maria di Angelo. She was from Venice, but her father was a diplomat in Washington, D.C. That's where I met her. When you and your sister were young, it was a bad time to be children of Hades. World War II was brewing. A few of my, ah, *other* children were leading the losing side. I thought it best to put you two out of harm's way."

"That's why you hid us in the Lotus Casino?"

Hades shrugged. "You didn't age. You didn't realize time was passing. I waited for the right time to bring you out."

"But what happened to our mother? Why don't I remember her?"

"Not important," Hades snapped.

"*What?* Of course it's important. And you had other children—why were we the only ones who were sent away? And who was the lawyer who got us out?"

Hades grit his teeth. "You would do well to listen more and talk less, boy. As for the lawyer . . ."

Hades snapped his fingers. On top of his throne, the Fury Alecto began to change until she was a middle-aged man in a pinstriped suit with a briefcase. She—he—looked strange crouching at Hades's shoulder.

"You!" Nico said.

The Fury cackled. "I do lawyers and teachers very well!"

Nico was trembling. "But why did you free us from the casino?"

"You know why," Hades said. "This idiot son of Poseidon cannot be allowed to be the child of the prophecy."

I plucked a ruby off the nearest plant and threw it at Hades. It sank harmlessly into his robe. "You should be helping Olympus!" I said. "All the other gods are fighting Typhon, and you're just sitting here—"

"Waiting things out," Hades finished. "Yes, that's

correct. When's the last time Olympus ever helped me, half-blood? When's the last time a child of *mine* was ever welcomed as a hero? Bah! Why should I rush out and help them? I'll stay here with my forces intact."

"And when Kronos comes after you?"

"Let him try. He'll be weakened. And my son here, Nico—" Hades looked at him with distaste. "Well, he's not much now, I'll grant you. It would've been better if Bianca had lived. But give him four more years of training. We can hold out that long, surely. Nico will turn sixteen, as the prophecy says, and then *he* will make the decision that will save the world. And I will be king of the gods."

"You're crazy," I said. "Kronos will crush you, right after he finishes pulverizing Olympus."

Hades spread his hands. "Well, you'll get a chance to find out, half-blood. Because you'll be waiting out this war in my dungeons."

"No!" Nico said. "Father, that wasn't our agreement. And you haven't told me everything!"

"I've told you all you need to know," Hades said. "As for our agreement, I spoke with Jackson. I did not harm him. You got your information. If you had wanted a better deal, you should've made me swear on the Styx. Now, go to your room!" He waved his hand, and Nico vanished.

"That boy needs to eat more," Demeter grumbled. "He's too skinny. He needs more cereal."

Persephone rolled her eyes. "Mother, enough with the cereal. My lord Hades, are you sure we can't let this little hero go? He's awfully brave."

"No, my dear. I've spared his life. That's enough."

I was sure she was going to stand up for me. The brave, beautiful Persephone was going to get me out of this.

She shrugged indifferently. "Fine. What's for breakfast? I'm starving."

"Cereal," Demeter said.

"Mother!" The two women disappeared in a swirl of flowers and wheat.

"Don't feel too bad, Percy Jackson," Hades said. "My ghosts keep me well informed of Kronos's plans. I can assure you that you had no chance to stop him in time. By tonight, it will be too late for your precious Mount Olympus. The trap will be sprung."

"What trap?" I demanded. "If you know about it, do something! At least let me tell the other gods!"

Hades smiled. "You are spirited. I'll give you credit for that. Have fun in my dungeon. We'll check on you again in—oh, fifty or sixty years."

EIGHT

I TAKE THE WORST
BATH EVER

My sword reappeared in my pocket.

Yeah, great timing. Now I could attack the walls all I wanted. My cell had no bars, no windows, not even a door. The skeletal guards shoved me straight through a wall, and it became solid behind me. I wasn't sure if the room was airtight. Probably. Hades's dungeon was meant for dead people, and they don't breathe. So forget fifty or sixty years. I'd be dead in fifty or sixty minutes. Meanwhile, if Hades wasn't lying, some big trap was going to be sprung in New York by the end of the day, and there was absolutely nothing I could do about it.

I sat on the cold stone floor, feeling miserable.

I don't remember dozing off. Then again, it must've been about seven in the morning, mortal time, and I'd been through a lot.

I dreamed I was on the porch of Rachel's beach house in St. Thomas. The sun was rising over the Caribbean. Dozens of wooded islands dotted the sea, and white sails cut across the water. The smell of salt air made me wonder if I would ever see the ocean again.

Rachel's parents sat at the patio table while a personal

chef fixed them omelets. Mr. Dare was dressed in a white linen suit. He was reading *The Wall Street Journal*. The lady across the table was probably Mrs. Dare, though all I could see of her were hot pink fingernails and the cover of *Condé Nast Traveler*. Why she'd be reading about vacations while she was on vacation, I wasn't sure.

Rachel stood at the porch railing and sighed. She wore Bermuda shorts and her van Gogh T-shirt. (Yeah, Rachel was trying to teach me about art, but don't get too impressed. I only remembered the dude's name because he cut his ear off.)

I wondered if she was thinking about me, and how much it sucked that I wasn't with them on vacation. I know that's what *I* was thinking.

Then the scene changed. I was in St. Louis, standing downtown under the Arch. I'd been there before. In fact, I'd almost fallen to my death there before.

Over the city, a thunderstorm boiled—a wall of absolute black with lightning streaking across the sky. A few blocks away, swarms of emergency vehicles gathered with their lights flashing. A column of dust rose from a mound of rubble, which I realized was a collapsed skyscraper.

A nearby reporter was yelling into her microphone: "Officials are describing this as a structural failure, Dan, though no one seems to know if it is related to the storm conditions."

Wind whipped her hair. The temperature was dropping rapidly, like ten degrees just since I'd been standing there.

"Thankfully, the building had been abandoned for

demolition," she said. "But police have evacuated all nearby buildings for fear the collapse might trigger—"

She faltered as a mighty groan cut through the sky. A blast of lightning hit the center of the darkness. The entire city shook. The air glowed, and every hair on my body stood up. The blast was so powerful I knew it could only be one thing: Zeus's master bolt. It should have vaporized its target, but the dark cloud only staggered backward. A smoky fist appeared out of the clouds. It smashed another tower, and the whole thing collapsed like children's blocks.

The reporter screamed. People ran through the streets. Emergency lights flashed. I saw a streak of silver in the sky—a chariot pulled by reindeer, but it wasn't Santa Claus driving. It was Artemis, riding the storm, shooting shafts of moonlight into the darkness. A fiery golden comet crossed her path . . . maybe her brother Apollo.

One thing was clear: Typhon had made it to the Mississippi River. He was halfway across the U.S., leaving destruction in his wake, and the gods were barely slowing him down.

The mountain of darkness loomed above me. A foot the size of Yankee Stadium was about to smash me when a voice hissed, *"Percy!"*

I lunged out blindly. Before I was fully awake, I had Nico pinned to the floor of the cell with the edge of my sword at his throat.

"Want . . . to . . . rescue," he choked.

Anger woke me up fast. "Oh, yeah? And why should I trust you?"

"No . . . choice?" he gagged.

I wished he hadn't said something logical like that. I let him go.

Nico curled into a ball and made retching sounds while his throat recovered. Finally he got to his feet, eyeing my sword warily. His own blade was sheathed. I suppose if he'd wanted to kill me, he could've done it while I slept. Still, I didn't trust him.

"We have to get out of here," he said.

"Why?" I said. "Does your dad want to *talk* to me again?"

He winced. "Percy, I swear on the River Styx, I didn't know what he was planning."

"You know what your dad is like!"

"He tricked me. He promised—" Nico held up his hands. "Look . . . right now, we need to leave. I put the guards to sleep, but it won't last."

I wanted to strangle him again. Unfortunately, he was right. We didn't have time to argue, and I couldn't escape on my own. He pointed at the wall. A whole section vanished, revealing a corridor.

"Come on." Nico led the way.

I wished I had Annabeth's invisibility hat, but as it turned out, I didn't need it. Every time we came to a skeleton guard, Nico just pointed at it, and its glowing eyes dimmed. Unfortunately, the more Nico did it, the more tired he seemed. We walked through a maze of corridors filled with guards. By the time we reached a kitchen staffed by skeletal cooks and servants, I was practically carrying

Nico. He managed to put all the dead to sleep but nearly passed out himself. I dragged him out of the servants' entrance and into the Fields of Asphodel.

I almost felt relieved until I heard the sound of bronze gongs high in the castle.

"Alarms," Nico murmured sleepily.

"What do we do?"

He yawned then frowned like he was trying to remember. "How about . . . run?"

Running with a drowsy child of Hades was more like doing a three-legged race with a life-size rag doll. I lugged him along, holding my sword in front of me. The spirits of the dead made way like the Celestial bronze was a blazing fire.

The sound of gongs rolled across the fields. Ahead loomed the walls of Erebos, but the longer we walked, the farther away they seemed. I was about to collapse from exhaustion when I heard a familiar *"WOOOOOF!"*

Mrs. O'Leary bounded out of nowhere and ran circles around us, ready to play.

"Good girl!" I said. "Can you give us a ride to the Styx?"

The word *Styx* got her excited. She probably thought I meant *sticks*. She jumped a few times, chased her tail just to teach it who was boss, and then calmed down enough for me to push Nico onto her back. I climb aboard, and she raced toward the gates. She leaped straight over the EZ-DEATH line, sending guards sprawling and causing more alarms to blare. Cerberus barked, but he sounded more excited than angry, like: *Can I play too?*

Fortunately, he didn't follow us, and Mrs. O'Leary kept running. She didn't stop until we were far upriver and the fires of Erebos had disappeared in the murk.

Nico slid off Mrs. O'Leary's back and crumpled in a heap on the black sand.

I took out a square of ambrosia—part of the emergency god-food I always kept with me. It was a little bashed up, but Nico chewed it.

"Uh," he mumbled. "Better."

"Your powers drain you too much," I noted.

He nodded sleepily. "With great power . . . comes great need to take a nap. Wake me up later."

"Whoa, zombie dude." I caught him before he could pass out again. "We're at the river. You need to tell me what to do."

I fed him the last of my ambrosia, which was a little dangerous. The stuff can heal demigods, but it can also burn us to ashes if we eat too much. Fortunately, it seemed to do the trick. Nico shook his head a few times and struggled to his feet.

"My father will be coming soon," he said. "We should hurry."

The River Styx's current swirled with strange objects—broken toys, ripped-up college diplomas, wilted homecoming corsages—all the dreams people had thrown away as they'd passed from life into death. Looking at the black water, I could think of about three million places I'd rather swim.

"So . . . I just jump in?"

"You have to prepare yourself first," Nico said, "or the river will destroy you. It will burn away your body and soul."

"Sounds fun," I muttered.

"This is no joke," Nico warned. "There is only one way to stay anchored to your mortal life. You have to . . ."

He glanced behind me and his eyes widened. I turned and found myself face-to-face with a Greek warrior.

For a second I thought he was Ares, because this guy looked exactly like the god of war—tall and buff, with a cruel scarred face and closely shaved black hair. He wore a white tunic and bronze armor. He held a plumed war helm under his arm. But his eyes were human—pale green like a shallow sea—and a bloody arrow stuck out of his left calf, just above the ankle.

I stunk at Greek names, but even I knew the greatest warrior of all time, who had died from a wounded heel.

"Achilles," I said.

The ghost nodded. "I warned the other one not to follow my path. Now I will warn you."

"Luke? You spoke with Luke?"

"Do not do this," he said. "It will make you powerful. But it will also make you weak. Your prowess in combat will be beyond any mortal's, but your weaknesses, your failings will increase as well."

"You mean I'll have a bad heel?" I said. "Couldn't I just, like, wear something besides sandals? No offense."

He stared down at his bloody foot. "The heel is only

my *physical* weakness, demigod. My mother, Thetis, held me there when she dipped me in the Styx. What really killed me was my own arrogance. Beware! Turn back!"

He meant it. I could hear the regret and bitterness in his voice. He was honestly trying to save me from a terrible fate.

Then again, Luke had been here, and he hadn't turned back.

That's why Luke had been able to host the spirit of Kronos without his body disintegrating. This is how he'd prepared himself, and why he seemed impossible to kill. He had bathed in the River Styx and taken on the powers of the greatest mortal hero, Achilles. He was invincible.

"I have to," I said. "Otherwise I don't stand a chance."

Achilles lowered his head. "Let the gods witness I tried. Hero, if you must do this, concentrate on your mortal point. Imagine one spot of your body that will remain vulnerable. This is the point where your soul will anchor your body to the world. It will be your greatest weakness, but also your only hope. No man may be completely invulnerable. Lose sight of what keeps you mortal, and the River Styx will burn you to ashes. You will cease to exist."

"I don't suppose you could tell me Luke's mortal point?"

He scowled. "Prepare yourself, foolish boy. Whether you survive this or not, you have sealed your doom!"

With that happy thought, he vanished.

"Percy," Nico said, "maybe he's right."

"This was *your* idea."

"I know, but now that we're here—"

"Just wait on the shore. If anything happens to me . . . Well, maybe Hades will get his wish, and you'll be the child of the prophecy after all."

He didn't look pleased about that, but I didn't care.

Before I could change my mind, I concentrated on the small of my back—a tiny point just opposite my navel. It was well defended when I wore my armor. It would be hard to hit by accident, and few enemies would aim for it on purpose. No place was perfect, but this seemed right to me, and a lot more dignified than, like, my armpit or something.

I pictured a string, a bungee cord connecting me to the world from the small of my back. And I stepped into the river.

Imagine jumping into a pit of boiling acid. Now multiply that pain times fifty. You still won't be close to understanding what it felt like to swim in the Styx. I planned to walk in slow and courageous like a real hero. As soon as the water touched my legs, my muscles turned to jelly and I fell face-first into the current.

I submerged completely. For the first time in my life, I couldn't breathe underwater. I finally understood the panic of drowning. Every nerve in my body burned. I was dissolving in the water. I saw faces—Rachel, Grover, Tyson, my mother—but they faded as soon as they appeared.

"Percy," my mom said. "I give you my blessing."

"Be safe, brother!" Tyson pleaded.

"Enchiladas!" Grover said. I wasn't sure where that came from, but it didn't seem to help much.

I was losing the fight. The pain was too much. My hands and feet were melting into the water, my soul was being ripped from my body. I couldn't remember who I was. The pain of Kronos's scythe had been nothing compared to this.

The cord, a familiar voice said. *Remember your lifeline, dummy!*

Suddenly there was a tug in my lower back. The current pulled at me, but it wasn't carrying me away anymore. I imagined the string in my back keeping me tied to the shore.

"Hold on, Seaweed Brain." It was Annabeth's voice, much clearer now. "You're not getting away from me that easily."

The cord strengthened.

I could see Annabeth now—standing barefoot above me on the canoe lake pier. I'd fallen out of my canoe. That was it. She was reaching out her hand to haul me up, and she was trying not to laugh. She wore her orange camp T-shirt and jeans. Her hair was tucked up in her Yankees cap, which was strange because that should have made her invisible.

"You are such an idiot sometimes." She smiled. "Come on. Take my hand."

Memories came flooding back to me—sharper and more colorful. I stopped dissolving. My name was Percy Jackson. I reached up and took Annabeth's hand.

Suddenly I burst out of the river. I collapsed on the sand, and Nico scrambled back in surprise.

"Are you okay?" he stammered. "Your skin. Oh, gods. You're hurt!"

My arms were bright red. I felt like every inch of my body had been broiled over a slow flame.

I looked around for Annabeth, though I knew she wasn't here. It had seemed so real.

"I'm fine . . . I think." The color of my skin turned back to normal. The pain subsided. Mrs. O'Leary came up and sniffed me with concern. Apparently I smelled really interesting.

"Do you feel stronger?" Nico asked.

Before I could decide *what* I felt, a voice boomed, "THERE!"

An army of the dead marched toward us. A hundred skeletal Roman legionnaires led the way with shields and spears. Behind them came an equal number of British redcoats with bayonets fixed. In the middle of the host, Hades himself rode a black-and-gold chariot pulled by nightmare horses, their eyes and manes smoldering with fire.

"You will not escape me this time, Percy Jackson!" Hades bellowed. "Destroy him!"

"Father, no!" Nico shouted, but it was too late. The front line of Roman zombies lowered their spears and advanced.

Mrs. O'Leary growled and got ready to pounce. Maybe that's what set me off. I didn't want them hurting my dog. Plus, I was tired of Hades being a big bully. If I was going to die, I might as well go down fighting.

I yelled, and the River Styx exploded. A black tidal wave smashed into the legionnaires. Spears and shields flew everywhere. Roman zombies began to dissolve, smoke coming off their bronze helmets.

The redcoats lowered their bayonets, but I didn't wait for them. I charged.

It was stupidest thing I've ever done. A hundred muskets fired at me, point blank. All of them missed. I crashed into their line and started hacking with Riptide. Bayonets jabbed. Swords slashed. Guns reloaded and fired. Nothing touched me.

I whirled through the ranks, slashing redcoats to dust, one after the other. My mind went on autopilot: stab, dodge, cut, deflect, roll. Riptide was no longer a sword. It was an arc of pure destruction.

I broke through the enemy line and leaped into the black chariot. Hades raised his staff. A bolt of dark energy shot toward me, but I deflected it off my blade and slammed into him. The god and I both tumbled out of the chariot.

The next thing I knew, my knee was planted on Hades's chest. I was holding the collar of his royal robes in one fist, and the tip of my sword was poised right over his face.

Silence. The army did nothing to defend their master. I glanced back and realized why. There was nothing left of them but weapons in the sand and piles of smoking, empty uniforms. I had destroyed them all.

Hades swallowed. "Now, Jackson, listen here. . . ."

He was immortal. There was no way I could kill him, but gods can be wounded. I knew that firsthand, and I figured a sword in the face wouldn't feel too good.

"Just because I'm a nice person," I snarled, "I'll let you go. But first, tell me about that trap!"

Hades melted into nothing, leaving me holding empty black robes.

I cursed and got to my feet, breathing heavily. Now that the danger was over, I realized how tired I was. Every muscle in my body ached. I looked down at my clothes. They were slashed to pieces and full of bullet holes, but I was fine. Not a mark on me.

Nico's mouth hung open. "You just . . . with a sword . . . you just—"

"I think the river thing worked," I said.

"Oh gee," he said sarcastically. *"You think?"*

Mrs. O'Leary barked happily and wagged her tail. She bounded around, sniffing empty uniforms and hunting for bones. I lifted Hades's robe. I could still see the tormented faces shimmering in the fabric.

I walked to the edge of the river. "Be free."

I dropped the robe in the water and watched as it swirled away, dissolving in the current.

"Go back to your father," I told Nico. "Tell him he owes me for letting him go. Find out what's going to happen to Mount Olympus and convince him to help."

Nico stared at me. "I . . . I can't. He'll hate me now. I mean . . . even more."

"You have to," I said. "You owe me too."

His ears turned red. "Percy, I told you I was sorry. Please . . . let me come with you. I want to fight."

"You'll be more help down here."

"You mean you don't trust me anymore," he said miserably.

I didn't answer. I didn't know what I meant. I was too stunned by what I'd just done in battle to think clearly.

"Just go back to your father," I said, trying not to sound too harsh. "Work on him. You're the only person who might be able to get him to listen."

"That's a depressing thought." Nico sighed. "All right. I'll do my best. Besides, he's still hiding something from me about my mom. Maybe I can find out what."

"Good luck. Now Mrs. O'Leary and I have to go."

"Where?" Nico said.

I looked at the cave entrance and thought about the long climb back to the world of the living. "To get this war started. It's time I found Luke."

NINE

TWO SNAKES SAVE
MY LIFE

I love New York. You can pop out of the Underworld in Central Park, hail a taxi, head down Fifth Avenue with a giant hellhound loping along behind you, and nobody even looks at you funny.

Of course, the Mist helped. People probably couldn't see Mrs. O'Leary, or maybe they thought she was a large, loud, very friendly truck.

I took the risk of using my mom's cell phone to call Annabeth for the second time. I'd called her once from the tunnel but only reached her voice mail. I'd gotten surprisingly good reception, seeing as I was at the mythological center of the world and all, but I didn't want to see what my mom's roaming charges were going to be.

This time, Annabeth picked up.

"Hey," I said. "You get my message?"

"Percy, where have you been? Your message said almost nothing! We've been worried sick!"

"I'll fill you in later," I said, though how I was going to do that I had no idea. "Where are you?"

"We're on our way like you asked, almost to the Queens–Midtown Tunnel. But, Percy, what are you planning?

We've left the camp virtually undefended, and there's no way the gods—"

"Trust me," I said. "I'll see you there."

I hung up. My hands were trembling. I wasn't sure if it was a leftover reaction from my dip in the Styx, or anticipation of what I was about to do. If this didn't work, being invulnerable wasn't going to save me from getting blasted to bits.

It was late afternoon when the taxi dropped me at the Empire State Building. Mrs. O'Leary bounded up and down Fifth Avenue, licking cabs and sniffing hot dog carts. Nobody seemed to notice her, although people did swerve away and look confused when she came close.

I whistled for her to heel as three white vans pulled up to the curb. They said *Delphi Strawberry Service*, which was the cover name for Camp Half-Blood. I'd never seen all three vans in the same place at once, though I knew they shuttled our fresh produce into the city.

The first van was driven by Argus, our many-eyed security chief. The other two were driven by harpies, who are basically demonic human/chicken hybrids with bad attitudes. We used the harpies mostly for cleaning the camp, but they did pretty well in midtown traffic too.

The doors slid open. A bunch of campers climbed out, some of them looking a little green from the long drive. I was glad so many had come: Pollux, Silena Beauregard, the Stoll brothers, Michael Yew, Jake Mason, Katie Gardner, and Annabeth, along with most of their siblings. Chiron came out of the van last. His horse half was compacted into his magic wheelchair, so he used the handicap lift. The Ares cabin wasn't here, but I tried not to get too angry about that. Clarisse was a stubborn idiot. End of story.

I did a head count: forty campers in all.

Not many to fight a war, but it was still the largest group of half-bloods I'd ever seen gathered in one place outside camp. Everyone looked nervous, and I understood why. We were probably sending out so much demigod aura that every monster in the northeastern United States knew we were here.

As I looked at their faces—all these campers I'd known for so many summers—a nagging voice whispered in my mind: *One of them is a spy.*

But I couldn't dwell on that. They were my friends. I needed them.

Then I remembered Kronos's evil smile. *You can't count on friends. They will always let you down.*

Annabeth came up to me. She was dressed in black camouflage with her Celestial bronze knife strapped to her arm and her laptop bag slung over her shoulder—ready for stabbing or surfing the Internet, whichever came first.

She frowned. "What is it?"

"What's what?" I asked.

"You're looking at me funny."

I realized I was thinking about my strange vision of Annabeth pulling me out of the Styx River. "It's, uh, nothing." I turned to the rest of the group. "Thanks for coming, everybody. Chiron, after you."

My old mentor shook his head. "I came to wish you luck, my boy. But I make it a point never to visit Olympus unless I am summoned."

"But you're our leader."

He smiled. "I am your trainer, your teacher. That is not the same as being your leader. I will go gather what allies I can. It may not be too late to convince my brother centaurs to help. Meanwhile, *you* called the campers here, Percy. *You* are the leader."

I wanted to protest, but everybody was looking at me expectantly, even Annabeth.

I took a deep breath. "Okay, like I told Annabeth on the phone, something bad is going to happen by tonight. Some kind of trap. We've got to get an audience with Zeus and convince him to defend the city. Remember, we can't take no for an answer."

I asked Argus to watch Mrs. O'Leary, which neither of them looked happy about.

Chiron shook my hand. "You'll do well, Percy. Just remember your strengths and beware your weaknesses."

It sounded eerily close to what Achilles had told me. Then I remembered Chiron had *taught* Achilles. That didn't exactly reassure me, but I nodded and tried to give him a confident smile.

"Let's go," I told the campers.

A security guard was sitting behind the desk in the lobby, reading a big black book with a flower on the cover. He glanced up when we all filed in with our weapons and armor clanking. "School group? We're about to close up."

"No," I said. "Six-hundredth floor."

He checked us out. His eyes were pale blue and his head was completely bald. I couldn't tell if he was human or not, but he seemed to notice our weapons, so I guess he wasn't fooled by the Mist.

"There is no six-hundredth floor, kid." He said it like it was a required line he didn't believe. "Move along."

I leaned across the desk. "Forty demigods attract an awful lot of monsters. You really want us hanging out in your lobby?"

He thought about that. Then he hit a buzzer and the security gate swung open. "Make it quick."

"You don't want us going through the metal detectors," I added.

"Um, no," he agreed. "Elevator on the right. I guess you know the way."

I tossed him a golden drachma and we marched through.

We decided it would take two trips to get everybody up in the elevator. I went with the first group. Different elevator music was playing since my last visit—that old disco song "Stayin' Alive." A terrifying image flashed through my mind of Apollo in bell-bottom pants and a slinky silk shirt.

I was glad when the elevator doors finally dinged open. In front of us, a path of floating stones led through the clouds up to Mount Olympus, hovering six thousand feet over Manhattan.

I'd seen Olympus several times, but it still took my

breath away. The mansions glittered gold and white against the sides of the mountain. Gardens bloomed on a hundred terraces. Scented smoke rose from braziers that lined the winding streets. And right at the top of the snow-capped crest rose the main palace of the gods. It looked as majestic as ever, but something seemed wrong. Then I realized the mountain was silent—no music, no voices, no laughter.

Annabeth studied me. "You look . . . different," she decided. "Where exactly did you go?"

The elevator doors opened again, and the second group of half-bloods joined us.

"Tell you later," I said. "Come on."

We made our way across the sky bridge into the streets of Olympus. The shops were closed. The parks were empty. A couple of Muses sat on a bench strumming flaming lyres, but their hearts didn't seem to be in it. A lone Cyclops swept the street with an uprooted oak tree. A minor godling spotted us from a balcony and ducked inside, closing his shutters.

We passed under a big marble archway with statues of Zeus and Hera on either side. Annabeth made a face at the queen of the gods.

"Hate her," she muttered.

"Has she been cursing you or something?" I asked. Last year Annabeth had gotten on Hera's bad side, but Annabeth hadn't really talked about it since.

"Just little stuff so far," she said. "Her sacred animal is the cow, right?"

"Right."

"So she sends cows after me."

I tried not to smile. "Cows? In San Francisco?"

"Oh, yeah. Usually I don't see them, but the cows leave me little presents all over the place—in our backyard, on the sidewalk, in the school hallways. I have to be careful where I step."

"Look!" Pollux cried, pointing toward the horizon. "What is *that*?"

We all froze. Blue lights were streaking across the evening sky toward Olympus like tiny comets. They seemed to be coming from all over the city, heading straight toward the mountain. As they got close, they fizzled out. We watched them for several minutes and they didn't seem to do any damage, but still it was strange.

"Like infrared scopes," Michael Yew muttered. "We're being targeted."

"Let's get to the palace," I said.

No one was guarding the hall of the gods. The gold-and-silver doors stood wide open. Our footsteps echoed as we walked into the throne room.

Of course, "room" doesn't really cover it. The place was the size of Madison Square Garden. High above, the blue ceiling glittered with constellations. Twelve giant empty thrones stood in a U around a hearth. In one corner, a house-size globe of water hovered in the air, and inside swam my old friend the Ophiotaurus, half-cow, half-serpent.

"*Moooo!*" he said happily, turning in a circle.

Despite all the serious stuff going on, I had to smile.

Two years ago we'd spent a lot of time trying to save the Ophiotaurus from the Titans, and I'd gotten kind of fond of him. He seemed to like me too, even though I'd originally thought he was a girl and named him Bessie.

"Hey, man," I said. "They treating you okay?"

"*Mooo,*" Bessie answered.

We walked toward the thrones, and a woman's voice said, "Hello again, Percy Jackson. You and your friends are welcome."

Hestia stood by the hearth, poking the flames with a stick. She wore the same kind of simple brown dress as she had before, but she was a grown woman now.

I bowed. "Lady Hestia."

My friends followed my example.

Hestia regarded me with her red glowing eyes. "I see you went through with your plan. You bear the curse of Achilles."

The other campers started muttering among themselves: *What did she say? What about Achilles?*

"You must be careful," Hestia warned me. "You gained much on your journey. But you are still blind to the most important truth. Perhaps a glimpse is in order."

Annabeth nudged me. "Um . . . what is she talking about?"

I stared into Hestia's eyes, and an image rushed into my mind: I saw a dark alley between red brick warehouses. A sign above one of the doors read RICHMOND IRONWORKS.

Two half-bloods crouched in the shadows—a boy about fourteen and a girl about twelve. I realized with a start that the boy was Luke. The girl was Thalia, daughter of Zeus. I was seeing a scene from back in the days when they were on the run, before Grover found them.

Luke carried a bronze knife. Thalia had her spear and shield of terror, Aegis. Luke and Thalia both looked hungry and lean, with wild animal eyes, like they were used to being attacked.

"Are you sure?" Thalia asked.

Luke nodded. "Something down here. I sense it."

A rumble echoed from the alley, like someone had banged on a sheet of metal. The half-bloods crept forward.

Old crates were stacked on a loading dock. Thalia and Luke approached with their weapons ready. A curtain of corrugated tin quivered as if something were behind it.

Thalia glanced at Luke. He counted silently: *One, two, three!* He ripped away the tin, and a little girl flew at him with a hammer.

"Whoa!" Luke said.

The girl had tangled blond hair and was wearing flannel pajamas. She couldn't have been more than seven, but she would've brained Luke if he hadn't been so fast.

He grabbed her wrist, and the hammer skittered across the cement.

The little girl fought and kicked. "No more monsters! Go away!"

"It's okay!" Luke struggled to hold her. "Thalia, put your shield up. You're scaring her."

Thalia tapped Aegis, and it shrank into a silver bracelet. "Hey, it's all right," she said. "We're not going to hurt you. I'm Thalia. This is Luke."

"Monsters!"

"No," Luke promised. "But we know all about monsters. We fight them too."

Slowly, the girl stopped kicking. She studied Luke and Thalia with large intelligent gray eyes.

"You're like me?" she said suspiciously.

"Yeah," Luke said. "We're . . . well, it's hard to explain, but we're monster fighters. Where's your family?"

"My family hates me," the girl said. "They don't want me. I ran away."

Thalia and Luke locked eyes. I knew they both related to what she was saying.

"What's your name, kiddo?" Thalia asked.

"Annabeth."

Luke smiled. "Nice name. I tell you what, Annabeth— you're pretty fierce. We could use a fighter like you."

Annabeth's eyes widened. "You could?"

"Oh, yeah." Luke turned his knife and offered her the handle. "How'd you like a real monster-slaying weapon? This is Celestial bronze. Works a lot better than a hammer."

Maybe under most circumstances, offering a seven-year-old kid a knife would not be a good idea, but when you're a half-blood, regular rules kind of go out the window.

Annabeth gripped the hilt.

"Knives are only for the bravest and quickest fighters," Luke explained. "They don't have the reach or power of a sword, but they're easy to conceal and they can find weak spots in your enemy's armor. It takes a clever warrior to use a knife. I have a feeling you're pretty clever."

Annabeth stared at him with adoration. "I am!"

Thalia grinned. "We'd better get going, Annabeth. We have a safe house on the James River. We'll get you some clothes and food."

"You're . . . you're not going to take me back to my family?" she said. "Promise?"

Luke put his hand on her shoulder. "You're part of *our* family now. And I promise I won't let anything hurt you. I'm *not* going to fail you like our families did us. Deal?"

"Deal!" Annabeth said happily.

"Now, come on," Thalia said. "We can't stay put for long!"

The scene shifted. The three demigods were running through the woods. It must've been several days later, maybe even weeks. All of them looked beat up, like they'd seen some battles. Annabeth was wearing new clothes—jeans and an oversize army jacket.

"Just a little farther!" Luke promised. Annabeth stumbled, and he took her hand. Thalia brought up the rear, brandishing her shield like she was driving back whatever pursued them. She was limping on her left leg.

They scrambled to a ridge and looked down the other side at a white Colonial house—May Castellan's place.

"All right," Luke said, breathing hard. "I'll just sneak in and grab some food and medicine. Wait here."

"Luke, are you sure?" Thalia asked. "You swore you'd never come back here. If she catches you—"

"We don't have a choice!" he growled. "They burned our nearest safe house. And you've got to treat that leg wound."

"This is your house?" Annabeth said with amazement.

"It *was* my house," Luke muttered. "Believe me, if it wasn't an emergency—"

"Is your mom really horrible?" Annabeth asked. "Can we see her?"

"No!" Luke snapped.

Annabeth shrank away from him as though his anger surprised her.

"I . . . I'm sorry," he said. "Just wait here. I promise everything will be okay. Nothing's going to hurt you. I'll be back—"

A brilliant golden flash illuminated the woods. The demigods winced, and a man's voice boomed: "You should not have come home."

The vision shut off.

My knees buckled, but Annabeth grabbed me. "Percy! What happened?"

"Did . . . did you see that?" I asked.

"See what?"

I glanced at Hestia, but the goddess's face was expressionless. I remembered something she'd told me in the woods: *If you are to understand your enemy Luke, you must understand his family.* But why had she shown me those scenes?

"How long was I out?" I muttered.

Annabeth knit her eyebrows. "Percy, you weren't out at all. You just looked at Hestia for like one second and collapsed."

I could feel everyone's eyes on me. I couldn't afford to

look weak. Whatever those visions meant, I had to stay focused on our mission.

"Um, Lady Hestia," I said, "we've come on urgent business. We need to see—"

"We know what you need," a man's voice said. I shuddered, because it was the same voice I'd heard in the vision.

A god shimmered into existence next to Hestia. He looked about twenty-five, with curly salt-and-pepper hair and elfish features. He wore a military pilot's flight suit, with tiny bird's wings fluttering on his helmet and his black leather boots. In the crook of his arm was a long staff entwined with two living serpents.

"I will leave you now," Hestia said. She bowed to the aviator and disappeared into smoke. I understood why she was so anxious to go. Hermes, the God of Messengers, did not look happy.

"Hello, Percy." His brow furrowed as though he was annoyed with me, and I wondered if he somehow knew about the vision I'd just had. I wanted to ask why he'd been at May Castellan's house that night, and what had happened after he caught Luke. I remembered the first time I'd met Luke at Camp Half-Blood. I'd asked him if he'd ever met his father, and he'd looked at me bitterly and said, *Once.* But I could tell from Hermes's expression that this was not the time to ask.

I bowed awkwardly. "Lord Hermes."

Oh, sure, one of the snakes said in my mind. *Don't say hi to us. We're just reptiles.*

George, the other snake scolded. *Be polite.*

"Hello, George," I said. "Hey, Martha."

Did you bring us a rat? George asked.

George, stop it, Martha said. *He's busy!*

Too busy for rats? George said. *That's just sad.*

I decided it was better not to get into it with George. "Um, Hermes," I said. "We need to talk to Zeus. It's important."

Hermes's eyes were steely cold. "I am his messenger. May I take a message?"

Behind me, the other demigods shifted restlessly. This wasn't going as planned. Maybe if I tried to speak with Hermes in private . . .

"You guys," I said. "Why don't you do a sweep of the city? Check the defenses. See who's left in Olympus. Meet Annabeth and me back here in thirty minutes."

Silena frowned. "But—"

"That's a good idea," Annabeth said. "Connor and Travis, you two lead."

The Stolls seemed to like that—getting handed an important responsibility right in front of their dad. They usually never led anything except toilet paper raids. "We're on it!" Travis said. They herded the others out of the throne room, leaving Annabeth and me with Hermes.

"My lord," Annabeth said. "Kronos is going to attack New York. You must suspect that. My *mother* must have foreseen it."

"Your mother," Hermes grumbled. He scratched his back with his caduceus, and George and Martha muttered *Ow, ow, ow.* "Don't get me started on your mother, young lady. She's the reason I'm here at all. Zeus didn't want any of us to leave the front line. But your mother kept pestering him nonstop, 'It's a trap, it's a diversion, blah, blah, blah.' She wanted to come back herself, but Zeus was not going to let his number one strategist leave his side while we're battling Typhon. And so naturally he sent *me* to talk to you."

"But it *is* a trap!" Annabeth insisted. "Is Zeus blind?"

Thunder rolled through the sky.

"I'd watch the comments, girl," Hermes warned. "Zeus is not blind *or* deaf. He has not left Olympus completely undefended."

"But there are these blue lights—"

"Yes, yes. I saw them. Some mischief by that insufferable goddess of magic, Hecate, I'd wager, but you may have noticed they aren't doing any damage. Olympus has strong magical wards. Besides, Aeolus, the King of the Winds, has sent his most powerful minions to guard the citadel. No one save the gods can approach Olympus from the air. They would be knocked out of the sky."

I raised my hand. "Um . . . what about that materializing/teleporting thing you guys do?"

"That's a form of air travel too, Jackson. Very fast, but the wind gods are faster. No, if Kronos wants Olympus, he'll have to march through the entire city with his army and take the elevators! Can you see him doing this?"

Hermes made it sound pretty ridiculous—hordes of monsters going up in the elevator twenty at a time, listening to "Stayin' Alive." Still, I didn't like it.

"Maybe just a few of you could come back," I suggested.

Hermes shook his head impatiently. "Percy Jackson, you don't understand. Typhon is our greatest enemy."

"I thought that was Kronos."

The god's eyes glowed. "No, Percy. In the old days, Olympus was almost overthrown by Typhon. He is husband of Echidna—"

"Met her at the Arch," I muttered. "Not nice."

"—and the father of all monsters. We can never forget how close he came to destroying us all; how he humiliated us! We were more powerful back in the old days. Now we can expect no help from Poseidon because he's fighting his own war. Hades sits in his realm and does nothing, and Demeter and Persephone follow his lead. It will take all our remaining power to oppose the storm giant. We can't divide our forces, nor wait until he gets to New York. We have to battle him now. And we're making progress."

"Progress?" I said. "He nearly destroyed St. Louis."

"Yes," Hermes admitted. "But he destroyed only *half* of Kentucky. He's slowing down. Losing power."

I didn't want to argue, but it sounded like Hermes was trying to convince himself.

In the corner, the Ophiotaurus mooed sadly.

"Please, Hermes," Annabeth said. "You said my mother wanted to come. Did she give you any messages for us?"

"Messages," he muttered. "'It'll be a great job,' they told me. 'Not much work. Lots of worshippers.' Hmph. Nobody cares what *I* have to say. It's always about other people's *messages*."

Rodents, George mused. *I'm in it for the rodents.*

Shhh, Martha scolded. *We care what Hermes has to say. Don't we, George?*

Oh, absolutely. Can we go back to the battle now? I want to do laser mode again. That's fun.

"Quiet, both of you," Hermes grumbled.

The god looked at Annabeth, who was doing her big-pleading-gray-eyes thing.

"Bah," Hermes said. "Your mother said to warn you that you are on your own. You must hold Manhattan without the help of the gods. As if I didn't know that. Why they pay her to be the *wisdom* goddess, I'm not sure."

"Anything else?" Annabeth asked.

"She said you should try plan twenty-three. She said you would know what that meant."

Annabeth's face paled. Obviously she knew what it meant, and she didn't like it. "Go on."

"Last thing." Hermes looked at me. "She said to tell Percy: 'Remember the rivers.' And, um, something about staying away from her daughter."

I'm not sure whose face was redder: Annabeth's or mine.

"Thank you, Hermes," Annabeth said. "And I . . . I wanted to say . . . I'm sorry about Luke."

The god's expression hardened like he'd turned to marble. "You should've left that subject alone."

Annabeth stepped back nervously. "Sorry?"

"SORRY doesn't cut it!"

George and Martha curled around the caduceus, which shimmered and changed into something that looked suspiciously like a high-voltage cattle prod.

"You should've saved him when you had the chance," Hermes growled at Annabeth. "You're the only one who could have."

I tried to step between them. "What are you talking about? Annabeth didn't—"

"Don't defend her, Jackson!" Hermes turned the cattle prod toward me. "She knows exactly what I'm talking about."

"Maybe you should blame yourself!" I should've kept my mouth shut, but all I could think about was turning his attention away from Annabeth. This whole time, he hadn't been angry with me. He'd been angry with *her*. "Maybe if you hadn't abandoned Luke and his mom!"

Hermes raised his cattle prod. He began to grow until he was ten feet tall. I thought, Well, that's it.

But as he prepared to strike, George and Martha leaned in close and whispered something in his ear.

Hermes clenched his teeth. He lowered the cattle prod, and it turned back to a staff.

"Percy Jackson," he said, "because you have taken on the curse of Achilles, I must spare you. You are in the hands of the Fates now. But you will *never* speak to me like that again. You have no idea how much I have sacrificed, how much—"

His voice broke, and he shrank back to human size. "My son, my greatest pride . . . my poor May . . ."

He sounded so devastated I didn't know what to say. One minute he was ready to vaporize us. Now he looked like he needed a hug.

"Look, Lord Hermes," I said. "I'm sorry, but I need to know. What happened to May? She said something about Luke's fate, and her eyes—"

Hermes glared at me, and my voice faltered. The look on his face wasn't really anger, though. It was pain. Deep, incredible pain.

"I will leave you now," he said tightly. "I have a war to fight."

He began to shine. I turned away and made sure Annabeth did the same, because she was still frozen in shock.

Good luck, Percy, Martha the snake whispered.

Hermes glowed with the light of a supernova. Then he was gone.

Annabeth sat at the foot of her mother's throne and cried. I wanted to comfort her, but I wasn't sure how.

"Annabeth," I said, "it's not your fault. I've never seen Hermes act that way. I guess . . . I don't know . . . he proba bly feels guilty about Luke. He's looking for somebody to blame. I don't know why he lashed out at you. You didn't do anything to deserve that."

Annabeth wiped her eyes. She stared at the hearth like it was her own funeral pyre.

I shifted uneasily. "Um, you didn't, right?"

She didn't answer. Her Celestial bronze knife was strapped to her arm—the same knife I'd seen in Hestia's vision. All these years, I hadn't realized it was a gift from Luke. I'd asked her many times why she preferred to fight with a knife instead of a sword, and she'd never answered me. Now I knew.

"Percy," she said. "What did you mean about Luke's mother? Did you meet her?"

I nodded reluctantly. "Nico and I visited her. She was a little . . . different." I described May Castellan, and the weird moment when her eyes had started to glow and she talked about her son's fate.

Annabeth frowned. "That doesn't make sense. But why were you visiting—" Her eyes widened. "Hermes said you bear the curse of Achilles. Hestia said the same thing. Did you . . . did you bathe in the River Styx?"

"Don't change the subject."

"Percy! Did you or not?"

"Um . . . maybe a little."

I told her the story about Hades and Nico, and how I'd defeated an army of the dead. I left out the vision of her pulling me out of the river. I still didn't quite understand that part, and just thinking about it made me embarrassed.

She shook her head in disbelief. "Do you have *any idea* how dangerous that was?"

"I had no choice," I said. "It's the only way I can stand up to Luke."

"You mean . . . *di immortales*, of course! That's why Luke didn't die. He went to the Styx and . . . Oh no, Luke. What were you thinking?"

"So now you're worried about Luke again," I grumbled.

She stared at me like I'd just dropped from space. "What?"

"Forget it," I muttered. I wondered what Hermes had meant about Annabeth not saving Luke when she'd had the chance. Clearly, she wasn't telling me something. But at the moment I wasn't in the mood to ask. The last thing I wanted to hear about was more of her history with Luke.

"The point is he didn't die in the Styx," I said. "Neither did I. Now I have to face him. We have to defend Olympus."

Annabeth was still studying my face, like she was trying to see differences since my swim in the Styx. "I guess you're right. My mom mentioned—"

"Plan twenty-three."

She rummaged in her pack and pulled out Daedalus's laptop. The blue Delta symbol glowed on the top when she booted it up. She opened a few files and started to read.

"Here it is," she said. "Gods, we have a lot of work to do."

"One of Daedalus's inventions?"

"A lot of inventions . . . dangerous ones. If my mother wants me to use this plan, she must think things are very bad." She looked at me. "What about her message to you: 'Remember the rivers'? What does that mean?"

I shook my head. As usual, I had no clue what the gods were telling me. Which rivers was I supposed to remember? The Styx? The Mississippi?

Just then the Stoll brothers ran in to the throne room.

"You need to see this," Connor said. *"Now."*

The blue lights in the sky had stopped, so at first I didn't understand what the problem was.

The other campers had gathered in a small park at the edge of the mountain. They were clustered at the guardrail, looking down at Manhattan. The railing was lined with those tourist binoculars, where you could deposit one golden drachma and see the city. Campers were using every single one.

I looked down at the city. I could see almost everything from here—the East River and the Hudson River carving the shape of Manhattan, the grid of streets, the lights of skyscrapers, the dark stretch of Central Park in the north. Everything looked normal, but something was wrong. I felt it in my bones before I realized what it was.

"I don't . . . hear anything," Annabeth said.

That was the problem.

Even from this height, I should've heard the noise of the city—millions of people bustling around, thousands of cars and machines—the hum of a huge metropolis. You don't think about it when you live in New York, but it's always there. Even in the dead of night, New York is never silent.

But it was now.

I felt like my best friend had suddenly dropped dead.

"What did they do?" My voice sounded tight and angry. "What did they do to my city?"

I pushed Michael Yew away from the binoculars and took a look.

In the streets below, traffic had stopped. Pedestrians were lying on the sidewalks, or curled up in doorways. There was no sign of violence, no wrecks, nothing like that. It was as if all the people in New York had simply decided to stop whatever they were doing and pass out.

"Are they dead?" Silena asked in astonishment.

Ice coated my stomach. A line from the prophecy rang in my ears: *And see the world in endless sleep.* I remembered Grover's story about meeting the god Morpheus in Central Park. *You're lucky I'm saving my energy for the main event.*

"Not dead," I said. "Morpheus has put the entire island of Manhattan to sleep. The invasion has started."

TEN

I BUY SOME NEW FRIENDS

Mrs. O'Leary was the only one happy about the sleeping city.

We found her pigging out at an overturned hot dog stand while the owner was curled up on the sidewalk, sucking his thumb.

Argus was waiting for us with his hundred eyes wide open. He didn't say anything. He never does. I guess that's because he supposedly has an eyeball on his tongue. But his face made it clear he was freaking out.

I told him what we'd learned in Olympus, and how the gods would not be riding to the rescue. Argus rolled his eyes in disgust, which looked pretty psychedelic since it made his whole body swirl.

"You'd better get back to camp," I told him. "Guard it as best you can."

He pointed at me and raised his eyebrow quizzically.

"I'm staying," I said.

Argus nodded, like this answer satisfied him. He looked at Annabeth and drew a circle in the air with his finger.

"Yes," Annabeth agreed. "I think it's time."

"For what?" I asked.

Argus rummaged around in the back of his van. He brought out a bronze shield and passed it to Annabeth. It looked pretty much standard issue—the same kind of round shield we always used in capture the flag. But when Annabeth set it on the ground, the reflection on the polished metal changed from sky and buildings to the Statue of Liberty—which wasn't anywhere close to us.

"Whoa," I said. "A video shield."

"One of Daedalus's ideas," Annabeth said. "I had Beckendorf make this before—" She glanced at Silena. "Um, anyway, the shield bends sunlight or moonlight from anywhere in the world to create a reflection. You can literally see any target under the sun or moon, as long as natural light is touching it. Look."

We crowded around as Annabeth concentrated. The image zoomed and spun at first, so I got motion sickness just watching it. We were in the Central Park Zoo, then zooming down East 60th, past Bloomingdale's, then turning on Third Avenue.

"Whoa," Connor Stoll said. "Back up. Zoom in right there."

"What?" Annabeth said nervously. "You see invaders?"

"No, right there—Dylan's Candy Bar." Connor grinned at his brother. "Dude, it's open. And *everyone* is asleep. Are you thinking what I'm thinking?"

"Connor!" Katie Gardner scolded. She sounded like her mother, Demeter. "This is serious. You are not going to loot a candy store in the middle of a war!"

"Sorry," Connor muttered, but he didn't sound very ashamed.

Annabeth passed her hand in front of the shield, and another scene popped up: FDR Drive, looking across the river at Lighthouse Park.

"This will let us see what's going on across the city," she said. "Thank you, Argus. Hopefully we'll see you back at camp . . . someday."

Argus grunted. He gave me a look that clearly meant *Good luck; you'll need it*, then climbed into his van. He and the two harpy drivers swerved away, weaving around clusters of idle cars that littered the road.

I whistled for Mrs. O'Leary, and she came bounding over.

"Hey, girl," I said. "You remember Grover? The satyr we met in the park?"

"WOOF!"

I hoped that meant *Sure I do!* And not, *Do you have more hot dogs?*

"I need you to find him," I said. "Make sure he's still awake. We're going to need his help. You got that? Find Grover!"

Mrs. O'Leary gave me a sloppy wet kiss, which seemed kind of unnecessary. Then she raced off north.

Pollux crouched next to a sleeping policeman. "I don't get it. Why didn't we fall asleep too? Why just the mortals?"

"This is a huge spell," Silena Beauregard said. "The bigger the spell, the easier it is to resist. If you want to sleep millions of mortals, you've got to cast a very thin layer of magic. Sleeping demigods is much harder."

I stared at her. "When did you learn so much about magic?"

Silena blushed. "I don't spend *all* my time on my wardrobe."

"Percy," Annabeth called. She was still looking at the shield. "You'd better see this."

The bronze image showed Long Island Sound near La Guardia. A fleet of a dozen speedboats raced through the dark water toward Manhattan. Each boat was packed with demigods in full Greek armor. At the back of the lead boat, a purple banner emblazoned with a black scythe flapped in the night wind. I'd never seen that design before, but it wasn't hard to figure out: the battle flag of Kronos.

"Scan the perimeter of the island," I said. "Quick."

Annabeth shifted the scene south to the harbor. A Staten Island Ferry was plowing through the waves near Ellis Island. The deck was crowded with *dracaenae* and a whole pack of hellhounds. Swimming in front of the ship was a pod of marine mammals. At first I thought they were dolphins. Then I saw their doglike faces and the swords strapped to their waists, and I realized they were telkhines—sea demons.

The scene shifted again: the Jersey shore, right at the entrance to the Lincoln Tunnel. A hundred assorted monsters were marching past the lanes of stopped traffic: giants with clubs, rogue Cyclopes, a few fire-spitting dragons, and just to rub it in, a World War II–era Sherman tank, pushing cars out of its way as it rumbled into the tunnel.

"What's happening with the mortals outside Manhattan?" I said. "Is the whole state asleep?"

Annabeth frowned. "I don't think so, but it's strange. As far as I can tell from these pictures, Manhattan is totally asleep. Then there's like a fifty-mile radius around the island where time is running really, really slow. The closer you get to Manhattan, the slower it is."

She showed me another scene—a New Jersey highway. It was Saturday evening, so the traffic wasn't as bad as it might've been on a weekday. The drivers looked awake, but the cars were moving at about one mile per hour. Birds flew overhead in slow motion.

"Kronos," I said. "He's slowing time."

"Hecate might be helping," Katie Gardner said. "Look how the cars are all veering away from the Manhattan exits, like they're getting a subconscious message to turn back."

"I don't know." Annabeth sounded really frustrated. She *hated* not knowing. "But somehow they've surrounded Manhattan in layers of magic. The outside world might not even realize something is wrong. Any mortals coming toward Manhattan will slow down so much they won't know what's happening."

"Like flies in amber," Jake Mason murmured.

Annabeth nodded. "We shouldn't expect any help coming in."

I turned to my friends. They looked stunned and scared, and I couldn't blame them. The shield had shown us at least three hundred enemies on the way. There were forty of us. And we were alone.

"All right," I said. "We're going to hold Manhattan."

Silena tugged at her armor. "Um, Percy, Manhattan is huge."

"We *are* going to hold it," I said. "We have to."

"He's right," Annabeth said. "The gods of the wind should keep Kronos's forces away from Olympus by air, so he'll try a ground assault. We have to cut off the entrances to the island."

"They have boats," Michael Yew pointed out.

An electric tingle went down my back. Suddenly I understood Athena's advice: *Remember the rivers.*

"I'll take care of the boats," I said.

Michael frowned. "How?"

"Just leave it to me," I said. "We need to guard the bridges and tunnels. Let's assume they'll try a midtown or downtown assault, at least on their first try. That would be the most direct way to the Empire State Building. Michael, take Apollo's cabin to the Williamsburg Bridge. Katie, Demeter's cabin takes the Brooklyn–Battery Tunnel. Grow thorn bushes and poison ivy in the tunnel. Do whatever you have to do, but keep them out of there! Conner, take half of Hermes cabin and cover the Manhattan Bridge. Travis, you take the other half and cover the Brooklyn Bridge. And no stopping for looting or pillaging!"

"Awwww!" the whole Hermes cabin complained.

"Silena, take the Aphrodite crew to the Queens–Midtown Tunnel."

"Oh my gods," one of her sisters said. "Fifth Avenue is *so* on our way! We could accessorize, and monsters, like, *totally* hate the smell of Givenchy."

"No delays," I said. "Well . . . the perfume thing, if you think it'll work."

Six Aphrodite girls kissed me on the cheek in excitement.

"All right, enough!" I closed my eyes, trying to think of what I'd forgotten. "The Holland Tunnel. Jake, take the Hephaestus cabin there. Use Greek fire, set traps. Whatever you've got."

He grinned. "Gladly. We've got a score to settle. For Beckendorf!"

The whole cabin roared in approval.

"The 59th Street Bridge," I said. "Clarisse—"

I faltered. Clarisse wasn't here. The whole Ares cabin, curse them, was sitting back at camp.

"We'll take that," Annabeth stepped in, saving me from an embarrassing silence. She turned to her siblings. "Malcolm, take the Athena cabin, activate plan twenty-three along the way, just like I showed you. Hold that position."

"You got it."

"I'll go with Percy," she said. "Then we'll join you, or we'll go wherever we're needed."

Somebody in the back of the group said, "No detours, you two."

There were some giggles, but I decided to let it pass.

"All right," I said. "Keep in touch with cell phones."

"We don't have cell phones," Silena protested.

I reached down, picked up some snoring lady's BlackBerry, and tossed it to Silena. "You do now. You all know Annabeth's number, right? If you need us, pick up a random phone and call us. Use it once, drop it, then borrow another one if you have to. That should make it harder for the monsters to zero in on you."

Everyone grinned as though they liked this idea.

Travis cleared his throat. "Uh, if we find a really nice phone—"

"No, you can't keep it," I said.

"Aw, man."

"Hold it, Percy," Jake Mason said. "You forgot the Lincoln Tunnel."

I bit back a curse. He was right. A Sherman tank and a hundred monsters were marching through that tunnel right now, and I'd positioned our forces everywhere else.

Then a girl's voice called from across the street: "How about you leave that to us?"

I'd never been happier to hear anyone in my life. A band of thirty adolescent girls crossed Fifth Avenue. They wore white shirts, silvery camouflage pants, and combat boots. They all had swords at their sides, quivers on their backs, and bows at the ready. A pack of white timber wolves milled around their feet, and many of the girls had hunting falcons on their arms.

The girl in the lead had spiky black hair and a black leather jacket. She wore a silver circlet on her head like a princess's tiara, which didn't match her skull earrings or her *Death to Barbie* T-shirt showing a little Barbie doll with an arrow through its head.

"Thalia!" Annabeth cried.

The daughter of Zeus grinned. "The Hunters of Artemis, reporting for duty."

There were hugs and greetings all around . . . or at least Thalia was friendly. The other Hunters didn't like being around campers, especially boys, but they didn't shoot any of us, which for them was a pretty warm welcome.

"Where have you been the last year?" I asked Thalia. "You've got like twice as many Hunters now!"

She laughed. "Long, *long* story. I bet my adventures were more dangerous than yours, Jackson."

"Complete lie," I said.

"We'll see," she promised. "After this is over, you, Annabeth, and me: cheeseburgers and fries at that hotel on West 57th."

"Le Parker Meridien," I said. "You're on. And Thalia, thanks."

She shrugged. "Those monsters won't know what hit them. Hunters, move out!"

She slapped her silver bracelet, and the shield Aegis spiraled into full form. The golden head of Medusa molded in the center was so horrible, the campers all backed away. The Hunters took off down the avenue, followed by their wolves and falcons, and I had a feeling the Lincoln Tunnel would be safe for now.

"Thank the gods," Annabeth said. "But if we don't blockade the rivers from those boats, guarding the bridges and tunnels will be pointless."

"You're right," I said.

I looked at the campers, all of them grim and determined. I tried not to feel like this was the last time I'd ever see them all together.

"You're the greatest heroes of this millennium," I told them. "It doesn't matter how many monsters come at you. Fight bravely, and we will win." I raised Riptide and shouted, "FOR OLYMPUS!"

They shouted in response, and our forty voices echoed off the buildings of Midtown. For a moment it sounded brave, but it died quickly in the silence of ten million sleeping New Yorkers.

Annabeth and I would've had our pick of cars, but they were all wedged in bumper-to-bumper traffic. None of the engines were running, which was weird. It seemed the drivers had had time to turn off the ignition before they got too sleepy. Or maybe Morpheus had the power to put engines to sleep as well. Most of the drivers had apparently tried to pull to the curb when they felt themselves passing out, but still the streets were too clogged to navigate.

Finally we found an unconscious courier leaning against a brick wall, still straddling his red Vespa. We dragged him off the scooter and laid him on the sidewalk.

"Sorry, dude," I said. With any luck, I'd be able to bring his scooter back. If I didn't, it would hardly matter, because the city would be destroyed.

I drove with Annabeth behind me holding on to my waist. We zigzagged down Broadway with our engine buzzing through the eerie calm. The only sounds were occasional cell phones ringing—like they were calling out to each other, as if New York had turned into a giant electronic aviary.

Our progress was slow. Every so often we'd come across pedestrians who'd fallen asleep right in front of a car, and we'd move them just to be safe. Once we stopped to extinguish a pretzel vendor's cart that had caught on fire. A few minutes later we had to rescue a baby carriage that was rolling aimlessly down the street. It turned out there was no baby in it—just somebody's sleeping poodle. Go figure. We parked it safely in a doorway and kept riding.

We were passing Madison Square Park when Annabeth said, "Pull over."

I stopped in the middle of East 23rd. Annabeth jumped off and ran toward the park. By the time I caught up with her, she was staring at a bronze statue on a red marble pedestal. I'd probably passed it a million times but never really looked at it.

The dude was sitting in a chair with his legs crossed. He wore an old-fashioned suit—Abraham Lincoln style—with a bow tie and long coattails and stuff. A bunch of bronze books were piled under his chair. He held a writing quill in one hand and a big metal sheet of parchment in the other.

"Why do we care about . . ." I squinted at the name on the pedestal. "William H. Steward?"

"Seward," Annabeth corrected. "He was a New York governor. Minor demigod—son of Hebe, I think. But that's not important. It's the statue I care about."

She climbed on a park bench and examined the base of the statue.

"Don't tell me he's an automaton," I said.

Annabeth smiled. "Turns out most of the statues in the city are automatons. Daedalus planted them here just in case he needed an army."

"To attack Olympus or defend it?"

Annabeth shrugged. "Either one. That was plan twenty-three. He could activate one statue and it would start activating its brethren all over the city, until there was an army. It's dangerous, though. You know how unpredictable automatons are."

"Uh-huh," I said. We'd had our share of bad experiences with them. "You're seriously thinking about activating it?"

"I have Daedalus's notes," she said. "I think I can . . . Ah, here we go."

She pressed the tip of Seward's boot, and the statue stood up, its quill and paper ready.

"What's he going to do?" I muttered. "Take a memo?"

"Shh," Annabeth. "Hello, William."

"Bill," I suggested.

"Bill . . . Oh, shut up," Annabeth told me. The statue tilted its head, looking at us with blank metal eyes.

Annabeth cleared her throat. "Hello, er, Governor Seward. Command sequence: Daedalus Twenty-three. Defend Manhattan. Begin Activation."

Seward jumped off his pedestal. He hit the ground so hard his shoes cracked the sidewalk. Then he went clanking off toward the east.

"He's probably going to wake up Confucius," Annabeth guessed.

"What?" I said.

"Another statue, on Division. The point is, they'll keep waking each other up until they're all activated."

"And then?"

"Hopefully, they defend Manhattan."

"Do they know that we're not the enemy?"

"I think so."

"That's reassuring." I thought about all the bronze statues in the parks, plazas, and buildings of New York. There had to be hundreds, maybe thousands.

Then a ball of green light exploded in the evening sky. Greek fire, somewhere over the East River.

"We have to hurry," I said. And we ran for the Vespa.

We parked outside Battery Park, at the lower tip of Manhattan where the Hudson and East Rivers came together and emptied into the bay.

"Wait here," I told Annabeth.

"Percy, you shouldn't go alone."

"Well, unless you can breathe underwater . . ."

She sighed. "You are *so* annoying sometimes."

"Like when I'm right? Trust me, I'll be fine. I've got the curse of Achilles now. I'll all invincible and stuff."

Annabeth didn't look convinced. "Just be careful. I don't want anything to happen to you. I mean, because we need you for the battle."

I grinned. "Back in a flash."

I clambered down the shoreline and waded into the water.

Just for you non-sea-god types out there, don't go swimming in New York Harbor. It may not be as filthy as it was in my mom's day, but that water will still probably make you grow a third eye or have mutant children when you grow up.

I dove into the murk and sank to the bottom. I tried to find the spot where the two rivers' currents seemed equal—where they met to form the bay. I figured that was the best place to get their attention.

"HEY!" I shouted in my best underwater voice. The sound echoed in the darkness. "I heard you guys are so polluted you're embarrassed to show your faces. Is that true?"

A cold current rippled through the bay, churning up plumes of garbage and silt.

"I heard the East River is more toxic," I continued, "but the Hudson smells worse. Or is it the other way around?"

The water shimmered. Something powerful and angry was watching me now. I could sense its presence . . . or maybe *two* presences.

I was afraid I'd miscalculated with the insults. What if they just blasted me without showing themselves? But these were New York river gods. I figured their instinct would be to get in my face.

Sure enough, two giant forms appeared in front of me. At first they were just dark brown columns of silt, denser than the water around them. Then they grew legs, arms, and scowling faces.

The creature on the left looked disturbingly like a telkhine. His face was wolfish. His body was vaguely like a seal's—sleek black with flipper hands and feet. His eyes glowed radiation green.

The dude on the right was more humanoid. He was dressed in rags and seaweed, with a chain-mail coat made of bottle caps and old plastic six-pack holders. His face was blotchy with algae, and his beard was overgrown. His deep blue eyes burned with anger.

The seal, who had to be the god of the East River, said, "Are you *trying* to get yourself killed, kid? Or are you just extra stupid?"

The bearded spirit of the Hudson scoffed. "You're the expert on stupid, East."

"Watch it, Hudson," East growled. "Stay on your side of the island and mind your business."

"Or what? You'll throw another garbage barge at me?"

They floated toward each other, ready to fight.

"Hold it!" I yelled. "We've got a bigger problem."

"The kid's right," East snarled. "Let's both kill *him*, then we'll fight each other."

"Sounds good," Hudson said.

Before I could protest, a thousand scraps of garbage surged off the bottom and flew straight at me from both directions: broken glass, rocks, cans, tires.

I was expecting it, though. The water in front of me thickened into a shield. The debris bounced off harmlessly. Only one piece got through—a big chunk of glass that hit my chest and probably should've killed me, but it shattered against my skin.

The two river gods stared at me.

"Son of Poseidon?" East asked.

I nodded.

"Took a dip in the Styx?" Hudson asked.

"Yep."

They both made disgusted sounds.

"Well, that's perfect," East said. "*Now* how do we kill him?"

"We could electrocute him," Hudson mused. "If I could just find some jumper cables—"

"Listen to me!" I said. "Kronos's army is invading Manhattan!"

"Don't you think we know that?" East asked. "I can feel his boats right now. They're almost across."

"Yep," Hudson agreed. "I got some filthy monsters crossing my waters too."

"So stop them," I said. "Drown them. Sink their boats."

"Why should we?" Hudson grumbled. "So they invade Olympus. What do we care?"

"Because I can pay you." I took out the sand dollar my father had given me for my birthday.

The river gods' eyes widened.

"It's mine!" East said. "Give it here, kid, and I promise none of Kronos's scum are getting across the East River."

"Forget that," Hudson said. "That sand dollar's mine, unless you want me to let all those ships cross the Hudson."

"We'll compromise." I broke the sand dollar in half. A ripple of clean fresh water spread out from the break, as if all the pollution in the bay were being dissolved.

"You each get half," I said. "In exchange, you keep all of Kronos's forces away from Manhattan."

"Oh, man," Hudson whimpered, reaching out for the sand dollar. "It's been so long since I was clean."

"The power of Poseidon," East River murmured. "He's a jerk, but he sure knows how to sweep pollution away."

They looked at each other, then spoke as one: "It's a deal."

I gave them each a sand-dollar half, which they held reverently.

"Um, the invaders?" I prompted.

East flicked his hand. "They just got sunk."

Hudson snapped his fingers. "Bunch of hellhounds just took a dive."

"Thank you," I said. "Stay clean."

As I rose toward the surface, East called out, "Hey, kid, any time you got a sand dollar to spend, come on back. Assuming you live."

"Curse of Achilles," Hudson snorted. "They always think that'll save them, don't they?"

"If only he knew," East agreed. They both laughed, dissolving into the water.

Back on the shore, Annabeth was talking on her cell phone, but she hung up as soon as she saw me. She looked pretty shaken.

"It worked," I told her. "The rivers are safe."

"Good," she said. "Because we've got other problems. Michael Yew just called. Another army is marching over the Williamsburg Bridge. The Apollo cabin needs help. And Percy, the monster leading the enemy . . . it's the Minotaur."

ELEVEN

WE BREAK A BRIDGE

Fortunately, Blackjack was on duty.

I did my best taxicab whistle, and within a few minutes two dark shapes circled out of the sky. They looked like hawks at first, but as they descended I could make out the long galloping legs of pegasi.

Yo, boss. Blackjack landed at a trot, his friend Porkpie right behind him. *Man, I thought those wind gods were gonna knock us to Pennsylvania until we said we were with you!*

"Thanks for coming," I told him. "Hey, why do pegasi gallop as they fly, anyway?"

Blackjack whinnied. *Why do humans swing their arms as they walk? I dunno, boss. It just feels right. Where to?*

"We need to get to the Williamsburg Bridge," I said.

Blackjack lowered his neck. *You're darn right, boss. We flew over it on the way here, and it don't look good. Hop on!*

On the way to the bridge, a knot formed in the pit of my stomach. The Minotaur was one of the first monsters I'd ever defeated. Four years ago he'd nearly killed my mother on Half-Blood Hill. I still had nightmares about that.

I'd been hoping he would stay dead for a few centuries, but I should've known my luck wouldn't hold.

We saw the battle before we were close enough to make out individual fighters. It was well after midnight now, but the bridge blazed with light. Cars were burning. Arcs of fire streamed in both directions as flaming arrows and spears sailed through the air.

We came in for a low pass, and I saw the Apollo campers retreating. They would hide behind cars and snipe at the approaching army, setting off explosive arrows and dropping caltrops in the road, building fiery barricades wherever they could, dragging sleeping drivers out of their cars to get them out of harm's way. But the enemy kept advancing. An entire phalanx of *dracaenae* marched in the lead, their shields locked together, spear tips bristling over the top. An occasional arrow would connect with their snaky trunks, or a neck, or a chink in their armor, and the unlucky snake woman would disintegrate, but most of the Apollo arrows glanced harmlessly off their shield wall. About a hundred more monsters marched behind them.

Hellhounds leaped ahead of the line from time to time. Most were destroyed with arrows, but one got hold of an Apollo camper and dragged him away. I didn't see what happened to him next. I didn't want to know.

"There!" Annabeth called from the back of her pegasus.

Sure enough, in the middle of the invading legion was Old Beefhead himself.

The last time I'd seen the Minotaur, he'd been wearing nothing but his tighty whities. I don't know why. Maybe he'd been shaken out of bed to chase me. This time, he was prepared for battle.

From the waist down, he wore standard Greek battle gear—a kiltlike apron of leather and metal flaps, bronze greaves covering his legs, and tightly wrapped leather sandals. His top was all bull—hair and hide and muscle leading to a head so large he should've toppled over just from the weight of his horns. He seemed larger than the last time I'd seen him—ten feet tall at least. A double-bladed axe was strapped to his back, but he was too impatient to use it. As soon as he saw me circling overhead (or sniffed me, more likely, since his eyesight was bad), he bellowed and picked up a white limousine.

"Blackjack, dive!" I yelled.

What? The pegasus asked. *No way could he . . . Holy horse feed!*

We were at least a hundred feet up, but the limo came sailing toward us, flipping fender over fender like a two-ton boomerang. Annabeth and Porkpie swerved madly to the left, while Blackjack tucked in his wings and plunged. The limo sailed over my head, missing by maybe two inches. It cleared the suspension lines of the bridge and fell toward the East River.

Monsters jeered and shouted, and the Minotaur picked up another car.

"Drop us behind the lines with the Apollo cabin," I told Blackjack. "Stay in earshot but get out of danger!"

I ain't gonna argue, boss!

Blackjack swooped down behind an overturned school bus, where a couple of campers were hiding. Annabeth and I leaped off as soon as our pegasi's hooves touched the pavement. Then Blackjack and Porkpie soared into the night sky.

Michael Yew ran up to us. He was definitely the shortest commando I'd ever seen. He had a bandaged cut on his arm. His ferrety face was smeared with soot and his quiver was almost empty, but he was smiling like he was having a great time.

"Glad you could join us," he said. "Where are the other reinforcements?"

"For now, we're it," I said.

"Then we're dead," he said.

"You still have your flying chariot?" Annabeth asked.

"Nah," Michael said. "Left it at camp. I told Clarisse she could have it. Whatever, you know? Not worth fighting about anymore. But she said it was too late. We'd insulted her honor for the last time or some stupid thing."

"Least you tried," I said.

Michael shrugged. "Yeah, well, I called her some names when she said she still wouldn't fight. I doubt that helped. Here come the uglies!"

He drew an arrow and launched it toward the enemy. The arrow made a screaming sound as it flew. When it landed, it unleashed a blast like a power chord on an electric guitar magnified through the world's largest speakers. The nearest cars exploded. Monsters dropped their weapons and clasped their ears in pain. Some ran. Others disintegrated on the spot.

"That was my last sonic arrow," Michael said.

"A gift from your dad?" I asked. "God of music?"

Michael grinned wickedly. "Loud music can be bad for you. Unfortunately, it doesn't always kill."

Sure enough, most monsters were regrouping, shaking off their confusion.

"We have to fall back," Michael said. "I've got Kayla and Austin setting traps farther down the bridge."

"No," I said. "Bring your campers forward to this position and wait for my signal. We're going to drive the enemy back to Brooklyn."

Michael laughed. "How do you plan to do that?"

I drew my sword.

"Percy," Annabeth said, "let me come with you."

"Too dangerous," I said. "Besides, I need you to help Michael coordinate the defensive line. I'll distract the monsters. You group up here. Move the sleeping mortals out of the way. Then you can start picking off monsters while I keep them focused on me. If anybody can do all that, you can."

Michael snorted. "Thanks a lot."

I kept my eyes on Annabeth.

She nodded reluctantly. "All right. Get moving."

Before I could lose my courage, I said, "Don't I get a kiss for luck? It's kind of a tradition, right?"

I figured she would punch me. Instead, she drew her knife and stared at the army marching toward us. "Come back alive, Seaweed Brain. Then we'll see."

I figured it was the best offer I would get, so I stepped out from behind the school bus. I walked up the bridge in plain sight, straight toward the enemy.

When the Minotaur saw me, his eyes burned with hate. He

bellowed—a sound that was somewhere between a yell, a moo, and a really loud belch.

"Hey, Beef Boy," I shouted back. "Didn't I kill you already?"

He pounded his fist into the hood of a Lexus, and it crumpled like aluminum foil.

A few *dracaenae* threw flaming javelins at me. I knocked them aside. A hellhound lunged, and I sidestepped. I could have stabbed it, but I hesitated.

This is not Mrs. O'Leary, I reminded myself. *This is an untamed monster. It will kill me and all my friends.*

It pounced again. This time I brought Riptide up in a deadly arc. The hellhound disintegrated into dust and fur.

More monsters surged forward—snakes and giants and telkhines—but the Minotaur roared at them, and they backed off.

"One on one?" I called. "Just like old times?"

The Minotaur's nostrils quivered. He seriously needed to keep a pack of Aloe Vera Kleenex in his armor pocket, because that nose was wet and red and pretty gross. He unstrapped his axe and swung it around.

It was beautiful in a harsh *I'm-going-to-gut-you-like-a-fish* kind of way. Each of its twin blades was shaped like an omega: Ω—the last letter of the Greek alphabet. Maybe that was because the axe would be the last thing his victims ever saw. The shaft was about the same height as the Minotaur, bronze wrapped in leather. Tied around the base of each blade were lots of bead necklaces. I realized they were Camp Half-Blood beads—necklaces taken from defeated demigods.

I was so mad, I imagined my eyes glowing just like the Minotaur's. I raised my sword. The monster army cheered for the Minotaur, but the sound died when I dodged his first swing and sliced his axe in half, right between the hand-holds.

"Moo?" he grunted.

"HAAA!" I spun and kicked him in the snout. He staggered backward, trying to regain his footing, then lowered his head to charge.

He never got the chance. My sword flashed—slicing off one horn, then the other. He tried to grab me. I rolled away, picking up half of his broken axe. The other monsters backed up in stunned silence, making a circle around us. The Minotaur bellowed in rage. He was never very smart to begin with, but now his anger made him reckless. He charged me, and I ran for the edge of the bridge, breaking through a line of *dracaenae*.

The Minotaur must've smelled victory. He thought I was trying to get away. His minions cheered. At the edge of the bridge, I turned and braced the axe against the railing to receive his charge. The Minotaur didn't even slow down.

CRUNCH.

He looked down in surprise at the axe handle sprouting from his breastplate.

"Thanks for playing," I told him.

I lifted him by his legs and tossed him over the side of the bridge. Even as he fell, he was disintegrating, turning back into dust, his essence returning to Tartarus.

I turned toward his army. It was now roughly one hundred and ninety-nine to one. I did the natural thing. I charged them.

You're going to ask how the "invincible" thing worked: if I magically dodged every weapon, or if the weapons hit me and just didn't harm me. Honestly, I don't remember. All I knew was that I wasn't going to let these monsters invade my hometown.

I sliced through armor like it was made of paper. Snake women exploded. Hellhounds melted to shadow. I slashed and stabbed and whirled, and I might have even laughed once or twice—a crazy laugh that scared me as much as it did my enemies. I was aware of the Apollo campers behind me shooting arrows, disrupting every attempt by the enemy to rally. Finally, the monsters turned and fled—about twenty left alive out of two hundred.

I followed with the Apollo campers at my heels.

"Yes!" yelled Michael Yew. "That's what I'm talking about!"

We drove them back toward the Brooklyn side of the bridge. The sky was growing pale in the east. I could see the toll stations ahead.

"Percy!" Annabeth yelled. "You've already routed them. Pull back! We're overextended!"

Some part of me knew she was right, but I was doing so well, I wanted to destroy every last monster.

Then I saw the crowd at the base of the bridge. The retreating monsters were running straight toward their reinforcements. It was a small group, maybe thirty or forty demigods in battle armor, mounted on skeletal horses. One of them held a purple banner with the black scythe design.

The lead horseman trotted forward. He took off his helm, and I recognized Kronos himself, his eyes like molten gold.

Annabeth and the Apollo campers faltered. The monsters we'd been pursuing reached the Titan's line and were absorbed into the new force. Kronos gazed in our direction. He was a quarter mile away, but I swear I could see him smile.

"Now," I said, "we pull back."

The Titan lord's men drew their swords and charged. The hooves of their skeletal horses thundered against the pavement. Our archers shot a volley, bringing down several of the enemy, but they just kept riding.

"Retreat!" I told my friends. "I'll hold them!"

In a matter of seconds they were on me.

Michael and his archers tried to retreat, but Annabeth stayed right beside me, fighting with her knife and mirrored shield as we slowly backed up the bridge.

Kronos's cavalry swirled around us, slashing and yelling insults. The Titan himself advanced leisurely, like he had all the time in the world. Being the lord of time, I guess he did.

I tried to wound his men, not kill. That slowed me down, but these weren't monsters. They were demigods who'd fallen under Kronos's spell. I couldn't see faces under their battle helmets, but some of them had probably been my friends. I slashed the legs off their horses and made the skeletal mounts disintegrate. After the first few demigods took a spill, the rest figured out they'd better dismount and fight me on foot.

Annabeth and I stayed shoulder to shoulder, facing opposite directions. A dark shape passed over me, and I dared to glance up. Blackjack and Porkpie were swooping in, kicking our enemies in the helmets and flying away like very large kamikaze pigeons.

We'd almost made it to the middle of the bridge when something strange happened. I felt a chill down my spine— like that old saying about someone walking on your grave. Behind me, Annabeth cried out in pain.

"Annabeth!" I turned in time to see her fall, clutching her arm. A demigod with a bloody knife stood over her.

In a flash I understood what had happened. He'd been trying to stab me. Judging from the position of his blade, he would've taken me—maybe by sheer luck—in the small of my back, my only weak point.

Annabeth had intercepted the knife with her own body.

But why? She didn't know about my weak spot. No one did.

I locked eyes with the enemy demigod. He wore an eye patch under his war helm: Ethan Nakamura, the son of Nemesis. Somehow he'd survived the explosion on the *Princess Andromeda*. I slammed him in the face with my sword hilt so hard I dented his helm.

"Get back!" I slashed the air in a wide arc, driving the rest of the demigods away from Annabeth. "No one touches her!"

"Interesting," Kronos said.

He towered above me on his skeletal horse, his scythe in one hand. He studied the scene with narrowed eyes as if he could sense that I'd just come close to death, the way a wolf can smell fear.

"Bravely fought, Percy Jackson," he said. "But it's time to surrender . . . or the girl dies."

"Percy, don't," Annabeth groaned. Her shirt was soaked with blood. I had to get her out of here.

"Blackjack!" I yelled.

As fast as light, the pegasus swooped down and clamped his teeth on the straps of Annabeth's armor. They soared away over the river before the enemy could even react.

Kronos snarled. "Some day soon, I am going to make pegasus soup. But in the meantime . . ." He dismounted, his scythe glistening in the dawn light. "I'll settle for another dead demigod."

I met his first strike with Riptide. The impact shook the entire bridge, but I held my ground. Kronos's smile wavered.

With a yell, I kicked his legs out from under him. His scythe skittered across the pavement. I stabbed downward, but he rolled aside and regained his footing. His scythe flew back to his hands.

"So . . ." He studied me, looking mildly annoyed. "You had the courage to visit the Styx. I had to pressure Luke in many ways to convince him. If only *you* had supplied my host body instead . . . But no matter. I am still more powerful. I am a *TITAN*."

He struck the bridge with the butt of his scythe, and a wave of pure force blasted me backward. Cars went careening. Demigods—even Luke's own men—were blown off the edge of the bridge. Suspension cords whipped around, and I skidded halfway back to Manhattan.

I got unsteadily to my feet. The remaining Apollo campers had almost made it to the end of the bridge, except for Michael Yew, who was perched on one of the suspension cables a few yards away from me. His last arrow was notched in his bow.

"Michael, go!" I screamed.

"Percy, the bridge!" he called. "It's already weak!"

At first I didn't understand. Then I looked down and saw fissures in the pavement. Patches of the road were half melted from Greek fire. The bridge had taken a beating from Kronos's blast and the exploding arrows.

"Break it!" Michael yelled. "Use your powers!"

It was a desperate thought—no way it would work—but I stabbed Riptide into the bridge. The magic blade sank to its hilt in asphalt. Salt water shot from the crack like I'd hit a geyser. I pulled out my blade and the fissure grew. The bridge shook and began to crumble. Chunks the size of houses fell into the East River. Kronos's demigods cried out in alarm and scrambled backward. Some were knocked off their feet. Within a few seconds, a fifty-foot chasm opened in the Williamsburg Bridge between Kronos and me.

The vibrations died. Kronos's men crept to the edge and looked at the hundred-and-thirty-foot drop into the river.

I didn't feel safe, though. The suspension cables were still attached. The men could get across that way if they were brave enough. Or maybe Kronos had a magic way to span the gap.

The Titan lord studied the problem. He looked behind him at the rising sun, then smiled across the chasm. He raised his scythe in a mock salute. "Until this evening, Jackson."

He mounted his horse, whirled around, and galloped back to Brooklyn, followed by his warriors.

I turned to thank Michael Yew, but the words died in my throat. Twenty feet away, a bow lay in the street. Its owner was nowhere to be seen.

"No!" I searched the wreckage on my side of the bridge. I stared down at the river. Nothing.

I yelled in anger and frustration. The sound carried forever in the morning stillness. I was about to whistle for Blackjack to help me search, when my mom's phone rang. The LCD display said I had a call from Finklestein & Associates—probably a demigod calling on a borrowed phone.

I picked up, hoping for good news. Of course I was wrong.

"Percy?" Silena Beauregard sounded like she'd been crying. "Plaza Hotel. You'd better come quickly and bring a healer from Apollo's cabin. It's . . . it's Annabeth."

TWELVE

RACHEL MAKES A BAD DEAL

I grabbed Will Solace from the Apollo cabin and told the rest of his siblings to keep searching for Michael Yew. We borrowed a Yamaha FZ1 from a sleeping biker and drove to the Plaza Hotel at speeds that would've given my mom a heart attack. I'd never driven a motorcycle before, but it wasn't any harder than riding a pegasus.

Along the way, I noticed a lot of empty pedestals that usually held statues. Plan twenty-three seemed to be working. I didn't know if that was good or bad.

It only took us five minutes to reach the Plaza—an old-fashioned white stone hotel with a gabled blue roof, sitting at the southeast corner of Central Park.

Tactically speaking, the Plaza wasn't the best place for a headquarters. It wasn't the tallest building in town, or the most centrally located. But it had old-school style and had attracted a lot of famous demigods over the years, like the Beatles and Alfred Hitchcock, so I figured we were in good company.

I gunned the Yamaha over the curb and swerved to a stop at the fountain outside the hotel.

Will and I hopped off. The statue at the top of the

fountain called down, "Oh, fine. I suppose you want me to watch your bike too!"

She was a life-size bronze standing in the middle of a granite bowl. She wore only a bronze sheet around her legs, and she was holding a basket of metal fruit. I'd never paid her too much attention before. Then again, she'd never talked to me before.

"Are you supposed to be Demeter?" I asked.

A bronze apple sailed over my head.

"Everyone thinks I'm Demeter!" she complained. "I'm Pompona, the Roman Goddess of Plenty, but why should *you* care? Nobody cares about the minor gods. If you cared about the minor gods, you wouldn't be losing this war! Three cheers for Morpheus and Hecate, I say!"

"Watch the bike," I told her.

Pompona cursed in Latin and threw more fruit as Will and I ran toward the hotel.

I'd never actually been inside the Plaza. The lobby was impressive, with the crystal chandeliers and the passed-out rich people, but I didn't pay much attention. A couple of Hunters gave us directions to the elevators, and we rode up to the penthouse suites.

Demigods had completely taken over the top floors. Campers and Hunters were crashed out on sofas, washing up in the bathrooms, ripping silk draperies to bandage their wounds, and helping themselves to snacks and sodas from the minibars. A couple of timber wolves were drinking out of the toilets. I was relieved to see that so many of my friends had made it through the night alive, but everybody looked beat up.

"Percy!" Jake Mason clapped me on the shoulder. "We're getting reports—"

"Later," I said. "Where's Annabeth?"

"The terrace. She's alive, man, but . . ."

I pushed past him.

Under different circumstances I would've loved the view from the terrace. It looked straight down onto Central Park. The morning was clear and bright—perfect for a picnic or a hike, or pretty much anything except fighting monsters.

Annabeth lay on a lounge chair. Her face was pale and beaded with sweat. Even though she was covered in blankets, she shivered. Silena Beauregard was wiping her forehead with a cool cloth.

Will and I pushed through a crowd of Athena kids. Will unwrapped Annabeth's bandages to examine the wound, and I wanted to faint. The bleeding had stopped but the gash looked deep. The skin around the cut was a horrible shade of green.

"Annabeth . . ." I choked up. She'd taken that knife for me. How could I have let that happen?

"Poison on the dagger," she mumbled. "Pretty stupid of me, huh?"

Will Solace exhaled with relief. "It's not so bad, Annabeth. A few more minutes and we would've been in trouble, but the venom hasn't gotten past the shoulder yet. Just lie still. Somebody hand me some nectar."

I grabbed a canteen. Will cleaned out the wound with

the godly drink while I held Annabeth's hand.

"Ow," she said. "Ow, ow!" She gripped my fingers so tight they turned purple, but she stayed still, like Will asked. Silena muttered words of encouragement. Will put some silver paste over the wound and hummed words in Ancient Greek—a hymn to Apollo. Then he applied fresh bandages and stood up shakily.

The healing must've taken a lot of his energy. He looked almost as pale as Annabeth.

"That should do it," he said. "But we're going to need some mortal supplies."

He grabbed a piece of hotel stationery, jotted down some notes, and handed it to one of the Athena guys. "There's a Duane Reade on Fifth. Normally I would never steal—"

"I would," Travis volunteered.

Will glared at him. "Leave cash or drachmas to pay, whatever you've got, but this is an emergency. I've got a feeling we're going to have a lot more people to treat."

Nobody disagreed. There was hardly a single demigod who hadn't already been wounded . . . except me.

"Come on, guys," Travis Stoll said. "Let's give Annabeth some space. We've got a drugstore to raid . . . I mean, visit."

The demigods shuffled back inside. Jake Mason grabbed my shoulder as he was leaving. "We'll talk later, but it's under control. I'm using Annabeth's shield to keep an eye on things. The enemy withdrew at sunrise; not sure why. We've got a lookout at each bridge and tunnel."

"Thanks, man," I said.

He nodded. "Just take your time."

He closed the terrace doors behind him, leaving Silena, Annabeth, and me alone.

Silena pressed a cool cloth to Annabeth's forehead. "This is all my fault."

"No," Annabeth said weakly. "Silena, how is it your fault?"

"I've never been any good at camp," she murmured. "Not like you or Percy. If I was a better fighter . . ."

Her mouth trembled. Ever since Beckendorf died she'd been getting worse, and every time I looked at her, it made me angry about his death all over again. Her expression reminded me of glass—like she might break any minute. I swore to myself that if I ever found the spy who'd cost her boyfriend his life, I would give him to Mrs. O'Leary as a chew toy.

"You're a great camper," I told Silena. "You're the best pegasus rider we have. And you get along with people. Believe me, anyone who can make friends with Clarisse has talent."

She stared at me like I'd just given her an idea. "That's it! We need the Ares cabin. I can talk to Clarisse. I *know* I can convince her to help us."

"Whoa, Silena. Even if you could get off the island, Clarisse is pretty stubborn. Once she gets angry—"

"Please," Silena said. "I can take a pegasus. I *know* I can make it back to camp. Let me try."

I exchanged looks with Annabeth. She nodded slightly.

I didn't like the idea. I didn't think Silena stood a chance of convincing Clarisse to fight. On the other hand, Silena was so distracted right now that she would just get herself hurt in battle. Maybe sending her back to camp would give her something else to focus on.

"All right," I told her. "I can't think of anybody better to try."

Silena threw her arms around me. Then she pushed back awkwardly, glancing at Annabeth. "Um, sorry. Thank you, Percy! I won't let you down!"

Once she was gone, I knelt next to Annabeth and felt her forehead. She was still burning up.

"You're cute when you're worried," she muttered. "Your eyebrows get all scrunched together."

"You are *not* going to die while I owe you a favor," I said. "Why did you take that knife?"

"You would've done the same for me."

It was true. I guess we both knew it. Still, I felt like somebody was poking my heart with a cold metal rod. "How did you know?"

"Know what?"

I looked around to make sure we were alone. Then I leaned in close and whispered: "My Achilles spot. If you hadn't taken that knife, I would've died."

She got a faraway look in her eyes. Her breath smelled of grapes, maybe from the nectar. "I don't know, Percy. I just had this feeling you were in danger. Where . . . where is the spot?"

I wasn't supposed to tell anyone. But this was Annabeth. If I couldn't trust her, I couldn't trust anyone.

"The small of my back."

She lifted her hand. "Where? Here?"

She put her hand on my spine, and my skin tingled. I moved her fingers to the one spot that grounded me to my mortal life. A thousand volts of electricity seemed to arc through my body.

"You saved me," I said. "Thanks."

She removed her hand, but I kept holding it.

"So you owe me," she said weakly. "What else is new?"

We watched the sun come up over the city. The traffic should've been heavy by now, but there were no cars honking, no crowds bustling along the sidewalks.

Far away, I could hear a car alarm echo through the streets. A plume of black smoke curled into the sky somewhere over Harlem. I wondered how many ovens had been left on when the Morpheus spell hit; how many people had fallen asleep in the middle of cooking dinner. Pretty soon there would be more fires. Everyone in New York was in danger—and all those lives depended on us.

"You asked me why Hermes was mad at me," Annabeth said.

"Hey, you need to rest—"

"No, I want to tell you. It's been bothering me for a long time." She moved her shoulder and winced. "Last year, Luke came to see me in San Francisco."

"In person?" I felt like she'd just hit me with a hammer. "He came to your house?"

"This was before we went into the Labyrinth, before . . ." She faltered, but I knew what she meant: *before he turned into*

[200]

Kronos. "He came under a flag of truce. He said he only wanted five minutes to talk. He looked scared, Percy. He told me Kronos was going to use him to take over the world. He said he wanted to run away, like the old days. He wanted me to come with him."

"But you didn't trust him."

"Of course not. I thought it was a trick. Plus . . . well, a lot of things had changed since the old days. I told Luke there was no way. He got mad. He said . . . he said I might as well fight him right there, because it was the last chance I'd get."

Her forehead broke out in sweat again. The story was taking too much of her energy.

"It's okay," I said. "Try to get some rest."

"You don't understand, Percy. Hermes was right. Maybe if I'd gone with him, I could've changed his mind. Or—or I had a knife. Luke was unarmed. I could've—"

"Killed him?" I said. "You know that wouldn't have been right."

She squeezed her eyes shut. "Luke said Kronos would use him *like a stepping stone.* Those were his exact words. Kronos would use Luke, and become even more powerful."

"He did that," I said. "He possessed Luke's body."

"But what if Luke's body is only a transition? What if Kronos has a plan to become even more powerful? I could've stopped him. The war is my fault."

Her story made me feel like I was back in the Styx, slowing dissolving. I remembered last summer, when the two-headed god, Janus, had warned Annabeth she would have to make a major choice—and that had happened *after* she saw Luke. Pan had also said something to her: *You will play a great role, though it may not be the role you imagined.*

I wanted to ask her about the vision Hestia had shown me, about her early days with Luke and Thalia. I knew it had something to do with my prophecy, but I didn't understand what.

Before I could get up my nerve, the terrace door opened. Connor Stoll stepped through.

"Percy." He glanced at Annabeth like he didn't want to say anything bad in front of her, but I could tell he wasn't bringing good news. "Mrs. O'Leary just came back with Grover. I think you should talk to him."

Grover was having a snack in the living room. He was dressed for battle in an armored shirt made from tree bark and twist ties, with his wooden cudgel and his reed pipes hanging from his belt.

The Demeter cabin had whipped up a whole buffet in the hotel kitchens—everything from pizza to pineapple ice cream. Unfortunately, Grover was eating the furniture. He'd already chewed the stuffing off a fancy chair and was now gnawing the armrest.

"Dude," I said, "we're only borrowing this place."

"Blah-ha-ha!" He had stuffing all over his face. "Sorry, Percy. It's just . . . Louis the Sixteenth furniture. *Delicious.* Plus I always eat furniture when I get—"

"When you get nervous," I said. "Yeah, I know. So what's up?"

He clopped on his hooves. "I heard about Annabeth. Is she . . . ?"

"She's going to be fine. She's resting."

Grover took a deep breath. "That's good. I've mobilized most of the nature spirits in the city—well, the ones that will listen to me, anyway." He rubbed his forehead. "I had no idea acorns could hurt so much. Anyway, we're helping out as much as we can."

He told me about the skirmishes they'd seen. Mostly they'd been covering uptown, where we didn't have enough demigods. Hellhounds had appeared in all sorts of places, shadow-traveling inside our lines, and the dryads and satyrs had been fighting them off. A young dragon had appeared in Harlem, and a dozen wood nymphs died before the monster was finally defeated.

As Grover talked, Thalia entered the room with two of her lieutenants. She nodded to me grimly, went outside to check on Annabeth, and came back in. She listened while Grover completed his report—the details getting worse and worse.

"We lost twenty satyrs against some giants at Fort Washington," he said, his voice trembling. "Almost half my kinsmen. River spirits drowned the giants in the end, but . . ."

Thalia shouldered her bow. "Percy, Kronos's forces are still gathering at every bridge and tunnel. And Kronos isn't the only Titan. One of my Hunters spotted a huge man in golden armor mustering an army on the Jersey shore. I'm not sure who he is, but he radiates power like only a Titan or god."

I remembered the golden Titan from my dream—the one on Mount Othrys who erupted into flames.

"Great," I said. "Any good news?"

Thalia shrugged. "We've sealed off the subway tunnels into Manhattan. My best trappers took care of it. Also, it seems like the enemy is waiting for tonight to attack. I think Luke"—she caught herself—"I mean Kronos needs time to regenerate after each fight. He's still not comfortable with his new form. It's taking a lot of his power to slow time around the city."

Grover nodded. "Most of his forces are more powerful at night, too. But they'll be back after sundown."

I tried to think clearly. "Okay. Any word from the gods?"

Thalia shook her head. "I know Lady Artemis would be here if she could. Athena, too. But Zeus has ordered them to stay at his side. The last I heard, Typhon was destroying the Ohio River valley. He should reach the Appalachian Mountains by midday."

"So at best," I said, "we've got another two days before he arrives."

Jake Mason cleared his throat. He'd been standing there so silently I'd almost forgotten he was in the room.

"Percy, something else," he said. "The way Kronos showed up at the Williamsburg Bridge, like he knew you were going there. And he shifted his forces to our weakest points. As soon as we deployed, he changed tactics. He barely touched the Lincoln Tunnel, where the Hunters were strong. He went for our weakest spots, like he knew."

"Like he had inside information," I said. "The spy."

"What spy?" Thalia demanded.

I told her about the silver charm Kronos had shown me, the communication device.

"That's bad," she said. "Very bad."

"It could be anyone," Jake said. "We were all standing there when Percy gave the orders."

"But what can we do?" Grover asked. "Frisk every demigod until we find a scythe charm?"

They all looked at me, waiting for a decision. I couldn't afford to show how panicked I felt, even if things seemed hopeless.

"We keep fighting," I said. "We can't obsess about this spy. If we're suspicious of each other, we'll just tear ourselves apart. You guys were awesome last night. I couldn't ask for a braver army. Let's set up a rotation for the watches. Rest up while you can. We've got a long night ahead of us."

The demigods mumbled agreement. They went their separate ways to sleep or eat or repair their weapons.

"Percy, you too," Thalia said. "We'll keep an eye on things. Go lie down. We need you in good shape for tonight."

I didn't argue too hard. I found the nearest bedroom and crashed on the canopied bed. I thought I was too wired to sleep, but my eyes closed almost immediately.

In my dream, I saw Nico di Angelo alone in the gardens of Hades. He'd just dug a hole in one of Persephone's flower beds, which I didn't figure would make the queen very happy.

He poured a goblet of wine into the hole and began to chant. "Let the dead taste again. Let them rise and take this offering. Maria di Angelo, show yourself!"

White smoke gathered. A human figure formed, but it wasn't Nico's mother. It was a girl with dark hair, olive skin, and the silvery clothes of a Hunter.

"Bianca," Nico said. "But—"

Don't summon our mother, Nico, she warned. *She is the one spirit you are forbidden to see.*

"Why?" he demanded. "What's our father hiding?"

Pain, Bianca said. *Hatred. A curse that stretches back to the Great Prophecy.*

"What do you mean?" Nico said. "I have to know!"

The knowledge will only hurt you. Remember what I said: holding grudges is a fatal flaw for children of Hades.

"I know that," Nico said. "But I'm not the same as I used to be, Bianca. Stop trying to protect me!"

Brother, you don't understand—

Nico swiped his hand through the mist, and Bianca's image dissipated.

"Maria di Angelo," he said again. "Speak to me!"

A different image formed. It was a scene rather than a single ghost. In the mist, I saw Nico and Bianca as little children, playing in the lobby of an elegant hotel, chasing each other around marble columns.

A woman sat on a nearby sofa. She wore a black dress, gloves, and a black veiled hat like a star from an old 1940s movie. She had Bianca's smile and Nico's eyes.

On a chair next to her sat a large oily man in a black pin-stripe suit. With a shock, I realized it was Hades. He was leaning toward the woman, using his hands as he talked, like he was agitated.

"Please, my dear," he said. "You *must* come to the Underworld. I don't care what Persephone thinks! I can keep you safe there."

"No, my love." She spoke with an Italian accent. "Raise our children in the land of the dead? I will not do this."

"Maria, listen to me. The war in Europe has turned the other gods against me. A prophecy has been made. My children are no longer safe. Poseidon and Zeus have forced me into an agreement. None of us are to have demigod children ever again."

"But you already *have* Nico and Bianca. Surely—"

"No! The prophecy warns of a child who turns sixteen. Zeus has decreed that the children I currently have must be turned over to Camp Half-Blood for *proper training*, but I know what he means. At best they'll be watched, imprisoned, turned against their father. Even more likely, he will not take a chance. He won't allow my demigod children to reach sixteen. He'll find a way to destroy them, and I won't risk that!"

"*Certamente*," Maria said. "We will stay together. Zeus is *un imbecile*."

I couldn't help admiring her courage, but Hades glanced nervously at the ceiling. "Maria, please. I told you, Zeus gave me a deadline of *last week* to turn over the children. His wrath will be horrible, and I cannot hide you forever. As long as you are with the children, you are in danger too."

Maria smiled, and again it was creepy how much she looked like her daughter. "You are a god, my love. You will protect us. But I will not take Nico and Bianca to the Underworld."

Hades wrung his hands. "Then, there is another option. I know a place in the desert where time stands still. I could send the children there, just for a while, for their own safety, and we could be together. I will build you a golden palace by the Styx."

Maria di Angelo laughed gently. "You are a kind man, my love. A generous man. The other gods should see you as I do, and they would not fear you so. But Nico and Bianca need their mother. Besides, they are only children. The gods wouldn't really hurt them."

"You don't know my family," Hades said darkly. "Please, Maria, I can't lose you."

She touched his lips with her fingers. "You will not lose me. Wait for me while I get my purse. Watch the children."

She kissed the lord of the dead and rose from the sofa. Hades watched her walk upstairs as if her every step away caused him pain.

A moment later, he tensed. The children stopped playing as if they sensed something too.

"No!" Hades said. But even his godly powers were too slow. He only had time to erect a wall of black energy around the children before the hotel exploded.

The force was so violent, the entire mist image dissolved.

When it came into focus again, I saw Hades kneeling in the ruins, holding the broken form of Maria di Angelo. Fires still burned all around him. Lightning flashed across the sky, and thunder rumbled.

Little Nico and Bianca stared at their mother uncomprehendingly. The Fury Alecto appeared behind them, hissing and flapping her leathery wings. The children didn't seem to notice her.

"Zeus!" Hades shook his fist at the sky. "I will crush you for this! I will bring her back!"

"My lord, you cannot," Alecto warned. "You of all immortals must respect the laws of death."

Hades glowed with rage. I thought he would show his true form and vaporize his own children, but at the last moment he seemed to regain control.

"Take them," he told Alecto, choking back a sob. "Wash their memories clean in the Lethe and bring them to the Lotus Hotel. Zeus will not harm them there."

"As you wish, my lord," Alecto said. "And the woman's body?"

"Take her as well," he said bitterly. "Give her the ancient rites."

Alecto, the children, and Maria's body dissolved into shadows, leaving Hades alone in the ruins.

"I warned you," a new voice said.

Hades turned. A girl in a multicolored dress stood by the smoldering remains of the sofa. She had short black hair and sad eyes. She was no more than twelve. I didn't know her, but she looked strangely familiar.

"You dare come here?" Hades growled. "I should blast you to dust!"

"You cannot," the girl said. "The power of Delphi protects me."

With a chill, I realized I was looking at the Oracle of Delphi, back when she was alive and young. Somehow, seeing her like this was even spookier than seeing her as a mummy.

"You've killed the woman I loved!" Hades roared. "Your prophecy brought us to this!"

He loomed over the girl, but she didn't flinch.

"Zeus ordained the explosion to destroy the children," she said, "because you defied his will. I had nothing to do with it. And I did warn you to hide them sooner."

"I couldn't! Maria would not let me! Besides, they were innocent."

"Nevertheless, they are your children, which makes them dangerous. Even if you put them away in the Lotus Hotel, you only delay the problem. Nico and Bianca will never be able to rejoin the world lest they turn sixteen."

"Because of your so-called Great Prophecy. And you have forced me into an oath to have no other children. You have left me with nothing!"

"I foresee the future," the girl said. "I cannot change it."

Black fire lit the god's eyes, and I knew something bad was coming. I wanted to yell at the girl to hide or run.

"Then, Oracle, hear the words of Hades," he growled. "Perhaps I cannot bring back Maria. Nor can I bring you an early death. But your soul is still mortal, and I *can* curse you."

The girl's eyes widened. "You would not—"

"I swear," Hades said, "as long as my children remain outcasts, as long as I labor under the curse of your Great Prophecy, the Oracle of Delphi will never have another mortal host. You will never rest in peace. No other will take your place. Your body will wither and die, and still the Oracle's spirit will be locked inside you. You will speak your bitter prophecies until you crumble to nothing. The Oracle will die with you!"

The girl screamed, and the misty image was blasted to shreds. Nico fell to his knees in Persephone's garden, his face white with shock. Standing in front of him was the real Hades, towering in his black robes and scowling down at his son.

"And just what," he asked Nico, "do you think you're doing?"

A black explosion filled my dreams. Then the scene changed.

Rachel Elizabeth Dare was walking along a white sand beach. She wore a swimsuit with a T-shirt wrapped around her waist. Her shoulders and face were sunburned.

She knelt and began writing in the surf with her finger. I tried to make out the letters. I thought my dyslexia was acting up until I realized she was writing in Ancient Greek.

That was impossible. The dream had to be false.

Rachel finished writing a few words and muttered, "What in the world?"

I can read Greek, but I only recognized one word before the sea washed it away: Περσεύς. My name: *Perseus*.

Rachel stood abruptly and backed away from the surf.

"Oh, gods," she said. "*That's* what it means."

She turned and ran, kicking up sand as she raced back to her family's villa.

She pounded up the porch steps, breathing hard. Her father looked up from his *Wall Street Journal*.

"Dad." Rachel marched up to him. "We have to go back."

Her dad's mouth twitched, like he was trying to remember how to smile. "Back? We just got here."

"There's trouble in New York. Percy's in danger."

"Did he call you?"

"No . . . not exactly. But I *know*. It's a feeling."

Mr. Dare folded his newspaper. "Your mother and I have been looking forward to this vacation for a long time."

"No you haven't! You both hate the beach! You're just too stubborn to admit it."

"Now, Rachel—"

"I'm telling you something is wrong in New York! The whole city . . . I don't know what exactly, but it's under attack."

Her father sighed. "I think we would've heard something like that on the news."

"No," Rachel insisted. "Not this kind of attack. Have you had any calls since we got here?"

Her father frowned. "No . . . but it is the weekend, in the middle of the summer."

"You *always* get calls," Rachel said. "You've got to admit that's strange."

Her father hesitated. "We can't just leave. We've spent a lot of money."

"Look," Rachel said. "Daddy . . . Percy needs me. I have to deliver a message. It's life or death."

"What message? What are you talking about?"

"I can't tell you."

"Then you can't go."

Rachel closed her eyes like she was getting up her courage. "Dad . . . let me go, and I'll make a deal with you."

Mr. Dare sat forward. Deals were something he understood. "I'm listening."

"Clarion Ladies Academy. I'll—I'll go there in the fall. I won't even complain. But you have to get me back to New York *right now*."

He was silent for a long time. Then he opened his phone and made a call.

"Douglas? Prep the plane. We're leaving for New York. Yes . . . immediately."

Rachel flung her arms around him, and her father seemed surprised, like she'd never hugged him before.

"I'll make it up to you, Dad!"

He smiled, but his expression was chilly. He studied her like he wasn't seeing his daughter—just the young lady he wanted her to be, once Clarion Academy got through with her.

"Yes, Rachel," he agreed. "You most certainly will."

The scene faded. I mumbled in my sleep: "Rachel, no!"

I was still tossing and turning when Thalia shook me awake.

"Percy," she said. "Come on. It's late afternoon. We've got visitors."

I sat up, disoriented. The bed was too comfortable, and I hated sleeping in the middle of the day.

"Visitors?" I said.

Thalia nodded grimly. "A Titan wants to see you, under a flag of truce. He has a message from Kronos."

THIRTEEN

A TITAN BRINGS ME
A PRESENT

We could see the white flag from half a mile away. It was as big as a soccer field, carried by a thirty-foot-tall giant with bright blue skin and icy gray hair.

"A Hyperborean," Thalia said. "The giants of the north. It's a bad sign that they sided with Kronos. They're usually peaceful."

"You've met them?" I said.

"Mmm. There's a big colony in Alberta. You do *not* want to get into a snowball fight with those guys."

As the giant got closer, I could see three human-size envoys with him: a half-blood in armor, an *empousa* demon with a black dress and flaming hair, and a tall man in a tuxedo. The *empousa* held the tux dude's arm, so they looked like a couple on their way to a Broadway show or something—except for her flaming hair and fangs.

The group walked leisurely toward the Heckscher Playground. The swings and ball courts were empty. The only sound was the fountain on Umpire Rock.

I looked at Grover. "The tux dude is the Titan?"

He nodded nervously. "He looks like a magician. I hate magicians. They usually have rabbits."

I stared at him. "You're scared of bunnies?"

"Blah-hah-hah! They're big bullies. Always stealing celery from defenseless satyrs!"

Thalia coughed.

"What?" Grover demanded.

"We'll have to work on your bunny phobia later," I said. "Here they come."

The man in the tux stepped forward. He was taller than an average human—about seven feet. His black hair was tied in a ponytail. Dark round glasses covered his eyes, but what really caught my attention was the skin on his face. It was covered in scratches, like he'd been attacked by a small animal—a really, *really* mad hamster, maybe.

"Percy Jackson," he said in a silky voice. "It's a great honor."

His lady friend the *empousa* hissed at me. She'd probably heard how I'd destroyed two of her sisters last summer.

"My dear," Tux Dude said to her. "Why don't you make yourself comfortable over there, eh?"

She released his arm and drifted over to a park bench.

I glanced at the armed demigod behind Tux Dude. I hadn't recognized him in his new helmet, but it was my old backstabbing buddy Ethan Nakamura. His nose looked like a squashed tomato from our fight on the Williamsburg Bridge. That made me feel better.

"Hey, Ethan," I said. "You're looking good."

Ethan glared at me.

"To business." Tux Dude extended his hand. "I am Prometheus."

I was too surprised to shake. "The fire-stealer guy? The chained-to-the-rock-with-the-vultures guy?"

Prometheus winced. He touched the scratches on his face. "Please, don't mention the vultures. But yes, I stole fire from the gods and gave it to your ancestors. In return, the ever merciful Zeus had me chained to a rock and tortured for all eternity."

"But—"

"How did I get free? Hercules did that, eons ago. So you see, I have a soft spot for heroes. Some of you can be quite civilized."

"Unlike the company you keep," I noticed.

I was looking at Ethan, but Prometheus apparently thought I meant the *empousa*.

"Oh, demons aren't so bad," he said. "You just have to keep them well fed. Now, Percy Jackson, let us parley."

He waved me toward a picnic table and we sat down. Thalia and Grover stood behind me.

The blue giant propped his white flag against a tree and began absently playing on the playground. He stepped on the monkey bars and crushed them, but he didn't seem angry. He just frowned and said, "Uh-oh." Then he stepped in the fountain and broke the concrete bowl in half. "Uh-oh." The water froze where his foot touched it. A bunch of stuffed animals hung from his belt—the huge kind you get for grand prizes at an arcade. He reminded me of Tyson, and the idea of fighting him made me sad.

Prometheus sat forward and laced his fingers. He looked earnest, kindly, and wise. "Percy, your position is weak. You know you can't stop another assault."

"We'll see."

Prometheus looked pained, like he really cared what happened to me. "Percy, I'm the Titan of forethought. I know what's going to happen."

"Also the Titan of crafty counsel," Grover put in. "Emphasis on *crafty*."

Prometheus shrugged. "True enough, satyr. But I supported the gods in the last war. I told Kronos: 'You don't have the strength. You'll lose.' And I was right. So you see, I know how to pick the winning side. This time, I'm backing Kronos."

"Because Zeus chained you to a rock," I guessed.

"Partly, yes. I won't deny I want revenge. But that's not the only reason I'm supporting Kronos. It's the wisest choice. I'm here because I thought you might listen to reason."

He drew a map on the table with his finger. Wherever he touched, golden lines appeared, glowing on the concrete. "This is Manhattan. We have armies here, here, here, and here. We know your numbers. We outnumber you twenty to one."

"Your spy has been keeping you posted," I guessed.

Prometheus smiled apologetically. "At any rate, our forces are growing daily. Tonight, Kronos will attack. You will be overwhelmed. You've fought bravely, but there's just no way you can hold all of Manhattan. You'll be forced to retreat to the Empire State Building. There you'll be destroyed. I have seen this. It *will* happen."

I thought about the picture Rachel had drawn in my dreams—an army at the base of the Empire State Building. I remembered the words of the young girl Oracle in my dream: *I foresee the future. I cannot change it.* Prometheus spoke with such certainty it was hard not to believe him.

"I won't let it happen," I said.

Prometheus brushed a speck off his tux lapel. "Understand, Percy. You are refighting the Trojan War here. Patterns repeat themselves in history. They reappear just as monsters do. A great siege. Two armies. The only difference is, this time you are defending. *You* are Troy. And you know what happened to the Trojans, don't you?"

"So you're going to cram a wooden horse into the elevator at the Empire State Building?" I asked. "Good luck."

Prometheus smiled. "Troy was completely destroyed, Percy. You don't want that to happen here. Stand down, and New York will be spared. Your forces will be granted amnesty. I will personally assure your safety. Let Kronos take Olympus. Who cares? Typhon will destroy the gods anyway."

"Right," I said. "And I'm supposed to believe Kronos would spare the city."

"All he wants is Olympus," Prometheus promised. "The might of the gods is tied to their seats of power. You saw what happened to Poseidon once his undersea palace was attacked."

I winced, remembering how old and decrepit my father looked.

"Yes," Prometheus said sadly. "I know that was hard for

you. When Kronos destroys Olympus, the gods will fade. They will become so weak they will be easily defeated. Kronos would rather do this while Typhon has the Olympians distracted in the west. Much easier. Fewer lives lost. But make no mistake, the best you can do is slow us down. The day after tomorrow, Typhon arrives in New York, and you will have no chance at all. The gods and Mount Olympus will still be destroyed, but it will be much messier. Much, much worse for you and your city. Either way, the Titans will rule."

Thalia pounded her fist on the table. "I serve Artemis. The Hunters will fight to our last breath. Percy, you're not seriously going to listen to this slimeball, are you?"

I figured Prometheus was going to blast her, but he just smiled. "Your courage does you credit, Thalia Grace."

Thalia stiffened. "That's my mother's surname. I don't use it."

"As you wish," Prometheus said casually, but I could tell he'd gotten under her skin. I'd never even heard Thalia's last name before. Somehow it made her seem almost normal. Less mysterious and powerful.

"At any rate," the Titan said, "you need not be my enemy. I have always been a helper of mankind."

"That's a load of Minotaur dung," Thalia said. "When mankind first sacrificed to the gods, you tricked them into giving you the best portion. You gave us fire to annoy the gods, not because you cared about us."

Prometheus shook his head. "You don't understand. I helped shape your nature."

A wiggling lump of clay appeared in his hands. He fashioned it into a little doll with legs and arms. The lump man didn't have any eyes, but it groped around the table, stumbling over Prometheus's fingers. "I have been whispering in man's ear since the beginning of your existence. I represent your curiosity, your sense of exploration, your inventiveness. Help me save you, Percy. Do this, and I will give mankind a new gift—a new revelation that will move you as far forward as fire did. You can't make that kind of advance under the gods. They would never allow it. But this could be a new golden age for you. Or . . ." He made a fist and smashed the clay man into a pancake.

The blue giant rumbled, "Uh-oh." Over at the park bench, the *empousa* bared her fangs in a smile.

"Percy, you know the Titans and their offspring are not all bad," Prometheus said. "You've met Calypso."

My face felt hot. "That's different."

"How? Much like me, she did nothing wrong, and yet she was exiled forever simply because she was Atlas's daughter. We are not your enemies. Don't let the worst happen," he pleaded. "We offer you peace."

I looked at Ethan Nakamura. "You must hate this."

"I don't know what you mean."

"If we took this deal, you wouldn't get revenge. You wouldn't get to kill us all. Isn't that what you want?"

His good eye flared. "All I want is respect, Jackson. The gods never gave me that. You wanted me to go to your stupid camp, spend my time crammed into the Hermes cabin because I'm not important? Not even recognized?"

He sounded just like Luke when he'd tried to kill me in the woods at camp four years ago. The memory made my hand ache where the pit scorpion had stung me.

"Your mom's the goddess of revenge," I told Ethan. "We should respect that?"

"Nemesis stands for balance! When people have too much good luck, she tears them down."

"Which is why she took your eye?"

"It was payment," he growled. "In exchange, she swore to me that one day *I* would tip the balance of power. I would bring the minor gods respect. An eye was a small price to pay."

"Great mom."

"At least she keeps her word, unlike the Olympians. She always pays her debts—good or evil."

"Yeah," I said. "So I saved your life, and you repaid me by raising Kronos. That's fair."

Ethan grabbed the hilt of his sword, but Prometheus stopped him.

"Now, now," the Titan said. "We're on a diplomatic mission."

Prometheus studied me as if trying to understand my anger. Then he nodded like he'd just picked a thought from my brain.

"It bothers you what happened to Luke," he decided. "Hestia didn't show you the full story. Perhaps if you understood . . ."

The Titan reached out.

Thalia cried a warning, but before I could react, Prometheus's index finger touched my forehead.

Suddenly I was back in May Castellan's living room. Candles flickered on the fireplace mantel, reflected in the mirrors along the walls. Through the kitchen doorway I could see Thalia sitting at the table while Ms. Castellan bandaged her wounded leg. Seven-year-old Annabeth sat next to her, playing with a Medusa beanbag toy.

Hermes and Luke stood apart in the living room.

The god's face looked liquid in the candlelight, like he couldn't decide what shape to adopt. He was dressed in a navy blue jogging outfit with winged Reeboks.

"Why show yourself now?" Luke demanded. His shoulders were tense, as if he expected a fight. "All these years I've been calling to you, praying you'd show up, and nothing. You left me with *her*." He pointed toward the kitchen like he couldn't bear to look at his mother, much less say her name.

"Luke, do not dishonor her," Hermes warned. "Your mother did the best she could. As for me, I could not interfere with your path. The children of the gods must find their own way."

"So it was for my own good. Growing up on the streets, fending for myself, fighting monsters."

"You're my son," Hermes said. "I knew you had the ability. When I was only a baby, I crawled from my cradle and set out for—"

"I'm not a god! Just once, you could've said something. You could've helped when"—he took an unsteady breath, lowering his voice so no one in the kitchen could overhear—"when she was having one of her *fits*, shaking me and saying crazy things about my fate. When I used to hide in the closet so she wouldn't find me with those . . . those glowing eyes. Did you even *care* that I was scared? Did you even know when I finally ran away?"

In the kitchen, Ms. Castellan chattered aimlessly, pouring Kool-Aid for Thalia and Annabeth as she told them stories about Luke as a baby. Thalia rubbed her bandaged leg nervously. Annabeth glanced into the living room and held up a burned cookie for Luke to see. She mouthed, *Can we go now?*

"Luke, I care very much," Hermes said slowly, "but gods must not interfere directly in mortal affairs. It is one of our Ancient Laws. Especially when your destiny . . ." His voice trailed off. He stared at the candles as if remembering something unpleasant.

"What?" Luke asked. "What about my destiny?"

"You should not have come back," Hermes muttered. "It only upsets you both. However, I see now that you are getting too old to be on the run without help. I'll speak with Chiron at Camp Half-Blood and ask him to send a satyr to collect you."

"We're doing fine without your help," Luke growled. "Now, what were you saying about my destiny?"

The wings on Hermes's Reeboks fluttered restlessly. He studied his son like he was trying to memorize his face, and suddenly a cold feeling washed through me. I realized Hermes *knew* what May Castellan's mutterings meant. I wasn't sure how, but looking at his face I was absolutely certain. Hermes understood what would happen to Luke someday, how he would turn evil.

"My son," he said, "I'm the god of travelers, the god of roads. If I know anything, I know that you must walk your own path, even though it tears my heart."

"You don't love me."

"I promise I . . . I do love you. Go to camp. I will see that you get a quest soon. Perhaps you can defeat the Hydra, or steal the apples of Hesperides. You will get a chance to be a great hero before . . ."

"Before what?" Luke's voice was trembling now. "What did my mom see that made her like this? What's going to happen to me? If you love me, *tell* me."

Hermes's expression tightened. "I cannot."

"Then you don't care!" Luke yelled.

In the kitchen, the talking died abruptly.

"Luke?" May Castellan called. "Is that you? Is my boy all right?"

Luke turned to hide his face, but I could see the tears in his eyes. "I'm fine. I have a new family. I don't need either of you."

"I'm your father," Hermes insisted.

"A *father* is supposed to be around. I've never even *met* you. Thalia, Annabeth, come on! We're leaving!"

"My boy, don't go!" May Castellan called after him. "I have your lunch ready!"

Luke stormed out the door, Thalia and Annabeth scrambling after him. May Castellan tried to follow, but Hermes held her back.

As the screen door slammed, May collapsed in Hermes's arms and began to shake. Her eyes opened—glowing green—and she clutched desperately at Hermes's shoulders.

"*My son,*" she hissed in a dry voice. "*Danger. Terrible fate!*"

"I know, my love," Hermes said sadly. "Believe me, I know."

The image faded. Prometheus pulled his hand away from my forehead.

"Percy?" Thalia asked. "What . . . what was that?"

I realized I was clammy with sweat.

Prometheus nodded sympathetically. "Appalling, isn't it? The gods know what is to come, and yet they do nothing, even for their children. How long did it take for them to tell you *your* prophecy, Percy Jackson? Don't you think your father knows what will happen to you?"

I was too stunned to answer.

"Perrrcy," Grover warned, "he's playing with your mind. Trying to make you angry."

Grover could read emotions, so he probably knew Prometheus was succeeding.

"Do you really blame your friend Luke?" the Titan asked me. "And what about you, Percy? Will you be controlled by your fate? Kronos offers you a much better deal."

I clenched my fists. As much as I hated what Prometheus had shown me, I hated Kronos a lot more. "I'll give you a deal. Tell Kronos to call off his attack, leave Luke Castellan's body, and return to the pits of Tartarus. Then maybe I won't have to destroy him."

The *empousa* snarled. Her hair erupted in fresh flames, but Prometheus just sighed.

"If you change your mind," he said, "I have a gift for you."

A Greek vase appeared on the table. It was about three feet high and a foot wide, glazed with black-and-white geometric designs. The ceramic lid was fastened with a leather harness.

Grover whimpered when he saw it.

Thalia gasped. "That's not—"

"Yes," Prometheus said. "You recognize it."

Looking at the jar, I felt a strange sense of fear, but I had no idea why.

"This belonged to my sister-in-law," Prometheus explained. "Pandora."

A lump formed in my throat. "As in Pandora's box?"

Prometheus shook his head. "I don't know how this *box* business got started. It was never a box. It was a *pithos*, a storage jar. I suppose Pandora's *pithos* doesn't have the same ring to it, but never mind that. Yes, she did open this jar, which contained most of the demons that now haunt mankind— fear, death, hunger, sickness."

"Don't forget me," the *empousa* purred.

"Indeed," Prometheus conceded. "The first *empousa* was also trapped in this jar, released by Pandora. But what I find curious about the story—Pandora always gets the blame. She is punished for being curious. The gods would have you believe that this is the lesson: mankind should not explore. They should not ask questions. They should do what they are told. In truth, Percy, this jar was a trap designed by Zeus and the other gods. It was revenge on *me* and my entire family—my poor simple brother Epimetheus and his wife Pandora. The gods knew she would open the jar. They were willing to punish the entire race of humanity along with us."

I thought about my dream of Hades and Maria di Angelo. Zeus had destroyed an entire hotel to eliminate two demigod children—just to save his own skin, because he was scared of a prophecy. He'd killed an innocent woman and probably hadn't lost any sleep over it. Hades was no better. He wasn't powerful enough to take his revenge on Zeus, so he cursed the Oracle, dooming a young girl to a horrible fate. And Hermes . . . why had he abandoned Luke? Why hadn't he at least warned Luke, or tried to raise him better so he wouldn't turn evil?

Maybe Prometheus was toying with my mind.

But what if he's right? part of me wondered. *How are the gods any better than the Titans?*

Prometheus tapped the lid of Pandora's jar. "Only one spirit remained inside when Pandora opened it."

"Hope," I said.

Prometheus looked pleased. "Very good, Percy. Elpis, the Spirit of Hope, would not abandon humanity. Hope does not leave without being given permission. She can only be released by a child of man."

The Titan slid the jar across the table.

"I give you this as a reminder of what the gods are like," he said. "Keep Elpis, if you wish. But if you decide that you have seen enough destruction, enough futile suffering, then open the jar. Let Elpis go. Give up Hope, and I will know that you are surrendering. I promise Kronos will be lenient. He will spare the survivors."

I stared at the jar and got a very bad feeling. I figured Pandora had been completely ADHD, like me. I could never leave things alone. I didn't like temptation. What if *this* was my choice? Maybe the prophecy all came down to my keeping this jar closed or opening it.

"I don't want the thing," I growled.

"Too late," Prometheus said. "The gift is given. It cannot be taken back."

He stood. The *empousa* came forward and slipped her arm through his.

"Morrain!" Prometheus called to the blue giant. "We are leaving. Get your flag."

"Uh-oh," the giant said.

"We will see you soon, Percy Jackson," Prometheus promised. "One way or another."

Ethan Nakamura gave me one last hateful look. Then the truce party turned and strolled up the lane through Central Park, like it was just a regular sunny Sunday afternoon.

FOURTEEN

PIGS FLY

Back at the Plaza, Thalia pulled me aside. "What did Prometheus show you?"

Reluctantly, I told her about the vision of May Castellan's house. Thalia rubbed her thigh like she was remembering the old wound.

"That was a bad night," she admitted. "Annabeth was so little, I don't think she really understood what she saw. She just knew Luke was upset."

I looked out the hotel windows at Central Park. Small fires were still burning in the north, but otherwise the city seemed unnaturally peaceful. "Do you know what happened to May Castellan? I mean—"

"I know what you mean," Thalia said. "I never saw her have an, um, episode, but Luke told me about the glowing eyes, the strange things she would say. He made me promise never to tell. What caused it, I have no idea. If Luke knew, he never told me."

"Hermes knew," I said. "Something caused May to see parts of Luke's future, and Hermes understood what would happen—how Luke would turn into Kronos."

Thalia frowned. "You can't be sure of that. Remember Prometheus was manipulating what you saw, Percy, showing you what happened in the worst possible light. Hermes *did* love Luke. I could tell just by looking at his face. And Hermes was there that night because he was checking up on May, taking care of her. He wasn't all bad."

"It's still not right," I insisted. "Luke was just a little kid. Hermes never helped him, never stopped him from running away."

Thalia shouldered her bow. Again it struck me how much stronger she looked now that she'd stopped aging. You could almost see a silvery glow around her—the blessing of Artemis.

"Percy," she said, "you can't start feeling sorry for Luke. We all have tough things to deal with. All demigods do. Our parents are hardly ever around. But Luke made bad choices. Nobody forced him to do that. In fact—"

She glanced down the hall to make sure we were alone. "I'm worried about Annabeth. If she has to face Luke in battle, I don't know if she can do it. She's always had a soft spot for him."

Blood rose to my face. "She'll do fine."

"I don't know. After that night, after we left his mom's house? Luke was never the same. He got reckless and moody, like he had something to prove. By the time Grover found us and tried to get us to camp . . . well, part of the reason we had so much trouble was because Luke wouldn't be careful. He wanted to pick a fight with every monster we crossed. Annabeth didn't see that as a problem. Luke was her hero. She only understood that his parents had made him sad, and she got very defensive of him. She still *is* defensive. All I'm saying . . . don't you fall into the same trap. Luke has given himself to Kronos now. We can't afford to be soft on him."

I looked out at the fires in Harlem, wondering how many sleeping mortals were in danger right now because of Luke's bad choices.

"You're right," I said.

Thalia patted my shoulder. "I'm going to check on the Hunters, then get some more sleep before nightfall. You should crash too."

"The last thing I need is more dreams."

"I know, believe me." Her dark expression made me wonder what she'd been dreaming about. It was a common demigod problem: the more dangerous our situation became, the worse and more frequent our dreams got. "But Percy, there's no telling when you'll get another chance for rest. It's going to be a long night—maybe our *last* night."

I didn't like it, but I knew she was right. I nodded wearily and gave her Pandora's jar. "Do me a favor. Lock this in the hotel vault, will you? I think I'm allergic to *pithos*."

Thalia smiled. "You got it."

I found the nearest bed and passed out. But of course sleep only brought more nightmares.

I saw the undersea palace of my father. The enemy army was closer now, entrenched only a few hundred yards outside the palace. The fortress walls were completely destroyed. The temple my dad had used as his headquarters was burning with Greek fire.

I zoomed in on the armory, where my brother and some other Cyclopes were on lunch break, eating from huge jars of Skippy extra-chunky peanut butter (and don't ask me how it tasted underwater, because I don't want to know). As I watched, the outer wall of the armory exploded. A Cyclops warrior stumbled inside, collapsing on the lunch table. Tyson knelt down to help, but it was too late. The Cyclops dissolved into sea silt.

Enemy giants moved toward the breach, and Tyson picked up the fallen warrior's club. He yelled something to his fellow blacksmiths—probably "For Poseidon!"—but with his mouth full of peanut butter it sounded like "PUH PTEH BUN!" His brethren all grabbed hammers and chisels, yelled, "PEANUT BUTTER!" and charged behind Tyson into battle.

Then the scene shifted. I was with Ethan Nakamura at the enemy camp. What I saw made me shiver, partly because the army was so huge, partly because I recognized the place.

We were in the backwoods of New Jersey, on a crumbling road lined with run-down businesses and tattered billboard signs. A trampled fence ringed a big yard full of cement statuary. The sign above the warehouse was hard to read because it was in red cursive, but I knew what it said: AUNTY EM'S GARDEN GNOME EMPORIUM.

I hadn't thought about the place in years. It was clearly abandoned. The statues were broken and spray-painted with graffiti. A cement satyr—Grover's Uncle Ferdinand—had lost his arm. Part of the warehouse roof had caved in. A big yellow sign pasted on the door read: CONDEMNED.

Hundreds of tents and fires surrounded the property. Mostly I saw monsters, but there were some human mercenaries in combat fatigues and demigods in armor, too. A purple-and-black banner hung outside the emporium, guarded by two huge blue Hyperboreans.

Ethan was crouched at the nearest campfire. A couple of other demigods sat with him, sharpening their swords. The doors of the warehouse opened, and Prometheus stepped out.

"Nakamura," he called. "The master would like to speak to you."

Ethan stood up warily. "Something wrong?"

Prometheus smiled. "You'll have to ask him."

One of the other demigods snickered. "Nice knowing you."

Ethan readjusted his sword belt and headed into the warehouse.

Except for the hole in the roof, the place was just as I remembered. Statues of terrified people stood frozen in midscream. In the snack bar area, the picnic tables had been moved aside. Right between the soda dispenser and pretzel warmer stood a golden throne. Kronos lounged on it, his scythe across his lap. He wore jeans and a T-shirt, and with his brooding expression he looked almost human—like the younger version of Luke I'd seen in the vision, pleading with Hermes to tell him his fate. Then Luke saw Ethan, and his face contorted into a very inhuman smile. His golden eyes glowed.

"Well, Nakamura. What did you think of the diplomatic mission?"

Ethan hesitated. "I'm sure Lord Prometheus is better suited to speak—"

"But I asked *you.*"

Ethan's good eye darted back and forth, noting the guards that stood around Kronos. "I . . . I don't think Jackson will surrender. Ever."

Kronos nodded. "Anything else you wanted to tell me?"

"N-no, sir."

"You look nervous, Ethan."

"No, sir. It's just . . . I heard this was the lair of —"

"Medusa? Yes, quite true. Lovely place, eh? Unfortunately, Medusa hasn't re-formed since Jackson killed her, so you needn't worry about joining her collection. Besides, there are much more dangerous forces in this room."

Kronos looked over at a Laistrygonian giant who was munching noisily on some french fries. Kronos waved his hand and the giant froze. A french fry hung suspended in midair halfway between his hand and his mouth.

"Why turn them to stone," Kronos asked, "when you can freeze time itself?"

His golden eyes bored into Ethan's face. "Now, tell me one more thing. What happened last night on the Williamsburg Bridge?"

Ethan trembled. Beads of perspiration were popping up on his forehead. "I . . . I don't know, sir."

"Yes, you do." Kronos rose from his seat. "When you attacked Jackson, something happened. Something was not quite right. The girl, Annabeth, jumped in your way."

"She wanted to save him."

"But he is invulnerable," Kronos said quietly. "You saw that yourself."

"I can't explain it. Maybe she forgot."

"She forgot," Kronos said. "Yes, that must've been it. *Oh dear, I forgot my friend is invulnerable and took a knife for him. Oops.* Tell me, Ethan, where were you aiming when you stabbed at Jackson?"

Ethan frowned. He clasped his hand as if he were holding a blade, and mimed a thrust. "I'm not sure, sir. It all happened so fast. I wasn't aiming for any spot in particular."

Kronos's fingers tapped the blade of his scythe. "I see," he said in a chilly tone. "If your memory improves, I will expect—"

Suddenly the Titan lord winced. The giant in the corner unfroze and the french fry fell into his mouth. Kronos stumbled backward and sank into his throne.

"My lord?" Ethan started forward.

"I—" The voice was weak, but just for a moment it was Luke's. Then Kronos's expression hardened. He raised his hand and flexed his fingers slowly as if forcing them to obey.

"It is nothing," he said, his voice steely and cold again. "A minor discomfort."

Ethan moistened his lips. "He's still fighting you, isn't he? Luke—"

"Nonsense," Kronos spat. "Repeat that lie, and I will cut out your tongue. The boy's soul has been crushed. I am simply adjusting to the limits of this form. It requires rest. It is annoying, but no more than a temporary inconvenience."

"As . . . as you say, my lord."

"You!" Kronos pointed his scythe at a *dracaena* with green armor and a green crown. "Queen Sess, is it?"

"Yesssss, my lord."

"Is our little surprise ready to be unleashed?"

The *dracaena* queen bared her fangs. "Oh, yessss, my lord. Quite a lovely sssssurprissse."

"Excellent," Kronos said. "Tell my brother Hyperion to move our main force south into Central Park. The half-bloods will be in such disarray they will not be able to defend themselves. Go now, Ethan. Work on improving your memory. We will talk again when we have taken Manhattan."

Ethan bowed, and my dreams shifted one last time. I saw the Big House at camp, but it was a different era. The house was painted red instead of blue. The campers down at the volleyball pit had early '90s hairstyles, which were probably good for keeping monsters away.

Chiron stood by the porch, talking to Hermes and a woman holding a baby. Chiron's hair was shorter and darker. Hermes wore his usual jogging suit with his winged high-tops. The woman was tall and pretty. She had blond hair, shining eyes and a friendly smile. The baby in her arms squirmed in his blue blanket like Camp Half-Blood was the last place he wanted to be.

"It's an honor to have you here," Chiron told the

woman, though he sounded nervous. "It's been a long time since a mortal was allowed at camp."

"Don't encourage her," Hermes grumbled. "May, you *can't* do this."

With a shock, I realized I was seeing May Castellan. She looked nothing like the old woman I'd met. She seemed full of life—the kind of person who could smile and make everyone around her feel good.

"Oh, don't worry so much," May said, rocking the baby. "You need an Oracle, don't you? The old one's been dead for, what, twenty years?"

"Longer," Chiron said gravely.

Hermes raised his arms in exasperation. "I didn't tell you that story so you could *apply*. It's dangerous. Chiron, tell her."

"It is," Chiron warned. "For many years, I have forbidden anyone from trying. We don't know exactly what's happened. Humanity seems to have lost the ability to host the Oracle."

"We've been through that," May said. "And I know I can do it. Hermes, this is my chance to do something good. I've been given the gift of sight for a reason."

I wanted to yell at May Castellan to stop. I knew what was about to happen. I finally understood how her life had been destroyed. But I couldn't move or speak.

Hermes looked more hurt than worried. "You couldn't marry if you became the Oracle," he complained. "You couldn't see *me* anymore."

May put her hand on his arm. "I can't have you forever,

can I? You'll move on soon. You're immortal."

He started to protest, but she put her hand on his chest. "You know it's true! Don't try to spare my feelings. Besides, we have a wonderful child. I can still raise Luke if I'm the Oracle, right?"

Chiron coughed. "Yes, but in all fairness, I don't know how that will affect the spirit of the Oracle. A woman who has already borne a child—as far as I know, this has never been done before. If the spirit does not take—"

"It will," May insisted.

No, I wanted to shout. *It won't.*

May Castellan kissed her baby and handed the bundle to Hermes. "I'll be right back."

She gave them one last confident smile and climbed the steps.

Chiron and Hermes paced in silence. The baby squirmed.

A green glow lit the windows of the house. The campers stopped playing volleyball and stared up at the attic. A cold wind rushed through the strawberry fields.

Hermes must've felt it too. He cried, "No! NO!"

He shoved the baby into Chiron's arms and ran for the porch. Before he reached the door, the sunny afternoon was shattered by May Castellan's terrified scream.

I sat up so fast I banged my head on somebody's shield.

"Ow!"

"Sorry, Percy." Annabeth was standing over me. "I was just about to wake you."

I rubbed my head, trying to clear the disturbing visions. Suddenly a lot of things made sense to me: May Castellan had tried to become the Oracle. She hadn't known about Hades's curse preventing the spirit of Delphi from taking another host. Neither had Chiron or Hermes. They hadn't realized that by trying to take the job, May would be driven mad, plagued with fits in which her eyes would glow green and she would have shattered glimpses of her child's future.

"Percy?" Annabeth asked. "What's wrong?"

"Nothing," I lied. "What . . . what are you doing in armor? You should be resting."

"Oh, I'm fine," she said, though she still looked pale. She was barely moving her right arm. "That nectar and ambrosia fixed me up."

"Uh-huh. You can't seriously go out and fight."

She offered me her good hand and helped me up. My head was pounding. Outside, the sky was purple and red.

"You're going to need every person you have," she said. "I just looked in my shield. There's an army—"

"Heading south into Central Park," I said. "Yeah, I know."

I told her part of my dreams. I left out the vision of May Castellan, because it was too disturbing to talk about. I also left out Ethan's speculation about Luke fighting Kronos inside his body. I didn't want to get Annabeth's hopes up.

"Do you think Ethan suspects about your weak spot?" she asked.

"I don't know," I admitted. "He didn't tell Kronos anything, but if he figures it out—"

"We can't let him."

"I'll bonk him on the head harder next time," I suggested. "Any idea what surprise Kronos was talking about?"

She shook her head. "I didn't see anything in the shield, but I don't like surprises."

"Agreed."

"So," she said, "are you going to argue about me coming along?"

"Nah. You'd just beat me up."

She managed a laugh, which was good to hear. I grabbed my sword, and we went to rally the troops.

Thalia and the head counselors were waiting for us at the Reservoir. The lights of the city were blinking on at twilight. I guess a lot of them were on automatic timers. Streetlamps glowed around the shore of the lake, making the water and trees look even spookier.

"They're coming," Thalia confirmed, pointing north with a silver arrow. "One of my scouts just reported they've crossed the Harlem River. There was no way to hold them back. The army . . ." She shrugged. "It's huge."

"We'll hold them at the park," I said. "Grover, you ready?"

He nodded. "As ready as we'll ever be. If my nature spirits can stop them anywhere, this is the place."

"Yes, we will!" said another voice. A very old, fat satyr pushed through the crowd, stumbling over his own spear.

He was dressed in wood-bark armor that only covered half of his belly.

"Leneus?" I said.

"Don't act so surprised," he huffed. "I *am* a leader of the Council, and you *did* tell me to find Grover. Well, I found him, and I'm not going to let a mere *outcast* lead the satyrs without my help!"

Behind Leneus's back, Grover made gagging motions, but the old satyr grinned like he was the savior of the day. "Never fear! We'll show those Titans!"

I didn't know whether to laugh or be angry, but I managed to keep a straight face. "Um . . . yeah. Well, Grover, you won't be alone. Annabeth and the Athena cabin will make their stand here. And me, and . . . Thalia?"

She patted me on the shoulder. "Say no more. The Hunters are ready."

I looked at the other counselors. "That leaves the rest of you with a job just as important. You have to guard the other entrances to Manhattan. You know how tricky Kronos is. He'll hope to distract us with this big army and sneak another force in somewhere else. It's up to you to make sure that doesn't happen. Has each cabin chosen a bridge or tunnel?"

The counselors nodded grimly.

"Then let's do it," I said. "Good hunting, everybody!"

We heard the army before we saw it.

The noise was like a cannon barrage combined with a football stadium crowd—like every Patriots fan in New England was charging us with bazookas.

At the north end of the reservoir, the enemy vanguard broke through the woods—a warrior in golden armor leading a battalion of Laistrygonian giants with huge bronze axes. Hundreds of other monsters poured out behind them.

"Positions!" Annabeth yelled.

Her cabinmates scrambled. The idea was to make the enemy army break around the reservoir. To get to us, they'd have to follow the trails, which meant they'd be marching in narrow columns on either side of the water.

At first, the plan seemed to work. The enemy divided and streamed toward us along the shore. When they were halfway across, our defenses kicked in. The jogging trail erupted in Greek fire, incinerating many of the monsters instantly. Others flailed around, engulfed in green flames. Athena campers threw grappling hooks around the largest giants and pulled them to the ground.

In the woods on the right, the Hunters sent a volley of silver arrows into the enemy line, destroying twenty or thirty *dracaenae*, but more marched behind them. A bolt of lightning crackled out of the sky and fried a Laistrygonian giant to ashes, and I knew Thalia must be doing her *daughter of Zeus* thing.

Grover raised his pipes and played a quick tune. A roar went up from the woods on both sides as every tree, rock, and bush seemed to sprout a spirit. Dryads and satyrs raised their clubs and charged. The trees wrapped around the monsters, strangling them. Grass grew around the feet of the enemy archers. Stones flew up and hit *dracaenae* in the faces.

The enemy slogged forward. Giants smashed through

the trees, and naiads faded as their life sources were destroyed. Hellhounds lunged at the timber wolves, knocking them aside. Enemy archers returned fire, and a Hunter fell from a high branch.

"Percy!" Annabeth grabbed my arm and pointed at the reservoir. The Titan in the gold armor wasn't waiting for his forces to advance around the sides. He was charging toward us, walking straight over the top of the lake.

A Greek firebomb exploded right on top of him, but he raised his palm and sucked the flames out of the air.

"Hyperion," Annabeth said in awe. "The lord of light. Titan of the east."

"Bad?" I guessed.

"Next to Atlas, he's the greatest Titan warrior. In the old days, four Titans controlled the four corners of the world. Hyperion was the east—the most powerful. He was the father of Helios, the first sun god."

"I'll keep him busy," I promised.

"Percy, even you can't—"

"Just keep our forces together."

We'd set up at the reservoir for good reason. I concentrated on the water and felt its power surging through me.

I advanced toward Hyperion, running over the top of the water. *Yeah, buddy. Two can play that game.*

Twenty feet away, Hyperion raised his sword. His eyes were just like I'd seen in my dream—as gold as Kronos's but brighter, like miniature suns.

"The sea god's brat," he mused. "You're the one who trapped Atlas beneath the sky again?"

"It wasn't hard," I said. "You Titans are about as bright as my gym socks."

Hyperion snarled. "You want bright?"

His body ignited in a column of light and heat. I looked away, but I was still blinded.

Instinctively I raised Riptide—just in time. Hyperion's blade slammed against mine. The shock wave sent a ten-foot ring of water across the surface of the lake.

My eyes still burned. I had to shut off his light.

I concentrated on the tidal wave and forced it to reverse. Just before impact, I jumped upward on a jet of water.

"AHHHHH!" The waves smashed into Hyperion and he went under, his light extinguished.

I landed on the lake's surface just as Hyperion struggled to his feet. His golden armor was dripping wet. His eyes no longer blazed, but they still looked murderous.

"You will burn, Jackson!" he roared.

Our swords met again and the air charged with ozone.

The battle still raged around us. On the right flank, Annabeth was leading an assault with her siblings. On the left flank, Grover and his nature spirits were regrouping, entangling the enemies with bushes and weeds.

"Enough games," Hyperion told me. "We fight on land."

I was about to make some clever comment, like "No," when the Titan yelled. A wall of force slammed me through the air—just like the trick Kronos had pulled on the bridge. I sailed backward about three hundred yards and smashed into the ground. If it hadn't been for my new invulnerability, I would've broken every bone in my body.

I got to my feet, groaning. "I really *hate* it when you Titans do that."

Hyperion closed on me with blinding speed.

I concentrated on the water, drawing strength from it.

Hyperion attacked. He was powerful and fast, but he couldn't seem to land a blow. The ground around his feet kept erupting in flames, but I kept dousing it just as quickly.

"Stop it!" the Titan roared. "Stop that wind!"

I wasn't sure what he meant. I was too busy fighting.

Hyperion stumbled like he was being pushed away. Water sprayed his face, stinging his eyes. The wind picked up, and Hyperion staggered backward.

"Percy!" Grover called in amazement. "How are you *doing* that?"

Doing what? I thought.

Then I looked down, and I realized I was standing in the middle of my own personal hurricane. Clouds of water vapor swirled around me, winds so powerful they buffeted Hyperion and flattened the grass in a twenty-yard radius. Enemy warriors threw javelins at me, but the storm knocked them aside.

"Sweet," I muttered. "But a little more!"

Lightning flickered around me. The clouds darkened and the rain swirled faster. I closed in on Hyperion and blew him off his feet.

"Percy!" Grover called again. "Bring him over here!"

I slashed and jabbed, letting my reflexes take over. Hyperion could barely defend himself. His eyes kept trying to ignite, but the hurricane quenched his flames.

I couldn't keep up a storm like this forever, though. I could feel my powers weakening. With one last effort, I propelled Hyperion across the field, straight to where Grover was waiting.

"I will not be toyed with!" Hyperion bellowed.

He managed to get to his feet again, but Grover put his reed pipes to his lips and began to play. Leneus joined him. Around the grove, every satyr took up the song—an eerie melody, like a creek flowing over stones. The ground erupted at Hyperion's feet. Gnarled roots wrapped around his legs.

"What's this?" he protested. He tried to shake off the roots, but he was still weak. The roots thickened until he looked like he was wearing wooden boots.

"Stop this!" he shouted. "Your woodland magic is no match for a Titan!"

But the more he struggled, the faster the roots grew. They curled about his body, thickening and hardening into bark. His golden armor melted into the wood, becoming part of a large trunk.

The music continued. Hyperion's forces backed up in astonishment as their leader was absorbed. He stretched out his arms and they became branches, from which smaller branches shot out and grew leaves. The tree grew taller and thicker, until only the Titan's face was visible in the middle of the trunk.

"You cannot imprison me!" he bellowed. "I am Hyperion! I am—"

The bark closed over his face.

Grover took his pipes from his mouth. "You are a very nice maple tree."

Several of the other satyrs passed out from exhaustion, but they'd done their job well. The Titan lord was completely encased in an enormous maple. The trunk was at least twenty feet in diameter, with branches as tall as any in the park. The tree might've stood there for centuries.

The Titan's army started to retreat. A cheer went up from the Athena cabin, but our victory was short-lived.

Because just then Kronos unleashed his surprise.

"REEEEET!"

The squeal echoed through upper Manhattan. Demigods and monsters alike froze in terror.

Grover shot me a panicked look. "Why does that sound like . . . It can't be!"

I knew what he was thinking. Two years ago we'd gotten a "gift" from Pan—a huge boar that carried us across the Southwest (after it tried to kill us). The boar had a similar squeal, but what we were hearing now seemed higher pitched, shriller, almost like . . . like if the boar had an angry girlfriend.

"REEEEEET!" A huge pink creature soared over the reservoir—a Macy's Thanksgiving Day Parade nightmare blimp with wings.

"A sow!" Annabeth cried. "Take cover!"

The demigods scattered as the winged lady pig swooped down. Her wings were pink like a flamingo's, which matched her skin beautifully, but it was hard to think of her as *cute* when her hooves slammed into the ground, barely missing one of Annabeth's siblings. The pig stomped around and tore down half an acre of trees, belching a cloud of noxious gas. Then it took off again, circling around for another strike.

"Don't tell me that thing is from Greek mythology," I complained.

"Afraid so," Annabeth said. "The Clazmonian Sow. It terrorized Greek towns back in the day."

"Let me guess," I said. "Hercules beat it."

"Nope," Annabeth said. "As far as I know, *no* hero has ever beaten it."

"Perfect," I muttered.

The Titan's army was recovering from its shock. I guess they realized the pig wasn't after them.

We only had seconds before they were ready to fight, and our forces were still in a panic. Every time the sow belched, Grover's nature spirits yelped and faded back into their trees.

"That pig has to go." I grabbed a grappling hook from one of Annabeth's siblings. "I'll take care of it. You guys hold the rest of the enemy. Push them back!"

"But, Percy," Grover said, "what if we can't?"

I saw how tired he was. The magic had really drained him. Annabeth didn't look much better from fighting with a bad shoulder wound. I didn't know how the Hunters were doing, but the right flank of the enemy army was now between them and us.

I didn't want to leave my friends in such bad shape, but that sow was the biggest threat. It would destroy everything:

buildings, trees, sleeping mortals. It had to be stopped.

"Retreat if you need to," I said. "Just slow them down. I'll be back as soon as I can."

Before I could change my mind, I swung the grappling hook like a lasso. When the sow came down for its next pass, I threw with all my strength. The hook wrapped around the base of the pig's wing. It squealed in rage and veered off, yanking the rope and me into the sky.

If you're heading downtown from Central Park, my advice is to take the subway. Flying pigs are faster, but way more dangerous.

The sow soared past the Plaza Hotel, straight into the canyon of Fifth Avenue. My brilliant plan was to climb the rope and get on the pig's back. Unfortunately I was too busy swinging around dodging streetlamps and the sides of buildings.

Another thing I learned: it's one thing to climb a rope in gym class. It's a completely different thing to climb a rope attached to a moving pig's wing while you're flying at a hundred miles an hour.

We zigzagged along several blocks and continued south on Park Avenue.

Boss! Hey, boss! Out of the corner of my eye, I saw Blackjack speeding along next to us, darting back and forth to avoid the pig's wings.

"Watch out!" I told him.

Hop on! Blackjack whinnied. *I can catch you . . . probably.*

That wasn't very reassuring. Grand Central lay dead

ahead. Above the main entrance stood the giant statue of Hermes, which I guess hadn't been activated because it was so high up. I was flying right toward him at the speed of demigod-smashing.

"Stay alert!" I told Blackjack. "I've got an idea."

Oh, I hate your ideas.

I swung outward with all my might. Instead of smashing into the Hermes statue, I whipped around it, circling the rope under its arms. I thought this would tether the pig, but I'd underestimated the momentum of a thirty-ton sow in flight. Just as the pig wrenched the statue loose from its pedestal, I let go. Hermes went for a ride, taking my place as the pig's passenger, and I free-fell toward the street.

In that split second I thought about the days when my mom used to work at the Grand Central candy shop. I thought how bad it would be if I ended up as a grease spot on the pavement.

Then a shadow swooped under me, and *thump*—I was on Blackjack's back. It wasn't the most comfortable landing. In fact, when I yelled "OW!" my voice was an octave higher than usual.

Sorry, boss, Blackjack murmured.

"No problem," I squeaked. "Follow that pig!"

The porker had taken a right at East 42nd and was flying back toward Fifth Avenue. When it flew above the rooftops, I could see fires here and there around the city. It looked like my friends were having a rough time. Kronos was attacking on several fronts. But at the moment, I had my own problems.

The Hermes statue was still on its leash. It kept bonking into buildings and spinning around. The pig swooped over an office building, and Hermes plowed into a water tower on the roof, blasting water and wood everywhere.

Then something occurred to me.

"Get closer," I told Blackjack.

He whinnied in protest.

"Just within shouting distance," I said. "I need to talk to the statue."

Now I'm sure you've lost it, boss, Blackjack said, but he did what I asked. When I was close enough to see the statue's face clearly, I yelled, "Hello, Hermes! Command sequence: Daedalus Twenty-three. Kill Flying Pigs! Begin Activation!"

Immediately the statue moved its legs. It seemed confused to find that it was no longer on top of Grand Central Terminal. It was, instead, being given a sky-ride on the end of a rope by a large winged sow. It smashed through the side of a brick building, which I think made it a little mad. It shook its head and began to climb the rope.

I glanced down at the street. We were coming up on the main public library, with the big marble lions flanking the steps. Suddenly I had a weird thought: Could *stone* statues be automatons too? It seemed like a long shot, but . . .

"Faster!" I told Blackjack. "Get in front of the pig. Taunt him!"

Um, boss—

"Trust me," I said. "I can do this . . . probably."

Oh, sure. Mock the horse.

Blackjack burst through the air. He could fly pretty

darned fast when he wanted to. He got in front of the pig, which now had a metal Hermes on its back.

Blackjack whinnied, *You smell like ham!* He kicked the pig in the snout with his back hooves and went into a steep dive. The pig screamed in rage and followed.

We barreled straight for the front steps of the library. Blackjack slowed down just enough for me to hop off, then he kept flying toward the main doors.

I yelled out, "Lions! Command sequence: Daedalus Twenty-three. Kill Flying Pigs! Begin Activation!"

The lions stood up and looked at me. They probably thought I was teasing them. But just then: *"REEEEEET!"*

The massive pink pork monster landed with a thud, cracking the sidewalk. The lions stared at it, not believing their luck, and pounced. At the same time, a very beat-up Hermes statue leaped onto the pig's head and started banging it mercilessly with a caduceus. Those lions had some nasty claws.

I drew Riptide, but there wasn't much for me to do. The pig disintegrated before my eyes. I almost felt sorry for it. I hoped it got to meet the boar of its dreams down in Tartarus.

When the monster had completely turned to dust, the lions and the Hermes statue looked around in confusion.

"You can defend Manhattan now," I told them, but they didn't seem to hear. They went charging down Park Avenue, and I imagined they would keep looking for flying pigs until someone deactivated them.

Hey, boss, said Blackjack. *Can we take a donut break?*

I wiped the sweat off my brow. "I wish, big guy, but the fight's still going on."

In fact, I could hear it getting closer. My friends needed help. I jumped on Blackjack, and we flew north toward the sound of explosions.

FIFTEEN

CHIRON THROWS A PARTY

Midtown was a war zone. We flew over little skirmishes everywhere. A giant was ripping up trees in Bryant Park while dryads pelted him with nuts. Outside the Waldorf Astoria, a bronze statue of Benjamin Franklin was whacking a hellhound with a rolled-up newspaper. A trio of Hephaestus campers fought a squad of *dracaenae* in the middle of Rockefeller Center.

I was tempted to stop and help, but I could tell from the smoke and noise that the real action had moved farther south. Our defenses were collapsing. The enemy was closing in on the Empire State Building.

We did a quick sweep of the surrounding area. The Hunters had set up a defensive line on 37th, just three blocks north of Olympus. To the east on Park Avenue, Jake Mason and some other Hephaestus campers were leading an army of statues against the enemy. To the west, the Demeter cabin and Grover's nature spirits had turned Sixth Avenue into a jungle that was hampering a squadron of Kronos's demigods. The south was clear for now, but the flanks of the enemy army were swinging around. A few more minutes and we'd be totally surrounded.

"We have to land where they need us most," I muttered.

That's everywhere, boss.

I spotted a familiar silver owl banner in the southeast corner of the fight, 33rd at the Park Avenue tunnel. Annabeth and two of her siblings were holding back a Hyperborean giant.

"There!" I told Blackjack. He plunged toward the battle.

I leaped off his back and landed on the giant's head. When the giant looked up, I slid off his face, shield-bashing his nose on the way down.

"RAWWWR!" The giant staggered backward, blue blood trickling from his nostrils.

I hit the pavement running. The Hyperborean breathed a cloud of white mist, and the temperature dropped. The spot where I'd landed was now coated with ice, and I was covered in frost like a sugar donut.

"Hey, ugly!" Annabeth yelled. I hoped she was talking to the giant, not me.

Blue Boy bellowed and turned toward her, exposing the unprotected back of his legs. I charged and stabbed him behind the knee.

"WAAAAH!" The Hyperborean buckled. I waited for him to turn, but he froze. I mean he *literally* turned to solid ice. From the point where I'd stabbed him, cracks appeared in his body. They got larger and wider until the giant crumbled in a mountain of blue shards.

"Thanks." Annabeth winced, trying to catch her breath. "The pig?"

"Pork chops," I said.

"Good." She flexed her shoulder. Obviously, the wound was still bothering her, but she saw my expression and rolled her eyes. "I'm fine, Percy. Come on! We've got plenty of enemies left."

She was right. The next hour was a blur. I fought like I'd never fought before—wading into legions of *dracaenae*, taking out dozens of telkhines with every strike, destroying *empousai* and knocking out enemy demigods. No matter how many I defeated, more took their place.

Annabeth and I raced from block to block, trying to shore up our defenses. Too many of our friends lay wounded in the streets. Too many were missing.

As the night wore on and the moon got higher, we were backed up foot by foot until we were only a block from the Empire State Building in any direction. At one point Grover was next to me, bonking snake women over the head with his cudgel. Then he disappeared in the crowd, and it was Thalia at my side, driving the monsters back with the power of her magic shield. Mrs. O'Leary bounded out of nowhere, picked up a Laistrygonian giant in her mouth, and flung him into the air like a Frisbee. Annabeth used her invisibility cap to sneak behind the enemy lines. Whenever a monster disintegrated for no apparent reason with a surprised look on his face, I knew Annabeth had been there.

But it still wasn't enough.

"Hold your lines!" Katie Gardner shouted, somewhere off to my left.

The problem was there were too few of us to hold

anything. The entrance to Olympus was twenty feet behind me. A ring of brave demigods, Hunters, and nature spirits guarded the doors. I slashed and hacked, destroying everything in my path, but even I was getting tired, and I couldn't be everywhere at once.

Behind the enemy troops, a few blocks to the east, a bright light began to shine. I thought it was the sunrise. Then I realized Kronos was riding toward us on a golden chariot. A dozen Laistrygonian giants bore torches before him. Two Hyperboreans carried his black-and-purple banners. The Titan lord looked fresh and rested, his powers at full strength. He was taking his time advancing, letting me wear myself down.

Annabeth appeared next to me. "We have to fall back to the doorway. Hold it at all costs!"

She was right. I was about to order a retreat when I heard the hunting horn.

It cut through the noise of the battle like a fire alarm. A chorus of horns answered from all around us, echoing off the buildings of Manhattan.

I glanced at Thalia, but she just frowned.

"Not the Hunters," she assured me. "We're all here."

"Then who?"

The horns got louder. I couldn't tell where they were coming from because of the echo, but it sounded like an entire army was approaching.

I was afraid it might be more enemies, but Kronos's forces looked as confused as we were. Giants lowered their clubs. *Dracaenae* hissed. Even Kronos's honor guard looked uneasy.

Then, to our left, a hundred monsters cried out at once. Kronos's entire northern flank surged forward. I thought we were doomed, but they didn't attack. They ran straight past us and crashed into their southern allies.

A new blast of horns shattered the night. The air shimmered. In a blur of movement, an entire cavalry appeared as if dropping out of light speed.

"Yeah, baby!" a voice wailed. "PARTY!"

A shower of arrows arced over our heads and slammed into the enemy, vaporizing hundreds of demons. But these weren't regular arrows. They made whizzy sounds as they flew, like *WHEEEEEE!* Some had pinwheels attached to them. Others had boxing gloves rather than points.

"Centaurs!" Annabeth yelled.

The Party Pony army exploded into our midst in a riot of colors: tie-dyed shirts, rainbow Afro wigs, oversize sunglasses, and war-painted faces. Some had slogans scrawled across their flanks like *HORSEZ PWN* or *KRONOS SUX*.

Hundreds of them filled the entire block. My brain couldn't process everything I saw, but I knew if I were the enemy, I'd be running.

"Percy!" Chiron shouted across the sea of wild centaurs. He was dressed in armor from the waist up, his bow in his hand, and he was grinning in satisfaction. "Sorry we're late!"

"DUDE!" Another centaur yelled. "Talk later. WASTE MONSTERS NOW!"

He locked and loaded a double-barrel paint gun and blasted an enemy hellhound bright pink. The paint must've been mixed with Celestial bronze dust or something, because as soon as it splattered the hellhound, the monster yelped and dissolved into a pink-and-black puddle.

"PARTY PONIES!" a centaur yelled. "SOUTH FLORIDA!"

Somewhere across the battlefield, a twangy voice yelled back, "HEART OF TEXAS CHAPTER!"

"HAWAII OWNS YOUR FACES!" a third one shouted.

It was the most beautiful thing I'd ever seen. The entire Titan army turned and fled, pushed back by a flood of paintballs, arrows, swords, and NERF baseball bats. The centaurs trampled everything in their path.

"Stop running, you fools!" Kronos yelled. "Stand and ACKK!"

That last part was because a panicked Hyperborean giant stumbled backward and sat on top of him. The lord of time disappeared under a giant blue butt.

We pushed them for several blocks until Chiron yelled, "HOLD! On your promise, HOLD!"

It wasn't easy, but eventually the order got relayed up and down the ranks of centaurs, and they started to pull back, letting the enemy flee.

"Chiron's smart," Annabeth said, wiping the sweat off her face. "If we pursue, we'll get too spread out. We need to regroup."

"But the enemy—"

"They're not defeated," she agreed. "But the dawn is coming. At least we've bought some time."

I didn't like pulling back, but I knew she was right. I

watched as the last of the telkhines scuttled toward the East River. Then reluctantly I turned and headed back toward the Empire State Building.

We set up a two-block perimeter, with a command tent at the Empire State Building. Chiron informed us that the Party Ponies had sent chapters from almost every state in the Union: forty from California, two from Rhode Island, thirty from Illinois . . . Roughly five hundred total had answered his call, but even with that many, we couldn't defend more than a few blocks.

"Dude," said a centaur named Larry. His T-shirt identified him as BIG CHIEF UBER GUY, NEW MEXICO CHAPTER. "That was more fun than our last convention in Vegas!"

"Yeah," said Owen from South Dakota. He wore a black leather jacket and an old WWII army helmet. "We totally wasted them!"

Chiron patted Owen on the back. "You did well, my friends, but don't get careless. Kronos should never be underestimated. Now why don't you visit the diner on West 33rd and get some breakfast? I hear the Delaware chapter found a stash of root beer."

"Root beer!" They almost trampled each other as they galloped off.

Chiron smiled. Annabeth gave him a big hug, and Mrs. O'Leary licked his face.

"Ack," he grumbled. "Enough of that, dog. Yes, I'm glad to see you too."

"Chiron, thanks," I said. "Talk about saving the day."

He shrugged. "I'm sorry it took so long. Centaurs travel fast, as you know. We can bend distance as we ride. Even so, getting all the centaurs together was no easy task. The Party Ponies are not exactly organized."

"How'd you get through the magic defenses around the city?" Annabeth asked.

"They slowed us down a bit," Chiron admitted, "but I think they're intended mostly to keep mortals out. Kronos doesn't want puny humans getting in the way of his great victory."

"So maybe other reinforcements can get through," I said hopefully.

Chiron stroked his beard. "Perhaps, though time is short. As soon as Kronos regroups, he will attack again. Without the element of surprise on our side . . ."

I understood what he meant. Kronos wasn't beaten. Not by a long shot. I half hoped Kronos had been squashed under that Hyperborean giant's butt, but I knew better. He'd be back, tonight at the latest.

"And Typhon?" I asked.

Chiron's face darkened. "The gods are tiring. Dionysus was incapacitated yesterday. Typhon smashed his chariot, and the wine god went down somewhere in the Appalachians. No one has seen him since. Hephaestus is out of action as well. He was thrown from the battle so hard he created a new lake in West Virginia. He will heal, but not soon enough to help. The others still fight. They've managed to slow Typhon's approach. But the monster cannot be stopped. He will arrive in New York by this time tomorrow. Once he and Kronos combine forces——"

"Then what chance do we have?" I said. "We can't hold out another day."

"We'll have to," Thalia said. "I'll see about setting some new traps around the perimeter."

She looked exhausted. Her jacket was smeared in grime and monster dust, but she managed to get to her feet and stagger off.

"I will help her," Chiron decided. "I should make sure my brethren don't go too overboard with the root beer."

I thought "too overboard" pretty much summed up the Party Ponies, but Chiron cantered off, leaving Annabeth and me alone.

She cleaned the monster slime off her knife. I'd seen her do that hundreds of times, but I'd never thought about why she cared so much about the blade.

"At least your mom is okay," I offered.

"If you call fighting Typhon *okay*." She locked eyes with me. "Percy, even with the centaurs' help, I'm starting to think——"

"I know." I had a bad feeling this might be our last chance to talk, and I felt like there were a million things I hadn't told her. "Listen, there were some . . . some visions Hestia showed me."

"You mean about Luke?"

Maybe it was just a safe guess, but I got the feeling Annabeth knew what I'd been holding back. Maybe she'd been having dreams of her own.

"Yeah," I said. "You and Thalia and Luke. The first

time you met. And the time you met Hermes."

Annabeth slipped her knife back into its sheath. "Luke promised he'd never let me get hurt. He said . . . he said we'd be a new family, and it would turn out better than his."

Her eyes reminded me of that seven-year-old girl's in the alley—angry, scared, desperate for a friend.

"Thalia talked to me earlier," I said. "She's afraid—"

"That I can't face Luke," she said miserably.

I nodded. "But there's something else you should know. Ethan Nakamura seemed to think Luke was still alive inside his body, maybe even fighting Kronos for control."

Annabeth tried to hide it, but I could almost see her mind working on the possibilities, maybe starting to hope.

"I didn't want to tell you," I admitted.

She looked up at the Empire State Building. "Percy, for so much of my life, I felt like everything was changing, all the time. I didn't have anyone I could rely on."

I nodded. That was something most demigods could understand.

"I ran away when I was seven," she said. "Then with Luke and Thalia, I thought I'd found a family, but it fell apart almost immediately. What I'm saying . . . I *hate* it when people let me down, when things are temporary. I think that's why I want to be an architect."

"To build something permanent," I said. "A monument to last a thousand years."

She held my eyes. "I guess that sounds like my fatal flaw again."

Years ago in the Sea of Monsters, Annabeth had told

me her biggest flaw was pride—thinking she could fix any-thing. I'd even seen a glimpse of her deepest desire, shown to her by the Sirens' magic. Annabeth had imagined her mother and father together, standing in front of a newly rebuilt Manhattan, designed by Annabeth. And Luke had been there too—good again, welcoming her home.

"I guess I understand how you feel," I said. "But Thalia's right. Luke has already betrayed you so many times. He was evil even before Kronos. I don't want him to hurt you any-more."

Annabeth pursed her lips. I could tell she was trying not to get mad. "And you'll understand if I keep hoping there's a chance you're wrong."

I looked away. I felt like I'd done my best, but that didn't make me feel any better.

Across the street, the Apollo campers had set up a field hospital to tend the wounded—dozens of campers and almost as many Hunters. I was watching the medics work, and thinking about our slim chances for holding Mount Olympus. . . .

And suddenly: I wasn't there anymore.

I was standing in a long dingy bar with black walls, neon signs, and a bunch of partying adults. A banner across the bar read HAPPY BIRTHDAY, BOBBY EARL. Country music played on the speakers. Big guys in jeans and work shirts crowded the bar. Waitresses carried trays of drinks and shouted at each other. It was pretty much exactly the kind of place my mom would never let me go.

I was stuck in the very back of the room, next to the

bathrooms (which didn't smell so great) and a couple of antique arcade games.

"Oh good, you're here," said the man at the Pac-Man machine. "I'll have a Diet Coke."

He was a pudgy guy in a leopard-skin Hawaiian shirt, purple shorts, red running shoes, and black socks, which didn't exactly make him blend in with the crowd. His nose was bright red. A bandage was wrapped around his curly black hair like he was recovering from a concussion.

I blinked. "Mr. D?"

He sighed, not taking his eyes from the game. "Really, Peter Johnson, how long will it take for you to recognize me on sight?"

"About as long as it'll take for you to figure out my name," I muttered. "Where are we?"

"Why, Bobby Earl's birthday party," Dionysus said. "Somewhere in lovely rural America."

"I thought Typhon swatted you out of the sky. They said you crash-landed."

"Your concern is touching. I *did* crash-land. Very painfully. In fact, part of me is still buried under a hundred feet of rubble in an abandoned coal mine. It will be several more hours before I have enough strength to mend. But in the meantime, part of my consciousness is *here*."

"At a bar, playing Pac-Man."

"Party time," Dionysus said. "Surely you've heard of it. Wherever there is a party, my presence is invoked. Because of this, I can exist in many different places at once. The only problem was finding a party. I don't know if you're aware how serious things are outside your safe little bubble of New York—"

"Safe little bubble?"

"—but believe me, the mortals out here in the heartland are panicking. Typhon has terrified them. Very few are throwing parties. Apparently Bobby Earl and his friends, bless them, are a little slow. They haven't yet figured out that the world is ending."

"So . . . I'm not really here?"

"No. In a moment I'll send you back to your normal insignificant life, and it will be as if nothing had happened."

"And *why* did you bring me here?"

Dionysus snorted. "Oh, I didn't want you particularly. Any of you silly heroes would do. That Annie girl—"

"Annabeth."

"The point is," he said, "I pulled you into party time to deliver a warning. We are in *danger.*"

"Gee," I said. "Never would've figured that out. Thanks."

He glared at me and momentarily forgot his game. Pac-Man got eaten by the red ghost dude.

"Erre es korakas, Blinky!" Dionysus cursed. "I will have your soul!"

"Um, he's a video game character," I said.

"That's no excuse! And you're ruining my game, Jorgenson!"

"Jackson."

"Whichever! Now listen, the situation is graver than you imagine. If Olympus falls, not only will the gods

[267]

fade, but everything that is connected to our legacy will also begin to unravel. The very fabric of your puny little civilization—"

The game played a song and Mr. D progressed to level 254.

"Ha!" he shouted. "Take that, you pixelated fiends!"

"Um, fabric of civilization," I prompted.

"Yes, yes. Your entire society will dissolve. Perhaps not right away, but mark my words, the chaos of the Titans will mean the end of Western civilization. Art, law, wine tastings, music, video games, silk shirts, black velvet paintings—all the things that make life worth living will disappear!"

"So why aren't the gods rushing back to help us?" I said. "We should combine forces at Olympus. Forget Typhon."

He snapped his fingers impatiently. "You forgot my Diet Coke."

"Gods, you're annoying." I got the attention of a waitress and ordered the stupid soda. I put it on Bobby Earl's tab.

Mr. D took a good long drink. His eyes never left the video game. "The truth is, Pierre—"

"Percy."

"—the other gods would *never* admit this, but we actually *need* you mortals to rescue Olympus. You see, we are manifestations of your culture. If you don't care enough to save Olympus yourselves—"

"Like Pan," I said, "depending on the satyrs to save the Wild."

"Yes, quite. I will deny I ever said this, of course, but the gods *need* heroes. They always have. Otherwise we would not keep you annoying little brats around."

"I feel so wanted. Thanks."

"Use the training I have given you at camp."

"*What* training?"

"You know. All those hero techniques and . . . No!" Mr. D slapped the game console. "*Na pari i eychi!* The last level!"

He looked at me, and purple fire flickered in his eyes. "As I recall, I once predicted you would turn out to be as selfish as all the other human heroes. Well, here is your chance to prove me wrong."

"Yeah, making you proud is real high on my list."

"You must save Olympus, Pedro! Leave Typhon to the Olympians and save our own seats of power. It must be done!"

"Great. Nice little chat. Now, if you don't mind, my friends will be wondering—"

"There is more," Mr. D warned. "Kronos has not yet attained full power. The body of the mortal was only a temporary measure."

"We kind of guessed that."

"And did you also guess that within a day at most, Kronos will burn away that mortal body and take on the true form of a Titan king?"

"And that would mean . . ."

Dionysus inserted another quarter. "You know about the true forms of the gods."

"Yeah. You can't look at them without burning up."

"Kronos would be ten times more powerful. His very presence would incinerate you. And once he achieves this, he will empower the other Titans. They are weak now, compared to what they will soon become, unless you can stop them. The world will fall, the gods will die, and I will never achieve a perfect score on this stupid machine."

Maybe I should've been terrified, but honestly, I was already about as scared as I could get.

"Can I go now?" I asked.

"One last thing. My son Pollux. Is he alive?"

I blinked. "Yeah, last I saw him."

"I would very much appreciate it if you could keep him that way. I lost his brother Castor last year—"

"I remember." I stared at him, trying to wrap my mind around the idea that Dionysus could be a caring father. I wondered how many other Olympians were thinking about their demigod children right now. "I'll do my best."

"Your best," Dionysus muttered. "Well, isn't *that* reassuring. Go now. You have some nasty surprises to deal with, and I must defeat Blinky!"

"Nasty surprises?"

He waved his hand, and the bar disappeared.

I was back on Fifth Avenue. Annabeth hadn't moved. She didn't give any sign that I'd been gone or anything.

She caught me staring and frowned. "What?"

"Um . . . nothing, I guess."

I gazed down the avenue, wondering what Mr. D had meant by nasty surprises. How much worse could it get?

My eyes rested on a beat-up blue car. The hood was badly dented, like somebody had tried to hammer out some huge craters. My skin tingled. Why did that car look so familiar? Then I realized it was a Prius.

Paul's Prius.

I bolted down the street.

"Percy!" Annabeth called. "Where are you going?"

Paul was passed out in the driver's seat. My mom was snoring beside him. My mind felt like mush. How had I not seen them before? They'd been sitting here in traffic for over a day, the battle raging around them, and I hadn't even noticed.

"They . . . they must've seen those blue lights in the sky." I rattled the doors but they were locked. "I need to get them out."

"Percy," Annabeth said gently.

"I can't leave them here!" I sounded a little crazy. I pounded on the windshield. "I have to move them. I have to—"

"Percy, just . . . just hold on." Annabeth waved to Chiron, who was talking to some centaurs down the block. "We can push the car to a side street, all right? They're going to be fine."

My hands trembled. After all I'd been through over the last few days, I felt so stupid and weak, but the sight of my parents made me want to break down.

Chiron galloped over. "What's . . . Oh dear. I see."

"They were coming to find me," I said. "My mom must've sensed something was wrong."

"Most likely," Chiron said. "But, Percy, they will be fine. The best thing we can do for them is stay focused on our job."

Then I noticed something in the backseat of the Prius, and my heart skipped a beat. Seat-belted behind my mother was a black-and-white Greek jar about three feet tall. Its lid was wrapped in a leather harness.

"No way," I muttered.

Annabeth pressed her hand to the window. "That's impossible! I thought you left that at the Plaza."

"Locked in a vault," I agreed.

Chiron saw the jar and his eyes widened. "That isn't—"

"Pandora's jar." I told him about my meeting with Prometheus.

"Then the jar is yours," Chiron said grimly. "It will follow you and tempt you to open it, no matter where you leave it. It will appear when you are weakest."

Like now, I thought. Looking at my helpless parents.

I imagined Prometheus smiling, so anxious to help out us poor mortals. *Give up Hope, and I will know that you are surrendering. I promise Kronos will be lenient.*

Anger surged through me. I drew Riptide and cut through the driver's side window like it was made of plastic wrap.

"We'll put the car in neutral," I said. "Push them out of the way. And take that stupid jar to Olympus."

Chiron nodded. "A good plan. But, Percy . . ."

Whatever he was going to say, he faltered. A mechanical drumbeat grew loud in the distance—the *chop-chop-chop* of a helicopter.

On a normal Monday morning in New York, this would've been no big deal, but after two days of silence, a mortal helicopter was the oddest thing I'd ever heard. A few blocks east, the monster army shouted and jeered as the helicopter came into view. It was a civilian model painted dark red, with a bright green "DE" logo on the side. The words under the logo were too small to read, but I knew what they said: DARE ENTERPRISES.

My throat closed up. I looked at Annabeth and could tell she recognized the logo too. Her face was as red as the helicopter.

"What is *she* doing here?" Annabeth demanded. "How did she get through the barrier?"

"Who?" Chiron looked confused. "What mortal would be insane enough—"

Suddenly the helicopter pitched forward.

"The Morpheus enchantment!" Chiron said. "The foolish mortal pilot is asleep."

I watched in horror as the helicopter careened sideways, falling toward a row of office buildings. Even if it didn't crash, the gods of the air would probably swat it out of the sky for coming near the Empire State Building.

I was too paralyzed to move, but Annabeth whistled and Guido the pegasus swooped out of nowhere.

You rang for a handsome horse? he asked.

"Come on, Percy," Annabeth growled. "We have to save your *friend.*"

SIXTEEN

WE GET HELP FROM A THIEF

Here's my definition of *not fun*. Fly a pegasus toward an out-of-control helicopter. If Guido had been any less of a fancy flier, we would've been chopped to confetti.

I could hear Rachel screaming inside. For some reason, *she* hadn't fallen asleep, but I could see the pilot slumped over the controls, pitching back and forth as the helicopter wobbled toward the side of an office building.

"Ideas?" I asked Annabeth.

"You're going to have to take Guido and get out," she said.

"What are *you* going to do?"

In response, she said, "Hyah!" and Guido went into a nosedive.

"Duck!" Annabeth yelled.

We passed so close to the rotors I felt the force of the blades ripping at my hair. We zipped along the side of the helicopter, and Annabeth grabbed the door.

That's when things went wrong.

Guido's wing slammed against the helicopter. He plummeted straight down with me on his back, leaving Annabeth dangling from the side of the aircraft.

I was so terrified I could barely think, but as Guido spiraled I caught a glimpse of Rachel pulling Annabeth inside the copter.

"Hang in there!" I yelled at Guido.

My wing, he moaned. *It's busted.*

"You can do it!" I desperately tried to remember what Silena used to tell us in pegasus-riding lessons. "Just relax the wing. Extend it and glide."

We fell like a rock—straight toward the pavement three hundred feet below. At the last moment Guido extended his wings. I saw the faces of centaurs gaping up at us. Then we pulled out of our dive, sailed fifty feet, and tumbled onto the pavement—pegasus over demigod.

Ow! Guido moaned. *My legs. My head. My wings.*

Chiron galloped over with his medical pouch and began working on the pegasus.

I got to my feet. When I looked up, my heart crawled into my throat. The helicopter was only a few seconds away from slamming into the side of the building.

Then miraculously the helicopter righted itself. It spun in a circle and hovered. Very slowly, it began to descend.

It seemed to take forever, but finally the helicopter thudded to a landing in the middle of Fifth Avenue. I looked through the windshield and couldn't believe what I was seeing. Annabeth was at the controls.

I ran forward as the rotors spun to a stop. Rachel opened the side door and dragged out the pilot.

Rachel was still dressed like she was on vacation, in

beach shorts, a T-shirt, and sandals. Her hair was tangled and her face was green from the helicopter ride.

Annabeth climbed out last.

I stared at her in awe. "I didn't know you could fly a helicopter."

"Neither did I," she said. "My dad's crazy into aviation. Plus, Daedalus had some notes on flying machines. I just took my best guess on the controls."

"You saved my life," Rachel said.

Annabeth flexed her bad shoulder. "Yeah, well . . . let's not make a habit of it. What are you *doing* here, Dare? Don't you know better than to fly into a war zone?"

"I—" Rachel glanced at me. "I had to be here. I knew Percy was in trouble."

"Got that right," Annabeth grumbled. "Well, if you'll excuse me, I have some injured *friends* I've got to tend to. Glad you could stop by, Rachel."

"Annabeth—" I called.

She stormed off.

Rachel plopped down on the curb and put her head in her hands. "I'm sorry, Percy. I didn't mean to . . . I always mess things up."

It was kind of hard to argue with her, though I was glad she was safe. I looked in the direction Annabeth had gone, but she'd disappeared into the crowd. I couldn't believe what she'd just done—saved Rachel's life, landed a helicopter, and walked away like it was no big deal.

"It's okay," I told Rachel, though my words sounded hollow. "So what's the message you wanted to deliver?"

She frowned. "How did you know about that?"

"A dream."

Rachel didn't look surprised. She tugged at her beach shorts. They were covered in drawings, which wasn't unusual for her, but these symbols I recognized: Greek letters, pictures from camp beads, sketches of monsters and faces of gods. I didn't understand how Rachel could have known about some of that. She'd never been to Olympus or Camp Half-Blood.

"I've been seeing things too," she muttered. "I mean, not just through the Mist. This is different. I've been drawing pictures, writing lines—"

"In Ancient Greek," I said. "Do you know what they say?"

"That's what I wanted to talk to you about. I was hoping . . . well, if you had gone with us on vacation, I was hoping you could have helped me figure out what's happening to me."

She looked at me pleadingly. Her face was sunburned from the beach. Her nose was peeling. I couldn't get over the shock that she was here in person. She'd forced her family to cut short their vacation, agreed to go to a horrible school, and flown a helicopter into a monster battle just to see me. In her own way, she was as brave as Annabeth.

But what was happening to her with these visions really freaked me out. Maybe it was something that happened to all mortals who could see through the Mist. But my mom had never talked about anything like that. And Hestia's words about Luke's mom kept coming back to me: *May Castellan went too far. She tried to see too much.*

"Rachel," I said, "I wish I knew. Maybe we should ask Chiron—"

She flinched like she'd gotten an electric shock. "Percy, something is about to happen. A trick that ends in death."

"What do you mean? Whose death?"

"I don't know." She looked around nervously. "Don't you feel it?"

"Is that the message you wanted to tell me?"

"No." She hesitated. "I'm sorry. I'm not making sense, but that thought just came to me. The message I wrote on the beach was different. It had your name in it."

"Perseus," I remembered. "In Ancient Greek."

Rachel nodded. "I don't know its meaning. But I know it's important. You have to hear it. It said, *Perseus, you are not the hero.*"

I stared at her like she'd just slapped me. "You came thousands of miles to tell me I'm not the hero?"

"It's important," she insisted. "It will affect what you do."

"Not the hero of the prophecy?" I asked. "Not the hero who defeats Kronos? What do you mean?"

"I'm . . . I'm sorry, Percy. That's all I know. I had to tell you because—"

"Well!" Chiron cantered over. "This must be Miss Dare."

I wanted to yell at him to go away, but of course I couldn't. I tried to get my emotions under control. I felt like I had another personal hurricane swirling around me.

"Chiron, Rachel Dare," I said. "Rachel, this is my teacher Chiron."

"Hello," Rachel said glumly. She didn't look at all surprised that Chiron was a centaur.

"You are not asleep, Miss Dare," he noticed. "And yet you are mortal?"

"I'm mortal," she agreed, like it was a depressing thought. "The pilot fell asleep as soon as we passed the river. I don't know why I didn't. I just knew I had to be here, to warn Percy."

"Warn Percy?"

"She's been seeing things," I said. "Writing lines and making drawings."

Chiron raised an eyebrow. "Indeed? Tell me."

She told him the same things she'd told me.

Chiron stroked his beard. "Miss Dare . . . perhaps we should talk."

"Chiron," I blurted. I had a sudden terrible image of Camp Half-Blood in the 1990s, and May Castellan's scream coming from that attic. "You . . . you'll *help* Rachel, right? I mean, you'll warn her that she's got to be careful with this stuff. Not go too far."

His tail flicked like it does when he's anxious. "Yes, Percy. I will do my best to understand what is happening and advise Miss Dare, but this may take some time. Meanwhile, you should rest. We've moved your parents' car to safety. The enemy seems to be staying put for now. We've set up bunks in the Empire State Building. Get some sleep."

"Everybody keeps telling me to sleep," I grumbled. "I don't need sleep."

Chiron managed a smile. "Have you looked at yourself recently, Percy?"

I glanced down at my clothes, which were scorched, burned, sliced, and tattered from my night of constant battles. "I look like death," I admitted. "But you think I can sleep after what just happened?"

"You may be invulnerable in combat," Chiron chided, "but that only makes your body tire faster. I remember Achilles. Whenever that lad wasn't fighting, he was sleeping. He must've taken twenty naps a day. You, Percy, need your rest. You may be our only hope."

I wanted to complain that I *wasn't* their only hope. According to Rachel, I wasn't even the hero. But the look in Chiron's eyes made it clear he wasn't going to take no for an answer.

"Sure," I grumbled. "Talk."

I trudged toward the Empire State Building. When I glanced back, Rachel and Chiron were walking together in earnest conversation, like they were discussing funeral arrangements.

Inside the lobby, I found an empty bunk and collapsed, sure that I would never be able to sleep. A second later, my eyes closed.

In my dreams, I was back in Hades's garden. The lord of the dead paced up and down, holding his ears while Nico followed him, waving his arms.

"You *have* to!" Nico insisted.

Demeter and Persephone sat behind them at the break-fast table. Both of the goddesses looked bored. Demeter poured shredded wheat into four huge bowls. Persephone was magically changing the flower arrangement on the table, turning the blossoms from red to yellow to polka-dotted.

"I don't *have* to do anything!" Hades's eyes blazed. "I'm a god!"

"Father," Nico said, "if Olympus falls, your own palace's safety doesn't matter. You'll fade too."

"I am not an Olympian!" he growled. "My family has made that *quite* clear."

"You are," Nico said. "Whether you like it or not."

"You saw what they did to your mother," Hades said. "Zeus killed her. And you would have me *help* them? They deserve what they get!"

Persephone sighed. She walked her fingers across the table, absently turning the silverware into roses. "Could we *please* not talk about that woman?"

"You know what would help this boy?" Demeter mused. "Farming."

Persephone rolled her eyes. "Mother—"

"Six months behind a plow. Excellent character build-ing."

Nico stepped in front of his father, forcing Hades to face him. "My mother understood about family. That's why she didn't want to leave us. You can't just abandon your family because they did something horrible. You've done horrible things to them too."

"Maria died!" Hades reminded him.

"You can't just cut yourself off from the other gods!"

"I've done very well at it for thousands of years."

"And has that made you feel any better?" Nico demanded. "Has that curse on the Oracle helped you at all? Holding grudges is a fatal flaw. Bianca warned me about that, and she was right."

"For demigods! I am immortal, all-powerful! I would not help the other gods if they begged me, if Percy Jackson himself pleaded—"

"You're just as much of an outcast as I am!" Nico yelled. "Stop being angry about it and do something helpful for once. That's the only way they'll respect you!"

Hades's palm filled with black fire.

"Go ahead," Nico said. "Blast me. That's just what the other gods would expect from you. Prove them right."

"Yes, please," Demeter complained. "Shut him up."

Persephone sighed. "Oh, I don't know. I would rather fight in the war than eat another bowl of cereal. This is boring."

Hades roared in anger. His fireball hit a silver tree right next to Nico, melting it into a pool of liquid metal.

And my dream changed.

I was standing outside the United Nations, about a mile northeast of the Empire State Building. The Titan army had set up camp all around the UN complex. The flagpoles were hung with horrible trophies—helmets and armor pieces from defeated campers. All along First Avenue, giants sharpened their axes. Telkhines repaired armor at makeshift forges.

Kronos himself paced at the top of the plaza, swinging his scythe so his *dracaenae* bodyguards stayed way back. Ethan Nakamura and Prometheus stood nearby, out of slicing range. Ethan was fidgeting with his shield straps, but Prometheus looked as calm and collected as ever in his tuxedo.

"I hate this place," Kronos growled. "*United Nations.* As if mankind could ever unite. Remind me to tear down this building after we destroy Olympus."

"Yes, lord." Prometheus smiled as if his master's anger amused him. "Shall we tear down the stables in Central Park too? I know how much horses can annoy you."

"Don't mock me, Prometheus! Those cursed centaurs will be sorry they interfered. I will feed them to the hellhounds, starting with that son of mine—that weakling Chiron."

Prometheus shrugged. "That weakling destroyed an entire legion of telkhines with his arrows."

Kronos swung his scythe and cut a flagpole in half. The national colors of Brazil toppled into the army, squashing a *dracaena.*

"We will destroy them!" Kronos roared. "It is time to unleash the drakon. Nakamura, you will do this."

"Y-yes, lord. At sunset?"

"No," Kronos said. "Immediately. The defenders of Olympus are badly wounded. They will not expect a quick attack. Besides, we know this drakon they cannot beat."

Ethan looked confused. "My lord?"

"Never you mind, Nakamura. Just do my bidding. I want Olympus in ruins by the time Typhon reaches

New York. We will break the gods utterly!"

"But, my lord," Ethan said. "Your regeneration."

Kronos pointed at Ethan, and the demigod froze.

"Does it seem," Kronos hissed, "that I *need* to regenerate?"

Ethan didn't respond. Kind of hard to do when you're immobilized in time.

Kronos snapped his fingers and Ethan collapsed.

"Soon," the Titan growled, "this form will be unnecessary. I will not rest with victory so close. Now, go!"

Ethan scrambled away.

"This is dangerous, my lord," Prometheus warned. "Do not be hasty."

"Hasty? After festering for three thousand years in the depths of Tartarus, you call me hasty? I will slice Percy Jackson into a thousand pieces."

"Thrice you've fought him," Prometheus pointed out. "And yet you've always said it is beneath the dignity of a Titan to fight a mere mortal. I wonder if your mortal host is influencing you, weakening your judgment."

Kronos turned his golden eyes on the other Titan. "You call me weak?"

"No, my lord. I only meant—"

"Are your loyalties divided?" Kronos asked. "Perhaps you miss your old friends, the gods. Would you like to join them?"

Prometheus paled. "I misspoke, my lord. Your orders will be carried out." He turned to the armies and shouted, "PREPARE FOR BATTLE!"

The troops began to stir.

From somewhere behind the UN compound, an angry roar shook the city—the sound of a drakon waking. The noise was so horrible it woke me, and I realized I could still hear it from a mile away.

Grover stood next to me, looking nervous. "What was that?"

"They're coming," I told him. "And we're in trouble."

The Hephaestus cabin was out of Greek fire. The Apollo cabin and the Hunters were scrounging for arrows. Most of us had already ingested so much ambrosia and nectar we didn't dare take any more.

We had sixteen campers, fifteen Hunters, and half a dozen satyrs left in fighting shape. The rest had taken refuge on Olympus. The Party Ponies tried to form ranks, but they staggered and giggled and they all smelled like root beer. The Texans were head-butting the Coloradoans. The Missouri branch was arguing with Illinois. The chances were pretty good the whole army would end up fighting each other rather than the enemy.

Chiron trotted up with Rachel on his back. I felt a twinge of annoyance because Chiron rarely gave anyone a ride, and never a mortal.

"Your friend here has some useful insights, Percy," he said.

Rachel blushed. "Just some things I saw in my head."

"A drakon," Chiron said. "A Lydian drakon, to be exact. The oldest and most dangerous kind."

I stared at her. "How did you know that?"

"I'm not sure," Rachel admitted. "But this drakon has a particular fate. It will be killed by a child of Ares."

Annabeth crossed her arms. "How can you possibly know that?"

"I just saw it. I can't explain."

"Well, let's hope you're wrong," I said. "Because we're a little short on children of Ares. . . ." A horrible thought occurred to me, and I cursed in Ancient Greek.

"What?" Annabeth asked.

"The spy," I told her. "Kronos said, *We know they cannot beat this drakon.* The spy has been keeping him updated. Kronos knows the Ares cabin isn't with us. He intentionally picked a monster we can't kill."

Thalia scowled. "If I ever catch your spy, he's going to be very sorry. Maybe we could send another messenger to camp—"

"I've already done it," Chiron said. "Blackjack is on his way. But if Silena wasn't able to convince Clarisse, I doubt Blackjack will be able—"

A roar shook the ground. It sounded *very* close.

"Rachel," I said, "get inside the building."

"I want to stay."

A shadow blotted out the sun. Across the street, the drakon slithered down the side of a skyscraper. It roared, and a thousand windows shattered.

"On second thought," Rachel said in a small voice, "I'll be inside."

* * *

Let me explain: there are dragons, and then there are *drakons*.

Drakons are several millennia older than dragons, and *much* larger. They look like giant serpents. Most don't have wings. Most don't breathe fire (though some do). All are poisonous. All are immensely strong, with scales harder than titanium. Their eyes can paralyze you; not the *turn-you-to-stone* Medusa-type paralysis, but the *oh-my-gods-that-big-snake-is-going-to-eat-me* type of paralysis, which is just as bad.

We have drakon-fighting classes at camp, but there is no way to prepare yourself for a two-hundred-foot-long serpent as thick as a school bus slithering down the side of a building, its yellow eyes like searchlights and its mouth full of razor-sharp teeth big enough to chew elephants.

It almost made me long for the flying pig.

Meanwhile, the enemy army advanced down Fifth Avenue. We'd done our best to push cars out of the way to keep the mortals safe, but that just made it easier for our enemies to approach. The Party Ponies swished their tails nervously. Chiron galloped up and down their ranks, shouting encouragement to stand tough and think about victory and root beer, but I figured any second they would panic and run.

"I'll take the drakon." My voice came out as a timid squeak. Then I yelled louder: "I'LL TAKE THE DRAKON! Everyone else, hold the line against the army!"

Annabeth stood next to me. She had pulled her owl helmet low over her face, but I could tell her eyes were red.

"Will you help me?" I asked.

"That's what I do," she said miserably. "I help my friends."

I felt like a complete jerk. I wanted to pull her aside and explain that I didn't mean for Rachel to be here, that it wasn't my idea, but we had no time.

"Go invisible," I said. "Look for weak links in its armor while I keep it busy. Just be careful."

I whistled. "Mrs. O'Leary, heel!"

"ROOOF!" My hellhound leaped over a line of centaurs and gave me a kiss that smelled suspiciously of pepperoni pizza.

I drew my sword and we charged the monster.

The drakon was three stories above us, slithering sideways along the building as it sized up our forces. Wherever it looked, centaurs froze in fear.

From the north, the enemy army crashed into the Party Ponies, and our lines broke. The drakon lashed out, swallowing three Californian centaurs in one gulp before I could even get close.

Mrs. O'Leary launched herself through the air—a deadly black shadow with teeth and claws. Normally, a pouncing hellhound is a terrifying sight, but next to the drakon, Mrs. O'Leary looked like a child's night-night doll.

Her claws raked harmlessly off the drakon's scales. She bit the monster's throat but couldn't make a dent. Her weight, however, was enough to knock the drakon off the side of the building. It flailed awkwardly and crashed to the sidewalk, hellhound and serpent twisting and thrashing. The drakon tried to bite Mrs. O'Leary, but she was too close to the serpent's mouth. Poison spewed everywhere, melting centaurs into dust along with quite a few monsters, but Mrs. O'Leary weaved around the serpent's head, scratching and biting.

"YAAAH!" I plunged Riptide deep into the monster's left eye. The spotlight went dark. The drakon hissed and reared back to strike, but I rolled aside.

It bit a swimming-pool-size chunk out of the pavement. It turned toward me with its good eye, and I focused on its teeth so I wouldn't get paralyzed. Mrs. O'Leary did her best to cause a distraction. She leaped onto the serpent's head and scratched and growled like a really angry black wig.

The rest of the battle wasn't going well. The centaurs had panicked under the onslaught of giants and demons. An occasional orange camp T-shirt appeared in the sea of fighting, but quickly disappeared. Arrows screamed. Fire exploded in waves across both armies, but the action was moving across the street to the entrance of the Empire State Building. We were losing ground.

Suddenly Annabeth materialized on the drakon's back. Her invisibility cap rolled off her head as she drove her bronze knife between a chink in the serpent's scales.

The drakon roared. It coiled around, knocking Annabeth off its back.

I reached her just as she hit the ground. I dragged her out of the way as the serpent rolled, crushing a lamppost right where she'd been.

"Thanks," she said.

"I told you to be careful!"

"Yeah, well, DUCK!"

It was her turn to save me. She tackled me as the monster's teeth snapped above my head. Mrs. O'Leary body-slammed the drakon's face to get its attention, and we rolled out of the way.

Meanwhile our allies had retreated to the doors of the Empire State Building. The entire enemy army was surrounding them.

We were out of options. No more help was coming. Annabeth and I would have to retreat before we were cut off from Mount Olympus.

Then I heard a rumbling in the south. It wasn't a sound you hear much in New York, but I recognized it immediately: chariot wheels.

A girl's voice yelled, "ARES!"

And a dozen war chariots charged into battle. Each flew a red banner with the symbol of the wild boar's head. Each was pulled by a team of skeletal horses with manes of fire. A total of thirty fresh warriors, armor gleaming and eyes full of hate, lowered their lances as one—making a bristling wall of death.

"The children of Ares!" Annabeth said in amazement. "How did Rachel know?"

I didn't have an answer. But leading the charge was a girl in familiar red armor, her face covered by a boar's-head helm. She held aloft a spear that crackled with electricity. Clarisse herself had come to the rescue. While half her chariots charged the monster army, Clarisse led the other six straight for the drakon.

The serpent reared back and managed to throw off

Mrs. O'Leary. My poor pet hit the side of the building with a yelp. I ran to help her, but the serpent had already zeroed in on the new threat. Even with only one eye, its glare was enough to paralyze two chariot drivers. They veered into a line of cars. The other four chariots kept charging. The monster bared its fangs to strike and got a mouthful of Celestial bronze javelins.

"EEESSSSS!!!!!" it screamed, which is probably drakon for *OWWWW!*

"Ares, to me!" Clarisse screamed. Her voice sounded shriller than usual, but I guess that wasn't surprising given what she was fighting.

Across the street, the arrival of six chariots gave the Party Ponies new hope. They rallied at the doors of the Empire State Building, and the enemy army was momentarily thrown into confusion.

Meanwhile, Clarisse's chariots circled the drakon. Lances broke against the monster's skin. Skeletal horses breathed fire and whinnied. Two more chariots overturned, but the warriors simply leaped to their feet, drew their swords, and went to work. They hacked at chinks in the creature's scales. They dodged poison spray like they'd been training for this all their lives, which of course they had.

No one could say the Ares campers weren't brave. Clarisse was right there in front, stabbing her spear at the drakon's face, trying to put out its other eye. But as I watched, things started to go wrong. The drakon snapped up one Ares camper in a gulp. It knocked aside another and sprayed poison on a third, who retreated in a panic, his armor melting.

"We have to help," Annabeth said.

She was right. I'd just been standing there frozen in amazement. Mrs. O'Leary tried to get up but yelped again. One of her paws was bleeding.

"Stay back, girl," I told her. "You've done enough already."

Annabeth and I jumped onto the monster's back and ran toward its head, trying to draw its attention away from Clarisse.

Her cabinmates threw javelins, most of which broke, but some lodged in the monster's teeth. It snapped its jaws together until its mouth was a mess of green blood, yellow foamy poison, and splintered weapons.

"You can do it!" I screamed at Clarisse. "A child of Ares is destined to kill it!"

Through her war helmet, I could only see her eyes—but I could tell something was wrong. Her blue eyes shone with fear. Clarisse never looked like that. And she didn't *have* blue eyes.

"ARES!" she shouted, in that strangely shrill voice. She leveled her spear and charged the drakon.

"No," I muttered. "WAIT!"

But the monster looked down at her—almost in contempt—and spit poison directly in her face.

She screamed and fell.

"Clarisse!" Annabeth jumped off the monster's back and ran to help, while the other Ares campers tried to defend their fallen counselor. I drove Riptide between two of the creature's scales and managed to turn its attention on me.

I got thrown but I landed on my feet. "C'MON, you stupid worm! Look at me!"

For the next several minutes, all I saw were teeth. I retreated and dodged poison, but I couldn't hurt the thing.

At the edge of my vision, I saw a flying chariot land on Fifth Avenue.

Then someone ran toward us. A girl's voice, shaken with grief, cried, "NO! Curse you, WHY?"

I dared to glance over, but what I saw made no sense. Clarisse was lying on the ground where she'd fallen. Her armor smoked with poison. Annabeth and the Ares campers were trying to unfasten her helmet. And kneeling next to them, her face blotchy with tears, was a girl in camp clothes. It was . . . Clarisse.

My head spun. Why hadn't I noticed before? The girl in Clarisse's armor was much thinner, not as tall. But why would someone pretend to be Clarisse?

I was so stunned, the drakon almost snapped me in half. I dodged and the beast buried its head in a brick wall.

"WHY?" The real Clarisse demanded, holding the other girl in her arms while the campers struggled to remove the poison-corroded helmet.

Chris Rodriguez ran over from the flying chariot. He and Clarisse must've ridden it here from camp, chasing the Ares campers, who'd mistakenly been following the other girl, thinking she was Clarisse. But it still made no sense.

The drakon tugged its head from the brick wall and screamed in rage.

"Look out!" Chris warned.

Instead of turning toward me, the drakon whirled toward the sound of Chris's voice. It bared its fangs at the group of demigods.

The real Clarisse looked up at the drakon, her face filled with absolute hate. I'd seen a look that intense only once before. Her father, Ares, had worn the same expression when I'd fought him in single combat.

"YOU WANT DEATH?" Clarisse screamed at the drakon. "WELL, COME ON!"

She grabbed her spear from the fallen girl. With no armor or shield, she charged the drakon.

I tried to close the distance to help, but Clarisse was faster. She leaped aside as the monster struck, pulverizing the ground in front of her. Then she jumped onto the creature's head. As it reared up, she drove her electric spear into its good eye with so much force it shattered the shaft, releasing all of the magic weapon's power.

Electricity arced across the creature's head, causing its whole body to shudder. Clarisse jumped free, rolling safely to the sidewalk as smoke boiled from the drakon's mouth. The drakon's flesh dissolved, and it collapsed into a hollow scaly tunnel of armor.

The rest of us stared at Clarisse in awe. I had never seen anyone take down such a huge monster single-handedly. But Clarisse didn't seem to care. She ran back to the wounded girl who'd stolen her armor.

Finally Annabeth managed to remove the girl's helmet. We all gathered around: the Ares campers, Chris, Clarisse, Annabeth, and me. The battle still raged along Fifth Avenue, but for that moment nothing existed except our small circle and the fallen girl.

Her features, once beautiful, were badly burned from poison. I could tell that no amount of nectar or ambrosia would save her.

Something is about to happen. Rachel's words rang in my ears. *A trick that ends in death.*

Now I knew what she meant, and I knew who had led the Ares cabin into battle.

I looked down at the dying face of Silena Beauregard.

SEVENTEEN

ᕕᑐᕗ

I SIT ON THE
HOT SEAT

"What were you thinking?" Clarisse cradled Silena's head in her lap.

Silena tried to swallow, but her lips were dry and cracked. "Wouldn't . . . listen. Cabin would . . . only follow you."

"So you stole my armor," Clarisse said in disbelief. "You waited until Chris and I went out on patrol; you stole my armor and pretended to be me." She glared at her siblings. "And NONE of you noticed?"

The Ares campers developed a sudden interest in their combat boots.

"Don't blame them," Silena said. "They wanted to . . . to believe I was you."

"You *stupid* Aphrodite girl," Clarisse sobbed. "You charged a drakon? *Why?*"

"All my fault," Silena said, a tear streaking the side of her face. "The drakon, Charlie's death . . . camp endangered—"

"Stop it!" Clarisse said. "That's not true."

Silena opened her hand. In her palm was a silver bracelet with a scythe charm, the mark of Kronos.

A cold fist closed around my heart. "You were the spy."

Silena tried to nod. "Before . . . before I liked Charlie, Luke was nice to me. He was so . . . charming. Handsome. Later, I wanted to stop helping him, but he threatened to tell. He promised . . . he promised I was saving lives. Fewer people would get hurt. He told me he wouldn't hurt . . . Charlie. He lied to me."

I met Annabeth's eyes. Her face was chalky. She looked like somebody had just yanked the world out from under her feet.

Behind us, the battle raged.

Clarisse scowled at her cabinmates. "Go, help the centaurs. Protect the doors. GO!"

They scrambled off to join to fight.

Silena took a heavy, painful breath. "Forgive me."

"You're not dying," Clarisse insisted.

"Charlie . . ." Silena's eyes were a million miles away. "See Charlie . . ."

She didn't speak again.

Clarisse held her and wept. Chris put a hand on her shoulder.

Finally Annabeth closed Silena's eyes.

"We have to fight." Annabeth's voice was brittle. "She gave her life to help us. We have to honor her."

Clarisse sniffled and wiped her nose. "She was a hero, understand? A hero."

I nodded. "Come on, Clarisse."

She picked up a sword from one of her fallen siblings. "Kronos is going to pay."

* * *

I'd like to say I drove the enemy away from the Empire State Building. The truth was Clarisse did all the work. Even without her armor or spear, she was a demon. She rode her chariot straight into the Titan's army and crushed everything in her path.

She was so inspiring, even the panicked centaurs started to rally. The Hunters scrounged arrows from the fallen and launched volley after volley into the enemy. The Ares cabin slashed and hacked, which was their favorite thing. The monsters retreated toward 35th Street.

Clarisse drove to the drakon's carcass and looped a grappling line through its eye sockets. She lashed her horses and took off, dragging the drakon behind the chariot like a Chinese New Year dragon. She charged after the enemy, yelling insults and daring them to cross her. As she rode, I realized she was literally glowing. An aura of red fire flickered around her.

"The blessing of Ares," Thalia said. "I've never seen it in person before."

For the moment, Clarisse was as invincible as I was. The enemy threw spears and arrows, but nothing hit her.

"I AM CLARISSE, DRAKON-SLAYER!" she yelled. "I will kill you ALL! Where is Kronos? Bring him out! Is he a coward?"

"Clarisse!" I yelled. "Stop it. Withdraw!"

"What's the matter, Titan lord?" she yelled. "BRING IT ON!"

There was no answer from the enemy. Slowly, they

began to fall back behind a *dracaenae* shield wall, while Clarisse drove in circles around Fifth Avenue, daring anyone to cross her path. The two-hundred-foot-long drakon carcass made a hollow scraping noise against the pavement, like a thousand knives.

Meanwhile, we tended our wounded, bringing them inside the lobby. Long after the enemy had retreated from sight, Clarisse kept riding up and down the avenue with her horrible trophy, demanding that Kronos meet her battle.

Chris said, "I'll watch her. She'll get tired eventually. I'll make sure she comes inside."

"What about the camp?" I asked. "Is anybody left there?"

Chris shook his head. "Only Argus and the nature spirits. Peleus the dragon is still guarding the tree."

"They won't last long," I said. "But I'm glad you came."

Chris nodded sadly. "I'm sorry it took so long. I tried to reason with Clarisse. I said there's no point in defending camp if you guys die. All our friends are here. I'm sorry it took Silena . . ."

"My Hunters will help you stand guard," Thalia said. "Annabeth and Percy, you should go to Olympus. I have a feeling they'll need you up there—to set up the final defense."

The doorman had disappeared from the lobby. His book was facedown on the desk and his chair was empty. The rest of the lobby, however, was jam-packed with wounded campers, Hunters, and satyrs.

Connor and Travis Stoll met us by the elevators.

"Is it true?" Connor asked. "About Silena?"

I nodded. "She died a hero."

Travis shifted uncomfortably. "Um, I also heard—"

"That's it," I insisted. "End of story."

"Right," Travis mumbled. "Listen, we figure the Titan's army will have trouble getting up the elevator. They'll have to go up a few at a time. And the giants won't be able to fit at all."

"That's our biggest advantage," I said. "Any way to disable the elevator?"

"It's magic," Travis said. "Usually you need a key card, but the doorman vanished. That means the defenses are crumbling. Anyone can walk into the elevator now and head straight up."

"Then we have to keep them away from the doors," I said. "We'll bottle them up in the lobby."

"We need reinforcements," Travis said. "They'll just keep coming. Eventually they'll overwhelm us."

"There are no reinforcements," Connor complained.

I looked outside at Mrs. O'Leary, who was breathing against the glass doors and smearing them with hellhound drool.

"Maybe that's not true," I said.

I went outside and put a hand on Mrs. O'Leary's muzzle. Chiron had bandaged her paw, but she was still limping. Her fur was matted with mud, leaves, pizza slices, and dried monster blood.

"Hey, girl." I tried to sound upbeat. "I know you're

tired, but I've got one more big favor to ask you."

I leaned next to her and whispered in her ear.

After Mrs. O'Leary shadow-traveled away, I rejoined Annabeth in the lobby. On the way to the elevator, we spotted Grover kneeling over a fat wounded satyr.

"Leneus!" I said.

The old satyr looked terrible. His lips were blue. There was a broken spear in his belly, and his furry goat legs were twisted at a painful angle.

He tried to focus on us, but I don't think he saw us.

"Grover?" he murmured.

"I'm here, Leneus." Grover was blinking back tears, despite all the horrible things Leneus had said about him.

"Did . . . did we win?"

"Um . . . yes," Grover lied. "Thanks to you, Leneus. We drove the enemy away."

"Told you," the old satyr mumbled. "True leader. True . . ."

He closed his eyes for the last time.

Grover gulped. He put his hand on Leneus's forehead and spoke an ancient blessing. The old satyr's body melted, until all that was left was a tiny sapling in a pile of fresh soil.

"A laurel," Grover said in awe. "Oh, that lucky old goat."

He gathered up the sapling in his hands. "I . . . I should plant him. In Olympus, in the gardens."

"We're going that way," I said. "Come on."

Easy-listening music played as the elevator rose. I thought about the first time I'd visited Mount Olympus, back when I was twelve. Annabeth and Grover hadn't been with me then. I was glad they were with me now. I had a feeling it might be our last adventure together.

"Percy," Annabeth said quietly. "You were right about Luke." It was the first time she'd spoken since Silena Beauregard's death. She kept her eyes fixed on the elevator floors as they blinked into the magical numbers: 400, 450, 500.

Grover and I exchanged glances.

"Annabeth," I said. "I'm sorry—"

"You tried to tell me." Her voice was shaky. "Luke is no good. I didn't believe you until . . . until I heard how he'd used Silena. Now I know. I hope you're happy."

"That doesn't make me happy."

She put her head against the elevator wall and wouldn't look at me.

Grover cradled his laurel sapling in his hands. "Well . . . sure good to be together again. Arguing. Almost dying. Abject terror. Oh, look. It's our floor."

The doors dinged and we stepped onto the aerial walkway.

Depressing is not a word that usually describes Mount Olympus, but it looked that way now. No fires lit the braziers. The windows were dark. The streets were deserted and the doors were barred. The only movement was in the parks, which had been set up as field hospitals. Will Solace and the other Apollo campers scrambled around, caring for the wounded. Naiads and dryads tried to help, using nature magic songs to heal burns and poison.

As Grover planted the laurel sapling, Annabeth and I went around trying to cheer up the wounded. I passed a satyr with a broken leg, a demigod who was bandaged from head to toe, and a body covered in the golden burial shroud of Apollo's cabin. I didn't know who was underneath. I didn't want to find out.

My heart felt like lead, but we tried to find positive things to say.

"You'll be up and fighting Titans in no time!" I told one camper.

"You look great," Annabeth told another camper.

"Leneus turned into a shrub!" Grover told a groaning satyr.

I found Dionysus's son Pollux propped up against a tree. He had a broken arm, but otherwise he was okay.

"I can still fight with the other hand," he said, gritting his teeth.

"No," I said. "You've done enough. I want you to stay here and help with the wounded."

"But—"

"Promise me to stay safe," I said. "Okay? Personal favor."

He frowned uncertainly. It wasn't like we were good friends or anything, but I wasn't going to tell him it was a request from his dad. That would just embarrass him. Finally he promised, and when he sat back down, I could tell he was kind of relieved.

Annabeth, Grover, and I kept walking toward the palace. That's where Kronos would head. As soon as he made it up the elevator—and I had no doubt he would, one way or another—he would destroy the throne room, the center of the gods' power.

The bronze doors creaked open. Our footsteps echoed on the marble floor. The constellations twinkled coldly on the ceiling of the great hall. The hearth was down to a dull red glow. Hestia, in the form of a little girl in brown robes, hunched at its edge, shivering. The Ophiotaurus swam sadly in his sphere of water. He let out a half-hearted moo when he saw me.

In the firelight, the thrones cast evil-looking shadows, like grasping hands.

Standing at the foot of Zeus's throne, looking up at the stars, was Rachel Elizabeth Dare. She was holding a Greek ceramic vase.

"Rachel?" I said. "Um, what are you doing with that?"

She focused on me as if she were coming out of a dream. "I found it. It's Pandora's jar, isn't it?"

Her eyes were brighter than usual, and I had a bad flashback of moldy sandwiches and burned cookies.

"Please put down the jar," I said.

"I can see Hope inside it." Rachel ran her fingers over the ceramic designs. "So fragile."

"*Rachel.*"

My voice seemed to bring her back to reality. She held out the jar, and I took it. The clay felt as cold as ice.

"Grover," Annabeth mumbled. "Let's scout around the palace. Maybe we can find some extra Greek fire or Hephaestus traps."

"But—"

Annabeth elbowed him.

"Right!" he yelped. "I love traps!"

She dragged him out of the throne room.

Over by the fire, Hestia was huddled in her robes, rocking back and forth.

"Come on," I told Rachel. "I want you to meet someone."

We sat next to the goddess.

"Lady Hestia," I said.

"Hello, Percy Jackson," the goddess murmured. "Getting colder. Harder to keep the fire going."

"I know," I said. "The Titans are near."

Hestia focused on Rachel. "Hello, my dear. You've come to our hearth at last."

Rachel blinked. "You've been expecting me?"

Hestia held out her hands, and the coals glowed. I saw images in the fire: My mother, Paul, and I eating Thanksgiving dinner at the kitchen table; my friends and me around the campfire at Camp Half-Blood, singing songs and roasting marshmallows; Rachel and me driving along the beach in Paul's Prius.

I didn't know if Rachel saw the same images, but the tension went out of her shoulders. The warmth of the fire seemed to spread across her.

"To claim your place at the hearth," Hestia told her, "you must let go of your distractions. It is the only way you will survive."

Rachel nodded. "I . . . I understand."

"Wait," I said. "What is she talking about?"

Rachel took a shaky breath. "Percy, when I came here . . . I thought I was coming for you. But I wasn't. You and me . . ." She shook her head.

"Wait. Now I'm a *distraction*? Is this because I'm 'not the hero' or whatever?"

"I'm not sure I can put it into words," she said. "I was drawn to you because . . . because you opened the door to all of this." She gestured at the throne room. "I needed to understand my true sight. But you and me, that wasn't part of it. Our fates aren't intertwined. I think you've always known that, deep down."

I stared at her. Maybe I wasn't the brightest guy in the world when it came to girls, but I was pretty sure Rachel had just dumped me, which was lame considering we'd never even been together.

"So . . . what," I said. "'Thanks for bringing me to Olympus. See ya.' Is that what you're saying?"

Rachel stared at the fire.

"Percy Jackson," Hestia said. "Rachel has told you all she can. Her moment is coming, but your decision approaches even more rapidly. Are you prepared?"

I wanted to complain that no, I wasn't even close to prepared.

I looked at Pandora's jar, and for the first time I had an urge to open it. Hope seemed pretty useless to me right now. So many of my friends were dead. Rachel was cutting me off. Annabeth was angry with me. My parents were asleep down in the streets somewhere while a monster army surrounded the building. Olympus was on the verge of falling, and I'd seen so many cruel things the gods had done: Zeus destroying Maria di Angelo, Hades cursing the last Oracle, Hermes turning his back on Luke even when he knew his son would become evil.

Surrender, Prometheus's voice whispered in my ear. *Otherwise your home will be destroyed. Your precious camp will burn.*

Then I looked at Hestia. Her red eyes glowed warmly. I remembered the images I'd seen in her hearth—friends and family, everyone I cared about.

I remembered something Chris Rodriguez had said: *There's no point in defending camp if you guys die. All our friends are here.* And Nico, standing up to his father, Hades: *If Olympus falls,* he said, *your own palace's safety doesn't matter.*

I heard footsteps. Annabeth and Grover came back into the throne room and stopped when they saw us. I probably had a pretty strange look on my face.

"Percy?" Annabeth didn't sound angry anymore—just concerned. "Should we, um, leave again?"

Suddenly I felt like someone had injected me with steel. I understood what to do.

I looked at Rachel. "You're not going to do anything stupid, are you? I mean . . . you talked to Chiron, right?"

She managed a faint smile. "You're worried about *me* doing something stupid?"

"But I mean . . . will you be okay?"

"I don't know," she admitted. "That kind of depends on whether you save the world, hero."

I picked up Pandora's jar. The spirit of Hope fluttered

inside, trying to warm the cold container.

"Hestia," I said, "I give this to you as an offering."

The goddess tilted her head. "I am the least of the gods. Why would you trust me with this?"

"You're the last Olympian," I said. "And the most important."

"And why is that, Percy Jackson?"

"Because Hope survives best at the hearth," I said. "Guard it for me, and I won't be tempted to give up again."

The goddess smiled. She took the jar in her hands and it began to glow. The hearth fire burned a little brighter.

"Well done, Percy Jackson," she said. "May the gods bless you."

"We're about to find out." I looked at Annabeth and Grover. "Come on, guys."

I marched toward my father's throne.

The seat of Poseidon stood just to the right of Zeus's, but it wasn't nearly as grand. The molded black leather seat was attached to a swivel pedestal, with a couple of iron rings on the side for fastening a fishing pole (or a trident). Basically it looked like a chair on a deep-sea boat, that you would sit in if you wanted to hunt shark or marlin or sea monsters.

Gods in their natural state are about twenty feet tall, so I could just reach the edge of the seat if I stretched my arms.

"Help me up," I told Annabeth and Grover.

"Are you crazy?" Annabeth asked.

"Probably," I admitted.

"Percy," Grover said, "the gods *really* don't appreciate people sitting in their thrones. I mean like turn-you-into-a-pile-of-ashes don't appreciate it."

"I need to get his attention," I said. "It's the only way."

They exchanged uneasy looks.

"Well," Annabeth said, "this'll get his attention."

They linked their arms to make a step, then boosted me onto the throne. I felt like a baby with my feet so high off the ground. I looked around at the other gloomy, empty thrones, and I could imagine what it would be like sitting on the Olympian Council—so much power but so much arguing, always eleven other gods trying to get their way. It would be easy to get paranoid, to look out only for my own interest, especially if I were Poseidon. Sitting in his throne, I felt like I had the entire sea at my command—vast cubic miles of ocean churning with power and mystery. Why should Poseidon listen to anyone? Why shouldn't he be the greatest of the twelve?

Then I shook my head. *Concentrate.*

The throne rumbled. A wave of gale-force anger slammed into my mind:

WHO DARES—

The voice stopped abruptly. The anger retreated, which was a good thing, because just those two words had almost blasted my mind to shreds.

Percy. My father's voice was still angry but more controlled. *What—exactly—are you doing on my throne?*

"I'm sorry, Father," I said. "I needed to get your attention."

This was a very dangerous thing to do. Even for you. If I hadn't looked before I blasted, you would now be a puddle of seawater.

"I'm sorry," I said again. "Listen, things are rough up here."

I told him what was happening. Then I told him my plan.

His voice was silent for a long time.

Percy, what you ask is impossible. My palace—

"Dad, Kronos sent an army against you on purpose. He wants to divide you from the other gods because he knows you could tip the scales."

Be that as it may, he attacks my home.

"I'm *at* your home," I said. "Olympus."

The floor shook. A wave of anger washed over my mind. I thought I'd gone too far, but then the trembling eased. In the background of my mental link, I heard underwater explosions and the sound of battle cries: Cyclopes bellowing, mermen shouting.

"Is Tyson okay?" I asked.

The question seemed to take my dad by surprise. *He's fine. Doing much better than I expected. Though "peanut butter" is a strange battle cry.*

"You let him fight?"

Stop changing the subject! You realize what you are asking me to do? My palace will be destroyed.

"And Olympus might be saved."

Do you have any idea how long I've worked on remodeling this palace? The game room alone took six hundred years.

"Dad—"

Very well! It shall be as you say. But my son, pray this works.

"I am praying. I'm talking to you, right?"

Oh . . . yes. Good point. Amphitrite—incoming!

The sound of a large explosion shattered our connection.

I slipped down from the throne.

Grover studied me nervously. "Are you okay? You turned pale and . . . you started smoking."

"I did not!" Then I looked at my arms. Steam was curling off my shirtsleeves. The hair on my arms was singed.

"If you'd sat there any longer," Annabeth said, "you would've spontaneously combusted. I hope the conversation was worth it?"

Moo, said the Ophiotaurus in his sphere of water.

"We'll find out soon," I said.

Just then the doors of the throne room swung open. Thalia marched in. Her bow was snapped in half and her quiver was empty.

"You've got to get down there," she told us. "The enemy is advancing. And Kronos is leading them."

MY PARENTS GO COMMANDO

By the time we got to the street, it was too late.

Campers and Hunters lay wounded on the ground. Clarisse must've lost a fight with a Hyperborean giant, because she and her chariot were frozen in a block of ice. The centaurs were nowhere to be seen. Either they'd panicked and ran or they'd been disintegrated.

The Titan army ringed the building, standing maybe twenty feet from the doors. Kronos's vanguard was in the lead: Ethan Nakamura, the *dracaena* queen in her green armor, and two Hyperboreans. I didn't see Prometheus. The slimy weasel was probably hiding back at their headquarters. But Kronos himself stood right in front with his scythe in hand.

The only thing standing in his way was . . .

"Chiron," Annabeth said, her voice trembling.

If Chiron heard us, he didn't answer. He had an arrow notched, aimed straight at Kronos's face.

As soon as Kronos saw me, his gold eyes flared. Every muscle in my body froze. Then the Titan lord turned his attention back to Chiron. "Step aside, little son."

Hearing Luke call Chiron his *son* was weird enough, but

Kronos put contempt in his voice, like *son* was the worst word he could think of.

"I'm afraid not." Chiron's tone was steely calm, the way he gets when he's really angry.

I tried to move, but my feet felt like concrete. Annabeth, Grover, and Thalia were straining too, like they were just as stuck.

"Chiron!" Annabeth said. "Look out!"

The *dracaena* queen became impatient and charged. Chiron's arrow flew straight between her eyes and she vaporized on the spot, her empty armor clattering to the asphalt.

Chiron reached for another arrow, but his quiver was empty. He dropped the bow and drew his sword. I knew he hated fighting with a sword. It was never his favorite weapon.

Kronos chuckled. He advanced a step, and Chiron's horse-half skittered nervously. His tail flicked back and forth.

"You're a teacher," Kronos sneered. "Not a hero."

"Luke was a hero," Chiron said. "He was a good one, until *you* corrupted him."

"FOOL!" Kronos's voice shook the city. "You filled his head with empty promises. You said the gods cared about me!"

"Me," Chiron noticed. "You said *me*."

Kronos looked confused, and in that moment, Chiron struck. It was a good maneuver—a feint followed by a strike to the face. I couldn't have done better myself, but Kronos was quick. He had all of Luke's fighting skill, which was a lot. He knocked aside Chiron's blade and yelled, "*BACK!*"

A blinding white light exploded between the Titan and the centaur. Chiron flew into the side of the building with such force the wall crumbled and collapsed on top of him.

"No!" Annabeth wailed. The freezing spell broke. We ran toward our teacher, but there was no sign of him. Thalia and I pulled helplessly at the bricks while a ripple of ugly laughter ran through the Titan's army.

"YOU!" Annabeth turned on Luke. "To think that I . . . that I thought—"

She drew her knife.

"Annabeth, don't." I tried to take her arm, but she shook me off.

She attacked Kronos, and his smug smile faded. Perhaps some part of Luke remembered that he used to like this girl, used to take care of her when she was little. She plunged her knife between the straps of his armor, right at his collar-bone. The blade should've sunk into his chest. Instead it bounced off. Annabeth doubled over, clutching her arm to her stomach. The jolt might've been enough to dislocate her bad shoulder.

I yanked her back as Kronos swung his scythe, slicing the air where she'd been standing.

She fought me and screamed, "I HATE you!" I wasn't sure who she was talking to—me or Luke or Kronos. Tears streaked the dust on her face.

"I have to fight him," I told her.

"It's my fight too, Percy!"

Kronos laughed. "So much spirit. I can see why Luke

wanted to spare you. Unfortunately, that won't be possible."

He raised his scythe. I got ready to defend, but before Kronos could strike, a dog's howl pierced the air somewhere behind the Titan's army. *"Arroooooooo!"*

It was too much to hope, but I called, "Mrs. O'Leary?"

The enemy forces stirred uneasily. Then the strangest thing happened. They began to part, clearing a path through the street like something behind them was forcing them to.

Soon there was a free aisle down the center of Fifth Avenue. Standing at the end of the block was my giant dog and a small figure in black armor.

"Nico?" I called.

"ROWWF!" Mrs. O'Leary bounded toward me, ignoring the growling monsters on either side. Nico strode forward. The enemy army fell back before him like he radiated death, which of course he did.

Through the face guard of his skull-shaped helmet, he smiled. "Got your message. Is it too late to join the party?"

"Son of Hades." Kronos spit on the ground. "Do you love death so much you wish to experience it?"

"Your death," Nico said, "would be great for me."

"I'm immortal, you fool! I have escaped Tartarus. You have no business here, and no chance to live."

Nico drew his sword—three feet of wicked sharp Stygian iron, black as a nightmare. "I don't agree."

The ground rumbled. Cracks appeared in the road, the sidewalks, the sides of the buildings. Skeletal hands grasped the air as the dead clawed their way into the world of the living. There were thousands of them, and as they emerged, the Titan's monsters got jumpy and started to back up.

"HOLD YOUR GROUND!" Kronos demanded. "The dead are no match for us."

The sky turned dark and cold. Shadows thickened. A harsh war horn sounded, and as the dead soldiers formed up ranks with their guns and swords and spears, an enormous chariot roared down Fifth Avenue. It came to a stop next to Nico. The horses were living shadows, fashioned from darkness. The chariot was inlaid with obsidian and gold, decorated with scenes of painful death. Holding the reins was Hades himself, Lord of the Dead, with Demeter and Persephone riding behind him.

Hades wore black armor and a cloak the color of fresh blood. On top of his pale head was the helm of darkness: a crown that radiated pure terror. It changed shape as I watched—from a dragon's head to a circle of black flames to a wreath of human bones. But that wasn't the scary part. The helm reached into my mind and ignited my worst nightmares, my most secret fears. I wanted to crawl into a hole and hide, and I could tell the enemy army felt the same way. Only Kronos's power and authority kept his ranks from fleeing.

Hades smiled coldly. "Hello, Father. You're looking . . . young."

"Hades," Kronos growled. "I hope you and the ladies have come to pledge your allegiance."

"I'm afraid not." Hades sighed. "My son here convinced me that perhaps I should prioritize my list of enemies." He glanced at me with distaste. "As much as I dislike certain *upstart* demigods, it would not do for Olympus to fall. I would miss bickering with my siblings. And if there is one thing we agree on—it is that you were a TERRIBLE father."

"True," muttered Demeter. "No appreciation of agriculture."

"Mother!" Persephone complained.

Hades drew his sword, a double-edged Stygian blade etched with silver. "Now fight me! For today the House of Hades will be called the saviors of Olympus."

"I don't have time for this," Kronos snarled.

He struck the ground with his scythe. A crack spread in both directions, circling the Empire State Building. A wall of force shimmered along the fissure line, separating Kronos's vanguard, my friends, and me from the bulk of the two armies.

"What's he doing?" I muttered.

"Sealing us in," Thalia said. "He's collapsing the magic barriers around Manhattan—cutting off just the building, and us."

Sure enough, outside the barrier, car engines revved to life. Pedestrians woke up and stared uncomprehendingly at the monsters and zombies all around them. No telling what they saw through the Mist, but I'm sure it was plenty scary. Car doors opened. And at the end of the block, Paul Blofis and my mom got out of their Prius.

"No," I said. "Don't . . ."

My mother could see through the Mist. I could tell from her expression that she understood how serious things were. I hoped she would have the sense to run. But she locked eyes with me, said something to Paul, and they ran straight toward us.

I couldn't call out. The last thing I wanted to do was bring her to Kronos's attention.

Fortunately, Hades caused a distraction. He charged at the wall of force, but his chariot crashed against it and overturned. He got to his feet, cursing, and blasted the wall with black energy. The barrier held.

"ATTACK!" he roared.

The armies of the dead clashed with the Titan's monsters. Fifth Avenue exploded into absolute chaos. Mortals screamed and ran for cover. Demeter waved her hand and an entire column of giants turned into a wheat field. Persephone changed the *dracaenae*'s spears into sunflowers. Nico slashed and hacked his way through the enemy, trying to protect the pedestrians as best he could. My parents ran toward me, dodging monsters and zombies, but there was nothing I could do to help them.

"Nakamura," Kronos said. "Attend me. Giants—deal with them."

He pointed at my friends and me. Then he ducked into the lobby.

For a second I was stunned. I'd been expecting a fight, but Kronos completely ignored me like I wasn't worth the trouble. That made me mad.

The first Hyperborean giant smashed at me with his club. I rolled between his legs and stabbed Riptide into his backside. He shattered into a pile of ice shards. The second giant breathed frost at Annabeth, who was barely able to stand, but Grover pulled her out of the way while Thalia went to work. She sprinted up the giant's back like a gazelle, sliced her hunting knives across his monstrous blue neck, and created the world's largest headless ice sculpture.

I glanced outside the magic barrier. Nico was fighting his way toward my mom and Paul, but they weren't waiting for help. Paul grabbed a sword from a fallen hero and did a pretty fine job keeping a *dracaena* busy. He stabbed her in the gut, and she disintegrated.

"Paul?" I said in amazement.

He turned toward me and grinned. "I hope that was a monster I just killed. I was a Shakespearian actor in college! Picked up a little swordplay!"

I liked him even better for that, but then a Laistrygonian giant charged toward my mom. She was rummaging around in an abandoned police car—maybe looking for the emergency radio—and her back was turned.

"Mom!" I yelled.

She whirled when the monster was almost on top of her. I thought the thing in her hands was an umbrella until she cranked the pump and the shotgun blast blew the giant twenty feet backward, right into Nico's sword.

"Nice one," Paul said.

"When did you learn to fire a shotgun?" I demanded.

My mom blew the hair out of her face. "About two seconds ago. Percy, we'll be fine. Go!"

"Yes," Nico agreed, "we'll handle the army. You have to get Kronos!"

"Come on, Seaweed Brain!" Annabeth said. I nodded. Then I looked at the rubble pile on the side of the building. My heart twisted. I'd forgotten about Chiron. How could I do that?

"Mrs. O'Leary," I said. "Please, Chiron's under there. If anyone can dig him out, you can. Find him! Help him!"

I'm not sure how much she understood, but she bounded to the pile and started to dig. Annabeth, Thalia, Grover, and I raced for the elevators.

NINETEEN

WE TRASH THE
ETERNAL CITY

The bridge to Olympus was dissolving. We stepped out of the elevator onto the white marble walkway, and immediately cracks appeared at our feet.

"Jump!" Grover said, which was easy for him since he's part mountain goat.

He sprang to the next slab of stone while ours tilted sickeningly.

"Gods, I hate heights!" Thalia yelled as she and I leaped. But Annabeth was in no shape for jumping. She stumbled and yelled, "Percy!"

I caught her hand as the pavement fell, crumbling into dust. For a second I thought she was going to pull us both over. Her feet dangled in the open air. Her hand started to slip until I was holding her only by her fingers. Then Grover and Thalia grabbed my legs, and I found extra strength. Annabeth was *not* going to fall.

I pulled her up and we lay trembling on the pavement. I didn't realize we had our arms around each other until she suddenly tensed.

"Um, thanks," she muttered.

I tried to say *Don't mention it*, but it came out as, "Uh duh."

"Keep moving!" Grover tugged my shoulder. We untangled ourselves and sprinted across the sky bridge as more stones disintegrated and fell into oblivion. We made it to the edge of the mountain just as the final section collapsed.

Annabeth looked back at the elevator, which was now completely out of reach—a polished set of metal doors hanging in space, attached to nothing, six hundred stories above Manhattan.

"We're marooned," she said. "On our own."

"Blah-ha-ha!" Grover said. "The connection between Olympus and America is dissolving. If it fails—"

"The gods won't move on to another country this time," Thalia said. "This will be the end of Olympus. The *final* end."

We ran through streets. Mansions were burning. Statues had been hacked down. Trees in the parks were blasted to splinters. It looked like someone had attacked the city with a giant Weedwacker.

"Kronos's scythe," I said.

We followed the winding path toward the palace of the gods. I didn't remember the road being so long. Maybe Kronos was making time go slower, or maybe it was just dread slowing me down. The whole mountaintop was in ruins—so many beautiful buildings and gardens gone.

A few minor gods and nature spirits had tried to stop Kronos. What remained of them was strewn about the road: shattered armor, ripped clothing, swords and spears broken in half.

Somewhere ahead of us, Kronos's voice roared: "Brick

by brick! That was my promise. Tear it down BRICK BY BRICK!"

A white marble temple with a gold dome suddenly exploded. The dome shot up like the lid of a teapot and shattered into a billion pieces, raining rubble over the city.

"That was a shrine to Artemis," Thalia grumbled. "He'll pay for that."

We were running under the marble archway with the huge statues of Zeus and Hera when the entire mountain groaned, rocking sideways like a boat in a storm.

"Look out!" Grover yelped. The archway crumbled. I looked up in time to see a twenty-ton scowling Hera topple over on us. Annabeth and I would've been flattened, but Thalia shoved us from behind and we landed just out of danger.

"Thalia!" Grover cried.

When the dust cleared and the mountain stopped rocking, we found her still alive, but her legs were pinned under the statue.

We tried desperately to move it, but it would've taken several Cyclopes. When we tried to pull Thalia out from under it, she yelled in pain.

"I survive all those battles," she growled, "and I get defeated by a stupid chunk of rock!"

"It's Hera," Annabeth said in outrage. "She's had it in for me all year. Her statue would've killed me if you hadn't pushed us away."

Thalia grimaced. "Well, don't just stand there! I'll be fine. Go!"

We didn't want to leave her, but I could hear Kronos laughing as he approached the hall of the gods. More buildings exploded.

"We'll be back," I promised.

"I'm not going anywhere," Thalia groaned.

A fireball erupted on the side of the mountain, right near the gates of the palace.

"We've got to run," I said.

"I don't suppose you mean *away*," Grover murmured hopefully.

I sprinted toward the palace, Annabeth right behind me.

"I was afraid of that," Grover sighed, and clip-clopped after us.

The doors of the palace were big enough to steer a cruise ship through, but they'd been ripped off their hinges and smashed like they weighed nothing. We had to climb over a huge pile of broken stone and twisted metal to get inside.

Kronos stood in the middle of the throne room, his arms wide, staring at the starry ceiling as if taking it all in. His laughter echoed even louder than it had from the pit of Tartarus.

"Finally!" he bellowed. "The Olympian Council—so proud and mighty. Which seat of power shall I destroy first?"

Ethan Nakamura stood to one side, trying to stay out of the way of his master's scythe. The hearth was almost dead, just a few coals glowing deep in the ashes. Hestia was nowhere to be seen. Neither was Rachel. I hoped she was okay, but I'd seen so much destruction I was afraid to think about it. The Ophiotaurus swam in his water sphere in the far corner of the room, wisely not making a sound, but it wouldn't be long before Kronos noticed him.

Annabeth, Grover, and I stepped forward into the torchlight. Ethan saw us first.

"My lord," he warned.

Kronos turned and smiled through Luke's face. Except for the golden eyes, he looked just the same as he had four years ago when he'd welcomed me into the Hermes cabin. Annabeth made a painful sound in the back of her throat, like someone had just sucker punched her.

"Shall I destroy you first, Jackson?" Kronos asked. "Is that the choice you will make—to fight me and die instead of bowing down? Prophecies never end well, you know."

"Luke would fight with a sword," I said. "But I suppose you don't have his skill."

Kronos sneered. His scythe began to change, until he held Luke's old weapon, Backbiter, with its half-steel, half-Celestial bronze blade.

Next to me, Annabeth gasped like she'd suddenly had an idea. "Percy, the blade!" She unsheathed her knife. *"The hero's soul, cursed blade shall reap."*

I didn't understand why she was reminding me of that prophecy line right now. It wasn't exactly a morale booster, but before I could say anything, Kronos raised his sword.

"Wait!" Annabeth yelled.

Kronos came at me like a whirlwind.

My instincts took over. I dodged and slashed and rolled,

but I felt like I was fighting a hundred swordsmen. Ethan ducked to one side, trying to get behind me until Annabeth intercepted him. They started to fight, but I couldn't focus on how she was doing. I was vaguely aware of Grover playing his reed pipes. The sound filled me with warmth and courage—thoughts of sunlight and a blue sky and a calm meadow, somewhere far away from the war.

Kronos backed me up against the throne of Hephaestus—a huge mechanical La-Z-Boy type thing covered with bronze and silver gears. Kronos slashed, and I managed to jump straight up onto the seat. The throne whirred and hummed with secret mechanisms. *Defense mode,* it warned. *Defense mode.*

That couldn't be good. I jumped straight over Kronos's head as the throne shot tendrils of electricity in all directions. One hit Kronos in the face, arcing down his body and up his sword.

"ARG!" He crumpled to his knees and dropped Backbiter.

Annabeth saw her chance. She kicked Ethan out of the way and charged Kronos. "Luke, listen!"

I wanted to shout at her, to tell her she was crazy for trying to reason with Kronos, but there was no time. Kronos flicked his hand. Annabeth flew backward, slamming into the throne of her mother and crumpling to the floor.

"Annabeth!" I screamed.

Ethan Nakamura got to his feet. He now stood between Annabeth and me. I couldn't fight him without turning my back on Kronos.

Grover's music took on a more urgent tune. He moved toward Annabeth, but he couldn't go any faster and keep up the song. Grass grew on the floor of the throne room. Tiny roots crept up between the cracks of the marble stones.

Kronos rose to one knee. His hair smoldered. His face was covered with electrical burns. He reached for his sword, but this time it didn't fly into his hands.

"Nakamura!" he groaned. "Time to prove yourself. You know Jackson's secret weakness. Kill him, and you will have rewards beyond measure."

Ethan's eyes dropped to my midsection, and I was sure that he knew. Even if he couldn't kill me himself, all he had to do was tell Kronos. There was no way I could defend myself forever.

"Look around you, Ethan," I said. "The end of the world. Is this the reward you want? Do you really want everything destroyed—the good with the bad? *Everything?*"

Grover was almost to Annabeth now. The grass thickened on the floor. The roots were almost a foot long, like a stubble of whiskers.

"There is no throne to Nemesis," Ethan muttered. "No throne to my mother."

"That's right!" Kronos tried to get up, but stumbled. Above his left ear, a patch of blond hair still smoldered. "Strike them down! They deserve to suffer."

"You said your mom is the goddess of balance," I reminded him. "The minor gods deserve better, Ethan, but total destruction isn't *balance*. Kronos doesn't build. He only destroys."

Ethan looked at the sizzling throne of Hephaestus. Grover's music kept playing, and Ethan swayed to it, as if the song were filling him with nostalgia—a wish to see a beautiful day, to be anywhere but here. His good eye blinked.

Then he charged . . . but not at me.

While Kronos was still on his knees, Ethan brought down his sword on the Titan lord's neck. It should have killed him instantly, but the blade shattered. Ethan fell back, grasping his stomach. A shard of his own blade had ricocheted and pierced his armor.

Kronos rose unsteadily, towering over his servant. "Treason," he snarled.

Grover's music kept playing, and grass grew around Ethan's body. Ethan stared at me, his face tight with pain.

"Deserve better," he gasped. "If they just . . . had thrones—"

Kronos stomped his foot, and the floor ruptured around Ethan Nakamura. The son of Nemesis fell through a fissure that went straight through the heart of the mountain—straight into open air.

"So much for him." Kronos picked up his sword. "And now for the rest of you."

My only thought was to keep him away from Annabeth.

Grover was at her side now. He'd stopped playing and was feeding her ambrosia.

Everywhere Kronos stepped, the roots wrapped around his feet, but Grover had stopped his magic too early. The roots weren't thick or strong enough to do much more than annoy the Titan.

We fought through the hearth, kicking up coals and sparks. Kronos slashed an armrest off the throne of Ares, which was okay by me, but then he backed me up to my dad's throne.

"Oh, yes," Kronos said. "This one will make fine kindling for my new hearth!"

Our blades clashed in a shower of sparks. He was stronger than me, but for the moment I felt the power of the ocean in my arms. I pushed him back and struck again—slashing Riptide across his breastplate so hard I cut a gash in the Celestial bronze.

He stamped his foot again and time slowed. I tried to attack but I was moving at the speed of a glacier. Kronos backed up leisurely, catching his breath. He examined the gash in his armor while I struggled forward, silently cursing him. He could take all the time-outs he wanted. He could freeze me in place at will. My only hope was that the effort was draining him. If I could wear him down . . .

"It's too late, Percy Jackson," he said. "Behold."

He pointed to the hearth, and the coals glowed. A sheet of white smoke poured from the fire, forming images like an Iris-message. I saw Nico and my parents down on Fifth Avenue, fighting a hopeless battle, ringed in enemies. In the background Hades fought from his black chariot, summoning wave after wave of zombies out of the ground, but the forces of the Titan's army seemed just as endless. Meanwhile, Manhattan was being destroyed. Mortals, now fully awake, were running in terror. Cars swerved and crashed.

The scene shifted, and I saw something even more terrifying.

A column of storm was approaching the Hudson River, moving rapidly over the Jersey shore. Chariots circled it, locked in combat with the creature in the cloud.

The gods attacked. Lightning flashed. Arrows of gold and silver streaked into the cloud like rocket tracers and exploded. Slowly, the cloud ripped apart, and I saw Typhon clearly for the first time.

I knew as long as I lived (which might not be that long) I would never be able to get the image out of my mind. Typhon's head shifted constantly. Every moment he was a different monster, each more horrible than the last. Looking at his face would've driven me insane, so I focused on his body, which wasn't much better. He was humanoid, but his skin reminded me of a meat loaf sandwich that had been in someone's locker all year. He was mottled green, with blisters the size of buildings, and blackened patches from eons of being stuck under a volcano. His hands were human, but with talons like an eagle's. His legs were scaly and reptilian.

"The Olympians are giving their final effort." Kronos laughed. "How pathetic."

Zeus threw a thunderbolt from his chariot. The blast lit up the world. I could feel the shock even here on Olympus, but when the dust cleared, Typhon was still standing. He staggered a bit, with a smoking crater on top of his misshapen head, but he roared in anger and kept advancing.

My limbs began to loosen up. Kronos didn't seem to notice. His attention was focused on the fight and his final victory. If I could hold out a few more seconds, and if my dad kept his word . . .

Typhon stepped into the Hudson River and barely sank to midcalf.

Now, I thought, imploring the image in the smoke. *Please, it has to happen now.*

Like a miracle, a conch horn sounded from the smoky picture. The call of the ocean. The call of Poseidon.

All around Typhon, the Hudson River erupted, churning with forty-foot waves. Out of the water burst a new chariot—this one pulled by massive hippocampi, who swam in air as easily as in water. My father, glowing with a blue aura of power, rode a defiant circle around the giant's legs. Poseidon was no longer an old man. He looked like himself again—tan and strong with a black beard. As he swung his trident, the river responded, making a funnel cloud around the monster.

"No!" Kronos bellowed after a moment of stunned silence. "NO!"

"NOW, MY BRETHREN!" Poseidon's voice was so loud I wasn't sure if I was hearing it from the smoke image or from all the way across town. "STRIKE FOR OLYMPUS!"

Warriors burst out of the river, riding the waves on huge sharks and dragons and sea horses. It was a legion of Cyclopes, and leading them into battle was . . .

"Tyson!" I yelled.

I knew he couldn't hear me, but I stared at him in amazement. He'd magically grown in size. He had to be thirty feet tall, as big as any of his older cousins, and for the first time he was wearing full battle armor. Riding behind him was Briares, the Hundred-Handed One.

All the Cyclopes held huge lengths of black iron chains—big enough to anchor a battleship—with grappling hooks at the ends. They swung them like lassos and began to ensnare Typhon, throwing lines around the creature's legs and arms, using the tide to keep circling, slowly tangling him. Typhon shook and roared and yanked at the chains, pulling some of the Cyclopes off their mounts; but there were too many chains. The sheer weight of the Cyclops battalion began to weigh Typhon down. Poseidon threw his trident and impaled the monster in the throat. Golden blood, immortal ichor, spewed from the wound, making a waterfall taller than a skyscraper. The trident flew back to Poseidon's hand.

The other gods struck with renewed force. Ares rode in and stabbed Typhon in the nose. Artemis shot the monster in the eye with a dozen silver arrows. Apollo shot a blazing volley of arrows and set the monster's loincloth on fire. And Zeus kept pounding the giant with lightning, until finally, slowly, the water rose, wrapping Typhon like a cocoon, and he began to sink under the weight of the chains. Typhon bellowed in agony, thrashing with such force that waves sloshed the Jersey shore, soaking five-story buildings and splashing over the George Washington Bridge—but down he went as my dad opened a special tunnel for him at the bottom of the river—an endless waterslide that would take him straight to Tartarus. The giant's head went under in a seething whirlpool, and he was gone.

"BAH!" Kronos screamed. He slashed his sword through the smoke, tearing the image to shreds.

"They're on their way," I said. "You've lost."

"I haven't even started."

He advanced with blinding speed. Grover—brave, stupid satyr that he was—tried to protect me, but Kronos tossed him aside like a rag doll.

I sidestepped and jabbed under Kronos's guard. It was a good trick. Unfortunately, Luke knew it. He countered the strike and disarmed me using one of the first moves he'd ever taught me. My sword skittered across the ground and fell straight into the open fissure.

"STOP!" Annabeth came from nowhere.

Kronos whirled to face her and slashed with Backbiter, but somehow Annabeth caught the strike on her dagger hilt. It was a move only the quickest and most skilled knife fighter could've managed. Don't ask me where she found the strength, but she stepped in closer for leverage, their blades crossed, and for a moment she stood face-to-face with the Titan lord, holding him at a standstill.

"Luke," she said, gritting her teeth, "I understand now. You have to trust me."

Kronos roared in outrage. "Luke Castellan is dead! His body will burn away as I assume my true form!"

I tried to move, but my body was frozen again. How could Annabeth, battered and half dead with exhaustion, have the strength to fight a Titan like Kronos?

Kronos pushed against her, trying to dislodge his blade, but she held him in check, her arms trembling as he forced his sword down toward her neck.

"Your mother," Annabeth grunted. "She saw your fate."

"Service to Kronos!" the Titan roared. "This is my fate."

"No!" Annabeth insisted. Her eyes were tearing up, but I didn't know if it was from sadness or pain. "That's not the end, Luke. The prophecy: she saw what you would do. It applies to you!"

"I will crush you, child!" Kronos bellowed.

"You won't," Annabeth said. "You promised. You're holding Kronos back even now."

"LIES!" Kronos pushed again, and this time Annabeth lost her balance. With his free hand, Kronos struck her face, and she slid backward.

I summoned all my will. I managed to rise, but it was like holding the weight of the sky again.

Kronos loomed over Annabeth, his sword raised.

Blood trickled from the corner of her mouth. She croaked, "Family, Luke. You promised."

I took a painful step forward. Grover was back on his feet, over by the throne of Hera, but he seemed to be struggling to move as well. Before either of us could get anywhere close to Annabeth, Kronos staggered.

He stared at the knife in Annabeth's hand, the blood on her face. *"Promise."*

Then he gasped like he couldn't get air. "Annabeth . . ." But it wasn't the Titan's voice. It was Luke's. He stumbled forward like he couldn't control his own body. "You're bleeding. . . ."

"My knife." Annabeth tried to raise her dagger, but it clattered out of her hand. Her arm was bent at a funny angle. She looked at me, imploring, "Percy, please . . ."

I could move again.

I surged forward and scooped up her knife. I knocked Backbiter out of Luke's hand, and it spun into the hearth. Luke hardly paid me any attention. He stepped toward Annabeth, but I put myself between him and her.

"Don't touch her," I said.

Anger rippled across his face. Kronos's voice growled: "Jackson . . ." Was it my imagination, or was his whole body glowing, turning gold?

He gasped again. Luke's voice: "He's changing. Help. He's . . . he's almost ready. He won't need my body anymore. Please—"

"NO!" Kronos bellowed. He looked around for his sword, but it was in the hearth, glowing among the coals.

He stumbled toward it. I tried to stop him, but he pushed me out of the way with such force I landed next to Annabeth and cracked my head on the base of Athena's throne.

"The knife, Percy," Annabeth muttered. Her breath was shallow. "Hero . . . cursed blade . . ."

When my vision came back into focus, I saw Kronos grasping his sword. Then he bellowed in pain and dropped it. His hands were smoking and seared. The hearth fire had grown red-hot, like the scythe wasn't compatible with it. I saw an image of Hestia flickering in the ashes, frowning at Kronos with disapproval.

Luke turned and collapsed, clutching his ruined hands. "Please, Percy . . ."

I struggled to my feet. I moved toward him with the knife. I should kill him. That was the plan.

Luke seemed to know what I was thinking. He moistened his lips. "You can't . . . can't do it yourself. He'll break my control. He'll defend himself. Only my hand. I know where. I can . . . can keep him controlled."

He was definitely glowing now, his skin starting to smoke.

I raised the knife to strike. Then I looked at Annabeth, at Grover cradling her in his arms, trying to shield her. And I finally understood what she'd been trying to tell me.

You are not the hero, Rachel had said. *It will affect what you do.*

"Please," Luke groaned. "No time."

If Kronos evolved into his true form, there would be no stopping him. He would make Typhon look like a playground bully.

The line from the great prophecy echoed in my head: *A hero's soul, cursed blade shall reap.* My whole world tipped upside down, and I gave the knife to Luke.

Grover yelped. "Percy? Are you . . . um . . ."

Crazy. Insane. Off my rocker. Probably.

But I watched as Luke grasped the hilt.

I stood before him—defenseless.

He unlatched the side straps of his armor, exposing a small bit of his skin just under his left arm, a place that would be very hard to hit. With difficulty, he stabbed himself.

It wasn't a deep cut, but Luke howled. His eyes glowed like lava. The throne room shook, throwing me off my feet. An aura of energy surrounded Luke, growing brighter and brighter. I shut my eyes and felt a force like a nuclear explosion blister my skin and crack my lips.

It was silent for a long time.

When I opened my eyes, I saw Luke sprawled at the hearth. On the floor around him was a blackened circle of ash. Kronos's scythe had liquefied into molten metal and was trickling into the coals of the hearth, which now glowed like a blacksmith's furnace.

Luke's left side was bloody. His eyes were open—blue eyes, the way they used to be. His breath was a deep rattle.

"Good . . . blade," he croaked.

I knelt next to him. Annabeth limped over with Grover's support. They both had tears in their eyes.

Luke gazed at Annabeth. "You knew. I almost killed you, but you knew . . ."

"Shhh." Her voice trembled. "You were a hero at the end, Luke. You'll go to Elysium."

He shook his head weakly. "Think . . . rebirth. Try for three times. Isles of the Blest."

Annabeth sniffled. "You always pushed yourself too hard."

He held up his charred hand. Annabeth touched his fingertips.

"Did you . . ." Luke coughed and his lips glistened red. "Did you love me?"

Annabeth wiped her tears away. "There was a time I thought . . . well, I thought . . ." She looked at me, like she was drinking in the fact that I was still here. And I realized I was doing the same thing. The world was collapsing, and the only thing that really mattered to me was that she was alive.

"You were like a brother to me, Luke," she said softly. "But I didn't love you."

He nodded, as if he'd expected it. He winced in pain.

"We can get ambrosia," Grover said. "We can—"

"Grover," Luke gulped. "You're the bravest satyr I ever knew. But no. There's no healing. . . ." Another cough.

He gripped my sleeve, and I could feel the heat of his skin like a fire. "Ethan. Me. All the unclaimed. Don't let it . . . Don't let it happen again."

His eyes were angry, but pleading too.

"I won't," I said. "I promise."

Luke nodded, and his hand went slack.

The gods arrived a few minutes later in their full war regalia, thundering into the throne room and expecting a battle.

What they found were Annabeth, Grover, and me standing over the body of a broken half-blood, in the dim warm light of the hearth.

"Percy," my father called, awe in his voice. "What . . . what is this?"

I turned and faced the Olympians.

"We need a shroud," I announced, my voice cracking. "A shroud for the son of Hermes."

TWENTY

WE WIN FABULOUS
PRIZES

The Three Fates themselves took Luke's body.

I hadn't seen the old ladies in years, since I'd witnessed them snip a life thread at a roadside fruit stand when I was twelve. They'd scared me then, and they scared me now—three ghoulish grandmothers with bags of knitting needles and yarn.

One of them looked at me, and even though she didn't say anything, my life literally flashed before my eyes. Suddenly I was twenty. Then I was a middle-aged man. Then I turned old and withered. All the strength left my body, and I saw my own tombstone and an open grave, a coffin being lowered into the ground. All this happened in less than a second.

It is done, she said.

The Fate held up the snippet of blue yarn—and I knew it was the same one I'd seen four years ago, the lifeline I'd watched them snip. I had thought it was my life. Now I realized it was Luke's. They'd been showing me the life that would have to be sacrificed to set things right.

They gathered up Luke's body, now wrapped in a white-and-green shroud, and began carrying it out of the throne room.

"Wait," Hermes said.

The messenger god was dressed in his classic outfit of white Greek robes, sandals, and helmet. The wings of his helm fluttered as he walked. The snakes George and Martha curled around his caduceus, murmuring, *Luke, poor Luke.*

I thought about May Castellan, alone in her kitchen, baking cookies and making sandwiches for a son who would never come home.

Hermes unwrapped Luke's face and kissed his forehead. He murmured some words in Ancient Greek—a final blessing.

"Farewell," he whispered. Then he nodded and allowed the Fates to carry away his son's body.

As they left, I thought about the Great Prophecy. The lines now made sense to me. *The hero's soul, cursed blade shall reap.* The hero was Luke. The cursed blade was the knife he'd given Annabeth long ago—cursed because Luke had broken his promise and betrayed his friends. *A single choice shall end his days.* My choice, to give him the knife, and to believe, as Annabeth had, that he was still capable of setting things right. *Olympus to preserve or raze.* By sacrificing himself, he had saved Olympus. Rachel was right. In the end, I wasn't really the hero. Luke was.

And I understood something else: When Luke had descended into the River Styx, he would've had to focus on something important that would hold him to his mortal life. Otherwise he would've dissolved. I had seen Annabeth, and I had a feeling he had too. He had pictured that scene Hestia showed me—of himself in the good old days with

Thalia and Annabeth, when he promised they would be a family. Hurting Annabeth in battle had shocked him into remembering that promise. It had allowed his mortal conscience to take over again, and defeat Kronos. His weak spot—his Achilles heel—had saved us all.

Next to me, Annabeth's knees buckled. I caught her, but she cried out in pain, and I realized I'd grabbed her broken arm.

"Oh gods," I said. "Annabeth, I'm sorry."

"It's all right," she said as she passed out in my arms.

"She needs help!" I yelled.

"I've got this." Apollo stepped forward. His fiery armor was so bright it was hard to look at, and his matching Ray-Bans and perfect smile made him look like a male model for battle gear. "God of medicine, at your service."

He passed his hand over Annabeth's face and spoke an incantation. Immediately the bruises faded. Her cuts and scars disappeared. Her arm straightened, and she sighed in her sleep.

Apollo grinned. "She'll be fine in a few minutes. Just enough time for me to compose a poem about our victory: 'Apollo and his friends save Olympus.' Good, eh?"

"Thanks, Apollo," I said. "I'll, um, let you handle the poetry."

The next few hours were a blur. I remembered my promise to my mother. Zeus didn't even blink an eye when I told him my strange request. He snapped his fingers and informed me that the top of the Empire State Building was now lit up blue. Most mortals would just have to wonder what it meant, but my mom would know: I had survived. Olympus was saved.

The gods set about repairing the throne room, which went surprisingly fast with twelve superpowerful beings at work. Grover and I cared for the wounded, and once the sky bridge re-formed, we greeted our friends who had survived. The Cyclopes had saved Thalia from the fallen statue. She was on crutches, but otherwise she was okay. Connor and Travis Stoll had made it through with only minor injuries. They promised me they hadn't even looted the city much. They told me my parents were fine, though they weren't allowed into Mount Olympus. Mrs. O'Leary had dug Chiron out of the rubble and rushed him off to camp. The Stolls looked kind of worried about the old centaur, but at least he was alive. Katie Gardner reported that she'd seen Rachel Elizabeth Dare run out of the Empire State Building at the end of the battle. Rachel had looked unharmed, but nobody knew where she'd gone, which also troubled me.

Nico di Angelo came into Olympus to a hero's welcome, his father right behind him, despite the fact that Hades was only supposed to visit Olympus on winter solstice. The god of the dead looked stunned when his relatives clapped him on the back. I doubt he'd ever gotten such an enthusiastic welcome before.

Clarisse marched in, still shivering from her time in the ice block, and Ares bellowed, "There's my girl!"

The god of war ruffled her hair and pounded her on the back, calling her the best warrior he'd ever seen. "That drakon-slaying? THAT'S what I'm talking about!"

She looked pretty overwhelmed. All she could do was nod and blink, like she was afraid he'd start hitting her, but eventually she began to smile.

Hera and Hephaestus passed me, and while Hephaestus was a little grumpy about my jumping on his throne, he thought I'd done "a pretty bang-up job, mostly."

Hera sniffed in disdain. "I suppose I won't destroy you and that little girl now."

"Annabeth saved Olympus," I told her. "She convinced Luke to stop Kronos."

"Hmm," Hera whirled away in a huff, but I figured our lives would be safe, at least for a little while.

Dionysus's head was still wrapped in a bandage. He looked me up and down and said, "Well, Percy Jackson. I see Pollux made it through, so I suppose you aren't completely inept. It's all thanks to my training, I suppose."

"Um, yes, sir," I said.

Mr. D nodded. "As thanks for my bravery, Zeus has cut my probation at that miserable camp in half. I now have only fifty years left instead of one hundred."

"Fifty years, huh?" I tried to imagine putting up with Dionysus until I was an old man, assuming I lived that long.

"Don't get so excited, Jackson," he said, and I realized he was saying my name correctly. "I still plan on making your life miserable."

I couldn't help smiling. "Naturally."

"Just so we understand each other." He turned and began repairing his grapevine throne, which had been singed by fire.

Grover stayed at my side. From time to time he would break down in tears. "So many nature spirits dead, Percy. So *many*."

I put my arm around his shoulders and gave him a rag to blow his nose. "You did a great job, G-man. We *will* come back from this. We'll plant new trees. We'll clean up the parks. Your friends will be reincarnated into a better world."

He sniffled dejectedly. "I . . . I suppose. But it was hard enough to rally them before. I'm still an outcast. I could barely get anyone to listen to me about Pan. Now will they ever listen to me again? I led them into a slaughter."

"They will listen," I promised. "Because you care about them. You care about the Wild more than anyone."

He tried for a smile. "Thanks, Percy. I hope . . . I hope you know I'm really proud to be your friend."

I patted his arm. "Luke was right about one thing, G-man. You're the bravest satyr I ever met."

He blushed, but before he could say anything, conch horns blew. The army of Poseidon marched into the throne room.

"Percy!" Tyson yelled. He charged toward me with his arms open. Fortunately he'd shrunk back to normal size, so his hug was like getting hit by a tractor, not the entire farm.

"You are not dead!" he said.

"Yeah!" I agreed. "Amazing, huh?"

He clapped his hands and laughed happily. "I am not dead either. Yay! We chained Typhon. It was fun!"

Behind him, fifty other armored Cyclopes laughed and nodded and gave each other high fives.

"Tyson led us," one rumbled. "He is brave!"

"Bravest of the Cyclopes!" another bellowed.

Tyson blushed. "Was nothing."

"I saw you!" I said. "You were incredible!"

I thought poor Grover would pass out. He's deathly afraid of Cyclopes. But he steeled his nerves and said, "Yes. Um . . . three cheers for Tyson!"

"YAAARRRRR!" the Cyclopes roared.

"Please don't eat me," Grover muttered, but I don't think anyone heard him.

The conch horns blasted again. The Cyclopes parted, and my father strode into the throne room in his battle armor, his trident glowing in his hands.

"Tyson!" he roared. "Well done, my son. And Percy—" His face turned stern. He wagged his finger at me, and for a second I was afraid he was going to zap me. "I even forgive you for sitting on my throne. You have saved Olympus!"

He held out his arms and gave me a hug. I realized, a little embarrassed, that I'd never actually hugged my dad before. He was warm—like a regular human—and he smelled of a salty beach and fresh sea air.

When he pulled away, he smiled kindly at me. I felt so good, I'll admit I teared up a little. I guess until that moment I hadn't allowed myself to realize just how terrified I had been the last few days.

"Dad—"

"Shhh," he said. "No hero is above fear, Percy. And *you* have risen above every hero. Not even Hercules—"

"POSEIDON!" a voice roared.

Zeus had taken his throne. He glared across the room at my dad while all the other gods filed in and took their seats. Even Hades was present, sitting on a simple stone guest chair at the foot of the hearth. Nico sat cross-legged on the ground at his dad's feet.

"Well, Poseidon?" Zeus grumped. "Are you too proud to join us in council, my brother?"

I thought Poseidon was going to get mad, but he just looked at me and winked. "I would be honored, Lord Zeus."

I guess miracles do happen. Poseidon strode over to his fishing seat, and the Olympian Council convened.

While Zeus was talking—some long speech about the bravery of the gods, etc.—Annabeth walked in and stood next to me. She looked good for someone who'd recently passed out.

"Miss much?" she whispered.

"Nobody's planning to kill us, so far," I whispered back.

"First time today."

I cracked up, but Grover nudged me because Hera was giving us a dirty look.

"As for my brothers," Zeus said, "we are thankful"—he cleared his throat like the words were hard to get out—"erm, thankful for the aid of Hades."

The lord of the dead nodded. He had a smug look on his face, but I figure he'd earned the right. He patted his son Nico on the shoulders, and Nico looked happier than I'd ever seen him.

"And, of course," Zeus continued, though he looked

like his pants were smoldering, "we must . . . um . . . thank Poseidon."

"I'm sorry, brother," Poseidon said. "What was that?"

"We must thank Poseidon," Zeus growled. "Without whom . . . it would've been difficult—"

"Difficult?" Poseidon asked innocently.

"Impossible," Zeus said. "Impossible to defeat Typhon."

The gods murmured agreement and pounded their weapons in approval.

"Which leaves us," Zeus said, "only the matter of thanking our young demigod heroes, who defended Olympus so well—even if there are a few dents in my throne."

He called Thalia forward first, since she was his daughter, and promised her help in filling the Hunters' ranks.

Artemis smiled. "You have done well, my lieutenant. You have made me proud, and all those Hunters who perished in my service will never be forgotten. They will achieve Elysium, I am sure."

She glared pointedly at Hades.

He shrugged. "Probably."

Artemis glared at him some more.

"Okay," Hades grumbled. "I'll streamline their application process."

Thalia beamed with pride. "Thank you, my lady." She bowed to the gods, even Hades, and then limped over to stand by Artemis's side.

"Tyson, son of Poseidon!" Zeus called. Tyson looked nervous, but he went to stand in the middle of the Council, and Zeus grunted.

"Doesn't miss many meals, does he?" Zeus muttered. "Tyson, for your bravery in the war, and for leading the Cyclopes, you are appointed a general in the armies of Olympus. You shall henceforth lead your brethren into war whenever required by the gods. And you shall have a new . . . um . . . what kind of weapon would you like? A sword? An axe?"

"Stick!" Tyson said, showing his broken club.

"Very well," Zeus said. "We will grant you a new, er, stick. The best stick that may be found."

"Hooray!" Tyson cried, and all the Cyclopes cheered and pounded him on the back as he rejoined them.

"Grover Underwood of the satyrs!" Dionysus called.

Grover came forward nervously.

"Oh, stop chewing your shirt," Dionysus chided. "Honestly, I'm not going to blast you. For your bravery and sacrifice, blah, blah, blah, and since we have an unfortunate vacancy, the gods have seen fit to name you a member of the Council of Cloven Elders."

Grover collapsed on the spot.

"Oh, wonderful," Dionysus sighed, as several naiads came forward to help Grover. "Well, when he wakes up, someone tell him that he will no longer be an outcast, and that all satyrs, naiads, and other spirits of nature will henceforth treat him as a lord of the Wild, with all rights, privileges, and honors, blah, blah, blah. Now please, drag him off before he wakes up and starts groveling."

"FOOOOOD," Grover moaned, as the nature spirits carried him away.

I figured he'd be okay. He would wake up as a lord of the Wild with a bunch of beautiful naiads taking care of him. Life could be worse.

Athena called, "Annabeth Chase, my own daughter."

Annabeth squeezed my arm, then walked forward and knelt at her mother's feet.

Athena smiled. "You, my daughter, have exceeded all expectations. You have used your wits, your strength, and your courage to defend this city, and our seat of power. It has come to our attention that Olympus is . . . well, trashed. The Titan lord did much damage that will have to be repaired. We could rebuild it by magic, of course, and make it just as it was. But the gods feel that the city could be improved. We will take this as an opportunity. And you, my daughter, will design these improvements."

Annabeth looked up, stunned. "My . . . my lady?"

Athena smiled wryly. "You *are* an architect, are you not? You have studied the techniques of Daedalus himself. Who better to redesign Olympus and make it a monument that will last for another eon?"

"You mean . . . I can design whatever I want?"

"As your heart desires," the goddess said. "Make us a city for the ages."

"As long as you have plenty of statues of me," Apollo added.

"And me," Aphrodite agreed.

"Hey, and me!" Ares said. "Big statues with huge wicked swords and—"

"All right!" Athena interrupted. "She gets the point.

[349]

Rise, my daughter, official architect of Olympus."

Annabeth rose in a trance and walked back toward me.

"Way to go," I told her, grinning.

For once she was at a loss for words. "I'll . . . I'll have to start planning . . . Drafting paper, and, um, pencils—"

"PERCY JACKSON!" Poseidon announced. My name echoed around the chamber.

All talking died down. The room was silent except for the crackle of the hearth fire. Everyone's eyes were on me—all the gods, the demigods, the Cyclopes, the spirits. I walked into the middle of the throne room. Hestia smiled at me reassuringly. She was in the form of a girl now, and she seemed happy and content to be sitting by her fire again. Her smile gave me courage to keep walking.

First I bowed to Zeus. Then I knelt at my father's feet.

"Rise, my son," Poseidon said.

I stood uneasily.

"A great hero must be rewarded," Poseidon said. "Is there anyone here who would deny that my son is deserving?"

I waited for someone to pipe up. The gods never agreed on anything, and many of them still didn't like me, but not a single one protested.

"The Council agrees," Zeus said. "Percy Jackson, you will have one gift from the gods."

I hesitated. "Any gift?"

Zeus nodded grimly. "I know what you will ask. The greatest gift of all. Yes, if you want it, it shall be yours. The gods have not bestowed this gift on a mortal hero in many centuries, but, Perseus Jackson—if you wish it—you shall be made a god. Immortal. Undying. You shall serve as your father's lieutenant for all time."

I stared at him, stunned. "Um . . . a god?"

Zeus rolled his eyes. "A dimwitted god, apparently. But yes. With the consensus of the entire Council, I can make you immortal. Then I will have to put up with you forever."

"Hmm," Ares mused. "That means I can smash him to a pulp as often as I want, and he'll just keep coming back for more. I like this idea."

"I approve as well," Athena said, though she was looking at Annabeth.

I glanced back. Annabeth was trying not to meet my eyes. Her face was pale. I flashed back to two years ago, when I'd thought she was going to take the pledge to Artemis and become a Hunter. I'd been on the edge of a panic attack, thinking that I'd lose her. Now, she looked pretty much the same way.

I thought about the Three Fates, and the way I'd seen my life flash by. I could avoid all that. No aging, no death, no body in the grave. I could be a teenager forever, in top condition, powerful, and immortal, serving my father. I could have power and eternal life.

Who could refuse that?

Then I looked at Annabeth again. I thought about my friends from camp: Charles Beckendorf, Michael Yew, Silena Beauregard, so many others who were now dead. I thought about Ethan Nakamura and Luke.

And I knew what to do.

"No," I said.

The Council was silent. The gods frowned at each other like they must have misheard.

"No?" Zeus said. "You are . . . turning *down* our generous gift?"

There was a dangerous edge to his voice, like a thunderstorm about to erupt.

"I'm honored and everything," I said. "Don't get me wrong. It's just . . . I've got a lot of life left to live. I'd hate to peak in my sophomore year."

The gods were glaring at me, but Annabeth had her hands over her mouth. Her eyes were shining. And that kind of made up for it.

"I do want a gift, though," I said. "Do you promise to grant my wish?"

Zeus thought about this. "If it is within our power."

"It is," I said. "And it's not even difficult. But I need your promise on the River Styx."

"What?" Dionysus cried. "You don't trust us?"

"Someone once told me," I said, looking at Hades, "you should always get a solemn oath."

Hades shrugged. "Guilty."

"Very well!" Zeus growled. "In the name of the Council, we swear by the River Styx to grant your *reasonable* request as long as it is within our power."

The other gods muttered assent. Thunder boomed, shaking the throne room. The deal was made.

"From now on, I want you to properly recognize the children of the gods," I said. "All the children . . . of *all* the gods."

The Olympians shifted uncomfortably.

"Percy," my father said, "what exactly do you mean?"

"Kronos couldn't have risen if it hadn't been for a lot of demigods who felt abandoned by their parents," I said. "They felt angry, resentful, and unloved, and they had a good reason."

Zeus's royal nostrils flared. "You dare accuse—"

"No more undetermined children," I said. "I want you to promise to claim your children—all your demigod children—by the time they turn thirteen. They won't be left out in the world on their own at the mercy of monsters. I want them claimed and brought to camp so they can be trained right, and survive."

"Now, wait just a moment," Apollo said, but I was on a roll.

"And the minor gods," I said. "Nemesis, Hecate, Morpheus, Janus, Hebe—they all deserve a general amnesty and a place at Camp Half-Blood. Their children shouldn't be ignored. Calypso and the other peaceful Titan-kind should be pardoned too. And Hades—"

"Are you calling me a *minor god*?" Hades bellowed.

"No, my lord," I said quickly. "But your children should not be left out. They should have a cabin at camp. Nico has proven that. No unclaimed demigods will be crammed into the Hermes cabin anymore, wondering who their parents are. They'll have their own cabins, for all the gods. And no more pact of the Big Three. That didn't work anyway. You've got to stop trying to get rid of powerful demigods. We're going to train them and accept them instead. All children of the gods will be welcome and treated with respect. That is my wish."

Zeus snorted. "Is that all?"

"Percy," Poseidon said, "you ask much. You presume much."

"I hold you to your oath," I said. "All of you."

I got a lot of steely looks. Strangely, it was Athena who spoke up: "The boy is correct. We have been unwise to ignore our children. It proved a strategic weakness in this war and almost caused our destruction. Percy Jackson, I have had my doubts about you, but perhaps"—she glanced at Annabeth, and then spoke as if the words had a sour taste—"perhaps I was mistaken. I move that we accept the boy's plan."

"Humph," Zeus said. "Being told what to do by a mere child. But I suppose . . ."

"All in favor," Hermes said.

All the gods raised their hands.

"Um, thanks," I said.

I turned, but before I could leave, Poseidon called, "Honor guard!"

Immediately the Cyclopes came forward and made two lines from the thrones to the door—an aisle for me to walk through. They came to attention.

"All hail, Perseus Jackson," Tyson said. "Hero of Olympus . . . and my big brother!"

TWENTY-ONE

BLACKJACK GETS JACKED

Annabeth and I were on our way out when I spotted Hermes in a side courtyard of the palace. He was staring at an Iris-message in the mist of a fountain.

I glanced at Annabeth. "I'll meet you at the elevator."

"You sure?" Then she studied my face. "Yeah, you're sure."

Hermes didn't seem to notice me approach. The Iris-message images were going so fast I could hardly understand them. Mortal newscasts from all over the country flashed by: scenes of Typhon's destruction, the wreckage our battle had left across Manhattan, the president doing a news conference, the mayor of New York, some army vehicles riding down the Avenue of the Americas.

"Amazing," Hermes murmured. He turned toward me. "Three thousand years, and I will never get over the power of the Mist . . . and mortal ignorance."

"Thanks, I guess."

"Oh, not you. Although, I suppose I should wonder, turning down immortality."

"It was the right choice."

Hermes looked at me curiously, then returned his

attention to the Iris-message. "Look at them. They've already decided Typhon was a freak series of storms. Don't I wish. They haven't figured out how all the statues in Lower Manhattan got removed from their pedestals and hacked to pieces. They keep showing a shot of Susan B. Anthony strangling Frederick Douglass. But I imagine they'll even come up with a logical explanation for that."

"How bad is the city?"

Hermes shrugged. "Surprisingly, not too bad. The mortals are shaken, of course. But this is New York. I've never seen such a resilient bunch of humans. I imagine they'll be back to normal in a few weeks; and of course I'll be helping."

"You?"

"I'm the messenger of the gods. It's my job to monitor what the mortals are saying, and if necessary, help them make sense of what's happened. I'll reassure them. Trust me, they'll put this down to a freak earthquake or a solar flare. Anything but the truth."

He sounded bitter. George and Martha curled around his caduceus, but they were silent, which made me think that Hermes was *really* really angry. I probably should've kept quiet, but I said, "I owe you an apology."

Hermes gave me a cautious look. "And why is that?"

"I thought you were a bad father," I admitted. "I thought you abandoned Luke because you knew his future and didn't do anything to stop it."

"I *did* know his future," Hermes said miserably.

"But you knew more than just the bad stuff—that he'd

turn evil. You understood what he would do in the end. You knew he'd make the right choice. But you couldn't tell him, could you?"

Hermes stared at the fountain. "No one can tamper with fate, Percy, not even a god. If I had warned him what was to come, or tried to influence his choices, I would've made things even worse. Staying silent, staying away from him . . . that was the hardest thing I've ever done."

"You had to let him find his own path," I said, "and play his part in saving Olympus."

Hermes sighed. "I should not have gotten mad at Annabeth. When Luke visited her in San Francisco . . . well, I knew she would have a part to play in his fate. I foresaw that much. I thought perhaps she could do what I could not and save him. When she refused to go with him, I could barely contain my rage. I should have known better. I was really angry with myself."

"Annabeth did save him," I said. "Luke died a hero. He sacrificed himself to kill Kronos."

"I appreciate your words, Percy. But Kronos isn't dead. You can't kill a Titan."

"Then—"

"I don't know," Hermes grumbled. "None of us do. Blown to dust. Scattered to the wind. With luck, he's spread so thin that he'll never be able to form a consciousness again, much less a body. But don't mistake him for dead, Percy."

My stomach did a queasy somersault. "What about the other Titans?"

"In hiding," Hermes said. "Prometheus sent Zeus a message with a bunch of excuses for supporting Kronos. 'I was just trying to minimize the damage,' blah, blah. He'll keep his head low for a few centuries if he's smart. Krios has fled, and Mount Othrys has crumbled into ruins. Oceanus slipped back into the deep ocean when it was clear Kronos had lost. Meanwhile, my son Luke is dead. He died believing I didn't care about him. I will never forgive myself."

Hermes slashed his caduceus through the mist. The Iris-picture disappeared.

"A long time ago," I said, "you told me the hardest thing about being a god was not being able to help your children. You also told me that you couldn't give up on your family, no matter how tempting they made it."

"And now you know I'm a hypocrite?"

"No, you were right. Luke loved you. At the end, he realized his fate. I think he realized why you couldn't help him. He remembered what was important."

"Too late for him and me."

"You have other children. Honor Luke by recognizing them. All the gods can do that."

Hermes's shoulders sagged. "They'll try, Percy. Oh, we'll all try to keep our promise. And maybe for a while things will get better. But we gods have never been good at keeping oaths. You were born because of a broken promise, eh? Eventually we'll become forgetful. We always do."

"You can change."

Hermes laughed. "After three thousand years, you think the gods can change their nature?"

"Yeah," I said. "I do."

Hermes seemed surprised by that. "You think . . . Luke actually loved me? After all that happened?"

"I'm sure of it."

Hermes stared at the fountain. "I'll give you a list of my children. There's a boy in Wisconsin. Two girls in Los Angeles. A few others. Will you see that they get to camp?"

"I promise," I said. "And I won't forget."

George and Martha twirled around the caduceus. I know snakes can't smile, but they seemed to be trying.

"Percy Jackson," Hermes said, "you might just teach us a thing or two."

Another god was waiting for me on the way out of Olympus. Athena stood in the middle of the road with her arms crossed and a look on her face that made me think *Uh-oh*. She'd changed out of her armor, into jeans and a white blouse, but she didn't look any less warlike. Her gray eyes blazed.

"Well, Percy," she said. "You will stay mortal."

"Um, yes, ma'am."

"I would know your reasons."

"I want to be a regular guy. I want to grow up. Have, you know, a regular high school experience."

"And my daughter?"

"I couldn't leave her," I admitted, my throat dry. "Or Grover," I added quickly. "Or—"

"Spare me." Athena stepped close to me, and I could feel her aura of power making my skin itch. "I once warned you, Percy Jackson, that to save a friend you would destroy the world. Perhaps I was mistaken. You seem to have saved both your friends and the world. But think very carefully about how you proceed from here. I have given you the benefit of the doubt. Don't mess up."

Just to prove her point, she erupted in a column of flame, charring the front of my shirt.

Annabeth was waiting for me at the elevator. "Why do you smell like smoke?"

"Long story," I said. Together we made our way down to the street level. Neither of us said a word. The music was awful—Neil Diamond or something. I should've made that part of my gift from the gods: better elevator tunes.

When we got into the lobby, I found my mother and Paul arguing with the bald security guy, who'd returned to his post.

"I'm telling you," my mom yelled, "we have to go up! My son—" Then she saw me and her eyes widened. "Percy!"

She hugged the breath right out of me.

"We saw the building lit up blue," she said. "But then you didn't come down. You went up *hours* ago!"

"She was getting a bit anxious," Paul said drily.

"I'm all right," I promised as my mom hugged Annabeth. "Everything's okay now."

"Mr. Blofis," Annabeth said, "that was wicked sword work."

Paul shrugged. "It seemed like the thing to do. But

Percy, is this really . . . I mean, this story about the six hundredth floor?"

"Olympus," I said. "Yeah."

Paul looked at the ceiling with a dreamy expression. "I'd like to see that."

"Paul," my mom chided. "It's not for mortals. Anyway, the important thing is we're safe. All of us."

I was about to relax. Everything felt perfect. Annabeth and I were okay. My mom and Paul had survived. Olympus was saved.

But the life of a demigod is never so easy. Just then Nico ran in from the street, and his face told me something was wrong.

"It's Rachel," he said. "I just ran into her down on 32nd Street."

Annabeth frowned. "What's she done this time?"

"It's where she's gone," Nico said. "I told her she would die if she tried, but she insisted. She just took Blackjack and—"

"She took my pegasus?" I demanded.

Nico nodded. "She's heading to Half-Blood Hill. She said she had to get to camp."

TWENTY-TWO

I AM DUMPED

Nobody steals my pegasus. Not even Rachel. I wasn't sure if I was more angry or amazed or worried.

"What was she thinking?" Annabeth said as we ran for the river. Unfortunately, I had a pretty good idea, and it filled me with dread.

The traffic was horrible. Everybody was out on the streets gawking at the war zone damage. Police sirens wailed on every block. There was no possibility of catching a cab, and the pegasi had flown away. I would've settled for some Party Ponies, but they had disappeared along with most of the root beer in Midtown. So we ran, pushing through mobs of dazed mortals that clogged the sidewalks.

"She'll never get through the defenses," Annabeth said. "Peleus will eat her."

I hadn't considered that. The Mist wouldn't fool Rachel like it would most people. She'd be able to find the camp no problem, but I'd been hoping the magical boundaries would just keep her out like a force field. It hadn't occurred to me that Peleus might attack.

"We've got to hurry." I glanced at Nico. "I don't suppose you could conjure up some skeleton horses."

He wheezed as he ran. "So tired . . . couldn't summon a dog bone."

Finally we scrambled over the embankment to the shore, and I let out a loud whistle. I hated doing it. Even with the sand dollar I'd given the East River for a magic cleaning, the water here was pretty polluted. I didn't want to make any sea animals sick, but they came to my call.

Three wake lines appeared in the gray water, and a pod of hippocampi broke the surface. They whinnied unhappily, shaking the river muck from their manes. They were beautiful creatures, with multicolored fish tails, and the heads and forelegs of white stallions. The hippocampus in front was much bigger than the others—a ride fit for a Cyclops.

"Rainbow!" I called. "How's it going, buddy?"

He neighed a complaint.

"Yeah, I'm sorry," I said. "But it's an emergency. We need to get to camp."

He snorted.

"Tyson?" I said. "Tyson is fine! I'm sorry he's not here. He's a big general now in the Cyclops army."

"NEEEEIGGGGH!"

"Yeah, I'm sure he'll still bring you apples. Now, about that ride . . ."

In no time, Annabeth, Nico, and I were zipping up the East River faster than Jet Skis. We sped under the Throgs Neck Bridge and headed for Long Island Sound.

It seemed like forever until we saw the beach at camp. We thanked the hippocampi and waded ashore, only to find

Argus waiting for us. He stood in the sand with his arms crossed, his hundred eyes glaring at us.

"Is she here?" I asked.

He nodded grimly.

"Is everything okay?" Annabeth said.

Argus shook his head.

We followed him up the trail. It was surreal being back at camp, because everything looked so peaceful: no burning buildings, no wounded fighters. The cabins were bright in the sunshine, and the fields glittered with dew. But the place was mostly empty.

Up at the Big House, something was definitely wrong. Green light was shooting out all the windows, just like I'd seen in my dream about May Castellan. Mist—the magical kind—swirled around the yard. Chiron lay on a horse-size stretcher by the volleyball pit, a bunch of satyrs standing around him. Blackjack cantered nervously in the grass.

Don't blame me, boss! he pleaded when he saw me. *The weird girl made me do it!*

Rachel Elizabeth Dare stood at the bottom of the porch steps. Her arms were raised like she was waiting for someone inside the house to throw her a ball.

"What's she doing?" Annabeth demanded. "How did she get past the barriers?"

"She flew," one of the satyrs said, looking accusingly at Blackjack. "Right past the dragon, right through the magic boundaries."

"Rachel!" I called, but the satyrs stopped me when I tried to go any closer.

"Percy, don't," Chiron warned. He winced as he tried to move. His left arm was in a sling, his two back legs were in splints, and his head was wrapped in bandages. "You can't interrupt."

"I thought you explained things to her!"

"I did. And I invited her here."

I stared at him in disbelief. "You said you'd never let anyone try again! You said—"

"I know what I said, Percy. But I was wrong. Rachel had a vision about the curse of Hades. She believes it may be lifted now. She convinced me she deserves a chance."

"And if the curse *isn't* lifted? If Hades hasn't gotten to that yet, she'll go crazy!"

The Mist swirled around Rachel. She shivered like she was going into shock.

"Hey!" I shouted. "Stop!"

I ran toward her, ignoring the satyrs. I got within ten feet and hit something like an invisible beach ball. I bounced back and landed in the grass.

Rachel opened her eyes and turned. She looked like she was sleepwalking—like she could see me, but only in a dream.

"It's all right." Her voice sounded far away. "This is why I've come."

"You'll be destroyed!"

She shook her head. "This is where I belong, Percy. I finally understand why."

It sounded too much like what May Castellan had said. I had to stop her, but I couldn't even get to my feet.

The house rumbled. The door flew open and green light poured out. I recognized the warm musty smell of snakes.

Mist curled into a hundred smoky serpents, slithering up the porch columns, curling around the house. Then the Oracle appeared in the doorway.

The withered mummy shuffled forward in her rainbow dress. She looked even worse than usual, which is saying a lot. Her hair was falling out in clumps. Her leathery skin was cracking like the seat of a worn-out bus. Her glassy eyes stared blankly into space, but I got the creepiest feeling she was being drawn straight toward Rachel.

Rachel held out her arms. She didn't look scared.

"You've waited too long," Rachel said. "But I'm here now."

The sun blazed more brightly. A man appeared above the porch, floating in the air—a blond dude in a white toga, with sunglasses and a cocky smile.

"Apollo," I said.

He winked at me but held up his finger to his lips.

"Rachel Elizabeth Dare," he said. "You have the gift of prophecy. But it is also a curse. Are you sure you want this?"

Rachel nodded. "It's my destiny."

"Do you accept the risks?"

"I do."

"Then proceed," the god said.

Rachel closed her eyes. "I accept this role. I pledge myself to Apollo, God of Oracles. I open my eyes to the future and embrace the past. I accept the spirit of Delphi, Voice of the Gods, Speaker of Riddles, Seer of Fate."

I didn't know where she was getting the words, but they flowed out of her as the Mist thickened. A green column of smoke, like a huge python, uncoiled from the mummy's mouth and slithered down the stairs, curling affectionately around Rachel's feet. The Oracle's mummy crumbled, falling away until it was nothing but a pile of dust in an old tie-dyed dress. Mist enveloped Rachel in a column.

For a moment I couldn't see her at all. Then the smoke cleared.

Rachel collapsed and curled into the fetal position. Annabeth, Nico, and I rushed forward, but Apollo said, "Stop! This is the most delicate part."

"What's going on?" I demanded. "What do you mean?"

Apollo studied Rachel with concern. "Either the spirit takes hold, or it doesn't."

"And if it doesn't?" Annabeth asked.

"Five syllables," Apollo said, counting them on his fingers. *"That would be real bad."*

Despite Apollo's warning, I ran forward and knelt over Rachel. The smell of the attic was gone. The Mist sank into the ground and the green light faded. But Rachel was still pale. She was barely breathing.

Then her eyes fluttered open. She focused on me with difficulty. "Percy."

"Are you okay?"

She tried to sit up. "Ow." She pressed her hands to her temples.

"Rachel," Nico said, "your life aura almost faded completely. I could *see* you dying."

"I'm all right," she murmured. "Please, help me up. The visions—they're a little disorienting."

"Are you sure you're okay?" I asked.

Apollo drifted down from the porch. "Ladies and gentlemen, may I introduce the new Oracle of Delphi."

"You're kidding," Annabeth said.

Rachel managed a weak smile. "It's a little surprising to me too, but this is my fate. I saw it when I was in New York. I know why I was born with true sight. I was meant to become the Oracle."

I blinked. "You mean you can tell the future now?"

"Not all the time," she said. "But there are visions, images, words in my mind. When someone asks me a question, I . . . Oh no—"

"It's starting," Apollo announced.

Rachel doubled over like someone had punched her. Then she stood up straight and her eyes glowed serpent green.

When she spoke, her voice sounded tripled—like three Rachels were talking at once:

Seven half-bloods shall answer the call.

To storm or fire, the world must fall.

An oath to keep with a final breath,

And foes bear arms to the Doors of Death.

At the last word, Rachel collapsed. Nico and I caught her and helped her to the porch. Her skin was feverish.

"I'm all right," she said, her voice returning to normal.

"What was that?" I asked.

She shook her head, confused. "What was what?"

"I believe," Apollo said, "that we just heard the next Great Prophecy."

"What does it mean?" I demanded.

Rachel frowned. "I don't even remember what I said."

"No," Apollo mused. "The spirit will only speak through you occasionally. The rest of the time, our Rachel will be much as she's always been. There's no point in grilling her, even if she has just issued the next big prediction for the future of the world."

"What?" I said. "But—"

"Percy," Apollo said, "I wouldn't worry too much. The last Great Prophecy about *you* took almost seventy years to complete. This one may not even happen in your lifetime."

I thought about the lines Rachel had spoken in that creepy voice: about storm and fire and the Doors of Death. "Maybe," I said, "but it didn't sound so good."

"No," said Apollo cheerfully. "It certainly didn't. She's going to make a wonderful Oracle!"

It was hard to drop the subject, but Apollo insisted that Rachel needed to rest, and she did look pretty disoriented.

"I'm sorry, Percy," she said. "Back on Olympus, I didn't explain everything to you, but the calling frightened me. I didn't think you'd understand."

"I still don't," I admitted. "But I guess I'm happy for you."

Rachel smiled. "Happy probably isn't the right word. Seeing the future isn't going to be easy, but it's my destiny. I only hope my family . . ."

She didn't finish her thought.

"Will you still go to Clarion Academy?" I asked.

"I made a promise to my father. I guess I'll try to be a normal kid during the school year, but—"

"But right now you need sleep," Apollo scolded. "Chiron, I don't think the attic is the proper place for our new Oracle, do you?"

"No, indeed." Chiron looked a lot better now that Apollo had worked some medical magic on him. "Rachel may use a guest room in the Big House for now, until we give the matter more thought."

"I'm thinking a cave in the hills," Apollo mused. "With torches and a big purple curtain over the entrance . . . really mysterious. But inside, a totally decked-out pad with a game room and one of those home theater systems."

Chiron cleared his throat loudly.

"What?" Apollo demanded.

Rachel kissed me on the cheek. "Good-bye, Percy," she whispered. "And I don't have to see the future to tell you what to do now, do I?"

Her eyes seemed more piercing than before.

I blushed. "No."

"Good," she said. Then she turned and followed Apollo into the Big House.

The rest of the day was as strange as the beginning. Campers trickled in from New York by car, pegasus, and chariot. The wounded were cared for. The dead were given proper funeral rites at the campfire.

Silena's shroud was hot pink, but embroidered with an electric spear. The Ares and Aphrodite cabins both claimed her as a hero, and lit the shroud together. No one mentioned the word *spy*. That secret burned to ashes as the designer perfume smoke drifted into the sky.

Even Ethan Nakamura was given a shroud—black silk with a logo of swords crossed under a set of scales. As his shroud went up in flames, I hoped Ethan knew he had made a difference in the end. He'd paid a lot more than an eye, but the minor gods would finally get the respect they deserved.

Dinner at the pavilion was low-key. The only highlight was Juniper the tree nymph, who screamed, "Grover!" and gave her boyfriend a flying tackle hug, making everybody cheer. They went down to the beach to take a moonlit walk, and I was happy for them, though the scene reminded me of Silena and Beckendorf, which made me sad.

Mrs. O'Leary romped around happily, eating everybody's table scraps. Nico sat at the main table with Chiron and Mr. D, and nobody seemed to think this was out of place. Everybody was patting Nico on the back, complimenting him on his fighting. Even the Ares kids seemed to think he was pretty cool. Hey, show up with an army of undead warriors to save the day, and suddenly you're everybody's best friend.

Slowly, the dinner crowd trickled away. Some went to the campfire for a sing-along. Others went to bed. I sat at the Poseidon table by myself and watched the moonlight on Long Island Sound. I could see Grover and Juniper at the beach, holding hands and talking. It was peaceful.

"Hey." Annabeth slid next to me on the bench. "Happy birthday."

She was holding a huge misshapen cupcake with blue icing.

I stared at her. "What?"

"It's August 18th," she said. "Your birthday, right?"

I was stunned. It hadn't even occurred to me, but she was right. I had turned sixteen this morning—the same morning I'd made the choice to give Luke the knife. The prophecy had come true right on schedule, and I hadn't even thought about the fact that it was my birthday.

"Make a wish," she said.

"Did you bake this yourself?" I asked.

"Tyson helped."

"That explains why it looks like a chocolate brick," I said. "With extra blue cement."

Annabeth laughed.

I thought for a second, then blew out the candle.

We cut it in half and shared, eating with our fingers. Annabeth sat next to me, and we watched the ocean. Crickets and monsters were making noise in the woods, but otherwise it was quiet.

"You saved the world," she said.

"We saved the world."

"And Rachel is the new Oracle, which means she won't be dating anybody."

"You don't sound disappointed," I noticed.

Annabeth shrugged. "Oh, I don't care."

"Uh-huh."

She raised an eyebrow. "You got something to say to me, Seaweed Brain?"

"You'd probably kick my butt."

"You *know* I'd kick your butt."

I brushed the cake off my hands. "When I was at the River Styx, turning invulnerable . . . Nico said I had to concentrate on one thing that kept me anchored to the world, that made me want to stay mortal."

Annabeth kept her eyes on the horizon. "Yeah?"

"Then up on Olympus," I said, "when they wanted to make me a god and stuff, I kept thinking—"

"Oh, you *so* wanted to."

"Well, maybe a little. But I didn't, because I thought— I didn't want things to stay the same for eternity, because things could always get better. And I was thinking . . ." My throat felt really dry.

"Anyone in particular?" Annabeth asked, her voice soft.

I looked over and saw that she was trying not to smile.

"You're laughing at me," I complained.

"I am not!"

"You are *so* not making this easy."

Then she laughed for real, and she put her hands around my neck. "I am never, *ever* going to make things easy for you, Seaweed Brain. Get used to it."

When she kissed me, I had the feeling my brain was melting right through my body.

I could've stayed that way forever, except a voice behind us growled, "Well, it's about time!"

Suddenly the pavilion was filled with torchlight and campers. Clarisse led the way as the eavesdroppers charged and hoisted us both onto their shoulders.

"Oh, come on!" I complained. "Is there no privacy?"

"The lovebirds need to cool off!" Clarisse said with glee.

"The canoe lake!" Connor Stoll shouted.

With a huge cheer, they carried us down the hill, but they kept us close enough to hold hands. Annabeth was laughing, and I couldn't help laughing too, even though my face was completely red.

We held hands right up to the moment they dumped us in the water.

Afterward, I had the last laugh. I made an air bubble at the bottom of the lake. Our friends kept waiting for us to come up, but hey—when you're the son of Poseidon, you don't have to hurry.

And it was pretty much the best underwater kiss of all time.

TWENTY-THREE

WE SAY GOOD-BYE, SORT OF

Camp went late that summer. It lasted two more weeks, right up to the start of a new school year, and I have to admit they were the best two weeks of my life.

Of course, Annabeth would kill me if I said anything different, but there was a lot of other great stuff going on too. Grover had taken over the satyr seekers and was sending them out across the world to find unclaimed half-bloods. So far, the gods had kept their promise. New demigods were popping up all over the place—not just in America, but in a lot of other countries as well.

"We can hardly keep up," Grover admitted one afternoon as we were taking a break at the canoe lake. "We're going to need a bigger travel budget, and I could use a hundred more satyrs."

"Yeah, but the satyrs you *have* are working super hard," I said. "I think they're scared of you."

Grover blushed. "That's silly. I'm not scary."

"You're a lord of the Wild, dude. The chosen one of Pan. A member of the Council of—"

"Stop it!" Grover protested. "You're as bad as Juniper. I think she wants me to run for president next."

He chewed on a tin can as we stared across the pond at the line of new cabins under construction. The U-shape would soon be a complete rectangle, and the demigods had really taken to the new task with gusto.

Nico had some undead builders working on the Hades cabin. Even though he was still the only kid in it, it was going to look pretty cool: solid obsidian walls with a skull over the door and torches that burned with green fire twenty-four hours a day. Next to that were the cabins of Iris, Nemesis, Hecate, and several others I didn't recognize. They kept adding new ones to the blueprints every day. It was going so well, Annabeth and Chiron were talking about adding an entirely new wing of cabins just so they could have enough room.

The Hermes cabin was a lot less crowded now, because most of the unclaimed kids had received signs from their godly parents. It happened almost every night, and every night more demigods straggled over the property line with the satyr guides, usually with some nasty monsters pursuing them, but almost all of them made it through.

"It's going to be a lot different next summer," I said. "Chiron's expecting we'll have twice as many campers."

"Yeah," Grover agreed, "but it'll be the same old place."

He sighed contentedly.

I watched as Tyson led a group of Cyclops builders. They were hoisting huge stones in place for the Hecate cabin, and I knew it was a delicate job. Each stone was engraved with magical writing, and if they dropped one, it would either explode or turn everyone within half a mile into a tree. I figured nobody but Grover would like that.

"I'll be traveling a lot," Grover warned, "between protecting nature and finding half-bloods. I may not see you as much."

"Won't change anything," I said. "You're still my best friend."

He grinned. "Except for Annabeth."

"That's different."

"Yeah," he agreed. "It sure is."

In the late afternoon, I was taking one last walk along the beach when a familiar voice said, "Good day for fishing."

My dad, Poseidon, was standing knee-deep in the surf, wearing his typical Bermuda shorts, beat-up cap, and a real subtle pink-and-green Tommy Bahama shirt. He had a deep-sea fishing rod in his hands, and when he cast it the line went way out—like halfway across Long Island Sound.

"Hey, Dad," I said. "What brings you here?"

He winked. "Never really got to talk in private on Olympus. I wanted to thank you."

"Thank me? You came to the rescue."

"Yes, and I got my palace destroyed in the process, but you know—palaces can be rebuilt. I've gotten so many thank-you cards from the other gods. Even Ares wrote one, though I think Hera forced him to. It's rather gratifying. So, thank you. I suppose even the gods can learn new tricks."

The Sound began to boil. At the end of my dad's line, a huge green sea serpent erupted from the water. It thrashed and fought, but Poseidon just sighed. Holding his fishing pole with one hand, he whipped out his knife and cut the line. The monster sank below the surface.

"Not eating size," he complained. "I have to release the little ones or the game wardens will be all over me."

"Little ones?"

He grinned. "You're doing well with those new cabins, by the way. I suppose this means I can claim all those other sons and daughters of mine and send you some siblings next summer."

"Ha-ha."

Poseidon reeled in his empty line.

I shifted my feet. "Um, you *were* kidding, right?"

Poseidon gave me one of his inside-joke winks, and I still didn't know whether he was serious or not. "I'll see you soon, Percy. And remember, know which fish are big enough to land, eh?"

With that he dissolved in the sea breeze, leaving a fishing pole lying in the sand.

That evening was the last night of camp—the bead ceremony. The Hephaestus cabin had designed the bead this year. It showed the Empire State Building, and etched in tiny Greek letters, spiraling around the image, were the names of all the heroes who had died defending Olympus. There were too many names, but I was proud to wear the bead. I put it on my camp necklace—four beads now. I felt like an old-timer. I thought about the first campfire I'd ever attended, back when I was twelve, and how I'd felt so at home. That at least hadn't changed.

"Never forget this summer!" Chiron told us. He had healed remarkably well, but he still trotted in front of the fire with a slight limp. "We have discovered bravery and friendship and courage this summer. We have upheld the honor of the camp."

He smiled at me, and everybody cheered. As I looked at the fire, I saw a little girl in a brown dress tending the flames. She winked at me with red glowing eyes. No one else seemed to notice her, but I realized maybe she preferred it that way.

"And now," Chiron said, "early to bed! Remember, you must vacate your cabins by noon tomorrow unless you've made arrangements to stay the year with us. The cleaning harpies will eat any stragglers, and I'd hate to end the summer on a sour note!"

The next morning, Annabeth and I stood at the top of Half-Blood Hill. We watched the buses and vans pull away, taking most of the campers back to the real world. A few old-timers would be staying behind, and a few of the new-comers, but I was heading back to Goode High School for my sophomore year—the first time in my life I'd ever done two years at the same school.

"Good-bye," Rachel said to us as she shouldered her bag. She looked pretty nervous, but she was keeping a promise to her father and attending Clarion Academy in New Hampshire. It would be next summer before we got our Oracle back.

"You'll do great." Annabeth hugged her. Funny, she

seemed to get along fine with Rachel these days.

Rachel bit her lip. "I hope you're right. I'm a little worried. What if somebody asks what's on the next math test and I start spouting a prophecy in the middle of geometry class? *The Pythagorean theorem shall be problem two.* . . . Gods, that would be embarrassing."

Annabeth laughed, and to my relief, it made Rachel smile.

"Well," she said, "you two be good to each other." Go figure, but she looked at *me* like I was some kind of troublemaker. Before I could protest, Rachel wished us well and ran down the hill to catch her ride.

Annabeth, thank goodness, would be staying in New York. She'd gotten permission from her parents to attend a boarding school in the city so she could be close to Olympus and oversee the rebuilding efforts.

"And close to me?" I asked.

"Well, someone's got a big sense of his own importance." But she laced her fingers through mine. I remembered what she'd told me in New York, about building something permanent, and I thought—just maybe—we were off to a good start.

The guard dragon Peleus curled contentedly around the pine tree underneath the Golden Fleece and began to snore, blowing steam with every breath.

"You've been thinking about Rachel's prophecy?" I asked Annabeth.

She frowned. "How did you know?"

"Because I know you."

She bumped me with her shoulder. "Okay, so I have. *Seven half-bloods shall answer the call.* I wonder who they'll be. We're going to have so many new faces next summer."

"Yep," I agreed. "And all that stuff about the world falling in storm or fire."

She pursed her lips. "And foes at the Doors of Death. I don't know, Percy, but I don't like it. I thought . . . well, maybe we'd get some *peace* for a change."

"Wouldn't be Camp Half-Blood if it was peaceful," I said.

"I guess you're right . . . Or maybe the prophecy won't happen for years."

"Could be a problem for another generation of demigods," I agreed. "Then we can kick back and enjoy."

She nodded, though she still seemed uneasy. I didn't blame her, but it was hard to feel too upset on a nice day, with her next to me, knowing that I wasn't really saying good-bye. We had lots of time.

"Race you to the road?" I said.

"You are so going to lose." She took off down Half-Blood Hill and I sprinted after her.

For once, I didn't look back.

ACKNOWLEDGMENTS

As the first Camp Half-Blood series draws to a close, I have so many people to thank: My editor, Jennifer Besser, who has championed Percy Jackson since the very beginning; all the great people at Disney-Hyperion; my agent, Nancy Gallt, who helped bring the series to the world; my family—Becky, Haley and Patrick—who are my most understanding and patient supporters; and of course my readers—no author could ask for a more dedicated and enthusiastic group of fans. You all have a place at Camp Half-Blood!

RICK RIORDAN is also the author of the previous books in the *New York Times* #1 best-selling series Percy Jackson and the Olympians—Book One: *The Lightning Thief*; Book Two: *The Sea of Monsters*; Book Three: *The Titan's Curse*; and Book Four: *The Battle of the Labyrinth*. His previous novels for adults include the hugely popular Tres Navarre series, winner of the top three awards in the mystery genre. He lives in San Antonio, Texas, with his wife and two sons.